NEW YORK REVIEW BOOKS
CLASSICS

THE RECOGNITIONS

WILLIAM GADDIS (1922–1998) was born in Manhattan and reared on Long Island. He attended Harvard during World War II, but left without a degree in 1945. He was a fact-checker at *The New Yorker* for a little over a year, during which time he began writing short stories. In 1947 he embarked on a course of travel, living in Mexico, Panama, Spain, and France, while starting his first novel. *The Recognitions* was published in 1955 to largely negative reviews, though it found an underground following. Over the next twenty years, Gaddis was employed by various companies as an industrial writer, and taught part-time while working on his second novel, *J R*, which was finally published in 1975, winning the National Book Award. Ten years later he published his third novel, *Carpenter's Gothic*, which was also well received, and nine years later published his fourth novel, *A Frolic of His Own*, which won the National Book Award in 1994. Just before his death in 1998 he finished a novella, *Agapē Agape*, which was published in 2002 along with a collection of his essays, *The Rush for Second Place*. He was the recipient of grants and awards from the Rockefeller Foundation, Guggenheim Foundation, MacArthur Foundation, and Lannan Foundation, and was a member of the American Academy of Arts and Letters. His letters were published in 2013, and his work has been the subject of more than a dozen books and numerous essays. In addition to *The Recognitions*, New York Review Books also publishes *J R* as part of its Classics series.

TOM McCARTHY is the author of four novels—*Remainder, Men in Space, C,* and *Satin Island*—and several works of criticism, including *Typewriters, Bombs, Jellyfish* (2017), a collection of essays published by New York Review Books. In 2013 he was awarded the inaugural Windham-Campbell Prize for Fiction by Yale University. He lives in Berlin.

WILLIAM H. GASS (1924–2017) was a novelist, short-story writer, essayist, critic, and professor of philosophy. NYRB Classics reissued his book-length essay *On Being Blue: A Philosophical Inquiry* and his short-story collection *In the Heart of the Heart of the Country* in 2014.

THE RECOGNITIONS

WILLIAM GADDIS

Introduction by
TOM McCARTHY

Afterword by
WILLIAM H. GASS

NEW YORK REVIEW BOOKS

New York

THIS IS A NEW YORK REVIEW BOOK
PUBLISHED BY THE NEW YORK REVIEW OF BOOKS
435 Hudson Street, New York, NY 10014
www.nyrb.com

A portion of Chapter II of this book appeared originally in *New World Writing*, 1952, in slightly different form.
First published as a New York Review Classic in 2020.

Library of Congress Cataloging-in-Publication Data
Names: Gaddis, William, 1922–1998, author. | McCarthy, Tom, writer of introduction. |
  Gass, William H., 1924–2017, writer of afterword.
Title: The recognitions / by William Gaddis ; afterword by William H. Gass.
Description: New York : New York Review Books, 2020. | Series: New York Review
  Books classics
Identifiers: LCCN 2020005676 (print) | LCCN 2020005677 (ebook) |
  ISBN 9781681374666 (paperback) | ISBN 9781681374673 (ebook)
Classification: LCC PS3557.A28 R4 2020 (print) | LCC PS3557.A28 (ebook) |
  DDC 813/.54—dc23
LC record available at https://lccn.loc.gov/2020005676
LC ebook record available at https://lccn.loc.gov/2020005677

ISBN 978-1-68137-466-6
Available as an electronic book; ISBN 978-1-68137-467-3

The publishers wish to thank Steven Moore for his assistance in preparing this volume.

Printed in the United States of America on acid-free paper.
10 9 8 7 6 5 4 3 2 1

INTRODUCTION
From Deeds to Seeds and Back Again

WHAT BETTER place to start than with a repetition—with a double repetition, one whose innate non-originality pulls the rug out from underneath all claims of "starting" or originating? I'm thinking of the hapless Otto, one of this novel's many would-be writers. While his contemporaries sign other authors' books, or slip their DIY dust jackets over these, or delude themselves into believing that they've penned the first lines of the *Duino Elegies*, Otto at least gathers enough snippets of overheard wisdom to patch together into his own play. The problem is that his potential publisher-producers, on reading the manuscript, find it so familiar that they're certain they've read it before, that it's plagiarized, although none of them can put their finger on the source.

The situation's emblematic: William Gaddis's work forces every writer into this uncomfortable position; it makes Ottos of us all. When the first novel I wrote was eventually (after two of its successors) published, a *New York Times* reviewer praised it as a tribute to *The Recognitions*—which I hadn't read but, when I subsequently did, discovered had the same core plot. Thomas Pynchon hadn't read *The Recognitions* when he wrote *V.*, yet aren't his Whole Sick Crew, yo-yoing back and forth between New World and Old in search of some elusive grail, chips off the block of Gaddis's degenerate yet driven New York demimonde? And what must the Pynchon of *Vineland* have thought when he came across Ellery's throwaway mention of a man who jumps through windows as a TV stunt? Or the Vladimir Nabokov of *Ada*, with its quick-change alternation of originals and duplications, real flowers posing as fake ones in a Francophone copy shop's clutter, when he stumbled on the Bosch-topped table Reverend Gwyon passes as a copy so as to sneak it out of Spain, which his son, Wyatt, copies and exchanges with a dealer before heading off to Paris's carnival of replay in which, everything already having been done, there remains "no bud of possibility which had not opened in the permanent bloom of artificial flowers"?

It's not just literature either. Isn't Andy Warhol's painterly output reprised in advance by Gaddis's vision of modulating repetition in lined-up canvases, "the same picture from different angles, the same painting varying from easel to easel as different versions of a misunderstood truth," of studios "more an assembly line than a manufactory" turning out "mass-produced artifacts" of the world we live in—or, indeed, his filmic output by the looping, overlapping monologues of Gaddis's drugged-up art-world partygoers? Nor does it stop there: it reaches well into the future. Picture, if you will, Flavor Flav thumbing his copy of *The Recognitions* backstage at a 1990s Public Enemy gig, dipping into the same 1950s party scenes, gasping and double-taking at the entrance of Mr. Feddle, a luminary who goes about with an alarm clock strung around his neck...

Then again, the preemptive doubling, the originary non-originality, works two ways: like Otto's name, it runs backward as well as forward. The name of the novel's fraud-orchestrating lynchpin, Basil Valentine, appears in "Social Error," a Damon Runyon story published two full decades earlier: it belongs to a character who, in a move that will seem familiar to Gaddis's readers, in order to pass himself off as a legendary New York gangster when he's nothing of the sort, agrees to shoot a "rival" gangster with blank cartridges, only to have the blanks switched for real ones by a scheming *actual* rival of the "rival." The art-forgery career of Wyatt, the novel's protagonist, whose first drawing, "a picture, he said, of a robin, which looked like the letter *E* tipped to one side," not to mention that of Jim the Penman and many other counterfeiters in *The Recognitions*, is anticipated by that of Shem the Penman, James Joyce's own embedded writer-avatar who copies other writers' signatures "so as one day to utter an epical forged cheque on the public for his own private profit" in *Finnegans Wake*—a 1939 work whose hero is represented by, that's right, the letter *E* tipped to one side. But Gaddis hadn't read *Finnegans Wake* when he wrote his book. Nor, despite his novel's affirmation of experience relived or regained, had he read Proust. Had he, when he sketched his panning urban sweeps, visual-verbal collages of newspaper headlines, faces of subway passengers, and snatches of dialogue, read Alfred Döblin's 1929 groundbreaker *Berlin Alexanderplatz*? Had he read Jules Laforgue? Or H.D.? Who knows.

It strikes me that, while academically interesting, these questions are, at base, *fausses pistes*, red herrings. You don't need to have read Sophocles, or even Freud, to have an Oedipus complex, after all. If Gaddis's work both sends out and is racked by shock waves moving fore and aft and on all sides around it, this is because it's engaging—rigorously, unreservedly—with structures, processes, and patterns that are, have been, and always will be central to

Western art and thought; not least, those that turn around the perennial fetish of *authenticity* and its flip side, the fraught issue of the copy.

For Plato, only *eidos*—abstract, ideal "form"—is real. Everything else, including the entire physical, embodied world around us, is a mere reflection of that ideality, recast in the mold of *hyle* (corrupt matter). As for literature and art, they're even worse, a copy of a copy. Christianity imbibes and divinizes that thought: only God is real or "true"; the highest, truest form of knowledge is of God—and since humans, descended into bodies, fallen flesh, are de facto carnal, sinful, and in every way corrupted, it would be thoroughly hubristic to presume we could attain, much less originate, that knowledge.

The Recognitions forcefully restates this philosophical and theological schema, most notably through the figure of Aunt May. To young Wyatt's earliest artistic efforts (that tipped-*E* robin) she retorts by warning him not to usurp God's place: "Our Lord is the only true creator, and only sinful people try to emulate Him." She attempts to scare him with the cautionary Mother Goose rhyme about a "man of double deed, who sows his field without a seed," which Gaddis skillfully proceeds to interweave with the story of Origen, "that most extraordinary Father of the Church, whose third-century enthusiasm led him to castrate himself so that he might repeat the *hoc est corpus meum, Dominus*, without the distracting interference of the rearing shadow of the flesh . . . sowing his field without a seed" (although when we revisit the rhyme, some seventy pages and twenty-odd years after its recital by Aunt May, the opening has been amended to "There was a man of double deed / Sowed his garden full of seed"). Thus a complex set of concerns, around fathering, reproducing, doubling, and conjuring up ex nihilo—acting as origi/en—are brought into alignment, all around the dual stars of some kind of sleight-of-hand-induced overabundance (on the one hand) and (on the other) barrenness, castration.

This is pretty much the orbit in which Wyatt's, and the novel's, transits and returns will move. His early-adult bid to gestate his own art career is cut off by the corrupt critic Crémer, who makes his way by cultivating gardens not of his own planting (demanding a percentage of all future sales in exchange for good write-ups). Even as a child, though, Wyatt has found that, paradoxically, while original artworks of his making are "vulgar" and tainted by "blemish," his copied ones near "that perfection to which only counterfeit can attain." His Munich tutor Koppel provides a more formal framework for this intuition, decrying "That romantic disease, originality, all around we see originality of incompetent idiots, they could draw nothing, paint nothing, just so the mess they make is original....When you paint you do not try to be original...you do not invent shapes, you know them, auswendig wissen Sie, by heart..." The statement is half Marxist critique of bourgeois subjectivity, laying the ground logic for brazenly appropriative later artists and writers such as Sherrie Levine and Kathy Acker (both of whom, being female, stand ab ovo in a different relation to seeds and fatherhood), half sacred affirmation of devotional submission: for religious-icon painters, the "event" of a work was not its newness but the opposite, its plugging into an ongoing and staggered series of pulsing reiterations. Through Wyatt's pilgrim progress from aspiring artist to art forger, Gaddis effects an inversion, or implosion, of the entire rationale separating paternity or authorship from derivation or redoubling. As Valentine notes: "Most original people are forced to devote all their time to plagiarizing."

As I suggested earlier, these concerns are both classical and foundational. You can see them playing out in Shakespeare, for example, whose oeuvre (with its many lines copied straight from Ovid, Plutarch, or the authors of the previous *Leir*s and *Henry*s he reworked) demonstrates a near-obsession with questions of paternity versus illegitimacy or "bastardliness." Deploying a strikingly similar register to Gaddis's, Shakespeare writes, in *Venus and Adonis*:

> Seeds spring from seeds, and beauty breedeth beauty;
> Thou wast begot; to get, it is thy duty.

Urging the mystery male addressee of his *Sonnets* to start making babies, he argues that Nature

> ... carved thee for her seal, and meant thereby
> Thou shouldst print more, not let that copy die.

Later in the sonnet sequence, though, he has decided that his own craft as a poet can regenerate his loved one's beauty better than Nature herself:

> All in war with Time for love of you,
> As he takes from you, I engraft you new.

Engraft: the term neatly combines the world of horticulture with that of image-carving and printing or writing. Through the brilliance of his pen, Shakespeare guarantees that "in eternal lines to time thou growest." Wyatt, though, finds no such neat artistic synthesis or resolution through his work. Rather, it fills him with a dissonance that drives him first to drink and then to near-psychotic fugue states in which all artistic and subjective coherence slips away, "Like when a clay reproduction is made of an original statue, and then they take the copy and cut it behind the head with fine wire, and behind the arms and the legs, and those are all moved and it's cast again." It's at the moment of *signing*, of attaching a name to a piece Wyatt genuinely experienced, while (re)making, as his "own," that everything unravels: "I attach the signature," he tells Valentine, "and . . . lose it." Accordingly, Gaddis sees to it that, after two and a half chapters, neither he the author nor any of his characters will "sign" for Wyatt, write or speak his name. From here on (as though the text weren't hard enough to parse already—although if you're after a quick, easy read you probably won't have picked up *The Recognitions* in the first place), Wyatt's presence will merely be implied through mirroring and reverse POV, his very lodging indicated by "the bell with no name."

As for Wyatt, so for all the others. Names, acts, whole identities are switched, misappropriated, doubled, or simply lost. By the end, the secondary cast has spawned two extra sets of people with their titles, though in some cases lost the use of these titles for themselves (that's when they haven't already swapped them out for liquor brand names earlier). It's not just nomenclatural; it's a general condition. Everyone repeats everyone else's quips, rethinks their thoughts. Even their problems are "plagiarisms" of each other's. The text itself, right at the level of the sentence, turns at times into a kind of pastiche in which all actions and words are secondhand: Janet watches the unnamed Wyatt's homecoming "with a look of familiar wonder," recycling lines of scripture, while the Town Carpenter regurgitates snatches of poetry, the entire scene playing out as replay, as a form of ritualized reenactment. Experience thus cut loose from any innate (rather than imitative) moorings, we see not only characters but also existence *tout court* flailing about for some kind of coagulant, anchor, or compass: something to hold them together, to hold on to or just recognize . . .

This vertigo, this casting loose into inauthenticity, is opened or precipitated through the realm of art. But it plays out, too, through another prime arena, one that Gaddis would go on to explore further in his next novel, *J R*: money. Not only does *The Recognitions* contain multiple digressions on the history of counterfeit coinage, it uses all currency, both fake and "real" (all coins and banknotes, being symbols stamped on matter, multiply redoubled signs exchangeable for something else, or just for one another, are by their nature artificial), as another fault line along which the Platonic-Christian category of the ideal or divine is shaken and brought crashing down. As a child in church at collection time, Wyatt tries to "circumvent surrender of the coin in the wet palm of his hand" while "a voice singing, he believed, from Heaven" (but which turns out to belong to a boardinghouse keeper) describes what he understands as God's credit-and-debit scam, His issue and recall of everything, and wonders "what use that covetous heavenly host could have for a nickel." Canonization is assessed in terms of its cost (three million lire for the hire of St. Peter's alone!). Metaphysics, as a nameless girl lying on a bed in Paris quips, is at base simply economics, "heaven...paying for...hell."

On a more phenomenological scale, too, within the metric and dimension of being situated in the space-time of a city, Being reveals itself, through Gaddis's extraordinary prose, to be both generated and sustained by processes of coining, spending, and, of course, counterfeiting. Thus we see Mr. Pivner, in one of the book's most brilliant passages, hurrying through New York streets in which

> No fragment of time nor space anywhere was wasted, every instant and every cubic centimeter crowded crushing outward upon the next with the concentrated activity of a continent spending itself upon a rock island, made a world to itself where no present existed. Each minute and each cubic inch was hurled against that which would follow, measured in terms of it, dictating a future as inevitable as the past, coined upon eight million counterfeits who moved with the plumbing weight of lead coated with the frenzied hope of quicksilver, protecting at every pass the cherished falsity of their milled edges against the threat of hardness in their neighbors as they were rung together, fallen from the Hand they feared but could no longer name, upon the pitiless table stretching all about them, tumbling there in all the desperate variety of which counterfeit is capable, from the perfect alloy recast under weight to the thudding heaviness of lead, and the thinly coated brittle terror of glass.

One of Gaddis's more telling anecdotes from the well-researched history of economics narrates how, "like so many of the mystic contrivances devised by priesthoods which slip, slide, and perish in lay hands," the early establishment of sovereign credit turned into an American cottage industry as tradesmen, barbers, and barkeeps issued money, while inspectors traveling from bank to bank to verify their currency's securitizing were thwarted by banks shifting the same pile of bullion from one on to the next a step ahead of them. The tale is allegorical: in this novel in which sovereignty of all types—artistic, personal, ontological—is slipping, sliding, perishing at every moment, it's not so much that there is no gold standard (although there isn't) as that the very *notion* of one, let alone attempts to exercise or ratify it, is continually thwarted by its substrate of misprision, by its grounding in sleight of hand, in double-deeded seed capital that's at once excessive and unguaranteed: a stock bubble or Ponzi scheme. Of course, we get our crashes; even when the system's working, though, it's operating through an endless set of slippages, exchanges unfixed by any index other than that of exchange itself...

If this seems abstract, let's dive into a specific audit by looking more closely at a section in which Gaddis's dexterity—the deftness and inventiveness with which he shifts his signs and stocks and markers from depository to depository, shuttles them around his novel's trading floor—is on full, glorious display. Chapter 5 of part 2 begins with a quotation from President Lincoln's Treasurer, addressed to the director of the Mint, urging that "The trust of our people in God should be declared on our national coins"—an act he calls a "national recognition." (Ezra Pound's father, interestingly, was also the director of the Mint; Pound, describing visiting his workplace as a child, likens the testing of silver to "an aesthetic perception, like the critical sense ... the habit of testing verbal manifestations." His later anti-Semitism would be tied up, like that of Shakespeare's Antonio in *The Merchant of Venice*, with his revulsion for usury, the practice of making money breed more money out of nothing.) We then see Frank Sinisterra, the self-same counterfeiter who, posing as a doctor earlier, caused the death of Wyatt's mother. He's prepping, donning wig and makeup, for a meeting at which he'll hand over a supply of counterfeit twenty-dollar bills to an underground (and previously unencountered) contact in a hotel lobby; having already forged the money, he's now busily forging himself. As he does so, amidst back-and-forth with his long-suffering wife about Judaism versus Christianity, he bemoans the arrest of Jim the Penman, "the greatest artist that there ever was," and boasts of his own artisanal skill, claiming that no more than a half dozen men "can pick up engraving tools and do what I can do."

We then cut to Mr. Pivner, setting out to meet, for the first time in decades, his estranged son, Otto, in the same hotel lobby. Pivner, too, is on a path of self-creation, with the help of Dale Carnegie's *How to Win Friends and Influence People*, with its credo of virtue, faith, and other values "oriented toward the market place," of constructed authenticity ("I am talking about a real smile," we read over Pivner's shoulder). Then we see Otto, waiting for Pivner as arranged, mistaking Sinisterra for his father, preparing to "receive from that hand the clasp of recognition, pledge fealty, inherit the signet and the kingdom its seal perpetuated." Sinisterra, mistaking Otto for his contact, hands him the fake twenties, which Otto interprets as a paternal gift. Thus fatherhood and sovereignty (the kingdom) embark on a dance of comical misrecognition over the lit-up disco floor of artifice, the whole thing paid for, underwritten by fake currency. (The next day, Otto and his actual father will stand side by side in the same hotel's urinal, their generative members out, each completely unaware of who the other is; later still, Pivner will "adopt" the office boy Eddie Zefnic, before being accused of being a counterfeiter himself.) Otto, suddenly flush, goes about town flashing his (unbeknown to him, fake) cash, pretending to have sold his (unattributably "plagiarized") play, while Sinisterra and his actual intended contact (whom he belatedly connects with) follow him around in an attempt to get their money back, only to see him picked up for soliciting yet another made-up or "counterfeit" figure, an undercover policewoman. Realizing how awry his plans have gone, Sinisterra ends up hurrying off to church to confess to the sin of pride and light a candle for the recently deceased master forger Johnny the Gent, who "had humility."

This last sequence is exemplary of how *The Recognitions* works: through an endless out-of-joint-ness, people and stories wander from their posts, encroach and interlope on situations not their own, scale up from low-lying levels (that of anecdotal aside, say) to momentous (grand-symbolic or plot-central) ones, or tumble down the other way, to turn into a background detail in another plot: slip, slide, and perish indeed. In Gaddis's galaxy, celestial objects heave into *mis*alignment, not alignment, with each other—and then, even that is only temporary; any reading we take at one point of transit will be out of date ten pages later. Navigating this book, then, involves a kind of sidereal tracking of the paths of moving bodies, of signs being transported from one context to another, fading, bursting, re-amalgamating elsewhere.

I would invite you to see this stellar ballet and its machinations as a kind of mise-en-scène of a process and mechanism central to the book, to literature itself—that is, to view it as a large-scale enactment of the very essence and machinery of *metaphor* (a term that, literally, means transporting or transposing, carrying across: ΜΕΤΑΦΟΡΑΙ is written on the side of every truck in Greece). Itself a category, or more accurately another fault line, in the history of philosophy, metaphor's consideration prompts Nietzsche to assert that truth itself is no more than (and note, once more, the Gaddis-like language here) "a mobile army of metaphors, metonymics, anthropomorphisms . . . a sum of human relations . . . poetically and rhetorically intensified . . . illusions of which one has forgotten that they *are* illusions . . . coins which have their obverse effaced and now are no longer of account as coins." Jacques Derrida, in "White Mythology: Metaphor in the Text of Philosophy," weighs Nietzsche's passage against Aristotle's earlier (equally Gaddis-like) assessment of metaphor, specifically the example of it proffered by Plato's student in his *Poetics*: the sun casting forth light like a sower casting forth seeds—a construct that (as Derrida points out), relies on "a long and hardly visible chain" of associations. All metaphors, claims Derrida, are "heliotropic," since like sunflowers they turn toward what is supposedly "true," present, and visible, the superior, extra-linguistic, sun-like origin and source of visibility. Yet, conversely (he continues), it's from inside language itself, its tropes and transpositions, that the illusion of absolute, transcendent presence is projected in the first place. Metaphor, properly understood, is doubly heliotropic; it involves a double transport: both the movement of sunflowers as they turn after a sun that slips from the horizon *and* the turning of the (always metaphorical) "sun" itself within language. While sub- or post-Platonic metaphysics keeps on turning and returning in its bid to point toward a true, absolute, or (as it were) "gold-standard" sun, a radical, poetic version of philosophy would instead attempt to collapse the sun down into a sunflower and disgorge it, letting its seeds gush out without limit. This image, in turn, leads Derrida to consider the remarkable philosopher (and keeper of the Bibliothèque Nationale's coin collection) Georges Bataille, who describes, in his short 1930 essay "Sacrificial Mutilation and the Severed Ear of Vincent van Gogh," the Dutch artist's "solar obsession," the "overwhelming relations he maintained with the sun." The Arles sower paintings, which depict sunsets so vivid that they're virtually unbearable, or the sunflower series, whose subjects seem to writhe and wrench themselves apart, lead Bataille to suggest that the essence of van Gogh's auto-mutilation, and the truth of sacrifice in general, lies in the desire "to resemble perfectly an ideal term, generally described in mythology as a solar god who rips and tears out his own organs."

These are complex, sexy thoughts—but what concerns us most about them here is the way they intersect so vividly with Gaddis's own concerns. *The Recognitions* is, of course (as we have seen), constructed around an elaborate set of metaphors (sowing, "counterfeit" of all types, etc.), of metonymic chains (those series of associations and substitutions); of sums, whole networks, of human relations, poetically intensified. It's also awash with solar obsession: with the Mithraism that erupts through the weak skin of Gwyon's Christianity ("to teach them to observe Sunday, and keep sacred the twenty-fifth of December as the birthday of the sun. Natalis invicti, the Unconquered Sun... to worship the sun.... Herakles star-adorned, king of fire, ruler of the universe, thou sun, who with thy far-flung rays art the guardian of mortal life, with thy gleaming car revolving the wide circuit of thy course..."); or the mysticism of old alchemists who "had seen in gold the image of the sun, spun in the earth by its countless revolutions, then, when the sun might yet be taken for the image of God." The sun, too, is interwoven with the history of Origen ("under the cauterizing brilliance of the summer sun, reared up now as the winter sun struck from the south . . . short memories reached back, struggling toward Origen"), and thus with (church) fathering and its de-seeded flip-side non-progeniture. When "Dick," Gwyon's replacement as minister, visits him in the psychiatric institution to which he's been confined, the doctor mistakes him for "the son," repeating to Nurse Inch "The son . . . the son"—to which she, noting the sunshine outside, replies, "It's a beautiful day, doctor . . ."

This solar obsession, these overwhelmingly maintained sun relations, go hand in hand—as for Bataille's van Gogh—with sacrifice and (striking, cauterizing) mutilation: it starts with the slaughtering of Heracles, the ape who shares the sun-god's name, a ritualized exchange or payoff made by Gwyon to ransom his sick child back from the clutches of death; then, in similarly Mithraic fashion, there's the killing of the sun-god bull who's just coupled with Janet in her reenacted role as Helios's daughter Pasiphäe. Soon after, Anselm will replay Origen's automutilation, cutting his own genitals off with Gwyon's razor in a subway bathroom. In performing this last act, Anselm *literalizes* or becomes the end point of a metaphor chain that not only has run through the whole book but which was itself *already* and inherently, at least in its Mother Goose version, *about* chains of metaphor:

> *When the seed began to grow,*
> *'Twas like a garden full of snow;*
> *When the snow began to melt,*
> *'Twas like a ship without a belt;*
> *When that ship began to sail,*
> *'Twas like a bird without a tail . . .*

Etc. The procession of *'Twas likes* goes on and on until "a penknife in my heart" and the literality of "death and death and death indeed" put a stop to the poetic transpositions. Gwyon's Mithraic substitutions and transubstantiations, too, are ended when he finds *himself* sacrificed by his institutional cellmate who decides to replay the crucifixion with, or on, him. Thus metaphor flips over, via the desire for perfect resemblance of an ideal term, into its opposite, literality, fed back in an implosion, a collapse of metaphysics into matter, bodies, acts. Pivner may eat meat "that had got its succulent redness from sodium sulphite rubbed into it when it had turned toxic gray the day before," but there's nothing fake about the "fine gray texture . . . practically turning red" of the bread Wyatt and the others in the Spanish monastery chew on at the end: it's Gwyon's conflagrated, packaged, and postmarked flesh and blood, unwittingly consumed in a Sadean Eucharist.

For a novel that is so relentlessly profane, *The Recognitions* is (as we have also seen) exceedingly steeped in religion. Or, rather, in religions: Calvinism, Catholicism, their pre-Christian feeds; Judaism; Buddhism, Jainism, Hinduism.... In the melting pot of the mid-1950s, with the emergence of the patchwork or pick-and-mix belief systems so prevalent today, these blur together and with other categories such as lifestyle and aesthetics: "Do you know this new word, *Caprew*...? It's made up of the first two letters of Catholic, Protestant, and..." one tourist "pilgrim" in Spain asks another, to which the second replies: "Christ no, I just came over to see the art here."

It may be from early Christianity that Gaddis takes his title—from Saint Clement of Rome's third-century "theological romance" of the same name—but the term, in typical Gaddis fashion, far transcends its source context to wander, encroach, and interlope on scores of other situations. Art, even when earnestly copied, involves (as the devout Stanley understands) "that sudden familiarity, a sort of...recognition"; Wyatt, in his own inchoate artistic manifesto, claims that "the recognitions go much deeper, much further back, and I...this...the X-ray tests, and ultra-violet and infra-red, the experts with their photomicrography and...macrophotography, do you think that's all there is to it? Some of them aren't fools, they don't just look for a hat or a beard, or a style they can recognize, they look with memories that...go beyond themselves, that go back to...where mine goes." Pivner, reading the newspaper, scans his memory "for recognition" of its stories; Gwyon, after his wife's death, accepts "funerary offers of drink" as "recognitions..." As Steven Moore's invaluable (and online—use them!) annotations point out, variants on the word appear no fewer than eighty-one times in the text. Overall, it forms the book's core concept—or, to revert to theological diction, dogma. In the intellectual framework of the Jewish mystical tradition, "recognition" might approximate to Walter Benjamin's notion of "constellation," that revelatory (and revolutionary) moment at which all things coalesce into a legible assemblage; in that of Puritanism, to a vision of the prewritten (by God) "script" at work behind the world, a sensibility that runs from Marvell all the way to Burroughs and Pynchon (who renames it "paranoia"); in that of Catholicism, to a Joycean metempsychosis in which word becomes flesh and both can be assimilated through ingestion (as the artist Margarita Gluzberg puts it, "Catholics eat death for breakfast"). In a "pure" literary framework, it's not far off what Proust is trying to chart: not memory itself but rather the whole network of patterns, and the process of patterning, for which, poetically tapped, memory serves as the portal.

In his own working notes, Gaddis, too, explicitly links his title term with the word "pattern"—a coupling that, as a prompt for how to think this novel through, is spot-on. In virtually every setting, and at every scale (individual, institutional, technological, commentarial), the fundamental tendency or drive is toward pattern recognition, toward an apperception of the many patterns, macro and micro, that surround and shape us. What is Bicknall's *Counterfeit Detector*, the tome used by Sinisterra as a professional measuring stick or handbook, if not a pattern-recognition manual? What is Bernie the tourist's light meter, that he adjusts to correlate with "the bleak even color of the day," if not (like Wyatt's experts' gizmos) a pattern-recognition device? Or day itself, "laid out, shreds of its first reluctance to appear still blown across its face . . . exposed passive and foolish at the lifting of chaos," challenging its human occupants "to blunder upon its familiar features, its ribs and hollows . . . like the blind man identifying with a memory-sensitized hand the body of a familiar in what they had both called life"? Consciousness, at the base cognitive level, is (according to neuroscience's "fool theory about recognition" that Wyatt recaps to his father) nothing more than the forepart of the brain receiving an impression an instant before the other half. "When it reaches the second half the brain recognizes it!"

Mr. Feddle, fixing the book a critic acquaintance is reviewing (but not reading) "with a look of myopic recognition," notes its "pattern of bold elegance," the "stark configurations" of its cover's letterings which "intimate the origin of design." Bernie the tourist, too, has a book's cover, or title, forced upon his consciousness: he's made to write it out, letter by letter, on a train by a gun-toting Wyatt whom Bernie's wife (but not he, busy fiddling with that light meter and trying, Rorschach-like, to decipher the contours of his necktie) will later recognize. It's *Transcendental Speculations on Apparent Design in the Fate of the Individual*, Schopenhauer's great tome on pattern and agency, in which Schopenhauer makes the claim "that the systematic connectedness which we believe to have apprehended in the events of our lives is no more than an unconscious effect of our regulative and schematizing fantasy." Wyatt, here, could be Gaddis, holding us all to ransom, shoving his book, and all the other books it has ingested, transubstantiated, in our faces, confronting us with its impassioned central claim: that everyone is a reader, moving at confusing speed across a landscape it behooves us to get some kind of traction on; that pattern recognition is the task, the stake, and the goal of all existence—on top of which, it also presents (through our propensity to over-recognize) a lure, a danger, one of many will-o'-the-wisps along the pilgrim path.

That these exhortations and admonitions written (constellated, scripted, offered sacrificially to us who have for the most part, like Bernie or the critic, stubbornly resisted reading them) so brilliantly more than fifty years ago should (in their turn) find such powerful traction on our present moment shouldn't, given their transhistorical nature, surprise us. All the same . . . wow. In an age of diagnostic and predictive algorithms, QR codes, and facial recognition software, pattern recognition has become both *nomos* and *agon* of contemporary existence. And counterfeit, fraudulence, has become (or remains) its currency. It would be too easy to point out that at the time of this essay's writing, the most powerful office in the world is occupied by a grotesquely made-up con man who makes Sinisterra look decidedly sincere. More nuanced, perhaps, is the story of the strategist behind his rise, the double-shirted speculator who made his millions by buying out a *World of Warcraft* gold-farming company (that is, a platform that hires low-paid workers to amass in-game currency and sell it onward for real money to wealthier gamers), then reselling that to Goldman Sachs for $60 million (as Issie Lapowsky, the *Wired* journalist who reported on this story, commented: "Surely there's a metaphor in there somewhere"). This, in turn, might point us backward, via Pound, and prompt us to recall that *his* beloved fascism, in its first, Italian version, derived its imagery and title from a Roman symbol—the *fasces* or bound wooden rods—that was also to be found on the reverse side of the US Mercury dime. But maybe that would just be connectedness projection, false speculation.

More urgent, perhaps—and more in the spirit of Gaddis—would be to think our way through and out of this moment, to navigate it. One knee-jerk strategy, when faced with overwhelming and oppressive fraudulence in every walk of life, might be to call for a "return to authenticity." Yet as Theodor Adorno cautioned, authenticity, as ideological construct, is *itself* a core part of the problem. In a seminal 1964 essay of the same name, Adorno warns against "the jargon of authenticity" that "extends from philosophy and theology . . . to pedagogy, evening schools, and youth organizations, even to the elevated diction of the representatives of business and administration. . . . Whoever is versed in this jargon does not have to say what he thinks, does not even have to think it properly. The jargon takes over this task and devaluates thought" (note, yet again, the economic metaphor). More sinisterly, Adorno suggests that authenticity, as Weltanschauung, has intimate ties to fascism, furnishing the language that in turn "provides it [fascism] with a refuge." This last insight is vital to an understanding of our present political quandary: every single far-right power seizure of the last few years, from that of Trumpists in America to Brexiters in Britain to the Law and Justicers in Poland, has (just like those of the 1930s) been initiated and driven through by a sustained invocation of authenticity—"real Americans," the "true voice" of the "authentic British/Polish people"—and by demands for a supposedly lost "sovereignty." A political, intellectual, and aesthetic—or, indeed, ethical—strategy of opposition to these tendencies, I'd suggest, should consist of a turn *away from* sovereignty and its associated credos (uniqueness, "purity" of national and cultural mettle, etc.), and an embrace of the very type of commingled interdependence that the sovereignty fetishists abhor. As Giorgio Agamben, one of our more astute contemporary philosophers, puts it: "Ethics begins only when ... the authentic and the proper have no other content than the inauthentic and the improper."

Gaddis, of course, knows all this in advance. He is at pains to point out that "recognition" is *not* the same as authenticity; nor is it the same as any other type of resolution or transcendence; nor as the negation, on any scale or level, individual or collective, of a basic fallenness; nor rescue from a given state of errancy. At the climax of the novel, as the deluded tourist pilgrims fawn over miracles of "rigorously authentic origin" and the assassin Inononu discusses the "authenticity" of Sinisterra's mummified Egyptian, Wyatt's trajectory is brought—briefly and strategically—into conjunction with that of yet another novelist, the "distinguished" middlebrow author Ludy, whose success lies in "explaining, not man to himself, but men to each other." Ludy, who picks up none of Wyatt's literary or theological allusions, longs for just this type of transcendent resolution, for this rescue, spending his time in the monastery waiting for "a religious experience" that he might then package in digestible paragraphs for his many readers, answering his key market demand—as he puts it to Wyatt, using a register that combines Platonism, Christianity, and nascent New Age vagueness, "A need for spiritual ... something more spiritual than typewriters ..."

Ludy may be "just" a literary figure, and a rather one-dimensional one at that, but he stands in for the doctrines of authenticity and self-redemption as they play out in all areas of life. If Gaddis steers his protagonist right up against these doctrines, it's in order to forcefully and pointedly veer him away from them again. In his new inauthentic guise as the fugitive art restorer "Stephen," Wyatt finishes off Ludy's attempt to describe the way one might encounter beautiful things without "shouting" about them with the words (theologically overtoned but also profanely accepting of an endless, pained worldly experience from which there's no release): "You suffer them." A few pages later, Stephen/Wyatt literally brings Ludy crashing down as, ejected from the monastery's inner haven, he (Wyatt) delivers his own counterdoctrine, claiming that the ultimate pilgrim trajectory, rather than beating open the doors of the sovereign kingdom and being gathered up into some kind of personal, artistic, and metaphysical salvation, follows instead another path: that of "going back and living it through." The path, in other words, of being cast out once more into lived (*relived, doubled, slipping, sliding, perishing*) existence—which, being precisely that sphere which is *not* redeemed into divinely sanctioned unity, belongs de facto to the realm of the irresolubly inauthentic. The path of being cast, through art and consciousness (or, pace Proust, through consciousness of consciousness), back out into the world, compelled to navigate and recognize its multiples and replications all over again, even when we who navigate and recognize are *ourselves* made up of nothing other than these very multiples and replications. This impossible situation is the basis of all possibility. To requote Agamben, who here seems to be speaking as one with Wyatt:

> We can have hope only in what is without remedy. That things are thus and thus—this is still in the world. But that this is irreparable, that this *thus* is without remedy, that we can contemplate it as such—this is the only passage outside the world. (The innermost character of salvation is that we are saved only at the point when we no longer want to be. At this point, there is salvation—but not for us.)

—Tom McCarthy

THE RECOGNITIONS

Nihil cavum neque sine signo apud Deum.
—Irenaeus, *Adversus haereses*

For Sarah
The awakened, lips parted, the hope, the new ships

PART I

I

THE FIRST TURN OF THE SCREW

MEPHISTOPHELES (*leiser*): Was gibt es denn?
WAGNER (*leiser*): Es wird ein Mensch gemacht.

—GOETHE, *Faust* II

EVEN CAMILLA had enjoyed masquerades, of the safe sort where the mask may be dropped at that critical moment it presumes itself as reality. But the procession up the foreign hill, bounded by cypress trees, impelled by the monotone chanting of the priest and retarded by hesitations at the fourteen stations of the Cross (not to speak of the funeral carriage in which she was riding, a white horse-drawn vehicle which resembled a baroque confectionery stand), might have ruffled the shy countenance of her soul, if it had been discernible.

The Spanish affair was the way Reverend Gwyon referred to it afterwards: not casually, but with an air of reserved preoccupation. He had had a fondness for traveling, earlier in his life; and it was this impulse to extend his boundaries which had finally given chance the field necessary to its operation (in this case, a boat bound out for Spain), and cost the life of the woman he had married six years before.

—Buried over there with a lot of dead Catholics, was Aunt May's imprecation. Aunt May was his father's sister, a barren steadfast woman, Calvinistically faithful to the man who had been Reverend Gwyon before him. She saw her duty in any opportunity at true Christian umbrage. For the two families had more to resent than the widower's seemingly whimsical acceptance of his wife's death. They refused to forgive his not bringing Camilla's body home, for deposit in the clean Protestant soil of New England. It was their Cross, and they bore it away toward a bleak exclusive Calvary with admirable Puritan indignance.

This is what had happened.

In the early fall, the couple had sailed for Spain.

—Heaven only knows what they want to do over there, among all those ... those foreigners, was one comment.

—A whole country full of them, too.

—And Catholic, growled Aunt May, refusing even to repeat the name of the ship they sailed on, as though she could sense the immediate disaster it portended, and the strife that would litter the seas with broken victories everywhere, which it anticipated by twenty years.

Nevertheless, they boarded the *Purdue Victory* and sailed out of Boston harbor, provided for against all inclemencies but these they were leaving behind, and those disasters of such scope and fortuitous originality which Christian courts of law and insurance companies, humbly arguing ad hominem, define as acts of God.

On All Saints' Day, seven days out and half the journey accomplished, God boarded the *Purdue Victory* and acted: Camilla was stricken with acute appendicitis.

The ship's surgeon was a spotty unshaven little man whose clothes, arrayed with smudges, drippings, and cigarette burns, were held about him by an extensive network of knotted string. The buttons down the front of those duck trousers had originally been made, with all of false economy's ingenious drear deception, of coated cardboard. After many launderings they persisted as a row of gray stumps posted along the gaping portals of his fly. Though a boutonnière sometimes appeared through some vacancy in his shirt-front, its petals, too, proved to be of paper, and he looked like the kind of man who scrapes foam from the top of a glass of beer with the spine of a dirty pocket comb, and cleans his nails at table with the tines of his salad fork, which things, indeed, he did. He diagnosed Camilla's difficulty as indigestion, and locked himself in his cabin. That was the morning.

In the afternoon the Captain came to fetch him, and was greeted by a scream so drawn with terror that even his doughty blood stopped. Leaving the surgeon in what was apparently an epileptic seizure, the Captain decided to attend the chore of Camilla himself; but as he strode toward the smoking saloon with the ship's operating kit under his arm, he glanced in again at the surgeon's porthole. There he saw the surgeon cross himself, and raise a glass of spirits in a cool and steady hand.

That settled it.

The eve of All Souls' lowered upon that sea in desolate disregard for sunset, and the surgeon appeared prodded from behind down the rolling parti-lit deck. Newly shaven, in a clean mess-boy's apron, he poised himself above the still woman to describe a phantasmagoria of crosses over his own chest, mouth, and forehead; conjured, kissed, and dismissed a cross at his calloused fingertips, and set to work. Before the mass supplications for souls in Purgatory had done rising from the lands now equidistant before and behind, he had managed to put an end to Camilla's suffering and to her life.

The subsequent inquiry discovered that the wretch (who had spent the rest of the voyage curled in a coil of rope reading alternatively the Book of Job and the Siamese National Railway's *Guide to Bangkok*) was no surgeon at all. Mr. Sinisterra was a fugitive, traveling under what, at the time of his departure, had seemed the most logical of desperate expedients: a set of false papers he had printed himself. (He had done this work with the same artistic attention to detail that he gave to banknotes, even to using Rembrandt's formula for the wax ground on his copper plate.) He was as distressed about the whole thing as anyone. Chance had played against him, cheated him of the unobtrusive retirement he had planned from his chronic profession, into the historical asylum of Iberia.

—*The first turn of the screw pays all debts,* he had muttered (crossing himself) in the stern of the *Purdue Victory,* where the deck shuddered underfoot as the blades of the single screw churned Boston's water beneath him; and the harbor itself, loath to let them depart, retained the sound of the ship's whistle after it had blown, to yield it only in reluctant particles after them until they moved in silence.

Now he found himself rescued from oblivion by agents of that country not Christian enough to rest assured in the faith that he would pay fully for his sins in the next world (Dante's eye-witness account of the dropsical torments being suffered even now in Malebolge by that pioneer Adamo da Brescia, who falsified the florin, notwithstanding), bent on seeing that he pay in this one. In the United States of America Mr. Sinisterra had been a counterfeiter. During the investigation, he tried a brief defense of his medical practice on the grounds that he had once assisted a vivisectionist in Tampa, Florida; and when this failed, he settled down to sullen grumbling about the Jews, earthly vanity, and quoted bits from Ecclesiastes, Alfonso Liguori, and Pope Pius IX, in answer to any accusatory question. Since it was not true that he had, as a distant tabloid reported, been trapped by alert Federal agents who found him substituting his own likeness for the gross features of Andrew Jackson on the American twenty-dollar note, Mr. Sinisterra paid this gratuitous slander little attention. But, like any sensitive artist caught in the toils of unsympathetic critics, he still smarted severely from the review given his work on page one of *The National Counterfeit Detector Monthly* ("Nose in Jackson portrait appears bulbous due to heavy line from bridge . . ."); and soon enough thereafter, his passion for anonymity feeding upon his innate modesty amid walls of Malebolgian acclivity, he resolved upon a standard of such future excellence for his work, that jealous critics should never dare attack him as its author again. His contrition for the death which had occurred under his hand was genuine, and his penances sincere; still, he made no connection between that accident in the hands of God, and the career which lay in his own. He was soon at work on a hand-engraved steel plate, in the prison shop where license number tags were turned out.

For the absence of a single constellation, the night sky might have been empty to the anxious eye of a Greek navigator, seeking the Pleiades, whose fall disappearance signaled the close of the seafaring season. The Pleiades had set while the *Purdue Victory* was still at sea, but no one sought them now, that galaxy of suns so far away that our own would rise and set unseen at such a distance: a constellation whose setting has inaugurated celebrations for those lying in graves from Aztec America to Japan, encouraging the Druids to their most solemn mystery of the reconstruction of the world, bringing to Persia the month of Mordad, and the angel of death.

Below, like a constellation whose configured stars only hazard to describe the figure imposed upon them by the tyranny of ancient imagination, where Argo in the southern sky is seen only with an inner eye of memory not one's own, so the ship against the horizonless sea of night left the lines which articulated its perfection to that same eye, where the most decayed and misused hulk assumed clean lines of grace beyond the disposition of its lights. "Obscure in parts and starless, as from prow / To mast, but other portions blaze with light," the *Purdue Victory* lay in the waters off Algeciras, and like Argo, who now can tell prow from stern? Vela, the sails? Carina, the keel? where she lies moored to the south celestial pole, and the end of the journey for the Golden Fleece.

The widower debarked in a lighter that cool clear November night, with one more piece of luggage than he had had when he set out. Gwyon had refused to permit burial at sea. He faced strenuous difficulties entering the port of Spain, most of which hung about an item listed as "Importación ilegal de carnes dañadas," difficulties surmounted only by payment of a huge fee covering the fine, duties, excises, imposts, tributes, and archiepiscopal dispensation, since the cadaver was obviously heretical in origin. The cumbrous bundle was finally sealed in a box of mahogany, which he carted about the country seeking a place suitable to its interment.

Eventually, on the rise behind the village of San Zwingli overlooking the rock-strewn plain of New Castile, Camilla Gwyon was sheltered in a walled space occupied by other rent-paying tenants, with a ceremony which would have shocked her progenitors out of their Calvinist composure, and might have startled her own Protestant self, if there had been any breath left to protest. But nothing untoward happened. The box slid into its high cove in the bóveda unrestrained by such churnings of the faithful as may have been going on around it, harassed by the introduction of this heretic guest in a land where even lepers had been burned or buried separately, for fear they communicate their disease to the dead around them. By evening her presence there was indigenous, unchallenged, among decayed floral tributes and wreaths made of beads, or of metal, among broken glass façades and rickety icons, names more ornate than her own, photographs under glass, among numerous children, and empty compartments waiting, for the moment receptacles of broken vases or a broken broom. Next to the photograph of a little cross-eyed girl in long white stockings, Camilla was left with Castile laid out at her feet, the harsh surface of its plain as indifferent to memory of what has passed upon it as the sea.

The Reverend Gwyon was then forty-four years old. He was a man above the middle height with thin and graying hair, a full face and flushed complexion. His clothing, although of the prescribed moribund color, had a subtle bit of dash to it which had troubled his superiors from the start. His breath, as he grew older, was scented more and more freshly with caraway, those seeds often used in flavoring schnapps, and his eyes would glow one moment with intense interest in the matter at hand, and the next be staring far beyond temporal bounds. He had, by now, the look of a man who was waiting for something which had happened long before.

As a youth in a New England college he had studied the Romance languages, mathematics, and majored in classical poetry and anthropology, a series of courses his family thought safely dismal since language was a student's proper concern, and nothing could offer a less carnal picture of the world than solid geometry. Anthropology they believed to be simply the inspection of old bones and measurement of heathen heads; and as for the classics, few suspected the liberties of Menander ("perfumed and in flowing robe, with languid step and slow…"). Evenings Gwyon spent closeted with Thomas Aquinas, or constructing, with Roger Bacon, formidable geometrical proofs of God. Months and then years passed, in Divinity School, and the Seminary. Then he traveled among primitive cultures in America. He was doing missionary work. But from the outset he had little success in convincing his charges of their responsibility for a sin committed at the beginning of creation, one which, as they understood it, they were ready and capable (indeed, they carried charms to assure it) of duplicating themselves. He did no better convincing them that a man had died on a tree to save them all: an act which one old

Indian, if Gwyon had translated correctly, regarded as "rank presumption." He recorded few conversions, and those were usually among women, the feeble, and heathen sick and in transit between this world and another, who accepted the Paradise he offered like children enlisted on an outing to an unfamiliar amusement park. Though one battered old warrior said he would be converted only on the certainty that he would end up in the lively Hell which Gwyon described: it sounded more the place for a man; and on hearing the bloody qualifications of this zealous candidate (who offered to add his mentor's scalp to his collection as guaranty), the missionary assured him that he would. But the tall men around him would have none of his ephemeral, guilt-ridden prospects, and continued to beatify trees, tempests, and other natural prodigies. In solemn convocation, called in alarm, his superiors decided that Gwyon was too young. He was certainly too interested in what he saw about him. He was called back to the Seminary for a refresher course, and it was at that time that he developed a taste for schnapps, and started the course of mithridatism which was to serve him so well in his later years.

As a youth in college he had also got interested in the worldly indulgence of the theater (though it was not true, as some had it years later when he was locked up, defenseless, that he had made pocket money while in Divinity School playing the anonymous end of a horse in a bawdy Scollay Square playhouse). As he observed, no theater can prosper without popular subscription; which may well have been why the sincere theatricals of religions more histrionic than his own appealed to him. It was why he donated a resplendent chasuble, black with gold-embroidered skulls-and-bones rampant down the back, to the priest at San Zwingli in Spain (whom he would have costumed like an archbishop had the poor fellow dared let him). It was why he had given money for a new plaster representation of the canonized wraith (though, as the priest said, what they dearly needed was a legitimate locally spawned patron saint) who watched over the interests of the multitude: to them he gave Camilla's clothes, and an assortment of tambourines. And that was why, in Christian turn, they reciprocated with the festival which committed the body he had shared to rest on earth, and cajoled the only soul he had ever sought toward heaven.

In the next few months, various reports were received at home concerning the pastor's sabbatical: rococo tales, adorned with every element but truth. It was not true that, to exercise the humility struck through him by this act of God (in later years he was heard to refer to the "unswerving punctuality of chance"), he had dressed himself in rags, rented three pitiful children, and was to be encountered daily by footloose tourists in a state of mendicant collapse before the Ritz hotel in Madrid; it was not true that he had stood the entire population of Málaga to drinks for three days and then conducted them on an experimental hike across the sea toward Africa, intending that the One he sought should manage it dry-shod; it was not true that he had married a hoary crone with bangles in her ears, proclaimed himself rightful heir to the throne of Abd-er-Rahman, and led an insurrection of the Moors on Córdoba. It was not even true that he had entered a Carthusian monastery as a novice.

He had entered a Franciscan monastery as a guest, in a cathartic measure which almost purged him of his life.

The Real Monasterio de Nuestra Señora de la Otra Vez had been finished in the fourteenth century by an order since extinguished. Its sense of guilt was so great, and measures of atonement so stringent, that those who came through alive were a source of embarrassment to lax groups of religious who coddled themselves with occasional food and sleep. When the great monastery was finished, with turreted walls, parapets, crenelations, machicolations, bartizans, a harrowing variety of domes and spires in staggering Romanesque, Byzantine effulgence, and Gothic run riot in mullioned windows, window tracings, and an immense rose window whose foliations were so elaborate that it was never furnished with glass, the brothers were brought forth and tried for heresy. *Homoiousian*, or *Homoousian*, that was the question. It had been settled one thousand years before when, at Nicæa, the fate of the Christian church hung on a diphthong: Homoousian, meaning of *one* substance. The brothers in faraway Estremadura had missed the Nicæan Creed, busy out of doors as they were, or up to their eyes in cold water, and they had never heard of Arius. They chose Homoiousian, of *like* substance, as a happier word than its tubular alternative (no one gave them a chance at Heteroousian), and were forthwith put into quiet dungeons which proved such havens of self-indulgence, unfurnished with any means of vexing the natural processes, that they died of very shame, unable even to summon such pornographic phantasms as had kept Saint Anthony rattling in the desert (for to tell the truth none of these excellent fellows knew for certain what a woman looked like, and each could, without divinely inspired effort, banish that image enhanced by centuries of currency among them, in which She watched All with inflamed eyes fixed in the substantial antennae on Her chest). Their citadel passed from one group to another, until accommodating Franciscans accepted it to store their humble accumulation of generations of charity. These moved in, encumbered by pearl-encrusted robes, crowns too heavy for the human brow with the weight of precious stones, and white linen for the table service.

They had used the place well. Here, Brother Ambrosio had been put under an iron pot (he was still there) for refusing to go out and beg for his brethren.

There was the spot where Abbot Shekinah (a convert) had set up his remarkable still. There was the cell where Fr. Eulalio, a thriving lunatic of eighty-six who was castigating himself for unchristian pride at having all the vowels in his name, and greatly revered for his continuous weeping, went blind in an ecstasy of such howling proportions that his canonization was assured. He was surnamed Epiclautos, 'weeping so much,' and the quicklime he had been rubbing into his eyes was put back into the garden where it belonged. And there, in the granary, was the place where an abbot, a bishop, and a bumblebee . . . but there are miracles of such wondrous proportions that they must be kept, guarded from ears so wanting in grace that disbelief blooms into ridicule.

They got on well enough, even with the Holy See, the slight difficulties which arose in the seventeenth century being quite understandable, for who could foresee what homely practice would next be denounced as a vice by the triple-tiered Italian in the Vatican. The Brothers were severely censured for encouraging geophagous inclinations among the local nobility, whose ladies they had inspirited with a craving for the taste of the local earth, as seasoning, or a dish in itself: it was, after all, Spanish earth. But the commotion died. The ladies were seduced by salt (it was Spanish salt, from Cádiz), and peace settled for two more centuries, broken only by occasional dousings of the church altar with flying milk by peasants who chose this fashion of delivering their tithes, or monks knocked senseless by flying stones when they were noticed beyond the walls.

No one had ever got round to installing central heating, or any other kind. In summer, no one thought of it; in winter the good Brothers were immobilized, stagnating round heavily clothed tables with braziers underneath which toasted their sandaled feet, warmed them as far as the privities, and left them, a good part of the time, little better than paraplegics. The winter Reverend Gwyon appeared was a particularly harsh one in Estremadura. He was admitted as a curiosity, for few had ever seen a living Protestante, let alone one of their caudillos. But for Fr. Manomuerta, the organist, their guest might have been invited elsewhere: had not the confessor to the young king recently declared that to eat with a Protestante was to nominate one's self for excommunication? not vitando, perhaps, but at the least implying the consequence of working for a living. Curiosity prevailed. And at Christmas, Fr. Manomuerta reported to his fraternity that he had witnessed (through the large keyhole) their heretic guest administer the Eucharist to himself in his room, a ceremony crude and lonely compared to their own. —He is a good man, Fr. Manomuerta told the others, —there is some of Christ in him . . . But a few of those others wanted Gwyon castigated for defiling their rite, and even those who did not credit him with an actual Black Mass felt there was no telling how much damage might have been done simply by his tampering. Fr. Manomuerta understood some of the English language and assured them no such thing had happened, but for those whose suspicions were not allayed, reward seemed imminent some days later.

Gwyon had impressed his hosts with his capacity for their red wine, inclined to sit drinking it down long after they had finished eating, wiped their silver on their linen napkins and hidden it, and padded away. But he finally succumbed to a bronchial condition which threatened to become pneumonia and give him opportunity to pay the highest of Protestant tributes to Holy Church by dying on the good Brothers' hands. In a small room whose window lay in the countenance of the church façade overlooking the town's muddy central plaza, he developed a delirium which recalled the legends of the venerated Eulalio Epiclautos to some, to others (better read) the demoniacal persecution of Saint Jean Vianney, the Curé d'Ars, whose presbytery was in a continual state of siege, demons throwing platters and smashing water jugs, drumming on tables, laughing fiendishly and even, one night, setting fire to the curtains round the curé's bed. Gwyon himself was a big man. It was considered wise to leave him alone during these visitations.

So he lay alone one evening, perspiring in spite of the cold, almost asleep to be wakened suddenly by the hand of his wife, on his shoulder as she used to wake him. He struggled up from the alcoved bed, across the room to the window where a cold light silently echoed passage. There was the moon, reaching a still arm behind him, to the bed where he had lain. He stood there unsteady in the cold, mumbling syllables which almost resolved into her name, as though he could recall, and summon back, a time before death entered the world, before accident, before magic, and before magic despaired, to become religion.

Clouds blew low over the town, shreds of dirty gray, threatening, like evil assembled in a hurry, disdained by the moon they could not obliterate.

Next day the Brothers, in apprehensive charity, loaded Gwyon onto a mule, and after conducting him as far as the floor of the valley, Fr. Manomuerta Godsped him with benediction and the exhortation to return. Following a horrendous journey, Gwyon was delivered to the best hotel in the country, where he was left to recover.

At night, his was the only opened window in Madrid. Around him less than a million people closed outside shutters, sashes, inside shutters and curtains, hid behind locked and bolted doors themselves in congruent shapes of unconsciousness from the laden night as it passed. Through that open window he was wakened by lightning, and not to the lightning itself but the sudden absence of it, when the flash had wakened him to an eternal instant of half-consciousness and left him fully awake, chilled, alone and astonished at the sudden darkness where all had been light a moment before, chilled so thoroughly that the consciousness of it seemed to extend to every faintly seen object in the room, chilled with dread as the rain pounding against the sill pounded into his consciousness as though to engulf and drown it. —Did I close the study window?... The door to the carriage barn? Anything... did I leave anything out in the rain? Polly?... a doll he had had forty years before, mistress of a house under the birch trees in the afternoon sun, and those trees now, supple in the gale of wind charged inexhaustibly with water and darkness, the rest mud: the sense of something lost.

On the hill in San Zwingli the rain beat against the figure crucified in stone over the gate, arms flung out like a dancer. It beat against the bóveda, vault upon vault, bead flowers and metal wreaths, broken stems and glass broken like the glass in a picture frame over a name and a pitiful span of years where the cross-eyed girl in white stockings waited beside Camilla, and the water streamed into the empty vaults. Outside another wall enclosed a plot of grass long-grown and ragged over mounds which had sunk from prominence, to be located only by wooden triangles and crosses, unattended and askew in that fierce grass, unprotected like the bodies beneath whom poverty denied a free-standing house in death as it had in life, and faith alone availed them this disheveled refuge of consecrated ground, wet now.

Gwyon bounded out of bed in sudden alarm, his feet on the cold tile woke him to himself in Madrid and he stood shivering with life, and the sense of being engulfed in Spain's time, that, like her, he would never leave. He dressed with his usual care but more quickly, drank down a glass of coñac, and went out. The rain was over, When the huge gates were opened he walked into the formal winter wastes of the Retiro Park, waiting for the late sunrise, menaced on every hand by the motionless figures of monarchs.

In that undawned light the solid granite benches were commensurably sized and wrought to appear as the unburied caskets of children. Behind them the trees stood leafless, waiting for life but as yet coldly exposed in their differences, waiting formally arranged, like the moment of silence when one enters a party of people abruptly turned, holding their glasses at attention, a party of people all the wrong size. There, balanced upon pedestals, thrusting their own weight against the weight of time never yielded to nor beaten off but absorbed in the chipped vacancies, the weathering, the negligent unbending of white stone, waited figures of the unlaid past.

Gwyon fingered the stick under his arm, extended it, struck at a leaf which he missed. He looked again. Like his family they waited; and he stood in every moment of his blood's expenditure a stranger among them, and guilty at the life in him, for like these figures of stone, each block furrowed away from the other so that the legs were an entity, the cuirassed torso another, the head another, his family had surrounded him in a cold disjointed disapproval of life. As the statues bore the currents of the seasons his family had lived with rock-like negligence for time's passage, lives conceived in guilt and perpetuated in refusal. They had expected the same of him.

Each generation was a rehearsal of the one before, so that that family gradually formed the repetitive pattern of a Greek fret, interrupted only once in two centuries by a nine-year-old boy who had taken a look at his prospects, tied a string round his neck with a brick to the other end, and jumped from a footbridge into two feet of water. Courage aside, he had that family's tenacity of purpose, and drowned, a break in the pattern quickly obliterated by the calcimine of silence.

—Lost: one golden hour, set with sixty diamond minutes . . . Quoted in an oft-quoted sermon of his father's. Anything pleasurable could be counted upon to be, if not categorically evil, then worse, a waste of time. Sentimental virtues had long been rooted out of their systems. They did not regard the poor as necessarily God's friends. Poor in spirit was quite another thing. Hard work was the expression of gratitude He wanted, and, as things are arranged, money might be expected to accrue as incidental testimonial. (So came the money in Gwyon's family: since he disapproved of table delicacies, an earlier Gwyon had set up an oatmeal factory and done quite well. Since his descendants disapproved of almost everything else except compound interest, the fortune had grown near immodest proportions, only now being whittled down to size.)

Gwyon had married Camilla the year after his father's death. Everything was in order at the wedding except for an abrupt end to the wedding march on a triumphal high note. Miss Ardythe, who had attacked the organ regularly since a defrauding of her maidenhood at the turn of the century, had dropped stone dead at the keyboard with her sharp chin on a high D. Then there was also Aunt May's disapproval of Camilla's father, the Town Carpenter, who was said to have Indian blood, and had a riotous time at the wedding. Aunt May preferred to exclude him from her scheme, since he had been baptized in Christian reason and his salvation was his own affair, unlike a harried group of Laplanders who were even then being pursued by representatives of one of the Societies through which she extended her Good works. Those heathen were a safe distance away, not likely to be found rolling down Summer Street at unseemly hours, singing unchristian songs.

Camilla had borne Gwyon a son and gone, virginal, to earth: virginal in the sight of man, at any rate. The white funeral carriage of San Zwingli was ordained for infants and maidens. For the tainted and corrupt there was a ponderous black vehicle which Gwyon had turned his back on the moment he saw it. —She would never ride in that, he murmured in English, speaking not to San Zwingli's priest who stood beside him, but as though to someone inside himself. And before they closed that casket for the last time, Gwyon had stopped them, to reach in and remove Camilla's earrings, heavy Byzantine hoops of gold which had contrasted the fine bones of her face all these last years of her life. In the first week of his marriage, a friend, an archaeologist whom he had not seen since, had shown them to Camilla, and noting the delicate pricks in her ears (done with needle and cork years before), said laughing, —You may have them if you can wear them..., not knowing Camilla, not knowing she would run from the room clutching the gold hoops, and surprised (though Gwyon was not) when she burst in again with wild luster in her eyes, wearing the gold earrings, blood all over them.

Now, with a few delicate lies and promise of a carboy of holy water from a notorious northern font, he secured the white carriage to bear her up the hill, renovated like that remontant goddess who annually clambered forth from the pool with her virginity renewed. In that perennial innocence, —If there had only been time... He could hear her voice in this wistful complaint all of her life. —If only there were time..., she would have asked him for instructions. —What shall *I* do, in a Purgatory?...where they all speak Spanish? I've never been in any kind of Purgatory before, and no one...I'm not afraid, you know I'm not afraid but...if you'll only tell me what I should do...

Gwyon struck vaguely at the woman's profile on the stone shield of Don Felipe V, who stood above him casting back from the concave surface of a noseless face the motionless cold fallen from the white peaks of the Sierra de Guadarrama to the north, down upon the city. —El aire de Madrid es tan sutil, que mata a un hombre y no apaga a un candil, he had read somewhere, and that deadly cold seemed to come not from outside but to diffuse itself through his body from the marrow in his bones. False dawn past, the sun prepared the sky for its appearance, and there, a shred of perfection abandoned unsuspecting at the earth's rim, lay the curve of the old moon, before the blaze which would rise behind it to extinguish the cold quiet of its reign.

A feeling of liberation came over Reverend Gwyon. Whether it was release from something, or into something, he could not tell. He felt that a decision had been made somewhere beyond his own consciousness: that he must follow its bent now, and discover its import later. There would be time.

There would be time: just as the sun sped up over the margin of the earth in the miracle of its appearance and then, assured in its accomplishment, climbed slowly into day.

Reverend Gwyon packed his things and moved slowly about the peninsula. He saw people and relics, motion and collapse, the accumulation of time in walls, the toppled gateways, mosaics in monochrome exposure brought to colors of Roman life when a pail of water was dashed over them, the broken faces of cathedrals where time had not gone by but been amassed, and they stood not as witnesses to its destruction but held it preserved. Walking in cities, he was pursued by the cries of peddlers, men buying bottles, selling brooms, their cries the sounds of men in agony. He was pursued down streets by the desperate hope of happiness in the broken tunes of barrel organs, and he stopped to watch children's games on the pavements, seeking there, as he sought in the cast of roofs, the delineations of stairs, passages, bedrooms, and kitchens left on walls still erect where the attached building had fallen, or the shadow of a chair-back on the repetitious tiling of a floor, indications of persistent pattern, and significant form. He visited cathedrals, the disembow-eled mosque at Córdoba, the mighty pile at Granada, and that frantic Gothic demonstration at Burgos where Christ shown firmly nailed was once said to be fashioned from a stuffed human skin, but since had been passed as buffalo hide, a scarcer commodity, reminiscent, in his humor, of the mermaid com-posed from a monkey and a codfish. He collected things, each of a holy inten-tion in isolation, but pagan in the variety of his choice. He even got to a bullfight when the season opened.

In all this, he encountered few people who knew San Zwingli. Those who had heard of it recalled the only event which had distinguished that town in a century's current of events. Twelve years before, an eleven-year-old girl had been brutally assaulted on her way home from her first communion. She died a few days later. The man who had done it was found to be infected with a disease which he believed such intercourse with a virgin could cure, and since everything about her appearance confirmed her probable virginity, he stalked the little cross-eyed bride to this simple curative end. He was in prison.

San Zwingli appeared suddenly, at a curve in the railway, a town built of rocks against rock, streets pouring down between houses like beds of unused rivers, with the houses littered like boulders carelessly against each other along a mountain stream. Swallows dove and swept with appalling certainty at the tower of the church, and the air was filled with their morning cries, with the sound of water running and the braying of burros, and the distant voices of people. Gwyon had climbed to the pines behind the town, pausing to breathe and smell the delicious freshness of manure, to realize how his senses had fallen into disuse under the abuses of cities. The day deepened weightlessly, a feast day, crowds wandering through the streets, groups singing and playing, in one a boy with half an arm supporting a broken anis bottle played scratching accompaniment on that corrugated glass surface.

He rarely smoked, but he sat with a cigar after dinner, charging its exhaled smoke with the quickening breath of coñac, as he spoke with Señor Hermoso Hermoso about Spain and the giant Antaeus, whose strength was invincible as long as he stayed on earth, and Hercules, discovering this, lifted him up and crushed him in the air. —Spain..., Gwyon said, —the self-continence, and still I have a sense of ownership here, but even now...to outsiders, it seems to return their love at the moment, but once outside they find themselves shut out forever, their emptiness facing a void, a ragged surface that refuses to admit...there, Spain is still on the earth and we, in our country, we are being crushed in the air...

—What we are most in need of here, said Señor Hermoso, who had been listening politely, —is of course a patron saint of our own. Perhaps you note the lack during your visit? Perhaps our kind priest drew it to your attention...? Señor Hermoso taught foreign languages, or would have, if anyone had found such preposterous instruments necessary, and he ran an approximation to a drugstore. His face was round, its limp flabby quality belied by an exquisite mustache and penetrating eyes. The part in his hair cut clean separation from the back of his neck through his widow's peak. —But such a thing costs money, so much money you know, he went on, raising his voice above the strident chords of a barrel organ which had stopped before their café. —Such sums of money that perhaps only someone of your position could understand? Too much, perhaps, it is to say, for these poor and ignorant people who need the blessed care of a patron saint so much... He paused, sniffed his coffee with forlorn expectation, but Gwyon did not interrupt. —Then I feel certain, like these people who are so good, perhaps our Little Girl (here he referred to that unfortunate child done in twelve years since) —was sent us for this purpose. The Lord does not err, true? Verily, as your Bible says, true? Verily, she was a saint, a little saint among us. Asking nothing for herself, living on the simplest fare, beans and rice, she... Señor Hermoso stopped, as though he might have lost his place in a speech carefully prepared and memorized beforehand. —Though, perhaps that was because she was so poor...? he went on, reasoning helplessly, trying to recover his lines.

Gwyon tossed his cigar out to the street, where it was caught before it touched the ground. He mumbled something about Antaeus and straightened up, but Señor Hermoso took hold of his sleeve. —I remember so well, Señor Hermoso persisted, —you know, she would not use an unclean word. "My tongue will be the first part of me to touch the Host..." que fervorosa luna de miel para esta pequeña esposa de Jesús!...when she is so cruelly struck down by all that is base in man...

Gwyon got out to the steps which led down to the plaza. The streets were thronged, sparsely and dimly lit. —But there are ways, true? he left Señor Hermoso saying. —Our Lord points to us the right one? Many thousands of pesetas, millions of lire, he whispered, clasping his plump hands, forsaken, as Gwyon went down the steps. —There are ways...

In the streets below, Gwyon was hailed by sundry extremes of his wife's wardrobe, worn with sportive and occasionally necessitous disregard for original design. Her favorite long flowered evening skirt passed on three distinctly different little girls. Then one woman appeared wearing three of her dresses, each a pattern of holes, what remained of one supplying the lack in the others. Her green cloche hat, her Fifth Avenue hat looking as though it had been slept in and eaten out of, was jammed at a warlike angle on the head of the local match-seller. After the feast celebrated that morning, most of the paraphernalia had been put away, since the holy oils, holy water, and fly-specked holy wafers were kept under lock and key for fear they be stolen and used in sorcery.

But other holy appliances were kept handy, for a rousing ceremony to speed the foreign visitor who rested up on the hill. Reliquaries were opened, censers swung in dangerous arcs, beads fingered and psalters thumbed, water scattered, bells clattered, tapers lit, candles burned and gutted, Latin jumbled and coughed in monody. In this perfectly ordered chaos, over the black waves rising and falling in genuflection, the tide of sound ebbing and flooding, Gwyon was told that it was, really, a pity (lástima) that there was no patron saint to defend their rights and advance their cause by direct intervention. The new tambourines, though slightly out of place, were used to brilliant effect: their clamor enhanced the spirit of impatience in which, presumably, the wistful laboring shade of Camilla Gwyon waited to be sprung to the gate of Paradise.

They never forgave him for not bringing the body home. And Gwyon thought it wiser, or at least less complicating, never to brief the families on the extravagant disposition that had been made of the soul. —It certainly would have weighed a lot less, said Aunt May (speaking of the body), —than all this rubbish he brought back. The rubbish included a number of un-Protestant relics soon to darken the parsonage, among them a tailless monkey (it was a Barbary ape from Gibraltar, being held in quarantine) which the distracted woman had not yet seen.

Wyatt was four years old when his father returned alone from Spain, a small disgruntled person with sand-colored hair, hazel eyes which burned into green on angry occasion, and hands constantly busy, clutching and opening on nothing, breaking something, or picking his nose. He was in celebrant spirits that spring day, and observed the solemn homecoming by emptying the pot on which he meditated for an hour or so each morning into a floor register. Aunt May was there a moment later. She gave him a hard slap on the bottom, realized her mistake, and pondered with some bitterness the end of this Christian family while she washed her hands. She had just come from the father, who had told her about the impatient piece of luggage waiting in quarantine. Leaving his room brusquely, to take this revelation away and try to fit it into the hectic tangram of recent events, she had hardly reached the newel at the stairhead when she heard a crash. She returned to find the Reverend swaying unsteadily among the breakage of a Bennington ware pitcher, a peculiarly ugly thing of which she'd been very fond. The Reverend, who'd been about to change, now trying to pull his trousers back up, said something about the roll of a ship, and losing his balance when the chiffonier failed to move over and support him. If her sniff was meant simply to express disdain, a sharp attentive look came to her face as she repeated it, and she was about to speak when, from below decks, rose the hilarious sound of metal being banged against metal. Down the wide golden-oak front staircase vaulted Aunt May, traveling at a great rate but retaining the glasses clamped to her nose, thus her dignity.

—It's certainly reached the furnace by this time, she said when the child's father appeared, drying her hands on an old dishcloth. —You can smell it all over the house, she added in unnecessary comment to heighten the effect, and turned on Wyatt with, —Why did you do such a nasty thing? He stood looking behind her, at the picture of his mother on the mantel, a photograph made before Camilla was married. Aunt May gripped his small-boned shoulder in her hand and shook him. She was his Christian mentor. It was she who had washed his mouth out with laundry soap after the rabbit episode. —Do you enjoy the sme-ll? she went on, drawing the word out so that it seemed laden with odor itself.

—You'd better go to your room, said his father, in a voice stern only with effort, for this sudden demand for discipline was confusing.

—To his room! said the woman, as though she would lop off a hand as a lesson. —Why that boy...

—Go to your room, Wyatt. Reverend Gwyon was stern now, but for her, not the child; and Aunt May swept out of the room to write a hurried note rescinding a tea invitation to the ladies of the Use-Me Society. The father and son faced one another across the stark declivity of their different heights, the man staring wordless at this incarnation of something he had imagined long before, in a different life; the child staring beyond at his virgin mother.

Gwyon recovered himself, but before he could speak the sound which was not yet a word in his throat Wyatt had turned away and walked slowly up the stairs to his room, to a chair beside a closed window where he sat looking out upon the unfulfilled landscape of the spring, picking his nose, and seeming not to breathe.

Beyond the roof of the carriage barn, clouds conspired over Mount Lamentation. He looked there with open unblinking eyes as though in that direction lay the hopeless future which already existed, of which he was already fully aware, to which he was conclusively committed. His shoulders were drawn in, as though confirmed in the habit of being cold.

For one dedicate in the Lord's service, as Aunt May assured him that he was, Wyatt seemed already to have piled up a tidy store of sin. He could move in few directions without adding to it. His most remarkable accomplishment had occurred right after Hallowe'en. He was in his mother's sewing room going through the button drawer, in the afternoon when he should have been taking his nap, when she came in. She was dressed in white, and although she appeared to be looking for something, she did not seem to see him. He ran toward her, crying out with pleasure, but before he could reach her she turned and went out, at the instant Aunt May came through the door. —She was here, where did she go? Mother was here . . . , he started to Aunt May, with barely another word when that flesh-and-bloodless woman picked him up and took him to his bed, to force him down there with little more than a turn of her wrist, and leave him to "beseech the Lord" to help him stop lying. It was days later when Aunt May called him to her, shaking, with an opened letter in her hand, and had him repeat that lie in detail. Quivering like the letter he stared at in her hand, he spoke with frightened reluctance, as though this were a device, logical for Aunt May, to promote more punishment. But when he was done Aunt May had him kneel beside his bed and pray to the Lord to help him forget it, pray to the Lord to forgive him. She even knelt with him.

The Lord had not helped him: he remembered it very well. There was some confusion in his mind when his father returned, for somehow his father and the Lord were the same person and he almost asked his father to help him forget it. That would not do, because Aunt May had told him never to tell his father. Didn't his father know? And if the Lord was everywhere, hadn't *He* seen Camilla come in, dressed in a white sheet, looking for something?

Aunt May never mentioned that again. But she lost no time telling his father about the rabbit. —I scarcely know how to tell you, she commenced, and when Gwyon looked satisfactorily alarmed she went on, —Your son has learned, somewhere, to swear. It's scarcely surprising, with a grandfather who talks to him just the way he talks to his cronies in the saloon, and fills him full of all kinds of drivel... She went on to explain that she had taken a toy away from Wyatt every time this happened (being lenient), until he was left with only one, a cloth rabbit. (For the truth of that, the words which cost him those treasures were *darn* and *heck*: she seemed to know their euphemistic derivation well enough.) —And then, the last straw, I... I can scarcely repeat his words. Though Heaven knows how they are engraved on my memory. He knew I was in the room, he was sitting on the floor with his last toy, this rabbit, and he said... your son said, as clearly as I'm speaking now, he said, "You're the by-Goddest rabbit I ever damn saw!" At which, hearing herself speak this, Aunt May almost sobbed crying out, —What kind of a Christian mi... mish... minister do you think he will make?

Wyatt was, in fact, finding the Christian system suspect. Memory of his fourth birthday party still weighed heavily in his mind. It had been planned cautiously by Aunt May, to the exact number of hats and favors and portions of cake. One guest, no friend to Wyatt (from a family "less fortunate than we are"), showed up with a staunchly party-bent brother. (Not only no friend: a week before he had challenged Wyatt through the fence behind the carriage barn with —Nyaa nyaa, suckinyerma's ti-it-ty...) Wyatt was taken to a dark corner, where he later reckoned all Good works were conceived, and told that it was the Christian thing to surrender his portion. So he entered his fifth year hatless among crepe-paper festoons, silent amid snapping crackers, empty of Christian love for the uninvited who asked him why he wasn't having any cake.

On Sunday mornings he would sit tugging buttons or strands of horsehair from the pew's upholstery, trying to work out a way to circumvent surrender of the coin in the wet palm of his hand. But the untoward moment always arrived, heralded by a voice singing, he believed, from Heaven, —All things come of Thee O Lord and of Thine own give we back to Thee. He later learned that it was no heavenly voice at all, but Mrs. Dorman, a dumpy deep-chested boarding-house keeper, strategically placed somewhere up in the vicinity of the bell tower. The rest of the congregation was being victimized by this ruse, and he might have enlightened them but for the prospect of the yellow bar of laundry soap. And aside from the actual buying power of five cents, it was the notion that it had once belonged to the Lord he resented: what use that covetous heavenly host could have for a nickel... —Praise God from whom all blessings flow, burst the choir, and the money was carried away in a wicker basket never to be seen on earth again.

Now, even before the day was out, Wyatt was back staring through his window. After the near-silent midday meal, Aunt May sent him to his room for singing an indecent song.

—Singing? Gwyon demanded.

—He was humming it.

—But . . . humming? How . . .

—He knows the words well enough. It's a saloon song, he learned it from that . . . that dirty old man.

The Town Carpenter had left his daughter's upbringing to an aunt and a silent cousin named Mary. He was a floridly untidy fellow, lopsided from pushing a plane, so he said, and could usually be found in the Depot Tavern when his working day was done, around eleven in the morning. Some years before, his own mother's death had robbed him of his main occupation: retrieving her from the foot of the granite Civil War monument in the center of town where she went when the house oppressed her, and squatted there in any weather cross-legged under a blanket. The Town Carpenter's one accomplishment to date had been fathering Camilla. As for the course of recent events, this man having taken her on as a spiritual and economic responsibility and then left her inoperative in a land surrounded by foreigners, mountains, and the sea: he was somewhat muddled. What he could make out with little difficulty was the disapproval of his dead wife's sister and the silent cousin, both of whom wanted the body back. From convenient habit he disagreed with them. This gave him good excuse for staying away from home. It was in the Depot Tavern that he received condolences, accepted funerary offers of drink, and, when these recognitions were exhausted, he sank into the habit of talking familiarly about persons and places unknown to his cronies, so that several of them suspected him of reading. Vague as it had been, his period of mourning did not last long for his temper was not suited to it, and he was never known to mention his daughter's name, in the Depot Tavern at any rate, again.

In the immediate family, blood proved thicker than three thousand miles of sea water; and prospect of scandal precluded any schismatic activities the Gwyon blood might not have taken care of. They faded in thin-lipped silence, though there were a few, wavering souls haunted by Darwinian shadows of doubt, who, when the mocking companion from Gibraltar was discovered, made it known to one another that they had no intention of forgiving him, in this world or the next.

In the late spring Reverend Gwyon returned to the pulpit of the First Congregational Church. The people inherently respected him, for their fathers had held his father in almost as high regard as they held their own. The name had the weight of generations behind it since, two centuries before, Reverend John H. Gwyon had been butchered by disaffectionate Indians whose myth he had tried to replace with his own. Most of that congregation pointed out pillars of Puritan society among their forebears, who had never permitted maudlin attachment to other human beings to interfere with duty. To suffer a witch to live was as offensive to the God of Calvin, Luther, and Wesley, as it was to That of the Pope of Rome; and as though bent on surpassing the record of the Holy Inquisition in the neighborhood of Toulouse, where four hundred were burned in half a century, these stern hands kept the air of the New World clean the same way, and might well have been locked up had they appeared among this present posterity, but were wisely exiled in death. They had done their work, passed on the heritage of guilt. The rest was not their business.

This congregation admired the Reverend's bearing up, as they called it, under his suffering (though there were an evilly human few who envied him his Providence) and they had never had the full details of the Spanish affair. Enough to know that their minister was of familiar lineage, had suffered sore trials, and was now returned from temporal disasters to lead them unfaltering, by word and example, in the ways of Christian fortitude.

His sermons took up a lively course. In his loneliness, Gwyon found himself studying again. With the loss of Camilla he returned to the times before he had known her, among the Zuñi and Mojave, the Plains Indians and the Kwakiutl. He strayed far from his continent, and spent late hours of the night participating in dark practices from Borneo to Assam. On the desk before him, piled and spread broadcast about his study, lay Euripides and Saint Teresa of Avila, Denys the Carthusian, Plutarch, Clement of Rome, and the Apocryphal New Testament, copies of *Osservatore Romano* and a tract from the Society for the Prevention of Premature Burial. *De Contemptu Mundi, Historia di tutte l'Heresie, Christ and the Powers of Darkness, De Locis Infestis, Libellus de Terrificationibus Nocturnisque Tumultibus, Malay Magic, Religions des Peuples Noncivilisés, Le Culte de Dionysos en Attique, Philosophumena, Lexikon der Mythologie.* On a volume of Sir James Frazer (open to the heading, Sacrifice of the King's Son) lay opened *The Glories of Mary*, and there underlined, —There is no mysticism without Mary. Behind the yew trees, whose thickly conspired branches and poison berries guarded the windows, night after night passed over him, over the acts of Pilate, Coptic narratives, the *Pistis Sophia*, Thomas's account of the child Jesus turning his playmates into goats; but the book most often taken from its place was *Obras Completas de S Juan de la Cruz*, a volume large enough to hold a bottle of schnapps in the cavity cut ruthlessly out of the *Dark Night of the Soul*.

In church his congregation attended his sermons out of stern habit, and occasionally with something uncomfortably like active interest they were swayed. They even permitted him to regale them in Latin, and later, with growing incidence as years passed, he dashed their petrous visages with waves from distinctly pagan tongues, voluptuous Italian, which flowed over their northern souls like sunlit water over rocks. They had not much use for that slovenly race. He exhorted them to breathe out when they prayed, ... or was it breathe in? No one, alone with God afterward, was certain. And when unrest showed on those gray shoals, he put them at dismal ease once more by reminding them that they were, even at that moment, being regarded from On High as a stiff-necked and uncircumcised generation of vipers: they found such reassurances comforting.

He even managed to re-institute wine for the grape juice prescribed by temperate elders in the celebration of the Eucharist, rousing his flock one sunny morning with the words, —Drink no longer water, but use a little wine for thy stomach's sake and thine often infirmities. That upset Aunt May, and though she could not presume to argue with Saint Paul the Apostle, it was at moments like this that she suspected him of never having really got over being Saul the Jew of Tarsus, with a nose like Saint Edmund, and those dirty intemperate habits Jews are famous for. Unlike her charity and that of her Societies, which never ventured south of the sixtieth parallel except for forays into darkest Africa, Gwyon's troubled everyone by reaching no further than the sound of his own voice for objects worthy of mercy. Janet, a girl with a tic which drew her head to one side in bright affirmative inclinations of idiocy, exemplar of a lapse from Puritan morality on the part of her mother (done in by a surgical belt salesman from New York), was found sharing a slap and tickle with the church janitor behind the organ one night after choir practice. Janet had been born a number of minutes after her mother's death, which some including Aunt May regarded as a bad sign from the start. The incident behind the organ proved it, and Aunt May said something about the stocks and the pillory, a shame they'd gone out of fashion. —A shame to deprive us all of that satisfaction, Gwyon agreed. She was wary. —What do you mean? —The great satisfaction of seeing someone else punished for a deed of which we know ourselves capable. —But I . . . —What is more gratifying than this externalizing of our own evils? Another suffering in atonement for the vileness of our own imaginings . . . —Stop it! cried Aunt May, —I'm sure I have never had such thoughts. —Then how can you judge her crime, if you have never been so tempted? he asked quietly. —You . . . you are speaking like a heretic, Aunt May brought out, —a heretic from your church and your . . . and from your family . . . ! and she left the room.

The text for the following Sunday's sermon was taken from the Sermon on the Mount (Matt. 7:1), and Janet became kitchen girl in Reverend Gwyon's household.

There were a few, of an intuitive nature seldom bred in such a community, who suspected his charity to be a mask behind which he dissembled a sense of humor to mock them all. The Town Carpenter was one of these. He commenced to appear regularly on Sunday mornings in the dimmer sections of the church, dressed in policeman suspenders and shirts so respectfully modest that they even concealed the usually prominent top button of his underwear.

The parsonage was a clapboard house whose interiors were done in dark paper and wainscoting. Most of the downstairs windows were darkened by outside trees. As the master unpacked, its character changed, realizing itself for the first time in sympathy with the obscurity. Watts's painting of Sir Galahad, in the hall leading to the study, was replaced by a small cross bearing a mirror in each extremity. A robin, a thrush, and a bluejay (mounted by a distant cousin who had found taxidermy the Way Out and was last seen in the Natural History Museum in Capetown, South Africa, drinking himself to death in a room full of rigid hummingbirds he had stuffed himself) gave up their niche to the defaced stone figure of a Spanish saint, Olalla. A picture of an unassuming elk skulking among empty trees was replaced by a copy of a painting by the elder Breughel; and Saint Anthony's insanity manifest in the desert was hung over the unfaded square caused and covered by a painting of Trees (done by a maiden relative long since gone to earth, and rescued now by Aunt May).

A large low table appeared under the window in the dining room. It was the prize of this incipient collection, priceless, although a price had been settled which Gwyon paid without question to the old Italian grandee who offered it sadly and in secret. This table top was the original (though some fainaiguing had been necessary at Italian customs, confirming it a fake to get it out of the country), a painting by Hieronymus Bosch portraying the Seven Deadly Sins in medieval (meddy-evil, the Reverend pronounced it, an unholy light in his eyes) indulgence. Under the glass which covered it, Christ stood with one maimed hand upraised, beneath him in rubrics, *Cave, Cave, D^s videt* . . .

—Catholic! said Aunt May, sounding anathema in her voice. She added something about Catholic, or Spanish, vanity anent the mirrors in the arms of the cross. Reverend Gwyon thought it best not to explain their purpose.

As for the distinctly heathen monkey, it was forced to live in the carriage barn.

It is the bliss of childhood that we are being warped most when we know it the least. In the medievally construed parsonage Wyatt graduated from the potty to more exalting porcelain eminence, and learned to pick his nose with his forefinger instead of his thumb. He spent more time indoors than out, and there was a chill in those dim corridors which no change of season dispelled, passages where he was often found wandering aimlessly, or simply standing still, gazing at the grooves in the wainscoting or up at the concave molding, to listen to the creaks that came from the sharp angles of woodwork, to talk to himself repeating words and phrases over and over, and then to move as though he were being watched. He could stand until interrupted by the opening of the study door behind him, and his father's garbled exclamation of surprise at finding him there staring up at the cross mounting the four small mirrors, though he never asked about it; and there was only one hall he avoided, or hurried when he had to pass through it to the dining room, even then with a quick look over his shoulder at Olalla watching, noseless, from her niche, the hand upraised, which he fully expected to strike him from behind as he passed.

—Al-Shira-al-jamânija..., he whispered.

—What? What is it you're saying? Aunt May demanded, rounding a corner.

—Al-Shira-al-jamânija...the bright star of Yemen...

—Where do you hear things like that? she scolded. —Yemen indeed! And she turned him toward the stairs, and sent him up to read in Foxe's *Book of Martyrs*, one of the books provided to prepare him for the Lord's work. From the first time he was asked, —Do you love the Lord Jesus? he was uncomfortably embarrassed; and since hate is an easier concept to embody than love, the Pope trod in far more substantial reality through the frightened corridors of his mind than did the Lord. At such an age, the Blood of the Lamb provoked no pleasant prospect for bathing; and resurrection a dispensable preoccupation for one who had not yet lived. If it was (as she said) in the way of God that he walked with Aunt May, he might only have protested that her horny feet prepared her where his did not: only the exclusive atmosphere of this thorny expedition proved for a time unwholesomely attractive, that, and promise that his mother had already arrived in that intermediate Elysium where he would join her, whither, even then, Aunt May led by a dead reckoning of Orphic proportion. To say nothing of fear, and less of terror, for the jealous God wielded by Aunt May made the sinner's landscape of after-Death more terrible even than his happy life on earth. —The devil finds work for idle hands, she taught him, and —In Adam's fall / We sinned all, with the grim penitence of one who had never had opportunity.

The two of them, father and son, grew away from her in opposite directions. Wyatt grew forward, escaping for the most part in casual innocence any who would hold him back with the selfish nostalgia of love. And his father seemed to find the adventure of daily life more and more trying. Reverend Gwyon retreated from it, by centuries, whenever he could escape to his study, where he sank, inhumed until her voice struck with the sharpness of a gravedigger's pick. As men whose sons are born to them late in life do often, he regarded Wyatt from a wondering distance, saw in his behavior a phantasy of perfect logic demonstrating those parts of himself which had had to grow in secret. It is true they shared confidences, but even these usually centered about oddments from the forepart of Gwyon's mind, topics he might have left a minute before in his study, from Ossian, or Theophrastus, to the Dog Star, a sun whose rising ushered in the inundation of the Nile, Al-Shira-al-jamânija, the star of heat and pestilence, which Gwyon spoke of familiarly when he found himself forced to conversation by the abrupt and even more shy presence of this fragment of himself he kept encountering. He even spoke his son's name unfamiliarly. (But there was reason for that. Months before the boy's birth, he and Camilla had agreed, if it were a son, to name him Stephen; and not until months after their son was born, and Aunt May had peremptorily supplied the name Wyatt from somewhere in the Gwyon genealogy, did they remember. Or rather, Camilla remembered, and though it might have been a safe choice, for the name's sake of the first Christian martyr, even to Aunt May, neither of them mentioned it to her, for baptism had already taken place.)

When questions of discipline arose, Gwyon's face took the look of a man who has been asked a question to which everyone else in the room knows the answer. Or when his son sat whining in disobedience Gwyon stood over him clutching his hands as though restraining the impulse to kill the child, then took him up foreignly by a hand and a foot and swung him back and forth in labored arcs until Wyatt shouted with pleasure.

It was Aunt May who kept the stern measure of the present, unredeemed though it might be, alive to practical purposes, binding the two of them together like an old piece of baling wire.

—Go and ask your father, she said often enough, when questions came up in the reading she thrust upon him. —Ask your father what Homoousian means ... But a good half-hour later she found him, standing still in the hall outside the study door, whispering, —Homoousian? ... Homo-oisian? ...

—What's the matter? Why haven't you ... what is the matter?

And a few minutes later Wyatt was sent to bed for saying he could not move, as though the mirrors in the arms of the cross on the wall had gripped him from behind.

Gwyon came out looking confused, and she explained petulantly. —He comes up with all sorts of fabrications, she went on, seeing her chance, —things he invents and pretends they are *so*, things he picks up Heaven knows where. He's told me about seven heavens, made out of different kinds of metal, indeed!

Last night he said the stars were people's souls, and sorcerers could tell the good from the bad. Sorcerers! He must pick up this drivel from that dirty old man, that...grandfather, indeed! Telling him all sorts of things, witches drawing the moon down from the heavens...

—Umm...yes, Gwyon muttered, his hand on his chin, looking down thoughtfully. —In Thessaly...

—What?

—Eh? Yes, the umm...Thessalian witches, of course, they...

—Do you mean to say you...you're telling him this...filling him full of this nonsense?

—Well, it's...Vergil himself says umm...somewhere in the *Bucolics*...

—And I suppose that you told him that pearls are the precipitate of sunlight, striking through the water...

—The eighth *Bucolic*, isn't it, Carmina vel caelo...

—And he has you to thank, she went on, raising her voice in the dim hall, —for that idiotic story about the Milky Way being the place where light shows through because the solid dome of heaven is badly put together?

—Theophrastus, yes, umm...

—And that tale about the sky being a sea, the celestial sea, and a man coming down a rope to undo an anchor that's gotten caught on a tombstone?...

Gwyon had been attending her with the expression of a man who's come on a bone in a mouthful of fishmeat; now he looked up as though understanding the tenor of her conversation for the first time. He began in a defensive mutter, —Gervase of Tilbury...

—His own father! and a Christian minister, telling him...and I've blamed that foolish old man.

—Why...

—Yes, why shouldn't he be foolish? Falling down a well, and coming up to say he'd seen the stars in broad daylight. Indeed! Of course I thought I had him to thank for that story about evil spirits who keep the path to Paradise dirty, and the path to...to Hell clean to fool good people!

Gwyon, backing into his study, commenced, —Among the Wathi-wathi...

—Wathi-...wathi! she cried out. —Is that a thing for a Christian...

—Is it any worse, Gwyon broke out suddenly, his back to the door, his figure filling the doorway; then he lowered his head and spoke more evenly, —any worse than some of the things you give him to read, the man who jumps into the bramble bush and scratches out both his eyes...

—Children...

—The man of double deed, who sows his field without a seed...

But she'd turned away, her heels already in piercing conflict with the sharp creaks of the wood around her: so her trenchant mumbling almost soothed the chill it rode on, summoning not this but fragments of an earlier conversation she'd luckily interrupted, the Town Carpenter with the boy cornered on the porch, confiding —Your Father thinks the Dog Star is a sun, but I've seen it, of course. I've seen it in daylight. I've seen it in broad daylight, I've seen all the stars in broad daylight, that day I fell into the well. There's too much light during the day, the air's full of it, but get to the bottom of a well, why, I go there still, to look at them, one day I'll take you down with me and you can see them too, the stars in broad daylight...

She got up the stairs, passed a closet jammed with the empty square tin boxes made and stamped with the labels of better days, when the family oatmeal factory had flourished, there she sniffed, settling the glasses on her nose, but did not pause, to enter her room, steady herself in her chair with the first book to hand, and she called Janet, for supper to be brought her there. The book unfortunately proved to be Buffon's *Natural History*, but she sat bound to it, sprung open upon the magot, "generally known by the name of the Barbary Ape. Of all the apes which have no tail, this animal can best endure the temperature of our climate. We have kept one for many years. In the summer it remained in the open air with pleasure; and in the winter, might be kept in the room without any fire. It was filthy, and of a sullen disposition: it equally made use of a grimace to show its anger, or express its sense of hunger: its motions were violent, its manners awkward, and its physiognomy rather ugly than ridiculous. Whenever it was offended, it grinned and showed its teeth..."

That evening Reverend Gwyon ate alone, staring out vacantly over the large dining-room table toward the low table under the window, where his son had finished a little while before.

Unlike children who are encouraged to down their food by the familiar spoon-scraped prize of happy animals cartooned on the bottom of the dish, Wyatt hurried through every drab meal to meet a Deadly Sin. Or occasionally he forgot his food, troubled by the presence of the underclothed Figure in the table's center, which he would stare at with the loveless eyes of childhood until interrupted. After he had been told the meaning of the rubric, he could be heard muttering in those dark hallways, —Cave, cave, Dominus videt.

Even Aunt May, despite her closely embraced anti-Papal inheritance, did not dispute this litany, for she still, like all the women before her, planned another respectable minister in the family. Recent revelations had only prompted her to renew her efforts. Wyatt overheard her one day discussing his future with Janet. The question was whether he would grow up sturdy enough to weather the winters of Lapland, where he would be carrying the Gospel. After that, he never asked the Lord to make him strong and healthy again.

There were several sides she found herself obliged to shield for him, and possible influences to anticipate and combat, in addition to Rome, which he was taught was the greatest agent of evil, poison, and depravity on earth (Aunt May seemed to know the full history of the Papal court at Avignon, the only time she was ever known to use the word brothel). She rehearsed him in the exquisite careers from the *Book of Martyrs*, read aloud to him from Doctor Young's *The Last Day*, and had him read aloud *The Grave* of Blair. Together, they read aloud Bishop Beilby Porteus, *Death*, while she discouraged him from spending time with Janet, from visiting the tenant in the carriage barn, and from going for walks with his grandfather. The parsonage was not a door or two from the church, as is usual, but exposed on a rise almost two blocks away, at the opposite end of town from the direction of the Depot Tavern, an approach guarded by a curve in the highway whose warning arrow pointed the wrong way. It was almost a mile from there to the parsonage, through the short decorous nave of the main street, a mile which the Town Carpenter accomplished quite often and, when he was able and permitted, took his grandson on walks to a recently abandoned bridge works, managing, on these brief excursions, to contribute heavily to the store of "nonsense" which Aunt May battled so valiantly. Between the two men, she could never be quite sure where Wyatt picked up his prattle about griffins' eggs, alchemy, and that shocking, disgusting story about the woman and the bull; but when his curiosity turned upon great voyages, and figures like Kublai Khan, Tamerlane, and Prester John, she knew she had the Town Carpenter to thank.

Now, in the middle hours of a late fall afternoon, she stood on the west porch, pursing her lips, her elbows drawn up in her palms, watching the sky darken above Mount Lamentation. A piercing tinkle from down the hill caused her to draw her elbows in, and close her lips even more tightly. She did not move when she saw Wyatt come round from the entrance to the carriage barn and start up the hill toward her.

It was neither known, nor did anyone (except perhaps the Town Carpenter) trouble to wonder why the Reverend had named the Barbary ape Heracles. Most, in fact, took the easy way of ignorance, and believed the name of the tenant in the carriage barn to be Hercules, easy enough to explain for he was a sturdy fellow over three feet high, light yellowish-brown with a darker line along his cheeks, and parts of his hands and feet naked of hair. He was active, good-tempered, and took up a whole end of the barn with his cavorting and singing. He slept in an old sleigh. When he thought it was mealtime, when he wanted company, or sometimes it seemed had simply the effervescence of some message to communicate, he rang the sleighbells furiously. A white rabbit given him for company proved his gentle nature mawkish. He sat with it cradled in his arms, singing. But his best friend was still the child who came down to give him cod-liver oil from the same bottle and spoon he used himself (a tie Aunt May did not know of), and spent hours devoting confidences to him. Heracles scratched his chin thoughtfully when asked questions, bowing his head in much the same manner, if anyone had noticed it, as Reverend Gwyon did. For at other hours Gwyon came too, always alone, always smelling better than anyone else, the faint freshness of caraway. He asked questions too.

But as he grew older, Heracles sang less often. He took to sitting sullenly in the sleigh looking far beyond the walls of the barn, as though dreaming of days under the Moroccan sun, in another generation, stealing from the gardens of the Arabs. He had never met Aunt May. He knew her thin shape, appearing to hang clothes on the line (where she inclined to hang male and female garments separately, or directed Janet to do so), or coming out alone with a trowel and scissors to tend the hawthorn tree on the edge of the upper lawn. He knew her singing voice too, and he hated it. She had never seen Heracles, and never mentioned him, but drew her lips tightly together and looked in another direction when his name came into conversation. So disquieting to her Christian scheme that she had never mentioned it, nor admitted it even to herself, was the sense that this monkey had replaced Camilla.

—Now where have you been? she demanded as Wyatt came up the steps, but her voice was almost gentle. —And what is the matter, have you been crying? He rubbed his eyes, and then drew his hand down over his face, but did not answer a word. —You look feverish, she said as he took her skirts in the sudden self-effacing embrace of childhood, and thus hobbled, she led him into the house. —Today is your mother's birthday, she said, once inside, and then, —You have dirt all over your hands.

—What is a hero? he asked abruptly, separating himself and looking up at her.

—A hero? she repeated. —A hero is someone who serves something higher than himself with undying devotion.

—But . . . how does he know what it is? he asked, standing there, grinding one grimy hand in the other before her.

—The real hero does not need to question, she said. —The Lord tells him his duty.

—How does He tell him?

—As He told John Huss, she answered readily, seating herself, reaching back with assurance to summon that "pale thin man in mean attire," and she started to detail the career of the great Bohemian reformer, from his teachings and triumphs under the good King Wenceslaus to his betrayal by the Emperor Sigismund.

—And what happened to him then?

—He was burned at the stake, she said with bitter satisfaction, as footsteps were heard in a hall from the direction of the study, —with the Kyrie eleison on his lips...Here, where are you going? What have you been up to...? He had turned away, but Gwyon stood filling the doorway, and between them the child started to cry. Gwyon raised a hand nervously, uncertain whether to punish or defend, and Aunt May took up, —What have you done? I know that guilty look on your face, what is it?

—Go to your room, Gwyon brought out, trying to rescue him.

Aunt May started from her chair with, —To his room!...but Gwyon's upraised hand seemed to halt her, and she turned on the small retreating figure with, —To your room, go to your room then, and read...read what we've been reading, and I'll be up before supper to see if you know it.

—What have you been reading? Gwyon asked her, a strain in his voice.

—He's learning about the Synod of Dort.

—Dort? Gwyon mumbled, dropping his hand.

—Dort. The final perseverance of the saints. Good heavens, you...

—But...the child...

—Did you see the guilty look on his face? His sinful...

—Sinned! Where has he sinned...already...

—That you, as a Christian minister, can ask that? You...Suddenly she came closer to Gwyon, who stepped back into the hall away from the assault of her voice. —Not his sin then, but the prospect, she came on in a hoarse breathless voice, near a whisper, as though she were going to cry out or weep herself, —the prospect draws him on, the prospect of sin.

She stood there quivering, until the sound of Gwyon's footsteps had disappeared back down the hall. Then she sniffed, biting her lower lip, and stepped into the hall herself.

Later that evening Reverend Gwyon stood over the littered desk in his study, staring through the glass at the darkness beyond. —The final perseverance of the saints! he muttered. Then he turned to the door, as though he had heard a sound there. He waited, a hand out to the doorknob, for the faint knock to be repeated, but there was nothing. He had just turned away when he heard a creaking in the corridor, but whether it was someone moving slowly and carefully away, or only renewed betrayal of the constant conflict among those sharp angles of woodwork, he never knew.

The house was large and, perhaps it was the unchanging, ungratified yearning in the face of Camilla on the living-room mantel, eyed from the wall across by the dour John H., it held a sense of bereavement about it, though no one had come or gone for a long time.

While even Aunt May's medieval posture could not credit her stomach as a cauldron where food was cooked by heat from the adjacent liver, she sought evidences of the Lord's displeasure in foreign catastrophes and other people's difficulties, and usually found good reason for it. Among provinces where He retained sway was that of creativity; and mortal creative work was definitely one of His damnedest things. She herself had never gone beyond a sampler, atoning there in word and deed for any presumption she might have made, at the age of ten, in assuming creative powers:

> Jesus permit thy gracious name to stand
> As the first effots of an infants hand
> And while her fingers o'er this canvass move
> Engage her tender heart to seek thy love
> With thy dear children let her share a part
> And write thy name thy self upon her heart

That absent *r* was not, like the flaw in Oriental carpets, an intentional measure of humility introduced to appease the Creator of perfection: she had been upset about it now for half a century, and would have torn out her mistake with her teeth as a child, had not a weary parental hand stopped her. (So she worked NO CROSS NO CROWN in needle-point, still hung unfaded in her room.)

But it was why Wyatt's first drawing, a picture, he said, of a robin, which looked like the letter *E* tipped to one side, brought for her approval, met with —Don't you love our Lord Jesus, after all? He said he did. —Then why do you try to take His place? Our Lord is the only true creator, and only sinful people try to emulate Him, she went on, her voice sinking to that patient tone it assumed when it promised most danger. —Do you remember Lucifer? who Lucifer is?

—Lucifer is the morning star, he began hopefully, —Father says...

—Father says!... her voice cut him through. —Lucifer was the archangel who refused to serve Our Lord. To sin is to falsify something in the Divine Order, and that is what Lucifer did. His name means Bringer of Light but he was not satisfied to bring the light of Our Lord to man, he tried to steal the power of Our Lord and to bring his own light to man. He tried to become original, she pronounced malignantly, shaping that word round the whole structure of damnation, repeating it, crumpling the drawing of the robin in her hand, —original, to steal Our Lord's authority, to command his own destiny, to bear his own light! That is why Satan is the Fallen Angel, for he rebelled when he tried to emulate Our Lord Jesus. And he won his own domain, didn't he. Didn't he! And his own light is the light of the fires of Hell! Is that what you want? Is that what you want? Is that what you want?

There may have been, by now, many things that Wyatt wanted to do to Jesus: emulate was not one of them. Nonetheless it went on. He made drawings in secret, and kept them hidden, terrified with guilty amazement as forms took shape under his pencil. He wrapped some in a newspaper and buried them behind the carriage barn, more convinced, as those years passed, and his talent blossomed and flourished with the luxuriance of the green bay tree, that he was damned. Once, digging back there, he came upon the rotted remains of the bird he had killed that day he had burst into tears at Aunt May's conjectural challenge and punishment, the vivid details of the Synod of Dort: even that evening he had gone to his father's study to try to confess it, for it had, after all, been an accident (he had thrown a stone at the wren, and could not believe it when he hit it square, and picked it up dead). But when there was no answer to his first faint tapping on the study door, he retreated. Just as now, he almost went to his father to confess, in a last hope of being saved; but he had since learned from Aunt May that there was no more hope for the damned than there was fear for the Elect. And his father, withdrawing into his study with a deftness for absenting himself at crucial moments akin to that talent of the Lord, had become about as unattainable.

The earth behind the carriage barn was broken often enough that Wyatt, burying there still another package of drawings, would turn up the moldering guilt of years before. Even as he grew older, and might have burned them, he found himself unable to do so. He continued to bury them, around near the kitchen midden, as though they might one day be required of him.

Eventually Aunt May permitted him to copy, illustrations from some of the leather-bound marathons of suffering and disaster on her shelf; but even she had no notion of the extent of his work. It was hardly original, but derived from the horror of the Breughel copy in his father's study, and the pitilessness of the Bosch, promoting an articulate imagination which any Flemish primitive might have plumbed to advantage. Unlike the healthy child who devises ingenious tortures for small animals, Wyatt elaborated a domain where the agony of man took remarkable directions, and the underclothed Figure from the center of the Bosch table suffered a variety of undignified afflictions.

Transportation and communication advanced, bringing to Aunt May's door the woes of the world, a world which she saw a worse thing daily.

She put aside the Bible only for excursions among the *Lives, Sufferings, and Triumphant Deaths of the Primitive Protestant Martyrs from the Introduction of Christianity to the Latest Periods of Pagan, Popish, and Infidel Persecutions* ("embellished with engravings"), and such recent prophets as stood her in stead of newspapers. She read interpretations of the eleventh-century Malachi prophecy (on the Popes, of which only seven remained to come, and with the seventh the destruction of Rome) with the avidity of someone reading the morning's news, the same enthusiasm she brought to the *Penetralia* of Andrew Jackson Davis (who could see the interior of objects), the same hunger that she brought to William Miller, satisfied as he was a century before that the end of the world was at hand, as evidence continued to "flow in from every quarter. 'The earth is reeling to and fro like a drunkard.' At this dread moment look! The clouds have burst asunder; the heavens appear; the great white throne is in sight! Amazement fills the Universe with awe! He comes! He comes! Behold the Saviour comes!"

She waited, thumbing the Revelation of Saint John the Divine, which she read as a literal transcription of the march of science, a parade led off by Darwin which had trod on simian feet throughout her life. She spent more time with Janet; or rather, she had Janet spend more time with her. After her original disapproval of the kitchen girl had been firmly established, Aunt May worked her toward salvation with every discouragement she could supply. Janet was willing. She was, indeed, far on the way to that simple-mindedness which many despairingly intelligent people believe requisite for entering the kingdom of Heaven. This quality might prevent her from grasping some of the more complicated arcana which Aunt May tendered, still there was room for the residence of terror in the collapsing tenement of her mind. Darwin soon became as real to her as the Pope, the one resembling Heracles, the other triple-headed. From the carriage barn, the jingle of sleighbells reached them both. Aunt May, believing that she shut them out, hid them from herself in that part of her mind which turned upon her in dreams; Janet seemed to rush out to meet the hellish tinkling, and it was only on waking that her dreams began. But of all the distress that Janet endured, most persistent was her body's revenge on her attempt to disdain it. At first, hardly knowing how man and woman differed, she accepted the changes which grew upon her with no more regret than life itself produced. It was Aunt May who called her attention to the darkening of her chin, and asked questions of such profound delicacy that, when confirmed, the consternation which descended upon the questioner was only equaled in that household by her reception of the news of the Scopes trial in distant Tennessee. Of that she could hardly speak, but sat shaking her head over Buffon's *Natural History*, reading again and again the article there on the animals called pygmies, and waiting, as though what she was waiting for was a secret from everyone but herself and her Creator.

Aunt May gradually withdrew from the affairs of the household, reading the Bible aloud to herself in her room, her voice only a sound barely broken by articulation. In this monotone it became so familiar a part of the house, that one paused when it was deflected, hearing it rise in pleading argument to the challenge of absolutes, —*I am* the Resurrection and the Life..., so plaintive that it seemed querulous, fearful not of doubting but of even admitting for an instant such existential possibility. Then the glimpse of humility was done, and the voice recovered the somnambulance of certitude.

She waited, her hair bobbed (not worn so for fashion from the outside world, where flappers were ushering it into smart society from the bawdy houses, where all fashions originate, but) in the clean shingles of a state hospital, always in the same trim arrangement, raising a clinically unsympathetic mirror to snip hairs from her nostrils. —This would be your grandfather's birthday, she told Wyatt, on May Day. —He would be eighty-six today, if he were alive, she added. She had been talking about John Huss a minute before, and looking the lean pale boy up and down, when he, for whom King Wenceslaus in that story bore striking resemblance to the Town Carpenter, broke out,

—But Grandfather, I ... I saw him yesterday...

—Your father's father, she corrected him sharply, but her voice broke, almost bitter as she looked away, not for the death of her brother but to insinuate that he had abandoned her in this bondage of mortality. She talked to Wyatt familiarly of death, as though to take him with her would be the kindest expression of her love for him possible: still, she never spoke directly of death, never named it so, but continued to treat it with the euphemistic care reserved elsewhere for obscenity.

—And this? she appeared one morning in the study door poised rigid, dangling forth a pamphlet between forefinger and opposable thumb, —tell me how *this* got among *my* things? As though there might have been movement in the air, the pamphlet fluttered open, quaking its suspended title: *Breve Guida della Basilica di San Clemente.* In his chair, Gwyon startled, to reach for it, but stayed held at bay by her unpliant arm, and unyielding eyes which had fixed the distance between them. With a single shudder he freed his own eyes from hers and fixed them on the pamphlet, to realize that it was indeed not being offered in return but rather in evidence: not an instant of her stringent apparition suggested surrender. —Another souvenir from Spain! she accused, a page headed in bold face *La Basilica Sotterranea Dedicata alla memoria di S Clemente Papa e Martire* fled under her thumb. —Pictures of

Spanish idols, ... fragments of Byzantine fresco captioned *Nostra Signora col Gesù Bambino* almost caught her attention, —Catholic images ... Another page fell over from the hand quivering at her arm's length, and bringing her foot a step past the sill she held it out that space closer to him: nothing moved. But the sill's sharp creak underfoot penetrated, a signal for her to hurl it at him, or down; for him to leap and snatch it. But nothing moved until she retired recovering her advance, and spoke with bitter calm, looking square at the thing, —A nice ... place of worship! The illustration pinioned by her gaze was captioned *Il Tempio di Mitra*. —Look at it! a dirty little underground cave, no place to kneel or even sit down, unless you could call this broken stone bench a pew? She got her breath when he interposed, —But ... —And the altar! look at it, look at the picture on it, a man ... god? and it looks like a bull!

—Yes, a pagan temple, they've excavated and found the basilica of Saint Clement was built right over a temple where worshipers of ...

—Pagan indeed! And I suppose you couldn't resist setting foot inside yourself? Did you? Again she paused, getting breath she appeared to prepare requital for his answer, admission or denial, and when he withdrew mumbling only —Set foot inside myself ... ? she snapped immediately, —At least I have finally had the satisfaction of hearing you call the Roman Catholic Church *pagan!* She filled her grievous gaze a moment longer with the picture, and finishing with —Now that we all know what the inside of a Catholic church looks like, ... she was gone, holding the abhorrent memento at arm's length, her eyes alert upon it, as though it might take life and strike.

Gwyon came slowly forward in his chair, hands clenched on nothing, listening to her sharp footsteps receding toward the kitchen. He waited until he heard them on the stairs, then hurried to the kitchen himself. Janet came in a few minutes later to find him sifting through the kitchen trashbin; but he went out without a word, and empty-handed. And when at lunch he once or twice faltered toward questioning her she looked up and beyond him and the room, as though listening to a confidence, or a summons, from far away.

For the most part, conversation seemed to pass over her, when she would stop it in its tracks to rescue something which struck her. Few things seemed to stir her pleasantly but news of unhappy occurrences in Italy: whether storms or strikes or railway accidents, she saw imminent in them the fall of Rome. She waited, contemplating wholesale damnation for the whole non-Christian world with an eye as level as that of Saint Bonaventura: no more mother than he, the prospect of eternal roasting for millions of unbaptized children did not bring the flutter of an eyelash: "The sight of the pains of the damned heaps up the measure of the accidental joys of the righteous," and with his words on her own lips, she firmly expected to see Saint Bonaventura heaping her own measure in the Life ahead. But even that torrid landscape chilled and shattered, pierced by the sleighbells, more pointed for their infrequency, to stop her breath if she were speaking, or raise her voice to the defense when she read.

—It's all right indeed, all right for a man who goes to bullfights! she brought out next day at table, summoning this distant detail to interrupt the conversation between father and son. —Bringing a . . . a creature like that back from Africa, there should be a law against it.

—Creature? Gwyon repeated.

—That creature you brought back, that's what you're talking about isn't it. Isn't it?

—I was telling . . . talking about that painting, there, the table under the window.

—There ought to be a law against it, bringing back creatures like that.

—Oh, oh Heracles, yes, you mean, it's forbidden, yes, taking them from Gibraltar, he commenced, confused, answering.

—Breaking the law, proud of yourself! Her glasses went blank with light as she returned her attention to her plate; and Wyatt, after the pause of her absenting herself, asked:

—How were you certain it was the original? Suppose . . .

—That took some . . . umm . . . conniving, getting it through customs. It's prohibited, you know, taking works of art out of Italy . . .

—Italy! Aunt May cut in across the table. —You never told me you had been in Italy! Never. You never told me that!

—Strange I never mentioned it, Gwyon said.

—Mentioned! You never told me, she said getting up from the table.

—What earthly difference . . .

—Earthly! No earthly difference, as you say. No earthly difference, at all. For someone who tells stories about evil spirits who deceive good people by keeping the path to Paradise littered with filth, no earthly difference at all, she went on nearing the door. —At least you spared Camilla that! she finished, and was gone. Gwyon left the table a moment later, with a mutter of apology to his son, though he did not look up at him, and went out to the porch, where he stood looking straight up at the sun.

On pleasant days, such as this was, Aunt May still went out to tend her hawthorn tree. This afternoon, when she came in from it, she was impressively silent. Gwyon might have thought it was the Italian incident, but she said quietly, —I saw a moor hen this afternoon. (The moor cock was their family crest.) —And no male anywhere in sight. I have not seen a male moor hen for years.

Though slow, she still moved with energy. Her world had finally shrunk to her books and her hawthorn tree. When questions of foreign suddenness were asked she looked up startled and afraid, as though some worldly circumstance might intrude upon her preparations for departure. As the days passed, she sang in a weak voice which she believed maintained a tune, a hymn which, as she remembered, came to her from John Wesley, expressing her divine longing, ready sometimes, it seemed, like Saint Teresa, "to die of not being able to die."

—O beautiful aspect of death
What sight on earth is so fair
What pageant, what aspect of life
Can with a dead body compare,

came her wail on the vivid spring air to the ears of living things.

She put an old smock over her housedress and tied a shielding bonnet to her head. Over the morning grass alive with creatures smaller than its own blades her old garden shoes trod. A robin took to the air before her as she approached the hawthorn tree, torn from the ground and lying flat, pink blossoms among the weeds. Her voice in its singing stopped in disbelief. Frantically she raised the tree and pushed it back into the open earth at a dead angle. Then she came back to the house, and before she reached it the tree had fallen again.

Heracles had got loose the night before. The Town Carpenter, who met him outside the Depot Tavern, brought him back, and tried to replant the tree. But it was no good. The tree was dead before the week was out, and so was Aunt May.

She was sixty-three. It was not, in her case, a ripe age, but quite the other way, a systematic reduction of unfertile years and thoughts, disapprobation, generally a life bounded by terms of negation, satisfied with its resistance to any temptation which might have borne fruit. Better to marry than to burn, but she had not been forced to that pusillanimous choice: gnarled, she stepped from one virginity to another without hesitation. Here, three centuries after Dort, her face wore a firm look of Election, as though she knew where she was going, had visited there many times before. She seemed in a hurry to be gone from that body, as any vain soul well might have been, the still fingers faded under the framed flush of NO CROSS NO CROWN. Surrounded by closed books, with Buffon's *Natural History* on the floor, they found that body in her chair where she had left it when she fled, unequivocally abandoned, as though not even the last trumpet could summon her to take it up again. Her last words were, —I believe I put it in the top bureau drawer. They looked there afterward, but found only the white round shell box with a hole in its top, into which she had used to put dead hair when she combed it out.

Wyatt was twelve, and deeply impressed by the funeral sermon his father spoke over that anonymous box where Aunt May, in a lavender gown she had never before worn, lay with the lid closed, a stipulation as importunate as that of the Blessed Umiliana (another devotee of quicklime) having her socks put on, with her last breath, so that the crowd could not venerate her nude feet.

—"O man, consider thyself! Here thou standest in the earnest perpetual strife of good and evil," Reverend Gwyon thundered the lines of William Law down upon the gray faces (whose owners, years later when he was locked up, defenseless, recalled it as the last truly Christian sermon he had ever read). —"All nature is continually at work to bring forth the great redemption; the whole creation is travailing in pain and laborious working to be delivered from the vanity of time; and wilt thou be asleep? Everything thou hearest or seest says nothing, shows nothing to thee but what either eternal light or eternal darkness has brought forth; for as day and night divide the whole of our time, so heaven and hell divide all our thoughts, words, and actions. Stir which way thou wilt, do or design what thou wilt, thou must be an agent with the one or the other. Thou canst not stand still, because thou livest in the perpetual workings of temporal and eternal nature; if thou workest not with the good, the evil that is in nature carries thee along with it. Thou hast the height and depth of eternity in thee and therefore, be doing what thou wilt, either in the closet, the field, the shop or the church, thou art sowing that which grows and must be reaped in eternity."

Three years later, that partisan Deity whose most recent attention to the family had been Aunt May's rescue from mortality, acted in Wyatt's direction (though, as the boy and his father independently suspected, perhaps it was a different God altogether). Wyatt was taken with a fever which burned him down to seventy-nine pounds. In this refined state he was exhibited to medical students in the amphitheater of a highly endowed hospital. They found it a very interesting case, and said so. In fact they said very little else. Physicians, technicians, and internes X-rayed the boy from every possible angle, injected his arms with a new disease they believed they could cure, took blood by the bottleful from one arm to investigate, and poured the blood of six other people into the other. They collected about his bed and pounded him, tapped his chest, thrust with furious hands for his liver, pumped his stomach with a lead-weighted tube, kneaded his groin, palped his spleen, and recorded the defiant beats of his heart with electric machinery.

He was embarrassed by the flocks of fingers exploring for cancer, or something as satisfactory, and mortified when photographed in despoiled nudity by a handsome nurse. The hands of these young women were the first ever to reach him with the succor of indifferent love; and two he would never forget, though he never saw her to whom they belonged. He lay in an operating room staring at the lamp above him, reading the circle of words in its center, *Carl Zeiss, Jena, Carl Zeiss Jena Carl Zeiss*... while a surgeon's insistently clumsy fingers dug in an incision under his arm for a node which slipped from their grasp. The hands of the nurse at his head wiped his face with a damp cloth, and when he fainted were there with aromatic spirits to revive him: so the woman's hands kept him, and the man's eventually caught the node, took it out, sewed up that hole and descended to make another in the leg where they paused on the surface to slice off a piece of mottled skin, then entered to probe and remove a fragment of muscle. A zealous young interne, Doctor Fell, ran a needle into his backbone and tapped that precious fluid. Week after week, he continued to provide an outlet for this conspiracy of unconscionable talents and insatiable curiosity.

Reverend Gwyon took all this in a dim view. As his son lay dying of a disease about which the doctors obviously knew nothing, injecting him with another plague simply because they had it on familiar terms could only be the achievement of a highly calculated level of insanity. Wyatt's arms swelled at each point of injection. The doctors nodded, in conclave, indicating that science had foreseen, even planned, this distraction. From among them came Doctor Fell with a scalpel in his hand and a gleam in his eye seldom permitted at large in civilized society, a gleam which the Reverend recalled having seen in the eye of a Plains Indian medicine man, whose patient regarded it respectfully as part of the professional equipment assembled to kill him. With the bravura of a young buck in an initiation ceremony, he slashed the arms open at each point of infection. Dr. Fell did a good job. They drained for two months.

Winter thawed into sodden spring, cruel April and depraved May reared and fell behind, and the doctors realized that this subject was nearing exhaustion, might, in fact, betray them by escaping to the dissection table. A few among them bravely submitted, in the interests of science, new experiments and removals; but during Wyatt's prolonged residence many comparatively healthy people had been admitted to the hospital, and were waiting in understandable impatience to make their own vital contributions to the march of science. With serious regret, the doctors drew their sport to a close, by agreeing on a name for it: *erythema grave*. After this crowning accomplishment they completed the ritual by shaking hands, exchanging words of professional magic, mutual congratulation and reciprocal respect, and sent the boy home to die.

In the parsonage, Wyatt lay perspiring freely in his sheets. At one moment his muscles and the joints of his body were so filled with pain that he would deliberate for minutes before moving a limb, or turning over. At other times he was feverishly awake, and the books stacked round him could not hold his exhausted attention. Their titles ran from Doughty's *Travels in Arabia Deserta* to *A Coptic Treatise Contained in the Codex Brucianus*, the *Rosarium Philosophorum*, two books of Dante's *Divine Comedy*, Wyer's *De Præstigiis Dæmonum*, Llorente's *Inquisition d'Espagne*, the pages of these and all the rest littered in the margins with notations in Reverend Gwyon's hand. Gwyon had brought them up, one by one, meaning them to serve for conversation, which he found difficult; but once arrived in the sickroom he would stand passing the book nervously from one hand to the other until asked about it. He would look down, as though surprised to find it in his hands, a moment later be talking about it with a fervor which gradually became agitation, until he left off altogether and handed it over, as shy at the idea of trying to press on his son things which so interested him, as he was excited at the possibility of sharing them with him. Then he might simply stand, trying to keep one hand still in the other behind him, while he stared at the floor, in the acute embarrassment of this intimacy which the sickness had created between them. On the other hand, Wyatt read as much as he could, to prepare for these conversations which gave his father such pleasure, to break the silences whose strain showed so readily in that flushed face, and the short exhalations tainted with the sweet freshness of caraway. Sometimes Gwyon simply turned and rushed out of the room, with as much restraint as he could manage until he reached the door, as he did one day when he espied a stained familiar pamphlet among his son's papers on the floor. —Where did this come from! he demanded snatching it up open on a picture of a wreathed papal monogram tied at the foot with an anchor. —I found it, in the rubbish, on the rubbish heap, Wyatt faltered, —the kitchen midden years ago, behind the carriage barn. He stared at the covetous look on his father's face. —I didn't know... —And you've kept it, yes, all this time, kept it for me? Gwyon brought out without looking up from it, turning the spotted pages. —Did you read it? —Just, the Italian was difficult, I didn't know all the words, but the pictures... that? that monogram, with the anchor? —Yes, Gwyon murmured catching it under his thumb, —Clement's monogram, he was martyred, yes here, gettato a mare con un'ancora ...they tied an anchor to his neck and threw him into the Black Sea.

—Yes into the sea with an anchor? like the man you told me about? The anchor caught on a tombstone, and the man coming down the rope in the celestial sea to free it, and he drowned? Listen,... But Gwyon, fearing the insistent monotone that crept into the boy's voice for the delirium it might forebode, hurried out of the room studying the picture of the subterranean sanctuary discovered beneath the basilica of Saint Clement of Rome, a sudden light in his eyes as though his senses were afloat with vapors from two thousand years before.

Gwyon's entrances were often as precipitous as this escape; and there were times Wyatt pretended to be asleep when he heard his father's approach upon the stairs.

When he could not read, he painted, with an extraordinary deftness which consumed his whole consciousness, and often left him so tense that he passed into delirium. —Listen, I . . . what was it? Listen . . .

It was the deliria that Gwyon feared, which left him doubly helpless, trying to conceal his anxiety behind his back in one hand twisting the other, and he hastened to call Janet who was, a good part of the time now, the only moving thing in the house. She remained, gibbering testimony to Aunt May's inquisition.

So far as anyone knew, she never left the house. Her voice had gained the timbre of that of a grown man when she raised it in the full volume of speech. But this was infrequent. She usually spoke in a hoarse whisper, lubricated by a salivary flow which she had difficulty controlling (and caused, though she did not know it, by a medicine compounded of mercury which she'd found in Aunt May's cabinet, renewed and taken reverently in uniform overdose since Aunt May's death). Her shoulders were broad, thighs narrowed, and with squarely muscular hands she plied an emery cloth to remove the fine filaments which darkened her chin.

In any other native household, her regular absences from her work, or those occasions which found her insensibly rigid before an empty window, or prostrate on the kitchen floor, might have been taken for organic disorders; and, like the Venerable Orsola Benincasa, whose sixteenth-century childhood was visited by innumerable misinterpreted ecstasies, she might have been bruised black-and-blue, pricked with needles, and burned with exposed flames to rouse her. But Reverend Gwyon remarked to himself that her derelictions from duty had occurred most notably during Easter week of that year: that about eight o'clock on Thursday evening, in the midst of serving his dinner, she was numbly entranced before the kitchen stove; and the following afternoon at three he almost upset her in the dark passage outside his study door, where she stood limbs immobilely extended before the cruz-con-espejos.

When modern devices fail, it is our nature to reach back among the cures of our fathers. If those fail, there were fathers before them. We can reach back for centuries. Gwyon appreciated the extended hands of his people less and less as the months passed. The doctors refused him information of any direct nature, guarding the frail secrets of their failing magic as carefully as Zuñi priests planting prayer sticks. And then there was that hallowed tribal agreement among them never to admit one another's mistakes, which they called Ethics.

On the other, the spiritual, hand, the congregation breathed out stale prayers for the boy's recovery. But in the end they always gave their God full leave to do as He wished, to remove the lad if such were His sacred whim, loading the fever-stricken boy with the guilt it had taken them generations to accumulate. They called this Humility.

The sermons thundered at them from the pulpit of their peaceful church increased in violence, and embraced expiatory petitions to the Lord their God less and less frequently. Still the gray faces continued to appear, drawn by duty and (though none but the Town Carpenter might have admitted it) a sort of perilous curiosity. The tension mounted, until the sermon on the evils of vivisection, on the morning of June twenty-fourth, after which the Reverend retired for the rest of the summer.

That Sunday morning, Saint John's, or, as the Reverend reminded them in a deceptively peaceful voice, Midsummer Day, the simple altar was decorated with flowered sprigs of oak trees. The warm light of the sun stretched in long empty patterns from the diamond-shaped panes across the congregation. Someone's liver-and-white hound appeared and tussled briefly with the bell-rope, came part way down the aisle, and then sensing something turned and fled.

The sermon, meanwhile, had progressed from vivisection to the Mojave Indians, —among whom it is humbly understood, and I quote from foremost authority, "to be the nature of doctors to kill people in this way just as it is in the nature of hawks to kill little birds for a living." Among the Mojaves, it is believed that everyone dead under the doctor's hand falls under his power in the next life. Superstition? It is what we, gathered here today in the sight of God, call superstition. We call such people as those benighted savages, and send missionaries among them, to enlighten them with the word of Truth we are gathered together to worship here today. For centuries, missionaries have brought back stories to make us blanch with horror, stories of human sacrifice practiced in the interests of religion on the bloodstained altars of the Aztecs. Yet we support in our very midst a highly respected class of men who are Aztecs in their own right. Like ourselves, they may throw up their hands at the thought of murdering a maiden on a stone altar. But it is only that this was done to serve a god different from their own, that shocks them. We may find them wringing their hands in reproach against those who roasted Saint Lawrence on a gridiron: Is it the roasting they regret? Is it the suffering of Saint Catherine on the wheel? The choking cries of Tyndale being strangled? The muffled words of forgiveness on the lips of John Huss at the stake . . . those of Our Lord on the Cross . . . O Sancta simplicitas! No! They regret simply that none of these experiments was carried out under the scientific conditions of a medical pathological laboratory. (He had already gone ten minutes beyond the time usually allotted to the sermon, but the gray faces were bound in wonder.) —Tell me, how did Asclepius end? he demanded, reaching his turning point. —Asclepius, the Greek god of medicine. Why, Zeus slew him with a thunderbolt! But we mortals, what are we allowed? Not even as little as John of Bohemia, who threw his surgeon into the river when he failed to cure the king's blindness. No terms, like the Hungarian king five centuries ago, who could promise full reward to the surgeon who cured his arrow wound, with death if he failed. No, we turn them loose, with money in their pockets, and expressions of deep respect for their failures. The same trust, and confidence, perhaps, that Saint Cyril had for the physician who cut out his liver and ate it, . . . that Pope Innocent VIII had in the physician who prescribed the blood of three small children for His Holiness' nerves, . . . of Cardinal Richelieu, on his deathbed, given horse dung in white wine . . . Have you noticed, he went on, lowering his voice, leaning toward them over the high pulpit, —the charm that doctors wear? A cross? No. In the very name of Heaven, no! It is a device called the caduceus. Look closely . . . two serpents coupling round a wand, the scepter of a pagan god, the scepter of Hermes. Hermes, the patron of eloquence and cunning, of trickery and theft, the very wand he carried when he conducted souls to Hell. (The organist, an alert young man, fingered the pages of the next hymn and made sure there was air in the bellows.) And when Reverend Gwyon hit the pulpit with the flat of his hand and raised his voice from the crisp confidence he had just given to commence a new inventory of the achievements of the medical profession, beginning with —Who was it that suggested the use of the guillotine in the French Revolution, but a doctor who died under its own blade! . . . there was a cheer from the far end of the nave, a moment of unholy silence, and the organ lusted into *Rock of Ages* as the Town Carpenter left hurriedly from one end of the church (in the direction of the Depot Tavern), and Reverend Gwyon, shaking but steadily, left from the other.

A stirring sermon, everyone agreed; as they agreed that their minister was tired, and might do well to rest for the summer. He was undergoing a severe trial, and they gave him credit for that, as practicing Christians magnanimously sharing their sins approve the suffering of another.

*

Janet's jaw dropped with concentration, —Listen. When the seed began to blow, 'Twas like a garden full of snow, I . . . didn't . . . mean . . . Father? A safe-conduct from the Emperor Sigismund, but you see how they betrayed him? Keeping the road to Paradise littered with filth, to deceive good people. Limited atonement, total depravity, . . . wait. Unconditional election, limited atonement, total depravity, ah . . . ahhm . . . irresistibility of grace, I didn't mean . . . Father? I . . . what was it? Listen . . .

—The power of God to guide me, Janet whispered, —the might of God . . .

—If you want proof, if you want proof, listen Father. That . . . and that wren, I didn't mean . . . Father? Father? . . .

—The wisdom of God to teach me, the eye of God to watch over me, Janet went on, leaving the bedside to run down the stairs and pound on the study door, a thing she had never done, but this time she brought Reverend Gwyon bounding back up after her, to listen to his son's broken disjointed confession of killing the wren that day, a confession which broke off and left the boy sitting bolt upright in the bed, his teeth chattering, blazing green eyes fixed on his father. Gwyon started to put a hand out, but withdrew it, saying, —A wren though, a wren? My boy, that . . . why, a wren, you know, the missionaries themselves, the early Christian missionaries used to have it hunted down, hunted down and killed, they . . . the wren was looked on as a king, and that . . . they couldn't have that, . . . around Christmas . . . they couldn't have that, he finished, withdrawing slowly, his voice trailing off as his son sank back on the bed, and Gwyon turned abruptly and hurried back downstairs to his study, where he bolted the door and reached to a bookshelf for the works of Saint John of the Cross.

—The ear of God to hear me, the word of God to speak for me . . . Janet paused, at the bedside, to listen to the church bell ringing the hour. But like those on the pillow before her, her lips kept moving.

Hidden from people and the declining sun by the heavy green of the yew trees, Gwyon kept to his study. He was reaching back.

The longest day of the year was passed, and long past the annual Midsummer Day magic of bonfires to impel the sun on its suddenly flagging course, a measure despaired of, when religion took the reins, faith the ritual, and the day was turned over to Saint John Baptist who, in return for these same bonfires, rid cattle of sickness and banished the witches who caused it, raised splendid harvests, and even brought rain in Russia to the families of women who bathed on his day there (though faith had not quite won the day there:

if drought continued, rain could certainly be brought by tossing into the nearest lake the corpse of a villager who had drunk himself to death). But in New England rain fell according to the caprice of a Divine who was to be propitiated only by making good use of it, and feast days, such as this Sunday, were best spent in the reverent complacency of sitting still. The outdoors was still light after suppertime, though Gwyon had refused supper from behind his study door, and Wyatt ate scarcely a bite before he lay back, whispering at the ceiling, leaving Janet contorted in prayer beside him. All day she had moved through the halls, on the stairs, to the kitchen in near silence, the only sounds to betray her to man the slavering lisps of her higher devotion which she exercised now: —The hand of God to protect me, the way of God to lie before me, the shield of God to shelter me, the host of God to defend me, Christ with me Christ before me Christ behind me Christ within me . . .

Birds ran on the empty lawns of the parsonage pecking at fallen irregular shapes of unripe crab apples. Swallows cut silent erratic courses above the carriage barn. The only clear sound was the sound of the sleighbells.

—Christ beneath me Christ above me Christ at my right Christ at my left Christ in breadth Christ in length Christ in height . . . Wyatt lay full length on his back, listening without hearing, staring without seeing at the familiar lines on the ceiling, a network of cracks which had formed an Arabian camel in childhood, since become Bactrian and grown a long tail. The windows were opened, and the whole house so silent that the warmth of day seemed even to have penetrated the dim corridors and set at rest the creaking contention among those dark angles of woodwork. Thus the sound from the carriage barn came inside interrupted only by its own impatient pauses. It was these clinking splinters of sound which suddenly seemed to penetrate Janet, raise her from her bedside attitude and lift her away to her own room, where no one but she had entered bodily since she first entered it herself. Her door closed, closeting the stifled sound which escaped her as she sank to the floor.

It was almost an hour from dark. Gwyon stared at the branches arm's length through the study window. From beyond those lacings of yew came the sound of the sleighbells, seeming more insistent with the approaching darkness. His arm rested as though lifeless on the Egyptian *Book of the Dead;* and he tapped the hard closed cover of the *Malleus Maleficarum* with his fingertip. Hardly moving in his chair, he took the flask from its cavity in the *Dark Night of the Soul,* and drank down half a tumblerful of schnapps. He placed the empty glass on the level surface of a volume of the *Index,* and said aloud, after a few minutes had passed so, —Make full proof of thy ministry. But the book open before him was not the Bible, nor the words Saint Paul's.

"Close to the outskirts of every big village a number of stones may be noticed stuck into the ground, apparently without order or method. These are known by the name of *asong*, and on them is offered the sacrifice which the Asongtata demands. The sacrifice of a goat takes place, and a month later that of a *langur* (*Entellus* monkey) or a bamboo-rat is considered necessary. The animal chosen has a rope fastened round its neck and is led by two men, one on each side of it, to every house in the village. It is taken inside each house in turn, the assembled villagers, meanwhile, beating the walls from the outside, to frighten and drive out any evil spirits which may have taken up their residence within. The round of the village having been made in this manner, the monkey or rat is led to the outskirts of the village, killed by a blow of a *dao*, which disembowels it, and then crucified on bamboos set up in the ground. Round the crucified animal long, sharp bamboo stakes are placed, which form *chevaux de frise* round about it. These commemorate the days when such defences surrounded the villages on all sides to keep off human enemies, and they are now a symbol to ward off sickness and dangers to life from the wild animals of the forest. The *langur* required for the purpose is hunted down some days before, but should it be found impossible to catch one, a brown monkey may take its place; a hulock may not be used."

He walked up the stairs slowly. Wyatt slept, the sheet covering him rose to points on the bony protrusions of his body. Only faintly aware of the trouble in his mind over the apparent extreme shortness of the boy's legs, Gwyon suddenly brought this terrible impression straight up into his consciousness and, doing so, realized that the points of the sheet were not Wyatt's feet but his knees, so thin they stood up like feet. He moved quickly. He turned down the stairs, and walked from one room to another in the darkened parsonage, past the small butler's pantry where Aunt May had stood weeping silently and alone that day her hawthorn tree had been found torn from the ground. He passed Olalla, her nose broken off a century before by a suppliant whose prayers had gone unheeded, her arm raised in her niche as though to stay him. For an instant fragments of his passing were reflected in the powerful clear mirrors of that cruz-con-espejos said to have been used by Sor Patrocinio, the Bleeding Nun, whose pullulating stigmata upset Spanish politics and the throne to such extent that she inclined to wear mittens. Gwyon glanced in at the low table in the dining room, mesa de los pecados mortales, —Cave, cave, Dominus videt. Abscondam faciem meam ab eis et considerabo novissima eorum, not reading those words but repeating under his breath, as though to give himself strength, words of that fourteenth-century translator of the Bible who died in bed, only to be dug up and burned, already rewarded for his labor of Divine Love with the revelation, —In this world God must serve the devil.

In the living room, he turned away from Camilla's picture, where he had stopped, and took John H. down from the wall across. That portrait he put in a broom closet, muttering that the ancestor had probably got just what he deserved. All this time it seemed that Gwyon was putting off a decision which had already been made. He even stopped to cover a large mirror with a table-cloth. Finally he walked out to the back veranda of the house, and down onto the lawn.

Perhaps it was prospect of the white moon's rising which had upset Her-acles. The sleighbells sounded furiously, and then stopped, leaving an urgent silence. Gwyon was perspiring freely as he paced toward the arbor and back, in spite of the cool night air mounting around him. Then he stopped for a full minute to look toward the shadowed hulk of Mount Lamentation.

When he went in at the carriage-barn doors, Heracles stood still, quivering his long arms slightly, and then came up to his full height, waving a piece of bread. Gwyon took the leash from the wall, fastened it to the animal's neck and together they walked up the lawn toward the house.

Afterwards Wyatt could not distinguish reality in these days, and the nights of the weeks just past. Deliria embraced in his memory, and refused to discriminate themselves from one another, from what had happened, and what might have happened. Memories of pain were lost between waking and sleep, and but for the merciless stabbing in his feet that night, no longer identified themselves with definite parts of his body. Prolonged hours of wakefulness, when all he sought was sleep, might turn out to have been sleep when he waked: but most insupportable was the sensational affair which went something like this: consciousness, it seemed, was a succession of separate particles, being carried along on the surface of the deep and steady unconscious flow of life, of time itself, and in fainting, the particles of consciousness sim-ply stopped, and the rest flowed on, until they were restored: but this was the stoppage, the entire disappearance of that deeper flow which left the particles of consciousness suspended, piling up, ready any instant to shatter with noth-ing to support them. Still, at such times everything was in order, of shape and color to mass and distance, of minutes accomplishing hours by accumulation just as the clock itself stayed on the table where it was if only because it had been accumulating there for so long: that was the reassurance of weight. But had a voice, even his own, quoted, —"With regard to Saint Joseph of Coper-tino Rapture was accompanied by Levitation"? The grating cry of Janet rang in his ears still: had he chased her down the brick wall of someone's garden, where she turned on him transformed into a black man, and escaped? Had his father come in with Heracles, shaken him in his bed and pounded the walls saying words he could not understand, and turned to drive the animal out before him and down the stairs? And then a faint cry from the carriage barn below: had he leapt from his bed toward the pale casement of the window, forgetting that he had been so long off his feet that they were useless, their function totally forgotten, so that he fell screaming at the pain in them? For he woke on the floor with his father beside him, holding him up by the shoulders, his father whom he did not recognize, wild-eyed in that dim light. Then he broke open sobbing at the memory of the pain which had just torn up through his body. —In my feet, he cried, —it was like nails being driven up through my feet, as he was laid back on the bed blood-spotted at the shoulders, by this shaking man who could hardly walk from the room.

A few days later, Wyatt began to recover. He regained the weight of his body by meticulous ounces. That fever had passed; but for the rest of his life it never left his eyes.

The Town Carpenter came to call, and stood looking round the room at the wallpaper. The convalescent's bed had been moved to the sewing room, since its windows faced east and south and those of his own smaller room to north and west, away from the sun. Her sewing cabinet, with its long drawer still full of a thousand buttons, stood to one side of a window, and over it a shelf with a few books she had never opened since leaving school. There was nothing else of Camilla in the room, though here it was she had come at the moment of death, seeking something. —What was it? he whispered sometimes, looking up and around as though he expected her again, though her presence had always been one silent and expectant, often even while she was in the room it had seemed empty.

Camilla had chosen the wallpaper. It was pink, with beaded bands of light blue running to the ceiling and rows of roses between them. Her father had papered the room, and behaved very professionally about it though his pleasure showed through at the privilege of doing it for them: showed through so well that he had got the paper on upside down. And only now, as he lay on his back and followed its lines up the wall, did Wyatt realize that the roses were roses, not the pink dogs' faces with green hats he had taken them for as a child, and never questioned since. When she stepped into the room that first time, Camilla could not see what had gone wrong. Then she did; but there stood her father with a smile of pride beside her, and she threw her arms over his crooked shoulders and thanked him, and never told him. It was the way things had of working out for her from the start.

—It looks fine, it still looks fine, the Town Carpenter said now, backing into a chair stacked with paintings and sketches and knocking the whole thing over, which immediately put him at his ease by giving him something to do. He admired each piece separately as he picked them up. —The detail! The detail! he said over and over, of these souvenirs of Wyatt's illness by now become permanent fixtures in his life. Of these fragments of intricate work most were copies. Only those which were copies were finished. The original works left off at that moment where the pattern is conceived but not executed, the forms known to the author but their place daunted, still unfound in the dignity of the design.

—Look! said the Town Carpenter, waving a book from the floor. —Balloons! . . . Then he added, —Damn them, the French. Someone's written it in the French language. He stood turning the pages, muttering, —They do that to confuse people, of course. The French covet a truth when they come upon it, you know . . . He stayed an hour or so, talking himself most of the time, a proclivity he'd developed since he started to become hard of hearing and people tired of the effort of talking to him. Now, he gave a rough précis of the *Odyssey* (Gwyon had sent him off one day with Chapman's translation), and as though the voyage had suddenly grown too short, had just introduced Odysseus to Prester John at Ogygia, when Janet came in with Wyatt's supper. The Town Carpenter behaved with all the courtly grumbling of a shy hero, retiring before her, waving from the door to the boy on the bed and calling out, as though across a chasm, —And they've made me the sexton at the church, you know. The Reverend your father made me the sexton, over their dead bodies if you follow me . . . And he escaped with both volumes of Tissandier's *Histoire des ballons*.

Thus the bells ringing in the morning hours were usually right on time; but after eleven in the morning they commenced to fall off a bit, for it was a good fifteen-minute walk from the Depot Tavern to the church.

Waking in this room of roses upside-down was a new experience, the dawn red from the roses of Eden (as one of those books at his bedside had it from the Talmud), after the days' ends in his own room red from the fires of Hell. Here, after the throbbing flow of the night was broken by the first particles of light in the sky, he often pulled a blanket from the bed and crept to the window, to sit there unmoving for the full time it took until the sun itself rose, the unmeasured hours of darkness slowly shattered, rendered into a succession of particles passing separately, even as the landscape separated into tangible identities each appraising itself in a static withdrawal until everything stood out separate from the silent appraisals around it.

He passed the months of convalescence painting, and with increasing frequency broke his gaze at the window to get to work. He was most clear-headed, least feverish, in these early hours when, as unsympathetically as the daylight, his own hand could delineate the reasonable crowded conceits of separation.

Only once, going to the window before it was light, he was stopped in his tracks by the horned hulk of the old moon hung alone in the sky, and this seemed to upset him a good deal, for he shivered and tried to leave it but could not, tried to see the time on the clock but could not, listened, and heard nothing, finally there was nothing for it but to sit bound in this intimacy which refused him, waiting, until the light came at last and obliterated it.

Then, mornings just before sunrise he could hear his father's steps on the east porch below. And though he heard the voice speaking sometimes, he never made out a word.

Wyatt missed the sound of sleighbells. On his first attempt at a long walk outside, he went down to the carriage barn and found it locked and silent.

—Yes, his... his time came, Gwyon said, clearing his throat and pulling at one hand with the other behind him.

—But you... no one told me.

—Well, we... you were sick, while you were sick I didn't want to upset you.

—But, then what did you do?

—Yes, I... I buried him, down there, down behind the barn there.

—How did it happen, did he just... It's funny, some of the things I... sometimes I think I remember things that are... that couldn't... like... He looked up earnestly, pausing now as though he expected to be prompted, to see his father watching him with eyes which, had he known it, blazed with the same wild intensity as his own in fever. —It's... sometimes it's bewildering..., he faltered, looking down as Gwyon looked away, turned his back and showed his twisting hands behind him. But only for a moment. Gwyon swung round, looking very different, reassured, and tried to smile with,

—You're well? You're well now, almost well? Yes, it's bewildering, bewildering... He changed the subject clumsily. —Like the bulls. Yes, people say they're kept in a dark cell before they're let into the arena, into the bright sun, to confuse them, but that... that... you should see their confidence, their grandeur when they come in, a great moment, that, when they come in, they... their heads up, tossing their heads when they come in... He paused to look up and see if he'd relaxed Wyatt's attention, then went on enthusiastically, —It's after that, after they stick those... the banderillas in the shoulders, you can hear them rattling in the bull's shoulders, a regular dance of fury, it's after that their legs start to cave outward, after that they just stand, bewildered, looking around... before the sword, the... they say you don't kill with the sword but with the cape, the art of the cape... He relaxed himself as he spoke, moving about the room until he got near the door, talking as though in a hurry to be gone, but he paused there to finish with, —The sword, when the sword is in and the bull won't drop, why, they use the cape then, to spin him around in a tight circle so the sword will cut him to pieces inside and drop him. His legs stiffen right out when they stab him in the brain. Do you want anything? But you're up, you're up now. Do you want anything? I'll send Janet up, Gwyon finished and got out to the stairs.

When Janet arrived, Wyatt had her help him out and down the stairs, but he left her in the house when he went down the lawn with his cane. A large stone had been pushed into place against the hole in the hillside, among thorn bushes now bearing early blackberries. The place had been the kitchen midden for as long as he could remember. In his weakness he could not move the stone from its place, for it was very great; and when he started back for the house he tripped against a row of small stakes, driven into the ground there without evident purpose. He climbed unsteadily to his feet from the blemished earth and stones and walked as quickly as he could manage back up the open lawn. There was something defiled about that place which frightened him.

From her window above, Janet watched him stagger back into the open, and was down to help him climb to the porch and in, without a word between them. He went upstairs and got to work without a pause.

Every week or so he would begin something original. It would last for a few days, but before any lines of completion had been drawn he abandoned it. Still the copies continued to perfection, that perfection to which only counterfeit can attain, reproducing every aspect of inadequacy, every blemish on Perfection in the original. He found a panel of very old wood, nearly paper-thin in places but almost of exact size, and on this he started the Seven Deadly Sins: Superbia, Ira, Luxuria, Avaritia, Invidia...one by one they reached completion unbroken by any blemish of originality. Secrecy was not difficult in that house, and he made his copy in secret.

His father seemed less than ever interested in what passed around him, once assured Wyatt's illness was done. Except for the Sunday sermon, public activities in the town concerned him less than ever. Like Pliny, retiring to his Laurentine villa when Saturnalia approached, the Reverend Gwyon avoided the bleak festivities of his congregation whenever they occurred, by retiring to his study. But his disinterest was no longer a dark mantle of preoccupation. A sort of hazardous assurance had taken its place. He approached his Sunday sermons with complaisant audacity, introducing, for instance, druidical reverence for the oak tree as divinely favored because so often singled out to be struck by lightning. Through all of this, even to the sermon on the Aurora Borealis, the Dark Day of May in 1790 whose night moon turned to blood, and the great falling of stars in November 1833, as signs of the Second Advent,

Aunt May might well have noted the persistent nonappearance of what she, from that same pulpit, had been shown as the body of Christ. Certainly the present members of the Use-Me Society found many of his references "unnecessary." It did not seem quite necessary, for instance, to note that Moses had been accused of witchcraft in the Koran; that the hundred thousand converts to Christianity in the first two or three centuries in Rome were "slaves and disreputable people," that in a town on the Nile there were ten thousand "shaggy monks" and twice that number of "god-dedicated virgins"; that Charlemagne mass-baptized Saxons by driving them through a river being blessed upstream by his bishops, while Saint Olaf made his subjects choose between baptism and death. No soberly tolerated feast day came round, but that Reverend Gwyon managed to herald its grim observation by allusion to some pagan ceremony which sounded uncomfortably like having a good time. Still the gray faces kept peace, precarious though it might be. They had never been treated this way from the pulpit. True, many stirred with indignant discomfort after listening to the familiar story of virgin birth on December twenty-fifth, mutilation and resurrection, to find they had been attending, not Christ, but Bacchus, Osiris, Krishna, Buddha, Adonis, Marduk, Balder, Attis, Amphion, or Quetzalcoatl. They recalled the sad day the sun was darkened; but they did not remember the occasion as being the death of Julius Caesar. And many hurried home to closet themselves with their Bibles after the sermon on the Trinity, which proved to be Brahma, Vishnu, and Siva; as they did after the recital of the Immaculate Conception, where the seed entered in spiritual form, bringing forth, in virginal modesty, Romulus and Remus.

If the mild assuasive tones of the Reverend offended anywhere, it was the proprietary sense of his congregation; and with true Puritan fortitude they resisted any suggestion that their bloody sacraments might have known other voices and other rooms. They could hardly know that the Reverend's powers of resistance were being taxed more heavily than their own, where he withstood the temptation to tell them details of the Last Supper at the Eleusinian Mysteries, the snake in the Garden of Eden, what early translators of the Bible chose to let the word 'thigh' stand for (where ancient Hebrews placed their hands when under oath), the symbolism of the Triune triangle and, in generative counterpart so distressing to early fathers of the Church, the origin of the Cross.

Janet did not go to church. There was no disaffection, but she seemed to have attained some unity of her own. And she was no longer found benumbed on the kitchen floor; but might interrupt any household drudgery to hurry to her room where rapturous gasps could have been heard from behind the closed door, if anyone had listened. For the most part she went about her work happily, detached, padding through the dim passages in soft slippers, and ordering the kitchen with dark-gloved hands. Occasionally she kept to her bed.

Gwyon's interest in his son's painting was perfunctory when it did occur, slightly distracted and puzzled as he became now for anything intruding upon him from worlds that were not his own. He only broke through this withdrawal once, when he sustained a shock at seeing an unfinished approximation to the picture of Camilla on the living-room mantel. It was done in black on a smooth gesso ground, on strong linen, a stark likeness which left its lines of completion to the eye of the beholder. It was this quality which appeared to upset Gwyon: once he'd seen it he was constantly curious, and would stand looking away from it, and back, completing it in his own mind and then looking again as though, in the momentary absence of his stare and the force of his own plastic imagination, it might have completed itself. Still each time he returned to it, it was slightly different than he remembered, intractably thwarting the completion he had managed himself. —Why won't you finish it? he burst out finally.

—There's something about a . . . an unfinished piece of work, a . . . a thing like this where . . . do you see? Where perfection is still possible? Because it's there, it's there all the time, all the time you work trying to uncover it. Wyatt caught a hand before him and gripped it as his father's were gripped behind the back turned to him. —Because it's there . . . , he repeated.

Gwyon turned back to the unfinished panel muttering, —Yes, yes . . . Praxiteles . . . and his voice tailed off as he returned and stood following the line of the nose, bringing it back round the broken circle of a Byzantine hoop of gold, while behind him his hands opened and closed on nothing.

The table of the Seven Deadly Sins was unfinished. It remained unfinished for some years, when Wyatt went away to study. It was still hidden and untouched when he came home from Divinity School, where he had completed a year's work.

Something was wrong then. His father knew it, but Reverend Gwyon by this time lived immersed in himself. He shied from talking with Wyatt about his studies. From his flushed face and his agitated manner, it seemed that one word could summon in him histories and arguments of such complexity that they might now take hours, where they had in truth taken centuries, to unravel: but he seemed at pains to dismiss them as quickly as he could, commenting directly, then obliquely, and then changing the subject entirely. —Mithras? Of course, he answered to some question of Wyatt's. —It didn't fail because it was bad. Mithraism almost triumphed over Christianity. It failed because it was so near good. He mumbled something, and then added, —That's the trouble today. No mystery. Everything secularized. No mystery, no weight to anything at all . . . , and he got up and left the room, as he did often in the middle of conversation. Especially these questionings grown from Wyatt's studies. —Pelagianism? he repeated over a plate of disintegrated white lima beans (for Wyatt seldom saw him but at meals). —If it hadn't been Pelagius it would have been someone else. But by now we...too many of us may embrace original sin ourselves to explain our own guilt, and behave...treat everyone else as though they were full-fledged...umm...Pelagians doing just as they please...He did not elaborate, but sat drumming his fingers on the mahogany dining-room table top.

—Free will...Wyatt commenced, but his father was not listening. In all these discussions there seemed to be decisions he had made privately, and in the effort of suppressing them could at last say nothing at all. But as the weeks passed, Wyatt pressed him more and more for encouragement in his own study for the church. Sometimes Gwyon rose to this as though it were his duty to do so. He might manage, for instance, to discourse on the intricacies of transubstantiation without dissent, or even departure from orthodoxy; but as his references mounted, and his enthusiasm grew, reaching the doctrine, which he called Aristotelian, of God retaining the 'accidents' of the bread and wine (in order not to shock His worshipers, he added), and embarked upon a discussion of the 'accidents' of reality, and the redemption of matter, he left the table abruptly to get a reference, a paper or a book from his study, and did not come back. It was all as though he had no wish to push Wyatt into the ministry, like a man whose forebears have served all their lives on wooden ships, and he the last of them to do so, who will not force his son to serve on one knowing that the last of them will go down with him. Full proof of his ministry had begun. It was beyond his hand to stop it now.

Something was wrong. The summer fell away to fall, and Wyatt packed to leave. In the increasing amount of time he had spent painting, a plan formed of its own accord, so spontaneous of generation that he went on unaware of it, and it might seem only by chance that he did not stray from the confines of its design. He had called less and less frequently upon his father for encouragement toward the ministry, and Gwyon appeared to appreciate that, to become more relaxed, leading their conversations off in the direction of the past, the monastery in Estremadura, and Fr. Manomuerta to whom he still wrote, and sent packages of food; or the town of San Zwingli, the barrel organs in the streets, and the still uncanonized patron saint; the only bullfight he had ever seen: —And you don't kill with the sword, but with the cape, the art of the cape..., he said following his son up the stairs, to the sewing room where Wyatt was packing.

The room was littered with sketches, studies, diagrams and unfinished canvases. A large panel stood face to the wall, and Wyatt, who'd entered first, suddenly backed up against it and stood there staring at the floor as though overcome by an idea, something he had known all along, but only now dared bring to consciousness.

—What is it, what did you bring me up to show me? Gwyon asked, looking over the litter. —Some painting, is it, you've done? Finished? At that he took a step toward the large panel, and Wyatt threw out his arms as though to protect it. —Eh? Gwyon stopped. —What is it? What's the matter? Didn't you have something to show me?

—Yes, yes, but I . . . I did, but . . . here. Wyatt's eyes had been darting about the floor, then he stooped abruptly and snatched up a paper. —Yes, here, he said holding it out, —you see, this . . . this is what I've been . . . doing. He held the paper out, his face in a blank expression which fused into desperate appeal as he looked up at his father.

—This? All these lines? Gwyon said, taking it.

—Yes, it's studies in perspective.

—I see, all these lines, coming together here at one point.

—Yes, Wyatt mumbled, backing away toward the panel again. —The vanishing point. That's called the vanishing point. He was staring wide-eyed at his father, but he withdrew his eyes quickly when Gwyon looked up, and waited there, shaking throughout his frame, until his father left the room. Even then he did not move, but waited until the heavy footfalls sounded to the bottom of the stairs. Then he swung round to the panel, pulled it out from the wall, and looked at this finished copy of the Bosch painting with a new expression on his face.

At supper that evening, each of them tended his plate with more than the usual shy pretense to interest, nervously alert to one another, but silent until Gwyon called Janet in to open a bottle of wine. He seemed prepared to sit over that dark oloroso sherry all evening, starting sentences and leaving them unfinished, looking up at his son with the evasiveness of a conspirator, one, that is, involved in a conspiracy to which no one has confessed. For an instant their unblinking eyes locked with one another, then Gwyon turned away, and started to recount the brave deceit of the old Italian grandee, the Conte di Brescia, looking, as he spoke, at the table top of the Seven Deadly Sins under the far window, without a shadow on his features to suggest that he knew he was looking at an imposture, or hint at the memory of the meticulous and molding pictures he had found buried wrapped in newspapers behind the carriage barn, that evening of Midsummer Day years before.

When the bells struck noon next day, at about quarter past the hour, Janet followed Wyatt's departure as far as the front door, where her blessings engulfed him in a farewell bath of blood, the Precious Blood which seemed forever now upon her lips, —O Blood ineffable, burning burning blood which I have shed and bathed in with my Beloved ... and that door closed.

The luggage had gone to the station, where Wyatt and his father arrived and stood in the dust without speaking. The sky was a deep gray-blue, banded with the colors of rust seen under water. Gwyon looked nervously about to speak several times, towering over his son, fingers twitching in the pocket of his black waistcoat. Finally he blurted out, —Do you have that painting? Wyatt looked overcome, guilt reddened his face until his father interrupted his choking attempt to speak. —The ... her picture, the picture of your mother that you ... that you won't finish.

—That, yes, yes I have it, in that crate, that flat crate there, Wyatt brought out breathless, trying to indicate the crate with casual innocence. —It's there, with ... you know, a lot of other pictures.

—You must finish it, you must try to finish it, Gwyon told him, —finish it, or she will be with you, he paused, looking at his son's face where so few traces betrayed his own, come under self-dominance so long before. —Or she will be with you always, Gwyon said suddenly withdrawing his fingers from the waistcoat pocket, drawing out those two large studded Byzantine hoops of gold. —Here, he held them out. —These were hers, these ... were hers.

Wyatt accepted them, hidden, large as they were, in his hand. He started to speak, but his father, looking away from him toward the east, made a sound, and they were both caught, as a swimmer on the surface is caught by that cold current whose suddenness snares him in cramps and sends him in dumb surprise to the bottom.

The sun showed their motionless shadows on the rough wood platform. Then the sun was obscured by a cloud, and the shadows disappeared. When the sun came out again the shadows were gone.

Days passed, then weeks, and Gwyon, restlessly leaving his study to pace those dim passages, the mirrors in the cruz-con-espejos clenching at him as he emerged, to pause beyond and confront Olalla silently, or listen for the creaking from the sharp angles of woodwork around him, muttering, —And he took my razor! He took my razor! ... And then, when he'd received the letter, —The final perseverance of ... yes, perspective, the vanishing point ..., before he'd even opened it. He gazed at the unfamiliar postage stamps, made out the postmark, München, and finally took it out with him, to read on a walk in the clear air of that season. He walked out, toward the abandoned bridge works, seen by no one, this man born on the yellow day in Boston when the volcano Krakatao had erupted on the other side of the earth and night came everywhere with a red sunset, only now in age approaching maturity, waiting, like Manto, while time circled him, to make full proof of his ministry.

The New England evening had taken on the chill of finished day, the chill of reality which follows sunset. All Saints' approached, and All Souls', when in France there would be picnics in the cemeteries, and in Spain they would be out to place chrysanthemums on the graves, against beaded wreaths and the ornate names of the dead, where Camilla's name stood out in cold vigilance, waiting.

—Guilt? he murmured, walking with the letter unfolded in his hand. —Because of guilt, my son cannot study for the ministry. Guilt...good God! are You hiding somewhere under this welter of fear, this chaos of blood and mutilation, these terrors of weak minds...A feeling of guilt, dear Heaven what other kind of Christian ministers do you send us? or have there ever been? The fool!...and I thought I could spare him. Perhaps, if he knew the truth...An abrupt shudder broke through his whole frame, and he stood as though he had been pierced, the shock of the past in that woman's voice perhaps, —Pagan indeed!...and his faltering withdrawal, —Set foot inside myself...? He sniffed, as though to clear his head of vaporous memories risen from some chill sanctuary deep in the basilica of the past; and squared his shoulders as he had coming forth from that subterranean Mithraeum under the church of Saint Clement of Rome. And suddenly he sought the empty sky for the sun.

But the sudden cooling of the air, and this letter, had startled the old man into the present, from which he turned and trudged back in a lucidity of memory against which he was defenseless. The memories became facts, including him unsparingly in their traffic but shut him unmercifully out from intrusion, left him walking slowly and impotent among their hard thrusts. The shrill cry of Heracles, echoed down from the house on two voices; and the dark-stained faces of the mirrors mounted in the cross. His discovery upon her corpse's head that Aunt May had worn a transformation, hidden from him those last years of her life with the care of Blessed Clara. That plain casket gone deep in earth, while the other stood a man's height above the earth, anticipating dehiscence, ready to shell in falling: Camilla, and her death of which he never spoke, the white carriage mounting the rock-studded road, its course marked by the stations of the Cross and droppings of animals still too fresh to be picked up for fuel, toward the cypress trees. That desolate Eucharist on Christmas Day at Nuestra Señora de la Otra Vez: the accidents of reality, Christ made of buffalo hide, or was it human skin? in the cathedral at Burgos. The bewilderment of the bulls, the port, and Columbus surrounded by lions. Then the trees of Tuscany in spired erection, the apologetic decay of the Conte di Brescia, the marble porch at Lucca so beautiful that no one ever stopped to look at it; and the image; and the words of William Rufus, to

Bishop Gundulf of Rochester, —*By the Holy Face of Lucca, God shall never have me good for all the evil that He hath wrought upon me!*

Tearing his eyes from the empty place in the sky where the sun had set, he stopped stumbling back by years and ran, vaulted through centuries. The letter he had torn in pieces lay on the moving air for an instant, was caught, spread up over the ground and blew away from him like a handful of white birds startled into the sky.

II

Très curieux, vos maîtres anciens. Seulement les plus beaux, ce sont les faux.

—PAUL EUDEL, *Trucs et truqueurs*

ON THE terrace of the Dôme sat a person who looked like the young George Washington without his wig (at about the time he dared the Ohio country). She read, with silently moving lips, from a book before her. She was drinking a bilious-colored liquid from a globular goblet; and every twenty or so pages would call to the waiter, in perfect French, —Un Ricard..., and add one to the pile of one-franc saucers before her. —Voilà ma propre Sainte Chapelle, she would have said of that rising tower (the sentence prepared in her mind) if anyone had encouraged conversation by sitting down at her table. No one did. She read on. Anyone could have seen it was *transition* she was reading, if any had looked. None did. Finally an unshaven youth bowed slightly, as with pain, murmured something in American, and paused with a dirty hand on the back of a chair at her table. —J'vous en prie, she said, lucid, lowering *transition*, waiting for him to sit down before she went on. —Mursi, he muttered, and dragged the chair to another table.

Paris lay by like a promise accomplished: age had not withered her, nor custom staled her infinite vulgarity.

Nearby, a man exhibited two fingers, one dressed as a man, one as a woman, performing on a table top. Three drunken young Englishmen were singing *The Teddy Bears' Picnic*. Three dirty children from Morocco were selling peanuts from the top of the basket and hashish from the bottom. Someone said that there was going to be a balloon ascension that very afternoon, in the Bois. Someone else said that Karl Marx's bones were buried at Highgate. Someone said, —I'm actually going to be analyzed. *Psycho*analyzed. A boy with a beard, in a state of black corduroy (*corde du roi*) unkemptness which had taken as long as the beard to evolve, said, —I've got to show these pictures,

I've got to sell some of them, but how can I have people coming up there with him there? He's dying. I can't put him out on the street, dying like that... even in Paris. A girl said that she had just taken a villa right outside Paris, a place called Saint Forget. —Of course it's a hideous place, and Ah had to pay a feaful sum to get the tiasome French family that was there out of it, but it's such a sweet little old address to get mail at. Another girl said, —My conçerage has been returning all my mail marked ankonoo just because I oney gave her ten francs poorbwar. People who would soon be seen in New York reading French books were seen here reading Italian. Someone said, in slurred (blasé) French, —Un café au lait.

Over this grandstand disposal of promise the waiters stared with a distance of glazed indulgence which all collected under it admired, as they admired the rudeness, which they called self-respect; the contempt, which they called innate dignity; the avarice, which they called self-reliance; the tasteless ill-made clothes on the men, lauded as indifference, and the far-spaced posturings of haute couture across the Seine, called inimitable or shik according to one's stay. Marvelous to wide eyes, pricked ears, and minds of that erectile quality betraying naive qualms of transatlantic origin (alert here under hair imitative long-grown, uncombed, on the male, curtly shorn on the girls) was this spectacle of culture fully realized. They regarded as the height of excellence that nothing remained to be done, no tree to be planted nor building torn down (they had not visited Le Bourget; found the wreckage up behind the Hôtel de Ville picturesque), no tree too low nor building too high (those telescoping lampposts on the Pont du Carrousel), no bud of possibility which had not opened in the permanent bloom of artificial flowers, no room for that growth which is the abiding flower of humility.

"A mon très aimé frère Lazarus, ce que vous me mandez de Petrus l'apostre de notre doux Jesus...," wrote Mary Magdalen. "Notre fils Césarion va bien...," wrote Cleopatra to Julius Caesar. There was a letter from Alexander the Great to Aristotle ("Mon ami..."); from Lazarus to Saint Peter (concerning Druids); from Pontius Pilate to Tiberius; Judas's confession (to Mary Magdalen); a passport signed by Vercingetorix; notes from Alcibiades, Pericles, and a letter to Pascal (on gravitation) from Newton, who was nineteen when Pascal died. But M. Chasles, eminent mathematician of the late nineteenth century, paid 140,000 francs for this collection of autographs, for he believed them genuine: they were, after all, written in French. So the Virgin appeared to Maximin and Mélanie at La Salette, identified Herself by speaking to them in French which they did not understand, broke into their local patois for long enough to put across Her confidences, and then returned to Her native language for farewell: any wonder that transatlantic visitors approached it with qualms? murmured in tones spawned in forests, on the plains in unrestricted liberty, from the immensity of mountains, the cramped measure of their respect, approached in reverence the bier where every shade of the corpse was protected from living profanation by the pallbearers of the Académie Française.

Before their displacement from nature, baffled by the grandeur of their own culture which they could not define, and so believed did not exist, these transatlantic visitors had learned to admire in this neatly parceled definition of civilization the tyrannous pretension of many founded upon the rebellious efforts of a few, the ostentation of thousands presumed upon the strength of a dozen who had from time to time risen against this vain complacence with the past to which they were soon to contribute, giving, with their harried deaths, grounds for vanity of language, which they had perfected; supercilious posturing of intellect, which they had suffered to understand and deliver, in defiance; insolent arbitration of taste, grown from the efforts of those condemned as having none; contempt for others flourishing from seedlings which they had planted in the rain of contempt for themselves; dogmata of excellence founded upon insulting challenges wrought in impossible hope, and then grasped, for granted, from their hands fallen clenching it as dogma.

From the intractable perfection of the crepusculous Île de la Cité (seen from the Pont des Arts) to the static depravity of the Grands Boulevards, it was unimpeachable: in superficiating this perfection, it absorbed the beholder and shut out the creator: no more could it have imitation than a mermaid (though echoes were heard of the Siren of Djibouti).

—Voici votre Perrier m'sieur: —Mais j'ai dit café au lait, pas d'eau Perrier... A small man in a sharkskin suit said, —Son putas, y nada mas. Putas, putas, putas... Someone said, —Picasso... Someone else said, —Kafka... A girl said, —You deliberately try to misunderstand me. Of course I like art. Ask anybody. Nearby, a young man with a beard received compliments on his recent show. It was a group of landscapes in magenta and madder lake. Très amusant, gai, très très original (he was French). It was quite a rage. He said he had walked four kilometers out of Saint Germain en Laye, found he'd forgotten all of his colors but magenta and madder lake, so he went ahead and painted anyhow. He said, —Quelquefois je passe la nuit entière à finir un tableau... Someone said that there was a town in Switzerland called Gland. Someone told the joke about Carruthers and his horse.

On the right bank, a lady said, —You'll like Venice. It's so like Fort Lauderdale. At the same table, a man said, —I'm going to look her up. She's lived here for years, right outside Paris, a place called Banlieu. At another table someone said, —By God, you know, they're almost as rude to us as they are to each other.

On Montmartre, someone looked up at the Sacré Coeur and said, —What the hell do you think they call *that?* The woman with him said, —Why bother to go all the way to the top, I haven't got my camera. A girl said, —Voulez vous voir le ciné cochon? Deux femmes...

Above, the thing itself towered exotic and uninvited, affording the consolation of the grotesque: that dead white Byzantine-Romanesque surprise which was heaped in bulbiferous pyramids atop the Hill of the Martyrs in the late nineteenth century, soon after the city had finished installing a comprehensive new sewage system. It was a monument (the church) not, as many had it, to the French victory over Prussia, but to the Jesuit victory over France. The birth of Ignatius of Loyola was early understood to have erred only in its location: Spain was origin, but none has ever excelled France in vocational guidance for the ideas of others, and it was obvious (in France) that his Society of Jesus could be best advanced through the medium of the French mind. In the mid-seventeenth century, the Society was having difficulty with the Jansenists, and the contributions of Pascal upset them almost as much as did the Miracle of the Holy Thorn, a relic which cured little Marguerite Périer of fistula lachrymalis: it was a Jansenist miracle. The Society recouped: found its own Marguerite and, with the kindly instruction and encouragement of Père La Colombière, her confessor, she revealed to the world a parade of the marvelous which shocked even those who were compelled to believe, an account which made a cure of fistula lachrymalis, never a pretty thought, pale into organic commonplace. The searing narrative of Marguerite Marie Alacoque passed from hand to hand for some two centuries until at last, in 1864, Pope Pius IX was assailed with a petition asking highest recognition for the Sacred Heart (the afflicted organ). In fact the petition itself participated in the miraculous, bearing as it did twelve million signatures forth from a country whose district records showed three-fourths of its brides and grooms unable to write their names. A bare decade after the beatification, papal decree consecrated the Universal Catholic Church to the Sacred Heart, and the Society has since defended its successful exploit against all comers with the same dexterous swashbuckling that was shown in its achievement: against the Virgin of La Salette, against promoters of the Devotion of the Perpetual Rosary, even against the prodigal (85 liters per minute) Virgin of Lourdes, whose bottled testimonials were soon flowing broadcast when proved not liable to the excise levies and export taxes of the Republic. Amid a crowd equaling the population of Afghanistan, the Sacré Coeur launched its church on the crown of that hill Saint Denis had once approached carrying his head under his arm. The new "public utility," so it was called, was dedicated by Cardinal Archbishop Guibert, disdaining insular mutterings which insinuated that the Society had plagiarized the Sacred Heart from England's leading philosophe, William Godwin, who thought of it first. And eventually, the Devotions within the favored land made truce: after all, as Monseigneur Ségur said, the Virgin shows very good taste in choosing France as the theater for her apparitions.

Near the Bourse, a lady said, —Des touristes, oui, mais des sales anglais, ... là, regardez ce type là ... She indicated a figure across the street, not a dirty Englishman, as she noted, but Wyatt, who lived nearby. With no idea of Paris when he arrived, he had been fortunate enough to find quarters in this neighborhood which maintained anonymity in the world of arts. Few people lived here. Activity centered around the stock exchange. On Sunday it was empty.

He knew few people, and them he saw infrequently. In three years, he had not written his father; and after a year in Paris he had finished seven pictures, working with a girl named Christiane, a blonde model with small figure and features. As she exposed the side of her face, or a fall of cloth from her shoulder, he found there suggestion of the lines he needed, forms which he knew but could not discover in the work without this allusion to completed reality before him. He had by now little money, and so in addition to his own work he did some restoring of old paintings for an antique dealer who paid him regularly and badly. He did not spend time at café tables talking about form, or line, color, composition, trends, materials: he worked on this painting, or did not think about it. He knew no more of surréalisme than he did of the plethora of daubs turned out on Montmartre for tourists, those arbiters of illustration to whom painting was a personalized representation of scenes and creatures they held dear; might not know art but they knew what they liked, hand-painted pictures (originals) for which they paid in the only currency they understood, to painters whose visions had shrunk to the same proportions. He might walk up there occasionally and see them, the alleys infested with them painting the same picture from different angles, the same painting varying from easel to easel as different versions of a misunderstood truth, but the progeny of each single easel identical reproduction, following a precept of Henner who called this the only way of being original. Passing, he showed all the interest for them he might have for men whitewashing walls.

Still, a dull day in the fall, a day which had lost track of the sun and the importunate rendition of minutes and hours the sun dictates, and that configuration on Montmartre stood out in preternatural whiteness, the ceremonial specter of a peak, an abrupt Alp in the wrong direction. Walking home alone, the cold bearing in a dread weight of anxiety, the sense of something lost, passing people closely he passed them with wonder as though he'd seen no one in years, looking into every face as though hoping to recognize something there. Could the cold differentiate? aside from the change in clothing where the trees and the people reciprocate, the people suddenly came out muffled, and what trees there were stood forth in the mottled dishabille of discolored leaves. But even the streets, and the lights showing along the streets looked different, recalling nakedness in angular displeasure, summoning the fabled argument between the sun and the wind, distending the brief Rue Vivienne into the crowded desolation of Maximilianstrasse, the secure anonymity of childhood recalled by the fall of the year, and a Munich which had known spring and summer only in the irretrievable childhood of the Middle Ages, that hence, forward, there was no direction but down, no color but one darker, no sky but one more empty, no ground but that harder, no air but the cold. —Bitte?... Propriety faded, the level decorum of French roofs might break into the fibrous fakery of Italian and French rococo, an occasional tumor of nineteenth-century Renaissance sparked by the Byzantine eye behind the Allerheiligen-Hofkirche's Romanesque façade. As lonely, or more lonely (so they say one is in a crowd), the buildings in Munich's modern town stood away from each other in their differences, made up to extremes like guests at a Venetian masquerade, self-conscious perpetrations of assertive adolescence, well-traveled, almost wealthy, déracinés, they had gathered as transcripts of their seducers who were not known in this land, and stood now stricken in erect silence up and down the aisles of the avenues, surprised that those they had known in conglomerate childhood had also traveled, had also been seduced, and that, in this shocked instant, by lovers more beautiful than their own. Like paralyzed barbs of lightning, hooked crosses in the streets had portended holocaust; while alone indigenous, hermaphrodite host and doubly barren, the Frauenkirche disembosomed impartial welcome from twin and towering domes at which the others railed but could not supplant. Empty pavilions colonnaded on a hill across the river witnessed the afternoon pleasure of a child who had been called away, and left this glittering plaything for the wind to tear.

Now, he painted at night. In the afternoon he worked at restoring old pictures, or in sketching, a half-attended occupation which broke off with twilight, and Christiane went on her way uncurious, uninterested in the litter of papers bearing suggestion of the order of her bones and those arrangements of her features which she left behind, unmenaced by magic, unafraid, she walked toward the Gare Saint-Lazare, unhurried, seldom reached it (for it was no destination) before she was interrupted, and down again, spread again, indifferent to the resurrection which filled her and died; and the Gare Saint-Lazare, a railway station and so a beginning and an end, came forth on the evening vision, erect in testimony, and then (for what became of the man who was raised?) stood witness to a future which, like the past, was liable to no destination, and collected dirt in its fenestrated sores.

He painted at night, and often broke off in a fever at dawn, when the sun came like the light of recovery to the patient just past the crisis of fatal illness, and time the patient became lax, and stretched fingers of minutes and cold limbs of hours into the convalescent resurrection of the day.

The streets, when he came out, were filled with people recently washed and dressed, people for whom time was not continuum of disease but relentless repetition of consciousness and unconsciousness, unrelated as day and night, or black and white, evil and good, in independent alternation, like the life and death of insects.

This can happen: staying awake, the absolutes become confused, time the patient seen at full living length, in exhaustion. One afternoon he went to sleep, woke alone at twilight, believed he had slept the night through, lost it, here was dawn. He went out for coffee. The streets were full, but unevenly. There was a pall on every face, a gathering of remnants in suspicion of the end, a melancholia of things completed. Wyatt, haggard as he was, looked with such wild uncomprehending eyes on a day beginning so, that he attracted the attention of a policeman who stopped him.

—Où allez-vous donc? —Chez moi. —Vos papiers s'il vous plaît. —Mon passeport? Je ne l'ai sur moi, c'est chez moi. —Où habitez vous? —Vingt-quatre rue de la Bourse. —Qu'est-ce que vous faites? —Je suis peintre. —Où donc? —Chez moi. —Où habitez vous? —Mais... —Avez vous des moyens? —Oui...Wyatt reached into his pocket, took out what francs he had, showed the money. —Alors, said the policeman, —il faut toujours en avoir sur soi, de l'argent, vous savez...

After a glass of coffee he climbed the stairs to his room. Someone was waiting in the dim light of the hall. As Wyatt approached the figure turned, put out a hand and murmured a greeting. —My name is Crémer, he said. —I met you last week, in the Muette Gallery. May I come in for a moment? He spoke precise English. Wyatt opened the door to his room, ordered and large, blank walls, a spacious north window. —You will be showing some of your pictures next week, I believe?

—Seven pictures, Wyatt said, making no effort to expose them.

—I am interested in your work.

—Oh, you've...seen it?

—No, no, hardly. But I see here (motioning toward the straight easel, where a canvas stood barely figured) —that it is interesting. I am writing the art column in *La Macule*. Crémer's cigarette, which he had not taken from his lips since he appeared, had gone out at about the length of a thumbnail. He looked rested, assured, hardly a likely visitor at dawn. —I shall probably review your pictures next week, he added after a pause which had left Wyatt smoothing the hair on the back of his head, his face confused.

—Oh, then, ... of course, you want to look at them now?

—Don't trouble yourself, Crémer said, walking off toward the window. —You are studying in Paris?

—No. I did in Munich.

—In Germany. That is too bad. Your style is German, then? German impressionism?

—No, no, not ... quite different. Not so ...

—Modern? German impressionism, modern?

—No, I mean, the style of the early Flemish ...

—Van Eyck ...

—But less ...

—Less stern? Yes. Roger de la Pasture, perhaps?

—What?

—Van der Weyden, if you prefer. Crémer shrugged. He was standing with his back to the window. —In Germany ...

—I did one picture in the manner of Memling, very much the manner of Memling. The teacher, the man I studied with, Herr Koppel, Herr Koppel compared it to David, Gheerardt David's painting *The Flaying of the Unjust Judge*.

—Memlinc, alors ...

—But I lost it there, but ... do you want to look at the work I've done here?

—Don't trouble. But I should like to write a good review for you.

—I hope you do. It could help me a great deal.

—Yes. Exactly.

They stood in silence for almost a minute. —Will you sit down? Wyatt asked finally.

Crémer showed no sign of hearing him but a slight shrug. He half turned to the window and looked out. —You live in a very ... clandestine neighborhood, for a painter? he murmured agreeably. In the darkening room the cigarette gone out looked like a sore on his lip.

—The anonymous atmosphere ... Wyatt commenced.

—But of course, Crémer interrupted. There was a book on the floor at his feet, and he moved it with the broad toe of one shoe. —We recall Degas, eh? he went on in the same detached tone of pleasantry, —his remark, that the artist must approach his work in the same frame of mind in which the criminal commits his deed. Eh? Yes ... He approached Wyatt slightly hunched, his hands down in his pockets. —The reviews can make a great difference. He smiled. —All the difference.

—Difference?

—To selling your pictures.

—Well then, Wyatt said looking away from the blemished smile, down to the floor, bringing his arms together behind him twisted until he'd got hold of both elbows, and his face, thin and exhausted, seemed to drain of life. —Yes, that . . . that's up to the pictures.

—It's not, of course, Crémer said evenly.

—What do you mean? Wyatt looked up, startled, dropping his arms.

—I am in a position to help you greatly.

—Yes, yes but . . .

—Art criticism pays very badly, you know.

—But . . . well? Well? His face creased.

—If you should guarantee me, say, one-tenth of the sale price of whatever we sell . . .

—We? You? You?

—I could guarantee you excellent reviews. Nothing changed in Crémer's face. Wyatt's eyes burned as he looked, turning green. —Are you surprised? Crémer asked, and his face changed now, expressing studied surprise, scorning to accept; while before him Wyatt looked about to fall from exhaustion.

—You? For my work . . . you want me to pay you, for . . . for . . .

—Yes, think about it, said Crémer, turning to the door.

—No, I don't need to. It's insane, this . . . proposition. I don't want it. What do you want of me? he went on, his voice rising as Crémer opened the door.

There was hardly light, not enough to cast a shadow, left in the room. As they had talked, each became more indistinct, until Crémer opened the door, and the light of the minuterie threw his flat shadow across the sill. —I regret that I disturbed you, he said. —I think you need rest, perhaps? But think about it. Eh?

Wyatt followed him to the door, crying out, —Why did you come here? Now? Why do you come at dawn with these things?

Crémer had already started down the stairs. —At dawn? he called back, pausing. —Why my dear fellow, it's evening. It's dinner time. Then the sounds of his feet on the stairs, and the light of the minuterie failed abruptly, leaving Wyatt in his doorway clutching at its frame, while the steps disappeared below unfaltering in the darkness.

Il faut toujours en avoir sur soi, de l'argent, vous savez . . .

Like lions, out of the gates, into the circus arena, cars roared into the open behind the Opéra from the mouth of the Rue Mogador. Around it this faked

Imperial Rome lay in pastiche on the banks of its Tiber: though Tiber's career, from the Apennine ravines of Tuscany, skirting the Sabine mountains to course through Rome and reach with two arms into the sea, finds unambitious counterpart in the Seine, diked and dammed across the decorous French countryside, proper as wallpaper. Nevertheless, they had done their best with what they had. The Napoleons tried very hard. The first one combed his hair, and that of his wife and brothers, like Julius Caesar and his family combed theirs. J. L. David (having painted pictures of Brutus, Andromache, and the Horatii) painted his picture looking, as best he could manage, like Julius Caesar; and Josephine doing her very best (the *Coronation*) to look above suspicion herself. Everyone rallied round, erecting arches, domes, pediments, and copied what the Romans had copied from the Greeks. Empire furniture, candlesticks, coiffures... somewhere beyond them hung the vision of Constantine's Rome, its eleven forums, ten basilicas, eighteen aqueducts, thirty-seven city gates, two arenas, two circuses, thirty-seven triumphal arches, five obelisks, four hundred and twenty-three temples with their statues of the gods in ivory and gold. But all that was gone. There was no competition now. Not since Pope Urban VIII had declared the Coliseum a public quarry.

As the spirit of collecting art began in Rome, eventually it began in Paris, reached the proportions of the astounding collection of that wily Sicilian blood the Cardinal Mazarin, murmuring to his art as he left in decline and exile, —Que j'ai tant aimé, French enough to add, —et qui m'ont tant coûté. If the Roman connoisseur could distinguish among five kinds of patina on bronze by the smell, French sensitivities soon became as cultivated. If, to please the Roman connoisseur, sapphires were faked from obsidian, sardonyx from cheap colored jasper, French talents were as versatile: "Un client désire des Corots? L'article manque sur le marché? Fabriquons-en..." (And one day, of Corot's twenty-five hundred paintings, seventy-eight hundred were to be found in America.) Even then they knew the value of art. Or of knowing the value of art. As Coulanges said to Madame de Sévigné, —Pictures are bullion.

Paris, fortunate city! by now a swollen third of the way into the twentieth century, still to be importuned by those who continued to take her at her own evaluation. Perhaps a kindred homage which rang across the sea was well earned (from a land whose length was still ringing with the greeting —Hello sucker!): perhaps fifty million Frenchmen couldn't be wrong. Four million of them, at any rate, were nursing venereal diseases; and among the ladies syphilis brought about some forty thousand miscarriages that year. "Paris": a sobriquet to conjure with (her real name Lutetia), it bore magic in the realm of Art, as synonymous with the word itself as that of Mnesarete, "Phryne," had once been with Love. Long since, of course, in the spirit of that noblesse oblige which she personified, Paris had withdrawn from any legitimate connection with works of art, and directly increased her entourage of those living for Art's sake. One of these, finding himself on trial just two or three years ago, had made the reasonable point that a typical study of a Barbizon peasant signed with his own name brought but a few hundred francs, but signed *Millet*, ten thousand dollars; and the excellent defense that this subterfuge had not been practiced on Frenchmen, but on English and Americans "to whom you can sell anything"... here, in France, where everything was for sale.

Under the eyes of Napoleon I (atop a column in the Place Vendôme, "en César") the Third Republic bickered on. Having established their own squalid bohemias, there was no objection to handing the original over to their hungry neighbor across the Maginot Line, who was busy scrapping the Versailles treaty, fragment by fragment, until the day when a German envoy would be shot in Paris, and, weeks later, a peace pact signed to prepare for a re-enactment of the bloodshed which had provoked this expression of faith from one killed in it, "Il y a tant de saints, ils forment un tel rempart autour de Paris, que les zeppelins ne passeront jamais." And Paris waited, as ever ready as Phryne beset by slanders and threats, to rend her robe and bare her breasts to the mercy of her judges.

In an alley, a dog hunting in a garbage can displayed infinite grace in the unconscious hang of his right foreleg. Little else happened that Saturday night in August. Saint Bartholomew's Day was warm. It was the dead heat of Paris summer, when Paris cats go to sleep on Paris windowsills, and ledges high up, and fall off, and plunge through the glass roof of the lavabo. The center of the city was empty. A sight-seeing bus set off from the Place de l'Opéra. A truck and a Citroën smashed before the Galeries Lafayette. At the Pont d'Auteuil, a man's body was dragged out of the Seine with a bicycle tied to it. Among the fixtures, tiled and marbled shapes remindful of a large outdoor bathroom, in the cemetery at Montrouge a widower argued with his dead wife's lover over who had the right to place flowers on her grave. In front of the Bourse, a deaf-mute soccer team carried on conversation in obstreperous silence. On the Quai du Pont Neuf, a Frenchman sat picking his nose. Then he put his arm around his girl and kissed her. Then he picked his nose. It was Sunday in Paris, and very quiet.

On the terrace of Larue, under the soiled stature of the Madeleine's peripteral imposture, Wyatt considered a German newspaper. Taxis limped past, bellicose as wounded animals, collapsing further on at Maxim's, late lunch. Unrepresentatively handsome people passed on foot. Some of them stopped and sat at tables. —In Istanbul in the summer, a lady said, —it was Istanbul, wasn't it? We used to take long rides in the cistern, in the summer...

Wyatt read slowly and with difficulty in *Die Fleischflaute*, an art publication. His show was over. No pictures had been sold. He had thrown away *La Macule* quickly, after reading there Crémer's comments: —Archaïque, dur comme la pierre, dérivé sans cœur, sans sympathie, sans vie, enfin, un esprit de la mort sans l'espoir de la Résurrection. But at this moment the details of that failure were forgotten, and the thing itself intensified, as he made out in *Die Fleischflaute* that there had just been discovered in Germany an original painting by Hans Memling. Crude overpainting had transformed the whole scene into an interior, with the same purpose that Holofernes' head had once been transformed into a tray of fruit on Judith's tray (making it less offensive as a 'picture'): this one proved to be a figure being flayed alive on a rack, since overpainted with a bed, and those engaged in skinning him were made to minister to the now bedridden figure. A fragment of landscape seen through an open window, said *Die Fleischflaute*, had excited the attention of an expert, and once it was taken to the Old Pinakothek in Munich and cleaned, the figure stretched in taut agony was identified as Valerian, third-century persecutor of Christians, made captive by the Persian Sapor whose red cloak was thrown down in the foreground before the racked body thin in unelastic strength, anguish and indifference in the broken tyrant's face, its small eyes empty with blindness. Possibly, the experts allowed, it might be the work of Gheerardt David, but more likely that of Memling, from which David had probably drawn his *Flaying of the Unjust Judge*. There followed a eulogy on German painters, and Memling in particular, who had brought the weak beginnings of Flemish art to the peak of their perfection, and crystallized the minor talents of the Van Eycks, Bouts, Van der Weyden, in the masterpieces of his own German genius.

Saint Bartholomew's Day in Notre Dame, reflecting commemoration of the medal which Gregory XIII had struck honoring Catherine de' Medici's massacre of fifty thousand heretics: the music surged and ebbed in the cathedral, and in the Parisian tradition of preconcerted effects the light suddenly poured down in fullness, then faded, together they swelled and died. At the end of the service, as the organ filled that place with its sound, the body of the congregation turned its many-faced surface to look back and up at the organ loft, and from the organ loft they formed a great cross so. Then the cross disintegrated, its fragments scattered over their city, safe again in the stye of contentment.

Paris simmered stickily under the shadowed erection of the Eiffel Tower. Like the bed of an emperor's mistress, the basin she lay in hadn't a blade or stitch out of place; and like the Empress Theodora, "fair of face and charming as well, but short and inclined to pallor, not indeed completely without color but slightly sallow...," Paris articulated her charm within the lower registers of the spectrum. So Theodora, her father a feeder of bears, went on the stage with no accomplishment but a gift for mockery, no genius but for whoring and intrigue. An empress, she triumphed: no senator, no priest, no soldier protested, and the vulgar clamored to be called her slaves; bed to bath, breakfast to rest, she preened her royalty. —May I never put off this purple or outlive the day when men cease to call me queen... She died of cancer.

Toward evening the shadow of the Eiffel Tower inclined to the Latin Quarter across her body. She prepared, made herself up from a thousand pots and tubes, was young, desperately young she knew herself and the mirror forgotten, the voice brittle, she lolled uncontested in the mawkish memories of men married elsewhere to sodden reality, stupefied with the maturity they had traded against this mistress bargained in youth. Revisiting, they could summon youth to her now, mark it in the neon blush uncowed by the unquerulous façades maintained by middle age, and the excruciating ironwork and chrome, the cancerous interiors.

At a bar in Rue Caumartin a girl said to an American, —Vous m'emmenez? Moi, je suis cochonne, la plus cochonne de Paris...Vous voulez le toucher? ici? Donnez moi un billet...oui un billet, pour le toucher...ici...discrètement...

A girl lying in a bed said, —We only know about one per cent of what's happening to us. We don't *know* how little heaven is paying for how much hell.

Someone said, —But you've been over here so *long*, to an American in a hotel room who was showing his continental savoir faire by urinating in the sink. He said, —I wanted to marry her, but you know, she's tied to her envirement. Someone said, —I never knew him very well, he's of the Negro persuasion. On the left bank, someone had just left his wife and taken up the guitar. It was at home in bed. —I dress it in her bathrobe every night, he said. Someone else suggested using a duck, putting its head in a drawer and jamming the drawer shut at the critical moment. A young gentleman was treating his friends to shoeshines for the seventh time that hour. He was drunk. The dirty Arab children sold peanuts from the top of the basket and hashish from the bottom. They spoke a masterful unintimidated French in guttural gasps, coming from a land where it was regarded neither as the most beautiful language, as in America, nor the only one, as in France. At that table someone said, —This stuff doesn't affect me at all. But don't you notice that the sky is getting closer? —Of course I love art, that's why I'm in Paris, a girl said. The boy with her said, —Je mon foo, that's French for... —Putas, putas, putas, muttered the man in the sharkskin suit. Someone said, —My hands are full, would you mind getting some matches out of my pocket?... here, my trouser pocket. Someone said, —Do you like it here? Someone else said, —In the morning she didn't want to, so I put it under her arm while she was grinding the coffee. A man in an opaque brown monocle said, —Gzhzhzhzhzt...hu... and fell off his chair. Someone told the joke about Carruthers and his horse.

On the quai, the man kissed his girl and returned to his more delicate preoccupation. Along the Rue de Montmartre stubby hands lifted glasses of red wine. These were the people, slipping, sliding, perishing: they had triumphed once in revolution, and celebrated the Mass in public parody; installing the Goddess of Reason with great celebration, she proved, when unveiled, to be a dancing girl with whom many had extensive acquaintance. The People, of whom one of their officers, Captain de Mun, said —"Galilean, thou hast conquered!" Ah, for them no mercy; they are not the people, they are hell itself!... But they knew what they wanted: Liberté, égalité, fraternité... evaded the decorous façades decreed by their elders, or betters, and gathered in public interiors of carnivorous art nouveau.

In Père Lachaise an American woman bought a plot so that she might be buried near...who was it? Byron? Baudelaire? In the Place Vendôme another transatlantic visitor overturned a stolen taxicab at Napoleon's feet, was jailed, fined, and made much of by his friends. In Notre Dame du Flottement a millionairess from Maine married her colored chauffeur and was made much of by his friends. On the terrace of the Dôme, beset behind the clattering bastion of her own Sainte Chapelle, the young George Washington read with silently moving lips, broke wind pensively and looked around to see if she had attracted notice. On the Boulevard de la Madeleine a girl walking alone, swinging her purse, paused to glance in at the feet showing below the shield of the pissoir, and waited to accost their owner. Someone, looking above, cried out, —What's that? What is it? —The balloons. The balloons have gone up. In the washroom of the Café de la Régence, someone scrawled *Vive le roi* over the sink.

To one side, a man read the *Tribune*. To the other, *Al Misri*. —Votre journal, m'sieur, the waiter called, waving *Die Fleischflaute*, —votre journal...

And the shadow he cast behind him as he turned away fell back seven centuries, to embrace the dissolute youth of Raymond Lully, and infatuation with the beautiful Ambrosia de Castello, which she discouraged; and if she seemed to succumb at last, offering to bare her breasts in return for a poem he had written to their glory, it was to show him, as he approached in that rapture of which only flesh is capable, a bosom eaten away by cancer: he turned away to his conversion, to his death years later stoned in North Africa, and to his celebration as a scholar, a poet, a missionary, a mystic, and one of the foremost figures in the history of alchemy.

III

First of all, then, he is evil, in the judgment of God, who will not inquire what is advantageous to himself. For how can anyone love another, if he does not love himself? ... In order, therefore, that there might be a distinction between those who choose good and those who choose evil, God has concealed that which is profitable to men.
—PETER, in the Clementine *Recognitions*

—WYATT...let's get married before we know too much about each other.
That was unlike Esther.

She liked to get things out in the open, find why they *happened*. Still, like other women in love, salvation was her original purpose, redemption her eventual privilege; and, like most women, she could not wait to see him thoroughly damned first, before she stepped in, believing, perhaps as they do, that if he were saved now he would never need to be redeemed. There was a historical genuineness about Esther, which somehow persisted in spite of her conscious use of it. In her large bones there was implicit the temporal history of a past, and a future very much like it. There was size to her. She had the power of making her own mistakes appear as the work of some supramundane agency, possibly one of those often vulgarly confused with fate, which had here elected her capable of bringing forth some example which the world awaited. Principal among these (and no less a mistake, somewhere, which she must live out as though it were her own) was being a woman. She worked very hard to understand all this; and having come to be severely intellectual, probing the past with masculine ruthlessness, she became an accomplice of those very circumstances which Reason later accused of being unnecessary, and in the name of free will, by which she meant conscious desire, managed to prolong a past built upon them, refurbished, renewed, and repeated. With great diligence, and that talent of single purpose with which her sex pursue something unattainable in the same fashion they pursue something which is, her search for Reason was always interrupted by reasons. Things happened for reasons; and so, in her proposal it may have been simply her feminine logic insuring a succession of happenings which reasonably might never have happened at all. Or being a woman, and the woman she was, her proposal may have been an infinite moment of that femininity which is one of humanity's few approximations to beauty, asking no justification and needing none to act in a moment of certainty with nothing to fear, one day to be recalled in a fearful moment threatened by certainty.

Left hand; right hand: they moved over her with equal assurance. Undistinguished here they raised her flesh, and Esther rose to reconcile them, to provide common ground where each might know what the other was doing.

A year later, they had been married for almost a year; which was unlike Wyatt. He had become increasingly reluctant wherever decisions were concerned; and the more he knew, the less inclined to commit himself. Not that this was an exceptional state: whole systems of philosophy have been erected upon it. On the other hand, the more he refused to commit himself, the more submerged, and the more insistent from those depths, became the necessity to do so: a plight which has formed the cornerstone for whole schools of psychology. So it may be that his decision to marry simply made one decision the less that he must eventually face; or it is equally possible that his decision to marry was indecision crystallized, insofar as he was not deciding against it.

Knowing that extraordinary capacity for jealous hatred which men so often have for a woman's past, Esther was in a way grateful that he never asked her about hers. Still, she did not disown it, though much as she wanted to go everywhere she had never been, she as fervently never wanted to revisit any scene in that past, a frantic concatenation whose victim she remained, projecting her future upon it in all the defiant resentment of free will, in a world where she had been victimized by every turn of the die since her father had first cast it. Where Esther's mind had gone since, her thighs had followed with errant and back-breaking sincerity, in civilized correspondence to that primordial cannibal rite performed by sober comrades who eat their victims in order to impart to themselves the powers with which those victims had, as enemies, threatened to overcome them. (It is not simply hunger: those driven by hunger alone have been heard to remark afterward, —I should have preferred pork.)

Not hunger? One of the more fastidious comments risen in her past had sported the phrase *vagina dentata*. Still it was not hunger, but an insatiability which took this hunger as its course, seeking, in its clear demand, to absorb the properties which had been withheld from her; and finding, in its temporary satisfaction, and the subsequent pain of withdrawal, insatiability. Year after year the emancipated animus of free will labored its spinneret, spun out this viscous fluid of causality which had rapidly hardened into strands fatal as those of the tarantula's silk-lined burrow here in the sandy soil of native hope. She did not question it; no more than the trap door which the tarantula leaves open at the top, or the victims who tumble in, affirming her woman's part in deep despair over their common lot, expressed in a resentment of men for the success of their casual fortunes where her devourings continued, but not for love.

At no time was Esther unprepared for those attempts which the lives around her made to rise to tragedy; though by the time they managed it, they had escaped it, and through their ascendance she had come rather to see herself as the conglomerate tragic figure, since it was she who was always left. It confirmed something. Esther had spent little time with women. She seemed to find in their problems only weak and distorted plagiarisms of the monstrous image of her own. Thus it seemed very odd to many who knew her that she should choose a woman analyst. It became a very deep attachment, so long before any completion of her analysis that it was evident to both of them who had the upper hand. When Esther met Wyatt, she asked if she should marry, and was forbidden. She demanded, and was pled with. She married, and her analyst was a suicide. It was a way things had of working out for Esther. It confirmed something.

Call him louder! Call him louder! Trumpets sounded, and the roll of drums.

—And why you like Handel, Esther said quietly after their argument, or to continue it. She had a cold, which broke her voice low with apparent emotion.

—Handel?

Is not His voice like a hammer...?

—Mozart... She coughed.

Like a hammer that breaketh the stone

She swallowed. There was a magazine open in her hands, as there was a book in his; but she was watching him, to see if the intent strain in his face were for his reading, or tense suspension waiting, borne upon the chords of music, for the next sound of constriction and release in her throat. He did not move. Her throat drew tighter, its strictures embraced, and she swallowed with difficulty. At that, as though it were a signal of release from restraint, a hand rose to hide the intent corner of his profile. —And *Tosca!...* she murmured, as her throat bound up again, and she swallowed quickly. He did not move. The book was a large one, but she could not make out its title. It might have been anything; just as his tension must be for her presence, since he appeared to read everything with the same casual concentration. When she interrupted, there was no way of knowing whether he was looking up from Diogenes Laërtius or *No Orchids for Miss Blandish*. She might be breaking a thread in Berkeley's *New Theory of Vision*, joining a rain of falling objects from the supercelestial geography of Charles Fort, or only echoing a voice in some cheap paper novel like *Les Damnés de la Terre*. Mendelssohn's *Elijah* continued from the radio. She swallowed. Immediately, he cleared his throat, a vicarious measure which left her unrelieved. If she asked, he might look up with, —Fort says, "By the damned, I mean the excluded"...but she would have to ask, —Excluded from what? —"By prostitution, I seem to mean usefulness..."

She studied him now as though he might not be reading at all, but peeping at her through fingers of the hand shielding his eye. She cleared her throat. There was no way, as *Elijah* came to a close, to reopen their discussion: unless the next composition should be something by Beethoven or Mozart. If the radio voice should announce, Mozart's Symphony Number 37, Köchel Listing 444...He turned a page. Since their discussions seldom lasted long, she often carried them on in her own mind, reconsidering now (and certain she saw the glint of his eye between his fingers) her thralldom to the perfection of Mozart, work of genius without an instant of hesitation or struggle, genius to which argument opposed the heroic struggle constantly rending the music of Beethoven, struggle never resolved and triumphed until the end. —Genius in itself is essentially uninteresting. —But the work of genius... —It's difficult to share in perfection. —You, to share? she'd commenced; but that was all. He was reading. She swallowed, and caught the glitter of an eye. *Elijah* was finished. Still in her mind, "By prostitution, I seem to mean usefulness," Esther said:

—What are you reading?

—Eh? His surprise was a look (she would think of it one day, remembering, or trying to remember) indigenous to his face, either that immediate anticipatory surprise, reflecting sudden foretaste of something past (as when she asked him when he'd been in Spain: —I? I've never been in Spain); or it was this look he had now, the surprise of one intruded upon. And year after year as their marriage went on, the first came less and the other more often, until one day, remembering him, or trying to remember, it would be this one which would come to her, this face of confusion, of one intruded upon, an anxious look. He said, —Nothing.

—Nothing? You can't read nothing.

—It's a book on mummies.

—Mummies?

—Egyptian mummies.

—Why are you reading a book on Egyptian mummies?

He cleared his throat, but said nothing.

—But what I gave you of mine, the story I'm writing, you haven't read that yet.

—Yes, I did read it.

—And...well? What did you think?

—It was...you seemed quite partial to the word atavistic.

—Well that, is that all?

—Well Esther, the um, and double adjectives, cruel, red anger; hard, thin lips; dark, secret pain...

—But...

—But women's writing seems to get sort of...Sharp, eager faces; acid, unpleasant odor...listen. He turned toward the radio, where a poet whose work they both enjoyed was about to read. She looked at him a moment longer, and the book which had gone closed in his hand the instant she'd spoken to him. It had happened as directly as when once she had said, —You have wonderful eyes, and he turned them from her. What was it? As though to protect whatever lay beyond them until he could solve it himself, betraying the fear that in one lax moment his eyes might serve her as entrances. Even taking up a book she had read (Esther admired Henry James, but she trusted D. H. Lawrence), he did so anxiously, as though he might find the pages blank, the words eaten away by that hunger.

—Do you want to follow it? she asked, coming toward him with the *Collected Poems* opened in her hand. He shook his head, but did not look up, listening; and she sat down nearer him.

The poet read, in modulated tones given a hollow resonance by the radio. Esther's thumb was drawn down the page, following one line to the next, bent over the book, and her lips moved, forming around the poet's words as he spoke them, clear separate syllables which her lips, meeting and parting, moistened by her tongue, allowing exhalations in vowels, wet clicks from the roof of the mouth on *d*, brought into viscous consonance with her absorbedness, unrestrained by those lips clamped tight beside her until he cleared his throat and suddenly got to his feet. Before she could speak he had reached a door.

—But what?...

—I have some work, he said quickly, and left her there sitting, hunched over the pages, staring after him, while the poet read on in clear separate syllables. She blew her nose, and returned to the page before her, but her lips did not move, for she did not hear another word of the reading. Neither did her eyes, for she was gazing at the backs of her hands.

The room Wyatt had entered was as large as the bedroom, but had only one window which would have opened on an airshaft if anyone had bothered opening it. During the first year or so, the room served various vague purposes. Though between them they hadn't a great number of books, not great enough, that is, to warrant a library (for a library, to Esther, was a roomful of books), it served as that for awhile. However, this was not practical, for reasons of which each privately accused the other in refusing to admit his own. Esther liked books out where everyone could see them, a sort of graphic index to the intricate labyrinth of her mind arrayed to impress the most casual guest, a system of immediate introduction which she had found to obtain in a number of grimy intellectual households in Greenwich Village. Her husband, on the other hand, did not seem to care where his books were, so long as they were where he put them. That is to say, separate. No doubt Boyle's *Skeptical Chemist*, Jalland's *The Church and the Papacy*, Cennino Cennini's *Libro dell' Arte*, or *La Chimie au Moyen Age* would have dressed up Esther's shelves; no doubt the *Grimorium Verum* and the *Turba Philosophorum* would have been dusted down their spines regularly. No doubt these were among the reasons he kept them on his own, or strewn among the litter which had gradually filled the undetermined room until it belonged to him. Things were tacked on the walls there haphazard, an arm in dissection from a woodcut in the *Fabrica* of Vesalius, and another sixteenth-century illustration from the *Surgery* of Paré, a first-aid chart called "the wound man"; a photograph of an Italian cemetery flooded by the Po; a calendar good for every day from 1753 to 2059; a print of a drawing of the head of Christ by Melozzo da Forlì; a ground plan of the Roman city of Leptis Magna; a mirror; and rolls of paper and canvases on stretchers leaning in the corners.

When he started to work at restoring paintings, in addition to his regular job, the littered room changed only slightly. There had always been piles of drawing paper, and canvases on frames, prepared and clean or the composition begun in black unfinished lines, most prominent, or most familiar among these the initiated portrait of Camilla. The gessoed surface had cracked here and there, and got unevenly soiled, but the composition was very clear in lines unaltered since he'd put them there some fifteen years before. Occasionally this was hung on one of the walls, as though being studied with an eye to completion. Other times it remained stacked with the other empty and besmirched canvases against a wall. There was a wide flat drafting table, and a heavy easel stood erect in the middle of the room under the bare electric bulb. But the most noticeable change was not to be seen: it lay heavily on the air, the smell of varnish, oils, and turpentine, quickened by the pervasive delicacy of lavender, oil of lavender which he used sometimes as a medium.

Esther had admired the drawing begun on that large soiled cracked surface, the fine-boned face (so unlike her own) whose fleshless quality of hollows was elevated by heavy earrings, archaic hoops of gold she had seen in a leather box where her husband kept odds and ends; admired the drawing not for what it was but, as she said, for what it could be. He stood looking at it, and they were silent, for he knew she was looking at him. The only work he had ever finished, those paintings shown in Paris years before, had ended up in a warehouse in New Jersey. Esther had never seen them. They seldom discussed painting, for like so many things upon which they might agree, they never managed to agree at the same moment; and as the conversations of the early months of their marriage went on, their ideas and opinions seemed to meet only in passing, each bound in an opposite direction, neither stopping to do more than honor the polite pause of recognition.

The poet's clear tones had given way to the ingratiating pillage of the announcer, and she rose, the charm broken, with no word of the poet in her head but, for no apparent reason, "By prostitution I seem to mean usefulness." She picked up *The Royal Mummies* and blew her nose as she crossed the room toward the half-open door, where she put her head in, and the book, saying, —Do you want this in there?

—What? Oh that, thank you.

—What are you doing?

—Nothing, just . . . this work. He motioned toward the plans pinned on the drafting table.

—Don't they give you enough time down there, to do your work? But he lowered his eyes from hers, shrugged and turned back to the table. —If it were something real, but this, going to this silly job every day, year after year.

—It's not a silly job, Esther, he answered soberly, without turning.

—Copying lines, copying plans, one bridge after another. Oh, all right, it isn't silly but you could do better, you could do more. Honestly Wyatt, the way you go day after day with your job and your reading and your . . . fooling around, and you could do more. It's not . . . you're not waiting to discover something, are you. Waiting to be discovered, aren't you? Oh I hate to go on like this, sounding like this . . . She paused, watching his narrow black-suited figure bend as a vertical line came down the paper. —It's this . . . seeing you like you are sometimes now, she went on slowly, —I see you with your head down and, I don't know, but it upsets me, it makes me unhappy to see you that way.

—Why? he asked in a voice near a whisper, his face close down to the paper.

—Because you look so lonely and that's what I can't bear, she brought out at his back. Then her eyes lowered to the floor when he did not turn, and she brought the damp knot of the handkerchief to her nose. —Don't you want anything... any of the things, that other people want?

—Other people? he demanded, turning.

—Oh..., her throat caught. —Never mind. There. I'll leave you with company.

—That? the mirror?

—I love that, you having a mirror in here.

—But that... to correct bad drawing...

—Good night, I'm going to bed when I've done the dishes.

—I'll do them, if you're tired, he offered. —Your cold...

—Don't be silly. I'll do them. She left him there, knotting a piece of string in his hand. A few minutes later, when she'd turned out the lights in the living room, the light from the half-open door drew her eyes and she saw him standing, running the fingers of his right hand over his rough chin, up one cheek and then the other, as though to wake after the night needing a shave made sense, but finding his face rough with growth after a day's well-lighted consciousness a strange thing. Then he said aloud, —How safe from accident I am!

She had once heard him mentioned, with little more than curiosity, by people whom neither of them knew now. Then, when she came to asking more pointedly about him, there were anecdotes enough (someone she met at a party had heard he'd jumped off the Eiffel Tower, and with drunken persistence marveled at his survival). In and out dodged the vagrant specter, careering through conversations witness to that disinterested kindness which other people extend to one who does not threaten them with competition on any level they know. Costumed in the regalia of their weary imaginations, he appeared and vanished in a series of images which, compacted, might have formed a remarkable fellow indeed; but in that Diaspora of words which is the providential nature of conversation, the fugitive persisted, like those Jewish Christians who endured among the heathen, here in the figure of a man who, it appeared at last, had done many things to envy and nothing to admire.

—Wyatt, what is it? What's the matter?

—A dream?...

—Only a dream?

—But...

—It's all right, darling, whatever it was it's all right now.

—It was...

—What was it?

—At home, in bed, that parsonage was a big empty house and I know every step in it, I woke up and I could hear footsteps. I woke up there hearing very heavy footsteps in an even tread and I knew where they were going, I heard them down the stairs and through the front hallway and into the living room, across the living room and through the back hall past the dining room toward the kitchen...

—But, was that all?

—But listen, what was terrible was that I know every step in that house, I know how many steps it takes to come down the stairs or to cross the living room, I can't tell you the number but I know, but these steps I heard in the darkness, they were regular and even, not in a hurry but what was terrible, they kept reaching places too soon. I know the sound, I know how the sounds change when you step from the front hall into the living room, or passing the dining room or off the last stair and... but these steps kept arriving too soon, not hesitating anywhere and not in a hurry, but if you take regular even steps, and there weren't enough of them.

—It is strange. And your voice, you sound like a child.

—It doesn't sound terrible does it, now.

—We'll talk about it in the morning, she whispered, and her hand moved down his body to find him and gently raise him into life. —There must be a reason...

—Reason! but, good God, haven't we had enough... reason.

Her hand twisted and her fingers, closed together, moved only enough to make themselves felt, to make their motion not an act but a sense, to arouse not simply the blood which rushed to meet them but, in a touch, something beyond it. —Why do you fight it all so hard, Wyatt?

—Women, he commenced, and then, —men rising to isolated challenges, he spends his life preparing to meet one, one single challenge, when he triumphs it's, they call it heroic, but you, I know how hard you try for me, women just go on, they just go on and I...

—They have to, Esther said beside him, as he came over half upon her in the darkness. —If we could get away from here, you've been everywhere, you've studied in Germany and in Paris and I... Wyatt, if we could travel... She felt his leg relax on hers. —And you don't want to, you don't want to travel.

—To voyage...

—With me?

—Charles Fort says maybe we're fished for, by supercelestial beings...

—Yes, without me. Alone.

—My grandfather, he fell down a well once, did I tell you? He talks of voyages, he's oriented by the stars. Orientation sidérale, the man who experimented with ants in the desert in Morocco... Then he seemed to tighten and hold her off suddenly, and she asked:

—What is it?

—In that dream, I just remembered my... my hair was on fire.

She felt him run his hand over his hair, and down his rough cheek in the darkness. —We'll talk about it in the morning, she said, —not now.

—Not flames, he said holding her again.

—You, you'd go to Morocco...

—But just burning, he whispered, almost wondrously, as she rose to engage the incredulous tension of his right hand, still murmuring:

—And be more... Moroccan... than the Moors.

Next morning Esther woke alone, to realize that she had been alone most of the night. She swallowed, and found her cold better. She smelled coffee and went to the kitchen, where half a pot of it was boiling furiously on the stove. She started to call out, felt a wave of nausea, and sat down and decided to eat something. She got out bread and butter and looked for an egg, but could not find one. Then she poured some of the boiling coffee into a cold cup, and the cup cracked; nonetheless she poured until it was full and took it into the living room.

Light showed from the studio, and she heard sounds behind the half-closed door. Then:

—Damn you, damn you... damn you!

—What? she brought out, at the door. —What a smell.

—Nothing. He stood facing her under the bare brilliance of the bulb, as though stricken, in the midst of some criminal commission, as lightning freezes motion.

—What is it?

—Nothing, I'm... talking to myself.

—Are you working? still working?

—Yes, yes, working, he answered. His empty hands opened and closed at his sides, as though seeking something to occupy them. Then he caught up a knife in one, and with the other pointed to the straight easel, —On that.

—That? She looked at the familiar thing on the easel. It was a late eighteenth-century American painting in need of a good deal of work, the portrait of a woman with large bones in her face but an unprominent nose, a picture which looked very much like Esther. She found it so, at any rate; and even when he'd said, —As a painting, it isn't very good as a painting, is it?... she standing behind him could see no further than the portrait, held by the likeness as happened so often but seldom so clearly, finding resemblances to herself everywhere as though she set out from the start seeking identity with misfortune, recognition in disaster.

He had backed away from her, holding the knife, as though he were guarding something, or hiding it, and when she looked behind him on the wall she

saw the black lines on the cracked soiled surface of the unfinished portrait.
—That, she said, —that's what you were working on?

—That. He made a stab pointing behind her with the knife, and she moved
to sink wearily against the door frame.

—A way to start the day, she said, looking at him. —I wish you'd stop
waving that knife. Start the day? I feel like you've been in here all night, like
you're always in here, and whoever it is that sleeps with me and talks to me
in the dark is somebody else.

—I woke up, he said putting the knife down, —I wanted to work.

—But this... if you wanted to work on that, you can tell me, you don't
have to pretend, ... this secrecy...

—Aunt May, when she made things, even her baking, she kept the blinds
closed in the butler's pantry when she frosted a cake, nobody ever saw anything
of hers until it was done.

—Aunt May! I don't care about Aunt May, but you... I wish you would
finish that thing, she went on, looking at the lines over his shoulder, —and
get rid of her.

—Rid of her? he repeated. From somewhere he'd picked up an egg.

—Finish it. Then there might be room for me.

—You? to paint you?

—Yes, if you...

—But you're here, he brought out, cracking the egg over a cup, and he
caught the yolk in his palm. —You're so much here. Esther... I'm sorry, he
said with a step toward her, the egg yolk rolling from one palm to the other,
threatening to escape. —I'm sorry, he said seeing the expression he'd brought
to her face. —I'm tired.

—Even this, she said lowering her eyes, and bringing them round to the
damaged likeness on the easel, —if you'd finish this.

—There's no hurry, he said quickly, —they've gone abroad, the people who
own it, they may not be back for some time.

—If they were gone ten years you'd take ten years. You could do work like
this in half the time you take, a tenth of the time, even if you won't paint
yourself you could settle down to restoring work and make something of it.
It's no wonder you don't sleep, that you're nervous and have bad dreams when
you're not doing what you want to do.

He stood bent over a cup, where he held the egg yolk suspended between
the squared fingertips of one hand, and a pin in the other, about to puncture
it, and he looked up at her. —But I am, Esther.

—If you could finish something original, she said. —You look like an old
man. Why are you laughing?

—Just then, he said straightening up, and the egg yolk still hanging from his fingers, —I felt like him, just for that instant as though I were old Herr Koppel, I've told you, the man I studied with in Munich. As though this were that studio he had over the slaughterhouse, where we worked, he'd stand with an egg yolk like this and talk, "That romantic disease, originality, all around we see originality of incompetent idiots, they could draw nothing, paint nothing, just so the mess they make is original... Even two hundred years ago who wanted to be original, to be original was to admit that you could not do a thing the right way, so you could only do it your own way. When you paint you do not try to be original, only you think about your work, how to make it better, so you copy masters, only masters, for with each copy of a copy the form degenerates...you do not invent shapes, you know them, auswendig wissen Sie, by heart..." The egg yolk fell, most of it went into the cup. —Damn it, he said, looking at it, —but it doesn't matter, these stale eggs... "Country eggs you must have, with stale city eggs you cannot make good tempera..."

—I might have had it for breakfast.

—But, was it the last one? I didn't...I'm sorry, Esther, I...here...He poured the white from one stained cup into what yolk there was in the other. —Here, it just isn't...it's clean, there just isn't as much yolk...

—Aren't you going to your office? You'd better shave if you are, she said and left him offering the cup in the direction of the damaged likeness on the easel.

Her coffee was cold. She poured it into the sink, and went down to get the mail. She read one letter on the stairs, and called out before she'd closed the door behind her, —Wyatt, something awful's happened. Where are you? Then she almost screamed, seeing him standing in the door of the studio with blood all over one side of his face and his neck. —What happened?

—What is it? he asked. —What awful thing...

—What's happened to you? she cried running up to him.

—What? He stood there with a straight razor opened in his hand.

—What are you doing?

—Shaving...

—Did you do that...shaving? What are you doing in there, shaving.

—Oh, he said running his fingertips over his chin, and looking at the blood on them. —It's a mess, I'm sorry, Esther. The mirror, I was using this mirror in here, you have the one in the bathroom covered...

—Covered! she burst out impatiently, twisting the letter in her hand.

—It has a cloth over it, I thought for some reason you might...

—It's a handkerchief drying, why didn't you just pull it off. And that, she went on, getting breath, —that terrible thing, it's dangerous to shave with, look at it, just because your father...You're like a child about it, this image of his...

—What was the letter?

—The letter? This? Yes, that warehouse, the place in New Jersey where you had your things, it burned. And here, they send you a check for a hundred and thirty dollars.

—Really? That's fine.

—Fine? Aren't you upset? Things like those paintings, they can't be replaced.

—No, they can't, he said quickly, a hand to his chin where the blood had already begun to dry.

—Where are you going?

—To wash. I have to hurry, I...I have some plans to take in.

She caught him again at the front door, where he paused with a roll of papers under his arm. —No coffee? Nothing?

—I had some earlier. He pulled at the knob, but she had a hand on his arm.

—I wish you could rest, she said, and when he turned, looking at her as though he had suddenly been stopped in a crowded street: —Are you all right?

—I? Why yes, yes I'm all right, Esther, I...you mustn't...Goodbye, he broke and hurried toward the stairs.

A few minutes later, when she was standing pouring coffee into the cracked cup, the doorbell rang. It was a delivery boy with a dozen eggs. She put them on the kitchen table, and then took out a handkerchief and stood, steadying herself with a hand on the table, staring at the coffee, whose surface was broken with the regular beats of her heart.

It was dark afternoon when Esther came in, bearing in the forefront of her mind fragments of a conversation she had left a little earlier (on Rilke, not Rilke's poetry but Rilke the man, who refused to be psychoanalyzed for fear of purging his genius); but over this, and through the rest of her mind, skated an image far more familiar, plunging and surfacing, escaping under the applied hand of her memory, reappearing when she turned elsewhere, echoing, among faces and lanterns and the prows of boats, —Maybe we're fished for..., an image whose apparition she waited even now. Though it was dark in the studio, she opened the door and looked in there. Then she took off her coat, turned the radio on, and sat down, oblivious to the soprano singing nel massimo dolore, —Sempre con fè sincera la mia preghiera...

The door rattled, with muttering beyond it. She sat still. Finally he entered,

in a state of some excitement. —I had trouble with the key, he said, and gave
her a broken self-conscious laugh. She wanted time to study him before she
spoke, but could not let him escape to the studio before she asked:

—Was it you I saw this afternoon? a little while ago?

—Me? Why? Where?

—Were you there, where they're showing Picasso's new...

—*Night Fishing in Antibes*, yes, yes...

—Why didn't you speak to us?

—Speak to who? You? Were you there?

—I was there, with a friend. You could have spoken to us, Wyatt, you didn't
have to pretend that...I was out with someone who...

—Who? I didn't see them, I didn't see you, I mean.

—You looked right at us. I'd already said, There's my husband, we were
near the door and you were bobbing...

—Listen...

—You went right past us going out.

—Look, I didn't see you. Listen, that painting, I was looking at the painting. Do you see what this was like, Esther? seeing it?

—I saw it.

—Yes but, when I saw it, it was one of those moments of reality, of near-
recognition of reality. I'd been...I've been worn out in this piece of work,
and when I finished it I was free, free all of a sudden out in the world. In the
street everything was unfamiliar, everything and everyone I saw was unreal,
I felt like I was going to lose my balance out there, this feeling was getting all
knotted up inside me and I went in there just to stop for a minute. And then
I saw this thing. When I saw it all of a sudden everything was freed, into one
recognition, really freed into reality that we never see, you never see it. You
don't see it in paintings because most of the time you can't see beyond a painting. Most paintings, the instant you see them they become familiar, and then
it's too late. Listen, do you see what I mean?

—As Don said about Picasso...she commenced.

—That's why people can't keep looking at Picasso and expect to get anything
out of his paintings, and people, no wonder so many people laugh at him. You
can't see them any time, just any time, because you can't see freely very often,
hardly ever, maybe seven times in a life.

—I wish, she said, —I wish...

How real is any of the past, being every moment revalued to make the
present possible: to come up one day saying, —You see? I was right all the
time. Or, —Then I was wrong, all the time. The radio is still busy with Puc-
cini, *Tosca* all the way through: from the jumble at the end of the second act,

Wyatt rescues her words, repeats them. —Questo è il bacio di Tosca! That's reality, then. Tosca's kiss, reality?

—I wish... she repeats (preferring *Don Giovanni*).

—Maybe seven times in a life.

Magic number! but she sits looking at him, waiting in the space populated by memory. One night when she was doing her nails, he came in. —Wyatt, you've never had a manicure? Never? Let me give you a manicure... But he said something in a tone apologetic, alarmed, and took his hands away one clutched in the other.

—But it can't really be that simple... (a discussion: did the coming of the printing press corrupt? putting a price on authorship, originality). —Look at it this way, look at it as liberation, the first time in history that a writer was independent of patrons, the first time he could put a price on his work, make it a thing of material value, a vested interest in himself for the first time in history...

—And painters, and artists? Lithography, and color reproductions...

—Yes, I don't know, if one corrupts the artist and the other corrupts... that damned *Mona Lisa*, no one sees it, you can't see it with a thousand off-center reproductions between you and it.

—But how...

—I don't know, I've tried to understand it myself. Spinoza...

Mozart? The air is full of him, you've only got to have a radio receiving set to formulize the silence, give it shape and put it in motion: *Sleigh Ride* hurtles from the grid and strikes her. She suffers the impact without surprise. —I know you've never said you didn't want children, but whenever I've mentioned it you just look... you just get a look on your face. He puts his hand there, his right hand to his forehead and draws it down with feverish application, as though in this to pull away the features so long forming, revaluing for this moment; but above his hand, his face comes back into shape, the forehead quickly rises and recovers its lines, then the brows, and the eyes vividly devious permit nothing to enter. —I wish we were in the dark, you can talk to me in the dark, in the light you tell me things like... Zero doesn't exist.

—But you asked me...

—Or bad money drives out good.

Esther watched him now, standing in the middle of the room, drawing his hand down over his face as though, again, to wipe out some past, how long ago, or how recent, or all of it? She did not know, but sought one area among the German festivals, Handel at Breslau, Shakespeare at Stuttgart, Beethoven at Bonn, all in May; *Egmont* at Altenburg, *Der Fliegende Holländer* at Nürnberg in June; *Die Ägyptische Helena* at München...

—Munich, she said, —when you were in Munich?

—What?

—You've never told me much about it.

—About Munich?

—And that boy you knew there that you spent so much time with.

—Han? I didn't spend a lot of time with him.

—You worked together, and drank together and traveled together.

—Traveled?

—That night you spent together at Interlaken, from what you've told me of that...

—We were there for almost a week, waiting for a look at the Jungfrau, it was hidden every day, I told you about that. And the day I left for Paris, early in the morning standing on the railway platform I looked up, and there it was as though it had come from nowhere, and at that instant the train came in right between us, good God I remember that well, that morning.

—But... But he had turned and gone into the studio, and she went to the kitchen, stopping only to change the station on the radio. They were silent through most of supper, as though in deference to a symphony of Sibelius which reached across the room to jar them into submission, for neither of them would have confessed, even privately, to liking it.

Sensing the thought, If he does not love me, then he is incapable of love, —I wish... she said. Moments like this (and they came more often) she had the sense that he did not exist; or, to re-examine him, sitting there looking in another direction, in terms of substance and accident, substance the imperceptible underlying reality, accident the properties inherent in the substance which are perceived by the senses: the substance is transformed by consecration, but the accidents remain what they were. The consecration has apparently taken place not, as she thought, through her, but somewhere beyond her; and here she sits attending the accidents.

Her lips did not move, neither did the words laid out there on the stillness of the white page: the faculty of reading suspended in her dull stare, the syllables remained exposed, hopelessly coexistent. Then one caught her eye, drew her on through another, and so through six, seven... When her wet tongue clicked *t*, she looked up and the poem died on the page. —Did you know he was homosexual? she asked.

—Ummm.

—I didn't know it until Don told me today.

—Who?

—Don Bildow, he edits this little magazine, the...

—He's homosexual?

—Oh no, he isn't, Don isn't, don't you listen? He told me that this...
this... She held up that *Collected Poems*, shunning to speak the poet's name.
—Did you know it?

—What? Yes, I've heard something like that.

—Why didn't you tell me?

He looked up for the first time. —Tell you?

—You might have mentioned it, she said and put the book aside with its
cover down.

—Might have... why would I mention it? What's that to do with...

—When we were sitting here listening to him read, it didn't occur to me,
it's funny, it never occurred to me about him, pictures I've seen of him, and
his poems, the things he says in his poems... and I'd wanted to meet him.
Esther's eyes had come to rest on the floor, and the shadow thrown there from
the chair, meaningless until it moved.

—And you're surprised?... upset over this?

—I'd wanted to meet him, she commenced, following the shadow's length
back to its roots.

—Meet him? And now a thing like this... I don't understand, you Esther,
you're the one who always knows these things about people, these personal
things about writers and painters and all the...

—Yes but...

—Analyzing, dissecting, finding answers, and now... What did you want
of him that you didn't get from his work?

Esther's eyes rose slowly from the floor the height of her husband's figure.
—Why are you so upset all of a sudden? she asked him calmly. —Just because
I'd mentioned Han...

—Han! he repeated, wresting the name from her. —Good God, is this
what it is! That stupid... Han, why he... after all these years, a thing like
this...

—And that painting you gave him, you've never given me...

—Gave him? It disappeared, that's what I told you. "You give it to me to
remember you, because we are dear friends, this Memlinc you are making
now..." He asked me for it, but it disappeared before it was even finished,
when they arrested the old man, Koppel, that's what I told you. He subsided,
muttering something, he'd picked up a piece of string and stood knotting it.

She murmured, her eyes back on the shadow's busy extremity, —You've
told me...

—That stupid... Han, he went on, —in his uniform, pounding his finger
with a beer stein, "You see? it couldn't hurt me..." At Interlaken, what else
was there to do but drink? Snowed in, waiting, "There's something missing,"

he says, he hadn't shaved for three days, the blank look on his face, "...if I knew what it is then it wouldn't be so missing..." I've told you...

—Oh, you've told me, she said, impatient, looking up at him for a moment, then back at the shadow. —I don't know what all you've told me, what little... New England, all right, you're the Puritan, all this secrecy, this guilt, preaching to me out of Fichte about moral action, no wonder a thing like this upsets you, when I mention a poet I've wanted to meet and he turns out...you don't want to talk about it, do you! she pursued him, where he had got almost across the room, about to escape into the studio.

But he stopped in that doorway, reaching a hand inside he snapped on the bright light which flung a heavier shadow across the floor to her. —Listen, this guilt, this secrecy, he burst out, —it has nothing to do with this...this passion for wanting to meet the latest poet, shake hands with the latest novelist, get hold of the latest painter, devour...what is it? What is it they want from a man that they didn't get from his work? What do they expect? What is there left of him when he's done his work? What's any artist, but the dregs of his work? the human shambles that follows it around. What's left of the man when the work's done but a shambles of apology.

—Wyatt, these romantic...

—Yes, romantic, listen...Romantics! they marry cows and all kinds of comfort, soon enough their antics betray them to what would have been fatal in the work, I mean being obvious. No, here, it's competence right here in the world that's rewarded with romantic ends, and the romantics battling for competence, something to eat and carfare home...Look at the dentist's wife, she's a beauty. Who's the intimate of a saint, it's her Jesuit confessor, and the romantics end up anchorites in the desert.

Esther stood up, turning her back as she spoke to him so that he could not evade her question with a look, or by turning away himself, but was left with, —Then tell me, what are you trying to do? And she picked up a magazine, and came back to a chair with it, not looking up to where he took a step toward her from the brightly lighted doorway.

—There's only one thing, somehow, he commenced, faltering, —that... one dilemma, proving one's own existence, it...there's no ruse people will disdain for it, and...or Descartes "retiring to prove his own existence," his "cogito ergo sum," why...no wonder he advanced masked. Kept a salamander, no wonder. Something snaps, and...when every solution becomes an evasion,...it's frightening, trying to stay awake.

Though his voice had risen, still Esther did not look up, but sat quietly turning the pages of the magazine, and when she spoke did so quietly and evenly. —You've told me, all your reasons for letting year after year go by this way while you...work? And even this, look. This magazine your company puts out, look at this picture, this bridge, it's something your company did, designed by Ben somebody, I can't pronounce it, the road bridge at Fallen Ark Gap.

—Do you like it? he asked, suddenly standing beside her, anxiety still in his face and sounding in his voice, but a different, immediate anxiousness.

—It's beautiful, she said. Then she turned and looked up to him. —Wyatt, you know you could do more, more than just the drafting, copying lines, wasting your time with...

—Look at it, he said, —do you see the way it seems to come out and meet itself, does it? He held his hands up in a nervous bridge, fingertips barely touching, the piece of string still hung from one of them. —Does it look that way to you? that sense of movement in stillness, that...tension at rest and still...do you know that Arab saying, "The arch never sleeps"?...

—Yes, it is dynamic. Wyatt, you, why can't you...Then her eyes, meeting his, seemed that abruptly to empty the enthusiasm from his face and his voice.

—It's derivative, the design, he said.

—Derivative?

—Of Maillart.

—I don't know him.

—A Swiss, there's a book of his work somewhere around here.

She looked at his hands, gone back to knotting the string, and watched a bowline form there. —Like a knot, she said, —pulling against itself.

—I'm going back to work, he said and turned away. She walked after him as far as the lighted doorway, and stood for a minute staring at the picture on the upright easel. —I've come to hate that thing, she said finally, and with no answer, left him removing corroded portions of the face with the sharp blade.

Most nights now Esther went to sleep alone, her consciousness carried in that direction by Handel and Palestrina, William Boyce, Henry Purcell, Vivaldi, Couperin, music which connected them across the darkness in the stream where everything that had once brought them together returned to force them apart, back to the selves they could no longer afford to mistrust. Sometimes there was a long pause between the records; sometimes one was repeated, over and over again.

She woke to the same exquisitely measured contralto, —*When I am laid...*, that had lost her to sleep what seemed so many hours before. She lay in the dark and saw herself as she had been, a week before was it? sitting with an open book. —Wyatt...? —What is it? When she said nothing he looked up at her. —What is it, Esther? She looked at him. —I just want you to talk to me. He looked at her; and looking at him she heard herself saying something she had said another time and wanted to repeat but there was no way to, for he simply sat, looking at her, and would not provoke it: —I wish you *would* lose your temper, she had said, —or *some*thing because this ... this restraint, this pose, this control that you've cultivated, Wyatt, it becomes inhuman ... He just looked at her.

The music, she realized now, was not the Purcell, not the contralto at all, but strident male voices in a Handel oratorio. Memories ran together, and she sat up in bed. Just her position, lying flat on her back, had advanced one memory, one evening and one conversation, into another, like streams commingling on an open plain. Bolt upright, everything stopped. She drew breath, and smelled lavender.

Esther got out of bed and went into the living room, where she sat down in the darkness. The door to the studio was open barely an inch. She sat, listening and remembering, as though he had been gone a long time. Would the music of Handel always recall sinful commission, the perpetration of some crime in illuminated darkness recognized as criminal only by him who committed it: Persephone, she sat now listening. And would the scent of lavender recall it? as it was doing now; for she felt that she was remembering, that this moment was long past, or that she was seated somewhere in the future, seated somewhere else and had suddenly caught the smell of lavender in the air, recalling this moment only in memory, that in another moment she would breathe deeply, destroying the delicate scent, that she would arise and go: queen of the shades, was her mother wandering in search of her? now where she waited, here on the other side of the door opening upon her husband's infernal kingdom.

She woke sitting straight up in the chair. The music was right where it had abandoned her: repeating? or had she been lost to it for no more than a transition of chords, as is the most alert consciousness. She stared at the shaft of light; and immediately she was up, and had pushed the door open.

Wyatt had modified his handwriting to a perverse version of Carolingian minuscule, in which the capital *S*'s, *G*'s, and *Y*'s were indistinguishable, and among the common letters, *y*, *g*, and *f*. The looked like *M*, and *p* a declined bastard of *h*. (Esther wrote in one continuous line, interrupted by humps, depressions, lonely dots and misplaced streaks, remarkably legible.) There were specimens of his writing strewn about the room; still, his childhood hand was apparent as the child father to the man. On the length of the table made from a door, on top of large sheets of unfinished lines drafted in origins of design pinned to the table, among opened books, and books with slips of paper profusely stuck between their pages, *The Secret of the Golden Flower*, *Problems of Mysticism and Its Symbolism*, *Prometheus and Epimetheus*, *Cantilena Riplœi*, beside an empty brandy bottle, lay open Foxe's *Book of Martyrs*, and there in the scrupulous hand of childhood, written on lined paper, a nursery rhyme which she suddenly had in her hand, standing alone in the room.

There was a man of double deed, it commenced,

> *Sowed his garden full of seed.*
> *When the seed began to grow,*
> *'Twas like a garden full of snow;*
> *When the snow began to melt,*
> *'Twas like a ship without a belt;*
> *When the ship began to sail,*
> *'Twas like a bird without a tail;*
> *When the bird began to fly,*

—Esther!

> *'Twas like an eagle in the sky;*
> *When the sky began to roar,*
> *'Twas like a lion at the door;*

—Esther...

> *When the door began to crack,*
> *'Twas like a stick across my back;*
> *When my back began to smart...*

—Esther, what is it? What are you doing here?

> *'Twas like a penknife in my heart;*
> *When my heart began to bleed,*
> *'Twas death and death and death indeed.*

—Esther...

—I just couldn't stop reading it, she said. He had her, supporting her with one arm.

—But what...why...

—Are you here now? she said, looking at him, into his eyes.

The music stopped, and the automatic arm lifted, paused, returned to the grooves it had just left. He reached over and turned it off.

—Wyatt...?

—I thought you were asleep, I just went out to get this, he said, holding up a bottle of brandy. He looked down quickly at his table, at the undisturbed plans and the books there. —I thought you were asleep, he repeated, looking at her. Then he saw what she had in her hand. —That, he said taking it from her, —what are you reading it for, it... it's just something I found here, here in this old book of Aunt May's. It's nothing, it's just something... He set the brandy down on the table. —Something she made me copy out.

He had no coat, and was dressed in a black suit. The bones in his face were smaller than Esther's. His hair was cut short, and his skull looked almost square. —Esther? . . . She put her arms around him. —Come to bed.

The dream recurs.

—Darling . . . the same one?

—Yes. The same. Exactly the same.

She thinks then, Perhaps . . .

—It doesn't really hurt, there isn't any pain and there aren't any flames, but just that my hair is burning . . .

Perhaps the consecration has not taken place yet after all, and the substance is still there, caught up in accident, waiting. Bedded in darkness she drew him over, and sweating he performed, and lay back, silent, inert, distant. —There are some cigarettes on the dresser, she said. He walked there in the dark, found them and lit one, sitting on the edge of the bed he smoked.

—Wyatt?

—What.

—How are you?

—Fine.

—I mean how do you feel?

—Empty, he answered.

She said nothing, but pretended sleep. After minutes of sitting abandoned he turned open the disrupted covers, and was asleep before she was, dwelling close up against the exposure of her back.

The lust of summer gone, the sun made its visits shorter and more uncertain, appearing to the city with that discomfited reserve, that sense of duty of the lover who no longer loves.

Then, as someone in a steam-heated room (it was a woman named Agnes) said while mixing gin with sweet vermouth, —Christmas is almost down our throats.

In another apartment, a tall woman put down the telephone and said to her husband, —A party. I did hope we'd get to the Narcissus Festival this year. The Hawaii one.

On Madison Avenue, two deer hung before a shop by their hind feet, bellies split and paper rosettes planted under their tails.

On Second Avenue, a girl in a south-bound bus (her surname appeared 963 times in the Bronx directory) said, —But he don't even know my name. —Who don't? —The lipstick man, he was in today. I found out he's single.

—Is he hansome? —He's not really hansome, he's more what you might say inneresting looking. With my hair and my complexion he says I ought to wear teeshans red. My favorite movie star...

On First Avenue, a girl in a north-bound bus (who used the same lipstick as her favorite movie star) said, —My doctor told me to ride this bus, he says maybe that'll bring it on.

In a Lexington Avenue bar, a man in a Santa Claus suit said, —Hey Barney, let's have one here, first one today. The bartender was saying —It's just the same as in Brooklyn, irregardless... —That's what I say, if you serve food you gotta have a rest room for ladies as well as men. A woman said, —Where do you come from? —Out on Long Island, Jamaica. —Jewmaica you mean. —Yeh? So where do you come from. —Never mind. —Yeh, never mind, I know where, it's nothing but a bunch of Portuguese and Syssirians up where you come from up there.

—Hey Barney, let's have another one here.

—OK Pollyotch, the woman called to Santa Claus.

—Hey Barney...

—Hey Pollyotch, don't start singin your ladonnamobilay in here.

—I need this drink like I need a hole in the head, said Santa Claus, interrupting the young man beside him who was staring at a dollar bill pinned on the wall, a sign which said, *If you drive your* FATHER *to drink drive him here*, and his own image in the mirror. He turned and nodded agreement. —You know what I mean? What's your name? —Otto. —You know what I mean, Otto? Otto held up his beer glass, half emptied, and nodded. —Can I buy you a drink Otto?

—He tole me ahedda time he's gonna get drunk, the woman said.

—Who's kiddin who?

—Some people never learn.

—Listen to this guy you'll go crazy.

—Can I buy you a drink?

—No, thank you, really. I feel just the way you do. I'm just waiting.

—You won't drink with me, hunh? You won't drink with me...?

—Hey Pollyotch...

—Like I say, it's just like in Brooklyn, irregardless...

The juke-box came to life, and played *The World Is Waiting for the Sunrise*. Fruit stores were busy. Taxi drivers were busy. Trains were crowded, in both directions. Accident wards were inundated. Psychoanalysts received quivering visits from old clients. Newspaper reporters dug up and wrote at compassionate length of gas-filled rooms, Christmas tree fires and blood shed under mistletoe, puppy-dogs hung in stockings and cats hung in telephone wires, in what were called human interest stories.

—Do I know him? We was like we was married together for four months, said a girl on Third Avenue. —I'm going to give him a presint this year, just for spite.

It rained; then it snowed, and the snow stayed on the paved ground for long enough to become evenly blackened with soot and smoke-fall, evenly but for islands of yellow left by uptown dogs. Then it rained again, and the whole creation was transformed into cold slop, which made walking adventuresome. Then it froze; and every corner presented opportunity for entertainment, the vastly amusing spectacle of well-dressed people suspended in the indecorous positions which precede skull fractures.

—Who made the first one? Will somebody tell me that? said The Boss at an office party in a suite at the Astor Hotel. His stiff dickey stood out like a jib as he flew before the winds of First Cause. —You may not have thought I'm a very religious guy, but I'll just ask that one question. *Who made the first one?* Then he dropped his glass on the carpet.

In a large private house on East Seventy-fourth Street, the girls entertained their gentlemen friends at a champagne breakfast. The gentlemen were away from home on business: at home, their aging children opened gifts bought by efficient secretaries, asked embarrassing questions, and were confounded to receive answers which common sense had told them all the time; they stared at their gifts, and awkwardly accepted this liberation from infancy, made privy to the reciprocal deceits which as children they had been taught to call lies. Miles away here, Daddy smiled munificently as the girl in the new housecoat ("Who gave you *that?*") said, —And even with my own name on it and all. Are they real di-mins?

Hundreds of thousands of doors closed upon as many single young women in single rooms: there, furnished with the single bed, the lamp, the chair, bookcase full of encouragement, radio, telephone, life stepped tacitly and took her where she never saw the sun. Who would send flowers? Not him! And relatives again? A handkerchief from a cold-nosed aunt. She telephoned her mother in Grand Rapids, and was surprised to note that Mother seemed to have been weeping even before she answered the telephone. The radio, unattended, played *The Origin of Design*. And she still had her hair to put up. Flub-a-dub-dub, she washed her girdle in the basin, singing alto accompaniment to the Christmas carols on another station. Every hour on the hour consciousness blanked, while the disembodied voice spoke with respectful disinterest of train wrecks, casualties in a far-off war, the doings of a president, an actress, a murderer; and then suddenly warm, human, confidential (if disembodied still) of under-arm odor. Hark the herald angels sing! she sang (alto) accompanying the body-odor song which followed very much the same tune. Flub-a-dub-dub went the girdle in the basin while she sang, not too loudly, fearful of missing something, of missing the telephone's ring. —Glory to the new-born King! she sang, waiting for the lipstick man.

As it has been, and apparently ever shall be, gods, superseded, become the devils in the system which supplants their reign, and stay on to make trouble for their successors, available, as they are, to a few for whom magic has not despaired, and been superseded by religion.

Holy things and holy places, out of mind under the cauterizing brilliance of the summer sun, reared up now as the winter sun struck from the south, casting shadows coldly up the avenues where the people followed and went in, wearing winter hearts on their sleeves for the plucking. Slightly offended by Bach and Palestrina, short memories reached back, struggling toward Origen, that most extraordinary Father of the Church, whose third-century enthusiasm led him to castrate himself so that he might repeat the *hoc est corpus meum, Dominus*, without the distracting interference of the rearing shadow of the flesh. They looked; but he was nowhere about, so well had he done his work, and the churches were so crowded that many were forced to suffer the Birth in cocktail lounges, and bars. So well had Origen succeeded, sowing his field without a seed, that the conspiracy, conceived in light, born, bred in darkness, and harassed to maturity in dubious death and rapturous martyrdom, continued. *Miserere nobis*, said the mitered lips. *Vae victis*, the statistical heart.

Tragedy was foresworn, in ritual denial of the ripe knowledge that we are drawing away from one another, that we share only one thing, share the fear of belonging to another, or to others, or to God; love or money, tender equated in advertising and the world, where only money is currency, and under dead trees and brittle ornaments prehensile hands exchange forgeries of what the heart dare not surrender.

—Hey Barney, let's have another here. First today.

—Hey Pollyotch, the woman called. —Hey Sanny Claus.

—Why don't you drop dead?

—Don't give me none of your hocus pocus.

—Yeh ...

—And who are you going to be miserable with New Year's Eve? asked Mrs. Bildow on the telephone. Esther, at the other end of the line, accepted this kind invitation for herself and her husband.

Mrs. Bildow laid the instrument back in its cradle and looked out the window of the sidewalk-level apartment. She could see four legs. —Don, she called. —Do you think she's all right with him? What's his name, Anselm? Outside, the four legs retreated, out of her sight.

It was a dark afternoon. To the north, the sky was almost black. Anselm rounded the corner with the little girl by the hand. He stopped there, met by a friend. —Hey Anselm, I've got one you'd like, old man.

—One what?

—Is it all right to kiss a nun?

—What do you mean, for Christ's sake?

—Sure it's all right, as long as you don't get into the habit.

—Ha, hahahaha . . . Anselm turned his thin face down to the little girl. She looked up. He had a bad case of acne. —Hahaha-haha . . .

—I knew you'd like that.

Anselm nodded, and looked serious again, as he had rounding the corner. He looked wistful.

—What's the matter with you, anyway?

—Afternoons like this, Anselm commenced, looking to the dark sky between the buildings to the north, —afternoons like this, he repeated, —I think about girls.

—Happy New Year, if you'll pardon the expression.

—Goodbye Esther, tell your husband . . .

—Good night, I . . .

—Happy New Year, if you're sure you can't come? . . .

—No, Esther's voice came back on the smoke with theirs, —we've decided to go to a little Spanish place Wyatt knows about, just the two of us, good night and thanks, happy New Year.

—Good night . . .

—And happy New Year, I . . .

Then the smoke in the room stopped moving, the door closed on the draft, and the room hung with silence; until Esther came back in, moving the smoke around her, and speaking, —Well, that's over. She stood unsteadily.

—If you wanted to go to their party, Esther . . .

—Party? . . . It's always so frightening we thought we'd just hide at home this year, that's what she said. If you call that a party.

—I wouldn't have minded staying here, if you'd wanted to . . .

—Go alone?

—Well, I . . . there's some work I wanted to finish.

—Work, she repeated dully.

—The woman called about that picture in there, it's all done, it just needs a coat of varnish.

—You were varnishing it when we came in.

—Yes, I did a little . . . as a matter of fact it's done, he admitted.

Esther sat slowly against the edge of a table. The brightness of her eyes fluctuated, glimmering to dull, as she fixed them on him and away. Finally she said, —It was like you were trying to . . . escape. He started a motion with his hand, but did not make a sound nor look up from the chair he sat in. —I didn't think you'd mind, they're not . . . they're a nice couple, and the boy with them . . .

—Who was he?

—I've never met him, his name's Otto something. He just showed up, he said he'd been at a party uptown, at some playwright's house, he left when it got too noisy and some woman kept calling him Pagliacci . . . you liked him, didn't you.

—Yes, he was . . . he's quite young, isn't he.

—You might have offered brandy to someone else, besides just him. And yourself, she added. Her idle hand reached the new typewriter on the table, a Christmas gift (she had given him an electric razor), and her finger made a speculative stab at a key she would never use: she looked at the paper, where she had imprinted ā. —Poor Don, you might have been a little nicer . . .

—Nicer? I talked to him, I tried to talk to him.

—I heard you, I heard you saying . . .

—Did you hear him? . . . An extensive leisure is necessary for any society to evolve an at all extensive religious ritual . . . did you hear all that? . . . You will find that the rationalists took over Plato's state *qua* state, which of course left no room for the artist, as a creative figure he is always a disturbing element which threatens the status *quo* . . . good God, Esther. Did you hear us discussing *quid*dity? and Schopenhauer's *Transcendental Speculations on Apparent Design in the Fate of the Individual*? and right into the Greek skeptics . . .

—And I heard you with this. Her voice rose, she held up a small stiff-covered magazine, —And I couldn't believe it, I thought you must be drunk or . . . I don't know what, I've never heard you that way, that . . . being rude. You're grinning now as if you still thought it was funny, pretending you didn't know he was an editor of this, that he wrote the piece in here on Juan Gris . . .

—Esther, please . . .

—And ran this whole symposium on religion they had. Wyatt, it just wasn't like you.

—What wasn't? People like that . . .

—All that about mummies, you know very well what I mean, when you said that ideas in these pages are not only dead but embalmed with care, respecting the sanctity of the corpse, I heard all of it. Some daring person appears in one issue to make the first incision, you said, and then runs off to escape stoning for his offense against the dead, and then the embalmers take over. The staff of embalmers, a very difficult clique to join, do you think he didn't know you meant him when you said that? Like good priests dictating canons for happy living they disdain for themselves. You were actually referring to his piece on Juan Gris, weren't you, when you said the corpse was drained, the vital organs preserved in alabaster vases, the brain drawn out through the nostrils with an iron hook, I heard all of it . . . the emptied cavities stuffed with spices, the whole thing soaked in brine, coated with gum, wrapped up and put in a box shaped like a man. Esther brandished the hard roll of paper, and then dropped it on the table, looking for a cigarette. —Why you picked on him . . .

—I don't know, Esther, there was something about that translucent quality of his, that round chin and thin hair and those plastic-rimmed eyeglasses, that brown suit . . .

—He can't help what he looks like.

—Hasn't he got a mirror? And that yellow necktie with palm-trees on it. There's just something about soft-handed complacent fools like that pontificating on . . .

—He's not complacent, Don suffers a good deal.

—I suppose he's given you every heart-rending detail.

—He talks to me. He talks to me more than . . . She stopped to sniff, and lit her cigarette.

—More than what?

—Never mind. Do you know what it looked like?

—What what looked like.

—It looked like all of a sudden you were trying to impress that boy Otto.

—Impress him?

—You were being . . . really, you were being just too clever and . . . coquettish.

—Esther, good God! Esther. He got to his feet.

—Do you think he's homosexual too? she asked calmly.

—Otto? How in heaven's name . . . what do you mean, too?

—Nothing, she said, looking down.

—Too? Listen . . . good God. His hands dropped to his sides.

—Well why you should be so nice to a conceited pretentious boy, and try to make a fool out of a nice person like Don when he wants to talk to you about things that interest you, and his wife . . .

—Well damn it, there it is, his wife. That woman! do you know her? Did you hear her?... As Don says in his piece in the religious symposium, he has a religion too though maybe you wouldn't suspect it because he's so philosophical...

—All right, let's forget about it.

—Forget about it? forget about her? peering out through her granulated eyelids... Esther tells us you're so original, you must tell me more about *your* work, you must know all the tricks... The tricks!

—Well she tries, Wyatt, you mustn't be unkind, and she tries to paint herself.

—She can paint herself red and hang on the wall and whistle, I don't care, but not here... Esther tells us... Esther says... good God! what have you told them?

—What's the matter? I've never seen you like this, Wyatt, she said sinking into a chair.

—Well what have you told them? About me, that I need psychoanalysis?

—I've had to talk to someone.

—Well... you... listen, he stood before her with his hands quivering in the air. —Damn it, if you think I need a psychoanalyst...

—Please don't swear at me.

—Listen, did you see her... reading my hands?... My, they're strong aren't they, but you must give me the left one too, I hope it does something to justify *this*... Did you see her, dragging her grubby little fingers over my palm?... There, the left one is so much better, but I've never seen such a complete dichotomy, she said,... that's one of Don's words, it means two things that describe each other like black and not black, and your right hand is so rough... Even when I got away from her she went on, did you hear her?... Your left hand is so gentle, so soft, it understands, and your right hand is so rough, that means your judgment is much better than your will, why do you try to follow your will as though it ran your life? Your left hand does, but you work against yourself, don't you, so stubborn, not happy, not happy, your left hand has love, what a lonely person you are, good God!

—Wyatt...

—And then,... is it possible? can a man be jealous of himself? Damn it, listen Esther, did you see what she tried to do? she almost kissed me goodbye? Why, she's insane. But she goes out on the street and nobody's surprised to see her, she talks and nobody's surprised to hear her. It's suffocating. Right this minute, she's talking. They're down there right this minute and that woman with the granulated eyelids is talking. You look up and there she is, people... the instant you look at them they begin to talk, automatically, they take it for granted you understand them, that you recognize them, that they have something to say to you, and you have to wait, you have to pretend to listen, pretend you don't know what's coming next while they go right on talking with no idea what they're talking about, they don't even know but they go right on, trying to explain who they are because they take it for granted you want to know, not that they have the damnedest idea as far as that goes, they just want to know what kind of a receptacle you'll be for their confidences. How do they know I'm the same person that...Who are they, to presume such intimacy, to...go right on talking. And they really believe that they're talking to me!

—Darling you shouldn't have let her upset you so, Esther said to him.

—Upset me! Did you hear her talking about her analysis with her husband? Her *lay* analysis?...Don's being analyzed, but we can't afford it for both of us, so he analyzes me. My paintings help, they're really pure symbols in the process of individuation Don says...Lay analysis! and she titters, one of those...little minds where naughtiness breeds intimacy, when she said to you, I've been trying to make your husband come out of his shell but he just won't *come*,...and she titters. She was sitting there...

—That's enough, Wyatt, really.

—No listen, she was sitting there watching the two of you, you and Don, sitting here with her knees hanging apart and Otto staring up her garter straps, He should have an affair now, she said. Don, he needs one now.

—Wyatt, please...

—He knew Esther before she was married, she said to me...Don knew Esther before she was married.

—Where are you going? Esther asked when he turned away. He did not answer but walked toward the studio door. —Wyatt, she said, getting up to follow, —please...

—It's all right, he said, going on through the doorway, and the bright light came on overhead.

A few minutes later Esther appeared in the door, her make-up freshened, her hair pushed up to where she thought it belonged. A drying lamp had been turned on the portrait, and she looked at it. He had done an excellent job and she, fresh from her mirror, stared at the flesh of the face on the easel as clear as her own. —I'll miss it, she said. —I'll be glad to see it gone but...but I'll miss it. Something moved. She turned, but it was not he. In the mirror ("to correct bad drawing...") she caught his reflection, and realized he was behind the table. —I'm sorry, these things happen, but now, you're not upset are you? now?

—No, no, it's just that...the rest of us...He drank down some brandy, and sat staring at some papers on the table before him. —I don't know, there are things we have to do, so we do them together. We have to eat, so we eat together. We have to sleep and we sleep together but ... all that? does it bring us any closer together?

—But you ... can't ... not ...

—But they're gone, he went on more calmly, looking back at the papers. —Thank God you thought of something, that excuse about our going somewhere else together, to get rid of them.

—But I ... I really wanted to go.

—Esther ... He got up quickly and came over to her. —Don't, don't, I'm sorry. Of course we'll go, if you want to, I didn't understand, Esther, but don't cry.

(For the first time in months) he put his arm around her; but his hand, reaching her shoulder, did not close upon it, only rested there. They swayed a little, standing in the doorway, still holding each other together in a way of holding each other back: they still waited, being moved over the surface of time like two swells upon the sea, one so close upon the other that neither can reach a peak and break, until both, unrealized, come in to shatter coincidentally upon the shore.

It was colder, outside where the deer still hung by their heels, and the rosettes still bloomed where they'd been planted. A small army of men moved through the streets, collecting twenty-five thousand tons of boxes and colored paper, beribboned refuse from Christmas.

Esther started.

—What is it?

—Just a chill, down my back. It's chilly here. She stared up at the pressed tin ceiling. —It's not the kind of place I expected.

—What, what did you expect?

—You said gypsy.

—Some greasy Hungarian dipping his violin bow in your soup?

—I didn't mean ... please. I didn't mean I don't like it, I like it. When were you in Spain?

—Spain? He looked up surprised. —I've never been in Spain.

—But you've told me ...

—My father, my father ...

—And your mother. To think you never told me.

—What?

—Your mother, buried in Spain. Why are you smiling?

—The music.

—It's exciting, isn't it. Exciting music. I wonder why the place is almost empty. No . . . , she stayed his hand tipping the bottle over her glass, —I can't drink any more of it, what is it? She tipped her head to read the label, —La Guita?

—Manzanilla.

—I don't feel very well, I shouldn't have had as much to drink earlier, martinis, and now this wine. I'm not used to just sitting and drinking so much wine. Wyatt?

—Eh?

—You've almost finished this bottle yourself.

—Yes, we'll order another.

—I wouldn't drink any more of it if I were you, Wyatt?

—Ah?

—I said . . . didn't you hear me?

—I was listening to the music.

—Can you understand it?

—The music?

—The words.

—Sangre negra en mi corazón . . . I can't speak Spanish.

—Wyatt, couldn't we go?

—You want to leave now?

—I mean go, go to Spain, couldn't we, together?

—What?

—Oh don't . . . never mind, no. You couldn't take me there traveling, with your mother there. No, you . . . Morocco, following ants through the desert to see if they're guided by the stars, more Moroccan than . . . I don't know, I wish . . . where are you going?

—Men's room.

She watched him cross the room unsteadily. He stopped at the bar. There was an elderly man with large features behind the bar, the waiter joined them, and then a stout and very pretty girl came from the kitchen. Esther watched them all talking and laughing, watched her husband buy them all three a drink, saw them raise their glasses, saw him pound his heels on the floor with the pounding heels from the music on the record in the dark juke-box; and a few minutes later the waiter approached the table opening another bottle. Earlier the waiter had stood over them and detailed the plot of a moving picture he'd seen that afternoon. His English was very choppy, and before they knew it he was describing the moving picture he'd seen the day before. These were very enthusiastic descriptions, as though they were details from his own life. He said his name was Esteban, and he came from Murcia.

—But . . . did we order this? Esther asked, as he pulled the cork from the bottle.

—Oh yes. El señor, your husband. Es muy flamenco, el señor.

—What?

—Is very flamenco, your husband.

They watched him, standing now bent over the dark juke-box beside the pretty stout girl from the kitchen, saw him straighten up, laugh, and pound the floor again with his heel.

—You understand what it mean, flamenco?

—Yes, she murmured, watching him cross the room toward her, with his head up. He paused to say something to Esteban, and came on, looking at the floor. A chill touched her shoulders, and was gone. When he sat down, she said speaking quietly under the music, —How handsome you were just then.

—What do you mean? He paused, filling his glass.

—The way you were standing there, when you hit your heels on the floor, with your head up. Were you doing it on purpose, looking so arrogant?

—You . . . make it sound theatrical.

—No, but that's it, it wasn't that, up on a stage, not just you being arrogant, not just your expression, it was . . . you had the back of your head thrown back and kind of raised but still your face was up and open in . . . I don't know, but not like you are sometimes now. She watched the glass shake slightly in his hand when he started to raise it, and he put it back on the table. —Wyatt, it's . . . sometimes when I come in and see you looking down and looking so lonely and . . . but just now, it was the whole man being arrogant, it was towering somehow, it was . . . it had all the wonderful things about it, that moment, all the things that, I don't know, . . . but all the things we were taught that a man can be. He said nothing, and did not look up, but took out some cigarettes. —Heroic, she said quietly, watching him light a cigarette with his head down, and then in the same tone, —Could I have one too?

—What? he asked, looking up quickly, and his burning green eyes shocked her.

—A cigarette? He gave her one; and filled her glass while she lit it. She stared at his squared fingers gripping the thin stem of the glass, and after a minute asked, —What does flamenco mean?

—Flemish.

—Flemish? I don't see . . .

—From the costumes the Spanish soldiers wore back, after the invasion of the Lowlands in the seventeenth century. He sounded impatient and nervous, answering her. —Strange clothes, . . . the gypsies took them over, so they . . . called them flamenco.

Esther leaned toward him at the table, with a smile of intimate confidence, and starting to put her hand to his said, —Do you know what, Wyatt? I didn't even know Spain had ever invaded ...

—Listen ..., he said. He'd withdrawn his hand on the table top automatically. —That's what it is, this arrogance, in this flamenco music this same arrogance of suffering, listen. The strength of it's what's so overpowering, the self-sufficiency that's so delicate and tender without an instant of sentimentality. With infinite pity but refusing pity, it's a precision of suffering, he went on, abruptly working his hand in the air as though to shape it there, —the tremendous tension of violence all enclosed in a framework, ... in a pattern that doesn't pretend to any other level but its own, do you know what I mean? He barely glanced at her to see if she did. —It's the privacy, the exquisite sense of privacy about it, he said speaking more rapidly, —it's the sense of privacy that most popular expressions of suffering don't have, don't dare have, that's what makes it arrogant. That's what sentimentalizing invades and corrupts, that's what we've lost everywhere, especially here where they make every possible assault on your feelings and privacy. These things have their own patterns, suffering and violence, and that's ... the sense of violence within its own pattern, the pattern that belongs to violence like the bullfight, that's why the bullfight is art, because it respects its own pattern ...

He stopped speaking; and after a moment Esther, who was looking down now too, repeated the word, —Suffering ... suffering? Why ... don't you think about happiness, ever?

—Yes, did you hear what that woman said? ... I think it's the artist is the only person who is really given the capability of being *happy*, maybe not *all* the time, but *some*times. Don't you *think* so? Don't *you* think so? ...

—And what did you say?

He put down his empty glass. —I said, there are moments of exaltation.

—Exaltation?

—Completely consumed moments, when you're working and lose all consciousness of yourself ... Oh? she said ... Do you call that happiness? Good God! Then she said, It was terrible about Esther's analyst, wasn't it, for Esther I mean ... No, good God no, people like that ...

From the other end of the room came the flamenco wail, —Sangre negra en mi corazón.

—Do you know that Spanish line, Vida sin amigo, muerte sin testigo?

—What does it mean? she asked quietly, her eyes still turned from him.

—Life without a friend, death without a witness.

—I don't like it, she said quietly; then she caught his hand before he could withdraw it: she felt it pull for an instant, then go rigid in hers. —I'm sorry they upset you, she said, —but they've been very kind to me, both of them, when I . . . needed friends. I have talked to them about you, I've talked to them about a lot of things, and things I can't talk to you about because you just won't talk to me.

—What things? he mumbled when she paused, as though obliged to.

—Well, my writing for instance, I know it's nothing to you but it is important to me, and what do you say? . . . partial to the word atavistic . . .

—All right, Esther, he said and suddenly got his hand back from her.

—If all you can say is . . .

—All right, listen, I have ideas but why should I oppress you with them? It's your work, and something like writing is very private, isn't it? How . . . how fragile situations are. But not tenuous. Delicate, but not flimsy, not indulgent. Delicate, that's why they keep breaking, they must break and you must get the pieces together and show it before it breaks again, or put them aside for a moment when something else breaks and turn to that, and all this keeps going on. That's why most writing now, if you read it they go on one two three four and tell you what happened like newspaper accounts, no adjectives, no long sentences, no tricks they pretend, and they finally believe that they really believe that the way they saw it is the way it is, when really . . . why, what happened when they opened Mary Stuart's coffin? They found she'd taken two strokes of the blade, one slashed the nape of her neck and the second one took the head. But did any of the eye-witness accounts mention two strokes? No . . . it never takes your breath away, telling you things you already know, laying everything out flat, as though the terms and the time, and the nature and the movement of everything were secrets of the same magnitude. They write for people who read with the surface of their minds, people with reading habits that make the smallest demands on them, people brought up reading for facts, who know what's going to come next and want to know what's coming next, and get angry at surprises. Clarity's essential, and detail, no fake mysticism, the facts are bad enough. But we're embarrassed for people who tell too much, and tell it without surprise. How does he know what happened? unless it's one unshaven man alone in a boat, changing I to he, and how often do you get a man alone in a boat, in all this . . . all this . . . Listen, there are so many delicate fixtures, moving toward you, you'll see. Like a man going into a dark room, holding his hands down guarding his parts for fear of a table corner, and . . . Why, all this around us is for people who can keep their balance only in the light, where they move as though nothing were fragile, nothing tempered by possibility, and all of a sudden bang! something breaks. Then you have to stop and put the pieces together again. But you never can put them back together quite the same way. You stop when you can and expose things, and leave them within reach, and others come on by themselves, and they break, and even then you may put the pieces aside just out of reach until you can bring them back and show them, put together slightly different, maybe a little more enduring, until you've broken it and picked up the pieces enough times, and you have the whole thing in all its dimensions. But the discipline, the detail, it's just . . . sometimes the accumulation is too much to bear.

Esther had been studying his face as he spoke, and did now, where nothing moved until she said clearly, —How ambitious you are!

He looked at her with an expression which was not a frown but had happened as an abrupt breaking of his features, an instant before apparently cast for good as they were but even now, in this new constriction, renewing an impression of permanence, as molten metals spilled harden instantly in unpredictable patterns of breakage. And Esther looked at him with the face of someone looking at a wound.

They left a few minutes later. —That seems like a lot of money to leave, Esther said to him.

—For the music.

—Well, I wouldn't tip so much if I were you, she said in the door.

—But you're not, he whispered hoarsely, holding it open.

It is a naked city. Faith is not pampered, nor hope encouraged; there is no place to lay one's exhaustion: but instead pinnacles skewer it undisguised against vacancy. At this hour it was delivered over to those who inherit it between the spasms of its life, those who live underground and come out, the ones who do not come out and the ones who do not carry keys, the ones who look with interest at small objects on the ground, the ones who look without interest, the ones who do not know the hour for the darkness, the ones who look for illuminated clocks with apprehension, the ones who look at passing shoe-tops with dread, the ones who look at passing faces from waist level, the ones who look in separate directions, the ones who look from whitened eyeballs, the ones who wear one eyeglass blacked, the ones who are tattooed, the ones who walk like windmills, the ones who spread disease, the ones who receive extreme unction with salted peanuts on their breath.

The moon had not yet entered the sky, waiting to come in late, each night waiting nearer the last possible minute before day, to appear more battered, lopsided, and seem to mount unsteadily as though restrained by embarrassment at being seen in such condition.

—You do hate the winter, don't you. There were no taxicabs in sight, and they walked hurriedly. —You always look so much colder than other people do.

—Other people! he muttered, as they walked east. The sky ahead was already

light. —Look at it! he said abruptly, catching her arm. —Can't you imagine
that we're fished for? Walking on the bottom of a great celestial sea, do you
remember the man who came down the rope to undo the anchor caught on
the tombstone?

Then she heard his name called. It seemed to come from a great distance,
like a cry in a dream, or under water: she might have imagined it; but it was
repeated. Then there stood the priest before them, in a black hat and coat and
the round collar, carrying a suitcase, —hurrying to catch a train, she heard
him say. She heard him, heard her husband's voice, her own for a moment
sounding especially loud, their greetings, the hurried slightly embarrassed
renewal of their acquaintanceship, all as though they were suddenly met in a
submarine landscape where only the others were at home, and she fighting
desperately to surface, as she had that one moment when her voice burst,
—How do you do... His name was John. She heard him say, —There was an
air of legend and mystery about you even then, Wyatt...

She swayed. And it seemed a long time before they were walking again,
and she heard her own voice, breathed again and controlled it as she spoke.
—An old friend? you studied with him? You? You studied for the priesthood?

—For the ministry, Esther. He... he's high church.

—You studied for the priesthood?

—It's...yes, there's no... mystery about it. It was quiet except for their
heels on the pavement, and sounds of constriction from Esther's throat. A
block ahead, the street was lit up by a blaze where a Christmas tree burned
in the gutter. —It's too warm to snow, he said. They walked on toward the
blaze.

—But that sounded like thunder. He turned to support her with both
hands. —Esther, Esther...They both swayed. —You have to *walk*. She let
herself back in a shallow doorway, and the light of the blaze covered her face.
It was a big tree.

—No mystery? she said. —No mystery? All the time he talked I could see
you standing there with blood all over your face. All the time he talked I could
see you dancing like a lunatic, all locked up like a...lock... She managed to
stop her eyes on his face. —Tonight I can believe everything I've ever thought
about you, she said. —And you never told me.

—Esther, now stop it. It never occurred...

—Why did you marry me? she demanded.

—Esther, I don't want to be unkind...

She looked at him, full in the face where nothing moved to betray the man
she had loved; then her eyes, moving quickly, searching, lost and found and
lost him again. —But you are, she whispered. —You are all the time. Her

voice rose dully, and then it broke. —You shouldn't know other people if you have nothing to share with them. You shouldn't even *know* them, she cried. And she sobbed, —You haven't . . . ever shared anything with me . . . you won't help me do things, you do them for me but you won't help me . . . you . . . offer to do the dishes, but you wouldn't help me do them, I know you'd do them if I said yes but you wouldn't help me . . .

—Esther . . . In the distance a siren whined.

—That . . . set of Dante you had, *we* couldn't have it, it was as though it couldn't exist without being yours or mine so you gave it to me, but it couldn't be ours. You . . . even when you make love to me you don't share it, you do it as though . . . so you can do something sinful. And you never told me . . . She raised her head which had fallen as she sobbed, and the blaze caught it again as the sirens, distinguishable now and punctuated by bells, approached nearer. —Why aren't you a priest? You are a priest! Why aren't you one then, instead of . . . me . . . they don't share anything.

—Priests don't share anything? he repeated, holding her.

—Nothing! Nothing, any more than you share love with me. They hold out something, offer it down. They even give it but they never share it, they never share anything . . . Her coarse hair stood away from her face in disarray as she looked at his profile in the fire's light, uneven shocks of flame as one branch blazed up and another fell glowing, which seemed to make his features move, though nothing moved but his hands, taking a closer grip from which she half twisted. —Precision of suffering . . . privacy of suffering . . . if that's what it is, suffering, then you . . . share it. She was looking down, and shook her head slowly. —If you can't share it, . . . you can't understand it in others, and if you can't understand it you can't respect it, . . . and if you can't respect it, if you can't respect suffering . . .

The firelight had suddenly been penetrated by the sharp white lights of a car, which stopped at the curb, its siren droning down too deep to be heard. Beyond, other sirens and the clangor of bells violated the night almost upon them.

—O.K. Jack, what d'you call this?

—I . . . we . . . it's nothing, officer.

—Is this here your campfire?

—I don't know anything about the fire, Wyatt said, turning to face him, still supporting Esther. —Do I look like I . . .

—O.K. Jack, take it easy. Who's the little lady?

—This is my wife.

—You live here?

—No, we live uptown. My wife has just had a little too much to drink.

—The both of you look like you've had a few too many. This your husband, lady?

—No.

—Esther...

—He *ain't* yer husband?

—Look at him, Esther said raising her eyes. —Can't you see? Look at his eyes, can't you see he's a priest?

—Esther...

Suddenly the night around them disappeared in a blaze of red and white lights and the harmonic explosion of the sirens and bells, as a hose truck, an emergency vehicle, and a hook and ladder arrived, it seemed at the same instant. The policeman turned his back on them in the doorway. —It's just somebody's friggin Christmas tree, he called out.

—Are them the ones that lit it? came a voice from behind a red beam.

—You better get home to bed, Jack, the policeman said, turning to Wyatt.

—There aren't any cabs...

—Come on. I'll give you a lift, Father.

They drove uptown, in silence except for the constant static voice on the radio at their knees repeating its esoterics, ——signal thirty, signal thirty... car number one three seven, signal thirty...

Wyatt handed the policeman a five-dollar bill when they got out, and the policeman said, —Happy New Year, Father.

As he fitted the key in the door, Esther murmured, —I feel so old. He let her in, to the darkness and the scent of lavender. She sat down and said, —Leave the light off, as he crossed to the bright shaft of light that came from the drying lamp set up before the portrait in the studio.

—Wyatt, she said, —can't you say something to me...? Even if you don't believe it?

He did not appear to have heard, standing over the portrait. He turned off the hot lamp, lifted a small ultra-violet hand lamp and stood tapping his foot, waiting for it to warm up. There were sounds of Esther standing in the dark room, and her footsteps. The violet light gradually rose to its lurid fullness, and showed his drawn face and level unblinking eyes turned upon the portrait. The smooth surface was gone under the violet light: in the woman's face, the portions he had restored shone dead black, a face touched with the irregular chiaroscuric hand of lues and the plague, tissues ulcerated under the surface which reappeared, in complaisant continence the instant he turned the violet light from it, and upon the form of Esther who had come, looking over his shoulder, and fallen stricken there on the floor without a word.

Wyatt picked her up, and carried her across the dark room to the bedroom.

—Don't try to carry me, she whispered, as he got her there and laid her down on the bed, losing his balance and coming down almost on top of her, where she suddenly held him. Then Esther reached out with one hand and turned on the soft bed lamp. He held her face between his hands, his thumbs meeting above her eyes, and drew his thumbs along her brows. Her eyes opened, bloodshot and the whites almost possessed by the flesh round them: his eyes above were still and hard, looking down unblinking. She reached up to catch his right hand and stop it, so that only his left thumb moved along her brow. —You look like a criminal, she said gently. His smile seemed to draw her lips together, her upper lip caught under her lower. —Why? she whispered. —Why do you fight it all so hard?

—There's still ... so much more to do, he answered, as his smile left his face.

—So much what? If ... you can't share your work with me ... but does that mean you can't share anything? She moved under him, and put one hand up to his rough cheek. He did not answer. —You looked like a little boy, with the flames all over your face, she whispered.

—It was terrible, he commenced, —and that woman ... !

—A lonely little boy, getting upset over silly people.

—But Esther ... when I realized how much you've talked to them, told them about me, about my father and ... my mother, and guilt complexes and that dream I have that comes back, and saying that I needed analysis badly, and all sorts of ... He paused. She was not crying.

—I had to talk to someone, she said. She scratched the palm of his right hand with her fingernails. —I wish ... she said, moving under him. His right hand closed on her fingers, and they stopped.

He stroked her hair.

Then she moved so quickly, raising herself on her elbows, that her dress tore. —Do you think it can go on like *this?* she said loudly. His tight black jacket, unpadded and unpressed, bound his arms, but he did not stop to take it off; and then her eyes closed, his thumbs on the lids, and they shared the only intimacy they knew.

—What do you think about? she asked him, as they undressed.

—Think about? he repeated, looking up confused.

—Just ... now, she said.

—Not thought. I don't *think* of anything, but ... He drew on his cigarette, which was half smoked away. —It was strange. There were sapphires. I could see sapphires spread out, different sizes and different brilliances, and in different settings. Though some of them weren't set at all. And then I thought, yes I did think, I thought, if only I can keep thinking of these sapphires, and not lose them, not lose one of them, everything will be all right.

She turned out the light. —That must mean something. Like your dream. Your dream isn't hard to understand. Certainly not . . . after tonight.

—There's always the sense, he went on, —the sense of recalling something, of almost reaching it, and holding it . . . She leaned over to him, her hand caught his wrist and the coal of tobacco glowed, burning his fingers. In the darkness she did not notice. —And then it's . . . escaped again. It's escaped again, and there's only a sense of disappointment, of something irretrievably lost.

He raised his head.

—A cigarette, she said. —Why do you always leave me so quickly afterward? Why do you always want a cigarette right afterward?

—Reality, he answered.

—Reality? Otto repeated. —Well I always think of it as meaning the things you can't do anything about. This was an argument which many women might have welcomed; and, from the way he raised one eyebrow, it might appear that many had. Nevertheless, Esther continued to stare into the cup before her. —I mean . . . Otto commenced.

—I think he thinks of it as . . .

—Yes? he asked, after pausing politely.

—As nothing, she said. —As a great, empty nothing.

Before Otto could look (or try not to look) as uncomfortable as this made him, he was startled by her looking him square in the face across the table, to ask, —Do you like him?

—Why, yes, he answered, looking down, in a tone which she might have taken for insincerity, had she not been able to see his embarrassment. —I mean, I don't really know him, he went on as she looked back into her empty coffee cup, —but I . . . he is sort of hard to get to know, isn't he.

Esther nodded. —Yes, she said, and looked up for what he would say next.

—I mean, I can't imagine that anybody really knows him really well. Except you of course, he added hastily, offering her a cigarette.

—I'd better not take time, she said.

—And I mean, Otto said, lighting a cigarette, —I think you can learn so much from him. I mean I think I can. I mean little things that you don't learn at Harvard. Like the way he was talking about the Saint Jerome in El Greco's painting being the real Saint Jerome, the neck and chest all sort of drained of decay, and the sort of lonely singleness of purpose of insanity. That kind of thing. And he doesn't talk down to me, he just sort of . . . talks, like . . . well we were talking about German philosophy, and he was talking about Vainiger,

and something about how we have to live in the dark and only assume postulates true which if they were true would justify...

—Romantic, German...Esther murmured.

—Yes but, and then Fichte saying that we have to act because that's the
only way we can know we're real, and that it has to be moral action because
that's the only way we can know other people are. Real I mean. But look,
there's something, I mean do you think he minds me...taking you to lunch
like this? Esther looked up and smiled across the table for the first time in
some minutes. —Because you know, I wouldn't want...

—I think he'll be grateful, she said.

Otto turned for the waiter, whom he'd been having trouble reaching since
they sat down. He'd brought her to a small restaurant which, with excess of
garlic in everything but dessert and coffee (though it lingered even there), and
very dry martini cocktails served by disdainfully subservient waiters one and
all in need of a shave, sustained a Continental fabric that would have collapsed
entirely without the expense accounts of the publishing world. —His mother
breathed for him before I married him, said the woman at the next table, who
was seated nearer to Otto than Esther was. —His job is to scrub the kitchen
and the bathroom...

Otto studied the bill.

—And thank you for the book, Esther said as she did her lips. —It was
kind of you to bring it, just because you heard me mention it the other evening.
Did you like it?

—As a matter of fact, he said, unable to interrupt himself so that he paid
the thirty-cent overcharge without question, —I haven't had a chance to read
it yet.

—Well then you take it back. She pushed it toward him.

—No, no, I brought it to you. But maybe, I might come up and borrow it
when you're done? I mean, if neither of you mind?

—I hope you will come up, she said. —He would too. I know he would,
because he...because you can talk to him. And you must, she said taking
Otto's hand in hers as they reached the sidewalk outside. Her eyes darted back
and forth, looking from one of his to the other. —And you...mustn't be put
off by the way he seems to withdraw. He does like you. And I'm glad you like
him. I'm glad you told me you did just now, because I told him you did last
night.

—What did he say? Otto asked anxiously.

Esther smiled. —It was funny, she said. —He said it made it like there
were three of us in the room where there should only have been two. He said
I shouldn't try to make explicit things that should be implicit. She was looking

beyond him as she said this, into the crowd of people passing on Fifth Avenue, looking searchingly. Then she looked quickly back at his face. —But you understand, don't you?

—Yes, I . . .

—You . . . it's as though you bring him to life.

Otto turned to watch her leave him. Then, a hand moving in his pocket, he counted his money by memory. Then he looked at his watch. Then he took a slip of paper from his pocket.

—Chr-ah-st. Otto. I mean what are you doing standing in the middle of the street writing a note?

—Oh Ed, I . . . it's just something I thought of for this play I'm working on.

—A play? Chrahst, how unnecessary. Who's in it? asked Ed, who, though he did not know it, was himself in the play, with the unlikely name of Max.

—Well no one yet, Otto said, returning to his pocket the slip of paper on which he had just written: Gordon says nt mke thngs explict whch shd be implict ie frndshp. —I haven't finished it. The plot still needs a little tightening up. (By this Otto meant that a plot of some sort had yet to be supplied, to motivate the series of monologues in which Gordon, a figure who resembled Otto at his better moments, and whom Otto greatly admired, said things which Otto had overheard, or thought of too late to say.) —The whole plot is laid . . .

—Chrahst what lousy weather, I mean I've been everywhere and wherever you go all you find out is that it's hot as hell in summer and cold as hell in winter. Got time for a drink?

—Why yes, yes fine, I . . .

—I mean Chrahst what else do they expect you to do? he said as they walked south.

—Are you going to the reunion?

—What reunion?

—Our class, the class reunion, it's going to be . . .

—My Chrahst, I mean who wants to go to a thing like that? I mean Chrahst you just get drunk with the same stupid guys you were drunk with for four years, except every year they manage some goddamn way to get a little stupider and lose their hair and bring their wives instead, and why go all the way up there to get drunk? I mean Chrahst it's as though you hadn't grown up any.

—Say, while we're near here I want to stop in at Brooks for a minute, Otto said. —I have to get . . .

—O Chrahst I might as well stop too. I've got to get some drawers. I mean, I'm going to get married next week, and I've got to get some drawers. We could take my car . . .

—But it's only four blocks away.

—I know, and I lost the goddamn car anyway.

—You lost it?

—Last night, I left it somewhere. I think it was uptown, but I mean Chrahst, you can't expect me to remember everything.

Pillaged by a cold wind about his midriff (for fashion confided that he might button only the bottom button of his jacket, hybrid heritage of the Guards, which forbade an overcoat), Otto reached their doorway. He paused there to look back up the street, and then take a slip of paper from his pocket. Gordon's speeches were becoming more and more profound. Gordon would soon be at home only in drama; and, though his author had not considered it, possibly closet drama at that. Otto often disappeared at odd moments, as some children do given a new word, or a new idea, or a gift, and they are found standing alone in some private corner, lips moving, as they search for the place where this new thing belongs, to get it firmly in place and part of themselves before they return to adult assaults, and the incredible possibility that they may one day themselves be the hunters. Like their lips, his pencil moved, getting the thing down before it was lost, not to himself but to his play; for once written, it need be reconsidered only for sound and character, and the scene it would best fit in, while he returned to the assaults and possibilities that only the hunter knows. In the past few months, Gordon had begun to lose his debonair manner, and become more seriously inclined; he tossed off epigrams less readily, but often paused and made abrupt gestures with his hands, as though to shape his wisdom in plain view of the large audience, halting between phrases to indicate the labor they cost him; he was liable to be silent, where he had chatted amiably; and where he had paused upstage, thoughtfully silent, he was liable not to appear at all. Grdn: We hate thngs only becse in thm we see elemnts whch we secrtly hate in rslves, Gordon's creator wrote, at the foot of a page almost covered with notations (one of which covered half the page, and only two of which were not Gordon). He paused for a moment, tapping his lip with the pencil; then, Grdn: Orignlty not inventn bt snse of recall, recgntion, pttrns alrdy thr, q. You cannt invnt t shpe of a stone. N. Mke Grdn pntr? sclptr? By now Gordon was some three or four inches shorter than he had been, and considerably less elegant. With this note that Gordon's profession was still open to change, Otto pushed at the outside door and found it open. He entered and climbed the stairs. He was commencing to envy Gordon.

A full minute passed before the door was answered. Even then, Esther returned quickly to her typewriter and sat over it biting a thumbnail, while he crossed the room to stand and look out the window, turned to stare into the empty studio, and finally sat on the couch and opened a book. It was a collection of plates of the work of early Flemish painters. A single snap of the typewriter brought him up straight. —What was that? he asked.

—A comma. She looked regretfully at the page before her. —It makes a lot of difference sometimes, a period or a comma. She suddenly looked round. —Where is he, he isn't with you?

—I just left him, we've been up at the Metropolitan. He said he wanted to take a walk.

—I knew he wasn't with you, she said sitting back and speaking more slowly, —and yet, by now sometimes I just don't know, I don't even know whether he's here with me or not.

Otto looked up, to see her staring at the floor, and he cleared his throat. —Is this his, this book on Flemish painters?

—No, it's mine, she said looking up vaguely. —He has something against reproductions.

—Yes, Otto agreed, open upon a Dierick Bouts, —but these are especially good, aren't they. This kind of stringency of suffering, this severe self-continence of suffering that looks almost peaceful, almost indifferent. But in a way it's the same thing, this severe quality of line, this severe delicacy and tenderness. She was staring at him, but he did not look up. He turned pages, and continued to speak with casual and labored confidence. —You can see how well these men knew their materials, using color like a sculptor uses marble, not simply filling in like cartoons but respecting it, using it as a servant of the pattern, the tactile values, . . . this, this van Eyck, the white headdress on Arnolfini's wife, how sharp the lines are, look at how smoothly they flow, it's perfect painting in stand oil, isn't it. It isn't difficult to see why Cicero says . . . what's the matter? He'd glanced up, to see her eyes fixed on him.

—Nothing, go on, she said, fascinated.

—Nothing, I was just going to say . . . that passage in Cicero's *Paradoxa*, where Cicero gives Praxiteles no credit for anything of his own in his work, but just for removing the excess marble until he reached the real form that was there all the time. Yes, the um . . . masters who didn't have to try to invent, who knew what . . . ah . . . forms looked like, the um . . . The disciple is not above his master, but everyone that is perfect shall be as his master.

—Who said that? she asked after a pause, still looking fixedly at him.

—Yes, Saint Luke. He was the patron saint of painters.

—Was?

—Well I mean I guess he still is, isn't he. Otto closed the book and stood up looking for a place to put it.

—Is that all? she asked finally.

—All what?

—About Flemish painters?

—Well Esther, I like them, and the . . . I mean the discipline, the attention to detail, the separate consciousnesses in those paintings, the sort of . . . I guess it's both the force and the flaw of those paintings, the thoroughness with which they recreate the atmosphere, and the, I mean a painter like Memling who isn't long on suggestion and inferences but piles up perfection layer by layer. But, well it's like a writer who can't help devoting as much care to a moment as to an hour.

—Otto . . . She got up and came toward him.

—But God devotes as much time to a moment as He does to an hour, Otto brought out abruptly, as though defending himself, or someone very close to him. She stood before him, looking into his face querulously.

—Esther . . .

—Do you have a cigarette? she asked, stepping back. He fumbled and gave her one, lit it for her, then got the package out and took one for himself.

—Esther, look, is something wrong? he asked as she sat down on the couch and started to turn pages of a book, without looking at the words.

—Nothing, it just gets . . . I don't know, she said, and started looking at the pages, running her thumb down the lines as though seeking an answer there. He stood over her, blowing out smoke, as though the cigarette were an occupation in itself, until she said, —Here's a lovely passage, it's something of Katherine Mansfield's, a review she wrote. She held it up and he took it as though he might find some solution there himself. —It's too bad, such a lovely thing hidden away in an old review.

—Yes, he said, covetously, and read it again. He got out his pencil. She saw the book in his pocket and asked what it was.

—Spinoza, Otto answered taking it out. —I'm glad you reminded me, he lent it to me a long time ago, and just asked me if I'd leave it here.

Esther thumbed the pages. —Did you get all the way through it?

—Well, I mean not all the way really. We were talking about quiddity once, and he . . .

—About what?

—Quiddity, what the thing is, the thing itself, and he said that Kant says we can never know . . .

—Is this all you talk about? Quiddity, philosophers . . .

—But Esther . . .

—Doesn't he talk about himself to you?

—Well, I mean in a way he's always talking about himself, but he, you know, for instance when he said, But aren't we all trying to see in the dark? I mean . . . you know.

—I know, she said, staring at her hands. —But he must say something about me?

Otto stood looking down at her hair, at her shoulders and the curve of flesh at her neck. He laughed, a slight, nervous, and confidential sound; and when he spoke his voice was more strained with casualness than before. —As a matter of fact, today he said sometimes he felt like the homunculus that ah, I forget, the Greek god of fire made, and then um another god criticized it because he hadn't put in a little window where they could see its secret thoughts. She did not move, and when she remained silent Otto repeated his nervous sound of a laugh. —I mean, he didn't mean anything, you know . . . What?

—I know, she repeated in a whisper.

—He didn't mean . . .

—Do you know what it's like?

—What what . . .

—Do you know what it's like? Living with someone like him, living with him, do you know what it's like? Do you know what it's like, being a woman and living with him?

—But Esther . . .

—To come into the room, and see him staring, without blinking, just staring, not an insane stare but just sitting and looking? Last night he was sitting there, that way, and the music on the radio, I can still hear the announcer's voice afterward because it was such a relief, it was the Suite Number One in C Major of Bach, and afterward all he said was, *such precision. Such precision.*

—But that's true, it's . . . Otto came down on the sofa beside her.

—Yes but it isn't human . . . He put a hand on hers. —It isn't a way to live, she said in the same dull voice, her hand dead under his. —It isn't . . . is it strange that he has ringing in his ears? Is this dream of his strange, this damned damned dream he has? That after an hour's silence he can say, The one thing I cannot stand is dampness . . . That's all, it took him an hour to work that out. Strange? that he can drink down a pint of brandy, and be just as he was before. Nothing happens. Nothing happens, except he blinks even less. Yes, a . . . man of double deed, I sow my field without a seed . . .

—Esther, you mustn't get so . . .

—When the seed began to blow / 'Twas like a garden full of snow.

—Look, it won't last, he said taking both her hands. —He can't just go on, like this.

—I know it, she said, moving her hands in his. —Sleeping, clutching his throat with both hands. I found him that way, when I got up in the night, sleeping on his face with both hands to his throat. I took them away, and when I came back, back from the bathroom he was like that again. Or jumping out of bed in the middle of the night, barefoot, and he comes back muttering something in Greek, apologizing, he'd gone to look up the word accusative. No, no, argue? We can't even argue, he goes into the studio there and finishes the argument alone, I hear him behind the door, answering me. Damn all this business, these shapes and smells, I heard him one night, and a wife, he said, trembling before everything that doesn't happen, weeping for everything we'll never lose. Do they really know each other, do they really give anything to each other? or is all they have to share this . . . same conspiracy against reality they try to share with me?

—And . . . then what? Otto asked, when she paused, and her hands stilled.

—He said, You can change a line without touching it. She was silent until Otto started to interrupt, then, —Is she surprised? I heard him say. Why, I have to tell her why, good God do I always have to use words when I talk to her? Is she surprised to see me when she comes in? when she wakes in the morning and sees me there? She's never been surprised. Everywhere, Esther said looking up slowly, —everything, as her eye caught a shiny magazine on the low table, —even there. There's a story in that about a girl who goes to Spain, during Holy Week she meets the mother of a man she was in love with, then one night when she's seen one of those holy processions with the Virgin in tears going by, she meets her old lover with his wife, the girl who took him away from her, and she forgives the girl.

—Yes, but that sounds . . .

—But all he could say is, What a . . . what rotten sentimentality, I can still hear his voice. What a vulgarizing of something as tremendous as the Passion, this is what happens to great emotions, this is the way they're rotted, by being brought to the lowest level where emotions are cheap and interchangeable. Has there ever been anything in history so exquisitely private as the Virgin mourning over Her Son?

—But Esther, don't you see that? Don't you feel this . . . this way we're all being corrupted, by . . .

—Don't you know that I love him? she cried. —Do you think that there's anything more . . . exquisitely private than . . . that, for me?

Otto found her head in his lap, and looking down upon it, stroked her hair. —Esther, he whispered, —Esther . . .

—To have him say, she commenced again, sitting up as suddenly, —if something, if I . . . if we talk about having children, and to have him look surprised, and then to, . . . once, once he said, A daughter, a daughter? he said, a daughter! and he said…I don't remember, and then it disappeared, then what we're talking about just disappears, it…He studied to be a priest. Did you know that? To be a minister, did he ever tell you that? He, and then that's what I say, I say that, and I ask him why aren't you then? Why aren't you a priest, if you are one! because, because I want him to…I want him to…

—Esther…Otto reached out to hold her, but she drew back.

—And then as though it was the most real thing in the world he says, Because I should rebe…I should believe in my redemption that way, because I should have to believe that I am the man for whom Christ died.

Otto took out a cigarette. He lit it, and taking it from his lips quickly said, —I'm sorry. Unprofaned, the word Christ embarrassed him.

She took it from his outstretched fingers. —You shouldn't apologize, she said. —You could at least pretend that you lit it for me.

He smiled, and leaned toward her. But his smile made hers suddenly the less real, less a smile as its life drained from behind it while the smile remained fixed on her lips; then her lips opened again and it disappeared. Esther stood up, away from him, smoking, and he took out another cigarette. —For a woman, she said, —do you think it's easy for a woman? She was turned toward the half-open door of the studio. —Reality! He talks about reality, despair. Doesn't he think I despair? Women get desperate, but they don't understand despair. Despair as a place to start from, he said to me. And that. And that. She turned on Otto, who looked uncomfortable and as quickly brought his cigarette to his lips. Hers hung forgotten in her hand, running the smoke up her wrist. —Just being a woman, do you know what a woman goes through? You don't, but do you? Can you imagine? Just trying to keep things going, just…A man can do as he pleases. O yes, a man! But a woman can't even walk into a bar alone, she can't just get up and leave things, buy a boat ticket and sail to Paris if she wants to, she can't…

—Why not? Otto asked, standing.

—Because they can't, because society…and besides, physically, do you think it's easy then, being a woman?

—No no, no I don't. Otto stepped back as though threatened with it.

—And do you know the worst thing? she went on. —Do you know the hardest thing of all? The waiting. A woman is always waiting. She's…always waiting.

He took a step toward her, where Esther had started toward the door of the studio. —Do you remember once, when you first knew us? she asked, —when you'd been out with…him, and seen a painting, a portrait of a lady, you said it was quite beautiful, a woman looking just beyond you, her hands folded across in front of her shutting you out, she was holding up a ring…

—Yes, yes I remember it, he said, relieved at the calm in her voice. —A…
um, Lorenzo di Credi, though he said as a painting…

—Do you want to see this picture of his mother? she demanded.

—I remember he said, that picture reminded him of his mother, on account
of the hands or something.

—Do you want to see it? she challenged. —Yes, she must have been a very
beautiful woman.

—Really? I mean, is there a picture of her?

Esther stood with a hand on the knob of the door, but moved no further.
—He has one he started, fifteen years ago. It's just hanging in there, she added
dully.

—Well… Otto stepped back. —No don't bother, it isn't important.

—Isn't important! He can't paint me, because of her we can't travel, to
Spain because she's there. She turned to the dark doorway. —At night, night
after night he works in there. Works? she repeated. —He's in there, night
after night. That music, night after night. She stared in. —And to hear him,
Damn you! damn you! Oh, talking to himself he said. Yes. He's in there now.

Otto came up behind her and took her shoulders. —Esther, he said, holding her. Then she coughed, his cigarette so close to her face. —I work at night
too, he said, trying to recover her reasonably.

—It's this crazy Calvinistic secrecy, sin…

—Esther it isn't the secrecy, the darkness everywhere, so much as the late-
ness. I mean I get used to myself at night, it takes that long sometimes. The
first thing in the morning I feel sort of undefined, but by midnight you've
done all the things you have to do, I mean all the things like meeting people
and, you know, and paying bills, and by night those things are done because
by then there's nothing you can do about them if they aren't done, so there
you are alone and you have the things that matter, after the whole day you
can sort of take everything that's happened and go over it alone. I mean I'm
never really sure who I am until night, he added.

—Alone! She moved, enough that he loosed his grasp.

—That sort of funny smell, he said, standing uncertainly, then he took a
step inside, as though he had left her of his own will, saw a piece of paper on
the floor and picked it up, as though it were that he was after all the time.
—And I mean things like this, he said holding it up, —these sort of magical
diagrams and characters and things he makes…

—That, she said looking at it, —it's just a study in perspective.

—Yes, but, when you look in there, don't you think of things like…

—It's nothing, it's just a study in perspective. The little x is the vanishing
point.

—Yes but, I mean today we were talking about alchemy, and the mysteries that, about the redemption of matter, and that it wasn't just making gold, trying to make real gold, but that matter... Matter, he said matter was a luxury, was our great luxury, and that matter, I mean redemption...

She swung him round. —Redemption!

—Esther... She had her arms round his neck. He held her, at the waist, so quickly that he withdrew his thumb which had touched her breast and stood with hands paralyzed, not daring to return it. —That sort of funny smell, he murmured after a moment.

—Lavender, she said to him. Then she asked, —And you too, you want to be alone?

He looked at her face which was very close, perhaps too close to appreciate the slight raising of his eyebrow, and the complementary urbanity of his faint smile. —It's rather difficult to shed our human nature, he said. She broke away from him, and stood in the center of the room looking at him. —Esther, what's the matter?

—That too, you got that from him too! Didn't you?

—Well, I... sort of, I mean...

—What. Go on.

—Well we were talking about a philosopher, Otto said helplessly, —Pyrrho, about Pyrrho of Elis, who said that one state was as good as another, and one day his students found him treed by a dog and they taunted him, and he said that, It's difficult to shed our human nature.

She let him finish, and then said, —You don't have to repeat all these things to impress me, Otto, I've heard them all, from him.

—But...

—About Flemish painting, and stringency of suffering, that God cares as much about a moment as he does for an hour, I've heard it all from him. She paused, looking Otto over, and then said, —Do you know what he asked me once? when we first met you?

—What? Otto asked, coming toward her.

—He asked me if I thought you could be homosexual.

Otto stopped. —But... what? What did he... and what did you say?

—I said I didn't know, you might be.

—But Esther, why should he, I mean you, you didn't, did you think that? I mean why would you ever think... He stopped, before her, beside the couch.

—You never tried to kiss me, she said.

—But I, he... I mean Esther, Esther. I love you, Esther. With that, Otto commenced a silence which he broke himself minutes later. —Esther, we can't, I mean not... suppose he should come in?

She drew her head back, resting it on the arm of the sofa, and looked at him. —Suppose he should? she said.

Late that night, Gordon stood poised in the doorway of a summer cottage, about to speak. (As a matter of fact, Gordon had been holding that screen door open for about a week now, laboring, as one hand shaped the air, to reduce Priscilla with some painful profundity.) Suddenly, in a rush of type-writer keys, he spoke. Gordon: Suffering, my dear Priscilla, is a petty luxury of mediocre people. You will find happiness a far more noble, and infinitely more refined state. Priscilla sobbed, and someone pounded on the floor from below, warning Gordon that he had said enough. There was, however, little chance of Gordon's going on tonight. At a stroke, Gordon had recovered his former assurance, and his former height. He had acquired a few new habits (could, for instance, put away a pint of brandy without showing it) but, for all urbane intents and purposes, his profundities were to be spoken with that withering detestable cleverness of old, delivered with his former ease, as he dressed with his former elegance. What was more: Gordon had discovered Art.

The screen door ~~slammed~~ closed behind him; and Otto got up to look in the mirror. Then his expression changed, as he took his eyes from its reflection, and he hurriedly picked up a pencil and scribbled, Gd crs as mch fr mmnt as fr hr—wht mean?

Zosimus, Albertus Magnus, Geber, Bernhardus Trevisanus, Basilius Valentinus, Raymond Lully, Khalid ben Yezid, Hermes Trismegistus, have they been transcended by our achievement? For today (at a cost of $10,000 an ounce) it is possible to transmute base metal into gold.

The alchemist, for Otto, was likely an unsophisticated man of a certain age assisting in a smelly hallucination over an open fire, tampering with the provenience of absolutes, as Bernard of Trèves and an unnamed Franciscan are pictured seeking the universal dissolvent in the fifteenth century with a mixture of mercury, salt, molten lead, and human excrement. Otto was young enough to find answers before he had even managed to form the questions; nevertheless, if anyone had stopped him just then as he hurried up Madison Avenue, and asked what he was thinking about, Otto (to whom thought was a series of free-swimming images which dove and surfaced occasionally near to one another) would have said, —Alchemy! without hesitation. True, like everyone else, he had never seen a copy of the *Chemā*, that book in which the fallen angels wrote out the secrets of their arts which they had taught to the women they married. As embarrassed by the mention of Christ as he was charmed by the image of gold, the only thing which kept him from dismissing alchemy as the blundering parent of modern chemistry (for a pair of plastic eyeglasses, or a white shirt made from coal-tar derivatives, were obviously more remarkable, and certainly more useful, than anything Bernhardus Trevisanus turned up) was this very image of gold. Coined or in heavy bars, or exquisite dust, it came into his mind, to be fashioned in that busy workshop in less time than it takes to tell (for it was more an assembly line than a manufactory) into cuff links, cigarette cases, and other mass-produced artifacts of the world he lived in, mementos of this world, in which the things worth being were so easily exchanged for the things worth having. Gone to earth alone, as lonely as they had been in life, were the accidents of Bernard and his Franciscan fellow; and gone to earth Michael Majer, who had seen in gold the image of the sun, spun in the earth by its countless revolutions, then, when the sun might yet be taken for the image of God.

All this may have been in the way of progressive revelation, that doctrine which finds man incapable of receiving Truth all of a lump, but offers it to him only in a series of distorted fragments, any one of which, standing by itself, might be disproven by someone unable to admit that he is, eventually, after the same thing. Thus the good Dominican Albertus Magnus said he had tested gold made by the alchemists, and found it unable to withstand seven exposures to fire; chronicling their incredible history, he did not leave the hardly less extraordinary paths of his own, but contributed a book on the care of child-bearing mothers, no less careful here, than there, to abjure accident (for his concern was not the suffering or possible death of the woman, but keeping the child alive long enough for baptism). But with the age of enlightenment those lonely men were left far behind, to haggle in darkness over the beams which they had caught, and clung to with such suffocating desire.

Anti-histamine, streptomycin, penicillin and 606: few may question but that Theophrastus Bombastus von Hohenheim ("better known as Paracelsus") was right. It was Paracelsus who emerged from the fifteenth century (castrated by a hog, so they said, in his childhood) to proclaim that the object of alchemy was not at all the transmutation of base metals into gold, but the preparation of medicines, thus opening the way for the hospitalized perpetuation of accident which we triumphally prolong, enlarge upon, finance, respect, and enjoy today. 3:3'-diamino-4-4'-dihydroxyarsenobenzine dihydrochloride, writes Doctor Ehrlich (after 605 tries), thereby dismissing the notion that syphilis might be a visitation upon that pleasure which, in its perennial variety, had until now afforded the gratification of which only sin is capable. For unlike progressive revelation, the enlightenment of total materialism burst with such vigor that there were hardly enough hands to pick up the pieces. Even Paracelsus was left behind (dead of injuries received in a drunken brawl); and once chemistry had established itself as true and legitimate son and heir, alchemy was turned out like a drunken parent, to stagger away, babbling phantasies to fewer and fewer ears, to less and less impressive derelicts of loneliness, while the child grew up serious, dignified, and eminently pleased with its own limitations, to indulge that parental memory with no doubt but that it had found what the old fool and his cronies were after all the time.

It was with some effort, then, that Otto took his eyes from the gold cube in the Madison Avenue window, a cube capable, at the flick of a thumb, of producing a flame, not, perhaps, the *ignis noster* of the alchemists, but a flame quite competent to light a cigarette. He looked at his stainless steel wrist watch, and hurried on. He was used to having engagements, which were always matters of fixed hours or half-hours, indicated, as he hurried to meet them, by this watch; thus he glanced at it now, as though it might confirm an engagement which he did not have. He forgot to notice the time, looked again, and almost bumped Esther who was coming out of the doorway. It was mid-afternoon.

—Otto!

—Are you just going out?

—Yes, but I'll be back in an hour or so. Do you want to wait?

—Is he up there?

—He's asleep. He didn't come in till about dawn.

—Is . . . I mean is everything all right?

—Yes, it is. I guess it is. Here, take the key and go on up, you can slip in without waking him. I have to run.

Otto had got in and closed the door quietly behind him before he heard anything; even then, he could hardly distinguish words. He stood uncomfortably looking round, toward the half opened door of the studio and away from it. —Like the eyes in the petals of the flower Saint Lucy holds in that Ferrara painting . . . he heard, quite clearly, and looked at his watch. He looked up again at the half-open door. —Like the swollen owl . . . watching Saint Jerome . . .

Otto turned to leave but had hardly taken a step when the door to the studio banged behind him. —This damned hole in the wall, he heard, and turned.

—Oh, I just . . . I mean I just . . .

—I didn't hear you come in.

—I'm sorry, I mean . . . I just sort of came in.

—I'm . . . I was just on my way out. For a walk, going for a walk.

—It . . . well I mean I was just out, and I mean it looks like it's going to rain.

—Yes. Well you . . . you stay and read, if you like. There are some . . . books here, he said, gesturing. —Here. You read French, don't you?

—Why...why yes, Otto said, —of course, I...

—Here. Take this. Keep it. Read it. He picked up, as though from nowhere, a small book whose spine was doubly split, the thin leather facing, torn around the edges from the cardboard, of olive green almost entirely covered with gold stamping of scrolls and fleurs-de-lis.

—*Adolphe*, Otto read, on the cover. —I don't think I...

—It's a novel, he said, —it's a good novel. You read it.

—Well thank you, I...

—I'll...get on with my walk now.

—Do you mind if I come along? Otto asked.

He had not looked surprised when he saw Otto; but he did now. He stood, his hands at his sides, opening and closing on nothing.

—I...I mean I wouldn't want to...well, you know, I...Otto put *Adolphe* into his jacket pocket as he spoke. —I...

—Well, let's get on then.

As they walked toward the park, Otto said, —You look tired.

—Tired?

Otto turned to look at him, as though this response invited him to do so, or permitted it, since he had, for two blocks, been looking from the corner of his eye, awaiting some change in the face beside him, though even now, as the single syllable left its lips, it relapsed into the expression of intent vacancy which it had not lost, even in the interruption of surprise, a peremptory confusion which had seemed, for that instant, to empty it even further.

—Yes, Otto said, —I know. I mean when I stay cooped up like that working, I mean staying inside working on this play, it gets...I mean I get...I mean it doesn't seem to sound right after awhile.

—Yes, yes. I imagine it might not.

Though the tone of this response was an absent one, Otto was encouraged to go on, looking away, just then, from something he would never forget, a detail, he would tell himself, of no significance or consequence whatever; still Otto would remember him unsurprised, his lower lip drawn, exposing his lower teeth, as he spoke and finished speaking. —I mean, trying to get everything to fit where it belongs, there's so much that...well you know what I mean, I mean you've talked to me about these things before, but...well, you've really taught me a great deal.

—Have I?

—Yes but, well I mean to know as much as you do, it must be...I mean you can really do anything you want to by now, I mean, you don't feel all sort of hedged in by the parts you don't know about, like I do. Otto finished speaking, and looked anxiously for response; there was none but a sound which indicated that he needn't try to repeat what he had said. They walked on in silence, but any silence was a difficult state for Otto, most especially in the company of another person it seemed an unnatural presence which must be assailed and broken into pieces, or at least shaken until it rattled. Finally he said, —I've been wondering, I mean are you on a vacation now? Or are you just sort of taking time off.

—From what?

—Well I mean from your job, the drafting…

—Oh that. That. I'm through with that.

—Really? That's wonderful. I mean, it is, isn't it? From what Esther's said, now you'll be able to… do what you want to do.

Attentive only to pools of water, the curbs, and shining bits of ice, they walked on. Before they reached the block they had set out from, Otto had looked at his watch a half-dozen times, and drawn only one response which he turned over in his mind, not to try to understand it immediately, face to face, for itself, nor the source from which it came, but fitting it to the lips of Gordon, through whom, though he did not know it, nor plan it so, he would one day overtake himself. As he walked he pictured Gordon in one after another setting, saying to one after another of the characters who were distinguished only by sex, —And if I cannot teach anyone how to become better, then what have I learned?

—It's just as though that dog's following us, Otto said looking back. He snapped his fingers. The black poodle bounded away. —But I mean, you don't see dogs like that running around loose in the streets. Otto looked up. It was the first time his companion had shown any interest in anything but the ground before them. —I mean, somebody must have lost it.

—Yes, she is odd. Running around us in circles, getting a little closer each time.

—Looking for its master probably, and all it sees is two strangers, Otto said. —But with all that fine trimming, that fancy coiffure and red collar, look at it, just another dog, crouching on its belly.

—Here. Come here.

—I've heard they're terrifically bright, though. The dog was off again. But when they got up the steps, they looked round to see the black poodle halfway up behind them.

Esther was putting her hat on when they came in. —What… wherever… she said, as the dog ran past her, entering as though it knew the house better, had more right there than she did.

—I thought you'd be just coming back, Otto said to her.

—I did, but the Bildows just called and asked us down for drinks. Do you want to come?

—Why yes, I mean if I . . .

—Well *he* wouldn't come, certainly, she said good-humoredly. —He's never forgiven her for trying to kiss him New Year's Eve. They both turned to include him on this, but he had stepped inside the door of the studio where he was fumbling with the phonograph.

—Esther, I . . .

—He . . .

—I'll just be a minute, she said going toward the bedroom.

Otto stood, examining his fingernails. Then he looked at his watch, and music burst upon him. —What is it? he asked, approaching the door of the studio.

—This? Something of Handel's, an oratorio *Judas Maccabaeus*.

—Oh. It's . . . it's splendid isn't it, Otto went on, unable to show his appreciation by listening. —*Lo the conqueror comes*, sang the bass.

—It always seems too bad when they have to translate these things. I mean, it must sound much more impressive in the original.

—The *original?*

—I mean . . . in German, he said, as Esther entered, emptying the unexamined jumble of one purse into another. She dropped a lipstick. Her skirt pulled tightly against the long line of her thigh as she stooped to pick it up. The day had begun to darken. The poodle watched them both without interest.

—Please don't let the dog mess up the house.

—Goodbye, I . . .

—Goodbye.

On the first landing of the staircase, Esther fumbled in her purse and got out a piece of paper. —Can you read it? She handed it over. —It's their address, I never remember it.

—What's this?

—No. The other side. God knows what that is, something of his.

—The equation of x^n plus y^n has no nontrivial solution in integers for n greater than 2.

—The other side. She pulled the outside door open herself.

—He is so . . . strange by now, Esther, Otto said catching up with her. —You can hardly . . . I mean all this time we were walking I couldn't reach him at all.

—I hardly know him at all now. It is strange. She looked up at Otto as they walked. —Do you know, there's something alike about you both.

—Yes, but...with his ability...

—With his ability and your ambition, she said taking Otto's arm, and looking away too soon to see the expression she brought to his face, —I'd have quite a remarkable man.

The poodle, lying on the floor with its forelegs extended, watched him drink down a glass of brandy. —The original! Good God, how can anyone clinging to such foolishness keep any hope in his head? He walked over to the window and stood before it, his back turned upon the room. Outside it had begun to rain. The room was warm, water clattered against the glass. As these minutes went by, the place took on the aspect of any quiet room on a winter's raining afternoon, the room cut away from everything else which the sun and opened windows allow, and here even the music an extensive furnishing which served rather to order the silence than to break it, building upon the impression that the room shall not be returned as part of the world until it has enclosed an assignation. —A boy, brittle as a preconception, I suppose I ought to thank him, I ought to thank him for getting me out of that damned feeling that...

The dog stretched its forelegs, and digging its nails into the floor pulled itself toward him, inclining its head slightly to one side as it listened. He turned, and they stared at each other, the man and the dog: and the dog saw a man whose appearance held nothing in the least remarkable, though dressed to confirm the fact that he looked some years older than he was. The dog raised its forequarters and sat, without taking its eyes from him, to watch him go over and turn the phonograph down until it was almost inaudible. He stood beside it for a moment, and then picked up a book. When he opened it, a slip of paper fell out, which he caught between his fingers. As he sat down to read, the dog's eyes caught his again, each eyed the other obliquely, he as though to discountenance the dog's presence, the black poodle to suggest that the book was a distraction unworthy of notice.

"The first discovery" (it was an account of the oracle at Delphos) "is said to have been occasioned by some goats which were feeding on Mount Parnassus near a deep and large cavern, with a narrow entrance. These goats having been observed by the goatherd, Coretas, to frisk and skip after a strange manner, and to utter unusual sounds immediately upon their approach to the mouth of the cavern, he had the curiosity to view it, and found himself seized with the like fit of madness, skipping, dancing, and foretelling things to come..."

—Damn you! he cried out as the dog barked. —If I have to share this room with you, he commenced, lowering his tone, though the black animal did not seem at all upset by his curse. —Damn you, he repeated, confirming it more quietly, and threw down the book, —skipping, dancing, and foretelling things to come . . . He got up and poured himself another glass of brandy. The dog watched him look around the room. The music was still going on, and he suddenly crossed to stop it, so suddenly that the dog reared as though ready to jump behind him. He stood beside the silent phonograph, looking at the slip of paper between his fingers. —I A O, I A E, he read, copied in a delicate Italian semi-gothic hand he'd once worked on. Before him, on the wall and in sight of the other room where the dog sat poised, watching him, hung the soiled beginning of Camilla on gesso. He stood looking at it; then something moved. He swung about. It was the dog's reflection in the mirror. But the dog sat still in the door. —Damn it, he said directly to its face, —what is it you have, or don't have, that you sit there completely self-contained, that you can sit and know . . . and know exactly where your feet are? Yes, that's what makes cats incredible, because you know they're aware every instant of where their feet are, and they know how much they have to share with other cats, they don't try to . . . pretend . . . He came out muttering, and drank down this third glass looking out the window at the rain. The black poodle had followed and was quite close upon him, sitting looking up at the back of his head. He did not realize it, and when he turned, he dropped his glass and it broke on the floor between them. The dog did not move. —What are you doing in here? he burst out. —What do you want here? What are you . . . what do you want of me? He swayed a little, wiped his cheek with his hand, and found he was perspiring freely. Then he suddenly wiped his cheek again. The dog watched him drop his hand slowly, met his eyes, and did not move.

—Move! he demanded. —Get out of my way, get out! The dog sat with the broken glass at its feet, looking up at him. The rain beat on the glass behind him. Then instead of pushing the dog aside he turned and went round the couch. He had started for the brandy bottle, there on the table where the dog blocked his way; but he stopped again at the door of the studio, and went through a pile of records on the floor. The dog came over and stood sniffing at the doorway. He put a record on the turntable, and stood with a fingernail in the groove as it turned. Then the dog startled for the first time, when he put the needle on the record and turned up the volume. The music was Arabic. The dog put its head on one side, then the other, watching him. —There are shapes, he murmured, raising his right hand to move it on the air as though shaping the line of the flute from the dissonance. The dog had laid its ears back, its mouth was closed, no longer panting, no longer exposing teeth. —There are shapes, and . . . exquisite strength . . . They both watched his hand move slowly between them. —Change a line without touching it . . . there's delicacy. The dog turned slightly to look up at his face, at his perspiring forehead, as though seeking there evidence or betrayal of the signs he made in the air between them. —Not a word. Not an instant of adultery. "You can really do anything you want to by now!" The dog bared its teeth at his harsh laughter, and watched his hand drop, all the way to snatch up the slip of paper he'd dropped a few minutes before. —I A O, I A E, in the name of the father and of our Lord Jesus Christ and holy spirit, iriterli estather, nochthai brasax salolam . . . yes, very good for cows in Egypt . . . opsakion aklana thalila i a o, i a e . . .

The dog growled at him. He crumpled the paper and hurled it, but it fell slowly, at the dog's feet. The dog stood up instantly and backed into the other room, which was already getting darker, though not yet as dark as the studio, where he'd sat down gripping the edge of the table, looking feverishly over the books and papers spread before him. He caught at Remigius' *Demonolatria* and pushed it aside, raised the cover of the *Libro dell' Arte*, and pushed it off to the floor, then found pen and paper, and the ink bottle already opened, and wrote, slow, and with great care and application,

Emperor

His lips moved over the letters, as the flute disappeared, the music broke, recovered, rose into collision, fell in clangor, and the dog in the other room commenced trotting in irregular circles, sniffing the air which the heat seemed to have weighed down the more heavily with lavender.

. . . *by the power of the grand ADONAY* . . . his lips were moving, over letters, then words,

. . . *to appear instanter, and by ELOIM, by ARIEL, by JEHOVAM, by AQUA, TAGLA, MATHON, OARIOS, ALMOAZIN, ARIOS, MEMBROT, VARIOS, PITHONA, MAJODS, SULPHÆ, GABOTS, SALAMANDRÆ, TABOTS, GINGUA, JANNA, ETITNAMUS, ZARIATNATMIX* . . .

He stopped and listened. Then,

A. E. A. J. A. T. M. O. A. A. M. V. P. M. S. . . .

The music stopped, leaving the sounds of the dog's nails clicking on the wood floor. Then as abruptly that stopped, and the pen hung in his hand over the wet black letters on the paper. A movement caught the corner of his eye; he turned his head quickly, saw the arm of the phonograph raise itself, pause. He looked through the door, unable to see the black poodle. —Dog, he whispered in a hoarse tone. —*Dog! Dog! Dog!* No sound contested his challenge, no recognition of men imprisoned in the past for spelling the Name of God backwards, no response to God, if not the Name, reversed three times in his whisper.

He jumped to his feet, slipped against the table, spilling the ink on the papers there, and in three steps was through the door to the other room. The dog lay in the darkened foyer before the front door, facing the door and apparently at rest. —Damn you! he said. —I'll...

The dog turned to look at him, as he threw his hands out before him. —Damned...animal out of hell are you...The dog, only partially distinguishable in the darkness, got up, the hair on its shoulders bristling as he took two steps closer, and paused. They both listened to the footsteps on the lower staircase, he with his hands still in the air as though counting the steps, heavy and even, neither casual nor hurried, reaching the hallway below, the foot of the stairs, and up the stairs with no more apparent effort than one step at a time, though too soon *knock knock knock*

The rain, silenced by inattention, took up its beating against the glass; then the dog whined and clawed the door, movement which broke the still arrangement where every object seemed tense in suspension. He walked to the door, and as he put his hand to the latch the hand on the other side, as though responding, moved too: *knock knock knock*. And he drew back as though threatened.

The dog clawed the door, and when he pulled it open the dog jumped so fast that he had no chance to restrain it. But the visitor who waited in the darkness had apparently expected the attack, for he caught at the red collar and held the black poodle down.

—Hello. Hello, said that voice in the shadow, a voice at once cheerful and unpleasant. —Some kids in the street saw you bring her in here.

He opened the door more widely. —Come in, he said, in a tone which seemed to reassure him, for he repeated it. —Come in...Who are you?

The visitor extended his hand as he entered, a stubby hand mounting two diamonds set in gold on one finger. —My name is Recktall Brown.

He took the hand and said his own name in reply, distantly, as though repeating the name of an unremembered friend in effort to recall him.

Recktall Brown entered and strode to the middle of the room, looking round it through heavy glasses which diffused the pupils of his eyes into uncentered shapes. —Good thing you brought her in, he said, and waved the diamonds at the dog where it lay on the floor, licking itself. —She hates the rain. Then he turned, a strange ugliness, perhaps only because it looked that a smile would be impossible to it.

—Would you...like a drink?

—No. Not now. Not now.

—Yes, but...there, yes, sit down.

Recktall Brown dropped into a heavy armchair facing the open door of the studio. He tapped the diamonds on the arm of the chair while he continued to look around the room, his head back, his face highly colored with the redness of running up flights of stairs; yet he breathed quietly, almost imperceptibly, for his stoutness absorbed any such evidence before it reached the double-breasted surface of his chest. —I know your name. He smiled, a worse thing than the original, turning for a moment to the man who stood watching him as he poured brandy into a glass, and said, —Yes, I . . . I think I know your name, but in what connection . . .

—A publisher? A collector? A dealer? Recktall Brown sounded only mildly interested. —People who don't know me, they say a lot of things about me. He laughed then, but the laughter did not leave his throat. —A lot of things. You'd think I was wicked as hell, even if what I do for them turns out good. I'm a business man.

—But . . . how did you know my name?

—What's your business?

—I'm a draftsman.

—And an artist? Recktall Brown was looking beyond him to the studio, and back at him as he approached and sat on the couch.

—I . . . do some restoring.

—I know.

—You know? He sat forward on the couch, holding the glass between his knees, and looked at his visitor and away again, as though there were some difficulty which he could not make out.

—You did some work for me.

—For you?

—A Dutch picture, a picture of a landscape, an old one.

—Flemish. Yes, I remember it. That painting could hang in any museum . . .

—It does. The hand which carried the diamonds was folded over the other before him. —You couldn't tell it had been touched. Even an expert couldn't tell, without all the chemical tests and X-rays, an expert told me that himself.

—Well, I tried, of course . . .

—Tried! You did a damn good job on it. He looked around the room with an air of detached curiosity, and finally asked what the funny smell was. Because the glasses obliterated any point in his glance, it was difficult to tell where he was looking, but he seemed aware that he was being watched with an expression of anxiety almost mistrust, not of him, but an eagerness to explain anything which might be misunderstood. His questioning was peremptory.

—Lavender. I use it as a medium sometimes. The smell seems to stay.

—A medium?

—To mix colors in, to paint with.

—You do a lot of work here, don't you.

—Well, I ... I've been doing some of my work at home. This drafting, bridge plans.

—No. The painting, the painting, Recktall Brown said impatiently.

—Oh, this restoring, this ... patching up the past I do.

—You don't paint? You don't paint pictures yourself?

—I ... No.

—Why not?

—I just ... don't paint.

Recktall Brown watched him wipe his perspiring forehead, and drink part of the brandy quickly. —All this work, all these books, you go to all this trouble just to patch up other people's work? How come you've never painted anything yourself?

—Well I have, I have.

—What happened, you couldn't sell them?

—Well no, but ...

—Why not?

—Well people ... the critics ... I was young then, I was still young.

—What are you now, about forty?

—Forty? Me, forty?

—Why not, you look forty. He took a cigar from his pocket, and continued his gaze at the man across from him. —So they didn't like your pictures. What happened, the critics laugh you out of town?

—Well they ...

—And you got bitter because nobody gave your genius any credit.

—No, I ...

—And you couldn't make any money on them, so you quit?

—No, it ...

—And you decided the only thing you could do was patch up other people's pictures.

—No, damn it, I ...

—Don't get mad, I'm just asking you. He had unwrapped the cigar, and he raised it to his ear, rolling it between fingers as thick as itself. —Don't you want me to ask you?

—Why yes, yes. And I'm not angry, but, damn it ...

—Why, do you want to tell me you can do more than patch up old pictures? There was no sound of dryness as he rolled the cigar, lowered it to trim the end off with a gold penknife, and thrust it among uneven teeth.

—Of course I can.

—But you won't, because they won't all stand up and cheer and pay you a big price.

—It isn't that, it isn't those things. They don't matter...

—Don't matter? Don't tell me they don't matter, my boy. That's what anybody wants, Recktall Brown said, lighting the cigar. —Everybody to stand up and cheer. There's nothing so damn strange about that.

—But it all... it isn't that simple now.

—Now?

—In painting, in art today...

—Art today? The uneven teeth showed in a grin through the smoke. —Art today is spelled with an *f*. You know that. Anybody knows it, he added patiently and waited, offering an oppressive silence which forced an answer.

—It's as though... there's no direction to act in now.

—That's crazy. You read too much. There's plenty to do, if anybody's got what you've got.

—It isn't that simple.

The smoke from a cigarette mingled with that of his cigar, and he asked, —Why not? and smiled patiently.

—People react. That's all they do now, react, they've reacted until it's the only thing they can do, and it's... finally there's no room for anyone to do anything but react.

—And here you are sitting here with all the pieces. Can't you react and still be smart?

—All right then, here I am with all the pieces and they all fit, everything fits perfectly and what is there to do with them, when you do get them together? You just said yourself, art today...

—Today? Maybe you put the pieces together wrong.

—What do you mean?

As the smoke rose before him, it became apparent what was wrong. It was the ears. They were hardly ear-shape at all, their convolutions nearly lost in heavy pieces of flesh hung to the sides of the head, each a weight in itself. —You look forty years old and you talk like you're born yesterday, Recktall Brown said. He stared through his glasses, and the voice he heard was more distant, hardly addressed to him in its first words, —In a sense an artist is always born yesterday.

—Come on now, my boy...

—Damn it, am I the only one who feels this way? Have I made this all up alone? If you can do something other people can't do, they think you ought to want to do it just because they can't.

Recktall Brown gestured with his cigar, and an ash fell from it like a gray bird-dropping. —So you're going to stay right here, drawing pictures of bridges, and patching up...

—Those bridges, those damned bridges.

—What's wrong with them.

—Who are they all, driving over those bridges as though they grew there. They don't...they don't...

—They don't give you the credit.

—No, it isn't that simple.

—I'm afraid it is, my boy.

—Damn it, it isn't, it isn't. It's a question of...it's being surrounded by people who don't have any sense of...no sense that what they're doing means anything. Don't you understand that? That there's any sense of necessity about their work, that it has to be done, that it's theirs. And if they feel that way how can they see anything necessary in anyone else's? And it...every work of art is a work of perfect necessity.

—Where'd you read that?

—I didn't read it. That's what it...has to be, that's all. And if everyone else's life, everyone else's work around you can be interchanged and nobody can stop and say, This is mine, this is what I must do, this is my work...then how can they see it in mine, this sense of inevitableness, that this is the way it must be. In the middle of all this how can I feel that...damn it, when you paint you don't just paint, you don't just put lines down where you want to, you have to know, you have to know that every line you put down couldn't go any other place, couldn't be any different...But in the midst of all this... rootlessness, how can you...damn it, do you talk to people? Do you listen to them?

—I talk business to people. Recktall Brown drew heavily on his cigar, watched the cigarette stamped out, the brandy finished.

—But...you're talking to me. You're listening to me.

—We're talking business, Recktall Brown said calmly.

—But...

—People work for money, my boy.

—But I...

—Money gives significance to anything.

—Yes. People believe that, don't they. People believe that.

Recktall Brown watched patiently, like someone waiting for a child to solve a simple problem to which there was only one answer. The cigarette, lit across from him, knit them together in the different textures of their smoke.

—You know...Saint Paul tells us to redeem time.

—Does he? Recktall Brown's tone was gentle, encouraging.

—A work of art redeems time.

—And buying it redeems money, Recktall Brown said.

—Yes, yes, owning it . . .

—And that's why you sit around here patching up the past. Recktall Brown leaned forward, resting his elbows on his broad knees. —That's why old art gets the prices, he said: —Everybody agrees on it, everybody agrees it's a masterpiece. They copy them right and left. You've probably done copies, yourself.

—Not since I studied. And who wants them? Who wants copies.

Recktall Brown watched him get up suddenly, and walk over to the window, there the rain streaked the glass into visibility. —Nobody wants copies. He ground out his cigar in an ashtray. —The ones who can pay want originals. They can pay for originals. They expect to pay. He paused, and then raised his tone. —As long as an artist's alive, he can paint more pictures. When they're dead, they're through. Take the old Dutch painters. Not even the best ones. Some small-time painter, not a great one, but known. Exclusive, like . . . like . . .

—The Master of the Magdalene Legend, came from across the room, blurred against the window.

—No chance of him not selling. Suppose some of his pictures, some of his unknown pictures, turned up here and there. They might turn up a little restored, like the kind of work you do. Look at that canvas in there, what is it? He did not look at the canvas inside the door of the studio where he motioned, but at the perspiring face that turned toward it.

—Nothing. A canvas I prepared two or three years ago. I never . . .

—Well just suppose, Recktall Brown went on, not allowing him to interrupt, —suppose you did some restoring on it. If you worked there for a while you might find an undiscovered picture there by Master what-ever-he-was. It might be worth ten thousand. It might be worth fifty. He got to his feet, and walked quietly toward the back turned on him. —Can you tell me you've never thought of this before?

—Of course I have. They were suddenly face to face. —It would be a lot of work.

—Work! Do you mind work? Recktall Brown reached out his two heavy hands, and took the arms before him. —Is there any objection you've made all this time, over all the work you have done, and can't do, that this doesn't satisfy?

—None, except . . .

—Except what?

—None.

Recktall Brown let go of him, and took another cigar out of his pocket. His mouth seemed sized to hold it, as he unwrapped it, trimmed the end, and thrust it there. —The critics will be very happy about your decision.

—The critics . . .

—The critics! There's nothing they want more than to discover old masters. The critics you can buy can help you. The ones you can't are a lot of poor bastards who could never do anything themselves and spend their whole life getting back at the ones who can, unless he's an old master who's been dead five hundred years. They're like a bunch of old maids playing stoop-tag in an asparagrus patch. His laughter poured in heavy smoke from his mouth and nostrils. Then he took off his glasses, looking into the perspiring face before him, and a strange thing happened. His eyes, which had all this time seemed to swim without focus behind the heavy lenses, shrank to sharp points of black, and like weapons suddenly unsheathed they penetrated instantly wherever he turned them.

When Esther came in alone she paused in the entrance to the living room, not listening to the music but sniffing the air. Then she jumped, startled. —I didn't see you, I didn't see you standing there . . . She sniffed again. —That funny smell, she said. The smell of the dog, weighted with cigar smoke, had penetrated everywhere. —Has someone been here? She turned on a light. —What's the matter, who was it? She stopped in the middle of taking off her wet hat. —Recktall Brown? she repeated. —Yes, I've heard something about him. What was it. Something awful. She coughed, and got her hat off. —I'm glad I can't remember what it was. As she crossed the room she said, —What *is* that music?

In the doorway of the bedroom she stopped. —Do you remember that night? she asked. —In that Spanish place? . . . She stood looking at his back, and finally said, —Oh nothing. She put her hand to her hair. —Nothing, she repeated, turning toward the bedroom, —but I liked you better flamenco.

"Most people make a practice of embellishing a wall with tin glazed with yellow in imitation of gold, because it is less costly than gold leaf. But I give you this urgent advice: to make an effort always to embellish with fine gold and with good colors, especially in the figure of Our Lady. And if you try to tell me that a poor person cannot afford the outlay, I will answer that if you do your work well, and spend time on your paintings, and good colors, you will get such a reputation that a wealthy person will come to compensate you for your poor clients; and your standing will be so good as a person who uses good colors that if a master is getting one ducat for a figure, you will be offered two; and you will end by gaining your ambition. As the old saying goes, 'Good work, good pay.' And even if you were not adequately paid, God and Our Lady will reward you for it, body and soul."

—What in the world are you reading?

—I don't know, Otto said closing the *Libro dell' Arte*, staring at its worn spine before he put it down. —It was something of his.

The telephone rang, and as she went in to pick it up he walked over to the mirror hung in the living room at his suggestion. He could hear Esther's voice from the bedroom, where she'd had the telephone moved. —Yes, yes, but... I don't know. To tell you the truth, it's... some time since I've seen him myself. But... what? Well, I think he's taken some sort of studio downtown, on the west side. I think it's Horatio Street. What? Oh. I don't know. To tell you the truth, honestly, I don't know.

—Who was that? Otto asked, ducking away from the mirror as she returned.

—Somebody named Benny, it's somebody from his office who's been trying to reach him for months.

—It's funny, isn't it, Otto said looking at the floor. —I mean it's strange, without him anywhere.

—Do you want to go out tonight? The Munks asked us down for a drink.

—Do you want to?

—If you do.

—Well I, I ought to stay and get some work done.

—I thought your play was going to be finished by the end of April.

—Well it is, sort of.

—Why don't you do something with it?

—Well it isn't really... it's all here, it holds together but... it doesn't seem to mean anything. But I've got to do something, he said gripping his chin in his hand. —I've got to get hold of some money. They were both silent. Otto walked over, picked up a magazine and sat down beside her. The magazine was *Dog Days*. —What's this doing here? he asked idly.

—That, it's something he brought in once, when we'd talked about having children. Oh, sometimes he used to be so... Oh!...

—What's the matter?

—The dream I had last night, I just remembered it, she said. —It was about my sister Rose, we were flying kites in a vacant lot like we used to, and some boys were there with a kite with broken glass on the edge of it, and they cut our kite right down out of the sky.

—But that doesn't sound so frightening.

—It was terrible, it was... Otto pulled her over and silenced her mouth with his. Finally she said, —Will you do something for me?

—Shave before I come to bed?

—How did you know?

Later, he called from the bathroom, —This handkerchief drying on the mirror, can I take it off and fold it up? It's dry... Esther? did you hear me? This handkerchief...?

—Yes yes, she cried out, suddenly, then caught her voice and controlled it. —Yes, take it down. She picked up Otto's jacket from the couch and went toward the bathroom where she heard the sound of the electric razor.

—It's all right if I use this isn't it?

—Why yes. Yes, of course. I'm glad you're using it.

—There's a straight razor here, he said turning to her where she stood in the doorway with his jacket, the machine whirring in his hand, —but I don't think I could manage it.

—I know, she said. —It's strange. That he left that. Then she went in to hang up the jacket. —What's this book in your pocket? she called out.

—That? Otto stopped to look at himself in the glass. —It's a novel, a French novel he gave me once.

—Have you finished it?

—Well, I... I haven't got all the way through it yet. It's a... I... Oh incidentally, I found a paper in it, he must have written it out when he was little. About the whole creation working to be delivered from the vanity of time, about nature working for this great redemption. It sounds like a sermon.

—A sermon of his father's, she said, hanging up the jacket as Otto came in and sat on the bed.

—But it's sort of nice. Even for a sermon, he said, taking off a shoe, which he sat there and held for a minute, staring at it.

It was a dark night, especially for spring or so it seemed on the lower West Side, near the river where there is little illumination, and day and night the air carries in far above the city's quota of black silt from the railway and the boats on the water. Sounds were few, for the later the night became the fewer were the sounds of wanton circumstance, the casual sounds of fortuity, the reckless sounds of accident; until all that rose on the silt-laden air were the sounds of necessity, clear and inevitable, which had earlier been so eagerly confused by those who had retired from the darkness now and slept, waiting for the dawn.

Still, now, the sky contained no suggestion of dawn, in its absence a chimera to be dreaded in actuality by loneliness, and even that forsworn and gone to earth, carrying with it that substance of which all things eventually are made, the prima materia it had sought to deliver from the conspiracy of earth, air, fire, and water binding it here in baseness. "For me an image slumbers in the stone," said Zarathustra, no more content to let it lie bound so than those since gone to earth, disappointed? or surprised were they? by fictions, and followers who summoned them back, vicars demanding of them vicarious satisfaction in life for that which they had suffered in the privacy of death.

Itinerant drunkards and curious neighbors sometimes saw him at night, near the docks, and the slaughterhouses a block away, gathering the wood of broken crates to carry back to the fireplace which squatted at one end of the sub-basement room. Benny had stopped in every doorway looking for the name, and could not find it. Then he saw a figure, knew it a block away, and ran toward it, to take an arm and stop him before he could step into one of the doors and disappear. —Thank God I found you! Benny said, when he caught him standing under a streetlamp with broken wood under his arm. —Where have you been? It's been months, we haven't seen you in the office for months.

Benny was an anxious man in gray flannel, single-breasted, a silk foulard tie which caught the wind, a cigarette in his hand.

—What's happened? What are you doing? Are you all right? You look fine, you look better than I've ever seen you, but wait, wait . . .

—But wait, wait a minute for me, listen to me, are you . . . have you done any plans, have you done any more of them?

—Bridge plans . . . don't you know who I am? Bridge plans, I have to have another one, I have to submit another one now.

—But listen, I know it, I hardly know what I'm saying, but listen. We have one up now, a very important one, and if I bring you the location and the problem will you do it?

—But listen to me. It's months since I've submitted anything. Once. Listen, I submitted a plan of my own and they laughed at me, they laughed at me, they thought it was a joke, they said, You're not serious with this are you Benny? After the Cooper City viaduct? and the bridge at Fallen Ark Gap? You used to be a genius Benny, what happened to you? Wait, listen to me, listen, just one more. Listen, old J. W. died last month, did you know that? He died. Don't you see? I can be a vice-president, and I'll never have to draw a plan again, a vice-president in charge of design, and I can do that. I can do that. You know I can do that. But it all depends on this, it all depends on this one new job, to show them.

—Just this one, this last one. And I'll pay you for this one, I know I never paid you before, but I'll pay you for this one, I'll pay you whatever you want.

—Listen maybe I never thanked you right for all you did, but you know how much it meant. I can pay you now. I can pay you. You've got nothing to lose, and I've got everything.

—Everything, and I . . . and you . . . Look at you. What is it? What are you doing, what are you doing to yourself? You like fine, I said you look fine but not like you, fine for somebody else but not like you.

Benny reached out to take his arm again, and a nail in one of the broken crates tore his sleeve.

—You're the only one who can do this for me. You're the only one who can save me. One more. And we can forget the whole thing, as though it never happened . . .

The silk foulard stirred on the wind. Then Benny turned away too, leaving the cone of light empty, to east and the city where the flood caught him and the ebb bore him away, as though from an empty beach and no trace on it at the feet of the figure pausing for an instant to look at the tide's recession and then going on, gathering driftwood.

When Esther came in alone she paused in the entrance to the living room; then she jumped, startled. —I didn't see you, I didn't see you standing there. She turned on a light, and stood in the middle of the room taking off her hat, looking at his back. —Posing there, she said finally, and dropped her hat on a table, —like he used to. Like an old man.

Otto turned from his reflection in the glass window, streaked into visibility by the spring rain. —Yes, he said, looking to the floor between them. —More than a year . . .

—What?

—And he used to warn me against youth. Did you know that? The trap of being young. He warned me about it. He said that youth is a trap that . . .

—Please, I don't want to hear any more about it.

—But . . . I just can't believe, a whole year's passed, and I'm still . . .

—Otto, if you spend all your time fretting and . . . fooling around . . .

—But I've got to get hold of some money.

—And this obsession you have about money . . .

—Yes but money, you need money to . . .

—You seem to take not having it as a reflection on your manhood.

—But money, I mean, damn it, a man does feel castrated in New York without money. And this, I mean you say he puts plenty in your checking account, but it, I mean for me to, well not take it out and use it but to let you actually pay . . .

—Otto, you know I've never understood why you've never looked up your father. If he lives right in New York, and you've never seen him. And I should think he could give you some money.

—But I don't...

—And it would probably help clear up this obsessional neurosis you have about...

Gordon: When we lose contact with the beloved one, we lose contact with the whole world.

—What are you writing?

—Just something I thought of. For this play. Otto had followed her in, and he sat on the foot of the bed which had become a refuge, no longer a beginning but a desperate end, no longer a vista of future conquest but sanctuary where failure in all else made this one possession unbearable, unearned and come too soon. —It's all like a play, a bad play with nothing but exits and entrances. And your work, your novel, he mumbled contentiously. —You haven't...

—My what?

He looked up at her. —Who is this guy Ellery that you keep seeing?

—He's in advertising, and he's very interested in analysis. Haven't you thought of going into...

—Analysis! Haven't we been over that enough?

—I was going to say advertising.

—Advertising! Do you think I've sunk that low? And what...what do you go out with him for anyhow? You're going out tonight?

—Yes.

—But why?

—It does me good to be seen in successful company.

Otto cleared his throat. He was staring at the floor between them. He raised his eyes, slightly, enough to reach her feet flattened on the floor with her weight. He mumbled, —Sometimes I wish I was old, an old man.

—Otto?

—What.

—You...Oh nothing but, I liked you better a boy, she said from the closet where she stood putting on her slip:

The women who admonish us for our weaknesses are usually those most surprised when we show our strength and leave them.

—I...

—We...

—You...

—Esther?

—Ellery?...Oh, Otto? Otto went away, says Esther from the closet where she stands, taking off her slip. —He went to Central America, to work on a banana plantation.

Images surround us; cavorting broadcast in the minds of others, we wear the motley tailored by their bad digestions, the shame and failure, plague pandemics and private indecencies, unpaid bills, and animal ecstasies remembered in hospital beds, our worst deeds and best intentions will not stay still, scolding, mocking, or merely chattering they assail each other, shocked at recognition. Sometimes simplicity serves, though even the static image of Saint John Baptist received prenatal attentions (six months along, leaping for joy in his mother's womb when she met Mary who had conceived the day before): once delivered he stands steady in a camel's hair loincloth at a ford in the river, morose, ascetic on locusts and honey, molesting passers-by, upbraiding the flesh on those who wear it with pleasure. And the Nazarene whom he baptized? Three years pass, in a humility past understanding: and then death, disappointed? unsuspecting? and the body left on earth, the one which was to rule the twelve tribes of Israel, and on earth, left crying out —*My God, why dost thou shame me?* Hopelessly ascendant in resurrection, the image is pegged on the wind by an epileptic tent-maker, his strong hands stretch the canvas of faith into a gaudy caravanserai, shelter for travelers wearied of the burning sand, lured by forgetfulness striped crimson and gold, triple-tiered, visible from afar, redolent of the east, and level and wide the sun crashes the fist of reality into that desert where the truth still walks barefoot.

—This place needs a good airing out. One look at that room in there and anybody can see that your husband . . .

—My husband . . .

—He . . .

—I . . .

The music is Mozart's, the Concerto Number Seven in F Major for three pianos. —I wish . . . Esther says. In a feverish conspiracy of order the notes of the music burst from the radio in the other room where it is dark. They thrust there in the darkness against hard surfaces and angles as sharp as themselves. Possibly molecules are rearranged, set dancing, in a sympathy which lasts no longer than the duration of the note; possibly not, but there is the lighted doorway, to be entered in a concerted rush, the naked soles of a man's feet hung over the end of the bed, calloused and unlikely targets. —I wish . . . Esther says. Her hand moves quickly, but too late, where she has been pausing, holding cloth. Her breast, bared, and not especially full but standing out, centered and still, is very real to her and to no one else: her hand moves there quickly but too late as a note from one of three pianos strikes with the purpose of a blade, and has entered with the cold intimacy of a penknife in the heart.

—I wish . . .

—You don't think he'd walk in, do you?

—*He?*

IV

Les femmes soignent ces féroces infirmes retour des pays chauds.

—RIMBAUD

IN THE dry-season haze, the hills were a deep blue and looked farther away than the sun itself, for the sun seemed to have entered that haze, to hang between the man and the horizon where, censured and subdued, it suffered the indignity of his stare. The heat of day was as inert as the haze which made it visible; and it only mitigated with the dissolution of the haze in darkness.

From that darkness outside the window came a bird cry, staccato, sound of a large alarm clock being wound in the next room late at night. Otto was sitting in a pair of underdrawers, writing. When his door was flung open and a man wearing only faded dungarees, with a bottle in one hand and a glass in the other, entered, Otto put down his pen and said, —Hello Jesse.

—Hello Jesse. How do you like that. Hello Jesse. What are you doin anyhow? said the tattooed man, and sat down on the other wooden chair.

—I'm writing.

Jesse put the bottle and glass on the table and looked around him. The corners of his mouth twitched, momentarily confused about something, but something which was going to be pleasurable. He looked over the table, littered with papers illegibly scribbled upon, and at the pictures on the wall.

—Do you want a cigarette? Otto asked him.

—Yeah, give me a cigarette. Jesse put out his hand, and then waved away the green package of MacDonald's Gold Standard. —What do you smoke those things for? That ain't even American-made stuff.

—I don't know, I . . . anyhow it is Virginia tobacco, I . . .

—Yeah what do you smoke those lousy things for? Why don't you smoke American cigarettes? He knocked one of Otto's clean socks from the corner of the table into the cuspidor with his elbow, and watched suspiciously while Otto got up and went behind him to retrieve it.

—What are you doin anyhow? Jesse asked. Then he said, —You're a religious bastid ain't you.

—Not exactly, why do you say…

—That. That's a religious picture ain't it?

—Why no, that's just a print of a painting, an Italian Renaissance…

—Looks like some friggin madonna, said Jesse, mistrustful, and looked back at Otto. Then he spat into the cuspidor. —Give me a cigarette, he said.

—All I've got are these, said Otto. He held forth a packet of Emu, locally manufactured.

—What do you smoke these lousy things for? Why don't you smoke American cigarettes? Jesse spat again, on the floor. Otto pushed the cuspidor nearer with his bare foot. —I didn't get any on me, did I? Jesse looked down at his chest, where a ship struggled through a mat of hair. Toward each brown nipple a bluebird dipped. On one shoulder, a peacock; on the other, a palm-tree seascape. The arms wore anchors, a tombstone with MOTHER on a scroll, and a dagger. The gallery swelled as he watched it. —That's pretty good, hunh? What do you think of that, hunh? He turned his head to one shoulder and then the other, admiring the rippling art there. Then he looked Otto over.

Otto lit a cigarette. It was too late to get up and put on a pair of trousers.

—Why don't you get out and build yourself up a little? Jesse Franks returned to his own splendor. —That's a real man, hunh?

—Yes, it's just…

—Hunh? What do you think of that, hunh? Then he looked at the scribbled papers sticking to his forearm on the table. —What's all this crap?

—That's my play.

—That's your play, hunh? There, he said, getting a handful of the papers and pushing them to Otto, —read me your play.

—Well I…this act isn't…

—Read me your play.

—"Gordon: Wit, my dear Priscilla, is the vulgar currency of wisdom.

"Priscilla: But darling, no one could accuse you of being vulgar. Though to tell the truth, there are moments when I feel absolutely suffocated by witty people.

"Gordon: You are surrounded by people who take a half-truth deliberately misunderstood to be one of the privileges of wit." It's not quite…I mean this act is…

—Read another act.

—"Priscilla: You know I love you, Gordon. Do you fear it?

"Gordon: Any rational person fears romance, my dear Priscilla.

"Priscilla: And so you will not marry me, because I love you.

"Gordon: Romantic love, my dear, romantic love. The most difficult challenge to the ideal is its transformation into reality, and few ideals survive.
Marriage demands of romantic love that it become a reality, and when an
ideal becomes a reality it ceases to be an ideal. Someone has certainly commented on the seedy couple Dante and Beatrice would have made after twenty
years of badly cooked meals. As for the *Divine Comedy*, it's safe to say that
the *Purgatorio* would have been written, though perhaps a rather less poetic
version. But Heaven and Hell rejuvenated, I think not, my dear. There is a bit
of verse somewhere on this topic concerning Petrarch and his Laura, but I
cannot recall it. But even Virginia, you may remember, preferred drowning
before the eyes of her lover to marrying him. Paul at least had the pleasure of
seeing her drown nude, but she knew what she was doing. A wise girl, Virginia.

"Priscilla: But then, what you're saying is . . ."

—What the hell is he saying?

—Well, Gordon is saying that love, I mean romantic love . . .

—That's all they do, talk?

—Well, it's a play, and I mean . . .

—When does he slip it to her?

—Well on the stage you can't very well . . .

—So they get married?

—Well no, I mean not really, but they . . .

—But he's been slipping it to her anyway, hunh?

—Well he . . . I mean . . .

—Who's Gordon, anyway?

—Well he's the hero of the play.

—The hero? He don't sound like much of a hero. Why don't you write
about Jesse?

—Well I . . .

—You want something to write about? O.K., take this down. Gordon was
the kind of guy that walked into . . . shouldered his way into a bar. He came
in and got what he wanted. If anybody wanted to make trouble . . . no. He was
a nice guy, but if anybody wanted to make trouble . . . you got that?

—Yes, Otto said with a pencil.

—If anybody was looking for trouble . . . no, that don't sound so good.
Leave that out. He watched Otto's pencil to be sure it was marking out. —O.K.
now start with this. I was around in Chilano Bay in Colombia with no money
of the country, see? I had some money, I had about a hundred dollars, but no
money of the country, see? But I have to have a little to get around the country. I was on a boat with a contraband cargo. So I run into a chuleta. You
know what a chuleta is?

—No, I...

—Then you're not so smart, are you. Just because you went to college. It's a money-changer, a guy who changes money and takes some out for himself. O.K. So a cayuga come out to the ship, wanting to buy her cargo. But no sell. Worth too much see? You got that?

—Yes I...

—O.K. now where was I?

—A cayuga came out to the ship...

—Yeah. So this guy is only wearing a pair of dungarees, tight-fitting, see? He's well-built, wearing a pair of tight-fitting dungarees. You got that?

—Yes.

—How do you say it?

—He was a well-built fellow wearing tight-fitting dungarees.

—O.K. So he goes into town and finds a girl in a bar. She wants to go into bed with him. But he can't take no chances on account of that cargo. The police, see? The girl visits him at his house, but he can't take no chances. So he tells her, take it easy... Jesse stopped and looked at Otto. —You're goin to get paid for this and I ain't goin to get nothin.

—I've never sold anything yet, Otto said.

—Yeah. Well you can sell this, see. This is what people like to read about. Where was I? O.K. So she wants to stay, but he wants everything he has in his mind for shark-fishing. Chilano Bay, that's the place for shark-fishing. So he dives for sharks. The white ones and the nigger sharks. Those are the black ones. They don't kill the white ones, but he'll do it, see? He's not scared. He'll dive for any shark. Period.

Otto waited.

—How's that? asked the author.

—Well it isn't quite a story yet...

—What do you mean it isn't a story. You think I don't know what a story is? This is what people like to read about, realism, real men doing something, not a lot of crap in fancy trimmings. You get me?

—Yes I...

—You're goin to get paid for it and I ain't goin to get nothin. Jesse returned to admiring his chest.

Otto stood up and walked over to the bed. He scratched his arm, to give his hand something to do.

—Yeah, you're pretty, all right. Where'd you get hands like that? They aren't men's hands.

—They just grew, Otto started to reason, —like yours did...

—Like mine! Jesse made a fist, as Otto sat down again. —Yeah, you got to wise up to yourself, see? Jesse approached with the flat bottle in the palm of his hand, and stopped, swaying over him. He made the motion of smashing the bottle in Otto's face, then stood laughing.

—I have to go to bed, Jesse.

—Yeah, you have to go to bed. Look, rabbit, I'm looking for a shack-job, see? Otto sat still.

—Get me?

—I get you.

Jesse stood swaying for a moment. Then he said, —I got to go dump my bowels.

—Well, I'm going to bed, said Otto. He stood, stretched as though at ease, yawned a feigned yawn. Jocularly, man-to-man, he said, —Good night, Jesse. I don't want to seem to throw you out, but . . .

—Throw me out! Why rabbit you couldn't throw me . . . you just try, if you want me to kick you from one end of this room to the other. Throw me out, rabbit, that's a good one . . . said Jesse, out the door carrying the bottle, leaving the dirty glass.

The plantation outside was quiet, the jungle held at distance by thousands of pert green erections rearing on the stalks of the banana plants. There were no poisonous snakes, no poisoned darts. Few years before, within every discouraged native memory, they had managed in primitive content selling a consistently inferior grade of sisal, hands of green bananas, and occasional loads of hardwood to ships which came in leisurely to trade. Then an American fruit company arrived, tired of buying thousands of hands of bananas, set on hundreds of thousands of stems. The Company replaced the shaky wharf in the port with two firm piers, cleared and planted a tremendous plantation; and while waiting for their own trees to mature offered eight dollars a stem to local growers, since the Company ships were ready to call regularly. The natives gathered bananas in frenzied luxuriance, and planted thousands more. Then the Company's crop started to ripen. The price dropped to three dollars. The Company's bananas were cut and loaded, filling the Company ships to capacity. The Company ships were the only ones to call, since the Company owned the two new piers which the people had been so proud of at first. The local banana market disappeared. It simply ceased to exist. Ships passing the coast sailed through the smell of the fruit rotting on the trees miles out to sea. (It was now said that a plywood company in West Virginia was planning new and similar benefits for these fortunate people, so recently pushed to the vanguard of progress, their standard of living raised so marvelously high that none of them could reach it.)

The single bare bulb swung on its cord so slightly that shadows on the floor moved with the faint reciprocity of breathing, inhaling and exhaling in swell and recession the bare boards over which Otto trod in silence picking up a shirt, then a necktie, seemed to breathe the silence of that sullen night before the rains.

The walls were white painted board. There was a metal bed with a discolored mattress on it, a metal chest of drawers with the mirror, table with two chairs, a long shelf and cuspidor. The room was high-ceilinged, with vents around the top to let what moving air there was circulate. It was through those vents that the strident crack ... crack-crack of his typewriter had first roused his neighbors against him, and after his first interview with Jesse he had settled to write his play in longhand, and transcribe it on the typewriter in the Company office on days when he was not working.

The mirror had a frame which looked like brown wood, but it was metal painted to appear so. This was because of the termites, which work so industriously in the tropics. A fifty-year-old Funk & Wagnall's dictionary the size of a suitcase standing on a rickety table in the telegraph office down in the port was eaten through by them, hardly a whole word remained. But this mirror frame retained its patina. It might as well have been a picture frame, by now it had enclosed his image so often that it would seem it could not accommodate anyone else. He looked out the window, and saw on the ground only his own shadow. Jesse's light had gone out. He returned to the mirror.

He was now wearing a white linen suit which Brooks Brothers, who kept his measurements two thousand miles away, had sent him. He was wearing a Brooks Brothers shirt of off-white Egyptian cotton, and a gray silk hound's-tooth pattern (Brooks Brothers) tie. One thing more. With a casual over-the-shoulder glance into the mirror he turned and walked across the floor, took a Canadian cigarette from the table and lit it, his mirrored reflection intent upon him. He smiled at himself in the mirror. He raised an eyebrow. Better. He moistened his lips, and curled the upper one. Better still. The smile, which had shown his face obsequious, was gone. He must remember this arrangement: left eyebrow raised, eyelids slightly drawn, lips moistened, parted, down at corners. This was the expression for New York.

Having recovered himself, he flicked his cigarette into the darkness beyond the open window, and glanced again at the shreds on his upper lip which would be a mustache by the time he left the job. Then with a sursum corda on his lips in farewell to the image abandoned in the mirror, he undressed again and lay down on his sweated mattress. Before he was asleep, it had begun to rain.

The specially prepared matches lit easily, but cigarettes fell apart between the fingers. Weeks went by with mortal slowness, parade of heat, insects, water, paper work, stupidity aggressive and fearful, and the scribbling on the play. Weeds grew luxuriously. The only way that Otto was certain that time was passing was the frequency with which he had to pare his nails. His shoes, left under the bed, turned green.

Red flowers drooped at the end of long stalks, then dropped revealing the fruit in infant impotence. Week by week the fruit grew larger, pointed outward, then upward, and was cut in the full erectile vigor of youth.

Then it was over, early that year; and the minute the wet season was done it was forgotten. Near the horizon the haze appeared and the sun, part in and part out, rose warped out of shape like a drunken memory of sunrise. Black ashes hung over the plantation houses from a fire some distance away. Next door, from a radio, Enesco's Third Rumanian Rhapsody was being played on a harmonica. Otto counted his money.

The months of waiting were over, the months of non-entity. Saint Paul would have us redeem time; but if present and past are both present in time future, and that future contained in time past, there is no redemption but one. This one Otto now pressed with his wrist to be certain that it had not disappeared while he was dressing, leisurely, like a tired Colonial on the stage of a West End theater, for he had returned his wallet to his inside breast pocket. The man with the kewpie doll tattooed on the inside of his forearm (signed up for two years) said, —Two years isn't long, not if you say it real fast. For those nomads who sold the time of their lives, time was either money being made or money being spent, and life a cycle of living and unliving, as the sailor's life loses the beginning, middle, and end of the voyage from port to destination and becomes repetition of sea and ashore, of slumber and violence. The hours of work were hours of vacant existence, but the minutes were pennies, and in each dollar was held captive the hour gone for it: here time was held in thrall, to be spent at a man's wish. So as misers keep years bound up in mattresses and old tin boxes, wrapped in newspaper, sewn into linings (and ashore they sing —What shall we do with a drunken sailor?), he came forth with months in his pocket, and himself to dictate their expenditure.

—I wouldn't reach up my ass for the whole city of New York, said the man with the kewpie doll tattooed on his forearm, who stood before a mirror in the communal lavatory eating cold chili out of a can. He ate before the mirror so that he could see where his mouth was, for he had been drinking for three days. He was not working because of the burn on his back, which he said he had got when someone took a chicken out of a boiling pot and threw it at him, in a brothel down in the port. The wound on his back was not the shape of a chicken. It had been painted with a purple solution, a great island the shape of Australia the first day, now contracted to the proportions of New

Zealand, the stroke of Tasmania out to sea for the doctor's hand was not a steady one.

—That's where I live, Otto said. He enjoyed coming into this lavatory, because the mirrors all in a row over the wash basins gave the pleasant illusion of passing one's self at many windows. —That sounds like quite a revolution they're having, Otto said washing his hands at the next basin.

—Them bastids don't know how to have a revolution, said the other, turning with such Anglo-Saxon indignance that the orange chili ran down his chin. —You know what I'd do if I was up there. All you got to do is get them dumb cops on their motorcycles, and string a good piece of piano wire across the road, then get down at the end of the road and take a couple of shots at them. They come after you on their motorcycles and zing zing zing there go their heads just like that. All you need, a good piece of piano wire. They don't know how to have a revolution. They're afraid somebody'll get killed. If I was up there...

—I've got to go pack, Otto said. —Have you seen Jesse?

—What do you want to see that dumb son of a bitch for?

—I'm leaving. I just wanted to tell him goodbye.

—You goin somewhere?

—New York. I told you. I'm going home.

—New York! What do you want to go there for? I wouldn't reach... But he was busy eating.

Otto had suddenly remembered his manuscript, the manuscript of his play. He was certain he had not packed it, for he had kept it out to look at until the minute before departure. It was nowhere in his room. All he found was a newspaper, in which he had been looking up sailings from nearby ports (knowing all the time that he would take the Company boat), found only a want ad for a male Chihuahua sought for breeding purposes. This paper he threw across the room, and with a cigarette in his fist like a smoking weapon he strode out, down the porch toward the shanty where the cleaning women settled about this time of day.

—Quién limpian mi cuarto mañana? he asked when he arrived, getting out in one breath the question it had taken him the distance of his walk to phrase in mistranslation.

An ancient timid hand went up among the women. —Yo, answered its owner, letting it drop. One by one they got to their feet before him.

—Hay visto una manuscripta aquí? Otto had made up the word manuscripta. One of the triumphs of his stay was his successful evasion of learning more than some thirty mispronounced words of the language.

—Qué dijo?

—La manuscripta de mi playa, said Otto forcefully. He knew that by adding *a* he could translate any English noun satisfactorily. The ladies were vastly confused. He turned from the doorway and set off toward his building. They followed.

—Qué dijo de *playa?* asked one, drawn on by the mystery of a man looking for a beach. None tried to answer her. They tramped up the dirt in silence. Inside his room Otto turned on the woman who had admitted to cleaning it. —El está para la máquina, he said pointing to the typewriter. —Esta mañana.

—Perdido, said one woman, satisfied that something was lost.

—Sí, perdido, said another equally agreeable. She started to look under the mattress.

—Qué cosa? asked the accused bravely.

—Papel, said the master. —Papel que yo escribo mi playa al máquina, finishing in triumphal confusion. —Mi playa, he repeated, menacing.

—Es muy misterioso, said one of the women.

—Sí.

—Muy misterioso, repeated the third, while the fourth let go the mattress (it was where she would have hidden anything) and stood silently marveling at this man who had lost a beach right here in the room.

—Titulito The Vanity of Time, Otto recommenced.

—No entiendo, the eldest came back at him, helplessly defiant.

—The Vanity of Time, he said more loudly. —La Vanidad del Tiemplo, God damn it, he almost shouted. Illiterate, illiterate old fools. He looked around for a pencil, found none, returned. —Tiene una...una... He made scribbling motions in the air. —Por escribo.

One held a pencil out to him. —Un lápiz, señor? she asked. Lápiz, of course; though anyone looking at it could see that it was a pencil. He took it from her and wrote, T H E V A N I T Y O F T I M E, in large letters. —Mucho papel, he said.

—Aïe... said the old one, dawning. —Pero sí, sí señor, with happy relief. She was uncomfortably familiar with this pile of paper. It had once been pointed out to her as mucho importante, and she had daily dusted the title page with care: the words were as unforgettably meaningless to her as the Latin legend circumscribing the largest local Virgin. —Aquí está, she said reaching to the top of a pile of linen on a shelf. —Lo pusé aquí cuando empacaba, todo estaba tan revuelto que tuve miedo de que se perdiera, o se ensuciara... she got out, in what sounded like one wildly relieved word.

Otto, breathing heavily, took it from her muttering, —Gracias, gracias, señoritas, without raising his eyes from the precious bundle. The four smiled, murmured —Nada, de nada, señor, and trundled out the door clustering about the acquitted for an explanation.

He carried the sheaf of clean papers over to a chair. The words were beautiful. The letters themselves were beautiful. His handwriting, in careful notes along occasional margins to give the thing a casual look, was beautiful. He read at familiar random, smiling to himself. Every page, beautiful, except one which would have to be retyped, he had killed a cockroach on it. Or perhaps, perhaps it had style in itself, that dark smudge. There were (though he had never seen one) tarantulas in Central America. Or was it black widows? And would a black widow make a brown smudge?

Then he raised his face to the empty door. The obsequious smile was gone. Left eyebrow up, lips moistened, slightly parted and curled, he waited while a producer approached, welcoming hand extended. Otto eyed the vision, nodded casually, reached for a cigarette. There were none in the linen suit. He was interrupted while he went to the dirty striped shirt for the necessary property; and returned to the chair the long way round the room, pausing (at the mirror) to light the cigarette. Putting the papers on the publisher's desk he fumbled a little, able to use but one hand. —Here, let me help you, the publisher said. —Nothing serious, I trust? —Nothing, nothing at all, Otto answered, elbowing the sling back under his jacket. —A scratch. Central America, you know.

He read a few lines in the second act and blew a perfect smoke ring on the quiet air. There was Esther. Where would he meet her? At the apartment? But he did not want to see her husband again. The thought of that man barely ten years his senior made him curl inside, the man who had seemed at first almost a father, then a fool, finally near maniac. It would be better to call Esther for a drink. Or for luncheon. Better still to meet her casually, by carefully prearranged accident.

—How wonderful you look, Otto.

—A little color... How have you been?

—Oh the same old things, you know, but without you it's been so dull and so lonely. But you, what about you? And what's happened to your hand?

—A revolution. Just one of those things, a regular occupational hazard down there. Possibly you saw something of it in the papers?

—Oh I never read them, you know that, not any more. But they tell me you've written a wonderful play.

And then as he took off his shirt and his trousers, —And you're so brown, all of you, and all in white...

Outside the sun poured its heat over the endless green of the fan-leaved banana trees. As Otto struggled down the porch carrying two suitcases and his typewriter, a voice came from an open door, —Hey come here, I want to show you some pictures.

—I've got to get the train for the port, he called to the man with the kew-pie doll tattooed on his forearm. —It leaves in twenty minutes.

—Come here. I want to show you some pictures.

Otto had, on occasion, pictured fine man-to-man farewells, close handclasps, and a few words of curt but constant friendship. He put his bags down in the door and entered. Snapshots of all sizes and degrees of fading surrounded the man sitting on the rumpled bedcover. —I'm putting them in an album, he said. He could hardly sit up. —See this one? This here is me with my first car, in Pennsylvania. He put glue all over the back of it, and then took an envelope of those black art corners used to mount snapshots in albums, and stuck them on the corners. As he licked them they came off in his mouth, and the glue on his chin, colored with dry chili. —See this one here? he went on, blowing the art corners out of his mouth and getting fresh ones. —This is me with my old man. That's my first car behind us. That was 1931, see that? A new car. Even then I wasn't doin so bad. On the pages he had completed, snapshots were firmly stuck with artistic disregard for angles, size, and number of art corners. All were consistent in one thing, however: —This is me. This is me in a bar in Brooklyn with some Greek sailors, one of them had a camera, I was workin in the Navy Yard. This is me in Panama, I worked in the Canal Zone before I came up here. This is me in Darien on a hunting trip with some Indians. Here, this is me with some Sand Blast Indians . . .

—I have to go, I have to get that train. It leaves in about ten minutes.

—Here, look at this one . . . By now he had got glue over most of his chin, and art corners stuck to his wrists and arms, framing the kewpie doll. —This is me . . . he started as Otto went toward the door. —Look can you hand me that bottle on the table before you go, I don't want to get up and make a mess of all this. My grandchildren . . .

As Otto started down the porch, there was the rending sound of breaking wind from the room behind him, and the voice, —There's a goodbye kiss for you, kid.

The fine particles of ash in the air settled on his white linen as he hurried.

The small town of the port might have had but one place in this world of time, and that to make itself presentable for Otto's departure, after which it could settle down to a long and uninterrupted decline. He walked in and out of its streets, looking about casually, pausing only when he saw his sudden reflection in a shop window. Stopping at the shops he appeared to be looking at the goods spread before him, while his stare got no farther than the image in the glass. Then he crossed to the shaded side of the street. On a veranda as he passed three black men were playing cards. When they saw him they pointed up, over their heads, smiling, nodding. On the open porch above a girl stood, as black and smiling as those below. She was wrapped only in a white towel, held together with one hand. He did not turn. —You want chikichig? one of the men asked. —Boy change you luck, called another after him where he walked on. —Pretty boy get all what he want...

The whiteness of the Company boat was a glitter in the strong sun. Few passengers were in sight, but the pier was crowded with people selling and begging and looking for a penny's worth of work. Their colors rose from a soft tan to hearty black. They were dressed in clothes which they had never seen new, and each carried something worthless, a basket of dolls made of straw, bundles of papers, inedible confections.

—La limpia, a child cried at Otto, pointing to his shoes, and then lost interest. Those shoes were perfect. The white linen suit had got becomingly crumpled on the trip down, and in this blazing light the gray tinge from the ashes did not show, clearly the definition of cultivated diffidence. He had a French book, labeled *Adolphe*, in a side pocket which he carried when he traveled and appeared to read in public places. As he started toward the dock with a boy who came barely to his waist carrying his bags, the sun cast his shadow striding with vain certainty before him.

Beside the boat, he took the change from his pocket to count. There were a few coins of the republic which he was leaving, mixed in with E Pluribus Unum dimes and quarters, odd-looking shiny coins (he had made certain to put aside new ones) which he would drop on New York bars, by mistake. He felt a hand touch his arm, and turned to see a black face of sudden age which held no beauty for him.

—Una limosnita, por el amor de Dios...The face had tufts of hair at chin and lips, so separately white that they looked to have been stuck there a moment before. Otto looked at his coins. The shiny two-and-one-half-cent piece looked like a dime. He felt that the beggar would make the same mistake, or think that he had made it unwittingly. He gave the lesser coin into the old hand and turned away. —Dios se lo pague, said the voice, in beneficent threat.

The luggage and its carrier disposed of, Otto walked through the town, into the wide open plaza of cement benches and palm trees. In the center was a dry fountain, and children who would seem to have nothing to laugh at laughed at nothing. They quieted for a moment when the priest passed. He was a long black-skirted affair with magenta buttons from throat to feet, five magenta buttons on each cuff. Around the largest part of him came a wide sash of glorious purple. His round black hat carried a purple corded band. He made no sign, marching toward the cathedral.

The broken face of that old building was covered with the sun. It was difficult to believe that it had ever been new, actually been built stone by stone under the surface of the plaster. The saints, some armless and headless, waited in still niches smoothed and quietened by the rain. The towers hung heavy with silent bells. But in places the plaster had come away, showing the walls built brick by brick, separated by lines of mortar laid by men's hands. Just inside the door waited a Virgin; the priest went in not glancing at her, passed her with proprietary certainty. When he was gone the children forgot him and remembered themselves. The birds, forgetting nothing and remembering nothing, dashed the benches with spots of white.

Otto walked more rapidly, for fear of one of them catching his linen, and was suddenly brought up face to face with a girl beside the waterless fountain. The darkness which she wore about her gave her an air of richness, her skin a color never burned by one sun; and in an evanescent instant he loved her. Recovering, he was as suddenly embarrassed, and got round her through the plaza.

Around the weight of the cathedral, the town looked transitory, brightly colored and haphazard, as though without that weight it might disintegrate, to wander off and be lost in the green hills.

The white boat slipped away from the pier, away from the black and brown and tan upturned faces, the hands extended for a last tossed coin and those few raised in farewell. The water was shallow and clear green. Slowly the heat of land fell away, and two people stood, a distance apart, at the boat-deck rail, watching the buildings lose their form and become smears of color, the palms lose their majesty and fade into the heavy green of the countryside. The harbor was still, nothing could be seen to move, and its sounds and cries were lost: there was only the throbbing of the boat, moving with certainty out upon water which became deeper and deeper blue. Otto, walking up to the bow, was taking the sun of this lost country with him.

He took a case out of his pocket, opened it, and caught his quivering lower lip with his teeth as a jarring of the boat hit his hand against the rail and sent the gold-rimmed dark glasses down into the white water. He stood clutching the emptied case tightly, looking over the bow to where it tore that water open, as though there must be some way of recovery.

—Too bad, said a cheerful voice beside him, a fiercely sun-pinkened American. —Looked like a nice pair of glasses. Otto closed the case and put it into his pocket. —Why don't you throw the case in too? asked his witness.

—I can use it for something, Otto said, surly, defensive.

—Carry pills in? said the traveler, and laughed again. —Hot as hell, isn't it. It'll cool down when we get out a ways.

—Possibly, said Otto, and walked aft.

The mirror in his cabin was smaller than he would have liked, framed in wood covered with thick green paint. He looked at his luggage. It was all there, with Wanted-on-Voyage tags tied to the handles. Then he thought to look at his fingernails. Not as a man does, the fingers turned in upon the palms, but like a lady, at the back of the extended hand so that she may admire the slim beauty of her fingers. Otto admired the taut dark figure of his hand, forgot to look at the nails and had to look back again (fingers turned in upon the palm). He was immediately troubled about covering that fine hand with a bandage. Still, injury might have been to the wrist: in which case the white gauze would go splendidly across the base of his hand, set off the dark length of the fingers like a lady's evening glove. He made certain that he had two extra packages of Emu which he would offer (preferably to ladies), casually indifferent to their choking fumes. He considered unpacking, but there was no hurry. The sling he had fashioned was in the top of the small suitcase. There would be time that evening to try it again, to decide where the bandage would go, where the wound was.

The sun moved down toward the sea, its redness heightened in hurry to be gone, moving as though pursued. The land was far behind, a soft haze behind the slowly curving wake of the boat, a white wake already floating with garbage where white birds dove and lifted themselves away. Otto saw none of this. He had started to post the Italian print on his wall (*Lady of the Junipers*), thought of Jesse's words, shrank, put it out of mind. He thought of his wallet, and pressed the bulge under his coat with his wrist. His hair, like his nails, was grown just the right length. The mustache, sparse and golden, the same. He tightened the knot in his tie and pulled down the skirt of his jacket. With the smoke from a fresh cigarette he blew a perfect circle against the hard surface of the mirror, where it clung growing larger and thinner around this image of his importunate face.

Up the coast of the New World the ship bearing ten million bananas ground out its course, every minute the waste heaving brokenly around it more brilliant as the moon rose off the starboard bow and moved into the sky with effortless guile, unashamed of the stigmata blemishing the face she showed from the frozen fogs of the Grand Banks to the jungles of Brazil, where along the Rio Branco they knew her for a girl who loved her brother the sun; and the sun, suspicious, trapped her in her evil passion by drawing a blackened hand across her face, leaving the marks which betrayed her, and betray her still.

V

America is the country of young men.

—EMERSON

—NOTHING, said Maude Munk.

—Nothing? Arny Munk repeated.

—Nothing, she confirmed, dropping ice cubes into a glass. —The same things. They ask the same questions they've been asking for three years. *Was I conscious after the accident, and if I wasn't how could I have reported it all to the police, and did I have pains in my back then, and if I did why don't the hospital records show it.* Then my doctor and their doctor argue, and my lawyer and their lawyer argue, and the cab driver who was driving the cab I was in lives in Detroit now. I wish you'd put your shoes away somewhere when you take them off.

—Well I could tell them your personality's changed. And you never used to drink before that accident. It used to upset you because I drank.

—It still does, Arny. Terribly. And you don't have pains, like I do. Today I even asked the judge, Would you have two operations and wear a spinal brace if you were malingering?

—Maude look, you're spilling your drink, he said, righting the glass which tipped toward him in her forgotten hand. The radio offered cocktail music, *When Buddha Smiles.*

—What is it? Are you tired? Arny? . . . Oh, I just wish you got tired doing something you liked.

—You don't make a living doing things you like.

—But selling . . . and year after year . . . and . . . things like last week.

—Maude.

—Does your father know about that? Or does he just pretend he doesn't know, and he's glad you've sold another order, playing cards in a hotel room where they send naked women in for your out-of-town buyers. And all the time your father's such a fine dignified old man. Why if my Daddy ever...

—Maude.

—Anyhow, my Daddy was a man.

—What do you mean by that? Just because I have a rupture...

—I don't mean your old rupture. It's just that... She looked at him a moment longer, got up and freshened her drink, and turned the dial on the radio. Finally she asked, —What are you reading? Arny? You're not even reading, are you.

—Maude.

—As though you were all alone. Sometimes I come into the room and you're sitting here with a book open, but you're not reading. You're just sitting looking at the page, but you're not reading? Are you lonely?

——that looks better, smells better, tastes better, and is better, said a young man's voice on the radio.

—But how can you be lonely? *I'm* here.

——the next number on our program, the Academic Festival Overture, by Tschaikovsky.

—Arny, have you filled out the papers?

—What papers?

—*The* papers, what other papers. For the Red Heart Adoption Center.

—It's the Sacred Heart. Red Heart's a dog food.

—Well anyway, have you?

—Yes Maude.

—And can we go up and get it in the morning?

—We may have to wait.

—How long?

—Maude, please don't have another drink.

—A little brand-new one, Arny. It will make everything different between us again, won't it? for you? I mean for me, it will make us more like we used to be, won't it?

—Is dinner ready?

—Do you want chutney?

—Chutney?

—With the curry.

—Yes.

—Then you'll have to go out and get it. There isn't any.

—Never mind then.

—But I want chutney.

—I'll wait while you go out and get it. The walk might do you good, he

added, looking up at his wife's eyes, wandering past him wed to nothing.
—There's someone at the door.

—Oh Herschel, I forgot, Herschel called and you can't get him off the telephone until you make some kind of date with him, he said he'd stop in . . .

—Are you going to answer the door?

—Herschel! . . . Arny, it's Herschel, and . . . he has a girl with him!

Outside the door stood a young lady adjusting a garter. Her companion watched. —Anyhow, come in, said Maude. Herschel waited until the garter was taken care of, the stocking smoothed over the knee, the skirt over the thigh. Then he said:

—Baby! looking up to see Maude for the first time, and he offered both his hands. Herschel was tall, and had always been handsome. He had been the handsomest boy in his home town, and the only one in that part of Ohio to own dinner clothes. His picture, in dinner clothes, still stood in the photographer's window on Front Street where, faded and fly-specked, it continued to exact a certain prestige, for it was some years since he'd been home. —I brought along a little two-legged friend, he said. —Arny and Maude, I want you to meet . . .

—Adeline, the blonde supplied.

—Adeline.

—How do you do, I'm sure, said Adeline.

—Baby is your name really Adeline? I had a nurse named Adeline, a black one, big West Indian black Adeline. One day under the apple tree I bit her right square . . .

—Herschel! . . . your head is brachycephalic, Maude said from where she'd gone to pour drinks, whisky with water (she'd heard soda was bad for the stomach lining). —It's the coming shape in heads.

—Aren't you kind, baby. No one's ever told me *that* before.

—Maude.

—Arny, it's true. Head shapes are very important. Arny thinks I'm silly, reading books about heads, that book there. Do you see the picture it's open to? That's a good domestic. That's why I want to look at the babies first, we don't want one that will be a domestic. On the next page there's one kind of sticking out in the back, that's the Intellectual. And the kind of big square one is a Leader of Men. We're going to have a baby, she said pausing on her way to the kitchen for more water. Adeline stopped her drink halfway to her lips and looked at the other woman's figure curiously. —Tomorrow morning. Adeline looked downright insulted.

—Oh God, baby, again? Herschel sank back in his chair.

—No, this time we're really going to get there, aren't we Arny? Tomorrow morning at nine. Oh, did you want a drink? I didn't know you wanted one, Arny.

—I shouldn't tell this, baby, but if you're shopping for a bargain...

Maude cried out from the kitchen. —Oh...a cockroach. I hate New York, no matter where you live, you have them. The people downstairs have them, they chase them up here and then I chase them back down, up and down the drain.

—Why don't you use D.D.T.?

—It's no good, it just makes them hysterical, Maude said, coming in with water. —They run around screaming.

—Cockroaches?

—Well you can't really hear them, but you can tell that's what they're doing, that's what you do when you're hysterical.

—Baby...

—Yes, tomorrow morning at nine. Have you finished that already, Arny?

—If you're not in a wild rush, Herschel said slyly, —I know someone who might help you. Someone who's going to have one. I mean really have one. Not just yet, though.

—A woman? But how does that help...?

—Because she doesn't want it, baby. Someone told me she was looking for a doctor, someone who must be nameless, and he asked me. Can you imagine *me* knowing such a thing?

—A doctor? I know so many doctors, what kind? Back doctors, bone doctors...

—No, a doctor to take *care* of it for her, one with an *in*-strument.

—Oh!

—Maude, you're spilling your drink.

—You know Esther, baby...well I'm not to tell but...

—I saw her on the street, Maude said. —She has such bad luck.

—She told *you* about it?

—About Rose?

—Oh no, everybody knows about Rose, that they've sent her sister Rose back from the tee-hee farm and Esther has to take her in. But this is something you mustn't tell, baby. This is for your tomblike little ears. She has a turkey in the oven.

—She has what?

—She's preg, baby.

—But...her husband?

—Her husband! No one ever sees him. I've never met him. I'm sure if he had ever said anything amusing I would have met him somewhere, but I understand that he lives underground. Or underwater. Some really absurd part of town. No one's ever been there.

—He used to paint, didn't he? used to paint things?

—Oh who didn't, so did I, said Herschel, —the naughtiest...

—No one's seen him since that boy Otto...do you remember Otto?

—Otto? Nobody's named Otto any more, he must be an impostor.

—Herschel, you've met him, silly. He used to show up everywhere with Esther before she and her husband...I mean after she and her husband...

—Oh I do remember him, Otto. He talked all the time. He was rather cute. Yes, I remember Otto, for almost a year he and Esther made half of a very pretty couple. You mustn't repeat this, but I was told that Otto and Esther's husband...

—Herschel, don't...

—Baby I'm not responsible for all the queer things that go on. It was all explained as a father complex or a mother complex or something vulgar. Why, no one has secrets any more.

—But Esther's husband, what...

—You mustn't tell, but he's mixed up with an international counterfeit ring, he makes gold down there, out of fingernail parings...

—Herschel, silly...

Adeline looked very interested.

—But baby everyone knows it. And there's a skinny little girl he keeps there...well, there are simply terrifying stories about *her*. It's known she takes dope. Known simply everywhere.

At that, Maude took out a small round Battersea enamel box, with the words *We Live in Hope* on the cover, and took out a pill. —Arny, not another drink, tomorrow morning...

—Don't you want another?

—No, I have a little headache.

—Don't be put out if I ask you this, Herschel commenced, —after all we all had the same analyst.

—I wish Arny had finished, I almost finished mine, Maude said. —He reminded me of Daddy. He introduced us, did you know that?

—You and Arny?

—Yes, he thought we could help each other, so he thought we should get married. I guess that's why we never finished. Analysis I mean. Arny you've almost finished that bottle of whisky. You know what happened Saturday.

—But...you can tell me, why don't you just go ahead and *have* a baby?

—It's easier...it's easier this way isn't it Arny, and besides how can you have a baby these days in a...a place like this, how can you...Maude looked suddenly about to cry. When the doorbell rang she ran to answer it, but stopped for a moment before she opened the door.

Outside stood a tan, summer-clothed, rather embarrassed young man. —Otto! she said. —Why Otto, how funny! It's Otto, she said into the room, and —How brown you are, following him in.

——I beg your pardon, ladies and gentlemen, that was the Academic Festival by Brahms. Our next number, by the French composer Clair...I mean Claude, Debussy, Alla-press, midi, dun-fon...

Otto raised an eyebrow, brandished his sling, and tripped over the pair of shoes by the table.

Arny got up and offered him a drink. Herschel got up and said, —Baby what are you doing in an outfit like that? You'll freeze to death. And Adeline looked at the golden mustache, and the arm-in-a-sling, and said nothing at all.

—I am, but I haven't any others. They're all following me, somewhere between here and banana land.

—Who's following you, baby?

—No, I mean my clothes. I've been on a banana pl...

—Oh yes, you were on a banana plantation, said Maude. —Esther told me. It sounded so...so quite hideous I'd tried to forget it.

—I didn't know people ran off to banana plantations any more. No, don't go to a banana plantation, baby. It's old hat.

—Herschel, silly. He's just come back.

—All the more reason. What are you wearing that thing for? Herschel pointed at the sling.

—My hand, I...

—Did something happen to it?

—There was a revolution. Why, they're regular occupational...

—I couldn't understand why you wanted to go down there in the first place.

—It wasn't so bad. In spite of the revolution I got a play written...

—Did you, asked Maude. —About bananas? Arny, please don't drink any more. Tomorrow morning at nine, we've got to be there this time. She turned to Otto who was busy raising an eyebrow at Adeline. —We're going to have a baby, she said.

—Really? That's wonderful, I...

—Tomorrow morning, we're going up and adopt one.

—That's wonderful, I...

—Do either of you want to come to a party? Herschel asked. —That's where we were on our way to.

—Whose party? Maude asked.

—I don't know, baby. It's a party for a painting. Somebody did a painting so they're giving a party so everybody can see it. Don't you understand?

—Where is it?

—I've got the address here. Somebody wrote it down for me. He took out a rumpled slip of paper with Memorandum across the top in bold face, and then in gothic characters, *United States Senate.* —Sullivan Street.

—I couldn't stand a Village party tonight. Could you Arny? They're always so quite ha…

—Hideous, Herschel supplied.

—I wasn't going to say that, silly. I was going to say harrowing. I couldn't stand one tonight, that special Village quality of inhuman ghastliness and dirt. And tomorrow morning, Arny please don't have another drink. No really, Herschel, it sounds too hideous.

—You're right of course, baby. Now you've made me feel awful about going myself. But everybody who goes feels the same way. Do you want to come down and see the painting? he asked Otto, who had just lit an angry black-tobacco cigarette with her help, beside Adeline's chair. —Oh, I am sorry. Adeline, this is Otto. Do you want to come down with us? The painting's called *L'Ame d'un Chantier.*

—Herschel, how silly. Really? Really. What's a Lom?

—I haven't a notion who's giving it, said Herschel. —It doesn't matter, you always see the same people.

—It means soul, said Otto. —The soul of a…

—And chantier is a singer, said Maude. —The soul of a singer.

—You coming baby? said Herschel, with his coat and Adeline's.

—Have you seen Esther recently? Otto asked, faltering slightly. —I mean, do you think we might…

—Not for months, said Herschel.

—Well, I used to know some people down there, I…

—Don't be afraid. Everybody has a Village past. The ones who stay down there just don't know it's past.

—No, that isn't what I meant, I…

—Arny, please. No more. You remember what you did Saturday night. Maude turned to them. —Arny sat up drinking late Saturday night here all alone, and when I got up Sunday I found he'd undressed and put all his clothes carefully into the refrigerator.

Up four flights of stairs, Herschel instructed Adeline. —They all talk about painting. Now remember, no matter what anyone says, you just comment on the solids in Uccello. You can say you don't like them, or say they're divine. Can you remember that? The *solids* in Oo*chel*lo, can you say that? They arrived at a room full of people who spent their lives in rooms.

Adeline directly sought the bathroom; Herschel lay against the doorjamb getting his breath; and Otto (thinking only of what it looked like to see Otto entering a room) entered. He was dressed comfortably for the temperature. It was not a large room. The established guests were too engrossed in talking, or waiting for opportunity to talk, to attend the new ones. Some of them glanced up, as residents of a railway coach glance up at a new passenger struggling down the aisle after a seat; but all maintained a composure which reflected the impertinence of the new arrivals for arriving at all. Everyone, that is, but the two policemen, who were disposed like clocks which must be stood at odd angles to tell the time.

On the gray chipped mantel lay a spray of flowers, which someone had gaily lifted from the door of a bereaved Italian family downstairs. Above it hung the painting. No one was looking at it. The unframed canvas was tan. Across the middle a few bright spots of red lead had been spattered. The spots in the lower left-hand corner were rust, above them long streaks of green paint, and to the upper right a large smudge of what appeared to be black grease. It looked as though the back of an honest workman's shirt had been mounted for exhibition, that the sleeves, collar, and tails might be found among the rubble in the fireplace.

A young man in tortoise-shell glasses, who clutched in his hand some papers entitled *Toilet Training and Democracy*, was saying, —But you've got to understand New York. New York is a social experience. Someone else said, —Don't tell me how sincere he is. He dabbles in Rome the way some people dabble in *The Joy of Cooking*. A bearded man was saying to a girl, —Since I've been married, I've never looked at another woman. Do you find me attractive? Someone cried out, —Queer! Even the cockroaches in his house are queer.

—Really, said Herschel, when he had his breath, —how artsy can we get.

—Yes, said Otto, who had stopped looking at the painting. —Who is that? A sun-tanned woman in a white dress had been exposed momentarily by an opening in the curtain of trouser seats round her, and as quickly hidden again. Her voice, however, carried on. —Darling, I was there for six weeks, and we didn't have dinner at home the whole time, except four or five times and those were dinner parties.

—Don't you know her? It's Agnes Deigh, she just got back from Puerto Rico. Thank God, she's plastered too.

—No I don't know her, I...

—Know her brother? You don't? He's the cutest...well! Of course *I've*

never really met him, she won't let me, for some girlish reason of her own. But
I've seen his picture, in a soldier suit, the cutest ... *Nothing* like her husband
Harry, he's just the most ... he's a writer too you know. "Publish and be
damned," the Duke of Wellington said, remember? Harry's in Hollywood,
spelled backward. Do you know what I mean? "Trade ye no mere moneyed
art," spelled backward. Oh never mind. After all, it's just the impurities in
gems that give them their exquisite luster isn't it. And their value! I mean
Shelley did drink laudanum by the gallon, didn't he. And of course Swinburne!
Dear! I feel so na-ked among all these people. It's like a masquerade isn't it.
Look! do you see her? the girl on the couch? looking just *too* like la noyée de
la Seine, that touching death mask they made from the face of some nameless
child who life was just too much for. I mean real life you know. And wasn't
it just so *french* to preserve her beauty when she was dead in a mask we could
all enjoy, instead of squandering money to keep her alive and let her get ...
just all the things that women *get*. There, do you see her? just too noyée for
words, why I'd run right out and drown myself tomorrow if I could be that
beautiful, wouldn't you? I feel so naked, don't you? among all these frightfully
masked people. Remember? de Maupassant, Guy de Maupassant of course,
writing to that Russian girl, "I mask myself among masked people." Remember? They'd never met, you know. They never did meet, did they. Of course
he was just as mad as a hatter, and her name was Marie Bashkirtseff. She
painted. She died too, you know, before she could gain three hundred pounds
in all the most obvious places and turn into a woman. She was Russian. And
there goes that awful boy who told me about Thomas à Becket. No, or was it
à Kempis? plagiarizing the *Imitation of Christ*, imagine! See him? him, with
the rather bad skin, he's cute isn't he. But imagine *pla*giarizing the imi-*ta*tion
of Christ. Why, Handel plagiarized the most delightful things, didn't he. But
then that was music, wasn't it. And he was finally stricken blind by the hand
of you-know-Who for being so cavalier with other people's work. Wasn't he.
But what about *you*. And so brown. Like a tootsie roll. For all the world ...

—Me? I ... Otto had taken a step back, looking about the room with restrained anticipation in his eyes, and presentiment of greeting in his features
as though he were searching for an old friend whom he had expected to see
here. He was looking for a mirror.

—like the Negro of the Narcissus!

—Huh?

—You have to be so careful below Fourteenth Street, baby. There are certain
words you just can't say. And imagine, you've known Agnes's brother all this
time and never introduced me! And were you a soldier-boy in the late hate too?

—I ... what?

—And I didn't know you knew her husband too. No one knows him. Even though he has the same name she has. The same last name, I mean. He took her last name when they were married, wasn't that sweet? because nobody could pronounce his. Before they were married she called him Mister Six-sixty-six, because that was the number of the first hotel room she took him to. Didn't you meet him then?

—No, is he here?

—Oh no, *no* baby. They haven't been out together since the gas stove exploded. When they got married they both wanted to write. Everything was fine until the books came out, then they found they'd written about each other. That was the only reason either of them wanted to get married, to study the other one. They used to sit and ask about each other's childhood, and all kinds of things, and they both thought the other one was doing it for love. Now they just watch each other's sales, and whoever's ahead takes all the cream at breakfast.

—Is she...

—When they *have* breakfast. Together.

Otto strained for another look. He heard her saying, —It's absolute heaven, the people are so poor they work for almost nothing. We had a maid who did the laundry too and do you know how much we paid her... Under the loosely fitted white dress she wore an open-top brassière (They all wear them like crazy down there, she said) bringing her front up to where it could be seen with little difficulty. On her browned wrist, complemented with gold in all the garrulous ugliness of the Modernism heresy, was a Mickey Mouse watch. Otto was perturbed by the flourishing color of her skin, which the dress and (the trouser-seat curtain parted again and he saw her fingernails) white nail polish set off to better effect than the rumpled linen and the black silk sling did his own. He ran a fingertip over his golden mustache. —She doesn't look like she quite belonged here, he said. —That white gown.

—Baby what about you in your jungle suit?

—That's not what I meant, in the Village I meant, in that gown, it's so sort of formal... Otto faltered to a finish, awaited comment, and only heard someone say, —That's the plot, briefly. Now do you think I can call myself a negative positivist? —I think you'd be safer calling yourself a positive negativist.

—Everyone knows why the Bildows stay married, said a deep voice. —He's impotent with anybody but her. —You know the real reason? she was challenged. —It's because neither of them wash.

—Is it true, Arny and Maude are going to adopt a baby? Otto asked.

—Poor Arny, they've been trying for years, but they always feel too awful in the morning, poor Maude...

—Boy or girl? demanded a girl's voice behind them.

—A boy. Oh Hannah, said Herschel, —Baby...He looked afraid and unhappy, as though this plainly unattractive girl were someone to escape and forget. She stood firm, in the peasant's dress of the Village, a soiled man's shirt tucked into denim pants on a bunchy figure composed of separate entities, calves, thighs, chest, and head, like a statue of soft stone whose blocks have been weathered apart.

—He's probably a homosexual, said Hannah.

—The baby? Herschel asked helplessly.

—No, the father. He's the one who wants a boy isn't he?

—Do you know Arny?

—Arny who?

—Arny Munk. He's the one who's going to be the father.

—No.

—Then how can you say...

—It's psychologically obvious, that's the only reason queer men want boy children, to perpetuate their own kind.

—Hannah, please...

Hannah muttered an unpleasant sound in greeting to a tall stooped figure in a green wool shirt, who was about to go on across the room when she saw the book in his hand. —What are you doing with that, *The Trees of Home?* Reading best sellers?

The stooped figure stopped plodding and turned on her; so did his stubby companion, who stood looking slightly injured (he was a poet, with eye trouble, and since everything but the printed page was brought to a focus before it reached him, the world was simply a series of vague images and threatening spectacles, which he faced with lowered eyes as though seeking a book at hand to explain it all); he said, —A best seller! The guy that wrote it submitted it to a board that showed it to a cross section of readers, the reading public. So the reading public doesn't like the lousy end, so he puts on the kind of lousy end they suggest, and it's published. A best seller, for Christ sake.

—I'm reviewing it, the stooped man said, and started to plod off.

—You read it?

—No, he said over his shoulder, —but I know the son of a bitch who wrote it.

—That poor bastard, Hannah said after him. —He wants to go to Europe. They both do, the poor bastards, ask them why. They won't see anything, they're both myoptic. Where you going? she said to Herschel.

—I was just...Hannah...

—Have you got your tattoo yet? she asked in a humorless tone.

—No.

—How's your writing?

—Movie magazines, simply all sex, Herschel answered, making an effort, —the most obvious perversions. I'm writing a whole series now on movie stars and God. They're all exactly the same. They all believe that *Some*thing is carrying us on *Some*where, and they simply reek with the most exquisite sincerity.

—You mean you interview them?

—Baby, I just make a few notes on them and write these heart-to-heart confessions. The publicity agent looks it over and signs her name to it. *She* never sees it.

—She? Otto asked.

—She. These are lady movie-stars.

—What happened to your senator? Hannah said.

—The last speech I wrote for him, he never saw it until it appeared in the Congressional Record, and I said simply all the wrong things. Now he's being investigated and he's quite put out at *me*. Imagine! I'm simply going to have to write a novel myself.

—You write a novel! Who'll read a novel with no women in it?

—But baby, there will be, I'll do it just like Proust did, write it about simply everyone I know and then just go through and change boys' names to girls, I know the perfect Odette...

—You ought to go back to analysis. Or have a vagotomy and get it over with. Just because your analyst killed himself...

—He didn't kill himself, it was an accident.

—An accident! He ties a rope around his neck and climbs out a window, but the rope breaks and he falls forty-six stories, so it's an accident?

—Hannah, I'm going, going to get a drink, Herschel said turning on the room, no idea where he was going, but away.

—I didn't know he was a writer, Otto said.

—Writer! He ghosts. He just ghosted some army general's autobiography. A writer!

Otto looked after Herschel. —I'd say he was a latent heterosexual, he said, immediately regretted wasting such an inspired line on Hannah, and resolved to repeat it later to someone who would repeat it as his own. He even tried to think quickly of a spot for it in his play.

—Dissociated personality, said Hannah soberly. —He's not sure who he is any more, whether he's anyone at all for that matter. That's why he wants a tattoo, of course. Simply a matter of ego-identification.

—So that when he wakes up he'll know it's the same person he went to bed with, said a young man who had been standing with his back to them, turning now his unshaven face.

Herschel was coming toward them, leading a nice-looking confused boy toward the door. —You'd better go, he was saying, —on account of Agnes. Come on, baby. She asked me to help you go, she says you bore the tits off her and you wouldn't want to do that... But as they reached the door Agnes Deigh was between them with an arm around the boy. —But darling where are you going? You're not leaving? You can't leave now, it's so early. She plucked this petal back, and Herschel, mumbling something about her bosom, stumbled confusedly after.

—Poor Charley, said Hannah.

—Was that Charley? Otto had noticed a scar across the boy's throat, and a glitter in his hair. —What's that in his hair?

—That's a silver plate, they put it there when they took the bullet out he tried to kill himself with. Did you see his throat? And his wrists are covered with scars. He was in the army, in a plane that dropped an atom bomb, and he has intense guilt feelings. He hated the army. It's a good thing he got out.

—I should think they would have sent him to a hospital if he's like this.

—Oh no, this wasn't the reason he was discharged, said Hannah. —When he was still in he stayed at the place I was staying one night on leave. The next morning he went out to get some coffee, but his own clothes were a mess because he'd been sick the night before so he put some of my warm underwear on under his uniform. The M.P.'s picked him up at Nedick's and when they took him in and found him with girls' underwear on they thought he was queer. He was discharged.

—Oh.

—I think he's going to have a lobotomy, said Hannah. —What do you think of the painting? she said, looking above the mantel.

—The colors are good. Very bright.

—Bright?

—Well, I mean the orange and the green. Of course, a painter is limited by his materials, isn't he. I mean, there are pigments you can't just mix together in certain mediums and expect them to bind. There are certain pigments you can't lay over others and expect them to hold, I mean of course they break up, you have to know your materials and respect them, but modern painting...

—I think it's the saddest thing Max has ever done. It's an epitaph.

—Léger, I mean Chagall...

—The emptiness it shows, it hurts to look at it. It's so real, so *real*.

—Soutine, of course, Chagall and Soutine, Otto continued, —there won't be one of them in sight anywhere in a hundred years, they'll break up and fall to pieces right on the canvas. Inherent vice, I believe they call it. There are certain pigments...

—I think it's the saddest thing Max has ever done.

Otto stopped speaking: who was Max? He remembered Max as someone he did not particularly like, someone he felt unsafe with. Aware of an unshaven face over his shoulder, he took out a package of his impressive cigarettes, and did not turn until the unshaven boy, not included in their conversation, went away rubbing a badly blemished chin. —Who was that?

—He's a drunk, Hannah said, —his name is Anselm. He gets all screwed up with religion.

In one corner of the room stood a thin young man with a heavy mustache which seemed to weigh his round head forward. At that moment it was being weighed toward a dirty window, which he studied wistfully. His coat was belted behind, and too short. His trousers fell in wrinkles, and dragged frayed cuffs on his shoe-tops. A candid look of guilt hung about him, as though he knew he should not be there, but saw no way of leaving but osmotically, through the translucent window glass. At his back a group, bulging with laughter, threatened to upset him. They were arguing. Then one of them called, —Is it "Ils vont prendre le train de sept heures" or "de huit heures," Stanley?

—Weet, he answered, and returned to the dirty window muttering, —How could it be anything but *weet*? Then he turned his eyes, and stared at whoever was seated on the couch, out of Otto's view.

—If modern painters won't study their materials, Otto took up, fingering the figure of the emu on the cigarette packet, and he spoke with urbane hesitations, indicating concurrent thought worthy of his words, —if they can't waste the time, a sculptor of course has to study every property of his medium before he...

—Do you know him? Hannah asked.

—settles down to his, what? Who?

—Stanley.

—No, is he a sculpt...

—Stanley? Why should he be a sculptor?

—No, but um... and as Praxiteles...

—What?

—I was just going to say, as Cicero says of Prax...

—Music, he writes music, organ music.

—Who?

—Stanley. Him. She pointed. —This one thing he's been working on a long time, a mass, he's trying to finish it in time to dedicate it to his mother. She's got diabetes, in the Hospital of the Immaculate something, it's around here, they just took her leg off, it had gangrene. She just lies up there with all these souvenirs in bottles around her, her appendix and her tonsils and something they took out of her nose, she wants to take them with her, she just lies there staring at her false teeth in an empty glass, gumming memories.

Otto offered a cigarette. Hannah did not smoke; and so the only way to impress her was to blow some in her direction. She coughed and stopped talking.

The funeral spray on the mantel had wilted, and the wires which held it taut were apparent. It had not been an expensive one. The clusters of guests moved vaguely before it and back like limp flowers dying in the earth where they had grown, shifting in the dust. Otto was looking over the room for someone he knew to talk with, or someone he did not know, to talk to. For just that moment he saw the face of a girl who was sitting alone on the couch, looking with a smile of newness over this moribund garden, allowing herself to be hidden by it. Then she was gone, with the silent consciousness of a painting obscured by a group of nattering human beings. He had stared at her in that moment of exposure: her eyes had been looking at him; and then they were not: and her smile went beyond him, like a face he knew so well he could never recall it to memory.

—She got fed up with him screwing the Sunday roast, so she shot herself, do you blame her? Anselm was saying suddenly at his elbow speaking, to Hannah, of the stooped man in the green wool shirt, whom he'd just left. —That's what breaks my heart, he added, and rubbed his chin.

—Who is it? Otto asked, turning.

—A half-assed critic, Hannah said, —he thinks he has to make you unhappy before you'll take him seriously.

—A three-time psychoanaloser, Anselm added, —for Christ sake. He just told me Bildow's going to sell The Magazine. Tragedy. Hannah reached for the yellow book he carried. —Have you read it, *Justine?* he asked, holding it back. —I brought it to show Stanley.

—Leave him alone tonight, Hannah said.

—There's a nice part, in this Benedictine monastery, where the abbot puts the holy wafer up her and defiles it . . .

—Listen, Anselm . . .

—Hey Stanley, come here, I got something to show you, Anselm called, and Hannah repeated, —Leave him alone, as Stanley worried his way toward them. Otto smoothed his own mustache with a fingertip.

—What are you reading? Anselm took the book from under Stanley's arm. —Malthus, for Christ sake. Do you want to get excommunicated, carrying that around in public? The next thing, you'll be peddling rubbers in the street.

—Malthus doesn't recommend . . . those, when he speaks of moral restraint . . .

—Moral restraint! Anselm laughed, waving his yellow book. —If you think the Church wouldn't do an about-face on contraceptives if it owned a block of stock in Akron rubber! And how much real estate do you think they own in this whorehouse of a world? Here, you ought to read this, he went on, opening *Justine*, —there's somebody in here you'd like, named Roland, he has a crucifix with a girl on it face-to . . .

—Listen, Anselm, Hannah commenced.

—can play hide-the-baloney . . .

—I heard you sold another book title, Stanley interrupted him.

—"Except for Fornication," fifty bucks. Matthew nineteen, nine, "Except it be for fornication . . ."

—I'm having a little difficulty, with a title, Otto lied.

—A novel?

—No, a play I've just finished. I've called it "The Vanity of Time."

—Corny, Hannah commented. —What a lousy party.

—It's from a sermon . . .

—Peanut butter, for Christ sake. Fifty million pounds of food a day eaten in New York, and what do I get? Peanut butter.

—Do you like the painting? Stanley asked her.

—The composition's good. Max is good with composition, he's successful with it, but he still works like painting was having an orgasm, he has to learn that it isn't just having the experience that counts, it's knowing how to handle the experience . . . what the hell are you smoking? she coughed, looking at the cigarette in Otto's brown hand.

Stanley turned and asked timidly, —And, Anselm? what are you doing now?

—I keep myself busy sawing toilet seats in half for half-assed critics, Anselm said without turning to him, without taking his eyes from the tall figure stooped in the green wool shirt.

Otto cleared his throat. —That ahm girl on the couch, she . . . do you know her? Anselm looked at him for the first time, and he added —I mean, and cleared his throat.

—That's Phryne. Anselm watched the lack of response on Otto's face. —Phryne. Don't you know Phryne, for Christ sake? I thought I just heard you talking about Praxiteles.

—Well yes I was but, I mean when Cicero says that Praxiteles, that all Praxiteles has to do is remove the excess marble, to reach the real form that was there all the time underneath, I mean inside . . .

—And he reached Phryne. Haven't you ever seen it?

—Seen what.

—Praxiteles' statue of Phryne. Who the hell do you think was hiding inside his block of stone but a high-class whore. They've got it in the Vatican with the rest of the high-class whores. I just wanted to be Eve before the Fall, Anselm mimicked in a whimper, —for Christ sake.

Stanley was staring fixedly at the floor.

Anselm wiped his mouth. —Look at Agnes, he said, —with all the little faggots around her. Christ. He looked vaguely in that direction for a moment, then returned to Stanley. —When are you going to Italy? he demanded, and as quickly turned on Otto, who drew up his cigarette like a smoking weapon of defense, but Anselm merely said, —There's this broken-down old church where he wants to play the organ, something he wrote he wants to play on their organ. "Seated one day at the organ," hey Stanley? How does it go, "weary and ill at ease"? And your fingers running idly over the ... hey! He was gone, after someone with a bottle. —Give me some beer.

Somewhere a sober voice said, —I suppose you might call me a positive negativist. Elsewhere, —Of course he'll never write another book, his bookshelves are crammed with books in different jackets and every one of them inside is that book of his. From a conversation on the excellent abstract composition in isolated fragments of Constable, rose Adeline's voice, —like the solids in Oochello ... Above them all the Worker's Soul hung silent, refusing comment; though the red lead recalled bridges built by horny hands, sexually unlike any that fluttered glasses beneath it now, the spots of rust a heavy male back straining between girders, generically different from any weaving here. For all its spatters of brightness, that canvas looked very tired, hanging foreign and forlorn over the sad garden. There, Anselm paused with a glass in one hand, treating his chin with a piece of (No. 1/2) sandpaper in the other.

Stanley turned to Hannah and asked with solicitude, —But what about your painting?

—They took it Monday.

—Took it? Otto repeated.

—I rented a Modigliani last month, I couldn't pay another month rent on it so they took it back. I can't live without that painting. I don't have any place to hang it, but I can't live without it, it was more beautiful than my mother. But what do *they* care? All they want is their lousy twenty dollars.

—But that much money, you could buy a good print, Otto commenced, —a Picasso ...

—Picasso, he paints like he spits.

—Well, of course ... Otto said uncomfortably, —and the ... I mean, if a painter is only after a um immediate effects ...

—Some of them have set out to kill art, Stanley said quietly looking at the floor. —And some of them are so excited about discovering new mediums and new forms, he went on, looking up, between the two people he was talking to, —that they never have time to work in one that's already established.

—Yes, and when they haven't studied their materials...

—Or they don't care, they just don't care. They don't. They accept history and they... they thumb their noses at it.

—While you sit around and try to write music like Gabrieli.

—If a painter knows his materials and respects them...

—Oh Christ, what are you talking about? Hannah broke in. —The kind of crap you buy now in tubes, how do you know what you get?

—Well of course, Otto agreed, moving his moist hand in the sling, —one can get more ink powder in a tube of cheap indigo than there is indigo, or no madder at all in rose madder, but...

—All right, what do you blame the painter for, if a system of enterprise like this one screws him up?

—Well you... I mean...

—You can buy as good colors today as have ever been made, Stanley said, —but there's a sort of a satisfaction grinding your own colors isn't there, here where everything you pick up is ready-made, everything's automatic. Where Henry James says, "to work successfully beneath a few grave, rigid laws..."

—Oh, stuff Henry James... Hannah commenced, and coughed. Otto had lit another cigarette. He turned upon her seriously unattractive face as though to accuse her of having made it so on purpose.

—Of course, when Vainiger says... he began, but she turned and set off toward a plate of crackers.

—Are you a painter? Stanley asked Otto.

—Me? Oh no, I just, I'm a writer, a playwright, I just finished a play.

—I thought from the way you talked maybe you were.

—A playwright?

—A painter.

—Well I, no, in fact I would have thought that you... And, but what does Hannah do?

—She really doesn't *do* so very much, Stanley admitted.

A face lowered behind them, to contribute, —Hannah knows *The Sound and the Fury* by heart.

—The sound and the fury? Otto turned.

—*The Sound and the Fury.* Faulkner's novel, haven't you ever read it?

—Of course I've read it, Otto said without an instant's hesitation.

—Hannah knows it by heart.

—She paints some, Stanley said in a vindicatory tone.

—Paints! Did you see the abstract she did for the Army Air Force? the face persisted. —For a psychological test, they used it to pick out the queers, if you were queer the painting didn't look like anything, if you weren't it looked like a snatch.

—A what?

—What's the matter, you queer?

—She painted still lifes, Stanley interposed helpfully.

—It took her so long the fruit got rotten.

—But Cézanne...

—Now she paints landscapes but she has to put telephone poles in all of them to get perspective. Linear perspective.

—How does she get on without working?

—She says work is death.

—People give her money?

—Work is death. She's too strong to ask for charity. When she really needs something, that's different, we all helped her when she got her front teeth knocked out. The ones she has now are made of cellophane. She washes and does all her laundry in a subway ladies' washroom.

—She's very... she has such integrity of purpose, Stanley said weakly.

—Purpose? Otto repeated. —What purpose.

—Just... purpose, Stanley said looking after their nameless companion. —I ought to leave, he added, shifting nervously, gazing toward that full-blown flower whose fey petals curled and yellowed round its white spore-bearing carpel, Agnes Deigh. She was reciting a limerick about Titian which ended, —climbed up the ladder and had 'er, to rhyme with rose madder.

—What is she, anyhow? Otto asked as they drifted in that direction.

—An agent, a literary agent, Stanley answered under his breath, and they arrived to fill a gap in the trouser-seat curtain around her. There was a silent moment: Agnes Deigh and Otto compared sun tans. Then she said, —I'm collecting members for Art for Labor and Democracy. It's a party.

—A party? someone from another cluster turned to ask.

—A political party, darling, she said, and he retired.

—I have no political interests, Otto said to her.

—But you don't have to do anything. You just give me two dollars, that pays your dues and they have another member.

—But why join if I'm not going to do anything?

—They need members. They just want your name, darling.

—I'm sorry, I'm afraid I really couldn't afford it.

—Two dollars?

—That isn't what I meant . . . But Agnes Deigh was talking to someone else. Otto retired, to recover composure with an eyebrow raised on nothing.

The funeral spray was on the floor; and in the sunless garden round it the flowers wilted one way and another, toward each other and away. There was music, briefly. A girl's voice counterfeited by the phonograph sang, "I sold my heart to the junkman . . ." until the needle broke and the song was lost in a whirr and momentary dimming of the electric light. A healthy baritone voice from a girl with a tubercularly collapsed chest said, —But it isn't really a good novel at all, the only perceptive chapter is where the boy discovers he's queer.

One, with an unconscionably persistent smile, his coat too long and trousers too short, was detailing the plot of his as-yet-unfinished novel, —slightly reminiscent of Djuna Barnes perhaps. A man is told that his girl is a lesbian, so he makes himself up as a girl and goes to a party where she'll be. He makes advances to her, she accepts, and he throws off his disguise and rapes her . . . The voice of Agnes Deigh rose, —But darling, you don't have to *do* anything.

Time, essential for growth, seemed to have forgotten the place, abandoned this garden which had never seen the sun, neither known the songs nor the fertilizing droppings of birds; still there might be worms, and one would hesitate to pry under to prove that there were not. In spite of not being tall, Otto looked loftily over the dusty scene, as he had upon the simmering market in the Central American port two weeks before. Here, as there, he poured disdainfully casual and acrid tobacco smoke over the traders, stood with one foot extended, an eyebrow raised. Occasionally he flicked at the ends of his new mustache, or affected difficulty with his sling. No one had mentioned either.

In spite of the fact that the couch was out of sight, he set off toward it, suddenly remembering the perennial hunt; and by now he had had enough to drink to encourage him toward the woman sought after in vain, die Frau nach der man sich sehnt (as Gordon called her in Act III). So he knew the eyes that looked beyond and did not acknowledge him, the hands which offered but protected, and these were the places one was forced to seek her in New York, no matter the shadows, the choking air, this Ewig-Weibliche, the Eternal Helen. Then he suddenly heard Jesse Franks's voice saying, —She looks like some friggin madonna, and, no more realizing the wonder in that remark than the man who had spoken it, shut it out.

—I haven't seen you for months, said someone beside him. They shook hands.

—I've been in Central America, said Otto, brandishing the sling.

—Were you? I didn't know it.

Otto recognized him: the young man who wore his coat too long and trousers too short. The unconscionable smile, Otto remembered unpleasantly, not a smile to make one feel cheerful in its presence and persistence. Rather its intimation was that the wearer knew all of the dismal secrets of some evil jungle whence he had just come, a place of surreptitious traffic in fetid sweetish air where the fruits hung rotten on the trees. —How do you like my painting? This, of course, was Max.

—The colors are good, said Otto warily to his host. The smile was not cold, but its very attempt to show itself open and honest revealed disarming calculation. It was a smile that had encouraged many to devote confidences, which gaining the cold air of outdoors they regretted, and mistrusted him accordingly. He dealt largely in facts, knowing for instance that most Hawaiian grass skirts are made in Switzerland, that Scottish Border ballads originated in the Pacific islands, that Scotch tartans are made in Switzerland, British army swords in Germany. It was for these moments that Otto wanted to carry a gun, not to flourish, certainly not to fire, simply to feel it heavily protective under his arm. —Did it take you long? he asked.

—Thinking it out was the main thing, said Max.

—It always is. I've just finished a play and ...

—Do you know Ed Feasley? He was at Harvard too, said Max, who had studied locally.

—Hello, said Ed. —Chrahst we were in the same class. You know, I called you up a couple of months ago. I looked you up in the phone book when I came to New York and called. I got some man. He seemed to know you, but he didn't know where you were.

—That must have been my father, Otto said.

There was the sound of collision across the room, as Anselm went down.

—That last time I saw you, said Otto. —you were playing golf down here, driving golf balls down Thompson Street.

—I was drunk, said Ed, whose father owned a battleship works. —Just happened to have some clubs in the car.

—What are you doing now?

—Not a God-damned thing. The old man told me he'd give me a ten per cent commission if I'd sell one of his God-damned boats, I think the old bastard's just kidding me. He wants me to go to work in one of his plants. Start from the bottom.

—What happened to that girl you were going to marry?

—O Chr-ah-st, Ed said wearily. His old-school drawl relieved him of the burden of blasphemy. —I've decided to write a book about her instead. He was a tall well-built fellow with a very small head, what was known as the university type before those institutions let down their barriers, now viewed by the frail round-heads who have penetrated as definite evidence of degeneration of the race.

—I guess we're all writing, Otto said cheerfully. —I've just finished a play...

—Wha'd you do to your hand anyway? Ed asked.

—I've been in Central America. A revolution...

—Wha'd you go down there for?

—I was working, but when this revolution started, well, you know, you get mixed up in things, before you know it. And to see a dozen policemen coming at you on motorcycles, after you've strung piano wire...

—Mister Feddle, said Max, —I'm so glad you came. This interloper was an old man, who seemed glad to be here.

—I feel young again, among all of you, he said. —And I must tell you since I know you'll be interested. My poems are being published.

—That's splendid. Congratulations. Things will be a lot easier for you and your wife now. Is she here?

Mr. Feddle looked out into the room. —She was, he murmured, —she was, as he tottered away.

—All you really need is a length of good piano wire...

—Did you say you were writing a novel? Max asked Ed Feasley.

—No, said Otto, —a play. I just finished a play, down in...

—Has anyone seen it? Max asked him.

—No, I...well...

—I'd like to read it, Max said.

—Would you? Let's see. I might get it to you tomorrow. It's one of those things, you can't really be sure of it until an outside person has seen it, said Otto explaining this sudden committal to himself and to them, as though he would show it to Max if he were uncertain. And Max smiled at Otto, as though he knew him very well, and had seen him often in another part of the jungle.

The sound of singing seeped through the smoke. The singer was not singing for the group, but to himself as in encouragement. If ever a tattered dahlia bloomed in that brown plot, it was Herschel. His lyrics remained the same, though the tune was under no such restriction:

—*I'm going down to Dutch Siam's, yes I am,...yes I am*

he sang from the floor, where he sat playing with his feet like any village idiot. He had not left his corner since introducing Max, Hannah, and Stanley, giving them all Christian names which he supplied himself, to a blonde Miss Adeline Thing. Those three were dumbfounded, then livid, and clamored to give Adeline their correct names; not bothering to ask hers they retired.

—*Yes I am* ... (he was very drunk), —*yes I am* ...

Miss Thing was across the room, as far as she could be from him in that place. —He is pretty far gone, isn't he? Otto said; and as they turned to look he added, —I'd say he was a latent heterosexual.

—I'm sorry, said an old lady at Max's arm. —Have you seen my husband? The old fool's probably drunk.

—Oh Mrs. Feddle, no he's not at all drunk. He looks fine. I was so glad to hear that things are working out. Life should be a lot easier for you now.

—Well, she said, weary, —it costs money to have things published, you know. She scanned the room, while Otto retreated to the bookcase.

When among people he did not know, Otto often took down a book from which he could glance up and note the situation which he pretended to disdain. One evening he had read seventeen pages in Thomas of Brabant's *On Bees* that way. Now he found himself staring at Robert Browning:

Well, and it was graceful of them: they'd break talk off and afford
—She, to bite her mask's black velvet—he, to finger on his sword,
While you sat and played Toccatas, stately at the clavichord?

—Oh God! Agnes Deigh screamed with delight. —Darling! Her laughter seemed to clear the room of the smoke that hung like marsh gas, for long enough to glimpse her abandon before the tall Swede who had just arrived to hand her a key. —It's to my box, he said, —and you mustn't lose it ever. I just don't trust myself, that's all. Why at any moment I'm liable to open that box and take out those divine dresses, those brrr beautiful bits of lingerie. Sometimes I just *have* to put them on. But if you have the key you won't let me give in, will you?

—But tell us about Rome, darling. Paris.

—I had the most divine trip back. You can't imagine anything more ghastly. On the very same boat with the right arm of Saint Ignatius of Loyola! Isn't that just too camp? You can't imagine, traveling with a relic. Victoria and Albert came with me. You can't imagine the contretemps we had when we landed ...

—...

—...?

—Tins of opium that he was trying to put onto himself with adhesive tape my dear, and in the heat of the cabin they blew up of course, simply blew up everywhere, and there they were covered with broken tins and that horrid sticky plaster *ev*erywhere, and poor Victoria had to drop a bottle of *Chanel* on the floor and smash it, just to cover up the *smell*. She's still sick with trench mouth. She got it kissing the Pope's ring.

—But what shall *I* do with the key, darling?

—Just keep it hidden until I come screaming to have it. Wasn't that wild? On the very same boat, my dears, with that odious right arm, I met the person who stole my passport in Venice. Can you imagine being introduced to yourself? You can't. Poor boy, they took him right off to prison, even though I offered to keep him in my custody. They wouldn't let me keep him. Isn't that divine? I hear the most touching stories about life in prisons.

—When did you get back?

—Just this very morning. And do you know the filthy trick they played? There I was, at Rudy's apartment, I left all my luggage there covered with the most adorable stickers from everywhere, my dears, every chic hotel you ever heard of. And when I came back tonight they had put all my bags out into the hallway, but do you know what they'd done? You cannot imagine. Simply torn off all those divine labels and stuck the most horrid vulgar things on, all over my beautiful bags, simply covered with labels from Shredded Wheat packages and Kotex boxes, isn't that the most vile thing?

—But Friday night. You'll have your dinner clothes?

—Never never again. I lent them to a divine young Sicilian boy on the way over. He committed suicide in them and I just didn't have the heart to ask for them back…

The smoke settled quickly, the guests were found again and knitted together with tendrils of conversation. The flat girl said, —A eulogy on a Wall Street man who lives in Westchester: Birth and commutation and death, that's all…

—Copulation, said Stanley, indignantly loud, cutting the asthmatic laughter she had earned. He was staring at the girl on the couch.

—Why Stanley, Agnes Deigh admonished from the chair below him, and reached a spray of white fingernails soothingly toward his face. But the consecrated mind thrust the vagrant heart aside. —It's "birth and copulation and death," he said to the profane girl.

—But she's joking, darling, said Agnes Deigh as her hand reached his trembling chin.

"Dust and ashes!" So you creak it, and I want the heart to scold.
Dear dead women, with such hair too—what's become of all the gold
Used to hang and brush their bosoms?

Otto looked up, avoiding the eyes of Max. She was watching him, suddenly, still hidden on the couch. Pretending he had not noticed her, he let a few pages slip under his finger and continued.

He never saw, never before today,
What was able to take his breath away,
A face to lose youth for, to occupy age
With the dream of, meet death with…

And she was alone. The sight of her had startled him: looking out at nothing, her lips silent and almost smiling while the rest chattered, her body still where everyone else shifted, conscious only in herself while all the others were only self-conscious. Alone on the couch, and alone in the room like the woman in that painting whose beauty cannot be assailed, whose presence cannot be discounted by turning one's back, but her silence draws him to turn again, uncertain whether to question or answer. Otto put the book back in the shelf, and started toward her. Then a tweed arm was around his shoulders. Beside him someone was saying, —There was a woman in Brooklyn who used to do it, but I think the police got her. She charged two hundred dollars. And someone else said, —Is this the first one she's ever had? You can't let it go much longer than two months. —She might make something on the side, a third person said, —You get two dollars an ounce for mother's milk these days.

—Someone has been very cru-el not introducing us, said the owner of the tweed arm. Otto freed himself and set off again, as someone in the other group said, —I'm surprised she's never been in a mess like this before.

Through the smoke, among the bumping buttocks and wasted words, he arrived. She looked up and smiled. —May I get you something? he asked her. He had taken out the cigarette package and put the last remaining cigarette between his lips, which were dry. —I'm sorry, it's my last, he said, struggling to light it, and then in confusion, —Oh I'm sorry, I should have … He stood gesturing at her with the fuming cigarette.

—I'd like a cigarette, she said.

—But I … here, take this. He had forgotten the casual stance, the raised eyebrows, lips moistened, slightly parted. His mouth was dry, and palms wet with perspiration. —I'm sorry. Let me get you one.

—No, I have some I think, she said, and reached for her bag on the floor. —My name is Esme, she told him when she sat up with a cigarette.

—Oh. Is it? said Otto, struggling to open a small match box with one hand. She helped him with the light, looking into the room beyond him. Her large eyes were exaggerated in their beauty by the hollows of her thin face, and the image he sought, distended afloat on their surfaces, drowned and was gone.

—Yes. And you?

—Me? Oh. My name's Otto, he said. A face to lose youth for, to occupy age, with the dream of, meet death with . . .

—But won't you sit down?

He sat.

The room was filled with smoke, dry worn-out smoke retaining in it like a web the insectile cadavers of dry husks of words which had been spoken and should be gone, the breaths exhaled not to be breathed again. But the words went on; and in those brief interruptions between cigarettes the exhalations were rebreathed. —I don't know, he told me he was a negative positivist. —Well he told me he was a positive negativist. —Incidentally have you read *Our Contraceptive Society?* —My dear fellow, I wrote it, for Christ sake. Adeline had been cornered by Ed Feasley, who was telling her that the trouble with America was that it was a matriarchy and had no fatherland myth. Someone said, —No one here really understands New York. It's a social experience. Max was discussing orgone boxes as though he had lived in one all of his life. Buster Brown had an arm around Sonny Byron, a young Negro said to be descended from an English poet of whom few in the room had heard. One of the policemen was asleep. The other sat holding his glass, making faces at no one. Anselm was working his way round the wall, so as not to lose his balance, toward the window. The chinless Italian boy was standing all alone, looking at the painting. Charles was in the bathroom looking through the medicine cabinet. Hannah was divided between intellect and emotion: on the one hand, arguing that D. H. Lawrence was impotent with a youth in eye-shadow who insisted that at heart he was a "raving queen"; on the other, she was trying to protect Stanley from Agnes Deigh, where he sat on the arm of her chair with the white fingertips dug into his knee.

—Sometimes I know just what it must be like, being the left arm of Saint Ignatius of Loyola, said the big Swede, who looked ready to weep.

—Baby, don't touch me, said Herschel, —my head is brackaphallic, and he began to sing as he sank back toward the floor.

Anselm managed to reach the window, which he opened, and crawled to the fire-escape, making a mess in someone's yard below.

The critic in the green wool shirt was stooped over the poet, saying —These snotty kids who come out of college and think they can write novels.

Mr. Feddle was busy inscribing the fly-leaf of a book.

Someone came in at the door with a manila envelope under his arm, and went over to the policeman who was making faces. —The radio in your patrol car is making a hell of a racket, he said. The policeman buttoned his tunic over the mangy red sweater and went out. Then the boy who had come in said, —It's snowing.

—Chrahst, how unnecessary, said Ed Feasley. He had just told Adeline that the literal translation of the German word for marry, *freien*, was to free; for aside from immediate intentions she was being considered as a character in forthcoming fiction. This Harvard boy who had never learned a trade watched her with indulgent curiosity.

—Ye haven't an arm and ye haven't a leg, Hulloo, hulloo...

sang Adeline's sometime escort from a far corner, with sudden cheer as though he'd just discovered the song.

Ye haven't an arm and ye haven't a leg,
Ye eyeless noseless chickenless egg,
Ye'll have to be put in a bowl to beg

(he sang, delighted with such a device), and an unlikely chorus followed:

I'm going down to Dutch Siam's, yes I am...

Then someone said loudly what everyone had been suspecting. —There's no more to drink. The room quieted. Even the eyeless noseless chickenless egg was abandoned, as its chorister struggled to an optimistically vertical position against the bookcase.

—Oh God, said Agnes Deigh. —Give me my bag will you darling? she asked an anonymous trouser seat, pulling at the coat which hung above but did not match. She handed a folded twenty-dollar bill to a boy wearing her racing colors and stood, saying —I've got to go to the can anyhow, where is it?

Hannah had been watching her. She felt in the pockets of the deep-seated denim pants, came up with nothing, and said, —What time is it? to Max, probably the only other sober person in the room.

—Three-fifteen, said Max, for whom time was also a matter of the clock.

She sniffed, as with a personal grievance. —It's disgusting, giving a string of Mozart operas as benefits so they can buy new scenery for *The Ring*. Mozart pimping for Wagner. And that old bag, she added, —with her Mickey Mouse watch. Then she looked down the room and asked, —Who's that skinny girl on the couch, with that... Otto?

—She writes poems, her name's Esme. I think she's been modeling for some painter. She hasn't got any stomach.

—I've heard about her, Hannah muttered. —On the needle. A schiz.

—Manic depressive, schizoid tendencies, Max elaborated. —Has anybody ever seen her child?

—Child? She's a mother, her? She's too fucking spiritual.

—She says she has one four years old.

—Christ. And look at Herschel, he's simple, but Stanley, this thing he has on the Church, that's why he's stuck on that old bag with the Mickey Mouse watch, he wants to bring her back to the Church he thinks. I wish he'd get off it.

—I wish he didn't smell, said Max. —I've told you before, he's an oral type. But if you want a real obsessive neurosis look at this, he said nodding to where Anselm approached on hands and knees, a beatific expression on his blemished face. —Have you read any of his poetry? I don't see why Bildow takes it.

—Why shouldn't he smell? Anselm demanded from below. —He doesn't wash.

—Screw, will you Anselm? Hannah said, with a step toward Stanley.

—What did Saint Jerome say? "Does your skin roughen without the bath?"

—Screw.

—"Who is once washed in the blood of Christ need not wash again."

Hannah reached Stanley and took his arm. —Don't you want to leave? Come on, I'll walk you as far as the subway.

—Yes...in a minute, he said looking down at the warm indentations Agnes Deigh had left in the chair.

Hannah muttered something. She was staring at Esme again, and suddenly said to Max, —She looks like she thinks she *is* a painting. Like an oil you're not supposed to get too close to.

—She's high right now, can't you see it? She's been on for three days.

Hannah snorted, and took Stanley's arm again. —Coming?

He looked down to see someone tugging at his trouser leg. —What kind of an ass-backwards Catholic are you? asked Anselm from the floor.

—Why...why...

—Shut up, Anselm, said Hannah. —For Christ sake, go home and take a nap.

—For Christ sake, you say to me! What do you know about Christ?

—Take a nap.

—Well I can't. Do you know why? Because of Christ. Because when I lie down and feel my hands against my own body, that's all I can think of, that thin body of Christ. I can feel it, with my own hands. Does that interest you?

—Please...said Stanley.

—Not a God-damned bit, said Hannah.

—Well don't try to talk to me about Christ then, said Anselm, and started away. Then he turned his head back to them. —Do you know who went around like this? Do you know that Saint Teresa went around on all fours, with a basket of stones on her back? and a halter? That's the ritu quadrupedis, if you think it's so God damn funny don't you. And do you know what Christ said to her? "If I had not already created Heaven, I would create it for thy sake alone." Don't try to talk to me about Christ, he said, and went toward the other end of the room, quadrupedis. Stanley stood still; and Hannah turned from him angrily.

Herschel was still propped against the bookcase, where he had left himself a while before. Hannah's approach woke him to a look of fear and no under-standing. —By now you probably don't even know what your name is, she said, her tone merciless sobriety.

—Hannah . . .

—No. I'm Hannah, and who are you? He stumbled past her to the other side of the room and interrupted Ed Feasley, who was telling Adeline that the literal translation of the German word for surrender, *niederlage*, is to lie under.

—Adeline, said Herschel. —*Baby*, drawing his breath through his open mouth, liquidly audible. —Is your name really Adeline? I had a nurse once named Adeline, a west black woman Adeline. One day I bit her right square under the apple tree. What do you think of that?

The white Adeline thought enough of it to stand away from him. Herschel swung before her, like a man whose feet were grounded on springs. —Is your name really Adeline? he pled, now with such insistence that if she would answer, or even allow the affirmative by silence, it would legitimize anything to follow. But the door opened upon them, and four late arrivals appeared, hazy-eyed, with willowy movements, the three boys unshaven and the girl unclean, smelling like lives from the swamp. —We've been having a ball, man, one of them said. —Have you got any tea?

A policeman, his tunic unbuttoned, appeared in the doorway to announce loudly that he had had a call from headquarters to answer a complaint at this address . . . a party . . . too much noise . . . have to quiet down . . . and could somebody get me another drink?

Otto took Esme's arm and helped her up, almost using that arm which lay helpless in the sling. He recovered enough of his wit to say, —May I take you home? Now you're supposed to say, Sure, where do you live? Esme looked up, smiled pleasantly, blankly. She did not understand; and sophistry, confronted by simplicity, was lost. —It seems like we've always been just here, she said.

Someone appeared before Otto with a manila envelope. —Here's the story, the one you said you'd send to your friend on a magazine for me, he said, and disappeared.

Herschel stood mumbling to himself. All sense of humor was gone, all sense of anything. His eyes, looking and finding nothing, had stopped seeking and lay open and empty. Only when Hannah reappeared, reflected in their glassy surface, they clouded. —Now I suppose you want to get your tattoo? she said. He nodded helplessly. —Herschel, don't be such a fool. Go back to analysis. Do you think a tattoo will solve everything?

—Hannah…baby…

—What are you going to have tattooed on you, anyhow? Names? Pictures?

—Leave me alone, he whispered.

A discussion of fierce intellectual intensity continued in one corner. Someone had said that everyone knew that Tennyson was a Jew. In the middle of the room two young men met. —I thought you'd gone home, one said. The other embraced him. —I was waiting for someone to ask me. The Swede sat on the windowsill, head in his hands. —Those horrid horrid vulgar labels, all over my bags, he sobbed. —But I could hear them laughing behind the door, behind the locked door, I could hear them laughing…The flat girl said, —Aren't you going to say good night to our host? And her escort, a full-blown woman, said, —God no, I never speak to *him*.

Agnes Deigh returned, straightening her skirt and loosening her waist. Then there was Stanley's voice saying, —No, I promised I'd go home with Hannah, the tone of the seven-year-old's loyalty to the squat and eternal mother. A boy in a bow tie thanked Agnes Deigh for the party, and she cried, —Darling it wasn't *my* party, I'm leaving too. Will you take me home? As she went out she stopped with Max, who stood smiling under the forgotten scars of the Workman's Soul. —There's somebody in the can darling, she said, —somebody passed out in the tub, somebody I've never seen before. You'd better go in and look at him, there's blood all over the place.

At their feet squatted the late guests, smoking something the size of a thumbnail which they passed among them, like a pitiful encampment of outcast Indians satisfying the wrong hunger. —This stuff doesn't really affect me, one said, —but don't you notice that the ceiling is getting closer?

The policeman who had been making faces put down an empty glass, and woke up his buddy. They left.

Otto felt strange, holding her thin wrist: that Esme could give all and lose nothing, for the taker would find she had given nothing; plundering her, the plunderer would turn to find himself empty, and she still silently offering. When she looked up, he was lost to himself as though the woman in that painting had turned her unchanging eyes on his helplessness, and he looked away from her eyes, at the straight darkness of her hair, and cowardly, down at her ringless fingers. Her eyes embarrassed him with their beauty, all at once as she showed them.

—Whore! said a voice at their feet, throaty, breathing heavily, as if there were indeed a load of stones on his back. Then in a clear hard voice Anselm called Esme a name which fell from his mouth like a round stone, and seemed to strike the floor and remain. She looked down at him. —Come on. Look out, Otto said, pulling her away. But she stood, for all her delicacy, firm, and smiling. —Anselm, she said, her voice gentle and quenching as she repeated the name. —Anselm.

—Succubus, said Anselm, his voice deep in his throat again. —*Ssucc*ubus, he hissed. —Devil in a woman's body, to lead a man in vile sin, abominable lusts, carnal pleasures, blasphemy, the filthy delights of copulation. Do you think I don't know? Do you think no one knows? Not for your own delectation, you get no pleasure from it, only to corrupt and pollute the soul and body of a mortal man. Succubus to a man, incubus to a woman... He reared his acned chin.

—Come on, Esme, said Otto. —Let's get out of here. But she stood, charmed, still gently smiling.

—Go home and read Saint Augustine. *On the Trinity*, said Anselm, turning his thin face up to Otto. —There you'll find that devils do indeed collect human seed. Not for delectation. Succubus to a man, incubus to a woman. Damn you, damn you, damn you. If devils fell from every rank, those who fell from the lowest choir are deputed to perform these abominations, these filthy delights. Not for delectation. Do you know about the monk Helias, and how the angels answered his prayers by castrating him? Do you know about Saint Victor?

Otto had moved Esme toward the door, where the Swede stood sobbing —Behind the locked door, I could hear them laughing...

Then Otto turned, feeling something spray on him. Anselm had flung up a hand wet with beer, and was shuddering, —I exorcise thee, unclean spirit, in the name of Jesus Christ; tremble, O Satan, thou enemy of the faith, thou foe of mankind, who hast brought death into the world... He gasped; and in that moment Otto heard clearly from across the room, in Max's voice:

—I'd say he was a latent heterosexual, and looked up to find Max's eyes upon him. He stood trapped for an instant in Max's smiling eyes, then sought others, saw Stanley sunk against a chair watching Anselm.

—Thou seducer of mankind, thou root of evil, thou source of avarice, discord, and envy...

—Esme, come on. He pulled her arm.

—Hey Stanley, Anselm called suddenly over his shoulder, —who's this coon with your girl? Hey Stanley, I am one, sir, that comes to tell you...

—Esme...

—Your daughter and the Moor are now making the beast with two backs.

—Damn it...

—Now be nice...the Swede whispered through his tears.

—For Christ sake Anselm...

—Go home and fornicate, came from the floor. —Only know that God for His own glory permits devils to work against His will. For His own glory...

And then a crash.

They looked to see Hannah getting up from the floor, and Max went to help her. Herschel stumbled and fell against a chair, where his whole body shook, heaving from its shallow depths. —I can't stand it, I can't stand it any more. She asked me who I was, and I told her and she said How do you know who that is, is it anybody at all and...Oh God, *Christ*, I hate hitting somebody I don't like.

On the floor before the fireplace lay the funeral spray, lifted gaily from the door of a bereaved Italian family downstairs, trampled so that its wires stood out naked. Time had been there. The garden which one had thought could not grow, had risen in rank luxuriance, like the plants on that plantation abandoned. For even bananas must be cut and hung to mature properly; left on the stalk, they swell and burst open, attract insects, develop an unpleasant taste, beyond the bounds of cultivation, beyond the plantation, in the jungle, where in the art of evil their near relatives, the orchids, blossom, not questioning the distant Greeks on how they got their name, deriving innocently from the devil's residence in man: that part which the angels cut from the monk Helias. Otto led Esme forth, and at the stairs she drew him down.

VI

"Father," he asked, "are the rich people stronger than anyone else on earth?" "Yes, Ilusha," I said. "There are no people on earth stronger than the rich." "Father," he said, "I will get rich, I will become an officer and conquer everybody. The Tsar will reward me, I will come back here and then no one will dare..." Then he was silent and his lips still kept trembling. "Father," he said, "what a horrid town this is."

—DOSTOEVSKI, *The Brothers Karamazov*

"WHY HAS not man a microscopic eye?" writes Alexander Pope; "For this plain reason: man is not a fly." What of Argus, equipped with one hundred eyes to watch over the king's daughter turned into a heifer by a jealous goddess; how many images of the heifer did he see? how many leaves to the bracken where she browsed? And after the death of Argus (his eyes transplanted to the peacock's tail), this wretched heifer, the metamorphosis of Io, was visited by a gadfly sent by the jealous goddess, and driven frenzied across frontiers until she reached the Nile. What did the gadfly see? And Argus, suffering the distraction of one hundred eyes: did he sit steady? or move distracted from distraction by distraction, like the housefly now dashing and retreating in frenzy against the windowpane, drawn to a new destination the instant it halted, from the shade-pull to the floor, from there to the lampshade, back to the baffling window glass. No Argus, this miserable Diptera, despite its marvelous eyes guardian of nothing; for where was the heifer? Below, perhaps. From the high ceiling the housefly careened to the molding across the room, thence to the lampshade, to a green muffler, a pair of socks on the floor, and so to the sleeping face which it attended with custodial devotion, until the blinking unmicroscopic eyes came open, and Otto lay awake.

—O God, what have I *done?* came borne on a girl's voice, sustained by a muted Rhadames singing before his judges from the lungs of a radio. Otto closed his eyes, not yet ready to return to this life. The fly rummaged about his cheek, remarking there the pitted damages of adolescence, an uneven surface affording foothold for claws laden with typhoid bacilli. Still, for a moment, the fly studied the caves of the nostrils leading into the crooked tanned peak of the nose. Otto threw his arm across his face. The fly rose, swirled, returned to walk across the cleft of the chin, and from that eminence sighted the convoluted marvel protruding across the way, and leaped silently to the ear.

—O God, what *have* I done? This was followed by a tearing sob.

Otto's hand moved quickly, to the ear; but by the time it reached there, the fly was trampling his eyebrow, its purpose of devilish torment unchanged since Io reached the Nile, where Egyptian mothers still hesitate to disturb flies settled on a sleeping child, awed by the fly god, Baal-zebub, evil and insect-breeding power of Baal, the sun himself, lover and quickener of nature.

—O God, *what* have I done . . . oouuuh . . . while in Egyptian background Rhadames was sealed up in the tomb, alive, where he finds Aïda waiting, sunless, and out in the sunshine metamorphosed by a pun Baal-zebub becomes Beelzeboul, the dung god, Prince of Devils.

So Otto, forced awake by three millenniums, a goddess, a princess, and a devil, swung once more at the housefly and sat up on the edge of his bed, his face anxiously distorted, listening. He waited.

—O God! *What* have I *done!* sounded through the thin wall.

He got up and lit an American cigarette.

December's thin sunlight came in at the window, hopefully revisiting this city despaired of the night before. In thousands of rooms, as many men intently removed minuscule stubble from pallid chins, with as much care for office appearance as though each worked under Saint Wulstan, whose holiness was so offended by beards that he carried a knife, and when a man so adorned knelt for his blessing the good Bishop of Wulster cut out a handful of it, threw it in the poor fellow's face, and told him to cut the rest off or go, quite literally, to Hell. Now they buttoned buttons for the thousandth time without question, absorbed in pragmatic interior monologues which anticipated the successes of the day to come fostered by the failures of the day before.

The city throbbed in gray effulgence, radiating motion, while silent pigeons swept the lower air, or walked grunting on the sills and cornices of the buildings, and on the sidewalks of open places. In Union Square, one of them attacked a bird of rare beauty, tropically plumed, which looked lost and unused to spreading its wings beyond the breadth of a cage.

Otto stumped about the small room, picking up his cigarette whenever it had rested for long enough to burn a brown scar on the woodwork, to liven its coal and find a fresh place to leave it. He was dressed in shorts. The linen suit was rumpled, and the morning light showed it less becomingly so than he had believed the night before. He examined a smudge on the elbow (where it had been dropped on Esme's floor), started to brush it out, and then did not. It remained, witness to what, try as he would, he could not clearly remember. Two suits and a jacket hung beside the linen, only the gray flannel carefully unpressed.

—O God! *What have I du-un*... huuuuh... came through the wall. —Haha. Haha. That's the way to do it... He sank back in the chair, still staring at the wall; but only the radio voice reached him: ——Ladies, if you are troubled by excess hair, write for a *free* brochure of our method, guaranteed to remove fifteen hundred hairs in a single hour...

Then he got up and dressed slowly. Buttoning his shirt, he looked vacantly at a book and some papers on the table, which had come under the attention of the fly. He took a towel from the bed and snapped it at the fly. The fly moved to the ceiling, and several of the papers to the floor. Picking up the local Spanish newspaper (which he carried in public and appeared to read), he muttered something; then, pulling on his trousers, he looked as absently at a scrap of notepaper on which was written, Gd crs as mch fr mmnt as fr hr—wht mean? The expression on his face started to change as he read that over, scratching his head as he filled in the vowels. But whatever that expression would have been, it failed: he stood looking at his fingernails, turned in upon the palm. Then barely glancing, crumpled the notepaper as he picked it up and threw it in the basket, to turn away buttoning his trousers, and sit down to count his money.

——And now friends, you've probably been hearing so much about this wonderful new protein diet... He looked up, having reached one hundred thirty. The dial in the next room was being turned.

——To take the odor out of perspiration. Fifty-two per cent more effective...

He gave up counting the money, thumbing over the rest before he put it away, and went to the mirror with a necktie. There he studied his eyes anxiously for a moment, then noticed that his skin appeared pale beneath the surface of color, and the mustache hairs were brought into separate and ragged prominence.

——And so friends, to get your free... Christ sent me not to baptize but to... That wonderful he-man aroma that girls really go for...

Then a pneumatic pavement-breaker started in the street below, some ten yards from where it had been torn up, and repaired, the week before. He considered leaving the sling where it was, empty, on the table, for it was proving more of an impediment than he had anticipated. But fearful of meeting someone who had seen him in it, he hung it round his neck, and went back to the mirror to arrange it.

The pavement-breaker below stopped just long enough for him to hear through the wall,

——You have just heard the oria from Gluck's Orfeoadoiradeechay . . . and he stood in his open door looking at the closed door just to his right. He raised a hand to knock; but glancing back as his own door came closed saw the large manila envelope on the table, returned to pick it up, and took the smaller less familiar one with it.

The morning was exceptionally fine, the streets still comparatively unlittered by those tons of ingeniously made, colorfully printed, scientifically designed wrappings of things themselves expendable which the natives drop behind them wherever they go, wary as those canny spirits down under cluttering the path to paradise.

As he walked toward the bus stop, he noticed that his watch was fourteen minutes slow. Turning the corner, he started to run; and the bus which had been waiting roared away as he arrived, bearing faces which looked with benign satisfaction on him catching breath in the exhaust fumes. He waited. A cab stopped right before him; and the next bus, unable to approach the curb, roared past. The taxi driver had looked at him questioningly, now disdainfully, and drove after the bus. The downtown bus he boarded a quarter-hour later was driven by a mustached man in a leather jacket, whose swashbuckling motions recalled the devil-may-care bomber pilots of the motion-picture screen. His cap, its wire frame removed, clung rakishly to the back of his oily head, as he guided his huge machine down the runway for another takeoff. Otto rocked back and forth, holding a strap, attempting to appear as vacant as the faces before him while he stared straight forward at

Take someone to church with you
next Sunday
You'll both be richer for it

The phantasies of the passengers were suspended, as they tore through clouds, shuddered at air-pockets, dove low over landmarks. Otto had finally turned round, and was staring at

1,500,000
Americans have
SYPHILIS or GONORRHEA
and don't know it

From their empty faces, none of the passengers resented the driver's incursion into their own phantastical domains: watching his weaving back, they appeared to respect his right to perform in allegory, to redeem, as best his numb imagination would permit him, the absurdity of reality.

Anselm said nothing; but smiled without recognition as they passed in Washington Square. Otto caught his breath and lowered his eyes quickly from the thin newly shaven face to the crimson-covered book under Anselm's arm, and went on to the doorway he had left only hours before. The stairs had the familiarity of a staircase descended in a dream. He had seen them last unlit, with other eyes than these of morning: now they interested him, for he could see himself climbing them, often and regularly, up and down. The door he approached was blank, anonymous. He knocked sharply: still it stood, no hint of what was resident behind it.

Knock knock knock. And more silence than before.

—Esme? he called.

—Who is it?

—Otto.

—*Who?*

—Otto.

—Oh. But it's so early.

The instant her voice stopped the door, flat, blank, regained its anonymity, and she was gone, nowhere.

—Otto?

—Hello?

—Will you come back in an hour?

—An *hour?*

—I have to take a bath.

—All right, he called at that resolute door, and went down the stairs.

A small hairy face turned to him from the lap of the blonde whom he sat beside at the drugstore counter. He ordered coffee, and started to tamper with the green ribbon on the dog's crown. The blonde straightened herself, looking the other way, the lhasa turned to stare at the Coca-Cola machine, and she bent forward to blow softly in its hair. On his left, the hairy-armed counterman rested his hands on the counter. —Yeh, I could write a book, he said to the girl sitting there —I bet it'd be banned in Boston, she said. She laughed. —Not oney in Boston, he said. They laughed. The blonde with the dog coughed, and moved down a seat. Otto blew more cigarette smoke straight before him, and put the packet of Emu on the counter.

Over his third cup of coffee, staring at the two manila envelopes, he suddenly remembered the smaller one which contained a short story written by a navy veteran, handed him at the party the night before after he said he had a friend with a magazine. That friend was the girl who had caused him untold misery three years before, by not marrying him. Having got all of the poetically incumbent recriminations out of his system, Otto remembered her now with condescending fondness. He wrote on a slip of paper, "My dear Edna: I enclose a copy of a story written by a friend of mine, because having read it over I thought it might go well in your magazine. If you can't use it, will you please return it to me, since he has no permanent address . . . ," which note he signed and clipped to the papers in the envelope without even having to bother to take them out.

Stanley said nothing; but hung his head without recognition as they passed in Washington Square. When Otto returned to Esme's door, he was uncertain whether to kiss her uproariously, formally, or not at all. The restraint of not-at-all would be best rewarded, eventually, for then she would believe that she wanted him to kiss her, and arrange an unequivocal opportunity. He adjusted his sling.

She opened the door and smiled at him, as she probably smiled at the janitor when he appeared there. Otto said good morning, and came in. He took off his green muffler and tossed it to a chair, where it fell on the floor behind. —How do you feel this morning? he asked her.

—Like I feel in the morning, Esme answered, smiling, unhesitating as a good child.

—I mean after last night.

—Morning is always after last night.

—No, I mean the party, and . . .

—Oh. I was . . . what did you call it? Plas-tered?

—You were pretty far gone. Otto stared at her face: how she must have scrubbed it, making its hollows more cleanly cut, and then applied the dark lines of the eyebrows and no other make-up. He reached for her waist. She moved away.

—Did you bring me home? she asked.

—Did *I* bring you home? Esme . . . He stared at her eyes, wide in innocent curiosity.

—Is something the matter? she asked.

—Don't you remember?

—What?

—Don't you remember *any*thing?

—The party? she asked, happily. —It was a lovely party. And then poor

Anselm was walking around like a dog and saying funny things, and then that poor young man hit that girl . . . She stopped.

—Herschel hit Hannah. And then?

—Yes, she said, —Herschel hit Hannah. She stopped.

—But Hannah, I mean Esme, is that all you remember?

—Yes, it was a lovely party, and you were standing there pretending to read that old book . . . She was reeking of honesty.

—Esme . . .

—And you kept fooling with that funny thing you wear around your neck . . .

—Esme.

—What, Ot-to?

—Don't you remember coming back here with me?

—Then you *did* bring me home. Why didn't you tell me, instead of teasing me like that?

Otto's forehead drew together; the sling quivered. What is a conquest which goes unacknowledged by the conquered? Here was where he had dropped his coat, there the ashtray he had overturned. —Esme . . .

knock knock knock

—But Esme . . .

—What is it? she said, on her way to the door, smiling.

— . . . ?!

—Chaby! Esme said, as though delighted with what came in at that door. —This, she said to Otto, —is Chaby Sin-is-ter-ra, as though she were making up the words syllable by syllable.

—How do you do, said Otto, not wishing to be told. Nor was he.

Chaby was small, sharply boned. His chin was small and sharp, so were his eyes, and his teeth: everything about him, in fact, but his hair, a shiny black pompadour which he wore like a hat and continually adjusted with an unclean pocket comb missing a tooth, which left a ridge on the otherwise smooth metaled surface. His mustache was a thin line of black hairs drawn from his nostrils along his upper lip. Otto ran a fingertip along the straggling fullness of his own, and sat down. —What a friggin night I had, said Chaby. And his fingernails were black.

Otto lit an Emu and sat apparently absorbed with it, indicating that its complete enjoyment required all of his attention. He blew a ring of smoke one way, another another way, and another to the floor, where it sank and settled upon the carpet. The carpet ended halfway across the room in an indecision of color and design, its surface the flat and slightly ribbed lay of Aubusson because of the uneven texture of the floor. Its intricate design, beginning under the daybed where Otto sat, gave way to abstraction, threatening even worse where it came suddenly to an end, a sense of delirium in the hand of the painter who had painted it there, cross-stroking the warp and the weft with a two-inch brush. Chaby tapped a shiny foot, accompanying an evil rhythm which played endlessly within. Esme sat down on the arm of his chair. He got up and went to the radio, which he turned on with the casual thoughtlessness of long habit. The room was filled with the throbbing hesitations of a tango. In silent disdain, so watered down that it approached charity, Otto contrasted his own attire to the padded, pleated affair swaying across from him, until he realized that Chaby had taken off his coat and drawn Esme's waist closely and somewhat below his own. They were dancing. Otto followed the first intimacies of that tango with painful intentness. He adjusted his sling, as though to indicate that but for this injustice he might dance or do battle. Then he yawned; but the yawn did not succeed, simply left him sitting with his mouth open. With his unharnessed hand he reached for a book.

The first at his hand was new: *In Dreams I Kiss Your Hand Madam*, "An Anthology of Romantic Stories from Seven Centuries, by forty-six authors, gathered from thirty-one countries... Edited by Recktall Brown." The first page was blank, the second repeated the title, the fourth the title and the elucidations on the jacket, but Otto studied the third: "To / ESME / whose unerring judgment / is responsible for whatever value / this book may have."

The tango ended in a long unwilling surrender on the radio, and a similar expression in the middle of the floor. Esme recovered. Laughing, she pushed her hair up from perspiring temples. —Chaby teaches dancing, she said to Otto, explaining what had just happened, smiling like the Baganda woman smiles in Central Africa, lain in the thick grass with a plantain flower between her legs, flower dislodged by her husband's rearing member before he takes her to dance in the gardens of friends, to encourage the plantain trees that grow in their gardens.

—Really, Esme said, —it must be illegal to dance like that. Her unruffled partner had opened his shirt to the waist, showing a silver medal swung on a chain from his neck.

—It should be, Otto muttered.

—What Otto? She sat beside him now, and said over his shoulder, —Isn't that awful? when she saw what he was reading.

—Who's Recktall Brown? he asked back.

—He did that because he wanted to go to bed with me, she said cheerfully.

—Who is he?

—A terrible fat man who does things like that.

—How can he give you credit for the merit in a Maupassant story? he said, thumbing the pages to *Bed Number* 29, laying the fault on her.

—Because he just does, she explained. —He's going to publish my poems.

—Same reason?

—Yes. Just because he wants to go to bed with me. Isn't that funny? Isn't that disgusting? she said laughing.

—Yes it is, Otto agreed soberly.

—What's that funny smell? said Chaby. —I always smell it up here.

—What smell? Esme asked.

—Don't you smell nothing? Some funny smell, like oily flowers.

—I noticed it, Otto said to Esme. —It's lavender, he explained, condescending to glance across the room where Chaby sniffed, audibly, formed his lips in a silent obscenity which indicated that he understood, and lit an extra-length cigarette. He had not even looked over at Otto.

—Is it perfume? or is it from your clothes? Otto asked her. —Sachet, I mean. She was looking out the window absently. She turned quickly and said, —Oh, from my clothes I guess. I guess it's from my clothes.

—I saw Anselm in the park, Otto said.

—What did he say, she asked.

—He didn't say anything. I just saw him. He'd shaved, anyhow.

—I know, Esme said, smiling again, —and he cut himself three times because he said the razor blade was dull.

—What do you mean?

—Because I didn't have any new razor blades, and he had to use the same one I shaved my legs with.

—You mean he shaved here?

—Yes. Anselm came in and shaved.

—But...

—What is a succubus? Esme asked. —Chaby, do you know what a *succubus* is?

—It sounds like somebody that sucks, said Chaby.

—You're *ter*rible, Esme said, laughing again and as if about to throw a book at him.

—What do you want to know for anyhow?

—Because Anselm says he called me one, and that he's sorry, he didn't mean to call me that, but I still *am* one.

—You're the best one I know, said Chaby, grinning. Esme got up, went over and shook him by the shoulders. —I hate you, you're being so bad this morning, she said, laughing, and her face flushed. —Isn't he being *bad*, Otto?

—Have you had breakfast, Esme? Otto asked her.

—No, have you, she asked, turning, —Mister Sin-is-ter-ra? still holding him by the shoulder with sisterly fondness, and the tone of two who shared all of one another's secrets.

They went down the stairs, all three. Otto (brandishing his sling) forgot his green scarf, left behind on the floor.

Seated at a counter, Chaby ate hungrily, Esme with little attention to what she was eating or how, Otto already floating nauseously on coffee smoldered silently over another cup. At one point he leaned over to Esme who sat between them, and said, —Esme, I want to talk to you about . . . well, alone.

—What is it? she asked, sitting back, offering the busy immediacy of Chaby. —Tell me. She was delighted by confidences, wanted to share them with everyone. Otto grimaced, lit another cigarette. —But you already have one, she said, pointing to the cigarette smoking in his saucer.

—Hullo, Stanley said in a dull voice behind them.

—Stanley! said Esme turning; and she had that tone of having waited for him for weeks.

—You seem happy, said Stanley, accusingly.

—Oh Stanley! I *am*. Has something else happened?

Stanley held out a paper. It was a letter, from an eye bank. Esme read it. —It's scandal-ous, Stanley, she said. She laughed. —Do they want you to deposit your eyes?

—I don't really understand *what* they want, Stanley said. —I think it's that if I die, they want my eyes sent to them immediately. There's a little coupon at the bottom you fill out.

—Well that's all right, isn't it? said Esme. —Then will they come and get your eye while it's still warm?

—Don't talk like that, Esme, it's . . .

—Why not?

—It's frightening, the thought of these complete strangers coming to get my *eyes* . . .

—But you won't *need* them . . .

—But I will. I might . . .

Otto leaned toward Esme. —Look, will you be home this afternoon? he said. —Alone? he added, as Chaby reached for a toothpick.

—Unless someone comes.

—Who?

—I don't know. People.

—They have bone banks too, Stanley said.

—I'll see you this afternoon, Otto said. —Alone. He took out a five-dollar bill, and carefully tore a corner off of it. Chaby watched, frowning. —Wha-tayadoin? he said.

Otto raised an eyebrow, took a step away, and paid for their breakfasts. —If she'd said I only gave her a dollar, I'd tell her to go through her money there until she found a five with this corner missing, he said, dropping the shred of evidence under the counter, and pocketing his change. Stanley looked troubled.

—Esme, Otto said, —I...

—In Russia I read that they even graft on...well, you know...onto soldiers who get wounded there,...

—Stanley!

—Esme...Otto rested a delicate hand on the counter for a moment more. Chaby was showing Esme a picture from his wallet, a tattered thing which at a glimpse showed only limbs indecently intertwined. Otto looked, as casually as he could; and as casually, the thing was turned from his gaze. Stanley looked away. —I don't want to see it, he said. Esme was laughing. Otto turned and left like an angry steam engine.

As he reached the door Esme called, —Goodbye, Otto...but he did not stop. Chaby did not even look around. —They spoiled a good whore when they hung a pair of nuts on him, he said. —Maybe they could help him out in Russia...

—Chaby Sin-is-ter-ra! Stanley, isn't he being *bad?* She was laughing.

Meanwhile, the winter sky had darkened. The blazing eye of the sun was gone, and the sky lowered upon the city with the weight of a featureless being smothering it against the earth. The peaks of its buildings reared against the sky seemed to hold that portentous weight at bay, in the great conspiracy of mother and son, the earth and the city, against the father threatening overhead; for it was Cronus the mother conspired with, to free the children suffocated between the intimately united bodies of their parents, where they could not see light.

Years had passed over the Titanic capital, as it grew to its full stature, and over the continent spread at its feet where a year's relief from love cost eighty-five million dollars in headache remedies; and for faith: 15,670,944,200 aspirin tablets, carried like phylacteries. The state, this Titan's namesake, breathed the smoke of forty billion cigarettes that year. Descending into the lungs of this reinforced concrete incarnation, the smoke circulated through steel lobules cushioned in pleural cavities of granite (though unlike the lungs of a good giant no concave inner surface was necessary for the heart), and from there it was exhaled through chromium-cartileged larynges to diffuse into the spew of grime with which the ungrateful child affronted his father above. Fly-ash, cinders and sand, tar, soot, and sulfuric acid: six tons a day settled on this neighborhood where Otto stepped forth, his faculties so highly civilized that he seemed not to notice the billions of particles swirling round him, seemed not to notice the flashing of lights, the clangor of steel in conflict, the shouts, and the words spoken, timorous, temerarious, eructations of slate-colored lungs, seemed to acknowledge nothing but his own purpose, which led him east.

The sky refused the encounter it threatened. The storm refused to break; but the dark being continued in menacing movement above, content to un-nerve its arrogant antagonist, to inspire foreboding, but declining the skirmish which would witness the spilling of its own blood in streaks of lightning. The inhabitants moved agitated, apprehensive, intent on immediacies. For the rest of the morning, Otto behaved impatiently in the streets, ruthlessly in the subway, merciless in revolving doors. Left arm tense, and occasionally com-bative in the sling, his right arm pressed against the presence of his wallet, he moved between immediate destinations, every address a destination until it was reached, when it offered simply a pause where the next step could be planned, time unbroken by leisure but instead brief spasmodic stretches of emptiness between activities, minutes parceled together by cigarettes. Leaving a glass of beer on the bar, Otto went back to the telephone booth. He dialed Max's number. It was busy. He sat staring through the dirty glass panel, where someone had drawn the letters of an obscene syllable on the glass with a dia-mond. He dialed again; got only brrk, brrk, brrk. He dialed two other num-bers, hoping to find someone free for lunch. No one was. He dialed Max again: brrk, brrk, brrk. Then he thought of a number which came to him almost out of habit, he had dialed it automatically that many times. What would he say? And if a man answered? But by this time he was unsettled enough to call that number without giving himself time to think of consequence. He could ask Esther to meet him now, for lunch. He dialed. The telephone at the other end was picked up. He said, —Hello? There was silence. —Hello? Hello? Silence. —Hello? Is Esther there? —No, said a voice in weak decision, as though re-lieved. —Hello. Who is this? —Rose. —Rose? Rose, are you the maid? Hello? —Rose, said the voice. —Hello? Then their humming silent contact was dead. Otto shook the hook up and down. —Hello, hello, say... The bartender was looking in at him. He hung up. He sat for another moment, staring at the word written on the glass. Then he dialed Max. He could hear the brrr which indicated that Max's telephone was ringing. There was no answer. He hung up. He dialed again, another number, this time found Maude Munk at home sounding as though she did not want to talk, not for a minute stopping. —Did you get it, Maude? —Get what? —I mean did you get to the adoption center? —Oh no, silly, we were both so hung over... I don't know which one of us really wants it anyhow...We decided it wasn't such a good idea; for today anyhow...What about your party, I hear it was quite hideous... —Say, do you know someone at Esther's house named Rose? She answered the phone... —Oh Rose, Rose, of course, silly, everyone knows about Rose... look would you mind calling me later, I've got to do something now... —But who's Rose? —Around five? Could you call around five...?

Otto returned to the bar. He remembered that his watch was fourteen minutes slow. He started to pull out the stem to reset it, looked up at the clock over the bar. That clock told the same time his watch did. —Is that the right time? he asked the bartender. —Yuh. Maybe it's a little fast. Another beer? Otto started to decline, then noticed the mirror behind the bar, and watched himself accept.

—It's funny, said a man beside him. Otto turned, to see a striped tie. Unsure what club it represented, he said, —What?

—This sunlight. I was just wondering where this sunlight could be coming from, from the west. Then I noticed it's a reflection from that window across the street.

—Yes, so it is.

—Can I buy you a beer? Let's have two beers here, he called to the bartender.

—I'm always surprised to see sunlight anywhere in New York, Otto said.

—Have ever crossed on the ferry? Have you ever seen the sun on the Statue of Liberty at seven o'clock in the morning? Here's your beer. Have you?

—Matter of fact, said Otto, resting his helpless arm on the bar, —I passed it on a ship just yesterday morning. Coming in from Central America.

—Central America, have you been down there?

—I just got back.

—You know, when I saw you, or when I heard you talk first, I thought you had some sort of accent. Not a foreign accent, more of a what you might call cosmopolitan.

—Well, I...

—Can you speak Spanish?

—Oh yes. Certainly, I picked it up down there.

—You did?

—It's not difficult. When you really live with the people.

—Not if you have a talent for languages. You must have one.

—Well, a bit perhaps. I...

—Say, do you know Central America very well?

—Fairly well, I . . .

—Peru and northern Bolivia, have you ever been there?

—I've never spent much time down that far.

—Have you ever done any writing?

—Yes, as a matter of fact that's the sort of work I do.

—Ever done motion picture work?

—Never directly, I . . .

—Here, will you take my card, and get in touch with me?

Otto took the card. It said SUN STYLE FILMS in large letters, and R. L. Jones in one corner. —I'm very glad to know you, Otto said, shaking hands. —My name is Otto . . .

—Just write it down here, the man said. Otto wrote.

—When I saw you first, or rather when I heard you talk. Another beer?

—Let me get it, Otto said, reaching in for his wallet. The man paid from his change on the bar.

—What were you doing down there? In South America?

—Writing. But those revolutions . . .

—You were covering a revolution?

Otto thrust his sling forward. —Things got pretty hot down there, he said.

—Is that where . . . something happened to your arm?

—Yes, I . . .

—I didn't want to ask you. You know, I thought it might hurt your feelings, I mean some people are sensitive about things like that.

—Oh, I don't mind talking about it. As a matter of fact, I . . .

—What time is it? said the man looking at his wrist watch. —Is that clock right? I've got to get going. He pulled his hat down in front.

—Haven't you got time for another beer? It's my turn . . .

—I've got to get to the office. Will you call me there?

—Yes, certainly, I'll be delighted . . .

—Don't forget, now. We may be able to work something out.

They shook hands. The man went out. Otto nodded to the bartender. —Could you give me a whisky and soda? he said, and opened his large manila envelope, to study a few pages of his play with minute appreciation. The bartender put a whisky sour down before him. —But I . . .

—Sixty cents, the bartender said. Otto paid.

The trip to MacDougal Street involved two crowded buses and a seething subway. Otto, in good spirits, planned to spend some time with Max, discussing the finer points of his play. Max was not at home. Otto tried to wedge the manuscript into the mailbox, but it was getting badly bent. Then the thought of it getting lost, or stolen (and produced with great acclaim under someone else's name) drove him to summon the janitor. After establishing the thing's value in that dull head he gave it over for delivery, slightly weakened at its loss.

Walking west, he stopped in an Italian grocery to buy cigarettes, was disregarded, tapped his foot loudly, and then pocketed a package from the counter and left.

Hannah passed without a word. She was talking with a tall Negro. Otto looked the other way.

Esme was alone. She had just stopped Chaby in her doorway, telling him it was cold, that he must wear a coat, warming his neck with her arms for a moment and then tying round it a green scarf she found on the floor behind the chair. He was gone when Otto appeared.

Otto and Esme sat quietly for a few minutes, for Esme a content quiet demanding nothing, for him a perilous one, the minutes building up upon themselves like a precarious house of cards waiting to be shattered. She walked about the room singing a frail song, whose words found nothing to bind them together but the free sale of her voice, separated, and were lost. She smiled at him, but shy, when she looked up and saw him watching her. Picking up papers, or hanging a skirt, or simply following the fragments of her song about the room, Esme seemed to show how easy it was being happily alive, to be beautiful, not to question.

Otto sat impatient. Finally he said, —I may have to go to South America.

—Really Otto? she said, charmed.

—Bolivia and northern Peru.

—That would be very nice, she said. —What a silly place to go, Otto.

—I don't see anything so silly about it.

—You must do what *you* want to do.

—It's not as silly as staying in New York. Spending time with people like Chaby. And half-wits like Anselm. And Stanley.

—They are very beautiful people, Esme said.

—Chaby? Beautiful?

—Yes, Otto, she said gently.

—He's a kind of a . . . there's something really low, really disgusting . . .

—He's very unhappy.

—That's his own damned business.

—Please don't swear at me, Otto.

—I wasn't swearing at you, Esme. I'm sorry, I didn't mean . . .

—He was hurt in the war, and that's where he got the bad habit.

—What bad habit?

—Of taking drugs, she said, sober and simple, staring at the floor where the rug ended.

—He's a drug addict? I might have known it.

—It wasn't his fault. They gave him morphine in the war when he was hurt, and that's the way he learned about it.

—Well, enough people came out of the war without being dope fiends.

—Chaby didn't, she said. She looked up, to watch Otto find an ant on the back of his hand, and crush it and roll it into a bit of lifeless dirt with his thumb. Then he said, —Is this one of your poems?

—Yes, she answered, seeing he had picked it up from the bookcase.

—Do you publish them?

—Sometimes. If I like.

He read it.

To a Child, beheld in summer raiment

Little girl, one lesser garment
Will suffice to clothe your crotch,
Hide that undiscovered cavern
Where old Time will wind his watch.

—Where did you get a word like crotch? Otto asked, his voice mocking, shocked (for he was shocked, and this dissembling the only way he knew to evade it).

—I got it.

—But don't you think it's sort of...vulgar? I mean, why crotch?

—It rhymes with watch, Esme explained. —It's a poem. Then, in the tone of a child conspiring, she said, —I wrote a poem for Recktall Brown. It's about him and me. Would you like to read it?

Otto, ready to sulk again, took it from her. —What does *Effluvium* mean?

—That's the title.

—Yes, I see. But what does it mean?

—Why should it mean anything? It's the title.

He read it through, stared at it, and finally managed to say, —I didn't know you knew words like perspicacious.

—It's just a word, Esme said.

—It's a very nice poem.

—It isn't nice at all.

—I'm afraid I don't understand it.

—Why should you understand it?

—But what does it mean?

—What does it *mean*. It just *is*.

One moment he thought she was laughing at him for finding no meaning; the next, that she took him a fool for looking for one. —It sounds hermaphroditic, he said, defensively.

—Her-maph-ro-dit-ic? What is that?

—Someone with the equipment of both sexes.

—Like a succubus?

—Queer. Queerer.

—Queerer than *queer*?

Even now, it was almost dark; and the daybed where he sat stood mounted on the surface of the painted rug, and she outside it, looking on as one looks at an odalisque. Alone in the chair she thought of this, and started to shiver. —What's the matter? he said, and started to get up.

—Don't, don't, she said quickly as though frightened. —Stay there, please. Please.

—But what's the matter?

—I just get cold sometimes, all of a sudden my feet get very cold.

—Esme, about last night . . .

—What did you want to see me about, alone? she asked, seemed to mock him.

—Well, about last night, I wanted to clear up . . .

She sat still, far out of his reach, one leg folded under her. She had lit a cigarette, and its smoke rose between them. He had no wish to clear up the events of the night before: only to repeat it, in the pall of half-light, but while there was still light, light, so he could see. He got up and came to her chair.

—Please sit down, please, where you were, she said, hiding her face. —If we're going to talk I have to be able to see you. The cigarette burned, a protective brand between them. He turned, silent, and looked around, on the chest, on the table. There he picked up a paper, covered with writing in her large open hand. He read, "Baby and I / Were baked in a pie / The gravy was wonderful hot. / We had nothing to pay / To the baker that day / And so we crept out of the pot." —Is this more of your poetry?

—Oh no, Otto. That's a nursery rhyme I used to know.

—What did you write it here for?

—Sometimes I just write things I know, things I remember, because I like to write lovely things.

—I don't see what's so lovely about being baked in a pie.

—Please sit down, she said. But when she put her cigarette out, he crushed his own quickly and reached her before she had time to do more than throw her elbow up before her eyes. He took her shoulders and turned them back until her face fell open to him. Her eyes were larger than he thought they could be, her lips quivering with fear, he kissed her crushing her down with his whole weight. Then like the pickpocket who calls attention to one's arm by bumping it, while his hand slips in to the billfold, Otto distracted the dress covering her breasts with one hand, while his other sought delicately, lower, until it came to uneasy rest in warmth and darkness.

—But your arm? she whispered.

—What arm? She pointed to that sling, come undone. —It's all right, he said, flushing. —It's all right. Esme's thin face had the look of a small terrified animal never assailed, never before held and forced, and now caught in a snare; but a face that asked no pity, no stopping now, only assault, until every terror was consummated. Then she hid her face. —Otto, that thing scratches.

—What thing?

—This, she said, pointing at his mustache, exposing herself, and they went down in the chair again. Something snapped. Esme reached to her shoulder, embarrassed at this interruption of reality. Then, blithe as a little girl who has a secret game, or hiding place, which she shows to only one (or as candidly, one at a time) she led him back to the daybed.

—Esther . . . Otto whispered, and buried himself more deeply on her, forced his head down over her shoulder, pressing the lips that lied into her neck. —*Esme . . .*

As in Chinese fencing, whose contractual positions eliminate the fetters of time, time passed.

—It's a song from *Tosca*, she said, waking in the dark.

—What is?

—The song you wanted to know the name of.

—Song? Then you were dreaming.

—Then I was, she said. —Was it a dream? He felt her feet, very cold, against him. And he held her close to him, smiling. —I dreamt . . . he said, —Now don't you smell it?

—What?

—Lavender. Don't you smell the lavender? A moment of silence, and she said, —What did you dream?

—I dreamt . . . I had a terrible dream. I was at a film with a woman I knew very well, and I was pretending to be blind, with my eyeballs looking way up under the lids. Then I really was blind, and I was walking with a stick with a retracting point. There was cloth over my eyeballs that scratched and hurt, but I didn't seem to be upset. And the woman with me threatened me if I tried to escape her. Then another woman came along, she was very full-breasted, in a tight sort of bodice. We went to the park, and there was someone else there. Who was it? I can't think who it was. But the woman with me led me down a long street, and we came to a movie palace. Then I realized I'd made myself blind. And then the stick split down the middle, and I was there alone. The woman had left me alone. It was terrible.

—I dreamt about someone.

—Who?

—Someone you don't know, she said. Then she said to herself, —He was in a mirror, caught there.

—Now I remember who it was I saw in the park, Otto said.

—Who?

—Someone I used to know, someone you don't know, he said, and saw that pale thin man standing in the park vividly silent, watching him without recognition as he approached, blind, with the stick and its retracting point. —A friend, I used to . . . it's funny, that I miss him.

—But why aren't you missing me! she cried out in a suffocated voice. —I'm here . . . In the dark he felt her shudder, and traced her brow with his finger.

Esme put her head under his chin. He held her, smiling. And in the darkness, he suddenly realized that she could not see his smile, and he relaxed his face, feeling what a strain the smile had been.

She straightened her clothes, getting up, and turned on a light. —Stop *looking* at me, she said.

—You have a lovely body, he said.

—That isn't true.

—It is, it's so slim, almost like a boy's body. Do you ever model?

—Sometimes I do, Esme admitted.

—For fashion magazines? She hesitated, and turned away, looking for a belt. —Yes, that's it, she said, and Otto pursued her no further, busy as he was tying up his bandage which had come loose, exposing a healthy, though pallid, length of forearm. —I like my body because it's just easy to wash, Esme said, and went out, to the communal bathroom.

His hair was rumpled; looking for a mirror, all he found was a medicine chest, the mirror's place filled by a painting of dark abstraction.

—Do you like the painting? she said, coming in behind him.

—Don't you have a mirror?

—Don't you see? There aren't any, she said.

—But why not?

—Mirrors dominate the people. They tell your face how to grow.

—Now Esme, really. Mirrors are made to look in.

—Made to look in? she said. —They are evil, she said, thinking of her own dream now. —To be trapped in one, and they are evil. If you knew what they know. There are evil mirrors where he works, and they work with him, because they are mirrors with terrible memories, and they know, they *know*, and they tell him these terrible things and then they trap him...She was speaking with hysteric speed.

—Esme, he said, holding her. —Now relax Esme, and she reached her arms around him, pulling him down to her as though never to let go.

—Is there a mirror in the bathroom? he asked as he let her go.

—Yes, she whispered.

He tried to take her round the waist again, but she twisted away. —Let me go. I have to hurry, she said.

—Why?

—I have to meet somebody.

—Who?

—Somebody you don't know, she said, suddenly recovered, and as though playing his game with him like a child.

In the communal bathroom, he felt for his wallet in his pocket, then caught his face's image in the mirror: crooked, out of proportion, it looked a stranger to him, because her face in this hour past, searching in it so deeply that his own face was forgotten, all faces other than hers forgotten, her face had become the very image, the definition of a face.

He pulled at the roll of paper on the wall, to wipe away a smudge on his cheek, and that paper rolled out to him with a great creaking, and one small brave passenger, a cockroach, riding like Palinurus piloting the ship of Aeneas, where he went to sleep at the helm and fell overboard, to be murdered by natives ashore.

VII

And as Jesus Christ, of the house of David, took upon himself human nature in order to free and to redeem mankind who were in the bonds of sin because of Adam's disobedience, so also, in our art, the thing that is unjustly defiled by the one will be absolved, cleansed and delivered from that foulness by another that is contrary to it.
—RAYMOND LULLY, *Codicillus*

THAT AFTERNOON, Fuller sat on a bench, his back turned to Central Park in December. Women scuttled past him the bulks of furs, bearing gold and precious ornaments which he watched without envy. He'd only to smile, to yawn, or frankly raise his upper lip and he could show more gold than any of them could wear, even in their most offensive aspirations to taste: jewels by the pound-weight, rings so heavy that they looked like weapons. The cold wind made continuous suggestion to his hat, a narrow-brimmed, imperially high-crowned straw, to join the fuzzy commotion that passed. The hat would have none of it. It was as firm on his head as his right hand on the umbrella, or his left hand holding the leash on the black poodle.

His face remained peacefully arranged until that leash tightened, and then the lines in Fuller's forehead and around his mouth tightened too. When they walked, the leash was taut like a bar holding them apart, instead of a binding tie. The black faces viewed one another with mistrust, but a weary mistrust which had by now settled down to resigned loathing. Though now as Fuller looked down at the dog, there was an element of glee in his expression of disgust. It was cold; and though Fuller was cold, the dog was shivering. Fuller too was inclined to shiver, but refused to give the dog that satisfaction. He sat quite tense, restraining himself, but staring directly at the dog, who could not stop shivering. But the disgust in Fuller's face was evident. He wanted to visit a dear friend, whose office was a bare six blocks off, and sat now considering whether he could get there and back to Mr. Brown's before the cocktail hour. Mr. Brown had gone to the doctor. Sometimes he was late, returning from the doctor. Fuller knew that *he* would be punished if *he* were late. On the other hand, he knew that Mr. Brown would hear about the visit, late or not. That was why Fuller looked at the poodle with troubled eyes now, for he was certain that this poodle and their master communicated, that if he went to see his friend, the poodle would tell on him.

Then he smiled. Today must be different, and he tried to evade the habit of fear. He had his ticket, and tomorrow he would be gone. Mr. Brown would shout for him, the poodle would bark, but he would be far away. This ticket which he carried deeply hidden was the most expensive he had ever got. Its destination must be much nearer home than any of the others.

He looked down to see that the poodle was watching him with that look which seemed to enter his mind and rummage in his memory. Was it learning about the ticket? Fuller stood, pulling the poodle to its feet roughly as it lunged toward a bird alighted near. He set off defiantly toward First Avenue, the witness a taut four feet away.

We would believe that Fuller had had a childhood only in helpless empiricism, because we all have. But it was as unreal to him by now as to anyone looking at his face, where time had long since stopped experimenting. That childhood was like a book read, misplaced, forgotten, to be recalled when one sees another copy, the cheap edition in a railway station newsstand, which is bought, thumbed through, and like as not left on the train when the station is called. The slow train of Fuller's life had made one express dash, when Recktall Brown had found him while on a Caribbean cruise, bought him from himself with something he had prized above life, not having it, this set of gold teeth, and a promise of magic unfulfilled: he was delivered at what seemed to be the last stop, Mr. Brown, Mr. Brown's dog, and Mr. Brown's apartment. That promise of magic, which had appealed so to youth, never materialized, though Fuller did not doubt but what Mr. Brown could make his skin white if he wanted to, a possibility which, grown older, he regarded now more as threat than redemption, and did not speak of it.

The dog hated his singing. Today, in easily understood levity (the ticket), he sang:

—Littel girl, please leave my bachelor room.
Littel girl, littel girl please leave my bachelor room,
You are so brazen, you are so free,
You must proteck your mo-ral-i-ty:
Littel girl, please leave my bachelor room,

as they walked toward Third Avenue, and the elevated train which the dog hated too. Fuller knew this, and always waited at the corner until a train was in sight, pretending to the dog that he was looking into a cigar-store window there.

—Hello mahn, how you goin? Fuller greeted his friend after the pleasant walk (there had been two trains, from opposite directions, passing above them in a roar).

The little mortician shook hands with him. —We had a big one, a . . . I mean we had a big one today, a funeral. Why I have more, there, do you see them all, all those at the end, those flowers, I have more flowers for you than you'll be able to carry, Fuller. He motioned at the tall erectly wired bank of lilies, browning a bit at the edges. Fuller looked distressed.

—I cannot go off with them, mahn.

—But why? I mean, why not?

—It's that Mister Brown, mahn, sayin to me Fuller don't you bring any more of your God-damned corpse bouquets in at this house.

—But in your own room, I mean even in your own room you can't have them?

—No mahn, and he find out some way too if I try. Like the birds, I believe he even know about the birds. Somebody inform on me, I know, he added, looking at the poodle.

—What birds?

—I tell you about that another time, when we not under surveillance. But the gloves? You reserved another selection of gloves for me?

—Yes, I mean I have eight pairs. Eight of them, I mean sixteen. Sixteen gloves, eight pall-bearers I mean. He fetched the gloves, and Fuller looked them over carefully.

—These are very choice, Fuller said holding up one pair. —Very clean and immaculate. I suppose he don't carry the coffin, just walk alongside to be respectable.

—But doesn't he mind the gloves? I mean Mister Brown, he doesn't mind you wearing these gloves that were used to carry the, a . . . well I mean there's no harm in it but some people are peculiar, I mean to serve things wearing these?

—He think I purchase them, said Fuller. —That is how I managin to finance my trip mahn. The money I save.

—Your trip?

—Yes, I fear this is sayin farewell to you. Tomorrow I will be a distance away, goin to my home.

—To the Barbados?

—I plan departin tomorrow in the morning.

—But Fuller, I mean not like the other times, I mean you've started out other times . . .

—I plan departin in the morning, Fuller repeated firmly, speaking to the dog. He put the gloves under his coat. —You still have your Armenium?

—Oh yes, I mean always, he'll always be here.

—It remain a great pity his family cannot have him back, down in the Armenium where they reside, put him in the nice groung of his homeland where he belong to be.

—Seven years. He's been there, I mean, here, seven years. He was here when I bought this store, I mean the business. I write letters to his family, but they can't send money out of Armenia to pay the rent, I mean to pay his . . . my keeping him here like this. I'm not even sure there is such a country as Armenia any more.

—I wish some day I could aid him to return to his homeland, Fuller said, as he put out his hand. —Goodbye, he said. —I leavin you to God to watch over and prokeck you. And the Armenium.

—Goodbye Fuller, come around Thursday night if you can, there's going to be a big . . . I mean . . . The little man had looked forward to the greatest day in his career when Fuller's master was given over to him for the last shave and costuming, and had no doubt Fuller would see that he got the commission. It had never been discussed between them. Nevertheless it was understood. Fuller had rehearsed the scene in his own impatient imagination many times. —Goodbye Fuller, he said, disappointment in his voice. —Send me a picture postcard, Fuller.

The black companions returned to hear their master's voice echoing the words God damn it down the halls. Fuller was greeted with the phrase when they appeared in the doorway.

—God damn it, Fuller. Do you know what time it is? The poodle ran up to his side, where it stood muzzling his hand. —You're late. Where the hell have you been? That God damn undertaker's? Fuller looked at the poodle, who was betraying him even as he stood there.

—I stop to say somebody hello, sar, he admitted.

—Bring in the glasses, Fuller. Then go to bed.

—But Mister Brown I don't mean to . . .

—Bring in the glasses, Fuller.

A few minutes later, Fuller entered, bearing the tray in white-gloved hands, with three glasses, two clean linen towels, and a bucket of ice. He put them on the bar across the room, behind Recktall Brown and Basil Valentine who were sitting before the fireplace. He stood fussing at the bar. Then Recktall Brown realized that he was still in the room, waiting like a hopeful shadow to be assigned some attachment in the light.

—Before you go to bed you'd better give me that ticket, Fuller.

—Ticket, Mister Brown?

—Give me that ticket you bought for Utica New York.

—Ticket please . . . Mister Brown?

—God damn it Fuller, give me that ticket you bought this morning for Utica.

—But Mister Brown I don't mean to . . . Fuller was shaking.

—Fuller!

Fuller reached down into an inside pocket, and drew the ticket out slowly, handed it over. —Now go to bed. And no lights. Remember, no lights.

Fuller looked, at him and then at the poodle, and turned to trudge up the stairs.

—Crazy old nigger's scared of the dark, Recktall Brown said. —He says he's "visited by the most terrible creatures in the whole of history," he laughed, tearing up the ticket to Utica. He threw the bits into the fireplace. —He thinks anywhere must be on the way to Barbados.

—Your occult powers are rather impressive.

—Occult? Recktall Brown grunted the word, and paused his cigar in the air between them abruptly so that its ash fell to the Aubusson carpet like a gray bird-dropping. He looked through his thick lenses and through the smoke: there were moments when Basil Valentine looked sixteen, days when he looked sixty. In profile, his face was strong and flexible; but, when he turned full face as he did now, the narrowness of his chin seemed to sap the face of that strength so impressive an instant before. Temples faintly graying, distinguished enough to be artificial (though the time was gone when anyone might have said premature, and gone the time when it was necessary to dye them so, instead now to tint them with black occasionally), he looked like an old person who looks very young, hair-ends slightly too long, he wore a perfectly fitted gray pinstripe suit, soft powder-blue Oxford-cloth shirt, and a slender black tie whose pattern, woven in the silk, was barely discernible. He raised a gold cigarette case in long fingers. Gold glittered at his cuff.

—How did you know, that he had a ticket for Utica?

—This morning he asks me very carefully, Mr. Brown, do they use United States of America money in a place called Utica? Recktall Brown laughed, and Basil Valentine smiled, took a cigarette from the case, and laid the case on the low table before him. There was a long inscription, worn nearly smooth, on the surface of the gold, and he ran a fingertip over it before leaving the case on the glass-covered painting, on the slender column separating the tableaux *Avaritia* and *Invidia*. He raised his eyes slightly when he lit his cigarette, to the table's center, and blew a stream of smoke toward the underclothed Figure there with its maimed hand upraised. —You keep it too warm in here, he said finally.

—I like it this way.

—Not for you, not for you. I wasn't thinking of you. The paintings, the furniture. This steam heat will warp everything you have.

—Not before I sell them. And what the hell? Whoever buys them puts them up in steam-heated places. Recktall Brown ground an Aubusson rose under heel, turning to cross the room toward the bar. It was a small hexagonal pulpit, furnished with bottles. The carved oak leaves, and the well-pinioned figure of Christ on its face (which gave him occasion to remark, —He was innocent, and they nailed him) were stained with tricklings of gin. —Gin?

—I'd prefer whisky. Basil Valentine did not look up from the magazine he'd drawn toward him and opened again on the table. He studied the reproduction on the two-page spread of the centerfold, and his lips moved. Then he pushed the open *Collectors Quarterly* away and stood abruptly, to demand: —Is he always this late? accepting the glass from the heavy hand mounting the two diamonds.

—Nervous? Brown laughed, a sound which stopped in his throat, and sank back in a chair. —With somebody like him you can't expect...

—You've been quite successful in your efforts to keep me from meeting him, Basil Valentine interrupted. —One might think...

—Just watch your step with him, Recktall Brown muttered from the chair he filled, and Valentine, muttering something himself, turned his back and flung his cigarette into the fireplace, and stood looking at the carved letters beneath the mantel.

The chimney piece was a massive Elizabethan affair, ponderous like the rest of the furniture, the chairs standing out from the carpeting which stretched from wall to wall, and the two refectory tables, giving the place the look of an exclusive gentlemen's club; but only at first glance: for Recktall Brown, owner and host, was implicit everywhere. More than one guest had been provoked to make obvious remarks on the generic likeness between the head of the wart hog, mounted high on one wall, and the portrait of the host hung across the room. And even though he had been rallied often enough over that portrait (when he had been drinking), Recktall Brown would not remove it. Instead he could pause and look at it with fond veneration. They looked, too, over his shoulder, but none could find the youth he reverenced there. Instead they saw an unformed likeness of the face turned from them, ears protruding but erect, only the hands too similar. There were other paintings, especially the Patinir on the other side of the doorway, in whose neighborhood this portrait would at best have been an intrusive presence; but there was something in the thing itself which made it absurd, though it took a moment to realize what had happened. It had been painted from a photograph (the sitter too busy to sit more than that instant of the camera's eye) in which his hands, found in the foreground by the undiscriminating lens, were marvelously enlarged. The portrait painter, directed to copy that photograph faithfully and neither talented, nor paid enough, to do otherwise, had with attentive care copied the hands as they were in the picture. And pausing, passing it hundreds of times in the years since, often catching up one hand in the other before him, his hands came to resemble these in the portrait, filling out large and heavy, so apparently flaccid that they had been referred to once, and repeated by other voices in other rooms, as prehensile udders. And the diamond ring? It appeared; though none but himself knew that its double gleam had been added long after the paint of the portrait was dry.

Year after year, the painting and the wart hog hung, avoiding each other's eyes across the waves of pestilential heat that always filled that room.

—Damn her! Valentine brought out, turning suddenly. —That dog, lying there, licking her . . . self, can't you discourage these disgusting little attentions in public? He stood looking impatiently at the black shape on the roses, as though expecting some sharp defense from her owner, and when there was none, brought his eyes for a moment to the cloud of smoke rising shapeless from the chair, and the dark amorphous pools behind the thick lenses: Recktall Brown just looked at him, and he brought his narrow black-shod feet together and sat down. A moment later he was leaning forward again, studying the reproduction in *Collectors Quarterly*, his hands drawn up under his chin, and he appeared to kiss the gold seal ring he wore on a little finger.

—What time is it? Brown asked abruptly.

—After four, Basil Valentine murmured, then looked up to repeat sharply, —after four. He's probably drunk somewhere.

—He doesn't do that kind of thing, going out on a drunk and getting into trouble, I already told you, he's . . .

—Yes, you've told me, you've told me what a . . . aren't you fortunate! Most artists have a great lunk of a man they trail around with them, they never know what to do with him, he gets drunk, gets into trouble with the law, women, money . . . yes. Aren't you fortunate! having a protégé with no animal self.

Recktall Brown started to speak, but subsided. His own hands embraced in his short wide lap, the diamonds glittering uppermost, he watched Valentine trace a contour in the picture with the tip of a little finger, then reach out to push away the ashtray whose smoldering cigar was sending an even current of smoke over the hand and up the arm: Valentine blew at the smoke pettishly, and asked, —How old is he?

—He's about thirty-three now. He looks more my age.

—He never goes to the showings, does he? When these paintings appear. I imagine I might have known him if he had.

—I don't know why not either. Brown laughed to himself, leaning forward with effort to take the cigar and throw it into the fireplace. —You'd think he'd get a kick out of them, seeing these important old maids blubbering over his pictures, these critics...

—Yes... Their eyes met for a moment, and Basil Valentine smiled. —It's heartbreaking to watch, isn't it. They are all so fearfully serious. But of course that's just what makes it all possible. The authorities are so deadly serious that it never occurs to them to doubt, they cannot wait to get ahead of one another to point out verifications. The experts...

—You said you came here for business. What is it? Brown said, not listening. He took off his glasses and lowered his sharp eyes to Basil Valentine who, as though knowing him to be near sightless this way, looked into Brown's eyes with a penetration which seemed to freeze the blue of his own.

—I'd prefer to wait until he gets here, he said calmly. —Strictly speaking, it's rather more than a matter of business, he went on as Brown rubbed his eyes and put his glasses on again. —It's really quite a challenge, a piece of work that will really challenge his genius.

Brown looked up through the thick lenses. —It damn near is genius.

—Talent often is, if frustrated for long enough. Today, at any rate, most of what we call genius around us is simply warped talent.

—Look, don't waste this kind of clever talk on me. Did you come here for business? or just because you want to meet...

—Of course, Valentine cut in, his voice stronger, —I am impatient to meet anyone capable of such work. Not an instant of the anxiety one always comes upon in... such work. To be able to move from the painstaking, meticulous strokes of Bouts to the boldness of van der Goes. Incredible! this... he motioned at the open reproduction, —slight uncertainty of a tremendous passion, aiming at just a fraction more than he could ever accomplish, poor fellow.

—Who?

—Van der Goes. He died mad, you know. Settled down in a convent, working and drinking. He believed himself eternally damned, finally ran about telling everyone about it. Such exquisite flowers he painted. And such, magnificent hands, Basil Valentine added, looking at his own.

Recktall Brown had taken out a cigar, and he opened his gold-plated pen-knife. —I don't want any slips, he said, trimming the cigar. —He's already done three by this same one, this van Gogh...

—Van Gogh!...

—You just said...

—Good heavens, Brown! Valentine stood up, with the gold cigarette case. —My dear fellow, he could no more paint van Gogh than he could fly. Valentine laughed, walking out into the room, watching his narrow black shoes on the carpet. —But the minute another van der Goes appears they rush off to compare it with the last one he did. They're never disappointed. You know, he added, turning away abruptly as he approached the black shape of the dog, —his work is so good it has almost been taken for forgery.

—What do you mean by that?

—By the lesser authorities, of course. The ones who look at paintings with twentieth-century eyes. Styles change, he mused, and stood looking up the wall behind the bar at the extensive wool tapestry hung there, originally intended to warm and decorate the bleak stone interior of some northern castle, here concealing well-heated paneling. The figures in this tapestry were engaged in some sort of hunt, or sylvan picnic, it was difficult to tell in this light. Their eyes were apparent, however, all turned in one direction, all staring at the portrait of Recktall Brown, as though arrested by its presence, and the gaze which it did not return: a flock of hard eyes, disdaining those fixed upon them now. And as though aware of their scorn, Valentine turned his back on them.

—Taste changes, he went on in an irritating monotone. —Most forgeries last only a few generations, because they're so carefully done in the taste of the period, a forged Rembrandt, for instance, confirms everything that that period sees in Rembrandt. Taste and style change, and the forgery is painfully obvious, dated, because the new period has discovered Rembrandt all over again, and of course discovered him to be quite different. That is the curse that any genuine article must endure. He had walked up behind the chair where Recktall Brown sat with thick calves extended baronially toward the fireplace, and stood looking down at the back of Brown's head and the heavy folds of flesh over the back of the collar. Nothing moved there, but for slight twitches of the cigar as it shifted among uneven teeth. Valentine ground the knuckles of one open hand in the palm of the other, and turned away. The quickness of his movements might have indicated an extreme nervousness, but for his restraint, moving away now with the disciplined motions of a diver, every turn to some purpose, though he simply walked down the room again, and came back saying, —And incidentally, you needn't give another thought to that contretemps with the Dalner Gallery.

—What happened?

—You remember, about three months ago they questioned one of his pictures, the small Bouts, said it was a palpable fake? Though what made them say that I cannot imagine, unless they wanted to discredit it and bring the price down. Dalner has done that before. At any rate, last week they questioned the authenticity of a di Credi belonging to a very important person, who shall be nameless. He sued for slander, and they're settling out of court.

The broken weights of Recktall Brown's laughter ascended in heavy smoke which rose to the silent spaces, and drifted toward the balcony across one end of the two-story room.

—Dalner won't say a word about these van der Goes'. These vulgar attempts at honesty prove too expensive, Valentine went on. —And as for where they come from, Dalner respects secrecy as much as we do. So long as people are afraid of being found out, you have them in the palm of your hand. And everyone is, of course. How touching...

—I just got hold of...

—How touching it is, when their secrets turn out to be the most pathetic commonplaces, Valentine finished from the middle of the room.

—I just got hold of a Memling. An original.

—Eh? How? Where?

—An original Memling, right from Germany. A guy I know in the army there, this thing has been marked down as lost on the reparations claims.

—You're certain it's genuine?

—Their Pinakothek over there has a stack of papers on it.

—Papers? You know how much papers mean.

—Don't worry, the papers on this are all right.

—Papers are always all right, when they're modern affidavits. Where is it now? If the experts...

—The experts! Brown said, and laughed again. He did not move, nor did his unpupiled eyes betray any surprise when Valentine moved from behind him with such sudden irritation that it might have been an assault, though he went no further than to pick up his drink from the table and finish it.

—You don't have to tell me, of course, Valentine said. —It's probably safe in your little private gallery behind that panel, he added, glancing beyond the refectory tables to the far end of the room as he crossed again to the bar.

—It's safe.

—This remarkable room, Valentine murmured, pouring whisky and looking round. —It's a pity, your taste, when you show any, seems to incline to German. He was looking at the polychrome figure of Saint John Baptist in a niche on the stairway, proportioned to stand on a pier of some German cathedral at considerable height, so that the head was unnaturally large and the eyes widened in what, at such closeness, amounted to a leer. The right arm, once extended in gesture of benediction, was broken off, leaving only the close-grained scar of the elbow's wooden marrow.

Recktall Brown shifted his weight; raised his glass, and his eyes to the balcony. —That suit of armor up there, it's Italian, it's not a fake either. That's my favorite thing here. Italian fifteenth century.

—I've looked at it. Pity it isn't all there.

—What do you mean, it's all there.

—But not all Italian. The footpieces. German. Clumsy German bear-paw as can be.

—It's my favorite thing here, Brown repeated, and put down an empty glass. Then he sat tapping his foot silently on the carpeted floor, and the fingers of one hand on the leather arm of the chair. He filled the air before him with smoke, a shapeless cloud of gray exhaled, through which the untasted smoke rising from the end of his cigar cut a clear blue line.

—You shouldn't inhale those things, Basil Valentine said, returning to his chair. —Throat cancer. And Brown laughed again, a single guttural sound which barely reached the surface. A weight seemed to slide back and forth between these two men; and though Basil Valentine will say, sooner or later, —We are, I suppose, basically in agreement . . . , affirming the fact that most argument is no more than agreement reached at different moments, it was these instants of reversal, when the weight was ready to return, that the one who rose to cast it off did so tensely, as though afraid that when it had fallen to him, it had slid for the last time. They talked now in tones which recognized those of the other, and treated with accordingly, desultory tones and cursory remarks which might come close upon but never touch the eventuality which both appeared to await.

—And what news of the publishing empire?

—If you mean that book about art you wrote, I've already sent out advance copies. Brown threw the half-finished cigar into the fireplace. The dog, on the floor beside his chair, started, at the sudden motion of his arm; and Valentine, as though drawn to it, put a hand forth to the open magazine as Brown, settling back, arrested the shiny pages with splayed fingers. —That's a nice reproduction, he said.

—No reproduction is nice. Valentine sat back, and folded his empty hands closely, one seeking the other before him. —Attempts to spread out two square feet of canvas to cover twenty acres of stupidity.

—All these God-damned little details, Brown muttered.

—Much more apparent in the Bouts he did, of course. Exquisite control of brilliant colors, the ascetic restraint in the hands and the feet. Valentine extended his legs, and crossed his ankles.

—They looked like every hair was painted on separately.

—It was, of course.

—This part is nice. Recktall Brown made a curve over the picture with the flat of his thumb. —The expression of her face.

—That...

—You...

—Please, your... thumb is rather like a spatula, isn't it. But here, Valentine went on quickly, before Brown could answer in a way that a shudder of his shoulders suggested, —the flesh tones in this are incredible, even in reproduction. This ashen whiteness, and the other large masses of color, a marvelously subdued canvas. This is the sort of thing he painted late in his life. When his mind was beginning to go.

—Who?

—Who do you think I mean, your protégé?

—I like this face. He ran his thumb over that portion. The diamonds glittered; and Basil Valentine raised a hand toward it, but restrained the hand and returned it empty to the other. Brown repeated the motion with his thumb.

—It's insured?

—For fire and theft.

—For fraud?

That brought Recktall Brown's face up. —Fraud? he repeated. —Fraud? Then he laughed. —They could never prove a thing. Nobody could. After these experts went over it with their magnifying glasses...

—I know, I watched them. I even helped them along, you know, Valentine smiled. —Examining a fragment the size of a pinhead with polarized light under a microscope, to determine whether it's isotropic or anisotropic, boring through the layers of paint...

—There's no way anybody could prove a God-damned thing wrong here. There's no proof anywhere. But the insurance, the only thing they won't insure against is if something happens to it all by itself. In the paint.

—Inherent vice.

—What?

—They hardly need worry about something this... old? The care that goes into these, still... the three-legged man of Velasquez? Never mind. As paint ages, it becomes translucent, and work which has been altered occasionally shows through. But of course no one will insure against inherent vice. A lot of our moderns make sudden changes dictated by the total uncertainty of what they're doing, which they call inspiration, and paint over them. The paint breaks up quite soon, of course.

Brown was looking down at the well-manicured fingertips which rested on the corner of the magazine as Valentine, his feet uncrossed and drawn together, twisted to look again at the reproduction. —What did you call it?

—Inherent vice, said Basil Valentine, looking up. His eyes were seized instantly by those which offered no centers to evade. —No one insures against inherent vice, he repeated evenly. *Collectors Quarterly* was abruptly shoved toward him. Recktall Brown sat back; one hand was closed like a fist round an unlit cigar.

—Sorry, Valentine said to him offering, with a gesture, to return the magazine, —if you're not finished?...

Recktall Brown looked at him, and asked suddenly, —That ring, what is it? Where'd you get it?

—This? My dear fellow, you've seen it a thousand times. A seal ring. It might be the seal of a very old family.

—Very old family! Brown muttered, looking away.

—With a motto, Valentine persisted, —like the one you're looking at now. Dominus providebit? He glanced at the chimney piece. —Yes..., sat back and lit a cigarette. He blew its light smoke out over the table, and extended his left hand on the arm of the chair. Golden hairs glistened faintly on the flesh there. —Gold rings were the peculiar ornament of Roman knights, you know. It was the way they distinguished themselves from the plebs.

Recktall Brown stood up. He was silent until he'd poured himself another drink. Then he demanded, —Why do you have to talk to him about this idea you've got? You didn't even talk to me about it yet.

—It's nothing to excite yourself about, yet. Simply an idea for another piece of work he might try, if he thinks he's up to it. Little good our talking about it until we know how he feels. You and he must be quite thick after all this time, he added as Brown returned across the room.

—I don't think he probably sees anybody but me any more.

—Scintillating social life. Do you talk?

—I can sit with him and not talk. Recktall Brown sat down, and stared at the low table before him. —I never knew anybody like that before. But we talk, he recovered. —When there's business, we talk.

Basil Valentine smoothed the hair-ends at the back of his head with his fingertips. —You must drive him mad, don't you? Insisting on business, business, business.

—Somebody has to nail him down to it. What the hell's wrong with that? When he looks like he forgets what he's doing. What the hell, when you're doing work like he is, you can lose contact with things, finally you don't have a real sense of reality.

—If he ever did, of course. You know, Brown, if by any stretch of imagination I could accuse you of being literary, I might accuse you of sponsoring this illusion that one comes to grips with reality only through the commission of evil. It's all the rage. Basil Valentine sat running his thumb over the worn inscription on his gold cigarette case, and looking at Recktall Brown, who had returned his gaze to his ankles, thick under black silk, with white clocks, before him. —How is it I haven't met him, in all this time? he asked finally.

—A lot of reasons.

—A lot of reasons?

—I don't want you to interfere with him, Recktall Brown said.

—Interfere?

—I just don't want you to get him mixed up, Brown said speaking rapidly. He strained forward to reach his glass.

—You know, Valentine said hunching behind his cigarette, —you speak as though he were a possession of some sort. Like Fuller . . . or this creature. He motioned at the dog, which had raised a leg and commenced to lick herself again. —The one really unbearable thing about females, isn't it. All of them, always so wet.

—I just don't want him upset from his work.

Basil Valentine stood up. —You do have some odd notions about me, don't you.

—I don't have any notions about anybody. This is work.

—You know, Brown, you seem to be under the same misapprehension that most people spend their lives under. That things stay as they are. I'm surprised at you, I am really. He sat back against the arm of his chair. —Tell me, he went on concisely, —just how would you expect me to interfere with him?

—I don't expect you to, so don't. Just don't get him started with your smart remarks, and these smart-aleck sayings in foreign languages the Jesuits taught you, that nobody understands but you, and . . . you know God damn well what I mean now. He has to stick to business. Recktall Brown drank, and sat holding his glass and looking straight ahead.

—You never have music here, do you.

—It makes me nervous.

—Yes. Yes, I think I understand. Tell me . . . Basil Valentine paused. —Do you think . . . Is he happy, do you think, doing this work?

—Happy? Brown asked, looking up for the first time in some minutes. —He has enough money to fly to the moon if he wants to.

Basil Valentine smiled, and nodded. —Carmina vel caelo, he commenced in precise syllables, as the doorbell rang, and Recktall Brown spilled his drink on *Invidia*, putting the glass down on the table of the Seven Deadly Sins.

—Charms can even bring the moon down from heaven. Sometimes, my dear fellow, he went on speaking to Recktall Brown's back as it receded across the room, —I cannot believe that you have ever really studied your Vergil. Then as he sat staring, his eyes again lost their liquid quality of agreeable indifference. He drew his hands up under his chin, so that the gold seal ring on the little finger of his left hand almost touched his lips. He did not move until he heard a voice in the outside hall. —What did you... why did you want me to get out, and come all the way up here?

—Business, my boy. Business.

By the time they entered, Basil Valentine had got to a downstairs bathroom, where he washed his hands. He dried them slowly, looking at himself in the mirror as he did so. Then he smoothed the hair at the back of his head with his fingertips, paused to pull downwards at the sides of his trousers (as a woman does before entering a room, straightening her girdle), and came out to them with his well-manicured hand extended in introduction.

For Basil Valentine, who was conscious of the disposition of every lineament of his face, and whose expressions were controlled to betray no more than he wished, a face to which surprise came with cultivated precaution, this face before him was a shock. Though still as his own, it seemed to be in constant movement, neither wonder nor bewilderment but the instant of surprise sustained, surprise perhaps not for the things and occurrences before it, but at its own constant exposure. The hand Valentine clasped was quickly withdrawn, recovered like a creature which its master dared not leave at large. —How do you do, I... I thought you were Fuller when I... just now. Recktall Brown stood with a hand on his shoulder. —I'm just... used to seeing Fuller here.

—I'm awfully sorry, I fear there's nothing I can do about that. Even Fuller's command of the language is quite beyond me, Basil Valentine said, and then the smile left his face, for he realized that the man had turned his back and was walking toward one of the chairs before the fireplace, where he stood looking down at the table, and placed there the book he carried before he sat down.

—Where is Fuller? he asked. He looked up at them, and Basil Valentine stopped, looking into the sunken green eyes staring from among the lines of the face which turned immediately from him to Recktall Brown, who said, —Fuller's busy.

—What are you... are you punishing him again?

—He's working on some crucifixes, Recktall Brown said to both of them.

—He's got twenty ivory ones up there, perfect thirteenth century, softened in vinegar to be cut, and hardened up in water. I told him if he wants his prayers to come true all he has to do is rub them with a sweaty hand. I guess a nigger's sweat will yellow them up as good as any.

—You're not concerned about Fuller's ... trustworthiness? Valentine said.

—He doesn't know what he's doing. I gave him a big frame and told him to rub bird crap into the wormholes and hang it up in this chimney, you should have seen him. Christ only knows where he gets the bird crap. He brings it in in little white packages. Recktall Brown stood, unwrapping a cigar as he spoke.

Basil Valentine offered a cigarette across the table, took one himself and laid the case there between them. Then he held a light, waiting.

—The eggs. He did get me the eggs, did he?

—Your fresh country eggs, laid yesterday. They're in the hall, but why the hell they have to be just laid within a matter of hours ...

—Yes, yes, they do. They do. They have to be fresh.

—Egg tempera? Basil Valentine asked, holding the light.

—Why ... why yes, how did you know? He looked at Valentine only long enough to get the light, and then turned to Recktall Brown with an expression which asked the same question. Brown was, for the moment, obscured by smoke himself. Basil Valentine took the opportunity to study the man seated across from him. His hair, closely cut, showed the lines of his skull clearly, a skull of squarish proportions. The dark unpadded jacket hung from shoulders which looked barely able to support it. The fingertips, too, were squared, tapping together in the smoke from the cigarette, the narrow tightly packed Virginia tobacco which Valentine preferred, lying in the ashtray between them.

Brown emerged from the cigar smoke and sat down unsteadily. —You look like hell, he said to him.

Basil Valentine watched him closely. He was staring down at the table, and his lips barely moved, shaping *Soberbia, Ira, Lujuria, Pereza* ... —That's because I'm ... I've been working like hell, he said looking at Basil Valentine, a quick anxious look cast up like his words which were separate immediate sounds. When neither of them spoke he said, —You keep it too hot in here, and looked up at Brown as though to provoke him to explain everything which this observation did not include. Brown grinned. —For the art? he demanded.

—It's just too hot. This dead steam heat. He looked down again.

—Now that you finally got here, Brown said, —we can get started.

—Yes, I was late. I was asleep.

—Sleeping now? Brown demanded.

—Yes, I ... I work at night, you know that, and I ... You can't imagine how hungry I get for the night to come sometimes, he said suddenly, looking up at them both. —Sometimes it seems like it...won't come at all, so I try to sleep. Waiting for it. When I was in school, a schoolboy, he went on rapidly, —we had this written on our report cards, "Here hath been dawning another blue day. Think! Wilt thou let it slip useless away?" Do you understand? That's...it's quite upsetting, that "another blue day"...Do you understand? he said, looking at Valentine. Then he looked down at the magazine opened in Valentine's lap. —That...I didn't know...I hadn't seen that reproduction.

—Sit down, my boy, relax, we...

—I...excuse me just a minute. He left them sitting there, and hurried toward the door where Basil Valentine had gone a few minutes before.

—You know, Valentine murmured, holding the color reproduction up before him, —it's not at all difficult to understand now, why he never comes to these showings.

—What do you mean?

—Look at this. He's stepped right out of the canvas.

—O.K., just don't get him started on it. You see what I mean about this, this "another blue day" stuff? You have to be careful, or he'll end up like this van...van... Recktall Brown motioned at the opened pages with the diamond-laden hand.

—It's all right, my dear fellow. You may say van Gogh. Van Gogh went mad too. Quite, quite mad. Valentine leaned forward and laid the magazine on the table.

They both glanced up when he returned, by way of the pulpit across the room where he stopped to get a bottle of brandy and a glass. These he placed on the table beside the book he had brought in, and picked up the *Collectors Quarterly*. He read the caption half aloud, —"...that most characteristic expression of the genius of Flemish art, which seems to enliven us with increased powers of eyesight, in this recently discovered painting, *The Descent from the Cross*, by the late fifteenth-century master Hugo van der Goes..." That's...well you can't really say "most characteristic," whoever...

—Valentine here wants to...

—But "increased powers of eyesight," I've seen that somewhere. Yes, it gives that sense of projecting illumination, instead of receiving it from outside, do you...don't you read it that way?

—Yes. I wrote it, said Basil Valentine, looking him in the eyes.

—You wrote it? he repeated.

—I meant it, too. I congratulate you.

—Then you know it's mine? That this is mine? He flattened his hand against the page on the table.

—My dear fellow, "If the public believes that a picture is by Raphael, and will pay the price of a Raphael," Valentine said, offering a cigarette, —"then it is a Raphael."

The cigarette was accepted heedlessly. —Yes, I . . . but the reproductions, they don't . . . I haven't seen this one, but they're a bad thing all round, they . . . here, you can see, this space right here, it loses almost all its value, because the blue, it doesn't quite . . . it isn't . . .

—Not bad, for a reproduction, Valentine said, watching him pour brandy into his glass. —But I've looked at the thing itself, and it is magnificent. It is, almost perfect. Perfect van der Goes.

—Yes, but I . . . it isn't that simple, you know. I mean, the thing itself, van der Goes, he repeated, his hand covering the sky behind the Cross, —this is . . . mine.

—Yours? Basil Valentine said, smiling, and watching him as he sat down. —You work at night, then, do you?

—Yes, I usually do now.

—This element of secrecy, it becomes rather pervasive, does it?

—No. No, don't start that. That's what they used to say, so don't say that. It isn't so simple. He drank off some of the brandy. —It's the same sense . . . yes, this sense of a blue day in summer, do you understand? It's too much, such a day, it's too fully illuminated. It's defeating that way, it doesn't allow you to project this illumination yourself, this . . . selective illumination that's necessary to paint . . . like this, he added, indicating the picture.

—Seeing you now, you know, it's answered one of the questions I've had on my mind for some time. The first thing I saw, it was a small Dierick Bouts, I wondered then if you used a model when you worked.

—Well I . . .

—But now, it's quite obvious isn't it, Valentine went on, nodding at the picture between them. —Mirrors?

—Yes, yes of course, mirrors. He laughed, a constricted sound, and lit a cigarette.

—You have one, you know, Basil Valentine said, watching him levelly as he started, looked at the cigarette in his hand, and crushed it out for the one he had just accepted. —You're very tired, aren't you.

—Yes. Yes, I am, I . . . I've been tired for a long time.

—Don't you sleep?

—I do, sometimes. During the day sometimes.

—Well, my dear fellow, Valentine said, sitting up straight and smiling, —I don't either. I think Brown here is probably the only one of us who does enjoy the sleep of the just.

—Do you dream? he asked abruptly.

—Dream? Good heavens no, not in years. And you?

—I? Why no. No, no. No, I haven't had a dream in ... some time.

—You haven't explained all this to me yet, you know, Basil Valentine said, raising his eyes from the picture, which he pushed forward with his right hand, and a glitter of gold at his cuff. —The Virgin.

—The Virgin? he repeated, staring across the table.

—Yes, here for instance. She really dominates this whole composition.

—Yes, she does. She does.

Valentine waited, watching him. —Exquisite repose in her face, he murmured, finally. —Do you find that with mirrors too?

—I ... she ... he stammered, picking up his glass.

Recktall Brown stood up, with great alacrity considering his stature and the heavy immobile presence he had presented, deep in the armchair, an instant before. He was a little unsteady on his feet, but his eyes swimming behind the glasses seemed to jell, and his voice rose sternly when he spoke. He had, all this time, been looking from one to the other of the two men before him, gauging their effect upon one another. —I'll answer that, and then we'll get down to business, he said. —This model he uses is a kid I got for him, she came up trying to sell us a book of crazy poems once. This repose she gets, she just isn't all there. He raised a naked hand. —Sit down, my boy, and be quiet. We've wasted half the God damn afternoon as it is, waiting for you. He turned to Basil Valentine, raising the left hand, with the diamonds, and the cigar which dropped its ash on *Gula*, gluttony, before him. —Valentine here has an idea for the next thing you're going to do, but first I want to know when you're going to finish the one you're fooling around with down there now.

—Fooling around? Fooling around?

—All right, my boy, God damn it, working on. Look, I've bought a farm up in Vermont. The family that built the place came over from England in the seventeenth century, they had plenty of money, they made bricks. They brought over everything they owned. There were about a dozen lousy paintings there when I bought the place, none of them worth more than twenty bucks, Valentine says, and some frames I want you to look at, little oak ones with red and green velvet in them around the inside, maybe you can squeeze something in. I'm going to stock this place and sell it at auction in two weeks, and this last thing of yours can be discovered there if you finish it in time. He paused. —What do you say?

Basil Valentine had started to rise, but let himself down in the chair again without making a sound, his lips open to show his teeth drawn tight together, and turned his eyes down to see the man across from him lower his eyes and seem to wilt, silent, and appearing not to breathe. Valentine waited, and then said gently, —The one you're working on now, another van der Goes?

—Yes, yes it is. He looked up, and drew a deep breath.

—What is it, the subject?

—I...I...it was going to be an *Annunciation*, that, because they're...well have you ever seen a bad one? I mean by any painter? He held his hands in the air before him, the fingertips almost touching. —It's almost as though...just the idea of the *Annunciation*, a painter can't...no painter could do it badly.

—The *Annunciation*? Valentine looked troubled.

—No, I...it isn't. I was going to, I wanted to, but then I got started on this other...this other idea took form and...

—What is it, then?

—It's a...the death of the Virgin.

—But there is one, you know, a splendid one of van der Goes, it's in Brussels I think, isn't it?

—Yes, yes, I know it, I know that one. It is splendid, that one. But this one, this one I've done is later, painted later in his life, when the shapes...

—Is it nearly done? Brown demanded, standing over them.

—Yes, it is. It's more than finished, really, he said looking up at Brown.

—More than finished?

—Yes, I...you know, it's finished, it has to be...damaged now.

—That must be difficult, Basil Valentine said.

—It is, it's the most difficult part. Not the actual damaging it, but damaging it without trying to preserve the parts that cost such...well, you know that's where they fail, a good many...painters who do this kind of work, they can't resist saving those parts, and anyone can tell, anyone can tell.

—You call me as soon as it's done then, do you hear me? Brown said, sitting down. He finished his drink quickly. —And we'll get started on the next one now. Valentine's here to...

—I...damn it, you can't just...He looked up at Basil Valentine. —He talks to me as though it was like making patent medicine. He...

—All right my boy, I...

—He heard a Fra Angelico had sold somewhere for a high price once, and he thought I should do a Fra Angelico, toss off a Fra Angelico...

—All right now...

—Like making patent medicine. He turned to Brown. —Do you know why I could never paint one, paint a Fra Angelico? Do you know why? Do you know how he painted? Fra Angelico painted down on his knees, he was on his knees and his eyes full of tears when he painted Christ on the Cross. And do you think I...do you think I...

—Control yourself now, for Christ sake. We have work to do.

—Work? Work? Do you think I . . . as though I spend my time down there flying balloons . . .

—"That vice may merit, 'tis the price of toil," Basil Valentine said, stretching his arms and smiling as he looked at both of them.

—All right, Valentine, what is it now? What is this thing of yours?

—Not mine, my dear Brown. Pope. Alexander Pope. "'But sometimes virtue starves, while vice is fed,' What then? Is . . ."

—Not that, God damn it. This idea . . .

The telephone rang. There was an extension in the hallway, as well as the one near the bar, and Recktall Brown went to the hallway extension.

—He would absolutely have to have Alexander Pope in a box, to enjoy him. He is beyond anything I've ever come upon. Honestly, I never in my life could have imagined that business could live so powerfully independent of every other faculty of the human intelligence. Basil Valentine rested his head back, blowing smoke toward the ceiling, and watching it rise there. —Earlier, you know, he mentioned to me the idea of a novel factory, a sort of assembly line of writers, each one with his own especial little job. Mass production, he said, and tailored to the public taste. But not so absurd, Basil Valentine said sitting forward suddenly.

—Yes, I . . . I know. I know.

—When I laughed . . . but it's not so funny in his hands, you know. Just recently he started this business of submitting novels to a public opinion board, a cross section of readers who give their opinions, and the author makes changes accordingly. Best sellers, of course.

—Yes, good God, imagine if . . . submitting paintings to them, to a cross section? You'd better take out . . . This color . . . These lines, and . . . He drew his hand down over his face, —You can change a line without even touching it. No, he went on after a pause, and Valentine watched him closely, —nothing is funny in his hands. Everything becomes very . . . real.

—Oh, he's given you some of his lectures too? "Business is co-operation with reality," that one? The one on cleaning fluid, a chemical you can buy for three cents a gallon, which he sold at a quarter a six-ounce bottle? His chalk toothpaste? The breakfast cereal he made that gave people spasms of the colon? Has he told you about the old woman who got spastic colitis from taking a laxative he made, a by-product of heaven knows what. They threw her case out of court. A riotous tale, he entertains with it when he's been drinking. He still makes a pretty penny from some simple chemical that women use for their menstrual periods, such a delicate necessity that the shame and secrecy involved make it possible to sell it at some absurd price . . .

—Yes, the secrecy.

—What?

—These paintings, selling these paintings, the secrecy of it.

Valentine chuckled. —Of course, he couldn't do any of it alone. Other people do his work for him, get his ideas for him. Who do you think launched this picture here in this country? He motioned to the open reproduction. —Did you read about it?

—Where?

—In the papers. No, you probably never see the newspaper, at that. He didn't tell you, then? He wouldn't, of course. It might interfere.

—Interfere? with what?

—With your work, of course, he's quite frantic about protecting you. I've gathered you're quite as dedicated as those medieval forgers of classical antiquities. Valentine was speaking rapidly and with asperity. —True to your art, so to say?

—True to . . . yes, that's like saying a man's true to his cancer.

—Don't be upset, don't concern yourself with him, with his explanations of reality.

—But that's what's so strange, it makes so much sense at first, and then if you listen, you . . . Yes, he understands reality.

—He does not understand reality. Basil Valentine stood up, still, grasping his lapels, and looked down to the lowered face across the table. —Recktall Brown is reality, he said, and after a pause where neither of them moved, turned on a toe and idled out into the room. —A very different thing, he added, over his shoulder, and stopped to light a cigarette.

Recktall Brown's voice reached them in the separate phrases of telephone conversation, —Not a dollar more, God damn it . . . , at one point, at another, —God damn it, not a dollar less.

—But let me tell you about discovering this van der Goes. It might amuse you. It was taken to London, secretly of course, and modified with tempera before it was brought back to America, a crude job of overpainting on a glue finish, which would wash right off. It was such an obvious bad job that even customs discovered it. As much as it pained them, poor fellows, since they collect ten per cent on anything they can prove is a copy or an imitation. But there was the genuine, duty-free, original work of art underneath. As a matter of fact, I was called in to help verify it. You see how much we trust your work. And of course everyone respected the owner's "business secret" about where he'd got it. After that incident people were predisposed to accept it.

—But . . . why? There's no law, is there, against . . .

—Not a question of law, my dear fellow, Valentine said returning to the table. —Publicity. Publicity.

—But, a thing like this, a ... painting like this ...

—A painting like this or a tube of toothpaste or a laxative which induces spastic colitis. You can't sell any of them without publicity. The people! Valentine turned away again, and commenced to walk up and down. He was talking more rapidly, in precisions of irritation as though he did not dare stop, for fear of an argument being rejected before he reached its point, or hesitate, and waste a precious instant before Brown's return. Even the Latin came with native sharpness from his tongue when he said, —You recall the maxim, Vulgus vult decipi, ergo decipiatur? Yes, if they want to be deceived, let them be deceived. Have you looked at his hands? he demanded, stopping abruptly at the edge of the table. —At Brown's hands, when he sits with them folded in his lap? And those diamonds? Like a great soft toad, "... ugly and venomous, wears yet a precious jewel in his head"?

—But, all this ...

—Yes, think of the tradition you have behind you, Valentine went on, turning his back. —Lucius Mummius, and that famous story in which he charges the men carrying his plunder from Corinth back to Rome, that any of the art treasures lost or broken would have to be replaced at the expense of the man responsible. No more idea of art than the people who surround us today, not a particle of appreciation, but they brought it back to Rome by the ton. Private collecting started, a thing the Greeks never dreamt of. It started in Rome, and forgery with it. The same poseurs, the same idiots who would buy a vase if they had to pay enough for it, the same people who come to Brown, in gray waistcoats, perhaps, instead of togas, the same people in Rome, the same people, the same hands ...

—But you, then you, if you feel this way ...

—Because the people, the people, they're bringing us to the point Rome reached when a court could award a painting to the man who owned the board, not the artist who had painted on it. Valentine stood with his knees against the edge of the low table. —Yes, when the Roman Republic collapsed, art collecting collapsed, art forging disappeared. And then what. Instead of art they had religion, and all the talent went into holy relics. Half the people collected them, the other half manufactured them. A forest of relics of the True Cross? Miraculous multiplication. Then the Renaissance, and they dropped the knucklebones of the saints and came back to art. His eyes, which were hard and blue now, settled on the radiant figure in the center of the table of the Seven Deadly Sins. —Intricate, cunning forgeries like this, he added, sweeping a hand with a glitter of gold over the whole table as he turned his back. —The people! he said, watching Recktall Brown approach. —Of course I loathe him.

—But it's not. This table, it's not a forgery.

—What's the matter? Brown demanded, coming up to them.

—This Bosch, it's not a forgery.

—Who the hell said it was? Look, Valentine . . .

—Listen . . .

—Have you got him all upset like this?

—Listen, this Bosch painting, it's not a forgery.

Basil Valentine sank back in his chair and clasped a knee between his hands. —It's not? he said quietly, with the beginning of a smile on his lips, and shrugged. —Not even a copy?

—You're God damn right it's not.

—It's not. It can't be.

—Why not? Valentine asked them. His eyes had recovered their light watery blue, agreeable indifference. —The story I heard, you know, he went on after a pause, —was that the original came from the di Brescia collection, one of the finest in Europe, most of them Flemish primitives in fact. The old man, the Conte di Brescia, found himself running out of money. He loved the pictures, and none of his family would have dared suggest he sell a single one, even if they'd known the state of their finances. Of course they were simply waiting for him to die so they could sell them all. Meanwhile they went right on living in the manner which centuries of wealth had taught them, watched the pictures go out to be cleaned and come back, none the wiser. When the old grandee died, they fell over themselves to sell the pictures, and found that every one of them was a copy. They hadn't been sent out to be cleaned, the old man had sent them out to be copied and sold, and the copies were brought back.

—That's right, sold, Brown said, —they sold the originals you just said, and I got this one. I got it ten or fifteen years ago.

—Where?

—Where? Never mind. Right here in America. I picked it up for just about nothing.

—The collection of copies was dispersed too, you know, Valentine said. —Soon after the scandal, in the late 'twenties. And this . . .

—But wait, listen . . .

—Don't get yourself upset, my boy, Brown said letting himself down in his chair; and Valentine looked across the table with the faint smile still on his lips.

—Listen, this is the original, it is.

—Don't get yourself so excited, God damn it my boy...

—How are you so certain? Valentine asked calmly.

—Because, listen. What happened was, I heard, I heard this somewhere, abroad, yes somewhere abroad I heard that what happened was, a boy, a boy whose father owned the original, he'd bought it himself, he bought it from the Conte di...Brescia, and the boy...the boy copied it and stole the original and left his copy in its place, and sold the original, he sold it in secret for... for just about nothing.

—How very interesting, Basil Valentine said quietly. The smile was gone from his lips, and he watched the quivering figure across the table from him without moving, without expression on his face.

—All right, that's enough of that. Didn't the two of you get started on this new thing he's going to work on while I wasn't here?

—Of course, Valentine said, his tone returned to its agreeable level, with an ingratiating edge to it as he turned to Brown and went on, —We decided to write a novel about you, since you don't exist.

Recktall Brown did look startled at that. But he recovered immediately to take off his glasses and turn his sharp eyes on Basil Valentine. —We're going to get down to business right now, he said.

—Brown doesn't exist, you must admit, Valentine went on. —He's a figment of a Welsh rarebit taken before retiring. A projection of my unconscious. Though a rather abiding one, I must confess.

—By God, Brown said, —if you don't settle down and be serious...

—But my dear man, I am being serious. I am the only person in this room who exists. You are both projections of my unconscious, and so I shall write a novel about you both. But I don't know what I can do with you, he said, turning to the other chair.

—With me? He almost smiled at Basil Valentine. —Why not?

—Because, my dear fellow, no one knows what you're thinking. And that is why people read novels, to identify projections of their own unconscious. The hero has to be fearfully real, to convince them of their own reality, which they rather doubt. A novel without a hero would be distracting in the extreme. They have to know what you think, or good heavens, how can they know that you're going through some wild conflict, which is after all the duty of a hero.

—I think about my work.

—But my dear fellow...

—God damn it Valentine, Brown broke in, —I'm as real as hell, and in just a minute...

—All right, to work, to work. Wait, there's something I've meant to ask.

Your own paintings, you have done work yourself, certainly. Are there any of them lying about anywhere?

—Why no, I...the only ones I had were destroyed in a fire.

—Good, good. If someone picked them up...you can't suppress all of yourself, you know. Valentine watched the brandy bottle raised and tipped over the empty glass.

—I know, he said, watching it himself. His hand quivered somewhat, and the bottle rattled against the edge of the glass.

—Now be careful, my boy, Recktall Brown said, watching him drink it down.

—Before we go any further with this, Valentine said, —I would like to know more about your work, because what I have in mind...The hard surface, for instance. Oil takes years to dry.

—Yes, that...getting the hard surface, it was one of the worst problems. He leaned toward them, his elbows on the table, clutching one hand in the other, and spoke rapidly but with effort. —I've tried everything, every different...I tried mixing my colors on blotting paper, to absorb the oil, and then mixing them with varnish but it dried too quickly, you see? It dried too quickly and it was unalterable. I tried a mixture of stand oil and formaldehyde, but it wasn't right, it wasn't what I wanted. I tried oil of lavender and form-aldehyde and I like it better, the oil with an egg tempera, and a varnish glaze. In those two Bouts pictures, in those when I prepared the canvas I laid linen threads on the gesso when it was still wet, you see? in the pattern I wanted for the crackle. Then I baked it, and when it came out of the oven the threads came off and left the pattern. But the best thing, here, I used it here, he said, motioning at the van der Goes reproduction which still lay open on the table, —a thin layer of gesso, over and over on the canvas, and it cracks of its own volition, because of the atmosphere, the changes, you see? This painting is whole egg and oil of lavender, and then glue, dilute glue and the varnish. This one, this is amber varnish, the undercoat of dilute glue shrank faster than the varnish when they dried and cracked it, you see? And a little India ink in the cracks and when that dried there were only particles, like dirt, when the experts came...

—Now take it easy, my boy, sit down, sit down.

—And then the experts came, you see? he said, standing, and rubbed his hand over his eyes, and his chin, leaving a broad smile quivering there when he reached down for the bottle again. —There isn't one test they don't know, and not one that can't be beaten. Not one. That...that's why I couldn't use that varnish medium, it dried so fast that I had to paint too fast, and you can't do that, you can't paint that fast and control these...these things that have to be controlled, do you understand? And an X-ray would have shown up those abrupt strokes, he added. He lifted the glass, and threw back his head to drink it down. —You see, this … controlling this damned world of shapes and smells …

—Sit down, my boy, Recktall Brown said as he started to walk away from them.

—But I haven't told you, after all this work, this … fooling around. Do you know what the best medium is? It's so simple I never dared try it, it's that simple. Glair, the liquid that settles to the bottom when the whites of egg are beaten, with dry powdered pigments, and a layer of clean white of egg over it and the varnish, it's so simple it doesn't need anything, it doesn't need to be baked, it crackles by itself beautifully, as though years, hundreds of years had passed over it. And that, it's … and then the experts come, with their little bottles of alcohol, to see if they can dissolve the fresh paint, but the glue … You never have music here, do you. Never, in all this time …

—Come back here and sit down. We can't talk to you way the hell out in the middle of the room.

—This glair, Basil Valentine said to him. —You sound as though you consider it practically foolproof.

—Yes, that's the word, foolproof. Foolproof, he said, coming back to them.

—That is what we need, Basil Valentine said, his hands drawn up beneath his chin. —The fools are the ones we must be most careful of. Most secrets are discovered by their accidents, very few by design. Very few, he repeated, looking up. —Foolproof enough, would you say, for a van Eyck?

Brown seemed to be awaiting some violent reaction to this, if it were, as he believed from Valentine's casual tone, the challenge. But he looked up to see it greeted with no more than a shrug.

—Easily, the perfect medium for him, for Jan van Eyck, but he's been done so often …

—Yes, yes, Basil Valentine interrupted impatiently, —there are probably more badly faked Jan van Eycks then any of the others. Hubert, on the other hand …

—Hubert van Eyck?

—It might be the art discovery of the century, if it were absolutely perfect, signed and documented …

—Yes, yes it might, it probably would be.

—If you could do it …

—If I could do it? If I could do it? he said, raising his head.

—How much? Recktall Brown demanded.

—It depends entirely on the picture. Perhaps as much as you got for all the rest put together.

—That much! What the hell have we been doing fooling around with these...

—If he could do it.

—If I could do it! Of course I can do it, he said more calmly, looking down at the van der Goes reproduction. —But listen, they have no right to do this, he went on, crumpling the reproduction into his hand as it tore from the magazine. —You have no right to do this, he said, as Valentine put a hand on Recktall Brown's arm.

—To do what, my dear fellow?

—This...these reproductions, they have no right to try to spread one painting out like this. There's only one of them, you know, only one. This... my painting...there's only one, and these reproductions, these cheap fakes is what they are, being scattered everywhere, and they have no right to do that. It cheapens the whole...it's a calumny, that's what it is, on my work, he said, standing with the thing wadded up in his hand.

Basil Valentine took the thin cigarette from his lips and spoke coldly. —Forgery is calumny, he said. —Every piece you do is calumny on the artist you forge.

—It's not. It's not, damn it, I...when I'm working, I...Do you think I do these the way all other forging has been done? Pulling the fragments of ten paintings together and making one, or taking a...a Dürer and reversing the composition so that the man looks to the right instead of left, putting a beard on him from another portrait, and a hat, a different hat from another, so that they look at it and recognize Dürer there? No, it's...the recognitions go much deeper, much further back, and I...this...the X-ray tests, and ultra-violet and infra-red, the experts with their photomicrography and...macrophotography, do you think that's all there is to it? Some of them aren't fools, they don't just look for a hat or a beard, or a style they can recognize, they look with memories that...go beyond themselves, that go back to...where mine goes.

—Sit down, my boy.

—And...any knock at the door may be the gold inspectors, come to see if I'm using bad materials down there, I...I'm a master painter in the Guild, in Flanders, do you see? And if they come in and find that I'm not using the... gold, they destroy the bad materials I'm using and fine me, and I...they demand that...and this exquisite color of ultramarine, Venice ultramarine I have to take to them for approval, and the red pigment, this brick-red Flanders pigment...because I've taken the Guild oath, not for the critics, the experts, the...you, you have no more to do with me than if you are my descendants, nothing to do with me, and you...the Guild oath, to use pure materials, to work in the sight of God...

—You've had enough of this stuff now, my boy, Recktall Brown said, reaching, too late, for the brandy bottle. —You need to keep a steady hand for what you're doing, all these God damn tiny little details . . .

Basil Valentine sat, watching him.

—A steady hand! he said, and drank down the brandy. —Do you think that's all it is, a steady hand? He opened the rumpled reproduction. —This . . . these . . . the art historians and the critics talking about every object and . . . everything having its own form and density and . . . its own character in Flemish paintings, but is that all there is to it? Do you know why everything does? Because they found God everywhere. There was nothing God did not watch over, nothing, and so this . . . and so in the painting every detail reflects . . . God's concern with the most insignificant objects in life, with everything, because God did not relax for an instant then, and neither could the painter then. Do you get the perspective in this? he demanded, thrusting the rumpled reproduction before them. —There isn't any. There isn't any single perspective, like the camera eye, the one we all look through now and call it realism, there . . . I take five or six or ten . . . the Flemish painter took twenty perspectives if he wished, and even in a small painting you can't include it all in your single vision, your one miserable pair of eyes, like you can a photograph, like you can painting when it . . . when it degenerates, and becomes conscious of being looked at.

Recktall Brown stood up, and came toward him.

—Like everything today is conscious of being looked at, looked at by something else but not by God, and that's the only way anything can have its own form and its own character, and . . . and shape and smell, being looked at by God.

Recktall Brown stood beside him, the heavy naked hand on his shoulder.

—And so when you're working, it's your own work, Basil Valentine said.
—And when you attach the signature?

—Leave him alone, God damn it Valentine, he . . .

—Yes, when I attach the signature, he said dropping his head again, —that changes everything, when I attach the signature and . . . lose it.

—Then corruption enters, is that it, my dear fellow? Basil Valentine stood up smiling. He lit a cigarette. —That's the only thing they can prosecute you for in court, you know, if you're caught. Forging the signature. The law doesn't care a damn for the painting. God isn't watching them. He put a hand on the other shoulder, the hand with the gold seal ring, and his eyes met those of Recktall Brown. The liquid blue of them seemed to freeze and penetrate the uncentered pools behind the thick lenses, and to submerge there as Recktall Brown said, —Let go of him.

They stood that way for a number of seconds, any one of which might have contained the instant that one would pull him from the other; until he stepped back himself and said, —I know. I know.

Then Basil Valentine shrugged, and sauntered the few steps back to his chair. —You are mightily concerned with your own originality, aren't you, he said, standing behind the chair, turned toward them.

—Originality! No, I'm not, I . . .

—Come now, my dear fellow, you are. But you really ought to forget it, or give in to it and enjoy it. Everyone else does today. Brown is busy with suits of plagiarism all the time, aren't you Brown? You see? He takes it as a matter of course. He's surrounded by untalented people, as we all are. Originality is a device that untalented people use to impress other untalented people, and protect themselves from talented people . . .

—Valentine, this is the last time . . .

—Most original people are forced to devote all their time to plagiarizing. Their only difficulty is that if they have a spark of wit or wisdom themselves, they're given no credit. The curse of cleverness. Now wait, Brown. Stop. Stop there where you are and relax for a moment. We still have some business to straighten out. He needs to talk or he'll come to pieces, isn't that what you told me before he got here? Well let him talk, he's said some very interesting things. But don't let him talk to himself, that's all he's been doing, that's all he does when he talks to you and you don't listen, he knows you don't. Let him talk, then, but listen to him. He may not say anything clever, but that's just as well. Most people are clever because they don't know how to be honest. He paused. —Come, my dear fellow. If you don't say anything I shan't be able to use you in this novel, the one in which Brown figures so monumentally since everyone thinks he's honest because he doesn't know how to be clever.

Recktall Brown had started toward him; but as Basil Valentine's voice rose, Brown stopped beside the pitcher of martini cocktails and watched him carefully. A vein stood out on Valentine's temple, and he raised his hand to ascertain it there with his fingertips, an impulsive gesture as though he had once done it to suppress. He touched the place, and continued his hand round to the back of his head where he smoothed the over-long ends of his hair. —Yes, he will figure monumentally, Valentine went on. —That portrait there, he said, flinging a hand toward it, —do you know why he keeps it? To humanize him, as evidence of youth always does, no matter how monstrous.

Basil Valentine watched them. When neither of them spoke he straightened up and walked across the room, watching his feet, to the low pulpit, where he turned and sat against it, drumming his long fingers against the oak leaves carved there.

—"Another blue day," eh? he said, looking beyond Brown, at the fever-stricken eyes fixed upon him. —"Another blue day," he repeated. And then, —Brown tells me you have another self. Oh, don't be upset, it's not uncommon you know, not at all uncommon. Why, even Brown has one. That's why he drinks to excess occasionally, trying to slip up on it and grab it. Mark me, he's going to get too close one day, and it's going to turn around and break his neck for him. He picked up the whisky bottle. —Have you heard Brown talk about the portraits he sells? Nineteenth-century portraits of blond men with strong chins that he sells for ten times their price, he tells me, to precarious Jews who want nice ancestors, he said, pouring the whisky into a glass. He sat against the pulpit again, drew a foot up, and it swayed slightly, with the sound of bottles ringing together like the sound of bells in the distance. —To the same purpose, you know. And they believe it, when the portraits have hung about long enough, common ancestor to their vulgar selves that every-one else knows, and this other . . . more beautiful self who . . . can do more than they can, he finished, swirling the whisky in the bottom of the tumbler.

In the middle of the Aubusson carpet, the dog licked itself. That was the only sound. Then Basil Valentine put the glass of whisky down and left it there. —Where do you keep him, Brown? he demanded, looking at them, around the walls, up to the balcony.

Recktall Brown turned back to his chair. He looked up at the man whom his bulk no longer separated from Basil Valentine. —Sit down, my boy, he said, and then abruptly to Valentine, —Where are you going?

—I'm simply going in to wash my hands, if no one objects.

Recktall Brown took out a cigar. He unwrapped it, trimmed the end with his penknife, thrust it among uneven teeth, and lit it. He shook the match out in the air, and tossed it toward the ashtray. It fell to the carpet, and lay smoking on a rose. —When most people ask where the washroom is, they really mean they want to go to the toilet. He just goes in there to wash his hands. Sit down, my boy. We'll be done in a few minutes. Recktall Brown filled the air before him with smoke. —What's the matter? he asked, as the smoke rose, and the figure before him remained unmoved and unchanged.

—Oh, I . . . I don't know, he said, looking down at Brown and seeming to recover. —I suppose I was surprised, when you let him go on like that.

—Never interrupt people when they're telling you more than they know they are, no matter how mad they make you.

—Telling you?

—About themselves, my boy. Recktall Brown drew heavily on the cigar, and the smoke broke around the discolored teeth as he spoke. —I never do business with anyone until I've had them investigated, I never sign a thing until I've been through a report by a good private detective agency. I know a lot about Basil Valentine. I know about him with the Jesuits, I know what happened there, and I know what happens now, I know what his private life is. Be careful of him...

—He...studied for the priesthood?

—He's not out of it yet.

—But then me? Even me? You had them...you had detectives...finding out about me?

—Of course I did, my boy. It's all right, it's all right. You're all right, but just keep on the way you are, Brown said, laying a heavy hand on the wrist before him, —don't let anybody interfere with you, and be careful, be God damn careful of that pansy.

—That's funny, then you...we both studied...

—What have you two accomplished? they heard behind them. —Dear, just sitting here and holding hands. I thought we had fearfully pressing business. Basil Valentine approached rubbing his hands together. He kicked the crumpled reproduction on the floor, and paused over it to smooth it out with the narrow toe of his black shoe. —Oil of lavender, eh? he said, looking down at it. —Mansit odor, posses scire fuisse deam, he said kicking it aside. —You must remember your Ovid, my dear Brown? He touched his smooth temple and smiled as he sat down. —"An odor remained, you could tell that a goddess had appeared." He took his eyes from Brown, and looked across the table. —But what are you looking at me that way for? Come, we have work to do. Hubert van Eyck...

—Why should he rate a quarter of a million? Brown interrupted.

—I was about to tell you: because he never existed.

—But he did, he did, came sharply across the table.

—All right, my dear fellow...

—He did, he did, of course he did, who...why, the Ghent altarpiece, the Steenken *Madonna*...?

—Who the hell, what is this? Who? He never existed but he painted the what?...sting...

—All right, have it your way, Valentine went on, speaking across the table, paying Brown no attention. —After all, we will have to have it your way, won't we. If one of his paintings is to appear?

—But he did.

—All right, he did, Brown broke in again, sitting forward. —Now that's settled.

—It's not settled, yet. But it will be.

—But to say he didn't exist, to say Hubert van Eyck didn't exist?

—God damn it, stop. Stop arguing with him, Valentine. You're just trying to upset him.

—Don't you understand? But don't either of you understand? Basil Valentine brought both hands up before him. —There are authorities who still insist that Hubert van Eyck is a legend, that he never lived at all, that Jan van Eyck never had an older brother. As a matter of fact, I'm one of them myself, but, wait. He held up an arresting palm. —Now don't you understand? If a painting appears, a signed, fully documented painting by Hubert van Eyck, they'll be proved wrong. The others, the…experts and art historians who have been insisting that there was a Hubert van Eyck will pounce on this new picture. They won't question it for a moment, because it will prove their point, and that's all they care about. It will prove that they've been right all this time, and that's all they care about. The painting itself doesn't matter to them, their authority is all that's important. And the dissenters? He dropped his hands, sank back in the chair and smiled across the table. —Even I may be brought around, you see.

Recktall Brown grunted an assent, and Valentine took out a cigarette and passed his case open across the table. It was snapped closed, and the worn inscription caught the light. —This? what's this? may I read it?

—If you can, Valentine said.

—Yes, it's difficult…Varé tava soskei me puchelas…cai soskei avillara catári…Gypsy?

—Why yes, a Hungarian dialect. Valentine's face almost showed surprise, as he took the thing back and slipped it into an inside pocket. —But you don't understand it? "Much I ponder why you ask me questions, and why you should come hither." A gift, he added, cleared his throat, shifted in his chair, and went on speaking as though to find recovery in his own words. —Van Eyck? and what did you think I was going to suggest? another Jan van Eyck?

—But, no but…

—Yes, another *Virgin and Child and Donor?* You could do that. Paint Brown in the place of Chancellor Rolin. Lovely! on his knees at a prie-dieu, before the Virgin and Child. A pious monument to his Christian virtue as a patron of art. We'd have to take off his glasses, and get him a haircut. You wouldn't mind running around in a tonsure for a while, Brown? But that ring…His eye caught the double gleam of the diamonds. —We could hardly have such vanity flaunting…

—What are you talking about? Brown demanded. —We decided he exists, this Herbert…

Valentine shrugged wearily, and went on in his irritating monotone, —Yes, we are, I suppose, basically in agreement. Now here is the point. Some time ago the will of a man named Jean de Visch was found. It is in the public domain, available as substantiation of this . . . project. The will mentions a picture by Hubert van Eyck, which goes to prove, supposedly, that such a picture was painted. Another Virgin of some sort. Proves it well enough for your purpose, at any rate. Now when they tore down that house in Ghent they hoped to find some of Hubert's work, hidden somewhere. They didn't. But there was a scrap of paper. It was regarded as a curiosity, and then it disappeared and was forgotten. It was a letter signed by Jodoc Vyt, the man who commissioned the Ghent altarpiece, commissioning a work by Hubert van Eyck. I can get hold of it for two thousand dollars.

—You can get it for less, Brown muttered.

—Perhaps I shall. Basil Valentine smiled at him. —You never begrudged me a commission?

—How do I know it isn't faked?

—You haven't made a habit of doubting my word either. But look at it this way. If it is not genuine, why should it exist at all?

—If it exists, why should I buy it?

—You are inclined to oversimplify, aren't you Brown? To insist on carrying us back to Rome, where for all their ingenious vulgarity they never managed to evolve blackmail, at least there's no word for it in Roman jurisdiction. They depended so heavily on the Greeks, and the Greeks apparently had no word for it either. No, it's taken our precocious modern minds to devise this delicate relationship between human beings. You might call this blackmail in reverse. You see, if you don't buy this slip of paper it will be destroyed.

—And he can't paint the picture without this scrap of paper?

—He can. Of course he can. But with this attached to it, it will be irreproachable. He paused. —This isn't a thing to scrimp on, and you know it.

—All right.

—Well?

They both looked across the table. —It isn't the first time I've thought of it, he said, watching the brandy he swirled in the bottom of his glass. —A *Virgin* by Hubert van Eyck.

—An *Annunciation*.

—Yes, he said, holding the glass up. —Isn't that an exquisite color? The color of the sixth heaven, jacinth. I remember a story my father told me, about the celestial sea. Instead of bedtime stories he used to read to me. The same things he was reading.

—Now this Herbert picture, Recktall Brown said, interrupting.

—When I was sick in bed, he read to me from *Otia Imperialia*. The twelfth century, Gervase of Tilbury, when people could believe that our atmosphere was a celestial sea, a sea to the people who lived above it. This story was about some people coming out of church, and they saw an anchor dangling by a rope from the sky. The anchor caught in the tombstones, and then they watched and saw a man coming down the rope, to unhook it. But when he reached the earth they went over to him and he was dead... He looked up at both of them from the glass. —Dead as though he'd been drowned.

—All right, my boy, is there anything else? Anything you need to go ahead with this? I had to buy him a God damn expensive egg-beater a couple of months ago, Brown said, turning to Basil Valentine, who stood up saying, —I have a number of photographs, blown-up details of the brushwork, you know. The foreground figures in the Ghent altarpiece, the Steenken *Madonna*...

—Or imagine heaven and earth joined by a tree, he went on, as Valentine reached over and picked up the book he had laid before him, some time before. —The sky is a roof, with windows in it for rain to fall through. People live up there, you see. And if you climb up high enough you can visit them. They're just like you are, he said, turning to Recktall Brown.

—The hell they are, Brown said, getting to his feet. —Do you want to talk any more about this Herbert picture you're going to do, or...

—But I am, he said. —I am. He looked from one of them to the other, from Recktall Brown to Basil Valentine, who stood over him. He looked bewildered. —Someone, who was it? said maybe we're fished for?

—Come along, my dear fellow. I'm going downtown, I'll drop you off.

—Or the seven heavens of the Arabs, he said decisively, making a hemisphere with one hand, which trembled as he held it forth. —Emerald, white silver, white pearls, then ruby, then gold, red gold, and then yellow jacinth, and the seventh of shining light...

Recktall Brown looked at his cigar. It had burned on the bias. —Look at this God-damned thing, he muttered. —This is the way they make cigars today. It's the way they do everything today, he said, and threw it into the fireplace. —Everybody but him, he added, and, walking over, put a hand on his shoulder as he got up.

—That vase, he said, motioning toward a glass-enclosed bookcase.

—That's not a fake, it's real. Early Netherlands ceramic.

—Can I take it? For a week or two.

—What do you need it for, it's damn valuable, Brown said.

—Lilies...

—Lilies, they're expensive here too, Brown went on, leading him toward the door slowly. —Fuller used to bring them in here by the armload, all held up by wires. I don't like them, they make me sick to my stomach. I told him to quit it. Nobody likes lilies much, why don't you use some other kind of a flower?

—In an *Annunciation* . . .

The dog followed them on one side, Basil Valentine on the other.

—Those little oak frames I got, I'll show them to you the next time, the ones with velvet inside them.

Basil Valentine held out the book he had picked up from the table before the fireplace. —Your Thoreau?

—Why . . . why yes, I . . .

—Hardly fifteenth-century reading. Though I'm as far in the other direction, I'm afraid. Valentine picked up the book which lay with his coat. —Dear Tertullian, he muttered. —And I suppose you're going to have your usual vulgar gathering this Christmas eve, Brown?

—I get more business done at those than a month in an office. This picture you've got now, he went on, turning, —as soon as you're done with it call me, I'll send down for it. And be careful with that vase. It's going to be a damn good auction, he said to Valentine. —You remember that Queen Anne sofa upstairs? There was enough perfect inlay in that to make two sofas and two chairs, part of the original in each one. Some smart guy says it's a fake, and you show him the original piece.

—Rather like Osiris, Basil Valentine said, pulling on his coat.

—What's that?

—They cut Osiris up in fourteen pieces, and later Isis modeled his body fourteen times, with an original piece in each one.

—Like a saint?

Basil Valentine smiled, lifting his coat by the lapels as he straightened it. —Precisely, my dear fellow.

Recktall Brown had taken a pigskin pad from his pocket. —Glassware, he mumbled, —for this auction. I've got some beautyful glassware, it's been in a manure pile out in the country, gives it that nice glittery effect, colors like you see in bubbles, that old glass has. Some wop taught me that trick.

—Italia irredenta. Basil Valentine reached down his hat. —That fine Italian hand, he said wearily, —which has taught us to make antiques by inflicting every possible indignity and abuse upon beautiful objects. He walked on toward the outside door.

Brown put the pad back into his pocket. —Be careful of that vase now, he muttered. —And don't forget what I told you. He nodded ahead of them. —Be careful of him.

—I . . . I wish you hadn't said what you did, he said, as Brown put the diamond-laden hand on his shoulder. —About her.

—About who?

—Her. Esme.

—Come on, my boy. Is she a good model for you?

—Yes, yes, she . . . why she can sit for three hours without moving.

—No needle marks on your Annunciation's arm, now.

—But you . . .

—She's a nice little piece, my boy, I know that too. But don't let that get in the way of your work. Don't let nothing get in the way of it. Here, don't forget your eggs.

—She says it's because she hasn't got any stomach, he said, smiling.

—Who?

—Esme. She says that's why she's a good model, because she hasn't got any stomach.

Recktall Brown stood in the hall, tapping his foot, until the outside door closed. Then he turned and went back to the vast room they had just left. The dog watched him approach, and got up when he came near, moving her stump of a tail slowly; but he stopped before he reached her, and she sat down. In the middle of the room, Recktall Brown took out a cigar and looked around him. He looked at the extensive wool tapestry on the wall to his right; but all their eyes were looking past him, in the other direction. He looked at the refectory table, where books and publications lay accounted for, and nothing moved. Then he turned abruptly, as though someone in the room with him had gone the instant his broad back was turned; but his youthful portrait was there, hanging silent as everything else. He raised his head, and looked up at the balcony where he saw the back of a rosewood chest, and the suit of armor standing patiently before the deed it had waited centuries to commit.

—Fuller! he shouted.

Then he turned toward the fireplace, and raised his cigar to the array of uneven teeth that had framed his cry. He looked at the Latin inscription over the fireplace, and bit off the end of the cigar. At his feet lay the crumpled reproduction from *Collectors Quarterly*. He noticed it, as he did anything which broke the pattern of the Aubusson roses, and with some effort he stooped over and picked it up. In four steps, he reached one of the leather chairs, where he sat down on the arm and raised his leg far enough to lay the crumpled paper against it. The unlighted cigar made erratic motions as it moved in his teeth, and he stared through the thick lenses, smoothing the picture out against his broad knee and its ample trouser with a wide thumb, which he exchanged, abruptly, for the edge of his hand.

His cry had risen to the balcony and beyond, into other rooms and withered, finding them empty, down a corridor then, to break against the wall and rebound, fractured, into the last crevice where it found asylum, embraced, however unwillingly, by Fuller's consciousness. Having written REKTIL BROWN on a piece of paper and put it into his drawer some time earlier, Fuller sat on the edge of his bed in the windowless room, in sagging white underclothes, rubbing a yellow figure (drawn against the prospect of a cross) with his moist palm in the darkness.

—Don't tell me you've come out without a coat?

—Yes, I ... I must have left it behind.

—Or don't own one, is that it?

They walked toward the corner. It was almost dark. Basil Valentine talked. —There was an eighteenth-century Spanish bishop named Borja, who said "I don't speak French," when he was addressed in Latin. I think of him whenever I meet our remarkable benefactor. That portrait, you know. Did you notice the ears? How erect and sharp they are, sticking right out. He tried to have them corrected, brought closer to his head, years ago. A cheap operation, and he goes to the plastic surgeon every week now, sitting under a green lamp there for hours. The cartilage is gone. It's quite useless.

He silenced as two young men passed. One of them was saying, —tsa great sperchul achievement ...

—You see what I mean. Valentine hailed a cab. —It seems to follow quite consistently, he went on as they got in, —people so bound to reality usually have something physically out of order about them.

Black-shod feet together on the shifting floor of the cab, he moved closer and took the vase. —It's a fake, you know, he said holding it up in both hands. —Are you surprised?

—In a way, it ... but it is beautiful.

—Beautiful? Valentine lowered it to his lap. —It suggests beauty, perhaps. At the sudden draft on him, he looked up. —Yes, do roll your window down. You don't look well at all.

—I just ... had to have some air.

—Are you free for dinner?

—Well, I don't usually ... don't you have anything else?

—My dear fellow, there's only one engagement that cannot be broken, and I don't plan it for some little time. Come along up to my place for dinner then, and you can pick up these photographic details.

The cab halted, started off as though to accomplish a mile in a minute, and halted abruptly twenty yards on, where the driver exchanged twilight expletives with a bus driver. The sea of noise poured in, striking the leather seats, penetrating the occupants with thrusts of chaos, sounds of the world battling with night, primordial ages before music was discovered on earth. —I know your name. I've tried to think where.

—The *Collectors Quarterly*? Basil Valentine suggested easily; but his eyes turned, incisive, searching.

—No. Longer ago. Further away than that. But I've lost it now.

—You don't mean the ninth century Pope? Valentine sat back, relaxed, his tone cordial. —There was one by that name, but alas! he said, turning, to smile, —he reigned for barely forty days. He took out the cigarette case, and it opened in his hand. —Well?

—Brown told me, you see, he mentioned that you were...that you had studied with the Jesuits.

—Dear heaven! Basil Valentine almost laughed aloud. —For Brown, that probably has the most weird connotations, the most frightening implications. My dear fellow...

—But you did...for awhile you did train for the priesthood?

—In a manner of speaking. You have something of the priest in you yourself, you know.

—Damned little.

—Far more of that than the renegade painter.

—Are they so...separate then?

—My dear fellow, the priest is the guardian of mysteries. The artist is driven to expose them.

—A fatal likeness, then.

—A fatal dissension, and a fatal attraction. Tell me, does Brown pay you well?

—Pay me? I suppose. The money piles up there.

—Why?

—The money? It...binds the contract. It's the only thing he understands.

The clear eyes of drained blue no longer darted with assumed pleasure but glittered steadily, like water frozen so quickly. Valentine clutched Tertullian in his narrow lap. —You don't dislike him, do you.

—No.

—No. In fact you rather like him. And this contract?

—Contract? Yes, a debt...a debt which the person to whom you owe it refuses to acknowledge, is impossible to bear.

—And the money?...Valentine was studying every line in the face beside him, details suddenly broken with a constricted sound like laughter,

—The money? you...can't spend love.

The cab had stopped at a light and people were passing around it: the voice of a girl penetrated in clear Boston accents, —Somerset Maugham? Haha, hahahahaha, Somerset Maugham my ahss…

—Money buys privacy, my dear fellow, said Basil Valentine, leaning across his lap to roll up the window. —It frees one from the turmoil of those circumstances which the vulgar confuse with necessity. And necessity after all… what are you laughing at?

—Something earlier, something I thought of earlier but I didn't laugh then, when I thought of, when you were talking about, a novel? Writing a novel, We don't know what you're thinking, you said. I thought of Momus and Vulcan, I thought of my wife then. You remember the homunculus that Vulcan made? and Momus said, You should have put a little window in him, so we could see his innermost thoughts. And I remembered… listen,

—You're married?

—What happens? In this novel?

—What happens? Basil Valentine turned his full face.

—To me. The cab jolted to a start.

—Why, to you? Good heavens, I haven't the faintest notion. Valentine laughed shortly, looking ahead again. —I was about to say earlier, of necessity… but tell me, when you were a child…

—Necessity, yes. Yes, a hero? John Huss…

—Huss? Hardly, today, eh? John Huss? Someone's said, you know, anyone who accepts a martyr's part today is a coward. And you? what happens to you? he went on hurriedly. —I suppose you… well, let's say you eat your father, canonize your mother, and… what happens to people in novels? I don't read them. You drown, I suppose.

—That's too romantic.

—Novels are romantic.

—As though, death could end it?

—Have it your way, there is a step after death then. Valentine sat back and clasped his knee with folded hands. —After all, my dear fellow, you are an artist, and nothing can happen to you. An artist does not exist, except as a vehicle for his work. If you live simply in a world of shapes and smells? You're bound to become just that. Why your life, the way you live…

—Yes, I don't live, I'm… I am lived, he whispered.

Valentine turned to see him gripping his face in the breadth of a hand, whose finger-ends had gone white at the temple. —But, do you know how I feel sometimes? The hand dropped to clutch Valentine's arm, and Valentine looked up into the feverish eyes. —Like… as though I were reading a novel, yes. And then, reading it, but the hero fails to appear, fails to be working out some plan of comedy or, disaster? All the materials are there, yes. The sounds, the images, telephones and telephone numbers? The ships and subways, the ... the ...

—The half-known people, Valentine interrupted easily, —who miss the subways and lose each other's telephone numbers? Cavorting about dressed in the absurd costumes of the author's chaotic imagination, talking about each other...

—Yes, while I wait. I wait. Where is he? Listen, he's there all the time. None of them moves, but it reflects him, none of them ... reacts, but to react with him, none of them hates but to hate with him, to hate him, and loving... none of them loves, but, loving...

—Loving?

The cab swerved suddenly. Basil Valentine was thrown against the window beside him, where he caught himself on his elbow. The man they had almost hit had seemed to hang in the air before them, the empty face a terrible exposure of nakedness.

—*Idiot!*

Basil Valentine's face in profile showed the vein standing out beneath the hat-brim, a face strong, unsympathetic, bearing all of the force which sympathy lacks, in lineaments (shaded now under the black brim of this Homburg) which belied childhood and youth.

—Idiot, he repeated, sitting back, unaware of the feverish stare fixed upon him.

Then the driver burst out over his shoulder, —You just try drivin a cab, Mac, if you think it's such a fuckin easy job.

Basil Valentine leaned forward. He was livid; but his voice was controlled. —I have no faint intention of wasting an instant considering such an absurd pastime. Now turn around and keep your obscenities to yourself, before you do run down someone as stupid as yourself.

—Listen Mac, don't give me any of that, who the hell are you, this is a fuckin free country...

—Pull up over here, driver.

The cab came to a precipitous stop. Basil Valentine looked at the vase, the eggs, the books, and chose the books to be seen with, carrying in the street. He read the meter as they got out, and was reaching deep into his change pocket when the cab roared away.

—But you ... you really hate people, don't you, came the voice beside him.

—You see? Valentine said, not listening. He took out his cigarette case. —When I exclaimed, "idiot," of course I meant the ... idiot whom we almost ran down. You see? They're the same, the ones who construct their own disasters so skillfully, in accord with the deepest parts of their ignorant nature, and then call it accident. He stood looking after the cab, a light poised before his cigarette.

—But . . . you really hate other people.

—My dear fellow, remember Emerson's advice, Basil Valentine said, and paused. There was a crash at the corner. From where they stood they could see that the cab had hit a bus. —We are advised to treat other people as though they were real, he said then, lighting his cigarette, —because, perhaps they are.

—I . . . I have to go.

—We're not dining, then?

—No, I . . . I have to get to work, I . . . it's late.

—But my dear fellow, of course I understand. And the van Eyck details, I'll drop them off at your place some time, shall I?

—Oh no, no don't, don't come down there, don't bother, I . . . goodbye, goodbye . . .

—Not goodbye, Basil Valentine said, extending his hand. —People don't say goodbye any more. You look up and they're gone, missing. You hear of them, in a country with exotic postage stamps, or dead at sea. I'll see you very soon. He smiled, and held the hand in his as though it were a creature he would suffocate.

In another cab a minute later, Basil Valentine found two books in his lap instead of one. He picked up the copy of Thoreau, and looked out of the rear window; but there, almost a block behind, people merged from all directions, and all that he could see at the point where they had separated were the tops of some lilies on a flower cart, stopped in the neon glow of a bar.

He faced forward again, thumbing the pages of the book, gold glittering at his cuff as he paused to glance at occasional sentences. The cab had turned east. As it stopped at a corner, the smile of a great and private pleasure drew out his lips, and he looked out the closed window. People who passed, passed quickly and silently, leaving behind a figure barely taller than the barrel organ mounted on a stick, whose handle he turned, his only motion, the hand, clockwise, barely more enduring than the sounds he released on the night air, sounds without the vanity of music, sounds unattached, squeaks and drawn wheezes, pathos in the minor key and then the shrill of loneliness related to nothing but itself, like the wind round the fireplace left standing after the house burned to the ground.

When the cab started again, he returned his eyes to the words underlined on the page before him: *What you seek in vain for, half your life, one day you come full upon, all the family at dinner. You seek it like a dream, and as soon as you find it, you become its prey.* And he was still looking at this line, and he was still smiling, when the cab stopped before his door.

—Seven lilies?

Seven celestial fabrics, seven spheres, the colors of the seven planetary bodies: all these revolved above the flower cart. But above seventh heaven, we are told, there are seven seas of light, and then the veils, separating the Substances seven of each kind, and then, Paradise: seven stages, one above the other, canopied by the Throne of the Compassionate, discreetly remote from the tumult going on here in the middle distance. The lights changed, traffic moved, and waves of figures crested with faces dumbly unbroken, or spotted with the foam of confusion, or shattering their surfaces with speech, ebbed and flowed on a sea of noise, disdaining the music of the spheres.

The moment of evening loss is suggested in restricted portions of the sky which only suggest infinity, and that such an intimacy is possible when something rises from inside, to be skewered on the peaks or continue to rise untrammeled: a desperate moment for those with nowhere to go, the ones who lose their balance when they look up, passing on all sides here, invited nowhere, enjoying neither drink nor those they drank with but suddenly desolated, glancing up, stepping down from the curb alone, to seek anywhere (having forgot to make a date for "cocktails," asylum of glass, brittle words, olives from across the sea, and chromium) a place to escape this transition from day to night: a grotesque time of loneliness, for what has been sought is almost visible, and requires, perhaps, no more than a priest to bring it forth. Restricted above the seven lilies, the sky lay in just such a portion as the Etruscan priest might have traced with his wand when, building the temple, he outlined on the sky the foundation at his feet, delivering the residence of deity to earth.

Seven days, seven seals, seven bullocks in burnt offering; seven times Jacob bowed before Esau; seven stars the angels of the seven churches, seven lamps which are the seven spirits, seven stars in his right hand; seven years in Eden; and seven times seven years to the jubilee trumpet; seven years of plenty, seven years of famine; so Nebuchadnezzar heated the furnace seven times more than it was wont to be heated, to purge the three who refused to bow down before the golden image sixty forearms (counting to the end of the middle finger) high, and six wide; and when they came through unscathed and unscorched, the king exclaimed, —Blessed be the God of Shadrach, Meshach, and Abednego, and quite sensibly joined them in their fearful subscription to a Hostility Who could afford no other gods before Him, and would seem to have triumphed in this fracas which took place not too far distant from India, where things remained quiet enough that many heard a serene voice saying, *Even those who worship other gods worship me although they know it not.*

—A priest?

—You remember me.

—Look out, chum. Look out of the way, said the flower-cart man.

—Don't you remember me?

—Here wait, I . . . could you sell me these lilies?

—Hurry up then, there's a cop coming. I'll leave you have all seven for a dollar, said the flower-cart man.

—Your face, yes, your face, but . . .

—Come on, chum. Talk to your friend here or give me a buck. There's a cop coming, the flower-cart man interrupted.

—I knew your face, but the round collar . . .

—And I knew you half a block away. But up close you don't look like yourself at all. It must be two years . . . ?

—Two years?

—Since I saw you, that night, New Year's Eve, with your wife in the street. John picked up his suitcase again. It was a large, and apparently heavy Gladstone bag, which he'd put down to shake hands, stood with his palm open, extended, and withdrawn it when the confusion his gesture had caused threatened upset among the driving currents of people, the threat of smashed eggs, fallen lilies, and a broken vase, which he stood over now protecting with his large black-coated frame, ballasted by the heavy bag. —But I have to make a train, he said. He took half a step back. Then his face streamed crimson: for a full second his large features were at once exposed stilled by surprise and swimming in the harsh brilliance of the three neon letters above. He recovered his half-step, dropped the bag with another step forward and brought up a supporting arm. —What's the matter? Are you all right? His eyes fell under the shadow of the soft black hat-brim, and were gone as the lower part of his face, the moving lips, shone livid under the letters BAR blazing green. —Are you all right?

—Yes, good night. Good night.

—But I can't just leave you . . .

—Your train, your train.

—But what is it? You're shaking. John's features showed no shape now, his whole face shaded under the soft black hat-brim as his shoulders and both extended arms were caught again in the blazing letters, and an empty hand, then two, as the laden figure turned from his support. —But here . . .

—Good night. Your train. And you can't come in here. It's a bar.

—Bar? Certainly I can, I'll help you. John caught up his bag with one hand, and caught an elbow with the other. A lily dropped.

—Wait!

—What?

—The lily?

—I'll get it. Now, here...be careful of the door.

In the dim-lit end of the bar, shadows were contorted in the effervescent illumination of the juke-box; which also played *Let's Do It*. John cleared his throat and spoke in an attempted convivial tone, —What are you doing with lilies and, eggs is it?

—Yes, a little brandy.

—Overwork? Here. Do you feel better? Take a lesson from the lilies. John smiled, and extended a hand. —They toil not...The wrist on the bar was jerked away from him. —Are you all right? he asked again, seeking for some sign in the profile of the face turned from him, and he found none, and faced forward himself. There his eyes rose to the mirror behind the bar, where a fevered stare pinioned them for an instant.

—Did either of you guys...excuse me, father, did either of you gentlemen put in a call to Miami? the bartender intruded between them and the mirror. John shook his head; and when the bulk of the bartender moved on, he saw the reflection of his own face overcome with youth in such proximity to one who looked twice his age. —When I mentioned to your father...he commenced.

—My father!

—Yes. I mentioned I'd seen you, I didn't say...

—You saw my father?

—Why yes, traveling. On church business, I happened to stop in your town, and saw him.

—What did he say?

—What did he say? Why...John repeated. —He didn't say...we talked church business, that's about all. He smiled again, but drew back.

—But my father?

—Church business, John faltered, and cleared his throat again. —You see, I do a good deal of traveling, among out-of-the-way parishes where enrollment has fallen down, it's part of the revival in religious...interest going on all over the country, a lot of it is inter-denominational...

—But my father? What did he say?

—Well to tell you the truth, John commenced, and looked down again, catching a cuff against his coat to draw it back and look at his wrist watch, —to tell the truth...he's quite old, isn't he. And he wasn't...very co-operative. The pressing necessities of the times...

—But what did he say?

Looking up, John's face startled more at finding itself uncomposed in the glass. —It was strange, he said, and paused at the apparently unfamiliar resonance in his own voice, going on, —I got there on Sunday, Sunday morning. I thought, Why not go in and hear his sermon? That's always a good way to get a picture of the problems a congregation . . . a minister may be up against, but . . . It was strange. When I went into church, there was almost the feeling the sunlight had stopped. He's a big man, but it was his voice. He towered over the pulpit, he was holding onto it with both hands when I came in, and afterward I looked around at the faces . . . the sermon, his sermon was on some primitive Australian religion, but you see, to tell the truth . . .

—What?

John looked up. The lilies on the bar were browning at the edges. He shifted his eyes only far enough to reach the image beside his own in the mirror, but found only a stare of feverish continence which was lost below the mirror's edge. —I remember every word of that Australian . . . legend, the parallel he was drawing with . . . Christianity, I can't get it out of my mind. John had clutched the edge of the bar, lowering his voice and slowing his words, —*Boyma big man; very budgery man. Him sit on big glass stone. Him son Grogoragally can see everything and go everywhere. See budgery man, like him; see bad man, plenty too much devil devil. Likes budgery man; no likes bad man: he growl too much. Budgery man die, Grogoragally tell Boyma; Boyma say, "Take him Ballima way, plenty budgery place." Bad man die; Boyma say, "Take him Oorooma way, plenty too hot, him growl there." Grogoragally plenty strong, him not so strong as Boyma* . . .

Several people in the bar were looking in their direction. One detached himself and set out toward them, slowly, with the care of a navigator. Before him, his hands composed a shivering binnacle for what served, on this voyage, as a compass, a glass of whisky, perilously plumb between the gimbals of his fingers.

—It was strange, it was as though he could lead every good Protestant there . . . Oorooma way, if he wanted to. And then, when I walked home with him he would hardly talk about it, he would hardly talk about any of the things that a . . . man with the pressing responsibilities . . .

—Say, gentlemen, said a voice behind them. —I enjoyed your sermon. It was the figure from down the bar, a dilapidated bark indeed, heaving in toward shore now and seeking anchorage.

—But . . . me? He didn't ask about me?

—Well, to tell the truth I . . . scarcely mentioned . . . I said I'd seen you, and he asked in an absent way . . . it's an absent way he seems to have about everything, everything except when I saw him in the church. When I was talking to him, I'd turn to see he'd stopped, standing staring straight up at the sun …

—Gentlemen, I have a religion too, said the voice. —I'm a drunkard. Would you like to join my church?

—But you, John said, bringing a hand up, and the wrist beside the lilies on the bar did not draw away from his touch, —you need a rest, don't you. As his arm had come up, the sleeve drew back to expose the face of his wrist watch. —I have to hurry, but I wish … to tell the truth, when I saw you out there on the street I thought I recognized you and then I thought No, it can't be, it's an old man.

—Gentlemen …

—I have to hurry now, I have to make that train. Will you be all right?

—Gentlemen, I have a religion too …

—If you could come up to visit us, you and your wife? We could talk like we did when we were … because I've wondered about you, I've thought about you, I've wished you hadn't changed your mind about …

—Gentlemen …

—Here, don't forget your eggs. Will you be all right now?

—Would you like to join my church?

Down from the surface of earth led the steps of the subway, one creation beneath another: the earth upon water; the water upon rock; the rock on the back of the bull; the bull on the bed of sand; the sand on the fish; the fish upon a still suffocating wind; the wind on a vale of darkness; the darkness on a mist.

And there beneath the mist? Jahennem, which consists of seven stages, one beneath another.

—The story about the lady saint, do you remember. You told me about her. So precious little you have told me, Esme said, —so precious little … running her fingers down the edge of a drawn shade, her back turned on the basement room. The bare electric bulb in the center of the low ceiling cast her shadow before her on the shade; she moved her hand to follow the outline of that dark shape laid there upon the light. —The lady saint they followed in the convent, for she left behind her a sweet odor clinging to the flags. The odor of sanc-tity. That is what you told me, she said turning to where her profile became almost apparent in the shadow. —What are you doing? What are you doing now?

Air never came through the room; but now, behind her a fresh new smell penetrated the weight of the others which had filled the air so long, resting there on the heavy smell of boiled stand oil risen from what looked like a pot of honey, to support the scent of lavender which was even now being driven away by something more fresh and pungent. —This color, he murmured.

—What color? She came across the room quickly to look into the pan where Venice turpentine was being heated with verdigris.

—The green, the green forming here.

—It is beautiful green. Beautiful green from a long time ago, before us. And before my mother, but it is not the blue. How quiet it is for now, she went on. —What was her name? She watched him take the pan from the hot coil to the table beside the empty easel, off near another wall where canvases were stacked, some unprepared, and some begun; behind them, two panels of thin aging oak; and then the mirrors. —And everything she touched held the delicious odor of sanctity days after she had touched it. What was her name? Esme sat on a stool in front of the fireplace, her chin in her hand, watching him. He seldom talked to her; she sat now where she had sat silent times she could not number while he studied her in the strong artificial light, not (he once explained) to find what was there, but to find what he could put there, and take away: for at first, wanting to hide her face, fearing close scrutiny, she had behaved as though someone from outside might discover something in her she did not know about herself, so unprepared was she to conceal or defend it. But the paintings done of her not to be of her at all, she found; and sat now, watching his lips move silently, and hers moved silently. Not to be of her at all, —but my bones and my shadows those of someone so long since dead, dead if she ever lived at all. Esme abandoned this exhibit of herself entirely, permitting what she showed to be indeed a counterfeit creature: the things she wore were nothing Esme would ever have worn: here half in profile, the blue cloth of velvet broken over her shoulder and across her breasts, and her hair drawn straightly down, she was safe away, her uninhabited face left in austere perfection, for him to search with clinical coldness, —but not to discover me here; rather academic disinterest, technical intensity, —not the eyes of a lover.

—Saint Catherine de Ricci, he said aloud, speaking the words of the pattern his lips had rehearsed. —A Dominicaness. She was a stigmatist, he added in a murmur.

—A stig-ma-tist? Saint Catherine de Ricci, a stig-matist.

Littered about the room were details of paintings, magnified reproductions of details from Bouts, van der Weyden, van der Goes; and some photographs of such high magnification that few experts could have told whose work they represented, details of brushwork.

—You did not tell me where those old flowers came from. You cannot paint them. They are almost dead. But I like the vase you brought. It is a very lovely vase.

—You...you may have it, he said quickly. —Yes, when I'm done with it, you may have it if you like. He stood beside the end-table whose top served as a palette.

—And the flowers too. Yes, and the flowers, too?

—Then they will be dead.

—Yes, they will. Where did you find them? How?

—A man sold them. A man in a hurry to be given a dollar. A policeman's coming, he says to me. A cop's coming.

—Is it against the law, then, to sell lilies? She waited. She looked up from them to him. He had only murmured, answering, busy over the table. She looked back down at them. —They are the flower of pur-i-ty, she said.

He stopped and looked up. —Lilies in India, he said clearly. —Great heart-shaped leaves on a fourteen-foot stem, and a dozen white flowers stained with purple... He broke off, and returned to what he was doing.

—Why did you go to In-dia?

—No. No, I didn't.

—And the lilies there?

—I remember them, he said, not looking up.

—I know, like I remember Baby and I were baked in a pie. And sometimes I try to write a poem and I cannot; and so I write down something I remember. It is the same feeling. I wrote down the poem about Baby and I were baked in a pie and some silly boy thought it was my po-em! Then she said, —I dreamt about you. She paused. —I dreamt you came to visit me. But when you knocked on the door, I opened the door and there was no one there. No one was there.

He was grinding something in a mortar. He did not stop.

—But I dreamt about you again. That was a terrible dream and I will tell you about it now because the mirrors are put away. Do not put them up again.

—Why not? He glanced up, because even across the room her shudder came, and the braying pestle stopped.

—Because they have terrible memories. There you were, as you are when you paint. With a long piece of rough brown cloth draped round your shoulders like you were, holding a stick that was the long handle of a spade, and unshaved too on your face, leaping from one mirror to another which held you whenever you stopped to fix it in the paint, flesh drawn over the hard bones, fixing only something lost and curious to be found again, staring out four times from the paint, reflecting itself in age and emptiness, so curious to be rescued each time you stopped. That big mirror was almost behind you, you kept looking over your shoulder like you do, pursuing yourself there, and then it caught you, you were caught in the mirror. And I could not help you out. Could that happen? Could that happen? I could not help you out.

He put down the mortar, and the pestle into it, and raised his hand to his eye, and rubbed his eye with the heel of his hand.

—Could that happen? she whispered.

The easel, erect between them, was empty. He looked beyond it to her and said, —Why have you put that . . . that blue thing on you now?

—So you may work, she said. —So that I am the lady in the picture.

—But I . . . I'm not working now, not on that. No, isn't it finished? Isn't it finished? he said suddenly, loudly. He went to the wall, and moved two books on the floor with his foot, to turn the large surface of the painting out. —Yes, yes. Yes it is, I thought it was. Good God, I thought it was. He brought it out and leaned it on the floor against the easel. —Now I . . . I have to work on it now. But it's finished. He looked up to her. —I . . . I didn't notice that you'd . . . that you thought you were going to sit tonight. Yes, yes, that's why I was surprised when you came. When you came I thought, maybe it wasn't finished.

—Then I am not to be the lady in the painting any more? The blue cloth slipped from her shoulder, taking the strap of her slip with it. She drew it back slowly. —And then I must . . . dress like they are now.

—You . . . you . . . what you like, he said turning away, to look for a knife on the table.

—To play you the lute, she said, getting down all of a sudden, —like you said they did for him. In the convent where he came, they tried to soothe and comfort him, playing the lute, she said gently, standing near to him. He looked up. —You told me, she said, gently, as though defending herself against the eyes he turned upon her.

—And did it help, their damned lute? And did it help?

—You told me, it did not, she said. She took three steps past him. —You don't need me then?

—I don't need you.

—Shall I go away?

He did not answer.

—Shall I go away?

Then he said, —Is there someone there, waiting?

—If there is no one there, and there is no one here?

He said nothing; but stood before the painting with a sketch of it in one hand, a sketch on which large blemishes were indicated.

She picked a book up from the floor. —I could read to you, she said. His lips parted, but he did not speak. He tapped his thumb on the knife blade. She sat on the edge of the low bed, running her fingertips over the print on the page. Then she commenced, —In den alten Zeiten, wo das Wünschen noch geholfen hat, lebte ein König, dessen Töchter waren alle schön, aber die jüngste war so schön, dass die Sonne selber, die doch so vieles gesehen hat, sich verwunderte, so oft sie ihr ins Gesicht schien. She looked up, smiling.

—But you read it beautifully. I ... I didn't know you could.

—Nor did I, she said.

—Where did you learn it, to read German?

—Just now, she answered.

—You don't understand it?

—Not the words, she answered. —It is very beautiful.

—I learned in this book, he said, taking it from her, and he stared at the cover. —Die Brüder Grimm ... He handed it back. —Shall I tell you what they mean, the words?

She smiled to him, in answer.

—"In olden times, when wishes still availed, there lived a king, whose daughters all were fair, but the youngest was so fair ..."

Her lips followed his voice from the page, —aber die jüngste war so schön, dass die Sonne selber ...

—"That the sun itself ..." He stood over her, looking down at her shoulder, and he stopped. —Wait, he said. —Have you ... have you got ... you don't have to go now?

—No, she said looking up, her eyes widely open. —I'm here.

—Will you sit up there for a minute? He gestured to the far stool, and went to the wall where he pulled one canvas after another aside.

She sat, her head half turned; and her face emptied of the curiosity and life of an instant before. If anything of life was left, it was a vague look of yearning, but that without expectation. All that moved in the room were his eyes, and his arm, touching with a pencil at the monochrome on the soiled surface of the gesso, pausing, rubbing the lines away with his thumb.

Suddenly she turned. —What's that?

—Be quiet. What?

—That. You were working on a piece of wood, and here is a piece of canvas.

—Linen, he said. —Be quiet. Turn your head back. Where it was. Where it was, damn it.

—When?

—There. Yes, yes, he said in a hoarse whisper. She was silent, beyond the outlines which she fitted perfectly enough to have cast them there in a quick reflection done without intent, without knowing. Some time passed. With each motion of his hand the form under it assumed a reality to exclude them both, to empty their words of content if they spoke, or, breathing, their breath of that transitory detail of living measured to one end; but left them, his motions only affirmations of this presence which projected her there in a form it imposed, in lines it dictated and colors it assumed, and the accidents of flesh which it disdained.

—Draw the cloth up, he said. —There, draw it up there. Just that part.

She turned, as quickly as a thing is dropped, and broken. His eyes were fixed part closed as though looking into a strong light. —A part every day, she cried, laughing, for his arm had stopped moving. —That's the way you wash when you have no tub, you wash a part every day, Monday is for the feet, Tuesday is knees day, Wednesday is thighs day... She stopped speaking, and hid her face away from him in embarrassment. He had not been looking at her arm or shoulder, or the line of the bone around her eye, not just a part but at her.

—Thursday? he asked, smiling, from the stool where he sat.

She got up, shedding the length of blue cloth to the dirty floor between them. She came and stood over him. She stood with a hand on his shoulder, gripping him there, bending over him, and her small breast spilled toward him, breaking its shape easily.

—It's my picture! You're making a picture of me!

—Do you think so? he asked quietly.

—Why does it look so old? A picture of me that looks so old.

—It's a study. The next picture, the next ... painting I'm going to do, this ... little ...

—You ...

—I ...

She had both arms around his shoulders; and the breath denied by the form before them came the more quickly. He straightened up and stood, straightened her to her feet and turned away from her. —That's all, he said. —We'll stop for today, very much the way he always said it. He took the soiled thing down from the easel. —I have to work on this, he said, approaching the large finished painting which stood on the floor almost between them. —Can you help me lift it up.

She stood staring at him, as though to stop his motions with the seizure of her eyes.

—Esme?

She lifted the other end of the thing, and they raised it. He picked up the knife again.

Kinder- und Hausmärchen lay at her feet, one of half a dozen books in the place. —How beautiful she is, no longer me, Esme said, looking at the prolonged figure in the painting, —for she is dead.

Over the emphatic drawing and the underpainting, translucent colors were fixed in intimate detail upon the established forms, colors added separately, unmixed on the palette, layer upon layer, constructed from within as necessity disposed these faces emptied in this perfect moment of the transient violence of life.

Round the closed eyes of the Virgin, where she looked now, the highlights were not opaque colors on the surface, but from the light underpainting tinted with ultramarine.

—Dead before death was defamed, she said, —as it is by those who die around us now, dying absurdly, for no reason, in embarrassment that the secret, the dirty secret kept so long, is being exposed, and they cannot help it, cannot hide it longer, nor pretend as they have spent their life in doing, that it does not exist. Yes, the blue, the beautiful blue of Her mantle there. How abashed they are to leave us, making up excuses and apologies with every last breath, so ashamed are we to die alone. How shocking it will be to see the day come again, out where they are, where the law does not permit him to sell lilies.

She moved away, to pull on a dress, and a coat, and treading on the length of blue cloth she approached him again from behind, where he stood in the strong light with the knife, and raised it to the face laid with closed eyes near the top of the composition.

—Before death was dishonored, she said, watching his hand move, —as you are dishonoring it now.

He continued to work. For some minutes there was no sound but the scratching of his blade. Then he turned round, raising his eyebrows in a mild surprise at the empty room, drawing his nostrils at the delicate scent which had returned and remained (for the brief pungence of the Venice turpentine had penetrated and was gone), as affirmative of recognition as the sight of blood, as the blood gushing on every Friday from the stigmata of Francesca de Serrone, blood with the odor of violets.

On the door, locked and bolted, she pinned a sign: *Do Not Disturb Me   I Am Working   Esme*. What worse thing could have happened, than had happened that morning. She had hidden the needle, the good silver (No. 22) needle with the glass syringe, in the black metal box on the wall over the sink. Who would think of looking there? Who, but a man in uniform. He entered carrying a flashlight, to walk past her and open the black box there on the wall over the sink without hesitating. He turned his light into the box, wrote something on a pad, then took the needle out and handed it to her. —You shouldn't put things in here, ma'am. It's liable to interfere with the meter. He saluted her hand-to-cap and went away.

She sat with a piece of white paper before her, the penholder's end in her mouth like a child told to write a letter home, being watched writing it, the letter to be read by her familiar jailer before it is mailed home. Over the paper she followed the course of an ant, pursuing its frantic flight with the scrupulously cruel point of the pen, leaving behind a trail of black crossing and re-crossing until the ant escaped to the rust-colored arm of her chair.

How were they all so certain? calling her "Esme": they knew she was *Esme* when she did not know, who she was or who Esme, if both were the same, every moment, when they were there, or when she was alone, both she. But she could not deny that they were right, for who would be making that denial? and if *who* could not be *no one*, it must be Esme. She thought now of undressing; and the thought was too much to bear, to undress alone, and stand there naked alone; with nothing, even shadows in this bare room, to cover her.

Across the bottom of the page where the terror of the ant was drawn she wrote, *An ant going home who does not live anywhere.*

Worse had been two nights before: asked her age, earlier, she had told it: twenty-nine. (That was the way she did, adding a year to this slow number when May appeared, and passed, taking another year with it.) Then alone at night, she had thought of the indelible year of her birth, subtracted it from this year whose number she shared with everyone, and come out with thirty. A year missing? She turned on the light, and covered three pages with numbers: the year, and her age opposite; and then the year and the month and her age; then the year, the month, her age, and where she had been and what doing. Still a year lacked, unaccounted for. And when she put down the year of her daughter's birth and worked toward it from the past and the present, *it* was the year missing. Was her daughter unborn? Whence was the year missing? from her life? or from time? Unsolved, it became a part in that world where she lay alone, unasleep at night, her limbs cold and her feet almost blue (though the room was not cold) she saw before she turned out the light: moving none of her body (thinking about other things) and then with abrupt horror remembered her body which she could not feel, all awareness gone from her legs. Was one resting against the other? or alone? The slightest move would tell, were they there? would have told immediately, if she had moved immediately this doubt came. But not having turned a foot, nor thrown back a hand in that instant of doubt the doubt grew, deepened and she in it engulfed in paralytic terror, unable to see in that darkness whether those limbs had melted into an amorphous mass, or into nothing; unable to turn on the light, without moving, then she would try to think of something else, and move unconsciously; but she was unable to deceive herself so, unable to move until some extreme of her moved itself in exhaustion.

Esme stared at a fresh page of paper. Her face, more and more forgotten as effort worked through her, took a sulking look: one of fear, remembering now a sculpture of her head and bust made once by a student who did not know that, when the plaster dried, it would shrink one-tenth the size he had modeled it, so that he made the cord tight which supported the neck, and when it dried they found death's excellent likeness of her head pendent, swinging gently with the door they had opened upon it. She hated herself for the fear which rose and choked her at that instant: the same terror that came at other times when, almost asleep, she woke suddenly with a deep breath of life, and the certainty that she had not been breathing, had recovered herself with her breath at the last instant of living possible: and then hating herself for her direct thankfulness at recovery, she who never wanted to recover.

She wrote slowly, with no effort apparent but as from memory, in confident trust as poetry is written,

> Who, if I cried, would hear me among the angelic
> orders? And even if one of them suddenly
> pressed me against his heart, I should fade in the strength of his
> stronger existence. For Beauty's nothing
> but beginning of Terror we're still just able to bear,
> and why we adore it so is because it serenely
> disdains to destroy us. Each single angel . . .

Then a knock sounded on her door, and drew her cold limbs abruptly in to her, startled and afraid.

PART II

I

A thousand accidents may and will interpose a veil between our present consciousness and the secret inscriptions of the mind; accidents of the same sort will also rend away this veil; but whether veiled or unveiled, the inscription remains forever; just as the stars seem to withdraw before the common light of day; whereas in fact we all know that it is the light which is drawn over them as a veil, and that they are waiting to be revealed when the obscuring daylight shall have withdrawn.

—Thomas De Quincey

Mr. Pivner stepped out of his office building, to the street. He moved warily, for not long before he had almost been knocked down by a cab. The December sky was gray, and the air dissolved in rain. To the south, however, lay a small portion almost rectangular in shape and extravagantly blue. It was banded by an arrogant streak of purple. He walked into the street without disturbing himself to verify the color of the sky, exposing his face and the pinched knot in his necktie to the rain which he could hear drumming on the brim of his hat. At three o'clock in the afternoon Eddie Zefnic, the office boy who daily during summer observed Mr. Pivner's wilting collar with the greeting, —Hot enough for you Mister Pivner? stopped to brood beside one of the long office windows. He stared out on the city until Mr. Pivner reached that critical point in his signature, the capital "P," which he liked to make a figure of dashing individuality even on order forms. As the pen touched paper, —It's a real winter day out all right Mister Pivner, interrupted. He looked up, startled, botching the initial miserably. In other parts of the world, as unreal as New York was inevitable, the sky may have been sporting snow, sleet, cumulus clouds and thunderheads, the consoling pattern of a mackerel sky, or only itself, tenanted by a sun in the vastness of even blue so immense that it would seem darkness had never existed. But when Mr. Pivner returned to his signature, the sky was settled for him. It was a lowering but safely remote, dull and unconscious gray.

Consequently there was no reason for him to stand idly in the wet, looking about and questioning the sky, when he came out of that office building. Little good would it have done him had he bothered. Tons of concrete and other opaque building materials stood between him and that impudent portion of blue.

In the fragment of sky which the buildings permitted above him flags were being lowered. For the full day they had floated, as much as the rain would allow, heraldic devices of marvelous power, far more impressive than a fiery cross, or the six balls of the Medici. A great bell signaled a telephone company which was omnipotent. Three strokes of white lightning on a blue ground hailed an electric company which controlled the allegiances of an office force equal to the medieval duchy of Mantua. The whole scene was lit by electricity, escaping statically in incandescent bulbs and, in splendidly colored fluidity adding a note of metaphysical (Bergsonian) hilarity to the air of well-curbed excitement, in tubes of glass cleverly contorted to spell out cacophonous syllables of words from a coined language, and names spawned in the estaminets of Antwerp. Any natural light which fell in from the sky, pale in impotence, was charitably neglected; but that sky, as has been noted, was a safe distance away.

Beneath these failing banners, these crippled ensigns depressing earthward under their own sodden weight, Mr. Pivner walked through the streets, head covered but bowed. Marvelous constructions passed him: a blackened truck with blackened men and pails hanging from every projection, dragging a cart bellied with open fire under a tub of molten asphalt, came almost over his feet. He barely glanced at it. The names AJAX and HERCULES borne in gold thundered by at an arm's reach, but Mr. Pivner did not appear to read. He stepped back, respectful as all ages of the expedition of heroes.

He had made this trip, a distance never measured in miles but in minutes, hundreds of times. Fortunately he had formed it as habit, for he accomplished it without thinking for a moment of where he was going, leaving his mind emptily cordial to the reflections of vacancy in the faces which stared with the same incurious anxiety at his own. If he had not rehearsed the trip many times, he might more easily have found himself among the flaming piles of rubble on a nearby city dump, which was a comparable distance away, far easier to reach, and whose central incineration plant had won a prize in functional architecture only ten years before.

Over and under the ground he hurried toward the place where he lived. No fragment of time nor space anywhere was wasted, every instant and every cubic centimeter crowded crushing outward upon the next with the concentrated activity of a continent spending itself upon a rock island, made a world to itself where no present existed. Each minute and each cubic inch was hurled against that which would follow, measured in terms of it, dictating a future as inevitable as the past, coined upon eight million counterfeits who moved with the plumbing weight of lead coated with the frenzied hope of quicksilver, protecting at every pass the cherished falsity of their milled edges against the threat of hardness in their neighbors as they were rung together, fallen from the Hand they feared but could no longer name, upon the pitiless table stretching all about them, tumbling there in all the desperate variety of which counterfeit is capable, from the perfect alloy recast under weight to the thudding heaviness of lead, and the thinly coated brittle terror of glass.

The subway stopped under a river. It stayed there for minutes, while the occupants looked at one another, surreptitiously, appraising the company with whom they were trapped to meet disaster. One or two, not alone, started explanations for the delay, —Lines wet... —Somebody probly jumped... and stopped speaking, embarrassed at the sounds of their own voices. It stayed there for minutes, as though to iterate to their consciousness that they were unprotected, unknown, that they did not exist singly but only in aggregate, material for headlines. Mr. Pivner stared at an advertisement which, like 90 per cent of the advertisements he read, had no possible application in his life. He had no sewer; but with glazed attention he read, "Look, darling, he found my necklace," spoken by a lady, of the Roto-Rooter Service man, who offered to come "to Razor Kleen that clogged sewer... No charge if we fail..." The subway stayed there for long enough to send one woman (who looked foreign, they said later at dinner tables) into hysterics, moaning that her head was swelling, tugging the tight hatband away from it and running down the car to thrust her head into people's faces, couldn't they see it was swelling? And they withdrew, abashed at this articulation of their own terror. Then the subway started and flashed its way into rock.

Mr. Pivner came out upon the street, to see a crowd gathering at the far corner. He turned his coat collar up again and pulled his hat down. When he reached the crowd, he looked where they were looking, up: at a man poised on a ledge eight stories above. Lights shone on him. Figures leaned from nearby windows. The crowd shifted impatiently. —Don't he know it's raining? I wish he'd get it done, if he's going to do it, a man said to Mr. Pivner. Mr. Pivner only stared. As he did, the rhythm of the crowd's voice took shape. They chanted, —Jump...jump...jump... and the figure above drew back. —JUMP ...JUMP...JUMP... they chanted. A priest appeared at the window nearest him. —JUMP...JUMP...JUMP... The figure drew back, further, toward the priest. A young man leaning from the door of a car with a *Press* card in the windshield said to his companion, —The son of a bitch isn't going to jump . . .

Two blocks further on, Mr. Pivner stopped to buy a newspaper. There a man was arguing with the news-vendor, hatless, weaving slightly. He had started to leave, but turned saying, —Now don't start to get obnoxious . . .

—Hello, Jerry, Mr. Pivner said, taking a paper. Jerry said, —Wet enough for you? Mr. Pivner said, —What's the matter with that fellow?

—Him? Aw, drunks get lonely sometimes. You know, he don't care what he says, he oney wants to talk to somebody.

—You're quite a philosopher Jerry, said Mr. Pivner, and went on, stopping in anxious habit at curbs, turning corners, glancing at passing shoe-tops, stockinged legs and trouser legs. Then with the city's suddenness someone was walking beside him. Their steps matched in a precise off-beat, ordained syncopation of doom on the wet pavement. Mr. Pivner walked faster, from fear was it? or revulsion? and still the man came on, beside and just behind him. Could he stop to light a cigarette? or for an untied shoelace? But the rain beat down around him and he walked on, again quickening his footsteps as they were echoed close upon him. When he turned down his street he looked back. The other continued straight, hat pulled down against the rain.

That street was quiet. There were no leaves dead and blowing in the gutters, because there were no trees within hope of the most boisterous wind. But there were forlorn bits of paper, candy wrappers, newspaper, paper bags, as satisfactorily dead and unmercied as winter's brown leaves in any village side street.

Like the others, Mr. Pivner spent little time at ground level. He was usually moving rapidly beneath it, or taking his spurious ease some ells above. Up he rose in the elevator, out into the passage, and he opened his door with one of a number of keys he carried, a satisfaction no one can know who does not keep a secret and private self locked away from eight million others. He stood for a moment in his open doorway, as he always did, lighting the rooms with the button at his hand and looking through the rooms in that instant of anxiety which waited always to be expanded into full terror at finding the place burgled, finding under the hand of the careless burglar the intimate slaughter of his secret self. But everything was in order, silently waiting to affirm him, holding there the sense of the half-known waiting for eventual discovery in a final recognition of himself. He took off his hat and shook it (having hurried home as though his own coronation were waiting), and moved now with the slow deliberation of lonely people who have time for every meager requirement of their lives. He took off his coat, shook it, and looked at the spots he had made on the wallpaper.

The small apartment was as inoffensive as himself. Like the defiantly patternless botch of colors he wore upon his necktie, signal of his individuality to the neckties that he met screaming the same claim of independence from the innominate morass of their wearers, the apartment's claims to distinction were mass-produced flower- and hunting-prints, filling a need they had manufactured themselves, heavy furniture with neither the seductive ugliness of functional pieces nor the isolate dumb beauty of something chosen for itself: in matching, they fulfilled their first requirement, as did the hopeless style of his brown pleated trousers which matched his brown coat, double-breasted over a chest resigned to be forever hidden like a thing of shame, whitening to yellowness with the years so that to show it now would be indeed offensive. It was a part of the body which he had never learned to use, never having been so poor that he was forced to feel the strain and growth of its muscles in the expansion of labor; nor rich enough to feel it liberated in those games (requiring courts, eighteen-hole courses, bridle-paths) which rich people played. Totally unconscious of itself except when something went wrong, that body served only to keep his identity intact, and was kept covered, like this room, to offend no one.

He turned the radio on, and adjusted his hearing, so that he heard only a comforting confusion of sound. An electric reading lamp, capable at a turn of a finger of three degrees of intensity, stood (just out of reach) beside a large chair. Behind was a veneered secretary of anonymous century and unavowed design, holding protected behind glass an assortment of books published by the hundred-thousand, treatises on the cultivation of the individual *self*, prescriptions of superficial alterations in vulgarity read with excruciating eagerness by men alone in big chairs, the three-way lamp turned to its wildest brilliance as they fingered those desperate blazons of individuality tied in mean knots at their throats, fastened monogrammed tie-clasps the more firmly, swung keys on gold-plated monogram-bearing ("Individualized") key-chains, tightened their arms against wallets in inside pockets which held the papers proving their identity beyond doubt to others and in moments of Doubt to themselves, papers in such variety that the bearer himself became their appurtenance, each one contemplating over words in a book (which had sold four million copies: How to Speak Effectively; Conquer Fear; Increase Your Income; Develop Self-Confidence; "Sell" Yourself and Your Ideas; Improve Your Memory; Increase Your Ability to Handle People; Win More Friends; Improve Your Personality; Prepare for Leadership) the Self which had ceased to exist the day they stopped seeking it alone.

——I knew it couldn't work out. I knew he was too good. I should have known . . . said a girl's voice on the radio, ——O God, what have I *du-un* . . .

On the end-table stood a ship model, a square-rigged man-o'-war set with so much sail (it was all metal) that it would have tumbled stern-over-prow in the idlest wind, furnished with so many guns that one of its own broadsides would have sent it heeling over to the bottom. The telephone was here too, and it was here that Mr. Pivner suddenly appeared from the bathroom, to pick up the receiver. —Hello? Hello? There was nothing. He dialed. —What number were you calling, ple-as? —I thought I heard the telephone ring, operator. Did you ring my telephone? —Excuse it, ple-as. —Hello? Hello?

——then and only then do you decide. The decision, my friends, rests with *you*. First come, first served. Don't wait, don't delay, don't hesitate. And re-member, you are under absolutely no obligation . . . said the radio.

Mr. Pivner returned from the bathroom with a bottle and a hypodermic needle, which he put down beside a photograph album. No one had opened the album for months. Shut in it were mean-sized prints, snapshots taken on vacations, of himself and other refugees. Some enclosed views of water, shreds of mountains, corners of sky, taken to remind him at moments like this of an outdoors whose wonders he was permitted to see some fifteen days in four hundred. But he had forgotten, not that sunsets did occur, but what a sunset was; or the flight of a bird; the movement of water against a shore; the fresh-ness of air consciously breathed; distances seen over land; the sound of wind in a green tree; or the silent, incredible progress of a snail.

And his camera photographs, having cast these phenomena into static patternless configurations of gray, recalled nothing. They served, waiting locked up in undimensional darkness here, as witnesses: that he had had more hair twelve years ago; that he had started to wear (rimless) glasses nine years before; that his brown suit was seven, not five, years old.

——Ladies, now is the time to save and save. Women are flocking to . . .

He sat down, and before filling the needle took a letter from his pocket which he put on the chair arm and did not read. He had read this brief letter enough times, at his desk and in the office lavatory, over coffee and over meals. He would read it again after supper, study his own name in counterfeit sig-nature at the bottom. Otto wrote to say that he would call to arrange a meet-ing place; but gave no number where he might be reached. Therefore there was nothing to do but wait. Some months before there had been a call, a drunken boy's voice shouting for Otto, asking him who the hell *he* was anyhow. Mr. Pivner took up the bottle and read the directions. Diabetes is a serious disease. No one can afford to take chances; there is no reason to take them, when the marvels of medical science are worked out to the most minute point, making the notion of hazard contemptible, if only one follows the directions on the bottle. True, he had had four attacks in these past seven years, suddenly rendered helpless in public, going down with the reeling fall of a drunkard: but those had been moments of excitement. One had only to be careful, keep hold of one's self. That poor woman in the subway tonight, for instance... (he had for the moment forgot the man on the ledge). One had only one's self to blame for catastrophe, with Science concentrating its huge forces on bettering the human lot. (Had he not read, only the week before in a newspaper, of a new medicine which would prolong human life? Men might live to be two hundred years old, unclothed perhaps and unfed since there would be so many, but Science took care of details when they arose (had he not read only this week that very palatable foods were being made from seaweed, coal, and cotton? and clothing: the same article said that very durable cloth could be made from soy beans, meat extracts, and vegetable products). Two hundred years old! and, as he understood it, alive.)

After the injection, he picked up his newspaper. The Sunday edition, still in the rack beside him, required fifty acres of timber for its magic transformation of nature into progress, benefits of modern strides in transportation, communication, and freedom of the press: public information. (True, as he got into the paper, the average page was made up of a half-column of news, and four-and-one-half columns of advertising.) A train wreck in India, 27 killed, he read; a bus gone down a ravine in Chile, 1 American and 11 natives; avalanche in Switzerland, death toll mounts... This evening edition required only a few acres of natural grandeur to accomplish its mission (for it carried less advertising). Mr. Pivner read carefully. Kills father with meat-ax. Sentenced for slaying of three. Christ died of asphyxiation, doctor believes. Woman dead two days, invalid daughter unable to summon help. Nothing escaped Mr. Pivner's eye, nor penetrated to his mind; nothing evaded his attention, as nothing reached his heart. The headless corpse. Love kills penguin. Pig got rheumatism. Nagged Bible reader slays wife. Man makes own death chair, 25,000 volts. "Ashamed of world," kills self. Fearful of missing anything, he read on, filled with this anticipation which was half terror, of coming upon something which would touch him, not simply touch him but lift him and carry him away.

Every instant of this sense of waiting which he had known all of his life, this waiting for something to *happen* (uncertain quite what, and the Second Advent intruded) he brought to his newspaper reading, spellbound and ravenous. Man fights lion in zoo, barefisted. Cow kills woman. Rooster kills woman. Dogs eat Eskimo. As he turned the pages, folding them smartly back over the bulk of the newspaper, he relaxed a little at his comparative safety away from the news, drew comfort from the train wreck (he was not in it), the bus accident in Chile (nor in that), the meat-ax slaying (he had not done it), the headless corpse (not his), and so the newspaper served him, externalizing in the agony of others the terrors and temptations inadmissible in himself. Even though the evening paper repeated the news of the morning paper, he read attentively again, reworded, of the hunt for the unknown person who was releasing birds from an uptown zoo, of the discovery of two priceless art treasures, original paintings of Dierick Bouts, in a pawnshop in Hell's Kitchen, of the murder trial in Mouth, Mississippi, where just that morning the husband's heart had been exhibited in court. All of these civilized wonders were brought together, he was made to feel, expressly for him, by the newspaper. True, they kept him in such a state that he often bought late editions of the same newspaper, seeing different headlines than those tucked under his arm, only to read the story from column six suddenly elevated to a banner across columns one to four. True, often the only way he could know whether he had read a newspaper was to turn to the comic strips, where life flowed in continuum; and recognizing them, he knew that he must have read everything else closely and avidly, that nothing had evaded his eye, nor penetrated to his heart round which he had built that wall called objectivity without which he might have gone mad. As the tales of violence seemed daily to increase it hardly occurred to him that he was living in such unnatural density of population that it daily supported disasters sufficient for a continent. Added to this came the blood of the world, piped in on wires, and wireless, teletype, undersea cables, and splashed without a drop lost in transit upon Mr. Pivner, who sat, hard, patient, unbending, wiped it from his eyes, and waited for more.

Mr. Pivner elevated himself slightly upon one narrow ham and broke wind, a soft interrogative sound which went unanswered. Then he sagged and stared at the newspaper, untroubled by the notion that this might have been a demon leaving its residence inside him. Not only would he, albeit embarrassed, scoff at this medieval reality; but he could, in all reason, believe that even had he lived then, he would have scoffed. Incubae and succubae, the shriek of the mandrake root pulled from the ground which drove a man mad if he heard it, chloroform a decoy of Satan, smallpox a visitation of God: all those, and many more, he could believe that he would not have believed, but would have stood forth, as he was submerged now, in Reason. It was true, there were things he did not understand, realms where Science advanced upon the provinces of God, where he felt rather uncomfortable, looking forward, secretly, to the day when Science would explain all, and vindicate the Doubt which he kept hidden in case it should not.

His thumb over the headline, Campanile at Venice Periled, his eyes blinked closed behind the glasses which were steadily weakening them, until one day they might be as little good in light as they were now in darkness: his trouble had been diagnosed as nyctalopia, caused, he was told, by a vitamin deficiency (and not, "like people used to think," from sleeping in the moonlight). He had a shelf-full of bottles (labeled Afaxin, Pancebrin, Natola, Multi-Vi Drops, Vi-Dom-A Pillettes, and others) to help correct this condition; but he had got the glasses "just to make sure." Nonetheless, he still stumbled in the dark.

Now, the headlines had commenced to run together before his eyes. He had read the letters written to the editors (written by the editors), and the columns of the columnists, an assortment of aggressive ulcerated men, self-appointed authorities who wrote intimately of people they had never seen and places they had never been, or colyumists with the "common touch," who simulated and encouraged the average reader's lack of intelligence, talent, and sensitivity. But now, Holy See Bans Psychoanalysis..., Giant Robot Runs Amok..., Lobotomy to Cure Man of Writing Dud Checks..., the black letters swam before his eyes, and he started to doze over the news that the bell tower of Saint Mark's was in danger of falling, cracked in the cool nights of summer after the scorching sun of the days.

——The Rootsicola Company now brings you the correct time. The time is six P.M. Have you tried Rootsicola? Rootsicola tastes better *and* is better for you, and remember, friends, Rootsicola keeps its flavor twice as long, and you get twice as much Rootsicola in the familiar big bottle...

(Better than what? he wondered faintly. Twice as long as what? Twice as much as what?)

——Rootsicola. That's right, friends. Remember the *root*. Rootsicola, for the smile of happiness... the uprooted voice went on, bursting with aggressive vitality, leveling Mr. Pivner's weariness to chronic decrepitude. True, he it was to whom they all appealed; and he did try, with all the attention his consciousness could muster under the attrition of the sameness of their words, to maintain his responsibility as a citizen. He listened to the radio during periods of political heat, the speech in which one senator told the truth about another (this was known as a "smear campaign"); and then the raucous gathering where people were paid in five-dollar bills to shout, clap, parade, and otherwise indicate the totally irrational quality of their enthusiasm for a man they had never met to take office and govern them. Occasionally, it is true, Mr. Pivner slipped into listening to these conventions in much the same spirit as benighted members of certain Latin cultures listen to the drawing of the National Lottery; but even when this expression disappeared he had as much difficulty reconciling his sense of public duty and responsibility with his feeling of total helplessness as a Central American Indian might, upon being told that he shared the responsibility for the number drawn in Panama on Sunday afternoon; and as far as that goes, the Indian could call in powers which Mr. Pivner knew nothing about, dreams and spells, magic numbers and meretricious deities, a seedy band to call in where Reason reigned, however staunch they might prove as allies there where the Indian sat silent with his radio on a peak in Darien.

Science assures us that "If man were wiped out, it is extremely improbable that anything very similar would ever again evolve." Threat and comfort: we need only turn the particle of the earth's crust read with such eager pride to make one of the other. Here in the foremost shambles of time Mr. Pivner stood, heir to that colossus of self-justification, Reason, one of whose first accomplishments was to effectively sever itself from the absurd, irrational, contaminating chaos of the past. Obtruding over centuries of gestation appeared this triumphal abortion: Reason supplied means, and eliminated ends.

What followed was entirely reasonable: the means, so abruptly brought within reach, became ends in themselves. And to substitute the growth of one's bank account for the growth of one's self worked out very well. It had worked out almost until it reached Mr. Pivner, for so long as the means had remained possible of endless expansion, those ends of other ages (which had never shown themselves very stable) were shelved as abstractions to justify the means, and the confidently rational notion that peace, harmony, virtue, and other tattered constituents of the Golden Rule would come along of themselves was taken, quite reasonably, for granted.

Retirement? the word shook him hollow, left him in a void where nothing remained to be done. With survival a triumph, the means themselves had become an end constantly unfulfilled; and now the specter of retirement formed its expression, leering within sight. He found himself surrounded by the rights of others who had ceased to grow more recently than himself, having earned that right the instant they mastered some fundamental technique of making a living, which they called education. Assured that they were under no obligation, and would do very well as they were, they advanced to take his place and relive his dilemma.

——and do you feel run down at the end of the day? that dull logy tired feeling that just seems to creep through you? Well friends, modern science has developed . . .

It was to him that these voices appealed, siding with him in this conspiracy against himself, citing him splendidly satisfactory just as he was, heralding his privileges, valuing the mass of his concurring opinion with guarantee of his protection against dissenters, justifying his limitations, and thus proving, by their own successful existence, that he was obliged to seek no further than himself for the authority which justified them both, pledged at last to secure and defend him in all these things, which they called his rights.

The newspaper now lay open to a feature story (*exclusive*) on the imminent canonization of a Spanish child, a feature not because the little girl was soon to be a saint, but because she had been raped and murdered. He stared, started, and felt suddenly for the keys in his pocket, always terrified that, losing them, the finder would know to whom they belonged, what they guarded. The newspaper tipped in his hand, and lay quiet on his lap, as the tic which came in his lip when he was tired pulled his mouth out of line. His half-opened eyes met those of the two faces before him, both pictures indistinct because they had been sent by radio, not that there was any hurry, but to show that this newspaper afforded its readers the most modern news service possible. He summoned his attention to read the article, for it was in such "features" that he found the satisfaction which life never suggested, that of a beginning, a middle, and an end. (Though occasionally one beginning got confused with other middles and other ends, he knew that these events were really taking place; and he even had the sense that he was slightly ahead of them, with evening papers out in the morning, and next morning's papers out that night.)

His eyes met the penetrating eyes of the murderer, fixed in a round face whose limp flabby quality was belied by a exquisite mustache and a sharp cleft in the widow's peak of black hair. He read the man's name, and that of his victim, confusions of foreign syllables which he did not try to align, and then details of the crime so rewardingly grisly and sharp that it might have happened the day before, instead of four decades. "Very soon after her death, the village of San Zwingli, its façades splashed blue with vine-spray, where the peasants live a mixed life with their goats, chickens, and burros, became the scene of a series of miracles. There were miraculous cures among sick peasants who insisted on attributing them to the little girl who appeared to them in visions, in a mist, carrying lilies of purity..." Even the criminal testified, "'I see her against the light, coming to me with lilies in her hands. But when she offers them to me they become flames. It is in these flames that I find remorse and penitence, and peace!...'" Through his drooping eyes, Mr. Pivner stumbled on to an interview with the priest who had promoted recognition of the child's sanctity, "A candle gave an extra flicker and lit up his face, the color and texture of antique parchment, surmounted by the black satin biretta..." With a gesture of "his pale El Grecoesque hands..." he went on, "'The Devil's Advocate took the information and after two years' study passed it to the Preparatory Congregation, which was held in the presence of the Cardinals. The following year, the Pope was present at the General Congregation, with his Cardinals, Prelates, and consultative Padres. They all cast votes in favor of the Martyrdom . . . We started without a single lira, and it takes a great deal of money to promote a saint. Apart from the expenses of bringing witnesses to Rome and making out the documents, it costs 3,000,000 lire to hire Saint Peter's for a canonization . . .'"

There the little girl stood before Mr. Pivner in long white stockings, and stared out at his dozing face wistfully, for the harsh newspaper reproduction, sent by radio, made her look cross-eyed.

——Friends, don't take our word for it. You owe it to your own health . . .

The newspaper slipped to the floor, and Mr. Pivner sat up as though called. A half-pound of ground beef waited in the kitchen, for his supper. (—Is it all beef? he had asked insistently; and assured that it was, did not ask how old it was, and so was not told that it had got its succulent redness from sodium sulphite rubbed into it when it had turned toxic gray the day before.)

——Exhaustive scientific tests have proved . . .

He breathed, a sigh, and sat back, his senses glazed, insulted and injured, a brave man, assailed on all sides, supporting with his last penny those things which tore from him the last sacred corner of his privacy, and with it the dignity which churchmen called his soul.

——Prominent medical specialists agree . . .

He looked at that letter again, on the chair arm, and his eyes widened as the stain of perfect metal in his alloy cried out for perfection.

——tastes better, looks better, smells better, and is better for you . . .

And that perfect particle was submerged, again satisfied with any counterfeit of itself which would represent its worth amongst others. As his eyes closed again, the letter slipped from the chair arm to the floor, and with it the precious metal of youth which it had suggested, alloyed in age with weariness, doubt and dread, circumstances constantly unpropitious to any approach to perfection. Gold was never seen, never passed from one hand to another, no longer currency, not only unexpected but against the law: only the compromises worn smooth which Exchangers do not even bother to ring but pass on, giving and receiving or losing and taking reciprocally their leaden counterparts.

Worth his weight in gold, Mr. Pivner would have brought seventy-four thousand and four dollars (at the official rate; $105,720 on the black market). But somewhere in the shadowy past, in that penumbra of Science called chemistry, lay the assurance that his body was worth ninety-seven cents: a faint sigh led him nearer sleep, a sound of anticipation, as though awaiting the strategic moment to sell out.

Even in sleep, he was waiting, a little tense like everyone waiting within reach of a telephone, for it to ring. And still, even in sleep, he knew there would be time. Adam, after all, lived for nine hundred thirty years.

Beside the empty cradle of the white telephone, a vase held erect against green six bird-of-paradise flowers, *Strelitzia reginae*, also called wild banana in South Africa where they grow naturally profuse, blue-tongued exotic orange protrusions from the deep purple-green bill, silently mating there among the native white pear, the red ivory, black stinkwood, and umzimbiti.

Mickey Mouse pointed to four o'clock.

—Am *I* in a state of Grace? But darling… Agnes Deigh paused, to reach beyond the oval-framed miniature of a young man in uniform, for the cigarettes on her desk. She got one and put it into her mouth at an extreme angle and, lighting it, listening, looked for that moment like a billboard picture into whose lips someone has stuck a cigarette. —Yes I know, that's sweet but I can't pray for you, she went on, the cigarette bobbing. —I know, darling, another time. But thank you for the divine flowers just the same.

When she'd hung up she sat staring for a moment at the news clipping one of the girls had sent in as a joke: Offer Husband's Heart in Evidence. A woman named Agnes Day of Mouth, Mississippi, was on trial for stabbing her husband to death. It was not funny. She crumpled it to throw in the basket, and rummaged in her bag, took out a French enameled thimble case, set it aside, and looked until she found another pill box. Then as she poured water from the carafe, she stared at the miniature in the oval frame. It was her brother, whom she'd known only in the intent intimacy of childhood, before he ran away, before she was sent away to school; and she found herself again counting the months since he'd been listed missing in a war which no one spoke of but as a political blunder. She turned her chair away from the desk to take her pill.

Across the court from Agnes Deigh's office there were two windows she could look directly into. One, she was certain, was a psychoanalyst. The Venetian blinds were usually drawn, but she had seen the couch, and the sight of its familiar length upset her. Her own analysis had taken three years, under one of the best analysts (he had made a name for himself with a paper he had published on one of his patients, a nun, who became a bear trainer when he had done with her). But there were still moments, when she thought of her husband, or when she looked at the picture in the oval frame, when Agnes Deigh was unsure whether she had correctly reassembled the parts he had spread out before her, as when a novice dismantles a machine, and putting it back together finds a number of parts left over, each curiously shaped to some definite purpose.

The other window was a dentist. Late every afternoon he appeared there in an undershirt, to shave before the mirror hung in the window frame. For some reason she always thought of her husband, Harry, when she looked across at him. But he never noticed her, he never glanced across the court, never anywhere but the mirror, not even when, one day, exasperated at his sloven obduracy, she had stood at her window with her blouse undone, pretending, as a breast slipped into conspicuous sight while she watched him from her eye's corner, to be adjusting an undergarment. He'd neither looked over nor seemed consciously to keep from doing so, but went on to shave, the flesh of his arms hanging loosely, suspenders dangling to his knees. Every time she looked up he was there, absorbed in some activity of the body, his own or someone else's, now washing his hands, now drying them, talking to someone unseen.

She returned to her desk to put down the glass of water, took a macadamia nut from the jar there, and sat exposing a face where time weighed out unconscious of exposure, a face even she herself had never seen in her mirror. Then her telephone rang.

—Yes? she whispered, and then, getting her voice, —Send him in.

Otto had left a copy of his play for her to look at (one of four made at alarming expense by a public stenographer, which he carried in a proportionately expensive pigskin dispatch case). When he arrived late that afternoon, he could hear her voice from an office or two away, ringing from the dark green walls, ricocheting off the white plaster approximations to tropical plants which were the indirect lighting fixtures, glancing from one unsympathetic modern surface to another, skipping across the edges of other sounds to attempt escape through the jalousies of the Venetian blinds, caroming off the absurd angles of the hats on other women who infested the place and who, themselves, rebounded among telephones. The whole scene, on the long-piled dark green carpet bore grotesque parody to those earlier caricatures of Nature sponsored by shades of the Sun King, where women of exhausted French sophistication dressed as shepherdesses to toil weary sins in new silks across carpets of false grass.

—Simpotico, came that voice, —I say they're so simpótico . . . what? Harry? Oh God no, not for months, he's still in Hollywood where they're filming his novel . . . yes, it was changed a little. What? . . . yes, the homosexual boy to a Negro and the Jew to a cripple. Sensitive minorities . . . Of course I'm interested in politics . . . Don't be tiresome, I couldn't care less about Harry using me in his ghastly book, but giving me a name like Seraphina . . . No, of course I don't need the money, I'm just suing him because money is the only language he understands . . .

—She's frightfully busy, said one of the hats to Otto. —She's on the phone, and she has someone in there now. Have you an appointment?

Some minutes later, during which Otto almost set fire to his sling trying to light a cigarette, Agnes Deigh appeared with an immaculate boy before her, saying to him, —But you will hurry with it? Buster Brown's third book will be out in the spring, and he's only twenty-three.

—Buster twenty-three! Agnes, he's twenty-eight if he's a day. And really, how can he pretend to write about depravity, why I told him myself about Leda and the swan, do you know what he said? Human beins cain't copulate wif bihds, silly...Really, he's a very wicked boy. You're coming to the party tonight? I'll tell you who I'm going to be or you'll never know me, Cleopatra!...

Otto followed her into her office, after her incurious smile and a glance, not at him but his fading suntan. Hers glistened richly. —Now...she paused behind her desk, —what was it? You are...

—*The Vanity of Time*, my play, my name...

—Oh yes. Sit down? She found it, under things, and sat a long silence staring at it. When he cleared his throat to speak, she said, —Well *I* liked it a great deal, you know...as though to indicate that no one else had. —But we've talked about it...Apparently no one else had. —It's not really that it isn't a good play, you do have an admirable eye for dramatic situation, and some very sensitive perceptions. But...possibly the theme is a little ambitious for someone your age? When you've really lived these things...as they happen...it isn't really topical, you see. If you look carefully at the plays and novels that are successful now...The white telephone rang. —Yes, Monday? sixish? Just drinks, yes, I want to talk to you about it. He left a moment ago, he said he'd have a copy for you in two or three weeks, and frankly I think it's worth ten thousand simply in pre-publication advertising, after all he is just the sort of thing we've made popular. I?...no, I haven't had a chance to read it yet myself.

As she spoke she twisted forward, looking past him, lips distorted to accept the cigarette he offered round the Strelitzia ambush. But before he could manage to light it, she'd hung up and held a flaming silver machine across to him. —There is something else I should mention, she went on as he sank back. —All of us had the feeling that parts of it were familiar, I hardly know how to say...She coughed, looked at the cigarette, and put it out. —No, I didn't mean to say you'd stolen it, not at all, but there was the feeling...some of the lines were familiar...The telephone rang. —Thank you for letting us look at it, she said lifting the telephone, and then lowering her eyes to vacancy as he stood. —Of course I have your key darling, the one to your box?...but you told me I wasn't to let you have it...She smiled down at space. —Oh, for the party tonight?... She looked up, and spoke around the telephone mouthpiece, —But you'll show us anything else you do, won't you...? her voice followed him, out the gate, across the greensward among those shepherdesses gesticulating their telephone crooks, up the garden path.

One of them passed him, carrying a letter to the office he'd just left, a letter which quivered, open, in Agnes Deigh's hand a few moments later. It was from the War Department, to inform her that the body of her brother had been recovered and identified. Did she want it? Please check *yes* or *no*.

—Darling, is something the matter?

—Please...just...

—What...?

—Leave me alone...for a minute. Then the slight sound of the letter quivering in her hand roused her from the numbness which had diffused itself through every sensible part of her body. —Not so cruel, she murmured, —but...how can they be so stupid?...Then she let go the paper and swung her chair away abruptly to face the window, to deny the familiar room, and the picture on her desk, seeing her wipe her eyes. She did that; and sat staring through the glass.

Check yes or no

Although she could not hear across the court, it was evident that the dentist was shouting. She could make out a girl of about twenty. Then Agnes Deigh leaned forward. She got up and went to the window and stared. He had hit her. He had hit the girl and he hit her again. He had the razor strop in his hand, and he brought it down against the arms protecting her bosom. Agnes Deigh's hand shook with excitement as she turned and lifted the white telephone, opening the directory with her other hand, to say, —Get me Spring seven three one hundred...Hello? Yes, I want to report a case of malicious cruelty. Or sadism. Yes, sadism. What? Of course, my name is Agnes Deigh...

As she spoke she stared at the Strelitzia; and as she spoke the words of an earlier conversation rehearsed in her mind. —Your flowers are lovely, are they for Christmas?

> (—Yes Agnes but I sent them because I knew they'd amuse you, aren't they sweet, they're so ob*scene*, but Agnes darling you know I'm mercenary, really quite venial, and I want someone to pray for something for me, darling *are* you in a state of Grace...?)

Immediately she had hung up she stood, put on her hat slowly, her coat quickly, and went through the door. *Check yes or no* In how many years? she thought, no one has sent me flowers for love.

She'd gone direct to the bank of elevators, but turned suddenly to the figure behind a near desk, and brought out, breathless, confused, not the words she expected, not, Are you Catholic? but, —Do you believe in God?

—Why yes, darling... in a way...

—Will you go to Saint Vincent Ferrer?... and have them say...you, you can go tomorrow, yes, go on your lunch hour?...The elevator doors opened behind her, and she said more clearly over her shoulder as she turned, —And put it on your expense account.

In the street she walked briskly, not a stitch or line out of place, her make-up set in a mask. An unshaven cripple, who'd come forth with an open hand, to be charitably avoided by a turn of her hips, retired saying to a passer-by, —You couldn't take her out in the rain.

She went into a bar, and ordered a martini.

—With pumpkin seeds in it?

She just stared at him. The girl next to her had one beside her book. She was reading *The Compleat Angler*.

"What is mine, then, and what am I? If not a curve in this poor body of mine (which you love, and for the sake of which you dotingly dream that you love me), not a gesture that I can frame, not a tone of my voice, not any look from my eyes, no, not even now when I speak to him I love, but has belonged to others? Others, ages dead, have wooed other men with my eyes; other men have heard the pleading of the same voice that now sounds in your ears. The hands of the dead are in my bosom; they move me, they pluck me, they guide me; I am a puppet at their command; and I but reinform features and attributes that have long been laid aside from evil in the quiet of the grave..."

The dead lilies stood beside her in a fruit jar, where she read, slowly as though bringing these words into concert for the first time herself.

The sign pinned to her door said, *Do Not Disturb Me I Am Working Esme*: and she had closed that door and bolted it, delighted to be alone. But as the afternoon passed, she moved less excitedly and less often. For a few minutes she sewed at a dress she was making, singing one of her own songs. Then she got up, with a cigarette, and walked about the double room, replacing things. Then she sewed again, sitting like a child of five sewing, and like a five-year-old girl singing unheard. But before that sewing was done she was up, rearranging her books with no concern but for size. There was, really, little else their small ranks held in common (except color of the bindings, and so they had been arranged, and so too the reason often enough she'd bought them). Their compass was as casual as books left behind in a rooming house; and this book of stories by Stevenson, with no idea where she'd got it, she hadn't looked into it for years, now could not put it down, and to her now it was the only book she owned. Even so she had never read for the reasons that most people give themselves for reading. Facts mattered little, ideas propounded, exploited, shattered, even less, and narrative nothing. Only occasional groupings of words held her, and she entered to inhabit them a little while, until they became submerged, finding sanctuary in that part of herself which she looked upon distal and afraid, a residence as separate and alien, real or unreal, as those which shocked her with such deep remorse when the features of others betrayed them. An infinite regret, simply that she had seen, might rise in her then, having seen too much unseen; and it brought her eyes down quick. It was Otto's expression, when his cigarette had burnt a cleft on her table, and he recovered it and looked up sharply to see if she'd noticed. It was Max's expression, when he'd taken a paper with her writing on it, whatever it was, she didn't know, but taken it from the table and slipped it into a pocket away from her, looking up with his smile to see if she'd seen him, his smile fixed and barely breaking as he started to talk hurriedly, looking at her with eyes which sent hers to the floor lest she weep for the lie in his.

The sole way, it seemed to her often enough when she was working at writing a poem, to use words with meaning, would be to choose words for themselves, and invest them with her own meaning: not her own, perhaps, but meaning which was implicit in their shape, too frequently nothing to do with dictionary definition. The words which the tradition of her art offered her were by now in chaos, coerced through the contexts of a million inanities, the printed page everywhere opiate, row upon row of compelling idiocies disposed to induce stupor, coma, necrotic convulsion; and when they reached her hands they were brittle, straining and cracking, sometimes they broke under the burden which her tense will imposed, and she found herself clutching their fragments, attempting again with this shabby equipment her raid on the inarticulate.

So for instance she stole *comatulid*, and her larceny went unnoticed by science which chose it to mean "a free-swimming stalkless crinoid..." and *crinoid:* lily-shaped (though this word belonged to the scientists too, Crinoidea, a large class of echinoderms). And the phylum Echinodermata she left far behind, left the starfishes, the sea urchins, and their allies to grope in peace in the dark water of the sea. *Comatulid* lay on the paper under her pen; while she struggled to reach it through the rubble amassed by her memory.

It was through this imposed accumulation of chaos that she struggled to move now: beyond it lay simplicity, unmeasurable, residence of perfection, where nothing was created, where originality did not exist: because it was origin; where once she was there work and thought in causal and stumbling sequence did not exist, but only transcription: where the poem she knew but could not write existed, ready-formed, awaiting recovery in that moment when the writing down of it was impossible: because she was the poem. Her hand tipped toward the paper, black stroke the pen made there, but only that stroke, line of uncertainty. She called her memory, screamed for it, trying to scream through it and beyond it, damned accumulation that bound her in time: *my* memory, *my* bed, *my* stomach, *my* terror, *my* hope, *my* poem, *my* God: the meanness of *my*. Must the flames of hell be ninety-story blazes? or simply these small sharp tongues of fire that nibble and fall to, savoring the edges and then consume, swept by the wind of terror at exposing one's self, losing the aggregate of meannesses which compose identity, in flames never reaching full roaring crescendo but scorch through a life like fire in grass, in the world of time the clock tells. Every tick, synchronized, tears off a fragment of the lives run by them, the circling hands reflected in those eyes watching their repetition in an anxiety which draws the whole face toward pupiled voids and finally, leaves lines there, uncertain strokes woven into the flesh, the fabric of anxiety, double-webbed round dark-centered jellies which reflect nothing. Only that fabric remains, pleached in the pattern of the bondage which has a beginning and an end, with scientific meanness in attention to details, of a thousand things which should not have happened, and did; of myriad mean events which should have happened, and did not: waited for, denied, until life is lived in fragments, unrelated until death, and the wrist watch stops.

The pen quivered over the paper, added *inae* to *comatulid*, and then carefully crossed out that free suffix; and then brought *comatulid* into the tangle of black ink, as she moved toward that world not world where the needle took her. It was the uncircumscribed, unbearable, infinitely extended, indefinitely divisible void where she swam in orgasm, soaring into a vastness away from the heaving indignity of the posture she shared; the world of music so intensely known that nothing exists but the music; it was the world of ecstasy they all approximated by different paths, one world in which temporary residence is prohibited, as the agonies of recall attest: "Love's dart" that wounds but does not kill; the ill complained of, but prized above every joy and earthly good; "sweet cautery," the "stolen heart," the "ravished understanding," the "rape of love": in Provençal, *conoscenza*. Thus Saint Teresa, quadrupedis, "dying of not being able to die."

What did the devil teach Gerbert, Archbishop of Ravenna, in exchange for his soul which Gerbert bartered to learn all, and become Pope? The devil taught him algebra and clock-making, for a world where there is no space, only distances; no time, only minutes and hours; where things are numbered, and even Christ bowed with finite care when he gave SS Elizabeth Matilda Bridget a written account of the kicks, blows, and wounds he had received, numbered the skull fractures 100, the drops of blood 38,430 (though another girl was later to receive a letter through her guardian angel numbering those drops of blood 3,000,800). The world in which the Virgin's titles number 305; and Sir Arthur Eddington decides that the electron is not subject to scientific law. The cosmos of Sir James Jeans, reigned over by a deity whose symbol is the square root of minus one, where in closed rooms they argue the weight of the crucified man sufficient to cause strangulation, and the Irish mathematician Sir William Rowan Hamilton calculates that Jesus in assumption, being drawn up through space at a moderate rate, would not yet have reached the nearest of the fixed stars.

When the devil appeared to Gerbert, to claim his soul, Gerbert resisted; and disappeared in a fork of flame.

The tracking point of the pen moved on the paper, and it was gone, Esme had lost it, and lay in the agonized exhaustion of this recovery of her temporal self. Still, on the edge of the chasm into which she could not fall, Esme quivered with anticipation of a sound which would interrupt, waiting fearfully for the signal to recall her from that edge. In the silence of waiting, she recovered herself; slow, she stepped back; silence, she began to talk with herself; stillness, she moved with exaggeration as though she were being watched, needed to be watched suddenly, to have another consciousness present, aware of her, containing her, to assure her of her own existence. There was no one. Even her voice sounded with a disembodied quality which frightened her. She sat there quiet again with the pen over paper, reduced in despair, her face expressing nothing but empty misunderstanding at being alone.

Across the air shaft from her closed window a woman ironed on a board. A man in underclothes appeared to stand beside her for a moment, talk silently and disappear. Then with no change in her expression Esme was crying and she turned her face from the window where she had been watching unbeknown. On the paper she wrote,

> In a nicely calcimined
> Apartment is a left-behind
> Opera chair against the wall
> Masquerading for a ball,

an exercise as significant as those ceremonies carried out at the insistence of the people during papal interdicts in the medieval Church, when saying the Mass was forbidden, but "the brethren had only to ring their bells, and play their organ in the choir; and the citizens in the nave were quite happy in the belief that Mass was being said behind the screen."

Esme wrote regretfully, pouting,

Your name is said in a far-off place
By someone alone in a room
You do not hear it

but it was spent. And the miracle of transubstantiation? only a glimpse; and only the fragrance of its death remained, the heavenly fragrance, as of lilies, which rose from the body of Saint Nicolas of Tolentino, after he had reproved his sorrowing brethren who brought him a dish of doves on his sweltering deathbed, and with a pass of his hand restored their plumage and sent them flying out of the window of his cell; only the scent of lilies, rotting in the fruit jar beside her.

She lit a spirit lamp, and sat beside it for a moment before finding a teaspoon in which to liquefy an injection of heroin, staring into the flame, and the lilies beyond it. —If I am not real to him, she said aloud, staring at the dead lilies, —then where am I real? And the book of Stevenson, which she had laid open on a pile of books beside the lamp, threatened to catch fire. She took it down, and read there, again, "You are a man and wise; and I am but a child. Forgive me, if I seem to teach, who am as ignorant as the trees of the mountain; but those who learn much do but skim the face of knowledge; they seize the laws, they conceive the dignity of the design—the horror of the living fact fades from their memory. It is we who sit at home with evil who remember... and are warned and pity..."

knock knock knock sounded on her door, in ruthless precision of recall to time in its aseptic succession of importunate instants. Her lips tightened. —Who is it? she called.

—Chaby.

—Jesis Christ why don't you put some lights on? he said when she let him in. He walked past her to the light cord.

—Because I'm alone, Esme said. Her weight hung on him, and without a word he bore her down.

As the afternoon ended, Otto was walking alone, south, on Madison Avenue, his own face expressing an extreme of the concentration of vacancy passing all around him, the faces of office messengers, typists turned out into the night air, dismally successful young men, obnoxious success in middle age, women straining at chic and accomplishing mediocrity who had spent the afternoon spending the money that their weary husbands had spent the afternoon making, the same husbands who would arrive home minutes after they did, mix a drink, and sit staring in the opposite direction. With his dispatch case, and an unkind thought for everyone he knew, Otto carried his head high. Affecting to despise loneliness, still he looked at the unholy assortment streaming past him as though hopefully to identify one, rescue some face from the anonymity of the crowd with instantly regretted recognition, and so rescue himself. He even strongly considered conversation with strangers; and with this erupted the thought of his father whom he had arranged to telephone, and appoint a place for their first meeting. With this, Otto took sudden new interest in every very successful middle-aged man who passed, coveting diamond stick-pins, a bowler hat, an ascot tie, and even (though he would have been shocked enough if this were "Dad") a pair of pearl-gray spats. It was a problem until now more easily left unsolved; and be damned to Oedipus and all the rest of them. For now, the father might be anyone the son chose. The instant their eyes met in forced recognition, it would be over.

—I must call the Sun Style Film man, he thought suddenly. —Peru, and northern Bolivia . . . Someone beside him was asking him how to get to Vesey Street. Otto held the impatient man with long and intricate explanation, two sets of alternate routes and was commencing a third when the poor fellow retreated down wind, thanking him, retiring to a policeman to ask directions for Vesey Street.

On the corner a tall black man with an umbrella towered in a hat of unseasonal straw, though on him no more out of season than the permanent attire of a statue. He stood as far as possible from the black poodle dog as their leash would allow, atolls of a formidable reef casting the white-caps to one side and the other. —He's very handsome, Otto said of the strangely familiar animal.

—I takin her to the veterinary, said Fuller, not looking at this young man whom he did not know but at the dog. —Seem like she sufferin with the worms, he added with relish, looking at the dog which ignored him.

—That's a shame, said Otto. —Beautiful dog.

—Yes, mahn, said Fuller, looking up and back at the poodle, —seem like she sufferin from the worms, he repeated, watching her face as though hoping to see discomfort and embarrassment cloud it.

The light changed, and the sea moved reuniting its currents, bore the reef away north and Otto south toward Esme. He had left her late the night before after what might have been an argument, except that he found no way to argue with Esme. He had worked for so long to develop his weak capacity for dialectic into equipment for a sophistical game that he was useless now against her blank simplicity. When she had asked him not to spend the night with her there, —because it's so Greenwich Village... he realized that none of his cleverness would change her mind. Still he was jealous enough of her: she had a way of bending one shoulder down almost upon the table and looking up across at him, laughing, which rose into his mind now, and he hurried toward the pit of the subway.

—Wait a minute, Esme called, after he had climbed her stairs wearily. Chaby was still fastening his clothes when he knocked.

Otto and Chaby did not exchange any greeting. They had come to behave together like two animals of different zoological classes in a private zoo, each wondering at their owner for keeping the other. Otto made it evident that he was waiting. Esme treated the three of them together as though they were well-met friends, or as happily, thorough strangers, while Otto smoked industriously. Chaby left, after keeping Esme at the door in a conversation audible enough to drive Otto to turning on the radio, which he did with an air of long habit. After Chaby had gone, Esme sat down beside the truculent smoker on the daybed. He suggested that they go to dinner, making the invitation in a tone tired but duty-bound, as a gentleman, a concept which labored mightily in his mind as it does in many, who find it the last refuge for insipience.

She agreed readily; at which he sulked more oppressively still. When she drew off her dress to change it, he tried to put his arms around her. —You don't do that to ladies who are dressing themselves, she said to him. —Besides your funny bandage gets in the way.

—I may have to go to Bolivia and northern Peru, Otto said soberly, and as though in direct answer. —Soon enough, he added, somewhat menacing. While she sought another dress, he opened his dispatch case and took out the play with business-like aversion. He separated the pages quickly to Act II scene iii, and immediately found the line. Enough times he had found it with a fond smile. Now he took his pen and drew it blackly through

PRISCILLA (*with tragic brightness*): But don't you understand, Gordon? These are the moments which set the soul yearning to be taken suddenly, snatched out of the heart of some fearful joy and set down before its Maker, hatless, disheveled and gay, with its spirit unbroken.

He wrote in:

Don't you understand the sudden liberation that's come over me?

and sat pouring smoke down on the wet ink.

Out on the street, Otto said, —How does it feel to be with a gentleman for a change?

—Ot-to.

—But he is such a ratty little creature, Chaby. How can you stand him.

—Isn't he bad? she said laughing, on Otto's arm. —Do you know what he did when I first knew him? He had something in his hands, and he told me to reach into his pants pocket and get some matches, and I reached in and he'd cut the bottom of the pocket off, my hand just went in and in. Wasn't that bad?

—Yes. What did you do then?

—I didn't do anything.

—Well what did he do?

—I don't remember.

—Where do you want to have dinner?

—At the Viareggio?

—Esme, that place is always so full of...well, I don't know, all the rags and relics below Fourteenth Street. It's like Jehovah's Witnesses when you sit down at a table there, everybody comes over. Why do you go there anyhow?

—I don't go there.

—Esme!

—People take me there, she said. And by now they were at the door of the Viareggio, a small Italian bar of nepotistic honesty before it was discovered by exotics. Neighborhood folk still came, in small vanquished numbers and mostly in the afternoon, before the two small dining rooms and the bar were taken over by the educated classes, an ill-dressed, underfed, overdrunken group of squatters with minds so highly developed that they were excused from good manners, tastes so refined in one direction that they were excused for having none in any other, emotions so cultivated that the only aberration was normality, all afloat here on sodden pools of depravity calculated only to manifest the pricelessness of what they were throwing away, the three sexes in two colors, a group of people all mentally and physically the wrong size.

Smoke and the human voice made one texture, knitting together these people for whom Dante had rejuvenated Hell six centuries before. The conversation was of an intellectual intensity forgotten since Laberius recommended to a character in one of his plays to get a foretaste of philosophy in the public latrine. There were poets here who painted; painters who criticized music; composers who reviewed novels; unpublished novelists who wrote poetry: but a *poet* entering might recall Petrarch finding the papal court at Avignon a "sewer of every vice, where virtue is regarded as proof of stupidity, and prostitution leads to fame." Petrarch, though, had reason to be irritated, his sister seduced by a pope: none here made such a claim, though many would have dared had they thought of it, even, and the more happily, those with younger brothers.

—Is that really Ernest Hemingway over there? someone said as they entered. —Where? —Over there at the bar, that big guy, he needs a shave, see? he's thanking that man for a drink, see him?

—I suppose you'd call me a positive negativist, said someone else.

—Max seems to have a good sense of spatial values, said a youth on their right, weaving aside to allow Esme to pass, —but his solids can't compare, say, with the solids in Uccello. And where is abstract without solids, I ask you?

While Otto looked dartingly for Max, Esme entered with flowing ease, and pleasure lighting her thin face as she smiled to one person after another with gracious familiarity. —There he is, Otto said, as they sat down. The juke-box was playing *Return to Sorrento*. Otto adjusted his sling, and smoothed his mustache. Esme sat, looking out over this spectral tide with the serenity of a woman in a painting; and often enough, like gallery-goers, the faces turned to look at her stared with vacuity until, unrecognized, self-consciousness returned, and they looked away, one to say, —I know *her*, but God knows who *he* is; another to say, —She was locked up for months, a couple of years ago; and another to listen to the joke about Carruthers and his horse.

At Max's table, among his and six other elbows, a number of wet beer glasses, a book titled *Twit Twit Twit* and a copy of Mother Goose, lay *The Vanity of Time*. Max rose, and came over with it.

—What did you think of it? Otto asked, pleasantly, not getting up. He rescued the pages, and wiped off a couple of spots which were still wet.

—Well Otto, it's good, Max said doubtfully.

—But what? What did you think?

—Well, I'll tell you the truth. It was funny sometimes, reading it. Like I'd read it before. There were lines in it . . .

—You mean *you* think it's plagiarized? Otto named the word.

—Well, Max said, laughing like a friend.

—Look, you had it out, I mean, at the table. Did they . . . I mean, did all those other people see it?

—They were looking at it. I didn't think you'd mind, and you see, I did want to ask them what they thought, about . . . recognizing it.

—Well? Otto opened his dispatch case, turning it away from view so that it was not apparent that the play went in to join its duplicates.

—What did they think? Pretty much the same thing, I think, Max admitted. —George said he felt like he could almost go right on with one of the . . . one of the lines. And Agnes . . .

—Agnes Deigh? You mean you talked to *her* about it?

—Well, it came up in conversation. I was up at her office this morning, talking with her about my novel. It's coming out in the spring. She's trying to arrange the French rights now.

—But what did you think it was plagiarized *from*, if you're all so sure I stole it.

—Nobody said you'd stolen it, Otto. It was just that some of the lines were a little . . . familiar.

—Yes but from *what*?

—That's the funny thing, nobody could figure it out, one of us would be just about to say, and then we couldn't put our finger on it. But don't worry about it, Otto. It's a good play. Then he straightened up, taking his hands from the table where he'd rested them, and said, —I'm showing some pictures this week, can you come to the opening?

—Yes, but . . .

—Thanks for letting me read it, Otto . . .

—There was one line I borrowed, I mean I put it in just to try it out . . . Otto called after him, but Max was gone to his table, where he talked to the people seated with him. They looked up at Otto.

Esme ate quietly, across from Otto's silent fury, weighted now to sullenness with four glasses of whisky, before his veal and peppers had appeared.

—Hello Charles, Esme said looking up, kindly. —You look very well tonight. Charles smiled wanly. Silver glittered in his hair. His wrists were bandaged, his glass empty. —Do you want my glass of beer, Charles? Because I can't drink it. She handed it to him, and murmuring something, without a look at Otto, he left.

—Really, Esme.

—What is it, Otto? she said brightly.

—Well I mean, I can't buy beer for everybody in the place.

She smiled to him. —That's because you don't want to, she said.

—You're damned right I don't, he said, looking round, and back at his plate.

—Of course I know it's near Christmas, said someone behind him. —For Christ's sake, what do you want me to do about it, light up?

There was a yelp from the end of the bar; and a few, who suspected it of being inhuman, turned to see a dachshund on a tight leash recover its hind end from a cuspidor. The Big Unshaven Man stepped aside. —I'm God-damned sorry, he said. —Oh, said the boy on the other end of the leash, —Mister Hemingway, could I buy you a drink? You are Ernest Hemingway aren't you?

—My friends call me Ernie, said the Big Unshaven Man, and turning to the bar, —a double martini, boy.

Though the place appeared crowded beyond capacity, more entered from the street outside, crying greetings, trampling, excusing themselves with grunts, struggling toward the bar.

—Elixir of terpin hydrate with codein in a little grapefruit juice, it tastes just like orange Curaçao. What do you think I was a pharmacist's mate for.

—When I was in the Navy we drank Aqua Velva, that shaving stuff. You could buy all you wanted on shipboard.

—Yeah? Well did you ever drink panther piss? the liquid fuel out of torpedoes?

The juke-box was playing *Return to Sorrento*. A boy with a sharp black beard sat down beside Esme. —Have you got any tea? he asked her. She shook her head, and looked up at Otto, who had not heard, had not in fact even noticed the person sitting half behind him. —Sometimes I really hate Max, he said, then noticed the beard. —I mean, I mistrust him. There were no introductions. —That poor bastard, said the beard. —He's really had it, man. So has she.

—Who? Otto asked incuriously.

—His girl, she's getting a real screwing. She wanted to marry him last year but she wanted him to be analyzed first. Max didn't have any money so she paid for it. Now his analyst says he's in love with her for all the neurotic reasons in the book. It don't jive, man. He's through with her but he can't leave her because he can't stop his analysis.

—Does she know it?

—Who, Edna? She...

—Edna who?

—Edna Mims, she's a blonde from uptown. He used to bring her down here to shock her, and then take her home and ball her...

—*Edna?* said Otto, unable to swallow. —With *him?*

Everyone silenced for a moment at a scream of brakes outside, anticipating the satisfaction of a resounding crash. They were disappointed. Instead, as their conglomerate conversation rose again, Ed Feasley rode in upon its swell. Behind him a blonde adjusting a garter followed with choppy steps like a dory pulled in the wake of a yawl on a rough sea. —Get a drink, was all Ed Feasley could say, as he sat down at Otto's table.

Mr. Feddle was there. He stood with difficulty, his hand on the hip of a tall light-haired girl, her delicately modeled face and New England accent manifest of good breeding. —His mother is the sweetest little Boston woman, she said, —*awf*ully interested in dogs, *awf*ully anti-vivisection. They were looking at Anselm, who looked about to drop to his knees. Behind her, Don Bildow said, —He is an excellent poet, when he tries. He's been taking care of my daughter when we're out, my wife and I. I haven't looked at another woman since we were married. Then with his hand on the man's-shirted shoulder of the light-haired girl, —Do you find me attractive?

The beard at Otto's table said, —Is that Hemingway? Ed Feasley looked over at the Big Unshaven Man, who had just said, —No queer in history ever produced great art. Feasley looked vague, but said, —There's something familiar about him.

—That's the damnedest thing I ever heard, Otto said, looking at Max, partially recovered. He motioned for another drink. When he had finished it he said, —I've got to make a phone call. I may have to go to Peru and northern Bolivia.

—Tonight? said Feasley. —You going to fly down? I'd like to go with you, but... say, if you can wait until tomorrow afternoon... I've got to go to a wedding tomorrow, but...

—No, I mean I've just got to call my father now, Otto said casually as though he had known that man all his life.

—Say hello to the old bastard for me, Ed Feasley called after him.

Otto called, made a rendezvous for a week later with the anxious voice at the other end of the line. They would meet in the lobby of a midtown hotel, at eight (—If you'll wear that green scarf I sent you for Christmas two years ago, Otto, I have one just like it. We'll know each other that way. And I wear glasses... said the voice, murmuring, after the telephone at the other end of the line was hung up, —Should I have said *rimless* glasses?). Otto had agreed quickly, he didn't know where his green muffler was but to push the thing further would have been too much, bad enough to need recourse to such a device to know your own father.

There were seven people at the table when he returned to it. The painters could be identified by dirty fingernails; the writers by conversation in labored monosyllables and aggressive vulgarities which disguised their minds. —Yeh, I'm doing a psychoanalysis of it, said one of them, tapping Mother Goose on the table.

—I tell you, there's a queer conspiracy to dominate everything. Just look around, the boy with the red hunting cap said. —Queers dominate writing, they dominate the theater, they dominate art. Just try to find a gallery where you can show your pictures if you're not a queer, he added, raising a cigarette between paint-encrusted fingers. —What do you think women look so damned foolish for today? It's because queers design their clothes, queers dictate women's fashions, queers do their hair, queers do all the photography in the fashion magazines. They're purposely making women look more and more idiotic until nobody will want to go to bed with one. It's a conspiracy.

Near their table, the tall dark girl who had been talking with Anselm said to someone she knew, —Do you know that girl? I want to meet her.

With his hand on Esme's shoulder, Otto leaned down to say, —Let's get out of here. Ed Feasley looked up to say, —You want to go to a party? A big ball a bunch of queers are giving up in Harlem.

—Drag? someone asked.

—What's drag?

—Where they all dress like women.

—This ball is drag, someone else said. —High drag.

There was a loud yelp. Anselm, on all fours, had met the dachshund, and had one of its ears in his mouth. The tall dark girl looked up at the doorway to see a timid Italian boy with no chin start to enter, and get pushed aside. —God, she said, —there's my stupid cousin. I'm going next door. —I've got a doctor for her, a young man was saying. —He'll do it for two hundred and fifty, but I can't get hold of her. Every time I call all I get on the phone is Rose, her crazy sister Rose.

Otto and Ed Feasley, with Esme between them, moved toward the door. The Big Unshaven Man turned away when Feasley passed. —Of course I know him. A damn fine painter, Mr. Memling, he was saying, as he took a quart flask out of his pocket. —Would you mind filling this up with martinis? Yes, what you read about me is true, I like to have some with me. Sure, I'll look at your novel any time, he finished, as the boy handed a ten-dollar bill across the bar.

—I sure as Chrahst know him from somewhere, Feasley said.

—That's because he's Ernest Hemingway, said a voice nearby.

—Paris? said the light-haired girl. —I wouldn't reach up my ahss for the whole city.

Mr. Feddle was being pushed out the door ahead of them. There they met Hannah. —Is Stanley in there? she asked. —Haven't seen him. —He had to go to the hospital to see his mother, said Hannah. —She just won't die. Then Hannah melted into the stew, where the juke-box was playing *Return to Sorrento*.

—Where's Adeline? Otto asked.

—I don't know. The hell with her, Feasley said.

They found Adeline asleep in the car. Fortunately it was a new model, with a low chassis and a low center of gravity, which saved it from overturning at the corners. They had some difficulty getting in to the party, when Ed Feasley offered to fight anyone who kept them out. They were saved when a crapulous Cleopatra appeared, waving a rubber asp at Esme and Adeline, thought it knew them, squealing in rapturous welcome that their costumes were *divine*.

It was quite a party. There must have been four hundred.

They arrived as a beautiful thing in a strapless white evening gown finished a song called *I'm a Little Piece of Leather*, followed on the stage by a strip-tease in two parts. The first performer was all too obviously a woman, gone to fat. This tumbled about in the spotlights, wallowed a great unmuscled expanse of rump and bounced a mammoth front at the audience, jeering with laughter, railed off the stage in grisly flounces of flesh. Then towering loveliness appeared, bowed to thunderous applause, and moving with perfect timing slipped off one after another garment to reveal exquisite limbs (hairless but a trifle muscular) with long gathering motions of blond hair to the waist, serpentine caresses rising over the spangled brassière. Ed Feasley, who had muttered with virile disgust at the first, watched this exhibition with wondering pleasure, until, in finale, the brassière was waved aloft leaving a chest uninhabited, leaving Feasley sitting forward in astonished indignation, leaving the stage through a curtain of wild applause.

—Are you *really* a girl? a young Bronzino in velvet asked Esme, punching in disbelief at her small bosom. She laughed, and Otto turned to brandish his sling; like Infessura, perhaps, writing of the papal court of Sixtus IV, "puerorum amator et sodomita fuit," he ordered a drink.

There was, in fact, a religious aura about this festival, religious that is in the sense of devotion, adoration, celebration of deity, before religion became confused with systems of ethics and morality, to become a sore affliction upon the very things it had once exalted. Quite as festive, these halls, as the Dionysian processions in which Greek boys dressed as women carried the ithyphalli through the streets, amid sounds of rejoicing from all sexes present, and all were; glorious age of the shrine of Hercules at Coos, where the priests dressed in feminine attire; the shrine of Venus at Cyprus, where men in women's clothes could spot women immediately, for they wore men's clothes: golden day of the bride deflowered by the lingam, straddling the statue of Priapus to offer her virginity to that god who, like all gods, even to the Christian deity who exercised it with Mary in the form of the Holy Ghost, had jus primae noctis, and no subterfuge permitted. So enough of these young brides had backed up upon the Priapean image and left their flowers there. So a voice said now, —Then let's go to Vienna, they've announced that you can wear drag in the streets if you don't offend public morals! Isn't that sweet? To which a dark-haired person in an evening gown of green watered silk said, —More than once I've dressed as a priest, just so no one would be troublesome about my wearing skirts. Sometimes I just can't *breathe* in trousers.

So priests down through the ages, skirted in respectful imitation of androgynous deities who reigned before Baal was worshiped as a pillar, before

Osiris sported erection, before men knew of their part in generation, and regarded skirted women as autofructiferous. When they made this discovery, the sun replaced the moon as all-powerful, and Lupercalia came to Rome, naked women whipped through the streets around the Palatine hill, and the cross became such a glorious symbol of the male triad that many a religion embraced it, so notorious that when the new religion which extolled the impotent man and the barren woman triumphed over a stupefied empire, the early skirted fathers of the Church forbade its use.

So even now, under a potted palm with silver fronds, a youth making a solemn avowal held another youth by that part where early Hebrews placed their hands when taking oaths, for it represented Jahveh.

Ed Feasley had a hand on a smooth chocolate shoulder which rose from a lavender evening gown in organdy, standing in the less-lighted shelter of a pillar.

There were women there. At a large table near the dance floor one sat, with broad tailored shoulders, flat grosgrain lapels, short-cut hair and heavy hands (she looked rather like George Washington without his wig, at about the time he married Martha Dandridge (Custis) for her money), recently in trouble, someone said, over kidnaping a seal for immoral purposes. She had not spoken to a *man* for sixteen years. Somewhere submerged in childhood lay a little girl's name which had once been hers. Only her bankers knew it now. Friends called her Popeye. Now she was saying, to an exquisitely pomaded creature whom thousands knew as a hero of stage, screen, and radio, —I wish I *were* a little boy, so that I could dance with *you*. They were interrupted by Big Anna, in dinner clothes. —*Have* you seen Agnes? said the Swede. —My dear she has the key to my *box*, and simply *ev*erything's locked up in it. The most delicious gown Jacques Griffes made for me especially to wear *tonight*, and I've had to come in this silly tuxedo suit, simply everyone thinks I'm a *woman* ...

The second in order of the strip-tease performers stood beside them, dressed now in silver lamé. —Rudy! the Swede said, —your dance was ex*cru*ciating.

—I feel simply ghastly, Rudy said. —I've been having hot flashes all evening. What divine perfume. Have you seen a book of mine?

—It's only *My Sin*, I borrowed it from Agnes. Is this your book? Rudy reached for it. —But what are *you* doing reading Tertullian?

—For my work of course. I'm designing sports costumes for an order of nuns, and I've been told that their ears simply must be kept covered, by a very dear friend. He lent me this book, Rudy said, fondling Tertullian. —*De Virginibus Velandis*, on the necessity of veiling virgins. Val told me the most divinely absurd stories this afternoon. Do you know why nuns must have their ears covered? My dear, so they won't conceive! The Virgin conceived that way, the Logos entered her ears. I have no idea what a *logos* is, but it doesn't sound at all nice does it. Val quoted Vergil and all sorts of dead people. Why, they all used to believe that all sorts of animals conceived that way. They thought that mares were made pregnant by the wind. And so I have to read this to really know what on earth I'm doing, covering their ears, because evil angels are waiting to do the *nas*tiest things to them. Can you imagine conceiving on the badminton court?

—It sounds really celestial, said Big Anna. —But what perfume are *you* wearing?

—I can't tell you, really. A very dear friend makes it himself. *Fuisse deam*, that's what he calls it. An aroma remained, you could tell a goddess had just appeared, Rudy said, waltzing toward the dance floor.

—I'd prefer French, Big Anna muttered, looking bitterly after Rudy's silver lamé. —*Where* is Agnes, he said, wringing his hands.

Otto was trying to order another drink. He stared on the festival with glazed eyes, and had decided for safety's sake to sit still until he could summon energy to leave. He waved with a heavy hand at a passing mulatto whose black hair stood out four inches behind his conical head in anointed streamlining, and that one was gone with his tray. Instead Cleopatra fluttered up to ask him for Maude Munk's telephone number, —because she's getting the most gorgeous baby by air mail from Sweden, and we want one so *much*…With the concentration of applied memory, Otto invented a telephone number. —Do you want to dance? Cleopatra asked him. Adeline returned to the table alone.

—I was dancing with some guy and he suddenly let go of me and said, You *are* a girl, aren't you, and left me right in the middle of the floor. See him, that big handsome boy, he looks like he went to Princeton.

—He probably did, Otto mumbled. Then he swung around at Cleopatra. —Will you get that God-damned thing out of my sling? he said, and the queen removed the asp, alarmed. —That's the cutest disguise you wear, said Cleopatra, and then, abruptly, and as indignant —Aren't *you* queer?

—Of course not, Otto said, indignantly unoriginal.

—What a *shame*, said Cleopatra. —I must find my barge.

Otto looked for Esme, did not see her. He looked for Feasley, did not see him. He was about to speak to Adeline when she left the table and went toward the dance floor saying, —I see a gentleman.

A voice said, —I've never seen so much bad silk on so many *divine* bodies. Another said, —Let's elope. And another, —You can't *touch* me, because I'm in a state of Grace. I'm going to be received tomorrow, only think! *Tomorrow…*

—Pony boy, a voice crooned.

—But I thought Victoria and Albert Hall were going to be here. Have you read her book? Have you seen his play? Where are they? said Big Anna, looking, as he had each minute of the evening, nearer to weeping. —Oh Herschel! Herschel! Will you stop that singing and console me?

—What is it, baby?

—It's Agnes. She has my *key*.

—Yes, baby, Herschel said. He was almost immobile, but still standing. —I have to get home to work, he said in a voice which was more a liquid presence and barely escaped his throat. —Work. Work. Work.

—What work?

—Haf to write a speech. Have you ever read *The Trees of Home?* It stinks, baby. It's a best seller. I've been writing speeches for the author of the best seller *Trees of Home*, baby. Moral regeneration, insidious influences sapping our very gzzzhuu huuu I'm going down to Dutch Siam yes I am … he sang.

—I haven't seen you since the boat docked! At this, Big Anna turned around. —Victoria! Where's Albert? I'm so glad to *see* you baby.

—He's dancing with an archbishop. But darling tell me have you seen a tall dark girl here? Her name is Seraphina di Brescia, I just hoped she might be here, I know she's in New York. I met her at the Monocle in Paris …

—No, but have you seen Agnes? Agnes Deigh?

—You're joking, darling. Tell me, did you ever get your little what-was-his-name over from Italy?

—Little Giono! said the Swede, wringing his hands again. —No, and I've been after the immigration people, but they won't help. Why he'll be fif*teen* by the time I can get him over here, and he won't do for a *thing*. I'm going to have to adopt him, it's the only way out. But before I adopt him I have to join the Church my dear, think of it. He has to have a Catholic *parent*. I'm going back next week.

—To Rome?

—Oh yes, I can't bear it here a moment longer.

Otto, seeing Feasley approach, struggled to his feet. —Let's get out of here, he said. —Where are Esme? and Adeline?

—The hell with them. Just wait a minute. There's a little colored girl here I want to take along. See if you can find her while I go to the head. She's in a purple dress.

—We met in Paris, someone said, —in the Reine Blanche …

—In the Carrousel …

—In Copenhagen …

—The Drap Dead …

—The Boof on the Roof …

—Seraphina? The one they call Jimmy? I know she has money, but what does she spend it all on? —Don't be silly. She spends it on girls.

—Yes darling, said Adeline's dancing partner into her blond hair resting against the grosgrain lapels. —We have to follow Emerson's advice to treat people as though they were real, because, perhaps they are...

From somewhere in the middle of the floor, in a quailing voice, —Baby and I were baked in a pie, the gravy was wonderful hot...

—Of course there's time, Agnes Deigh's voice said, —just take the key and *hurry*. And don't let me forget to give you my mother's address in Rome...

—And the address of Monseigneur Fé, he has his own chapel right near the Vatican where he performs the most divine *marriage* ceremonies...

So they danced, as though ridden with the conscience of the Tarahumara Indian, whose only sin can be not having danced enough.

Feasley said, —Come on, let's get out of here, not stopping as he passed the table. —Chrahst, I found her, the girl in the purple dress. Standing right beside me at the next urinal...

—I hate women, a voice said. It paused. Then, —I hate men too.

And so, as the Lord prophesied through the Greek Clement: *I am come to destroy the work of the woman, that is, concupiscence, whose works are generation and death.*

It broke up and spread itself, in couples and threes and figures of stumbling loneliness, into the streets, into doorways, they all went into the dark repeating themselves and preparing to meet one another, to reassemble, rehearse their interchangeable disasters; and the place looked like a kingdom stricken by papal anathema, as when Philippe Auguste, cunning pitiless monarch of France, was excommunicated for marrying Agnes while his wife Ingeborg still lived, and in his kingdom under the interdict there was neither baptism, marriage, nor burial, and corpses rotted on the high road.

—Wasn't it *fun*, said Agnes Deigh leaning against a garbage can. Herschel, scratching the sotted front of an evening shirt beside her, agreed, with the sound of a thing drowning. He excused himself, and when he had thrown up in an empty doorway returned singing. No doubt about it: tonight he was going to manage it. —Your strip-tease danse was *shock*ing, Rudy, he said. —Where's Tertullian? I can't lose *him*, Rudy said, and slipped a white hairless arm through Herschel's, pulled the evening cape tighter and with almost masculine exasperation thrust the long blond hair out over the fur. —Call a cab, baby, for God's sake. I feel awful. I feel like I was going to have a miscarriage.

Agnes Deigh returned a moment later, from between two parked cars. She was talking. But there was no one to talk to. There was no one there at all. The sound of thunder approached from the street's corner, a Department of

Sanitation truck stopping every ten or twelve yards to open the huge maw at its back and masticate the immense portions left out to appease it with gnashings of reckless proportions, glass smashed and wood splintered between its bloodless gums. Agnes, leaning alone there, was suddenly frightened less than ten bites away. She was, as much as her haze of consciousness would allow her, terrified, and set off up the street in the opposite direction, loping in frantic steps as though dodging among trees, an injured doe in a landscape of Piero di Cosimo fleeing the patient hunter. She reached a lighted doorway, struggled into the vast and empty interior, and collapsed into a pew.

Ed Feasley and Otto were moving at seventy-three miles an hour. But neither of them wanted to go to Connecticut, and when they realized that they were taking that direction the car swung about with a scream, and was saved from what might have been a fatal skid by hitting its sliding rear against a lamppost. It headed south. —I want to see how fast I can make that ramp around Grand Central, Ed said, full of spirit. As long as he was conscious, he liked to have a good time. He had been having one, continuous, for years, and never a moment of craven doubt in any of it. He was not afraid: not a grain of that fear which is granted in any definition of sanity. In college, he had entertained himself and others, quiet evenings in his rooms when his allowance was cut off, by beating the back of his fist with a stiff-bristled hairbrush, then swinging his hand in circles until the pressure of descending blood broke small capillaries and spotted the rug and ceiling with spots turned brown by morning; or standing before a mirror with thumb and forefinger pressed against his carotid arteries until his face lost all color and he was caught by consciousness as he fell; or dropping lighted cigarettes into the trouser turn-ups of a friend's two-hundred-dollar suit; or setting fire to his hand dipped in lighter fluid; or setting fire to the extended newspapers of people in subways just before the doors closed, leaving him on the platform overcome with laughter at the fugitive conflagration. He liked a Good Time.

The car stopped so suddenly it might have hit a wall. Otto straightened up from the dashboard holding his head. They were in front of a hospital. —What is it? he asked, brushing at a spot on his sleeve until he realized that it was a band of light from the streetlamp above.

—I've always wanted to pat a stiff on the head. They shave them, Ed Feasley said. A minute later they were in a basement corridor of the hospital, talking to the watchman. He was lonely. They just wanted to know how to get to Connecticut. They were told. The watchman left on his round.

In a large refrigerated room, Ed Feasley raised a sheet and stroked a smooth pate. He groaned with pleasure. Otto opened drawers, and closed them. Then he turned with his prize. It was a leg, small enough to be a woman's, quite old, slightly blackened around some of the toes and its detached end neatly bound with tape. But Ed's felicitous imagination had been busy too: with some effort, he had brought together two lonely corpses of opposite sex, erected now in the act of life. But even that mortal pleasure failed to change their expressions, leveled into disconsolate similitude by their shaven heads.

Otto was having trouble keeping the leg wrapped. —You ought to get rid of that sling, Ed Feasley said. —It's just a gag anyway, isn't it? Here, give me the leg, and he left with it partially wrapped in the bit of blue cloth under his arm.

The car roared south in the dawn's early light. —We have to *do* something with it, said Feasley, nodding back at the fragmentary passenger in the back seat. —We ought to give it to somebody. Somebody who needs it.

—There's a girl I'd like to give it to, Otto said. —I'd like to give it to Edna Mims, God damn it, in a box, a nice long white flower box from Max Schling.

—That's *it!* said the driver. —She's the girl you used to go around with in college? She's a good lay. We've got to get the box now.

The sudden light of Madison Square showed day approaching rapidly, though the sky was not yet colored with dawn; but with this clearing sky above, and the knock he had got on the head, sobriety and trepidation descended upon Otto. —We'd better not, he said.

—No, come on, it's a fat idea.

They thundered into Washington Square. Otto tried desperately to think of an alternative, something safer, someone defenseless. Then he said, —Stanley.

—Stanley?

—We'll tell him it's a relic. He's a Catholic, and he must want a relic. We'll give him the Pope's left leg.

—He won't believe it.

—He'll believe it.

—I wouldn't believe it, even if I was Catholic.

—He's a Catholic. He'll believe it. How does he know what the Pope's leg looks like?

—How does anybody know, except the Pope?

—Except the Pope. There's more than one pope.

—The rest are dead.

—All right, they're dead. This is from a dead one.

—Well then he can't have been dead very long.

—Look, we don't have to tell him it's a pope's leg. Stanley lives in a basement apartment. All we have to do is break the lock on the grating, we can do that some way, and slip it into bed with him. He'll wake up and think it's the Pope.

—The Pope in bed with him?

—But then he'll find that there's no one attached to it. Then he'll know.

—What'll he know?

—Why then he'll know that the Pope is dead.

The car turned toward Sixth Avenue.

At four in the morning, the nurse told Stanley that his mother was sleeping well, that he had better go home and get some rest, they would get in touch with him immediately if anything happened. Mother lay in one of those bed machines which can be cranked and warped in any direction, to accommodate whatever vagary of accident or human ill. But even now, though the black beads lay quiet in her fingers, she was not asleep. Not at all. After a reassuring look at her teeth in the glass she had closed her eyes and pretended sleep, so that they would go away, mortally tired she was of all of their quietened voices in hope that she would live, their faces drawn in dolefulness trusting that she would not die when that, in unequivocal reason, was all she wanted.

For one thing, she was certain that somewhere along the way they had left a pair of scissors inside her. For another, they had played music to her when they made the amputation (this was called therapy), and she could not get the tune out of her head. When she thought of her missing limb, she remembered the tune; then as her weary unmusical mind dragged her helpless through that tune, she remembered the leg, which would at this point begin to itch. When she inclined to scratch it, it was not there. And as she bent her body, the scissors would shift. Then the tune would commence again. Could she wait? while one after another of her parts was carried away, in a bottle, in a glass, on a tray. What shabby presentation would she make, when she appeared at her final Destination? Her thumb twitched on the crucifix, and a lonely movement of the sheet toward the end of the bed betrayed her wakefulness, where her foot tapped against a metal rung. No one noticed it. Stanley went home.

He let himself into his room, bolted the door and fixed the chain, and lay down on his back, fully dressed, staring at the crack in the ceiling above. At first, he had only measured that crack once a week, but in these last few months he measured it every evening, and since the beginning of December, two ways: along its broken length, and the straight distance from the corner of the room to the end of the crack. In twenty months it had lengthened one and five-eighths inches. How long could it go on? before that ceiling, with the sudden impatience of inanimate things, would yawn open over him, and fall with the astonished introduction of the lives above into his own. Who could live in a city like this without terror of abrupt entombment: buildings one hundred stories high, built in a day, were obviously going to topple long before, say, the cathedral at Fenestrula, centuries in building, and standing centuries since. A picture of that cathedral hung on the wall across the room, and when he lay down it was either to stare at the ceiling, or, on his side, at that print, the figure which seemed to be gathered toward heaven in the spired bulk of the cathedral. Fenestrula! If ever he should get to Italy, it was in that cathedral that he wanted to play the organ; a lonely ambition, solitary epiphany. Meanwhile he carried concealed a small hammer and chisel, escape tools, and tried to avoid travel underground.

On the ceiling grew the graph of Stanley's existence, his central concern: Expendability.

Everything wore out. What was more, he lived in a land where everything was calculated to wear out, made from design to substance with only its wearing out and replacement in view, and that replacement to be replaced. As a paper weight, on the pile of lined music composition paper tattered by erasure, lay a ceramic fragment from the Roman colony at Leptis Magna in North Africa. It was slightly conical, a triangular shape, dull, unglazed, and thumb prints were almost discernible in the scalloped edge: valueless as objet d'art, it had what might be credited as tactile value, and little else, except that it had been made to *last*. And Stanley, eating in the neighborhood with pressed metal cutlery, drinking from paper cups and plastic cups, often sat silent at table for minutes, weighing the dishonest weight of a plastic salt shaker, considering Leptis Magna, still standing on the Libyan shore of the middle sea. Phonograph needles? razor blades? thrown away entire, when their edges and points were worn. Automobile batteries? someone had told him that batteries in European cars lasted for years, but here companies owned those long-life patents, and guarded them while they sold batteries to replace those they had sold a year before. But there was more to it than gross tyranny of business enterprise; and advertising, whose open chancres gaped everywhere, only a symptom of the great disease, this plague of newness, this febrile, finally paretic seizure dictated by a beadledom of time monitored by clocks, observatories, signals on the radio, the recorded voice of a woman (dead or alive) who dissected the latest minute on the telephone when you dialed NERVOUS.

Stanley looked at his wrist watch. He was almost never seen in any but frayed and soiled clothing, but he owned others. In the closet at his head, which was locked, were three suits, two almost new and the third never worn. There were two pairs of shoes, brown and black, which he took out and dusted every week. He had two hundred new razor blades, and a porous stone on which he could get old ones almost sharp, which accounted for his half-shaven look. (Some day he hoped to own a Rolls razor; but he understood their sales were discouraged here by American razor blade manufacturers.)

Those were the outward signs. But like every legitimate terror, this obsession with expendability ran through every instant of his body's life. Stanley had haircuts infrequently, and even then only a trim. He did not wash often. People must suspect this. What did they think? But better, perhaps: let them think what they would. Every abrasive contact with the wash cloth and caustic soap *must* wear down the body a little. But here came another enigma: if washing wore things out, what of clothes? He always wore a shirt just one more day, not only making it last but keeping his supply of clean ones (and some never worn) *ready*. But when, eventually, the one he wore went to the laundry, wasn't it necessary to use the most harsh soaps and treatment to get it clean? Therefore wasn't it wearing out faster?

Still, he was most upset in these calculations over the prospect of the Last Moment. Would he have time to wash himself to perfect newness, dress in unworn, uncreased garments? Perhaps not. Perhaps he would be snatched up as he was! a picture so discomfiting that when it really came upon him, he would surprise everyone by appearing spotless for a day or two, leaving unanswered (except in his own apprehension) the cordial question, —Where are you going, Stanley? Perhaps what had happened to him when he went for an army physical examination was meant to be a lesson: told to undress, he was so mortified at the dirt on him that he went to the bathroom where the only place he could find to wash in privacy, in secret if you will, was the toilet bowl itself. Would he have time?

The perfect naked death of a baby (right after baptism).

What of Saint Catherine? appeared in pieces, did she? rolling that wheel before her. But there, she *had* that wheel, Saint Lawrence the gridiron, as witness to their unseemly appearances. But not in this world: things wore out, and you lost them in a thousand ways, preposterous and unconnected with any notion of devotion, martyrdom, sacrifice . . . What of Mother? a thought which had been running under the surface of all these others. What of *her*?

And at that moment a stab of pain penetrated a tooth, and slowed to a blunt ache as he turned his face to the wall, and his eyes to the crucifix there. The dull throbbing persisted, he took his jaw in his hand of cold thin fingers and turned his face again. On a low table near his head, under gathering dust and black flecks from the river and a railroad shunting track, were newspaper clippings, sequestered for no reason but to avoid throwing them away, unmatching pictures and unrelated information one shred of which might, at some extremity, be demanded. On top lay the most recent, the feature story on the Spanish girl to be canonized in the Easter week of the year ahead. The pain in his jaw subsided as he stared at her picture upside-down hanging from the table's edge, and his mind confused its thoughts and images, more vivid and irrelevant, as it did always when he lay this way, as unable to sleep at night as he was torpid during day.

He shuddered at Esme, seduced by an apprehension in a world real enough to her: appalled one day when an airplane moving with the speed of sound had disemboweled the heaven above them and eviscerated its fragments in nausea from their bodies walking below. Alone, he might have thought nothing of it, but shut it out as he did all the frenzied traffic of the world. But her terror shook him; and she was right. And if on the other hand, they'd met that early Jesuit Father Anchieta in the street on a sunny day, sheltered under the parasol of birds he summoned to hover over him and keep pace, she would have appreciated such resourcefulness without profane curiosity, probably not have repeated what she'd seen to a soul. But the airplane! Had she met Saint Peter of Alcántara, Saint Peter Nolasco, Saint Peter Gonzalez, walking, as they did, upon the waves of the sea, why, there was more reason in those excursions than that streak of cacodaemonic extravagance sundering the very dome of heaven.

Stanley moved suddenly, sitting up as though to break a spell. He sat rigid on the edge of the bed, clenching his teeth as though to discipline the activity of his mind, which he could hardly stir during the day when he tried to work. How could Bach have accomplished all that he did? and Palestrina? the Gabrielis? and what of the organ concerti of Corelli? Those were the men whose work he admired beyond all else in this life, for they had touched the origins of design with recognition. And how? with music written for the Church. Not written with obsessions of copyright foremost; not written to be played by men in worn dinner jackets, sung by girls in sequins, involved in wage disputes and radio rights, recording rights, union rights; not written to be issued through a skull-sized plastic box plugged into the wall as background for seductions and the funnypapers, for arguments over automobiles, personalities, shirt sizes, cocktails, the flub-a-dub of a lonely girl washing her girdle; not written to be punctuated by recommendations for headache remedies, stomach appeasers, detergents, hair oil ... O God! dove sei Fenestrula?

Still he did not get up, but sat staring toward the dim shape of the print of the cathedral. Beneath it was the table where he worked, a cardboard practice keyboard in the center, piled at both ends with papers in uneven stacks, one weighted with the ceramic fragment, another with the *Liber Usualis* opened upon the *Missae pro Defunctis*, his own cramped scribblings in the margins of majestic words between the bars, —Quántus trémor est futúrus, Quando júdex est ventúrus... And one page was marked with a tattered piece of notepaper. It was a *Misereris omnium*, and on the paper was written this piece of verse by Michelangelo, and beside it Stanley's broken attempt at translation:

O Dio, o Dio, o Dio,	O God, O God, O God,
Chi m'a tolto a me stesso	Who has taken me from myself
	from me myself
Ch'a me fusse più presso	Who was closest (closer) to me
O più di me potessi,	And could do more than I
	most about me
che poss' io?	What can I do?
O Dio, o Dio, o Dio.	

Specks of dirt on the floor caught his attention from the corner of an eye, and as was his habit he reached out and flicked at them, to see if any moved of their own volition. The tooth throbbed; and as he lay back he thought again of his mother, to whom his work was to be dedicated when it was finished. He looked at his wrist watch, turned off the light, and in closed eyes embraced a vision of the antiphonic brass of Giovanni Gabrieli pouring forth from the two choir lofts in Saint Mark's, to meet over the heads of those congregated below.

His work, always unfinished, was like the commission from a prince in the Middle Ages, the prince who ordered his tomb, and then busied the artist continually with a succession of fireplaces and doorways, the litter of this life, while the tomb remained unfinished. Nor for Stanley, was this massive piece of music which he worked at when he could, building the tomb he knew it to be, as every piece of created work is the tomb of its creator: thus he could not leave it finished haphazard as he saw work left on all sides of him. It must be finished to a thorough perfection, as much as he humbly could perceive that, every note and every bar, every transition and movement in the pattern over and against itself and within itself proof against time: the movement in the *Divine Comedy*; the pattern in a Requiem Mass; prepared against time as old masters prepared their canvases and their pigments, so that when they were called to appear the work would still hold the perfection they had embraced there. Not what was going on around him now, a canvas ready when it had been stretched and slavered with white lead, or not prepared at all, words put on paper, flickering images on celluloid, with no thought but of the words and the image and the daub to follow. (Stanley's work was done on scrap paper which he ruled himself and on envelope backs, old letters, or old scores which he had erased. He was saving a pile of new paper for the final composition.)

As dawn neared outside he was still fully awake, lying under the crack in the ceiling, under the yellowed ivory (thirteenth century) crucifix over the bed. He heard the truck collecting rubbish at the far end of his block. Christmas so near, again? Suddenly he looked at the watch strapped to his wrist, a rage of figures battling through his mind. He saw Anselm, and shuddered; Esme, and moaned: what unholy thing was that? what knowledge of evil did they share? for so they did, antipodal, but embracing in his mind, images profaning his love in their coupling. He stretched his arms above his head. Did one wear a watch in the tomb? A long walk, he decided; and then he would go to Mass. Why had Agnes Deigh refused to go to Mass with him, one day when they had met; it was just time, and near enough. —I've got to have drinks with someone, business is business darling, he could hear her voice again. Then her profane images shouldered his missionary intentions aside, and the more he thought of her.

He had turned his face to the window just above him, where uncertain light entered to show things as they had been left in each other's shadows the night before, shadowless now, older, wearing out separately and all together. This window he had to keep open in summer, so that passers-by could look in, upsetting to him, as though the friction of their glances might wear things down further; the window open in summer so that things might be thrown in, as some children one day, playing, had thrown something a dog had done on the sidewalk in behind the radiator.

There was a slight tapping on the door, as though someone were knocking who did not want to be answered to, knocking to find no one instead of someone there. Stanley sat up on the edge of his low couch, the door handle turned a slow quarter-circle, and back.

—Who is it? he cried out. —Who is it out there?

—Stanley? A girl's voice: it was Hannah, he let her in. —It's so cold, she said, —I'm sorry, but can I sleep in your chair?

—Stay here, he said. —Lie down, Hannah. I'm going out.

—But no, don't leave for me. Go back to bed. But you're all dressed?

—Yes, stay here. I'm going out.

—Is everything all right, Stanley? Has anything...

—Nothing has changed. Go to bed here, Hannah. I'm going out to Mass.

In the hall, where he stopped in the communal toilet, he was troubled again by the problem in arithmetic penciled on the wall there. Someone had multiplied 763 by 37, and got 38,231. He had checked it, idly, two years before;

then carefully, at every sitting since. Who had made the mistake? Was it too late to find them and tell them? 10,000...what? Had that person gained it? or lost it? Was it too late? Stanley looked at his wrist watch. He walked out into the cold morning asking himself this heretical question: Can you start measuring a minute at any instant you wish?

—I'll go in and try the door first, said Otto.

Feasley got out to follow, returned to get the leg out of the back seat, and rejoined him. The door was locked. —There's somebody awake inside, Otto said. Out on the sidewalk, he twisted the lock on the window grating. Feasley said, —I'll get a wrench, handed the leg to Otto and went back to the car. Suddenly the window shade shot up in Otto's face, the sash after it.

—What are you doing here?

—Oh, I...Hannah, I...I mean we...

—What are you doing here at this window anyhow?

—Why nothing I...Hannah was dressed only in a shirt, for all he could see. —We just...well, so long Hannah. See you later, he called as he heard the car's engine racing behind him, and he ran toward it, the bare foot waving his goodbye to Hannah from under his arm.

—He's got a girl in there, Hannah's sleeping with him, said Otto as they roared away. —Say listen, he said looking round him, —have you seen a little tan bag, a pigskin dispatch case? Suddenly frantic, he turned to look behind them in the car. The car slid around a corner, leaned to one side in a skid, recovered, skidded in the other direction, and Feasley was cursing as it went head-on into a pole. They got out. Otto looked, found nothing but the leg. —Come on. The hell with it.

—But what about this thing? Otto said, wrapping the cloth around it more tightly as they walked fast up Little West Twelfth Street.

—O Chrahst put it in an ashcan.

He started to, but three men rounded the corner, and he tucked it back under his sling. They got a subway, vapidly curious people appearing on all sides around them.

Stanley had taken a long bus ride, returning to the neighborhood of the hospital, and been walking for some time, it seemed, when he heard six o'clock strike nearby. Following the direction of the bells, he found the church and went in, mind seething as he stopped and genuflected. He moved toward a pew in the back, and had almost knelt beside her when he recognized Agnes

Deigh. He clutched at her wrist. She started in terror away from him, awakened.

—*Stanley?*

—You're *here*, he whispered.

—Oh God. Her head lolled forward and away from him. —Take me home.

—But you're here, at *Mass.*

—I know it. Take me home. Stanley, now.

—Look, we can't carry this thing all over town in broad daylight. It's beginning to smell, too.

—Let's have a look. Chra-ahst, it's turning gray.

Across from them a woman stared, but did not see them, her mouth working, her fingers working at her beads. It was the first car of the train, and at stops a voice rose, where at the glass which looked forward into the tube a woman talked, so close to her own image in that glass that it was steamed by her breath. —They told us all about it, there it is in letters where anyone can read it, everyone knows, they're killing each other, boys killing each other millions of American boys are being killed you can read all about it . . .

The roar of the train drowned her out.

—What shall I do with it?

—Leave it on the seat, there in the corner. We'll get off at this stop.

—he cut them both up and put them in suitcases and those are the people who travel on airplanes . . . The doors clapped to behind them, and they waited on the platform for another train. —My old man's going to get me this time, for mucking up that God-damned car again.

A girl stood in front of them, waiting for the next train, on her way to work in a chewing-gum factory: Hestia, Vesta, virgin-sworn, the hearth and the home (a cheap fluff of a jabot she wore, imitation coral earrings, crippling shoes, under a thin elbow a tabloid catalogue of the day's misinformation). —Chrahst, I don't know whether it's a boy or a girl, after that little nigger at the party last night. Hey honey, do you want to make thirty-five cents?

—No, I'm really *not* a Catholic any more, I just put that picture of Cardinal Spellman up there because that corner of the room needs a little *red*, said Agnes Deigh, almost recovered. —Do you want a drink?

—*Now?*

—Stanley, you look exhausted too, she said. —Here, drink this, it will warm you. She handed him a glass of port, and swallowed down, herself, almost choking, some whisky. —What a God-awful mess this place is. He must have got here. Agnes looked around, at her own underclothing scattered broadcast in the living room. One of her best gowns was hung over her sunlamp, which was turned on.

—It is warming, Stanley said, drinking, —I can feel it all through me.

—God, I'm so tired, she said, beginning to undress. —Will you help me? He followed her into the bedroom. —Thank God you found me.

—What's this? Stanley said, aghast holding up a card he'd taken from the table, reading in a whisper —"Christ has come!"

—Oh Stanley, you're not supposed to see that. It's a Christmas card.

—*Christmas* card! But who...

—Don't be upset, Stanley. From that Swedish boy they call Big Anna.

—But it's...disgusting, this picture...

—I know, Stanley. But these things happen in the world. Throw it in the wastebasket. No, don't tear it up, just throw it in the basket.

—But...why do you *know* those people?

—Oh Stanley, she said, and paused bent double over a rolled-down stocking. —Don't you see, Stanley, sometimes people like that are...are easier for a woman. They're safer somehow... She had taken off her stockings then, in the pause, and stood up dressed only in her slip. She picked up a plant, and carried it into the other room. —I just can't stand to have anything living and breathing in the same room where I'm trying to sleep. She sat down on the bed again with a glass of water, and laid two sleeping pills beside it. —God, what a smell of perfume he left in the place. He must have dropped the bottle. Oh, come Stanley, sit here. You do understand about people like that don't you? Just don't think about them. You've got to be philosophical, darling. Thank God you found me in that church.

—Yes, thank God, who led you there.

—But Stanley dear...

—You were at Mass, he said.

—I'm *not* a Catholic any more, I tell you.

—You will always be a Catholic. It is not for you to say. But why have you strayed so far? he asked, sitting beside her.

—Even when I was a child, I was frightened out of it, it seemed. Once in my convent school, I remember when we were all sent to look at a reliquary. It was...I don't know, a splinter of the Cross, or a crumb of something. They even had one that they said contained a bit of the original darkness that Moses called down on the world, imagine. Yes, I think it was a crumb, from the biscuit that bled when it was trampled by Zwingli's soldiers. But I didn't go, I went to a movie instead. The next day in class I was told to get up and

describe the reliquary, and I gave a wonderful description, about it being big
and fancy and gold, with a peep-hole and a magnifying lens so you could see
the speck inside. Then they whipped me, and told me that it hadn't even been
on exhibit, it was away being cleaned...

—But these things are our trials as children to prepare us...

—And I used to chew the wafer, she went on, almost somniloquent, in an
arrested whisper. —I couldn't hold it in my mouth without chewing it. The
more I knew it was sinful, the more I chewed His Body, I *had* to chew it...

—These sins we commit as children...

But now Agnes had breathed deeply and sat back. She glimpsed her face
in a boudoir mirror and said, —Don't I look awful, my eye...

—What happened to it?

—At that party, that terrible party, in the ladies' room, another woman
hit me with her hand bag. This has gone far enough, she said. She didn't think
I was really a...she thought I was one of the people in costume. Agnes was
staring at the floor. Then she sniffed and turned to Stanley with a smile forcing her lips. —But analysis is safer, and you have the same confessional.

—But don't you understand what happened this morning? he brought out
fervently. —You didn't know you were coming to Mass, but you were directed
there, as I was, as He led me there to...

She put an arm around his shoulders, and her strap came undone. Mickey
Mouse pointed to 6:45. —Stanley, she said. —You're such a boy.

Dawn, somewhere beyond the incinerator plant which had won first prize in
functional architecture a decade before: Fuller was busy in Mr. Brown's bathroom, picking up every piece of Mr. Brown's hair he could find and putting it
into an envelope. Esme wakened for a moment in a strange bed, looked at the
arm round her, could identify neither its owner nor its sex, and went back to
sleep. Esther woke, hearing sounds which seemed to have been going on for a
long time; as though she'd heard a key turn in the lock hours before, and footsteps, and the sound of a voice, or voices. But she lay still, and closed her eyes,
as she did always on the dull sounds of Rose's dreams. In the street below, young
policemen raced the engines of their motorcycles to arrogant pitch, and roared
to duty. In the East Fifty-first Street station-house, Big Anna sat on a bench
weeping. —But nobody even saw my *gown*, he cried. —We saw it, Jack, said
the man behind the desk, turning to another policeman in shirtsleeves, —Is
he known? Anselm was descending the steps of the I.R.T. West Side subway,
on all fours. Adeline had just closed a door behind her, having wakened beside
someone with short-cut hair and heavy hands, whom she remembered having

taken for a man the night before. Herschel was not to be wakened until some hours later, by two sailors in a Chelsea hotel room, where he lay bandaged over chest and back, the protective gauze of Dutch Siam, tattoo artist.

Dawn, just as it came to Australian skies, a woman of bad character in a cloak of red possum skins.

What Stanley marveled at most was the wealth of her that had appeared as her garments came off. There was so much *of* her. She stood, wiping the make-up from her face turned away, and he stared at her thighs from behind, as a collector stares at the fine patina glazed over the courses of worms, for those vast vermiculated surfaces were furrowed so. Terror struck him. He started to rise from the bed and reach for his shirt. Too late. She was there, tumbling the marvelous cucumiform weights down upon a chest which looked as though it would cave in under such manna. —Look, she said, joy of this world recovered, raising herself so that her front swung pendulant over him, unequaled, and unequal lengths untouched by baby's hand, —you can play telephone with them.

Trains from great distance over barbarous land, ships from civilized shores and airplanes from nowhere aimed at the island, dived at it, into it, unloaded lives upon it. Far uptown Mr. Pivner lay, unconscious arabesque in nervous imitation of sleep (he was, in fact, enduring a train wreck in Rajputana), that part of him already vigilant which would reach the control of the alarm clock an instant before it went off.

In Harlem, walking alone, Otto looked at his watch, forgot to see the time and looked again, as he sought the scene of Saturnalia where he hoped to recover the pigskin dispatch case.

The streets were filling with people whose work was not their own. They poured out, like buttons from a host of common ladles, though some were of pressed paper, some ivory, some horn, and synthetic pearl, to be put in place, to break, or fall off lost, rolling into gutters and dark corners where no Omnipotent Hand could reach them, no Omniscient Eye see them; to be replaced, seaming up the habits of this monster they clothed with their lives.

The newspaper quivered in Basil Valentine's hands, clasped behind him. Music, from another corner, plucked at his back. It was a pavan by a dead Spaniard.

Hungary to Sell Famed Paintings...Vienna...Diplomatic sources here said today that Hungary was attempting to sell in the West masterpieces from Budapest's National Art Gallery. The Gallery included paintings by Raphael, Tintoretto, Murillo, and others collected by the Austro-Hungarian emperors and princes. The informants said some of the paintings were being shipped to the United States as diplomatic luggage in the hope of interesting American art collectors.

He brought the newspaper up before him and read that again in the dull light of the dawn where he stood at the windows.

The desk in the far corner of the room was still littered with the papers he had spent the night over, finally snapped off the light and sat in a deep chair with his fingertips resting against his eyelids, and his head erect. The Vulliamy clock on the mantel had struck three times gently, at regular intervals, before he moved; and then, only his fingers moved, to remain arched before his face, meeting their tips in gothic contemplation, his eyes clear as though he'd done no more than blink them.

Now he gave an impatient sigh, dropped the newspaper on the window shelf, and stood looking straight out at the gray sky. —Another blue day? he murmured, as the stately strokes of the harp came to an end, and he turned from the window.

The letterheads among the sheaf of papers on his desk witnessed important oppositions in the world, languages as various as the devices and crests which adorned them. He sat down and hurriedly checked over a coded message against its original, —Put Inononu in touch immediately, have received necessary information...which he crumpled in his hand. He slipped the rest of the papers into a dispatch case, and was gone for a moment into the bedroom to lock it in a wall safe behind the chest. Then he went to the bathroom, dropped the crumpled note into the basin and put a match to it, washed the ashes down the drain, washed his hands slowly and with care, and went in to make tea.

There was exquisite correspondence between the Sèvres cup and the back of his hand, where blue veins showed making the flesh appear translucent: it was not a reflection of mutual fragility, but rather the delicacy of the porcelain completed a composition enhancing, as it did, the tensile strength of the hand which raised it. In the other, he opened a book, and read. Now and then his lips moved, as he turned the pages of Loyola's *Spiritual Exercises* which he had, contrary to habit, lent out (for this was not the only, certainly not the nicest copy he had). A fly landed on the print, and he struck at it. The fly rose and crossed the room to settle busily upon a golden figure, a bull lowering its jewel-collared head to thrust with its horns at the egg floating in the rock cavity before it. The figure was small, and stood on a column at the end of the couch.

He turned another page. A fine-sprung coil of brown hair lay in the inner margin. Basil Valentine leaned down to blow at it. The hair did not move. He made a sound with his lips, and flicked it away with a finger. Then he read for less than a minute more, closed the book abruptly and bent down, searching the floor for the coil of hair. He found it on the carpet, put it into an ashtray, opened the book again and gazed at the page. There was a faint hum, from the corner where the phonograph had shut itself off. His gaze shifted to the ashtray. Then he moved quickly, to stand, take the coil of hair from the ashtray, into the bathroom and drop it into the bowl. He flushed the toilet and washed his hands, studying his face in the mirror as he did so.

The expression of anxiety which he had worn all this time did not leave him as he returned to the living room, tightening the cord of his dressing gown, and taking the gold cigarette case from its breast pocket. Snapped open, without taking out a cigarette he snapped it closed again and stood looking at the inscription worn almost smooth on its surface. —Damn him, he whispered. —Damn him. He turned to look at the Vulliamy clock. It was adorned with a cupid. He loosened the cord of his dressing gown.

A few minutes later Basil Valentine had exchanged his black pumps for a pair of equally narrow black shoes, the dressing gown for a blue suit, and he returned pulling at the foundations under his trousers. Among the books at the back of his desk, he pushed aside *La nuit des Rois* and quickly found the copy of Thoreau. He pulled on his coat, and on his way out opened a panel closet and took out a large flat envelope. He paused in the doorway to look the room over quickly, and then locked the door with two keys, leaving the *Spiritual Exercises* of Saint Ignatius of Loyola open on the desk, where the fly had already alighted before the second key turned in the lock.

In the street door below, he paused to look in all directions. A slight drizzle had commenced. He came forth damning the wind, the hand with the gold seal ring holding his hat on as he hailed a cab with the other.

The wind from the river was quite strong. It was, in fact, strong enough to support a man; and this, at a corner on Gansevoort Street, is exactly what it was doing. The man himself, on the other hand, did not seem grateful. He was talking to the wind; and, as occasional words took shape from the jumble of sounds he poured forth, it became evident that he was calling it foul names. At this, the wind became even more zealous in its attentions to him. He hit at the skirt of his tattered coat as it flew up around him, addressing it somewhat like this, —Gway gwayg…yccksckr…until, its caprice satisfied, the wind flung him round a corner and went on east.

Abandoned, he swayed, and fortunately found a wall with the first throw of his hand, instead of the face of the man who approached, for he had struck out at just about that level.

—Here, my good man. Could you tell me whereabouts Horatio Street… good heavens.

Thus called upon, he took courage: the sursum corda of an extravagant belch straightened him upright, and he answered, —Whfffck? Whether this was an approach to discussion he had devised himself, or a subtle adaptation of the Socratic method of questioning perfected in the local athenaeums which he attended until closing time, was not to be known; for the answer was,

—Stand aside.

—Here, don't goway. Here, how do youfffk…He licked a lip and commenced again, putting out a hand. —My name Boyma…he managed, summoning himself for the challenge of recognition. —And you must be Gro… go…raggly!

He seemed to have struggled up on that word from behind; and he finished with the triumph of having knocked it over the head. He did in fact look down, as though it might be lying there at his feet. It was such a successful combat that he decided to renew it. —Go…gro…gorag…His hand found a wrist, and closed thereon. Bells sounded, from a church somewhere near. —Go…ro…grag…But the sharp heel of a hand delivered to the side of his head stopped him, and he dropped against the wall with no exclamation of surprise whatever.

The door was opened to the length of a finger.

—You…!

—I…

—How…how did you find me?

—It hasn't been easy. You might put *Rouge Cloître* out here on your bell, at least.

—Rouge…put what?

—The name of the convent that took van der Goes in, you know. May I come in?

—Oh, why…yes, yes come in.

—I'm not disturbing you? Basil Valentine asked, entering the room. —Coming at such an odd hour?

—Yes it is, but no, not if…you don't need the sleep?

—Unfortunately I do, I need it badly, Valentine answered with a smile. —Here, I brought down these van Eyck details. And your Thoreau. I went off with that quite by mistake.

—That, thank you for that. And you...your...

—My coat? Yes, it's wet. I'll take it off in a moment. First I'd like to wash my hands, Valentine went on, turning toward a door, —I had a rather disagreeable encounter on my way here. The room was the kitchen; and with one look at the sink, he returned to say, —Are you aware that there's something growing in here? A delicate plant, growing right up out of the drain?

—Oh no, but that, it must be a melon then. Some melon seeds washed down...here, here's the bathroom here.

A minute later, Valentine's voice came from there. —A towel?

—Yes, here, use this.

Valentine came out, drying his hands on a wad of cotton waste. —It's pretty stuff, isn't it, he said smiling again, and threw it into the fireplace. —And tell me, it's your habit to cover up mirrors? as they do in a house where someone's died?

—The one in the bathroom? it's only...something drying. But you, he asked Valentine suddenly, —don't you get tired of the image you dodge in mirrors?

—I don't dodge. Valentine had not lost his smile. He took off his coat, and put it with his hat on the bed, where he sat on the unmade edge and leaned back against the rumpled covers, hands clasped round one knee. —So, you're working, are you? he said agreeably. —You've been at it all night?

—All night, I've been working all night. I just finished it.

—What? could I see it?

—It's this one, this big one here.

Valentine got up to help him move it out from the wall, and stand it face out against the inside of the door. He offered his cigarette case, lit their cigarettes, and studied the painting for some time before he said, —Brown won't like this, you know. The face there, how badly you've damaged it.

—But the damage? It isn't as though I'd done that. A hand was flung up before him. —The painting itself, the composition took its own form, when it was painted. And then the damage, the damage is indifferent to the composition, isn't it. The damage, you know, is...happens.

Valentine shrugged. —I know, of course, he said. —But I doubt that Brown will. It will cut the price down badly.

—The price! What's that to do with...

—Good heavens, I don't care about it. But your employer is rather sensitive about those things, you know. After another pause, without taking his eyes from the painting, Valentine stepped back, and the figure behind him moved as quickly as his own shadow in the glare of the bare light above them. —It's magnificent, isn't it, Valentine said quietly. He stood entirely absorbed in it, and when he spoke murmured as he might have talking to himself. —The simplicity... it's the way I would paint...

There was no sound after his voice, and nothing moved to move him; until his eyes lowered to the shadow streaking the floor beside him: at that Basil Valentine turned abruptly and cleared his throat. —Yes, a splendid sense of death there isn't there, he went on in the tone usual to him, more forceful and more casual at once. —Death before it became vulgar, he went on, walking down the room away from the painting, —when a certain few died with dignity. And the others, the people who went to earth quietly like dung. Eh? he added, turning. He threw his cigarette into the fireplace, lit another without offering one, and blew the thin smoke out compulsively in a steady stream. —Yes, there is what you wanted there, isn't there, in this painting?

—Almost...

—Almost? Valentine repeated. He brought up the cold brilliance of his own eyes, to drive the feverish stare fixed upon him down to the floor between them. —Almost what?

—The ... strength, the delicacy, the tenderness without...

—Weakness, yes. Valentine kicked a book on the floor at his feet. —Pliny? what, for his discourse on colors? Yes thanks, I wouldn't mind a little of that myself, cognac is it? He held out the unwashed glass he was given while the bottle-neck clinked against it, but still looking at the damaged painting. —You do work fast, don't you. Yes, van der Goes was a fast painter himself, but one, the Portinari triptych I think it was, took him a good three years. But after all this is rather different isn't it, you know where you're going all the time. None of that feeling of, what was Valéry's line, that one can never finish a work of art? one only abandons it? But here there's none of that problem, is there. Eh? What's the matter.

—If one minute, first you say, or people say It's beautiful! and then if, when they find out it isn't what they were told, if it's a painting when they find out it was done by, or rather when they find out it wasn't done by who they thought...

—No, no, not this evening, or not today is it? No, really, we won't settle that here now. It's not ... not the point, is it. Drawn by his eyes, Valentine faltered for the first time. —Or if it is the point? the whole point? And he looked away, to the damaged painting.

—What you said, about signing a picture? About that, that being all they care about, the law...

—Modern forgeries, forgeries of modern painters, Valentine dismissed him quickly, but looking about the room found only the man and the damaged painting to draw his eyes. —And be careful, he said, forcing the ease in his voice. —If Brown should decide that there's as much money in modern painters as there is in his old masters, no, it's not funny, he's already threatened you with van Gogh ... He had commenced to pace the room, and paused to draw to him, with a toe of a black shoe, a detailed drawing which he picked up and studied. He held it up between them and said, —A remarkable likeness.

—A study, from the ... last work.

—Yes, I see. And reversed, the mirrors? Backwards, like a contact print. Exactly like, and yet a perfect lie. The thing dropped from his fingers and he laughed. —You? the, what was it you said, the shambles of your work? What a pitifully selfish career! being lived, as you said? by something that uses you and then sheds you like a husk when its own ends are accomplished?

—Yes, but if the gods themselves ...

—Is it worth ...

—If they cannot recall their ... gifts, to ... redeem them, working them out, do you understand? living them through ... ?

And Valentine turned quickly from those eyes back to the damaged painting leaned against the door, to murmur, —On second thought I believe I would have put another figure or two there in the lower left, the sense of ascendance in the upper part of the composition would gain a good deal ...

—You?

—and the blue is rather light isn't it. I think if I'd done it myself I would have used a more ...

—But you didn't.

Basil Valentine turned on him slowly, and studied him for a few moments before he spoke. —My dear fellow, he brought out finally. —If you are this sensitive to any sort of criticism, I didn't come down here to ...

—Why did you come down here?

—I came down to ask a favor of you. But if you are so painfully sensitive to criticism, such a self-conscious artist that ...

—No I, it's just, listen, criticism? It's the most important art now, it's the one we need most now. Criticism is the art we need most today. But not, don't you see? not the "if I'd done it myself ..." Yes, a, a disciplined nostalgia, disciplined recognitions but not, no, listen, what is the favor? Why did you come here?

Basil Valentine had dropped a cigarette on the stained floor; and stooping to get it, a suspender button at the back of his trousers came off, and he straightened up feeling half his trouser-seat hanging and the other half binding high. —That Patinir? he said. —The painting that Brown has just inside the door, hung opposite that idiotic portrait. I wanted to ask you if you'd mind making a copy of it for me. He put his hands in his pockets, to hitch his trousers up square, and spoke rapidly. —It wouldn't even have to be a perfect copy, you know, since the original doesn't exist. You didn't know? Brown had the painting heavily insured, and it was destroyed in a fire. At least he had the evidence that it was when the insurance company's experts came. He'd sawed off one end of it and he showed them that, pretty badly charred but not so much that it couldn't be identified as all that was left of the original, which he's waiting now to dispose of again, "in secret" of course. Yes, what's the matter? what's funny?

—These. I've done the same thing with these.

—What do you mean, the same thing? sawed the ends off and . . .

—Kept them.

—What? What for?

—Proof.

—Proof? Basil Valentine stepped aside quickly as he passed, and watched him pull canvases away from the wall.

—This! he said holding one up. —Do you see? It was going to be a study, it was a study for this . . . this new work, this van Eyck.

—But what? The *Annunciation?* Valentine hitched up the sagging side of his trousers. —And it's not turning out what you wanted? But it's an old thing. On linen? What is it? and this, these, earrings? Who is she? These old Byzantine-looking hoops, what is it? Who is she? This? a study for a van Eyck?

—No, but for what I want.

—What are you talking about? And this, what is it? It's exquisite, this face, the reproach, like the faces, the Virgin in other things you've done, the reproach in this face. Your work, it's old isn't it, but a little always shows through, yes something, semper aliquid haeret? something always remains, something of you. But what are you talking about? Valentine found the feverish eyes fixed on him. —Here, this . . . I've brought down these pictures, these photographic details of, here, if you're going to bring the critics back to believing in Hubert van Eyck? And the, why we may enshrine your arm in a casket right over the door here? in Horatio Street? like Hubert van Eyck's right arm over the portals of the church of Saint Bavon's in Ghent? But what is it? what's the matter? what are you talking about, this proof? to prove what? Valentine demanded.

—Listen, this, if I wanted to go on with this work, myself? And to clear up the other things I've done? The Bouts, the van der Goes? If I want to tell them, and I have the proof, off every one of them, a canvas or a panel, I cut a strip off the end when it was done, and I have them.

—Where? Valentine asked quickly.

—Yes, they're safe.

—Where? Valentine repeated.

—And that will be proof, won't it.

—Proof? Valentine stood up. —Do you think it's going to be that easy? Yes, do you think they want to be told? Any more than Michelangelo's Cardinale di San Giorgio? Yes, he'd kept aside an arm from his "antique" cupid, and he went to get the Cardinal's help starting his career, showed him the arm from the statue to prove he'd done it, do you think the Cardinal thanked him? Valentine picked up his glass and finished it. —Do you think it's that simple? Why... He put a hand out to the shoulder before him. —That you can do it alone, that simply? He withdrew his hand slowly. —But you're wet, your jacket's damp. You've been out?

—Earlier, just before you came, for a walk...

—But you told me, when I came in you said you'd been working here all night.

—Yes, but, I went out, I'll tell you, I went out, I took those fragments, those strips from the ends of the paintings, where they'd be safe.

—Where? Valentine demanded.

—I took them up... where I used to live.

—Where you haven't lived for, two years is it? To your wife, your wife, so you trust her? You trust your wife to watch over them?

—She doesn't even know. She wasn't there. Only her sister, yes her sister, we hid them.

But Basil Valentine had turned from him, to pace to the end of the room, where he stood looking at him, at his impatient eyes, and the crumpled damp black jacket hanging from his shoulders. —Your wife, eh? He paused, but spoke more rapidly as he went on, —The Rouge Cloître? Yes, and where's the mother superior? Who keeps house for you here, then? This floor, how do you keep it so dirty? Why... so you trust her with it, do you? these fragments that are so important. And here, this van der Goes, what happens to her face in that, eh? All the rest of them, yes, the men, you out of your mirrors, you're there half a dozen times, backwards? Drawing death and modeling it under your own hand, but what happens to her face? Oh, the damage doesn't respect the composition? No, not a bit, not a bit of it. He stopped; the vein stood out like a bulb at his temple. He touched it with a fingertip, dropped his shoulders back against the empty irregular brick mantel, and lit a cigarette. Immediately the draft caught its smoke and drew it up the flue behind him. —And this, who's this in this study on the easel? It's old, isn't it. Your wife?

Standing under the bare bulb, facing Valentine, he started to speak, but all he said was, —She...

—Yes, or your mother?

—Yes. My mother, he admitted in a whisper, looking back at the picture on the soiled gesso, his face drawn up in lines of confusion as though he had just remembered.

—Yes, is it? Valentine muttered. —The *Visitation*, then? He laughed. —A *Stabat Mater?* No. No more, thank you. Suppose . . . like Nicodemus I come down here? Yes, the Pharisee Nicodemus in Saint John, that . . . least reliable of the gospels? "Except a man be born again"? Yes, verily, ". . . Nicodemus saith unto him, How can a man be born when he is old? can he enter the second time into his mother's womb, and be born?" Valentine coughed and cleared his throat. He'd snatched up his, coat before he seemed aware of the clouding of anxiety which had risen in the eyes fixed on his sudden movements, an expression near a wince drawing up the face, and the figure seated unbalanced on a high stool, retreated there from avoiding him with the alert caution of a shadow, the crumpled shoulders sunk unevenly and still. Nonetheless Valentine pulled on his coat, but slowed, and his voice recovered its sharp ease.

—You want to get on with this work, don't you. But we might go up together sometime, and have a look at that *Eden?* The snake there, he laughed, gripping his lapels and lifted his overcoat into shape at the front. —The snake of consciousness? And there she is, Eve, the woman. The same woman, personalizing everything. Good Christians, good targets for advertising, because they personalize everything. A deodorant or a crucifix, they take it and make it part of them. He picked up his hat, dropping his voice to an irritating monotone. —What was it, in Ecclesiastes? God hath made man upright, but the women have sought out many inventions . . . ?

—Wait . . .

—Eh?

—Do you think . . . here, do you want some more brandy?

—I'll get along, I don't want to keep you, Valentine said, in his voice a tone of cordial deference; and back a step, something rolled away from his foot, and he stooped to retrieve it. —Rose madder? he read from the label.

—Oh that, it's nothing. Rose madder, it's too late.

—Too late? Valentine looked up pretending surprise at the eager distress in the voice, and the unsteady hand where he surrendered the packet.

—I got it for a Bouts, the first Dierick Bouts, but these colors, . . . madder lake wasn't used until the sixteenth century. And Bouts was dead. Dierick Bouts, he . . . he was dead. Wait . . . listen, do you think something might go wrong?

—Go wrong?

—If I try to tell them, about these pictures?

—Have it your own way, Valentine shrugged. —If you think you can do it alone.

—But the proof? even with that?

—You're sure they're safe? Valentine's lips drew to a thin smile.

—Well, wait then. Wait. If you . . .

—I? If I could help you?

—Yes, these fragments . . .

—Bring them along, then, if you like. We'll work this thing out. Basil Valentine put on his hat; and his eyes, gone hard under the black brim, were drawn over the wrinkled shoulder from the lined face before him to the clear face on the easel, as he added, —Bring them up to my place, then. Do you hear? There's no room for mistakes. He stood like that, staring at the picture up on the easel whose unsurprised eyes looked beyond him; and finally, murmuring, —Your mother, eh? he took his eyes from it with abrupt effort. —A *Stabat Mater*? Not a girl, not a woman at all.

He turned on his heel and pulled open the door. —It's going to smell strange out there, after this . . . odor of sanctity? The gold seal ring shone against the edge of the open door, glittering softly in the light of the bare electric bulb, as the slow light of day entered behind him with the sound of bells. —Hear Saint Bavon's? Another blue day. I'll be waiting for you. And many thanks for the cognac.

There was not a cab in sight.

—Blood is all they know, every hour boys being killed, an airplane just crashed and who was surprised, forty-one people killed, though there is some hope that the stewardess, who survived, will be able to tell police, because it is all there in the newspapers that anyone can read . . .

What was it?

Stanley sat down. Across from him a woman stared into his face, lips moving, fingers moving on her beads. He clutched the chisel in his pocket, the first time in years he had been on the subway, as though overcome with the necessity to dive down into darkness and not emerge until he reached home. He was not shivering from the cold, though it was cold in the subway. He was still buttoning his shirt. What was it she had cried to him when he asked her to kneel beside him, beside the bed; and then as he retreated through one door, fled toward another, escaped naked with all of his clothes in his hand, out into the hall where her voice died but the smell of her perfume followed him. He pulled his necktie's knot to his throat. The train roared into its rock firmament where lights twinkled in warning ahead of this front car and the woman's voice disappeared while her lips still moved, steaming the glass before them, and Stanley realized that he was on the wrong train, going in the wrong direction.

He looked up anxiously; as though another passenger might have made his mistake and, confirming him, prove everyone else misguided, misdirected. (It was an expression Stanley wore much of the time.) Standing across from him, gazing as though able to see through the dirty glass, a tall man stood with a handkerchief held to his nose and mouth. Gold glittered at his cuff. Then a woman of an uncertain age and massive shifting proportions trod on Stanley's foot, and swung, with grand inertia, into a white pole.

—You never see Jews drunk like that, said the person next to Stanley.

—Yehhh? the woman shouted, turning to them. The train was nearing a station. Stanley got up and went to the door where the tall man stood with his handkerchief to his face, turned, now, to the car. —Yehhh? the woman shouted, swinging round with Stanley. Both her hands were free. —Is that what you want? That's what you want is it? she cried, and as she did gripped the hem of her dress, and it became immediately apparent that it was the only garment she had on.

Stanley staggered into the tall man with the handkerchief, whose eyes had frozen in a cold blue horror, who whispered, —Good God! . . .

—Here! Come and get it! Come and get it!

Then a commotion started in the other end of the car, where a shabby old man had found something: but the commotion was his, only two others got up to look; the others stared in dreadful scorn, just as these seated near Stanley stared, not at the woman, but at him and the man beside him.

—Come on, both of you, you scared . . . ? The train lurched, approaching a station, and her skirt sagged and dropped as she caught a pole. The doors opened, and she kept shouting after them, —Come on, come on, you . . . throw a toilet seat around your heads and we'll all use it . . .

HE WAS WOUNDED
for our
transgressions,
he was bruised
for our iniquities:
. . . and with his
stripes we are
healed,

read the placard against which the tall man steadied himself. Across the top someone had scribbled, *Jesus a co-*

munist. He stood there with his handkerchief covering his face, and Stanley stopped, himself beside a placard which called public attention to a lower East Side knishery, where someone had penciled, *Hitler was right.* The handkerchief came down slowly, and the man caught a glimpse of a dirty shade of himself in the mirror of a chewing-gum vending machine. —Excuse me...are you all right? Stanley ventured.

The handkerchief was withdrawn, and he said in a level voice to Stanley, —Those, my dear young man, are the creatures that were once burned in witch hunts.

When Basil Valentine got home, he ran his bath immediately; and as the warm water closed over his shoulders, and one dry hand supported a cigarette, he exhaled, looking up at the clean ceiling, and his lips moved as though, all this time since he had taken his fingertips from his eyelids, seated out there in the big chair waiting for the dawn, he had been talking to himself.

Trucks were moving, loaded, toward the docks, and loaded away from the market as Stanley hurried toward his locked place, already assaulted. Why had he let Hannah stay? the last person he wanted to explain to now: even running, the odor of perfume from Agnes Deigh's nakedness rose to him. Birds clustered loudly at a horse trough. It was daylight.

His room was empty when he got there. Immediately, he noticed that the window over the bed was open, but he had no strength to pull it down. He dropped on the bed and lay still in the cold. What was it she had cried out as he ran, the cry and the voice of her a thing almost tangible hurled through the air between them, which entered and froze him in flight, as though an eternal abstraction were materialized in cast metal and bone, and Love showed its scarred steel jaws edged with broken teeth.

What was it? With his ear against the mattress, he stared at the cathedral of Fenestrula; and the beats of his heart were magnified in the bedsprings and sent back to him with the regular clattering resonance of snare drums. Crang, crang, crang, they went in regular familiar rhythm, missing a beat, or doubling one, in faithful accompaniment to something.

On the walk outside, a man approached unsteadily rubbing a rough cheekbone with a rough hand. The lucidity of the blue day rising over him seemed to prompt him to clarify the immediate issue of that turbid pool which, if questioned later on, he would call his memory, but found now resident in his cheekbone, where the blood was already dry. —He was Boyma, the man muttered, —then I must be Go...ro...gro...go...

Crang...crang...crang What was it? With his last breath of consciousness he realized that he had left his glasses on the table beside her uptown bed. *Crang crang crang* came the drums over the hill and into sight. They were playing *Onward Christian Soldiers*.

Two feet away from Stanley, the man stopped in the shallow covert that the window afforded to commit a nuisance, never glancing down at the face which lay in exhaustion under the open window at his feet.

II

This is as if a drunk man should think himself to be sober, and should act indeed in all respects as a drunk man, and yet think himself to be sober, and should wish to be called so by others. Thus, therefore, are those also who do not know what is true, yet hold some appearance of knowledge, and do many evil things as if they were good, and hasten to destruction as if it were salvation.

—The Clementine *Recognitions*, Book V

—I MEAN to tell her about the toast, this morning putting butter upon his toast, and the toast spoke with me, Fuller said, his voice in the near-inaudible confidence of intimacy. —But though I pause to listen very close, the toast conversed in a language with which as yet I remain unacquainted. Perhaps it was instructin me? he added, and his hand stopped its motion, the dirty polishing rag came to rest on the lance-rest, and he peered into the dark eye-slit of the helmet. Nothing moved. The armor stood at attention to his confidences, as it had been doing for some years. Polishing every hinge and joint, every plate and vent, had long since established his close informal acquaintance with this figure which, on first meeting, had posed no such possibility. It was some time before Fuller penetrated the cold reserve, and gained the ascendancy over the formidable hauteur with which it had greeted his reluctant advances. Left to himself, he would certainly have avoided it, and at best passed it with that respect inspired by mistrust, regarding it as his oppressor's ally. But as so often happens under the hands of tyrants, it was Mr. Brown himself who had brought them together. In his insistence that this, his favorite, be kept spotless and irreproachable, Mr. Brown had fostered a conspiracy right under his own nose.

—I already tell Adeline that the drawer method apparently destined to no great success, he went on, as the polishing rag moved again over a palette. He was recounting a recent visit to a woman of his own age, color, and forebears (but substantially heavier) whom he consulted, hands extended but not touching across a polished wood table top, concerning his affliction. Adeline, in turn, consulted her daughter Elsie, who had died when only three and was now going to school on the other side, but willingly played truant in this good cause. —I assure her, every time I enter my room I write his name upon a piece of paper and secrete it in the drawer. But when she learn that I spell his name in a variety of ways, there lies the hindrance. Perhaps you already brought misfortune to others whose names you spelt unwitting, she reprimand me.

The polishing cloth had by now reached the breastplate, which Fuller saved until last because of its flat accessibility, the directness of the encounter it permitted, and the rewarding way in which it shone. —Next we contemplate tryin the hair method, he continued, sounding slightly troubled. —She direck me to gather an envelope of his hair, which Elsie will proceed to treat the secret way, and return to me to burn sayin over it certain words from the mysteries she resides party to. Fuller rubbed hard, showing severe vexation in his sudden energy, bent lower, addressing now not the patient helmet but his own darting reflection in the breastplate. —I suggest perhaps this method reek of a kind of magic, I hesitate to do an unchristian act even upon him. But she hasten to assure me this method is Christian because I employ it against the forces of evil. Then she proceed to recount to me what Saint Louis instruck, this in the olden time of course, when a Jew have the best of you in controversy, to thrust a sword into his belly right up to the handle. He stopped and stood back to look at his work, but added, —Seem when Elsie die, ten thousand people die that same moment, nine thousand nine hundred ninety-five depart to hell direckly, four to the purgaratory, only Elsie carried straight to heaven. Thus she appear highly recommended, he reassured the impassive figure before him. They faced each other silently for a moment. Then darting the rag forward for another quick rub at the beaver, Fuller said, —I must hurry, to return in ample time, and he straightened up, and went to his room.

On his way back, the thick envelope deep in an inside pocket, he peered round the door onto the balcony, first to the head of the stairs, to see if the black dog were watching. He ventured to the rail, and there it lay below, a still blot on the Aubusson roses. With a glance of intrepid calm at his lustrous confidante, he turned to the stairs looking somewhat harried, but satisfied. Fuller was a good head taller than that suit of armor; and surely, on short acquaintance, his heart would have filled with foreboding suspicions toward one so anxious at his own safety, so apprehensive of others, that all his beauty lay in his defense. But year by year, polishing every plate and vent, every joint and hinge, Fuller had discovered every weak link in the mail, every chink in the armor, and he saw it now as a weaker demonstration of his own more elastic resistance, a hollow hope, but one which held its gauntleted hand forth, and a face which no longer glittered with disdain, but where, in their moments of confidence, familiarity had bred content.

Some time later Fuller entered with what he considered great stealth. He had not got far in the dark front hall, however, before he tripped on something. The large flat package fell flat on the floor. Fuller remained suspended before it. Then he saw two black eyes fixed upon him. The moment he looked up, the dog turned and trotted away. —You goin to write it down in your report, Fuller muttered, and straightened the package up again. —Some day I goin to discover where you keep it and destroy every page, he went on. —Rescue many good people from grief and vexation. Notably myself, he finished, entering the vast living room.

There, rising from one of the chairs before the fireplace, he saw a thin column of blue smoke. He retreated, put the straw hat in a very small panel closet in the hall, and approached again. Then, with great relief, he said, —Oh, it is you, sar. Good afternoon.

—Yes, it is, Fuller. For the moment, anyway. Who did you think…

—I take for granted maybe it's goin to be Mister Valentine, sar. I fallen into the habit of expectin the worst durin my residence here.

—We all have, we all have. Bring me some brandy, will you Fuller? Bring in the bottle of cordon bleu. The bottle with the blue ribbon on it.

—Yes sar, but Mister Brown, sar…

—When he sees me drinking the best he's got, I know it. Bring it in anyhow.

—Yes sar. A few minutes later, Fuller came in with ice and a glass, siphon, and the bottle of cordon bleu. —Could I mix somethin up for you, sar? he asked from the pulpit, where he stood, white-gloved. Given permission, he came across the carpet bearing a tumbler of brandy and ice in one hand, the siphon bottle in the other. He stepped with care. —A curious thing, he said upon arrival, —seem I always inclined to avoid steppin upon the flowers. Though he got no response, he continued to stand there, white hands swinging slightly above the table of the Seven Deadly Sins. Finally he said, —Thahss your package I encounter in the hallway, sar? and brought his eyes about in what he considered a surreptitious glance, if only because of the oblique angle of the steady stare which he lowered upon the face before him. —I trust I not responsible for any damage to the contents when it fall downward at my feet. We have a small collision there in the darkness. After another prolonged pause, Fuller said, —Upon my enterin the room seem like there not a soul present but myself. Mister Brown still occupied at the office, I presume.

Siphon was blown into the glass; and at last the voice said, —What is it, Fuller? What have you got on your mind?

Fuller's chest rose; at the same time his voice lowered to a tone consonant with the commonplace topics through which he planned to approach his question. —You tell me then, sar, is there such a thing as octopus?

—Yes. Of course.

—You have really observed one, sar?

—Well, I . . . not actually, no. But enough pictures of them, photographs.

Fuller looked at him with respectful disbelief. —Yes sar, I encounter the pictures myself upon occasion. Sar? Does there exist such a thing as mermaids, sar?

—That's legend, Fuller. They don't really exist, no.

Fuller looked at him with respectful disbelief. Nevertheless, he went on, —Are you acquainted with Saint Louis, sar?

—I've never been there.

—No sar, this one to which I refer is a mahn, sar, a kind of ghost-mahn they havin in the church. Fuller paused, and was rewarded with what appeared to be a look of reminiscence.

—The Crusader, who bought the original crown of thorns.

—Most likely the very same gentlemahn, Fuller said, raising his white hands. —Sound very reliable.

—For what purpose, Fuller?

—For wise counsel upon the problem I been rackin my understandin some time now, sar. If a mahn try to lead the good Christian life, and he find his path vexed by what he consider evil, sar, . . . can he righteously and justly have a recourse to the bahd method to combat the adversary?

Fuller waited eagerly. He even added —Sar? in encouragement. But his answer was simply, —Fuller, that is one of the oldest questions in the world.

—Yes sar. So it seem to me very old when I contemplate it. So the answer got to be very old too, no question but have his answer, for if you have got no answer you have got no question.

—Fuller, this is dialectics you're getting into.

—Yes sar, Fuller answered and withdrew a step. —These problems continue to vex me, sar, he went on. —Like the mermaids, sar.

—Fuller, Fuller . . . keep your mermaids, if they please you.

—Yes sar. But it remain complex, sar, for if they mermaid womans they got to be mermaid mahns too. For the first time the face which Fuller was, by now, staring directly at, turned to him with a smile.

—I suppose you're right, God knows, Fuller.

—Yes sar. God keep Himself very well informed upon these subjecks.

—Fuller...?

—Sar?

—You...you've never seen a picture of God, have you Fuller?

—No sar. If some artist paint His picture it become quite a hindrance to the faith, sar.

—Yes, yes, Michelangelo tried it.

—What appearance he give to Him, sar?

—An old man.

—Seem like the foreign people find a comfort makin these pictures... Fuller took a quick step back, and almost fell over the table, when the figure suddenly rose from the heavy chair. —I don't mean to disturb you, sar, comin forward with my vexations when you sittin quiet and peaceable enjoyin you... refreshment. Fuller took a step toward him, in the middle of the room.

—No, Fuller, it isn't... damn it, if these were just your problems we could lock you up and forget you.

—Yes sar, Fuller said, taking the step back. —That eventuality I preparin myself for daily.

—No, no, I didn't mean... I simply meant that...we all have the problems you ask about.

—Yes sar, Fuller said, looking relieved. —It seem an impractical measure, to lock up the whole world.

—Yes, but...you lock it out. You can lock it out.

—Can you, sar? Fuller looked up at the face suddenly turned upon him. —Seem like such a measure serve no good purpose, sar. Then the mahn lose everything he suppose to keep, and keep everything he suppose to lose. Fuller stood still, a conscious stolidity, as though to offset the movement before him, the shoes stepping heedlessly upon the roses. —It seem a very general inclination to contemplate God as an old mahn until the mahn become old himself, he said to the moving figure.

—I suppose it does, was all the answer Fuller got; nevertheless he went on, —Seem like the foreign people find a comfort makin these pictures.

—And you find them unnecessary, do you?

—If it give them comfort and sustain them...

—No, but for you. For you.

—No sar, it make itself an obstacle for me.

—And you just believe God is there.

Fuller answered, —We don't see him, sar, but we got to believe he there. And Fuller made wild anxious motions with his white hands in the space between them, like someone waving farewell to a friend on a departing ship, a friend constantly obscured by the waving arms and figures of other people. —So the preacher say...

—The preacher?

—Sar?

They were both silent. Fuller's hands fumbled in the white gloves, at his sides, as though in caricature of the hands he was watching, opening and closing on nothing. —The preacher, sar, the Reverend Gilbert Sullivan, thahss the preacher whose meetin I attend upon occasion. Finally he become a hindrance too.

—Reverend Gilbert Sullivan?

—Yes sar. The Reverend Gilbert Sullivan a very highly trained preacher, but it seem like when he acquirin his high trainin he lose somewhere along the way the first thing he require to be a preacher to us. Fuller had pulled the white hands together behind him, and stood with his eyes lowered, as though finished. But then he looked up anxiously to add, —Not that I presume to make the judgment upon him...

—But what requirement, Fuller? What requirement?

—Why sar, requirin the Reverend Gilbert Sullivan to believe he the mahn for whom Jesus Christ died.

—And you...you can believe that, Fuller? With no trouble, just that simply, you can believe it?

—Oh no, sar. It remain a challenge to believe, always. Not so simple to accept, like the mermaids.

—The mermaids...the mermaids...

—Yes, sar.

—And you can...accept the mermaids, without much difficulty?

—Yes, sar, though they remain the complication of the mermaid mahns.

—Yes, there does. There does.

—But the mermaid womans...

—Yes, the women...you can believe in the women...

—Oh yes sar, Fuller said, and then after a pause, —Woman bring you into the world, you got to stick with her.

—Wasn't it woman brought evil into the world, then?

—Sar?

—Yes. When she picked the fruit from the forbidden tree; and gave it to the man to eat?

—So the evil already there provided, and quite naturally she discover it.

—Yes, yes, and she gave it to the man...

—She share it with him, sar, said Fuller. —Thaht the reason why we love her.

The black poodle, which had been biting its nails, raised its head, then got up and went toward the hall doorway. Fuller looked at the back turned toward him, silent. Then he straightened his lapels, and followed the dog.

—*Effluvium?* Brown muttered, under his breath.

> Sweet Norah Winebisquit bedewed with sleep
> Swept down through sooted flues of chimney-sweep.
> And where? she cried, can be this sceptered rod
> That men call Recktall Brown, and I call god.
> Straight through a frosted glass-partitioned door
> They led her, and she doubted now no more.
> (The fair, the chaste, and unexpressive she)
> Might no more question wherewithal of he:
> Dreadful he sat, bastioned in golden oak,
> The humanizing of some dirty joke
> The gods tell one another ere they stand
> To attend the last obscenity, called man.

His wide sleeve covered the rest of this work on the clear mahogany surface where, their right hands extended but not touching, the thin yellow hand shifting nervously, his own couching the weight of the diamonds, Recktall Brown faced a wild-eyed youth with one arm in a sling, who said —I hope you do find it, I mean find a copy, I need it, if you don't need it, I mean if you don't think you can use it?... There was hope in that last.

Brown raised his eyes from the poem, still muttering, the pools behind the lenses disturbed as he brought his attention up. —What are you asking me about a copy of it for? What makes you think you sent it to us? Ask the secretary.

—But I sent copies to... I know I sent one here, your secretary... and your secretary isn't here today, she...

—We get things from agents, and send them back to agents. Ask your agent. Then Brown appeared to notice that the reddened eyes of this young man, who looked enough in keeping with that stereotype of disheveled insanity suddenly assembled so often associated with genius, eyes strained open to abnormal width, were fixed on the scrawled page protruding from under his sleeve. He pulled some papers toward him, partially covering it, to return to the day's business correspondence. But the voice went on, the words coming out brokenly, —Yes sir, but, since I'm here . . . A new intensity brought Brown's eyes up again. —There's one thing, something I want to know, if I could ask you what you thought, because some people have said, or I mean they've intimated, that they think I've . . . well that it really isn't mine, that I'd used some other . . . that I'd . . . plagiarized it.

—Plagiarized? Recktall Brown sat back. With a quick look over his desk, locating a manuscript, he pushed it forward with one hand and took off his glasses with the other. He fixed the figure across from him with his sharp eyes, and laughed. —Take a look at this, he said, as the quivering yellow fingers received it. —This is lifted. The whole God-damned novel is lifted. One of our readers spotted it the first thing. A lawyer went over it, and it's safe. A couple of things changed around, it's safe and it's good, and it will sell.

Wild Gousse Chase, Otto read on the title page.

—So you picked up a few things here and there for yours, what the hell? What hasn't been written before? You take something good, change it around a little and it's still good.

Otto was staring at Max's name on the title page of *Wild Gousse Chase*.

—You just take the words and string them around a little different, Brown went on, raising his glasses again.

—But . . . but words, Otto murmured helplessly. He looked up. —Words, they have to have a meaning.

—Let me give you some advice, boy, Brown said, standing. —Don't you worry about that. It's right when the idea's missing, the word pops up. You can do anything with the same words. You just follow the books, don't try to get a lot of smart ideas of your own. Brown pressed a button under his finger. There was belligerence and triumph in his voice; but it was belligerent solicitude as he finished, —It's all right there, you just take it out and write it down as though Jesus Christ himself dictated it.

—But this play, the retreating figure kept on, —it can't be lost, I'm sure a copy came here, she . . . it isn't plagiarized, I didn't steal it, I wrote it myself . . .

But Recktall Brown was seated again; and, when a secretary appeared, already returned to muttering over the rest of the open scrawl which his sleeve, drawn to him, had uncovered.

> Heaven's crown, brown-bought, fell lightly on his brow,
> Lay heavy on her perspicacious Now.
> (Still on the dreadful teeth of time she trod,
> And marveled at the maleness of god.)

Sweet Norah Winebisquit, bedewed with sleep,
Awoke this decorated painted heap
Of present woman: could she doubt her sin?
Sought furiously for the flame within,
Presented in a naked leaping cry
The burning plunder of the present I.
Pride drew her garments up, and swathed her face
In lineaments incapable of disgrace.
Slipped then away, her face bedewed with do,
Beyond the glass, and knowing all, she knew
That the immortals have their ashcans too.

—Yes sir?

—What is this thing? Where the hell did it come from? Brown demanded, waving the paper in the air. He held it out to her.

—I don't know, sir. It was in your mail this morning, I thought it might be something... literary.

—And him, how the hell did he get in here?

—I'm sorry, sir. Miss Mims is away this week, and ... She cleared her throat. —Mister Valentine to see you, sir, she said, retreating.

—Friends? Otto heard as he came out. The tall man in gray pinstripe gave him barely a glance, from a face entirely empty whose eyes affirmed, clearly and immediately, that they did not know each other. —Of course, choose your friends with as much care as you choose your clothes, the man continued, speaking to someone no more than Otto's age. —Infinite care at the outset...

In the outside hall, the pencil scribbling Chse frnds lk clthes suddenly stopped: he had just seen Gordon, and he had no place to put him.

Down below, Otto came out upon the street muttering imprecations of a general, pointless nature, until the wind hit him, and provided an object for his curses as it blew him along, mussing his hair from behind.

—Did I hear you giving some future Menander advice? Basil Valentine asked, entering. —And did I hear the word, plagiary?

Brown finished trimming a cigar before he answered, —You heard it. You can hear it again.

—Again? Valentine had not sat down. He commenced to idle up and down the room. —How do you mean?

—I mean I just saw an advance review of your art book, some half-ass critic takes it apart.

Valentine paused, lighting a cigarette. He held the match before him, looking at the flame. Then he blew it out. —How do you mean, takes it apart?

—He takes your own words out of it, and quotes them to...

—Yes, to condemn me. I see what you mean, Valentine said coldly. —He does sound rather...half-assed, as you so graphically describe him.

—Not only that...

—My dear Brown, nothing amuses me more than that, exactly that, Valentine interrupted. —Why do you suppose I put them there? To give your... half-assed reviewer opportunity to expose his own total lack of resources, in what he considers an exemplary demonstration of his own cleverness. Can you imagine the satisfaction that gives someone who has never done anything himself? Our great half-assed priesthood, so to speak, he finished with asperity, turning on Brown, or rather the cloud of cigar smoke that rose between them.

—Not only that, Brown went on with belligerent satisfaction as Valentine paced the floor away from his desk. —He says you plagiarized just about the whole thing, that you lifted...

—Plagiarized! Valentine turned, and controlled his voice with a thin smile. —You make me feel like Vergil, when someone saw him carrying a copy of Ennius, and implied...

—He says you lifted...

—I'm simply plucking the pearls from Ennius' dunghill, was Vergil's answer.

—If you think you can lift whole parts out of somebody else's...

—And now what? Valentine brought out quickly. —Making me out another...Chrysippus? Seven hundred five volumes, he went on, recovering the forced dilatory calm of his voice as he spoke. —But the work of others pleased him so, that one of his books contained a play of Euripides almost entire. The...drudgery of such a career would be appalling, he added in a mutter and turned away. Brown watched his nervous tread, and noticed a gesture familiar elsewhere: Valentine's hands, opening and closing on nothing at his sides. At the far end of the office, Valentine stopped, looking over the array of books and magazines on the table there. The slow-rising clouds from Recktall Brown's cigar seemed to accentuate the silence between them, and finally Valentine turned holding up a small stiff-covered magazine. —A symposium on religion! he read from the cover. —A rather old issue. I gather you've bought it?

—Where'd you hear that?

—The only possible reason you could have a copy lying around. You must be buying the whole thing.

—It's no secret, Brown said. —I picked it up for nothing.

—It's about time you breathed some life into it, I suppose, Valentine said, dropping the thing on a chair by his coat. —It's become quite a dismal affair, a frightened little group who spend all their time criticizing each other's attempts in terms of cosmic proportions, and then defend each other against the outside world. Even the fiction, the stories they write are about each other, they don't know anyone else. A sort of diary of dead souls.

—A bunch of second-hand Jews... Brown began, if only to interrupt.

—I doubt the windows of their editorial offices have been opened in decades, Valentine went on, in a monotone whose only purpose was to establish its authority to continue. —If there are any. What future do you plan for these... critics?

—Critics! Brown muttered. —They call themselves critics just because they never learned how to make a living. It's got a lousy circulation of about five thousand, but it's got a reputation. Intellectual. I'm going to bring it around to where even a half-wit can feel intellectual reading it. The circulation will be twenty times what it is now.

Valentine laughed quietly, walking away again; and only when his back was turned did Brown, shifting in his chair, show impatience. He seemed prepared to let Valentine go on, wasting time until whatever had brought him here, and strained his nervous presence now, broke forth.

—Like that incredible book you published, what was it? Valentine went on, looking over the array on the table. —"Soul-searching" the reviewers called it. By some poor fellow who joined a notorious political group, behaved treasonably? And after satisfying that peculiar accumulation of guilt which he called his conscience by betraying everyone in sight, joined a respectable remnant of the Protestant church and settled down to pour out his...

—It's already sold half a million, Brown said patiently. —That's what people want now, soul-searching.

—Soul-searching! Valentine repeated. —People like that haven't a soul to search. You might say they're searching for one. The only ones they seem to find are in some maudlin confessional with the great glob of people they really consider far less intelligent than themselves, they call that humility. Stupid people in whom they pretend to find some beautiful quality these people know nothing about. That's called charity. No, he said and shrugged impatiently, turning with his hands clasped behind him. —These people who hop about from one faith to another have no more to confess than that they have no faith in themselves.

Brown watched him carefully through the thick lenses, ambling slowly with head lowered, a slim hand raised to the strong profile of his chin, to stop again at the table and flick open the cover of a book there. —*In Dreams I Kiss Your Hand, Madam*, he read. —Really... "Selected and edited, with an introduction by..." yourself? All the world loves...

—There's no plagiary in that, Brown said. —Everybody who wrote something's got his name on it.

—You couldn't have sold a single copy if it weren't. But here, Esme? who the devil . . . ?

—Who?

—"To ESME, whose unerring judgment is responsible for whatever value this book may have . . ." Your humility is really quite touching.

—Some girl in the office pulled those together for me, Brown said, drumming his fingers more rapidly, as his lowered eyes caught the edge of the poem scrawled under his sleeve. —Now what . . .

—Your modesty is overwhelming, as always.

—You came up here to talk about my modesty? Brown broke out at last.

—Hardly. Valentine turned on him. —I dropped in to talk to you about your . . . most successful protégé. He smiled.

—What about him? What have you been up to with him?

—I? Nothing, nothing at all. If Valentine's composure had seemed to suffer, it was totally recovered; but Brown continued to look at him, hands splayed on the desk, as though nothing were more familiar than composure which was serene only when it had something to dissemble.

—You've seen him? What about?

—Let me see, Valentine answered vaguely. —As I remember, we discussed the Lex Cornelia, an ordinance against Roman matrons who poisoned . . .

—I told you, I wasn't going to have any of your crap interfering. Valentine raised his eyebrows. —My what?

—Yes, God damn it. I've allowed you a lot of things, but this time . . . Look here, there's a lot of things about you I know, that maybe you don't know I know, Recktall Brown said leaning forward over the desk, looking at him with the centerless eyes in those thick lenses.

—My private life is hardly any concern . . .

—Not just your private life. A God damn lot of other things.

—Other things? Valentine repeated blandly.

—What about a trip you made to Paris about six months ago? For a week in Paris. Where did you go from Paris?

—The Midi, as I told you. A pleasant town near . . .

—Midi hell. Do you want me to tell you where you went?

—Not especially, said Basil Valentine, tapping his chin.

—I could tell . . .

—But you wouldn't, would you, Valentine said, resting the finger on his chin, and looking up, as Recktall Brown looked down.

—I told you the day you met him, Brown repeated, —I don't want any interference from you.

—You know, I believe you rather like him. It must be an odd sensation for you.

—We're in business.

—Tell me, just how interested in him are you?

—Right now, a quarter of a million dollars. I'm not going to lose interest, either.

—I suppose not, Valentine said, taking out another cigarette, and pausing until he'd lit it. —Tell me, suppose something happened to sever this partnership of yours?

—Something like that over my dead body, Brown said evenly.

—And if these forgeries were discovered?

—What do you mean, discovered.

—I might have said, exposed.

—So that's it! Brown stood up, his hands remained planted on the desk. —You know God damn well, nobody could prove a thing.

—But if he...

—*He?*

—As you've told me, one cannot insure against inherent vice.

—What do you mean?

—Never mind, Valentine said. —I'm glad I understand you. Yes, for you he doesn't exist except as an investment?

—And for you he doesn't exist except as...

—We've had quite enough of this, Valentine cut in. —Now, this joint bank account you put his money into for him...

—It's safe enough, Brown muttered, sitting down. —Nobody even knows about it, nobody could touch it but us, you and him and I. Then Brown looked up. —That's what you're thinking? to reach in there and take out...

—Good heavens, Valentine laughed. —You know me better than that. All I could do would be to stop payment anyway, you know. But he... Valentine stood looking down at the reflection of the diamonds in the mahogany. —With his genius...

—With his genius and your ambition, I'd have...

—Why, Valentine interrupted again, looking up at him. —Perhaps you should settle down and raise a family. I can't imagine a prouder father than you might make.

—Listen, Recktall Brown said standing again, —we're not going to have any more of this. You're going to forget all this crap about exposing these pictures and ruining him.

—*Him?* But suppose... suppose it were he who had this notion himself?

—You think he's crazy? Maybe in other ways, but . . .

—But you cannot imagine anyone being crazy when it comes to making a million dollars. Basil Valentine picked up his coat. He stood looking round the large office as he pulled it on. —You know, you might start a novel factory here, he said. —It's been done before. And after the success of that "soul-searching" book. And that remarkable abomination, *The Trees of Home* was it? A regular assembly line. Incidentally, he went on in an agreeable tone, pulling up his lapels, —what ever happened to that boy who was up here with a book of poems to sell you? The one with a rather bad case of acne, whom I stumbled on sandpapering his cheeks in the lavatory? Arthur something . . .

—He's still around, with his God damn poems. Religious poems.

—They weren't awfully bad. You might allow him some money on them, you know, some chance to live like a human being.

—Do human beings write poetry? Recktall Brown demanded, looking up. Then his pointless gaze fell to the paper under his cuff. —Poets do.

Basil Valentine stood looking at the heavy bowed head for a moment. Then with his hat he picked up the stiff-covered little magazine from the deep chair. —I wish you luck with this, he said, tossing it over before Brown's hands on the desk, where it slid toward the mass of hand mounting the diamonds, which withdrew with instant volition. The cigar had almost gone out in the ashtray, but continued to give off a faintly noxious emanation. Brown did not look up. He stared at *Effluvium* and mumbled something about how popular religion was now, and something about —those poor intellectual bastards.

—Perhaps they all ought to be crucified? Basil Valentine suggested, pulling the door open behind him. —That might give them some idea of religious experience.

—But this book is about religion, said a sub-editor, standing aside for the tall man in the black Homburg to pass. —It's Buddhism.

—But it's by a Jew, said the other, standing aside.

—Well, I've told him if he'll change his hero from a Jew to a homosexual, we might accept it.

—But that's the way it was in the first place.

Recktall Brown entered to demand, —Who the hell is the Reverend Gilbert Sullivan, and what the hell does he want here? When he got no answer (though he paused no longer than it took to shift himself from the outside door to another) Recktall Brown entered a large roomy closet, and hung his coat among many others of the same size, and shape, and style. The dog, moving its stump of a tail slowly, met him, and he reached down to give it a single pat on the head which seemed to please it greatly.

—Sar...

—Why the hell don't you answer the door, Fuller? Recktall Brown said, advancing. —Instead of...who is this Reverend Gilbert Sullivan, what...

—Oh no sar, Fuller said, backing into the room before him. —The Reverend not present here, I alone here...

—Then why the hell don't you answer the door instead of talking to yourself.

—Oh no sar not exackly alone sar I...

—Well who the hell...Well, my boy. I'm glad to see you. God damn glad to see you. Fuller, bring me the pitcher over here. Recktall Brown stood by the chairs before the fireplace, watching Fuller get across the room to the pulpit.

—Fuller? he said suddenly.

—Sar...?

—What have you been up to, Fuller?

—Sar? Nothin, sar. I been most peaceable and quiet of late.

—See you stay that way. Recktall Brown glanced down at the table, and Fuller glanced down at the dog.

—Fuller?

—Sar?

—Isn't there any more regular brandy?

—Yes sar but...

—I told him I wanted this. You can take it out of my next check.

—It's all right my boy, relax. I just thought that dumb nigger made a mistake. He gets vexed by liquor, he says, don't know one from another. Recktall Brown settled down in a chair, and looked across the table. —You look tired, my boy. Tired as hell.

—Little dogs in the street bark at me.

—What the hell, my boy. What the hell. You can't blame them.

—You mean if you were a little dog in the street, you'd bark at me?

—Now listen, my boy, what the hell...

—That damned congenitally damned glowing fiend of a dog of yours is the only one that doesn't bark at me. This is good cognac.

—Listen, my boy, I want to talk to you. Now what about this picture you're working on?

—That's why I'm here. It's out in the hall.

Recktall Brown had been sitting forward in the big chair with his hands turned in upon his knees. He shifted so that flesh rolled over the back of his collar, and shouted, —Fuller!

—Sar?

—Bring in that big package in the hall, bring it in here. Is that it, my boy? he asked, turning. He got no answer, and shifted again to watch Fuller advance, carrying the thing, picking his way among the roses.

—Hurry up, Fuller. What the hell are you doing, playing hopscotch? Now lay it out here and open it and be careful, be God damn careful. As the brown wrapping paper came away Recktall Brown was saying, —I told you not to bring these God damn things up here on the subway. I told you to call me and I'd send a car down for it. Look at here, you already banged up a corner. Then he stopped speaking, and gathered his breath to say, —What the hell!

Fuller had taken three careful steps backward, and stood now staring with a look which another face might have refined into anxiety, but on his was simple expectant terror. The explosion was not for him, however; but however, he remained bound.

—Where the hell is her face?

—Sar?

—I'm not asking you, Fuller, God damn it. Where the hell is her face?

—Appear she deprived of it by the many centuries passin respectfully over...

—Fuller! By God, Fuller! Have both of you gone crazy? Get out of here. The pools behind the thick lenses quivered like water disturbed by wind. —This is... by God. Now here. Tell me where the hell is her face.

—As Fuller says, it appear she deprived of it by the attrition of many respectful years passing their loving hands...

—Stop! Recktall Brown lowered his voice, and then his bulk into a chair. He was perspiring. —I'm tired too, God damn it. Now just tell me simply why the hell you damaged it like this. Fuller, I told you to get out of here.

—Yes sar.

—Ah, to dictate to the past what it has created is possible; but to impose one's will upon what it has destroyed takes a steady hand and rank presumption. My wife told me once, that I looked like a criminal.

—What you've done to this picture here, it's a crime.

—A supralapsarian criminal.

Recktall Brown sat forward gripping his knees. —You mustn't laugh like that, my boy.

—Why not? Tell me, tell me. Some time I haven't laughed.

—It just don't sound right, Recktall Brown muttered, and looked down at the damaged picture. Then he looked up again. —Are you all right, my boy?

—Yes, well. There is often now the sensation of weightlessness, or weighing

very little. There. Weightless but well. When you live where I do, upsets of
the liver are seldom occurrences.

—It wasn't your liver I'm thinking about, Recktall Brown said looking
down again. —Look, you got to paint this face in here again, the face on this
woman. Ten thousand dollars you've taken right off the price right there.

—And dishonored death into the bargain, so they tell me. Could I have a
cigar?

—You?

—A cigar.

—My boy...

Recktall Brown watched him tear the cellophane cover away, and commence to trim the end with his thumbnail. —Here, take this, he said and
offered the penknife. —Don't just stare at it, my boy. Trim the end of the
God damn cigar with it.

—Indeed.

—My boy...

—Nothing moves in this room. If you had music...

Nevertheless, the smoke rises.

—There! something moved, intimate movement there on the far wall...
He recovered with a shudder, to draw a hand over his eyes and whisper, —Never
mind. I thought I saw Patinir hanging there, I keep forgetting he's in mortmain,
gone home and taken his wages. You see how the prospect draws us on? Making perfect dice. They have to be perfect before you can load them. Goodness!
what beautiful diamonds. How their impurities dance with life! Not deceit
just skin-deep, like this intricate, cunning field full of fraud separating us here,
seven and deadly. It's not even a very good copy. He stared unblinking at the
table, and suddenly came forward to pick at the edge of it with the penknife.

—Here! Brown lunged his naked hand out. —It's real, this table picture,
stop scratching it. Don't worry, right after Valentine shot his mouth off about
it I had some real experts look it over. Don't worry, Brown grunted belligerent
satisfaction, looking down at it. —It's the genuine original.

—I can see, it is not, came the whisper distinct across the table of the Seven
Deadly Sins. —Christ! to have copied a copy? and that was how it began!

—My boy, says Recktall Brown, and stands to his feet to light his own
cigar and jam it among uneven teeth. The youthful portrait hangs still as he
approaches it, and perhaps, as Basil Valentine remarked, serves in some measure to humanize the fragments of motion which compose his progress toward
it. Immediately upon arrival there, Recktall Brown turns his back upon it, a
gesture which leaves its expression unchanged as he obscures it with the one
which has superseded it. —Maybe you need a girl.

—A girl?

—How long is it since you've had one?

—Had one?

—I don't mean a God damn wife hanging around all the time. I mean just a girl. You can't go around month after month with all this piling up inside you. Of course, hell anybody can see that will drive you crazy as hell. You got to release that once in a while, or it drives anybody crazy. Do you want me to send you a nice girl down there for a couple of nights?

—But the cost.

—The cost? Each foot planted upon a rose, Recktall Brown's laughter might seem to rise the entire distance of his frame, a laborious journey, complicated by ducts and veins, cavities and sedulous organs whose functions are interrupted by the passage of this billowing shape which escapes in shambles of smoke. —You can pay for anything in this town.

—Barefoot on that vast acreage, for love or money.

—God damn it, my boy. God damn it...

—Without love?

—Do I fall in love with the barber when I get a haircut? God damn it, my boy.

—Reverend Gilbert Sullivan...

—God damn Reverend Gilbert Sullivan!

—Exactly.

Recktall Brown starts to turn away; his reversal is remarkable for its quickness, a feat of muscular co-operation which happens before his eyes can contain the reason. They do, though; his voice too. —Put that damn bottle down now and sit down.

—A hindrance to the working of reality. Ah, Brown, Brown, your daughters all were fair. But the youngest...

—Are you getting anything from Esme?

—There remains the complication of the mermaid men.

—Sit down. We're both going to sit down and figure this out. Did he put you up to all this crap?

—I hear singing.

Sinking, on heavy tones into the depth of the vast room, come these weights, ——Littel girl

              ——My bachelor room

—Fuller!

—Sar? drops from above.

—Stop that God damn noise.

—You and I, Brown. You and I. You are so damned familiar.

—You've got to get hold of yourself, my boy.

—If we are, as he says, projections of his unconscious. Then the intimacy is not at all remarkable, is it.

—Stop it. You got to stop talking this way. Valentine does the same God damn thing to me, he tries to wear me down. Did he . . . has he been bothering you, my boy? Now damn it talk to me, let's get all this straight. What's on your mind?

—The equation of x to the power of n plus y to the power of n has no nontrivial solution in integers for n greater than two.

—Sit down.

—That is Fermat's last theorem.

—Sit down. What the hell's the matter, is there . . . have you got a pain in you? The motion reflected on the thick lenses (and entering through aqueous chambers to be brought upside-down and travel so, unsurprised, through vitreous humors to the confining wall of the retinas, and rescued there, and carried away down the optic nerves to be introduced to one another after these separate journeys, and merge in roundness) emerges upon his consciousness in the constraint of slowed motion. —What are you grunting for?

—I'm pretending I weigh three hundred pounds.

—Sit down. Stop this. Give me that God damn bottle.

—It isn't difficult.

—Sar?

Nothing moves but the intimate landscape of Patinir, a self-contained silent process which demands no attention, for the prevailing color there is blue.

—Sar? What I goin to do with these relics?

A full dozen of crosses lie massed in Fuller's arms.

—Fuller, says Recktall Brown, with stolid deadly patience, —you take those little men you been rubbing and nail each one of them on a cross, and get them right side up, and do it quietly, and get the hell out of here, now.

—The little Jesus-men, sar?

—Get out. Get out. Get out.

—Saint Peter, upside-down. Wait, Fuller. Confirm me. Isn't there, in every one of us, a naked man marching alone down Main Street playing a bass drum?

Recktall Brown limbers the heavy extensions which support him, and rises. —Did you hear me, Fuller? Are you crazy too? Did you hear me?

—I think perhaps in the condition he enjoyin now sar he can understand the language the toast . . .

—Get out!

Fuller and Recktall Brown diverge. The old crucifer treads with care and mounts the hill of stairs. Recktall Brown reaches a corner, where he takes off his glasses, and from eyes sharp and open as those of undersea he stares into the soft diffusion of the room. —No, he says toward the fireplace; and then pursues his word. —You can't do this, my boy. You can't go crazy on me now.

—Now? Now?

—God damn it, my boy. Not before you finish this Herbert picture. Wreathed in smoke, he stands above his property. —How's it coming along?

—Beautifully. Excitingly. Wondrously.

—Good. Good, my boy. Good.

—But not van Eyck.

—What do you mean?

—Not Hubert.

—What do you mean, my boy? What the hell do you mean? The smoke itself hung on diffracted planes, and Recktall Brown sat down. —You want the credit for it, do you? Is that it?

—But not from you, and not from them, from the thing itself.

Recktall Brown rolled the cigar between thick fingers. Then he put it to his lips, and without relinquishing hold upon it, rolled it there. —You can't do this, my boy. He paused. —You know God damn well if you tried to sell one of these pictures as your own it's worth about forty dollars. Now wait, my boy. Don't laugh like that. It don't sound right.

—Suppose...

—God damn it, my boy. Did we make a bargain or didn't we. We're in business, you and me. Do you see that book over there on the shelf there, the yellow one? *The Trees of Home.* That guy is in business, and he's in business with me. And you...

—I...

—You knew when you started, said Recktall Brown, —you couldn't stop.

They were silent. The lines of their stares formed two sides of a triangle, that was all.

—God damn it, my boy, if it wasn't for being in business with me, you'd float away. This God damn world of shapes and smells you say you live in, you'll turn into one of them. Look at you, you almost have already. By God, Recktall Brown said, standing, so that the look from his eyes no longer needed cross the distance between them, seated, but fell like a weight with his words, —you can't go crazy now. I won't let you. He threw his cigar into the fireplace; and took out another. —Do I have to send Christ down there to model for you? His voice was rising again. —Do I have to send the Virgin down there to spread her...

—It's too late now.

—Too late for what. Go on. Talk to me. I feel like I'm talking to myself here.

—The Steenken *Madonna*. Well there. When Hubert van Eyck painted that, it wasn't just a man, painting a picture, of a woman.

—Well then what the hell was it, tell me.

—Feeling? Belief? Say sensation, then. Ask Caligula.

—Belief necessary? So is money, and look how many people have it, for Christ sake. You leave feelings to other people, you do the thinking. Look at them. They'd rather feel than think, and look at them. You let them do your feeling and believing for you, and you do their thinking for them, or you'll end up the same creek all of them are. In his throat, the two veins, either of them vital, pulsated under rolls of flesh. The two before him stood out in invitation to any passing blade.

—It is too late now. "The finest painting, and perhaps the culminating achievement of the fifteenth-century genius Dierick Bouts." You see? I have to tell them.

Recktall Brown lowered his voice. —Like you say, my boy, It isn't that simple. Do you think they want to know? Recktall Brown did not take out his penknife, nor even look for it in the pockets swung against his belly, where it was a familiar tenant. He bit off the end of his cigar, and began to pace before the fireplace. —Eminent scientists agree, after exhaustive tests, that a fifteen-cents-a-gallon chemical in a fancy bottle with a lot of scientific words on it is proven superior. So they pay a dollar a bottle because they want to. These pictures of yours, do you think you could get two hundred dollars for one? No. But these poor bastards crawl all over each other trying to get them away from me for prices in the thousands. They don't know, they don't want to know. They want to be told. This guy whose picture you print with a stethoscope in his hand, he's the same as your half-assed authorities. They want credit for discovering one of these old pictures. So just like the people who are proud to pay a dollar a bottle for this chemical, the same God damn people are proud they can hire an eminent authority to tell them what they ought to buy for art. If there aren't enough pictures to go round...

—We sanction Gresham's law.

—Don't talk to me now about law, just listen to me. Who would gain anything if you ran around telling people you painted these things? They'd all be mad as hell at you, most of all the people who bought them. Do you think they'd even admit they paid forty or fifty thousand for a fraud? Do you think anybody would thank you?

—I'll trade my cigar for that bottle of brandy, that bottle of cognac for this half-smoked Havana cigar which I am not enjoying.

—Do you think they'd even believe you? They'd lock you up, my boy. You could get up there and paint these things all over again, and they wouldn't

believe you. They'd think you're crazy. That's what they'd want to think. My
boy you've fooled the experts. But once you've fooled an expert, he stays fooled.
Wait a minute. Sit down. I'm not finished. Who put you up to this?

—The midget who married the tall woman. Have you heard that one?

—Valentine's doing this, is he? Answer me. I warned you about him, didn't
I? God damn it, I warned you about him. He's jealous of you, my boy, can't
you see that?

—You and he are very close, Mister Brown and Basil Valentine.

—I know him, Recktall Brown said, looking down at the cigar in his hand.
Its leaf had started to unroll, and he threw it so into the fireplace. —It's a long
time now I know him, and the one thing I know, he went on looking up, —you
can't trust him. Nobody can. He's mixed up in a lot of things. Brown was
fumbling in his pocket down front. —In God damn near everything. He's
too smart for his own good. Have you got that knife? Don't get up, don't get
up, just hand it to me here.

—A brilliant man?

—He's got the best education money can buy, I'll tell you that.

—If we are priests, conspiring against you, do not be surprised.

—I . . . God damn it, I told you not to laugh that way.

—What is laughter?

—It makes me nervous.

—You don't think about me when I'm not here. Well, should I be surprised
at that?

—Where are you going now?

—To be with my wife. Sheer enterprise, as you will understand. I wonder,
when I step out of doors, how the past can tolerate us.

Recktall Brown came round the chairs, and their paths converged. He
raised his arm, and it came to rest. —I can feel your bones right through your
shoulder. Don't you eat anything?

—Your reassurance strengthens me, for I have sensed I felt them there
myself. But no one has confirmed me in some time. Would it have been beyond
temptation then, to take a knife and dig for them, and prove they're there?

—Christ, my boy, you've got to get hold of yourself.

—Small choice, then, to take what others leave.

—You feel better now, do you? Take a rest. After this Herbert picture,
take a rest. And just forget these crazy things you've said. Hell, you can
paint this picture and you know it. And as for what you said about . . . well
hell, we'll just forget the other things but don't forget, just keep away from
Valentine.

—You are so damned familiar, Brown.

—Why Jesus Christ, my boy, I've known you quite awhile now. I want to watch out for you. And keep away from him, do you hear?

—So damned familiar.

—I'd trade him for you any day. Now take care of yourself. You'll feel better when you get yourself back to work.

In the hall doorway, the weight of the arm remains extended for another moment, and the cumbrous diamonds, hanging beside the rough cheek. Behind, the dog lay licking her belly. Beside hung the portrait, udder-like hands to the front. The weight of the arm and the diamonds, the milkless mamma, malfeasant, even at pendulant rest, that and the sound of the dog, licking, licking, in pestilential heat, as inertly oppressive as the hand, shaded in insensible intimacy to suffocation; and had Recktall Brown not, just then, patted the shoulder which he released, saying, —Get hold of yourself and finish up this last one, my boy, and then take a rest. You just need a rest... the shadow which united them, after an instant's complication, might have been simplified by one-third.

———Hi, gang! Your friend Lazarus the Laughing Leper brings you radio's newest kiddies' program, *The Lives of the Saints*, sponsored by *Necrostyle*. Before we hear from your friend Lazarus, just let me ask you a question. Does Mummy have trouble sleeping? If she does, and ha ha what Mummy doesn't, ask her if she knows about *Necrostyle*, the wafer-shaped sleeping pill. Remember the story Laughing Lazarus told you last week, kids? About the saint who didn't sleep for the last eight years of her life? That's right. Agatha of the Cross. But Mummy's not a saint, is she. Mummy needs her sleep. Tell her about *Necrostyle*, if she doesn't already know. Don't forget, kids, *Necrostyle*, the wafer-shaped sleeping pill. No chewing, no aftertaste...

—Ellery, Esther interrupted.

—Just a second. Ellery sat forward with a newspaper rolled in his hand, his head down, listening to the radio. —This is a new account.

———your friend Laughing Lazarus will be here in just a minute, but listen kids. Here's one real confidential question I want to ask you first, just between us. Do you have enough brothers and sisters? I know, you love big brother or little Janey, don't you. But too many can spoil your chances. Look at it this way. When you have pie for dessert, how many ways does it have to be divided up? Do you get your share? If you have enough brothers and sisters, or even if you don't have any and don't want any, tell Mummy about *Cuff*. *Cuff*, the new wonder preventative. *Cuff* is guaranteed not to damage internal tissues or have lasting effects. But you don't have to remember all those long words, just tell Mummy to ask about *Cuff* next time she visits her friendly neighborhood druggist. Remember, *Cuff*. It's on the *Cuff*.

—I feel ill, Esther said.

—Listen.

——and *Zap*. But I'll be back to tell you more about *Zap* later on. Now, here's your friend Laughing Lazarus, ha ha, who's going to tell us about what happened to Blessed Dodo of Hascha, when he...

—Can you turn it off now? Esther asked, resting her head back, her eyes closed.

—Rose wants to hear it. I'll just turn it down, Ellery said. He walked over to the radio with the laborious movements of a football player demonstrating that simply the act of being physical is one of high achievement. Ellery was lithely, easily built. He handled himself and everything round him with an air of clumsy familiarity. When he walked it was with an air of patient indifference to where he was going, though he never arrived anywhere else. Clothes looked well on him: he was what tailors with a sporting bent had in mind when they designed loose-fitting jackets and pleatless narrow-legged trousers. Cigarettes smoked from between his fingers lifelessly, forgotten, leaving him unresponsible for the ashes which dropped to the rug when they grew heavy enough. Smoking, he blew rings heavy with disdain which seemed to jar wherever they hit. He looked at things and at faces with patient boredom, and he shrugged his shoulders. Sometimes he winked, as he did now at Rose who sat on the floor, cowered against the loudspeaker of the radio. Ellery turned the volume down. Rose stared at him.

So did Esther. —Sometimes... I hear those things and I just can't believe them, she said.

—It's a big account, Necrostyle Products. That's the way to get at them, through the kids.

—But it... how can it be so vulgar? She breathed that last word heavily. She had opened her bloodshot eyes to stare at the ceiling.

—Vulgar? That's what people like. That's what vulgar means, people.

—Ellery, but I don't see why... I don't see why...

—You told me that yourself. They didn't teach Latin at Yale.

She lowered her eyes to look at him. In her lap, Esther held the kitten too close, threatening the strain of life in it with her attention.

—Not that I ever knew of, anyhow. He shrugged his shoulders. —How many people have you got coming to your party?

—Twenty or so, she said wearily.

—It's a hell of a time for a party. For you to give a party.

—I know it is, do you think I feel like it?

—Why don't you just call it off, then? Because you've already invited this great poet you've always wanted to meet. I know why, too, honey. But believe me, it won't help your writing any.

—I wish... She was staring at her typewriter and its silent litter.

—Isn't one enough?

—I wish you wouldn't talk this way now, please. We've got to find a doctor, Ellery, quickly.

—There's a call I have to make, he said, and went into the bedroom where the telephone was with the newspaper rolled in his hand. His voice broke above the radio. —Just a second, operator. It's the Hospital of the Immaculate some damn thing, hang on a minute... He opened the newspaper on the bed.

Rose turned from Blessed Dodo of Hascha. —Someone is at the door, she said to her sister. —Blessed Dodo, Blessed Didée, Blessed Bartolo of San Gimignano...

—Rose!

—Or even Doctor Biggs of Lima Peru.

—You...? Embracing his weariness in her own voice, Esther opens.

—Don't disturb, don't disturb. Only to find some things I left here, for safekeeping, they say. I enter sparingly.

—And Rose? says Rose.

—Rose.

—Rose of Lima, Peru. Saint Rose of Lima. Then you... Don Diego Jacinto Paceco...

—Rose, now, that's enough, says Esther. —She is... but you...?

(—Yeh, that's the guy, honey, he jumped out a window but the newspaper says he only broke a few ribs...)

—My wife God love you, even now some Mozart especially. Symphony Number Thirty-seven especially. Four four four.

—But you, you... here you are.

—Kind words then, while it's still daylight. Have you kept my secrets, then? I've come to get them.

(—Visiting hours, two to four and seven to eight. Thanks honey.)

—You look... are you... is everything all right? Esther comes alive; even her eyes seem to clear. —I have so much... there must be some way to... is it drinking has you this way?

—Its powers of magnification embrace us all, do they not, or do they not. Well, into the study, for I've trusted you there.

—Well you...

—I...

—Oh, this... is my husband, Ellery?

—How do you . . .

—This is a . . . friend, Ellery.

Lighting a cigarette with the hand he had used to shake the hand he had been offered, Ellery sat down. —I fixed it up, he said to Esther. —It's a cinch.

She looked at him, her eyes wide, daring relief. Ellery drew heavily on his cigarette, and then sent a smoke ring rolling toward Rose curled before the radio. Rose cringed at its approach. —She's like a kid, isn't she. I could probably get a good audience reaction from her on this program. Ellery picked up a magazine. It was an issue of *Dog Days* devoted to Doberman pinschers which had been here when he came.

§ ANNOUNCEMENT §
As a Token of his Appreciation
To every bitch who presents him with a Champion heir
Dictator will give an additional service
with his compliments

Ch. Dictator von Ehebruch was offered at stud ("to bitches for whom only the best is good enough") for one hundred fifty dollars.

—My eyes. May I show him my eyes?

—Sit down, Rose. Rose has been upset, Esther said, standing with the kitten. —She had a job in Bloomingdale's for the Christmas rush, and she was victimized. They fired her. Let's . . . sit down?

—Somebody pulled the old twenty-dollar-bill switch on her, Ellery said looking up from his magazine. —Somebody comes in and pays for something with a twenty with the corner torn off, then another guy comes in and pays with a buck, and when he gets change for only a buck he raises hell, see? He says he paid with a twenty, and he's got the torn corner to prove it, he got it from the other guy outside . . .

—It's a shame, Esther interrupted. —All she could tell police about the first one was that he had a hair-line mustache.

—And his hair! Rose burst in, —that he wore like a hat. She stared at them, and then returned to the radio and left them there abandoned to each other's vacancy like three children met in a summer bungalow colony where the plumbing in each ugly cottage is the same, the beds sagged in discouragement, used only for supporting sleep, where the heat of the sun serves only to excuse the appearance of white-skinned parents in offensive states of undress while they pretend that there is something new under this sun and they have come to find it; while the children know that there are no new secrets, and so they are satisfied to keep the old ones from each other.

—What day is it? Esther asked, pushing the switch on the table lamp beside her.

—Wednesday.

—Thursday, Ellery corrected, damning a day later, and she winced.

—What is it, Rose?

—How old you all looked, when the light went on. How quickly you grew up together, Rose said from shadow.

—I just read the Pope uses an electric razor, said Ellery. —I wonder what make it is, how much do you think he'd take for a testimonial.

Looking across the room Esther said, —But . . . can I get you something? Are you all right?

—Just for a minute, I was dizzy just for a minute. But here, I've come for other things . . .

—Are you . . . have you been working lately?

—Not lately, no. Not lately.

Ellery got up suddenly, dropping *Dog Days;* and he picked up another magazine as he crossed the room. —Esther tells me you've done a lot of painting, and I've got something for you if you want something like this. He held forth a page of advertisements. —This here, this is one of our accounts. He indicated the largest. Over a saccharine line drawing of a woman, her head covered, eyes raised, *YES, the Mother of God WILL relieve Your Pain, Disease, Distress* . . . The name of the Virgin Mary is making the headlines in today's newspapers . . . Write today for your free copy . . .

Beneath, another ad said, STIR UP YOUR LIVER BILE

Beneath, another ad said, Are YOU troubled with STICKY HOT SORE FEET?

—I just thought of this, Ellery went on. —I'll bet you could do it, and it would pay you good money. They're spending a hell of a lot on publicity. See, at first here we were going to have reproductions of some old masters, you know, pictures of the Virgin Mary like you see in museums. But this is better. It's more modern, catches the eye. And if you could paint a couple of pictures for us, the Virgin doing . . . something, whatever the hell she does, but a real arty picture . . .

—Ellery, please . . . Esther said weakly.

—They've got a lot of money behind them, religion's getting popular all over again. It would be a good deal for you, and I can . . .

—Ellery, wait. Let him go, Esther said. —It isn't . . . he wouldn't . . .

—All right, the hell with it, Ellery said, returning to his chair. —I just thought maybe he could do it, but he didn't need to be so damn rude did he? Ellery picked up *Dog Days* again, watching the door to the studio come half closed. —I just thought maybe I could help him out. He returned to Ch. Dictator von Ehebruch, and his chest filled as he studied the Doberman.

Esther did not hear; but sat staring at the door half closed upon her: Persephone then, and Proserpina now, the same queen in another country, she stared at the doorway to his kingdom and faltered forward.

—What is it? Can I help you? she asked, entering. —Rose has been sleeping in here, that's why it's different.

—Well, I trust Rose then. What are these marvelous things?

—Oh, those are pictures of eyes. Rose does them. She likes ... eyes.

—Somewhere, strips of canvas, somewhere strips of wood, painted upon. Hidden, Rose helped.

—Then you were here? You were here last night?

—Or was it?

—Because she said, Rose, said, she'd seen you in the mirror. And we ... I didn't understand. I was worried for Rose.

—The mirror, there?

—I've seen you in it too.

—To correct bad drawing. There.

—Under here? She put the kitten on the floor, stooping, reared the long lines of her thighs, and recovered a package wrapped in newspaper. —This?

Then face to face so abruptly that she startled back, her lips move before she can speak. —You don't look well, is all she finds to say.

—Not myself?

—Not yourself? When you loved me, then ...

—When you loved me?

—I was a whole dimension larger then, and now...

—This is where I sleep, said Rose putting her head in the doorway. —Because it smells so nice in here. This is where I sleep.

—Goodbye, for I have to leave.

—This is ... you've got what you want? Esther asked, following him. —What you came for?

—And can carry away.

—Hey wait a minute, before you go, Ellery said, standing, —there's a book here I wanted to borrow but Esther said it was yours.

—Ellery, don't ...

—It's all right, here, Ellery said, raising Aunt May's copy of the *Book of Martyrs*. He read from the title page, —*A History of the Lives, Sufferings, and Triumphant Deaths of the Primitive Protestant Martyrs from the Introduction of Christianity to the Latest Periods of Pagan, Popish, and Infidel Persecutions* ...

—But in the name of God...?

—Another program like this one, see? Ellery waved his hand toward the radio. —But for different denominations, like Catholics and Protestants. Stuff like this. Listen. "In Arethusa, several were ripped open, and corn being put into their..." wait, here... "scourged, put to the rack, his body torn with..." here, "Martha Constantine, a handsome young woman, was treated with great indecency and cruelty by several of the troops, who first ravished her, and then killed her, by cutting off her breasts. These they fried, and set before their..."

—Esther, goodbye, please God...

—Here, there's another about the guy they tie little bags of gunpowder... it's for kids, this is what kids like.

—Esther, please God, this man is mad and dangerous.

Ellery came forward with the book. —What, is he gone? Is he gone already?

—Yes. Yes, gone.

—Well what about this book. He is a weirdy, all right. Drunk?

—Oh take it, take it, take it.

Ellery returned to say, —Turn the radio up, to Rose, who sat immersed in the sounds it shaped from the silence she maintained.

—What was it, that phone call, Ellery. You said it was all fixed up. You found a doctor?

He looked at her, vaguely, shoulders hunched unevenly like a man deformed from holding a plow down in a thousand furrows. —A doctor? Oh, that call, no, I meant it was all fixed up about this guy who jumped out a window.

—What...?

—Never mind, it's something for a TV promotion stunt.

—Ellery, you've got to find one.

Ellery put down John Foxe's *Book of Martyrs*. He scratched the back of his head and looked uncomfortable. As he sat down he picked the book up again and said, —Martin Luther was struck by lightning, did you know that? He was knocked down and this guy with him was killed, that's why he entered the hermits, see? Imagine that on TV, the Combined Electric program...

—Ellery, *for the love of God*...

He looked up at her, then. —Don't worry, he said, hunched, perhaps, now like Blessed Catherine de Racconigi, suffering curvature of the shoulder from the blessed burden she was allowed to wield. —Listen.

——*Zap*, approved by doctors everywhere. Tell Mummy about *Zap*, the wonder-wakener, one *Zap* first thing in the morning and she'll zip into the day. So don't forget, gang. Tell Mummy about these new scientific aids to modern family living. *Necrostyle*, the wafer-shaped sleeping pill, swallowed just like a wafer, no chewing, no aftertaste. *Zap*, the wonder-wakener. And *Cuff*. Remember, it's on the *Cuff*.

—Spelled backwards. Spelled backwards, of course, the Holy Sacrament turned inside out, you know. Basil Valentine stood with his eyes closed, the telephone resting on his shoulder. —Yes, the redemption of women, if you like, he went on, forcing a wearied patience in his voice. —Eve, the curse Christianity had put on her. What?... Yes, the priestess and the altar too, the Mass performed on her open loins, I've come across something about the bread being baked on her loins, the wafer for profaning the Eucharist, but what in heaven's name do you want to know this sort of thing for? A novel? But...yes, perhaps he can, if he thinks it will do any good. But you can tell your friend Willie that salvation is hardly the practical study it was then. What?...Why, simply because in the Middle Ages they were convinced that they had souls to save. Yes. The what? The *Recognitions*? No, it's Clement of *Rome*. Mostly talk, talk, talk. The young man's deepest concern is for the immortality of his soul, he goes to Egypt to find the magicians and learn their secrets. It's been referred to as the first Christian novel. What? Yes, it's really the beginning of the whole Faust legend. But one can hardly... eh? My, your friend is writing for a rather small audience, isn't he. Incidentally, the next time you borrow Loyola... So I gathered, but that's hardly the place to read Loyola. Do they have what in the Vatican? A mold for fig-leaves?...

He stood for a moment, his eyes closed still, after he'd hung up the telephone, and murmured, —What can drive anyone to write novels? but thinking not of novels nor the Black Mass nor even the mold for fig-leaves kept in the Vatican museum; thinking instead and vainly of the dream which this telephone call had broken, though he could not recapture it, re-enter it, could not alter, even in that wishful fabric, events of a quarter-century before.

Eyes closed, attempting to revive the dream, it shut him out, escaped him; eyes open, he walked into the front room to stare at the face of the Vulliamy clock on the mantel, the gilt cupid atop oriental alabaster, and the dream pursued him. The shade of the boy whom he had not seen since they were boys together (Martin was Father Joseph's "suck") lived on the air as though they had parted only minutes before. —It's true then? We're not supposed to understand? Whether thirty seconds or thirty years ago he could not tell; and only memory rehearsed his own words spoken in childhood's shadows under the tower of Saint Ignatius where they met daily, met for the last time when he said, —Weeping will not help you. There is no place for weakness among us. You will grow up to be a fool, Martin, but I shall not. Obedience is the first servant of love. It was for love I did it.

Basil Valentine forced his feet into the black leather pumps and drew his dressing gown tight. He went into the bathroom where he washed his face with cold water, and stood for a moment looking into his own eyes reflected in the glass as the soft towel revealed them. The clock struck in the other room, and he dropped the towel and returned to the papers spread on his desk. —Idiots, he murmured, gathering papers together. —Ten million babbling idiots. He thrust the papers into a dispatch case and was standing with a cigarette unlit, looking at the gold case absently, when a sharp continuous bell severed the sentence, *Much I ponder*... Basil Valentine muttered, and crossed the room to the telephone connecting the downstairs entrance. —Who is it? he demanded.

—The Reverend Gilbert Sullivan? Yes, my dear fellow, come right up.

Then at the door he said, —Good heavens, come right in. Where have you been?

—I? With my dear wife, listening to Mozart. Sie kocht schlecht, my wife. It is some time since I have heard music.

Basil Valentine stood lighting his cigarette, watching the motion before him carefully; care, that is, which extended from every part of himself, to correspond with the movements he repeated, bearing them out, as he followed into the room, weighing the cigarette which distinguished him.

—I have been in the rotting room, to tell heaven's truth. The pudridero, where Charles the Second sits out his last days surrounded by his dead and Spanish family. Good God, now, some preservative is indicated.

—Sit down, my dear fellow. Cognac? Valentine glances at the irregular newspaper-wrapped package laid on the marble top of the coffee table; and hands over the decanter.

—Precision of shape and smell, and the sixth heaven all enclosed. Basil Valentine watches the decanter tipped over the crystal globe, seconds too long, and his right hand shifts, stopping it; while it continues to pour. —Not the seventh, of shining light, but a cigar, perhaps, to weigh me down.

—And perhaps some music? Here, do sit down, where I can see you.

—Music? To leave my heels swinging free in the air? No. I'm obliged to take refuge in fabrication as it is, where I can see you. It's the accumulation, you see. The accumulation. We are all in the dumps, for diamonds are trumps, the kittens have gone to Saint Paul's, do you remember that one? The babies are bit, the moon's in a fit, and the houses are built without walls. Well, you wouldn't remember it, without a childhood you wouldn't. As for me, I've just left a round dozen of crucifixions. Allegro ma non troppo.

—Do come over here and sit down.

—There's nothing I'd rather do, but it doesn't help. Here, would you believe me if I told you that Martha Constantine . . .

—Please, don't touch anything on that desk.

—And do you fall in love with the barber when you go for a haircut?

—My dear fellow . . . Valentine crossed the room quickly. —Put down those papers.

—Here, here, Hungarian . . .

—Give me that book.

—Magyar, isn't it bad enough without coding it?

—This . . . a dictionary, obviously, Basil Valentine said, taking the plain-cover book and jamming it into the dispatch case with the papers.

—Transdanubia . . .

—Do go over there and sit down, now. Valentine snapped the lock on the case.

—Buda Pest, they tell me, was the most civilized city in the world. And within living memory.

—And they are right, Valentine said curtly. Close upon the figure before him, he followed as though to enclose and drive it before him toward the couch. —Now sit down and tell me what you've been up to.

—Down to, consorting with mermaids in the bottom of a tank where the troll king lives (here a cough interrupted; and Basil Valentine held his breath) —God love him. I had willingly fastened the tail to my back, and drank what he gave me, you know, but there, when he tried to scratch out my eyes. "I'll scratch you a bit till you see awry; but all that you see will seem fine and brave."

—So you've been to see Brown, have you? Basil Valentine leaned down and pulled open the loose newspaper package. —And this?

—There they are, from A to izzard, from under the watchful eyes of Rose . . . protected, cautious, circumspect, eyes in every variety, but mostly those of children.

Valentine looked up from the painted fragments, and poised, the lines in his forehead wove concern. —What's the matter, what's the matter? he said suddenly, —groaning like that, what is it?

—I'll explain . . . as soon as I . . . yes . . . get settled . . .

—My dear fellow . . .

—It's a liberty I'm taking today, pretending I weigh three hundred pounds. Damn it, will you allow it? "I min Tro, i mit Håb og i min Kjærlighed" . . . eh? No, it didn't work out that way, I tell you. There's Solveig locked up with a dangerous man, human and industriously mad, he may save me yet like Luther saved the Papacy. Good God, today I dishonored death for ten thousand dollars. I'll die like Zeno then, strangling himself at ninety-eight because he fell and broke a finger coming out of school.

—Now relax a bit, my dear fellow. Tell me, what did Brown say to you.

—Took the bottle away from me just like you're doing, and he swore if he were a dog he'd bark at me in the streets. Then he went on to ask me about my liver, and he offered me work selling a bottled chemical in the streets to some lowland consumers dead four centuries. But good God, I'd just come in from the streets, you know. The streets were filling with people like buttons, and you can't sell anything to them. Someone once told them the best things in life are free, and so they've got in the habit of not paying. So I simply warned him and came on my way. He was so kind and fatherly, I left him with a warning and came away.

—Tell me what you mean, you warned him.

—Oh yes, yes. Warned him the priests are conspiring against him, and he hasn't a chance. You, and I, and the Reverend Gilbert Sullivan.

—Now wait a moment . . .

—What chance has he, old earth, when hierophants conspire. Especially three like you, and I, and Reverend Gilbert Sullivan. He believes us three, at any rate. How he will dance when he finds that we are projections of the Reverend Gilbert Sullivan's unconscience. You and I.

Basil Valentine had been seated. He stood up now, his hands clasped behind him and walked toward the window, his head down (watching the toes of his black shoes on the plain carpet) and back. As the voice sounded he would raise his head, and lower it again immediately.

—Or like Cleanthes then? Gums swelling, and two days' laying off from food, the doctors' orders. With leave to return to his diet, I'm far along on my journey now, he says to them, and starves. There's dieting to extinction, that's the thing. People stop too soon. Doubled in one century, from a billion to two. We're being devoured. Here, let me walk up and down the room with you. We'll see better that way.

—Sit down, Basil Valentine snapped, behind him.

—I've brought my report. In the year two thousand and forty, four billion. Twenty-one forty-one, eight billion. Twenty-two forty-two, sixteen billion. Those are statistics. What are we to do to civilize them? Centuries of art and celibacy, plagues and wars and abusive acts of God, religious ascetics howling in the desert and cultured mermaid men whispering sweet absolutely nothings on the beach, and good God they won't learn they're not wanted. One pair of human beings, there, a man and a woman at the rate of love of one per cent per annum, could equal our population in nineteen hundred years. Our work's laid out for us. Stamp out polygamy, I say. That's the first thing. Our exemplary

African missions have shown us the way. Why, good God, as a result of their fine work we're able to spend twenty thousand pounds sterling on syphilis in the Uganda alone. Perhaps we should have been doctors then, you and I, instead of what we are. Cardinal Richelieu drinking horse dung in white wine on his death bed, it's not hard to see why France is first son of the Church. And in Egypt...

—My dear fellow...

—We treated sore eyes with the urine of a faithful wife. Today of course we're forced to buy drugstore make-shifts.

Basil Valentine had walked down to the windows and returned to the couch from behind, the fingers of one hand tapping the palm of the other: there was more to it than the agitation his face betrayed, for every moment he seemed to become more aware of his own physique, and the weight of its members extended in space. Most oppressive, however, became the respiratory system; not a sense of constriction (though it might amount to that if it went on so) but an acute sense of what was going on there, among fibro-elastic membranes and cartilaginous rings. He was having difficulty in swallowing. He put his left hand to his throat, manifesting in gold the cricoid cartilage within, its seal turned behind. There was no one on the couch. Basil Valentine swung around. —What...what are you doing prancing behind me here. Good...good heavens, my dear fellow, come along now, and sit down again.

Basil Valentine turned a light on, and herded the figure before him like a shadow. —Put your feet up and relax, if you like. But I want to talk to you seriously.

—Seriously? Then talk to Richelieu. I've only been ordained a matter of months. Or years, is it? I can't distinguish now, I've come so far, tempted by the daughters of Mara disguised as beautiful women. That was before Buddhism was corrupted by idolatry. Where is that good cigar you gave me?

—Take one of these and sit down, Valentine said, holding out the gold case.

—Varé tava soskei...soskei...I can't sit down with one of these things. I'd float away. Here, what's this thing over here, this gold bull busting an egg.

Basil Valentine breathed more easily as the figure before him seemed to weary and wither a little. —An altar figure, my dear fellow.

—Well that's apparent, that's apparent.

—A small copy of one that stood in the Miaco pagoda, in Japan, Valentine went on, watching the hand stroking the gold of the bull's back. —The time of Chaos, you know, before creation, and the world concealed in an egg floating on the waters. And the bull here, the symbol of creative force, breaking the egg to give birth to the earth.

—Is that what the Jesuits are teaching now? Good God! How far back do

you go, anyhow? Before death came into the world? Before the time of Night
and Chaos? Before good and evil, before magic, before religion. There, religion
is the despair of magic . . . no, that's not you Jesuits, is it. Religion is the mother
of sin. I like that. That's Lucretius. You do keep occupied, don't you. Books,
papers, a griffin's egg? You can't manage without one of those. All the churches
had griffin's eggs hanging around. Hung them on the lamp ropes so the rats
couldn't get down and eat the oil. Exterior brown and hairy, white inside and
the yolk a clear liquid. Tell them about the egg that Leda laid, and make them
laugh.

—My dear fellow, Basil Valentine said, approaching, with his arms extended
(triceps, biceps, semi-lunar fascia all conscious). —this is enough, you know.
You must . . .

—Let me loose. Just give me a good book to read, and I'll improve my mind
while you're out preaching. Here we are, *Die Geschichte der fränkischen Könige
Childerich und Chlodovec*. Christmas day, the year four hundred ninety-six,
and Clovis is baptized in Rheims. A white dove flew down from heaven with
a vial of holy oil for that express purpose. Did you know that? His wife converted him. Clotilda. That's exactly what she did. She brought him round, in
the middle of a battle. He gave up the sun for that. Mithra, the sun god, and
Clovis threw him over. Why, even the Stoics believed the sun was animated
and intelligent, and Clovis throws him over eight hundred years later, just
like that. Why I remember, a child in church (the voice went on, as Basil
Valentine gently guided the shoulders before him back toward the couch)
—sitting reading the *Pilgrim Hymnal*. "Deliver me from bloodguiltiness, O
God, the God of my salvation," my father reads out. "For Thou desirest not
sacrifice, else I would give it," we all shout back at him. "For Thou delightest
not in burnt offering," he goes on, "the sacrifices of God are a broken spirit."
"A broken and a contrite heart, O God, Thou wilt not despise," we agree.

As the weight, at which Valentine was surprised, lowered to the couch, he
noticed that the eyes before him were closed. —But what I remember is the
countryside then, the brilliance of outdoors and outwindows, and the sunlight
streaming through the lozenge shapes of glass, and we were locked away from
it, locked inside to worship. And there was the sun out there for everyone else
to see. Good God, tell me that Clovis wasn't lonely at dawn. Tell me he wasn't
sick at the sunset.

—But what is it? What is it? For heaven's sake tell me, Valentine said, and
his own shoulders quivered too, —instead of this . . . babbling, what is it?
What is the matter?

—Thank God you love people. Thank God you love people. Thank God
you love people.

—I?

—But the night you caused that cab crash...why didn't you go down and look. I've wondered. I've wondered.

—Caused? I caused it?

—As sure as Mother Shipton. Good God, are prophets guiltless?

Basil Valentine sat back with his cigarette. He spoke with some strain, as though to convince and repress some part of himself. —If one pauses to enjoy vulgar satisfactions, you know, one loses sight of one's objectives.

The eyes were raised to him. —I know why you don't like them. They have too many hands, is that why? For each heart there are ten thousand hands, is that it?

—Precisely, Valentine said, and crushed out his cigarette, and stood. He walked toward the windows again, each step more composed, and each word, as he spoke, more calm. —Hands, hands, hands, he said. —Dirty hands picking things up, and dropping them, beautiful things, defiling them. Hands pushing, hands grabbing, hands outstretched, hands knotted up in violence, hands dangling in helplessness, hands...on you. He stood at the window, looking out on the city. —Hands...he repeated.

—Yetzer hara, the evil heart, were Adam and Eve in love? What I mean is, do we only know things in terms of other things? Well then, I'll die like Socrates, there's dignity .

—Will you now? Valentine turned his back to the window, though he remained there, and almost smiled. —A condemned felon. Do you think they'll let you? He turned to the window again. —Hands dropping pennies at the newsstand, in exchange for a picture of a man strapped in the electric chair, the faces gaping over the papers in the subway until every car looks like a traveling asylum. Thick heads bent over the radio, waiting for the news that the switch has been pulled in the death-house.

It was silent; and remained so some minutes. Basil Valentine stood looking out the window, as it was his habit when alone.

—Tell me, have you ever fallen in love with someone already engaged away, and then won the beloved away from your rival? And then as time goes on, you begin to suspect that you look like him? Him whom you hated and found ugly.

—No, my dear fellow, I can't say I have, Valentine said, sauntering back to the couch.

—Well, let me tell you what happened to me. When still a boy I read Novalis, and there was great appeal, you know. But after a few more years of study I understood the mistake I'd made, the romantic mistake I'd almost made, I saw eventually how Novalis had appealed to all the most dangerous parts of me, all the romantic and dangerous parts, so I settled down to extinguish them. After two or three years I emerged triumphant, to tell the truth quite pleased with myself, to be rid of all those romantic threats which would have killed me if they had taken me unawares. Thus cleansed, I went on in the rational spirit, easily spotted romantic snares and stepped aside. One day I picked up the work of a man named Friedrich von Hardenberg, and my rational mind became quite inflamed, with the logical answers to just the things I'd been questioning... since I'd turned my back on Novalis, and all he stood for.

Valentine sat down. He tapped a cigarette, commenced to smile, and look up, and say, —My dear fellow... when the figure before him leaped from the couch.

—Damn it! Damn it! Good God, can't you see what I mean? When you see yourself... when you see yourself... The hands before him quivered in the air, the fingertips almost touching. Then one hand seized the other. —And you know you'll do it again... and again.

Before Basil Valentine could stand, he found himself alone. He held the unlit cigarette, tapping it with his index finger, and heard a crash in his kitchen, and footsteps, and the bathroom door. He paused only to light the cigarette, and then quickly picked up the loose newspaper-wrapped package, and his dispatch case as he passed the desk on the way to his bedroom. He'd got them both in the safe, and was back, standing before the windows, before he heard another sound.

—They tell me there's no scene in all Greek literature should make us more ashamed of our Christian culture, came in a calm voice behind him.

—And they are right, Valentine said, turning, to see him sitting nonsensically on the empty marble top of the coffee table. —Now, my dear fellow, let's be sensible, Valentine said, approaching. —You look better, a good deal better than when you arrived. Now sit down and tell me just what you propose to do with yourself.

—Play *The Stars and Stripes Forever* and I'll march up and down the room. Play the *Thunder and Lightning Polka*. I'll dance.

—What did you say to Brown?

—I asked him, What's laughter.

—And I suppose he told you it distinguishes us from beasts.

—He said, It makes the present. He said, it must be shared, and being so, makes the present. Laughter.

—I imagine, Valentine muttered. —But... what did you and he...

—We laughed. Brown and me, and that damned, congenitally damned... He sat muttering to himself, then he looked around slowly, and had begun to subside when something caught his eye. —What's that? He half rose, pointing to a painting on a corner wall.

—That? Valentine repeated, and smiled. —Valdés. Juan de Valdés Leal. You know him?

—Where'd you get it?

—It was among the worthless pictures that Brown got in that country house. I asked it of him, because we are such . . . friends.

—And he gave it to you?

—Of course. Since Brown was assured it was worth no more than twenty dollars, he gave it to me for fifty . . . Watching the eyes staring fixed on the Valdés painting, as though it recalled something, Valentine pursued calmly, —And now, getting back to work are you? Have you thought any more about that favor I asked of you? The Patinir?

—It's all over, he shuddered. —I swear, by all that's ugly it's done. But you . . . He'd suddenly begun pinching up rolls of flesh on the back of one hand. —Why are you doing this to me? he demanded without looking up. —When you know it doesn't exist? to ask me to copy it? Like he . . . restoring an empty canvas, yes. He scratched me a bit, I'll tell you. Until today, God! that damned table. God's watching? Invidia, I was brought up eating my meals off envy, until today. And it was false all the time! He spoke with more effort than he had yet made to control his voice. —Copying a copy? is that where I started? All my life I've sworn it was real, year after year, that damned table top floating in the bottom of the tank, I've sworn it was real, and today? A child could tell it's a copy, he broke off, wrenching at the folds of flesh and veins on his hand, and he dared look up.

Valentine was watching him closely, the watery blue of his own eyes hardened, the narrowed lids sharpening interest into scrutiny: he saw what appeared as a weak attempt at a smile, but no more, a quirk on that face and it was gone while the voice picked up again, —Now, if there was no gold? . . . continuing an effort to assemble a pattern from breakage where the features had failed. —And if what I've been forging, does not exist? And if I . . . if I, I . . .

—Perhaps if you could listen to me for a minute . . .

—Listen! He was bolt upright, broken through by a shudder and left rigid there, as lightning freezes motion. —Do you hear? he whispered. Nothing moved. Valentine stared, until he saw the lips commence to tremble in sharp tugs, —two, three-four-five, sixseven . . . hear? you, you're wearing the watch? hear it? racing with the clock, hear them racing? tick, tick-tick-tick, tick tick . . . there! the watch is ahead. Is it? listen!

—Now really, if you can't . . .

—Listen! I say . . . And then he sank back slowly. —No, it's over. You ruined it, interrupting. But didn't you hear them? racing? Tick. Tick-tick. Zeno wouldn't have, Zeno...what I mean is add one, subtract anything or add anything to infinity and it doesn't make any difference. Did you hear? how they were chopping time up into fragments with their race to get through it? Otherwise it wouldn't matter. But Christ! racing, the question really is homo- or homoi-, who's who, what I mean is, who wins? Christ or the tortoise? If God's watching,...Christ! listen, O my sweet gold! why were we born so beautiful? That's why we're here, an alchemist and a priest, without blemishes, you and I. It's true? You've never seen a cross-eyed priest? an ordained ampu- tee? No, never! By all that's ugly, it's done! He sat, pinching up folds on the back of his hand. —Now, remember? Who was it, "gettato a mare," remember? an anchor tied to his neck? and thrown, caught by kelpies and martyred, re- member? in the celestial sea. Here, maybe we're fished for.

Valentine muttered, —What are you trying to...

—Making a mummy, but, what I mean is which came out first? the heart or the brain. Why, the brain with the optic lobes, pulled out through the nose by the nates...But the heart, didn't come out till very late. He sat quivering, lips still moving over that last, —Very late. He paused; and then his lips scarcely appeared to move when he took up, —By the damned, I mean the excluded and...keeping the path to hell clean, to fool good people. Fished for? why, fished for...Have you read Averroes? What I mean is, do we believe in order to understand? Or understand in order to be...be fished for.

Basil Valentine stood over him a moment longer, then shrugged, turned away, and spoke both humoring and impatient, —If you remember Saint Anselm, Credo ut intelligam...

—Yes, yes, that's it. That's it! Flesh, remember? flesh, how thou art fishified. He'd jumped to his feet. —Listen, do you understand? We're fished for! On this rock, remember? and I shall make thee a fisher of men?

—Where are you going?

—Philippi. Yes, the first...with Paul, to Philippi.

—You're not going anywhere. Sit down and tell me what you propose to do. If it's a rest you need, there's money.

—Ish Kerioth bought a cemetery with his...thirty pieces, do? do? he went on loudly. —While there's still time, we...follow our training, there's no way out. I'll go to North Africa, and tempt Arab children to believe in the white Christ by giving them candy. That's accepted procedure. They're prejudiced. They accept Him as a prophet of their own Prophet. That's worse to fight than if they never heard of him at all. Charity's the challenge.

—If it's simply some childish obsession with the priesthood...?

—And you? for you the priesthood is just, spreading damnation?

—Nothing can be given, which cannot also be withheld.

—By all that's ugly... yes, if they had but one neck? Do you remember the seventeenth-century messiah Shabbetai Zebi, but... he faltered, backing to a doorway, —What's that to do with... Dominus ac Redemptor.

—What's that? Valentine asked quickly, surprised, but he sat down.

—Yes, Clement the fourteenth, his brief suppressing the order? Remember? I know... the Church must punish, to prove it has the power to punish? But you... you...?

—You remind me of a boy I was in school with, Valentine said quietly. —You and Martin. The ones who wake up late. You suddenly realize what is happening around you, the desperate attempts on all sides to reconcile the ideal with reality, you call it corruption and think it new. Some of us have always known it, the others never know. You and Martin are the ones who cause the trouble, waking suddenly, to be surprised. Stupidity is never surprised, neither is intelligence. They are complementary, and the whole conduct of human affairs depends on their co-operation. But the Martins appear, and cause mistrust...

—There's Lent! Martin's? Martins? you killed him with much cherishing?

—I was a syndicus then. Martin was below me. In such a school the first thing one learns is obedience. Not encouraged to think for one's self, because one is not yet ready to do so. And you understand, one is encouraged to report the... breaches committed by others.

—A spy system! ac redemptor, I know. And you! he cried out from the doorway where he stood. —For you, if you hate their hands, and you hate their faces, and you hate their suffering... and you a priest! You... you... yes, a pope... a pope's...

The telephone rang behind him.

—Ici Castel Gandolfo... A Mister Inononu calling the SS Basil Valentine... hurry... the forty days is almost done...

Basil Valentine wrested the telephone from him, and he went through the doorway taking the lamp to the floor with him. The phone was dead in Valentine's hand, but he stood holding it, staring in the dark.

—*The Triumphal Car of Antimony*. Now I remember your name, Basil Valentine, the alchemist who watched pigs grow fat on food containing stibium, wasn't it... you tried it on some fasting emaciated monks and they all died...

Valentine dropped the telephone into its cradle, and the figure retreated before him, its back to the window.

—And so they named it antimony, anathema to monks...

Basil Valentine stood still in the near darkness, feeling every physical detail of his body, every one but his eyes; for the figure against the window was indistinct, its shape and size ambiguous, but for the eyes. —Preach to them, then, my yetzer hara, speak to, then, my evil heart. While I fly like a piece of cloth on the wind, or the color itself, the street is filling with people like buttons in Galilee. Speak to the Am-ha-aretz, preach to them, pray. Tell them, as the composer predicted, there's nothing left but knowledge and evidence, and art's become a sort of tailbone surviving in us from that good prehensile tail we held on with then. Tell them that Peter died an old man, and right side up. Tell them that Mary broke her vows to go off with a soldier named Panthera, and wandered away to give birth to his son. Tell them, the ones who are conscious of what happens to themselves only in terms of what has happened to themselves, who recognize only things they have seen with their eyes, tell them the whole thing hangs on a resurrection that only one lunatic saw, one and then twelve and then five hundred, for visions are contagious, and resurrections were a stock in trade, and the streets were full of messiahs spreading discontent, that Jesus Christ and John the Baptist would both be arrested on the street today, and jailed, and for the same reason. Tell them the truth, then, that Christ was thrown into a pit for common malefactors, tell them the truth, then, not that power corrupts men, but men corrupt power. My yetzer hara, speak to them, preach to them, my evil heart, to the ones who look out the window and are not surprised to see the sun, burning itself out, ninety-three million miles away, the ones who dream of the dead and expect themselves to be dreamt of, the Am-ha-aretz, filling the streets and seeking authority and no further, write with a brass pencil on a clean tin plate, I A O, I A E, corruption is no more than knowledge that comes too soon, tell them of Atholl's coronation with a red-hot iron crown, and of how the Egyptians burned red-haired men and scattered their ashes with winnowing fans, tell them of Justinian's pavement made like an ocean and destroyed when the roof of Saint Sophia fell in, and of the son of the ruler of Cairo, Ibn Tulun, sleeping on an inflated feather-bed on a lake of quicksilver, tell them of Antiope and the goat, of Pasiphaë and the bull, and the egg that Leda laid to make them laugh if they'll listen. The Am-ha-aretz, whose memories include nothing but their own failures, tell them their suffering belittles them, tell them that, my yetzer hara, tell the ones who trade only in false coin where they can buy clothes to wear when they are alone. That is all, and Gresham's law, and Gresham's law, and Gresham's law for love or money. Go out among them and tell them that their nostalgia for places they have never been is sex, the sweating Am-ha-aretz, and when they hear music, tell them it is their mother, tell Nicodemus, tell him there is no other way to be born again, and again and again and again of a thousand other mothers of others-to-be, tell him, my yetzer hara, tell them, tell them my evil heart, that they are hopeless, tell them what damnation is, and that they are damned, that what they have been forging all this time never existed.

On the couch, Basil Valentine rested a hand on his forehead, and moved it gently. —You are feverish, he said. He got up to turn on a soft light near the windows, and returned to the couch. —Just lie still, he said. —A little cognac ...there...

—Yes, you see...? You see?

—Don't try to talk now for a minute. And close your eyes. Basil Valentine held the hot squared sides of the skull between his hands, and rested his thumbs softly on the eyelids. —There's no need to say a word. You're safe here.

—You see, if...I became the one who could do more than I could.

Valentine moved his fingertips gently against the temples throbbing beneath them. He shifted slightly; and loosened his dressing gown. —And the one you left behind? he whispered, —the one you lost?

—Yes, yes, came the answer in a whisper. —Yes, I miss him...

Valentine lowered his face slightly, out of the light from over the back of the couch; and both his hands moved against the skull. —We're safe here, he said.

The telephone rang. Basil Valentine's hands drew together for an instant, pressing the skull between them. He raised his hands, and the eyes remained closed.

He got over to the telephone quickly, glanced back round the corner of the door, and picked it up, talking in a low voice, facing the wall directly before him, his eyes lowered. —Yes, it's all right, he said, —but...this telephone? Of course it may, no private telephone is safe...Meg van az informacio ami kell, itt vannak a papirok. Eh...? nem most, hivjon holnap reggel...

At that he hangs up, and stands for a moment with his weight resting on the instrument. Then in to wash his hands, where his face and the one in the glass exchange confirmation at the speed of light, as palms abrade knuckles and thumbs fret cuticles under warm water.

He walks back slowly, registering resolution in his steps, watching them placed before him in a path between there and the windows, does not raise his head until he stands looking out, movement compassed by the soft lamp in a black leap on the ceiling. —Even down among them, he says, —the stupid, thick-handed people, is there any one of them who doesn't know him, who has not suffered the indignity of his stare, and heard the mockery of his laughter, this other self, who can do more, who always escapes, but...now you are here, my dear fellow, and we...Basil Valentine pauses, to seat half his weight on the window shelf. —Would you be surprised, if I told you about myself, as much about myself as I know about you? Why I know that I hate them, where you wish you could love them. Direct in his view, ascendant in lights, the Empire State Building rears its stiff glans fourteen hundred seventy-two feet above the street. —There is their shrine, their notion of magnificence, their damned Hercules of Lysippus that Fabius brought back to Rome from Tarentum, not because it was art, but because it was big. S P Q R, they all admired it for the same reason, the people, whose idea of necessity is paying the gas bill, the masses who as their radios assure them, are under no obligation. Under no obligation whatsoever, but to stretch out their thick clumsy hands, breaking, demanding, defiling everything they touch.

Though his tone remains calm, he raises his hand to his temple and finds the vein standing out there, suppresses with two fingertips the life pulsating through it, and lowers his hand to his knee rearing half his weight in the window.

—We live in Rome, he says, turning his face to the room again, —Caligula's Rome, with a new circus of vulgar bestialized suffering in the newspapers every morning. The masses, the fetid masses, he says, bringing all his weight to his feet. —How can they even suspect a self who can do more, when they live under absolutely no obligation. There are so few beautiful things in the world, Basil Valentine says, taking a step toward the back of the couch, where it is quiet, where he has not yet raised his eyes, —that they must be protected. He stands looking down, to say the few more words, as though they were simply that, appended, when all this time he has been making toward, —The pity which none shall have who demands it. I called your work calumny once, so it was. But the face of Christ in your van der Goes, no one could call that a lie. And now, he says, advancing again, —here you are, and I shall teach you, I shall teach you the only secret worth knowing, the secret the gods teach, the secret that Wotan taught to his son... His hand reaches for the gold cigarette case and finds the pocket empty. When he looks up he notices first not the empty couch, but the empty pedestal where the gold bull stood: the egg is still there, unbroken.

Then Basil Valentine put a hand to his throat, as though to stem the rising nausea; and he leaned forward, still with the hand to his throat, the hard rings shifting on nothing in a rise and a fall between a thumb and a finger, swallowing, while the shadow on another wall and clear because unobserved, figures a steady hand pouring cognac.

A swallow of the stuff crystal-bound in his hand, and he clears his throat with abrupt loudness. —Of course the Athens of Socrates was a phenomenon, he says, glancing at the couch he passes, —the most civilized thing that has ever happened on earth, while the rabble of the Roman Republic, he goes on, nearing the windows, —Rome, you know…

Three stars in his belt, Orion lay out of sight beyond tons of opaque building material now dissolved in darkness, serving only to support fixed points of light, the solid firmament of early Jews where stars were nailed lest they fall; beyond, the flight of seven doves Orion hunts, out of sight.

Look darling he found my necklace
(The capacity of this bus
The new Wonder Gems   Developed in the laboratory
(Please do not speak to driver while bus is in motion
More brilliant than diamonds
(Expectorating in or from this omnibus is a punishable offense
(Step down to open doors

Above hung the cliff that Alexander climbed in India, the cliff studded with diamonds, hung with chains of red gold, five hundred steps to the house of the sun, to paradise.

Though Sir John Mandeville (in his *Travels*, among the earliest and most heroic of plagiaries in the French) confessed, "Of Paradise I cannot speak properly, for I was not there": what matter? Here above, the concrete cliffs had disappeared, only their lights studding darkness which posed as space and postured firmament.

—John!

—You?…bumping into you again on the street like this? But I have to hurry, I have to get a train.

—Yes, a train, a train.

Lights flashed past, their beams tangled in darkness to confirm it.

—Are you all right? What's that you're carrying? is it real gold? Where are you going?

Through the world of night, lost souls clutching guidebooks follow the sun through subterranean passage gloom, corridors dark and dangerous: so the king built his tomb deep in earth, and alone wanders the darkness of death there through twenty-four thousand square feet of passages and halls, stairs, chambers, and pits. So Egypt.

—Back.

Red in the west as it set, because of the fires of hell says the Talmud: red in the east from the roses of Eden.

—Back where?

—Can we stop for a minute? a glass of brandy?

—I have to make this train.

—Gentlemen...

Few anywhere disagreed, but that the sun and the moon and the planets issued from a hole in the east, descended into one in the west and returned, by night, through a subterranean passage.

—Gentlemen, I have a religion too. I'm a drunkard.

Raging up and down the sky like a beast in a cage, says the Talmud, and unable to escape, enclosed in the firmament, the gates of its entrance and exit only at opposite ends.

—All right, yes, a train. Wait.

—Gentlemen...

—Hurry...

Down: down went Tammuz (slain by the boar's tusk), entering at Babylon, the center of the earth, for there was the lid-stone to the lower world.

Thus the Assyrians invoked the bull who guarded the gates: O great bull, O very great bull, which stampest high, which openest access to the interior...

Please show your ticket at gate

—Leaving on track seven

Their death pursuing its descent, the Piute Indians followed the sun to that hole where it crawled in at the end of the earth, creeping constricted to earth's center, there to sleep out the night, and to waken and creep on to the eastern portal. The sun emerges, eating the stars its children as it rises, its only nourishment; and those on earth at the dawn see only its brilliant belly, distended with stars.

This ticket is your receipt and baggage check. Please keep it with you until you reach destination.

May the bull of good fortune, the genius of good fortune, the guardian of the footsteps of my majesty, the giver of joy to my heart, forever watch over it! Never more may its care cease.

(So reads the inscription of Esar-Haddon, whose father, the murdered Sennacherib, had destroyed Babylon; and he, the son, returned to restore the sacred city, to rebuild the temple of Baal, and refurbish its gods.)

Thrown open, the gates on the eastern face of the temple meet the dawn as the golden tips of the obelisks burn, and the red rim appears from the underworld. Those on earth prostrate before it, and the gates close upon Baal, Who has entered His Temple.

III

It was a man, sure, that was hang'd up here;
A youth, as I remember: I cut him down.
If it should prove my son now after all—
Say you? say you? —Light!

—KYD, *The Spanish Tragedy*

ABOVE the trees, the weathercock atop the church steeple caught the sun, poised there above the town like a cock of fire rising from its own ashes.

Few witnessed this inviolate miracle, for reverence here subscribed to roofs: worship was, as childhood had noted, an affair of defensive indecent enclosure, and few indeed the eyes raised on high unless assured the protective embrace of beams. As a matter of fact few eyes were ever raised at all, but rather lowered in consecrated embarrassment, finally closed in severe chagrin as the voice intoned, —The Lord's mercy is from everlasting to everlasting unto those that fear Him.

When the eyes opened it was to stare at the back of the neck of another similarly occupied; and if the eyes were raised no further, the voices were: O God be-neath Thy guid-ing hand   Our ex-iled fa-thers crossed the sea, they sang under that roof which rose to the level of the treetops outside, mounting New England gothic toward the white spire alerted by the weathercock which caught his eye, as he climbed the hill toward the Post Road. But even he, when he reached it, walked with his eyes lowered up the silent nave.

On either hand, the visages of the houses watched him pass, self-contained façades indifferent to his presence, but watching still, guarded, as he passed immediately before the panes and fanlights; and when with seven more steps he escaped their line of vision, they did not turn in indecorous curiosity but continued to stare out straight ahead. Unconcealed by walls, or coy behind hedges, sober-mouthed some of them with columns Ionic and Doric (with never the cheer of Corinthian), these miens of narrow clapboard and eighteenth-century brick looked upon the passer-by without deviation or interruption, with stares neither crooked nor circuitous, the lineal stare of propriety.

(Beyond, there were, to be sure, occasional cupolas, sportive relics of nineteenth-century profligacy.)

He passed the Civil War monument which thirty years before had spiked the sky, and stood now dwarfed in deference to greater wars. (And the resolute iron cannon at its foot was replaced by a mobile 75, albeit crippled by loss of one of its wheels.)

As he reached the transept, the spire behind him burned at its tip with the light of the sun, and from it the bell labored the early hour. Beyond the lucent spire the sky was patched with small clouds which did not move, no more than the ragged-edged patches of snow, reflecting here that celestial course of the sun which he trod on earth.

Past the highway's curve (and the arrow there, pointing the wrong way to delude barbarians), the mile from the railway station, and he had not paused; nor so much as raised his eyes but once when they were raised by the trans-figuration of the gold cock in the sun. Mirabile dictu: another blue day. What a narrow chin in his hand, when he raises his hand there, then taps two fingers on his lips and looks over the shoulder quickly. Bells, from far down the nave there. —God of our fa-thers, known of old, Lord of our far-flung bat-tle line (fingers stifle the lips) hymn no 383. Singing way, over the shoulder elders from preference heard no music, alarm it was for it set something living in them, and would that their children believe no such thing existed, to hang their heels on the air. But they heard, they heard and what's more without humil-ity and nor lightened nor lost set instanter to compose, whipped their children to practice as they'd been done for discovery. The bell again. Again. Adeste —ad esse fidelis: hymn no 223 larynges distended A,M,D,G, infra dig dom-inocus: Oh for a Faith that Will Not Shrink.

Demons the motes in a sunbeam, said Blessed Reichelm (though serious statisticians precisely populated hell's habitant host at 1,758,064,176): the Saxons driven through a river blessed upstream by bishops (kept their sword-arms dry). Blessed Leo X, could nicht anders, the 95 Thæces stuck to the door, in the beginning this end:

Town founded 1666 annus mirabilis Oh gosh Oh gee h-Holy Cowrist w-We got a big job ahead of us interdenominational infra supra sub threw the inkpot: Nunnery lecture, illustrated, Pagan ceremony, robed priests, Nuns, high altar, &c. A wail from the tomb. See girl in dungeon. Uncle Sam to the rescue. Public invited. Collection 50¢ leadeth us not into temptation.

Surprise! to be kissed on the cheek so. After all that time. There, over the shoulder describe necessity without touching me. Abscondam faciem meam

white Christ the fugitive. Consider me with my nose gone, knock on wood,
—or ask Helen for a piece, she found it: rub it, Aladdin, Constantine, Nicodemus blown back by the wind from the river m-Mthrfckr et considerabo
novissima eorum (sic)

The birth of a nation. Let in the light   Open the nunneries And save the
girls. Free lemonade, Mineral water, Shower baths Coming! to Haggard's
Gospel Tent   A drama of eighteen live people   This is a clean high-class
lecture exposing the whole Roman Catholic Religion from the Confession
Box to the Nunneries, High Priests, Mother Superior, Altar Boy, Six Nuns,
Holy Altar, Holy Candles, Holy Water, Holy Gods   Just as it looks in
Catholic Churches everywhere. With the mother giving her daughter to the
church for a supposed more holy life, daughter taking the Carmelite nun vow
(Black Veil) buried alive, thrown into a dungeon and how are they to be rescued

He stopped to cough, and courteously caught the cough away from the air
in his open palm and walked on again. Courteous, to this flood of unspeak-
able hyperduliacs, and why? to be rescued and wear a stinking merkin for a
beard? If she is only a woman (but a good cigar is a smoke) with Eve caught
by the furbelow, Hae cunni (the oldest catch we know): Dido a dowdy,
Cleopatra a gypsy, Helen and Hero hildings and harlots, praebeat ille nates
(I seem to mean usefulness), but Thisbe's gray eye on Alfonso Liguori —There
is no mysticism without Mary. Stabat Mater shrouded in the decent obscurity
of a learned language, fœmina si furtum faciet mihi virque puerque: dolorosa
while Origenal sin wields the blade. Carnelevarium (the heart came out very
late) reveling in lavish polymastia (Zwei Brüste wohnen, ach! in meiner Seele)
now, in Martinmas, Saint Martin's given or only Lent to SS Pelagia & Mary
of Egypt, thence to Thaïs, Kundry, Salome, and even Saint Irene; Costanza
(D^s ac Redemptor, S.J.), Valeria Messalina, Marozia in the garden, in the
Garden, Messalina in the gardens of Lucullus hic jaceted age 26 years, Thrawn
Janet's black man gone down the garden wall, and the men et ardet: Anaxagoras pre-empted in contemptu Christianae fidei; Lucretius (dead of an
overdose of love philter) preempted, —Religio peperit scelerosa atque impia
facta. I.e., exhomologesis (c. 218) by Calixtus I. Pelagic miles distant, on the
Rock, resident Barbary apes pelt stones at the local Y.M.C.A. In Spain Ignatius'
militant limp and Xavier 4'6" exhomolojesuis abhor the shedding of blood,
and the Inquisitor De Arbues describes Love ex hac Petri cathedrâ without
raising a Welt. Amor perfectissimus explaining what is dark by what is darker
still: Who then was the gentleman? (I mean the excluded.) Not Philo, De
Exsecrationibus! not Philo, certainly not Aristobulus busy-handed Alexandrine
Jew to prove plagiarism: Pythagoras Socrates Plato Homer & Hesiod, all
plagiarized from Moses, one and all. Pues díme Sigismundo, dí: El delito

mayor del hombre es haber nacido. Calixtus, then, after all? Politicking, No, no, don't listen to them 1870! Nono the winner: infallible (what is that racket?). The College of Cardinals turns to look. —It's Arkansas, crying Non placet.

The snow had hardened into reefs along his path and he narrowly avoided falling a number of times, even though he looked nowhere now but there where he walked. Schizophobic, how near the edge can he approach? how much longer disdain simple ruses? —Give me force and matter, and I will refurbish the world! Blame Descartes, then! resisting with some fortitude the purchase of a bowler hat, and wearing a cigar, and even then preferring perhaps a dry Brazil-filled, Java-bound, Sumatra-wrapped panatella: but soggy all-Havana is more weighingful, and; temptation to stop along the way, weary, damned weary, damned weary of it passing the campfires so many tents pitched with such care to the pegs insisting permanence when (God blind me) by their nature they are tents and Lord love me by the nature of things they will blow away, by the nature of force and matter blown away and the God-damned Cartesian with them. Mauled by luxuries, asking now no more than some well-chronicled illness to stir the viscera into affirming its existence within, the member without. Caveat: —On which side do you dress, Job? Mauled by luxuries, Oh doctor Æsculapius found out the hard way lightningstruck. Reality defined by the (luxury) gratuitous crime. Peace by (luxury) war. Love by (luxury) mugging, rape, Senta retires with Sabine smile of satiety, Thankyou ma'am. —E ucciso da una donna! M'hai tu assai torturato?! Su! Parla! Odi tu ancora? Guardami! . . . Son la Tosca! Son la Diva! . . .

Arsk Saint Bernard about women, their face is a burning wind, he'll tell you, arsk him, their voice the hissing of serpents, he'll tell you.

(fa un ultimo sforzo:) Soccorso! . . .

In rehearsal: Chrysippus. Cleanthes. Zeno. Pyrrho. Again, the story of Hipparchia's courtship, spare no details (the dress of Telephus and Crates then the groom are especially amusing) but one: —Kissed on the cheek after years, was it? A,M,D,G, sequence of unsurprise (Lao-tse's 84-year gestation), right Nicodemus? right? under a burning bush (I lost my wife) Ad Mariam Dei Genetricem, dixIt, pinxIt.

Sang, —Varé tava soskei . . . soskei . . . Mermaid mahn stole my heart away. (verso:) Ti soffoca il sangue? . . . il sangue? . . .

Configuring shapes and smells (damnation) sang —Yetzer hara, in the hematose conspiracy of night When they shout gfckyrslf Come equipped her morphidite.

Arse Alexander VI for a loan of his concave emerald, watching the rape of (Christian) girls through it. —Ah! è morto! . . . Or gli perdono! . . . E avanti a lui tremava tutta Roma!

Then he fell. He fell twice. The first time, a stone turned under his foot as he reached a slope of the east lawn of the parsonage. He went down on one knee, got up immediately and three steps later he slipped again. The ground was hard, and he caught himself on the back of a hand, and remained, down, for a good half-minute, looking at the back of his hand where he'd torn it, not badly but enough to bring blood. He sat until he'd got his breath; and the bull on the ground, its gold dull in the dull light, held his eyes, glistening themselves no more than the dulled jewels of its collar. For the first time, the sharp edge of the air startled him deeply, cutting his lungs as he breathed it. The hand with the blood to mark it he reached to the bull and rested it there; and his other he rubbed over his dry face, then to his bare head. That hand stopped there and the fingers drew together against the skull as though to wring out the occupant brain. He had a bad headache. It seemed to have been going on for some time, throbbing with permanence. His hand reached the back of his neck and closed again there, squeezing the muscles and tendons in its hold. They were sore. He spat on the ground. Then he coughed. The air was still. Cold came to him evenly. Again he hastened to get up, for his body was drawing the cold right up out of the earth.

His expression, which all this time had been one of confusion, drew gradually together as he rose, bringing the gold bull up with him, and under his arm. As the diffused look of bewilderment left him, his features lay in a concentration of anxiety, staring up toward the house. The sun had just touched the peak there and begun to descend; and again, for the first time, the sounds which he distinguished seemed to have been going on for some time. As long, that is, as he might have been within earshot: a regular ka-klack, ka-klack, ka-klack was the least sound, coming apparently from the house itself, and an irregular series of hammer blows from beyond. It was the voice, however, which arrested him. It was neither sharp nor loud, but lingered, and was gone, and rose again on this cold air, leaving off and rising like the smoke of a boat gone under a bridge, and emerging.

—Jupiter. Ammon. Adonis. Chemosh. Hercules. Osiris. Dionysus. Phoebus, Bacchus, Moloch, Baal . . .

The light of the sun spread over the face of the house, and its margin verged steadily lower toward the figure exposed on the open porch. The words lingered and were gone, leaving an emptiness which the silence rushed from all directions to fill. Then when he went on speaking his voice was lower, a tone of admonition which the silence retired before, but no great distance, as it had before the names of the sun. Now the silence withdrew barely to the point where the figure approached up the slope of the lawn, advancing with him, but hesitant, before then behind him, breaking the stream of the words, —man or woman...wickedness...transgressing his covenant, And hath gone and served other gods, and worshiped them, either the sun, or the moon, or any of the host of heaven...

Then as he climbed nearer the silence no longer infringed, but followed and closed in behind on the cold air, —And lest thou shouldst lift up thine eyes unto heaven, and when thou seest the sun, and the moon, and the stars, even all the host of heaven, shouldst be driven to worship them, and serve them, which the Lord thy God...

Reverend Gwyon was a big man. And, as the increscent light of the sun reached him and covered him, and he broke off speaking and stood exalted in the light, the sunlight and the silence seemed to augment him, actually to make him larger, standing alone up on the porch. Abruptly he cried out to the figure approaching him, —Turn around. There, turn around!

The sun stood emerged, glowing its great belly, motionless with the effort of emersion accomplished, paused, over the earth's rim, in confident prospect of the journey of the day. Suddenly breaking his own pattern of stillness Reverend Gwyon clattered down the porch steps, and stopped where he could get a full view of the sky. —A bad time of it, he muttered scanning the sky from one end to the other and back, east to west, to east and the sun itself. —A bad time of it today.

—Bad time of...what?

—Why there, the dirty sky, Gwyon said flinging a hand up. —He has a dirty path before him today. As he spoke he lowered his eyes, and what might, on a smaller face, have passed as a look of surprise, settled upon his own as one of curious, even inquisitive abstraction, a look which summoned every battery of history to bear simultaneously upon the immediate problem at hand.

Reverend Gwyon was a tall man; but it was his stance made him appear indomitable, that and the sense of a full meter of silence surrounding him which only he could penetrate, or roll back with the invitatory ardor of his own curiosity. His face was heavily lined, but lines in nowise the fortuitous tracings of disgruntled weariness with which one after another generation proclaims abrogation of responsibility for the future, and liability for the past. Venerable age had not, for him, arranged that derelict landscape against which it is privileged to sit and pick its nose, break wind, and damn the course of youth groping among the obstacles erected, dutifully, by its own hands earlier, along the way of that sublime delusion known as the pursuit of happiness.

Not to be confused with that state of political bigotry, mental obstinacy, financial security, sensual atrophy, emotional penury, and spiritual collapse which, under the name "maturity," animated lives around him, it might be said that Reverend Gwyon had reached maturity.

It must also be noted that, though his position in the community was appointed to justify the accumulated clutter of the things of this world in the eyes of the next, neither was there present in his face that benign betrayal of total incomprehension of the designs of eternity, and the concomitant suspension of the intellect, which so carefully separates this world from the next on Sunday mornings all over the country and, in asylums all over the world, every day of the week.

Gwyon's face was creased with lines of necessity. They sprang away from the eyes he lowered down from the clotted sky and right past the face before him, a face lined itself whose every lineament watched him anxiously. —Ahh, Gwyon said, —you've come . . . and his gaze settled on the gold bull. Then as Gwyon reached forth a resolute hand and rested it on the head of the bull figure, an unsteady and blood-streaked hand came up and took his arm and they stood like that, each looking at the hand of the other, when the sun was suddenly blotted out and they were left standing shadowless on the lawn.

The sky was becoming littered with fragments of cloud. They were being fed across it from a great bank in the north. The cloud bank was gray and motionless, and it did not diminish.

Gwyon shivered suddenly under his hand, and looked up at the impaired sunrise with an expression of severe indignation. Then the bull figure was lifted decisively from under his arm, and with it Gwyon turned before him and made with long strides for the house.

By the time they reached the porch the sun was unencumbered. It had already commenced to diminish in ascent, and to lose the fierce coloring of its violent entering into the sky.

At the top step Reverend Gwyon halted in front of him so abruptly that he almost lost his balance. —There, Gwyon said, making a sweeping motion with his free hand which included the porch and the sun behind them, —any fool can see what the churches lost when they put the entrances around facing the setting sun. His tone rang with the same direct and peremptory appeal that his face had reflected a moment earlier; but as he went on, rearing his great head to the presence he'd apparently expected to find beside him, surprised to find it moving unsteadily round behind, Gwyon's voice lowered as though talking to himself, and as though in the habit of so doing. —The Christian temple at Tyre, he muttered. —The propylaeum faced the rising sun, of course. Attracted passers-by with its glitter that way. Then he glanced quickly as though to secure that he was being followed in.

The hammering began again from the other side of the house, down in the direction of the carriage barn, clear sharp blows from a great distance it seemed; otherwise all was very quiet but for the heavy footfalls of Reverend Gwyon crossing the porch ahead of him. The muffled ka-klack ka-klack had ceased some time earlier. Watching Gwyon stoop before him to open the front door, he was inclined to do so himself, once inside the house, where it was darker and he had only the gold tail of the bull figure to guide him. Surely there was no danger of bumping a doorframe with his head nevertheless childhood still obtained and every portal was lower, and hallway more narrow, every turning closer and room smaller. Thus he hunched, past Olalla as though with cold and past the cruz-con-espejos into the dining room. The house was cold at that.

For some reason he went straight round to Aunt May's place at the dining-room table and sat down there. Gwyon poured two glasses of sherry wine. It was rich dark oloroso, a fresh bottle though the cork had been pulled. He put the bottle down between them and remained standing, one hand on the bull figure which he had not relinquished.

—What a trip, getting here.

—Yes, yes, Gwyon affirmed immediately, agitated. He emptied his own glass quickly and then, a moment later, looked down at it in his hand as though it were an unfamiliar object and he didn't know how it had got there. He put it on the table carefully. —You've come a great way . . . a great distance, he said looking up again at the figure seated there much, perhaps, as he might have looked upon the incarnation of some abstraction conceived long before, disturbed less by the actual epiphany and its haggard unsteady appearance than by its abiding and familiar permanence, in spite of the transient air it had assumed immediately he gained the weight of the gold bull figure into his own hand. Gwyon stood, with one hand still, heavy on the bull figure, the other busily contriving upon nothing at his side, configuring recourses in the air.

For this moment he seemed bound there, standing at his place at the head of the table. The sun by now was coming through the dining-room window which faced to east where the porch left off on that side of the house. —Here, this . . . Gwyon said to him, sitting there with his left side to the exposure where the sun entered, —for safekeeping, this had better be put away for safekeeping. Gwyon flourished the gold figure in a strain of sunlight and left him sitting there in the sun, his back to the buffet, looking at the empty place across the table. He looked up when Gwyon turned out of the room, but too late to see more than the departing back, that most prominently distinguishing feature of Reverend Gwyon.

He sat still for a moment, then raised a hand to his forehead and found it smooth. Inside, the headache persisted, its insistence ignominious, calling attention to tenancy and no more, devising, perhaps, a quantum theory of memory upon the departure of the old man gone, step by step, ushering the gold bellowless bull, Oorooma way? Gone Krakatao and the yellow day in Boston, the Grand Climacteric and Valerian, Ballima, way? while he sat here in the full of the morning sun warming Aunt May's side of the face at the breakfast table, looking as she did never across at an empty place. (To right was the dark corner where all Good works were conceived.) —Cave, cave, he got to his feet, —dominus vulgus vult. His eyes were cooled; the sun itself did not warm them, lowering them from the glory there through the window to the low table beneath, and the faded figure in the table's center shivered for an instant, underclothed, and remained still as he passed, shoulders drawn, listening, under surveillance, abruptly considering Tyndale strangled and burned for his labor of love. —The devil finds work for idle hands, here, without music, where reverberations of the human voice weary in recall with generations of fruitless exhaustion, denied the very possibility of music. A sharp unfriendly sound from the kitchen confirmed the silence and the vigilant conspiracy of inanimate things, watching for any break in the pattern. A movement broke it, his hand reaching forth to put his glass at his place at the table; and he stood in suspense sustaining the trust thrust upon his frame by the static details of dark woodwork, maintaining the inert vigil which belied music: music as ideal motion, a conceit in itself manifestly sinful, as the Serpent, gliding in the Garden, moved with unqualified motion, as the sound of a lute, struck here now, would move upon undulant planes never before explored, to be cornered and quickly killed by the ruthless angles of the room, proving that those planes had never existed, affirming, in sharp consentaneous silence, the illusion of motion, the sin of possibility, the devil-inspired absurdity of indetermination.

Above, another blue day, (upstairs) the room papered with green-capped pink-faced dogs, and the button drawer, only apparitions move to perfection, there! Pray the Lord to keep you from lying, there, O spectral stabat mater may I go out and play the violin outside to the town wearing its sinside inside and not a soul in sight. Church bells inspissated the air, dropping it in sharp fragments. He sat down in his place at table, excused by the falling weights of the bells, and motionless when they had done. There, old vicary, congratulate my refuge, the saneside outside sheltering the insane inside: to present the static sane side outside to another outside saneside, to be esteemed for that outsane side while all the while the insaneside attacks your outsane side as though we weren't both playing the same game, and gone down Summer Street (singing unchristian songs) the inane sinside, pocketing a cool million wearing the shoutside outside and the doubtside inside, the vileside inside and the violinside outside skipping dancing and foretelling things too come all ye faithful, of thine own give we back to thee.

He swallowed some of the oloroso sherry, and its warm course sent an imbrication of chills over his back. Still, there under the window, the low table looked to be faded, a parody of perfection more Bosch than Hieronymus, the seven deadly sins in meddy-evil indulgence, painted with damning care round the maimed hand upraised in the caveat, as below the brown wainscoting, and the fabricated angles above where the molding met in soiled beaded intimacy, the uneven patches faded on the walls between, and even an unfamiliar floor lamp standing beside him with the cold intentness of an unknown sentinel, watching, patient at all events with his prolix presence now the years of waiting were done, rewarded to find him twice-size, twice as difficult of concealment. No part of the room he could not see now, points and attentive angles he had never seen from his chair, saw him now.

He raised his glass. The streak of blood on the back of his hand was dried to a hard ridge of dirt's appearance, hypostasis on the outside and the skin drawn to it in mortal amends, a clot of the essential sediment crusted on the surface, hypostatic scab of the world of shapes and smells provided force and matter to touch a line without changing it, here, untormented by music, where as everywhere matter whetted its appetite for form and was easily pleased, circumspice, low levels of perfection issuing the remorseful timbre of the monogenetic voice, *The prosperity of the godly shall be an eyesore to the wicked,* Psalm 112, —*Wealth and riches shall be in his house: and his righteousness endureth forever,* moaning, lowering over the printed page (head bowed), Psalm 112, —*GLORIA!* sings Handel's soprano, —*Gloria!* across an ocean and centuries, *gloria!* far away.

A sharp bell from the kitchen shivered the air for an instant. Then as his fingers loosened on the emptied glass and he rested his elbow on the table and with it his arm and his shoulder and that whole side of him, one after another disposal of muscles went out of use, and contrary to usual sense of awareness in flex and strain (so the man chopping wood the first time in his life, a hand clutching tight right up under the ax-head, measuring the length of the haft between closed hands, right down it goes, neither hand moves on the haft so smoothed from sliding hands, the blade strikes a knot, the end of the haft his knee, and he looks up, pleased though, to say, —Say, using muscles . . . (by that night he'll have pulled a tendon in some unconcerned part of his body he'll tell you and not unproudly) . . . using muscles I never knew I had . . . and not in the stroke but recovery he finds them), so now right down from the neck muscles and tendons recovering from usage so long fell in unusual awareness one after another and one after another satisfied now he was asleep.

Reverend Gwyon returned to the breakfast table empty-handed. He startled slightly upon seeing the empty chair to his left, and looked no more composed upon seeing the one to his right occupied. So Reverend Gwyon sat alone there at the head of the table as he did every morning, with a second, a third, and a fourth glass of the dark oloroso from Spain and the look on his face of a man who's just come on a bone in a mouthful of fishmeat.

—"Ah, that dear old mother's Bible, Wherein my name she wrote, And marked me many sacred texts, Which once I well could quote..."

These words, rising on the clear New England morning air, were neither loud nor clear, for the Town Carpenter was absorbed in his work, and the five ten-penny nails he had clamped between his gums did not serve song as teeth, even so few, might have done. He continued to hammer, and word by word the next stanza became clearer, as nail by nail was taken to be driven into the wood. By the time he reached the last stanza, and stood back to look at his work, his mouth was quite empty of anything but song, which came out quite clear, and the small dog lying there raised its head to attend,

> —So who'll bid for a Bible?
> A purchaser I crave.
> Live while we may, we'll drink today:
> There's no drinking in the grave.

With that, he threw his hammer in the dog's direction. The dog moved as fast as the hammer, gained its feet, and followed him up the lawn wagging its tail.

Janet was there in the kitchen, older, square-shouldered, her face dark about the chin and faintly blue the rest of it from that mercuric compound of Aunt May's prescription renewed year after year. She strode to the stove, where two pots stood over the fire. The one she stirred, with a large spoon worn off square with stirring, was Scotch oatmeal. The other pot bubbled on, and Janet paid it no attention but to sniff the rising steam and turn away the large features of her face, drawing down her upper lip so that that gum was almost covered, and appearing not to breathe, careful and troubled about many things.

When the Town Carpenter arrived she was to her knees on the floor there and he, hearing the sharp tinkle of a bell as he got near, had slowed his uneven pace, and paused in the door respectfully. He waited for her to rise before he advanced into the kitchen with, —"Nymph in thy orisons, be all my sins remembered," crossing then to the other pot on the stove, —as Tom Swift has it, he added.

—Not that fork, not that fork! Janet said, coming to take away the fork he'd picked up.

—There ... now, he said to her, looking helpless until she thrust a piece of lath in his hand where she'd got the fork from.

—But this, it's got paint on it, he said waving the stick in the air.

—Old old paint, years and years old and hard and dry and it was white, she said sounding weary, speaking dry and low in no effort to make herself heard but giving him anyway the satisfaction of seeing her lips move. Then she turned away, stooped, cumbered with much serving.

He bent absorbed over the other pot; from it he raised a steaming length on the end of the stick. —There now, he muttered, let it drop back and stirred it a bit. —A month of underwear can't come clean in a minute.

—Four days it's been there, Janet said absently, —four days in the year, lamenting the daughter of Jephthah four days in the year...

He continued to stir at his pot. —You were late this morning, he interrupted finally, as she drew breath to go on and fight the battles of Ammon and Gilead, to follow the daughter of Jephthah bewailing her virginity in the mountains. She did not answer but with three sharp raps of the spoon on the rim of the saucepan.

—Three minutes late when I heard your press commence this morning, the Town Carpenter went on, to the square of her back. —How many pages did you print, tell me.

—You don't print them one two three four five, she answered not turning, —six seven eight nine ten eleven...

—How many? He tried to see her lips as she reached a bowl down.

—Eight one five four at a time, Janet said in the same dull tone, —two seven three six at a time...

—There now, he mumbled, shaking his head and looking back into his own pot on the stove. —We all have our work to do.

—The Lord keep us, until we finish it, Janet said.

The shape of those first two syllables on her lips seemed to strike him, familiar; and the Town Carpenter drew his own lips close, bridling the argument which lay impatient behind them, not, however, before its invitation had escaped. —A man...

—The Lord...

—A man takes his own chances, he got out quickly. Janet looked at him, her brow and lip drawn up, troubled.

—There now, I meant nothing. No disrespect to you, he said, twice her age but no more serious for all that even now, turning slow with his arms hung down and the top button of his underwear standing out like a creased stud against his informal attire. —After it all, he brought out soberly, —after your healing miracle then, restoring me the use of my legs, well, there now, I couldn't be disrespectful to you after that.

—Not to me, but to our Lord He healed you.

—There now, he mumbled in assent, —not after that.

—You must not talk so about these things, she said. —You must not, he must not, they must not...

—Do you recall the queer little salesman selling brushes, the Town Carpenter began, opening a new conversation since he'd lost track of the old one, —and told Reverend he was a Manichee...

Janet carried a bowl of oatmeal away through the door. Directly she was out he got the fork she'd taken from him and came back to his pot on the stove. He leaned down to blow off the steam, and then speared twice, each time coming up with a boiled potato. He quick wiped the fork on his trouser knee, then looked at it, and at the spot on his trouser knee, with a look near guilt, and thrust the tines of the fork under his shirt to wipe them clean there. When Janet came back, the fork was where she'd laid it; but she took no notice of him eating the one or the dog standing over the other boiled potato waiting for it to cool. She stood, wringing one hand in the other, and her eyes were very wide.

—There now, what is it? the Town Carpenter demanded, watching.

—He's come.

—What is it, now?

—He's here. As he said he would come.

The Town Carpenter hung there, imbibing Janet's excitement. She sought another bowl.

—Another bowl? he demanded, confused. —Someone's here?

—He's come back.

—So it's not the weightless show of a priest was here, him or the Manichee brush salesman. Is it... is it...

—He...

—Prester John?

—Prester John! Janet repeated. —If Prester John is young and old, and warm and cold, and breathes and does not breathe alive, wears blood on the hand, and sees with eyes not open. Maran-atha!

—He's come! There now, the Town Carpenter said. —Feed him. Feed him well, it's a long journey. Here, a potato, take a potato... But she was gone, with another bowl of oatmeal. —There now, no disrespect after that, the Town

Carpenter muttered going toward the outside door. —He'll come down. I'll wait for him there, he said to himself; but he paused in the door till Janet returned to the kitchen. —There, he murmured to her, —no disrespect, you know. "I am but a lump of clay, but I was placed beside a rose and caught its fragrance..." He stood a minute looking at Janet busy over the metal sink, squinting his eyes up with looking at her. Then the dog followed him out the door and down the lawn toward the carriage barn, carrying its hot potato.

He'd only got halfway down there when her voice on the air stopped him, and he turned. —And he, has he eaten? she cried.

—That one, he won't come near, the Town Carpenter called back to her, and he motioned toward the fence below which led away from the carriage barn and coursed the pasture's bounds. Title to that piece of land, long disputed with a neighbor, fell to his bull who spent the days there and had gradually become a familiar, encouraged by the girl and the old man with a feed box and even, finally, a stall in the carriage barn. Now Janet came out unwrapped in the cold morning and down the slope with long strides to the fence, where she made a moaning sound that brought the bull from out of sight immediately. The bull was all black, the weight well up in its forequarters sustaining those swells of muscle mounting in the great swell of the neck. Its approach was effortless, not a movement wasted, because every bit of it was in movement, movement which absorbed the weight of it and became motion coming forth here on legs as slender as they looked as a man's wrists swinging beneath. It came on at an angle to its path, which gave it a sense of drift as though suffering the wind to carry it along from behind; and the great weight of it was not apparent until it came close by, when even its breath dashed on the cold air fell with weight, and a hoof no longer adrift, but exerted to break the crust of the winter ground, made its force volitive, standing still.

Janet had watched its advance with a look of familiar wonder which almost broke her face into a smile. Now it was before her she stirred the feed in the box there with a square hand of hers and gazed with two eyes into one; and which of them made the gentle sound that rose between them wasn't clear as she caught a finger in a curl above the eye, and then left the bull at the feed box, sobering her face as she turned back for the house, and the bull raised its head, and watched her go.

The Town Carpenter raised a two-by-four, and nailed it carefully slightly out of line. —O pirate ships of the drunken main! O monster cruisers of wicked gain!... there now. He's finally got here.

Once in, Janet made across the kitchen for the dining room, there picked up the empty oatmeal bowl from the empty place at the head of the table, and stood staring at the figure across. —He's come, she murmured, and advanced an empty hand in the air. Then her gaze shortened to her hand there, which she squared round to meet it, to look at the palm, and return to the kitchen. She put the empty bowl in the sink. Then she slipped on a pair of gloves, took a slip of emery cloth from her skirt pocket and knelt rubbing her chin, her cheek, and her upper lip.

The sun was high enough now to fill the dining room with its light, over the dark dining table, and the low table under the window, and warm on the back of his neck when he woke moving nothing but his eyelids, opened upon the bowl of cold oatmeal before him, and nothing there else but a spoon. He did stare at the bowl and the spoon for a moment, or a minute, in that waking suspension of time when co-ordination is impossible, when every fragment of reality intrudes on its own terms, separately, clattering in and the mind tries to grasp each one as it passes, sensing that these things could be understood one by one and unrelated, if the stream could be stopped before it grows into a torrent, and the mind is engulfed in the totality of consciousness. Al-Shira-al-jamânija, consider the Dog Star: death? or Islam. Then perfect diamonds, and so across that brink of unbearable loneliness, and fully awake, startled only with the quiet, and the sunlight bearing flecks of silent motion. If there had been a dream, it was gone back where it came from, to refurbish its props, to be recast probably, possibly rewritten, given a new twist to put it across, make it memorable to the audience and acceptable to the censor, all that, but the same old director, same producer, waiting to dissemble the same obscenities before the same captive audience, waiting, again, the first curtain of sleep. He smiled, looking at the oatmeal, and as he did so reached up a hand as though to feel the smile on his face, and fix it there; it was gone when he looked up to the end of the table and saw it empty, and as immediately occupied it from memory but memory which, so suddenly assailed, leaped too far back, and brought forth the Emperor Valerian blinded, in taut agony, flayed under the hand of Sapor, the Persian emperor who battled Christianity in the name of the sun prophet Zoroaster, whose god, Ormazd, lord of light and goodness, wars ceaselessly against Ahriman, and the hosts of evil.

This house had a sense of bereavement about it; though no one had come or gone in a long time. The corridors rang with oppressive familiarity and, perhaps it was the distance that each step covered, the sense of diffusion persisted, diffusion from essential childhood, moving too fast too slowly, rested physically, arriving too soon without expenditure or the pulsations of effort, filling too much space and thus less instead of more powerful, less capable of hiding.

He was inclined to pause, passing the maimed hand upraised of the noseless Olalla, with his hand upon things, affirming their mass; and each weighed enough in return, resisting his touch, to affirm its reality, to belie, that is, the realities which had taken its place.

Suffer barbaric childhood to give and receive remorselessly; civilized age learns to protect what it has, to neither give nor accept freely, to trust its own mistrust above faith, and intriguing others above the innocent. Intrigue, after all, is rational, something the mind can sink its teeth into, and defeat it with the good digestion of reason, a hopeless prospect for the toothless heart, and God only knows what innocence will do next. So prudence rescues the emotions, and exiles them out of reach, countenancing only anxious glances from what another hero came forth from the desert to call "the hesitating retinue of finer shades."

In the unilluminated hallway where Olalla stood in her niche, he paused the ball of a thumb on the saint's broken nose, and smiled, the same involuntary smile of recognition that had lightened his face, and left it and come back, remaining each time a little longer and more fully extended, trying the unfamiliar terrain, since his arrival.

Childhood, the plain-dealer: nothing approached it but upon intimate terms. It's the shades of experience that afford shadows of fear, but the black-and-white of childhood discovers the intimacy of terror. Here, benign Olalla suffers the plunder of her face with wistful gravity in her stone eyes, empty now of the vengeful malice with which they had threatened blind justice upon unwary passers-by; and the hand, once poised to smash a passing skull, now lay flat up in benediction. What greater comfort does time afford, than the objects of terror re-encountered, and their fraudulence exposed in the flash of reason? Triumph! as though it were any cleaner, or happier, or more bare of disappointment, than the deadening shock of re-encounter with the object of love.

Songs of innocence and experience fill the head so empty of aching that the ache is forgotten, a brawl, but an orderly one, a sequence of decorous violence as neatly carried forth as the fight between the Pleasant and the Unpleasant Thoughts in Handel's *Almira*.

There were no clocks anywhere in sight or hearing.

—And hmmm...he did, did he? And he took away the horses that the kings of Judah had given to the sun, at the entering in of the house of the Lord, by the Chamber of Nathan-melech...hmm, Melech? Melich? the chamberlain, which was in the suburbs, and burned the chariots of the sun with fire...

This came, borne from behind the study door on the pungent vehicle of caraway, into the hall where he stood about to knock.

—And he put down the idolatrous priests, and hmmm whom the kings of Judah had ordained to burn incense in the high places in the cities of Judah, and in the places round about Jerusalem; them also that burned incense hmmm hmmmph unto Baal, to the sun, and to the moon, and to the planets, and to all the host of heaven...

Though the words stopped, the caraway came on, unladen but maintaining a belligerent calm out into the hall where he lowered his hand without knocking. Then as he turned from the door he said to himself aloud,

—How safe I am from accident here.

—In the precious blood of...

—Janet!

—Yes, she answered in a loud clear whisper, —I knew you would return. She stood before him with her gloved hands clasped, and her eyes shining with what light there was in the hall. He started past her, saying —My father...

—Still awaits you, she assented, eager. —Our Father...

—Janet, he said getting by her, and smiling to her, to calm the great agitation which threatened, as she came after him close as could be without touching him, to break out in some more vehement expression of welcome, —yes, I have come back.

—Rabboni, they doubted, she said. —I did not.

—Yes, seeing you here, and... he faltered, —I... my father... backing from her, —back...

—From the tomb! she whispered clear.

—Yes, it... in a way, he mumbled, reaching the door, —recovering from... good God, I... He fumbled with the handle behind him; and she held off, reflecting the vigilant angles of woodwork beyond her.

—The... reassuring feeling... he went on, figuring his hand in the air between them, —being home again... though the scraping of the door obscured his words to her, —here, to feel myself again, here...

—They will not know you.

—The reason I came back...

—Shall I tell them, it is you, come back?

The chill of outdoors embraced him from behind. —I... I... He commenced to shiver against it.

—Or will you tell them, in your own time? she asked with a step toward him.

—Yes, yes, he said, getting the door closed between them, and shutting her intensively submissive, conspiratory affirmation into the dim hall with her.

The scraps of cloud which the dawn had found out, drifting with no apparent purpose, met here and there now the sky was light. A delegation of them moved round to east, toward the sun; and others, darkly separate in the west, conspired together over Mount Lamentation, where he raised his eyes. It was the most prominent of an ascendance of rolling hills, drawn up against the only clear horizon; and that simply, it had been the horizon beyond which lay destiny. Again, the cold air stabbed with each breath. No matter the direction on a map, it was beyond Mount Lamentation Lapland lay, waiting for the Gospel. From one step to the next he dropped his weight, jarring, as his feet hit, restraining him down the hard slope toward the carriage barn; and remarkable here, as indoors, the distance a few steps covered, each one a familiar measurement of compulsion, but without the sense of motion, of the dash which this precipitous decline had once insisted down.

The Town Carpenter stood on his platform, with a slightly vacant but still expectant expression on his face. Much, perhaps, like good King Wenceslaus of Bohemia looking out on his still capital, prostrated before him by papal interdict, the Town Carpenter looked upon the town laid out here under the still cold, provoked by its sedulous silence; and here, as there, to the approach of the pale thin man in mean attire.

But however the shade of John Huss may have leaped here from beyond Lamentation to find itself animate, teeth a-clatter, shoulders hunched forward, and even the hands thrust down seeking warmth in empty pockets colder against hard shivering limbs of the moving frame within the cloth: too hard, perhaps, and worse, too familiar, a prospect too mean for even that most mettlesome martyr, on such a cold day, ahead one expression effaced another (the Town Carpenter leaned back to spit off the platform), and Wenceslaus IV, "the vacillating," abdicated and was gone, and the shade of the martyr gone with him.

—Here, don't bark at him, by God don't you bark at him! the Town Carpenter shouted, as the dog leaped forward over a heap of bull dung, barking. —Don't pick her up, he went on, coming down from the platform. —She'll pee all over you. There now, he finished, and standing over his visitor he looked at him with frank and eager curiosity. —There now, he repeated, —that you look tired, it's not surprising to me. Here from Ethiopia and the three Indies.

—Ethiopia! Good God yes, I feel like I'd come that far.

The Town Carpenter's eyes glistened, as he listened and pretended to hear. —Sooner or later, of course, I knew you'd arrive, he said. —And are you alone? He bent close, intent for the nod he received. —I knew you would be, of course, he went on at that. —To voyage today with ten thousand knights, and one hundred thousand footmen, it might clutter things up.

Nevertheless, the Town Carpenter looked slightly disappointed.

—Being back, I...well, thank God I'm back.

The Town Carpenter watched him draw a hand across his chin, and smile.
—Back, the Town Carpenter repeated, standing off to look above them at
the sky, —when we get back, of course, we can take up such proper customs
again. But here . . . he swept a hand out before him, —here, of course, they've
no idea of a hero. I live surrounded by people who've no idea what a hero is.
And do you know why? Why, because they've no idea of what they're doing
themselves. None! Not an idea in this world or the next of what they're doing
on God's green earth. Oh, it's a strange land you've come visiting to see me
here. With no idea of a hero, you see, but they need them so badly that they
make up special games, hitting a ball with a stick and all kinds of nonsense,
and the men who win the games are their heroes. And then, he went on,
warming to what was apparently a severe preoccupation of his, —when that
gets stale, they arrange whole wars which have no more reason for existing
than the people who fight in them, and a boy may become a hero fighting for
a life that's worth something for the first time, threatened with loss of it, that
or dying to save the lives of people who've no idea what to do with them.
Fortunately, he went on, and inclined his head nearer, —there's a way out for
most of them. They make money, the Town Carpenter whispered hoarsely.
—And a good thing such a recourse lies open, it gives them something to do,
keeps them out of our way. He straightened up, looking at his balloon ascension stand, his arms still folded, and dingy underwear elbows protruding from
his sleeves. He drew his lips tight together over the gums, and nodded. —Fortunately men like you and myself appear every century or so, to keep the way
open. But, he called as he walked to the corner of the barn and stood there
undoing the front of his clothes, —we must watch out for them, you know,
trying to intrude. Here, he said, waving his free hand at the balloon stand,
—they try to intrude. Traveling in their trains and their airplanes they try to
intrude on the greatest career of the hero. Why, travel's become the great
occupation of people with nothing to do, you find second-hand kings and all
sorts of useless people at it. There now, it's always the heroic places you find
them intruding, trying to have a share in the work of great men, looking at
fine paintings and talking as though they knew more of the thing than the
man who painted it, and the same thing listening to fine music, because they
suspect the truth but they won't pay the price, they all suspect that a man
needs something to do, he finished, standing over the light cloud of steam he
left rising from the gray boards of the barn.

—Something to do? Most of the trouble in the world is made by people
finding something to do.

—There now, the Town Carpenter said, buttoning himself up as he straightened round, and nodding as though he had heard. —Of course they misuse

things, every fine thing we have and make and discover, and the finest things get the most abuse. The generals and the missionaries and . . . but we cannot waste time on them, he said raising his eyes from the balloon stand to the sky, —there's but one thing you can do with a balloon.

—Going up? There's only one thing to do when you get up there.

—Danger? They don't know the meaning of it, sitting up there in their airplanes, and surprised when they drop out of the sky. Why, they haven't time to be frightened, they're so surprised, brought up so carefully, insured against accident. Why, their heads are smashed like melons before they know what's happened to them, sitting up there in their business suits at sixty miles an hour wondering if their fountain pens will leak, and then there they are spread all over twenty acres of somebody else's land. No, not the danger. The loneliness. It's the loneliness, the price they won't pay. The Town Carpenter remained abstracted for a minute or so; and the wind which had just come up sounded around the corner of the barn. He gazed up at the sun, which had become involved with a cloud much the shape of a camel, an odd-legged one to be sure, but as the Town Carpenter was quick to point out, —Bactrian. They watched it. The sun entered almost between the two humps and then, from the speed of things up there, looked to be attempting an escape, its body visible along the fleeting edge, as though every instant it would break away. —See him go, see him go, the Town Carpenter said, standing there lopsided. Then he turned and said in a tone of confidence, and commiseration, —The great misfortune of the sun, it has no history. That's why it never gets lonely up there.

Then with a surprising agility he had gone round behind the balloon stand, and from there he called, —This? did you see it? I keep it inconspicuous, they're all very interested in it, the American Legion . . . He swung about a length of two-inch pipe mounted on a swivel. —I've seen them sneaking around to look through it, but when they find no lenses in it, they think I've dismantled it. Of course there's no lenses in it in the first place, they'd only confuse things.

—Then, what is it?

—Yes, since they don't know what they're looking for, of course they don't see anything, wandering around in the daylight. There's so much daylight you can't see anything up there, unless you cut a path through it. Why, in good weather, one afternoon I saw Aldebaran, the red Eye of the Bull, keeping watch on the Pleiades, you know. That means it's a very old star, being red like that. Yes, the red Eye of Taurus, he muttered coming back, —keeping a watch on them. They bear some watching, the Pleiades . . . Do you know? One night I was assailed in the darkness. A man struck me, square across the eyes, and do you know, from that blow? the force of it brought light to my eyes? and I identified him afterward, I saw him plain as could be. His American Legion cap showed as plain as could be. Then he looked round evasively. —Tell me, he said, close by again, —did you bring your great Mirror?

—Mirror...?

—There now, it's not easy to transport, I imagine. The great mirror in which you can see all that goes on in your kingdoms. But...we need it here, he said bending closer, and with another quick look round, —the American Legion. They watch me all the time, you know. Very interested, very interested in this of course. He included the balloon stand in a gesture. —Though it's no secret. Why, more than one night they've come and picketed the house here. With your great mirror, we could keep an eye on them, the Town Carpenter finished, and watched intently the pockets searched before him until the gold cigarette case was brought out, empty. —For the messages! he exclaimed, taking it. —And with the secret inscription. There now, later you will explain it to me, he said, running his thumb over the words; then in a sudden feat of conjuring the gold case was gone inside the frontal folds of his clothing, and he stood with a large watch snapped open in his hand. —Of course I'd have known you anywhere, he said raising his brilliant eyes from the watch face. —There now, eleven-thirty. Later on we shall simplify things. Why, all the others are drowning in details. That's what happens to them, you know. That's where we'll outwit them. We must simplify...

His words were caught on the wind. The dog followed him. Before he was out of sight, there was the sound of thunder, rolling like a body to rest in the south. The Town Carpenter shook his fist at it, but did not diminish his step.

The wind had come up quite sudden. It commenced to blow with that terrible quality peculiar to the winter wind, pointless, and the more bitter. March winds make a boisterous kind of sense, blowing seeds and seed-pods, blowing off the white pustular symptoms of winter, awakening, preparing for growth; and a vengeful sense in the fall, so long as a leaf remains where it grew, but the winter wind blows nothing, and blows that nowhere, blows with destructive violence where there is nothing left to destroy, vindictive and viciously fingered to leave no crevice untouched. Looking up, even the balloon stand is testament to something, erect with the stupid patience of objects so violated, testimony found futile as the wind itself in the envy as quickly rejected as it is longed after. The clouds conspired over Mount Lamentation had lost their distinct edges, and mounted in a dark mass as though what lay beyond there were already suffering what the wind, if simply to justify itself, threatened to bring closer. It blew round the corners of the carriage barn, over the snow clotted against the mound of what had been the kitchen midden for as long as he could remember, over the snow crusted on the ground behind the barn, showing its surface here and there as though that ground had never been disturbed, as though the surface were all of it that existed.

He drew his shoulders closer together still, and almost lost his balance as he turned away from this desolation where something moved with the sudden effortless ease of an apparition, unconcerned with inertia, unrestricted by the ingenious arrangement of muscle and tendon, weight and intention whose failure to coincide threatened to upset him now. He made the gesture he might have made if he had had a stick in his hand, and expected it to support him; and then twisted like a man menaced on one hand by the very thing he has turned to escape on the other. Whether the empty carriage barn had put forth the shade of Heracles, caroling a missionary jaunt beyond the mountains, or John Huss had approached from that distant direction to urge those already baptized against false miracles, ecclesiastical greed, and seeking tangible evidence of Christ's presence instead of in His enduring word; and whether the two met on the horizon to merge, to vie, or simply compare wares, there was no time to consider, for he looked up to see the bull, its great head thrown up against the wind and the storm it threatened, the great rounds of the eyes wide open, fixed on webs of red veins. Where it had come from, or to what purpose, its casual properties and the questions which might have been asked on a day in June, none of that was provoked by the bull's appearance. Its back end wheeled as it came to the fence and stopped there, in a halt of defiance which challenged the wind and left it to be consumed in its own violence.

—That day is a day of wrath, a day of trouble and distress, a day of wasteness and desolation, a day of darkness and gloominess, a day of clouds and thick darkness . . . Janet read, alone in her room, the prophet Zephaniah, as any passing her closed door might have heard. None did. —And I will bring distress upon men, that they shall walk like blind men, because they have sinned against the Lord: and their blood shall be poured out as dust, and their flesh as the dung . . . The paranoid wind shivered the pane at her back. —Gather yourselves together, yea, gather together, O nation not desired . . . The unwavering quality of her voice sustained the relish of the prophet whose benisons she followed here, near breathless with being a step ahead of him, far and away from the New Testament wail down these same halls which had catechized and left her to work out her own excursions among the alarms of the Old. —The Lord will be terrible unto them: for he will famish all the gods of the earth; and men shall worship him, every one from his place, even all the isles of the heathen.

Zephaniah gets his business done quickly. Three chapters suffice; and he makes way for Haggai, whose nose is just as out of joint. In spite of her absorption, Janet read with the assurance of the Old Testament reader who knows that the New will follow, is, in fact, in hand with its more temperate prospects; just as she could read the New Testament without trepidation, knowing that any insinuations of wavering charity on the part of its engineers were bolstered by a Figure Who brooked no nonsense, lurking, "ravin in tooth and claw," at the ready, among the unalterable jots and tittles of His seventy-two-letter masquerade in the Old. Haggai anticipates Him shaking the earth, the heavens, the sea, the dry land, the nations, phenomenal antics still dignified as acts of God set forth with such strenuous diligence that the tenth minor prophet is drained in two chapters; but Janet had for the moment enough of a good thing with —when I turn back your captivity before your eyes, saith the Lord. Her blue lips finished, they repeated while she stood and gazed through that glass, a window tucked high on the house looking down to the carriage barn.

The wind had reached a height of delusion. Now, right before her eyes, it was given something to do: particles of snow appeared, conjured by the wind's own madness. Janet drew closer to the window. Standing with both palms flattened against the glass, her upper lip rose slowly as she stared below, to see the figure between the carriage barn and the bull's enclosure reel as though attacked on both sides, gain his balance and pause, steadying himself, and set out with what at first appeared extreme difficulty walking, until he broke into a run, up toward the house and out of her sight. —He is come, her blue lips made out; but the upper one was drawn down to the line of her bite, giving her a slightly perplexed look, as she turned to emerge, leaving two irregular near-translucent blots on the glass behind her.

Down on the porch, Reverend Gwyon stood staring at the sky, reflecting in his attitude and expression the bull's disdain for what was going on up there. In Gwyon's case, however, the simple grandeur of the bull's impersonal contempt for the storm was impaired by lines of fierce indignation, as though to indicate that this celestial turmoil had been got up as a personal affront to him, or one for whose honor he was jealous. Gwyon did not lower his eyes to the figure approaching up the lawn until the porch steps clattered immediately beneath him; at that, he broke off his engagement, muttering, and turned hastily to open the front door.

—There! . . . I mean, here! sounded behind him, teeth a-clatter.

—Whoo . . . what is it? Gwyon got out, looking wide-eyed over his shoulder, with the door open.

—Terror coming both ways . . . like being a child again. Yes, there, get the door closed . . .

Reverend Gwyon got the front door closed with a bang, rattling the bell in it. Then he started to turn down the hall, but his way was blocked. Though neither of them moved, a regular creaking had been set up in the hallway and sounded all around them.

—Why, it's . . . this whole house is saturated with priesthood, with . . .

—Priesthood? Gwyon repeated, looking for an opening.

—Ministry, the ministry then, eh? Yes, here we are, no exception, except I'm late. Late coming. Here, every creak, do you hear them? Every creak one of doubt, generations of it, so I'm no exception, except I'm late. But I . . . that's what I was trained for, after all, isn't it. Here, it's so familiar, all so familiar here . . .

Reverend Gwyon found an opening and got through it. Immediately he started to talk, striding down the hall. —Familiar, yes, he commenced, gauging his words to the distance ahead of him. —Science, science has a fool theory about recognition. Half the forepart of the brain receives an impression, they say, an instant before the other half. When it reaches the second half the brain recognizes it! A lot of bosh, of course, he paused a step to confide, —but it gives these fool scientists something to do, keeps them from meddling in important matters that don't concern them.

Reverend Gwyon had timed this observation perfectly; for as he reached the last phrases he had turned the corner to his study. The still surfaces of the mirrors in the cruz-con-espejos were alerted by his passage, but too late to hinder it, for with the last word he was inside, leaving them empty but vigilant now. Alone among books and papers in precarious piles, Reverend Gwyon sat down. There were books open and closed, some with twenty bits of paper between their pages; passages underlined, written in, crossed out. There were periodicals, and ribbons of newspaper littered everywhere. Near one knee a headline said, *Science Shows There's a God, Pope Declares.* Gwyon rested an elbow on *Osservatore Romano.* ("Who is capable of fixing his eyes on the shining sun?" It was that issue in which Cardinal Tedeschini testified to the Papal vision: "But he was able to do so, and during those days could witness the life of the sun under the hand of Mary.") Gwyon reached Saint John of the Cross down from a shelf. ("The agitated sun was convulsed and transformed in a picture of life, in a spectacle of heavenly movements, and it transmitted silent but eloquent messages to the Vicar of Christ.") This caught the corner of Gwyon's eye, which narrowed, and he grunted impatiently and covered it with another paper, the *Scientific American* for 11 April 1891. There, for a moment, he stared at a picture of Doctor Variot and a colleague consulting beside a baby skewered on an electrode in an electro-metallurgic bath. ". . . Rather than to rescue our cadavers from the worms of the grave," he read half aloud, with idle satisfaction, and sat back, staring at the door.

The gold figure of the bull lay on its side among some papers on his desk.

Beyond, through the windows, the wind whipped the branches of yew with snow. But Reverend Gwyon's was not an empty stare, arrested by that blank surface. He looked as though he saw straight through the door, and was fully aware of the two eyes which, at that instant, were looking square on a line with his own from the dark hallway, where the clear mirrors of the cruz-con-espejos on the wall behind had seized, and held, dim fragments of the arm raised to knock.

Gwyon waited for a moment; then he opened the book in his lap, and thrust his hand into the cavity cut ruthlessly out of *The Dark Night of the Soul.*

> *—Drink, drink! Drain, drain!*
> *Another link for the Devil's Chain,*

sang the Town Carpenter into the white teeth of violation. He left off, for an anxious moment, as he approached the Civil War monument, which he never passed in bad weather without a look of uneasy solicitude, though near half a century had passed since his mother's last obstinate bivouac there.

The wind was pursuing its career with extravagant glee, now it had one. The snow was driven to places which only this paranoid force could care to oppress so; though, to be striding forth in it was to assume the delusions of the storm itself, becoming the object of its hostility, and thus abruptly render a validifying dimension to this manic phase of a reality which would, left to itself, blow itself out in senselessness. Therefore, to redeem these absurd extravaganzas, which is after all the way of a hero, requires a worthy goal; then the gratuitous violence threatens only that path, and as the wind rises, the more worthy the goal then, and the more heroic the journey.

The Depot Tavern was presided over by the head of a twelve-point buck, whose look of resignation implied understanding of the fact that his antlers would never again be shed and renewed, a fate tempered by a festoon of Christmas tree bulbs which were, momentarily, seasonal, though he wore them with great forbearance whatever the solstice. Otium cum dignitate, the chipped lips posed up there, and with great dignity, considering his circumstances, the buck gazed down through dust-filmed eyeballs upon the present.

Just now this present was being cajoled toward a disfigured future by a man with a woman tattooed on his left arm. She reposed there so long as he talked or listened; but when he interrupted to raise his glass, she was strangled. Though she had been suffering this treatment for many years, she bore it with the same surprise contorting her blue face whenever it was repeated; and when it was done, she returned to the same pose of unsuspecting tranquillity. (True, she was not entirely innocent: turned at another angle, and a portion of her covered up, she was capable of a pose which none who did not know her might have suspected from her placid countenance.) —The Resurrectionists! said he; and she was strangled.

—The Resurrectionists? What would it have to do with grave-robbers? It was the sermon on medicine made from mummies. Mummies ground up in a powder for medicine, said a man as far from the weather as possible, at the far end of the bar.

—Not that any of you have ever heard one of his sermons, said a small man in the middle. —Relying on what your wives repeat to you.

—And you was there, I suppose, imperson?

—I was. It was the sermon in which the Swiss rooster is condemned to burn to death for laying an egg.

—Fourteen seventy-four. I know that one myself.

There was an air of grudging conspiracy over all this; and if voices rose in argument the overtones were slightly quelled, suggesting, as in any totalitarian society, walls with ears, the ubiquitous dictator long in residence hic, et ubique, disputing no passage, for He was going nowhere. —But that little man selling brushes...

—A manic...

—Manichee...

—He was sent here, but Reverend saved us from that. If good and evil was absolutes, we would all of us be Manichean heretics, says the Reverend. I was there, you see. If it wasn't for evil being a depraved qualification of good, says the Reverend, we should all be Manicheans like the little brush salesman.

—Selling unchristian brushes to honest people...

—Ha! there you're wrong, for Manichees was Christian. For them, says the Reverend, the sun itself was the visible symbol of Christ.

—They was not.

—It was so. How could you have the sun...

—They was not, and what's more...

—Here is the sexton coming now, he was there.

—They was not, and what if he was, he goes to church and makes up his own sermon, and afterward he'll tell you such and such was the Reverend's sermon which nobody heard but himself. Like the sermon on the American Legion... him, he's as deaf as that coconut.

Every head but the buck turned to see the door thrown open, shaking the plate of glass and the configuration ИЯƎVAT TOꟼƎᗡ between the men and the storm. The Town Carpenter entered, pursued by a distant peal of thunder. —That damned racket, he said, shutting it out.

—It's rare, that you have thunder with snow, said the small man in the middle, appeasing.

—May it roll away and take my curse with it, the Town Carpenter growled, arrived at the bar. He squared his shoulders, reared his head, and looked round him. —Now do you know, after the Great Deluge there was no God? Well, there was not. With the world wet for a hundred years, there was no thunder, and men went around with their heads up, alone and unafraid they went, like heroes should, you know. Then it all dried off and the atmosphere up there recovered. He paused to kick the snow from his feet against the bar; and the dog waited till that was done to lie at his feet. —And then that damned thunder started, and scared them all so much, looking up to see nothing, that they took the images of terror right out of their own minds and hung them up there in the empty space above their empty heads. He drank down his glass. —There now, he said, putting it empty on the bar, and he reared his head, as though the buck's were the only face he would countenance. —I have a very important visitor, finally he brought out.

—Tom Swift, it must be, the strangler muttered, watching the Town Carpenter narrowly.

—To see him, you might not guess at the hero he is. Of course I recognized him immediately.

—A strange fellow got off the morning train, said the man in the middle. —Neither hat nor coat. Oh, you never know, you never know. Drunk perhaps. You never know.

Stealthily, the Town Carpenter looked at these two, his expression one of cunning. It was a look with which they were all familiar; and for its astute divining quality (that and the subsequent logical parallel of his conversation) he was often accused of perfect hearing. —There now, he said, pulling a filled glass to him, —you'd be surprised to see him perhaps, a man waited on by seven kings at a time, sixty dukes and a count for every day in the year, so modest and quiet as him.

—That train come in from the city, said the small man with beer.

—I've seen them, city people in the country, said the strangler. —I know them, terrified when they see things move without ticking or smoking.

—A man who sits with twelve archbishops on his right hand and twenty bishops on his left.

—They live in cities where nothing grows. Did you know that? Nothing grows in the city. Even their minds they keep steam-heated. Their horizons are dirty windowsills.

—Drunk, perhaps. You never know.

—Whose chamberlain is a bishop and king, and his chief cook a king and an abbot, he couldn't stoop to taking such titles as those.

—Do you know what happens to people in cities? I'll tell you what happens to people in cities. They lose the seasons, that's what happens. They lose the extremes, the winter and summer. They lose the means, the spring and the fall. They lose the beginning and end of the day, and nothing grows but their bank accounts. Life in the city is just all middle, nothing is born and nothing dies. Things appear, and things are killed, but nothing begins and nothing ends.

—His domains lay from the three Indies to the ruins of Babylon, from Farther India to the tower of Babel. That's the voyage we're going to make. Waited on hand and foot by kings, from his humble looks you wouldn't believe it, from his quiet ways you'd never know. Of course I knew him immediately.

—You don't get heroes out of the cities. A city man is spread out too much.

—If you've ever watched the ground for a mole, tried to follow the silent movement of the course of his burrow and nothing moves, nothing but separate blades of grass, each of them moving for no good reason, and then the ground moves, and moves again, why that's the kind of a face he has.

—A simple man who is up against it, a man who knows what he's up against. You have to go to the country to find him. Out to the country or out to sea.

—In his dominions there are no poor, no thieves or robbers, and no dissension. Where he has come from there are no vices, no misers or flatterers, and no lies.

Snow whirled against the glass. The blue woman was held contorted for full half a minute. The Town Carpenter licked his lips, and gazed up at the movement on the cracked lips of the twelve-point buck who remained, unperturbed by the fly, looking down through glazed convexities of dust.

Streaks of sound pierced the woodwork, from the cavetto molding to stab through the stained ribs strained tongue-in-groove wainscoting the hallway, as though there were movement there.

—So, he burnt the throne of the sun with fire, did he? The throne of the sun! ... nine ... six, Reverend Gwyon muttered, standing over his littered desk, flinging over the pages of Job with the flat of three fingers. —Which shaketh the earth out of her place, and the pillars thereof tremble. Tremble, do they? Which commandeth the sun, and it riseth not; and sealed up the stars. Riseth not, does it? Which maketh Arcturus, Orion, Pleiades, and the chambers of the south, does he! Gwyon looked up impatiently, no more than to take his eyes from the book laid open on top of the *Letters* of the Emperor Flavius Claudius Julianus. His clear eyes struck the door, and held there a moment, waiting. Then he returned to the pages before him. —Nineteen . . . four . . . In them hath he set a tabernacle for the sun, which is a bridegroom coming out of his chamber, and rejoiceth as a strong man to run a race. His going forth is from the end of the heaven, and his circuit unto the ends of it: and there is nothing hid from the heat thereof . . . that's better, now, he muttered, turning pages. —Seven . . . eleven . . . and by it there is profit to them that see the sun . . . uhm . . . eleven . . . seven . . . Truly the light is sweet, and a pleasant thing it is for the eyes to behold the sun . . . yes . . . hmmmm . . . Truly the light is sweet, he repeated, raising his eyes now straight before him to the window, and the encumbered sky.

That impregnable meter of silence enveloped him directly he stopped speaking, and stood there erect and alone. There was nothing in his face to betray, or even suggest doubt; but his hands were not, as they might at first appear, resting their own weight and no more on the pages before him. As he stood unmoving so, the faint carnation under his nails became evenly fainter, draining away from the rims until they were, all together, blanched with the strain they sustained, streaked with the life that sustained them.

—One more day's dying, Gwyon murmured looking out at the sky. Would there be time? His fingertips regained their color. Even as they did, the lower part of his face drained of its fullness, as though the two were connected, or as though it were not two but one process, a continuous seepage down, and he caught his lower lip with concern. Would there be time? to make full proof of his ministry; and he searched the sky as though for answer. —One more day's dying, he repeated, searching the sky for the sun.

The parsonage was near a century old, and it was not strange that the wind should set it creaking so. Inside, however, and well in, beyond other evidences, the wind provided an arbitrary explanation and no more: as well say that the sharp angles of wall and wainscot, molding and baseboard complained so at the relentless obtrusion of one another's extremities where they were forced to meet; or that they creaked with effort, supporting the cross, and with vigilance for its prey, suspended there in the near darkness before the small mirrors which looked shined with work as though, leaving Sor Patrocinio stigmatized, they had begun again here. How John Huss would have vilipended the thing! as Aunt May had ruefully noted; but she had not prevailed against it, and inclined to avoid it. Gwyon, passing it many times a day, shocked it and banged the study door in its face before a fragment of his motion could be isolated and fixed. (True, more than once he had surprised Janet there; and often, when he thought of it, attempted stealthy glances at her ungloved palms, but in vain.) The creaking continued; still nothing moved in the dark hallway until the thin lips cracked apart, but still silent, —What was it? What am I supposed to ask? Am I the . . . Homoousian or Homoiousian? Am I the man that . . . What holds me back? . . . for whom . . . for whom . . . What was it? . . .

Reverend Gwyon gripped the lapels of his coat and peered at the inside of the door. —Damnation, he muttered, —what holds me back? And he commenced to rummage among the books and papers before him. The Old Testament and the *Letters* of Julian the Apostate were thrust aside, Origen's *Contra Celsum*, one after another he pushed the books back until they mounted in an unsteady pile about the gold bull figure. —Volume eighteen, he muttered, —PLANTS to RAYM . . . where . . . He paused, holding Tertullian's *De Coronâ*. Then he started through the discarded pile, muttering —*Cathemerinon*, but when he found it, and stood with it open, he spoke without looking at the page.

—Kindly Guide, Reverend Gwyon said to the sky without, —creator of the radiant light, who controllest the seasons in their fixed courses, if thy sun is hidden, grim chaos encompasses us, restore thy light O Christ to thy faithful followers . . . Gwyon paused, as though he had heard a sound. The sky before him darkened as he watched it; and as he watched, the book in his hand closed slowly, and the nails of his hand went white against the covers.

The knocks on the door were faint. Reverend Gwyon planted Prudentius firmly on the desk and turned; but when he reached the door he paused with a hand to the knob and stood that way, listening, the more intently, for something he had not heard.

On either side of the door they stood, a hand raised and a hand held forth, their extended arms abscissa and ordinate for the point of ordination where their eyes met on the inordinate curve of doubt.

There was a crash in the hallway. Reverend Gwyon threw the study door open. The cruz-con-espejos lay on the floor. Streaks of light pierced him from the sharp silvered fragments around it, and held him, blinded for a moment.

Rounding the corner from the kitchen, Janet collided with the figure coming in the other direction. She drew back aghast. —Has it begun? she managed to say, clutching one gloved hand in the other.

—Begun? Good God, I . . . I didn't . . .

—Is it time? she asked eagerly. —Time to tell them . . . you have come back?

—Yes, tell them, he said, getting round her with the speed of a shadow when a light is moved, —I came back to preach, but I . . .

—They doubted, she said drawing her upper lip down with the sudden modesty of veiling, —but I . . .

—Janet! Reverend Gwyon emerged, and pushed the cross aside with his foot. —Lunch, he said, advancing.

—Father... father, I...

Janet was gone. Reverend Gwyon, coming forth from the dark hallway, seemed to become larger as he approached the light, and the figure dancing backwards, still like a shadow retreating, went on, —Something I have to ask you, I... what was it?... you...

In this fashion they reached the dining room. With expletive —Thank God, once or twice, the voice had risen and went on more rapidly, drawing Gwyon on with the expression on his face of a man tormented by a question to which everyone else in the room knows the answer.

—You look like Valerian, very much, yes very much like the Emperor Valerian... the words came on, every syllable expletive and the more rapid, the sound sustaining itself in nimble surprise, alert for the right words, the right question when it came out to be rescued and repeated.

Reverend Gwyon reached the head of the table, and stood at his place. His nostrils worked for an instant. There did, in fact, issue from the kitchen the smell of frying fish.

—In the painting by Memlinc you know, the painting by Memling, Valerian in the painting by Memlinc...

—How many kings are there left in the world, then? Right now, today, how many kings are there left? The blue woman was drawn to full length, as her master extended an empty glass across the bar.

—I'd rather work for a living, said the small man with beer, staring up at the sign *Law forbids cashing welfare checks on these premises*.

—Counting the Pope of Rome? asked the man furthest from the storm, at the end of the bar.

—I said kings. He's no more king than that coconut, the Pope isn't.

—He's a kind of a king, the Pope is. Anyone who holds a temporal sway is a king, so the Reverend said.

—And when did he say that?

—In his sermon speaking on the Druids. That is why the Druids made the oak tree the king of trees, because it was so often struck by lightning, and that was a sign of divine favor.

—And when was the Pope of Rome struck by lightning?

—The divine right of kings, have you never heard tell of that? You may ask the sexton.

The Town Carpenter, who had been silent for some minutes, snared the word *kings* from somewhere, and lowered his eyes from the buck to find other, less dusty, glances directed toward him. —Kings, he responded, —second-hand kings and all sorts of useless people you find at it today. There now, just look at the way people travel today, they've no sense of voyages at all. I set off on a voyage myself a while ago, a voyage of discovery, you might say. The train was going a good sixty miles an hour and I got to my feet and pulled the emergency cord. You could see nothing at that speed. And do you know, they put me in prison? Yes they did, without a word of apology. It was in prison I lost these, he went on, motioning to his empty mouth. —I went to sleep, and the man in the prison with me, a dangerous man you could see in his eyes, he stole my teeth while I slept. Let him choke on them!

—Do you know how he holds his temporal power, the Pope of Rome? the strangler demanded, having choked the blue lady dry while the Town Carpenter spoke, taking advantage, now, of the gap while the Town Carpenter drank. —Money from right here in America, money from right here in the United States is what keeps him in power.

—Donations...

—Donations! Do you think he heats his fine Vatican palace, all the eleven hundred rooms of it, with donations? For one thing, he's sponsored by an American bread company, I know for a fact.

—Go to a train station yourself, the Town Carpenter continued, pushing forward his empty glass, —or a bus station. Go to an airport and look at them, the miserable lot of them with their empty eyes and their empty faces, and no idea what they're doing but getting out of one pot into another, weary and worried only for the comforts of the body, frightened only that they may discover something between now and the minute they get where they think they are going. There now, I've been to the airport myself, where the airplanes leave for Cairo and Damascus, and would you believe it to look at the people who go to Cairo and Damascus, the washed-out faces, and you see them come in from Cairo and Damascus and do they look any different? They might have been around to the corner grocer and no more, from the look of them. What they can tell of Cairo and Damascus is no more than I can tell of my train trip, sixty miles an hour and no toilet in sight, that is what they know of Cairo and Damascus. He recovered his glass, full, and raised it.

—Have you ever had trench mouth? asked the small man with beer. —At first I thought it was only a sore throat...

—He signed a contract for fifty thousand dollars a year, I know for a fact. When he gives the Lord's Prayer, now, every time he comes to the part about "give us this day our daily bread" he says, "Give us this day our daily slo-baked enriched oven-crust thin-sliced..."

—Ah, that's a joke, an old joke, said the man farthest from the storm.

—A joke! A joke, is it!

—Trench mouth can be fatal, they say, if it gets into your throat and the glands you have in there...

—I'll tell you the truth now, the Town Carpenter went on, his voice resonant with this confidence, —they've never been to Cairo and Damascus. With all their tickets and their passports, and their fine luggage all stuck up with advertising, they've never been out of their own bathrooms. It's so easy to go anywhere today, he said, and paused to look round, to see if any lips other than his own were moving, —that a fool can go anywhere, and it's the fools who do. There are men who have been around the world a dozen times, and they've never discovered anything but one inconvenience and one belly upset after another. Voyages have lost their meaning, it's so easy today, he finished, looking out over the top of the head of the small man with beer, whose eyes were on a level with the top button of his underwear, who said, —I should be in bed like the doctor told me, and no alcohol.

Beyond the glass three figures, who had crossed the street to avoid the Depot Tavern, passed in the storm. —The Ladies, someone said.

The Town Carpenter saw them too. —There they go, he said. —I offered to sing at their Christmas supper tonight at the church, a nice temperance song. *The Toast*. Do you know that one?

> —*By the woes of the drunkard's mother,*
> *By his children who beg for bread...*

he began in a low voice.

—I wouldn't dare go home now, said the small man with beer, gazing through the glass. —I'd catch my death.

—A joke? said the man farthest from the storm, studying the blue woman upside down. —Do you know the one about the little nigger boy meets the Catholic priest on the street and he says, Hello Father. So the priest says, Did you call me Father? The little nigger boy says Yes Father and the priest says, Are you a Catholic? So the boy says, I'm a nigger, ain't that bad enough?

Everyone laughed but the Town Carpenter. He'd gone to the men's room.

—You're carrying a dead body, the strangler retaliated, —and you ask him how much you owe him, and he says nothing. Is he dead?

—I'm the kind of a man that likes to be a poodle, said the small man with beer, watching the Town Carpenter return with the dog which had followed him in there, and waited.

—A poodle?

—If I'm going to be a dog I want to be something I like. He took a temperate sip of his small beer, and turned to the plate glass. The wind had gone down, and the snow continued to fall. —Do you think the sun will ever shine again? he asked no one.

The wind had gone down; and without its driving force the snow came on in residual particles, remnants of violence left moving loosely in the air, with no apparent direction. It had not settled heavily round the parsonage, because of the slight and exposed elevation, but every crevice and corner was packed as though the wind had come from every quarter in its brief paranoid career. The snow was packed round the dining-room window where, well inside, Reverend Gwyon's face reflected the slight clearing of the sky with raised eyebrows. The dining table, where he sat resting both hands before him, was an oval to which leaves might be added to accommodate a dozen people, though no such need had risen in years. Just the reverse, in fact, might better have served the interests of economy implicit everywhere, not a penurious economy but "sensible," sensible that is to waste, superfluity, extravagance, which might here have dictated that the table contract its surface even further, to the strict necessity of one man's setting: and for another man than this, it might well have done so (considering the withering glances of most of Gwyon's forebears, many of whom ate in the kitchen when alone, one of whom, long before the coming of the incandescent lamp, took his meals to a small upstairs closet, as its floor still showed, or the dour John H. (whose picture was nowhere to be seen) who, after he had reached his majority, was never known to eat indoors again). Not that Gwyon ever sat down to a groaning board, or ate with smörgasbord perambulation: there was seldom more than one monochrome dish at a time before him. But so much did his presence require this large open surface before him, that when he was joined at a meal he glanced up incessantly as though aware that the table was crowded, and, when his guest sat on his right hand, each time Gwyon turned his attention in that direction he would grip the edge of the table in the other, supporting the balance which this alien presence threatened, or sit staring straight ahead, steadying the thing with both hands planted flat upon it. So he sat now, muttering a steadying, —Hmmm, every few moments, and raising his glance like an eccentric weight, unsure where it would drop.

The expletive outburst which had issued in a tone of alternate expectation of the right thing, whatever it was, and surprise, when it did not come forth, had stopped as suddenly as it began. Now only breaks and brief beginnings came from one part of the room and then another, from the corner where all

Good works were conceived, to the low table under the window. —Superbia . . . Ira . . . Invidia . . . Avaritia, yes, there . . . "I would desire that this house and all the people in it were turned to gold, that I might lock you up in my good chest: O my sweet gold!" . . . do you remember that? I . . . well never mind, no matter. Covetousness, no matter . . . And the voice trailed off again.

Reverend Gwyon exhaled, sniffed caraway.

—Now, the priesthood . . . the ministry, I mean . . . yes, I heard about you, some time ago, John . . . John . . . what was it? He'd seen you, stopped in to see you, I mean hear you and then see you. A priest. John . . .

Their eyes met across the room for an instant. —Yes, yes, Gwyon said dropping his eyes quickly, speaking in a tone of dismissal. —No weight to him at all. Claimed to be a priest. No weight to him at all. He paused, holding the table down. —No mystery at all, he added in a mutter. But movement brought his eyes up again, he watched the hands embrace one another, break, reach out, a small pitcher picked up, juggled between them and almost lost, put down with one hand as the other caught up a streamer of newspaper, with —What's this?

The newspaper clipping slid across the table. —Yes, that's something I've been looking for, Gwyon said, reaching for it. —Some . . . figuring, a calculation.

Written in the margin, in pencil, was this:

$$\text{Μεἰθρας} = 40 + 5 + 10 + 9 + 100 + 1 + 200 = 365$$
$$\text{Αβραξάς} = 1 + 2 + 100 + 1 + 60 + 1 + 200 = 365$$

—Yes, there, Reverend Gwyon said, getting hold of it. He put it face down on the table, and covered it with his forearm. His lips were working. He stared straight ahead through the window at the sky.

Janet entered, to place two dishes on the table.

—Here, what's this? what's this? Gwyon demanded, looking at them.

—This is bread; and this is fish, said Janet, and raised her eyes across the table.

—Fish? Gwyon repeated.

—And bread, she confirmed, standing over the meager portion as though waiting for something to happen. Her upper gum lay exposed, forgotten.

—Bring me some eggs, Gwyon said curtly. She stood there. Reverend Gwyon brought his head up sharply. A quick baffled look at the food on the table, and the figure standing over it, and Janet was gone. A bell's tinkle followed, from the kitchen, and Gwyon clicked his lips at this signal of delay, fixing his elbows on the table as though to steady it while the figure beside him sat down.

—Fish!...

Gwyon shipped his oars; or sat, at any rate, as though he had done so, his hands drawn up before his face. There the fingers continued in agitated movement, dissembling the single persistent element in the variety of expressions passing over his face. Each expression embraced his features familiarly: each one was familiar to his face, but seldom had they followed one upon another in such swift succession, as the rate of his commutation between one past and another, the distant past and that more recent, increased; and the shocks of the present, those intervals when he was interrupted as he might have been changing vehicles, came more frequently. A gleam, however, persisted in Gwyon's eyes, a look of keen attention which commenced to glitter with something near cunning each time he turned it surreptitiously on his obstreperous passenger, now hunched over the plate of fish, eating ravenously.

Janet entered, bearing a single plate in her gloved hands. She was not looking where she put it down but straight across the table. The fish was almost gone. Reverend Gwyon lowered a hand and pushed the newspaper clipping aside to make room for the plate being lowered before him, noticing the clipping as he did so, recalling, —That food package, Janet? She said nothing; and Gwyon had to look up at her face to see her faint nod. Her face looked more blue than it did usually, for Janet had gone quite pale in the past few minutes. She went out saying, —There is no egg, over her shoulder, and left Gwyon staring into a plate of white navy beans.

The fish was gone, and the outburst commenced abruptly with, —That cross, you know, that cross, I've always... but I mean just now I didn't... The hand stopped in the middle of gesturing to the hall, where the cruz-con-espejos still lay on the floor.

Gripping the table edge with one hand, Gwyon snatched at the newspaper clipping with the other. He was too late; and could do no more than watch it picked up as though the wind had got it, and spread it out on the air between them. On one side a little girl in long white stockings stared out obliquely from an indistinct picture, on the other, the sharp eyes of a man from under the even division of a shiny widow's peak.

—This...

—That, said Gwyon, planting a hand on the paper as it fell back to the table, —is Señor Hermoso Hermoso. I don't understand it. I don't understand it at all. Confession of her attacker, it says here. Why, this is Señor Hermoso Hermoso. And this picture? taken when he was young of course, why this is Señor Hermoso Hermoso, a very respectable man in San Zwingli. I knew him there, Reverend Gwyon went on muttering, —years after the crime. Years after. His hand held the paper down flat on the table between them.

—Years after, Gwyon repeated, hiding the marginal calculations with his sleeve.

—Yes, but she ... she ...

—She? ... Gwyon looked up anxiously when he did not go on, to see him stopped, confused and preoccupied. It was a bone, in the last mouthful of fishmeat, and Gwyon's own face twitched, watching him remove it.

—But now, he went on more evenly, rid of the fishbone, —now I feel recovered. A lot recovered. Yes, here I am, he said, and though their eyes had caught one another's at a number of angles, he now looked Reverend Gwyon full in the face for the first time. —And I ... you must wonder what I've been doing, all this time?

Gwyon lowered his eyes. He started to make a steadying sound, but was interrupted as soon as his voice broke in his throat; and so he began to eat the navy beans.

—Yes, now here we are, and ... because down there, things got confused down there, dreadfully confused. I couldn't begin to tell you everything that happened, everything ... I hardly know myself, except ... I hardly believe it now, I hardly believe they actually did happen. And so I ... well there, so I just left it all there, it was getting to be so unreal anyhow that it ... and I ... well here, here to go on from where reality left off, to recover myself, and ... After all, it's what I was trained for, and I ... the ministry, a career with the times, in keeping with the times. He took a hand from the edge of the table to rub it over his face. —And all that ... fabrication, there's no reason to believe it ever existed, and she ... that city? If I fell among thieves? Why, there are places more real, there are places in books, there are people in plays more real than ... all that. It was turning into a ... a regular carnival. With a quick look up from his plate, Gwyon saw him shake his head slightly, four fingers pressed to a temple, then he broke out with the same constricted laugh. —Yes, a carnival, remember? O flesh, farewell! and he jumped up so suddenly that Gwyon dropped his fork and got hold of the table with both hands, like a man grabbing for the gunwales in fear of capsizing.

—But here, I feel like I'm being watched here. I always felt that way, but ... secure, being watched. He paused in the corner where all Good works were conceived. —You're watching me, aren't you! He caught Gwyon's glittering eye, and then turned toward the window, but did not reach it, he was stopped by the low table there and stared down at it. —It ... you see? he said turning, and his whole face was softened in a sickly smile, —this ... "in hell is all manner of delight" ... he coughed, —when the Seven Sins pay a call? But no matter, his features drew tight again and he looked away. —Not now, he whispered.

Gwyon, seated firmly, feet planted wide apart on the floor as though the hull were rolling, watched him standing there looking out through the glass. Outside the window, the snow fell in heavier smaller particles, at different angles to the earth, here in foreground from right to left, and beyond from left to right, not swirling but apparently on separate planes. There was a long pause before he spoke, more quietly, without turning from the glass, —And when the seed began to grow, 'twas like a garden full of snow...do you remember that?

Attentive as he was, Reverend Gwyon did not seem to be listening: all of his attention was in his eyes which, narrow and widen as they might with the expressions of his face, had not lost their gleam. Since the moment he had, as it were, almost tumbled into the tailsheets, he sat erect and more firm at the head of the table. His face, which had reflected coming forth from his own memory to the present, and then retreating to extreme confines of memory lying centuries beyond his years, now seemed to embrace them all in sudden intensity as he leaned forward.

At that moment Janet came in with a sail of wrapping paper. —If Reverend will write their name on this, she said, reefing it, —for I cannot write foreign, and she handed over the stub of a black crayon. Subdued, with a quick look at the fishbones and not elsewhere, she took that plate in a square gloved hand and went out, leaving Gwyon staring at the wrapping paper, the concentration in his face gone as suddenly as it had come there. Then his hand came up slowly and plotted the words of address to Estremadura. His lips moved, and seemed to draw the clear even whisper across the smooth table to themselves.

—And if beauty did provoke thieves, sooner than gold? The path I've come on, and you'd remember, here, how as an...ape to nature, I excelled. The path the foul spirits kept clean, but it's over. By all that's ugly, it's done.

Real Monasterio, Gwyon wrote, his lips moving, *de Nuestra Señora de la Otra Vez,* as the whisper came closer, and broke out in a voice over his head,

—What's this? Spain?

—Spain? Gwyon repeated. He dropped the crayon stub, looking up, and his large hand trembled over the newspaper clipping.

—Going to Spain?

—It doesn't snow there, Gwyon said lowering his eyes, until they fixed on the little girl in long white stockings. —But the cold, on the hill where...He shuddered. —That land! he broke out. —Damned, empty land, you're part of it when you're there. Part of it, that self-continent land, and when you're out, outside, shut out, and look back on it, you look back on its emptiness from your own, look over its ragged edges to its...its hard face, refuses to admit you've ever touched it. He was staring blankly at the newspaper clipping.

—But this isn't...you can't go now?

Gwyon looked him full in the face for the first time. —Spain is a land to flee across, he said, motionless, forcing the other face to lower in chagrin at the sight of his own undetermined features, as loss spread from his eyes out to the edges of his face, the emptiness in the eyepiece of a telescope where a point of light expands into a field of space and a worldless universe.

—She...They ejaculated at the same instant.

—She came to me there, Gwyon went on with somniloquent evenness, —in this monastery. I was almost asleep, and I felt her hand. I got up, I got to the window as fast as I could, and there, the moon had sent a stream of light in, across the room, right across the room to me. There it was in the sky. The moon...warm, like the moon...

—Yes but you can't...I'm not a child any more! and you can't...you used to tell me the Thessalian witches tried to draw it down...Gwyon watched him vacantly as he turned away, abrupt movements round the far end of the table as though evading the image, or a mock image of the figure Gwyon had conjured. —And if it's she standing over us...?

—"The moon is always in motion," says Arnobius.

—To hell with Arnobius.

—"According to your representation she is a woman, with a countenance that does not alter, though her daily variation carries her through a thousand forms," Gwyon finished, and his querulous voice failed.

—That...that, never mind all that! The words were harsh and uneven as he shook his head, shaking away the paraselene. —I came for you! he cried out at Gwyon.

—Yes...? Gwyon whispered, his hands finding one another before him on the table, as his features reformed and his eyes recovered their glitter.

—If I've come for the priesthood, and you...

—Yes, you...You brought the bull, the gold bull, Reverend Gwyon said leaning forward.

—The what? Yes, that, but listen...

—And you've come for the priesthood, Gwyon went on tensely.

—Yes I've come back, I've come to you, because you can tell me...what I must know. He lowered his eyes, then raised them gleaming before Gwyon could interrupt again. —Though why you, better than someone else, because I...then I'll be a minister, I'll know what I'm doing...I'll out-preach Saint Bernard. Mothers will hide their sons, wives will hide their husbands for fear my preaching will tempt them away. Yes, he broke up so many homes the deserted wives formed a nunnery. I'll form seventy-two nunneries. Yes, "And the brother shall deliver up the brother unto death, and the father the child:

and the children shall rise up against their parents, and cause them to be put to death..." Why, I'll go to Laodicea, and I... I'll be God's Fool Himself, he finished, swinging round to the windows again so abruptly that his hand cracked against the frame. He clutched it quickly in the other, then threw it out again. —Look! Look, the wren, do you see? he cried out.

A wren fluttered to an evergreen outside, its weight not enough to dislodge the snow on the spray where it landed.

—I'll go out like the early Christian missionaries did at Christmas, to hunt down the wren and kill him, yes, when the wren was king, do you remember, you told me...When the wren was king, he repeated, getting breath again, —at Christmas.

The wren had flown, as he turned from the window and approached with burning green eyes fixed on Gwyon. —King, yes, he repeated, —when the king was slain and eaten, there's sacrament. There's sacrament. Then at the side of the table he paused and lowered his head, a closed wrist couched in the back of his neck, mumbling, —Homo...homoi...what I mean is, Did He really suffer? And...no, that's not it, I mean...He stopped; and clinging to the edge, sank into his chair.

Reverend Gwyon sat high at the helm, steadying, hands stretched forth to the edge of the sail of wrapping paper, looking down at him as though he were trying to clamber aboard. Then, —Are you prepared? Gwyon brought out, his eyes gleaming with the challenge.

—Prepared?

—The priesthood. The trials before you, for the priesthood.

—Trials?

—There must be priests, strong and passionless, able to renounce the things of this world...Gwyon reached out and took his wrist, as though to pull him aboard. —To preach Him Who offers rest from sin, and hope beyond the grave. Born of the Rock, He comes forth to offer Remission of sins, and Everlasting Life.

—Yes...

—Priests to administer Baptism, the Oath, and the Sign on the Brow, and the Communion of Bread and Cup. To preach Redemption, Sacramentary Grace, and Salvation, through the Lord of Hosts, the God of Truth who rewards for acts of piety...

—Yes, yes...Gwyon's grip was tight as a closed vise on his wrist. It became tighter.

—To be his priest, are you prepared? Gwyon repeated. —To be inured to hardship? strengthened against temptation? and your body rendered passionless?

—But I...yes, good God, there's no passion left in me now.

—To renounce the things of this world?

—There's nothing here I want...Nothing.

—And when the crown is offered you...Gwyon came on, straining with intensity.

—Yes, the third temptation, "All these things will I give thee..." No, I'm through with that. He twisted in Gwyon's grip. —He offered me all that, and he's behind me. He gave me all that, and he's behind me. Just being here I've renounced him, just coming here, I've renounced all he gave me. He paused, and when Gwyon did not speak but continued to grip his wrist and fix all his attention, as he had before, with his eye, went on, —Do you think he didn't take me up on a high mountain, and show me all the kingdoms of the world? and the glory of them? and offer them to me? and give them to me? And here...now...if this is not Renunciation...

—Could you face fifty days of fasting? Gwyon demanded suddenly.

—Why...why yes, if...

—Could you stand two days exposed to extreme heat?

—But...

—And twenty days in the snow?

—But I...

—There are twelve trials of fortitude, Gwyon went on in a voice of intense confidence, —you must face heat and cold, hunger, thirst, and the terrors of drowning, before you take the sacramentum and be sealed on the forehead as his priest.

—But all this...

—You cannot be his priest without passing through all the disciplines, Gwyon said, relaxing his grip a little, speaking with an admonishing tone. —You must give proof of self-control and chastity, as Nonnus says in his *In Sancta Lumina*. To be rendered strong and passionless, in order to convert the army first, Gwyon went on, looking toward the window, his voice sinking to a reflective note.

—But Father...Father...

—Yes, Gwyon said closing his grip again, bringing his eyes back to the eyes which stared at him. —I have passed through all the grades, of course, to be the Pater Patrum. And then, he went on intent again, —after your death...

—My death?...

—After the cruciati you must die, of course, after the torments, when you have passed through all the disciplines, when you have attained Cryphius, and Miles, and Leo, and Perses, and Heliodromus...

—Die?...

—How else may the soul be relieved of the dread necessity of its lower nature? Gwyon demanded bending toward him.

—Father!...

—Yes, at my hands, Gwyon said looking at him steadily, —you must die at the hands of the Pater Patratus, like all initiates.

Gwyon's face was suffused with a flush which deepened as they sat locked rigidly hand and wrist together; and as it did the face that Gwyon looked into drained of all color until the skin was near translucent, so that it might have been not two processes but one continuous seepage of life. —No one can teach Resurrection without first suffering death himself. No one can be reborn without dying. No one can be Mithras' priest without being reborn...to teach them to observe Sunday, and keep sacred the twenty-fifth of December as the birthday of the sun. Natalis invicti, the Unconquered Sun, Gwyon finished, turning his face to the window.

—But I...you...to worship the sun?

Gwyon let go his wrist abruptly, and he drew it back.

—Nonsense, said Gwyon, brisk now. —We let them think so, he confided, —those outside the mysteries. But our own votaries know Mithras as the deity superior to it, in fact the power behind the sun. Here, his name you see...Gwyon revealed the marginal notes on the newspaper clipping. —Abraxas and Mithras have the same numerical value, the cycle of the year as the sun's orbit describes it. Abraxas, you know, the resident of the highest Gnostic heaven...

The scuffling of feet sounded on the porch outside. Janet passed through the room hurriedly, behind them. Gwyon reached for his wrist again. It was not there, and Gwyon's hand gripped the edge of the table. —"The gods are benevolent and regardful of the human race," says Elisæus, Gwyon said almost in a whisper. —"If only men acknowledge the greatness of the gods and their own insignificance, and take pleasure in the gifts of the earth distributed by the hands of the king..."

Janet's footsteps sounded in the front hall, and the door banged open, spilling voices into the house. Gwyon paused. His hand shook on the edge of the table, and his lip quivered. —Mithras means friend, he said, —mediator. Mithras is mediator between the gods and the lower world. He waited anxiously, as though for confirmation, as footsteps approached in the hall.

—Hell? the lower world, hell? came in distracted query.

—Our own earth, Reverend Gwyon answered, and was silent until Janet's voice broke in upon them from the doorway, and he leaped up.

—It's the Use-Me Ladies to see you, Reverend, said she.

Reverend Gwyon was through the doorway in the other direction before she'd finished her sentence, muttering —I'll...be a minute, as he passed her. The study door banged, and from inside the sound of a book hurled to the floor a moment later.

Janet fled to the kitchen, as footsteps sounded straight down the front hall to the dining room. Three ladies came in. The cold came in with them; it clung round them as they came to a stop.

—Reverend...

—Reverend...

—I beg your pardon. We have come to see Reverend Gwyon.

—Oh, I...I... He just went out.

—Went out?

—Went out?

—But in this kind of weather he never goes out. Reverend Gwyon is always irritable when the sky clouds over and we have bad weather.

—No, I mean...just out of the room. He'll be right back.

—I see.

—We'll wait. And are you visiting here?

—I? Why, you might say...

—It may have surprised you, when we mistook you for Reverend Gwyon.

—But there is a re*sem*blance.

—There *is* a resemblance. Of course Reverend Gwyon is a good deal bigger.

—A good deal older. But as you're dressed, you may see where we make our mistake. Are you in the Lord's work?

—I? why I...Yes, I'm...

—I can't see where I saw the resemblance.

—...the Reverend Gilbert Sullivan.

—But just for a minute...

—Just for a minute I saw it too. It may be that only this morning we were speaking of Reverend Gwyon's son.

—Who has been away a very long time.

—The prodigal son.

—But he has no brothers.

—Yes, the poor boy.

—Poor Camilla.

—May was really a mother to him.

—Poor May.

—It was a severe trial for everyone.

—He wasn't a strong boy.

—But then Camilla...

—Poor Camilla...

—Poor Camilla never was strong.

—Taken and left in foreign lands. Left to lie among Roman Catholics.

—I trust the Reverend Gilbert Sullivan is not a Roman Catholic priest? The name...

—The name...

—Me? Good God, no. I mean...

—The name suggests Irish extraction. Perhaps his forebears are *north* of Ireland?

—Perhaps we may ask Reverend Gilbert Sullivan to attend our Christmas supper tonight?

—Of course we may.

—Of course he may.

Hurraaaph!...—Look out, or by God I'll split your skull. Shake the snow off before you come inside. Oh, good day, ladies. I didn't see you, ladies. Don't mind us, the dog and me. We've been outdoors, as you can see. We've been working, both very tired. Up the stairs, now! Up the stairs!

—Working, indeed.

—Indeed!

—Indeed!

—Why I could smell him across the room.

—He wanted to sing at the supper tonight. One of his songs from the saloon.

—It is a disgrace to have him our sexton.

—It is a disgrace to have him living right here under the roof of the parsonage.

—But Reverend Gwyon...

—Reverend Gwyon...

—Reverend Gwyon always smells so *fresh*.

—Even his charity is stretched too far.

—Indeed it is. But I've been thinking...

—I've been thinking, don't misunderstand me, the very same thing. After all, the sexton is getting older.

—The Lord will deliver him.

—The Lord will release him.

—The Lord will have pity on the poor man.

—Why, Reverend Gwyon.

—Reverend Gwyon...

—We've come to ask you about our supper, the Christmas supper in the church tonight.

—Mrs. Dorman is going to sing. My sister is going to play the piano.

—And we've arranged for a visiting lecturer.

—A former Y.M.C.A. official. He is going to give a humorous talk.

—Nothing flighty. Nothing frivolous.

—Oh dear no, his talk will have some meat in it.

—I understand he has been in Africa. Not just traveling, wasting time. He was fully occupied with the Lord's work.

—And your guest will come.

—Yes, he is coming. We shall see both of you there tonight.

—Reverend Gwyon might like to hear our poem.

—Reverend Gilbert might like to hear our poem.

—Both of them might like to hear the poem we've written for the Christmas supper tonight.

—The last two verses. The rest will have to be a surprise!

So as members of the Use-Me
So as members of the Use-Me
So as members of the Use-Me

We hope to conquer all
We hope to conquer all
We hope to conquer all

Offering the fellowship of Jesus
Offering the fellowship of Jesus
Offering the fellowship of Jesus

To those who need him most of all
To those who need him most of all
To those who need him most of all

For when we get to heaven
For when we get to heaven
For when we get to heaven

A reward there will be in store
A reward there will be in store
A reward there will be in store

For those whose daily living
For those whose daily living
For those whose daily living

Has been "Use-Me evermore."
Has been "Use-Me evermore."
Has been "Use-Me evermore."

When they looked round, they were alone in the room. When they left, seeking their footprints, those were gone under the snow; and the prints of departure so quickly obliterated as to leave no witness that their visit had ever been made at all.

Though Reverend Gwyon, alone again in his study, found time to mutter, —There was a woman's grade in the Mysteries. Porphyry mentions it... hummn... He turned up open books on his desk. —Hyena. That was it. Hyena.

His gaze fell upon the Bible. —Near Christmas! Christmas! he said almost viciously, as his eye followed lines on the open page. —Then the moon shall be confounded and the sun ashamed... His hand flung over the pages of Isaiah. —The sun shall be no more thy light by day; neither for brightness shall the moon give light unto thee: but the Lord shall be unto thee an everlasting light, and thy God thy glory. Thy sun shall no more go down; neither shall the moon withdraw itself: for the Lord shall be...

Suddenly Gwyon's hand swept the Bible to the floor. He stood there quivering the length of his frame. Then he crumpled the newspaper clipping from *Osservatore Romano;* and after it, one by one, the books went to the floor, Tertullian's *De Præscriptione Hæreticorum,* Arnobius' *Adversus Nationes, De Errore Profanarum Religionum* of Firmicus Maternus... He did not stop until he came to Saint John of the Cross, which he opened, removed the contents, and dropped the hollow *Dark Night of the Soul* after the rest of them. Then he straightened the gold bull figure to its feet on his desk, and stood with his hands on its horns looking out at the darkening sky.

—Cannot they see, it is exhausted? he whispered. Thunder sounded, beyond Mount Lamentation, and it sounded again.

Then he broke out,

—Herakles star-adorned, king of fire, ruler of the universe, thou sun, who with thy far-flung rays art the guardian of mortal life, with thy gleaming car revolving the wide circuit of thy course... Belus thou art named on the Euphrates, Ammon in Libya, Apis of the Nile art thou by birth, Arabian Kronos, Assyrian Zeus... but whether thou art Serapis, or the cloudless Zeus of Egypt, or Kronos, or Phaëthon, many-titled Mithra, Sun of Babylon, or in Greece Apollo of Delphi, or Wedlock, whom Love begat in the shadowy land of dreams... whether thou art known as Paieon, healer of pain, or Æther with its varied garb, or star-bespangled Night—for the starry robes of night illuminate the heaven—lend a propitious ear to my prayer. He paused, then went on more loudly,

—O king, greatest of the gods, thou sun, the lord of heaven and earth, god of gods, thy breath is potent, if it seem good to thee, forward me on my way to the supreme deity who begat thee and formed thee, for I am the man Gwyon.

—I invoke thee, O Zeus the Sun-god Mithra Serapis, invincible, giver of mead, Melikertes, lord of the mead, abraalbabachaebechi . . .

He stood, his hand on the bull's horns, and the expression on his face of a man waiting for something which has happened long before.

Each time Janet's eyes reached the foot of the page, she returned them to the top, to verse eight of chapter twenty-four of the Gospel according to Saint Matthew, —All these are the beginning of sorrows, and read the column down again. She stood and bore this repetition silent for some time, until at last, after hanging for a moment on verse twenty-four, her gaze shortened to her bare hands clasped before her, and under the care of her eyes they opened, sustaining the shock of her pupils in two dark scars on the palms. The palms were clean, but the rest of her hands as she turned them, from the nails down along the ridges and jointures of the fingers, were not. Suddenly her left hand closed, and she dug the firm flesh on the back of it with her forefinger.

Through the window the snow fell fast and heavily, the leisured dignity of perfect flakes lost in bitter water-soaked streaks to earth, each moment passing in more frantic declivity until the artifice of its identity had entirely disappeared, and it was rain.

The sound of thunder drew her to the glass. She stood looking out. Then she raised her hands and tried to rub away the two blots on the windowpanes she had left earlier, but she could not, and her hands moved more and more slowly until they stopped, and left her staring down at the carriage barn, barely discernible below. As she looked, a hand came back to her face and commenced moving over it, not in caress along its surface, nor excitedly, but deliberately resting on her features in one position after another; until that hand stopped, the thumb along the ridge of her nose and the palm over her mouth, and she drew her left hand back to grasp the empty folds at her breast.

A minute later and she'd pulled the frame of type from the flatbed hand press in the corner, unlocked it and spilled the letters all over the floor, banged the Bible closed, hesitated a moment over it and then pushed it off into the pile of metal spellingless letters and come out her door. Her steps creaked in the hallway, but the Town Carpenter's voice came on from behind his door as she passed, evenly absorbed in reading aloud to the dog, —"While we go now to bring the Wanderer up, it should not be forgotten that the house, completely furnished, is awaiting him, and he has only to knock at the door, enter, and be at home"... (They were in volume I of Lew Wallace's *The Prince of India, or, Why Constantinople Fell*.)

At the other end of the hall Janet reached the empty sewing room and went straight in among the roses upside-down, the green-capped pink-faced dogs faded on the west wall behind the chaise longue where she suddenly saw him sitting rigidly erect, his drawn fist plunged into his neck so that his arm stood out like a wing, and his brows noticeable for being contracted so forcefully that they seemed to have seized the face and held it in this stifling grasp. Apparently he was asleep. Janet bent close, studying the thin face, the slightly crooked nose, the rough chin and bare throat. The left hand lay in his lap as rigid as the rest of him, the fingers doubled in upon themselves and the veins standing out around the clotted blood, where Janet reached and prodded the torn place with her forefinger. Not a muscle moved in his face, nor anywhere else about him; and Janet turned and ran out, down the hall, and the stairs, and out of the house, leaving him there in the darkening room, where he slept in this same tense numb position until the roses had faded to stripes, and the walls themselves had lost their boundaries.

He waked staring straight ahead to that full consciousness which only sheer horror attains: his blood stopped. For a prolonged instant everything stopped and the blood, without motion, was cast as a solid of unbearable weight and impenetrable density.

—*No one knows who I am.*

It was a full minute before he moved; and when he did he burst to his feet, as though to shatter this irregular surface of space enclosed by merciless solids. —No one in this house knows me, he brought out; but his mouth was so dry that the words came to pieces before he got them out where his own ear could resolve them, and he stood sucking the inside of his mouth in upon itself, plying the barren, abruptly unfamiliar hollow with his insensible tongue until its features dissolved, and he could repeat, —None of them knows who I am.

But even before these words were out, something else had assailed him. He began looking wildly round the room, where shapes refused to identify themselves, and endured only in terms of the others, each a presence made possible only by what everything else was not, each suffering the space it filled to bear it only as a part of a whole which, with a part standing forth to identify itself, would perish.

—Who was here? he whispered. Already the inside of his mouth was afloat with saliva, so that he swallowed, raised the pool on his tongue and exhausted its surface on the roof of his mouth and swallowed again. —She was here, he said, gripping his chin in his hand.

Starting again, the blood on its course had set every interior surface of his body stingingly aflame with the thrill of its own existence; and he stamped his feet, and shook his hands in the air. —This . . . this . . . he whispered hoarsely. Then he grabbed one hand with the other and gripped it tight as he could, until the balance of that was out and he exchanged them, gripping the second with the first, and finally got out of the room with his hands interlocked before him, the fingertips of each one straining in upon the bones of the other.

There had been a good deal of noise in this last hour or so, books thrown and dropped, the type-metal words smashed into their meaningless components, doors banging, and all these fragments were recapitulated now in the thunder, as he broke out into the hall and down the stairs repeating, —Don't you know me? Don't you know who I am? You know who I am. Don't you know who I am? . . . , words which broke the surface, and followed one another as discordant articulations of his heavy breathing.

Reverend Gwyon had gone out a minute before, hatless, across the bare boards of the porch so heavily that they seemed not yet to have recovered silence, when he reached them and made out Gwyon's great figure striding down the slope toward the carriage barn. He followed precipitously, sliding and slipping on the soaked pores of the snow as though it were the headlong incline of twenty-five years past; and before he'd reached the bottom he did fall, headlong, so that the crust of the snow gashed his cheekbone and, for the moment he lay there, smothered his rehearsal, —You know who I am. Don't you know who I am? Don't you know me? . . .

The rain was coming down the more heavily for the saturated surface which awaited it; and he was drenched when he gained his feet. Just then there was a crash of thunder.

Gwyon had already made the carriage barn and thrown the door open. There was electricity there, and Gwyon stood just inside, his great hand on the switch and his thumb jamming it back and forth, back and forth, with no consequence but a *snap*. —Damnation, Gwyon muttered; and then, aware of someone behind him, said, —The bull. I came down to make sure of the bull . . . But Gwyon had hardly got the words out of his mouth before his upraised arm was grasped in the dark so heavily that it almost pulled him over; and the lightning followed so fast on the words that followed, that both were gone, and the transformation was complete, when Gwyon heard,

—Father . . . *Am I the man for whom Christ died?*

Louder than laughter, the crash raised and sundered them in a blinding agony of light in which nothing existed until it was done, and the tablet of darkness betrayed the vivid, motionless, extinct and enduring image of the bull in his stall and Janet bent open beneath him.

Then it seemed full minutes before the cry, pursuing them with its lashing end, flailed through darkness and stung them to earth. Water fell between them, from a hole in the roof. The smell of smoke reached them in the dark.

With no warning uncertain flicker, the light came on. Before them, a metal wash-tub lay on the floor with a square hole riven through its bottom. The door was charred and smoking around the hinges and the lock.

Then the shadows round the walls were set dancing in duplication, each steady dark shape mocked by a distorted image leaping round it, as the Town Carpenter appeared with a lantern and stood swinging it in the door. —There now! he said; and though his voice was not loud it rang with confirmation, as he entered and walked over toward the bull's stall. —There! he said, swinging round, and the lantern with him, —There's a masterful pizzle for you!

The bull shifted on its feet, sounding its weight on the board floor, and turned its head from them and withdrew.

Gwyon was gone. They both turned to the door at the same moment to look; and by the time they reached the door together, Gwyon's figure showed halfway up the slope toward the house.

—There now, said the Town Carpenter, nodding and swinging the lantern out. His coat had come open to show long-underwear buttons to the waist. He'd pulled on his trousers and galoshes to come out, and the trousers were on backwards. —It's that I came down to look at, he said, swinging the lantern toward the balloon stand, which was as good as he'd left it. Then he held the lantern aloft, over the figure poised in the doorway of the carriage barn.

—There, he's fallen!

The Town Carpenter reached out and seized his arm. They could both see Gwyon on the ground up near the house.

—He's fallen. Will you let me go help him?!

—And would you humble him, the Town Carpenter answered without relaxing his grip, —by helping him back to his feet?

He hung there in the Town Carpenter's hand until Gwyon had recovered and mounted the porch steps. Then the Town Carpenter opened his hand slowly, eyes fixed on him, until he suddenly wrenched away and ran up the hill laughing.

The Town Carpenter lowered the lantern and looked into the barn again, murmuring. Then he snapped off the electric light, pulled the door closed, and trudged up the slope hitching the binding front of his pants as he went. At the kitchen door he raised the glass chimney, blew out the lantern and went in, pulling a light cord as he passed, straight over to his pot on the cold stove. There were voices, or a voice, in the dining room, or down the hall, he did not know and did not listen.

—"Away, to hell, to hell!" Do you remember that?

The Town Carpenter rolled up his sleeves, took a piece of yellow soap from the metal sink, and dipped his hands into the pot.

—"Oh, might I see hell, and return again, How happy were I then!" Yes, yes, that's it! Back there!

The Town Carpenter found the soap among folds in the bottom of the pot, lifted it out, and dried his hands. —Something amiss, he murmured as he pulled out the light, —we must simplify, as he tramped toward the back stairs.

Janet came from behind the door of the butler's pantry. She stopped when she heard the voice down the hall, or in the dining room, she could not tell, but stood for a moment listening, thoroughly wet, her skirt torn, her hair matted down. Then she came on.

—Yes, back there, that's the place! They're waiting! Yes, the harrowing of hell. That's it. Then wood splintered, in the dining room.

Janet found him alone there. He had just split the top of the low table under the window down the middle. —What is it? Janet asked calmly, coming closer.

—Damnation, he answered, backing round the table.

—Damnation? she repeated, clearly and quietly, as he got round and backed through the door.

—Damnation? he repeated questioning, and stopping as she came close, holding to the door frame.

—That is life without love, Janet said. —Who weeps for you?

He turned and broke down the hall.

—Whom do you weep for? she pursued him. He reached the front door and turned to stare at her, advancing in her torn blood-streaked skirt. —Do you not know that luxury, that most exquisite luxury we have? she kept on until she reached him.

—You... he burst out, holding a quivering hand before him, —were you... you down in the... barn?...

Janet was up beside him, so close that their rough cheeks almost touched. —No love is lost, she said, and kissed him on the cheek where the snow had torn it.

He stared at her an instant longer, and bolted out the front door.

The Town Carpenter had found a note under his door when he entered his room. He read it aloud to the dog, who raised her head from the pillow to listen. —Dawn tomorrow, a great deal of work to be done in the church.

It was on an outsize piece of paper, and signed *Gw*. At the foot it said, "Return vol. 18 Plants to Raym Britannica." All this was written in very large letters.

The Town Carpenter held it up to the light, and finding no other message he started to file it in a drawer which jingled with bottles when he opened it. But he turned with the paper still in his hand, took out his huge gold watch, weighed it for a moment without opening the case, and laid it on the dresser. Next he brought out a flat gold case and stood running his thumb over the inscription.

The dog whined; and a minute later the light was out, and the Town Carpenter's voice sounded weary in the darkness. —Move over, you're taking too much room. Did I brush your teeth? Here. Move over. Go to sleep. We have a lot of work to do tomorrow.

The Depot Tavern showed one of the few lights in that end of town.

—I wouldn't dare go out in this, said the small man with beer, staring through the glass into the clear night. —I'd go in over my head somewhere.

The man with the blue woman tattooed on his arm was about to comment when the door banged open, and the draggled figure who arrived demanded cognac before he reached the bar.

—No cognac, I got only some brandy here.

—All right, brandy. A glass of brandy. Here wait, I said a glass, not a ... not that thing.

A tumbler half-filled was put before him, and he took out a twenty-dollar bill.

The small man sipped his beer, and looked wonderingly at this extravagant diversion.

—Here, what's that? What's that?

—What? ...

—Right there behind you. In the glass.

—This here? This coconut?

—Good God ... it's a griffin's egg. Let me see it.

—This here's a coconut.

—Let me see it. Where did it come from?

—Some guy sent it to me, he was in the service ...

—Let me see it.

—You shake it, you can hear the milk inside rattling. Hear it?

—Yes, yes, I hear it. Good God ... will you sell it to me?

—Sell it?

—Here. Do you want more?

—Well, I . . . for a coconut I couldn't hardly ask you . . .

—Here, twenty more. Is this enough?

The small man's hand shook as he put his beer on the bar, silently, not to interrupt. The glass was almost opaque, spotted with fingermarks, for he had been holding it all the afternoon.

Further up the bar, the blue woman who had been reclining for some time was suddenly snapped up and strangled until her forehead almost met her knees.

—When's the next train?

—Where you going?

—Down.

—Down where?

—All the way.

—In a minute, in three or four minutes there's one, the small man brought out, greatly excited to hear himself speak. —In three or four minutes there's one, he repeated. —There's one in three or four minutes.

They held their breath until the door banged again, shivering the pane between them and the night. Then they stared at the empty glass, and the two twenty-dollar bills on the counter. Even the twelve-point buck seemed to have a dusty eye on it.

The train arrived in New York at eleven that night.

The cab slipped on the wet pavement, in and out of the slush in the gutters, thrusting itself ahead of everything else in the frenzied motion of the streets, tearing open the half-darkness of side streets with its lights and its noise.

When it pulled in at the curb he leaped out, thrusting uncounted bills into the driver's hand, and dropped his weight against the door as he reached for the bell. But the door was not locked, and he got into the downstairs hall. There he was stopped by a voice shouting in a fury from above,

—I tell you I goin to do it, Mister Brown . . . There was a heavy thud, and three more. —I tell you, I tell you I goin to kill you, and now I doin so . . . Mister Brown, and the sound of hitting, again and again, as he got through the vast living room, up the stairs past the polychrome wood saint in the niche extending the scar of the arm offered in benediction.

He switched on the light on the balcony, and there was silence. He looked into Recktall Brown's bedroom. It was empty. Then he ran down the hall, round the corner and on to the last doorway.

Fuller was alone. He was standing over his bed in his underwear with his broken umbrella in his hand, and the spread on the sagging bed rumpled and torn where he'd been beating it. —I caution him I goin to do it, Fuller said hardly looking round, the gold of his teeth a quick glitter in the light from the hall.

Two suitcases stood packed at the foot of the bed, both cardboard and tied with heavy twine. The high-crowned straw lay on top of them. On the table, among a number of cigar stubs, and the razor blade which Fuller used to pare them with, was the cigar whose wrapper had peeled when Recktall Brown had bitten off the end, now wrapped in a cologne-scented handkerchief. Under the table, all over the floor, bits of paper were scattered: RECKTIL BROWN, REKTELL BROWN, RECKTILL BROWNE ... covering the pile of crucifixes stacked against the wall.

—Where is he?

—Mister Brown take a short trip, say he will return tomorrow. Sometime when he vexed he become very unpredictable.

—What was it?

—He taken a ticket from me, Fuller answered, his chest shaking under the buttoned front of his underwear, yellowed by his life in it.

—But that smell? What's that awful smell? Like hair burning.

—That's what it is, an evil smell, Fuller said. —That's what evil smell like.

IV

"I've had a good dream, gentlemen," he said in a strange voice, with a new light, as of joy, in his face.

—DOSTOEVSKI, *The Brothers Karamazov*

——SEMPRE con fè sincera...la mia preghiera...ai santi tabernacoli salì...

No sound but this, the radio, behind Esme's door. Otto raised his clenched hand to knock again; and as his knuckles hit the door it came open an abrupt four inches. His smile warped into surprise, every line in his face converted to its contradiction.

Chaby faced him over the chain. Chaby had on a suède jacket, the collar turned up in back; and his hair looked like a pastry-cook's triumph.

——Nell'ora del dolore...perchè, Signore,
     perchè me ne rimuneri così?

—Is Esme here?

—No.

—Do you know where she is?

—Jesis how should I know. She went to get some coffee.

—Do you know where?

—Jesis how should I know where. Chaby did not slam the door until Otto had reached the stairs.

Esme was sitting at a counter eating toast. She wore no make-up but faint sharp lines on her eyebrows. She smiled, and held out her hand to Otto, who realized, as he sat beside her, that she was breakfasting with the heavy-necked person on her right. He was showing her pictures of snapshot size. —They came out nice, he said. —Much better than most of the girls we get, innocent-looking like. But look at these, look at these of me. The photographs showed him in theatrical attitudes. In one he held a knife. In another, a pistol. In another, a cord, ready for garroting. In all, he wore a hat (as he did now), and a cigarette stub stuck in the corner of his mouth (as one was now). —Whadda you say?

—It's very kind of you, Esme said smiling to him.

—I'll come see you Friday, huh?

—Who was *that?* Otto asked when the man left.

—He's a nice man who is going to act in movies, Esme said.

—What did he want from you?

—I think he wanted me to act in the mo-vies.

They had both smiled, and for a moment they were together. Then Otto said, —I just called at your apartment, and he withdrew his hand.

—And did you see Mister Sinis-ter-ra? she asked, still with her smile.

—Yes. What's he doing up there?

—He came to see me.

—So I gather. When, last night?

—Otto, that isn't nice, she said, sobered, disappointed.

—I'm sorry. Otto, suddenly, could not afford to be left so: he had withdrawn as a woman withdraws, to be followed. There was no pursuit in Esme's eyes, as she turned them from him. —Esme, I'm sorry.

—You're not sorry, Otto. You only say that. It is a habit. There was no admonition and no feeling of hurt in Esme's voice, she spoke to him simply.

—Esme . . . Oh look, that isn't what I meant . . .

—Why do you say he slept with me?

—That isn't what I meant at all, said Otto (and in that instant almost retorted, —Well did he?). Then Esme was smiling happily again. She was smiling at someone behind him.

—Hello Stanley, she said gently. —And do you know Otto?

Stanley nodded and said, —Hello, putting the book he carried from his right to his left hand, so that he could shake hands; but he got no further. His right hand dropped empty to his side.

—Poor Stanley. Why are you so dole-ful?

—I'm all right, Stanley said. He stood there, his only motion a slight weaving toward them, as though his mustache weighed him in their direction. Finally he said, —Did you hear about Charles?

—No, what?

—He's in Bellevue. They took him there last night.

Max came in. He was smiling. He greeted them, and ordered coffee. —How's your play, Otto? he said.

—Well as a matter of fact I'm sort of upset, Otto said. —I misplaced a copy or two of it. In a dispatch case. A pigskin dispatch case. You haven't heard anything? . . .

—No, I haven't heard a thing, Max said agreeably.

—I heard about your play, Stanley said.

—You *found* it?

—No, I mean I just heard about it.

—What did you hear, that it's plagiarized?

—No, I didn't mean that. I'd like to read it.

Otto murmured, —You would, would you... Esme said, —Otto has a guilty conscience, and Max raised his coffee cup and said nothing.

—I think I'd better get back uptown, Otto said in a strained tone, casual with great effort.

—Really, Otto? Esme said, surprised, as he took her breakfast check. —Then thank you for my breakfast.

—Did you have bacon and eggs and fruit and pastry?

—No, that was the gentleman from the movies, said Esme.

—All right, he said, crumpling the check in his hand.

—Thank you, Otto.

—Do you want me to go?

—But Otto why should I want you to go?

He lit a fresh cigarette and ordered another cup of coffee. They looked up and Stanley was gone. Esme turned to see him standing undecided outside, on the street corner. —Poor Stanley, she said gently, and smiled.

—He just needs a woman, Max said.

—He needs money, said Esme.

—Money is simply a substitute for the mother in Stanley's case. He has guilt feelings about her being in the hospital, and anyone who gave him money would be filling the mother's place, the nourishment substitute.

—I guess Hannah gives him what he needs, Otto said in morose confidence.

—She'd like to.

—Well she was sleeping with him a couple of nights ago.

—Where'd you hear that?

—She was there undressed at five in the morning. I don't know what else she was doing.

—Was Stanley there?

—Sure he was there, Otto said defiantly.

—Well, so she finally made him, said Max. He smiled and finished his coffee. —You haven't seen my pictures yet, have you Otto. The show opened two days ago. I'm going up to the gallery later, come along?

—Not now, Max. Otto looked at Esme.

—They've sold seven of them, Max said as he left.

—I hate him, Otto said when he was out the door.

—Otto, what a silly thing to say.

—I do, I... I just mistrust him so much. When he's around I'd like to have a gun in my pocket. Not to do anything with, just to have it there, he added, and brandished the sling.

—Yes, Esme said, suddenly putting her forehead in her hand and running her fingers into her hair. —Because he will survive.

—Esme, I want to talk to you. Esme . . . She looked up, surprised, and she looked frightened. —I want to talk to you.

—Talk to me, she said, and smiled.

—But not here, not in this place, I . . . We're liable to be . . . Someone's liable to . . . Will you go for a walk with me.

Otto paid for five breakfasts, and they went out. They walked toward Washington Square.

—What, Otto? she asked him, seated on a bench.

—I don't know. I mean, look.

—What did you do to yourself? she asked, pointing to his cheek.

—I cut myself with a lousy razor blade. Look, Esme. I mean, are you really with me? I mean, are you and I, well, together? I mean I always feel like I'm sharing you with everyone in sight.

—Otto, you make everything so difficult for yourself.

—*I* do?

—Yes, Otto. You push something and push it until it breaks.

—I don't want to do that, Esme. I don't mean to.

—And then you do all the more, Otto.

—I love you, Esme. I've kept telling you that. I love you.

—No you don't, Otto.

—I do. I love you.

—No you don't, Otto. You don't even know who I am.

Esme spoke to him calmly, explaining, as though to a child, an adult truth.

—But I do. And even if I don't, is that my fault?

—You had me all filled in before you met me, Otto. There was no room for me at all.

—Esme, don't be ridiculous.

—It is not ridic-ulous, Otto. It is only true, you do not know who I am.

—But I've . . . you've . . . and I don't even know if you've been faithful to me, he burst out.

—You can only be faithful to people one at a time, Otto.

He sat staring at her face turned half from him. Then he reached up and turned it to him with one hand. Esme looked frightened. —Why are you beautiful? he demanded. Her eyes opened more widely, and she tried to lower her face. —Why are you? he repeated, looking at her. She did pull her chin back, and lower her face, silent. —Because you . . . I look at your face, this flesh

and bone so many inches high and wide, and the nose sticking out and the ...
the punctures of nostrils, and your lips and I ... and those two things that are
eyes, and I ... why should that be beautiful, anyhow. What is it? ... and Otto's
voice was suddenly constricted, —What is beauty ... He cleared his throat,
—that your face should be beautiful? ...

—If it is not beautiful for someone, it does not exist, she said.

—Yes, well ... well ... he muttered, lowering his eyes. —Look, he said when
he raised them again. —Is it my fault if you haven't even let me know who
you are?

—But you never tried, Otto. No part of you ever tried.

—Look, I've done everything I ever could for you, haven't I? I ... I'm sick
and tired of all this foolishness, this ... I apologize for behaving the way I have
with some of your friends but ...

—You are the only one you make unhappy when you behave badly, Otto.
You become the victim of your own observations.

—Do you love me?

—It is not so simple, Otto.

—But you've said you did. She was silent. —I ... damn it, I get all mixed
up with other people, he broke out finally, clenching his free hand over the
hand protruding from the sling. —I ... it's like trying to tie a knot before a
mirror, I know just what to do and then do everything backwards. He sat
looking down. Then suddenly he raised his eyes and said, —Do you ... do I
look like Chaby?

Esme looked up at him. She did not smile, but her face cleared and it was
lightened, as a smile would have lightened it. —Otto, she said. —No. Why
did you ask me that?

—I don't know. Never mind, he said lowering his eyes again. —It's just
that I ... sometimes I feel my face and ... or I feel myself moving or looking
at something in a way that I ... well never mind, never mind that. Never mind
it then.

Suggestion of the smile she had not smiled faded from her face, and quietly
she said, —All right.

—But no, I mean, I don't know. Sometimes I do, sometimes I almost do,
and then I lose it. Like a story I heard once, a friend of mine told me, somebody
I used to know, a story about a forged painting. It was a forged Titian that
somebody had painted over another old painting, when they scraped the
forged Titian away they found some worthless old painting underneath it,
the forger had used it because it was an old canvas. But then there was something under that worthless painting, and they scraped it off and underneath
that they found a Titian, a real Titian that had been there all the time. It was

as though when the forger was working, and he didn't know the original was underneath, I mean he didn't know he knew it, but it knew, I mean something knew. I mean, do you see what I mean? That underneath that the original is there, that the real...thing is there, and on the surface you...if you can only...see what I mean?

She had rested her head back and closed her eyes. He put his arm over her shoulders, and she sat forward.

—Esme...The brief strokes of anxiety and sharp strokes of detail broke the fragments of expression on his face, and he seemed able to catch none of them and fix it congruent upon that image of original honesty which he clutched at so desperately beneath the surface, and the second surface, with each instant more confused in the succession of mocking streaks of parody which he could not control. A moment came when he might have thought, and even understood; but he had not time to embrace it, and it passed. —It's just...damn it, Esme...

—Please don't swear at me, she said dully, her lowered eyes on a pigeon passing before them.

—I'm sorry, but I...Then he laughed with abrupt hoarseness. —Do you remember once when...Look, don't you see? I mean, you can't just live this way, you can't...wait, where are you going?

—I have to go now, Otto.

—But don't, Esme please don't go, I want to talk to you.

—We have talked, she said, looking him in the face; and Otto reached up and drew an alterant stroke on his mustache.

—I want to marry you, Esme. I, you can't go on this way, I mean so insecure, the way you live, and I want to, if I can save you from...

—Save me from! she broke in, mocking. —It is always saving from, she said lowering her eyes, —and never saving for. Everyone fights against things, but people do not fight for things.

Otto stood unsteadily beside her, as though ready to curb her if she turned away. —And I...even if you don't love me now, I...like Saint John of the Cross said, "Where there is no love, put love, and take out love," and I...

She looked up at him, surprised, at that. Then she said, —Is that how he meant it? Before Otto could answer she went on, lowering her eyes again, —No, how did he know what he meant. When people tell a truth they do not understand what they mean, they say it by accident, it goes through them and they do not recognize it until someone accuses them of telling the truth, then they try to recover it as their own and it escapes. The saints were very mean people.

—Yes, I...yes that's it, and I...I want to marry you.

She looked up and smiled at him. —How could I marry you, if I haven't got any stomach?

—Esme, stop it, I really mean it. I mean, you know I'm sincere. I've always been sincere with you.

She put her hand on his. —Otto, she said. —Sincerity becomes the honesty of people who cannot be honest with themselves.

—Esme...

—I have to go away.

—All right then, damn it, go.

She turned and walked away from him. Then he was beside her again.

—Esme...

—What is it, Otto? she asked in a quiet voice, looking at him like a stranger whom she did not know.

—Esme, I ... look, please...

—Goodbye, Otto, she said gently.

—Esme...

She walked away from him easily. It was only eleven o'clock in the morning.

Gazing wistfully into a shop window filled with ladies' lingerie, including a brassière in black lace with black satin hands cupping the mannequin's composition bosom, Anselm stood with a six-year-old girl by the hand. In his other hand, Anselm had Tolstoy's *Kingdom of God*, but it was folded in a magazine with a girl and an umbrella, and nothing else, on the cover, so that all that showed of the small book was the spine. The little girl was looking up the street, in the direction of Stanley's approach, and she pulled her escort in that direction, but he hung back, rubbing the rough inflammations on his chin, and staring into the shop window.

Stanley might have gone on without disturbing that reverie, and so home to work (he was carrying his cardboard practice keyboard and a book), but Max was approaching from the other corner, pausing now to greet Otto, who came from the direction of the park.

Without a word Anselm took Stanley's book from his hand, looked at it and handed it back, muttering something. Then he said abruptly, —I dreamt about you last night. Stanley looked anxious. —I know it was you, it must have been you, Anselm went on, before the others came near. —I was crossing the street in this dream and somebody, somebody I knew well, it must have been you, was coming across the other way with something cradled up in his arms like a baby. It was wrapped in a black shawl, I just took for granted it's a baby, and then he said, then you said, I want you to meet my mother. I look and it was a tiny little old woman, this tiny little old woman was in the shawl . . .

—Yes, but . . . all right, but . . .

—What's the matter? Anselm was looking at him with intense curiosity.

—I just wish you wouldn't . . . Stanley looked one way and the other and down. —It's sort of . . .

—It was, it was strange, it was kind of a nightmare.

Stanley raised his eyes, and they looked at each other intently until Max was upon them. Then Anselm laughed suddenly, pulling the little girl round between them, and spoke as though carrying on the same conversation. —Come on, play us something. Look, Stanley brought his instrument, he said, brandishing his magazine at the practice keyboard which Stanley held defensively in front of him. —He's going to play us something by Vivaldi. Come on, Stanley, for Christ sake don't be so bashful, some of that nice Jesuit baroque music, be-do-be-boo, be-be, boody doody boo . . . did you hear the one about the boy who sat up on the rock? and fitted fiddle strings . . .

—Please . . . Stanley began.

—Here comes Otto, Max said.

—And with every erection he played a selection from Johann Sebastian Bach.

—I have to get home, Stanley said.

—To what, your five-fingered honeymoon?

—To . . . to work, Stanley said, as Anselm turned to look across the street, where a tall man hunched in a green wool shirt gave a nod of recognition slight enough to be disavowed if it were not returned. Max nodded back agreeably. —Who is that? Stanley asked Max.

—Some half-ass critic, Anselm said, —a three time psychoanaloser. He spat into the gutter. —With his fake conversion to the Church. You remember that little tiny girl that used to be around? she came about up to his waist. He used to take her home and dress her in little girl's clothes and rape her.

—Too much Dostoevski, Max said.

—The stupid bastard with his half-ass conversion, Anselm muttered, looking from the child who held his hand, glazedly at the sidewalk. —Christ, he said, rubbing his chin, —that's what kills me, a guy like that . . . as a colored girl, in a plaid skirt which Max identified from behind as the Stuart tartan, passed saying —Reading Proust isn't just reading a *book*, it's an experience and you can't reject an experience . . . to the boy she was with.

—It's the Black Watch, said Anselm, and turning to Stanley, —Why don't you change your luck, Stanley. You . . . God damn it what are you looking at me that way for? . . .

—I...I'm cold, Stanley said lowering his eyes. His jaw was shaking.

—Cold! You...you...What did you do to your face, anyway? What's the matter with your chin, anyway? Anselm burst out suddenly.

—I got mixed up this morning, Stanley said handling his chin, —and I shaved with the toothpaste instead of...

—With the toothpaste! Anselm said, withdrawing with a quick shock of a laugh. —You ought to try a cored apple filled with cold cream, you...

—And last night I had a terrible experience, Stanley went on, agitated, looking up at both of them. —I went into a delicatessen to get a can of soup and some bread, and the man behind the money...I mean behind the cash register was counting up the money and there was some in a paper bag on the counter, and I picked up the wrong bag and almost went out with the money, and when I went back with it and said I was sorry they...they weren't nice about it at all.

A blond boy in tight-fitted dungarees passed saying, —Zheeed...

—Well what the hell would you go back with it for?

—They almost called the police.

—Stanley's Christian spirit will undo us all, said Max, who had been standing back.

—Yeah, we'd make him a saint if it wasn't so God damn expensive, Anselm retorted, looking at Stanley. —Three million lire for a lousy canonization, he muttered.

—No, he won't do. Max stepped back and looked Stanley up and down. —He eats meat. His body would putrefy before they could get the halo on. Poor peasant girls from southern Europe make the best ones, brought up on beans.

—That's true, said Anselm, musing, looking down. Then he looked up querulously at Max.

From the drugstore behind them came a fat youth who looked, at this distance, to have his beard painted on. It dripped to a point at his chin. —If *she* won't pray for me, I don't know who *will*, he was saying animatedly, tossing the words about before him with plump fluttering hands. The boy with him took his arm as they crossed the street.

Max had nodded. —He gave my show a good write-up, Max explained.

—Do you know him? Stanley asked.

—You can't go to a single vernissage without seeing him. He says stupid things with a manner, you know, he has a certain style, so that people remember him as clever.

—People like that make me nervous, Stanley said.

—People like what.

—When they're so . . . queer.

—Queer! Anselm burst out, and continued to watch them cross the street.
—That one, queer? He's not a homosexual, he's a Lesbian. Max laughed; and
Anselm went on, —And that boy poet with him, for Christ sake. Poet! . . .
these limp flabby-assed little . . . boy poets who sit around waiting for somebody
to give them the business in their . . . Jesus Christ, these boy poets and their
common asphodel. Anselm laughed again, a tight constrained laugh looking
across the street at the receding couple. —Their common asphodel, he laughed,
taking the magazine from under Max's arm, and recovering the fit of abstraction he'd sunk into a moment before as he turned the pages.

—I liked your poem, Stanley said to Max. —The one they just published?
That line about Beauty, serenely disdains to destroy us?

—Yes, you . . . almost dropped this, Max interrupted quickly, righting the
practice keyboard which was gripped in Stanley's hands, with a quick glance
at Anselm. But Anselm had apparently not heard. He looked up from the
magazine to nod over his shoulder at the approaching figure, and said,

—Otto? He's the guy who's been laying Esme?

—She's been laying him, said Max.

Otto approached with his head down, as though it were weighed so by the
rampage going on inside, and his features declined to the edges of his face,
the look of one seeking something, or perhaps someone, a person he could
talk this over with, someone who had suffered good intentions put to bad use
by others, and would understand (by which Otto, talking to himself, meant
sympathize); someone sensitive (he meant weak) enough to appreciate, and
experienced (he meant bitter) enough to justify his dilemma. Stanley appeared
in the interior rampage, bowed, understanding, sensitive, experienced: he
raised his eyes and Stanley appeared, talking with (untrustworthy) Max and
(odious) Anselm.

—What does he wear that stupid sling around for? Anselm asked; but
Otto did not look affronted, for as he crossed into hearing they were talking
of Charles. —I saw him this morning, Anselm was saying. —Who was the
old bag with him?

—That was his mother, Max said. —She came from Grand Rapids to get
him out of Bellevue.

Stanley had stepped back looking pained, and as always, about to depart
but unable to do so. Otto and Max exchanged sounds, and Max reached for
the magazine sconced under Otto's slung arm, leaving a newspaper rolled
there. —I just picked that up, Otto said for no apparent reason, as Max opened
Collectors Quarterly.

—You had it this morning when I saw you, Max said, looking up to smile.

—Oh yes I . . . I saw you earlier, didn't I, Otto said discountenanced immediately, and sought a cigarette as though reaching for a shoulder holster.

—Christ! Look at this, will you look at this? Anselm brought out, holding up the magazine he'd taken from Max. It was large, on heavy coated paper, full of pictures, the most popular weekly in the country. The page Anselm exhibited was a fashion photograph. —Will you look at her? Can you imagine putting the boots to that? What man would want to lay her? He rolled the magazine and thrust it under Otto's arm, exchanging it for the newspaper. —Skinny, flat-chested, no hair on her head and no more in her pants than a ten-year-old boy, that's what they're trying to make women look like, these queer . . . what's that smell? He stopped and sniffed. He looked at his own shoes, then at Stanley's. —Did you step in it, Stanley?

—In what? Stanley asked helplessly.

—In what! Christ! . . . you wouldn't say shit if you had a mouthful. Then he glanced up to see that Otto had detached himself from them, and stood scraping his shoe on the curb. He started to say something more, but his eye caught the reproduction in *Collectors Quarterly* which Max held open. It was Velasquez, *Venus and Cupid*. A sound of admiration escaped Anselm. —Jesus, how'd you like to hang that on the wall and play hide-the-baloney every night? The little girl pulled his hand. He yanked her back, almost dropping the book folded in the magazine under his arm, and opened the newspaper to the front-page story. It was a vice probe, and he broke out again, —Look at this. In a city of eight million they find a half-dozen girls peddling their ass and it's the greatest clean-up in history. That kills me. Here, I don't want to look at the God damn thing, he finished, pushing it back under the slung arm as Otto returned, muttering to himself.

—I have to go, Stanley said.

—They did a great thing when they cleaned up the whorehouses out of New York City, a great thing for the high-school girls, Anselm said as the newspaper fell to the sidewalk. —If a nice girl isn't clapped up now before she's sixteen it's her own lousy fault. Then he turned on Otto, who attempted to raise his eyebrows as he straightened up, knocking the dirt from his newspaper. —How'd you like to go in business with me and Stanley? Anselm demanded abruptly.

—It hardly sounds . . .

—Artificial insemination, Anselm went on more loudly. —We bootleg the stuff. We're going to advertise in the movie magazines. Girls! Have a baby by your favorite movie star. I fill the barrels and Stanley peddles it . . .

Stanley had stepped back, looking down at the little girl whom Anselm pulled forward as he waved the nude with the umbrella in the air. —Which end of the business do you want to go in?

Otto muttered something, looking at his newspaper.

—Come on. I've got some nice pictures, Anselm went on more excitedly, —nice bodies with movie stars' heads montaged...

—Come off it, Max interrupted him.

Anselm turned to Max. —What's the matter, he said. The spots on his face had become inflamed by the wind blowing down from the north, and his hair was standing up. —You've never had it look up and spit at you?

—Come off it, for Christ sake. You're crazy.

—Who wouldn't be, in all... this, Anselm said breathlessly, waving the magazine so that the book folded inside it flew out. It slid along the sidewalk and went into the gutter. —Isn't any madness preferable to... all this?

Anselm stood there shaking. Then he saw Stanley going to pick his book from the gutter. —Leave it alone! he cried. —Leave it alone! Leave it alone! Leave it alone!

Stanley stopped and stood back, not before he had seen the title of the book. Anselm stooped before him to pick it up, hawking and spitting into the street as he straightened before Stanley. He wiped the book on his trousers, covering it with his hand as he did so. —For Christ sake, he muttered, getting his breath.

Stanley put his hand out with the palm up, and took a step toward him.

—And stop... stop being so... Anselm took a step back. —Stop being so God damn *h*umble, he said, as the little girl got his hand and drew him back another step. Max had taken Stanley's arm.

—You know God damn well that... that humility is defiance, Anselm went on disjointedly. —And you... that simplicity... simplicity today is sophisticated... that simplicity is the ultimate sophistication today...

They had turned their backs and stepped into the street. Max was guiding Stanley by the arm.

—Hey, what did the chicken say when she laid the square egg? Hey Stanley, I'll dream about you again tonight. Hey Stanley, I'll dream about you again tonight. What did the chicken say when she laid the square egg?... Anselm cried after them.

None of them spoke as they walked together, until Otto, after an apprehensive look over his shoulder, said —God, he is crazy, isn't he. He reached up to stroke his mustache, which was quivering, and asked, —Who's that little girl?

—Don Bildow's daughter, Anselm takes care of her sometimes.

—I wouldn't let a daughter near him if she was five. I wouldn't even if she was one, I wouldn't even trust him as a baby-sitter, you know? I'm not kidding, I wouldn't.

Max glanced up from *Collectors Quarterly* smiling. —That story he told about that fellow, dressing that girl up in child's clothes, that was him.

—Who? Stanley asked quickly, and stopped short.

—Anselm. He's the one who did it, himself.

Stanley came on with his head lowered, staring at the pavement, walking carefully. —Do you think it's true, that he lives on dog food? he asked finally.

Otto laughed unpleasantly. —Where'd you hear that?

—From him, he told me himself. Canned dog food, he said it isn't bad if you have enough catsup.

—Somebody ought to shoot him, Anselm, said Otto, —his crazy yammering about God.

—But have you ever read any of his poems? Stanley asked across Max, who walked between them with the magazine open. —There was one that was a beautiful poem, it was about Averroes, the Arab thinker in the Middle Ages, and should we understand in order to believe, or if we should believe in order to understand...

—Look at this, Max said holding up *Collectors Quarterly* open to a picture of a piece of sculpture by Lipchitz, titled *Mother and Child II.* —Who do you think writes these program notes? Listen, "It was some time after the sculptor began a series of studies of a woman's torso that he suddenly recognized in them a resemblance to the head of a bull. He developed the bull's head further until he achieved..."

—But there's more, Stanley broke in, —when he says...when Anselm says that God has become a sentimental theatrical figure in our literature, that God is a melodramatic device used to throw people in novels into a turmoil...

—Fairly obvious guilt feelings, Max murmured, lowering the magazine to look up as they approached the curb. On either side of him, they walked watching their way carefully; though Max, who scarcely glanced up from the pages, was the only one of them who knew where they were going.

—But it isn't that simple. Don't you wonder why...why everything is negative? Stanley craned round to look up at both of them. —Why just exactly the things that used to be the aspirations of life, those are just the things that have become the tolls? I mean, like...well like girls having babies? They used to be the fruit of love, the thing people prayed for above everything, and now, now they're the price of...Everything's sort of contraceptive, everything wherever you look is against conceiving, until finally you can't conceive any more. Then the time comes when you want something to work for you, the thing you've been denying all your life, and then it won't work...

And Stanley's voice fell behind them, as they crossed the street and he waited for a cab which turned in front of him. He caught up again saying,

—Everything is so transient, everything in America is so temporary... But Max was talking to Otto, who stopped at that moment wide-eyed on the opposite curb to demand,

—Her? I didn't even know you knew her. She needs a doctor? You mean, some man...?

—What do you think I mean, a duck? Max laughed. —That's what I've heard, anyhow, he added, walking on with the magazine open again. —I guess we were just lucky.

—Lucky? Otto repeated, pausing, then hurrying up beside Max. —You mean you...you've slept with her?

—Not for years, Max answered; and with a sidelong glance at Otto, went on in the same casual tone, holding up a two-page reproduction in *Collectors Quarterly*, —Look at this, they describe it as the "algebra of suffering," this Flemish painting. Hugo van der Goes. Otto muttered something, and looked at the picture if only because it was something to take his attention. But the confusion did not leave his face, and the lines round his eyes, gathered in a wince, became fixed so staring at the *Descent from the Cross* until Max turned the page.

—But... he murmured, commencing to raise a hand, commencing to speak (for though he had been seen carrying this magazine, which had cost a dollar, he'd only had it open once, and then, with chance venery, upon the Velasquez).

—This Dierick Bouts is remarkable, isn't it, Max went on of the reproduction on the next page, paraphrasing the caption, —the canniness, the control. Even in black and white, the rigid lines and the constrained attitudes, there is a sort of "algebra of suffering," isn't there.

—That van... the one on the page before, Otto commenced again.

—Van der Goes, there was an overwhelming uncertain passion about it, wasn't there, Max commented, turning a page, not back, but over to a portrait, —Van der Weyden, it's rather saccharine...

—Saccharine...? Stanley stayed his hand, with the first evidence that he was looking at the pictures over the other shoulder.

Max shrugged. —Ingratiating then, he said, lowering the magazine from Stanley's hand, to turn another page. —there's nothing like the perfect control... Max added and, having turned the page whose caption he was paraphrasing, went on, —There is a great sense of lucency and multiple perspective about these early Flemish...

—The separate multiple consciousnesses of the... things in these Flemish primitives, that is really the force and the flaw in these paintings, Otto said, —you might say, he added.

—What do you mean?

—Well, you might say that the thoroughness with which they feel obliged to recreate the atmosphere, and the . . . these painters who aren't long on suggestion, but pile up perfection layer on layer, and the detail, it's . . . it becomes both the force and the flaw . . .

—Where'd you get that? Max asked him; and when he got no immediate answer, looked up. Otto looked down immediately, but his expression did not change: it was fixed, like the dull compulsive tone in his voice which had come to it when he interrupted. —Like a writer who can't help devoting as much care to a moment as to an hour . . . he went on, now slightly more hurriedly, his voice, like the anxiety mounting with slight stabs in his face, straining an automatic effort of memory whose fullness he could not grasp, but only repeat its thrusts. —The perfection . . . Then he silenced, staring down ahead of him.

—There is an illusion of increased powers of eyesight, looking at these, even in reproduction. They're almost perfect, Max commented, flicking over pages. He glanced at Otto's averted profile, and turned to Stanley. —Isn't there, Stanley?

—Yes, but, Stanley began, faltering, —these men, these painters who were creating right out of themselves, and all of this, all this harmony with everything around them, with all the things, all the spiritual things around them that supported them, that they knew would be there tomorrow, and, in the Guild, why in the Guild it was the opinion of your fellow artists that mattered, not competition before a lot of people who didn't know anything but the price. The Guild even took care of your burial, he added plaintively.

Max laughed, his brief cordial mockery. —I'll bury you myself, Stanley. You can go home and make up all the music you want to now.

—But it isn't making it up, inventing music, it's like . . . remembering, and like, well van Gogh says about painting, when he would take a drawing of Delacroix as a subject and improvise with colors, not as himself, he says, but searching for memories of their pictures, the "vague consonance of colors," the memory that was himself, his own interpretation.

They stopped together at another curb. A store loudspeaker poured out upon them a vacuous tenor straining, —I'm dreaming of a white Christmas . . . with insipid mourning hope. And Stanley, escaping, abandoning his companions to that lugubrious assault, moved from the curb as though called forth by Cherubini: trumpets and the clash of brass: the horn sounded, and he leaped away from the immense and silent automobile guided by a brittle dame hung like some florid gothic tracery behind the steering wheel, her chin jutting just above it, sweeping round from Washington Square.

Max picked up the practice keyboard from the street and brought it up to him on the curb opposite, where he stood quivering. —What happened? he asked. —That moving Christmas music?

—Well it isn't . . . they have no right to . . . Stanley tried to speak, out of breath, accepting the cardboard keyboard like a delicate instrument.

—What do you want on Sixth Avenue, *The Messiah*?

—They have no right to . . . cheapen . . .

—Ask them to play, *Yes We Have No Bananas*, Max said, smiling. —That's from *The Messiah*, and it's more their line.

—What do you mean? Stanley was trying to wipe the tire marks from the length of the white keys.

—I mean *Yes We Have No Bananas* was lifted right out of Handel's *Messiah*. Come on, Max said taking his arm, and looking round for Otto. —What's the matter with both of you today?

—You don't have to . . . tell me things like that, Stanley said, pulling away.

A man standing with his back to a shop window said, —It won't snow, it's too warm to snow. And Otto, looking where the man was looking, over the buildings at the northern sky, realized that he was not shivering with cold, but simply shivering. And he heard Max say,

—You want everybody to be like you, that's your trouble Stanley.

—I want everyone to be like I want to be, Stanley answered.

Otto met Stanley's eyes. And though the sky was dull, and there was no such color in sight, they appeared green, brilliant, burning into green in that prolonged moment as Otto stood bound and apparently unable to mount the curb between them. But it was only a moment, the passage of a shadow, and Max's voice, breaking between them, brought Otto up.

—You might say that the man who wrote *Yes We Have No Bananas* was searching for memories? a vague consonance of sounds? . . . Max began good-humoredly. Then looking at Otto he said, —What's the matter, you look all disjointed.

—I don't know, but . . . yes, disjointed, Otto said mounting the curb, speaking unevenly as he fell in beside them. —Like . . . do you know what I feel like? Like when a clay reproduction is made of an original statue, and then they take the copy and cut it behind the head with fine wire, and behind the arms and the legs, and those are all moved and it's cast again.

—Why? Where'd you hear that?

—To be sold as part of a series, a series of the original, a series that never existed, I . . . I read about it in a book a friend of mine had, a friend a long time ago, he . . . listen . . . Otto groped.

As though spurred by his faltering confusion, Max interrupted, —I knew there was something I meant to tell you. That story you sent to Edna, for a magazine that publisher she works for owns, they're bringing out my book you know.

—What about the story, I sent it in for some guy I met at your party.

—She thinks you wrote it, Max told him. —That you wrote it and sent it under another name.

—She thinks *I* wrote it? But why would I have written it? I didn't even read it, I . . . why would I do a thing like that.

—I guess she thought you were playing it safe.

—But she . . . but God damn it . . . Otto brandished the sling.

—She says you used to be clever when you were in college, writing, but you sort of faded out, Max went on agreeably. —She says the reason you were clever was because you didn't know how to be honest.

—Well the only reason she's honest is because she's too God damn dumb to be clever, I mean if she was honest, but she . . . why the hell should she go around saying a thing like that about me? for no reason?

—No reason? Max repeated, and put a hand on Otto's shoulder. —Nobody resents you more than somebody who's loved you.

Otto twisted away from him, but unsteadily as though trying to retain the hand on his shoulder but turn his face to hide the trembling lip. —Why do I . . . why do people have to be so . . . so . . . he mumbled brokenly as detailed fragments of expressions broke over his face one after another until he grabbed with a whole hand round the eyes and drew the hand down, as though to wipe away these abrupt strokes on the surface which mocked the clear image of his anger beneath. Then he brought out a cigarette, and caught both lips round it.

—Forget it, Max said, and patting his shoulder before he removed his hand went on as cordially, —Say, I've meant to tell you again how much I liked your play, Otto . . . Otto mumbled something without looking up. —Because when other people have said they didn't like it, I've told them . . .

—You've told them what! Otto broke out. He looked up to see Max smiling at him.

—Don't be so touchy, Max said to him.

—It's just . . . all this . . . damned . . . Otto hunched again, looking down before him. —And when people say I stole it, that I plagiarized.

—Somebody, I can't think, who was it, Max appeared sympathetically thoughtful, —said they thought you'd lifted parts of *The Sound and the Fury*.

—The what?

—Faulkner's novel, *The Sound and the Fury*, that you'd plagiarized . . .

—I've never even read it, I've never read *The Sound and the Fury* damn it, so how the hell . . . Otto looked over to see Stanley look troubled and start to speak. —I mean, damn it . . .

—What's the difference? Max laughed. —I noticed a couple of little things you'd picked up, but what's the difference.

—What do you mean, what little things?

—Little things, lines here and there. That line of Ben Shahn's, "You cannot invent the shape of a stone" for instance.

—But . . . who the hell is Ben Shahn? That line, a friend of mine, a long time ago, somebody I used to know, said . . .

—What's the difference. Max smiled. —As Stevenson says, we all live by selling something. He raised a hand to Otto's shoulder again. —What's the difference. The money? You have a real complex about money don't you Otto, a real castration complex without it.

—Yes, the money, Otto muttered, —but, damn it . . .

—It doesn't have to be money, just money, Stanley broke in, —if he . . . if it's his work, if it's his own, and he wants . . .

—His own! Max repeated, and his laugh this time was sharper, more unkind, edged with contempt. —Look, he said to Otto, —that magazine of mine you've got there, open it. Max made no gesture of surrendering *Collectors Quarterly*, and taking the other magazine himself. —Just open it to . . . there, here it is, this thing on Sherlock Holmes, "the first authorized Sherlock Holmes story to appear" since Arthur Conan Doyle died. See? Authorized. It "was written after exhaustive study of Sir Arthur's literary methods . . ." he read, as Otto held the magazine before them. —See? these two men who wrote it, "They studied such minutiae as Doyle's sentence rhythms, his use of the comma, the number of words in the average Holmes sentence . . . The authors have felt no temptation to vary the pattern which Doyle usually observed . . . Special pains have been taken to reproduce certain Doylean literary tricks . . ."

—But what do you mean? Otto asked him.

—What's the difference? Max asked in return, bringing *Collectors Quarterly* up. —Authorized paintings by Dierick Bouts? van der Goes? Who authorizes them? Somebody says, One wishes there were more stories by Conan Doyle, somebody else wishes there were more paintings by Hugo van der Goes. So, after a careful study of the early Flemish painter's technique . . . such minutiae as his brush-stroke rhythms, his use of perspective, the number of figures in the average van der Goes canvas . . . What's the difference? You fake a Dürer by taking the face from one and turning it around, the beard from another, the hat from another, you've got a Dürer, haven't you?

—But only on the surface, Stanley said.

—On the surface! How much deeper do people go? the people who buy them?

—But this, this isn't a . . . forgery, Otto said holding out the large picture magazine. —It's no secret, they tell you right here . . .

—That's just what I mean, Max said impatiently. —What's the difference now? In our times? He laughed again, and folded *Collectors Quarterly* under his arm. —As long as it's "authorized." Isn't that right, Stanley?

Stanley answered immediately, —No.

—No? He studied Stanley's face with mock interest and shock. —Is there something diabolic about bringing Sherlock Holmes back to life?

—The devil is the father of false art, Stanley said quietly. He was walking carefully on the pavement along the edge, his face expressing a concentration which Otto's echoed, but a vague echo, as Otto walked staring at the pavement, not listening to them.

—Stanley believes in sin, don't you, Stanley? Max persisted.

—If we believe that love is weakness? Stanley brought out, —and people resent it, because they think it's an admission of weakness, and they draw away from it . . . and that's why you kill the thing you love, because it's your weakness personified. If you kill it, you kill your weakness before it kills you.

—I said sin, Max cajoled him.

—But, was there love? before sin, a sense of sin, made it possible? Stanley said in the same low tone, without looking up. —Before there was sin, to be suffered and forgiven?

—Love! You in love? Max laughed.

—Art is the work of love.

—Art is a work of necessity, Max said.

—Was it a good story? Otto asked finally.

—The Sherlock Holmes thing? It was lousy.

—No I mean, I mean, the one that I . . . that was sent up to . . . her.

—It was lousy too, Max answered.

—But isn't there a moment . . . Stanley went on, —a moment when love and necessity become the same thing?

They reached an open square where the sky was almost black, looking north, as most people were doing. Shops were lighted, and the lighted windows of the buildings stood out against the sky, holding it off, and themselves to earth.

—Where are we going, anyhow? Otto asked.

—I'm going right up here, Max said, nodding ahead. Then, noticing Stanley's careful walk again, he said, —Step on a crack, Break your mother's back . . .

and Stanley stopped. —Come on, Max laughed, and when Stanley came on, now obviously avoiding cracks in the pavement, Max said to him, —I can believe you'd really believe that, Stanley. What an unspotted soul for the devil to bid for. What do you think he'd give me, if I sold you to him?

—You couldn't, Stanley said.

—All right, we'll sell Otto. You wouldn't mind, would you Otto?

—Christ no, not at this point.

—You couldn't, Stanley said again.

—Well Faust did, damn it, Otto broke out morosely, —Faust sold his soul to the devil.

—No. That's a fallacy, Stanley said looking round at him soberly. —That evil can take entire possession of the soul like that. Evil is self-limited.

—Damn it, it was his soul, Otto said defiantly, —and he sold it to the devil.

—No. It was not his to dispose of. We belong to our souls, not our souls to us.

—Ontological dialectics, said Max, as they approached a subway entrance.

Otto stood unsteadily, as though afloat, away from them, as Max clapped Stanley jovially on the shoulder and said, —Stanley's fired by a divine spark. The words seemed to come from the great distance of sounds over water before a storm. He turned to Otto without breaking his smile. —But you and me . . . ?

Otto stood there, his arm shivering in the sling, the wind blowing his hair up from behind. —Yes, he said, raising his eyebrows, —sometimes it's difficult . . . he curled his lip slightly against its tendency to tremble, —it's difficult to shed our human nature. Then he turned away quickly and stepped back to the curb, where he stood with his back to them, scraping the edge of his shoe. He heard Max laugh, and call to him, —A little always sticks . . . And when he turned, Max was disappearing into the pit of the subway. There was only Stanley, frail against the dark sky.

—What's the matter? Stanley asked him as he approached slowly.

—There was something . . . Otto said, looking him in the face again, in the eyes, which were dull with the sky beyond. —Something . . .

—What? . . . Stanley looked at him anxiously.

—I don't know, earlier, that moment . . . Otto said, looking more confused. —For a moment, a feeling that you . . . that you and I . . . It was as though you were someone who had been . . . He faltered, broke off, and looked up, recovering. —Damn it. He's gone, Max?

—Yes, he's gone, down there, Stanley pointed.

—And this damned thing, he left me this and took *Collectors Quarterly*, it cost a dollar.

—Do you want it back? Stanley commenced helpfully. —If I see him...

—That painting, Otto murmured, looking down again. He rubbed his free hand over his face. —The Christ in that painting, I wanted to look at it, I wanted to look at it again, there was something...familiar...he went on vaguely, mumbling, —and the Virgin...

After a pause, Stanley said, —But there should be, Christ...

—Not that, not that, Otto waved him back, and stood gripping his temples in an open hand. Then he dropped his hand and shook his head. —Never mind, he said. Looking at Stanley, he tried a strained smile. —The divine spark...he muttered, at the anxious face being weighed toward him by the uneven mustache. —And what are you going to do with it, anyhow? he brought out in sudden derision.

—But that, Stanley said, coming a step nearer him, —that is what undoes us all. He stood before Otto looking into Otto's eyes, waiting; but saw them narrow.

—I hate him, Otto said, changing again as abruptly.

—Who?

—Him. Max.

—But, why?

—Yes...because he'll survive.

Every street she crossed, the black sky showed to her right, as though these were tunnels through to the "chilly hell" of the poet's *Elegy on the Thousand Children*, through to Boreas, and beyond the north wind. And so every time she stepped from the curb, going west, she tried not to look; and always had looked before she stepped up on the curb ahead.

As she came nearer the river, the pavement and the walks were wet with the light snow which had commenced since she started. She passed an empty baby carriage, and stopped, a step beyond it, to look back and make sure it was empty. Then she looked up and smiled at the woman who had been shaking a mop from the window above, and that woman only stared at her until she went on; and even then looked up, and a minute later stopped shaking the mop again, seeing her pause down the block and kneel on the wet walk to help a child with an entangled mitten-string, kneeling there, the narrow eyes of the woman in the window had it, a moment too long.

On a trestle at the far end of the street an engine smashed a coupling closed with a shattering sound which was gone immediately, leaving a wail from the river beyond suspended on the particles of silt in the air, to be exhausted slowly as they were borne to earth by the scales of snow shed from above.

Where a crate lay broken on the sidewalk she turned in at the doorway in this last block of Horatio Street. She sought the bell with no name and then, leaning against the door it came open before her finger found the bell, and his door was just inside. In front of it stood a wastebasket full: some bottles and tubes, electric-light bulbs, and that door was not tight closed.

—Asleep? she whispered, entering. And she closed the door behind her silently, a hand on the knob and her back against it, slowly, as she looked round. Then she coughed, and covered her mouth quickly, for the room was full of a bitter cluster of smells from the smoldering pile in the fireplace. In fact some of it had burned on the hearth and lay smoking spilled out on the floor, and she hurried over and kicked the burning pieces back up on the bricks seeing, as she did so, the blackened edges of photographs, details of brushwork highly enlarged.

There were torn bits of paper, torn pieces of canvas and splinters of wood, a few books, some eggshells, a small squirrel-hair brush, strewn among the bright pigmented spots on the floor. Beside the low bed, where she went and sat on the edge, was a broken glass, a box of Dutch cigars unopened, a coconut, and a leather box filled with cuff links, collar buttons, paper clips, two pen-knives, another knife, bladeless, and a knifeless blade, buttons, pen points, studs, a number of keys, some brass wood-screws, a single pearl earring, and prominently, two large archaically studded hoops of gold. She leant down and wiped her wet cheeks with the end of a blanket that trailed from the welter on the floor. Then she straightened, on the very edge of the bed, and turned putting a hand forth, gently. —You . . . she whispered.

She sat like that a minute more, seeming not to breathe, then she whispered again, —You . . . but more tartly, —if you keep your eyes closed, then where are you now without me?

The bare bulb glared on her standing up, and she said, —It is very warm in here, taking two, and three, and four steps, taking off her coat. She laid it on a high stool and looked round her again, stood singly beneath the bare bulb and casting no shadow until she turned and walked toward the only whole canvas in the room, turned face-to-wall, where her shadow fell on it and on a single plane expanded over the rough and soiled back of it. She got hold of the frame and turned it from the wall.

—Do you reproach me? she said, after a time of looking at it though their eyes did not meet, and then she extended her hand and traced its features. Then she whispered something and abruptly turned her back.

Frank, Bishop of Zanzibar, lay on the floor at her foot; and she kicked the book away. Then she walked over to where the hinged mirrors stood against another wall, turned them open and closed them again quickly.

—You ... she said again looking back to the bed, for she'd turned quickly.

There on the floor at her feet was a drawing, it was a meticulous self-portrait, and she took a step before she saw it, saw it was not a detail of brushwork that is, and leaned down to pick it up. —You, she said, —all upside-down. Then she righted it and repeated, —all upside-down.

She stood there staring somewhere between the bed and the drawing as though a hand were on her; and then turned and pulled the mirrors again. She cocked one leaf open with the toe of her right foot, holding the picture up with effort as though it were a great weight, and looked at the prompt emergences, settling her eyes on the even image, the same that she held in her hands; then raised her eyes to the second image of her own face, and let the leaf go closed with a clap, so that a part of it broke out and fell to the floor separating as soon as it sounded, to reflect the glare of the bulb in the ceiling back, in shapes of breakage, to the ceiling.

The room was filled with the odor of destruction: as though there might arise on the smoke a difference, when a storehouse of chemicals burned: here in the squat fireplace were chemicals, some of them inorganic, and the organic transmutations suffering oxidation with the immediacy of a chain reaction on the page of a chemistry text; but where, in this consummation, the law of the conservation of energy? Could brush strokes make the difference, then? Science in magnitude, biology and chemistry as triumphantly articulate as subordinates are always, offer no choice but abjure it in frantic effort to perfect a system without alternatives, the very fact of their science based on measure-ment; and measurement, designed to predicate finalities, refusing the truth which shelters in possibility: in the weight of the smell of the smoke there was more than the death of the body, the cellular sucking construction, hunger of tissues unconscious of any end but identical reproduction. But if strokes of creation fed the flames, strokes in whose every instant possibility had been explored for the finality which is perfection, torn apart in the attempt to free it into the delineation of that baffled enclosure of its own medium, here were brush strokes whose future had been dictated by the thwarting enclosure of the past, a past whose future was struck dying with every instant of the de-lineation of its everlasting life.

—You, she whispered, back seated on the edge of the bed, and then kick-ing out, —Go away egg... in a mocking voice as the coconut rolled away from her foot. She raised her eyes across the room again to the picture she'd turned from the wall; and faint under a single thin coat the Byzantine earrings showed through. —But...

—with your eyes closed, she whispered, turning back to the bed there. —I dream and wake up. The love I have from others is not love of me, but where they try to find themselves, loving me. I dream and I wake up, and then at that moment you are somewhere being real to other people; and they are a part of your reality; and I am not...But you are the only person I am real with...

She sat staring down.

—If you are the only person I am real with...

Her eyes strayed; and suddenly she had the leather box, spilling everything but the archaic hoops of gold which she held in a hand and was up, raising and dropping her shadow across the room in an instant as she crossed and went into the bathroom.

When she came out, wearing the Byzantine earrings, there was blood on them and on her shoulders, running down in singular unpaired lines over her bared breasts, breaking where they broke away from her, mocking their slightness by assailing it, respecting their fullness by parting above the two swollen stains whose color they ridiculed in passing, down, to delineate the unbroken rising below along the sharply broken lines that her walking so quickly forced with each step, to come apart and disappear where that rising fell away in the white hollow of her thighs.

—Then with your eyes closed, she whispered, pulling a blanket from the welter of blankets over her.

The fire had died under the steady censure of the electric glare, and its emanations contended bitterly until, one by one, their poisonous violence was exhausted by such severe emergency, and left only lavender to rise and spread in a diffusion which penetrated without edge, which cut without sharpness, impetuous without haste, filling without distending as a color deepens in saturation and exalts in brilliance at once.

—Oh yes...she whispered fiercely, —Oh yes, oh yes, oh yes...

As the fire died even the lavender became indistinct, and lay in with the smell of Venice turpentine, and stand oil, burnt photographic prints, burnt canvas and tortured gesso until, when she woke, there was neither triumph nor dissension in the air she breathed, standing, looking round her, back to the bed suddenly, and round her again.

She put on her coat, and sat on the stool where she'd got it from. She sat there for some time, almost under the light, so that her shadow lay steady and small over an irregular blow of verdigris on the floor, confining its elation within the clear and casual bounds of her retreat.

—Why did you not write to me? she said, still unmoving, not even to look toward the bed.

Then the green she had retired leaped out under the light as she stood, and began searching everywhere, pushing aside *Kinder- und Hausmärchen* with her foot, picking up a piece of paper, kicking Thoreau and a crumpled twenty-dollar bill, stepping on an eggshell, stooping again in a distracted pause to pick up an unopened container of indigo, kicking, again, *Frank, Bishop of Zanzibar*, and the broken glass, finding more paper, slipping, and almost falling in a pool of stand oil, picking up, with the same distracted pause, an unopened container of rose madder, and another piece of paper which she threw down because it was smeared on one side with blue paint, and on the other had written in large characters, *semper aliquid haeret*, and going on so until she had a number of pieces of paper in her hand, which she laid out on a drawing board and commenced to write with a broken penholder, and a point she got from the leather box.

—Here is the letter, she said sitting over it, and turning to look across the room. —Because you must not close your eyes now because you cannot, she said. —Because now you are alone, she said. Still looking over there she put down the broken penholder and picked up the rose madder, running her thumbnail to open it. —Because you cannot, she said, as the rose madder spilled into her hand, and she looked down at it, and shivered in the open coat.

Then she began to write. She wrote there for some time; and when she broke, between words, or in the middle of words, seldom between sentences or paragraphs, she would look over across the room, all the while, with the fingers of her left hand, applying the coarse rose madder to her lips, and the indigo around her eyes. She wrote for some time, and before she was done the rose madder was half gone, and the indigo had caked wetly round her eyes.

When the letter was finished she laid it in the middle of the floor, and looking round for something to weigh it down, found the coconut and stationed it there. Then going to the door she closed her coat, twice, each time after stooping and straightening from the floor, and went out. The crumpled twenty-dollar bill, which had stuck to her shoe with the stand oil she'd stepped in, came off before she reached the street.

Here is the letter she wrote, and left there.

You:

The demands of painting have the most astonishing consequences   In my life at this
    moment you are one of them

Perspective since De Chirico manipulated it plastically; resolved it in his painting
    paradigms, now exists in the mind; a nostalgia; a co-relative isolation; a plenary;
    a playa, where, one must, to see the water, go immediately after the rain, and to
    see the broad level ground, must visit before. Painting is exquisite as the punish-
    ment for the thinker: denied the thoughts of his grave-diggers, his own death-face

and his final curiosity, a vision of his bones—the skeleton: of which he was always aware, moment by moment emerging to that static release he, the thinker, cannot joyfully sit, a separated thing, shaking his bones Perhaps a heart petrified, or a brain, an eye, an unborn child, would roll deliciously inside it, to rattle there, the way a dead man rattles in the sea nor find a solution to deny all this, a solving, nor a solvent, to disappear those bones, make it an improbability the other's joy, nor to deny the priceless departure into death.

Since paintings are in the service of my desires, I can disdain no ruse to accomplish them.

To paint to intensify, to remember but what could I remember here, in this place, where, in truth, I have never been before? a street of accidents all designed to happen to me?

Chroniclers, replacing instinct, become us more and more to lose our sensibilities, but, how can I refuse this slan-derous name when I shall paint, and then insist upon it?

It would doubtlessly, be kinder not to insist so, or investigate less directly, more discreetly: ask my mother, not my brain; "what sort of little girl I was?" and lover: "what woman I became" in order to define the strange significance of the avowal of these episodes of paint, like circumstance divorced from motivation

This, though, would place it, in sum, upon another level of being, every delusion of my energetic brain engages itself alone, then, in this enterprise, this demonstration of itself.

The mere coincident of materials at one's disposal cannot make a painting, nor, even a journey where nothing had been selected, nor lost by traveling, a journey, indeed, that might as well never had been taken.

To paint without means, desire or justification—a dubious use, habit sloughed away from reason or, in an indecisive moment, "wasn't it good of it to rain?" or "who was it, came to see me at three in the afternoon?"

A law-maker, unable to formulate laws, can be a painter, or a land, where, laws when broken, punish, not the offender, but the law-makers, can produce painters. A painter in any other place must struggle to be what he is.

Rooted within us, basic laws, forgotten gladly, as an undesirable appointment made under embarrassing pressures, are a difficult work to find. The painter, speaking without tongue, is quite absurdly mad in his attempt to do so, yet he is inescapably bound toward this.

To recognize, not to *establish* but to *intervene*. A remarkable illusion?

Painting, a sign whose reality is actually, I, never to be abandoned, a painting *is* myself, ever attentive to me, mimicking what I never changed, modified, or compromised. Whether I, myself, am object or image, they at once, are both, real or fancied, they are both, concrete or abstract, they are both, exactly and in proportion to this disproportionate I, being knowingly or unknowingly neither one nor the other, yet to be capable of creating it, welded as one, perhaps not even welded but actually from the beginning one, am also both and what I must, without changing, modifying, or compromising, be.

The painter concerned for his mortal safety, indifferent because he fears to scrutinize, paradoxically sacrifices that very safety, for he will not be allowed to escape painting.

He will make paintings or they will revolt and make him, unhappy being in the grasp of them. He compulsively must, then, live them cold as they are, static, perversely with warmth and movement he cannot know but feel painfully, a bird with broken eggs inside.

On the other hand, a no-painter—resourceful as he may be, cannot paint. He cannot say, well, "I did not get the job but I shall say I got it anyhow"—by this distortion of fact he deludes, not himself, but other persons, until, that moment arrives to receive the reimbursement. With nothing of value to show the fact will disappear. There is no fact but value.

The painter knows, sadly enough, that experience does not suffice unto itself, has no proportion, dimension, perspective, mournfully he eats his life but is not allowed to digest it, this being reserved for others, not knowing, but who must somehow, at any sacrifice be made to know, then punished for the sight of this knowledge, by aiding it on its journey from brain to brain.

It does not seem unreasonable that we invent colors, lines, shapes, capable of being, representative of existence, therefore it is not unreasonable that they, in turn, later, invent us, our ideas, directions, motivations, with great audacity, since we, ourselves having them upon our walls. What rude guests they prove to be, indeed: although paintings differ from life by energy a painter can never be a substitute for his paintings, so complete so independent as reality are they. Imagine the pleasure they enjoy at this.

They by conversion into an idea of the person, do, instantaneously destroy him. A tragic gesture that actually leads to tragedy but diabolically exists only in an absence of tragedy, nevertheless procreating it, however, they are unreasonably enough, insufficient, because they are not made of ideas, they are made of paint, all else is really us.

Paintings are metaphors for reality, but instead of being an aid to realization obscure the reality which is far more profound. The only way to circumvent painting is by *absolute* death.

——Close your eyes for the next sixty seconds and try to walk around the room . . .

The man behind the bar reached up and turned it off.

—I got a friend he's got a glass eye with the American flag on it, said the man on the outside.

The man behind the bar poured whisky until it ran over his fingers. —This'll put lead in your pencil. He pushed it in a wet trail across the bar. —Now if you got somebody to write to you're all set.

—Here's Rose.

At the far end of the bar Otto stepped aside for the dumpy woman who came in the door. Her nose was red, so were her eyes.

—What's the matter, Rose? Cold enough for you?

Otto joined the cold coin on the bar with a warm one from his pocket, signaled with his empty beer glass, and put it back down beside the newspaper, folded there on the bar across one of the girls in the vice probe, whose dark glasses he had been staring at.

To his left, the mirror and the window conjoined at such an angle that vehicles on the street outside appeared to come into one another head-on. A bus telescoped and disappeared. He withdrew his bloodshot eyes and turned them straight before him; but he did not see his face for the sign FRANKS AND KRAUT *20¢* was pasted on the mirror just above his collar. Below, where his hands met sensitively on the empty beer glass, twitching somewhat, touching at the fingertips, frankfurters turned on hot rollers, slowly, receding and coming forward, passing each other forward and back with dull nudges like fat jointless fingers in meditation. He withdrew his left hand back into the loose sling.

—Here, pussy pussy pussy, said the dumpy woman.

—We got three of them.

—I lost mine, said the dumpy woman. —I raised him from this big. He had blood in his kidney.

—Human beings has to go too.

—I lost two husbands that way. Overnight.

Otto signaled with his empty glass. Then a tall blonde, in a fur cape, wearing dark glasses, walked to meet herself in the glass. Otto turned and looked out the window. He could not see her. He looked in the mirrored pillar behind him, and saw her coat-sleeve disappear. He looked before him, and saw her merge into herself. He looked out of the window again, and saw a man in a Santa Claus suit.

—Could I have a beer here? he said. He waited. Then he put down his empty glass and walked toward the back, taking out his wallet.

In the telephone booth a moment later he sat with the receiver to his ear, listening to a clock ticking in the Sun Style Film office. Finally a voice came through.

—Hello? Otto said, and named the man and himself in introductory greeting. —I'm sorry I've been so long calling you, but I . . . Yes, but . . . What? No, about Central America. You remember, I . . . When can we get together for a . . . No, it was Peru and northern Bolivia, you remember . . . Yes, I . . . What? But I . . . you . . . Well that bastard, he repeated to himself, leaning back against the wall of the booth. —"We have nothing to discuss." Well that bastard. That bastard. Then the sling gave way.

He came out with his wrist pressed against his wallet. He had forty-one dollars. —And why I gave a five-dollar bill to that Harlem nigger yesterday, to keep an eye out for that damn dispatch case. Damn it. That black bastard too.

The dumpy woman was drinking a manhattan. —I can feel it down to my toes, she said. Her stockings sagged over her broken shoe backs.

—Who you saving the cherry for, Rose?

The man behind the bar turned the radio on again, and left it while it warmed to strains of Mozart. Otto's glass was still empty, but he stood there as though unable to call and command, staring at the man's striped necktie, the signal of another final club which had not invited him to join.

—What's the matter, Rose? You blushing?

Otto waited a moment longer. Mozart continued, rising and gathering to exquisite pauses: and each of these apertures was obligingly filled by a saxophone. Otto picked up the two cold coins, and left the newspaper on the bar. Mozart measured a subtle withdrawal; and a voice from the saxophone world heralded,

——Here's an oldie, friends, Rudy Vallee singing, *Love Made a Gypsy Out of Me.*

—Hey Jack, you want your newspaper? the man behind the bar called after him.

—Never mind, Otto answered over his shoulder. —It's yesterday's.

The tropic breeze ruffled Otto's linen, boarding that banana boat, then standing on deck gazing out over the Caribbean, a whisky-soda in his free left hand, skin warm with memory of the sun: so he stood, serene and unapproachable, in the memory of the unsteady figure appearing now (wearing a new green muffler which enhanced the yellowness of his skin), an old friend whom Otto only now fully appreciated, and would like to see again. He passed the steamed windows lowering a handkerchief, where two black rings witnessed what desperate barriers are the fine hairs of the nostrils, and pulling open the door of the Viareggio, interrupted this with his entrance:

—Philogyny? I thought you said phylogeny.

—I said, misogyny recapitulates philogyny.

—Misogamy...?

—Never mind.

—What's the name of this book you're writing?

—Baedeker's *Babel*.

Noting only the striped tie on the taller of these two, Otto brought the handkerchief up again, and got by them.

—And you say you've become a misologist?

—Whisky-soda, Otto ordered at the bar, slurring his tone in casual rudeness as he imagined one used to command.

—Where's the head in this place? Someone bumped him. —Right through that door, it's called Tiffany's here.

—But I ordered whisky-and-soda.

—You said whisky sour. Sixty-five cents.

Max's back was turned to him at a near table, where a battered copy of *Collectors Quarterly* lay open to *Mother and Child II*, under the elbow of a man hunched in a green wool shirt who was saying to Max, —You had some work at the New School, well look. Would I have to prepare my lectures? or could I just bullshit. Otto took a step toward the table. He was blocked by a haggardly alert face, speaking to someone behind him, —She would have drownded herself if she could have found something to drownd herself in. And the response over Otto's shoulder, —She's been way out for a long time, man. You can't fool with horse without getting hooked.

—That magazine, Otto said to a girl standing behind the table, —do you know what happened...where it...

—A bear chewed it.

—What? I mean that...

—Oh I thought you meant this *Vogue*. She held up a tattered copy of *Vogue*. —A bear chewed this in Yellowstone Park, the craziest bear... She turned her back and went on with her conversation, —Oh very very very very *very* much...

—Hello. Can you buy me a beer?

—Hello Hannah, of course, I'd be glad to. Otto ordered it, handed her the dripping glass, and said, —Really, I've just had the most maddening...

—Thanks, said Hannah, and returned to the tall colored boy she'd been talking to, and shared her glass with him in the corner. At Otto's side a blond boy in dungarees said, —I tell you I felt just for all the world like Archimedes in his crwazy bathtub...But how could I? I tell you I was *stuck*. And at the near table, a green wool elbow knocked a glass of beer over *Mother and Child II*.

Otto winced, saw Stanley seated staring at a cup of coffee, started to approach, saw it was Anselm seated with him staring at nothing, and stopped.

The haggard boy came up to their table and dropped into a chair with neither invitation nor greeting.

—You know how I made her the first time I made her? Anselm went on.
—I described a wet dream to her, one I'd had about her, she listened as though it had really happened, and then before she knew it I was in again. He laughed, but sounded weary, not really interested in what he was talking about, and sat drumming blunt nail-bitten finger-ends on the table.

—She was probably high then, the haggard boy commented dully.

—You shouldn't ... Stanley commenced.

—What are you pretending you're worried about her now for? Christ, she didn't make it, did she?

—She could never make anything real, man. The gas was on all right, but there was air coming in all over the place.

—Just the same, Stanley appealed, —if her intention ...

—Her intention! what's that to you? Christ, wouldst thou be a breeder of sinners? She ought to get her ass into a nunnery.

Stanley said nothing. He lowered his eyes, sipped his coffee, and opened a newspaper.

—What does Saint Jerome say about women? Anselm persisted. —She's the gate of Hell. "A foe to friendship, an inescapable punishment, a necessary evil," says Chrysostom ... And he broke off, watching Otto's approach without recognition.

Otto got round the two young men whom he had interrupted with his entrance. —I'm doing for writing what Bruckner did for music, said one. —So what did Bruckner do for music? —Well put it this way, I'm doing *in* writing ...

—Freud! ... came borne in a pleasing Boston-bred voice from a tall girl.
—Hahaha ... Freud my ahss.

—You know what the trouble is, like Pascal says, all the malheurs in this world come from a man's inability to sit alone in a small room, said the taller of them. —Can I buy you a drink? He was wearing a tie from the first crossing of the *Queen Elizabeth*.

—But why ... ? why? Stanley repeated, plaintive and incredulous. —Why would Max say a thing like that? He'd know it's not true, that Hannah and I were ... sleeping together ... ? He looked up and included Otto in his appeal. Anselm was laughing. He shrugged.

—I am one to tell you, my lord, Stanley and a palindrome are making the beast with two backs, he said, and took Stanley's newspaper.

—But why do they ... people have to ... say such things?

—People? You sound like it's the first time in history somebody got laid, Anselm said, his tone musing and vague. —Das Unbeschreibliche, hier wird's getan... He did not look up, from the paper, whose pages he turned without apparent pauses to read. —Das ewig-Weibliche, for Christ sake, he mumbled.

Otto stood unable to turn away, bound by the hurt accusal in Stanley's eyes, which lowered uncertainly back to the table.

—The last time I saw her, the haggard boy said, —she had to have somebody around her all the time, so she could ask if she'd really done something or gone somewheres. She looked like she was going to flip then.

Anselm tore something out of the paper and pushed it across the table. —This ought to cheer you up, Stanley, he said. —The bell tower at Saint Mark's is ready to flip too.

—She told me once the reason her eyes bug out like that is some doctor gave her henbane, did you know that? She said she can even see the stars in the daytime. If she'd really wanted to make it she would have sliced her wrists like Charles...

—For Christ sake! will you... stop talking about it? Anselm broke out at the haggard boy suddenly, then looked at Stanley who was staring dumbly at the headline. —You better get over there before the whole thing falls down, Anselm said to him.

—Hannah... Otto interrupted, —tried to kill herself? I just saw her.

—Hannah! Anselm looked up and laughed at him.

—It was Esme, Stanley said quietly. —Last night.

—But what happened?

—You're spilling your drink. What are you drinking whisky sours for anyhow? Anselm demanded.

—She flipped, man. Chaby found her with the gas on. Then the haggard boy returned to Anselm. —Did you hear about Charles? His old lady came from Grand Rapids to take him back there, she's a Christian Science.

Otto put his glass on the table. He looked back as though minutes were hours, and the hours had been days since he'd seen her: he had driven her to it. His chest expanded as he got his breath and turned away.

—She came on all sweetness and light, you know man. She thought she could turn him on with Mary Baker Eddy, but she won't give him a penny unless he comes home with her. I don't blame him for flipping.

Anselm reached for Otto's glass as Otto hurried toward the door, pressing on between the two young men, interrupting

—Scatological?

—Eschatological, the doctrine of last things...

—Good lord, Willie, you are drunk. Either that or you're writing for a very small audience.

—So...? how many people were there in Plato's Republic?

*

Otto passed through the streets in a great hurry, but he was moving almost mechanically, one foot before the other and the load of the sling pounding against him, so that his excitement did not show until he passed the head of her stairs and stood breathless at her door. All the way his lips had been moving, and slight single sounds escaped them, chirps of forgiveness which he was trying to draw together.

Chaby opened the door. His sleeves were rolled up, and his shirt, the back of the collar turned up, was unbuttoned to the waist, showing a blue tattoo line which came, apparently, from the shoulder. Otto stared at the miraculous medal swinging from his throat, and then looked up at Chaby's small good teeth. —Is she...

Chaby nodded over his shoulder and turned away, leaving the door ajar. Otto pushed it open.

She came out to him from the other end of the double room. She wore a clean red cotton dress, and had a spotted blue coat on over it. She greeted him with almost a smile, her tranquil face looking as though she were going to smile, and then not.

—But you... are you all right? he asked going in to her.

—No. She must go to the doctor, she said to him. In her hand she held the book she had been reading, finger still between the closed pages. It was *Uncle Tom's Cabin*.

It was only as he came close that he realized how heavily made-up she was. From the door, there was an almost bluish look to her face, but this proved to be a reflection of the careful make-up on her eyes, which seemed to be diffused over her face by the paleness of her skin. Her lips were as carefully made-up, with a slightly softened but still brilliant red. On the wall where she had just come from hung a mirror, rather an unsquared piece of mirror going off to a sharp point at one side.

—There, Otto said, holding out an empty hand which he let fall slowly. —I'm sorry about... I can... She waited, with this same unachieved smile. —Are you all right?... he repeated, noticing the great hoops of earrings for themselves for the first time. Until that moment they simply served to complete her figure.

—She must go for a long walk, for today she has had nothing to eat, she said to Otto, —and the doctor put barium sul-phate in her stomach so that he can X-ray her and find out if she has a stomach. Isn't that silly? she added after a pause.

—Yes, but you . . . I mean I heard that you . . . that something happened to you last night . . .

—Last night, she repeated, looking away from him, —last night she did a very foolish thing, turning on the gas . . . She swung round to him suddenly, her tone mocking laughter and her eyes bright open: he looked from one to the other, saw in both his own distended reflection. —Turning on the gas, when the bill was so high already . . . ! And she allowed him a moment longer to stare at the image on the surface of her eyes, before she turned away to say, —But then Chaby came and everything was all right.

Otto rubbed his hand over his face and muttered something without turning round to Chaby (where she looked then, over his shoulder) who was seated smoking a cigarette in the room behind him. —Oh yes . . . he said and took a step away from her, dropping his hand, looking down to where the rug painted on the floor came to an end between them.

She went over to a drawer, looking for something, a handkerchief, and left him standing there looking round, but keeping his eyes from the room behind him. —I see you've finally got a mirror up, he said, rather distastefully, glancing into it to see his face shorn off at the jaw. When she said nothing he added, —You must need it, to get all that paint on your face.

—Oh no, the paint is not for the mirror, she said looking at him, half turned from the opened drawer and clinging to it. —But now a ghost lives here who is not happy. And when it comes she hides in front of the mirror where it cannot find her.

Otto muttered —Oh . . . , glanced in at the other room, and took a cigarette out. He lit it and tapped his foot on the floor, looking for a place to throw the match. —What's this? he said suddenly, over near the bookcase, turning a drawing round with his toe on the floor where he'd found it. —Why . . . who is this? he asked, and stooped over to pick it up and look at it close.

—Some one, she said.

—But where did you . . . how do you know him?

—It is just some one, she said.

—But it's . . . what's wrong with this? He stared at the face: it stared back, exactly like, but exactly unlike he remembered, faithfully precise but every honest line translated into its perfect lie, as a face seen from behind.

—It's a funny joke, she said suddenly, speaking more loudly, and she laughed but the laugh was gone by the time he looked up to her face.

—No, it isn't funny, he said, looking back at the picture. He started to hold it up before the mirror out of curiosity, and then abruptly he threw it down and turned to her. —Can you come out for a walk?

—She must go for a long walk with the chem-ical in her no-stomach, she said. She was pulling on gloves.

As they went out, she stopped in the door. —You will be here? she asked Chaby. Chaby nodded.

—But you *will*! . . . she said with a desperate step toward him.

—Sure, I'll be here, Chaby said from the chair, and he winked at her and smiled, hardly raising the ends of his hair-line mustache.

At that she lost her rigidity, and wilted against the edge of the open door, smiling at him.

Otto waited at the stairhead. As they went out he tossed an end of the green scarf over his shoulder and spoke as casually as he could, —Where'd you get those earrings, anyhow?

—She has always had them.

—I never saw them on you. I didn't even know your ears were pierced. She said nothing. —Don't they hurt? I mean, they're so big.

—Yes, she answered turning away, —they hurt her.

Otto thought of taking her arm, but he did not, yet. Also he was walking on her right, and could do no better than bump her with his slung elbow. He was thinking about the picture he had found, and left, on her floor; was, in fact, intensely curious about it, but put it off, as he was putting off taking her arm until they should be well away from her door (as though once into territory strange to her, she would be at the mercy of his protection): all this, though the self-portrait hung square before his eyes, as he said to her, —I have to meet my father in a little while, in an hour or so. When she did not comment, he added, —For the first time.

—That will be nice, she said.

—I don't know how nice it'll be, he said. —Imagine, being my age and meeting the old man for the first time. He paused as they turned the corner and sorted themselves out from strangers walking there. —Put off the old man, says the Bible, put on . . .

Suddenly she took his arm, his whole slung arm in hers. —Do you know? . . . she said.

—What? . . . He tried to reach his hand out the end of the sling, and snare her gloved hand, but he could not find it.

—I have discovered that there *is* no one, she said, in intimate confidence.

—No one?

—Last night there was a knock upon the door. I went and opened the door, and no one was there. No one was really there at my door. No one had come to call.

Otto mumbled and looked at her quickly, at the blue hollows of her eyes in the light of the street. —And...did no one come in? he managed to say, reaching across with his right hand to find hers.

—No, she said, and let him go as abruptly as she had caught him.

—Now look, you know...you mustn't get...you mustn't be too upset, you know, I mean after what happened...

—Do you know what happened too? she asked, looking up at him quite surprised.

Otto looked at her excitedly. It is true, he was confused; but she was with him, they were together after what seemed a very long time, and —All this... he said, —All this...

—He made love to her, and then she went away.

—What did you say?...

—Love that smelled like lilies of the Madon-na, she went on, her voice rising evenly to a plane of wonder and distance. —Yes, she said intently; then her voice dropped. —Like the pus of Saint John of the Cross.

He had started to get round and get hold of her, but she held him where he was with a look of infinite reproach.

—That smelled of Madon-na lilies, she said in this low tone, a tone of infinite regret.

—Now look, you...he *who?*...Otto burst round to the other side of her, started to take her arm and realized that she was still carrying *Uncle Tom's Cabin*. His mind churned a vast array of irrelevancies, from the faces passing them which turned here and there in dull curiosity to that incunabular joke which said that *Uncle Tom's Cabin* was not written by hand because it was written by Harriet Beecher Stowe...

—He in the mir-ror, -who, she said in her mocking tone.

—Now look, that photograph, and his...look, what is it?...Have you been modeling?...for him?

—Sometimes she did.

—But where is...but where are the pictures?

—He did not show them to her. Her voice was brisk with disappointment. They were passing outside a bar whose door just then came open and poured out a heavy broken stream of German music which was gone with their next step, leaving her face in the blue and red lights of the window sign for beer, exposed in the expression of fear he first remembered on it when he had gone down on her in the chair in the afternoon and something, somewhere, broke: but in this instantaneous conspiracy of lights and make-up that immaculate fear became terror, and jaded terror sustained beyond human years and endurance, and he shuddered at this hag before he knew it.

—When the witnesses come, she said to him, not taking his arm but touching it with her fingertips, —will they identify her? or will they turn from her to the pain-tings of her which are not of her at all, and shudder as you shudder and look away.

So he had looked away, passing the window of a fun store, a bright litter of novelties, of colors and false faces, pencils, puzzles, a kiddies' toilet seat, Christmas cards, ashtrays, a paint set, rings with false stones, a phosphorescent crucifix, —jingle all the wa-a-ay, came from the transom above.

—We are the gypsies, she said to him as he turned quickly back to her, and she spoke in that low tone of earlier, of deep remorse, —the Lost Egyptians, and we pay penance for not giving Them asylum, when They fled into Egypt. What harsh laws they make against us, she went on, her voice becoming dull. —They will not permit us to speak our own language, she said looking up at him again, —for they believe we can change a child white-into-black, and sell him into slavery! She laughed at that, suddenly, looking up at him; but with his hand tight closed on her wrist the laugh disappeared and left her surprised, staring into his eyes. They had come to a stop, and she took up walking again though he seemed to try to hold her back.

—Now look . . . he said. —Look . . .

—He even said once, that the saints were counterfeits of Christ, and that Christ was a counterfeit of God.

—Now look, where is he? I mean does he still have that studio? that place on Horatio Street.

—Perhaps he does, or he does not. She does not see him any more.

—I want to see him, I . . . but you, look can I see you later? at home.

—If you want to.

—Will he be there?

—She does not see him any more.

—I mean Chaby, will he be at your house?

—If he wants to be.

—But he . . . I mean damn it he's always there, he . . . what's he doing there anyhow?

—Now he is there doing bad things to himself with the needle.

—Look when will you be home?

After a long pause, when they'd reached a corner and she stopped there, under the streetlight, she said, —She does not know, she must take a long walk with the chemical in her stomach that is not there, and then she must go to the doctor.

—But the . . . I have to meet my father in a little while, but look, I want to see you. I mean, I have to talk to you, it seems like months since I've seen you, and you . . . and I still love you, even if . . .

He broke off, and gave her wrist which he still held such a quick tug that the book fell to the ground. He got it quickly, and came up with, —Because I've believed nothing, or I thought I didn't believe in anything and maybe I've been pretending I didn't believe in anything, but only tried to use my head and figure things out and . . . because that's the way everybody seems to have to be now, because you can't trust . . . and you . . . and now . . . and then when I found you, I found you really didn't, you really didn't believe in anything and you have to, you have to . . . he finished breathlessly and reached for her wrist again but she withdrew it and he stood with his free hand quivering on the air between them. Then he took a deliberate breath, deeply, and spent it all saying, —Do you love me?

—If there were time, she answered him looking him full in the face.

—Or . . . or . . . he started to falter again, raising his hand to the razor cut on his cheek and pressing his fingers there when he found it. —It's like . . . he commenced again, lowering his voice, and his hand, and he caught her wrist this time, —It's as though when you lose someone . . . lose contact with someone you love, then you lose contact with everything, with everyone else, and nobody . . . and nothing is real any more . . .

She stared at him, patient now in his grasp which loosened slightly as his voice ran out; though he found enough of it left to repeat, —Or things won't work. Then he drew breath again and stood looking at her under the streetlamp. She had relaxed in his hold; even taken half a step closer to him, and he studied her face in the light from above them, as it seemed a faint and expectant, and a receptive, anxiety spread over it; while his own slackened slowly over the cheekbones, and the excitement drained from his eyes as he marshaled his senses. He loosed her wrist, and lowered his hand, and stood before her as he had stood on the dock before the glare of that white fruit boat; and as he had counted out change for the beggar in whose face he saw no beauty, so suddenly had it come upon him, he computed his emotions, reckoning how much he could spare, and how much retain for himself. —You can depend on me, he said to her.

She withdrew; and there, like small coins slipping through his fingers, he began to lose what he had balanced and accounted with such practiced care, having given the two-and-one-half-cent piece, which looked like a dime. He whispered her name hoarsely, and raised his arm to put it round her.

—Don't.

—But I . . .

—Leave her alone.

The safety pin came undone, the sling dropped as he put both arms around her, and his hand opened, everything spilled. But she made no move, no effort to move, she stood and waited with her head drawn down as far as she could do. Then he closed his hands, looking beyond her, so quickly gathering up all that he had almost lost.

—You'll be all right alone? he said to her.

—Now she will.

Otto stooped and picked up the sling. —I'll see you later on, he said. Half a block apart, he turned and looked back, to see her walking away from him.

Balloons, a watch, a poopoo cushion, textile paints and stencils, a gold-finished silk-tasseled watch-case compact, Your portrait in oil (a genuine original oil painting) from favorite snapshot, 4 1/2 x 5 1/2 inch canvas, decorative wooden easel and palette free; a dusty imitation ink-blot; a dusty imitation dog spiral; a talking doll; Blessed Mother, Infant of Prague and Saint Joseph, 24K gold-plated, in pocket-identification case, 25¢; Venus de Milo with a clock in her belly; a sewing kit (resembles quality bone china) figurine; a Christmas card with 180-page genuine Bible postage-stamp size attached; a ventriloquist's dummy; a false face, mounted on another false face; all these, as well as many more durable, beautiful, useful, inspiring things lay stretched before Otto's gaze where he stopped to pin up the sling. The pin was gone. He knotted it, unsteadily stealthy with both hands, and felt for his wallet before he put his hand into his trouser pocket, for it was shaking. People passed in both directions. One bumped him below, and cried,

—Yaa, yaaaa ... The arm in the sling flew up in horror as he stared at his triumphant assailant, a person under three feet tall staring up at him with wide eyes, an immense red nose, and a great brush of a mustache all hung on by the empty wire glasses. With a few steps he was inside the bar where *Eine kleine Taverne im Golf von Napoli* was being played on the juke-box, and he ordered beer. He was suddenly very cold. He brought his hand out with a coin clenched in it, and tapped it on the bar, looking unwaveringly straight ahead, at the eyes of his image in a mirrored cabinet above the rows of bottles behind the bar. He was alone in the place, except for the bartender; and he lit his last cigarette.

The door opened again, and a man in a battered Santa Claus suit came in, beardless and hatless, but with a well-stubbled chin. He looked jovially down the bar at Otto and then said, —Pour us something with a smile in it, Jimmy. My special. Toot sweet, Jimmy ... He winked at Otto. —And the tooter the sweeter.

Unwinking, Otto turned back and put his forehead in his palm, that elbow on the bar and the coin in his slung hand, waiting. He closed his eyes for a moment.

The bartender came down empty-handed, opened the mirrored cabinet to take out a bottle of Old Heaven Hill Bourbon, and returned to the man in the battered Santa Claus suit.

Otto sniffed, and opened his eyes. On the shelf behind the bar, well out of reach, was a donation box for a Sacred Heart Society. Mounted on it was a colored print of Christ exposing the Sacred Heart, looking, from Otto's half-open eyes, like a C.I.D. man showing his badge. Otto stared at it and muttered something to himself. He sniffed again. It was his hair burning from the cigarette between his forefingers. —Damn, he said, and then, —damnation. He put the cigarette in an ashtray at arm's length, and looked up for the bartender who was just then coming with his beer.

—Fifteen, said the bartender. He waited while Otto fumbled through pockets, and finally joined the warm coin from his slung hand with a cold one from his jacket. —We only take American money here, Jack. The bartender tossed the cold shiny two-and-one-half-cent piece back to him and waited, looking absently at Otto's cigarette smoking in the tray until Otto found a dime. Then he took the coins, picked up the cigarette, and went back up the bar.

—But . . . Otto caught the word before it came out. He clenched his hand round the glass and stared straight ahead of him. And it took him a good half-minute to realize that neither the stubbled chin, nor the flattened nose, nor the bunched ears, nor the yellow eyes he stared into, were his own.

He turned and went straight back for the telephone booth. There he dialed SP 7-3100. —Hello? he said into the phone. —I want to report a case of drug-taking. Heroin. If you go to this address immediately . . . What? No, I'd prefer not to give my name.

The glassed doors came closed upon him slowly, and from outside he could be seen staring through the scribbled configuration uoY ƙɔuℲ on the glass, a dedication which might, under other circumstances, have recalled Sir Walter Raleigh's cunning advance upon Queen Elizabeth, scrawling "Fain would I climb, yet fear I to fall" upon a windowpane with a diamond.

The juke-box played *Fliege mit mir in die Heimat*. The bartender put out the cigarette half-smoked, as though it were his own. The man in the battered Santa Claus suit stood with his back to the bar and his elbows resting on it. —That's a nice muriel, he said, looking at the wall painting, where a moose stared out over an empty lake. But the clock, though hung high in the sky where the sun might have been at high noon in the fall weather of the moose's landscape, was running withershins, as a convenience to bar patrons who could see it right in the mirror.

—I knew a guy once, he had this muriel, said the man in the battered Santa Claus suit. —Except where it was, it was on the ceiling, he added reflectively, —And it was a dame.

V

"The trust of our people in God should be declared on our national coins. You will cause a device to be prepared, without unnecessary delay, with a motto expressing in the fewest and tersest words possible, this national recognition."
—ABRAHAM LINCOLN'S TREASURER, to the director of the Mint

—I CAN'T live with you and be a Christian, shouted the woman clinging to the edge of the dirty sink, answering the moaning from the next room, she whose ancestors had gathered at the foot of the Janiculum in ancient Rome, and sold whatever was for sale in the garlic-reeking interior of the Taberna Meritoria, that squalid inn on the Tiber bank.

—You're not a Christian, never were. And the moaning resumed.

—When are you going to stop that awful noise, she demanded, she whose ancestors strove with one another, asking, "How can this man give us his flesh to eat?"

—Be quiet. It's the only reason you married me. You wanted to marry a Christian, you wanted to marry a good Catholic. Well, leopards can't change their spots.

—Shut up! She turned the volume control of her hearing aid down.

Then there was silence. It lasted for a full minute, when both rooms were filled with a scream so ghastly as to stop the novice heart and breath and blood for the full eternal instant of its duration; a sound which, as the book said, once heard, can never be forgotten. The woman at the sink (she whose ancestors were kidnaped as children, to be brought up in the Faith, A.M.D.G.) clung to its sloped edge. The lines of her face were fallen, not in terror, but in weariness. Too late, she turned the volume control of her hearing aid down still further.

—How did that sound? asked her husband behind her, triumphant in the doorway. —That was an epileptic. I'm practicing.

—Oh Jesus and Mary, you've only been home this time for three weeks, and you've started again.

—What's the matter with it? Saint Paul was an epileptic.

—Can't you do anything else, Frank? Are you too old to do anything else?

It was true. Mr. Sinisterra was becoming an old man. Although he had been heard to say that he resented prison years no more than Saint Augustine resented the withdrawal he had made from the world when living near Tagaste; had, indeed, embracing the words of Saint Gregory ("the Contemplative Life is greater in merit and higher than the active"), spent a fair amount of time in solitary confinement ("the hole," as it was called, a place which, though cleaner and more dry, corresponded to the *in pace* of the convent, where, for their own good, medieval religious were occasionally immured for life), in spite of all this, and his commendable approach, prison years had not softened him, nor prolonged his youth. Life at Atlanta was not, as his son had been told on occasion, "a long vacation for Daddy," any more than Saint Giles's retirement to the desert resembled a tour from a travel folder. Now the retirement was over once more, and with the humility of the prophet Jeremiah, who longed for the contemplative life but was rooted out to "go and cry in the ears of Jerusalem," Mr. Sinisterra had returned again to shoulder the burdens of this world.

—I'm going out for awhile, he said in the doorway, looking suspiciously at his wife's hand as it lowered from the hearing-aid control pinned at her bosom. She stared at him. —You ought to learn self-control, like those yogis, she said.

—I should learn control. I! Me!

—That's a wonderful religion they got, that voodooism.

—Hopeless, he said, turning into the other room. —I was going to get you a book, but I don't think you even could read it if I did. There he sat down before a mirror, illuminated like a theatrical dressing-room mirror. Spread before him was an array of jars, tubes, colored pencils, and hair in bits and transformations which any star might have envied. On the wall hung a crucifix, a picture of Cavalieri as Tosca, some neckties representing better schools at home and abroad, and a reminder of a papal bull of Pius IX, the Pio Nono of many happy memories, in this case the *Bolla di Composizione* of 1866, granting pardon to the felon who devotes to pious uses three per cent (3%) of his plunder, permitting him to "keep and possess the remainder in good faith, as his own property justly earned and acquired."

On the table at his elbow, among bottles of aqua regia, alcohol, benzine, nitric acid, something known in the trade as "dragon's blood," a pair of shears, some beeswax, some resin, some mastic, some amber, some steel plates, and some oil of lavender whose springtime fragrance pervaded the room, lay two exotic passports, and a copy of the *Theologia Moralis* of Alfonso Liguori, on top of Bicknall's *Counterfeit Detector* for 1839. He had opened a large bottle of a solution of potassium permanganate, and sat now carefully daubing his face and neck with this brilliant purple, throwing the silver medal which hung at his throat over his shoulder.

—Thank God he took down his washing anyhow, he heard her mutter.

—What do you mean my washing? What washing?

—Them twenty-dollar bills you had hanging all over the place to dry.

—If you smeared any! He turned a face, which was minute by minute blooming with the flush of youth, threateningly to the doorway. —That's just the way they picked up the greatest artist that there ever was, he went on, returning to the mirror. —Jim the Penman, he drew every bill by hand, for twenty years he was a success. And what happens? Some dumb grocery clerk smudges one of them with a wet hand. When he was tried, you know what the defense was? He was an artist. Any of his work was worth more as a work of art than what the government was shoving. An artist, a real artist.

—Don't you worry, I didn't smear any of your worthless paper. Worthless, worthless paper, she muttered at the sink.

—*Worth*less! he cried. —Do you know how hard I worked on that? Do you know where I got the paper to print them? What do you think it was, old newspaper? Well it wasn't, there was two hundred and fifty dollars' worth of paper hanging up there. Do you think I'd do a cheap job after the work it was to make those plates? Did I ever do a cheap job? Worthless paper! That was two hundred and fifty one-dollar bills, bleached to print the twenties on. It took me almost eight years to make those plates, he added.

—That was a nice way to spend your time in prison, God knows.

—That's right, those are hand-engraved steel plates, you don't see them any more. None of your cheap photo-engraving. He started to fold a packet in brown paper, but appeared unable to resist taking out a bill, which he turned over in his hand murmuring, —You don't see work like this any more, as he looked into the challenging face of the seventh President. Under the packet lay the current issue of the monthly *National Counterfeit Detector*, where reviews of his work had not appeared in many years: in this work, anonymity advanced with worth, just as it did in the vignettes on the currency itself. The Father of His Country was crumpled, folded, and offered in the most piking and meretricious traffic millions of times a day, infinitely better known and worse treated than McKinley and Cleveland, far more readily summoned than the five thousand times remote Madison, still less than kin, ten thousand times removed, with Salmon P. Chase, if more than kind with him in coveting supreme office, a recognition never granted to that Secretary of the Treasury under Abraham Lincoln, who made the five hands down without even getting a haircut.

—You don't see work like this any more, he repeated. —Everything's cheap, everybody does things the quick cheap way. This is one of the only crafts left. Look at the eyes, there's none of that dead quality you see in a cheap job. Look at the sensitive lips, he murmured laying the bill back with the others. —I don't waste my time like a lot of people I know.

—Don't talk to me about wasting time, she came back at him. —If you had the kind of pains like I do. Go out and catch cancer yourself, and see how smart you are then.

—Cancer! Indigestion, that's what you've got.

—And another thing I want to talk to you about before you get yourself all made up like a circus clown. Where are you going anyway? she demanded, appearing in the doorway as he opened a bottle of eserine and took out an eyedropper.

—I'm going to make a meet, he answered shortly.

—To make a meat. That's nice.

He filled the eyedropper and turned to her with exaggerated patience. —I'm going out to meet a passer, to hand this stuff over to him. It's all arranged and paid for.

—Such nice friends you got. Socially I should meet them.

—You should meet them! I don't even know him myself, I don't want to know him, I don't want him to know me. They're the ones who get picked up first. If he doesn't know me, he doesn't know where he got the stuff, he can't talk. It's always trouble with the middleman and the passers that get you pulled in. I don't even have any middleman. Everything's middlemen. Everything's cheap work and middlemen wherever you look. They're the ones who take the profit. Thirty dollars a hundred while I get eight. After the way I work? Look at those three plates, that's hand-engraved on steel, they'll never wear out like these zinc plates in a cheap photo-engraving job. He tilted his head back and raised the dropper. —This guy I'm going to meet, he's going to identify me by I'm almost blind with my glasses . . . She watched a drop of eserine fall into his left eye, while he went on, —Do you think I can take chances? How many men do you think there are in this country who can pick up engraving tools and do what I can do? There's hardly half a dozen, and they can hardly come near me. Even them, they either work for the government or they're in jail. And do you think nobody knows who I am? The minute they spot a piece of this stuff, they've got it under a microscope. They've got work of mine they picked up thirty years ago, and they can compare it. They're not dumb, with a microscope in their hand, the Secret Service, they can find the smallest resemblance, even after thirty years they can see my own hand in there, a little of myself, it's always there, a little always sticks no matter what I do.

She stood supporting herself on the door jamb, and looked at him wearily; sniffed, and raised her eyes as though looking over distance in the landscape of his kingdom, the strong-scented landscape of Sheol. Finally she said, —So keep your friends to yourself, but let me tell you, when the doctor gives me morphine for my pains, what happens to it? Right out of the house it disappears. Who steals it? Your son, that's who steals it. From his mother yet.

—He's not mine, he's yours. I don't claim him. Does he ever go to church? No. He hasn't got any morals, he hasn't got any talent.

—So who ruined him? So who stood over him when he was a baby, and says, My ain't it wonderful his first two fingers are the same length, so he could pick pockets, trying to teach him how to make his fingers like scissors, picking pockets. So who stood over him and says, My, with sensitive fingertips like that I could feel the tumblers fall in any safe in the world. So who was it give him Daddy's signet ring, like he was a prince of somewhere, except this signet ring it's got a little knife in it, to cut pockets open yet.

Her husband turned to look at her. His was an odd look, for one pupil had shrunk almost to a pin-point, swimming in eserine which he wiped away. —Those things were primary courses, like any kid gets in his first grade school. Do you think I wanted him to be a bum? So I taught him some basic things, how to use his hands. Did he ever learn anything? Did he ever try? No. He never worked a day in his life, like his father. You had his moral side to bring up. That's a mother's work, all those years I was away you had him here to bring up his moral side. Look how it come out.

—So who's crying over spilled milk? It's no good to talk about, all I want is he stops stealing his mother's morphine. I go through his pockets, even, looking for it, what do I find, seasick remedy and chewing gum I find.

—So you think he's seasick? You know what he uses them for? He goes to the dog track, and dopes the dogs up with Mothersill's seasick remedy. The chewing gum he puts between their pads to slow them up. You think I taught him that?

—Anything bad he knows, you must have taught him.

She stood there, gazing at him, as he dropped eserine into his right eye. —Such a clown, yet, she said wistfully. —Anyhow he's never been in prison like his fine father who just come out again.

—You think I didn't figure that out? he said, turning from the mirror, to look at her with two pin-pointed pupils. —There was a war going on, and things are bad when there's a war. It's hard to get metal for the plates, it's hard to get the right inks, everybody you can depend on gets drafted, or they get a job in an airplane factory. Like prosperity, things get lousy. It's not so easy now.

But she just looked at him. —Frank, ain't it ever going to let up? Every time you go in this room, I don't know who's coming out. Two months go by, and everything gets chalk on them from your hands when you clean your plate. Everything smells all the time. Like I used to think lavender was flowers, but now I smell it somewhere all I think of is you doing this...this...

—I'm busy, he said, and returned to the table before him. —You're disturbing me on my nerves.

—Your nerves! she wailed, back at the sink. —So maybe I haven't got any nerves? Whenever you're away I think when you come back maybe it will be different, and then by the time you're back a month I almost wish you was away again. You'd be in there yet for that trouble you was in over the stamp, if it wasn't for a mistake they made.

—Mistake! If ever the hand of the Virgin watched over me it was that time. That conviction was thrown out because one of the jurymen was a Jew. He took his oath swearing on a New Testament. A mistake you call that. That was the Virgin Mary getting even for a mistake the Jews made two thousand years ago, that's what a mistake it was. He waited for her to answer, suspecting that she had turned off her hearing aid. Then he went on, nostalgically, looking at himself in the glass, —That stamp was beautiful, that one-penny Antigua stamp. It took me four months to make that plate. And do you think the color was easy? Do you think just anybody can make the color puce? That's why that kid is no good. Would he work hard on something like that? Do you hear me? He waited, suspiciously, to see if she had turned off her hearing aid, something he had not yet caught her at.

—I hear you, she said wearily, at the sink, and turned off her hearing aid.

—Well then stop talking to me like I was a common gangster. Did you ever see me with a gun? Did I ever hurt anybody, except once and that was a mistake, everybody knows it was, and you couldn't count the Masses I've had said for her. He crossed himself hurriedly, and chose his hair for the evening, a healthy black mop. —Not like that kid, he wouldn't have a Mass said for his own mother. He's slipshod and no good. Whenever I was home to give him the benefit of my study and experience, I tried to teach him. I taught him how to spring a Yale lock with a strip of celluloid. I taught him how to open a lock with wet thread and a splinter. I taught him how to look like he has a deformed spine, or a deformed foot. Nobody taught me all that. I learned it myself. It was a lot of work, and he had me right here to teach him, right here, his own father. So what does he learn? Nothing. He's never done a day's work in his life. You think a bum like that I'd claim him for my son? He's like everybody now, they don't study their work, they don't study their materials. Show me somebody who can get that color green so perfect, he went on, looking down at the back of a twenty-dollar bill. —It's not a place for bums to get into, it's a place for artists, for craftsmen.

Mr. Sinisterra paused to fit the black hair in place over his own, a thinning texture of early gray. Then he went on in a lower tone, —He has no ambition like his father. I tried to teach him how to make copper plates, zinc plates, glass plates. The only platinum plate I ever made he almost ruined it for me. Just once he tried it alone, he tried to make some Revenue stamps. I helped him right through it, like a old master, cleaning the copper plate with benzine, putting on the wax ground, softening it with a little lavender oil. He made a mess of it. I had to throw the whole thing out before he got us all in trouble. Even the color, do you think he could tell the difference of one green and another? He couldn't tell it from red even. His father's a craftsman, an artist, he's nothing but a bum.

Mr. Sinisterra dusted the black hair into place. There were sounds from the kitchen, but no answering words; only the clatter of pans. —It isn't like the old days, he said, looking at himself in the glass. —It isn't like when you could pass a gilded quarter for a ten-dollar gold piece. It isn't like the days of Pete McCartney and Fred Biebusch, and Big Bill the Queersman, the days when Brockway passed a hundred thousand just like that. It isn't like the days when Johnny the Gent melted down the Ascot Cup.

He went to the rack to choose a necktie. Flicking aside Eton and Harrow, he lifted the soft dark blue with jagged red streaks of the Honourable Artillery Company, considered it for a moment, and then replaced it beside the false arm hung on the rack. —It's not a place for bums to get into, it's a place for art. You know how big the spaces behind Hamilton on the ten are? Less than one one-hundred-twentieth of an inch. Do you call that a place for bums? That kid wouldn't even try, when he made those Revenue stamps. The acid got under the wax and made everything jagged. Do you think he cared? He didn't even know the difference. How sharper than a snake's tooth it is to have a kid like that, do you hear me? You never read a book in your life. Well never mind. It's a great disappointment for a father, when his son don't take an interest in his father's work and carry it on.

The pig, stamped upon the coins of Eleusis when she coined her first autonomous money in the fourth century B.C., the pig of purification, adorned the necktie which Mr. Sinisterra chose, and turned to the mirror to knot it about his neck with a manner of great tradition born. —It's a great disappointment when he don't appreciate our tradition, he said. —Our family wasn't just nobody in Salerno, every secret we have has been handed down from father to son for generations. Do you think he cares? My father was proud of me. He turned to put on his suit coat, flicking at its lapels, and buttoning it before the mirror. His chest filled as he looked at himself there.

Behind him lay the Protocols of the Elders of Zion; and the magnanimous grant of Constantine, though that emperor was some five centuries dead when the spirit of his generosity prevailed through forgers in Rome, to bequeath all of western Europe to the Papacy. Behind him lay decrees, land grants, and wills, whose art of composition became a regular branch of the monastic industry, busy as those monks in the Middle Ages were keeping a-kindle the light of knowledge which they had helped to extinguish everywhere else. Behind lay Polycrates, who minted gold-coated lead coins in his own kingdom of Samos; and Solon, who decreed death for such originality in his. Canute severed guilty hands; and England, escaping his empire and succumbing to the Normans not much later, removed not only hands but eyes, a lily flower of punishment gilded with castration which solved nothing, for even in the reign of Edward III it was found necessary to draw and quarter a number of talented ecclesiastics.

Historians, anxious to rescue some semblance of a system from the chaos of the past, point out that since the dawn of civilization, the center of civilization has moved westward: from Polycrates' Asian island and Solon's Athens to Constantine's Roman Empire nine centuries later, on to Charlemagne's Frankish labyrinth, ever onward to Canute the Dane at the millennium, across the Channel to the fourteenth-century England of Edward III it came, gathered its breath there (while word of renascence breathed behind in Italy) for three centuries, readying for the leap across the sea to shores of a New World, where early settlers (having thrown off that yoke of tyrannical ignorance, religious persecution) promoted a culture founded in pure reason, and introduced their civilized art to the Indians, forging wampum of porcelain and bone. They prospered. Hard work was the only expression of gratitude their deity exacted and money might be expected to accrue as testimonial; though Pennsylvania decreed the pillory, with the ears nailed to it and cut off, and a complement of thirty-nine lashes and a fine, these dedicated beings did not quail. But like so many of the mystic contrivances devised by priesthoods which slip, slide, and perish in lay hands, this too became a cottage industry: tradesmen, barbers, and barkeeps issued money, keeping up as best they could with the thousand different banks who were doing the same thing. Before the war which was fought to preserve the Union, a third of the paper money in circulation was counterfeit, and another third the issue of what were generously termed "irresponsible" banks. Meanwhile inspectors went from one bank to another, following the security bullion which was obligingly moved from the bank they had just inspected to the one where they next arrived; and the importunate public, demanding the same assurance, was satisfied with boxes rattling broken glass. Merchants kept "counterfeit detectors" under their counters, and every bill offered them in payment was checked against this list of all counterfeits in circulation, and notes rendered worthless by the disappearance of the evanescent banks which had issued them.

Mr. Sinisterra kept his copy of Bicknall's *Counterfeit Detector* for 1839 as a professional curiosity, much as a noted surgeon may exhibit a copy of Galen's *Anatomy*. And just as the noted cardiac surgeon may admire Galen's discovery that the arteries contain blood (and not air, as four centuries of the Alexandrian school had taught), but still smile patronizingly at his theory that the septum of the heart was pierced by imperceptible foramina (allowing passage of the blood from the right into the left ventricle); so Mr. Sinisterra mused over the ingenious devices of the century before him in Bicknall's, which listed 20 issues of money on fictitious banks, 43 banks whose notes were worthless, 54 banks which were bankrupt, 254 banks whose notes were counterfeited, and 1395 varieties of counterfeit notes in circulation. Thus he was becomingly proud of his tradition, which he had brought to the land of opportunity to exercise in the early part of the century, when the proportion of Italians to immigrants from less imaginative lands was about five to one: he whose consecration had helped to raise New York to its present reputation for being the greatest modern center of counterfeiting money of every currency in the world.

He crossed himself before the mirror, turned down his collar, and let his gaze rest upon the Siam National Railway's *Guide to Bangkok*, noting, as he did, that he must pick up a copy of Baedeker's *Spain*. He allowed himself a moment to dream, saw himself voyaging (for the Eternal City, in a Holy Year, lay before him) like those early pilgrims to the Holy Land, Lententide in Rome, Holy Week at Compostella while their families were left starving at home, where they eventually returned decked with cockleshells to recount their adventures, and receive the applause and reverent congratulations of their lesser neighbors who had cravenly remained at home to work for their living.

Into his pocket he thrust the *Theologia Moralis;* and, on second thought, a small sandy mustache with spirit gum stuck to it. He picked up the package of bills, and paused to gaze for a moment into the fearless eyes of Andrew Jackson before he folded the paper closed upon them, and secured it with two elastic bands. How could Jackson, fighting in the Battle of Hanging Rock at the age of thirteen, know that a hundred seventy-odd years later a man would be laboring over his portrait with the exquisite care of love Mr. Sinisterra showed for those eyes, those lips, that shag of hair? that more than a century later his rousing battle with wealth, and the Bank of the United States, would be taken up, if on slightly different grounds, by one so covetous of anonymity as this man who stood thrusting two hundred and fifty vignettes of the seventh President into his pocket now?

His wife did not turn around when he entered behind her, muttering —Seventy-two eighty-eight-hundredths of an inch apart! That's no work for a bum. He stopped, and said in a hoarse whisper, —Do you hear me? Still she did not turn. He raised his voice with the same question. Then he advanced upon her. She jumped, and let out a cry, clinging to the sink with one hand, fumbling at her bosom with the other. —You haven't heard a thing I've said all this time. You turned it off, didn't you? Didn't you! With that, he tore the hearing aid from her dress, and threw it on the floor. —There! he said, and stamped on it. —Now you don't have to listen to me.

She only stared at him, at his eyes pin-pointed, bearing blindness, through those dusty lenses. She shook her head, looking at his light reversible coat. —It's cold out, Frank.

—I know it, he said. —I won't be long.

—It's cold out, Frank. Here, you ought to take this around your neck. She went over to a chair, and picked up a green scarf which her son had thrown there. —Wear this. Probably it ain't his anyway.

Mr. Sinisterra stood while she put the scarf round his neck. —I'm sorry, he said, —but when you don't pay attention to me... Stupidity, I just cannot stand stupidity. She shook her head; and he left her there, stooping over to pick up the broken snarl of wire and plastic case at her feet. With that in her hand, she closed the door to his room which he had left open behind him, murmuring, —The smell... the smell gets everywhere, though no one heard her; and she could not be certain that she heard herself, echoing over Sheol.

hello.

Mr. Pivner gazed at a full-page advertisement in his newspaper... You can say "hello" to a man as you pass him on the street. But you can't sell him anything.

Mr. Pivner's reading embraced tangible things. He had not gone to college (but rather something which called itself a business school: he had studied "accounting"). True, even if he had, he might never have read Democritus, the sire of materialism (judged insane by his neighbors, true, those rare Abderites, who summoned Hippocrates to cure him). Mr. Pivner's attention rarely came upon things at first hand in any case. He preferred those mummifactory presentations called "digests," which reassured him about his own opinions before he knew what they were. Had he read Democritus, he might have discovered, in philosophy's first collection of ethical precepts, among portents of atheism, and the vision of his own soul composed of round, smooth, especially mobile atoms, that it is the unexpected which occurs.

Since life itself tried vigorously to teach him this, however, it was this knowledge that he resisted most successfully. In his reading (a serious pursuit, whether advertising or the Old Testament) he chose, not the disquieting road to serenity, but the serenely narrow path to eventual and total derangement. Nirvana? what sense could he make of a lifetime spent striving toward a goal where nothing was? what satisfaction with Buddhism even when it had reached its tangible (idolatrous) form, to sit in a vase-domed temple turning a prayer wheel before a gilded statue, muttering, —*Life is suffering*

What sense in the Buddhists? They who affirm.

What sense in the Gainas? They who say *Perhaps*

As far from the Prince of Kapilavastu (who brought hope that the chain of twenty-four lakhs of birth in the soul's migration might be severed), as he was from the Nazarene (who, agreeing with the Buddha that life was a sore thing, virility even worse, threatened resurrection), Mr. Pivner sat staring through rimless glasses at a kindly book-jacket face which returned his amorphous gaze. He was preparing to meet his son, to win him as a friend, and influence him as a person.

As Odysseus had Mentor, Jesus John the Baptist, Cesare Borgia Machiavelli, Faust Mephistopheles, Descartes Father Dinet, Schopenhauer's dog Schopenhauer, and Schiller his drawerful of rotten apples, Mr. Pivner had Dale Carnegie: he and four million other individuals, that is; among whom none dared suspect that (*perhaps*) Salome's mother was right.

Did Damon try to sell insurance to Phintias?

It is true, Mr. Pivner, sitting under his three-way reading lamp (turned to its highest brilliance), did not plan to sell insurance, nor even a half-million yards of upholstery fabrics (aggregate value $1,600,000) to the youth he planned to meet that evening, nor glean a Packard car from him in return for applying the "principles of appreciation" as the Connecticut attorney did on page 101. He had taken this most worn of his books from the shelf because it inspired in him what he believed to be confidence. As he read there (underscored), "Let me repeat: the principles taught in this book will work only when they come from the heart. I am not advocating a bag of tricks. I am talking about a new way of life." That was the wonderful thing about this book ("Regard this as a working handbook on human relations; and whenever you are confronted with some specific problem..."): if at first its approach seemed fraught with guile, subterfuge, duplicity, sophistry, and insidious artifice, that feeling soon disappeared, and one had...."Ah yes, you are attempting a new way of life."

True, Mr. Pivner might have read Descartes; and, with tutelage, understood from that energetic fellow, well educated in Jesuit acrobatics (cogitans, ergo sum-ing), that everything not one's self was an *IT*, and to be treated so. But Descartes, retiring from life to settle down and prove his own existence, was as ephemeral as some Roger Bacon settling down to construct geometrical proofs of God: for Mr. Pivner, a potential buyer (on page 95) who was head of the Hotel Greeters of America (and president of the International Greeters too!) was far more real.

True, he might have read the New Testament, and worked out a similar synthesis of Christly conduct and Cartesian method to Machiavellian ends; but how much more direct was this book in his narrow lap: for it was not a book of thought, or thoughts, or ideas, but an *action* book. It left no doubt but that money may be expected to accrue as testimonial to the only friendships worth the having, and, eventually, the only ones possible.

"I am talking about a real smile" (Mr. Pivner read), "a heartwarming smile, a smile that comes from within, the kind of smile that will bring a good price in the market place." An *action* book; and herein lay the admirable quality of this work: it decreed virtue not for virtue's sake (as weary Stoics had it); nor courtesy for courtesy (an attribute of human dignity, as civilized culture would have it); nor love for love (as Christ had it); nor a faith which is its own explanation and its own justification (as any faith has it); but all of these excellences oriented toward the market place. Here was no promise of anything so absurd as a void where nothing was, nor so delusive as a chimerical kingdom of heaven: in short, it reconciled those virtues he had been taught as a child to the motives and practices of the man, the elixir which exchanged the things worth being for the things worth having.

It was written with reassuring felicity. There were no abstrusely long sentences, no confounding long words, no bewildering metaphors in an obfuscated system such as he feared finding in simply bound books of thoughts and ideas. No dictionary was necessary to understand its message; no reason to know what Kapila saw when he looked heavenward, and of what the Athenians accused Anaxagoras, or to know the secret name of Jahveh, or who cleft the Gordian knot, the meaning of 666. There was, finally, very little need to know anything at all, except how to "deal with people." College, the author implied, meant simply years wasted on Latin verbs and calculus. Vergil, and Harvard, were cited regularly with an uncomfortable, if off-hand, reverence for their unnecessary existences. ("You don't have to study for four years in Harvard to discover that," Mr. Pivner read, with a qualm of superiority, for he understood that Otto had, indeed, gone to Harvard.) In these pages, he was assured that whatever his work, knowledge of it was infinitely less important than knowing how to "deal with people." This was what brought a price in the market place; and what else could anyone possibly want?

Here was Andrew Carnegie, who had only four years in school but garnered a million dollars for every day in the year. Here was Cyrus H. K. Curtis, "the poor boy from Maine ... starting on his meteoric career which was destined to make him millions ..." Here was George Eastman, who left a clerk's job at fifty cents a day to pull together a cool hundred million ... So it went on, with many lesser, but equally enthusiastic examples, each of whom seemed to know little or nothing about his work, but every exquisite channel in the minds of his workers, all expressed in a tone of such intimacy that the reader, if he could not rise (meteorically) to their levels, could take satisfaction in seeing them brought down to his own.

The carefully selected quotations were impressive, and from as many sources as the success stories, which included exemplary fraud practiced on a bed-wetting child (for his own good) and model deceit practiced on a great opera singer (for his own good). To prepare this handbook on human relations, the author had read "everything that [he] could find on the subject, everything from Dorothy Dix, the divorce-court records, and the *Parents' Magazine* ..." to three popular psychologists. He even hired a man to go to libraries and read everything he himself had missed. They spared "no time, no expense, to discover every practical idea that anyone had ever used throughout the ages to win friends and influence people." No wonder, thought Mr. Pivner, reading through these pertinently misunderstood half-truths, that it had succeeded. Here were Barnum and the Bible, Charles Schwab, Dutch Schultz, and Shakespeare, two Napoleons, Pola Negri, and the National Credit Men's Association, Capone, Chrysler, Two-Gun Crowley, and Jesus Christ, each in his own way posting the way to the market place. Even Jehovah appeared, if only in brief reversal ("Daniel Webster, who looked like a god and talked like Jehovah, was one of the most successful ...").

"You owe it to yourself, to your happiness, to your future, and TO YOUR INCOME!" Reference to "old King Akhtoi" of Egypt ("Old King Akhtoi said one afternoon, between drinks, four thousand years ago ...") made Mr. Pivner feel that the author had been right there, at cocktails, with that charming rascal, old King Akhtoi. The Socratic method was marvelously simplified ("His whole technique, now called the 'Socratic method,' was based upon getting a 'yes, yes' response"): the very essence of cornering, not truth which has no market value (and did, indeed, bring death to the cunning Greek), but a "good price in the market place." Christ and Confucius appeared, to recite the Golden Rule, and bow out, leaving Mr. Pivner (and four million other individuals) with the clever secret of humility which, carefully used, led the prey in the opposite direction to self-aggrandizement, the illusion of power: in fact, sometimes (when he was tired) Mr. Pivner felt that the sublime secret was to behave like a door mat, to present himself to the world as a cheerful simpleton with no ideas of his own, a good-natured half-wit turning the other cheek, to personify Nietzsche's idea of the Christian, a congenital idiot with nothing to gain (all the while, however, slipping a half-million yards of up-holstery fabric down his sleeve).

As a matter of fact, he was assured by the author that the only thing keep-ing him from being an idiot was five cents' worth of iodine in his thyroid gland (hardly a good price in the market place, even for humility). "A little iodine that can be bought at a corner drugstore for five cents..." Indeed, the general tone of the book was one of humility, a complacent and ungainly sort perhaps, proportioned as it was to the camel passing through the eye of the needle.

Mr. Pivner thumbed through the pages, glancing at the familiar chapter headings, *Fundamental Techniques in Handling People*... Six Ways to Make People Like You...Twelve Ways to Win People to Your Way of Thinking... and his head nodded. He was very tired. In the background, unattended, the radio poured out, subdued, the Reformation Symphony. Why so much atten-tion, so much time spent on this book resting in his narrow lap? Mr. Pivner found safety in numbers; any publication with a circulation of a million reas-sured him, and in a land where mental diseases tolled more people than all other human ills combined, a circulation of four million was more reassuring than anything else could be: for every twenty-five literate citizens over the age of fourteen, one had bought this book, not to guess at how many single dog-eared, underscored copies had circulated among the remaining twenty-four. Assuredly then, it was more than safe; it was an integral part of life around him, those who sneered notwithstanding (for they too were forced to share his life, to be won and to be influenced, no matter their faiths, their aspira-tions, no matter their reasons for courtesy, their grounds for love, how could they presume to distinguish what they offered from what they were given?); and those who decried and denounced it might be condemned out of hand as dangerous at best, bitter, ungrateful at the least, failing not virtue (which has no definition and no country) but that conspiracy of self-preservation known as patriotism.

The tic, which came in Mr. Pivner's lower lip just left of center when he was tired, came now, and waked him to a look of indecisive emotion. It would not stop, but pulled his lip down in quick throbs, as though he had abruptly been asked a question whose answer he knew, and feared to give. He looked suddenly at his watch. He raised it, and held it to his ear. He stood up (still holding the book, open) picked up the telephone, and dialed O, —I'd just like to know what time it is, he said. (—Do you want the time bureau?) —No, I just wanted to know if you had the time, please. (—I'm sorry, we're not permitted to give out that information...) He hung up, and looked at the radio, waiting. The Reformation Symphony made him nervous, as all such music (called "classical") did, as the word Harvard did; but sometimes he was struck with a bar of "classical" music, a series of chords such as these which poured forth now, a sense of loneliness and confirmation together, a sense of something lost, and a sense of recognition which he did not understand. It must be time to take his medicine, before he left to go downtown.

The symphony continued as he left it, and went into the bathroom. He preferred that music to which he did not have to listen. It was only the human voice on the radio that stopped him, that raised his head in expectation, as though it were about to impart something of great personal significance, to *him*. Indeed, that was always the tone in the voice, disembodied; and still listening, expectant, he would sit back, and wait. He had been laughed at, by someone who said, —But you don't *listen* to that stuff? Why do you let it bother you? and of advertising in print, —But you don't *read* that stuff, do you? What do you let it bother you for? What was this anomaly in him, that still told him that the human voice is to be listened to? the printed word to be read? What was this expectant look, if it was not hope? this attentive weariness, if it was not faith? this bewildered failure to damn, if it was not charity?

The room was filled with the strident ring of a telephone bell. It shivered the metal sails on the man o' war, brought forth an undisciplined tinkle of broken glass, and a frantic shade of movement concerted in seizure: breathing the hoarse aspirate initial of greeting, waiting, listening, everything stopped:

——Hello! This is Meribeth Watzon, speaking for the New York Telephone Company... the radio confided without changing the expression of its features, grill and knobs and a lighted smile; and what shadows moved in the room were slow about retiring, those that remained borne still on the walls including the black shape of the cradled telephone where he had dropped it dead, for almost a minute.

Mr. Pivner stood quivering. He'd just broken his last container of insulin. It was too late to go out and return.

——Friends, don't take my word for it. You owe it to yourself to get the details of our free offer. And listen, friends, the next time you...

True, the janitor in Mr. Pivner's office building did not yet call him by his first name. True, the divorce rate had almost doubled since the publication of the book before him. True, he read in headlines of men in the governments he helped to elect, men who might not know their work, but they certainly knew how to deal with people, men who strode forth from the front page in expensive clothes, smiling, the hand raised in bonhomie, on their way to appear before investigating committees interested in their remarkable incomes, withering the smiles which had brought a good price in the market place.

"...dashed off in a moment of sincere feeling..." As he put the green scarf around his neck, his lower lip pulled, and he tried to hold it tight. ——Friends, you owe it to your own health, and your family's...

And King David, what did he say in his chamber over the gate, after Joab had dispatched his son still hung in the branches of the terebinth tree?

Mr. Pivner pulled on his overcoat, and put the needle and syringe into a pocket. He turned off the radio, courteously, waiting until the voice had finished a sentence. He left the book of selective quotations out on the table, next the photograph album. True, one must select; impossible to quote all that Shakespeare ever wrote, to prove a point he never embraced; impossible to print the words of Rosalind, when she said, "But these are all lies: men have died from time to time, and worms have eaten them, but not for love."

Mr. Pivner stood in the doorway for a moment, looking back into the small apartment before entering the world of loss which came when he turned off the light. He remembered years back, when he had bought that book; and in the doorway, still lighted, a fragment of gold arrested him, gold now like the double eagle of the nineteenth century, bored as those words had pierced him, with the sound of the counterfeiter's drill, hollowing out the coin, and filling it with lead, and sealing it so, a very difficult counterfeit to detect. He had bought that book hoping to win friends. He wondered if other people had bought it for the same reason.

The button at his hand clicked, the place disappeared in darkness, as the days of faith were gone, all gone into the dark, gone to earth under Fort Knox, and in the cemetery at Hatton Gap, Arkansas, where, a bare half-century before, Moses had polled six votes in the presidential election, and John the Baptist, three.

And the Buddha?

And the Gainas?

And the morning? and the evening? Morning, evening, noontime, night: what was the shape of Mr. Pivner's soul? round, or oblong? And its atoms, worth as much as iodine atoms? worth five cents? Or were they of a different kind: round, smooth, and especially mobile?

And a good price in the market place, say . . . thirty pieces of silver?

—Whhhhassafuksamatter? This delicate question went unanswered, for the man who asked it was alone on the street corner. He waved his rolled-up newspaper at no one, and then stood smiling. —So. You wonanswer? Ascared? he challenged. The light above his head changed, on one side, from red to green, on the other from green to red. A bus approached. It stopped, and so he got on it. He put his fare in the box, and stopped halfway down the aisle, —MERRY CHRISTMAS!

No one answered. —Sgoddam too bad, he said. —I got on a funeral hearse. Snobody's funeral, snobody to bury. Merry Christmas in a cemetery. He sat down, and opened his newspaper. After a few minutes of patiently staring at the words there, he asked the man across from him, —Wherzis bus go?

—I don't know, said the other.

—Fine thing, you don't know. I congradulate you. You're the first man I've met in New York'll admit he don't know something. Congradulations. He extended a hand which swung emptily in the air between them. The bus stopped, and as his neighbor got off he called, —Look out, don't break your leg or we'll have to shoot you . . .

He sat back and stared at the newspaper. Across the top of it were printed chapters from Genesis, which was being serialized for the holiday season, as a public service. —I'll be damned, it's the Bible, he said loudly. —You get the Bible in the newspaper, he said, addressing the man who had sat down across from him, next to a lady with a baby in arms. —Whdyou think of that. You know why that is? He looked up and down the bus. —Sbecause any of these fine people would feel like a jerk reading the Bible in public, they'd be *ashamed* to. But if they're oney reading the newspaper, that's all right. Merry Christmas! You don't have to go to college four years to know that. Am I right? Am I right? he demanded of this man across from him.

—Yes, Mr. Pivner said, lowering his eyes from the card above the man's head, and raising them again, to read, Unbelievably Realistic See for Yourself $8.00 per carat

—Merry Christmas! the man threatened.

—Merry Christmas, Mr. Pivner answered him. He was very tired. He had stopped at a drugstore to buy his medicine, but not taken the time for the injection, fearful of missing his rendezvous, planning to take his injection in the men's room of the hotel, when he got there. Still, at this critical instant, his training did not fail him. He recalled chapter nine ("Wouldn't you like to have a magic phrase that would stop argument, eliminate ill feeling, create good will...? All right. Here it is...") —I don't blame you a bit for feeling as you do, said Mr. Pivner, recalling the words of John B. Gough, quoted on the following page ("...when he saw a drunken bum staggering down the street: 'There, but for the grace of God, go I.'"). Then he had a strange sensation on one leg. He drew it toward him, and looked, as the woman lifted the baby away from the large spot on his trousers. —You can't hardly blame the baby, can you? said the woman. Mr. Pivner stared at his trousers as he stood up. The tic in his lip pulled it down in quick throbs, and he said nothing.

—Sit down. Merry Christmas, said the man who sat beside the only empty seat in the bus. Mr. Pivner sat down. He was very tired, and nervous. He lifted the wet portion of his trouser away from his leg, and looked out the window. His destination lay some fifteen blocks on.

—I congradulate you. You're the first man I've met, said his companion. —D'you want to read the Bible? I got it right here. He disappeared for a moment under a flurry of newspaper.

The bus bore on, block after block. Chapter six, *How to Make People Like You Instantly:* ("So I said to myself: 'I am going to try to make that chap like me...What is there about him that I can honestly admire?'... I instantly saw something that I admired no end"), —What a wonderful head of hair you have, said Mr. Pivner. The man beside him looked at the thin hair on Mr. Pivner's head, and then clutched a handful of his own. —Lotsa people like it, he said. Then he sat back and looked at Mr. Pivner carefully. —Say what is this, are you queer or something?

Mr. Pivner's eyes widened. —I...I...

—Where you going?

—I get off here, said Mr. Pivner, and got out of the bus when it stopped, six blocks from his destination. It was a cold night, and the wind blew, concentrating on the wet spot on his trousers. How could he explain that, to his son? He walked on, suffering, more weary, against the wind, hoping now that the wind would dry that place before he reached the hotel.

He stopped outside its doors, to pull the green muffler from his coat. The wind helped him to whip it into plain sight.

—Whhhhelllll, here we are, said a familiar voice beside him. —My friend! Merry Christmas!

—Not now, said Mr. Pivner, quivering a hand in the air. He stepped toward the hotel.

—That's the idea. A drink for Christmas, said his companion, accompanying him. —Merry Christmas! You know, I've got a religion too, my friend.

Mr. Pivner paused at the revolving door. He said, —Go away.

—We're going to have a Christmas drink, friend. We're going to be friends. Like Damon and Pissyass, ha, hahahahaha...

The revolving door swung, emptying Mr. Pivner into the lobby where he stood weaving from the shock of the warm air, blinking his eyes, looking. The revolving door continued its round: —Whhhay, Merry Christmas!

Mr. Pivner reeled. He fell toward the tall bellboy, who caught him by the shoulders. He tried to speak; but he only gurgled. He was barely conscious. He was being taken out of the lobby.

—Whooooufff... I have a religion too gentlemen...

—Get them out of here, out the side door.

—Merry Christmas gentlemen...what's this, the policemen's ball?

—It looks bad for the hotel, taking them out the front way.

—I seen the little one, standing out in front there, fooling with his clothes, said the tall bellboy when quiet was restored.

—It's no good for the hotel, that kind of thing. Too early yet, said the manager. —Even so, you got to be charitable for them.

—He passed right out in my arms, just like my old man. Some of them you can't keep away from it, like my old man, you could blindfold him and tie him to the bed, but he always finds it.

They both stepped aside to let a breathless young man pass. One arm was concealed under his coat. He stopped to pull at his muffler, looking round him. Then he checked his coat and went into the bar with the muffler still around his neck.

—Don't tell me that kid ain't had one too many, said the tall bellboy.

—So it's Christmas, said the manager.

The mirror behind the bar was tinted, and of such a slight convexity that those who appeared within its confines wore healthy complexions, figures not distorted but faces slightly slimmer, and he appeared the more grave, she assumed delicacy, lost weight and the years gathered conspiring under the chin. Otto's pale lips, drawn in tension, appeared as thin dark lines of determination, the straggle of hairs on the upper lip a diffidently distinctive mustache. He raised an eyebrow. He moistened his lips, and curled the upper one. Left eyebrow raised, eyelids slightly drawn, lips moistened, parted, down at corners, his quivering hand anchored by the glass, he turned to look at the woman beside him. She was staring straight ahead. He returned to the mirror, where her eyes in ambush caught him and he felt tricked, out-maneuvered; and he quickly returned his eyes to their own reflection. Kettle drums rolled in some semi-classical pursuit from hidden untended amplifiers, rolling to crescendos which manifested capture, then withering as the prey escaped.

The blonde coughed. It was not the delicate unnecessary cough of a lady, drawing attention which she snares with her eyes, but a visceral sound of submission to reality. Nonetheless, looking at her he saw only her eyes as she turned and got down from the bar stool. She retreated in two directions at once, and Otto chose the mirror image to follow her short bobbing steps, and the ceding insinuation of her thighs. Among images of tables and portières she escaped in the tinted glass, but established him as the hunter and he drew breath, deeply, as though the air were fresh.

In the mirror again he saw himself as he had seen himself from two thousand miles away. —How brown you are, Esther said. —And all in white... There was still time.

As a child, Otto had had a phantasy which, in all of the childish good faith which designs such convictions, he passed for fact to himself and his friends. At about the time he learned that he had a father, or should have one, Albert, King of the Belgians, was killed mountain-climbing. It was not difficult to relate the two: he told that his father had been killed mountain-climbing, and so took upon himself the peculiar mantle of a prince.

Looking hastily round the room now, and down the bar, the sudden apprehension of royalty filled him, royalty about to be shoved from the throne room to the scullery, where the pretender belonged. For royalty's blunders always glisten with extraordinary foolhardiness, that makes them royal, distinguishes them from the common subjects who only make mistakes. And what blunderer more absurd than he who dethrones himself? So it has happened; a prince or a king may do it (but find a princess who would not at any cost be queen! a woman who would confess for no reason, who would step from shadows to), dare that reality which is the fabric of damnation, as men who have ruined themselves, for no reason, will tell you.

Down the bar, a man of better than middle age took Otto's attention. His suit was flannel, too light for the season, but bearing other seasons in other lands, as though it were spring now, in London, and he had stepped in from Saint James's Street for a drink; that when he walked out it would be to cross the Mall, and into Saint James's Park, across the turf, to pause for a moment and note the swans there, and other springtime foliage. (London and royalty wove close in Otto's mind.) The man signaled the bartender, raising a hand which caught Otto with the gold flash of a signet ring, an affirmation, a summons which drew taut the muscles in his legs, ready to stand and deliver, do homage, receive from that hand the clasp of recognition, pledge fealty, inherit the signet and the kingdom its seal perpetuated. Undeterred by the man's glance which turned to him, piqued quickly and moved on without curiosity or surprise (so the visage of monarchy, does not deign vulgar response), Otto looked and found resemblance. About the eyes, was it? the bridge of the nose? Clearer correspondence than the device hung from his own neck, wool proclamation of plebeian kinship, green signal of the multitude, its verdant undiscriminating growth.

He drank off the whisky in his glass, lightened the anchor which held him still. Beside his hand lay a pair of black gloves and a gold cigarette case, next to the half-finished cocktail in its long-stemmed glass, smeared red at the lip. Engraved on the gold in generous longhand was the word *Jean*. There was still time.

He lit a cigarette. His hand was weighted down with a full glass, and he relaxed slightly, looking down at his ringless fingers. He took the cigarette in his left hand and rested his slung-up elbow on the bar. The muffler got in his way. There was still time to destroy it. If he telephoned Esther, he might get her husband; if he called him, Esther. He looked quickly over the room again. There was still time to destroy the muffler before it sprang the trap which he had laid himself, before Procrustes appeared to fetter him, with no more than a shock of recognition, to the bed of reality, stretch him or cut him down to fit, release him then, and publish him abroad. He drank down half his drink, and tucked the green muffler under his jacket collar. Walking (so he believed, quickly) toward the telephone booth, his fingers sorting the change in his pocket for the right coin, he rehearsed his conversation. —Esther? Listen . . . yes, it's me, I told you I'd come back . . .

He rested against the side of the booth, and closed his eyes for a moment. Then he opened them, lifted the receiver and dropped his coin. Before he could dial, he heard

(—And so I says to him, you can't ever tell what *she*'s going to do, she's so psychological . . .

(—Nobody asked *me*, but *I* could have told you . . .

—Hello, Otto said. —Hello?

(—Hello, said another voice, a young woman, —darling, is that you?

—Hello? Hello?

(—I think we got a crossed wire, would the other parties mind hanging up? . . . So then he says to me . . . where was I . . .

Otto hung the receiver back on its hook, and clung to it himself. The door opened, and the light went out. Then as he started to the other telephone booth, he pressed his wrist against the breast pocket of his jacket, for assurance, the papers of identity, the money, the manhood implicit there. His wrist pressed against his chest. There was no interruption. There was no weight of that presence more familiar than his own bones, all he felt now with his wrist. The left hand leaped from the sling as he tore open his jacket with the other, and the bandaged wrist worked frantically down into the empty pocket, where his fingernails snagged rolls of dust. Then the left arm fell limp in the sling.

When he felt the empty pocket he had said *no*, quite clearly in the tone of *no*, of absolute rational denial. He repeated it again, this time not the thud of negation but *no* with a shape to it, rising in the middle, a convexity of complaint and disbelief. His upper lip quivered and he raised his right hand, and put his forefinger along its length to stop it. Then he turned quickly into the other telephone booth, dialed, and stood bent rigid before the mouthpiece. —Hello? he said. He gripped the receiver and listened. He heard a clock ticking. —Hello? hello? Then he heard a sound which froze his hand on the receiver, and he stood paralyzed with it jammed against his ear: it was the sound of someone salivating, lips opening and closing, the tongue dropping in fluid from the roof of the mouth.

He left the receiver swinging at the end of its cord, and turned seeking support, as he had in the subway threading a slow career down the veering deck where a man in shirtsleeves, swinging from pole to pole with tattooed arms, called out, —Hey buddy, could you tell me what's the name of this ship we're on? ... and a spattering of lights signaled their next port of call. He disembarked with the man's question filling his mind: unanswered and undiminished it lay there, static and insistent as a piece of ugly furniture, its place appointed, only to be dislodged by another more hideous when he stepped out on the quay, —Merry Christmas, hey, who got sick on your tie? ... and climbing the mole, —You're looking good too. Who's your embalmer?

—You're going to be the richest woman in the graveyard, said the bartender, smiling. —How long since you're back?

—Two days, she answered, turning her head, smoothing her blond hair back over the separate mink pelts swung at her shoulders. The upper part of her face was attractively drawn, the lines of her forehead and nose simple and sharp. Her mouth, and below her mouth, lay heavy, and the jaw no forceful prominence but thickset.

Lips parted, left eyebrow raised, he looked at her, but the eyes themselves stared out in an intent lunacy graduated by lust: he heard his own voice as one hears a voice far down the beach during a hesitation in the surf. The untended amplifiers threatened *Aïda*, and they drank. —My arm? he murmured. —Nothing, a scratch ... and as he lowered his glass swept his forearm along his chest to feel only the corrugations of his ribs. He offered a cigarette with cool clumsiness, brandishing the sling. —Yes ... they're a regular occupational hazard down there, you know.

The bartender laid the bill face down before him; and he glanced at it as though it were a splinter cast ashore, raising his eyes to the tinted horizon, and her indefinite profile afloat there, while his voice came on from far down the beach where the edge of the sea receded, to gather force from the mass and crash in again.

—As a matter of fact, I've just recently finished writing a play, he went on, and took his eyes from her image in the glass to that of the figure beside her whose familiarity he acknowledged without haste: rather, he approached it carefully, with the controlled enthusiasm of a painter advancing upon an unfinished portrait put away for months while he has, all that time, studied it and completed it in his mind. Slight alteration of an eyebrow, a touch at the lips, embellished with a slight flaring of the nostrils, and he'd turned and presented this portrait to her.

Her voice came in gusts, bringing them closer. —I don't think you really ought to read a play, it spoils it when you see it . . . But somehow when I own a book, it's almost like I'd read it . . . In the Modern Museum of Art, it was supposed to be a painting of a woman and he told me it was very valuable, but even my knees are better than hers were . . . The music had not stopped; had, in fact, been pounding its way into *Aïda* all this time, and by now reached "The dance of the little Moorish slaves." —Isn't just the word poem beautiful . . . ?

Staring into the loose top of her dress, he stroked his mustache with a fingertip, and sat closer, to hear, —I couldn't live without Christmas . . . as her knee came against his and lay there in warm confidence, like the plain gold cross whose stem sprang from between her breasts. —Yes, I turned into a Catholic when I got married . . . Shoulders drawn back, the cross climbed from between the cumulous embankments. —But then I got a divorce and I don't know if I'm still one or not. He gave me this . . . The cigarette case was snapped open and closed in metallic rumination. —It's all he ever gave me, it's supposed to be gold but I have to go and have it redipped every two or three months, I keep it because it's a kind of a sacred memory, that being the only time I was married and all.

—I know what you mean. He squeezed her knee in gentle affirmation. His eyes settled on the bill, and seeking something more pleasant rose to the tinted mirror which showed his hair mussed, the green muffler askew: but neither hand dared leave its duty, to the casualty, and the casual prey. —Back to Central America, he heard his voice echo, minutes later, —South America, really. Boru and northern Polivia . . . And he sat staring into the mirror at the person who had made this statement. He waited; as one may in polite conversation, for it to be corrected. But the figure he saw there in the glass made no such effort, simply sat, as though facing destiny on equal terms at last.

—Yes, my name's Jean, she repeated. —And you?

—My name? he said. —My name? His tongue clung to the roof of his dry mouth. He opened his lips and ran the end of his tongue over them. He started to raise his left arm to look at his watch, and the hampering sling surprised him as though he'd wakened bound. He did not look at his watch then, but thought he could hear it tick. He heard the sounds of his mouth recovering fluidity, heard his name but could not repeat it now, no more than the king who abdicates repeats the name he took when he assumed the crown. —Look… he murmured. She had a room in the hotel. The one next to it was empty. The bill for their drinks had mounted quite high: if he took the empty room he could sign for it. He looked down the bar quickly, to where the man in light gray flannel sat thoughtfully picking his nose with his thumb. —What time is it?

She leaned forward. —Your watch says twenty minutes of eight.

—Well then it's stopped, it must have stopped… He drew off the green muffler, and commenced to stuff one end in his pocket. —I'll see about the room. But he sat still for a moment longer, watching the man in light gray flannel, to see if he had been noticed during all this time. The man had no green muffler; and as Otto drew off his own, a contract of necessity disappeared: the Damastean robber took his bed and was gone, slain by Theseus, that hero who identified himself to his father with the sword his father had left behind, Aegeus, King of Athens.

Here the man in the light gray flannel suit signaled the bartender. The seal ring flashed, connoting monarchy; and turning away, the prince, to some extent, relaxed, as the Protean image of his father, after two decades of transforming itself, settled again prepared to change as soon as grasped, just as Proteus, rising from the sea at midday to sleep in the rock shade, assumed every possible shape and form to escape prophesying, when the curious caught him.

Otto let himself down from the bar stool slowly, intent intending dignity, posturing peril; and then he hung there, staring, as the revolving door swung into the lobby. Santa Claus entered, propelled with a whack from behind, and stood unsteadily for a moment. Then he saw what he was looking for, and started for the bar just as the tall bellboy caught him and inserted him again into one of the revolving compartments, pushing him back in as he came round again, and finally getting in with him to help him out the other side, and send the red-clad saint to other hearths. The dining room swayed gracelessly, and as Otto's feet rested upon the floor it seemed to shudder, like the deck of a ship as the hull lowers upon a ragged sea. He steadied himself for a moment; and then with his whole hand he felt for his inside breast pocket, as though the wallet must have been there all the time, its absence illusory, caused by witchcraft; and he glanced quickly at the blonde, as those medieval inquisitors, fingering the pages of the *Malleus Maleficarum* may have glanced at the witches who seemed to deprive men of their virile members, when they found that "such members are never actually taken away from the body, but are only hidden by a glamour from the senses of sight and touch."

But his hand pressed against bone. With that, he retired from the image of himself which had stepped down from the mirror above the bar, to dwell apart and watch it move across the room toward the lobby, prepared to applaud this vacant being if things should go well, to abandon it tinted and penniless if things should conspire against it. Even absolute, he mistrusted glamours; even so, he did not notice the green muffler trailing from his pocket as he walked across the floor.

—A single room for tonight?

—We have just one, sir. With bath. Nine-fifty.

—Fine. Fine.

—And your luggage, sir?

—Coming along behind me, you know. From the dock, following me.

—I'm afraid I'll have to ask you to pay in advance. A formality...

—I say, my travelers' checks are all in my small suitcase, you know, following me along here from the dock. Just recently arrived, I mean back in this country...

—I'm afraid we won't be able to...

—I haven't much time to...

—We might be able to hold a room for you until ten, unless someone else...

—Yes, well, that will do then. It will have to do, you know. Thank you, Otto finished, turning from the desk, the particles of his expression uncomposed, as though at the theater and temporarily confused by the course of the play; but as the theater-goer has redemption written on his ticket stub, and a sterile fragment of faith tells him that salvation is just around the corner as he takes his seat for the last act, so an anticipatory calm pervaded the materials of Otto's face.

Nevertheless the machinery of faith inclines to creak when the multitude boards; and the more the formidable tyranny of their privilege exerts itself, and love of spectacle demands effects, the more brazenly the machine is bared. Among Rome's earlier and more cheerfully dealt contributions to the decline of civilization was the gallant assistance she gave to the decadence of the Greek theater, where Roman eyes blinked in startled satisfaction as the god descended in a machine to dispense salvation on the stage, which faith, in the audience, had anticipated (while Democritus, succumbing in a measure to popular prejudice, granted to the upper air inhabitants "of the same form as men, but grander, composed of very subtle atoms, less liable to dissolution . . .").

As Jean was saying to Anatole in the bar, even then, —I just always kind of *expect* something nice to happen. And then it does.

The slung arm rose taut from the sling; the free one dropped its work of jamming the green muffler into a pocket, and collapsed as Otto stood, swaying gently as though suspended, like Absalom perhaps, hanging by his chin in the terebinth tree as the darts of Joab found his heart, and so smitten he came down to earth: the revolving door turned, and from it issued an apparition on a fragmentary blast too weak to do more than flutter the end of the green muffler.

It was too late to go out another door. The man had seen him. Otto finished jamming his own muffler down into his pocket, in mechanical denial of what was happening, and came forward with his hand extended.

—Hullo, he said, a sound which took all of his energy, left him unable to add the word, —*Father.*

—Uh huh, said the other, looking round him quickly through the thick glasses, pulling the cane up under his arm, hardly pausing to shake hands. —Everything all right? he murmured, going on in toward the bar.

—Why yes, I . . .

—You better take my arm. It looks better.

—Why yes. I'm sorry. Of course. Otto guided him in; and they paused. —Do you want to have a drink first? I mean, a drink at the bar? Otto managed to ask, staring over a sagging shoulder at the sagging charm of Jean at the bar.

—I don't drink. Too many people at the bar anyhow. We'll get a table.

Otto followed, looking back over his own sagging shoulder at the bar. —It isn't really crowded, he said.

His companion turned, and for the first time fixed him with sharp pupils which seemed to penetrate him. —You're not drunk, are you?

—Drunk? I? Why no, no I . . .

—That would be a nice stew.

A lonely waiter appeared, to show them to a table in one corner, felicitously almost dark. Otto walked with a slight limp, in time to the *March of the Sardar* which came from the hidden amplifiers. The cane before him kept similar time. Passing an occupied table, Otto looked with horror at the man seated there: not at the man, perhaps, but at his tie: the inquisitorial stripes still challenged him. He still felt eligible, or had until this moment. The glance of the man at the table was cursory, from Otto to the grotesque striding before him, the glance of the British resident as the two ruined nobles followed the crippled clamor of their music toward the south.

They were imprisoned, side by side, behind a table against the wall.

—You shouldn't have jumped like that, when you met me.

—Oh, did I?

—It just don't look good.

—I know, I...

—People notice things like that.

—I know. The waiter dropped menus before them and escaped. —I guess... well I mean we might as well start right off with dinner.

—You want to *eat*?

—Well, I mean I thought we were going to... I guess it doesn't really matter. It was difficult for Otto to study the figure beside him; nevertheless he tried, beyond the bushy hair and the heavy glasses. Otto wanted to see his teeth. —It's funny, he said. —You have such black hair.

—What's so funny about it?

—Well, I mean because mine is so light, Otto answered as the cane clattered to the floor.

—Is it on crooked? his companion asked in a low tone, raising his hand to his brow, and passing it delicately over his temple. —I been kind of rattled all evening, he said. —Since I left home.

—Why. I mean is anything wrong? at home?

—"He that is slow to wrath is of great understanding: but he that is hasty of spirit exalteth folly." I just done something sort of hasty, like the Bible says there. But stupidity gets me sometimes. I just blow up. He sat back, then, and appeared to relax. —That's dangerous in any business, let alone this one.

—Yes, said Otto. —Of course. He held the large menu card up as a screen for his confusion, increased now by a scent which crept up around him, a familiar fugitive aroma which he could not identify. He was not reading the menu, but anticipating, as though reality in any desperate measure would suffice to anchor his covetousness; and he did not dare look up the bar for Jean. Clams, gros, to start? or omelette aux truffes?

—But those things don't hardly seem to matter tonight. I feel in a nice mood. Coq au vin? Pigeon aux petits pois? Poularde au riz, sauce suprême?

—I always feel this way after a good job. And Christmas all over the place... The lonely waiter appeared, and he silenced.

Foie gras à la gelée de Porto? Poulet... Fonds d'artichauts... Salade à la grecque...

—Hamburger steak, sounded beside him; and the music was Mozart's *Turkish March*. Where had he found that? Otto realized that he was looking at the wine list. As he folded the huge card back upon itself, the voice said, —Same thing for you?

—Yes, I . . .

—Two hamburger steaks, well done. And hurry it up.

Albert, King of the Belgians, careening gloriously down among the crevices of rock, gone, never to reappear and interrupt legends offered about him, to suffer translation from the fiction of selective memories to the betrayal of living reality.

Otto looked at the heavy glasses, saw dust on the surfaces of the lenses. —I noticed your eyes. Are they . . . I mean, very bad? I mean, they really look . . .

—Eserine.

—Oh. Is it contagious? I mean, is it dangerous?

—Dangerous? It's not dangerous.

—But . . . is it painful?

—No. You can feel it, but it's not painful.

—Oh. Otto folded his hands before him. —Is it hereditary, do you know? he asked, looking up.

—Is it what?

—I mean, how did you get it?

—I got it from a friend of mine.

—Oh, said Otto, and sat a bit further away. Then he said agreeably, —I suppose you wonder what I've been doing with myself.

—Keeping busy I guess, was the answer, in an uninterested tone. Otto looked down at his hands, and reconsidered. —What have you been up to lately?

—I'm working on a passport now. It's no job for a beginner. It never was work for bums to get into. They ruin it for the real craftsman.

—Yes. I mean I guess it's like that in everything. But passports? I mean, what are you . . .

The lonely waiter bore down, a plate in each hand. —All right, can it.

—What? I mean, I just asked about passports, what are you . . .

—It's a very cold night out tonight, ain't it. Their plates were put before them, and the waiter went the way he had come. —What's the matter with you, anyway. Don't you know there's some things you just don't ask about like that? This is a public place.

—Oh. I'm sorry, Otto said, and watched his companion cross himself, and start to eat. —Are you *Cath*olic? he asked.

The eyes turned full upon him, penetrating the dust. He swayed, and looked down at his plate. —Am I Catholic! What do you think I am?

—Oh. I mean, that's fine. I was just sort of surprised. Seven thin slices of mushroom stuck to the top of the meat. Magic number: Otto cut into them. Somewhere (in exile, doubtless), the handsome young prince must be sitting, over cognac so fine it could hardly be swallowed, recalling legends of the king. Otto put a piece of the dry meat into his mouth, and could hardly swallow it. Beside him, he smelled lavender, and felt ill. He looked up to see the blond Jean leave the bar, carrying her bag. She glanced at the two of them without recognition or interest. Otto raised his face, his eyebrows, and his fork, to signal her.

—You know her? You know that woman?

—No, I . . . well, I talked to her while I was waiting.

—It's no time to get mixed up with women. Keep yourself out of trouble. He went on eating.

—Yes, well . . . I guess it was just Christmas, you know, I mean, the sort of Christmas feeling. Otto raised another shred of meat on his fork. —I've thought of it, you know. Joining the Church, I mean.

—Uh-phhm, was his answer, through a mouthful of bread.

—It's . . . it kind of gives a reason for things that otherwise don't seem to have any. I mean, it legitimizes . . . well, you know . . . life, sort of.

—You're either born into it or you're not. The fork beside him rested on the tablecloth. —There's too many people around joining it as if it was a sight-seeing party.

—But I . . .

—You got to be born into it.

—In a sense, I was, said Otto, with a slight laugh of confidence, waiting affirmation. There was none. He rested his fork on the table. He felt dizzy. From the corner of his eye he saw the figure beside him bowed over the plate, eating fast, moving the food only a matter of inches from the plate to his mouth. A fly descended upon the bread, and busied itself there. Otto's hand shook as he raised it with the fork. —I guess it's silly, that I should be nervous now, but I am I guess.

—Hide it the best way you can. It's all right to be nervous, anybody gets nervous in a thing like this sometimes. But you don't need to show everybody you're nervous. You look pretty young.

—Young? Well I guess I do *look* young. But I've been out of college for about three years now.

—College? You went to college? He wiped his mouth with his napkin, bowing his head to do so, and looked up.

—Yes, I thought you . . . I went to Harvard, Otto said, and for the first time noticed the man's necktie. —Why . . . you have on a Porcellian tie. Otto stared at the silk pigs' heads. —Were you P.C.? I mean, I didn't even know you went to Harvard.

—Me at college? You know where I studied. Attica and Atlanta.

—But . . . that tie, it is the Porcellian tie isn't it.

—Don't worry, kid. I know what I'm doing.

The fly lit on Otto's hand, and he shook it away. His legs were crossed, and he commenced rubbing his ankle up and down against what he believed to be the center leg of the table. The man in gray was leaving the bar. As he watched him go, Otto's hand rose with slow automatism to his chest, and his wrist pressed the vacancy there. Who could prove a thing? if he rose abruptly, dumping the table over if necessary, to turn square upon the upholstered shoulders beside him and cry, —Do *you* believe this? But then, who would pay the check? and the bar bill? There would certainly be no offer of a Christmas gift of money which Otto must, somehow, manage to suggest: a gift which might pay for the drinks he had enjoyed with Jean, for having seen the frayed trouser-cuffs when they walked to the table he could hardly expect more. Suddenly he imagined his hair furiously red, his skin dark, or eyes at a telltale slant: that would give the lie to this whole thing. But no: his nose was, really, quite like the one beside him, though Otto refused to recognize it as being absolutely so, derivative. Noses were, after all, noses, quite similar among Caucasians.

The most gross insult might simply be to say, —I trust there hasn't been some mistake? Better than that, to get up quietly from the table, cross the room quickly to the gentleman in light gray flannel (who also had a nose) and shake hands with him. But even now, the gentleman in light gray flannel was gone.

All this time, the sling had bumped between them without rousing curiosity. Now, he heard, —What are you wearing that sling for, you really got hurt?

—Well, in a way, I . . .

—I thought it was faked. You haven't learned how to handle it yet. You act like you're keeping a live squirrel in it.

—But it . . . I . . .

The music was the *Blue Danube* waltz. Otto rubbed his mustache with his fingertip, and looked into a distant mirror where he could see Santa Claus's strategic entrance, and stealthy approach to the door of the bar, where he was apprehended.

The fork beside him clattered to the plate. —I'm done.

—I think I've had enough, Otto said, barely half finished with the meal. He lit a cigarette, as the smell of lavender rose, heard a ringing in his ears from nowhere, wet his lips and heard forced salivation. Might it not all be rehearsed again, but differently, he thought, seeing a thin man of average height and quiet manner seated at a table in the middle of the room, finishing his dinner with a brandy: might Otto not have walked over and shaken his hand, and seated across from him, unsurprised, have listened to his intimacies with opera stars, artists, producers, over breast of guinea hen and wine?

The man in the club tie rose, looked at them, locking them together in his glance, and left. It was too late. Procrustes' bed was made: the only thing now was to get out of it the best way he could, which Otto did, more with weariness than pain. —It's kind of difficult, to talk about money, but...

—I've got it right here for you. You want to take it now? said the voice through a mouthful of bread. He was cleaning his fingernails with a tine of his salad fork.

—Take what?

—Twenties. Five G's in perfect twenties.

—Five what?

—Five thousand. Here, it's a thick packet. He motioned with his elbow to his side pocket.

—Five thousand *dollars?*

—Christ! Keep your voice down.

—But isn't that too much? I mean, even with Christmas...

—Listen, are you sure you're not drunk?

—Why no, *no*, I...

—I wouldn't give this stuff to you if you was drunk. You'd probably throw it all over town before the night's over. Lift it out of my pocket there.

—Oh I'll be very careful of it, ver-y care-ful of it... Otto said as he reached into the pocket and lifted the packet out, while the other sat silent and unconcerned, cleaning his nails with a tine of his salad fork. Otto wanted another glass of whisky. He opened the packet, and took out a twenty.

—Christ! Don't wave them around here! said the man beside him, and looked over the room quickly. But no one was near to notice them, and when he looked back he seemed unable to resist taking the bill from Otto and laying it on the cloth before him. —Beautiful, he said. —Beautiful, isn't it.

—Yess, Otto gasped.

—A real work of art. He stared into the face of the seventh President. —You know it takes six different artists to make one of these? That's what makes it tough. Six to one. Six against one, you might say. He turned it over, and ran a fingertip gently over the portico of the White House. —A real work of art, he said. —You don't learn that at Harvard.

Otto stared. He clutched the packet, as though it were liable to be wrenched from him at any instant.

—You know, they burn around six tons of this stuff a day, the true quill, down in the Bureau of Printing and Engraving. Worn-out bills. It's a crime.

—Yes, but...well...this...was all Otto could say.

The hand beside him rose to catch at a lapel, as the man sat back and stared upward, relaxed in nostalgia. —Johnny the Gent died the other day, he said. —You know him?

—No, I...

—He melted down the Ascot Cup. He was the first one to gild the sixpence, and passed them as half-sovereigns until they had to call them in. He knew so much about the Church that once he posed as Bishop of the Falkland Islands. He just died, Johnny. He had about ten dollars on him.

Otto appeared to listen; but he heard nothing but jarring syllables.

—He organized the best den London ever saw. He was even a Sunday School teacher for five years. He was a great man. I've thought of him a lot of times when I was sitting in the hole.

The waiter approached a nearby table. —Put that stuff away. Otto put the twenty into his pocket, and the packet between his knees.

—I miss him when a great artist dies like that. He was no bum. It's no place for bums to get into, but they're ruining it every day. There hardly is a single old master left, a real craftsman, like Johnny, or Jim the Penman. And me. I haven't had a notice in the *Detector* in fourteen years.

—The what? Otto asked, politely, but firm.

—*The National*... listen. Shut up and listen to that a minute. It is.

—What?

—Vissi d'arte, vissi d'amore, he murmured with the music, —non feci mai male ad anima viva... And they sat silent to the violent grief-impassioned end.

When it was done, Otto said, —That was very nice.

—*Nice?* Is that all you can say? But you're just a kid, you never heard Cavalieri do Tosca.

—No, I...

—I'm going to get out now. He stood, and found his cane.

—Well... but I mean, don't you want some coffee or something?

—No. I shouldn't have stayed this long anyhow.

Otto took the check. —I'll get this, he said graciously.

—All right, kid. Thanks.

—But thank you, I... Merry Christmas. Otto was left, the packet clutched against his parts, sniffing the delicious aroma of lavender, only half aware that the table had four legs. A fly landed on his hand, and he simply stared at it.

Two men went out the revolving door, the second a figure in a checked suit, who had been waiting for some time in the lobby. He caught the other by the arm. —This is you, isn't it?

—What do you mean?

—You're Frank? They told me I was going to meet you in the lobby. They kept me half an hour late, but you're an hour. Have you got the stuff? Five G's in queer?

—Jesus and Mary.

—I'm the pusher they sent, you know? Have you got the queer?

—Jesus Mary and Joseph.

—What's the matter with you, for Christ's sake?

—That kid. That fairy. He took every bit of it. He sat there rubbing his ankle against my leg...

—Where'd he go? We'll go in and get him. He's got the queer on him?

—We'll wait out here. We'll get him when he comes out.

—Where you going now?

—Right here in this doorway. The coat came off, was reversed, the black wig went into one pocket, green muffler and glasses into the other, and the sandy mustache appeared, stuck to his upper lip. —It's cold, said Mr. Sinisterra. —And stop calling it "the queer."

Otto had appeared at the desk briefly, to put down a ten-dollar deposit on his bill. He was taken to a room. There he sat on the edge of the bed. He tore the wrapping from the money, and started to count it. The sling got in his way. He ripped it off and threw it on the floor. Then he made piles of ten bills each, fanned out alternating backs and faces, on the bed cover. He stood looking at it, and then turned to the mirror, and ran his fingertip over his mustache. He called downstairs, and waited for the bellboy to come with a razor and "anything else that might come in handy," passing the time counting the money, in various positions. When the razor arrived, he shaved quickly and dressed. He reeled a little, putting four twenties with his change (which included a ten), and the rest into a drawer, hurriedly, for he heard stirring next door, remembering his neighbor. He turned off the light, closed his door, and stood outside 666, where he knocked and, unable to restrain himself, and as surprised to find the door unlocked, threw it open.

—Who...what do you want? Jean cried, pulling a sheet to her throat, uncovering her neighbor, whose light gray flannel suit lay on the floor.

—Why you...why...

—Get out, get out of here, what do you mean coming in a lady's room like that.

The door banged.

—Now just who the devil was that?

—Don't worry, honey, it's only a fairy I met down in the bar.

—A fairy?

—You know, queer. He said he was a writer, and they're always queer nowadays.

—There he goes, said the man in the checked suit. —Out the side door. Look out of the way, you dumb bastard.

—That's no way to talk to Santa Claus.

—Well get out of our way.

—Merry Christmas. Have you got a dime for old Saint Nick?

—Get the next cab in the line and follow him.

The two cabs pulled away from the curb half a minute apart, and a police car drew up before the hotel.

—I could sue you for false arrest, Mr. Pivner said when he got into the lobby, with a policeman, —if that would do any good. Do you know what you've done?

Behind him the policeman talked with the tall bellboy, who said, —Well Jesus, *I* thought he was drunk. The guy with him was. The policeman said, —We got him down to the station house and found a needle on him. We thought he was a junkie. He's real pissed-off.

—Do you know what you've done? Did you see him? A boy with a scarf like this on, he came here to meet me, that was my son, my son . . .

The policeman turned to the revolving door, and the tall bellboy said to him, —While you're at it, take Santy Claus along. He's driving us nuts out there.

The controversy in the sky, by this time, was no nearer settlement; there was really no promise of armistice at all, though the haggling might continue, precipitating fine rain for periods of monotonous variance, broken by impatient bursts of sleet. The skyline of the city was reduced to two dimensions. There was no depth; accustomed to mass, and there was no such sensation, but instead buildings in immediate isolation, their heights awhirl in the weather, their lights incredible in the night, their feat undiminished by comparison with the mass which had clung to their sides pretending support, cowering now out of sight, would be there next day if it were fair, pretending, and sharing the steep triumph of these hampered giants tonight abandoned in trial to their integrity.

The first cab turned into Jones Street; the second waited at the corner. —He's going into that doorway where all those cops are. What's he doing there. —How should I know what he's doing there. I never should have trusted him. —I wouldn't trust a fairy. —He's not a Catholic. I should have known. They watched Otto talk with one of the policemen, and get back into his cab. —How'd'ya ever *do* a thing like that? —It was pride, it was the deadly sin of pride, I was so proud of those...those...O Mary, pray for me...If I hadn't been so proud I would have watched my step... —Let's just let him go, said the man in the checked suit as Otto's cab left the curb. —The hell with him.

—Let him go? with all that? You think it's worthless, that paper? You think it's a cheap job I did? Driver follow that cab.

The juke-box played *Return to Sorrento*.

Someone said, —Have you read this? It's by a woman who spent the *entire* winter last year in Rome, she tells all about it here.

At hand, a limp wrist hung on air. —I was in Florida for two fearfully rainy weeks, and I didn't get browned very much...Laughter sprinkled up around him.

—I'm a drunkard, said one of two young men sitting at a table with Victoria and Albert Hall. —Nothing but a drunkard, he repeated despondently. —You think that's bad, I'm a drunk and I'm queer too, said the other, —an alcoholic *and* a homosexual. —So? demanded the paterfamilias. —I'm a drunk, a homosexual, and a Jew.

She looked them over calmly, and finished her drink. —I'm alcoholic, homosexual, and a Jew, she stated. —And I'm crippled. When the next round of drinks arrived, she was the toast.

—Have you heard the one about the muscular fellow named Rex? who had minuscular organs of sex?

—Do you know, Il y avait une jeune fille de Dijon?

—Es gibt ein Arbeiter von Linz?

—"The whole gripping story is founded on fact. Look at the beautiful girl shown in the accompanying cut..." Anselm read aloud. —Are you listening? "Note the cruel marks cut in her tender body by the lash of the cat-o'-nine-tails wielded by the hands of a heartless and Christless Mother Superior in whose heart all human sympathy had been assassinated by the papal system..." He lowered *The Moan of the Tiber* to look up at Stanley. —You're still brooding over that thing? he asked, seeing the torn strip of newspaper in Stanley's hand. —That's yesterday's paper, the whole of Saint Mark's is probably under water by now. What are you drinking so much coffee for?

—I have to stay awake, when I get home to work, Stanley said and looked anxiously at his wrist watch.

—To work! Anselm muttered. —What are you waiting for? But he appeared to have no interest in what Stanley might answer, or not. He sat slumped, looking sullenly out from the table at the evening victims of the Viareggio. The spots on his face were dulled, his eyes lit with a smoldering rancor now and then as he watched them, but his tone was vague when a tall girl with dark hair reaching her furpiece said to someone, —Well I have yet to see an animal reading a book...and Anselm mumbled, —How'd you like to get your hand in her muff? Then he brought a hand up, fingers turned in upon the palm, and commenced to bite his nails. A minute later he had slumped again, motionless, and started to whistle, dull and rasping through his teeth.

Stanley looked up. —What's that? What you're whistling.

—*Too Much Mustard.*

—Too much...what? No, what is it? It's familiar, it's Bach?

—Yes, it's called I can give you anything but love, Anselm answered without looking up. —Bach wrote it when he was three, he added, —for Mother's Day.

—Anselm, Stanley said inclining toward him slightly, —is there something, is something wrong?

—Is something wrong! Anselm turned at him. —That's the stupidest... But his voice tailed off, he lowered his eyes from Stanley, and scratched his head.

—If there's anything I could...do?

Anselm looked at the blunt black ridges of his nails, then held them out. —I've got a sycosis, see? Not psychosis, like these other crazy bastards. Plain sycosis. Scabs. And he went back to scratching his head.

Mr. Feddle entered, an alarm clock swinging from his neck on a piece of twine. In the doorway he bumped the man in the checked suit, whose companion said, —Go in and get him. —I couldn't just pull him out of there, said the man in the checked suit. —He won't stay long, he's too jumpy to hang around a dump like this. —Look out, there he goes!...—Goes, hell. He's going to the can.

As he stood, occupied, the mirror was beside him at his left shoulder, and Otto stared into it. He continued to stare as he turned a minute later, buttoning his trousers, weaving slightly, and allowed the smile to come to his face slowly as though savoring the renewal of an acquaintance long away, dead perhaps, for all they knew, in the jungles; returned now, and returned affluent. Then the smile left his face as slowly, and the same reckoned composure with which it had come: with all the sincerity of a suppliant before an icon he said, —If I were a character in a play...would I be credible? When the door banged open he was standing looking down at the pale left hand extended from his sleeve, and licking the strangely naked upper lip.

—What are you grinning about? You look pretty pleased with yourself.

—What? Oh...he spun around. —Max.

—What happened, you sell your play or something?

—My play? I...yes, yes that's it. How did you know? Yes...

—Good, Max said over his shoulder. Smiling, he added, —Look, I hope you didn't think I had anything to do with what people were saying.

—People? Otto repeated vaguely, going toward the door.

—You know, that you'd plagiarized...

—Oh, oh that, yes, no, no I wouldn't have thought that, Otto said, and left Max bound there to deepen the steaming gully in the cake of ice in the drain. He saw Stanley sitting at a table with Anselm, who was listlessly turning pages in a magazine which bore the picture of a girl sliding down a bannister, and the challenge, *Can Freaks Make Love?* on the cover. Anselm tore something out and pushed it across the table to Stanley who looked at it and then away quickly, his eyes searching the room for refuge until he lowered them to the floor.

—Hey, Hannah? Look at those two, said a tall round-headed young man in an expensive suit. —Did you ever see that Kollwitz print, *"Zwei Gefangene Musik hörend"*? That's what they look like, two prisoners listening to music.

—Stanley is a sort of prisoner, Hannah said half to herself.

—Anybody is who's always broke. He handed her the beer he'd got her.

—You can talk! Hannah turned on him, accepting the dripping glass. —You work for your money, so you don't have to worry spending it.

He stared at her; then cleared his throat and asked, —Say, is that really Ernest Hemingway behind me?

—What if it is, what would that make you?

—He, I...I'd like to meet him, I think he's a great writer.

—You think some of it will wipe off on you? You're still a salesman. Did you ever read Cummings' poem, *a salesman is an it that stinks to please*...and you want to write?

—I do in my spare time, I've taken a course...

—Go stink to please somewhere else.

—Yes, I...all right, all right...He turned two hundred dollars' worth of tweed on her, and said, —Mister Hemingway? My name is George...

—Glad to see you, George, said the Big Unshaven Man. —What are we drinking?

Otto paid for his whisky-and-soda with a twenty-dollar bill, and stood unsteadily looking about him.

—What are you mumbling about? Hannah demanded from just beneath the level of his gaze. He was looking at a tall blond girl who had just said, in Boston accents, that Paris was like a mouthful of decayed teeth.

—Hannah? I just sold my play, Otto repeated, but aloud this time, as though finding confirmation in what he heard.

—You sold your play? her query sustained him, but no further than, —Can you buy me a beer? as she put an empty glass on a table behind her. He struggled to the bar, got her a glass and handed it to her over someone's shoulder, but when he'd paid for it and turned again she was gone, leaving only her query echoing Max's, sanctioning what he had heard in his own words, and ratified now with a murmured yes and a smile of discovery. But immediately he saw Max, standing at the table with Anselm and Stanley, looking in his direction and talking through a smile, he felt unsteady again, called upon to defend himself, and his hand rose to the empty fall of his jacket as he approached them.

Max always looked the same, always the same age, his hair always the same short length, in his smile the humorless agreeability of one who could neither suffer friendship nor celebrate enmity, a parody on the moment, as his clothes caricatured a past at eastern colleges where he had never been.

—And if it's only through sin that we can know one another, and share our human frailty? Stanley went on, staring into his coffee. —And by doing that, we come to know ourselves . . .

—Crossing the Atlantic Ocean to get laid. He can't even get it up without a dose of methyltestosterone, Anselm interrupted, without looking up as Otto approached, without a pause in his speaking he tore something from his magazine and held it out to Otto, who read, "LONELY? 25¢ brings magazine containing pictures, descriptions of lonely sincere members everywhere, seeking friendship, companionship, marriage . . ." —What better reason is there to get out of this stupid white Protestant country, for Christ's sake. Yes, for Christ's sake. At least Catholic countries take sin as a part of human nature, they don't blow their guts when they find you've gone to bed with a woman. Somebody like him is scared to try it here, he'd rather go where nobody knows him, a bunch of stupid foreigners he doesn't have to respect because they don't speak English, and don't have any money, where nobody will point at him in the street if they see him coming out of a whorehouse. Christ. It breaks my heart. Somebody like that, it breaks my heart. But you know what breaks my heart? He looked up directly at Otto, who started, the smile jarred from his face, whose eyes, evading a wince, found Max's indulgent smile. —That that's sin! Anselm hissed, looking back at the table top. —That . . . Chhrist!

None of them spoke. Stanley clung to his coffee cup as though moored there. Otto tottered slightly. Max stood reflecting the vacant satisfaction he found in exposé.

—With all the . . . rotten betrayals around us, and that, that . . . that one moment of trust, is sin? Anselm whispered, looking at none of them.

None of them spoke until Anselm said, —You're spilling your God-damned drink, what's the matter with you? and Otto, righting his glass and licking his naked upper lip, came round to the other side of the table and the empty chair Max stood beside, bumping a girl who was carrying *Everybody Can Play the Piano* under her arm, and saying, —Well I thought his approach was rarther crude, just coming at me like that with a dollar bill wrapped around it...

—You're not sitting here? Otto asked Max, who stepped aside with the courtesy accorded infirmity. —Who's going abroad? Otto asked after a moment, seated. Stanley looked up at Anselm, as though to give him opportunity of answering, then said himself in a quelled tone, —Don Bildow... sounding as though he wanted to say more, but could find no more to say. And Otto looked up, over backs and shoulders, to see Don Bildow's white face bobbing behind the plastic-rimmed glasses; and heard, from someone falling toward the table, —Everything is either concave or convex... someone caught and raised to receive this intelligence, —Nothing, absolutely nothing, can convince me that all of us and everything isn't shrinking at the rate of one millimeter a minute...

—Has anybody seen Esme? Otto asked, his voice in an abrupt strain. —I just went by her house, he added hurriedly, and brought his glass to his lips.

—Nobody there? Max asked behind him.

—Well no, no not really, I mean no.

—Not even Chaby?

—No, he was... he wasn't there, no. I mean, I didn't see him, I didn't really go in, I... I just passed there, Otto finished looking up confused, rummaging his pale left hand, whose freedom no one had noticed, in a pocket, and seeing Stanley's ragged mustache, licking a lip whose nakedness no one had remarked. —Would anybody like a drink? he asked, and signaled a waiter who did not see him. Behind him, someone said, —A million people try to disappear in America every year, a million Americans try to erase themselves, that's a statistic and it doesn't include criminals either, a million a year, a million people a year...

The juke-box played *Return to Sorrento;* and nearby someone said that Saint Francis Xavier was only four and a half feet tall.

—"Does Drunkenness Threaten Your Happiness or Your Loved Ones? Our Remarkable New Discovery Quickly and Easily Helps Bring Relief from All Desire for Liquor!... No Will Power Is Necessary To Stop Drinking. This Is Strictly a Home Method!..." Anselm read, returned to his magazine and his dull tone.

—I'd just like some coffee, Stanley said.

—Have you got some money? Anselm asked. —If you do I'd rather eat. And he called a waiter.

—Yes, as a matter of fact I, yes I just sold my play, Otto said to them. He looked quickly from Anselm's shrug to the first sign of Stanley's approving pleasure but could not stop his eyes, and turned to Max for confirmation.

—Eggplant Parmigiana, Anselm ordered beside him, and Otto caught the waiter's arm as he departed, to order another whisky, and coffee for Stanley who looked up at that moment to ask, —Didn't you go to see Esme earlier?

—Well yes, earlier, I saw her earlier... The confusion in Otto's voice was reflected in his eyes. Escaping Stanley's simple question, he looked round at hazard for a new topic and unfortunately found it immediately. —There's Hannah, he said. —I just saw Hannah, she... I... The waiter appeared with their orders.

Anselm was laughing. —But I don't see why someone said what they said about me, about Hannah and me, Stanley brought out. And Otto, fleeing the appeal on this side, and the laughter on the other, looked to Max, whose smile was the conspiracy of an instant, an embrace confirmed in Stanley's discerning, and quickly lowered eyes.

—Stanley, you don't think... I didn't mean... Otto commenced, the lines of his face rising toward his brow in anxious entreaty, when Anselm interrupted, growling, with his mouth full, and Otto turned to him for deliverance.

Anselm ate rapidly, jamming pieces of bread into his mouth between forkfuls of the eggplant, as though he expected it all to be taken away at any moment. Still he managed to growl at Stanley, and crumbs flew from his mouth across the table. —The beast, Anselm gurgled, chewing, —the beast in the jungle. The beast with two backs, he growled and snarled and laughed at once. —Stalking, crouching, ready to spring, that's the number of the beast that's stalking you, the beast that's waiting to devour you, the beast with two backs, waiting to sspring!... and he lunged, blowing bread crumbs.

—Look, Anselm... Otto's voice quavered toward firmness.

But Anselm already appeared to have relented. He sat chuckling over his almost empty plate, looking down as though some imminent satisfaction filled his mind; while under the table out of their sight, his hands opened a small flat tin, took out an envelope, and unrolled its contents.

Meanwhile the waiter stood there with the bill, and Otto seized the interruption, taking a roll of money from his pocket. —Here, I'll get this, he said, as though it were necessary to forestall them, though neither moved until Anselm shot an arm forth unseen and dropped something into Stanley's coffee. And as Otto sat back, folding his money, Anselm asked him agreeably, —Could you lend me something?

—Why, why yes, sure, Otto said. —How much?

—Whatever you can.

—Yes, Otto repeated, hesitated, and turned to Stanley. —Do you need any right now, Stanley? Any money? because I'd be glad to, to lend you some?

—Maybe, five dollars? Stanley said. —I might need it, if I go to the dentist, I have a tooth...

—Here, take this, Otto said unfolding the bills again, and he held out a twenty. —Go ahead, you might need it.

—No, just five, that's all I'd need, just five.

—Give him five, I'll take the twenty, Anselm said quickly, putting a hand out. —You know the kind of a lousy life I have, I need it... But he watched Otto hand the clean twenty-dollar bill to Stanley, over another faint gasp of protest, and accepted himself a worn five, murmuring, —Thanks, I... thanks. And, have you got a cigarette? having trouble even then getting one from the pack with his blunt bitten finger-ends.

—I didn't know you smoked, Otto said to him.

—I do sometimes, Anselm said holding the cigarette unfamiliarly, and then he folded the five-dollar bill smaller and smaller, until it was a wad scarcely the width of his tortured thumbnail. He puffed the cigarette once or twice, then dropped it on the floor and stepped on it; and in that minute all of the sullenness of a little while before had returned, and he stared at the table as though he were sitting there alone.

Max had turned away to talk with a small elderly man dressed in black, with black rubbers and a black hat, carrying a black umbrella. He appeared to say nothing, nodded his head occasionally, and accepted the drink Max brought him, while Max talked. Max returned to identify the black figure as the art critic for *Old Masses*, said he had a very incisive wit, and had given his pictures very good notices, —which is what makes all the difference, Max added smiling.

—It's strange having the use of this left arm again, Otto said finally.

—Oh yes, you were wearing a sling, weren't you, Stanley said, looking up quickly at the hand motionless on the table. —It looks very white, he commented. —Did it leave a bad scar?

—Why don't you ask him to show you the scar? Anselm demanded. —I'll bet it was a nice hole. You envy him, for Christ sake.

—It isn't the wound that matters so much, getting it, Stanley said as Otto sat back and lowered the pale hand to his lap. —But the scar, the scar is a witness for all the wounds we get... all the wounds, all kinds of wounds. I heard about somebody once who had a scar and he bandaged it, every once in a while, to renew the wound.

—Scars, all Stanley wants is scars, to show people. Scars! Hey Stanley, did you hear about the reliquary they opened that was supposed to have Ignatius

Loyola's left arm in it? They brought it over on a boat, when they opened it they found an arm with a heart tattooed on it, with a bleeding dagger and the word *Mother*, ha, haha...

—That's not true, Stanley said promptly. —And it's not wanting to suffer, just for that, just to suffer, it's more...proving the right to it, to suffering.

—Come off it, man, said a haggard face rising over the back of a booth. —You're dragging us.

—He's right, for Christ sake, everybody suffers, the crime is in this world you suffer and it doesn't mean a God-damned thing, it doesn't fit anywhere. You can stand any suffering if it means something, Anselm went on rapidly, but still as though suppressing some specific thing which filled his mind. —The only time suffering's unbearable is when it's meaningless, he finished, muttering.

At that Otto raised an eyebrow and licked his lip, preparing to quote the lines with which Gordon reduced Priscilla toward the close of Act II, the scene in the doorway of the summer cottage which glittered before him even now, as though in production. GORDON: Suffering, my dear Priscilla, is a petty luxury of mediocre people. You will find happiness a far more noble, and infinitely more refined...

—You remember what Montherlant has to say, Max interrupted them.

—Le bonheur est un état bien plus noble et bien plus raffiné que la souffrance... His French was unprofessional and surprisingly clear. Otto muttered impatiently at being interrupted the moment he had started to speak, and turned to ask Stanley if he had ever read any of Vainiger, as Max finished, —le petit luxe des personnes de médiocre qualité.

—That's a lot of crap, Anselm said without looking up.

—When he says that life must be led in the dark, Otto pursued, —and that we must assume postulates to be true which, if they were true, would justify...

—Hey Stanley, I've got a song for you.

—Leave him alone.

—Hannah, sit down, sit down in Otto's place, he's delivering a lecture on *Die Philosophie des Als Ob*, Anselm advised her.

—On what? Otto demanded curtly.

—The buttons say U.S., So they just mean us I guess, Anselm sang, tearing something from his magazine which he handed to Hannah. —So they must just stand for me...and Mo-therrr...

"Get Male HORMONES   Science has discovered that domestic and business worries often disappear when male hormone deficiency is overcome... If you do not feel the return of that old-time activity, that keen love and zestful desire for life..." —Shut up and leave him alone, Hannah repeated, crumpling the paper but she did not drop it.

—Leave who alone? Otto and I are discussing Vaihinger, aren't we Otto? He's an expert on als ob, ich gebe Ihnen mein Wort, Hannah, an expert, ich bin ihm nicht gewachsen, Hannah...

—Shut up, she said to him, looking him straight in the face as he became more agitated. The spots on his complexion stood out vividly, and his hair was up as though a wind were blowing. He reached up and felt it, took out a dirty pocket comb and made cracking sounds combing his hair.

—Scabs, he said. —I'm sycotic. Do you know who I envy? I envy Tourette. He had a disease named after him, a very God-damned rare one.

—Are you drunk? If you're not why don't you shut up.

—When you have Tourette's disease you go around repeating dirty words all the time. Coprolalia. Everybody below Fourteenth Street has coprolalia. Then he opened his magazine and turned suddenly to Otto. —"Women are funny," he read. —"You never know whether you're making the right move or not. Avoid disappointment, heartbreak! Save yourself lots of tragedy. Don't be a Faux pas!"

—Anselm, Otto began quietly, —why don't you relax and...

—You're drunk. Why don't you try God? Four three-letter words, *Why Not Try God?* That's a book by Mary Pickford. Real coprolalia. You'd like that. Then he got breath and said, —You know who I envy? Never mind. The buttons say U.S....

—What's the matter with you tonight, is it on account of Charles? Hannah cut in, and Anselm stopped singing abruptly, and stared at her.

—I'm not... singing to you, he said after a moment, faltering, and he looked down at the dirty floor muttering something.

—Well why don't you...

—Well why don't you leave us alone!...you, God damn you, you...

—I meant to tell you how glad I am about your play, Stanley said to Otto. —I am, honestly.

—Thank you, I... I know you are, Otto said, and put a hand to his shoulder. —You're really good, aren't you Stanley.

—I wish I were. I wish everyone was.

—There'd be a lot of crazy priests out of work. Work! Hahaha...

—Anselm, you...

—Damn you Hannah, God damn you, is it any business of yours if I feel this way about Charles? And his mother coming here to get him and take him home to Grand Rapids and when he wouldn't go she left him here, with nothing? with his wrists...just like she found them, she...You remind me of her, maybe it's your God-damned smile. Maybe it's the way you try to get your hooks into Stanley, for his own good, for his own good!

—But what...

—It's the complacency I can't stand, Anselm burst out. —I can't stand it anywhere, but most of all I can't stand it in religion. Did you see Charles's mother? did you see her smile? that holier-than-thou Christian Science smile, she turns it on like... They're so complacent about this error of matter they've picked up, "It's nice because it's mine," that's the kind of a look they have, as if the old bag who started them off was the first one to think of the error of matter, didn't they ever hear of Catharism? or the Albigensians? or the Manichaeans? or even Bishop Berkeley? No, they stop thinking the minute they get hold of that thing *Science and Health*, they never read another book after that, they've got a corner on the Truth, everybody else is a Goy...

—So what have you got your balls in an uproar for? Hannah pressed him.

—Because Charles and I... I don't blame Charles a God damn bit for flipping. God is Love! We'd all flip, taking that from your own mother and you're lying there with your wrists slashed open. But love on this earth? Christ!... pity? compassion? That's why I've got my balls in an uproar if you want to know, talking about some kind of love floating around Christ knows where, but what did she give him? When he wouldn't go back to Grand fucking Rapids and be treated by Christian Science? She gave him one of those eternally damned holier-than-thou smiles and left him here. She left him here without a cent, to let Bellevue kill him, or let him try it again himself. God is Love, for Christ sake! If Peter had smiled like a Christian Scientist Christ would have kicked his teeth down his throat. He sat there whispering to himself, and then said, —At least the Catholics have some idea of humility, I have to admit.

—All right, Anselm, nobody...

—All right, all right, I'll shut up. But don't you understand me? He half rose from the table, looking at her with an insane intensity; and then shuddering through his frame, sank back in his chair, and she turned to Stanley.

—How is your mother? she asked him.

—You always ask me that, Hannah. Thank you for asking.

—But how is she?

—She's...waiting. She's still waiting very patiently. They're going to move her to another hospital.

—Catch my mother waiting patiently, Anselm muttered.

—Please don't talk disrespectfully of your mother, Anselm.

—She's a nut, Stanley, said Anselm calmly, looking up at him. —It's all right, I'm just stating a fact. She's a nut. An old nut. Right now she's probably down in the Tombs forcing a Bible on some poor bastard who just wants to be left alone with . . . alone. He was perspiring, staring at the dirty floor. —Do you care if He . . . a saint, kissing the leper's sores? he whispered to none of them; and then said, —Never mind, never mind, you don't . . . you can't . . . do you know who I envy?

Mr. Feddle's alarm clock swung like a pendulum as he almost fell, recovered, and tipped in the opposite direction. The swinging clock banged the edge of their table. —That old fool, Otto muttered, —except he's not funny.

—But very sad, Stanley said, drawing back as the clock swung in a dangerous arc, above the tabletop, and down. Someone cried, —Owwwww, as it cracked an ankle. —He's happy now because he's publishing something at last. People congratulate him, they're really laughing at him all the time because it's a vanity house, but he doesn't know that, that they're laughing at him. And his wife looks troubled and says, But publishing is expensive, isn't it, she doesn't know you're supposed to make money publishing something, she thinks any author has to pay to publish something of his own. At parties he used to go around autographing books from the bookshelves, he'd write a dedication and sign the author's name.

—That's good, Otto laughed, looking at Mr. Feddle's back which stood now stolid as a grandfather clock, only the pendulum swinging for he had just bowed and shaken hands. —It could go in a play.

—You shouldn't be cruel now, just when you've sold your play Otto.

—But even if I hadn't, Otto turned on Stanley. —Even if I hadn't . . .

—I envy Doctor Hodgkin. Anselm was cleaning his teeth thoughtfully with a folded match cover. —He had a disease named after him.

—What kind of disease?

—Hodgkin's disease, for Christ sake.

—A kind of cancer, said Max from behind them.

—Cancer hell. It's a kind of leukemia. If you want to know what it is, it's progressive hyperplasia of the lymphatic glands associated with anemia. Lymphadenoma.

—Where'd you hear that?

—I studied medicine, Anselm said, mumbling as he did usually when admitting to something favorable about himself; and as immediately embarrassed at so having drawn their attention, tore from his magazine "PILES! Amazingly fast palliative relief . . . No mess or sticky fingers! . . . It's Better, Faster, Easier to use! . . ." Beneath that: "GOD Wants You . . . Poor health? Money troubles? . . . A remarkable New Way of Prayer that is helping thousands to glorious New Happiness and Joys . . ." —Here Stanley, take your choice. It's all one anyhow, he said, rolling the cover closed on *Can Freaks Make Love?*

—You know, the trouble with you, you're all mothers' sons, Max said to them. Stanley stopped stirring his coffee and looked up, Anselm turned on him, Hannah had turned away. —You and Anselm and Charles, Max smiled agreeably to Stanley. —And Otto? he added, looking at Otto who said,

—As a matter of fact, I just finished dinner with my father a little while ago.

—Otto's part of a series of an original that never existed, Max said as though he had not heard.

—What do you mean, you...

—That's what you told me yourself yesterday, didn't you? Max drew him on.

—But no, Otto rubbed his hand over his eyes. —The series didn't exist but the original existed. The original did. It had to. He sat there looking glazed-eyed for a moment, then turned to Stanley. —I just had dinner with my father, he said, as though remembering back over a great distance, or attempting to separate a distant image from one which had recently supplanted it. —For the first time, he added.

—Did you like him? Stanley asked uncertainly.

—It's a funny feeling. It was strange, sort of... I feel like I'd lost something, like... I feel like nobody sort of... Staring straight ahead of him, he rubbed his forehead, and his wrist, descending, paused to press against his ribs, where no identity interrupted his contagion with himself. —I don't know, he mumbled, licking his naked lip, and went on in a low tone to Stanley, —Look, if you had a friend, somebody you haven't seen for a long time and he... someone else takes his place, but he still... I don't know. Never mind.

—You're drunk, Anselm offered.

—That's funny, Otto persisted without looking up at Max. —To say the original never existed! Look, he went on to Stanley, —Suppose you knew somebody who used to be a friend and who... and you found out he was, well like Mister Feddle, putting names on things that weren't his, I mean...

—You know who I envy? Anselm broke in on them impatiently. —I envy Christ, he had a disease named after him. Hahaha, hey Stanley?

Stanley pretended not to hear. He looked up from his cold coffee and said to Otto, —But if Mister Feddle saw a copy of a play by Ibsen, if he loves *The Wild Duck* and wishes he had written it, he wants to be Ibsen for just that moment, and dedicate his play to someone who's been kind to him, is that lying? It isn't as bad as people doing work they have no respect for at all. Everybody has that feeling when they look at a work of art and it's right, that sudden familiarity, a sort of... recognition, as though they were creating it themselves, as though it were being created through them while they look at it or listen to it and, it shouldn't be sinful to want to have created beauty?

—Why don't you go home and read Saint Anselm before you talk like this? said Anselm sitting forward, opening his eyes which he had closed as though attempting sleep here. —"The picture, before it is made is contained in the artificer's art itself," he said. "And any such thing, existing in the art of an artificer, is nothing but a part of his understanding itself."

—Saint Anselm. Dig him, said the haggard face bobbing over the back of the booth. —What are you trying to prove?

—I'm proving the existence of God, God damn you. Saint Augustine says a man who is going to make a box has it first in his art. The box he makes isn't life, but the one that exists in his art is life. "For the artificer's soul lives, in which all these things are, before they are produced."

—Where's God? In the box?

—You dumb son of a bitch . . .

—What's your favorite song, Anselm?

—*Nola.* Now screw, will you.

—I wish I had written *The Wild Duck*, Stanley said.

—I'm high, man.

—On what?

—On tea. We been balling all night. Have you got any? Hey Saint Anselm, have you got any charge? The haggard face hung over the back of the booth like a separate floating entity, rolling the eyes toward Max, to say, —He's in training. To be a saint.

—I notice he doesn't eat meat, is that the reason Anselm? Max asked. —So that your body won't . . .

—What God damn business is it of yours?

—Save the bones for Henry Jones . . . gurgled the haggard face.

—Anselm, preaching leftovers of the bleak ruin of Judaism, Max commenced with sententious ease, —a watered-down humanism . . .

—Cause Henry don't eat no meat. Hey Anselm, I got something for you.

—What are you supposed to know about religion? Anselm turned on Max.

—As Frazer says, Max explained indulgently, —the whole history of religion is a continuous attempt to reconcile old custom with new reason, to find sound theory for absurd practices . . .

—And what does Saint Augustine mean when he talks about the Devil perverting the truth and imitating the sacraments?

—This sacrament will go the way of all the rest of them, Max smiled. —It won't be long before they're sacrificing Christ to God as God's immortal enemy.

—Hey Anselm, listen to this, Daddy-o noster. Daddy-o, up in thy way-out pad. You are the coolest, and we dig you like too much . . .

—The god killed, eaten, and resurrected, is the oldest fixture in religion,

Max went on suavely. —Finally sacrificed in the form of some sacred animal which is the embodiment of the god. Finally everyone forgets, and the only sense they can make out of the sacrament is that they must be sacrificing the animal to the god because that particular animal is the god's crucial enemy, responsible for the god's death...

—Crucial!...Anselm spat out.

—Thy joint be right, the squares be swung...the haggard face continued, reading from a scrap of paper.

—And what does Justin Martyr mean, when he says "the evil spirits practice mimicry"? Anselm demanded. —Crucial!...

—Help us to score for some scoff today, and don't jump us salty if we come on like a drag, cause like we don't put down other cats when *they* goof...the haggard face went on in the silence straining between Anselm and Max. —For thine is the horse, the hash, and the junk...

—God damn you! give me that God-damned thing! Anselm burst out, swinging round and tearing the paper from the loose fingers; and the haggard face dropped out of sight, to bob up once more with, —Cause face it...and disappear again, as Anselm tore the shred of paper into smaller and smaller bits.

—Look Anselm, Max said coming up to him, —why don't you be reasonable? You'll end up like Charles, this pose of yours...

—Like Charles! And you, what...be reasonable! Anselm got to his feet. —This pose! this...Gott-trunkener Mensch, yes, you...be reasonable! That's what they called Spinoza, your prince of rationalists, damn him, you know what they offered Spinoza to conform? A thousand florins. "Conform outwardly" they told him, but what did he do, he changed his name from Baruch to Benedictus. The prince of rationalists!

Max had taken a step back, and another, smiling as though embarrassed for Anselm, as Anselm came on. —And what did they do, they damned him, the lens-maker Spinoza. They excommunicated him, right into the darkness of reason. The Schammatha, they damned him in the name that contains forty-two letters, they damned him in the name of the Lord of Hosts, and the Tetragrammaton, in the name of the Globes, and the Wheels, and the Mysterious Beasts...

Max was backing toward the door, toward the man in the checked suit who said, —To tell the truth I wouldn't dare go in there, they're all nuts. —I'm freezing to death, said his companion.

—In the name of Prince Michael and the Ministering Angels, Metateron, Achthariel Jah, the Seraphim, the Ofanim...Anselm went on shrilly as Max backed out into the night. —The trumpets dropped, they reversed the candles,

Amen, there's the Schammatha, damned right into the darkness of Reason ...
and he stood quivering in the empty doorway for a minute, indifferent to the
eyes turned on him. Then he spat in the street and came back to the table
where Otto had just stood preparing to leave. —Here, take this, Anselm said
to him, holding out his magazine. —There's a special article in it, *Can Freaks
Make Love?* with illustrations, a "rare photo of Chang and Eng, the original
Siamese twins, with two of their natural children ..." He slumped in his chair
again, and after a moment started to whistle, rasping through his teeth.

—What is that? what you're whistling, it's Bach isn't it?

He looked up at Stanley, and after a moment, —Yes, he admitted, —the
seventy-eighth cantata. His elbow rested on *The Moan of the Tiber.*

—An aria? Stanley asked to his empty face.

—"We hasten with feeble but diligent footsteps"... a duet, Anselm said
vaguely, watching Stanley stir the cold coffee, with a lifeless chill in his eyes.
—Sung by women, by women's voices ...

Stanley gasped, lifting the spoon from the coffee cup. —What is it? he
whispered, as the thing slipped back into the coffee. He raised it out again.

—Ha, ha, hahaha ...

The alarm clock strung to Mr. Feddle's neck went off.

—What is it? It's a ... he held it in the air, unable to move, staring at it.

—You can use it for a bookmark, Stanley. For when you read Malthus.
Hahahahaha ... look at what Stanley found in his coffee.

—Anselm, did you ...

—Hahahahahahahahaha

Mr. Feddle shut the clock off with one hand, finished his beer with the
other, bowed to three people, stumbling away from the hollow desperate
laughter behind him, out the door where he bumped the man in the checked
suit who said, —There, there he goes, out the other door, the side door.

Above emptied streets, the roseate heaving persisted; above bodies contorted
with sleep, strewn among the battlements erected in this common war without end, some wrenched as though in the last embrace, spoke with tongues,
untended and unattended, extended limbs and members to come up against
the thigh of another fallen, and be similarly still, or rise distended to enter
the warm nest again and swim in the dark channel, committing the final
assault in the anonymity of exhaustion, hearts emptied of prayer. But the
blood-luster of the sky witnessed that the battle was not done, though all were
slain: it shone like the sky over the Campagna where Attila's Huns met the
Romans in engagement so fierce that all were slain in deed, extreme but in-

conclusive, for their spirits continued the battle three nights and days over the field of unburied dead.

In the bar of a midtown hotel where the rear guard bivouacked among chrome and glass, scarred, alert, at battle stations (for there's no discharge in the war), Otto rested his left arm openly before him, raised one eyebrow, turned his lips down at the corners, flared his nostrils, and paid with a twenty-dollar bill. He spilled his drink. —Better give me another, he said. —Irish.

—You've had enough, Jack.

—Will you give me another drink?

—You've had enough tonight. Go home and sleep it off.

—Have I had enough? May I buy you a drink, madame?

—Come on, Jack, don't start any trouble. Leave the lady alone.

—I'm talking to her, not to you.

—Come on, fellow. Be a sport. Get the hell out of here.

The man in the checked suit came in the street door as Otto, clutching *Can Freaks Make Love?* rolled in his right hand, strode from the bar into the lobby of the hotel.

—You want to buy some pictures?

—Pictures? Otto asked, turning.

—Girls, you know?

—Just girls?

—Yeh, what'sa matter, you queer? He started to thrust back into the envelope the pictures he had half displayed, tangles of white limbs.

—Don't I know you? Otto stared at the young man, the hat on the back of his head, the extinguished cigarette stub in the corner of his mouth. —You don't know me, Mac, the young man said quickly. —You don't know me. You want these or not.

—Let's see them.

—What's the matter, you don't trust me? I can't bring them out here. A buck for the pack.

—All right, here. Here. Otto handed him a one-dollar bill.

In the men's room, he opened the envelope. A sailor banged the door, coming in, and Otto went into a booth. He stared at the first picture; and then sat down, staring at it. He turned it up, and looked at each one, his fingers quivering against their glossy surfaces, at each one quickly, ascertaining the face, unable to contain the whole figure in his apprehension, seizing at details, the unfamiliar maple chair she sat on, curled in, the Venetian blinds, the wallpaper, the upholstery pattern on the chair, her fingernails, the lines of her knuckles, the irregular dent of her navel and the two full blots swelling toward him, detailed blemishes on the expanse of her flesh, which delineated it but could not bring it to life in any variety of pose and exposure, obstacles at which his gaze stumbled, passing over the shadowed white in a silent mania of search which led him helplessly to her face, and deserted him there, fixed by the mouth which stigmatized his hunger, fixed by the eyes which knew him, and did not move.

Aware of silence, he stared at these blemished rubrics, WARNING! ALL SO-CALLED PROPHYLACTIC TUBES . . . NOT SANITU . . . GENU-INE!, on the metal door before him, conscious only now the sounds of it ceased that the sailor had been sick in a wash basin.

—Hey, come on out, you want a good browning?

He sat, paralyzed by silence, suddenly cold and in detailed motion, shivering. The metal door before him banged, and rattled on the latch. —Hey, come out of there, what are you doin in there, poundin your pork?

Another door banged.

—O.K., sailor. Be a sport. Get the hell out of here.

He heard that; and heard the scuff of shoes on the tile floor; and listening, heard nothing.

Out in the street, he paused as two men came toward him from one direction, a woman from the other. She walked slowly, looking at him in apparently careless interest, a look of appraisal.

—Pardon me, he said. She stopped. —Are you . . . are you . . .

—Trying to make a pick-up? she asked him.

—Yes maybe but it isn't that bad, it isn't that crude, it isn't just for that, it's that maybe you can . . . that I need . . .

The man in the checked suit stopped, stayed by Mr. Sinisterra's hand.

Otto stopped swaying, stayed by the woman's hand on his wrist. —Come along with me, she said. He started to withdraw his hand, to take her arm, and he felt his wrist caught in a chain. —But what's this? I . . . I mean you . . .

She gave the nippers a slight twist, and repeated, —Come along with me.

—I knew it, said Mr. Sinisterra, standing behind a refuse can.

—A cop?

—It sticks out all over her.

—It sure does. She's got a front like a cash register. We're screwed. If he has any of the queer on him we're really screwed. What are you going to do?

—Be quiet.

—Where you going?

—I'm going to church.

—What the hell are you going to church for?

—To confess.

—To confess *this*? to tell them…why Jeez what's the matter with you, them priests have a pipeline right into the cops…

—Be quiet. You think I'm a half-wit? I'm going to confess a *sin*.

—What sin, for Christ sake?

—Pride, said Mr. Sinisterra, removing the mustache from his lip, and putting it into his pocket. —And to burn a candle.

—For who you're goin to burn a candle, said the man in the checked suit, stepping back to look at his companion, his simple face falling into one of the few expressions it afforded, complete bafflement.

—For Johnny the Gent, said Mr. Sinisterra, walking on. —He had humility.

The music was the *Sorcerer's Apprentice*, threading into the lobby as though seeking a listener, for the bar was empty.

It came forth as though lunging from a coil hidden beyond the portières, trailing and lunging, as though these notes reaching the lobby now had been audible in the bar moments before; and, sitting in the bar, one might have followed the single course of the thing from behind, to behold it rearing over its prey.

Then it struck. Mr. Pivner stirred, started, woke in alarm, to recover all that he could in this unfamiliar chair, his newspaper, which had slipped to the floor as he read, ZOO ESCAPES INCREASE, HUNT MADMAN Police believe that they are on the trail of the man, apparently insane, who broke into the Bird House at Central Park Zoo last week in an attempt to turn loose the specimens on display there. Theft was discounted as the motive. The lunatic, described as a tall Negro of uncertain age, was seen by Bertha Hebble, a cleaning woman, as she passed…

—I beg your pardon sir, the young gentleman who you were waiting for has not come in yet. It is getting quite late, and…

—I must get home. I must get home, but I want to write a note, said Mr. Pivner, standing. He went to the desk, and the music lurked as he wrote. Then he put on his hat, which he had been carrying, and turned toward the revolving door, which the manager set in motion, and said —Good night, as the music towered in ambuscade's tense imitation of silence.

Sticking from an ashcan halfway down the block he saw a cane. He looked about him quickly, to establish his loneliness in fact; and when the four notes struck in finale he was beyond reach, moving slowly, escaping again in unconscious defiance of something which he did not understand, affirming with each step an existence still less comprehended, so crowded were its details, so clamorous of worth, until heeded, and then speechless as the night itself.

VI

"Des gens passent. On a des yeux. On les voit."

THE SKY was perfectly clear. It was a rare, explicit clarity, to sanction revelation. People looked up; finding nothing, they rescued their senses from exile, and looked down again.

Behind the bars which kept children out of their cages, the two polar bears moved continuously without touching each other, the male in an endless circuit, down to the front where he half reared, dropped and returned to his mate who stood swinging her head back and forth, timekeeper for their incarceration, clocking it out with this massive furred pendulum. —He's doin that every time I come here, swingin his neck, a little girl complained, straining at the outside bars. A little boy asked, —What's their *names?* The female turned toward the rock cave, exposing the people to the filth of her unformulated rear. A young Negro stood and stared. A fat man in a yellow and brown necktie aimed his light meter, and stepped back to adjust an expensive camera.

—You thought I'd gone to Lapland, didn't you.

—My dear fellow, I hadn't the faintest notion where you'd gone, Basil Valentine said without turning from the bears' cage. His voice sounded strained and a little weary. He was wearing a double-breasted gray coat, slightly fitted, fully buttoned, a gray hat with a rolled brim, gray gloves, and his tie was striped black and dark red. The polar bear approached looking him over, reared at the bars, sex apparent wobbling among fur drawn into spines by the water, and retired, gone green up about the neck. —But you do look rather better this morning, Valentine added, as though needing the makeshift of this observation to turn around, and look. —Where've you been?

—I? In a Turkish bath. Good God but it's cold.

—If you would put on an overcoat when you come out...

—What difference would that make, it would still be cold wouldn't it?

—You know, Valentine went on, as they came out of the arcade, —when

528

I look down to your feet, I'm almost surprised to see them there, on the ground. I half expect empty trouser-cuffs blowing in the wind.

—Yes. I hate the cold.

—Shall we go down and buy you an overcoat? To see you hunched up, with your hands in your pockets . . .

—An overcoat? No but listen, there's something. There's something. I went to the bank this morning, for some money. I went to get some money out, and they told me there's only a few hundred dollars. Why, there should be . . . there should be . . .

Basil Valentine pursed his lips, not as though coming forth to the subject at hand, but shifting from one preoccupation to another. —You've never known what sort of hand Brown kept on that account, have you.

—Why no, I . . . He put money in, and I took it out.

—And you haven't seen him . . . recently. Since your . . . the spree you went on?

—I interrupted his murder . . . but there. I'd just escaped my own.

—What do you mean? Valentine asked impatiently.

—Never mind. I won't try to explain it. Situations are fragile.

—Come now . . . what happened? Basil Valentine demanded, walking on with his head lowered as they approached steps leading down. He spoke no more loudly than he might have done asserting some demand upon himself, and as impatiently, knowing the question but finding it necessary to hear it in words, as though the answer, cogent as the query, were bound to follow upon it, —and enough of this foolishness, he added.

—No. No, I'm not joking. Who can tell what happened? Why, we have movement and surprise, movement and surprise and recognition, over and over again but . . . who knows what happened? What happened when Carnot was stabbed? Why, the fellow climbed into the carriage and stuck a knife in his belly, and no one would ever have known it if he hadn't stopped to shout, "Vive l'anarchie." All of our situations are so fragile, you see? If I meet you, by surprise? in a doorway? or come by invitation, for cocktails? or by carefully prearranged accident? Even that. No matter, you'll see. They're extremely fragile. And all this . . . all this . . .

A hand was waved before Basil Valentine where he paused to take off his gloves at the top of the steps. All this had been going on for some minutes, and Valentine was obviously annoyed. Indeed he did know of the anarchist Caserio's absurd blunder after assassinating the president of France, half a century ago, an image which assailed him now with all the vivid insistence of those irrelevant details which crowd a memory being probed for some calamity so alarming, or so disgraceful, that memory does not want to surrender it to consciousness until leavened by time, when the enormity of the deed may be appreciated at a distance, and, from this distance, dismissed. Basil Valentine got his gloves off, and stood looking at his hands for a moment there at the top of the steps as though recovering what the gloves had concealed, and verifying the left hand folded over the right with the glitter of the gold seal ring in the sun. Then, with the gray gloves clasped behind him, he descended.

—Did you see the moon last night?

—I can't say I noticed it, Valentine answered, looking quite old; though in profile his face maintained its look of strength, even heightened now by the severe preoccupation which his voice reflected.

—Yes, in its last quarter. The horned moon.

They had walked down near the seal pool in the center, where a child of about eighteen months stood blocking their way, gazing up at Basil Valentine who paused again to take out a package of Virginia cigarettes. The child was hatless, wet-nosed, and dripping steadily from the breech.

—Here, here...Valentine burst out, looking up. —I shouldn't touch it if I were you. He offered a distracting cigarette.

—Touch her! But she's lovely! And the rose...?

—You never know what they may have in their hair, and I shouldn't like to think where she got the flower. It's ruined, let her eat it, and come away. Valentine turned without looking back at the dripping figure, twisted to watch his retreat, chewing rose-petal. His effort to appear agreeable was being riddled by these thrusts, and he heard now beside him,

—Did you ever read the Grimm Brothers? the *Froschkönig*? No, never mind. Listen, those fragments? you have them? you still have them safe?

He stopped, to light their cigarettes. —I haven't forgiven you for running off with that cigarette case, you know. Where is it?

—I didn't ask you...that? that? Why, it's probably in Ethiopia by now. The three Indies. And the bull? Well damn it, I brought you back a griffin's egg, a much scarcer commodity, I found it in a secluded shrine in...

—You haven't yet told me where you've been. Hunched over his cigarette, Basil Valentine looked through its smoke without taking it from his lips; and they stood there motionless as plants, Valentine in epinastic curve as the expression on his face unfolded to immediacy, and bent him down over the growth from the lower surfaces before him. —You still hope to expose these fakes then, do you? he said calmly. The stem before him was uprooted.

—That's why I came back! I...

—Back? Valentine straightened up. —You went home, did you? he said, and seemed to appreciate the confusion this remark brought to the downcast face beside him as they walked on: it was at moments like this, absorbed in satisfaction, gleaned surreptitiously in a steady look from the corner of narrowed eyes, that Basil Valentine added ten, or even twice that many years to the face he showed to others. Even so, his silence evoked nothing as they walked toward the lion house, no response but an uneven cadence in the footsteps beside him, and he finally questioned, —That cut on your cheek? what is it?

—I fell in the snow, killing wrens. There. But this...

—You're done with that drunken inspiration for the priesthood, at any rate?... Eh? Tell me, what happened.

—What happened! What happened to Huss? John Huss, enticed by a salvoconducto up to Constance, where three bishops sat on his case, and he was burned...

—Anyone who hints that the Antichrist is to be found in Rome, my dear fellow, Valentine interrupted patiently, —and denies Peter as head of the Church...

—Burned and his ashes thrown into the Rhine, fishing for men, O sancta simplicitas!... yes, I've been off to see good old King Wenceslaus, there, and... my sainted mother! the women's voices... do you remember the Boyg? Why, I was almost pulled into the priesthood.

—And wasn't that why you went?

—And if it was! if it was! My sainted mother?... it's as though I'd left before she named me. Do you remember that story the poet tells? "I lay this destiny upon him, that he shall never have a name until he receives one from me"... never mind. The women's voices, and even that one, I left with her kiss on my cheek, see the scar?... there without so much as a talitha cumi I left that wise virgin.

—And now? The look from the corners of Valentine's eyes was the same concentrated appraisal of a few steps before. —The last time we talked...

—Yes, we talked about Shabbetai Zebi, didn't we. It's a way of getting acquainted, discussing the failings of mutual friends. A messiah? At Smyrna a letter from God falls out of heaven to confirm him. He's flogged and imprisoned. He denies he's the messiah, while the Jews outside are breaking their neck to free him, fasting, jumping naked into rivers, remember? They say he's never slept with a woman, though God knows he's been married for years. Before the Sultan, he denies it again, he's given the choice of death or Islam. Damnation! Sirius the Dog Star, the bright star of Yemen, Al-Shira... what was it? a sun itself where it rises with the color of ruby, then sapphire, emerald, amethyst, and then the most brilliant diamond... damn it, listen. In that immaculate place of yours, you... yes, immaculate, a thing like that would show up. It would show up immediately, a package like that wrapped up in old newspaper.

—You're still bent on this...suicide? Valentine asked, drawing on his cigarette, lowering his hand to take it from his lips. It stuck to his lips, and the coal burned his fingers as they slipped over it. The cigarette dropped to the ground, his lower lip trembled for that instant at losing control of it, his right hand came up clenched and behind him his left hand dropped a glove. —But here, he snapped, —will you walk up beside me where I can talk to you, instead of...

—Suicide!

They were approaching the steps to the lion house, passing a fat woman on a bench with two books in her lap, one gaudy but closed, *A Day with the Pope*, the other opened, *First Lessons in Italian*. With a hand mounting two mean pearls on a thin line of gold almost absorbed in the flesh, she drew an enameled nail down the page, and then wiped her nose, each time folding the piece of disposable tissue in half until she clutched only a wet wad, forming the words behind it, *mi piace*, with her lips, —mee piachay, mee piachay...

Three little girls had just deferred to the clamorous wishes of the smallest of them, and bought a balloon.

—It's been noted, of course, that the thought of suicide has got many a man through a bad night. Nietzsche, I believe...

—Suicide? this? Do you think there's only one self, then? that this isn't homicide? closer to homicide? that, listen...

Approaching the door, the lines on and around Basil Valentine's eyelids became apparent as he looked at the anxious face turned up to him; and, brought out of profile into the smiling duplicity of the full face, the strength seemed to drain out through the narrow chin. —It mayn't be so simple, you know. This so-called homicide of yours, he said. —This putting off the old man?

A child posted by the door pointed to a remarkably symmetrical dog spiral on the walk. —Look at that dog-do! the child said with intense admiration.

—Get out of the way, Valentine snapped, and pushed the child aside with a firm narrow foot. —Shall we go in? he asked, still smiling, with a step back to hold the door open.

The place was filled with noise coming from the opposite end, moaning which broke into a stifled scream, relapsed in a heaving sob, repeated, and repeated, interrupted by a hiss and spitting. The animals moved about their cages in the restless patterns of their lives, to turn their heads in that direction as they passed, across the front of the cage, round to the back, emerging again; and the tigers coming forth approached the bars as though they were coming straight through. Some of the animals did not move. A black panther, caged down across the way, stood watching, motionless but for the black tail whose weaving tip just cleared the floor. Other leopards sat waiting, and watched; an albino with pink eyes. The lion lay still, archetype of the calm of enduring vigilance, fore-paws extended. The racket went on, leaving only two apes, caged halfway down one side, generically unconcerned.

—And you don't hate Brown, do you? Basil Valentine asked abruptly. —For what he's done to you.

—Brown? hate him? for what he's done to me?

—There's a favor I have to ask of you, Valentine went on, as though he considered his question answered.

—That Patinir? I remember. You think I don't, but I remember.

—No. Something else, Valentine commenced, his tone both fresh and casual. —The *Stabat Mater?* What do you plan doing...

—She? ... bury her and marry her, after all, she ...

—No, no. That painting, the last one you were working on.

—Why?

—Well, if you are as you say, through with all this, I ... thought I'd rather like to have it. What's the matter?

—You? Yes, I told you, how fragile situations are! Every moment reshaping the past. You? you want it?

—If you'd give it to me, as a ... to a friend, a favor to an old friend? Valentine put a hand out to his shoulder, but he turned away.

—Everything down there's destroyed. I burned everything, I put everything into the fireplace and set fire to it.

—But not that? not that picture too?

—Why not? he demanded, turning.

—If it was, as you said, becoming ... not van Eyck, but what you want?

—What I want? he whispered, and shuddered. Moans from the other end rose above the broken echoes of human voices.

—The face, Valentine said. —The ... reproach in that face, it was very beautiful, I thought. Then Valentine felt his wrist gripped tightly.

—Yes, the reproach! That's it, you understand?

They were halfway down the tiers of cages.

—Gee lookit how *he* does it, said a boy before the apes' cage.

—That's a her ... and lookit her eat it, she's stoopin over and *eat*in it.

The caterwauling rose. The two pumas, as they would prove to be, were in the last cage to the right. Next to them, and separated by a metal wall, a white African lioness brushed the bars of her cage, stalked to the back, and came forth round a tree trunk in the center, its length torn by her claws and teeth. Her tail wove to one side and the other, and she twisted to bare her teeth and snap at it, making no pause when the cries in the next cage broke. —Weh weh

weh it's all right beautiful lady, yes, come on, you gonna eat it all up today? you gonna eat your tail all up? Yes...weh weh weh...said a woman before the cage, sharp-nosed, with too much make-up, she held out a skinny hand with a ring mounting a miserable stone, to the lioness.

—Listen. You see why it's important now?

Shocked as much by the smile fixed on him, as he was by the grip fastening his wrist, Valentine had started to withdraw. The instant his arm tightened the hazardous hand left it, but the smile persisted; and Valentine asked, —Why what's important?

—Yes, clearing up all this, these...those fragments, if they won't believe me. If you saw it too, in that face? The eyes turned away, the eyes not looking at you, but the forgiveness, the...grace? Yes, but even in that, the reproach. If you saw it too, that reproach? You understand, then, don't you. How I've felt since that dream? The Seven Sins, when they come to confess, and be shrived? The second dream, I don't remember the first one, but the second one, he wakes up but he goes to sleep again over his prayers, and there's Reason preaching, a "field full of folk"? And one by one, Superbia, Invidia...

—Damn it...!

—What?

—I've dropped a glove somewhere, Valentine said in a tone which penetrated the cry of the puma. Before him the lioness came forward with her head lowered and out to one side, waiting for him to appear in her view. Then their eyes met, and without turning from her as she did from him, passing the bars, he added, —Come now, what is all this...

—I'll tell you about it, listen. When I was away, I was dreamt, I mean I dreamt, I had two dreams I think, but the first one, I don't remember the first one. But the other one, sitting bolt upright in a chair, was it? And there she was, she touched me. Her lips were blue like indigo, and she...I didn't understand it then, but now, you can see, yes that reproach, if you saw it too. You can see that I can't just go to her, like this, after what I've done and, done to her. That I couldn't just go to her and offer her this...what's left.

—What is it, all this, this dream...? Valentine interrupted, not turning nor raising his voice, nor his attention which seemed to seethe and recede with the shape of the lioness looming toward the bars and retiring. —This she, this face in that study...?

—Yes, and you see why it's crucial. Why, when we've settled all this and we can leave...

—Leave! Valentine took a step back, without looking round his hand caught the wrist rising before him. —Tell me, what are you talking about?

—She...

—She? This . . . stabat Mater . . . dolorosa, it's she standing over you, is it? isn't it? Yes, you've told me, this blessed Queen of Heaven? . . . Valentine looked up quickly as the lioness turned away. The hissing in the next cage rose to broken cries. —Yes, your mother, isn't it? Your . . . "sainted mother"?

—My mother? He twisted in Valentine's hold, which was not tight but rigidly closed on his wrist. Beyond Valentine's shoulder, across the way, the rigid pattern of the bars was broken by dark blond hair and dark eyes, the abrupt, aware delicacy of a woman of undamaged beauty, who turned from the leopard cage to look for the child with her. She carried a fur coat over the arm of a tailored suit, and her expensive walking shoes lent purpose to the steps of her slender frame, deceptively fragile, full-bosomed and, again, so well tailored that that modesty was such only because she could afford simplicity, turning now to catch, for an instant, the eyes in the distraught face turned, for no reason, to her. He mumbled, or cleared a constricted throat, which was it? and she moved on quickly.

—Your . . . blessed Queen of Heaven? Basil Valentine seemed to force attention to his words as he stared into the cage where the lioness came forth again with her head lowered, turning, to look up, paused at the bars with forelegs crossed left over right, and then with no effort leaped to one side and was gone. —This woman, the "women's voices," and did I see the moon last night? this . . . good heavens, like Lucius in the *Golden Ass*, eh? Valentine faltered on, unwilling to pause and allow contradiction, postponing denial with whatever memory crowded upon him, casting up shattered shapes and fragments, shapes and smells. —And you, I suppose you went down and plunged your head seven times in the sea? You . . . "Little by little I seemed to see the whole figure of her body, bright and mounting out of the sea and standing before me . . ." One recalls her "odoriferous feet" but . . . yes, so it's not, then? Not your mother at all, that reproach and all the rest of it . . . ? Unwilling to stop until his hold was broken, unwilling to let go the wrist until it turned from his hand, unwilling to listen, until their embrace was sundered by laughter.

—My mother? why she . . . good God, she in the painting?

—Yes, you told me, you know . . .

A boy in the remnants, or perhaps the beginnings of a Boy Scout uniform had got between Valentine and the bars, and reached out over the rail. —Gimmeyatail, Zimba, he said. The sharp-nosed woman repeated, —Yes, weh weh weh . . . The lioness approached, looking beyond them.

—It's some girl you've picked up, is it? And all this talk about clearing things up, it's all some notion she's . . .

—No. Not that, all that is still itself, it's only part of itself.

—Really . . .

—Do you hear me?

—Really, and tell me, who is this . . . Solveig of yours? this Senta? The girl you've been using to model, I suppose, didn't Brown say he'd sent along something?

—Listen . . .

—And how is it I didn't see her? the night I dropped in on you.

—But she doesn't . . . we've never even . . .

—Gimmeyatail Zimba, the boy said between them and the cage.

—Or is it all in this phantasy of yours, eh?

—Yes, I'm working it out, and everything fits, everything fits so far, everything. And, that dream? I told you about that. Why, you've dreamt? and afterward, you meet them, who you dreamt of? What an advantage! . . . you know things they don't know, things about them they don't know that you know, things they've done, they never suspect you know. Why, they can go right on talking as though nothing had happened. Yes, like the saints, Rose of Lima? and what innocency of hers was woven into her past by her Jesuit confessor! What defense have they against our phantasies? And meeting her again, can she imagine what she's shared? where she's been enjoyed, in privacy? Can she imagine the postures and pleasures she's shared? And you know, all the time. What an advantage you have, over people you've dreamt of!

—Gimmeyatail gimmeyatail gimmeyatail . . .

—So you understand, how important this is? How crucial . . .

Basil Valentine turned and laughed in his face. —Really, really my dear fellow. No, he said, clutching the single gray glove before him. —The "somber glow" at the end of the second act, is it? the duet with Senta, is that it? . . . "the somber glow, no, it is salvation that I crave," eh! "Might such an angel come, my soul to save," your Flying Dutchman sings, eh? Good heavens! And up they go to heaven in a wave, or whatever it was? Really! And all that foolishness you were carrying on with the last time I saw you, that "I min Tro . . ." and the rest of it, that Where has he been all this time? and your Solveig answers In my faith? In my hope? In my, . . . good heavens! You are romantic, aren't you! If you do think you mean all this? And then what, They lived happily forever after?

—But listen, listen, she . . .

—No, no, it's too easy. After all, you know. With no interruption, Valentine paused, looking into the cage of the lioness. The lioness had come to the middle of the cage, watching him. She went round the tree trunk where her tail followed close, circling it. She stopped and moaned at the tail. She turned and bit at it. Then she moaned and faced him again. He did not speak until threatened by the voice beside him, then went on derisively, —And Saint Rose of Lima! Why, this sudden attempt to set the whole world right, by recalling your own falsifications in it? And then? Happiness ever after? Then you will be redeemed, and redeem her, and . . . good heavens knows what! And then, what next? First it's Shabbetai Zebi, now it's the Flying Dutchman? Listen to me, he went on, his voice dropping, —this lost innocence you're so frantic to recover, it goes a good deal farther back, you know. And this idea that you can set everything to rights at once is . . . is childish. I know what it's like with Brown, of course I know, I know you can't go on like that. But you and I, my dear fellow . . .

The broken cries from the next cage had stopped, given over to heaving and groans.

—What! You and I, what!

—Listen to me, Basil Valentine said, suddenly closing his grip on the wrist he'd recovered, without taking his eyes from those of the lioness. —Do you remember, when I told you that the gods have only one secret to teach? Neither was looking at the other. Over Valentine's shoulder, the blond woman reached the child who had run to her. She was bent down now, listening, her skirt drawn tight, her jacket full with the weight of her breasts, her face alive with attention. —Were they really fighting? she asked, still inclined over the child, being led back to the next cage where the pumas were, in her voice that tone children accept as awe, delighting to shock the innocence of those who awe them.

—That secret, do you remember? said Basil Valentine still holding him tight there and still looking, himself, into the cage of the lioness. —What Wotan taught his son? the only secret worth having?

—But how were they fighting?

—The power of doing without happiness, Basil Valentine said.

—See? said the child. She saw. She pulled the child to her, and looked quick into the other faces before the puma cage. They were all men. They all found her upturned face instantly, caught her dark eyes, one with a smile, one grinned an intimate recognition, until seeking escape she found herself looking into eyes familiar from a minute before, eyes not drawn to her by this instant of leveling, but still fixed on her, eyes which made no response at all. So she continued to stare at him, where he stood held in Valentine's grip there, for moments, finding sanctuary where she could recover all so abruptly assaulted, in eyes which shared nothing, recognized nothing, accused her of nothing: but those moments passed and, recovering, she groped for escape. But that lack of response held her, that lack of recognition no more sanctuary than the opened eyes of a dead man, that negation no asylum for shame but the trap from which it cried out for the right to its living identity. She clutched the child by the shoulder, as one essays handhold climbing from a pit, and turned to stare into the cage of the pumas, reddening over her face and neck and, though none knew it but she, to the very breaking-away of her breasts.

The sun was visible, white, in a sky which showed no premonition but in its fleeting neighborhood. The fat woman had followed it, from her chill seat near the seals to another, facing the sun, though she did not look up so far, no further than passing waist-levels, mouthing behind her damp wad, or the faces of children. —Frerra jacka, frerra jacka, dormay-voo? one sang. —What's that? asked the smallest. —Soney malatina, soney malatina... —What's that mean? asked the smallest, and the string of the balloon slipped from her finger. —It don't mean nothin stupid it's French, and lookit you lost the balloon already.

How old Valentine might have looked, to someone who'd shared with him the cruel familiarities of youth. Or are there moments of intimacy, of which only strangers are capable? of which those known, and suffered over years, could never conceive, so seeking for their own reflection in the attrition of familiarity. So the fat woman, mouthing —grot-zy, grot-sy... behind her damp wad looked up as though she might in that instant know the history of every line around his eyes but only lacked the time to set it down, set it down anywhere, even in her own; or set it down in prescience, not magic, not art, but only history before it happened: not age as mere accomplishment, but in performance, living out what would be lived out, age knowing itself, earning itself in that instant and gone. Until all she could have told, if she'd been interrupted a moment later, surprised? indignant? mouthing —grott-sy, probably all she could answer would be, —How old he looked just then, throwing that gray glove into the ashcan when he came out of the cat house.

—What now? the sun? A priest of Mithras, was it? Come along, my dear fellow, I'll tell you why Mithraism failed, the greatest rival Christianity ever had. It failed because it lacked central authority. It spread all over the country with the Roman Legions, but Christianity was a city religion, and power lies in cities, remember that. And what was it you said? A man's damnation is his own damned business? It's not true, you know. It's not true. Why, good heavens, this suicide of yours? Why, like Chrysippus then? feeding figs and wine to an ass, and dying of laughter? Look! look there, in the sky where it's still blue, that line? That white line the airplane's drawn, do you see it? how the wind's billowed it out like rope in a current of water? Yes, your man in the celestial sea, eh? coming down to undo it, down to the bottom, and they find him dead as though drowned. Why, this ... pelagian atmosphere of yours, you know. Homicide, was it? What was it Pascal said, There's as much difference between us and ourselves as between ourselves and others? ... no, but that was Montaigne wasn't it.

He stooped a little, finding his way up the steps to the street.

At the corner the three children stopped, to look at a deer hung there by its hind feet, to remark, —Lookit where they stuck the paper flower!

From down the block two women approached. —And I just haven't been the same since the *Morro Castle* ... the tall woman said, and laughed. —And I wish I could, but I can't, this dismal cocktail party tonight, my husband has to go, he's her editor, and I'm his wife. We're going to miss the Narcissus Festival in Hawaii again this year, I told him we'd just have one of our own ...

Basil Valentine's hands were clenched deep in his coat pockets. —Now? a Turkish bath? he muttered. —Well don't worry, those fragments, I'll be there tonight, I'll be at Brown's. And he looked up, as though watching something blown on the wind.

Ahead, the three children approached a figure sprawled on the sidewalk, and a little boy on a tricycle wheeling round it. —What's that? asked the smallest. —A man, what's it look like? —It looks like a Sanny Claus. What it's wearing, it looks like it was a Sanny Claus suit, don't it? —How could it be a Sanny Claus? It don't have a wite beard. —But it's getting a beard.

Valentine's look was not so steady: he raised it every three or so steps with that sort of blank surprise of a man glancing up to where he has been used to seeing a mirror upon entering a room, and finding a blank wall. —At Philippi? he murmured. —Yes ... Why, I will see thee at Philippi, then. Like the sky, his eyes remained unclouded, but (perhaps it was the sky beyond him that did it) simply darkened, evenly, assuming a hard solidity and the enduring texture of gray, as the sky itself was doing, as one might have seen, looking up at them both.

The tall woman turned her friend in at a door before the stubble-chinned figure sprawled on the walk in front of her house, —Right under the dining-room window, in fact, right here, as she remarked, —in front of God and everybody. She almost tripped over the tricycling child, but got the rail and down the steps to say, —My husband says that's when you have to be careful, around lunchtime, that's when most of them jump, when the streets are full of people, they do it then for the publicity.

Above her the sky darkened. She did not look at it, but went in with her eyes on her own hand laid out at elegant length on her friend's fur; while behind her, outside, the tricycle wove smaller and smaller circles, as its rider watched over the left shoulder how close the rear tire could come to the fingers on the pavement.

By late afternoon it was snowing.

The flakes were small, blown neither one side nor the other, nor falling direct to earth, but filling the air with continuous movement.

Mickey Mouse pointed to ten minutes of four.

The first thing she saw when she entered her apartment was the unnatural radiance of the sunlamp. Agnes Deigh paused there, still holding her keys, as though to appreciate fully the affliction before her, worse second by second as she hesitated, considering what might have happened had she not arrived; even perhaps that there was still time for her to leave, quietly as she had come, back into the transfiguring weather: but before she was able to contain this possibility sufficient to examine it, and find there one of those mortal shocks with which life rarely presents us opportunity to abandon the bonds of circumstances woven with such care, and start off upon any of a thousand alternative courses among which, like the needle in the haystack, lies the real one: habit betrays us, as it betrayed Agnes Deigh. She put a hand on the Swede's shoulder, and made a sound.

—Owwwayy...what...what...

—How long have you been asleep under this thing?

—What *time* is it?

—Almost four, she said, and finally turned the sunlamp off.

—Oh my God, my God, I've been here for...owwwww...what shall I *do*?...the Swede wailed.

—There's some butter. I'll get some butter.

So that is what she did. —I'll *die*...she heard him a minute later from the bathroom, applying it. —How could it *happen*? But just *look* at me!...

Instead she looked away, and said, —I wish you'd...But she had looked away in time, and broke off, biting her lip, her eyes fixed at the same level (staring at a table lamp) as though she could not raise them.

—Baby. *Ba*-by! Oooooooooo.

—I wish you'd put something around you, she said, recovered, looking up, and caught her lip again, for it had almost happened again: she had almost said what she did not know she meant, instead of what she meant to say; just as, that day in the office when she had intended to ask, Are you Catholic?... and had suddenly heard herself demand, Do you believe in God?

The Swede had got back into the bathroom. Agnes Deigh sat down, and opened the only letter that was waiting for her. She read,

Dear Madam... The case you reported to us as sadism and brutality reported by you to this precinct Tuesday December 20 at 10:17 A.M. resulted in false arrest for which you may be held responsible. Dr. Weisgall who you accused, was punishing his daughter in which case unless injury results no third party is obliged to intervene. This case is marked closed in our files but we feel it our duty to warn you that if at future date you accuse someone of criminal action that you investigate the facts thoroughly before reporting it to the Police. We also feel it our duty to warn you that Dr. Weisgall may be justified in communicating with you as agent of his unjust arrest, and any future action will take place between yourself and the injured party...

—Baby who sent you ros-es? The Swede had emerged, clothed.

Agnes looked up. She made a sound, almost told him, and bit her lip on that stark erect syllable. Then her telephone rang. —What? she said into it, shaken. —Hello?...

(—Hello, Mrs. Deigh?

—Baby I've got to find a *doc*tor.

—Yes, what is it? who is it?

(—I'm sorry, this is Stanley and I think I left my glasses at your house once, and when could I... how...

—I hate to run off like this baby but I'll call you, from the *hos*pital probably, but I can't go to the hospital on Christmas *Eve*...

—Stanley, Stanley, I... I'm so glad you called. Yes, I found them. I found your glasses, Stanley. But I won't be home now, I'm going to a party in a little while. But could you come there? Couldn't you meet me there?

(—But I'm getting a toothache, but yes, all right, I can come for a little while but I have to go up to this new hospital where they moved my mother...

—Yes here, here's the address... She read it to him; and almost a full minute passed after she'd hung up the phone and sat, staring at the letter she'd just received, before she looked up and realized she was alone.

Immediately she got pen and paper and started to write. "Dear Doctor Weisgall. I cannot begin to tell you how sorry I am for my recent mistake. How can I explain it to you so that you will forgive me? A woman's life is not..." She stopped and read that; as she would stop and read again, and again, until the letter on the edge of the wastebasket started, "Dear Doctor Weisgall. Perhaps it is not until late in life that we realize that we do not, ever, pay for our own mistakes. We pay for the mistakes of others, and they..." And the letter which fluttered to the floor, "Dear Sir. I trust that you are intelligent enough to distinguish between a vulgar act of meanness and revenge, which

God knows I have no reason to commit, and the act of a citizen and a human being doing what she believes…" when she got up to find two strips of tape. Then she stood at the window stretching the skin at her temples, sticking the tape there to discourage wrinkles while she rested. Unblinking, she stared out at the snowfall a minute longer; and when she turned on the room her moving eyes found the roses. They were full blown with the steam heat: and that instant her gaze struck them, three petals fell.

The snowflakes frolicked about the Swede's face, which was growing larger and more brilliantly red by the minute. He hit at them, as though they were a flight of insects sent to plague him. It did no good. They came from every hand until, seeing a bar, he fled from the white swarm inside, where patrons looked with impolite interest at his high buttered countenance. He got into the telephone booth, after only one drink, and dialed. —I came out in this blizzard to find a doctor but I don't know any doctors…

(—My doctor's away…on vacation…in prison…I can't think which… The tone was vague.

He dialed three more numbers, got no answer, and returned to the bar to try to think of telephone numbers.

—Nothing?

—Nothing. Nothing at all, except this…wet, said Maude, standing against the door she had closed behind her. Snow crystals melted and dripped from her coat to the floor. —I had to come home in a taxicab.

—The same judge?

—Oh yes, and I almost hate him even though he does look like Daddy.

—That's a good sound reason itself.

—Arny please don't be cruel, not today. It's Christmas Eve, Arny. I feel so awful. Even when my doctor said, Does she look like she's malingering to you? Would *you* undergo an operation on your spine if *you* were malingering? And their lawyer said he was sorry but…Oh Arny, I get so tired.

—Do you want a drink?

—No. My doctor gave me some morphine. Are you drinking this early?

—Just a couple before I have to start drinking at the party.

—Arny I wish you wouldn't drink so much. Have you filled out the papers?

—What papers?

—*The* papers. You know, the ones for the…I can't pronounce it, for Sweden. He planned to fill out these papers, declaring their fitness as parents, after the party. Now he poured the last of a bottle of whisky into his glass and sat down slowly, making a wry face, supporting the lower part of his abdomen with a hand inside his trouser pocket.

—I'm hungry, he said abruptly. —I didn't have any lunch.

—Do you want some spaghetti? Maude said vaguely.

—Spaghetti in the middle of the afternoon? he mumbled, as she went toward the kitchen. But what Maude thought was spaghetti turned out to be a box of waxed paper. She offered salad; but they were out of whisky. When he went out for some, she sped him with, —But get a quart, there's something sinful about a pint of whisky.

—Sinful?

—Well, naughty... She sat down wearily, and had hardly managed to assume that suspended look of a passenger on a railway train which came over her when alone, when the telephone and the doorbell both rang at once. She shuddered right through her frame, put out a hand in each direction, and finally got to the door. But when she'd let Herschel in, and picked up the telephone, all she could say was, —What?

(—Baby do you know a doctor? I need a doctor.

—A bone doctor? Maude managed. She looked helplessly at Herschel.

(—I've just had the most terrible accident...

—Baby are you in the hospital? Herschel answered, taking the thing.

(—No but I will be, if you'll just tell me a doctor.

—But where are you, baby? I always told you this would happen, no one can drive the way you do and go on living in *this* world...

(—But it isn't an automobile accident, I have sunstroke.

—Who *is* this?

(—It's *me*.

—Oh you! I thought it was you-know-who. *Sun*stroke? Are you drinking?

(—Second-degree burns at the very least, stop asking sillies.

—Listen baby we're going to a party. You just come there and we'll find you the cutest little doll-doctor you *ever*! Now listen, here's the address...

And when he'd hung up, Herschel turned to Maude. —And *I've* had the most...just *most* day, you cannot dream where I woke up! Can you tell I have this shirt on inside out?

—Who was that? Maude asked, motioning at the telephone.

—It was Rudy, I think he'd been in an auto crash, or something. He said the strangest things, he must have hit his head, and so I just told him to come right along to Esther's cocktail, baby is there a clean shirt? Because I can't possibly go anywhere in this. He followed her into the bedroom, where Maude opened a bureau drawer and took out Arny's last clean shirt.

When Arny arrived, with a full quart by the throat, Herschel was already revealing his latest arcanum: —Chavenet. It really doesn't mean anything, but it's familiar to everybody if you say it quickly. They mention a painter's style, you nod and say, Rather...chavenet, or, He's rather derivative of, Chavenet wouldn't you say? Spending the summer? Yes, in the south of France, a little villa near Chavenet. Poets, movie stars, perfume...shavenay, Herschel brayed becomingly.

The evening of this feast day, for so it was, perennially addressed to SS Adam and Eve, and the 40 Maidens martyred at Antioch, was brisk or cold, according to one's resources. The people in the streets had not changed; most of them, certainly, were the same people who might be seen passing the same points with the same expressions at the same hour on almost any of the three hundred sixty-five feast days of the year. Nevertheless, something had happened. There was a quality in the air which every passing figure seemed to intensify, a professional quality, as everyone became more consciously, more insistently, what the better part of the time he either pretended, or was forced to pretend himself to be. This was as true for each quantum in the bustling stream of anonymity, moving forth in an urgency of its own, as it was for such prodigies of the tyranny of public service as the policemen offering expressionless faces cut and weathered in the authority of red stone, and their contraries, a porous group in uniforms of low saturation and low brilliance gathered round something on the sidewalk before the American Bible Society, an object so compelling that it gave their diligent chaos the air of order. It appeared to be a gigantic male Heidi.

—Cross the arms on the chest, Maurice. All right there, get his feet. Wait a minute, don't lift yet until I tell you.

The policemen, busy elsewhere attending the smooth functioning of that oppressive mechanism which they called law and order, looked as unlikely of ever being seen in any other combination of lip, nostril, and cold eye, badge, uniform, and circumstance, as Saint-Gaudens' statue of the Puritan; in the same way the Boy Scouts hazarded neither past nor future, heirs to all the ages and the foremost files of time notwithstanding, they composed and expressed a pattern endowed with permanency.

—Look out f'his head, you want to break something?

—How'd it get so red?

—He's red all the way down. I looked.

—So how'd he get that way?

—You tell us, your father's a doctor.

Be Ye Doers of the word, and not hearers only, said a lighted sign behind them. In the window was a large loose-leaf book, whose lined pages were filled in a cramped round hand. A sign beside it said, *It took Mrs. Gille / 15 years to / copy the Bible // The Bible / was presented / to her son / at Christmas.* There was a picture of Mrs. William Gille, of New York City, and her hand-copied Bible.

—You passed First Aid, Maurice?

—Merit badge.

—What do you say?

—Artificialresperation?

—Right. Take his feet there and twist.

—He won't roll. He's big.

—*Twist.*

They stepped back, as the hulk rolled, and the nose hit the pavement.

—Cup the face in the arm, there.

—O.K. Get on him.

—*You* get on him.

—I'll get on him.

—We'll both get on him.

—O.K. Ready with your side? One two three go . . .

—Ughhh

—two, three . . . *push*, two, three . . . push,

—Sweet little boys.

—He's talkin. He said somethin.

—He's got me by the knee.

—Sweet little boys.

The police too were busy, in as serious, if less concerted pursuits. In the Fourteenth Street I.R.T.-B.M.T. subway station one of them reached Hannah. A policewoman handed that nomadic laundress over to the stronger arm of the law.

—You might at least have given me time to rinse them, Hannah said, a note of hauteur distinct in her voice as she gathered the wet clothes up under her arm. Earlier, she had gone to see Stanley. She had knocked at his door and found him not at home. Even going round to the front and peering through the bars of the grating and the dirty window, all she had been able to see was in order, that silent patient order of things abandoned. She could make out the picture of the cathedral at Fenestrula, the stacks of paper, palimpsests on the left, untouched to the right, twelve empty staves to a page but already dedicated and, she realized with a twinge of cold, as though the cold brought it to her clearly for the first time, not to her. Peering in she saw all this, even enough of the bed to ascertain that it, too, was empty. She could see everything in his room, in fact, except the crucifix, for it hung above the bed, next to the window through which she peered.

This willful insistence of finality was so pervasive that, on those occasions which seemed to resist, an element which might too easily have been called fateful intruded, heavy-handed some wheres as though fate had become exasperated; in others, no more than the cajoling hand of co-operation.

Stanley's mother had been transferred to a first-floor room in a large municipal hospital, pleading, the entire journey, for her possessions. After Stanley's visit, her attendants might have noted that there was something more than the usual immediate anxiety in her voice, which had deepened with her demands to a tone which implied that they would never have opportunity to separate her from another of them. Had they brought her appendix? her tonsils? her severed limb... and her teeth?

The denture was put into a clean glass on the bedside table, where the nurse, watching the doctor leave, poured the wrong solution into the glass without spilling a drop, and left her old patient gazing at that submarine chimera. Stanley's mother gazed. It moved gently, suspended, as though melting there before her eyes. She dug nut-sized knuckles into her eyes, and looked again. Gumming imprecations of an exhausted nostology, she slept.

She woke, jolted into consciousness by a belch, pulling her three limbs toward her, startled. What was it? She looked into the glass. There was nothing in the glass but a placid clear solution with a slight pink precipitation on the bottom. It was too much. She must get where she was going while there was still time.

Who but a priest, dead for a thousand years, could have read the words which formed themselves on those remnants of lips, as she made her way informally across the room, moving as though encouraged by fitful gusts of wind, weightless, like a sail without a ship, toward the windowsill. The window slid up easily; the shade rolled up like a shot. The forceps shifted, the music began, and she crossed herself, nightmare of the girl she had been two generations before, running to the water's edge, stopping for a breathless instant there to commend her own salvation before she dove in.

Transfixed below, the darkness unfurled upward, pierced by lights at each point in its ascendance until it hung, impaled, on the city. Over and under the ground he hurried home.

Mr. Pivner's lips moved as he walked. Perhaps it was this complement which gave him, as the seasonal festoons gave the pitted face of the city, this intense quality of immediate realization, real no longer opposed to ostensible but now in the abrupt coalescence of necessity, real no longer opposed to factitious nor, as in law, opposed to personal, nor as in philosophy distinguished from ideal, nor the real number of mathematics having no imaginary part, but real filled out to embrace those opponents which made its definition possible and so, once defined, capable of resolving the paradox in the moment when the mask and the face become one, the eternal moment of the Cartesian God, Who can will a circle to be square.

Mr. Pivner's monologue was neither gibberish nor absent mumbling. In a clear, if inaudible voice he was accounting for every one of his movements. It was difficult to know (and he might have had difficulty himself, saying) whether he was carefully preparing an explanation, or believed himself actually before a Tribunal where he had been summoned to account for his movements. What had once been anxious inclination was become severe practice; it might have been brought on by the hours he had so recently suffered at the hands of the police, an inquiry which had been, by the standards of almost everyone else who passed through the station house that day, an indifferent, even tedious procedure, in light of the compass of their own applied, and again detected, talents. For Mr. Pivner, it worked quite the other way; and it was, perhaps, just this quality of merciless boredom with which his captors treated him, the entirely disinterested manner with which their relentlessness pursued him, that impressed his own impersonal presence in the world most deeply upon him. Under their questioning, he began to see himself capable of almost anything, someone to be watched, and accounted for after those awkward incidents which composed the biography of the city whose turbulent diary he was accustomed to following in the newspapers.

He looked at his wrist watch, lowered it as his lips kept moving, and abruptly raised it again, first to his eyes, then his ear, and walked faster. He bought a newspaper, turned his corner, and it was not until he was mounting, motionless, in the elevator, that his lips stopped, finishing his account to the Tribunal as he approached his own door, and the locked-up disposal of witnesses waiting to confirm him. The key half in the lock, he paused, listened, and moved frantically, shaking the door to get it open and himself through, to strike at the light switch and reach the telephone which he seized and raised so quickly that it hit him in the eye. —Hello? hello? He heard that sound of patient vacancy which is called the "dial tone." —Hello? hello, operator? His hand quivered over the dial: he spun it all the way:

(—What number were you calling, ple-ase.)

—Operator? Oh, didn't this . . . I'm sorry, I thought I heard it ring.

He moved more slowly, returning to the hallway to remove his hat and coat, and pick up his newspaper. He placed the newspaper on the table beside his chair, turned on the radio, and went into the bathroom.

He came back carrying his medicine and a syringe, paused to change the station on the radio for no reason but to change it, and returned to his chair to relax into that state of spiritual unemployment which he called leisure.

Then her eyes caught his, staring out at him wistfully from the harsh newspaper reproduction where she stood patient in long white stockings; and Mr. Pivner looked confused, as though he'd been abruptly handed back among the classic peoples of pre-Christian times, whose dates, declining with the advance of time, had always given him the feeling that they had lived backwards. He picked up the paper, and his eyes followed automatically the feature story account of the little Spanish girl soon to be canonized, while his mind rummaged its rich embarrassment of glories and defeats no longer news, for recognition. He opened the page, and saw the headline on the bus gone down a Chilean ravine, killing one American and eleven natives, before he realized it was an old paper, and looked at the date to be sure. He folded it quickly and thrust it at a wastebasket behind him. He found the newspaper he'd just brought in, and settled back with a sigh, a weary sound suggesting a suspicion, if he had stopped to reconnoiter, that if the evil thereof is sufficient unto the day, so is it to a place. For had he known, no great disaster had occurred in that region of Chile where the bus crashed since the nineteenth century, when the cave-in of a burning church gave hundreds of bereaved families grief sufficient for decades; and these eleven new and sudden deaths were enough to be mourned for another score of years, deeply felt without publicity, realized in their full right as suffering and death, ungalled by the attrition of a world's tragedies circulated elsewhere on what had been, but remained, there, hectares of green trees.

If you can count, you can paint... he read, an advertisement in the evening paper. *New Subjects for your Paint-It-Yourself Collection*... and his lip drew in the tic which came when he was weary: for over this artistic suggestion loomed the specter of his retirement. "Yes, even if your artistic talents are zero, you'll be able to decorate your house, from wall to wall with fine paintings and be able to say: 'I did it myself.'"

The music was Francesco Manfredini's Christmas Concerto, approaching resolution in the last movement only to cease abruptly in favor of a voice, a voice laden with the viscous pauses of sincerity, feigning itself the last movement of that concerto interrupted with such confident presumption as though, in those minutes of music the listener had got, not bored but lonely, even alarmed at being left so long abandoned to the allurements of some possibility of beauty. Isolating in confident repetition the name of a product which had the distinction of never having been a word in any language, the voice came to the rescue, stickily compelling, glutinously articulate.

"Just match your numbered pre-planned canvas to the numbered pre-mixed paints. If you can count, you just can't miss..." he read, before he turned the page, this reasonable appeal, his head already nodding over retirement from the means which had become the only reasonable end. Still it was to him that they appealed; and a hand went to his pocket, where the past (his own, for there was no other) lay coined in justification.

With his last attention, he noted that the Burma Translation Society had published *How to Win Friends and Influence People*, and that U. Nu (Thakin Nu) hoped for more books, so that his nation would not "remain static as ignoramuses... This indeed is a matter of life and death to all of us." His eyes closed slowly; and when he thought, he fastened his hand on his extravasated heart, glad if only of recognition and familiarity, proof against Reason, and the cries of the mendicant Past.

When the doorbell rang; Mr. Pivner started violently, and grabbed the telephone. —Hello? hello? The doorbell rang again. —Oh... I'm sorry, he said to the sound of patient vacancy, —I thought...

He received the large package from the delivery boy, a wild-eyed figure about twice his own age who stood waiting dumbly for something more than his words of gratitude. —For *me*? *Piv*ner? Is it addressed to *me*? Oh, I... wait, he said, unnecessarily, —here... He fetched a quarter up from his pocket, which was accepted with a grunt. As the old man turned away, Mr. Pivner stopped staring at the package and cried out, —Wait! Here, I... merry Christmas. He handed over fifty cents.

The robe was too big. Nevertheless, the pattern was so conservative, and the material so fine, that this seemed rather a mark of luxuriance than some deliberate hebetude on the part of the giver; also in a way it marked the thing as a gift, for had he got it himself it would have fit perfectly. For that reason, any notion of exchanging it left his mind directly it arose there. The card said simply, "Merry Christmas from Otto."

And though he was surprised when he realized it, was it really any wonder at all that Mr. Pivner, whose world was a series of disconnected images, his life a procession of faces reflecting his own anonymity in the street, and faces sharing moments of severe intimacy in the press, any wonder that before he knew it, he had beseeched familiarity, and found himself staring at the image of Eddie Zefnic, as he sat running the end of his finger over the fine ridges of wool challis draped across his knee.

Wearing the robe, he stood up. He looked about him for something to do, something which, done while wearing the robe, would establish it as his own. First thing he noticed, there on the photograph album, was his syringe. He picked it up, noted that he had intended to attach a new needle, and went into his bedroom to get one. He opened a small upper drawer; and as he took a needle out the dull luster of gold caught his eye. He lifted the watch out by its chain, and dangled it there for a moment before he opened it. He pressed the stem with the heel of his palm, and caught the opening spring of the hunting case on his fingertips. Then he stood staring at that unchanged continent face, the hands stopped upon his father's forsaken past at XII; though whether noon or midnight, he did not know. The hunting case closed with a snap on this instrument which seemed, as his hand closed upon it, capable of containing time, time in continuum, where all things, even ends, might be possible of accomplishment. Mr. Pivner put the watch into the pocket of his robe, feeling, as he did so, Otto's card there. He put the card into the drawer, where the watch had been, and returned to the other room with the fresh needle.

Still, it was to him they appealed, (for that time coined dead in his pocket).

——In just a moment, *Necrostyle* will bring you the correct time. But first, friends, do you feel dull, logy, just not-up-to-much, first thing in the morning? Well ... Mr. Pivner took his injection with great care, as he always did. When he was finished, he was told that the correct time was six-thirty. He was startled at that; and on second thought he lifted the gold watch out of his pocket by its chain, opened it, and pulling out a lever on the side he turned the stem, and brought the gold filigree hands into concert with his own affairs.

——Every hour, on the half-hour, the latest news, brought to you by ...

He was suddenly in a hurry. He removed the robe with reluctant care and put on his jacket. He moved around the room, straightening things, or only touching them, as the voice rehearsed unimproved details of the war which no one talked about, commencing a summary of the same news summarized an hour before, which it had taken that hour to rewrite. He hung the robe carefully, and noticing its lopsidedness as he did so, removed the gold watch and put it into his vest pocket, not pausing to thread the chain through a buttonhole, for he was in a hurry, having intended to reach the hotel well before seven o'clock tonight. He put on his coat, and the green scarf, and had his hat in hand before he went to turn off the radio, waiting courteously, as he did from habit for the voice to finish a last-minute bulletin. ——In the metropolitan area, police are on the look-out tonight for a large man with a red, noticeably swollen face, who is believed to have abducted a group of seven Boy Scouts.

It had begun to snow again. Mr. Pivner hurried along the slippery sidewalk and caught a bus almost immediately. It did, in fact, wait for him, which put him in even better spirits as he sat down and looked out the window, allowing himself to marvel at this dreadnaught which bore him away to the south, and the wonders of science which made it, not simply possible, but ordinary. Then the bus drew to a stop, and moved again reduced to a crawl, a cautious hulk in the solid dark line of vehicles. Traffic in the other direction was stopped; and as though conducting tourists reverently past a venerable setting of martyrdom, the bus crept past the figure of a man on the glistening wet surface of the street. One of his feet was balanced up on the toe. His hat was four feet away, and all that moved was his smashed umbrella, its black festoons stirred by bits of wind. It was the image of the foot, so delicately awry, which held Mr. Pivner even as they went on. His bus passed another, stopped in line in the opposite direction. His driver leaned out, to call to the other driver, —Ya got a knockdown.

Mr. Pivner's lips were moving again. He opened his newspaper, and stared for a moment at the headline, *Minister Dies in 51-Day Fast Seeking "Perfect Will of God,"* trying to compose himself. Then he turned the pages looking for that ad, If you can count, you can paint... There were times when he had considered taking up a hobby, painting? or building ships in bottles; but something that would interest him. Seeking those words; I did it myself, his eye caught a picture: *Raise Chinchillas! in Your Own Home... No Mess! No Trouble!*

They all appealed to him, counting him excellently satisfactory just as he was; but if, on learning mistrust so late, he was not: how would they reward his ingratitude? how requite his betrayal?

Science assures us that it is getting nearer to the solution of life, what life *is*, that is ("the ultimate mystery"), and offers anonymously promulgated submicroscopic chemistry in eager substantiation. But no one has even begun to explain what happened at the dirt track in Langhorne, Pennsylvania about twenty-five years ago, when Johnny Concannon's car threw a wheel, and in a crowd of eleven thousand it killed his mother.

Mr. Pivner stared at the chinchillas. They looked warm.

"Here's to fire, not the kind that burns down shanties..." he found himself reading a few minutes later, bound by necessity before this scribbling on the wall. He shifted his eyes, chagrined at being seen staring with such attentive preoccupation at this, and the various graffiti surrounding it, even by the young man similarly preoccupied, and equivalently occupied, beside him. But the pictograph his eye caught was so alarming that he lowered his eyes, glimpsing in that brief embarrassed sweep, the face beside him, a haggard face drawn over a sharp profile which stared intently ahead. And his eyes were drawn slowly back up this figure his own height, near the same stature, slowly up, then snagged, drawn up short, and back, caught on a corner of green. And he was staring at that, down at the bit of wool protruding from the coat's pocket, waist-level, when the whole face turned on him, turned bloodshot eyes in a desolation of contempt.

Instantly Mr. Pivner returned square before him: "But the kind that burns in young girls panties." And after a shrugged fluster and buttoning beside him, he was alone.

—Is that old jerk going to come in here every night now, just sitting here in the lobby? the tall bellboy demanded as he emerged a moment later, and the night manager approached him. —Perhaps you would care to wait in the bar for the rest of the evening, sir?

—That young man, Mr. Pivner managed, —he, who just left?

—I believe he has been a guest of the hotel.

—Oh well yes, well then, no ... Mr. Pivner lowered his eyes to the shining tips of the night manager's shoes. —But ... ! he looked up suddenly: eyes as bright, and incurious as the shoetops, dismissed him.

—If the young man you have described ...

—Yes, thank you, thank you ... Mr. Pivner hurried into the bar, and there ordered orange juice. He sounded weary and unprepared for surprises, even one so familiar as the dim image already resident, awaiting but the raising of his eyes, in the tinted mirror. To one side of him, a blonde sagged slightly in his direction. Her elbow edged nearer to his own a gold cigarette case, and he politely averted his eyes to avoid reading the inscription, withdrawing, bumping the man on his right. Mr. Pivner cleared his throat, as one prepared to apologize. But the other merely darted a pin-pointed glance at him and turned away, straightening a lapel where hung a boutonnière shabby enough to appear, in this light, made of paper. And Mr. Pivner settled his rimless glasses back closer to his eyes to stare forth into the tinted glass whose length construed the three figures in vacancy, maintaining a dim reality of its own, embracing their shades in subterranean suspense.

To one side, the blonde opened her purse, and exchanged a muffled pleasantry with the bartender. From the other side came a gasp. Mr. Pivner cleared his throat, as though prepared to apologize but unable to think, so quickly, of anything specific to apologize for. But the sharp eyes gleamed at something beyond him, and with such intensity that his own were drawn in a reflex to look to where the blonde paid for her drink. But all Mr. Pivner saw, in the dim light, was a crisp twenty-dollar bill exchange hands: or so it looked to him, moonblind in the tinted gloom of that landscape where the three of them hung, asunder in their similarity, images hopelessly expectant of the appearance of figures, or a figure, of less transient material than their own.

VII

We will now discuss in a little more detail the struggle for existence.
—DARWIN, *The Origin of Species*

—IT REMINDS me rather of that convent, the one at ... Champigneulles, was it? Near Dijon, said a tall woman, looking round her. —The one that was turned into a madhouse.

—I know what you mean, said the girl beside her. —Everyone keeps changing size. The tall woman looked at her quizzically, and noted that both of her wrists were bandaged. She took a step back; the girl took a step forward. —What do you *do*?

—I? Why ... when?

—Write?

—Oh, said the tall woman, recovering, —I support my husband. *He* writes. He's an editor, you know. He's editing Esther's book.

—Who's Esther?

—Why, my dear, she's our hostess. There, talking with the tall fellow in the green necktie. She turned, as her husband approached with a martini. —What an *in*teresting group of people, she said. —And what *in*teresting music.

—It's Handel, he said, handing her a glass. —*The Triumph of Truth and Justice.*

She looked around her, and raised the glass to her lips. —Do you think *next* year we might get to the Narcissus Festival in Hawaii?

Drinks were spilled, another brown line burnt on the mantel, people collided, excused themselves and greeted one another, and Ellery, tucking the green silk tie back in his jacket, said, —Just stop talking about it for a while. Who's that? he added, nodding at a blond girl.

—I don't know. She came with somebody. She's going to Hollywood.

—I want another drink, Ellery said, and went toward the blonde.

—Ellery, please . . . But he was gone. She sat, holding her kitten.

—What does it mean, said a heavy voice near her. —The garbage cans in the street, the kids on the East Side playing in the gutters, swimming in that filthy river, see? What does *that* mean?

—Well *she* says Paris reminds *her* of a mouthful of decayed teeth, but *I* think Paris is just like going to the movies . . .

—A lovely little hotel near Saint Germain, I don't think I crossed the river more than twice all the time I was there. I really *lived* on the left bank, it's so much nicer, the architecture, the cloud formations over there . . .

—Of course if you like Alps. I found them a fearfully pretentious bore myself . . . I mean, what can you *do* with an Alp . . .

—He's still in Paris. He wrote that he's just bought one of those delightful Renaults . . .

—Oh yes, I do love them. An original?

Esther stood up. Her face was flushed. The music disturbed her because it seemed the records were being played at random, one stray side of Handel after another in haphazard succession. She started toward the room which had been the studio, where the music came from, and bumped into a person who was saying, —Do you mean you've never *heard* of Murti-Bing? Before she was halfway across the room, her way was blocked by an immense glistening countenance. —Baby they told me you were looking for a doctor, and . . .

—Do *you* know of one? Esther asked, too startled for poise.

—No but I'm looking for one too. Maybe we can find one together . . .

Esther found Rose sitting in the dark. —Isn't the music nice? *I'm* playing them, she said. —Yes, but perhaps, he wouldn't want any of them broken, Rose. —Oh, *I* won't break them, Rose said, smiling at her in the dark. Suddenly Esther put an arm around her: and then as abruptly withdrew it, and left her there with the phonograph.

—*Was*n't it silly of me. I tried to kill myself twice in two weeks. The second time I was out for two days. Sleeping pills.

—How many did you take?

—Twenty-three. Why?

—I just wondered. It's always a good thing to know.

Esther closed her eyes, as though shutting out sound, and moved on toward Don Bildow, whom she saw across the room talking with a gaunt man in an open-collar green wool shirt, and a stubby youth.

—Yes, I'm almost finished it, said a woman beside her, to the editor. —It's to be called *Some of My Best Friends Are Gentiles*. I'm so *weary* of these painful apologies from our sensitive minorities. I often think how nice it must be among dogs, a bulldog saying, there's a greyhound, there's a basset, a Pekinese, none of them mind at all. They're all dogs. Here all you have to do is say a word like Jew or Catholic or Negro or fairy and *some*one looks ready to cut you up...

—I'm sorry to interrupt, Esther said, —but who is that fellow talking to Don Bildow? The tall one.

—He's a critic. I can't remember his name. He used to do books on *Old Masses*.

—The other one calls himself a poet, said the woman who had been talking. —He's a professional Jew, if you know what I mean.

Nearby, a man smoking something from a box whose label said, "Guaranteed to contain no tobacco" spoke to a fluttering blond boy who, someone must eventually remark, resembled an oeuf-dur-mayonnaise. The tall woman indicated him to her husband, with the query, —And who is that perfectly weird little person? He's been talking for simply hours about the solids in Oochello. Wherever that is.

—He's one of our... more sensitive writers, her husband got out expelling air as though it were salt water.

—Yes, she murmured, —I can see he has a good deal to be sensitive about. She watched, as the object of her gaze halted a pirouette of departure to say, —But all my *dear* friends are exotic, just all twisted and turned like the ir*reg*ular verbs in any *civ*ilized language, and *all* from over-use!... The tall woman said thoughtfully, —Yes, and I tried to read his book. Didn't I? she added, turning to the other woman who, she noticed now, was wearing a maternity dress in collapsed folds, the pregnancy foiled. Then as though bringing a topic from nowhere she smiled and said, —Will you bring me a drink? to her husband; —I'm drinking for two now, to them both; and, —I don't know *how* he could have been so careless, to the other woman.

As Esther crossed the room, Herschel caught her arm. —Baby, you must hear what Rudy's given his maid for Christmas. A hysterectomy! Isn't that the most thoughtful thing you ever heard?

While the tall woman continued to stare toward the door, where the sensitive youth fluttered an escape against the current of entrants. —At least I think that's who it was, I remember the picture on the book jacket, posing with magnolias... She paused, to add, as he disappeared, —Or was that a book by Edna St. Vincent Millay...? And stepped aside for,

—Big Anna! but what happened baby? How did you get *here*?

—My Boy Scouts, I'll never speak to them again...

—But I'm really upset about Rudy, Herschel went on, —*that* one called and has been in an auto smash somewhere.

—I have to find a doctor...

—And you're so pretty tonight, and your nose, you know what they say about nos-es. Now you just drink this and we'll find you the cutest little doll-doctor...Oh! so pretty for Christmas Eve, all red and shiny like a candy cane.

In the doorway, Maude hung back. —Do you think we could just go join the baby and live in Sweden, Arny? —Same thing there, he said. —I'll get you a drink. Can you really tell I've got this shirt on inside out?

Someone was saying, —Rather like Pyramus and Thisbe, if you know what I mean, and of course everyone knows that he was so sensitive she had to put cotton in the bedsprings the first time so he wouldn't be embarrassed...That person quieted, nodding at who came in the door. Others turned to see Agnes Deigh, who said immediately, —It's really the most God-awful thing, will someone get me a drink? Is Stanley here?

—Who's Stanley?

—A funny boy with a mustache. She sat down, looking round her; but Stanley had not arrived, and she was soon enclosed behind a curtain of trouser-seats.

—I really prefer books. No matter how bad a book is, it's unique, but people are all so *or*dinary.

—I think we really like books that make us *hate* ourselves...

—But...why doesn't someone just write a *happy* book...Maude had said that; but no one heard her. —If you had a judge who looked like *your* Daddy wouldn't *you* trust him? she asked a youth who turned on her with, —Trust that old bastard? Chr-ahst, he doesn't even trust himself. Do you want to buy a battleship?

All Maude could say, looking round the room, was —How do all these people know each other?

—Chr-ahst only knows. Do you like the party?

—It's a little...chavenet. Don't you think?

—Chr-ahst yes.

Esther had retrieved her kitten, and stood holding it too tightly. At her elbow, someone said, —Well Ruskin dated his life from the first time he saw them. —Well, of course *Rus*kin, said the other. —He was in town just last week, wasn't he? said the tall woman. —I heard my husband talking about him. They had lunch together, I think...he's doing a book about stones...?

Across the room Ellery was turned toward her. He was talking to the blond girl, laughing, listening to her, she stood almost between them. The length of her back faced Esther. The heels were high, shoes narrow, legs slightly bowed. The whole of her figure up to the shoulders was slim as though waiting to be taken and turned, and bent downward and back: Esther felt heavy, resting against the door jamb, shapeless, and her head was tired, full, aching dully.

—All I want to do is rent a house in the south of France with four deaf mutes...
said someone near her. The room before her was clean; but in her own mind
it existed with the permanence granted only to shambles. Tenants whom she
had not met stood like fixed dwellers in her life, never to be dispossessed: they
had been borne to her as they were in their permanent blue suits and brown
suits and black dresses and eyeglasses, permanently standing and turning,
talking to and about one another, nourished and propagated by their own
sounds and the maneuvering of cigarettes, leaving the act of life outmoded,
a necessity of the past, a compulsion of ignorance: men raised cigarettes in
erect threat; women proffered the olive-tongued cavities of empty glasses.
—What's that music? someone asked her. —I don't know, it's something of
Handel's I think, said Esther, pausing to listen to the strains of celebration
written by the barber's son who had learned to play on a dumb spinet, as the
anachronistic morning-sickness rose in her, and she put an arm across her
sensitive breasts. Ellery blew a smoke ring toward her, a savage missile which
the blonde reached out and broke on the air.

—You'd better ask this nice lady right here, said a man who was fluttering
a pamphlet titled *Toilet Training and Democracy* in one hand, leading a seven-
year-old girl with the other.

—I'm the little girl from downstairs, the child said to Esther. —Mummy
sent me up to ask you could you give me some sleeping pills... Esther set off
with her to the bathroom, where they interrupted someone who was looking
through the medicine cabinet. —Oh, sorry... he said, —just wanted to see
if there were any razor blades here... He left with difficulty. Emerging a
minute later, she was caught forcefully by the wrist. —Look, you've got a
kitten, I've got to tell you the one about Pavlov and his kitten. You know
Pavlov, he had dogs. Pavlov rang a bell and whfffft, they salivated, remember?
The dogs I mean. Well this time Pavlov has a kitten... Voice and man were
swept away, and Don Bildow was not where she had seen him. But Ellery was
coming toward her smiling. She raised her face, smiling; and he stopped short,
at the couch between them, where sitting alone was a man whose profession
was as immediately obvious as that of the rickshaw boys of Natal, who white-
wash their legs. A bow tie of propeller proportions stood out over extra-length
collar bills on a white-on-white shirt, protected by many folds of a cloth which
somehow retained the gracious dignity of transatlantic origin in spite of the
draped depravity in its cut. —Benny! I'm glad you got here.

—Business is business, said Benny, raising his glass.

—What do you think of the idea?

—Terrific.

—I've got the guy all lined up. We're going to pay his family when he goes through with it, half now, half on delivery. But it's got to look accidental.

—Listen to this, said Benny. —I thought of this last night.

—What? An angle?

—Well, I didn't know whether you wanted to gag it up or make it arty or what. You know. We could have built a nice artistic number around it. Some ballet, with a story line in the background. Sweet. Or I thought if you wanted to gag it up we could make a kind of musical out of it. You know? Girls. Exploding cigars.

—Yeah but look, that's not quite . . .

—I know, we couldn't do that angle anyway, the cigars. We've got a couple of good cigar accounts that would yell. No. The more I thought about it, the more I thought, what you guys really want is stark human drama. The real thing. So listen to this. I thought of this last night.

—Yeh . . .

—From a church. He does it from a church steeple.

—Christ! Benny, you'll win the Nobel Prize for that. It's a natural.

—I figured how we can make it look accidental enough. There's this church up in the Bronx right across from a dancing school. We'll have the cameras up there doing a show on kids learning ballet dancing, see? Then when we get the word all we have to do is break in and dolly them around right out the window. Beautiful camera angle.

—But what about the priest? He might screw it up if he's around.

—He'll be around. He'll be busy inside, saying a Mass.

—It's terrific. That's all I can say. Ellery spoke with his eyes lowered, in thoughtful admiration. Then he raised them. —You deserve a drink. Where'd you think of it, alone or in a story conference?

—In church, said Benny.

—But Anna baby, came a voice from the end of the couch, filling the gap of Ellery's marveling silence, —they boiled Sir Thomas More's head for twenty minutes just so it would hold together, before they stuck it up on London Bridge . . .

—Right there, said the tall woman, nearer Esther, —in front of God and everybody. That's the way those things always happen. Do you think I have on too much perfume? I have sinus trouble and I never know. Isn't it *warm* in here.

—Well, your furpiece . . . Esther began, turning to face her.

—I know, my dear, but to tell you the truth I don't dare put it down anywhere.

—I'm sure it would be safe in my bedroom.

—Oh, then you're Esther. My dear I'm sorry, I didn't mean . . .

—It's all right, you're probably right. I don't know a lot of the people here myself.

—Tell me Esther, has *he* come yet?

—Who?

—Your guest of honor, of course . . .

—Do you know him?

—Hardly. But I've seen his picture so many times. And I own his book. I heard him speak once, about families, I mean about having children and that sort of thing. I can't bear them myself. I mean *bear* them, literally you know, she laughed. —A tipped uterus, you know. There seem to be so many nowadays, you run into a tipped uterus wherever you turn . . .

They both turned hopefully to look across the room, where the door opened. —My dear *he* is probably someone quite notable. You have to be, to go about with an alarm clock strung around your neck . . .

—Mendelssohn Schmendelssohn, someone else said. —I'm talking about *music*.

—Wasn't that silly of me, said the tall woman, watching Esther cross the room toward the couch. —Telling her a thing like that when here I am two months gone. It just goes to show what habit will do.

—I think Sibelius' fourth is his best.

—Fourth, schmorth; it's his *only*.

—It just goes to show that you can't trust nature.

Across the room, Mr. Feddle already was engaged, inscribing a copy of *Moby Dick*. He worked slowly and with care, unmindful of immediate traffic as though he were indeed sitting in that farmhouse in the Berkshires a century before.

Maude looked up and said, —Isn't it funny, how dark it seems over there, I mean where they are, do they make the corner dark or did they just gather there because it's dark there . . . Then she saw that the heavy-set man was in uniform, and said, —Oh. What are you? —Army Public Relations, he said, looking up again at the group in the dark corner. —They look like something out of a Russian novel, he said. —Chavenet, said Maude, looking up at him with wide unblinking eyes. —Yeh, him, said the officer. —Just because I'm not an intellectual don't mean I don't read books. Together they stared across the room; and Maude, feeling his warm hand on the back of her neck, relaxed somewhat.

A few years before, someone who had once seen one rather unfortunate print of Mozart (it was in profile, the frontispiece in a bound score of the

Jupiter Symphony printed in Vienna), and soon after looked once at the profile of the man now standing stoop-shouldered across the room in an open-collar green wool shirt, remarked that he looked (for all the world) like Mozart. Safe away by a century and a half, this was repeated often, most especially by those who persisted as his friends, wished to say something complimentary about him, and had never seen the frontispiece to the Vienna-bound Jupiter Symphony.

—I know him, the tall one, Maude said. —He's been around a long time.

He looked up, as though he might have overheard her, and he looked offended; but if she had seen him more often, anywhere, and in any circumstance, she would have realized that he always looked offended. Bildow, who was talking, looked slightly offended. So did the stubby young man whose belligerent interest was poetry. They might have been offended by the conversation immediately beside them, a group as unattractive as their own but in another way: crackling with brittle enthusiasm, these guests pursued one another from the Royale Saint Germain (across the street) to the Deux Magots; out to the Place des Vosges and back to the Flore; across the river to the Boeuf sur le Toit and back to the Brasserie Lipp (—It was Goering's favorite place in Paris you know); briefly to the Carnavalet and back to the Reine Blanche (—That's where *I* saw how tough the French police can be...).

—And laundry so expensive, eighty francs a shirt...

—Of course none of *us* had baths in our rooms, but there was a charming boy from Virginia whose bathtub was always free after eleven in the morning...

—I managed very well, just washing in the bidet...

Wherever encountered, it seemed that their one achievement had been getting across that ocean once, and getting back to retail wares which they deprecated but continued to offer, all they had in stock at present though a sparkling variety was on order (—Cyprus sounded like a marvelous place, I heard that they have these trumpets there, and at night when they go to bed they put one end out the window and the other end...).

—We didn't get time to *do* Italy this time, anyhow it's really more important to get to know *one* place really *well*, we were in Paris for almost a whole week...

Each one inclined from wistful habit to say, —Well I've only been back a couple of weeks, and...or, —I just got back recently, and...or, —Well I've only been back a little while, but..., realizing in the back of their minds that seasons had changed since their return, that the same season they had spent there was approaching again here, realizing, in spite of those vivid images which conversations like this one refurbished, that they were back, and their wares not for sale, but barter only, and in kind.

—I guess it *was* Corfu I meant, anyway when you walk down the street in the evening you hear these really mellifluous sounds from these trumpets...

—Well *we* were there when our ambassador laid a wreath on the grave of the unknown soldier. He dropped to his knees, and everybody in the crowd was so touched by his reverent act, then he fell flat on his face...

—You're talking about my *hus*-band! cried the one who had thanked Esther for her lovewy party, in passing, paused then to make a face at Don Bildow over their shoulders, and went on.

—I never saw anything like *that*, even at the Au Soleil Levant. What was it?

—The Duchess of Ohio.

Bildow turned his unimpressive back. —There isn't a good lay in this whole room, said their stubby companion, with a look as though recalling some severe unkindness done him privately years before. It was, in fact, a look he seldom lost. The tall stooped one undid the next button of his wool shirt, and said, —What about Esther, what about her?

—It's funny you never knew her. She was around a lot, before she got married. That summer your wife shot herself, Esther was all over the place.

—I was at Yaddo, said the critic. He smoothed the hair on the back of his head, but it stood up again immediately he lowered his hand; and the likeness to the Mozart print was remarkable again, not for the heavy and long upper lip, and the prominent nose, but the weight of the hair which he wore as consciously as the eighteenth-century man, though not for reason of that infestation of daunted vanity known as fashion, but for his own unintimidated reason: it made his head look bigger, inferring its contents to be a brain of the proportions which Science assures us we all might have, if we had wings. —I heard you sold out, he said to Bildow.

—What did I have to do with it? You know how much it costs to run a magazine.

He smoothed down and released his obedient hair. —Are you using my Dostoevski piece in this issue?

—Ahm...not in *this* one, but...

—Jesus Christ, you've had it up there for over a year. I'll finish the book before you print it, probably.

—Well, you know. There's politics up there like everywhere else.

—Who's out to get me?

—Well, you know that piece you did on Rilke last year, a lot of people...

—Jesus Christ, whose fault was that? Everybody knows I wrote that Rilke's references were occasionally *obscure*, and that dumb Radcliffe girl I had typed *obscene* when she copied it. I'd like to know who the hell copy-read that. And putting a *t* in genial...

—I was at Yaddo, said Bildow.

Someone from the neighboring international set tried to join them, offering, —Just imagine Victor Hugo wanting the whole city of Paris renamed for him! This credential earned cold stares, frightening, not for their severity, but for the very bleakness of the faces engaged.

—I hear you're going over, said Bildow's shorter friend, bleakly accusing.

—Yes, in a month or two. I want to see for myself, said Bildow, fingering his brown and yellow tie, bleakly defensive. Then he added, —It's funny that Max isn't here.

—What's so funny about it? That wise bastard...

—He usually shows up at these cocktail parties, said Bildow.

—What the hell ever made you print that poem of his, in the last issue? The one about Beauty disdaining to destroy him, that one.

—Well, we... It was...

—Did you see his paintings? Crap, all of them, even if he has got a sense of form.

—She looks like a good lay, said the stubby poet. —That blonde over there.

—Do you know who that is? It's that dumb God damn Radcliffe girl, Edna, the one who screwed me up on that Rilke piece, the one thing I've written that's worth everything else put together, because I understood Rilke, I understood him because he understood suffering, he respected human suffering, not like these snotty kids who are writing now... He put his glass down empty, saw another, full, and picked it up before its owner had finished saying, —It's like the movies because there's everything spread out for you, and you just have to react, like at the movies you don't have to pay with your *real* emotions, you don't have to *do* anything...

—And who's that over there, with all the queers around her? Agnes Deigh? Jesus Christ, I should think she'd get sick of playing mother to every God damn fairy in the city.

Esther had sat down on the couch because it was the only place in the room to sit. At one moment, she had thought that if she did not sit down, she might fall; but even now, sitting, she felt that she was falling, and she forced her back against the back of the couch, raising her chin as though trying to surface, for it was not a sense of tumbling through air, the limbs absurdly extended and unaccounted for, toward sudden impact which would so abruptly account for their ridiculous efforts in an unalterable pattern of incongruous torsions; but of falling in water where no bottom waited to delineate finality. With penetration peculiar to distance, every sound seemed to reach her, though it was perhaps her own doing, trying to escape the sounds nearest her by straining for those beyond.

—Malad*just*ed? To *this*? Well thank God I am. If I wasn't I'd go crazy, someone said across the room, while she listened.

—But you've got to under*stand* New York, it's a social ex*peri*ence.

—That's why I like her, she's part woman, came a tittering asthmatic voice; and someone else was whistling slightly delayed accompaniment to a stretch of Handel's *Water Music*. The door opened, and she raised her head in hopeful anxiety, still unaware of how he would appear, the writer whom she had invited, and as afraid that he would not; and she lowered her eyes in disappointed relief, for the man who came in was carrying a baby, and immediately met by the girl with the bandaged wrists. —What did you bring *it* for? she greeted him, then turned to say, —This is my husband. He's late because he's been tight-rope walking. He has one set up in the apartment and he says he can't practice when I'm around and I'm around most of the time...

In the middle of the room someone greeted the boy who had been looking for razor blades in the medicine cabinet with, —Charles Dickens, my God, they told me you'd gotten a job as publicity agent for the Hiroshima tourist bureau, Come see the Atom City and all that kind of thing...

The kitten tore at the arm of the couch. Esther caught it, and drew it to her, Ellery's voice still the clearest in the room. He was talking to the blonde a few feet away. —Hollywood's through, honey. Why go way the hell out there when TV's right here in town. What do you think, Benny? Don't you like her for a spot in Lives of the Saints when it goes on video...?

Esther realized that all this time the quiet seated presence beside her had been eating. He followed a stuffed egg with a small hot frankfurter, then a fresh carrot. —I beg your pardon, she said. He made a sound, eating. —Are you a friend of...

—Hors d'oeuvres. All I ever get, hors d'oeuvres. I keep thinking Benny will take me somewhere where we'll eat, an invitation to dinner somewheres, but all I get is cocktail parties, all we do is drink, all over town.

—Are you in television too?

—No, God help me. Benny and me went to school together. He coughed, and took another small hot frankfurter, as though annoyed at this interruption in his meal. —Benny and me went to school together, he repeated. —See this suit? This is Benny's. He gave it to me.

—It's a lovely suit, Esther said, looking at the gray flannel sleeve which came halfway down the man's forearm. —A very nice gift.

—Now it's too conservative for Benny, he can't wear things like this any more he says. Honest, you can't imagine a different guy than Benny when we went to school together, quiet and real serious. He was going to do great things then, he was going to design the most beautiful bridges you ever saw, and look at him now. Even a year ago I saw him and he was real, like the guy I used to go to school with. He isn't real any more. The tray was abruptly lifted away, and he grabbed two frankfurters and a stuffed egg. —Look at them, he said, watching casual hands pick up stuffed eggs, frankfurters, an occasional carrot. —You'd think they were hungry, the way they eat. Look at that woman with the white fingernails, does she look hungry? His meal was done, and he turned to Esther for the first time. —Do you know anything about player pianos?

—I'm afraid not, I've never really been interested...

—I've written a history of the player piano. A whole history. It took me two years, it's got everything in it. What's the matter with people. What do they want to read about, sex all the time? Politics? Why, did you know, he went on in a spicy tone, —the Crown Princess of Sweden, the Queen of Norway, the Sultan of Johore, all of them had piano players? And Anna Held, Julia Marlowe, President McKinley, they had player pianos. And Pope Pius X, the Wright brothers, the ships of the Russian navy...

—If you want something to eat, Esther interrupted, —I'm sure that out in the kitchen...

—*Any*thing, he said, but his eagerness was weary, for just then art had taken appetite's place. —Some day I'm going to have it printed myself, on Japanese onion-skin, bound in vellum...I don't know. Am I the only one that's hungry? Doesn't anyone else ever eat in New York? He stopped to pick some egg off the flannel sleeve. —White vellum with gold stamping...

—I'm sure that in the kitchen...

—Well, *here* you are! Benny stood over them, unsteadily, with a dripping glass in each hand. —Are you all right? He leaned over and spoke to Esther in a low tone, —Are you keeping my friend here supplied? He always needs a drink, poor fellow. We went to school together. I've had to take him to every party in town the last two weeks, I don't know what he does with himself when I'm up at the studio.

Esther felt that she had regained her strength, and stood as the arm beside her reached dutifully up for the glass. She did not see Ellery and the blonde, and started toward Don Bildow when Herschel took her arm. —Baby there is a kitchen here isn't there? Because we must have just a little but-ter... and baby, has Rudy come yet? You know Rudy don't you? You must, he designed this new Doukhobor dress, the one that comes off with a touch, isn't that fright-fully Tolstoy? And now he's designing sports clothes for nuns. Why, before he's through he'll end up in the Church himself! Isn't that too camp? Why even Agnes says...

—Bathysiderodromophobia. And that's only *one* of his troubles.

—But why does simply everyone join the Roman Church? When there are so many other divinely amusing religions around.

—I think sun worship would be the most divinely in*spir*ing thing, why just imagine everyone here running around without a stitch on ...

—I'd like to start right now ...

—*I* want a new messiah ...

—Baby we all do ...

—That tall stooped one in the open green shirt over there, I'd follow *him any*-where ...

—And it wouldn't do you a bit of good, said Agnes Deigh, leaning forward with a cigarette in her mouth, looking for a light. —He'd probably break every single little bone in your body.

—How fer-*wo*cious! Agnes introduce me, promise.

Of the three lights proffered, Agnes Deigh leaned over one and then sat back, lowering her cigarette. —Darling he's not any stronger than you are.

—But he looks so *in*-timate.

—He does, Agnes said, looking across the room. —That's because he has myopia.

—Agnes darling you sound *bit*-ter. What's *he* to Hecuba, baby?

—Oh God, let's not talk about it. I spent most of a year listening to his troubles with his wife, with his childhood, with religion, with his work, honestly, nursing him ...

—Agnes, how angrwy you are!

She had, indeed, got a stern look on her face which none of them had ever seen; but as quick as it had come, it softened to one of weary disappointment. Then she said thoughtfully, not looking at anyone, —The people who demand pity of you hate you afterward for giving it. They always hate you afterward. She watched him plod across the room as though in deep snow.

The front door was opened and closed three times in quick succession, the first draft catching the flower of Agnes Deigh's patronage to detach a frayed petal and waft it across the room. —Buster! —Sonny! —But how did you get here? The second was Stanley; and the third a dark-skinned man about five feet tall in a snappy gray sharkskin suit, who looked round cheerfully, raised his eyebrows, shrugged, and accepted a drink. (He was, in fact, the Argentine trade commissioner, at the wrong party.)

Maude sat with her eyes closed, moving her head slightly in the hand of the man in uniform. —I just don't do happy things any more, she was saying. —I guess because it's easier not to, because when you do, and then remember them, it's much worse than if you never did them, it's much better if you don't have happy things to remember, and then you don't remember them and get sad because you're not doing them any more, it's easier just not to have anything to remember . . . He leaned forward and blew softly into her hair.

—Who's looney now? someone said, as Mr. Feddle worked his way along the wall, with the care of coastal shipping not to venture into the open sea; his cargo was *Seven Pillars of Wisdom*, and he sought dockage where he might inscribe it in peace. Benny was approaching the very attractive girl who spoke with Boston accents. The tall woman said, —Then it's your husband who writes. What sort of thing? —God knows, said the girl with the bandaged wrists, —God and the Congregation of the Holy Office. Everything he writes goes right on the Index, and I can't read it. —Then you're Catholic? —My God yes.

The very attractive girl, indicating Benny, turned to Ed Feasley and said, —Tell your friend I'm a lost horizon, will you? —Chr-ahst, Feasley said, —I don't know him. He looks like a brush salesman in that outfit. Maybe I can sell him a suit. She raised her eyebrows. —Well Chr-ahst I've got to do something. Ever since I smashed this last car up I've been living on the free lunch at the Harvard Club, and going through the cushions of the big chairs there looking for change that drops out of those old bastards' pockets. Chr-ahst.

Benny turned unsteadily toward Agnes Deigh; but she had got up and gone to put an arm around Stanley, who shrank away. —Stanley, something awful has happened . . . she began, and looked over his shoulder to see the dark face of the critic. —Hullo, he said. —How is everything, Agnes?

—Well enough, I suppose, she answered, and took her arm from Stanley's shoulders. —I didn't know you knew Esther.

—I just met her, he said. His tone was dull.

—How's your own novel coming along? She sounded impatient.

—Well, I haven't finished it yet, but . . .

—And the autobiography of Dostoevski?

—Look Agnes, don't start that with me tonight, that autobiography crap.

—Relax, Agnes Deigh said. —Have another drink.

—All right. But just don't start . . .

—I'm not starting anything. Now relax.

—You must be having a good time here. I never saw so many queers in one room, queers and uptown fluff and cheap advertising . . .

Agnes Deigh turned her back. —Stanley, I have something I want to talk to you about, she said, and led him back to her chair. Benny walked toward the other side of the room, where Ellery stood with the blonde backed up against a cabinet, his hand in the shadows there, hardly moving. Benny's lip was trembling.

—Lady...lady... Esther felt her skirt being pulled, and looked down to see the little girl from downstairs. —Mummy sent me up to ask you for some more sleeping pills...—Just a minute, she said as she looked, and put her hand on the child's head. —You've got *lots* of friends, haven't you, the little girl said, looking up at her. —Mummy used to too, but not any more...

—You must meet Mister Crotcher, said someone to Esther, beside her. It was Buster Brown (whom she did not know either). The pair had approached like a depraved version of body and soul, the one on little cat-feet (as he himself remarked), the other in a brown suit of heavy material, nearer the floor with each step, as though wheeling a barrow full of cement. He shook Esther's hand with an air of great fatigue. —But you didn't tell us what you *do*, said Buster to him.

—I'm a writer, he answered.

—Oh. What sort of thing do you do? Esther asked, dropping the weight of his hand, and looking down as though she expected to see it drop to the floor.

—Write.

—Yes, but...ah...fiction?

—My book has been translated into nineteen languages.

—I must know it, Esther said. —I must know *of* it.

—Doubt it, said the modest author. —Never been published.

—But you said...

—I've translated it myself. Nineteen languages. Only sixty-six more to go, not counting dialects. It's Celtic now. A lovely language, Celtic. It only took me eight months to learn Celtic. It ought to go in Celtic.

—You mean be published?

—Yes, published in Celtic. Sooner or later I'll hit a language where they'll publish it. Then I can retire to the country. That's all I want, to retire to the country. Erse is next.

—It must be an awfully dirty book, said Buster.

Mr. Crotcher gave him a look of firm academic hatred which no amount of love, in any expression, could hope to erase. —It is a novel about ant life, he said.

—Lady, could you take me into the bathroom...

—You'll have to excuse me, Esther said, gripping the child's hand.

—Gee, lady, said the little girl as they crossed the room, —you ought to watch out for your baby.

—*What?*

—You ought to change his pants, she said pointing. Esther saw the baby on the floor, trying to climb the leg of a small dark-skinned man in light gray.

On the other side of the room the girl with bandaged wrists was saying to her husband, —What'd you do with it?

—Some girl borrowed it, he said. —You'll know her, she's got a green tongue.

—The baby's all right, if that's what you're talking about, said the tall woman. —A nice-looking man seems to be playing some sort of game with it. She turned to her husband and said, —Who do you suppose that flashy little dago is?

—But that's what's wonderful about France, someone said. —Simply *ev*rything is for sale.

—We've found the loveliest French restaurant, a girl said. —Everything is flavored with garlic, that's how you can tell... She was interrupted by the Duchess of Ohio who asked if her name were Maude.

—Why no. Why?

—They've told me that someone named Maude knows where you can get babies by post from Nor-way!

—Do *you* want one?

—Baby, I feel like I'm going to have one. The girl stared.

—There hasn't been anything like this since the *Morro Castle*, said the tall woman, looking round. —I expect everyone to burst into *Nearer My God to Thee* at any moment.

—Chr-ahst, what a party, said a young man to Esther, stopping her as she came from the bathroom, the little girl dodging obstacles, running for the door. —Could I get you a drink?

—It's my party, and you're very welcome, said Esther, feeling ill again.

—Oh Chrahst, I'm sorry. Ed Feasley was folding together four dirty five-dollar bills. He put them into his pocket. —Damned lucky bit of business, he said. —What? —You see that seedy-looking guy in the green shirt? —Oh yes, I know him, he's... —I just sold him a suit. —But... he doesn't look as though... your suits would fit him, Esther went on, automatically, making conversation. —I wouldn't sell him one of my old things, Feasley said. —I told him to go up and get a suit at Brooks. He can charge it to my old man. What else am I supposed to do? Sell a battleship?

They stood looking over the room. —How do you know all these people?

—I really don't, to tell the truth, Esther said, looking for any she could identify. There was James Leak, who said he had published a book called *With Gun and Camera in Flatbush and Greenpoint*, though no one had ever seen a copy, and was now at work exposing the Swiss conspiracy to dominate the world. There was Arthur, with a beard, who was writing a new life of Christ, to be published under another name, the same name he had used when he reviewed his first book, published under his own name, a satire on the Bible so badly received that he joined the chorus of its detractors and got even with himself by quoting Charles Reade and George Borrow, calling it an excrescence of over-refinement. —Yes, he was saying to a girl named Izarra (she had got that off a liquor bottle; her real name was Minna Vesendorf). —Of course it's going to be autobiographical. All books are.

Someone else was saying, —When I finish this psychoanalytic critique of Mother Goose I'm going right on to the Revelation of Saint John the Divine . . .

Someone else said, —*She* went into a cream dream talking about Ischia last night . . . Nearby, someone asked about a slim middle-aged man just out of earshot, who had been appointed instructor in one of the better eastern boys' boarding schools. —Well I don't think he really realizes what he's doing, he just lies beside them and kisses them . . .

—It's all right just so long as he doesn't turn them over . . .

—And where did you get those eyebrows? someone in that corner asked the Duchess of Ohio, who was waving an old magazine. —If I didn't have these eyebrows I couldn't look so fer-*wo*cious. The magazine was *Dog Days*, open to the picture of Ch. Dictator von Ehebruch.

—Of course I believe in Art, said a girl with a green tongue, near them. —But not just to look at.

—Chr-ahst, I mean, you know? I mean, Chrahst, don't you wonder what they're trying to do, all of them? I mean, look at this wild-eyed guy that just came in . . .

—God! said Esther, clutched his arm and thrilled him for an instant, left him dumb.

Esther crossed the room, her face flushed, as though this abrupt challenge temporarily suspended the consuming terror which had become the fabric of her own life, just as the flush in her cheeks replaced the transparent whiteness which had come over her face only hours before.

—Look, where's your kitten? Only someone who loves kittens could understand . . .

—Please, let go of me.

—But you've got to hear this. The kitten . . . I mean Pavlov had an experiment with lights, and when he rang a bell . . . whhffft

—Esther . . .

—Darling haven't you had enough? . . .

—Esther darling, the tall woman stopped her, —that music seems awfully loud, even for Bach . . . Darling where are you going? what's the matter?

The music was *The Great Elopement:* a chill horn raised her, twisted her up and exalted her for a moment; and then she was let go, and lowered evenly on strings. —He's here, Esther said, her flush already failing. —He's come . . . here.

—He has? . . . But I don't see anyone, said the tall woman looking over the room with her head cocked back, drawing her eyelids to the level of her lashes which did not move and she looked quite disdainful, —anyone who looks like a Kwa-ker, certainly . . . certainly no one whose picture I've ever seen on a book jacket . . . Then she lowered her face so quickly that the smooth proud hollows where her eyes lay became furrowed, drawn together by the brows, and —Who *do* you suppose? . . . she murmured, watching Esther hurry toward the door and there seize the arm of a figure with neither hat nor coat nor tie, immediately obscured by her back.

—You've come back . . . here? Esther said almost in a whisper.

—I didn't know you had a party. I . . . I won't interrupt.

—But you . . . come . . . Esther drew the arm she had seized to her in a convulsive gesture, then as though shocked at this she almost let it go, but did not, turning, toward the bedroom hall, trapped for an instant in the brown eyes of the critic upon her, a gaze she broke and went on, restraining the tension of the music in the wrist gone rigid in her hold. —Come in, in . . . into the bedroom. All these people, it's not . . . not . . . where have you been? she asked when they gained the cover of the hall.

—In a Turkish bath, he answered promptly.

—Oh no, you . . . I mean . . . close the door. She sat on the edge of the bed, holding with a hand on either side of her, and looked at him. He started toward the closet. Then she said, —You . . . and her voice quavered, so she stopped and made an effort to swallow, trying to draw together the great hollow behind her tongue. —Almost as though I knew you were coming, she said, and then added, —and expected you. At that he turned to her, and Esther shuddered, for his face was drawn in the mild surprise her memory knew so well, for here now, just as there, she had intruded upon him. There he was, in her memory, usually seated but sometimes standing at a window with his back turned, unaware of her approach so that no matter the circumstances or her intentions, she became stealthy, and might even try to retire and leave him there; but he always turned, like this, intruded upon, composing the lines of his surprise into expectation, looking at her, waiting.

But all this happened very fast, and sometimes, before she knew it she'd set fire to his hair, or saw it so, what was the difference? or saw him streaming blood down the side of his face (as he had that morning when they had news that the warehouse, where his early paintings were stored, had burned, and he came in with a razor cut on his cheek), and this same mild expectancy, waiting to be told.

But now he turned away. —I've just come to pick up some things, he said, and he stood there holding one hand in the other before him, looking down. She watched the lines of his face become confused again, and still sitting on the edge of the bed she asked him,

—What things?

—Well, the . . . there must be some clothes. Some clothes. Because this . . . He stopped again, holding a black wilted lapel, and looked at it.

—It's been so long, she said, starting to get up. But then she only clasped her hands around a knee, and stayed. —Are you going away? she asked him, and sorry she had for he looked bewildered and not at her. —You're not going to stay? she added abruptly.

—To stay? he repeated, and looked at her.

—You haven't come back to . . . to stay? . . . with me? Her knee slipped from her clasped hand.

—Why no I ssstopped in to . . . pick up some things, I . . . there's somewhere I have to go tonight, something I have to . . . do. He spoke each word as though intending another, misshaping them with his lips, and stood there uncertainly. —You see, I . . . he commenced again, but she interrupted briskly as she stood.

—It's all right, I simply wondered. A woman likes to know these things.

—But you . . .

—But you do look better than when you were up here a few days ago, don't you, she went on, her voice with an edge to it.

—Yes, I'm tired.

—Where have you been?

—A Turkish bath.

—All this time?

—No, I . . . yes.

—Why? Why? Why?

—Oh, they . . . do all sorts of things to you there. Heat and cold, and steam . . . and cold water, and they pound you, and you . . . and they . . . they do all sorts of things to you to make you . . . that you feel . . .

He turned toward the closet again, took a step and startled at his brief image in the mirror.

—Oh, but that . . . I'm sorry, she said, laughing, coming toward him around the foot of the bed.

—Well I didn't . . . think it was mine, he said, confused again, taking off the jacket he'd got from a closet hanger. Its bold plaid sleeves came down to his knuckles, the skirt well down over his thighs.

—I am sorry, Esther said and she quit laughing. —It's . . . someone left it here.

—But they're all like this, he said from the closet.

—Your things are in here, in these drawers. She stopped her going toward him, and pulled open a bottom drawer. When she straightened up she'd recovered her impatience. —When you're away for as long as you've been, she began. He was putting back on the wrinkled black jacket from the floor where he'd dropped it. —But here, Esther said, pulling folded clothes from the drawer, —surely there's something in here that will do better than . . . that.

But he buttoned the jacket in front, taking both hands to each button.

—This, she said.

He took from her the suit she held out, plain gray with a diagonal weave.

—Well, aren't you going to put it on?

He folded it and put it on the bed, at the same time making sure of the buttons on the jacket he wore, as though suddenly afraid to lose it.

—Aren't you going to wear this?

—I'll . . . I'll take it with me, and a shirt. Some shirts too. Then with a step he was nearer her, and another; and he stopped, bringing up his head, both hands open before him, open as though to come to grips except that he'd already fallen half a step back, and

She, straightening up with some shirts held forth on the flat of her hands raised her face to his, joining forces with the mirror behind her. —What is it?

But with that half a step back one image retired, and bearing his green eyes on her he recovered, the half-step and another with it so that Esther shrank back against the chest holding the shirts out farther still between them and she repeated —What is it?

The door opened, flung open. Music burst in.

—What do you . . .

—Sorry.

Broken shapes, gray Glen Urquhart mitigated by blond hair in a wild panache, shattered the wall; a peripheral pattern instantly restored as the door bangs, closed.

—What was it?

—Purcell.

—No. Her hands lay in his, under the squared white mass of the shirts, cold nails and soft lined joints against his hard palms.

—The music?

—No. Her thumbs out, and palms up with the weight on them, her shoulders relax, and her hands open further, to draw up as instantly there is no support, first his right hand gone, clearly gone, and then with an instant's paroxysm the left.

And then the weight of those shirts, lifted away, and her hands rise empty, round-fingered, untapering and separate.

The mass of the shirts broke on the bed as he dropped them there, and took his left hand in his right where veins stood out in swollen tributaries rising between the roughed mounds of the knuckles, breaking in detail on the fingers whose severity they articulated.

—That night... Esther said staring at his hands, her own withdrawn to shelter the hollows, heels on bone and the round ends of her fingers appointing that soft declivity which rose above them until her thumbs could not meet across her waist. —That night, she repeated, curling her finger-ends in upon the yielding bank, and the tips of her thumbs touched. —When I wanted to... manicure you? She looked up at his face, and with the effort smiled until she said, —And you... drew away just like that... each word draining the smile from her face, and she lowered her eyes, and her empty hands came down to her sides.

She waited, and heard no response, but watching saw his lips go tight. —What have you been doing all this time? she demanded of him, and sat on the bed.

He turned back to the shirts, which he'd just left stacked unevenly on the bed, and commenced to arrange them in a careful pile. —Nothing, he answered automatically.

—Nothing! she repeated, and sat up straight.

—A few things... working, sort of... experimental things.

—Painting? What kind of things, then?

—Yes, sort of... that kind of thing.

—Painting?

He looked up at her, quickly and away, back to what he was doing, squaring the pile between his hands. —Looking around us today, he said with effort, —there doesn't seem to be... much that's worth doing.

—Well what good is it then?... she burst out at him, —going on only to find out what's not worth doing?

—You find... he mumbled, —if you can find, that way...

—Are you very ill? Esther said.

—Ill? He looked up pale and surprised.

—Everything is just like it was, isn't it. Only worse. She started speaking rapidly again, as she got to her feet. —You've just got everything tangled up worse and worse, haven't you. Why the way you pulled your hands away from me just now, as though they were something...

—Esther...

—And your guilt complexes and everything else, it's just gotten worse, hasn't it, all of it. And the way you pulled your hands away from me just now, it was just like when we were first married and I hardly knew you, and the longer we were married the less you . . . won't you talk to me? even now, won't you talk to me?

—Really Esther, I . . . I didn't come here to argue with you. He sounded again himself she remembered, and she pursued,

—You won't argue, you'll say things like that but you won't argue, you won't talk . . . to me . . .

—Damn it, I . . . Esther, I just came in to get some things.

—Get them then! Take them! Take them!

He busied himself folding the shirts up with the gray suit, tightening his lips against the sounds which escaped her.

—Because there's no one, is there. You're alone now, aren't you. Are you alone now?

—Esther, good God . . . please . . .

—Ignorance and desire, you've told me . . . Oh, you've told me so many things, haven't you. All of our highest goals are inhuman ones, you told me, do you remember? I don't forget. But remorse binds us here together in ignorance and desire, and . . . and . . . not salt tears then, but . . . She gasped again, shuddered but would I not give in.

—And what is it now, this reality you used to talk about, she went on more quietly. —As though you could deny, and have nothing to replace what you take away, as though . . . Oh yes, zero does not exist, you told me. Zero does not exist! And here I . . . I watched you turn into no one right here in front of me, and just a . . . a pose became a life, until you were trying to make negative things do the work of positive ones. And your family and your childhood, and your illness then and studying for the ministry, and . . . when I married you we used to talk about all that intelligently, and I thought you were outside it, and understood it, but you're not, you're not, and you never will be, you never will get out of it, and you never . . . you never will let yourself be happy. Esther was talking rapidly again, and she paused as though to give effect to the softness of her voice as she went on, though her memory crowded details upon her and it was these she fought. —There are things like joy in this world, there are, there are wonderful things, and there is goodness and kindness, and you shrug your shoulders. And I used to think that was fun, that you understood things so well when you did that, but finally that's all you can do, isn't it. Isn't it.

He stood across the bed holding his bundle up before him, meeting her eyes, provoked, and he smiled, ready to speak.

—And your smile, she went on, —even your smile isn't alive, because you abdicated, you moved out of life, and you . . .

—But the past, he broke in, —every instant the past is reshaping itself, it shifts and breaks and changes, and every minute we're finding, I was right... I was wrong, until...

Esther plundered the fragments her memory threw up to her, taking them any way, seizing them as they rose and clinging to each one until she'd thrust it out between them. —The boundaries between good and evil must be defined again, they must be reestablished, that's what a man must do today, isn't it? A man! Wasn't it?... She paused, retaining hold on that for a moment longer, raising her hand to her forehead in fact as though doing so, considering its details and lowering her voice. —Yes, you couldn't have a world in which the problem of evil could be solved with a little cunning, she added, word by word, dully, —and you... Oh yes, by confessing, to set up order once more between yourself and the world... Esther's voice tailed off as she stared down at the bed between them.

—Yes, go on, go on with it, he said eagerly when she stopped, staring at her.

For as it happened, this point had come from a play she'd read shortly after Otto had sailed for Central America, a play by Silone called *And He Hid Himself*: but even now, looking up, Esther saw these words on the lips before her, slightly parted in expectation. She began again, —I wish...

—Yes, you understand, he burst in, —you understand, that's why this is crucial, you understand, don't you. How this is going to expiate...

—Expiate! She accepted him again, standing there with his hand out.

—And that it isn't just expiation, but... that's why it is crucial, because this is the only way we can know ourselves to be real, is this moral action, you understand don't you, the only way to know others are real...

A wave of nausea rose through her body, and Esther gripped the corner of the night table behind her, swaying a little, swallowing again. —If we had had a child... she murmured. —Yes, if we...

—And you understand it, his voice came on at her, —this moral action, it isn't just talk and... words, morality isn't just theory and ideas, that the only way to reality is this moral sense...

—Stop it! she cried out. —Stop it!... She caught herself, and took up the handkerchief again quickly for saliva was running from the corner of her mouth beyond the apprehension of her swallowing. —Moral sense! she repeated loudly at him. —Do you think women have a moral sense? Do you think women have... any morals? that... that women can afford them?

—Esther... He started toward her round the end of the bed.

—Oh no! she said. —No! Do you know how much she has to protect? and every minute more? And you make these things up, and force them on her, men take their own guilt, and call it moral sense and oppress her with it in the name of... She shrank back as he came close to her. —In the name of Christ why didn't you go on and ... stay where you came from, and be a minister where you came from, instead of... coming here where I ... she shuddered as he took her arm, —have so much to protect.

—Esther, he said to her, that close.

—But now you ... are here, she said to him in a whisper. The nausea had fallen away, abruptly as it had come, leaving her in his grip with her teeth chattering as she spoke, and her tears did not fall but spread evenly into the wetness of her cheeks. Two of her fingers sought his wrist, and tried to close on it. —You ... she articulated from a wild breath in his face, —now you are here to ... stay and protect...

They stood there with three senses locked in echo of the fourth, and she licked her lip.

—Sorry...

The door banged against the wall.

—They're still there only *talking*...

The door banged closed.

—Esther... you don't understand? His hand opened.

—You're not ... going to ...

—Not yet, because tonight, when I've done what I have to do...

—Not yet! She stepped away as though she had broken from him. The clothes bundle fell to the floor. He put a hand out, and then withdrew it slowly, and stooped to recover the clothes.

Esther stared at the wrinkled black of his bent unsteady figure only for a moment. Then she opened the handkerchief, wadded all this time in her hand, and blew her nose as she crossed the room to the mirror, and he backed toward the door.

—I'd better go, he said, from there.

She did not answer. She had picked up a lipstick, and stood contorting her mouth, drawing generous lips. Then a rush of sound broke over her, and she looked up quick as the door came open behind him, and he stood there in the course of the waves pouring in around him, his back to it, not straight but still as a rock secure against the flood, safe until the turn of the tide.

—Because this... one thing I have to do is ... crucial, Esther.

—*Crucial?* she repeated calmly, and still she did not turn from the mirror. —And you think it will work, well it won't. Whatever it is, it won't. She watched her lips as she spoke, paused to draw them in, purse them, separate them so that her large teeth showed, and smudge the handkerchief between them.

And she stopped, dry and silent, as the door came closed where he stood against it. —What are you going to do? she asked him. —I don't mean this...

thing you're up to now, this crucial thing, whatever it is, I don't care what it is, but after all this what are you going to do? What are you going to do?

—I don't know but I think... he started precipitously, and as he went on his voice was strained but for the first time there was no doubt in it, and no effort to control excitement, —if we go on... if we go on we're finally forced to do the right thing, but... and how can I say, now, where, or with whom... or what it will be.

Then he lost his balance and almost went over as the door came open behind him in someone else's hand.

—Rose!

—I saw you here.

—My razor, I forgot that, he said, between them, turning. —A straight razor with black handles, is it in the bathroom?

Rose followed him there. Looking for the thing, he paused half turned to her, seeming slightly confused at the scent of lavender she brought with her.

—Rose...

—I heard a poem, Rose said, —"A magnet hung in a hardware shop..."

—It's not here.

—Rose, Esther said, —that music is too loud, Rose.

Around them the sounds of voices reached separate crests, broke in spray, and lay in foam awash on the surface of the swells as the music rose and receded, and the faces themselves seemed to lift into a moment's prominence, immediately lost in the trough that followed. So Benny's face was raised, and stood out inflated with effort, and dropped from sight again.

—To find out what sex it is you just spread it out and *blow*.

Esther looked down to see the kitten, unfurled upside down between large thumbs. —Here, give it to me, give it to me, she said, rescuing it. The nausea startled up in her for a moment.

—It's the worst feeling in the world, said the tall woman beside her.

—What? Esther asked, drawing the kitten in to her.

—To know you've laid a cigarette down somewhere.

The little girl tugged at her skirt. —Mummy sent me up again... The tall woman laid a hand on her wrist. —You didn't tell me that *he* was coming tonight. Esther turned quickly, startled. —Do you know him?

—No, my dear, and I didn't know that you did.

—But... Oh, Esther said. Looking round to where he had been standing beside her she realized that the tall woman was talking about someone else.

—Did you like his book?

—What book? Esther asked, looking where the tall woman was looking, at a man in a tan suit who had just fallen over one end of the couch.

—Now don't tell me you don't know about *The Trees of Home?* Or are you snobbish about best sellers too?

—No, I . . .

—My husband says he stole the plot from the Flying Dutchman, whoever that is. My husband meets all sorts of people.

The man in the tan suit, back on his feet, was saying, —Why should I bother to write the crap for those speeches? I'm lucky I can stand up before the Rotary Club and deliver them. Some faggot writes them for me.

Near him, someone obligingly derived *faggot* from the Greek *phagein*. —Phag-, phago-, -phagous, -phagy, -phagia . . . the voice whined. —It means to eat.

Arny Munk, propped against a wall with Sonny Byron's arm around him, said, —Really ought to tell Maude, ought to tell her . . . huhhh . . . the University of Rochester has discovered huhhhh how to make synthetic morphine huhhhhp from coal tar dyes . . .

—I think you're sweet, said Sonny Byron, soberly.

Mr. Feddle was standing on a chair, reaching for a book on a high shelf. The swinging alarm clock hit a girl on the back of the head, and she stopped singing *I Can't Give You Anything But Love*.

Esther, listening intently beyond the tall woman's voice to escape it, heard only a whine, —the decay of meaning, and you can't speak a sentence that doesn't reflect it. You're enthusiastic over sealed-beam headlights. Enthousiazein, even two hundred years ago it still meant being filled with the spirit of God . . .

She would have gone direct to the couch and sat down, had not Benny caught her by both hands and turned her to face him. —Where did he go? Where is he? Who was that?

—Why . . . my husband. Do you know him?

—Where is he? What was he doing here?

—He just came to get . . . some things . . . Two or three people turned, curious at the tone in their voices, Benny's excitedly high, while Esther spoke with faltering intensity, as though forced to affirm, and repeat affirmation to this impersonal, circumstantial demand which was Benny. —You're hurting my wrists, she said.

—But . . . I thought I'd never see him again. Isn't that . . . isn't that . . . I never wanted to see him again, and now here he is and I want to see him, I have to see him, where is he?

—I can't believe he's really gone, she murmured as they took their eyes from each other and looked toward the door, saw only the young man whose heavy mustache seemed to weigh his round head forward, looking at them, innocent, anxious at their sudden scrutiny.

—Ellery, did you see him? I mean, he was just here, did you see him leave, Ellery?

—Sorry, old girl. He broke a leg. Had to shoot him.

—Really, Ellery, please. I've got to find him, is he still here? She had taken hold of Benny's arm; and who Benny was, or what he wanted, ceased in her grasp which held Benny forth, a dumb prodigy, to witness that the matter was not hers, but necessity's own.

—A shame to shoot him, a fine blooded animal like that ... It was difficult to know if the blonde beside Ellery was trying, but unable, to smile, or subduing that smile which is stupidity's cordial greeting to matters which its very nature excuses it from attempting to understand: so she looked, not at Esther, but at the silent phenomenon of Esther's evidence, as though there might be immediately apparent not only the evidence, but the very nature of the case itself, and its disposition not understanding, but dismissal.

—Ellery...

—The truck just came around from the Futtybrook Hunt Club, skinned him, cut him up, took him back to the kennels. Dog meat ... Benny tore from Esther's grasp, and, stepping forward, he said, —Ellery, what's the matter with you, good God Ellery will you ...

—Hell of an end for a thoroughbred.

—*Stop* it, will you tell us ... Benny commenced, raising his hands.

—Come on, Benny. You're drunk, Ellery said, grinning and looking at him, and the blonde looked at Esther, no longer plaintiff but witness herself to the relieving and obvious fact that there was really nothing to be concerned about after all. —He's gone, Ellery said easily. —I saw him leave a minute or two ago. He put a hand on Benny's shoulder. —Come on, Benny, Christ. Straighten up. I told you you deserved a drink, but not a whole bottle ... Benny drew away from him, without even looking at his face; and Ellery shrugged, took a deep inhalation from his cigarette, winking at the blonde as he turned away. Esther and Benny stood silent, as though both listening for denial of Ellery, for explanation of one another.

—That very odd girl with the green tongue has been telling me that it was really the Jews who discovered America, said the tall woman, her back to them. —Isabella's *jew*els didn't have a thing to do with it, backing Columbus I mean, it seems it was Isabella's *Jews*...

They both looked up, and both spoke at once. But Esther stopped.

—He was a draftsman, wasn't he. Were you married to him then? He was only a draftsman, and I was a designer. We worked together. He never mentioned me, did he. Well why, why should he, why should he have mentioned me to anybody, why...

Over his shoulder, Esther looked up to see the brown eyes of the critic; then she turned back to Benny with a different look on her face. —Don't you want to sit down somewhere? she said.

—He never talked about me, did he. And why should you care, what would it matter to you? And why should I care now, why should I want to see him, because anyhow everything's different now. And it's all different for him too, isn't it. Why should I want to see him now, any more than...why should we have even worked together then, what...because everything's different now, I'm fine now, I'm getting along fine, and is he? What's he doing now? Is he happy now? Is he getting along fine, like I am? Did everything change for him too, so that...Is he doing what he wanted to do now? or like me, is he doing what he can do, what he has to do...

—Why don't you just sit down here? Esther said as they reached the couch. —Can I bring you some coffee? She hesitated, and turned away.

—That's funny. That's funny, Benny said, sitting down slowly. —But you didn't tell me what he's doing now. That's funny. God. Benny blew his nose, and looked round him. He saw the back of his own flannel suit, and heard the voice of the man in it saying, —It's not really my line of work, I'm really a sort of historian, a musicologist, you might say, but I've been trying to get permission from the city to operate a public toilet concession in New York... Could you hand me those crackers?

The woman in the collapsed maternity dress said to someone, —And you see that person in the green shirt, you see that scar on his nose? Well I understand that he had his nose bobbed, an expensive plastic surgeon did it and some girl paid for it, didn't leave a mark, and then one night when he was in *bed* a radio fell off the shelf and gave him that scar, there's poetic justice... heh, heh heh heh...

—What's his name?

—Him? It's...I can't think of it, but it's one of those nice names, you know the kind they take, like White, White is a good nigger name.

Nearby, Mr. Crotcher had settled into an armchair, and begun moaning accompaniment to a harpsichord fraction of the *Harmonious Blacksmith*. He stopped to look down, and say, —Good heavens, good heavens, where did *you* come from? Get away. You're going to have an accident, get away, getaway getaway getaway...The baby, with a welt rising on its forehead, had begun to climb up his leg. Out of sight, the girl with bandaged wrists was saying, —After all, this is its first birthday, so this is kind of a birthday party for it too...

—Started to call himself Jacques San-jay when he went into interior decorating, someone said. —I knew him when his name was Jack Singer.

—So after that, the old man left me with nothing but fifty tons of sugar that I can't unload, and they're forcing me to take delivery. Do you think Esther would mind storing it here?

—Yess, said the dark man in the sharkskin suit, —I was told that the stock market in New York was a complex affair.

—Maybe I ought to have it dumped on the old man's doorstep. Chr-ahst, after a trick like that. Now all I have to do is sell one of his God-damned battleships . . .

—Ah? How fortunate, said the shark-skinned Argentine. —For a moment I thought I was at the wrong party.

—Dear God *no*, the tall woman was saying, —my husband hasn't got any friends. He doesn't have the time.

—Well look, it's obvious to any thinking person. The Swiss have banks all over the world. What's more necessary to a successful war than banks?

Mr. Feddle, concentrating on an open book (it was Frothingham's Aratos) was bumped aside by someone looking for an encyclopedia. —Got to look up a mutt named Chavenay. Sounds French.

—You have to really live there to understand why France has turned out so many great thinkers, and artists, a girl said. —Just live there for awhile and get a load of what they have to revolt against, and anybody would be great.

The boy who had got an advance on his novel said, —I wanted to sort of celebrate, but what the hell. Where are the nice places? They're all business lunchrooms, do you know what I mean? Expense accounts. They're all supported by expense accounts. It's depressing as hell.

—But my dear boy, why should all this bother you? said the tall woman, who had appeared. —*You* don't have to eat in these places all the time. Look at my husband, he *has* to.

—I know. But it's depressing as hell, where can you celebrate?

—I'd suggest Nedick's, said the tall woman.

—I'd suggest Murti-Bing, said the young man with no novel to advance.

—Oh, where is that? said the tall woman. —I don't believe I've ever eaten there.

—Fifty million tons of food a year eaten in New York, what does that *mean?*

—Something terrible happened, Stanley. Agnes put her hand on his.

—I'm sorry, Stanley said. —If you'll just give me my glasses . . .

—No, dear, I'm not talking about that, and that was so long ago, that night . . . She was looking in her purse. —Here, she said, —you'll have to read it yourself. What am I going to do, Stanley? Her hand shook as she dragged the letter from her bag. —It was a terrible thing to do, an unforgivable thing to do to this poor man but he's got to forgive me, and how can I . . . what can I do to . . . so he will?

Stanley unfolded the letter from the Police Department; and Agnes felt a gentle tap on the shoulder, and turned. —Did you see a kitty-cat here, lady?

—Why there was a kitten here somewhere, Agnes said, looking round her, —but I guess the kitty-cat has gone to bed. What are you doing up so late?

—My mummy sent me up to get some sleeping pills, but I can't find the lady who...

—Now don't you bother the nice lady, said Agnes, rummaging in the bottom of her large purse, taking out a French enameled thimble case. —I have some right here. Is three enough? You just take these down to Mummy. And I've already written him. She looked up at Stanley.

—Thank you, lady. Where'd you get the funny watch?

—Why, Mickey Mouse is my loyal faithful friend, said Agnes. —I can always trust *him*.

—What have you got the funny things sticking on your face for?

—Where... Agnes raised her hand, to feel the strip of tape at her temple, put there to discourage wrinkles when she lay down. —Oh my God, and they've been there... why didn't someone...

—What are they for, lady? the child asked as Agnes tore them off, and opened her compact.

—Go along down to Mummy now, for God's sake.

—He would understand, if you went to him, Stanley said, handing the letter back. —If you went to him and...

—I couldn't face him. To ask forgiveness...

—Is a sublime test of humility...

—And he's really rather an awful person I think...

—And from your inferiors an even greater trial.

—I want to do something, and... but don't you think I might just *send* him something? Maybe some sort of nice gift... yes, something nice and you know fairly expensively nice for his daughter?

—I think, Stanley commenced soberly, —that really, for your own good...

—Oh, let's stop thinking about it for a little while, she interrupted. —I just get so... tired of the terrible things I get in the mail. She smiled up at him briskly, and tightened her grasp on his hand. —Tell me about your music, Stanley, this long whatever-it-is that you've been working on for so long. Oh, and your tooth? I'm sorry, I forgot to ask.

—I think it went away, the toothache, it didn't last, but my work, it's an organ concerto but it isn't finished yet.

—But you've been working on it for months.

—For years, he said. —And you know, I look at the clean paper that I'm saving to write the finished score on, and then I look at the pile of... what

I've been working on, and, well I can see it all right there, finished. And yet, well ... you know I never read Nietzsche, but I did come across something he said somewhere, somewhere where he mentioned "the melancholia of things completed." Do you ... well that's what he meant. I don't know, but somehow you get used to living among palimpsests. Somehow that's what happens, double and triple palimpsests pile up and you keep erasing, and altering, and adding, always trying to account for this accumulation, to order it, to locate every particle in its place in one whole ...

—But Stanley, couldn't you just ... I don't know what a palimsest is, but couldn't you just finish off this thing you're working on now, and then go on and write another? She ran her hand over his, resting on the chair arm there; and Stanley called her by her Christian name for the first time. —No, that's ... you see, that's the trouble, Agnes, he said. —It's as though this one thing must contain it all, all in one piece of work, because, well it's as though finishing it strikes it dead, do you understand? And that's frightening, it's easy enough to understand why, killing the one thing you ... love. I understand it, and I'll explain it to you, but that, you see, that's what's frightening, and you anticipate that, you feel it all the time you're working and that's why the palimpsests pile up, because you can still make changes and the possibility of perfection is still there, but the first note that goes on the final score is ... well that's what Nietzsche ...

—All I know about Nietzsche is that he's decadent, that's what they say.

Stanley withdrew his hand, and it hung in air for a moment, like an object suddenly unfamiliar, which he did not know how to dispose of. —He was, because of ... well that's the reason right there, because of negation. That is the work of Antichrist. That is the word of Satan, No, the Eternal No, Stanley said, and put his hand in his pocket.

Agnes Deigh looked at her own hand on the arm of her chair. Two of the tanned fingers rose, and went down again; and when she looked over to where the critic had joined Benny on the couch, and sat, smoothing down the back of his hair, her face took the expression of the man she looked at, one of contemptuous, almost amused indulgence, though she did not have the dark hollows in her face, nor the brow and the forehead worn so with this expression that it looked natural; rather she looked uncomfortable, saying, —Those two look like they're discussing the same thing we are, and he should know, that one ...

—You know what I thought of immediately just now when I looked up and saw them? Stanley said, earnestly. —I thought of El Greco before the Inquisition, arguing the dimensions of angels' wings. He looks like an Inquisitor, that dark fellow. People laugh at arguments like that now, and how many angels can dance on the end of a pin. But it's not funny, it's very wonderful. Science hasn't explained it, and you know why, because science doesn't even understand the question, any more than science understands...You know, Agnes, this concerto I'm working on, if I'd lived three hundred years ago, why...then it would be a Mass. A Requiem Mass.

—Einstein...someone said.

—Epstein...said someone else.

—Gertrude...

—Of course you're familiar with Heisenberg's Principle of Uncertainty. Have you ever observed sand fleas? Well I'm working on a film which not only substantiates it but illustrates perfectly the metaphor of the theoretic and the real situation. And after all, what else *is* there?

—Who *was* it that said, "a little lower than the angels"?

—That? it's in that poem about "What is man, that thou art mindful of him." That was Pope.

—Which one?

At this point, Anselm, in a shirt torn at the shoulder, his hair tousled and on end, unshaven, and clutching a magazine and two books, appeared in the door. No one seemed to notice him; and he stood there silent for some time.

The music had got quite loud. —There, you see? said someone more loudly, —I told you. It *is* Handel. *The Gods Go A-Begging*, so there!

Benny's face was fleshy. Moreover, though it was not puffy, it seemed to be flesh recently acquired, and his expressions seemed, if such a thing were possible, to have difficulty in reaching the surface or, once arrived, to represent with conviction the feelings which had risen from within. So it appeared; though it may be that this want of precision pervaded the source itself, and his amorphous façade faithfully expressed confused furnishings, broken steps mounting deep stairwells, rooms boarded up, in disuse, and rooms of one character being used for new and timely purposes in the interior castle, whose defenses were not yet adjusted to the new tenancy but being constantly hastily altered in the midst of skirmishes, before that battle which would be the last.

—God is love, telling that to a Welsh Corgi in labor, isn't that divine? the girl with Boston accents laughed, and Benny, who had heard her remark about a lost horizon, drew away from where she toppled near his end of the couch, pulling the book to him as he did so. It was a book on bridge design, largely the work of Robert Maillart, and his finger marked a picture, diagram and description of the bridge at Schwandbach. He had picked it up after his words with Esther, and sat trying to appear absorbed with it while he collected himself. But he was interrupted by the figure in the green wool shirt who had joined him on the couch with, —I hear you're in TV. Smiling with effort, and already perspiring freely, Benny answered, —That's right, what can I do you for?... offering a cigarette, which was accepted without thanks.

They were being watched by the two who remained posted near the door, where they would be the first to greet, and snare, the guest of honor. Don Bildow, apparently supported upright by the lusty design of his necktie, watched through plastic rims. —What's he talking to him for, that television person? —He's just giving him a hard time, his companion answered, the same baleful satisfaction glittering under his brows, that poetic look of inner contemplation, charish, shot through with beams where some, his mirror among them, read a charismatic luster: all very well for the dust jacket of some slim volume (though no such had appeared), or the moment of inspiration itself, reflected in the eyes of someone else's wife, but, for moments like this, scarcely practical, for he could see nothing clearly more than a few feet away. —He said he was going to ask him for a job writing TV scripts.

It was evident that Benny was having a hard time. He'd just given his glass a brave, unsteady toss in his hand, and started to stand up, but he was stayed by the critic's hand, put forth in an annoying gesture as though to soothe where the irritating voice continued, speaking then of television as corrupting tragedy, now of the writer's integrity, of human suffering...

Benny had hardly looked at the face of the man who was talking to him: in contrast to his own it was a detailed fortification, every rampart erected with definite purpose, their parapets calculated to withstand repeated assaults from any direction, tried in innumerable skirmishes where many had approached so close as to tumble between scarp and counterscarp, an arrangement so long in the building that, though every bit of it had been erected for defense, in finished entirety it assumed aggressive proportions; inviting strategy, it might only be taken by storm.

All this time, Benny's smile had not failed. His smile was his first line of defense. But even as he'd started to his feet, that defense was being abandoned, and so it remained, unmanned, as empty as gaping breastworks relinquished before unexpected onslaught.

—So tell me the truth, the harassing voice went on, as its owner came far forth from his walls, openly besieging. —Do you guys really give this same crap to each other you're giving to me, pretending it's a cultural medium? or do you just admit you're all only in it for the money, that you've all sold out.

Benny's smile was gone. He sat silent for a moment, studying the features of this attack. Then he said, —Why do you hate me? Did I ever do you a favor?

The critic straightened up, unprepared for this sally, without time to recover his own walls, he withdrew instantly behind contravallations of mistrust.

—Tell me the truth, what do you want from me, you fine-haired son of a bitch, Benny said to him evenly.

—All right, for Christ's sake...

—What are you supposed to be, an honest man just because you don't have a necktie?

—Relax, relax...

—I will like hell relax. Who are you, anyhow?

—Now listen...

—You listen to me. I've just taken a lot from you. I've taken a lot from people just like you. Just like you. That's tough, isn't it, *just like you*, that this town is loaded with people just like you, the world is loaded with people just like you. The honest men who are too good to fit anywhere. You're one of the people, aren't you. Look at your hands, have you ever had a callus? You don't get them lifting glasses. Who are you, to be so bitter? Have you ever done one day of work?

—Look...

—And now I understand. And you talk to me about life, about real life, about human misery, Benny went on. He was not speaking loudly, nor fast, still the cold but vehement and level tone of his voice drew several people to turn around, and listen and watch. The other sat his ground with a patient sneer. —I offered you work, and you were too good for it. We buy stuff from guys like you all the time, writing under pen names to protect names that are never going to be published anywhere else, but they keep thinking they'll make it, what they want to do, but never quite manage, and they keep on doing what they're too good for. It's a joke. It's a joke, Benny repeated, and it was now that his voice began to rise. —I know you, I know you. You're the only serious person in the room, aren't you, the only one who *understands*, and you can prove it by the fact that you've never finished a single thing in your life. You're the only well-educated person, because you never went to college, and you resent education, you resent social ease, you resent good manners, you resent success, you resent any kind of success, you resent God, you resent Christ, you resent thousand-dollar bills, you resent Christmas, by God, you resent happiness, you resent happiness itself, because none of that's *real*. What is real, then? Nothing's real to you that isn't part of your own past, *real life*, a swamp of failures, of social, sexual, financial, personal, ... spiritual failure. Real life. You poor bastard. You don't know what real life is, you've never been near it. All you have is a thousand intellectualized ideas about life. But *life*? Have you ever measured yourself against anything but your own lousy past? Have you ever faced anything outside yourself? *Life!* You poor bastard. Benny started to laugh. He knocked an empty glass from the end of the couch, and Ellery put a hand on his shoulder. The stubby poet had come up beside the man at the other end of the couch, who was silent, looking at Benny, and the sneer almost squeezed from his face. Most of the people in the room were aware that something was happening, and had half turned, giving it half their attention, waiting to see if it deserved all. Benny started to stand up. —Come on, we'll get a drink, Ellery said to him, an arm across his shoulders. —All right, Benny said. Then suddenly he swung around again.

—Go on, you lush, said the stubby poet; but Benny did not regard him. He stood over the man who as quickly recovered his sneer to look up.

—How do you make your living? Benny demanded.

—Come on, Benny. Leave the poor bastard alone.

—I just asked how he makes his living.

—The hell with him. Come on, Ellery said.

—I just want to know how he makes his living, is there anything wrong with that?

—He's a critic. He writes about books, or some God damn thing. Now come on. But Benny pulled from Ellery's grasp on his shoulder. —How long is it since you've seen the sun rise? he demanded. Then he went on, —How you would have done it. That's the way everything is, isn't it. How you would have done it. Not how it should have been done, but how you would have done it. When you criticize a book, that's the way you work, isn't it. How you would have done it, because you didn't do it, because you're still afraid to admit that you can't do it yourself.

—Ellery, please . . . stop him, Esther said, in a low voice beside Ellery. He turned and looked at her, and he did, just then, have an expression very much like Benny's, one of tense impatience, which in that instant of exchange between them seemed to direct everything Benny had said, and was saying, at her. Everyone, within the bounds of what each considered either manners or sophistication, was watching; and most were watching the man on the couch. —Oh Chrahst I remember him, he's the guy that married Deedee Jaqueson, and they kicked her out of the little black book for it. Chrahst, what a co-incidence, Ed Feasley commented.

Rudy consoled a frightened group in one corner, with, —You know, he's the kind who knows art but doesn't know what he likes.

Don Bildow watched apprehensively from the other side of the room, where he had retired, and did not see Anselm who watched, silent and attentive. Mr. Feddle, clutching a book, had gained the front row. The back of Maude's neck was being manipulated by strong fingers, stronger perhaps but not so vigorous as those twisting Stanley's hand. He looked at Agnes and looked away quickly, as though afraid to provoke the tension in her face to burst in confidence to him.

A high voice broke the silence as Benny paused for breath. —So *there!* And that goes for your cat *too!* It was the Duchess of Ohio, who scurried back to cover.

The tall woman told someone that she and her husband were going to Spain in the spring, though she had hoped to be in Hawaii right now; someone said, —She rubs you the right way, does she? talking to someone else about someone else; Sonny Byron said, —Wake up, baby, the floor show's over, and stroked Arny Munk's forehead; the author of the best seller *Trees of Home*, who had kept his back turned to the room all this time, pretending conversation with Mr. Crotcher who was singing, said, to someone else, —How can I respect my readers when I know they're just trying to get a cheap psychoanalysis at my expense? and was told that they probably thought that he was getting one at theirs; the dark man in the sharkskin suit said, —Yes, I was warned about this sort of thing in New York. Now about these battleships...

—A dreadful crime she did commit, did all the world surprise, sang Mr. Crotcher to the baby, whose chin rested on his shoe, which he jarred in approximate 2/4 time. —Black beetles in walnut shells...

—And that dumb bastard's starting in again.

Ellery was holding Benny tight by one shoulder. —Come on, relax, forget the dumb bastard, he said. —Come on, Benny, take this. He held a full glass up, and Benny took it, and drank it down steadily and carefully. Then the empty glass hung in his hand like a weight.

—Get where I am, and then you can be bitter, Benny mumbled, staring into one of the few empty spaces in that room. —Do you think I like these clothes? Do you think I like double-breasted snappy clothes, like... Do you think I like this God-damned awful necktie, do you call it a necktie this thing? These glasses? He reached for them twice, and the second time a finger caught one of the broad bows and they fell to the floor. —I'm a success, that's why I've got a right to be bitter. God damn it. God damn it. How long do you think it is since *I've* seen the sun rise?

Though Mr. Feddle moved slowly, Benny raised his face as though the space before him had been materialized into an apparition. —Go on, said Mr. Feddle, hungrily. —Go on. I understand you. Go on.

—Isn't that right? Benny said to him, reaching an arm to him which made an irregular arc and dropped between them.

—Come on, forget that jerk, you'll be all right, Ellery said, supporting Benny. —You're making a fool of yourself.

—Why? *Why?*

—Go on. I understand you.

—That's what I've got a right to do, I've got a right to haven't I? Haven't I? Isn't that why I've worked, and worked, and...

—Go on...

—*Why?*

Mr. Feddle darted in and embraced him. —Do you remember Fedya, in *Redemption?* in Tolstoy's *Redemption?* he said, the alarm clock swinging between them. —"And you know..." His voice lowered, and he spoke more slowly, —"it's a funny thing, but we love people for the good we do them, and we hate them for the harm..." Do you remember?

Benny stared into his face, as they separated and Mr. Feddle braced himself with excitement. —Go on...!

—But...dishonest...then, but now? Now? I got into this and I found everybody believed what they were doing. They all believe it, and after awhile you believe it too. You live with it for awhile and you believe it too. Friends. Do you think I have any friends? Everybody I know...I...they want something from me or I want something from them. Somebody asked me if my wife is here. My wife? I go home and we just sit and look at each other. Home? My home looks like a cocktail lounge. I read all the books. I read all the books about self-improvement, master yourself, develop your personality, be a good God-damned Christian and get something for nothing...

—Go on...

—Forget...

—If you're doing something you hate, quit it while you still hate it...

—Go on...

—Relax...

—Because you were right the first time...

—Ellery, *please* stop him. Ellery looked down, to Esther hanging to his arm. —What can I do, he's...

—And you...Benny turned to her, —He was your husband, wasn't he. And you know, don't you. *Don't you.* You know who designed the bridge at Fallen Ark Gap...and the Cooper City viaduct...

—Why, I...Ellery, please. There's something wrong.

—Go on...

—That's what I wanted to do, that's all I ever wanted to do. Where did he come from, sitting there at a draftsman's table, and he could draw it as though he was making a sketch, but every tension was perfect, the balance was perfect, you can look at those bridges with my name on them and see them leap out to meet themselves, see them move in perfect stillness, see perfect delicate tension of movement in stillness, see tenderness in suspense . . . with my name on them, *I* designed them. Like hell I designed them. Do you know why? Benny looked into their faces, and suddenly took Mr. Feddle's arm. —It was like a part of me working, like part of myself working there. Do you understand?

—Yes. Go on . . .

—And I couldn't do it. He could do it and I couldn't do it. Do you understand?

—Yes, yes . . .

—I couldn't do it, Benny said; and for a moment the only sound was the ticking of Mr. Feddle's clock. And called upon, not by alarms but by this insistent and accurate silence, several people turned to hear Mr. Feddle say, —Yes, yes, do you remember him? Fedya? In Tolstoy's *Redemption?* "There was something terribly lacking between what I felt and what I could do . . ." Do you remember? Mr. Feddle had both hands on Benny's shoulders; but Ellery thrust his hands aside. —Come on, Benny, you'll be all right.

Benny had gone limp. He stood with the book on bridge design open, a page went over, and he was staring at a picture of Maillart's bridge at Salginatobel, a glazed distance in his eyes as though he were indeed gazing the full ninety meters to the foot of the valley below. Then his eye caught something, scribbled in the margin, *The arch never sleeps.* —Look . . . ! he said, and read it aloud, stared at it silently and read it aloud again. —He wrote that here, didn't he, I remember, I've heard him say that, he . . . yes . . . Suddenly he turned to Esther. —Could I ask you something? a favor? a gift from you? The pages of the book trembled in his hands. And if her tone was, —Yes, anything to silence you, to send you away . . . he did not notice. —Because this book . . . this book . . . ?

—Yes, she said. —Yes.

—Yes, he repeated, staring at it, he whispered —the arch never sleeps.

—Relax, Benny. You just need a drink, Ellery said. —You'll bounce back.

—Ellery, let him . . .

Benny stopped, and looked up at Ellery. —I know, he said. —That's what I can't stand. I know I'll bounce back, and that's what I can't stand. He looked at them all three. —Don't worry, he said. —This only happens once. That's the world I live in. You make one show, and when it's finished you throw it out. You give everything you've got to make one show, and then it runs for twenty minutes and you can never show it again, so you throw it out. This only happens once . . .

—Look, Benny . . .

—But could I have this? he went on, in the same loud tone, holding up the book. —Do you understand? Because I'm sentimental. That's why I have my job, because I feel what other people feel but more, the same things but more, but not too much, not too much like he did . . .

—Benny . . .

—Not too much. He relaxed against Ellery. —You're O.K., Benny. You just need a drink.

Benny looked up at him. —Don't you get tired?

—Yeh, we both need a good night's sleep.

—I mean tired of the whole thing.

Ellery looked at him. —I'll get you a drink, he said, and bumped into the tall woman, who had turned from this scene to say to her husband, —Now, do you see what I meant about Hawaii?

She was interrupted. —Do you see what I mean? But the man who made this demand turned from her to look at Esther, and looking at Benny he said to Esther, his forearm extending its own length from the gray flannel sleeve which Benny looked at with glazed familiarity, —Do you see what I meant? Do you see what I meant?

—That's what I hate. That's what I hate. That's what I hate.

—Do you see what I meant?

—Merry Christmas, someone said, raising a glass. —If you'll pardon the expression.

—Great God. Whatever made you think of *that*?

The girl with Boston accents looked at Benny and said, —What's he high on, man?

The stocky man in army uniform looked at the critic, still seated on the couch, and, saying, —A guy like that is dangerous, was, as usual, right for the wrong reasons.

—And the Swiss Guard at the Vatican? I suppose you know that the Pope has given them permission to practice shooting at a target range? And in plain clothes?

—And they say that the food in Spain is in*edi*ble, that is if you're used to eating like a civilized person, and so I'm taking *scads* of these marvelous reducing pills that simply take your appetite away.

—I finally got this new Cadillac, said the author of *The Trees of Home*, filling a hypodermic syringe with whisky. —I've just always wanted a brand new car, there's something about the way a brand new car smells inside, that new smell. It's something I've always wanted, it's been a regular phobia of mine.

The person with him was garnishing an unseasonal martini with Pernod from a pocket bottle, muttering —Just a drop in each one, there's some chemical reaction. But what's that? he added, looking up to see the needle fitted into place.

—You take it this way, you get just as drunk and you don't get hangovers, said the author of the best-selling book. —My analyst told me about it. He rolled up a sleeve. —Did I tell you about this new Cadillac I got? It's been a regular phobia with me...

Esther stood looking round her, nervously as though for something to demand her attention and relieve her of going where her attention was demanded: from the doorway, Don Bildow directed a plastic-rimmed appeal over the shoulder of a paunchy man whose familiar face had been so many times, and she realized now, so inadequately, photographed. At hand, the collar of the green wool shirt and the dark head above reared over the back of the couch. The critic and his stubby companion were looking in the same direction. —Christ...It was difficult to tell, from behind, which of them was muttering. —The guest of honor. Why can't he stay home to get drunk?

Across the room, Stanley had looked up and interrupted himself to say, —Look, he must have just come, isn't that...

—Somebody said he was coming, Agnes Deigh said. —Oh God, I don't want to listen to his soul-searching...

—But if we...

—Not from him. Not tonight. She looked up at Stanley.

—Black beetles in wal-nut shells, bound round her baby's eyes, Mr. Crotcher sang. —Do you like that?

—The Boeuf on the Roof...

—I haven't seen *her* since *Ischia*...

—It's in the Vatican, if you call *that* art...

—And don't let those medieval costumes fool you, you can carry fifteen rounds in a good codpiece, a grenade if you're underdeveloped...

—*She* says it happened right there in the Cappella Sistina, but you know *her*, it might as well have been the Cappella Paolina...

—I wonder what ever happened to old Deedee, Ed Feasley said to no one, and then, to the sharkskinned Argentine, —What was that about battleships?

Don Bildow brought his shoulders up to a hopeful slope as Esther approached, but they sagged again as her eyes and her smile passed him to embrace a haggard, red-eyed, rash-looking young man who had just come in.

The two on the couch watched her, though the shorter one did not stop talking. —I got a look at the manuscript, he said. —It's called *Wild Gousse Chase*, and I swear he's got you in it. A character named Hawthorn, and I swear it's you, just about the time you were mixed up with that same blonde, except he's got her having *you* psychoanalyzed just like she had him analyzed when he was trying to get rid of her and couldn't because she was paying for the analysis, so he's got this character that I swear is you screwed up like that with her. You could sue that wise bastard.

—Yuh. Hand me that glass, will you?

—Who's that that Esther's got her hands all over now?

—A stupid kid named Otto.

—He looks like a truck ran over him.

Benny was talking to the man in his old suit. —I'm going back tomorrow, he said. —I haven't been home for eleven years. That's a long time, to go back and try to take up where you left off. I haven't seen anything grow for eleven years. You forget that things grow. The vegetables you get in restaurants, you can't believe that they ever really grew anywhere, and the flowers, you never think of flowers growing, you see them one way, cut, and you can't think of them any other way except posing, dead. The trees here don't grow, they're ready-made like furniture, that puts on new slip-covers in the spring. My God, you forget, you forget...

—Benny...

—Why, I'll be there tomorrow morning, I'll be out on the side porch watching the sun come up Christmas morning, you see if I'm not...

Benny raised his head, looking around the room. Then, standing beside the door to the hall leading to the bedroom, he saw Ellery talking to the blonde; and when the man before him said, in the same tone he himself had been using a moment before, —Benny, would you take me along...? Benny said nothing.

Behind him, a girl said, to someone else, —So I started this personalidy course where they have you stand in front of a mirror and repeat your name over to yourself in a nice gentle tone... and now I'm Mister Wipe's personal secretary...

—So I said to her, you just go ahead and *be* pathological...

—So I said to them when we got back to Florence, of course there's no place I'd rather live than Siena if I had my analyst there with me...

—So he said to me, Oh, Sappho, he was queer too wasn't he...

No longer the garden, but, as Benny said, cut flowers posing dead, without past or future, in as great a variety of jealous identities assembled as the tenants of an expensive florist's window, lacking the careless grandeur of indigenous plants, arranged instead in that slightly frantic symmetry which dazed passers-by call artistic, and move on, never hazarding the senses to violation by wire and the treachery of paper petals. Even now, Herschel, perilously erect, posed blossomtime. —Of course, baby, I've never been better in my life...

but *no*, I couldn't *show* you the tattoo. Since you must know, the two friends I met that night played a *vile* trick on me, at least it seemed so when I saw it in the mirror, what they had tattooed on me I mean, I never saw *them* again. But now that I've lived with it for awhile I'm quite fond of it. It's *me*. Do you like foxes? I can't even tell you, it's so naughty, but it is rather cute, would you like to see it? Come into the bathroom...

Anselm watched all this in silence. Occasionally his lips moved, forming isolated syllables which were words in themselves, most often one which drew his lower lip under his front teeth, and released it on a sharp *k*. People made way for him, turning their backs, as he moved about the room with none but immediate goals, the half-emptied glasses put aside carelessly, and raised, empty, with surprise, when he had gone on. Someone, turning upon him too soon, challenged agreeably, —Why don't you ask for a full one? Anselm handed over the glass he had just emptied and said, —Why don't you ask for eight more inches? you'd still have a hole in your belly... and went on, the magazine rolled in his hand advertising trusses on its back cover.

—I don't know, Stanley, but it's as though everywhere I look, there's something, or someone... that I've failed to... Agnes Deigh paused, looking round. —Unintentionally maybe, even betrayed...

—It's because we've been led to believe today that we are self-sufficient, Stanley commenced, —that no transcendent judgment is...

—There, even there, do you see him? she said, starting a little in her chair. —The boy who just came in? He brought me a play he'd written, and I never got a chance to read it but I told him...

—Agnes, you...

—Stanley, I...

—*Esther*...

—Now listen, you're the lady with the kitten aren't you?...

—Esther, have you seen? fairies in the bottom of your garden? hehehe

—But this time he wasn't trying to teach the kitten to salivate...

—*Otto*... I'm so glad you're here.

—But I didn't know you were having a party, I just came up...

—But you're here, she said, and took his arm. —I knew you were back, she said, leading him slowly through the room, but not pausing. —But you look... I even heard you had your arm in a sling. Where have you been?

—I just got out of jail, he said rather jauntily.

—Out of what? jail? She did stop, and looked at him.

—It was nothing, he said to her. —A fifteen-dollar fine for... you know, fooling around. I was celebrating. I was lucky, I had just sixteen dollars on me... With a shock of anxiety, his hand went to a breast pocket, found the sharp confirming corner of the packet inside, and dropped. —I was lucky, I'd left all the rest of my money in a hotel-room bureau drawer, I was terrified it would be gone by the time I got back there, I ... Esther was looking at him, as though not listening, simply waiting for him to finish. —What's the matter? he asked uncertainly.

—You haven't said you were glad to see me.

—Oh but, I mean, of course I am, I just, everything's been so sort of ... you know, and I, and maybe ... someone's mentioned to you? about my play, I mean? he blurted out. She shook her head. —Well I mean, it's nothing, nothing really, but ... But she did not interrupt him, or no more than with the look in her eyes, waiting for him to ask what it never occurred to him to ask: about her, how she had been all of this time, how she was; what would have given him what he sought, had it occurred to him: the chance to bridle this runaway apology, which she did not require, this hazardous insistence, which he did not dare halt in this race with himself. His jauntiness was falling away, giving place to exhaustion and mounting anxiety. —And then, I met my father finally. I had dinner with him. I mean, do you remember how you used to ask me why I didn't look him up? And he ... so I did.

Esther's hand rested on his arm, she seemed to have wilted a little before him, and she asked quietly, —What was he like?

—Well he was fine, he was sort of stern, but I mean he was really very nice, and ... well sort of stern and brusque. And he was a Catholic, I mean not that that should make any difference, but it sort of surprised me, and ... well I don't know, to tell the truth I'm sort of mixed up ... Otto was rummaging in a pocket, and he brought out a note. —When I got back to the hotel finally, here was this note waiting from him. It's sort of pathetic, asking me to call him as soon as I can, and then he says he hopes I haven't been worried about him, right after I'd just seen him for the first time, maybe he means on account of his eyes, he didn't ... he doesn't see very well, and ... I don't know, I mean when I think of him that's what I remember, his glasses, the dust on his glasses, Otto persisted. And now, as the appeal in her face became more manifest, reaching further back, through unrelated privacies to the last embrace they had abandoned, the more he retreated, dodging among irrelevant images of himself. —And I haven't called him, I sent him a fancy robe this morning for Christmas, it seemed the least ... I mean, I thought I should do something like that, you know, for Christmas, he finished, running a finger of his pale hand across his smooth lip.

—Esther, Don Bildow interrupted them, giving Otto a bare glance, sufficient only to dismiss him. —I think you might come over and greet your guest ...

—That man standing over near the door, Otto commenced, recovering somewhat, —isn't that...?

—In a moment, Esther said to Don Bildow, who retired a polite step and waited. —Do you want to come over and meet him? she asked Otto.

—Well, I mean, I don't know...

—Do you remember? she asked, both hands on his arm now, —when you lent me his book? When we first knew each other, that first day at lunch?

—Yes, yes I remember, of course I remember, Otto said quickly, and then paused uncertainly. —But now...

—After all, Don Bildow recovered from his momentary lapse of politeness, —he is the only halfway interesting person here tonight, Esther. He started to turn his unimpressive back upon them.

—Wait, Esther said, and then to Otto, —You don't want to meet him?

—I guess not, Otto said, looking beyond her at the paunchy figure near the door, who had just covered his mouth with a handkerchief and looked like he was going to be sick into it; and the tall woman, who had just said, —*A*theism!...that charming word, I haven't heard it in years, turned looking for her husband murmuring, —Oh dear...have I said something wrong again?...—I guess not, thanks Esther, I mean what would we have to say to each other? he went on, as Esther was turned away on Bildow's urgent arm. —I used to...wanting to meet the poet, or the painter, or the writer or the tight-rope walker of the minute, as though you could sop up something from them in a handshake...Otto had lowered his eyes, over her thighs, and his voice until, having made a discovery in his own words, he was talking to himself. At that he raised his face, and with the brave refusal of one rejecting revelation for fear of examining the motives which conspired to breed it, went to seek a drink.

—Chrahst, I thought you'd gone to Peru.

Otto looked up to see Ed Feasley. —But I just saw you, a day or so ago.

—I know. Chrahst, wha'd you do, fly both ways? I mean, what are you doing here?

—I just heard there was a party here, Otto answered, and added, —I don't know, picking up a glass.

—I know, I mean Chrahst, you know? This crazy spic has been following me around all night. What's that they're playing anyway? He cocked his head numbly to a fragment of Handel's *Royal Fireworks Music*, which was being accompanied by Mr. Crotcher singing *Bye Bye Blackbird* from his armchair.

—I mean I wish they'd play *On the Sunny Side of the Street*, you know? There's been somebody tagging around after me all day, this marathon walker, I met him in a bar. Forty miles a day, you start at four A.M. and you get there at three P.M. and eat. You just have to have a destination, he told me. A marathon walker, I mean Chrahst, how unnecessary. And now this spic. I heard you sold your novel.

—My play, I...Otto commenced.

—Yes, Chrahst, you ought to try selling a battleship.

And the two young men finished their drinks and stood silent, staring vacant-eyed on the room, vaguely jarred by the words spattering around them.

—The one about the lady from the First Unitarian Church of Kennebunkport, M.E. who orders monogrammed napkins for a church luncheon and... Oh, I've spoiled it.

—And even barely more than a hundred years ago there weren't ten bathrooms in all the private houses in Paris...

—In a hundred years the population of Europe has tripled, what does that mean?

—And have you heard the Far Rockaway locker room story?

—I said to him, if you really believed what you wrote there, you'd be morally obliged to blow your brains out.

—Well *whis*ky's all right, said the girl with the bandaged wrists, —but for God's sake don't give it gin, gin stunts the growth, we tried it on a kitten.

Nearer by, the woman in the collapsed maternity dress said, —Cross-eyed people bring me bad luck.

—Not just cross-eyed, the tall woman went on, —but with a withered hand, on crutches, and an idiot. Can you imagine *one* person having all those things? *And* in a suit with a pleated, belted back?

—An embarras des richesses, or they would be for that woolly-headed boob over there on the couch. His main trouble is that he never finished his analysis, some girl was paying for it of course...There was a tug at her skirt. —And what do *you* want?

—Mummy sent me up for some more sleeping pills.

—What *are* you reading...?

—Oh I'm not readin this, the little girl said, holding up *Toilet Training and Democracy*. —Some man...

—Here, said the tall woman, opening her bag. —I have some right here. She took out a Chinese toothpick box, and worked with its intricate catch. —Oh wait a minute...my God, I almost gave you my Seconal. A friend of my husband's brings it from Mexico, she went on, rummaging. —Here you are, dear...

—Now you'd better march right downstairs and...

—Don't hurt the poor child's feelings.

—Another sensitive minority, children? If I hear once more...

—I mean Chrahst, sensitive minorities, you know? Ed Feasley took up, turning to Otto. —I mean it's really people like us, you and me, we're the persecuted minority. White, Protestant, male, over twenty-one, I mean we don't belong anywhere, you know? And finally we're all just parodies of each other. I mean Chrahst sometimes I wish I'd studied something in college. What's the matter? he broke off, seeing Otto's expression.

—Nothing. That girl, that blond girl, for a minute I thought... nothing.

—Her? I know her from somewhere, you want me to introduce you? Otto mumbled something, and reached for a full glass nearby. —You don't? I don't blame you, Chrahst why start all over again? I mean, it's just like that marathon walker, you know? What do you do when you get there? You eat and go to bed.

—I know, Otto said dully, looking at the floor. —It's funny, I used to think that to go to bed with a girl older than I was or bigger than I was, that made it all right. Then you know, when I was in Central America, it was funny, I thought that if you paid a girl, that made it all right, but if you paid a lot it was more sinful than if you paid a little, but it seemed more honest to pay with money than... than with pretending that you... than paying with... yourself, he finished vaguely, still looking at the floor.

—I know, you know? I mean imagine just starting in now. My old man says you're not a man until you're the head of a family. He's had it, Ed Feasley went on, as vaguely, looking at his shoetops. —There's this great big old house up in the Hudson River Valley. Cornwallis had his headquarters there, or maybe it was Lafayette or General Sherman, I don't know, but you can't go into the place without thinking about the parties they've had in it, ambassadors and presidents, you know, I mean it's historical as hell. And now my mother sits up there opening packages, that's the only thing she ever thinks about, whenever a package comes for anybody she gets so excited. I mean even the laundry. Even the groceries. You know? And now they've built this state hospital three miles away, it's full of feebs, feeble-minded people, and some niggers are building this crazy religious camp right across the river. I mean I've got nothing against niggers but Christ, you know? Ed Feasley finished his drink. —Whenever I go home, it's like everything's wearing out. I mean just imagine being the head of a family in that place now. Just starting in now. I mean Chrahst everything wears out, you know? People wear out, friends wear out, cars wear out, sometimes it's easier to smash them up while they're still new, and you don't have to watch them wear out.

They were being approached by a short shiny figure in a gray sharkskin suit who was, himself, being hounded by someone saying, —Are you the guy who's telling people that our company puts drugs in its dog food so dogs get addicted to our brand...?

—Oo, coño . . . I was warned about this sort of thing, the Argentine said, escaping in Ed Feasley's direction. —Excuse me, do I intrude? We became separated while speaking of . . .

—Battleships, said Ed Feasley wearily, and taken in charge, he left Otto staring into an empty glass. He did not even raise his eyes when someone beside him said, —She told me there was food in the kitchen, but I went in and there are two lunatics in there, one of them's almost naked and the other is buttering him.

Stanley's voice droned steadily as a distant undercurrent, —Yes but just let me finish . . . to Agnes Deigh. —I'm not trying to say I'm exempt from it, this modern disease, he went on with an insistence which prevented him from seeing that she was more than tired, was in fact exhausted in a sense so severe that it was physical only in its trembling expression. —That's what it is, a disease, you can't live like we do without catching it. Because we get time given to us in fragments, that's the only way we know it. Finally we can't even conceive of a continuum of time. Every fragment exists by itself, and that's why we live among palimpsests, because finally all the work should fit into one whole, and express an entire perfect action, as Aristotle says, and it's impossible now, it's impossible, because of the breakage, there are pieces everywhere . . .

Suddenly Otto's hand shot up to his inside breast pocket: one might have thought he'd been bitten, so involuntary had this reflex become.

—A nation of watchmakers, can you imagine any country better qualified to make atom bombs?

—Oh God, to be in Europe, anywhere in Europe, even in France . . .

—Maude, is this yours? Big Anna was wearing it under her shirt.

—Even in Mauberge, even in a coal mine.

Otto's face expressed nothing: unobserved, his features apparently had no reason to arrange themselves one way or another. His brow was level and without lines, his lips together and even. But slight marks of agitation drew up round his eyes when he raised them toward the door, where Esther stood with a woman wearing an orchid upside-down, and two or three others clustered about the guest of the evening, who afforded a spectacle of sartorial sloppiness and postural dilapidation consistent with the humility which he offered, in his soul-searching best-selling book, to share with others. At that moment Esther caught his eye with a querulous look which drew Otto's face up in immediate confusion, and widened his bloodshot eyes; though why, he could hardly have said, as he turned and pretended to be speaking with the woman in the collapsed maternity dress who had just said, —Monasteries are a good thing for America, they help keep the homosexuals off the streets.

Then Otto saw Anselm, who was whistling with soft harshness through his teeth, and watching Stanley. Otto looked away quickly, as though fearing to be recognized, and accused of something; but Anselm kept whistling, and watching Stanley.

—This self-sufficiency of fragments, that's where the curse is, fragments that don't belong to anything. Separately they don't mean anything, but it's almost impossible to pull them together into a whole. And now it's impossible to accomplish a body of work without a continuous sense of time, so instead you try to get all the parts together into one work that will stand by itself and serve the same thing a lifetime of separate works does, something higher than itself, and I... this work of mine, three hundred years ago it would have been a Mass, because the Church...

—But dear man... came from across the room, the woman with the orchid upside-down.

—And it would be finished by now, because the Church...

—But my dear Mister... Pott is it? her voice came on as she stood spilling part of her drink on his shoe and burning Don Bildow's sleeve with her cigarette, —I am a *birth*right Friend.

As Anselm approached behind him, Stanley heard the vague harsh whistle, half turned, and then talked more rapidly and more directly to Agnes Deigh, who listened with strained attention. Anselm walked with slow careless indifference, bumping people as though they were pieces of overstuffed furniture. —Come on baby, one more glass of nice gin and we'll find you the cutest doctor, why you look good enough to eat!... oww... Anselm bumped, bumped the girl with the bandaged wrists who went on, —We've been thinking of getting a two-toed sloth instead, they just hang on the shower-curtain rod all day and you don't have to do a thing.

—Hey Stanley, where's your instrument? Anselm asked coming up behind him. He'd taken out a dirty pocket comb with some teeth missing. —Here, middle C is missing, but if you can find some toilet paper I'll accompany you in "We hasten with feeble but diligent footsteps"... didn't you bring your instrument?

—And I don't read Voltaire of course, Stanley continued, his voice quavering as he forced it, —but somewhere I came across some words of his, "If there were no God, it would be necessary to invent him." That may sound irreverent, but...

—It sounds downright God-damned heretical, Anselm said behind him.

—But... even Voltaire could see that some transcendent judgment is necessary, because nothing is self-sufficient, even art, and when art isn't an expression of something higher, when it isn't invested you might even say, it breaks up into fragments that don't have any meaning and don't have any...

—You sound like Simon Magus, *invested*, for Christ sake, Anselm said, putting a dirty hand on Stanley's shoulder. —Why don't you go see his heart, they've got it in the Bibliothèque Nationale. You might understand him. By osmosis.

—Simon Magus? Stanley said, turning, confused.

—Voltaire, for Christ sake. He patted Stanley on the shoulder. —How's your crack, Stanley? he asked him. Two people turned, raising eyebrows in shocked interest. Agnes Deigh pretended to be looking for something in her large pocketbook.

—Why, what…

—The crack in your ceiling, what do you think I mean.

—Oh, I didn't know you…it's a little longer, three-eighths of an inch longer, I…

—What the hell have you got in your pocket? Anselm said, nodding at Stanley's side jacket pocket, which bulged, and weighed the jacket down on that side. —I'll be God damned, Anselm said, reaching into the pocket before Stanley could step away, —a cold chisel. I heard this but I wouldn't believe it.

—Well, I came up on the subway, and…

—Bathysiderodromophobia! What did I tell you! said an onlooker. Anselm looked up, his eyes narrowed. —And what's that in *your* pocket?

—A stethoscope, Anselm said, —what does it look like.

—Anselm! What are you doing here? They looked up to see Don Bildow. —Where is…you're supposed to be taking care of…

—I took her to a movie, and left her there until I come back.

—To a movie! But…what movie, where, where is she, how could you…

—All right, I'll tell you the truth…well, don't worry about her. It's a good show, it will do her good.

—But you can't…couldn't do a thing like that…

—Don, an excited young man interrupted, grasping his arm, and nodding at someone across the room, who stood looking at a copy of the small stiff-covered magazine. —That poem, that poem by Max, he says it isn't by Max at all, he says…well come over, quick.

Anselm said, —What poem? and followed them across the room, rolling his magazine now with the cover outside (*Pin-Up Cuties*) with one hand, picking up a drink with the other, and already showing the yellowed edges of teeth in a grin.

Stanley looked after them bewildered; then he saw Esther, whom he did not know, approaching Otto, and attempted an irresolute signal, saying —There's Otto, I still have the twenty dollars he lent me, I haven't needed it…His signal went unseen; he listened at a strain of music, and returned to

Agnes Deigh, whose eyes were closed. —And do you know what Handel had inscribed inside the cover of his harpsichord? Musica Donum Dei . . . they still have it, he finished in desolate consolation, looking up, embarrassed at the prospect before him, the flesh abandoned by the lights of the discriminating will.

Very near him, the tall woman had just caught her husband in time to prevent him from confessing (to some "total stranger" as she would tell him next morning) that he had two psychoanalysts, neither known to the other, whom he played off against each other and managed to keep ahead of them both himself. —Our bene . . . one of our dear friends, she interrupted, as Stanley attended with fugitive interest, —has the most exquisite Queen Anne sofa which he's hinted he might be willing to sell, for a *price* of course. Of course there's nothing we need less than a Queen *Anne* sofa, she went on pleasantly, including the total stranger and, with an icily cordial smile, Stanley's gape, and then she turned a rueful look on her husband, —but it might rather help things along, to buy something tonight from your employer . . . ?

The total stranger mumbled something about a Cadillac that smelled like a phobia inside; and Stanley, again abashed by the cordial dismissal in the tall woman's smile, and the weary bravery in the superciliary shadow of her look, sought refuge in more immediate terrain, anticipating it as unlit as he'd left it, and so doubly startled at being so sharply fixed in the illumination of both eyes upon him.

Beyond, someone was engaged in writing a criticism of a work which contained forty-nine one-syllable words to seven of two syllables; thirty-one words of Anglo-Saxon origin to five of Latin and one-eighteenth of Greek. It was *honest*, this person said.

And beyond, Otto fled himself from one of Esther's eyes to the other, and found himself in both. —You don't look well, she said to him. —Come, where we can talk . . . leading him across the room toward the door of the bedroom. —It's as though I knew you were coming . . . The bedroom door was locked. She turned to the other door, still holding his arm. —Oh Herschel, I'm sorry . . . She closed the bathroom door and they turned back. —What did you say?

—Like a jungle, Otto repeated, looking into the room beyond her. —A jungle where you've lived in the dry season, and you come back in a wet season . . . His voice tailed off and he stood there trying to assume no expression at all as her eyes searched his face, to find no betrayal but a quirked eyebrow which started to rise, and did not.

—What's happened to you? she asked him.

—Nothing, I . . . I'm tired.

—Nothing! She caught breath. —You're different. You've changed.

—I guess I'm just tired, he repeated.

—Do you want to stay here tonight?

—Here? he said, looking at her as though not understanding.

—Here. With me.

—But Esther, I . . . I don't think it would be . . .

—All right.

—I mean I just think it might . . .

—All right, I said.

—But . . .

—Please. If you don't want to then don't talk about it.

—Oh damn it Esther, I didn't come here to argue with you, he said in a hoarse whisper. —Why are you looking at me like that?

—Where have you been all this time? She asked him that gently, as though prompting him to the question he should have asked about himself, of her: for she had the answer ready enough, as he may have known, looking down at his own thumbnails instead of into her eyes where he might have read it.

—Just . . . around, he mumbled.

—But what have you been doing to yourself? she came on, forced to recover the moment.

—Nothing really, not much of anything, I . . . He looked up at her with an attempted smile. —Looking around, there just hasn't seemed to be much worth doing.

—Is it worth going on like this, alone? just to find out what's not worth doing? she demanded with an involuntary abruptness, and as he looked down again, —Even your smile isn't alive . . . and she stopped, lowering her own eyes as though someone else had spoken. Then she looked up quickly, as though to ascertain him there, before she went on, —And you, I suppose you have something . . . crucial, something crucial you have to do before you can . . . But Esther stopped speaking again, for in his face, she saw that he had not.

The place did present aspects of foliage, shifting and dank, the florist's window flooded perhaps, its tenants afloat in slithering similitude; or the jungle: for at that instant the room was pierced by a raptorial cry like that of the bird descending.

—That? that's Max's poem? Anselm laughed, crying out, —"Wer, wenn ich schriee . . ." that?

They looked toward the door, saw only the paunchy guest of the evening moving toward it, in an unsteady rasorial attitude as though following a trail of crumbs to the great world outside. Mr. Feddle approached, looking rather reckless, gripping *The Vertebrate Eye and Its Adaptive Radiation*.

Otto's hand jerked, and then moved furtively to his inside breast pocket as half a step back he looked frankly down Esther's figure. Her eyes drew him up quickly. —I just thought... remembered, you? are you all right? I mean, I heard...

—What?

—I don't know. Nothing. You hear things.

—What are you talking about?

—Well you, that you needed a doctor?

—A doctor came this afternoon, and... I saw him.

—But, and then, you're all right?

—I'd rather not talk about it.

—But all right, I'm sorry, I didn't mean...

He had started to move away from her but Esther was speaking to him, her voice going on as though she had not stopped, —Because you've done the same thing, you've spent all your time too, you've put all your energy up against things that weren't there, but you put them there yourself just to have something to fight...

—Esther...

—So you wouldn't have to fight the real things. She spoke with great rapidity at him. —And now you say you're tired? At your age, because you've been trying to make negative things do the work of positive ones...

—I wish I was an old man! he burst out at her, and then lowered his eyes again, his pale hand inside his coat holding the thick packet there. —Because... damn it, this being young, it's like he said it was, it's like a tomb, this youth, youth, this thing in America, this accent on youth, on everything belongs to the young, and we, look at us, in this tomb, like he told me it could be, like he said it was... And Otto raised his eyes to see nothing moving in her face.

—Yes, you came here for him, didn't you, she said quietly. —You only wanted to see him, didn't you. And you came here hoping to find him? Well he isn't here. He was here. But he isn't here now.

—Where, he was? here?

—I said he was, but he isn't here now, she answered steadily, watching Otto look everywhere round the room, waiting calmly until he brought his bloodshot eyes back to her, to say, —He's gone.

—Where, do you know where?

—No, she answered and paused, looking at him for seconds, before she said, —Yes I knew, you'd come for him, because, from the first it was like that, and you took me to get closer to him, to take what you thought was the dearest thing he had, and you... trusted him, didn't you...

—Do you think it's you I mistrust? he said suddenly looking up to her face; but then he looked away slowly, as from the light of a candle after knowing the light of a self-consuming indestructible sun, carefully as though in fear of extinguishing that candle, though it flare up in determined self-immolation, demanding to be saved from itself. —If I did then, he went on trying to speak clearly, —if I didn't trust you then, I mean mistrust you, then, I wouldn't have learned to mistrust myself and everything else now. And this, this mess, ransacking this mess looking for your own feelings and trying to rescue them but it's too late, you can't even recognize them when they come to the surface because they've been spent everywhere and, vulgarized and exploited and wasted and spent wherever we could, they keep demanding and you keep paying and you can't . . . and then all of a sudden somebody asks you to pay in gold and you can't. Yes, you can't, you haven't got it, and you can't.

—Where have you been asked to pay in gold? she asked quietly, when he finished the outburst which left him breathless staring down, as if uncertain if he knew what he'd said, and sought to recover it at their feet. —Otto? He looked up and stared at her. —Tell me, who's done this to you?

—I . . . he mumbled, looking away again, —I guess I've done it myself, he answered in a whisper, as Mr. Feddle bumped him, passing in the other direction, empty-handed.

And though aware of someone at her side demanding her attention, she waited, looking at him, waiting for his eyes to return to her.

—Esther, have you got a copy of the Diuno Elegies? Rilkey's Diuno . . . ?

—"Wer, wenn ich schriee, hörte mich denn aus der Engel Ordnungen?" Anselm repeated, in a rapture of delight, —"und gesetzt selbst, es nähme einer mich plötzlich ans Herz . . ."

—Shut up, Anselm.

—It can't be, Don Bildow repeated, staring at the open page of the small stiff-covered magazine in his hand, as the words of the first line under Max's name formed on his lips, "Who, if I cried, would hear me among the angelic . . ." —He wouldn't have dared.

—"Ich verginge von seinem stärkeren Dasein . . ." Hahaha, that's Max's poem? Die erste . . . haha, hahahahahaha, from the *Duineser Elegien* von Max Rilke, hahahaha

—Esther, have you got a copy of Rilke? these . . . elegies?

—I have, she faltered (for it was not true), —but I've lent it.

—But not Rilke, he wouldn't have dared, Don Bildow repeated, as though it might be a matter of opinion, or a rumor which, traced down, might yet be retracted.

—Ask him to show you his *Sonette an Orpheus*, you'd love it.

—Shut up, Anselm, said the stubby poet darkly, motioning to the man in the green wool shirt.

—*You* should have known, Bildow cried out at him as he slogged toward them.

—Whut?

—This, this . . . poem, this thing of Max's, you wrote that essay on Rilke last spring, you . . .

—Rilke, but that was on Rilke, Rilke the man, an essay on Rilke the man . . .

—Max Rilke. "Weisst du's noch nicht?" . . . Anselm howled, waving his magazine in the air, wrapping something around his neck. —Christ, don't you know Max by now? Like that shirt he cut up and framed, he called it a painting, "The Workman's Soul"?

—Shut up . . . was repeated, but Don Bildow was staring at Anselm dumbly. Then, —Shirt? he whispered.

—And these pictures he's showing now, the abstract paintings he's selling now, don't you know where he got them? Max Rilke Constable, Anselm went on, laughing. —Didn't you know where he got them? that they're all fragments lifted right out of Constable canvases?

—My God, my dear, excuse me, said the tall woman, —but that creature has my furpiece . . . She set off toward Anselm, sundering numerous conversations as she crossed that room.

—D'you know what happened when Caruso died? Science cut open his throat to see what made him sing. D'you know what *that* means?

—Do we know even half of what's happening to us?

—And do you know why the French are so honest? because there are so few words in their language they're forced to be.

Otto had moved slowly across the room, vaguely, sideways, steps backwards, picking up a glass half full, getting nearer the door of the studio, as though in that darkness might be the figure hidden there working, still there and silent from two years before.

—Hello, Rose said looking up to him with a smile.

—Oh! he startled, to see her there sitting on the floor. —And . . . you?

—Yes.

—And you, then you're Esther's sister?

—Rose. And she continued to smile while he looked at her almost wincing as though seeking something there in her face. Then, —You look like the doctor, she said. —Except the doctor was not so old.

—The doctor? You mean the doctor who came to . . . to see Esther?

—Yes, Rose said, and turned her face away suddenly. —To kill her beautiful baby.

—But the . . . I mean, they told you about it? Esther, about . . . a baby?

Rose looked up at him. She was smiling again; but it was a different sort of smile. —Not a real baby, she said, in a low tone of confidence. —For Esther made it up, she only made it up.

—Made it up? But I mean, is that what he said? the doctor? that it was a ... I mean, what do they call them, a hysterical pregnancy? Is that what he called it?

—Yes, Rose confirmed after a thoughtful moment, moving her lips as though fitting the words to them in recall. —So he said, when he killed it, for so he killed it. Those are the best babies, she said, as Otto looked away from her and stared out into the room. —Are they not? the best babies, for they do never grow up, she went on, —and when they die they go where nothing happens, and there they remain in suspense forever...

Her sigh lingered as he stared out into the room, listening to the tall woman, watching her attentively as though every word and movement of hers were extremely important, though he did not hear a thing she was saying, —Aren't they charming? Baby's breath ... taking a jeweled spray from her purse and fixing it to an earlobe. —My husband gave them to me, he says a woman can lie so much more convincingly when she wears jew-els, she went on, affixing the other. —I just gave him some money and told him to go out and buy himself something and promise not to look at it, she finished, snapping her purse. —We have to go on to another God-awful party later. She cleared her throat, looking round, and took up again, —Did you meet that very ... healthy-looking Boy Scout master? Except for his nose, possibly. I overheard him say that the Boy Scouts had hit him with a sidewalk.

Maude Munk had not moved. She said, —I haven't seen Arny for hours.

—Late hell, it's morning, said the man in uniform.

—It's always morning somewhere ... She looked at a windowless wall.

—That's Longfellow. I may not be an intellectual, but I know my American poets.

—Is it? she murmured, surprised without interest.

—That was *Hannah the Horror of Hampstead*, Mr. Crotcher intoned from his armchair bastion, to no one. —Shall I sing something else?

And the woman in the collapsed maternity dress, who had been talking to the tall woman, went right on to the girl with the green tongue, —You see all the fat ugly little men with beautiful girls? All the wrong people have the money now, that's because ugly people make money because there's no alternative. When you're ugly nobody spoils you, you see reality young and you see beautiful things as something separate from you you're going to have to buy. So you start right out thinking money. Since the old aristocratic system where you inherited looks and manners and taste with your money...

—Quick, gimme a piece of paper quick, Anselm said grabbing Otto by the shoulder. He wore the furpiece circling his face, knotted under his unshaven chin. —Hahaha, did you hear what just happened? I want to write something down, quick. He had jammed his rolled magazine into a hip pocket with the stethoscope. He was too excited with pleasure to notice Otto's face, an anxious expression, but a vacant anxiety, and the more abandoned for being features inured by conscious arrangements where, only now as in sleep, nothing happened. Otto's pale hand delved in his left jacket pocket, came up with his father's note, some papers, —Wait! . . . wait a minute, not that . . .

—Gimme that picture! . . . Everything about Anselm changed in an instant.

Papers dropped between them. And Otto stood staring, at the pale, quivering, empty left hand so long out of use.

—Where did you get it? Anselm demanded, half in a fury and half in a rage, as though he'd never seen, never before tonight, what was able to take his breath away: he picked it up from the floor staring at the glossy surface as though unable to contain the whole figure in his apprehension, seizing at details, the chair, the wallpaper, finally the delineating blemishes on the shadowed white, in a manic silence of search which led him to her face and left his own in a helpless show of fury and dismay. —I'd . . . you! . . . he hissed, looking up at Otto.

—Esther, I've just heard the campiest limerick about an a-*mee*ba and the queen of *She*-ba . . . a frail voice cried.

—You . . . Anselm hissed.

—But, listen . . . you can't . . .

—Are you the lady who wanted to hear about Pablo and his kitten?

—You . . .

—But how do you think I felt . . . ? Otto burst out at him, and reached to catch his naked trembling lip under a yellow forefinger.

—Pablo was this scientist . . .

—And it murmured, ich liebe, ich liebe.

Then Anselm laughed, a choking hysterical sound, broken for an instant with a whimpered, —Sssuccubus . . . until he got his voice, —And when they took her to Bellevue and she knew they were going to undress her, she stopped screaming long enough to take out her falsies, and then she started in again, there, there, there! . . . his face was almost touching Otto's.

—In . . . she in, Bellevue? The whisper burned both their lips.

Then a word ruptured Anselm's mouth in a concussive sound which laid them at arm's length: for both had brought up hands and stood so until, only Anselm did not move but followed his words with his eyes only, —yess, find her, find her, he hissed at the face gone in profile, and then that lost to hair and collar, and the soft convolution of an ear, —find her and be damned.

Sounds rose about him; still Anselm did not move. With another look at the likeness in his hand, he shuddered and stuffed it into a pocket, then stood there alone gazing with an expression of revulsion at the orchid wilting upside-down on the graceless trunk of the figure moving like something afloat, bearing the signature of the jungle deeper among its shadows.

—But nobody's ever physically proved that the earth *is* in motion.

—Einstein says *he* can't believe God plays dice with the universe.

—Well I have a friend who's a physicist, he's been converted. He writes songs now.

—Claims he's a serious musician. Be-bop, if you call *that* music.

—Just so what she writes rhymes, she calls it poetry.

—One of them goes, "With the Father, the Son, the Holy Ghost and you-hoo-ho-hoo, What wonders the five of us could do..."

—Painting like she was having an orgasm, if you call that art.

—If you call *this* living...

—If you call that love...?

Sounds echoing, not from the vibrant reaches of the jungle, but the jungle floor itself, constrictions in the peat bog, the specimens themselves in motion: —I feel like we've been here for simply ages, said the tall woman. —I feel like I was born here, murmured Maude. But neither plaint nor query sounded in their voices, and neither made a move to go. Those who had disappeared were gone silently, leaving only faint traces or none on their minute contributions to the origin of species: the others remained with the tenacity of creatures bound to work out natural laws of survival, thus prove the superiority of their various equipment in adapting to conditions which no memory was long enough to find anything but nature.

The dark poet reared his head with reptilian vigilance, looking from the dead orchid to Herschel, who had just come from the bathroom and posed, flourishing, in the door, an unfamiliar bloom sprung from the jungle floor, watched by these resentful close-focused eyes, turned away, at that moment, to a sound and flutter across the room, where the Duchess of Ohio soared on an outburst of tittering. The critic approached, moving with the steps of one in a familiar medium, disdaining claims of time past and future, both contained in this limicolous present.

—They're moving Father's grave...Mr. Crotcher sang, sunk in the armchair, indifferent as the oyster which, despite the evolutionary excursions going on above, has found no reason to change in two hundred million years. While all around, less abiding varieties kept in motion, as though this might in itself be proof against time. Arny Munk's head lolled in several directions, its sensory equipment unnecessary for he was being led by Sonny Byron whose tender voice belied the firm grip of his hand. —Come along, baby, be sweet, just for a minute, she'll never miss you . . . And they passed under the eyes of the Paleozoic poet, glittering open from features whose prehistoric simplicity was faintly shadowed with apprehension at the sight of the opportune mutations going on around him, denying, by their very existence, the finality of his old-world wisdom, and suggesting, as they took to the air manipulating the baubles so helplessly evolved with a pretense of having designed them themselves, that perhaps, for all his belligerent co-operation with environment, that environment itself was changing, and not only he, but the entire species upon which he depended while living, and rescue from anonymity, perpetuation afterward, was to become part of the sodden floor, and the mat, and finally only traces on the crust itself.

—Derive venereal, and see what you get, if you don't call *that* decay, said someone near the hunched critic, who turned away, looked down at his large hands, and shrugged.

Beyond, like some creature opportunely equipped to cope with situations which have not yet arisen or, indeed, even been suggested, Mr. Feddle scooted up a tier of shelved books, beyond the reaches of hagfish and lamprey, and other jawless progenitors babbling in apparent contentment below. From the surface there, the critic watched him, bringing up a hand to smooth his hair and for that moment betray the size of his head. His expression was as simple as resentment without understanding can be: now like plesiosaurus laboring all four limbs for the paddles they were, lifting a small head to see pterodactyl raise its absurd body on more absurd wings and with cumbrous scaling gain the sky, a ridiculous place to be, certainly, but for that moment he watched, disconcerting to plesiosaurus, to whom no such extravagance had ever occurred and who, by no feat of skill or imagination, could hope to accomplish it now.

—As for your Emerson . . . ! someone said: and indeed, there were those to satisfy that eclectic digger too, gliding not to eat, nor for love, but only gliding.

Esther, advancing, searched the shadows, but the speechless kitten was nowhere to be seen. Then looking for Ellery she raised her eyes, but their light remained untenanted until Benny's flickering image filled them, and he asked with forced cheer, —Have you seen a little blond number named Adeline?

Several people turned to see Mr. Feddle fall clattering to the floor; and in keeping with that refusal to be ruffled by disturbances, which they called good breeding, no one offered to help him up. For even those present who considered good breeding a pretension affected by a class they were vocationally in revolt against, substituting for it an obtuseness which they called honesty, watched with honest laughter.

—My dear, it's been lovely, the tall woman said to Esther. —I do wish I could give parties like this, but my husband...With one hand she was attempting to dislodge her husband from the shoal of furniture, where his hapteric glass anchored him. —But you're not upset? You have to learn to be philosophical about those things, my dear, just don't think about them. Now *I* have a real problem, just look at my furpiece...well it is insured, thank God. I spoke to him about it but I honestly don't believe he understands English. I can't repeat what he said to me. There is something almost prehistoric about him, wouldn't you say?...something almost attractive...wouldn't you say?

The furpiece had, in fact, lost the quality of being an assumed decoration. Nature's hand (which we are now assured is experimentally inclined) might have worked here to produce one of those severe mutations which (so Science goes on assuring us) are opportune, chancy arrangements with no particular purpose, included in the calculated risk of being born. Nonetheless, Anselm wiped his nose on a mink tail as casually as though the thing had grown there for that purpose. But his expression retained a livid suspension, as the lower lip was held sharply under an uneven yellow line of teeth. He was watching Stanley. From Rose's darkness came men's voices borne on music, *Judas Maccabaeus*. On one hand, Chavenet turned out to be the man who had first proved that the eye which forms the image could not possibly have worked until after it was complete. Seated on the other, that xenophobic accessory to monosyllabic criteria in honest writing, overheard the word hapteron from above, and swore. Anselm watched Stanley. And behind him, Don Bildow approached mustering as vengeful an expression as plastic rims would allow.

—There must be some place to hide for people who make mistakes, Agnes Deigh said holding Stanley's hand in both hers. She was staring there, where Mickey Mouse semaphored annul with yellow mittens. —It can't be that early, she murmured.

—But Agnes, the Church...

—That glass, the full one, could you hand it to me? she asked him then, looking up.

He did, hesitatingly, —But don't you think, for your own good?

—Isn't it when we make mistakes that we need love most? she said abruptly. She'd raised the glass in a quivering hand but did not drink, waiting.

—Yes but, he answered unsteadily, pretending not to see Anselm's approach as his voice picked up. —But not finite love that's as weak as we are, not just that, not...

—Stanley, she interrupted firmly, though her voice was faint. —I'm sorry. I'm sorry now for...about what I said to you that night, that night when you ran away Stanley, it was my fault, I shouldn't have said that to you, should I...He waited for her to go on, unable to answer. —It...I...I didn't know,

Stanley. I didn't know you didn't want to hear it, God knows I do, I mean . . . I thought we all did, I thought it was all anyone wanted, to hear that . . .

—Yes but . . . well, it's . . . I mean love has to be something greater than ourselves, and when it is then it is faith, and the Church . . .

Bildow clenched small fists, at the ends of his long arms. —I demand that you tell me where my daughter . . . he said loudly to Anselm.

—Shut up, this is a conversation about love. Did you ever read the great poet Suckling? Here's a poem of the English Cavalier poet Sir John Suckling for you, Stanley. "Love is the fart Of every heart; It pains a man when 'tis kept close; And others doth offend, when 'tis let loose." Do you like that? Hey come here, where you going?

Stanley looked helplessly at Agnes Deigh. —I have to . . . excuse me a minute, he said. She continued to stare at Anselm, who shifted his eyes from hers in sudden discomfort, finally said, weakly, —I'm . . . I mean he's scared . . . Isn't he . . . and turned away to where Bildow pulled him.

All this time, a figure had been moving about the room like a shadow, but a pale shade, if black light could cast such a wan shape in darkness. Occasionally Anselm had fixed inflamed eyes upon him, and looked away after a fiercely vacant exchange. He spoke to no one, hardly anyone had spoken to him, and fewer of him, until now the woman in the collapsed maternity dress noted, —Yes, the boy with the silver plate in his head, he looks like a sensitive minority of one to me. And that woolly-headed boob is trying to convert him, that's the trouble with converts . . . what is it, child? Mummy sent you up . . . I know, wait a minute, here . . . Wait, I almost gave you my Pubies . . .

—What are they for? the girl with the green tongue asked.

—I forget, but they help . . . And she looked back hungrily to where the hunched man in the green shirt had just said, —Just the same, you ought to get wise to yourself . . . when he was swung round with a dirty hand on his shoulder. Anselm looked him square in the eyes.

—Don't you get tired of hanging around like a spare prick?

—Why, why you . . . The hunched man quivered throughout his body, as though it were suddenly an unfamiliar arrangement which he could not call upon, at such short notice, to fight.

—Just don't give Charles a hard time, Anselm said to him calmly. —You'd be a God damn lot worse off than he is if you'd been through what he has. I heard this crap you were just giving him, your . . . and you can't argue that way, you can't discuss absolutes in relative terms. That's what screws you God-damned smart intellectuals up, trying to discuss absolutes in relative terms.

—I'll discuss it any way I want to, the critic said sounding firm because he spoke quickly.

—God damn it you will not! Anselm said desperately. —You can't, you can't do that with absolutes, you either accept them or you tell them to go take a flying fuck but you can't do what you're doing... Anselm stopped, breathless, close upon the man. Behind him Bildow stood where Anselm had broken from his grasp, looking at the pale face beyond them both. —And... and leave Charles alone, just... leave him alone, Anselm finished.

The other shrugged, taking green elbows in his heavy hands. —I was just trying to get a razor away from him, he said sullenly, turning away.

—A what? Anselm demanded, got no answer, and turned to the pale fading figure. —Did he? Have you? He grabbed a shoulder and shook him. —Where'd you get it? Give it to me. Give it to me. God damn you I said give it to me! He watched the thin wrist with its exaggerated rasceta disappear, and snatched the black-handled thing from the thin hand as it drew out of a pocket. —You... stupid bastard, you... what were you trying to do? Anselm went on, but his own voice was unsteady as he put it into his own pocket, and he did not look into the empty face before him. —You have no... God damn right to try things like this, you... stupid bastard... he finished bringing his voice to a whisper where he could control it. When he did look up their eyes held one another, Anselm's burning into that vacant embrace until he tore them away, and turning away himself sniffed and wiped his nose with his hand, muttering. Don Bildow stood in his path but did not interrupt him when he saw the orchid, fallen to the floor from an earlier caress, and went to pick it up. With it dangling between two fingers, Anselm turned, recovering, —Hey lady, he said, but the woman who'd worn it was not to be seen. —The lady lost her nuts, Anselm said to no one. He mumbled, —That's the world we live in, the ladies wear the nuts... choking forth convalescent laughter, coming on toward Stanley who had found the bathroom door locked and was returning to Agnes Deigh the long way round the room.

—And Pablov had this kitten...

—But Carruthers had a mare...

—Well she says she got pregnant by taking a bath right after her father, but I say...

—Omychrahst, I mean, youmeanyoureallywanttobuyone?

—Cómo? qué dice...?

—You. Really. Want. To. Buy. One.?

—That is the purpose of my trip to your country, in addition for picking up something of artistic for the Jockey Club in Buenos Aires.

—Oh Chrahst now look don't go away, I mean I haven't got one with me. Look tomorrow morning I'll come to your hotel and you come with me. I mean, you're not drunk are you?

—Drunk? I?

—Chrahst I'm sorry maybe I am, I mean I was, but I mean people don't just go around buying battleships.

Maude had been fumbling at her throat. —What's matter, you spilled something down your dress? The hand on the back of her neck stopped, the man leaned forward and looked, with her, down the front of her dress. —What's matter? But her fumbling hand failed, and she was staring at an encumbered limb before her. The attractive girl with the Boston voice, whose leg it was, looked down too. She had just said,

—It's not a bad kick, take two strips of benny and two goof balls, they get down there and have a fight. It's a good drive. She shook her leg. —Is this yours? she accused, looking up at Maude.

—Why I . . . I'll take her, Maude said reaching.

And the Boston girl pulled up her skirt at the waist and went on, —If you want to score tonight I know a connection uptown we can probably catch.

—Yes, I'll take her home now, Maude said and held the baby up before her, cupping one hand to the head, and she murmured, —A leader of men.

—Huuu, may I take you home? the uniform asked, still trying to gaze down into where Maude had sought what she had now forgotten.

—Where do you live? she asked vaguely, looking up at his face.

Agnes Deigh had taken Stanley's hand to say, —And every time people meet, they seem to just get a little further away from each other.

—These gulfs everywhere between everything and everybody, Stanley took up immediately, —it's this fallacy of originality, of self-sufficiency. And in art, even art . . .

—Didn't you know him? He died in my apartment in Paris when I was having my first one-man show.

—When art tries to be a religion in itself, Stanley persisted, —a religion of perfect form and beauty, but then there it is all alone, not uniting people, not . . . like the Church does but, look at the gulf between people and modern art . . .

—When I go abroad I want to see countries, who wants to see people? You can see people on the B.M.T.

—Damn fine music, Mozart, said the Big Unshaven Man. He had just finished making a whole pitcher of martinis, which he poured into a large pocket flask. —I tell you true.

—Well doesn't it seem to *you* like everybody's changing size?

And in spite of the torn orchid which lowered, and was dangling before his face, Stanley went on, —It isn't for love of the thing itself that an artist works, but so that through it he's expressing love for something higher, because that's the only place art is really free, serving something higher than itself, like us, like we are ...

And behind him, in a hoarse riot of whisper, —Oh this is mine! this is mine!

—And that's why you must stop staying outside Agnes, because the Church ...

—Yess, this is mine! ...

—There's no more to drink, said the woman he spoke to, but looking beyond him to that thin broken face. There yellow teeth tore sound into laughter.

—Tell them to fill the waterpots. Fill them up to the brim ...

—Anselm ...

—Mine hour is not yet come, Anselm returned, controlling the ragged edges to form words in Stanley's face, then getting breath, over Stanley's shoulder, he still laughed, —Woman! what have I to do ... Stanley bumped him, turning now his whole body against the shudders he shared, locked so as those yellowed teeth bit words out of the air between them, —For I am come to set man at variance against his father, and the daughter against her mother, and the daughter in law against her mother in law ... and a man's foes shall be they of his own household ...

Stanley licked his lips against the fever upon them; and he blinked against the burning eyes.

—Yes, there's your gulf, the hand of your everloving Christ!

With daring tenderness Stanley's hand came to the warm wrist, where a vein's blue ridge coursed the bone. —Why do you fight it so hard?

—You, you ... Anselm pulled away. Then he looked around frantically for an instant, pulling up breath before he could speak, —Yes, what a lousy time to be alive, yes isn't it? Yes, I ... and don't you wish it was the good old days, when Pope Urban sold his toenail parings as relics? and the ... yes, when you could choose between three assorted foreskins from the Lord's circumcision ...

—When I get drunk it means something, broke in upon them, broke long enough for Stanley's hand to reaffirm its hold, a frail enough articulation though, in closing so, it brought the veins on Anselm's hand to bursting prominence. —It doesn't help to talk this way Anselm, why do you do it?

—Because you can't ... I, yes ... Anselm threw his hand up, breaking the grasp with no effort. —These lousy apologies, these refuges from being alive, art and religion and God damn it you ... and philosophy, I ... and I was born with a veil over my head.

—With what? I don't ...

—Yes, a caul, God damn it, read an old cookbook, I, yes well what the hell, never mind. I studied medicine. I had a good lay this afternoon, Anselm went on disjointedly, pulling the stethoscope from his pocket. —I just go up to the hospital and I ...

—Please, don't talk about...

—No but listen, I've got to tell you, I go up to this hospital and they think I'm a special physician from outside, the nurses do, that's what I tell them, so then I go in to look over patients who think I'm connected with the hospital, that's what I tell them and you should see some of the handfuls I've had that way. This afternoon was the best yet. He brandished the stethoscope, the end flew past Stanley's chin. —This blonde, this terrific blonde, I gave her a three-and-a-half grain shot of sodium amytal and then I climbed in and gave her the business... Uninterrupted, he stood there staring at the uncoupled caducei of the stethoscope; then twisting them closed like metaled snakes in his hand he whispered, —That's what it is, that's all any of it is... But he could not break it, and he looked up and away, instantly found the blond girl earlier accused of putting a *t* in genial, made up, composed, as pretty (she would never be beautiful), as inanimate and stale as a photograph, once accused of taking the *v* out of live; now, of putting an *f* in lie: —Arse gratias artis, he muttered, —that's all any of it is.

—Anselm... Stanley put a hand forth to him again, —if... suffering...

—Yes, God damn it, my scars, do you want to see them, they... where's Otto? He'll show you his scars. Otto, hey Otto, come here, you, where the hell are you? Where the hell is he? He'll show you, he... he'll put up a real maudlin raree-show for you, he... maudlin! Yes, Mary Magdalene crying her eyes out for Christ. That's great. Can you see him crying his crazy eyes out for Christ?... Anselm shuddered. —Suppose you never see me again? he burst in Stanley's face. —Yes, what would you do, you wouldn't have, yes but Christ didn't have any friends did he? Is that what you mean? Yes, well you wouldn't even have a witness, you... because that's all He had, He... where the hell is he, he'll show you his scars, is that what you want? The Five Sacred Wounds. How would you like that, you could bleed all over the place. You might even get a good set of punctures with the Crown of Thorns, you... how about the Ferita? the real bloody heart-wound. Or a good sweat of blood in Gethsemane? you could out-Lutgarde Saint Lutgarde, you could out-pussy Blessed Catherine of Racconigi, if you want to suffer why don't you go somewhere where it will do somebody else some good instead of being so God-damned selfish about it like these crazy saints. Get a little cross with mirrors in it, that would be the nuts if you want to suffer your way, for Christ sake... Where the hell is he? yes, with his scars...? Anselm looked frantically round the room, clutching the stethoscope out before him, for some tangibility among the pale presences.

—If it is fear, Stanley whispered to him in confidence.

—Yes look! Anselm rescued the palest shade of them all in his gesture.

—Look at him, look at Charles for Christ sake, look at him! Love? I've heard you talking about love. He can tell you about love, about spiritual love, about your kind of love. Tell them, go ahead for Christ sake tell them, about your mother and the Pekinese that the pile of folding chairs fell on, she picked it up and breathed into its mouth, she kept it alive breathing her own life into it but for him? Would she give him one, breath of love? Or a lot of gas about love that has nothing to do with either one of them, for the love of Christ, for Christ sake, she left him here to cut his throat for Christ sake...

Figures had started to gather round them, and Anselm lost in his weight with every word, retreating in fury from every hand though none dared touch him. He tried to jam the twisted stethoscope into his pocket, instead knocked it and the rolled magazine to the floor, and came up with that. —Your sick... Lupercalia, he was muttering, as though the weight of words would keep them at bay, and the magazine came open on its back cover. And he burst out at Stanley for the last time, —Yes here, here's your peace and salvation, "If it slips, if it chafes, if it gripes, THROW AWAY THAT TRUSS!..."

—Shut up, the hunched critic said to him, close.

—"Literally *thousands* of Rupture sufferers *have* entered this *Kingdom of Paradise Regained*..."

—It doesn't help to talk this way, Anselm, Stanley said to him.

—Yes, here's your salvation, yes, thousands "have worn our Appliance without the slightest inconvenience. Cheap—Sanitary—Comfortable..."

—Anselm, it doesn't help to talk like this. Why do you do it?

—Because the one God-damned thing I can't stand is your God-damned... confidence. *Pin-Up Cuties* fell to the floor between them.

—But it's not confidence in myself, Stanley said quickly, —but faith, not confidence but faith in something greater than any of us.

—Why don't you shut up and get out of here? the critic said.

Anselm turned to him slowly, and formed his words slowly when he spoke, —Fuck a duck and screw a pigeon, that's the way you'll get religion. Then he spat in his face. —That's for your side-show conversion, he said.

—Leave him, Stanley said quickly. —Let him be. He put an arm around Anselm's shoulders.

Anselm hung there for a moment, or part of a minute, then came up in a shock, —And stop this damned... this God-damned sanctimonious attitude, he cried, twisting free, and they stood face to face. —Stanley, by Christ Stanley that's what it is, and you go around accusing people of refusing to humble themselves and submit to the love of Christ and you're the one, you're the one who refuses love, you're the one all the time who can't face it, who can't face loving, and being loved right here, right in this lousy world, this God-damned world where you are right now, right…right now. Anselm stood panting; and Stanley had withdrawn a step to stand with his insensible hand on the arm of Agnes Deigh's chair.

Anselm came toward him, crushing the orchid under foot, pulling in a pocket without moving his eyes from Stanley's. —Afraid of this, he came on, his voice lower, —this…ssuccubus, he came on, sibilant, —thiss, beast with two backs. He brought out the crumpled photograph. —This is it isn't it, isn't it…He forced it in Stanley's face. —Isn't it…! And then it crumpled in his hand, as though drawing itself in upon its own blemishes of betrayal while his hand closed on it, drawn by the loded hieroglyphs coursing the flesh blue in selfish sympathy. —If you should never see me again? Anselm's voice broke. —Do you know what it is? he came on, almost inaudible, looking at no one. —Und wir bewundern es so, weil es gelassen verschmäht…uns zu zerstören…

He stood with the orchid crushed underneath his foot: even Don Bildow could swing him round.

—Where is my daughter?

—Your daughter? Anselm repeated, and sounded about to gag. —She's all right.

—Where *is* she?

—She's in church, Anselm said. —I left her in church, he repeated helplessly. The critic advanced on him as he stood with his head rolling from side to side. —Go on, that's enough of you, you…go on, get out…

Anselm threw himself at the man but Bildow, clinging to his arm, afraid to let go, held him back. —Get out, get out, Anselm cried. —Go home alone. Alone. Alone…

—Shut up, you…

—Alone. Go home with your lover, old mister five fingers, haha, haha haha…here, he went on, snatching the magazine up from the floor and thrusting it in the face of the other, —here are some girls for you. *Here!* Do you think I don't know? do you think we all don't know, let's see the calluses on your right hand, old mister five fingers, hahahahahahahuhhhph…

Bildow let go of him as he sank to the floor from the comparatively light blow, an effort which had, nevertheless, exhausted his antagonist who stepped back and in the moment it took him to realize that Anselm was down, composed himself, in triumph.

Maude's voice was faint, but clear in the silence. —This isn't the way I remember Christmas Eve, she said.

Someone laughed.

—The Lord wouldn't like this…

—Well if this is the cultural center of the world you can give it right back to the Indians...

Someone else laughed.

—And so that one said to me, just ask God, baby, She'll protect you...

—Hehe, hehehe...

—*We* know what love is, don't we baby...

—Stanley, please...

—Just wait a minute, I want to... I have to help him.

—Leave me alone.

—Where is my daughter?

—Leave him alone for a minute. He shouldn't have hit him.

—Stanley please...

—Leave me alone. God damn you, leave me alone!

—But Agnes...

—Stanley...

—Chr-ahst...

—Yes I was told to expect this sort of thing in New York.

—Yes but I mean Chrahst don't go away, or we'll both go, let's both go to your hotel, I'll stay there tonight.

—But in another room.

—Chrahst yes.

—I was warned about that sort of thing in New York, his companion commented, adjusting his perfectly adjusted tie.

—Oh Rose, Esther said to where her sister sat on the floor in the dark with the records. —Aren't you tired?

—Are you having a nice party?

Esther put her face in her hands, and felt her sister's arm round her neck. —Oh Rose. Rose.

The hand under her became rigid, the paralysis ran up her arm, through her shoulders and neck, her face yellowing as the blood drained from behind its bronzed canvas. —Stanley!... Agnes Deigh whispered, staring at him bent over Anselm, an arm around Anselm.

—You see, it's all right now, Stanley said gripping his shoulder but unable to raise it from the floor. Anselm opened his eyes.

In the hand she drew from under her, the white nails clutched a limp cinnamon-colored body. —I thought... it was something, Agnes Deigh said weakly to herself. Then she looked around quickly, opened her bag and pulled handfuls of things out which she stuffed in her coat pocket, to snap it closed a moment later upon the lifeless kitten. She summoned her voice in, —Stanley...

—And now, you don't have to fight it any more, you... Anselm's arm was flung around him, and Anselm's unshaven face tore at Stanley's cheek with the kiss.

—Stanley! . . .

—You've got to listen carefully because it's very complicated, said someone dangling over her from behind, —Pavlov had dogs who salivated, but this time . . .

—*Stanley!* she cried out. Stanley looked up to her. —Stanley, please come here.

—But . . . Stanley said, rising and releasing Anselm, who sank back to the floor. —I can't leave him now, he said, taking a step toward her.

—God help me, Stanley, you must. She reached out and caught his wrist. —I think I'm going to be ill.

—But I can't leave him now, Stanley said, appealing to Don Bildow who stood beside them.

—Stanley, you can't leave *me.*

—But Agnes . . .

—Help me up.

—Where is he? Bildow burst out. —He's gone, he's gone, and where . . .

They looked around. Anselm was not there. Stanley staggered and braced himself as Agnes Deigh stood, clinging to his arm. His voice broke when he spoke. —But he was almost . . . I almost . . . what will he do now, alone?

Maude found the baby heavier than she had expected, when she stood with it. —Help me, she said.

—What's matter?

—We're going home.

—But that thing, you better leave it here, you better not take it, it might belong to somebody.

—Please, just . . . open the door.

—Calls himself Tree, does he? I knew him when his name was Tannenbaum, someone said.

—Spain? But everybody in Spain's been dead for *years* . . .

—I'm sorry, I'm going home with this gentleman, he's going to help me write a novel. I don't know *what* Mister Wipe will say . . .

A girl was being sick behind a bookshelf. —You gotto excuse her, she's not used to this. And the bathroom door's locked. Mr. Feddle, clutching *The Razor's Edge*, got to one side.

—That philodendron, that God damn cut leaf philodendron, that's the only thing I've seen growing in eleven years, if you call that growing . . .

Nearby someone obligingly derived philander, —Philos, *loving*, plus andros, *man* . . . the voice whined.

—It's my wife's, she pays more attention to it than she does to me . . . that's why I thought about the scythe, that's why I couldn't understand it, breaking a scythe . . . but tomorrow morning . . .

—You'll take me with you? Benny?

—She and Iphigenia, they're beginning to look like each other.

—Who's Iphigenia?

—The philodendron.

—What's that funny smell, I been smelling it all evening.

The heat, and the numbers of people, seemed to have heightened the scent of lavender which came from the dark doorway and pervaded the well-lighted room, except for the fragrant shade left by the tall woman, the trace of *My Sin* still clinging to the chair Agnes Deigh had left empty, and a sweet pungence rising in one corner where someone said to the Boston girl, —Don't smoke that stuff here, for Christ sake.

The music had, by now, become a fixture in the room; it was as though it had combined with the smoke and the incongruous scents into a tangible presence, the slag of refinement rising over the furnace, where the alchemist waited with a lifetime's patience, staring into his improbable complex of ingredients as dissimilar in nature as in proportion, commingling but refusing to fuse there under his hand, and as unaware of his hand as of their own purpose, so that some sank and others came in entirety to the surface, all that as though nothing had changed since the hand sifted the scoria of the Middle Ages for what all ages have sought, and found, as they find, that what they seek has been itself refined away, leaving only the cinders of necessity.

Esther started toward the dark doorway. Then across the room she saw Ellery coming from the bedroom passage. She turned toward him, but he appeared not to see her. When she got there the blonde was coming out. She smoothed her dress and smiled at Esther as she passed. Esther started to speak, but the blonde went on, smiling pleasantly, unhearing, fretting the quiescent cat that had swallowed whole the fled canary as she walked away.

In the bedroom Esther entered with her hand pressed against her belly, and turned on the hot light beside her mirror. She looked at the powder spilled on the dressing table. Then she turned, the heels of her hands buried in her eyes and sat down for a moment before she could look: the bedspread had been straightened with quick carelessness so that one corner hung to the floor, and the pillow lay half uncovered. She ran her hand through her hair, and looked up to say, —Rose? with dull loudness. From the next room all she heard was, —I've put a cigarette down somewhere . . .

—Rose?

—Well *I'm* proving that *Einstein* doesn't exist...

She got up and went back into the room.

—A million people a year in this country try to disappear, what does *that* mean?

—Pony boy, I feel light enough to skip all the way home.

—Aren't you going to even say good night to her?

—I stopped knowing *her* years ago.

—Oh Chrahst, Chrahst, you haven't seen a greasy-looking guy with shiny hair have you, because I mean Chrahst I can't have lost him.

—Is your name really Adeline? Herschel was asking the blonde as he left her. —Because baby I had a nurse once who looked just like you, I bit her... you-know-where! But you're going to Hollywood? Baby so am I, maybe I'll see you there and we'll have a nice teat-a-teat over old times... He was backing toward the roseate misery of the Swede, who was holding his swollen nose. —Now it's all right, baby...

—But those Boy Scouts! I'll never speak to a Boy Scout again.

—Don't cry, baby. Think about Rudy, I *know* something terrible has happened to *that* one, but I gave him this address when he called and said he was in an auto smash...

—Where's Bildow?

—He went to the police station.

—Why doesn't somebody just tell the French they're through.

—You'll like this song, said Mr. Crotcher to no one.

—This shiny-looking little guy with greasy hair, I mean Chrahst I can't have lost him, Chrahst.

—We'll just go where they've got some gone numbers on the box. We can order coffee and get high on benny.

—Come on, Ellery said to him. —I hate to see you like this, Jesus Christ Benny, you're my best friend, you're the best friend I got.

—That's all it is, Benny went on. —What's tragedy to you is an anecdote to everybody else. We're comic. We're all comics. We live in a comic time. And the worse it gets the more comic we are.

—Benny you're going to take me with you aren't you? the figure with flannel sleeves to his elbows broke in. —You are really going aren't you? We're really going, aren't we?

—We're comic because there isn't anything else that...that has to... anything else that has to be.

—Benny, relax, forget it, look, that church gimmick, you're in, you're made Benny... Ellery was supporting him, but he wrenched away when he saw Mr.

Feddle who had just finished inscribing the book he held, *with best wishes
from Benedict Arnold.*

—What happened to him? Benny demanded. —To him, Fedya, the one
you told me about. What happened to him? he pressed.

—Why, he killed himself, of course, said Mr. Feddle with relish. —He was
Russian. Benny had a hand on his wrist. —Yes, right after he said, "No need
to ask! I did it all myself. The design was mine, and the deed was mine…"
The hand fastened to his wrist loosed and fell away. —Right after he said,
"When the claw is caught, the bird is lost…" Mr. Feddle went on, muttering,
withdrawing, looking at his own hand. —Or was that *The Power of Darkness?*
Nikíta, in *The Power of Darkness*…?

—Benny, tomorrow morning Benny…

—In Rome I'll be at the Dingle. —The Dingle? —The Dingleberry, baby.
—What are you sailing on? —One of the Queens of course…

Esther did look in need of aid, returning across that room; so everyone
avoided looking at her. They renewed their assaults on one another instead.

—I can't imagine cutting my wrists in Pokheepsie.

—Hemingway? Well he said he's staying at the Ritz, but I say the Ritz was
torn down simply years ago…

—He joined the Church? I knew him when he joined the Yale Club.

—Then do we all get scared when we get old?

Esther reached the bathroom door as Arny Munk came out led by Sonny
Byron, who was saying, —We'll find her, and she doesn't need to know a thing
about it. Now tell the truth, wasn't it nice? while Mr. Crotcher sang, —Today
is the day they give babies away…

In the bathroom Esther leaned against the wall and wet a washcloth. She
stared at her mirror face until she realized that it could do nothing but stare
back, and then thrust the washcloth between her eyes and their image; as she
drew the wet cloth across her skin the bloodlines on the whites of her eyes
claimed the eyes for flesh, the firmness of the bones softened, the lines of life,
and the insistence of the mouth, all of it fused into one soft inanimate flesh.
She had already asked him to stay the night; now she turned to seek him.

In the room the critic turned, to the hand of the Duchess of Ohio. —I
can't just listen to this prwetty music without dancing, will you dance with
me?…The critic left him sprawled on the floor where he'd pushed him.

—And the oddest joke about the Pope, I don't understand it at all.

—I mean Chrahst, I can't have lost him.

—Flo-flo?

—Florence, baby.

She was not really surprised, in the bedroom, to see him lying there in the green wool shirt, that and nothing else. She turned quickly to close the door and bolt it: it seemed to take her an age to reach it.

—President McKinley had one

—I can play *The Stars and Stripes Forever*, or *Violets* lying *under* the piano

—The far lockaway rocker room story

—And the garbage cans

—The Pope

—The Swiss

—The Wright brothers and the ships of the Russian navy

—Loved *him*

—This time it was a kitten

—*Hated* her

Most penetrating, just outside the door she closed, unmocking, —Some sleeping pills that my mummy sent me up for, I know which bottle it is if you'll just lift me up.

Esther held to a corner of the bureau stepping out of her shoes, and she pulled off her skirt. Then she reached to turn out the light.

—Don't. Leave it on.

The woollen sleeve scratched her uncovered shoulders, her legs gave, soft against the hard tense muscles where she strained her hollowness to him. —Are you going to...take this off?

—Yes, in a...minute. His cold hand wrenched her shoulder down.

—But now, I don't know...whether I dare...

—No, you just...

—But what are you, I thought only little boys,

—It's all right, I,

—But what am I supposed to do? she cried.

—You, just...watch, he said breathlessly.

The long streets were straight tunnels of wind charged with snow which bit the skin of any out struggling against it, the paving hard-packed with that snow, its whiteness gone under a thousand dirty wheels, spotted and streaked from leaking oil-pans, dug here and there by a desperate heel. The undisciplined lights, most of them red for they hung before bars, shone through it, instructed by the tireless precision of the traffic lights turning green to red, red to green, halting precarious passage, releasing it.

Down the subway steps came a figure on all fours, and those who glanced at it looked away, or stopped to stare, almost as little able to stand up themselves though, if they had gone down like he was, they would have been as unable to move with his forceful ease, down, to drop his coin in the slot with his lips and pass through the stile, out onto the platform and, with hardly a minute's wait, onto a train.

—Arthur! What are you doing? Get up on your feet.

He turned his head, to look up and see a small woman in a black silk dress, tight up to her throat, a woman three times his age, who had lived twice the years she had given him since she gave him birth. He looked at her.

—Get up on your feet, I say. She clutched at the black-and-gold book in her lap, and nothing else moved but her thin lips as she spoke in low intensity, —Get up this instant. Where did you get that furpiece? You stole it! Get up this instant. Suddenly she reached out, and though he was very near her thin knees, with a motion as slight as an animal's evasion, and as seemingly careless, he avoided her hand. She clutched the book again. —Get up on your feet this instant, I demand. The train roared on. He looked at her.

Mickey Mouse semaphored annul. —It can't be that late. She held it to her ear. —I think it's stopped, she said. —He can't have stopped, she said, halting under a streetlamp.

—Wait here. There's a cab. Abruptly, she was alone, and she sank back against a building, watching him run toward the curb at the corner, where he slipped and fell. Behind her, one of the indistinct shadows articulated itself.

—Oh no, *stop!*

—What happened? he asked, brushing snow from himself with one hand, supporting her with the other.

—He stole my purse...

—But let me go, I can catch him...

—Oh no, she said, clinging to him. —He stole my purse. He stole my purse, she cried, all of her weight on him, laughing and crying at once.

He looked round desperately; then his whole expression, and his bearing, changed. He murmured something, and without much difficulty guided her up the cathedral's steps, and he took her in.

—Can you kneel? They were struck down by that vast silence, dropping like a weight from stone arches out of all reach; they struggled to the surface again, and it was penetrated with a bell's ringing like a rapier through stone. —I can't breathe, she said. She fell back in the pew, pulling at the front of her dress as her coat fell open.

He stared before him at serenity which, transfigured in light, seemed to move for him. —Could you take communion? he asked her, shaping the silence which lay between them, cutting a hard bit out of it to pierce her.

—I . . . it isn't . . . not now, she whispered, hacking his silence into shreds of shale, irregular fragments of its weight thrown against him. He started her to her feet, toward the liberation of the nave's channel which flowed in one direction from which the silence seemed suddenly to be gathered and hurled back with all its weight upon them.

—qui tollis peccata mundi, miserere nobis . . .

She fell over against him, dead weight.

—miserere nobis . . .

He supported her, as she regained her feet.

—dona nobis pacem . . .

He turned and followed her, where she ran from the rapier that struck behind them, out through the gigantic doors which spilled them together into that unholy night.

He might have caught her had he not fallen on the steps, a thing which she, for all her gyrations, somehow managed not to do. He did not reach her again until almost a block away where she stopped, breathing hard, under a red-lighted doorway. Even then, before he could hold her, she was inside the bar, where a battered man ran his hand over his uncared-for chin and stared at them, and the bartender came forward.

—Now I'd like a martini, she said, speaking clearly, seating herself.

—But Agnes . . .

—And you, sir?

—Nothing. A glass of water. Agnes . . .

She looked at him, glazed, without recognition.

—Agnes . . .

The bartender tapped his fingers on the bar, waiting.

—Agnes . . . He looked up at the bartender, surprised. —Oh, here, he said then, and handed over the twenty-dollar bill from his pocket. —I'm sorry, that's all I have. Agnes . . .

The bartender walked slowly toward the back of the bar, looking idly at the bill. —What'sa matter, you never saw American money before? said his battered client. —I see it alla time. I'm Santy Claus.

—Agnes, please . . .

—I'm going to a hotel, she said, straight before her, to no one, a she set down her empty glass. —I'll write him a letter.

The bartender had taken the bill over to hold it under a desk lamp which he turned on beside the cash register.

—Agnes, wait a minute . . . She got down from her stool.

—Wait a minute here, you two. Stanley turned. The bartender had him by the arm across the bar. —Wait a minute. Stop her.

—Agnes, *wait*...

—I can't stop her. I'm Santy Claus.

—Agnes, my glasses. You forgot to give me my glasses...

A few minutes later Stanley stood, eyeless enough in this reduction of Gaza, waiting for a patrol car. —You could tell it a mile away, the way the front of it's smeared, said the bartender to the patrolman who held Stanley's arm. —He had a dame with him, but she beat it. Thanks, Mac. He went back inside; and the patrolman turned his attention to his charge, to where the falling snow clotted the mustache, and gathered in the folds of hair on the back of the round head, silently, with a tourist's dull curiosity, the patrolman gazed as a tourist might upon the pitted figure of a saint in indefatigable stone, left insensibly exposed in the weather a century too long.

Roaring alight where the night never ended, underground, she said, —Arthur, get up on your feet. Don't you know me? Don't you know who I am?

He looked at her.

The train halted. Its doors opened, and before she could move they closed behind him and left her, recovering from her moment of indecision, seated and staring straight ahead.

On all fours, he trotted down the emptied platform. He paused for a moment and raised his head to look round him; then he went on, and bumped open the door to the men's room with his head. It was empty. He rose to his knees and reached into his pocket. The crumpled picture he threw into a toilet. With his other hand he undid his clothes, and opened the razor. He paused so, staring up at the dim illumination of the weak electric bulb, his voice audible only then, —In nomine... though his lips continued to move, without a tremor, as his hands worked quickly, with deft certainty, unseen.

—Why you could tell it a mile away.

—And the broad with him...

—The broad with him...

—You could have told her a mile away. Hello Jimmy. Merry Christmas. Come on in and have one for Christmas.

—Happy Yom Kipper. What're you doin.

—I'm drinkin, what's it look like I'm doin? Set one up for our friend here, Barney.

—It's a free country.

—Cozy fan tooty.

—The same to you. What does that mean?

—That's fuck you in Latin.

—That's not Latin.

—O.K., so why should it mean anything? Cozy fan tooty, that's just an expression.

—Well here's good luck. Happy Yom Kipper.

—That's how much you know, "happy yom kipper." Happy Yom Kippur was around Hallowe'en.

—So you're meine Yiddische Sendy Claus?

—That's no joke now, that's no joke. If it wasn't for the Jews there wouldn't be no Christmas.

—So you're a Jew?

—So I'm a Jew. Tell him Barney, ain't I a Jew?

—Come on, you're no more Jew than my dick.

—Quiet down, now. Quiet down.

—I been pissed off at him for five years.

—Yeah, well you ought to be good and wet then.

—Quiet down, now.

—O.K. Barney. Thanks for the beer. Just tell Santa Claus here to hold his water.

—You both better quiet down or go. It stopped snowing.

—It finally stopped snowing?

—You're not being a perfect host, Barney. You're supposed to be the perfect host.

—It finally stopped snowing? Well I'll be damned.

—Merry Christmas,

—And it finally stopped snowing,

—Happy Yom Kipper,

—Well I'll be damned.

VIII

Then Adam, seeing Enoc and Elias, says,
Say, what maner men bene yee,
That bodely meten vs, as I see,
And, dead, come not to Hell as we,
Since all men damned were?
When I trespassed, God hett me
That this place closed always should be
From earthly man to haue entry;
And yet fynd I you here.

—The Harrowing of Hell

UNDISCIPLINED lights shone through the night instructed by the tireless precision of the squads of traffic lights, turning red to green, green to red, commanding voids with indifferent authority: for the night outside had not changed, with the whole history of night bound up in it had not become better nor worse, fewer lights and it was darker, less motion and it was more empty, more silent, less perturbed, and like the porous figures which continued to move against it, more itself.

Mr. Inononu turned from the window and walked, apparently aimless in the suit which billowed silently about him, toward the fireplace, where something smoldered.

—Fas et Nefas ambulant, pene passu pari... He cocked his head for a moment and listened. —Prodigus non redimit vitium avari... He studied the face before him, as the words came on, —Virtus temperantia quadam singulari...

Mr. Inononu's nose was no more than two inches from the Vulliamy clock on the mantel. He stood peering into it as he did every face, an intent scrutiny of clinical exactness, brevity, and disposition. Then he raised his eyes to the gilt cupid, sniffed silently, lowered them to the fire smoldering in the grate, at which he sniffed audibly, and went on to the desk to examine its furnishings, the twitching fingers of his hands folded behind him the only signal of the agitation which the distant voice of his host provoked in him. Basil Valentine's voice continued, the book held in white hands above the clear water, reading in his tub.

Mr. Inononu stood a stolid five feet and four inches from the ground, draped in a brown suit which was some shades lighter, or at least softer, than his skin. His face reared in enigmatic blossom from the calyx of a sharp black beard. His brows were heavy and as black, doing little to hide or even temper the blacker eyes beneath them. The dark skin kept its patina to the back of his crown, where a black fuzz, gradually nourished into distinct hair, collared the back of his head and rose in slight peaks above his ears. Full face, as the Vulliamy clock had had him for a minute, there was something distinctly oriental about Mr. Inononu.

As he went on around the room, silent on the carpet, he seemed to have difficulty resisting putting out a hand and touching things. He was touching the gold egg atop the column near the couch when Basil Valentine entered, a book closed in one hand, the other holding closed the untied front of the blue dressing gown. —An egg?

—It's damaged, obviously, Valentine muttered.

—You are very nervous this evening, Mr. Inononu commented, turning from the column with a look which another face might have matched to his tone of solicitude, but his own reflected merely passive curiosity. His clothes were cut full; and for all the quiet alertness of his manner he seemed to billow in a wealth of folds and creases, moving to a bookshelf where he stood reading titles and touching the spines as he did so. —You are in the nineteenth century, he murmured running a thumb down *Az igazi pozitiv filozofia.* —And Móricz, side by side with Gárdonyi?...

—You came to discuss literature? You've already kept me waiting...

Mr. Inononu made a deprecative sound with his lips. —*A Véres költö...* you are fond of Kosztolányi? he asked, returning to the couch. —I would recommend to you Bródy? I do not see him on your shelf. His *Faust orvos,* his *Don Quixote kisasszony...*

—Have you looked at these papers? Valentine interrupted him impatiently. —You've already made me late for an important...

—I did not know which ones... still, you are not ready to leave yet.

—Which ones! They're right there in front of you, on the table there, if you'd simply looked, instead of poking around...

—I disturbed nothing on your desk, Mr. Inononu said, watching him look sharply over the books and papers spread out there. When Valentine turned, having difficulty inserting a cuff link, Mr. Inononu picked up the papers from the marble-top table and said, —This information deals with a Rumanian, Yák is his name?

—Among other things, Valentine answered shortly.

—He is presumed to be in Spain now?

—So they think. I think he's here, myself.

—You have information you have not communicated?

—I have no information, Valentine dismissed it quickly, going on to the other cuff link. —Even if he is, it will take them long enough to find him in this...chaos, he raised his eyes to the window. —Whatever name he's using now, he's certainly sold his passport, or burned it by this time if he has any sense, any sense of...you, Valentine brought out harshly under his breath. He stood there abruptly motionless, staring at the glass without seeing through it, his eyes fixed on the reflection, the pacific image of this guest who sat as though occupied with an academic treatise. —He's a scholar, you know, this Rumanian Yák, a scholar, and that means nothing...to you? he went on in dead monotone. —A scholar, a, a man you've never seen?

Mr. Inononu shrugged, turning the pages in his short lap. —You do a most neat job of the decoding, most orderly, he murmured, taking a notebook from his pocket. —Some of the information I am given...Then he commenced to read, closely and with extreme rapidity, pausing to make notes, or read aloud phrases which struck him with what appeared to be pleasure. —Yes, an accomplished scholar, of course...Coptic, Aramaic, of course...authority on the Demotic...Saite period, mummies...yes, something may be arranged around this...

—Will you do that too yourself? Valentine recovered irritably. —And you could have had this information in the usual way, he added, affixing a collar. —They know I don't like you coming here.

—I do as I am told.

—One would think you'd been told to keep an eye on me.

—This is entirely possible, Mr. Inononu agreed calmly, without looking up from his notes.

—What do you mean? Valentine's voice was as calm, but he'd spoken too quickly.

—Exactly as you suggest, Mr. Inononu said looking up at him.

—Yes, most likely! And if it were true, you would sit there telling me about it, eh?

—One never knows who will win.

—Who will win! what do you mean, who will win. Basil Valentine stood over him, a black tie strung tight between his hands. —Come, you've started this, now. What is being said?

—So many things, as always, said Mr. Inononu, closing the notebook and putting it in his pocket. —Stories, rumors . . . He paused; but when Valentine urged him with no more than the cold blue eyes, went on, —Of yourself? Of course, there have always been so many stories, as you know. Why, I have even once been told that when you first came to us, you could not bear friction of any sort? Soaking the feet in warm water and trimming the nails, and put on heavy socks before going to bed? But there are stories about all of us, of course . . .

Basil Valentine had turned away, and speaking with apparent calm, repeated, —What is being said now?

—Quite simply, that though the Roman Church believes you still to be acting to its interests, you came to us from the Jesuits some time ago. And that now, though we believe you to be in co-operation with the present regime, you are in truth working with those who would attempt to restore the monarchy of the Hapsburgs. Mr. Inononu folded the papers together. He had spoken disinterestedly, and did not even look up, as though to save Valentine the trouble of contriving some sign of indifference to this intelligence. —Of course, stories, rumors . . . he added.

—Oh yes, Valentine said then, wearily, pulling off the dressing gown. —First they expect me to work like, what was his name, the seventeenth-century primate, Pázmány? . . . converting the nobles first, sure that the people would follow. Now they say this. He shrugged, drawing the tie round his collar. —Come, there are stories about yourself, he went on agreeably. —One to match my abhorrence of friction "of any kind" as you say. I was once told that the reason for your rather oriental visage was, that a bank fell on you in a Japanese earthquake some years ago? An American bank, of course. And there were none but the local surgeons to operate on your face, who knew only the faces to which their own mirrors had accustomed them . . .

Mr. Inononu stood. His trousers, fully pleated at the waist, broke their crease two or three times before the shoetops, and almost touched the floor at his heels. He held forth the papers to Valentine, who motioned him to the fireplace, where he stooped before the grate and tried to prod the fire into life with the rolled papers before thrusting them in. —And I understand you shall go to Rome, yourself very soon? he asked, stooped there.

—I believe so, Valentine said. —How do you know?

—As I say, one hears things. Also I believe there is work contemplated there for me. A priest, though I am told far more important than the simple priest he pretends, perhaps you know of him, the name escapes, it is something Martin? Or Martin...

—Yes, I know of it, Valentine cut him short, and stood motionless looking at the floor until Mr. Inononu straightened up from the fire to say, —It is a very disagreeable smell, this smell of paint burning.

Basil Valentine glanced up at him and smiled for the first time. —Yes, isn't it, he said, commencing to knot the black tie.

On the mantel, the Vulliamy clock struck softly behind Mr. Inononu, who stepped away from it and picked up a book. —*De Omni Sanguine Christi Glorificato*, John Huss? You have curious reading habits, he said, and put it down again, his eye catching the newspaper clipping thrust in as a marker, as he did so.

—A personal matter, Valentine said, undoing the knot to pull one end slightly longer.

—And this? Hungary to Sell Famed Paintings, from the local newspaper?

—A tragedy, Valentine said thoughtfully, —an... absurd tragedy, as Inononu pushed the book away and sauntered billowing toward the windows.

—Of course, to say something like that, he began.

—Yes, put that in your report then! Valentine broke out abruptly, at his back. —Anyone who would say what I've just said, eh? must be working against the... present regime, eh?

—Do not be upset, Mr. Inononu said, without turning or pausing his slow course toward the windows. —You are a critic of art here, of course you are interested in such affairs. Tell me, is it enjoyable, your pose of the art critic in this culture?

Valentine cleared his throat and raised his chin, folding the knot. —There is always an immense congregation of people unable to create anything themselves, who look for comfort to the critics to disparage, belittle, and explain away those who do. And I might say, he added with slight asperity, —it's not entirely a pose.

—Still, other interests come first.

—Oh yes!...yes! And they send a...hired assassin to look after me, to make sure they do! Yes, like this Rumanian scholar, eh? A man you've never seen? and you're sent out to find him and kill him. Without asking questions, just find him and kill him. And if I say... there, does it surprise you? if I talk like this to... a hired assassin?

Mr. Inononu stood motionless before the windows. —And it should surprise you that I am? he brought out after a moment. His fingers twitched behind him, until his hands clasped one another. —Because I am a dead man already, he added quietly, and then, turning, —Like yourself…with an expression near a smile.

The knot broke in Valentine's hands; and a tremble touched his lip as he lost one end. He caught it up immediately, and at that moment the doorbell rang. Mr. Inononu stepped away from the windows instantly, and his hand went into the full breast of his jacket.

—It's nothing, Valentine said. —Someone downstairs. He was hurriedly gathering together the papers still spread on his desk, which he took, with the plainly bound book, through the door to the bedroom. —I'll just be a moment… And a moment later he appeared in the door pulling on a dinner jacket. —You're coming tonight then, are you? to keep an eye on me, eh?

—Let us say I come simply as an Egyptologist. I have in my leisure developed quite a monologue on the prophecies contained in the Great Pyramid of Cheops. At such a party, I might even encounter someone familiar with Egyptian culture. A Rumanian, familiar with the early dynasties?… I should think myself to be Turkish, since it is a culture with which I am familiar, and of course since, as you say, I look rather…oriental? But when he turned, Basil Valentine was not there. Then he heard running water, from the bathroom; and then Valentine's voice, —We'll go separately, you go along, I have an errand first.

The fingers of his clasped hands twitching behind him, Mr. Inononu returned to the window and stood looking out on the city. —You live very nicely here, he said, —it is very civilized. But most of these people live in squalor. I have been in the apartments of very respectable people, and they are squalor. He paused, and then his fingers still moving behind him he said, —Did you see what they did with our Molnár? what happened to *Liliom?* That was a beautiful thing, a beautiful ragged thing, *Liliom*, and they made it to music that sounds like all the other music I hear here, everything is smoothed round like everything else, it is sugar-coated suffering of the spirit here.

The doorbell rang again, in a long peal, and his hands stopped and held one another tightly behind him. As it went on, they relaxed.

—I have heard the radio, he said. —But since I can understand it, it is very depressing. It is spiritual squalor. Does it surprise you that I can talk this way? if you thought me no more than…that, he said and his hands came apart to gesture behind him, and fell together again.

—Do you know the novel of Mikszáth, *Szent Peter esernyoje?* Of course, if Saint Peter could come out today upon these streets below he would find all he could wish, voices from nowhere, music from unpopulated boxes, men ascending divine distances in gas balloons, and traveling at the speed of sound, apparitions from nowhere appear on the screen; the sick are raised from the dead, life is prolonged so that every detail of pain may be relished, the blind are given eyes and the cripples forced to walk, and there is an item which can blow a city of the beloved enemy into a place where their sins will be brought home to them, with of course as much noise as the trumpets on the walls of Jericho…

There was a heavy pounding on the door. Mr. Inononu swung round as he had before, his hand inside his coat. Basil Valentine came quickly from the bathroom, drying his hands on a linen hand towel. His coat and hat were laid out, and he picked them up. —Come, there's a back staircase, he said. Mr. Inononu got his own hat and coat from the deep chair near the windows.

The pounding continued on the front door as they went through the kitchen. —Do you know, there was a funny story about you that I heard, in the hospital in Székesfehérvár? They told me you had a radio transmitter sewn inside of you.

—A transmitter? Mr. Inononu demanded at the head of the service stairs. —A receiver perhaps, but a transmitter?

By the time that Basil Valentine appeared, it had all been going on for some time; and the voices of guests lay in monotonous layers on the pestilential heat, rising into the lighted regions, falling away to the dark beds of shifting infested silence. Someone had already remarked that Bruckner had been Hitler's favorite composer, someone else, that there was something wrong with any *young* person who really en*joy*ed the late Beethoven; someone had already confided that the soap business in America amounted to seven million dollars a year, someone else that advertising amounted to seven billion. Someone had already turned the radio on, and someone else turned it off though not before Mr. Schmuck (of Twentieth Century-Schmuck, here from the Coast on business for the holidays) had heard a catchy phrase of music, demanded of his assistant the name of the composer, been told, —I think the announcer said Kerkel… and finished, —Have him in my office Monday morning. Mr. Sonnenschein (here from the Coast for the holidays, on business) had already told his story about the girl who had dramatized a suicide attempt in the apartment next door to where he'd been invited to dinner the night before, —to get my attention for herself… had, in fact, told it four times and was finishing the fifth, —So I can't even finish my Baked Alaska. M. Crémer (here from the Continent, on business) with a cigarette end stuck to his lip like a sore, had already remarked the uncivilized lack of public toilets in New York, and a number of people had already remarked that the tall woman wore too much perfume. In one corner, under the Patinir, Miss Stein (she was with Mr. Sonnenschein) had already settled the future of American art with Mr. Schmuck's assistant, who had already developed his late-evening stammer which bespoke sincerity; just as the past of German art (—There was none, properly speaking, before Dürer) had already been settled in another, under the massive Christmas tree, a Norwegian spruce, reared before the critical eyes of the wart hog, which gave the impression that the host might have been ashamed of a tree grown of earth, for any natural green that could betray such coarse origin was obliterated in one grand festoon of tinsel, sparkling under three hundred twenty blue lights which Fuller had spent nine dizzy hours in arraying.

And something else had happened, as every face (except a few that had come after, like the tall woman) revealed in strained attempts to show, to one another, that it had not. (Though Mr. Schmuck had seen fit to repeat a number of times since, —Wherever you got art you got cranks, we got the same trouble out there.) All of their momentary discomposure, however, had accumulated, and remained unmollified in Fuller's face, as Basil Valentine saw directly they met when Fuller took his coat in the hallway.

—What is it, Fuller, he's been here already? he asked quickly.

—Yes sar.

—What happened?

—He accomplish very little, sar.

—Come now, what happened?

—Very little occur to happen, sar, Fuller commenced, having at first seemed eager to escape, and now as he talked unable to stop. —He enter a lit-tel wile ago, comportin himself very calm as he go about among the guests talkin very diligent to them, though I can tell in his eyes that he is in great extremity for they become very green, the eyes of each mahn, sar bein the windows of his soul . . .

—Come, get on with it, Valentine cut in, looking back from the great room beyond to Fuller, who stood before him staring at the hard surface which had come over the watery blue of his eyes.

—So he restrain himself very peaceable, all the wile wearin one suit atop the other one as he go about addressin the dignitaries gathered in there until no one take notice of what he so carefully speakin to them about, and then at long last so it seem to me he arise very excited to proclaim he can prove all this what he so perseverinly try to inform them of is the truth, and upon hastenin his departure say he goin in search of you, sar.

—And Brown? Brown, what about Brown? . . .

—Mister Brown, sar, Mister Brown behave quite vexed which is not altogether surprisin, though I try to wahrn him Mister Brown goin to be vexed . . .

—What do you mean, you tried to warn him? Valentine demanded, his mind already in the other room. Fuller had gone on as though he had forgot to whom he was speaking, which he probably had.

—I try to wahrn him...he drew himself up again, faltering, —such a projeck destin to no great success...He paused, and then added as a revelation, —Mister Brown behavin like it is not my fortune to see him heretofore. Seem like Mister Brown incline to drink quite heavily tonight, sar...But Basil Valentine had already turned away, and Fuller stood immobile holding his coat, and watched him out of sight into the great room beyond.

Someone had turned the radio on; and as it warmed to the finish of the Jupiter Symphony, someone else turned it off.

The tall woman returned across the room to her husband, looking affronted. —That rather...oriental creature told me that there were no female sphinxes in Egypt before Greek times, imagine! Is this drink for me? Good heavens but it is hot in here. Always the same people, or they look the same to me. There! who *do* you suppose that flashy little dago *is?*

—We want a goverment that will do something for Americans, said Mr. Schmuck, to the right, —and I don't mean the Indians.

Three men stood over the low table before the fireplace as Basil Valentine entered, fingertips suppressing, at that moment, the vein standing out at his temple. He approached them. Two of them were European, and the third was Recktall Brown.

—There is no place here for history to accumulate, said the tallest of them, taking the cigarette and pausing the lighted match as though to illuminate his synthesis, —and you call this progress.

—Good evening, Basil Valentine said as they turned to acknowledge his arrival; and while courtesies were being exchanged, he looked straight across the table.

There was something reckless about Brown's appearance. He had had his glasses on and off a number of times, and though they were on now, slightly crooked, the pupils swimming behind those thick lenses seemed to be wary of that constant renewal, sharpened to points, each time the glasses were removed, and nervously alerted against it. He was perspiring; and the cigar he held in his mouth burnt on a bias. At that moment he noticed it, taking it from among those uneven teeth, and threw it into the fireplace behind him. He had another out very quickly, unwrapped, and stood, vaguely marsupial, delving for the penknife in a pocket of his vest.

Basil Valentine wasted no manners in getting round beside him. —What happened?

And M. Crémer politely turned his back on them, and speaking to the tall man beside him managed to continue a conversation which had not yet begun.

—Mais cette peinture-là, je veux l'acheter, vous savez, mais le prix! . . . bien sûr que c'est Memlinc, alors, mais le prix qu'il demande, il est fou!

—Pas si bête . . . that one murmured, and together they crossed the room to look at a painting recently hung in the neighborhood of the vast tapestry. A lantern-jawed young man with a low forehead stared at them dumbly as they passed without a glance for him. He was quite used to being annoyed in public as a movie star. Now, hearing French, he muttered, —Fairies . . . and went for another drink.

—*Him* Byronic? Miss Stein demanded.

—I said *mo*ronic, said Mr. Schmuck's assistant. —We have to keep a tank of straight oxygen on the set to sober him up . . .

—What happened, I asked you.

—Nothing. Not a damn thing happened. Not a God-damned thing, Brown threw back unsteadily.

—You're in splendid shape this evening. Valentine stepped back, looking him over. —Splendid, he rasped.

Brown would not look round at him. Finally he did say, —He wants to buy that Memling.

—Who?

—This frog that was just here, he wants to buy it for nothing. Crazy frog.

—He is an idiot, I agree, Basil Valentine said, and supporting one elbow drew the hand up to his face, his chin lowered so that he seemed to kiss that gold seal ring, and they stood side by side, sustaining a perilous abeyance between them, and weighing the room before them in the balance.

Fuller entered, bearing glasses on a tray suspended at nose level between white hands, and altogether a harried look about him. They both watched Fuller until he arrived, without the mishap he appeared to expect, at the bar; but even when he'd set the tray down there safe, his expression did not change: it even seemed to summon itself to an exaggeration as he looked round to see them watching him from across the room, and the sounds and the movement about him fell away in the suspense of his own paralysis, an intolerable moment while they three were alone in the room, surrounded by shades, and waiting.

—Hey George, where's the can?

Fuller turned to Miss Stein. —I will direck you to the tilet, madam, he said, and set off before her.

Like undersea flora, figures stood weaving, rooted to the floor, here and there one drifting as though caught in a cold current, sensing in a greater or a less degree what one expressed as —Something submarine, as he paddled the air before him, and went on, —Agnes should be here, this is her world. Then he touched the beard which dripped to a point at his chin with two fingers, smirked at the stolid figure across the room whose somber presence he caricatured, and whined, —Where *is* that black Ganymede?...

Fuller was sitting on a white stool in the kitchen, bolt upright pretending to read a cruise guide he had found in a street trashbin. On the floor, the dog watched him. She swallowed. He did not move. She was watching him as though to see if the intent strain on his face were for his reading or tense suspension, waiting, for a sound from her. She growled. At that, as though it were a signal of relief from restraint, he brought a hand up to hide the intent corner of his profile, and peeked at her through his fingers. Sometimes this went on for what seemed hours to them both; though tonight the surveillant might be justified: she had seen him selling the evening's emptied liquor bottles, with their undamaged expensive labels, to a furtive shade at the service entrance.

Miss Stein returned to hear the lantern-jawed young man finishing what was apparently a familiar joke, for she laughed before it was done while the tall woman listened with polite anticipation to, —So one nurse says, And did you see he has the word swan tattooed on it? And the other nurse says (here Miss Stein burst into laughter), —That word's Saskatchewan.

The tall woman waited politely for a moment more, then she said agreeably, —Oh... that's in Canada, isn't it? They quit laughing and stared at her. —I'd better go look after my husband, she said. And turning, she gathered her features to return in kind an expression of vaguely startled curiosity from a tall white-haired man in gray, who was turning it everywhere in the room, though apparently in conversation with the hapless creature before him, to whom he had just said,

—Eh?

—Ail séd, ouî mest keep gôing ouor semmhouer naoû olouezz azz a séfté valv it izz valyouebel, ouith provijenn it dezz not spredd.

—Good heavens yes, daresay you're right, eh? Now if you'll just...

—Semm aoutt-ovv-dthe-oué pléce houer it dezz not interfîre ouith dthe civilise oueurld.

—Good heavens yes! Excuse me, there's a good mpphhht fellow.

—Ouonne ouor...

Nearby, someone overheard mention of Tuthmosis in another conversation, and going on, found it immediately useful in still another, —This is for your tomb-like little ears, *she* has something contagious called...

—Tuthmosis third, eh? Good heavens yes, remember him well, the white-haired man went on, now deep in confusion with a sharp-bearded "oriental sort of chap" as he would say when he escaped. —Probably the greatest Pharaoh of them mphht all, I daresay, eh? Had a very low forehead I remember, curious thing, eh? Looked a bit like this mphht chap here somewhere, works in pictures they tell me. Pitiful sort of mppht way to live eh? He finished and glanced up, startled again at the sharp eyes fixed on him.

—Ah yes . . . and the child princess Ink-naton, is she perhaps familiar?

—Ink . . . mphht . . . Ikhnaton, daresay that's who you mean, eh? Good heavens yes, very interesting chap he was, Ikhnaton. Put down the mphht what-do-you-call-ems, don't you know. Religious reform, all that sort of thing. Good heavens yes, had them all running round worshiping the sun. All very well, that sort of thing, don't you know, pushing out the mphht old gods, eh? But keep an eye on politics, eh? Keep an eye on politics. Not like this fellow what's-his-name we're talking about, building his temple out there on the edge of nowhere, eh? Spending everything he could get his hands on out there worshiping the mphht visible disc of the sun, eh? Won't do, won't do at all.

—This is perhaps your field of interest? Because it is mine also.

—Interest? Good heavens no, my dear chap, don't care a damn for the whole lot of them.

—You are very well informed, nevertheless?

—Oh, pick things up, don't you know, pick things up. Old school chum of mine, Lord mphht the devil, what the devil was his name, dug up old King Tut don't you know, not so long ago. Tutankhamen you know, the son of this fellow mphht Ikhnaton don't you know, who built Akhetaton out there on the edge of nowhere for his sun-worshiping, and let his politics go out the window. Go-od heavens yes, this white-haired man paused to grip his lapels and stare up with an air of recollection, —before the whole thing went to pot, don't you know, the Nineteenth Dynasty, eh? Too much gold, that was their difficulty, gold kicking around all over the place, and vulgarity everywhere, eh? Yes, that's what happens, that's when the decadence sets in, eh? Same damn thing running around today from the look of things, eh? Wasn't like this fifty years ago, eh? Good heavens no, people then who had money inherited it don't you know, knew how to spend it. Some sense of responsibility to their culture, eh?

—Nevertheless, I hear on the radio that gold to the amount of three-hundred fifty-six thousand dollars will bring a million dollars on the black market? . . .

—The radio? . . . good heavens yes, total loss in this country, don't you know. Turned it on meself and had some brazen idiot ask me how was the color personality of my house, eh? Who the devil puts up with all that nonsense do you spose. A pound a year we pay at home, don't you know, a pound a year to keep the airwaves clean, you might say. Cheap enough, eh? to keep that kind of infernal rubbish out of your house.

—Of course. But now, in the field of Egyptology, have you ever encountered a gentleman by the name...

—Good heavens, not my field at all, don't you know. I say, I've gut to get over and have a word with that chap, d'you mind? That offensive little Frenchman don't you know.

He almost stumbled over the Argentine Trade Commissioner, who had been worrying his way about that vast room for some time, and now approached the elbow of a man whom he apparently took for a countryman.

—Con permiso, señor... conoce Usted el Señor Brown?

—Iført den uovervinnelige rustning... eh?

—Nada... nada, gracias...

Even the tapestried eyes above avoided him.

At the foot of that sylvan enterprise, M. Crémer took out a blue coarse-paper packet, offered one of the harsh cigarettes, and took it himself when it was declined. —Oui, à vendre *à l'aimable*, vous savez, au prix d'un retable de... Hubert van Eyck. They turned again to look at the painting, hands in trouser pockets bunching the jackets behind. Crémer blew a steady stream of smoke at its surface. —Memlinc, bien sûr, he murmured again. —La force, voyez vous, encore plus la... tendresse.

The white-haired gentleman approached, side-stepping the argument going on behind them which went something like this,

—Roughly, .oooooooooooooooooooooooooooo6624

—Roughly! It's nearer to .ooooooooooooooooooooooooooooo6624

—Good heavens, eh? Lots of odd ducks here this evening. Crémer straightened round to him. —Just met some wog over there who talked me ear off about mphhht lot of dead Egyptians he carts about with him. You're buying this thing, are you? He leant over Crémer's shoulder to look close at the painting.

—I am interested in it, Crémer answered him, and then he introduced the two. The white-haired man was identified with a London gallery of some prominence, and Crémer was careful to add an R.A. after his name.

—Odd bit of business we had here earlier, eh? the R.A. said to them. —Funny sort of chap, storming in here like that, eh?

Crémer shrugged. —There are madmen everywhere.

—And he really had a go on this, didn't he, this Memlinc here, almost tore it from the wall, don't you know. I was standing nearby here, almost expected him to... attack me, don't you know, no reason on earth.

Crémer's shrug still hung in his shoulders, and he emphasized it with a twitch, throwing the exact lines of his neat blue suit off, for it was a thing of careful French construction, and fit only when the figure inside it was apathetically erect, arms hung at the sides, at which choice moment the coat stood up neat and square as a box, and the trousers did not billow as they did in walking, but hung in wide envelopes with all the elegance that right angles confer, until they broke over the shoes, which they were, fortunately, almost wide enough at the bottoms, and enough too long, to cover. —I saw him only this distance across the room, you know. But these spectacles, these spectacles you know… Crémer waved a hand before him as though he were going to take the cigarette from between his lips. —In America they are not uncommon. And this Memlinc, you know, it is beyond a doubt. He jerked his head back, dropping the long ash on the carpet, to indicate the painting hung behind him. —I am familiar with the origin, you see… et surtout, vous savez… there is no test to which it has not been subjected.

—That mmph what that curious fellow had to say about the sky here, don't you know, eh? Prussian blue, don't you know. 'T's what it is.

—Bleu de Prusse, alors. What difference?

—Mphh eighteenth-century color, don't you know.

—Bien alors, Crémer said wearily, —the hand of a restorer, you know. It is not uncommon. He shrugged again. The R.A. had been leaning over his shoulder, and straightened up now with a glance at Crémer which, if he had given himself to rudeness, might have been one of extreme distaste. Nevertheless, he said,

—Nevertheless, don't you know, a lovely thing, this. Ought to pick it up meself, I spose. Eh?

—I have no intention to bid against you, said Crémer, staring straight out into the room.

—Eh? Mphh… nothing like that, of course, I mean to say, don't you know. Good heavens! Quite out of my reach right now. I mphht special sort of taste for these Flemish things meself. So cleean, don't you know.

Crémer almost smiled, at that. Still looking across the room he murmured, —You should enjoy what Michel-Ange has to say about these painters, perhaps. Les tableaux flamands plaisent aux femmes, surtout aux vieilles et au très jeunes, ainsi qu'aux moines et aux religieuses…

—Mphh…

— …et enfin aux gens du monde qui ne sont pas susceptibles de comprendre la vraie harmonie…

—Mphht… The R.A. started to turn his back. —Eh? Don't keep up on these things much any more. Modern mphht attitudes, don't you know, modern art and all that sort of thing, eh? They try to say their paintings are the spirit of the times, don't you know, but good heavens aren't the times bad enough without having pictures of it hanging all over the place?

But M. Crémer, with the cigarette gone out and stuck like a sore on his lip, was looking across the room. —Your Monsieur Brown, you know, he is exceptional?

—Not mine, old fellow. Good heavens, not mine.

—See his feet behind the table, so small they are as he moves on them, it is a wonder he can find equilibrium. How he sways this evening. Pffft. On va faire des zigzags, eh?

Behind them, to one side, someone said something with the precise care of a radio announcer mispronouncing something from another language.

—Excuse me, said their companion, silent all this time, to their right now as they stood facing momentary exposures of the delicately detached balance which their host had broken, and restored, and maintained again with the man beside him across the depths of that room, —I am not here early for this ... contretemps? What happened?

And the guests drifted past on courses which left no more trace than water, glassy-eyed, with as little purpose apparent as movement undersea but, as there, interrupted by swift predatory sweeps, and darting search for cover. In striking differences of shape, and protective coloration, exotically helpless, deceptively dull, distinct varieties fed together in clusters, or tended to move separately, here and there raising wide-open eyes, and bumping the sides of the tank.

—We're shooting *Faust* now, a sort of bop version, we've changed him to this refugee artist, and Mephistopheles is ...

—But it's funny seeing pictures of yourself everywheres, starin out at you eatin things and drinkin things and smokin things you never heard of ... went on the one with no more forehead than a black bass; and in spite of the shocks of sound that broke the surface, a pelagian quiet drenched the whole place.

So the sprays at the ears of the tall woman shone like growths of some special nature, antennae perhaps, or merely lures, as she said to her husband, —You might ask him now, about that Queen Anne table? or was it a chair.

—And that ... person over there? with the beard?

—Oh yes, carries art to the masses, women masses, you know. A pontificator in ... Oh! Oh *that* one, calls himself Kuvetli, an Egyptian ... And where they turned their eyes, that denizen lurked and caught their glances instantly, though he went on talking to the person before him, and though, until that moment, he had not been looking in their direction at all.

—Of course, I do not concern myself with politics, or such triumphs of scientific ingenuity as your atom bombs and hydrogen bombs. All that I leave for the newspapers, it is so necessary to their self-importance to have all the answers. For me this war will be no more than a matter of academic interest, of course, a confirmation of the prophecies contained in the Great Pyramid of Cheops. As I say, we have entered the period . . . ahm, symbolized by the King's Chamber, in 1936, and it is only last year we have entered the period of final woe at last. But at this moment, he went on, pulling a stream of tinsel from the tree and winding it around his finger, —I am more interested in this mummy of which I speak, the mummy of Ink-naton. Of course she died when only twelve years of age, the Fourth Dynasty . . . of course it is too much to hope that I may encounter here someone who will be able to assist me with information? . . . And here he returned his black eyes, not to the man before him, to whom he spoke, but beyond him, directly across the room.

—What happened! What do you mean, what happened.

—You know very well what I mean, Valentine answered after all these minutes of silence which Brown was, finally, unable to sustain.

—You've seen him, Brown broke out, suddenly turning on Valentine.

—I give you my word, I haven't though.

—Your word! Recktall Brown muttered, turning away once more. —He went after you. He left here to go after you.

—So I understand.

—There! What do you mean, you didn't see him.

—My dear man, I haven't seen him in some time, please get that straight. Fuller mentioned that he'd gone off looking for me, why, I cannot imagine.

—You can't imagine! You God damn well can imagine. Valentine has the proof, he said to me right square in my face, I left it with him . . . so what the hell did he mean? Recktall Brown turned his heavy face up again; and Basil Valentine faintly smiled, and as faintly shrugged.

—You expect him back then?

—How the hell do I know. Sure I expect him back. Don't you?

—And nothing happened when he was here earlier? No one . . .

—Nobody would listen to him. Brown lowered his eyes again to the table before him. His cigar stood out between fingers as thick as itself in his left hand hanging beside him; and he raised his right hand to wipe his mouth.

—Still, it is rather embarrassing. You know, Basil Valentine said, falling into his familiar caustic tone, —you do sound rather disappointed?

Recktall Brown did not move. He did not even raise the cigar; but stood, staring down at that table. His forehead glistened.

—Now listen, Brown, I don't know what's got into you tonight besides a gallon of liquor, but you . . .

—That last picture he did, Brown interrupted, raising his cigar and looking over the room, —there's some people here who I want to have a look at it.

At that point Brown started round one side of the table, and Basil Valentine came rapidly after him round the other.

The cigarette in Crémer's mouth had gone out at about a thumbnail's length, and stuck there as he discussed a contemporary French painter, who was, he said, —Racinien, vous savez... le goût de l'en deçà. L'instinct de... de l'atticisme, alors. Comme Corot, comme Seurat, vous savez, il est racinien. Comme je viens d'écrire, suprême fleur du génie français et qui ne pouvait pousser qu'en France...With that Crémer stopped, raised an eyebrow, and carefully removed the blemish from his lip with a thumb and third finger, in anticipation of his host.

Recktall Brown swerved, as Valentine grabbed his arm when they met coming round the foot of the low table before the fireplace.

—Wait a minute now...

—Let go!...let go of my arm.

—Wait, listen!...you can't do this...

—God damn it let go of my arm. Recktall Brown stopped abruptly, and Valentine swung around almost before him.

—What's the matter with you tonight? What the devil's the matter with you?

—Not a God damn thing the matter with me...

—Listen now, listen to me, Valentine said, trying to take him by both arms now. —Don't be an idiot, you can't show another one now, you can't show this one so soon...

—Get out of the way.

—Do you think these men are fools? do you think they're children? And after what's just happened do you think you can take them in there and show them another van der Goes without...

Several people turned at Recktall Brown's laughter, which rose about him there in the middle of the vast room in an eructation of smoke. —And show them your face, hey? You think they'll laugh at your face, hey? Get out of the way.

Basil Valentine stepped back quickly. He opened a white handkerchief and paused to cough into it, as Recktall Brown went on. When he caught up, Crémer was saying, —Tell us, Monsieur Brown, for you which is the most beautiful...objet, in your present collection.

Recktall Brown stood before them with the cigar in one end of his mouth, uneven teeth discoloring his grin, the pupils of his eyes filling the lenses. He did not pause to consider but threw a hand up. Those before him startled back at this gesture; but Basil Valentine, arriving beside him, did not, and got the blow square in the face.

The handkerchief reddened as he held it up to his lip; but Brown did not even pause to look at the diamonds. —That! he said, pointing; and though they had started immediately to solicit Valentine on his injury, he had excused himself and was gone, and each of them was staring up at the balcony, and the suit of armor there, before he knew it.

Crémer recovered quickly. He took a loosely made cigarette from the battered blue packet and returned his eyes to his host. —Quelle drôlerie!

Recktall Brown looked back to see their eyes upon him, slightly quizzical, only Crémer looking at him with a penetration equal to that of Basil Valentine, whom, in a dismally obvious, badly dressed way, he rather resembled.

—You don't like it? Brown burst out, addressing himself directly to Crémer.

—Ah mais oui, mais . . . c'est charmant . . . Nevertheless Crémer took a step back now, and the smile faded from his face as he looked at Brown's.

Recktall Brown looked up at the other two men in quick turn, and then he suddenly took off his glasses and startled them all three with the sharpness of his eyes, which he lowered then, and wiped his forehead with the ends of his fingers. They were silent and attentive while he put the glasses back on, and said, peremptorily, —Come with me, I've got something to show you. He turned, signaling three or four other people with his nod, and they followed him toward the panel door in the other end of the room. Mr. Schmuck joined them, halfway across, Mr. Sonnenschein three-quarters, and Basil Valentine reached them before they were all through that door, and closed it behind him.

—They've gone in to look at dirty movies, said Miss Stein, watching them. —Art pictures the boss calls them. Too late, she had taken a step to follow.

The tall woman was deflected from her course by a plump hand which hit her in the breast. She did not pause for an apology; and the bearded youth did not pursue her to offer one. He went right on with, —No, the story was published over there, and of course I have every right to sue her, she's *ru*-ined my London reputation.

—But you've never been in London, have you?

—Well I might go . . . so there! No, don't you touch me . . . I'm going right over and discuss Martin Schoongauer's etchings with that exquisitely fifteenth-century-looking person.

The tall woman interrupted her husband, who was absorbed in saying nothing to anyone. —Oh dear, I always say the wrong thing, I just don't stand a Chinaman's chance . . . Then her voice stopped, as her eyes were halted by the man at her elbow whom she had met as Mr. Kuvetli. —A Chinese person's chance . . . she faltered on, bravely, —Oh dear, I do try . . .

And at the far end of that great room the panel door opened to upset someone who was depending upon it as part of the wall.

—Don't tell me that advertising does a cultural service by reproducing art, confusing the art and the product in people's minds, it corrupts the art by exalting the . . . ooops!

—Pardon, said M. Crémer, stepping back while this speaker picked himself up and renewed his attack. —So your hair oil reproduces the *Mona Lisa*, that's patronage . . .

—A magnificent work, Crémer went on, coming out, —bien entendu, le visage de la Vierge . . .

—Yes that, of course, said the white-haired man behind him, —but most obviously the work of some restorer. Rather serves to show up the excellence of the rest of the thing, though, you might say.

—Un sacrilège, ce visage-là, archaïque, dur comme la pierre, voyez vous, sans chaleur, sans cœur, sans sympathie, sans vie . . . en un mot, la mort, vous savez, sans espoir de Résurrection.

Last in the short line, Mr. Sonnenschein came out saying, —It's a price. It's a price. He looked over his shoulder, and started to say something, but the door closed in his face.

The white-haired man bumped Crémer, who'd stopped abruptly, one foot full on an Aubusson rose, to say, —Your Monsieur Brown, he is . . . typical?

Here the sharkskinned Argentine approached, to excuse himself and ask if any of them were Mr. Brown?

—He's right here . . . ummph . . . somewhere, the white-haired man said looking round over their heads. The Argentine looked, anxiously, with him.

—You are here on . . . business? Crémer challenged him.

—My official commission is completed earlier, the Argentine answered, —but I am here with the hope to secure something of . . . artistic? . . .

Crémer turned his back. —Il va sans dire, he said, pausing to chuckle, —comme tout le monde sait bien, les grands tableaux de Goya qu'on trouve dans le Jockey Club de Buenos Aires sont des . . . faux.

—A deodorant company reproduces the *Madonna of the Rocks* in an ad, and you call that . . . ooops!

Recktall Brown came through the panel door, with a fresh cigar in his mouth. He strode into the room and looked around with expectation, holding one heavy hand in the other behind him, and then the second in the first, his back turned to the direction he had come from, passing Crémer and the others so fast he had not seen them.

—A laxative company reproduces the portrait of Doctor Arnolfini and his wife in full color, and that's supposed to be . . . ooops!

Basil Valentine came through the panel door, and stood there, pulling it closed behind him slowly as he looked over the room, pale, his lips tight but moved by the tongue which caressed the broken tooth.

—Look, come on over to a safe corner, because I want to tell you that if there's one single cancer eating out this country, it's advertising.

Basil Valentine cupped his hands to light a cigarette, for the one he had held up with a match was quivering.

—But Doctor... Kuvetli is it? in the Fourth Dynasty the process of embalming and mummification...

—I beg you to excuse me for a moment... Valentine watched him approach, the cigarette poised at his mouth, where he pressed his upper lip with a fingertip.

—What is the trouble? what is happening?

—Nothing, Valentine answered in the same low tone.

—But there is something, you are very upset. How did you injure yourself?

—An absurd accident...

—But you must tell me what all this is, there is something very wrong here tonight...

—There is nothing wrong with anything but... with anything that concerns you, Valentine answered quickly.

—Ah, but you cannot...

—I can do anything I wish, Valentine said heatedly, turning his back on the room.

—I am most concerned to see you lose... to see you so disturbed, said the other, backed against the wall there. —It is never a good thing.

—I've lost control of nothing.

—And you expect some trouble?

—Nothing that... with which I am not familiar.

—Are you armed?

—Armed? Good heavens, do you expect someone to... attempt my life?

—Ah, but not so loudly...

Valentine backed a step from him. He looked the man up and down. —What the devil is all this...? Do you think you're here to... keep a watch on me? All this, I assure you, he went on, —I assure you it has nothing to do with any but personal concerns, do you understand me? And that man over there... he started to turn, nodding over his shoulder at Brown's heavy back. Then he suddenly closed in again. —And you, are you armed? he demanded. He had only a smile in return, a smile which did not spread beyond the lips, nothing else moved from the point of the beard to the sharp black eyes. —Give it to me, Valentine said.

—But if, as you say, this is all no more than a personal affair...

—Give it to me, I say.

—But in matters of this sort, your authority does not extend...

—Damn you! hand it over, and stop...The vein stood out, pounding in Basil Valentine's temple. —My authority extends where I take it, he said, opening his dinner jacket and shielding the figure before him as the square weight of an automatic pistol passed between them. —And now...

—Ah yes of course, I have read the book, a charmingly cynical thing of its kind. It is written with such...freshness...He stroked his beard with one finger, as Basil Valentine composed himself quickly, buttoning his dinner jacket and stepping back to allow the intrusion of a man whom neither of them appeared to know, —such naïveté, that one may imagine the author himself quite innocent of comprehending the full meaning of the deceit implicit in the scandalous behavior which he recommends, in order to win friends and, as it follows, influence people. Did you not have this feeling, Mister...Mister...?

Valentine had retired a step, and then another, about to turn. But he said, —Valentine. And now...

—Of course...He had not taken his sharp eyes from Valentine's face but for an instant. —Of course I have implicit faith in your judgment, in matters of this sort.

—Thank you, Valentine said, bowing quickly from the waist and excusing himself, —I must see our host for a moment.

—Of course...

—It proves no more than that the ends justify the means, and that eventually connivance is necessary to the accomplishment of good, said the intruder, carrying on with some perspicacity what he believed to be a conversation. —I believe that we can call its success in a society supposedly based in reason, as logical an outcome as the pragmatic approach of modern American psychoanalysis, he went on, though the man to whom he was now talking had favored him with the briefest scrutiny, and stood now looking over his shoulder toward the center of the room, where Basil Valentine collided with Fuller, who was retreating backwards with a loaded tray.

—You idiot! Idiot!

—Oh yes sar, yes sar...

—Here, what do you mean calling Fuller an idiot?

—Oh Mister Brown sar, Mister Valentine sar...

And if Basil Valentine was surprised, Fuller was astonished; if Valentine was discountenanced, Fuller was thoroughly alarmed at this guttural defense from the last source either of them might ever have expected.

Recktall Brown stood with his hands flattened across his belly one upon the other, the diamonds hidden beneath the thick joint of a finger. And as Valentine's eyes turned to the pools floating rash defiance in those thick lenses, Fuller made good his escape.

On the shifting surfaces of voices, rising, hesitating, and breaking, rolling deeply and fading away, moving in even swells, shattering in conflict, figures moved around them, as Recktall Brown took out a cigar with one hand, found the penknife with the other, and stood there, waiting.

—Whatever this game of yours is, it's gone far enough, Valentine got out finally.

Recktall Brown just looked at him. He began to trim the end of the cigar. Finally he said, —It's my party.

—But you can't...you can't...

—I can't what. Brown did not raise his eyes from what he was doing.

—Good God...

Brown raised his eyes at that, to stare at the face before him. He looked very tired: that was the only way to explain the expression on his face which he lowered quickly, as though his features, so familiar in the daylight of triumph, or wrath, or satisfaction, might betray him. He finished trimming the cigar, and folded the penknife closed in his hand. —What did you do that for? he asked quietly, as he raised his face, and with it the cigar, —about the money in the account? Like you just told me in the back room...the money I'd already paid him like he earned it. With the last word, he bit the cigar.

—What do you think I did it for?! Valentine stared. —And what are you suddenly so...My God, what's come over you?

—What did you do it for?

—To slow him down a little, to make him think twice before he went on with this...idea of his...But you...you...

—And he's trying it anyways. Recktall Brown turned away. Valentine got round in front of him, and broke out again,

—What's come over you? Why you...and that picture you just showed, in the back room, they know something's wrong. They won't say anything, they won't even say anything to each other but they know something's wrong. You couldn't have chosen a more stupid moment. What are you trying to do, see how far you can push them?

Recktall Brown lit the cigar, and then laughed in his face. —They know something's wrong all right. Who the hell told you to paint that face on it? They loved that, didn't they?

Then a man appeared before them and said, —Merry Christmas, Brown... holding out a glass across the table of the Seven Deadly Sins.

—What's this? Brown said, taking it.

—I don't know. Whatever you're serving.

—Listen, you go find Fuller, and tell him to bring out some of that good brandy, the ones with the blue ribbons on.

Whoever that was, was gone.

There he stood, staring, as his vision shrank from the gold and the wealth of colors and delicate forms of Hieronymus Bosch to the mass of his own hands. As Crémer and a few others came up behind him, he stood back and made a gesture with the spatula shape of his thumb. —That's a beautiful thing, he said.

—Sar?

—What does Ds videt mean?

—Sar? breaks in upon him again.

—God sees ... or is watching, Valentine murmurs with a sharp breath.

—Fuller?

—Sar a gentlemahn whom I do not recollect enter demandin me to open the bottles you keep so close with the blue ribbons upon them ...

—That's right, Fuller.

—Yes sar. Fuller stands before him, finally able to move his hands, which he takes one in the other, clasped before him, and with a wrenching motion turns his sagging figure away.

—Fuller!

—Sar? Fuller startles, with a flash of gold. Recktall Brown stands looking at him, the full of his lower lip moving as though behind it the tongue is searching for something on the face of the gum. And finally, —Stand up straight, Fuller, Brown said, and turned away.

M. Crémer was finishing a conversation as they approached. —Enfin, there is so little of fine art in the world, one should not question too closely ... ? As said Coulanges ... pictures are bullion.

Someone had turned the radio on; but there was still enough noise in the room to keep it unnoticed. Here and there, a few guests departed.

As they came up they were, in fact, again discussing the painting they had been shown privately a little earlier; discussing, that is, not the painting itself, but the face of the central figure, as though in that portion they had found a mutually satisfactory repository for peripheral doubts. —It is done with some taste, certainly, the R.A. mumbled.

—Taste! Crémer exclaimed, smiling at Brown and Basil Valentine to include them in the hind end, at any rate, of this conversation. —Taste is one thing, and the genius to create quite another. Eh? ... He glanced up, and stopped at the expression on Valentine's face which, whatever it might have been, was exaggerated by the swollen lip into one of extreme contempt.

And the white-haired man, who was not looking at Basil Valentine, took up agreeably, —Yes, when I was young, you know? I recall considering my work...as a sort of mmph...disciplined nostalgia for the things I umm... might have done. Eh? Yes. Yes...mmmph, he mumbled, looking down as Basil Valentine's expression turned upon him. Then he went on to break what he would later describe as an "awkward silence" with, —That face in there, don't you know...the face on the...ummph the figger in the van der Goes, the highlights round about the eyes, don't you know. Won't do, won't do at all.

—Won't do? Valentine demanded abruptly.

—Eh? Oh dear no, won't do at all. Zinc white, don't you know. Zinc white. I think you'll come upon that when you make an analysis of the pigments, don't you know.

—Zinc white?

—Oh dear, yes. An umm eighteenth-century color, don't you know.

Then (after what Crémer would later describe as un silence de mort) the older man bumbled on with, —Odd sort of fellow you had in here earlier... eh! Damned odd, eh? Bit of a lunatic, you might say, eh? Prancing about with mmph two suits of clothes on him, eh? I mean, you know? Rather...mmph. Ever seen the fellow before?

—Oh yes...Basil Valentine came in, his voice very level, and even and cutting. He offered a cigarette from a packet of Virginia. —Mad, of course, as you say. He drinks, you know...

—Oh yes, drinks, eh? Ummph...shouldn't be surprised.

—A morbid condition aggravated by drink, I suppose would be more to the point. He has all sorts of delusions about himself, Valentine went on, turning to Recktall Brown. —He's been quite a problem for some time, hasn't he.

—He wasn't drunk just now, when he was in here, Brown answered looking up at each of them.

—He wasn't eh? Oh dear, I shouldn't like to run on him drunk then, eh? Ho ho, hmmph...Oh dear no. Can't have that sort of thing.

—And if he comes back? Valentine's tone rang with a summons.

—If he comes back...Recktall Brown commenced, looking down before him.

—One has the police?...Crémer said with a shrug. —Après tout, chargé de défendre...

—Shouldn't hesitate a moment...mmph, calling them in. Might get about it right now. This sort of thing, don't you know. Can't have it, don't you know.

Basil Valentine murmured something, smiling with the slight distortion his lip compelled, and started to turn away. Recktall Brown swung on him and demanded, —Where are you going?

—If you can spare me for a moment, Basil Valentine rasped, —I thought I might put some ice on this... swelling. And he touched the lip with a fingertip and left them.

—My, he's a bit... mmph... rather touchy tonight. Eh? Mmhp...yes. We all are a bit... mmp... eh? I beg your pardon, miss. Eh?

—Is it true the British Museum has a toupee that George the Third had made for himself out of his mistresses'...

—I daresay... mmp! What was that, young woman? Ghood heavens! Ghood heavens!... He towered over Miss Stein for a moment and then got by her, though from the disparity in their presences and the haste he made in his escape, he might have stepped over her. —Ghood heavens... eh? he addressed Crémer's pinched back. —The damnedest... presumption. Mmmph... going upstairs are we, eh? Ummp. There's a pretty thing. German, I should think. Eh? Polychrome wood, fifteenth century or so. Saint John Baptist, eh? Ummp. Shame he's lost an arm here. Damn shame. He paused for a moment there on the landing, running a finger over the coarse-grained marrow of the break, and then followed the heels up the stairs before him muttering, —Eh?... The armor? good heavens, no one wants to look at armor...

Miss Stein returned to her companions to say, —Talk about how polite the English are supposed to be, he wouldn't even answer me. Just the same, I should think a thing like that would scratch. Wouldn't it? Wouldn't it?

There was a clanking sound from above, but no one turned to the balcony to see that the headpiece had been lifted from the suit of armor up there. No one, that is, except the sharply bearded sharp-eyed man at the other end of the room who, despite his attentive conversation, had been watching the activity aloft since it had begun.

The bearded young art critic was speaking in French, managing it with such urbanity, indeed, that his little friend (the one cheered on earlier as resembling an oeuf-dur-mayonnaise) told him later, with demure awe, that he had not been able to understand a word of it; no marvel of ignominy, really, for the harassed Lyonnais who was listening could not understand a word of it either, and attempted, at aspirate intervals, to swing things in his own direction with commentaries in a series of grotesque syllables which might, in Lyons, have passed for English by default.

This impressive bout drew the attention of someone who believed himself to be talking to an Egyptologist named Kuvetli, and (perhaps it was the fluttering of the plump hands over there, and the impassive mien before him) became so familiar as to draw a simile upon mimicry among the butterflies, citing, for his thesis, —The female of *Papilio cynorta*, in the Uganda...while over his shoulder the Egyptologist sought a face he could not locate. Basil Valentine had, all this time, been holding a cloth-covered ice cube against his upper lip, raising it now and then to look at the chipped tooth inside, and staring at his image in the mirror of the medicine cabinet.

Someone banged on the door, as someone had been doing at impatient intervals for some time, a guest apparently unable to make the stairs for he had directed them above with some irritation at the second assault, and now he cried out, —All right, damn you. He dropped the cold pack into the sink, saw the swelling gone down somewhat, peeled up the lip for another look at the tooth and then drew it down firmly, catching his own eyes in the glass. And since the intimacies of catoptric communion were by now as strange to him as any others (he was always prepared for, and satisfied with what he saw in the glass, in those numerous but brief encounters when he hunched toward it, washing his hands, his face an established proposition, his mind busied elsewhere with still mutable concerns), he stood now reflecting his face more absorbed than that most dubious mirror-gazer of our acquaintance; and it took another attack on the door to sunder Basil Valentine from this conspiracy of chin and eyes, the straight nose and high bones which were his face. He turned, adjusting himself behind, under the ventless jacket, and before at the weighted waist, and came out, without a look in either direction until he'd arrived among people.

He took some brandy immediately, and managed to avoid a conversation on whether the names of soft drinks spelled across the sky were desecrations of the House of God; a man who said, —In dthis kenntre no ouonne toks ovv dthe ouor becose ovv krissmess?...and a young woman who said something about King George III which he hoped, vaguely, he had not understood aright, as he looked anxiously over the room.

—Et ce vieux moricaud...où se cache-t-il?...

—Because Mister Schmuck wants to have one made just like George the Third...

Valentine stopped beside a dark man who barely reached his shoulder, and before he'd noted the peaked sharkskin suit or the glazed eyes asked, —Where's Brown? Have you seen Mister Brown?

—I fear you too are at the wrong party? Perhaps...

Basil Valentine moved quickly. He touched another elbow, —Have you seen Brown? Mister Brown?...

—Men den himmelske rustning...hey?

Then Valentine stopped short, staring more than half the length of the room at a stout fluttering figure, plucking the point of a black beard with one hand, disposing the other in riotous gestures on the air, and for all his apparent weight, moving with admirable agility upon his toes. —Good God! Good God no!

—Say, old man, where you been hiding, eh?... Missing all the fun, what?

—What?

—Jolly old rascal, isn't he! sweating up there like a... mmp. Just came down for a bit more of this cognac, eh? Good heavens yes, have to keep up, don't you know.

—Brown's... up there?

Some of the guests were leaving, with over-shoulder looks of last-minute anticipation, —We'd hate to *miss* anything... Some had left. Some appeared rooted; and even those that continued to move did so with a buoyant vagueness, sustained on the flood of heat filling that vast room like a natural element. Thus Basil Valentine's eyes, like those in the tapestry vacant, remained attached to the capering figure with the black beard beyond simply because it moved with such mimetic extravagance: a spell which he might break in an instant, as he well knew, by summoning his gaze to the right, near the Christmas tree, where a conversation on Cheops' prophecies, or the improbability of a Fourth Dynasty mummy (—There were none, properly speaking, until the Eighteenth...) was most certainly taking place. So much for his unbroken gaze; for now, in like manner, he was aware of sounds from the balcony above, scraping sounds, and the slight shocks of metal against metal, an affliction momentarily worse to whose relief the habit of intervention threatened to betray him, but he stood firm, giving the R.A.'s voice the same glazed attention his eyes gave the cavorting beard beyond, waiting, glamorized, for the shock which would break the spell. Even then, lapsing voices allowed the radio to penetrate with what sounded like dissonant caterwauling. (The music was Ravel, *L'Enfant et les Sortilèges*.)

—Is he up there, you say. Good heavens yes, with all his... mmmp. You'd think he wanted to climb into the thing, like that Don mmpht the Spanish fellow don't you know. Nice enough thing of its kind, I spose, but I mmp... never been very partial to armor meself. And good heavens, eh? Hardly the sort of thing to be seen running about in these days, eh? atom bombs and all that sort of thing popping off everywhere, eh? Not much protection, I shouldn't wonder, mmpht... like being roasted alive in a... I don't know what, eh? I say, hev you gut any more of thet Virginia about you? Smoking my brand, don't you know.

Basil Valentine's hand alerted, and he took out the packet of cigarettes as he continued to stare down the room.

—Lot of odd ducks kicking about this evening, eh? Oh yes, yes, thnks vry much.

—The armor? Basil Valentine said in a low tone, listening.

—Eh? Oh yes, rather a nice suit of its kind, I daresay, Italian, round about the fifteenth century looked like to me. Odd little fellows, the Italians, eh? I mean to say, small stature, don't you know, nothing Saxon about them at all, small-boned little fellows, fine Italian hand and all that sort of thing. Some of the more … mmmp less decorous guests up there egging him on. A regular carnival, don't you know. Good heavens, I daresay they'd hev a devil of a time getting him into it, eh? He's hardly a mmpt Renaissance figger, eh? The R.A. paused to light his cigarette, and then as though bound from having accepted it to the donor, who showed no inclination to move, he continued. —Not quite the … son métier, as that obnoxious little Frenchman says, eh? But then the French, eh? Good heavens. The French, don't you know. Can't do a thing with them. I mean to say, there's nothing I'd want to do with them, except mmmp … never mind, eh? Hardly go about doing that sort of thing. Good heavens, no. Not these days. He paused again, and made a clucking sound with his lips before he raised his glass there. From above came a dull thumping sound, the heels of hands on metal, forcing it down, pounding among strictures of laughter, and Basil Valentine raised his fingertips to the vein in his temple.

—Why good heavens, you'd hardly get the mmph what-do-you-call-ems down over his shoulders, the pauldrons I mean to say, eh? Made for some skinny little Italian … mmpht horse-soldier, don't you know. All bones, those little fellows, bones and sinews, you might say, eh? I daresay that's why it's such a delicate piece of craftsmanship, don't you know … all of a piece, as Dryden puts it somewhere. Good heavens yes … but not this suit, not this suit. A shame, too, lovely thing like that, to be mmmh … it's not my field, of course, so I've no right to interfere with my comments, eh? But good heavens, the feet, don't you know, a bit incongruous, having German feet wouldn't you say? I mean to say, that rather sort of delicate Italian line all the way down, and it ends up in a pair of German feet. Bear-paw type, don't you know, great wide clumsy German sort of things. Not that I'm carrying any ax to grind with the Germans, good heavens no. Much healthier heving a neighbor you can break out and hev a bit of a war with now and then, eh? Settle your differences right out in the open, eh? Instead of putting up with the mmpht absurd posturing of the French year after year, eh? What's the matter? …

Basil Valentine had startled suddenly, as the cigarette between his fingers burned down to meet the skin. He looked round at his interlocutor, as though fully aware of him there for the first time.

—Eh? You all right? I was just about to say...what the devil do you spose they're doing up there?...The sounds of metal on metal had become more noticeable, an irregular and subdued clatter; still Basil Valentine did not move to go. —Eh? You don't think that...good heavens no, why they couldn't even get the mmph what-do-you-call-ems over his calves, over his ankles, don't you know...the greaves I mean to say. Not my field, not my field at all. Though I did write a paper once, some occasion, what the devil was it...when I was studying, I suppose, eh? Some time ago, don't you know, though one doesn't just stop being a scholar, eh? like putting off Eton collars, eh? Good heavens no. Now that paper, what the devil was it...mmmpht. Oh yes yes yes...I was younger of course, it may sound a bit naive now, don't you know, but it was a rather original bit of thinking, I was told so at the time, at any rate, rather fresh approach, don't you know...but damn me if I can remember what it was...

And now, though very few faces turned to one side or the other, or up, to show they had noticed it, came the distraction of an even and metallic tread from above, and Basil Valentine turned his head slowly left, though he did not raise his face.

—Pfooo, the R.A. went over his glass, —yes, yes, here it is. The devil, wearing false calves, do you recall? Mephistopheles, don't you know, in mffft that ponderous thing by Goethe. Good heavens yes, wearing false calves, don't you know, to cover his cloven feet and his mphhht calves, yes. Well my thesis, don't you see, was that these things weren't simply a disguise, to fool people and all that sort of thing, but that some sort of mffft...aesthetic need you might say, some sort of nostalgia for beauty, don't you see, he being a fallen angel and all that sort of thing, rather...unpleasantly different in his mphhht appearance from mphhht...The white-haired gentleman stopped, looking at Basil Valentine square for the first time and, apparently for the first time, realizing that Valentine was not listening to a word he said. —Mphhht...a long time ago all that, eh? There, that's rather a nasty place you've got on your lip, eh? Going up like a balloon, eh? Good heavens...

Then, as Basil Valentine raised his hand to touch the broken swelling, his arm was pulled down.

—Ghood heavens! Ghood heavens! Ghood heavens!...D'you see? Here's your lunatic come back again. Eh? Do you see him there by the foot of the stairs?...looks like he's ready to...good heaven knows what...go up in flames, eh? Won't do, won't do at all...can't hev this sort of thing, invading a private gathering, eh? A man's home is his mphht what-d'you-call-it, don't you know, eh? Popping in here from nowhere in that sort of a get-up, good heavens no, no reason at all to run around in two suits of clothing, none that

I recall at this moment at any rate, don't you mpphhht ... I say, my dear fellow do be a bit more careful, you're spilling your drink all over me ...

The member of the Royal Academy stepped back, brushing cognac from his sleeve, and spilling what was in his own glass as he did so; and his immediate vicinity quieted somewhat, there under the balcony and round the foot of the stairs, as he stopped speaking. Then a number of people stopped talking, others to talk more loudly, some to turn their attention, and some their backs, on this diverting visitor who stood looking feverishly round, holding up a handful of charred wood, whispering, —Where is he? ... where is he? ...

Basil Valentine had stepped back. His finger remained at his lip, and he pressed it; suddenly aware of acute pain there, he pressed harder, and blood reached his tongue.

—Brown!

That end of the room silenced. Several people stepped away from the foot of the stairs, and the figure standing there, looking among them. Some of them looked up, to the shuffling sound of metal on metal. He saw them looking there, and turned himself; but there was nothing to see but the bend of the stairs, and the polychromed wood figure exposing the coarse-grained scar of the arm amputated in benediction.

Out in the room, voices continued. Flames moved unhurriedly up over a black wild cherry log in the fireplace. Muffled caterwauling came from the radio.

—Brown!

The panoplied figure reached the landing in one fall, taking a long time, so it seemed afterward to those who saw it happen; and making a good deal less of noise than they might have expected, hitting head-on at the turn, attacked by shadows leaping to meet it, withdrawing as it dropped away from the wall and hung, for a moment when the whole room silenced and all the eyes were brought into one equation, the quick eyes stilled, and the still eyes of the wart hog, the face in the youthful portrait, the blind eyes of Valerian stretched on his rack and the all-seeing eyes of the pale underclothed figure in the middle of the low table, those and the eyes in the tapestry, turned in the other direction, alerted.

—There, of course, I disagree with Dante, came on a voice from the far end, restoring the unconscious balance, rescuing what was alive from what was not; and enough voices to deliver one another from the isolation of separate identity took up and spread in a slow wave toward the broken weight poised on the edge of the landing, whose clinging shadows leaped away as it moved, and repeated their concerted attacks as it fell from one step to another, stifling it in their last embrace at the bottom.

—Good heavens!... they've knocked the thing down the stairs, d'you see? Heavier than one might have thought, eh? The white-haired gentleman approached. —Good heavens, I... daresay... there's someone in it.

Behind him, Basil Valentine crossed himself quickly with the third finger of his right hand; then touched the bend of his forefinger to his lips as he approached.

Clattering down the stairs in his grotesque shoes, which looked like they'd been built especially for participation in some sport, possibly one on snow, or in marshland, or some such sodden surface, that grimpen, perhaps, where is no secure foothold, came M. Crémer, to plant those remarkably equipped feet among the Aubusson roses, and hold forth the broad-bowed thick-lensed glasses which his host had left behind. He was talking at a great rate, and in his own tongue, so no one stopped, him, and no one paid him any attention.

Behind him, a tall unexaggerated man stood on the step holding a damp double-breasted suit coat; and there were others, crowding between this one and the polychrome amputee, as wide-open eyed, and as silent, a reticent concord which might have been mistaken for reverence but for the immoderate curiosity which had shone in the eyes of Saint John Baptist ever since he had first been put out in the weather some centuries before.

Then the tall woman reached up to catch a naked earlobe, and cry, —Oh!... I've lost my baby's breath... a line which did attract some attention.

Resounding in the regions beyond the staircase, the crash had straightened Fuller up on his kitchen stool forthwith. It was a minute before he could get out, for the dog wanted to get out too. It commenced to trot up and down the room, nervously sensing something amiss with that intuition which Fuller knew all too well, and seeing it active now, became the more alarmed. As the dog scratched at the door leading to the hall and the great room, Fuller slipped out another, up the kitchen stairs to the second-floor halls, round to the balcony and out slowly to the front stairs, where he paused at the newel and looked back, abruptly aware of a vacancy. Then his eye caught the cigar, half-smoked and gone out but not before it had burned a long scar on the rosewood chest. He picked it up, licked his thumb and rubbed the burnt place but it did no good: and at that moment, from the corner of his eye he realized what was missing at the end of the balcony, and carrying the half-smoked cigar he got to the stairs and almost fell in his hurry to get down them.

—Les pieds, voyez vous, les pieds de cette armure, il a trébuché vous savez... M. Crémer harangued his audience, so effectively that it grew moment by moment, as he waved the broad-bowed glasses in the air, and pointed with his other hand to the footpieces of the armor, —Et sans les lunettes alors...

Les pieds? les pieds, voyez vous? des Boches, pas vrai? Voyez vous quelle gaucherie allemande...

—Good heavens, said the R.A. somewhere in the shadows there under the balcony, —all well and good he tripped over his feet because they were German, don't you know, but how did he get into the damned thing to begin with? eh? eh? he demanded of no one.

Of all the figures gathered there beneath him, Fuller knew only two, meeting now over the headpiece where Basil Valentine knelt on one side to put forth a hand and withdraw it as quick, for the throat was covered with blood running from a corner of the mouth, though that was all of the face that could be seen, the throat, and the heavy chin, and a sagging corner of the small mouth. What had happened was, that in the fall one of the hooks which held the beaver in place had come undone; perhaps it was not fastened properly at the outset, or possibly it had not been fastened at all. And so the beaver of the helmet was knocked askew, and the visor above jammed even more tightly closed, as the figure still kneeling there when Valentine withdrew found out, trying desperately all of a sudden to get the thing open.

Fuller stared at Basil Valentine, down on one knee, the hand he'd pulled back from the unbroken throat resting now on the taces, those plates meant to afford a loose protection round the thighs where they clung now full and rigidly distended. The breastplate and the backplate had not been drawn together, though they were as tight as they could be, their gaps bulging with mounds of white shirting and a split side of the blue vest from which somehow the penknife had escaped, and lay there on the floor at Valentine's foot. And one of the greaves had come half off too, and the broad footpiece with it, exposing a small foot splayed in a silk sock, where the wrinkled white line of the clock on the black silk ridiculed the thickness of the ankle it covered, and it was there that Basil Valentine thrust two fingertips, waited a moment, shifted them and thrust them harder, behind the tendon there, waited again and withdrew them to figure a cross quickly at his chest as he stood away, taking a step back which Fuller repeated on the landing above; though both of them now were watching the figure still kneeling at the head, and both of them were in retreat, Fuller clutching the half-smoked cigar, up the stairs, down the hall, and Valentine stepping backward, slowly at first, when he started to speak. Waving the charred fragments before him, he took a step over the head and stood above it.

—Wait! Wait! he cried. —Wait!

The sound of this voice again, and the sight of him, worked on them immediately. The pool around him emptied, and no sooner did it flood from the rest of the room than it emptied again, the fraud of what had seethed for so long there as undersea discovered as the stopper of the tank was pulled and they poured out in a continuous stream, while he stood over the broken hulk shouting them on, —Wait! Listen! Wait!

Basil Valentine still clung in the shadows, watching him.

—Like me to stick around for a bit, old man? Anything I can mphht do d'you spose, eh? Before the mmmp who-do-you-call-ems come, eh? The R.A. stood at his elbow.

M. Crémer, on the other hand, was suddenly in a great hurry, but found time to say, —Il faut que je parte, je viens de me rappeler d'une . . . heh heh assignation vous savez, mais le Memlinc, voyez vous, le Memlinc, je veux l'acheter vous savez . . .

—Blasted little . . . mphht. Good heavens, eh? Probably willing to go as high as two and six at that . . .

—A n'importe quel prix, vous savez . . . Crémer cast back, being swept away now.

—Good heavens! the R.A. said, still at Valentine's elbow, —begins to sound like he might go to three shillings. I say, if there's nothing more I can do here but confuse things, don't you know, I mphht get on my way I spose . . . You seem to be in pretty close touch with this . . . mphht our host laid out here, eh? Ring me up tomorrow, let me know what hospital they stick him in, eh? There's a good fellow. Like to send along some flowers, don't you know. And that mppht van der Goes canvas in there . . . mphht like to mpht come to some terms, eh? Yes, well ghood night, eh? Ghood night . . . goo night, goo night, goo night . . .

A number of people, in fact, suddenly recalled other engagements and hurried off to fill them. Though the tall woman, as she described it to her husband next morning, simply led him off "as meek as Moses"; the bearded young art reviewer paddled away on a crest of enchantment, already repeating the story to people who had not been here to enjoy it, squeezing the hot little hand folded deep in his own; and the sharkskinned Argentine, his black hair high in a dorsal fin cutting the spray around him, fled murmuring —I was not warned about this sort of thing in New York . . . turning his glassy eyes for a last look at the bold spectacle on the floor, thankful, at least, that he was not, like M. Crémer, being hindered from leaving by the figure looming over it.

—Attention? eh? qu'est-ce que tu veux, alors! va donc . . . laisse moi passer . . .

—Yes, yes, yes . . . Crémer, yes. Yes, damn you. De l'argent, vous savez, damn you, il faut toujours en avoir sur soi . . .

—Eh bien, tu es fou, eh?

—Now listen, listen . . . the tone changed abruptly, —you've got to listen to me . . .

As the grip relaxed, Crémer wrenched away, brushing his neatly creased sleeve as he made for the door. There was some confusion at the large closet there, turned for this evening into a cloakroom; but M. Crémer emerged in short order wearing a voluminous camel's hair coat, enough sizes too big for him so that he considered it a perfect fit, and a Hollywood label inside, as he discovered a block or so away.

While here and there, inside the great room, eyes vaguely approaching the door were still caught by the eyes of the youthful portrait hung there, and turned away with such unconscious abruptness that they usually fled back to the broken thing on the floor for confirmation, and as quick there to avoid the half-face found refuge in the gauntleted hand flung out, its delicate lines palm up and open, and looked back to the portrait for denial.

The squat procession passed by, the third-in-line murmuring with the subdued reverence of a tourist speaking of something quite other than the hideous sarcophagus which he pretends to his guide he's come three thousand miles to see, —Tchikovsky you can almost take straight, but what can you do with Bach?... the second-in-line considering lighting, camera-angles, and the over-all general effect of the heavy figure in perfect grace despite its distension hurled down among roses, serving not contradiction but complement for the lighter one mounting over it, grown out of it and rising continuously in the tension of growth... distinct close-up possibilities there, the thin empty hand in a shape of its own ascending in wild emergency and the eyes the same... while their leader himself confirmed, —We oughda get ouda here... bad publicidy... And they advanced, suddenly remarkable for the fact that they all appeared a good half-head shorter than everyone else, except for the last of them, who, with a forehead, might have stood a half-head taller. They found the cloakroom and, considering their numbers, came out rather badly.

The R.A., who had resolutely sought the exit down near the Christmas tree for reasons buried near three-quarters of a century in his, or Sir Walter Scott's past (he had trouble distinguishing them), came forth over the empty field.

—Here now, don't you know!

—No listen, listen... you've got to listen to me, you've got to... to... wait... wait...

—Ghood heavens, my dear boy, I don't hev to wait for ennathing... here here now, turn loose, eh? You can't mphhht don't you know, eh? What the devil do you think I am, a mphhht...?

—No wait, if you'll listen, if you'll... listen to me.

—Here now, there's a good fellow, turn loose, eh? And mphht stop waving thet dirty hendful of mphhht whatever-it-is in my face, don't you know...

—Listen…Wait…

—Here now, my dear boy…The R.A. turned himself loose, but stood there a moment longer, —Nice hot bath, eh? Nice hot bath and a good night's sleep, eh? Thet'll straighten you up, eh? Ghood heavens yes, don't you know…And he got off quite nimbly, and spent hardly a moment in the cloakroom, for his threadbare tweed coat was one of the few garments left, and he would never have considered making off with the trenchcoat which hung beside it. So he was quite quickly out on the street, in a swank neighborhood, he noticed, for there was nothing in the refuse bins but empty bottles, and the elegantly long white boxes of florists.

The last stare Basil Valentine had matched, as he stepped back, one step, and another, startled him only because he had for so long been staring down the room at its counterpart the yellowed mimosa, and here his arm was taken in a tight hold, and —Come away, this is not a good place to stay now.

Valentine pulled away. —You…go on, eh? Go on. I'll be in touch with you tomorrow.

—But you…are too nervous now, you are not well, this is not a good time to leave you…alone?

—Alone? Go on. You go on, will you?…After a pause, in which Basil Valentine's face rehearsed every muscle the other restrained, he said, —What do you know about this? What do you know about…me?…

—Perhaps as much as you know about me. Yes. And the gun, now. You have no reason for it?

—Yes, I…leave it with me, I…I'll be in touch with you in the morning. Basil Valentine turned away, into the dark hall, and into the bathroom, where he locked the door.

He stood still on the tile floor, and he heard Fuller on the kitchen stairs. Then he went to the mirror, and stared at what he saw there. The swollen lip twitched, and he drew it into a smile. Then he raised a finger and pressed it, and looked into the eyes for as long as he could, and then to the soft shine of the gold signet ring. The weight at his waist was heavy as he thought what it was, and took the gun out and laid it on a hamper. Then he took off his jacket, and with a good deal of unfastening of buttons and buckles, and stretching of elastic, undid himself, and sat to a weak hypospadial stream. He stood, and saw bubbles on the surface he'd discolored, bubbles drawing into the features of a face. He flushed it, and swung on the mirror again, doing himself up (and that was the detail, the totally irrelevant detail, the floating face, which he remembered long afterward).

From the closed kitchen came the whine of the dog as Valentine emerged; and from the great living room, broken strains of music, as he approached, and stopped in shadow, watching, and licking his lip, and, as the voice came, listening.

—Yes, your daughters all were fair, and . . . your daughters all were fair, but the youngest . . . here, I didn't know you had a radio here? music here?

Basil Valentine first looked to the foot of the stairs, there saw nothing but the still caparisoned bulk. Then he saw the figure at the far wall, as still as everything else in the room, and his back turned on it, tuning the radio, stopping methodically along the stream that poured from it, bursts of brackish laughter, shreds of music, the human voice in aggressive counterfeit, lowered in counsel, raised in song, sincere in extolling absurdities, absurd parading devotion up and down the scale: a vapid tenor, widely known and loved, wound *Silent Night* round his throat, and strangled on it, into the brackish laughter again, and then from the north Beethoven's *Missa Solemnis* emerged, commenced to fill the place, and was gone into jazz, *When the Saints Go Marching In*. He left it at that, turned his back on it and walked vaguely across the room, empty-handed now. —You and I . . . he said approaching the foot of the stairs, —You and I . . . you were so damned familiar . . .

There, he went down on one knee, and tried to open the visor again but gave that up after a moment, and raised his hand to look at the blood he'd got on it. Then he looked back at the figure before him, and said quietly, breathing sharp in what sounded like a laugh, —Il sangue? ti soffoca il sangue? O yes, ecco un artista . . . Good God . . . Then he looked the figure up and down, and went off balance toward the feet, where he seized the exposed ankle and worked his fingers there seeking a pulse. —Yes, there's where they nailed the wren, there's where they nailed up . . . He pulled himself back to his knees again, staring suddenly feverishly at the chin and throat, his weight resting in a hand on the breastplate, where he turned his eyes and pushed it with the heel of his hand and all the weight he could give it. It sank a little, and came up again, and he rested there until his eyes caught the penknife on the rug across, and he reached over to pick that up and open it as he stood. —Yes . . . what chance had you, when hierophants conspired? . . . Then he walked away. —Good God, he said, wandering off toward the pulpit bar opening and closing the penknife blade in his hands, and the music continued, —I willingly fastened a tail to my back, and drank what you gave me, but damn it, there . . . He stopped and poured brandy into a glass, and with it turned and looked around the room. Then he put the glass down again without raising it to his mouth and took three steps, gone for a minute beyond the pulpit bar and out of sight for Basil Valentine who stood where he had stopped, tingling the tip of his tongue on the broken tooth and aware of a warm dampness filling the crotch of his trousers. A full minute of this, and Valentine prepared to step out, but put a foot back instead of forward as the figure emerged again, tucking something in an inside pocket, and, it sounded like whistling a broken delayed alto to the music, which he broke off with, —Oh yes, "I'll scratch you a bit till you see awry... But all that you see will seem fine and brave..."

Then he came rushing across the carpet toward the thing on the floor there crying, —Get up! Get up! When he reached it he stood over it, the penknife closed and gone inside one hand with the other closed round it, quivering, like his voice now, —Good God, you've... left me in midair, it's as though the... bottom has dropped out of time itself. Then he went to his knees and tore frantically at the visor trying to raise it. Finally he stopped, looking exhausted, staring down, and his hand still on the projecting chin. —What now?... good God, what now? You and I... you and I, you... were so damned familiar. He stared a moment longer, and then as he whispered —What a luxury you were!... and flung his face down bringing both hands in round the headpiece, Basil Valentine stepped forth and reached him very quickly. He lay there shaking.

—Here now... you know, Valentine said standing over him, surprised at the tremor in his own voice, and even more at the calm expression of the face raised to him. So they were silent, until Basil Valentine shifted half a step back and said, —You might... go in and wash, you know. You got... blood all over one side of your face just then... you know. At that Valentine stopped, unable to keep the tip of his tongue from the broken tooth, and more aware than he was of this face before him of the face he had left in the mirror minutes before as that image's smile returned, and he felt it distorting the lips in betrayal of the emotion he did not feel, as he summoned his voice and said, —My dear fellow... you're weeping, aren't you.

Still nothing moved.

—Come along now, my dear fellow, straighten up. It's a shock, but...

—Who are you?...

Basil Valentine stepped forward again, almost kicked the headpiece. —Now listen to me, he said firm for the first time, —there's been enough of all this... business. He sounded impatient. —Don't you think it's time to... wash up, and get into some fresh clothes, get a fresh start? Because all this... all this... Valentine raised his foot, and jarred the headpiece with his toe, at which the other stood up quickly and turned away, leaving the penknife dropped on the carpet where he'd knelt.

—After all, now, Valentine said to his back, —there will be some changes, won't there, without... now that there are just the two of us.

—I've got a headache, a... I've got a rotten headache. He stopped in the middle of the room, and Valentine came up on him where he stood pressing his forehead in his hands.

—I should think you might, you know. Basil Valentine put a hand gently on his shoulder, but he drew away quickly. Valentine stepped back. —And I suppose we should...call the police, you know, he said, licking his lip.

—They'll probably be here any minute.

—How do you mean?

—Where do you think I've been all this time? Good God, what do you think kept me from getting right back here before this...this...He shook a hand out at the scene behind them. —After I'd broken your door down, and was coming out...

—You broke my door down?

—Where the...what do you think those...pieces of...dirty...burnt wood, that...what do you think that is? I knew what it was, when I got in and saw the...saw something smoking in your grate, I knew what it was, I knew what you'd done, damn you...I knew what you'd done.

—Now listen to me, what is all this? The police are in my flat?

—I don't know, I don't know, I don't know where the police are. I know that two of them were taking me somewhere afterwards and I got away from them...and came here. How should I know where the police are? Why should I...care where the police are.

Basil Valentine had gone pale in the face; and now he touched his lower lip, tapped it with a fingertip. Then he looked up and said calmly, —There was really no reason for you to do a thing like that, you know. I...I've been trying to get hold of you since...yesterday morning, when you left me in the park there so...precipitously.

—You have! Then who did you think it was ringing your bell an hour or two ago?

—I've been out...for some time, Basil Valentine answered. —I've even been down to Horatio Street, you know, looking for you.

—You have! And what did you find there?

—No one at home, my dear fellow, obviously.

—No one at home! Yes, that's good...No one at home! Do you know what happened down there? Do you know what had happened when I went back down yesterday? It had burned. The whole place had burned, the whole building. It must have been that...I left some things burning there, in that fireplace, and there was oil and everything spilled everywhere, and something must have...the oil must have...Good God I don't know, but it's gone.

Basil Valentine had backed to the pulpit bar, where he leaned watching.

—That painting you were working on too, eh? he said after a moment. —The last one, the one I liked as it was, eh?

—What? The face turned to him in confusion from the abstract emptiness it had fallen into, staring down at the carpet.

—That *Stabat Mater*?

—What, she?

—Burned too?

—Good God! Good God! She wasn't ... she ...

—Here, my dear fellow, Basil Valentine said coming at him again. —Get hold of yourself, get hold of yourself. This time he did take both shoulders in his hands, to say, —We're both upset, there's no sense in all this now, and it's no time to try to talk rationally about it. If the place is burned, it's burned, and anything in it ...

—Oh yes, and the griffin's egg, that was there! Oh, that griffin's egg, damn it. That's why I went down there, to get it so I could ... Then he stopped and pulled from Valentine's hands again. —This last picture, he said, —the van der Goes, where is it?

—My dear fellow ...

—Where is it?

—Come back here ... listen ...

—Oh yes, it's in his privy chamber, isn't it. That's where he kept things like that, isn't it? Yes, in the genizah?

—Come here, listen ... And at that moment Basil Valentine's eye caught the painting behind him, just beyond the pulpit bar. —What's this! What's happened here?

—That ...

—Here, stop that laughter ... this, did you do this? Valentine stood running a finger over the hole, where the figure of the Emperor Valerian stretched on his rack had been cut neatly out.

—I? Good God no. Crémer, Monsieur Crémer, vous savez ...

—Stop that damned laughter ...

—Ah oui, qu'il voulait un souvenir, vous savez, un tout petit souvenir de sa vieille connaissance du monde des truqueurs ...

Valentine didn't answer, staring at the damage under his hand. He ran his finger along the edge where it was cut, as his tongue ran over his broken tooth, though he stopped that as he turned, to catch his lower lip under the broken place.

—Bleu de Prusse, alors, ça ne fait rien vous savez, le ciel en bleu de Prusse, retouché simplement vous savez ... the work of some incompetent restorer, un restaurateur vous savez ...

—Come here! Yes, and now you want to damage that ... van der Goes the same way ... come here!

—For the same reason, vous savez ...

—Come here! But Basil Valentine followed him to the panel door; and stood behind him as he stared at the painting hung inside.

—That face, that ... Good God, that face, where did it come from?

—The face? Valentine watched him, with hardly a look at the painting, —and ... what do you think of it? ...

—Think of it! Think of it? Good God, I ... I can't think of it, look at it, it's ...

—You don't care for it, eh? Valentine withdrew a step, and back outside the door. —You think it's bad, eh?

—Bad? No. No, it's not bad, it's funny. It's funny, do you know what I mean? he demanded turning on Basil Valentine. —It's funny, it's ... vulgar, he said holding a hand up between them.

—But you ... stop, my dear fellow, stop that laughing and come out.

—That's why it's funny, because it's vulgar, do you see?

—Damn it, come out of there.

He came out, and followed Basil Valentine across the room laughing. —Oh, and they ... said I dishonored death! Did you see that face? Then he stopped. —Where did it come from?

—My dear fellow ...

—No, tell me, who painted that face, tell me.

Basil Valentine stood taking a cigarette out, which he hung under the swollen lip. —Your benefactor there did it, he said, and motioned away.

—*He* did it? *He?*

—What do you think all this ... foolishness about climbing into a suit of armor was, this ...

—Oh no! No! No! The same thing, yes, oh yes, the same thing he wanted, but the only way he knew, but *you ... you* ...

Basil Valentine tasted blood. The cigarette paper had torn his lip again. He stood backed against the pulpit. But he could not turn away as he had in the lion house: for these were the same eyes on him, the same movements the lioness made, approaching, the head hung, one foot crossed over the other in a bound, and the eyes again on him in another approach, and no bars between them. The broken smile on Valentine's face yielded its weak incipience as he tried to draw his lips tight against a feeble sound that escaped them, initiating defense, or some proposal. Then he straightened up, a step from the pulpit. The threatening shadows had stilled, the figure retreated across the room to stand over the low table in the dull glow of the fireplace. —And you were the boy! Valentine said in a tone gone almost childish with recrimination. —The boy in your story? whose father owned the original? The boy who copied it, and stole the original, and sold it, for "almost nothing" to . . . him.

—To him! How did I know, I didn't know who bought it, I just sold it. The original! I thought . . . do you know what it was like, coming in here years later with him, and seeing it here? Waiting, seeing it here waiting for me? waiting to burn this brand of final commitment, as though, all those years, as though it was what I thought, instead of . . . a child could tell, even in this light . . .

—Perhaps you were right all the time, Valentine said quietly, coming closer.

—But this is a copy!

—Of course it is. When the old count sold his collection in secret, this was one of the copies he had made.

—And, the original? all this time . . . ?

—All this time, the original has been right where this one is now. Basil Valentine stood very near him by the table. —Of course it was the original here for so long, the one you sold him. And this, I picked this one up in Rome myself scarcely a year ago. Do you recall when we first met? right here, across the table? Of course that was the original. I said it was a copy simply to hear you defend it. I knew Brown would trust your judgment. And I knew Brown would be troubled enough to have it gone over again, by "experts." I brought the idea into his mind simply to let him kill it himself, so that once I'd exchanged the two, no matter who called this a copy, he'd simply laugh at them. He'd just made absolutely certain, hadn't he? And the original? It's on its way back to Europe where it belongs. I exchanged them quite recently. Do you think he knew the difference? And Valentine laughed, a sound of disdain severed by a gasp of pain at the shock in his lip.

—Yes, thank God! The figure across the table stood illumined at its edges with the steady glow of the fire. —Thank God there was the gold to forge!

Valentine smiled his broken smile, coming closer, as the other retreated a step up the room.

—And you wanted me to copy the Patinir, so you could steal it, so you could steal it from him too.

—Steal! Look at him, look at him over there. Steal from him? Look at . . . his hand on the carpet, Valentine shuddered. —Like a fat soft toad on the carpet, the ugly venomous toad with the precious jewel in its head, look at it. Hands like that, on these beautiful things? Then drawing his hands together before him as though in protection, Valentine's wrist pressed the weight at his waist. He stepped forward suddenly, keeping his arm there, and said, —Listen . . .

—Good God!

—It's all different, Valentine said, —it's different now, now that you and I are...alone.

—You...what do you want of me?

—And you! what do you want? Basil Valentine burst out, advancing again as this figure before him moved backwards up the room, not unsteady, but from side to side, back toward the staircase and the hulk flung at its foot. —Yes, your by all that's ugly! And you, handling you like a jewel, he went on, his voice rising. —You and your work, your precious work, your precious van der Goes, your precious van Eyck, your precious not van Eyck but what I want! And your precious Chancellor Rolin, look at him there, look at him. Yes, why didn't you paint him into a Virgin and Child and Donor? Do you think it's any different now? That that fat-faced Chancellor Rolin wasn't just like him? Yes, swear to me by all that's ugly! Valentine hissed, and got breath. —Vulgarity, cupidity, and power. Is that what frightens you? Is that all you see around you, and you think it was different then? Flanders in the fifteenth century, do you think it was all like the Adoration of the Mystic Lamb? What about the paintings we've never seen? the trash that's disappeared? Just because we have a few masterpieces left, do you think they were all masterpieces? What about the pictures we've never seen, and never will see? that were as bad as anything that's ever been done. And your precious van Eyck, do you think he didn't live up to his neck in a loud vulgar court? In a world where everything was done for the same reasons everything's done now? for vanity and avarice and lust? and the boundless egoism of these Chancellor Rolins? Do you think they knew the difference between what was bizarre and what was beautiful? that their vulgar ostentation didn't stifle beauty everywhere, everywhere? the way it's doing today? Yes, damn it, listen to me now, and swear by all that's ugly! Do you think any painter did anything but hire himself out? These fine altarpieces, do you think they glorified anyone but the vulgar men who commissioned them? Do you think a van Eyck didn't curse having to whore away his genius, to waste his talents on all sorts of vulgar celebrations, at the mercy of people he hated?

Blood flowed over his broken tooth. He'd turned away, but swung about again unable to stop. —Yes, I remember your little talk, your insane upside-down apology for these pictures, every figure and every object with its own presence, its own consciousness because it was being looked at by God! Do you know what it was? What it really was? that everything was so afraid, so uncertain God saw it, that it insisted its vanity on His eyes? Fear, fear, pessimism and fear and depression everywhere, the way it is today, that's why your pictures are so cluttered with detail, this terror of emptiness, this absolute terror of space. Because maybe God isn't watching. Maybe he doesn't see. Oh, this pious cult of the Middle Ages! Being looked at by God! Is there a moment of faith in any of their work, in one centimeter of canvas? or is it vanity and fear, the same decadence that surrounds us now. A profound mistrust in God, and they need every idea out where they can see it, where they can get their hands on it. Your ... detail, he commenced to falter a little, —your Bouts, was there ever a worse bourgeois than your Dierick Bouts? and his damned details? Talk to me of separate consciousness, being looked at by God, and then swear by all that's ugly! Talk to me about your precious van Eycks, and be proud to be as wrong as they were, as wrong as everyone around them was, as wrong as he was. And Basil Valentine flung out a hand to the broken hulk on the floor, toward which he backed the retreating figure before him. —Separation, he said in a voice near a whisper, —all of it cluttered with separation, everything in its own vain shell, everything separate, withdrawn from everything else. Being looked at by God! Is there separation in God? Valentine finished, and held out his hand again, but more slowly, less steady, to withdraw it immediately the two retreating before him came up, breaking the surface as the voice broke the silence he left.

—And that van der Goes? Who put the face on it? Who couldn't stand that emptiness? Who had to see it with his hands, then! Yes, what are you telling me all this for ... you ...

—Look out! Valentine spoke too late, and stopped still as the figure before him tripped over a gauntlet and was down to his knees again beside the shape on the carpet between them. Standing over it, Valentine said quietly, —Because, my dear fellow, you and I ...

—You and I what! You and I what!

—Because finally, you and I are together. And now ... here! what are you doing? What are you trying to do? He got no answer but what he saw, the hands straining again at the visor, blood spilled out on the rose beneath that gross chin and the back of a hand against the bloodied uneven teeth, and the hoarse whispered, —Damn it ... damn it ...

—Here now, leave ... leave all that alone.

—His eyes, I see his eyes shining through this ... thing. Do you see them? Do you see them?

—Stop it now, stop it ...

The visor came open. And they both drew breath suddenly, as though they had even now expected to see the youthful face of a Mantuan noble, and had been tricked, and were mocked, by this heavy forehead still wet, and the sharp protruding eyes in a stare unbroken by the quick interruptions of life.

Basil Valentine again made a cross on his chest, caught, now, his upper lip under whole teeth until it bled again, stepped back with a wave of the damp heat from his crotch rising, saw his own hand glittering with a shock of gold out before him, and below there a hand on the lower jaw, a thumb lapped over the bloody uneven teeth, and the other hand wiping the sweat away from the forehead.

—And now...Valentine said.

The moving hand stopped, and the eyes turned up to him.

—This man...

Valentine hung there over him, —What?...

—This man is your father.

Basil Valentine stepped back, his weight on one foot; and the other foot he put out, slowly, until it reached the headpiece. —You are mad, aren't you ... and with his toe he kicked the visor shut, and held his foot there.

The visor was jammed closed on the thumb which had opened it, jammed tight, as Valentine saw, crushing the white length between the joints, and Valentine moved nothing but his eyes, up, to the living eyes which burned green upon him. —But you and I, now, you and I...

The green eyes did not move, and Valentine withdrew slowly, withdrew his foot from the visor whose edge moved no more than the still thumb recovering its shape forced, for the thumb itself stayed.

—You know...Valentine said, getting his weight on both feet now, —all of this...He made a faint gesture over the room. —You and I...Then he watched the thumb withdrawn from the broken mouth, and that hand trailing a streak of watered blood down the breastplate. —You and I...listen. Listen...Valentine tried to smile; and was as instantly aware of the image he had left in the mirror returned to mock the cold lines of this face which he had learned so well to use and trust. —Listen...he said, watching the hand search between roses, and stop fingertips on the penknife, —Listen to me. You and I now, it won't be...the kind of thing that...it won't be vulgar... it won't be vulgar, he repeated with half a step back, watching the other hand come away from the half-opened visor, and as he saw the hands join on the penknife his own reached toward his waist but it hung at the weight there, —Because you're...part of me...damn you, damn you, damn you, he cried throwing both hands up before his face as the short blade stabbed him once, and again, and again, driven each time at the top of his chest, and he lost his balance and hit his head against the newel and went down.

A cry, or a yelp was it? came from the kitchen. And there Fuller walked over to the sink, none too steady, and washed his hands. Then he washed the butcher knife and dried it on a hand towel, dropped the towel in a hamper and put the butcher knife in the rack where it belonged, and then picked up the two cardboard suitcases which he'd been all this time tying closed. He turned off the kitchen light by stooping and catching the switch with his shoulder, and emerged into the great room with a bag in each hand.

—You, sar!

—Fuller! . . . I . . .

—But what occur sar? The bags in Fuller's hands sank to the floor. —And Mister Valentine, sar?

—Yes, yes I . . . I've just taught him the lesson . . . the only lesson the gods can teach, yes . . .

—But you, sar, you unharmed?

—I? Good God yes, I . . . I'm as free as the day I was born. Here! Here! . . . don't go near there, don't touch him.

—But maybe Mister Valentine in danger of recoverin, sar.

—But . . . no, don't touch him. You never know what they may . . . have in their hair. Then he laughed. —And you, Fuller? taking a vacation, Fuller?

—Yes sar. Where I belong to be, sar, after all the years of bondage. Then Fuller straightened up from the bags he'd returned to, saying, —Something enter my mind. He went over to a cabinet and took out a large flat cedar box. He opened it, passed a hand in, held it up and smelled its contents, and closed it again. When Fuller came back across that carpet, avoiding stepping on the roses, it was with an expression of guilty satisfaction. But he stopped to look up and say —What is it, sar? Fuller got no immediate answer, and stood watching him force the taces aside over the heavy buttocks, to get a hand into a trouser pocket and come out with some bills in a wet wad. Then he bent over the hand flung out there at his feet. Fuller by now was beside him, and they both stared at the diamonds embedded in the flesh of the finger.

—Sar . . . Fuller hesitated, —I believe by now the diamonds grow there, and to my eyes have lost their luster. Then he turned his face against his will to that staring up at him from the carpet.

—So the eyes, he said, and broke this hold for the last time, —the eyes look like that black dog one day havin the temperature taken.

—Good God!

—Sar? Fuller looked up, to see him pull open the dinner jacket and tug at the waist. The pistol fell out on the carpet, and he stood there wiping a hand across his forehead before he reached in and got the wallet, picked up the pistol, and put both into his pockets.

Fuller went back to his suitcases. —Seem I goin to enjoy the legacy of some excellent cigars, he said picking up the flat cedar case, unable to resist opening it wide enough to peep in, and sniff the contents. Then the dull jangle of the radio ceased, and Fuller watched him cross the carpet slowly, finishing the brandy he'd poured earlier. In the silence he stood looking down at the expanse of the table painting, the contour of his figure still before the fire until the movement of an arm broke it, and the empty glass shattered over the burning logs. Then the figure was all movement, sliding the glass top off of the table, smashing a foot down into the table's surface, hands rending the painted panel into one piece after another small enough to throw into the fire, while he whispered, —Cave, caveat emptor, Dominus videt, Christ! the original! . . . a whisper broken by laughter, —yes, thank God there was the gold to forge!

It was all the work of a few moments, and he was still again standing before the fire. The flames rose and moved quietly beyond his profile throwing a radiant edge to it and leaving the features in shadow and the streaks of blood indiscernible.

Fuller watched, cleared his throat, but did not interrupt. The fire rose with sharper cracks of insistence and sudden shocks of flame throwing longer shadows and Fuller moved like one of them toward his luggage, speaking softly. —So long ago, wen he tell me he goin to make me from a black man to a wite. He picked up his bags and got the cedar case of cigars under one arm. —Evidence of the great power watchin over me, that he did not succeed in his design. And after a moment's waiting, standing straight, Fuller started to the door without another look on that great room, startled, to be sure, passing the youthful portrait, as he went out to the hall and unloaded briefly to reach his hat down from the very small panel closet. Hat in hand he paused, readying to break the silence pouring out to him with his own voice in farewell perhaps, when the silence was broken, by a rattling of metal; and Fuller quickly busied himself with picking up his bags, embarrassed at eavesdropping on an intimacy which for the first time he understood, hearing now,

—Good God! what a luxury you were!

Out in the street Fuller waited. He stood and breathed deeply. Then when the door behind him opened again and closed he spoke without turning, looking toward the sky, —Seem we have the moon waitin to light us upon the way . . .

—The moon? the moon? where . . . They both sought the sky for it.

—A moment ago . . . Fuller commenced.

—Ah but it's all right, when we need it why, charms, yes charms can bring it down . . . Fuller, here, listen, this money. Will you take some of it? I don't know how much there is, but, where are you going now?

—First I must seek a telephone, inform a friend of the condition of these we leave behind, requirin his professional services. Then I believe escape from this vicinity to be desirable for many reasons. And you sar?

—Yes, to go. To go, but first, even if . . . it didn't turn out like I thought it would but, it turned out, it had its own design. Yes to go. where. But I have to get her first, you understand, you would understand, where I've been all this time. Fuller? the money...?

—Oh no sar, Fuller started to retreat, a pale shaft of light yellowing the life of the streetlights full upon him. —I quite sufficiently provided for as it is: in a smile his pink tongue fled delicate and in danger, into the darkness of that donjon keep as he closed the gold portcullis of his teeth.

The moon, and other lustrous blisters of heaven, were gone. It had commenced to snow again when the cab drew into Central Park, and the driver looked up into his mirror to see the figure slumped in back suddenly pull himself up at the apparition of trees and stare out, as though alarmed and uncertain where he was in the dark wood, until they came out of it.

The cab slurred up in the slush and stopped, and the driver twisted round in his seat. —Now look, Jack, we been riding around an hour now, I already told you an hour ago you can't just go into Bellevue this time of the night without something like you got your throat cut. Haven't you got a home somewheres you want to go? Haven't you got some dame you could go visit? Me, I got to get all the ways out to Astoria yet...what? Now you want to go back downtown? Horatio Street, that's down on the West Side? O.K., this is the last time, we'll go down, but this is the last time.

Above, windows were lighted, occasionally blocked by the shadows of incurious faces looking forth only in order not to look back, and her own back turned on this room of faded Edwardian elegance, motionless, heedless of the paper littering the carpet about her feet. The letter under her left foot opened, "I have written you a number of times now, and you have not answered me..." and its lines were streaked and awash, where a drink had spilled. She stared out into the dark chasm beneath her high window, unable to make out its depths from the laceration framing her figure in light, and turning away, the breath drawn so slowly was expelled in resolution as she crossed the strewn carpet. A moment later, the pen moved in upright strokes of vicious indignation: "Dear Doctor Weisgall. It may interest you to know that my mother and the Pope..."

Further down, in this concentric ice-ridden chaos, heavy wet snow was falling. The wind bellowed down fighting against itself in the dark gaping ruin where the building had been, and he turned slipping again in the slush, to see red lights streaming across the street further down, near the corner. He had to stumble round the dark edge of a pool to reach the bar, and even at that was forced to wait in the door, his entrance blocked by two beer barrels being rolled in opposite directions, meeting here head-on while the owner and the bartender swore at each other and rolled them back again. He came in muttering, felt for the sharp packet inside his coat, and ordered a drink. Someone ordered drinks all round. The place was foul-smelling, the floor awash and streaked with things spilled, and a clogged drain behind the door to the men's room. A small figure clutching a filthy dollar bill fixed him with a strabismic stare. He drank, breathing through his mouth to avoid the smell, and was trying to count the edges of the bills protruding from his inside pocket when a fight started and he withdrew, slowly for fear of being drawn in on their mud-spattered anger where they came on wildly at one another, hand and foot and a butting head which almost upset him before he recovered the darkness and the streets streaming red as though consumed with wet flame. The argument emerged behind him, as he set out to cross the dark lake.

—Look, Leroy...

—Dis city...

—Leroy...

—Dis

Across the chasm, the mirror reflected a brightly lighted and harsh reality, which included, immediately, two drunks busy in conversation. One of them, speaking from a twisted face, trod backwards upon Mr. Pivner's foot, forcing him to move slightly closer to his own companion, at whom, every few moments, he stole glances in the glass behind the bar.

—You know what I am? demanded the drunk on the far side. They were enjoying their discussion very much, each finding the other intelligent, witty, in all, a good companion, for neither was listening to what the other was saying. —I'm a male nurse.

—Well I say anybody can make a million dollars. You just have to start out thinking that way, and if you keep on, if you keep right on, you get into the habit and you can't help it.

—Well let me tell you what we had today. We had a c.a., do you know what that is?

—After awhile, you can't help it, you can't help making a million dollars. You know what I am? I'm a fortune teller. Hands, cards, I can read anything.

Mr. Pivner had taken off his wet hat when they came in, looked round, and put it on again. He felt well, but a little giddy. Their conversation was not hurried, he responded alertly enough, but found himself far behind: while listening, even while speaking, he was still examining the words of three or four sentences before. Speaking, —Well, what are you studying now?...he was still weighing his own embarrassed greeting when they'd met in the street, —I was going home, but, why no, no I'm not really in a hurry. Hearing, —I'm not studying anything special yet. It's pretty expensive going to night school, it's just the books that run into money, you'd be surprised how much they can cost. These are mostly books on science, that's mostly what I'm interested in...he was still savoring, —Merry Christmas, gee, I'm glad to see you sir. I was just going to midnight Mass...Savoring, again, —I'm glad to see you sir...he licked his lips, and looked to the mirror.

—This c.a., up in the hospital, you haven't never seen anything like it.

—Like a friend of mine, he's getting married, like I even foretold him he was going to. Tomorrow, Christmas, he's getting married. He was screwing this little Bronx girl regular, I foretold him he'd have to marry her.

—Now let me describe to you what a c.a. is.

—In a way you might say that this guy's lucky, in a way you might say maybe it's a good thing. A thing like that, when you put it off, after a wile you begin to get scared, but if it happens early like with this guy then there you are and you don't know no different, you get in the habit and you can't help it. Like I foretold him, I foretold him, you get in the habit and you can't help it. And with a step back, the fortune teller jostled the ribs behind him with an elbow.

There was already a similarity between their noses, so was the revelation in the glass; and if it were a negative one, that is, if neither his own, nor that which signaled the skinny face so close to his, was in any way exceptional, there was no time for such apprehension: it still seemed to be happening too fast. He heard himself speaking with the cordial restraint he had envisionedly prepared for his first conversations with his son; but it was a conversation which he had anticipated in such detail, in so many rehearsals, that now each channel and bend was cherished, not to be lost in the mutability of chance exchange, but clenched: yes, for in this instant the truth of it was, that doubt abided in the actuality: that this actuality urged the doubt, a featureless transient until now so abruptly given quiddity and a carnal selfishness of its own. Speaking, —But what I mean is, if you'd like...I mean I'd like to get these books for you, because if I can...if you and I...His lip twitched, but instead of looking away as he would usually have done, Mr. Pivner looked straight at Eddie Zefnic's face. —I think we can manage, he said. He smiled, and his lip stopped twitching.

—But gee Mister Pivner...

—And listen, Eddie. Here, Eddie, here there's something I want to give you. It may not seem...but it's Christmas Eve and, here, please I, think you should have it.

—You can't imagine what a mess it was, but you got to expect that with a c.a.

—So you see it come out just like I foretold him, there's certain things which you can't escape them.

—But gee!...a watch? and it's, gold? A gold watch?

—I think you should have it, because...

—But gee! sir. And gee, look it's almost twelve. You wouldn't want to come to Mass with me?

—But I don't think I'd know what to do.

—But if you're with me...

—It's that or religion.

—Or helping out to preform a c.a.

—Yes, if I'm with you...And Mr. Pivner blew his nose. He had almost thanked Eddie Zefnic for the robe.

Otto rounded a corner, walking the curb as though himself on the edge of a chasm, his back turned to the river whose wind followed him, momentarily dazzled by fire and pitch where a tub of asphalt stood in the street sentineled by kerosene flares. The snow had changed to sleet, to rain, and stopped; but his coat was wet, and hung heavy as lead from his shoulders.

—Otto!...Stanley appeared as though risen from an exposure of pavement. He shivered, his eyes were red, his mustache looked lopsided.

—Stanley, where are you going?...

—Otto why did you do that? Did you know? did you know?

—What, what, did I know what?

—I've been arrested, all this time, I've been in the police station since the last time I saw you.

—But what? what for? what happened?

—And the police, do you know what they're like, the police? like machines, they're so bored, they don't listen, they don't know who you are, but you can't do anything, you can't do anything...

—But what is this? what happened?

—You didn't know? That money you gave me, you didn't know? The money you lent me, that twenty-dollar bill, you didn't know it was no good?

—No good...?

—That it was counterfeit?

—Counterfeit?

—If you didn't know, thank God if you didn't know. I shouldn't have thought what I did, I shouldn't have thought you'd do that to me, I'm sorry, forgive me, forgive me for thinking that about you.

—But no...Otto whispered: —No. No, not all that...

—I'm sorry, forgive me, I'll pay it back to you. Forgive me, Otto. I have to go now.

—But wait, wait wait wait...

—I can't stay, I have a toothache, I've had it all day, I have to go, I have to go to midnight Mass now, and then I have to go see my mother, they moved my mother to a new hospital today and she'll wonder where I've been, and then I think the police might...

—The police, what did you tell them?

—About the money? I said I didn't know, I told them I didn't know where I got it, I don't know whether they believed me, they just look at you, maybe they're following me, I don't know, but it doesn't matter now, and forgive me, I'll pay you back...

—But no, Otto whispered.

—What is it? I have to go, will you come with me now? Do you want to come to Mass with me?

—No. No. Otto rubbed his forehead, then dropped his hand to the sharp weight in his jacket. —He couldn't have done that...

—Good night, good night...and I'll pay you back...

The wind from behind stood Otto's hair on end, and blew along before him an empty tin can, throwing it bounding over spots of snow, jingling it over bare stretches of pavement, to hurl it lost among the mutilated shadows as he turned the corner into her street and saw that he was not alone. He cried out loudly though the other figure was close upon him: they both halted before the encounter, but Otto came on instantly. —Thank God you're here, after all the...all that's happened, and now...Yes everything will be all right now. I've been looking for you, I've been looking everywhere, I just went over to Horatio Street looking for you but there was nothing there, the whole place is burned down, and I should have come here, I should have come here first anyhow shouldn't I, because you knew her, and she...you...

—Where is she?

—Where is she? why, she...she...why? Look, why are you looking at me that way? And what's happened to you? your face, what is it? is it blood on your face?

—Where is she?

—You're just looking for her? It's ... her you came for, then? His arms were moving in the dark as though he could scarcely keep himself upright in the thick gloom which seemed to have risen about them. —But I've been looking for you! he burst out. And then he did go off balance on the ice, taking a step back from the eyes which had penetrated him and emptied his face. —And she ... he got out, recovering his balance with another step back, —I don't know. I don't know where she is, he said, and repeated it slowly, but as clear, —I don't know where she is ... hesitated, and stood still. And when he raised his eyes, looking east toward the hospital, he was alone in the street. The wind had gone down, and the still cold was unbearable. He stood numb, surrounded by ice, among the frozen giants of buildings, as though to dare a step would send him head over heels in a night with neither hope of morning to come nor heaven's betrayal of its triumphal presence, in the stars.

IX

Vicisti, Galilæe.
　　—JULIAN, dying words

THE SUN rose at seven, and its light caught the weathercock atop the church steeple, epiphanized it there above the town like a cock of fire risen from its own ashes. In the false dawn, the sun had prepared the sky for its appearance: but even now the horned moon hung unsuspecting at the earth's rim, before the blaze which rose behind it to extinguish the cold quiet of its reign.

In the daylight's embrace, objects reared to assert their separate identities, as the rising sun rescued villagers from the throbbing harmony of night, and laid the world out where they could get their hands on it to assail it once more on reasonable terms. Shapes recovered proper distance from one another, becoming distinct in color and extension, withdrawn and self-sufficient, each an entity because it was not, and with daylight could not be confused with, or be a part of, anything else. Eyes were opened, things looked at, and, in short, propriety was restored.

Nonetheless, for here and there one drawing breath, with a conscious taste now letting it run to every sensible part, even as the daylight reinvested the furniture of out-of-doors with meaning, the rankling assurance, that is, that if it did not belong to one's self it did at least belong to someone else, here and there breath stopped abruptly as the ear took up the hour, attention pinioned upon sounds, and left so, more distraught at each repetition as the church bell rang in sevenths, an unresolved tone which set the listening nerves alert, a-jangle, a lamed tone leaving lips open at *ahh-*, repeating *ahh-*, confirming desperately irresolute *ahh-* seven times and forsaken there, incomplete at the last, still waiting hymnal resolution in ahh-*men*.

At that, several townsfolk summoned to mind their sexton, considered what he might know about bells in general, and how contrive toward setting this particular one to rights again; then, on second consideration, that he'd likely had something ingenious to do with its getting into this state in the first place, they pursed their lips and tried, with admirable Puritan fortitude, to put him out of mind until that time when he should be delivered from the extravagant snarl of his mortal coils, reckoning it, in all logic, a time not too far off, hoping it, in all charity, a race which he should win (for arrival at that glorious goal before him meant interment at his hands), and even now, in all good faith, quite unaware that that rescue had already been accomplished with all the intrepid serenity implicit in the Rescuer's reputation for order, quietly and in darkness: never in fact suspecting such a thing, what with the industrious hammering and clatter from inside the church since dawn of the day before, as they stood now, listening, drawn-lipped at the windows, and here and there leveled their eyes upon the still unilluminated bulk of Mount Lamentation, and the still-to-be-fulfilled landscape of Christmas.

Here and there they turned, to quietly ascertain that celebrated rubric on the calendar.

It is true, when that red-letter day was done, and its wealth of bits and pieces pruned and grafted, embellished, and laid gilded and gelded to rest in those private rotting-rooms called memories where, after rearranging things and tidying up a bit, the townsfolk sat down again among the corpses of the past, inhaling, and waiting; true that, when peace was restored that evening, and no more opportunities likely for the vigorous intervention of what was, with consentaneous relief, referred to as the hand of God; true, that is, that by about eight that evening, when even the hand of God inclined to decorous retirement, a number of the more exotic accounts of the day's main event, harried reports on the various epiphenomena, and exhibitions from among the souvenirs of the more dilapidated rotting-rooms, had shed their sources, and in currency gained credence.

Concerning the Reverend himself, for instance, by noon it was rumored that he had once traveled in Italy, and by one accepted that he had stopped in Rome; by two, rumored that he had in Spain entered a Carthusian monastery as a novice, and by three confirmed; by four, that he had once dressed himself in rags, rented three pitiful children, and attended in a state of mendicant collapse before the steps of the Ritz hotel in Madrid; by five, that he had stood the entire town of Málaga to drinks, conducted the male population on an experimental hike out on the sea toward Africa, seeking One who should manage it dry-shod; by six, that he had indeed married himself to a hoary crone with bangles in her ears, proclaimed himself heir to the throne of Abd-er-Rahman, and led an insurrection of the Moors on Córdoba; by seven, a score of people were to be found who had seen him on the roof of the church mid-morning of the day before; and by eight, even the tale told by an unpalatable fellow (whose general attitude toward life was sketched in a tattoo on his right forearm, and who had never been seen at any community-supported center but the police station, much less the church), a tale in which that very morning the Reverend had been seen abroad without a stitch on, albeit within the confines of his own lawns and pasture, a tale which might have ended that night under the twelve-point antlers of the buck in the Depot Tavern but for the main event of the day, or, again, if the buck had survived, or, indeed, even the Depot Tavern been left standing, by eight even this tale had made its way into a number of respectable parlors, a rococo affair, adorned, by this time, with elements which many now suspected might be the truth.

This fellow said that he was returning home (and a few suspected it right here at the outset, since he was known from the police blotter to reside at "no fixed address") from work, as he referred to the nightly periods he spent in the abandoned bridge works sleeping off drink, when, as he did every morning, he passed the parsonage, where he had become used to the reassuring spectacle of the Reverend greeting the dawn from the front porch, with increasing vehemence, it seemed, as recent dawns coincided with the end of the working day. This morning, however, and in spite of the fine sunrise, the Reverend was not to be seen at his station. The night watchman went on to relate how, glancing back over his shoulder as he descended the hill, he discerned what appeared to be an impressively large and white figure in the branches of a tree, down near the barn, the carriage barn at the foot of the back lawn. He paused, understandably, to await the next development, as the figure in the tree appeared to be doing also; and within a minute's time, the black bull appeared in the field below. The bull was readily enough identified; but it was here that the fellow's story assumed such proportions that credulity was strained, even among those enough offended by subsequent events, or injured in the trial of strength which ensued before the morning was out, to cherish every word, for he detailed a chase, and a capture, of such heroic dimensions, that only a few here and there, whom the pagan curiosity of youth had led into traffic with myths, could summon images to approximate his description, and none could match it. For once caught round the neck, at which point the captor's feet did, he admitted, leave the ground, he said that the bull was downed; and the more the time of the day passed, and the more he was given to drink, the more vociferously this fellow swore that he had seen the bull carried shoulder-high, and then dragged, by its hind legs, out of his sight, up the lawn toward the parsonage.

With contumely masked as charity on the one hand, and charity proffered as indifference by the other, the church-going and the Depot Tavern's public suffered one another at a distance, mutually exclusive, not, until that day, to say aloof (for by noon a few had crossed the line in both directions). And so, though a few gathered before the church that morning wore expressions of anxiety, on edge because of the bell which had been ringing the hour in irresolute sevenths since dawn, and even now called them to worship in the same breathless fashion, none was prepared for anything out of what, in extraordinary times, is called the ordinary. Of all the knot of soberly dressed children and somberly dressed adults, with here and there in the bright sunshine a voice like a tinkling cymbal, and another sounding brass, none even noticed from outside that the lozenge-shaped panes were boarded up from within; and none was prepared, upon entering, for the appearance of the interior of the church, though within a few minutes it was difficult to tell who was going in and who was coming out as they blocked the doorway describing the darkened place, the arrangement of the benches (for it proved later that a number of the pews had been hewn down to these modest proportions), the altar brought closer down with a gold bull figure mounted just out of a shaft of sunlight which struck from above. Still outside, a pale woman who never used scent, and so was highly responsive to such things, believed she smelled incense. And someone even noted the disappearance of the bronze tablet put up in loving memory of *John H.* —— (an item never recovered, and, as far as that goes, never replaced).

—Natalis Invicti Solis...

A burly man (he proved later, in daylight, to be commander of the local American Legion post) had climbed up and commenced to tear a board from a window, but he lost balance at the sound of this stern and still gentle voice.

—The birth of the Unconquered Sun...We are gathered here in the world cave before him born of the Rock, the one Rock hewn without human hands, in the sight of the shepherds who witnessed his birth, whose name signifies friend, and mediator, who comes with rest from sin, and hope beyond the grave... and offers the revival of the Sun in promise and pledge of his own...

A number of people were trying to get out, and others to get in; but, whatever the rearrangement of the obscure interior, it became increasingly evident that at best it would accommodate only fifty or sixty, and even that number only if they were familiar with the three-sided disposal of the benches.

—Transitus dei... the bull lies slain... and from the dying bull issues the seed of the world...

Possibly the familiar authority of the voice held them silent at first, standing in contorted positions and here and there sinking down on the benches.

—Cultores Solis Invicti Mithrae... gathered here wearied of the religions of the cities, the religions spoken of in the cities and practiced nowhere, the exhausted and pale, the frighted and forgotten, come before him who rewards for acts of piety more than he does for valor, the Lord of Hosts, the God of Truth...

Someone said later that the voice broke and took up with the gentle rush of smoke from a boat gone under a river bridge.

—We sacrifice unto Mithra, the lord of wide pastures, who has a thousand ears and ten thousand eyes, a God invoked by his own name.

—We sacrifice unto Mithra, the lord of wide pastures, who is truth-speaking, a chief in assemblies, with a thousand ears, well-shapen, with ten thousand eyes, high, with full knowledge, strong, sleepless, ever awake.

—We sacrifice unto Mithra, the lord of all countries...we sacrifice unto the undying, shining, swift-horsed sun.

—For his brightness and glory I have offered unto him a sacrifice worth being heard, unto Mithra the lord of wide pastures.

Later someone else said that here the voice quit and rose like the smoke of a train in and out of a tunnel,

—May he come to us for help. May he come to us for ease. May he come to us for joy. May he come to us for mercy. May he come to us for health. May he come to us for victory. May he come to us for good conscience. May he come to us for bliss. He, the awful and overpowering, worthy of sacrifice and prayer, not to be deceived anywhere in the whole of the material world, Mithra, the lord of wide pastures.

But by now, the sound which lay among them like a sound among stones, filling the cavern behind them, commenced to return in a murmur.

—On whichever side he has been worshiped first in the fullness of faith of a devoted heart, to that side turns Mithra, the lord of wide pastures, with the fiend-smiting wind, with the cursing thought of the wise.

The murmur rose, with the sound of an echo from a chasm, and started to disintegrate into separate voices. Someone said, —Just get hold of him...

—With a sacrifice in which thou art invoked by thine own name, with the proper words do I offer thee libations, O most beneficent Mithra. Should the evil thoughts of the earthly man be a hundred times worse, they would not rise so high as the good thoughts of the heavenly Mithra.

—Look out, be quiet...come on now, Reverend...

—Should the evil words of the earthly man be a hundred times worse, they would not rise so high as the good words of the heavenly Mithra.

—That's enough of this...get hold of him, shut him up...

—Should the evil deeds of the earthly man be a hundred times worse, they would not rise so high as the good deeds of the heavenly Mithra.

The shaft of sunlight struck the gold bull figure showing a hand grasping the horns, again and again, to be interrupted above by a visage which broke it and eyes blazing with the suddenness of lightning, as the voice at each flash became thunderous, and they struck at the same moment,

—To Mithra of the wide pastures, of the thousand ears, of the myriad eyes...

—Look out! Get his arms...

—the Yazad of the spoken name...

There was a crash, and a howl of pain.

—be sacrifice, homage, propitiation, and praise...

Someone finally managed to wrench a board from one of the windows. With the light, everyone looked in different directions. The howl of pain had come from a man now on the floor, and pinned there under the weight of the holy water stoup, drenched, having knocked it over in assailing the altar where it stood. The bell started again, and someone managed to turn off the mechanism. Someone else reached a telephone, and called a minister in a nearby town, inviting, and then entreating, him to come and restore the occasion they had gathered to observe.

Everyone looked in different directions; and afterward, outside, none of them could say for certain how the figure exhorting them had appeared, though two starry-eyed children turned nasty with one another over it, one describing Persian dress, and a turban, the other Assyrian, with a crown, becoming so vivid, indeed, that their schoolteacher, who was quivering nearby, confirmed that they had seen such pictures in a history primer the week before, though this did not deter their zeal for a moment.

One person said he'd been taken to hospital; another, back to the parsonage.

The brisk air was turning cold; and in the shelter of a clapboard buttress, where they'd already retired from the sun before the sky itself commenced to darken overhead, this rising chill embraced a small knot of ladies, uniting them so familiarly that they might have been the immediate source of it, and their voices the shocks of its emanation.

—At our supper last night we never suspected...

—Never imagined such desecration was taking place right over our heads...

—I heard hammering...

—Well *I* heard *ham*mering.

—I heard it too, but I never dreamt that something like this...

—Something like *this*!...

—I've had the feeling something like this was going to happen for quite a time now.

—Since the last time he went away for a rest. When we all agreed that a rest would be best.

—Ever since May...

—Since May?

—I've thought...

—Oh *May.*

—That was his last really Christian service. May's funeral service.

—How we have missed her.

—How we have needed her.

—How he has needed her guiding hand.

—May would be eighty-three this month.

—Someone ought to be notified. Someone ought to come immediately. Someone ought...

—The son...

—The son?

—The son has been gone for such a long time. A prodigal son.

—But he had no brothers. Poor Camilla...

—Poor Camilla never was strong. Taken and left in foreign lands.

—He wasn't a strong boy. When he took sick...

—The Lord did spare him.

—The Lord did spare him to do His work. To follow right in his father's footsteps. That is, of course...

—His fathers six generations back.

—To serve right here in his own community. The people he needs, who need him now.

—Now I shouldn't repeat this, but I heard...

—Do you know...

—I heard...

—Do you know what I thought, as I remembered, after that illness that lasted so long, the Lord didn't spare him. As I remembered...

—But I was certain...

—Well it's true, the past plays tricks when all we have to depend upon is mortal memory.

—Wait! Don't you smell something?

—I did in there, I smelled something burning.

—The terrible sweet smell of something burning.

Their words rose on bursts of wind, were fouled in the buttressed eddies, and sunk by metallic cries of nails being wrenched from wood inside, where they went themselves a moment later, for it had suddenly begun to snow.

The wind was still gentle enough, and the snow fell lightly; but through it, on the highway, gripping the steering wheel over which he could just see, a young man whose expression did something to redeem the otherwise vapid character of his face peered ahead between knuckles gone white with purpose, as he sped to answer the summons. His only sounds were bleating attempts to control his cold, now in its second, and most watery, day. The storm, as he would call it later, and as, later, it did indeed become, had blown up just as he left the town some ten miles off; and as though it had arisen as a challenge and a dare to his duty, he sped into the white flakes, making of their mild falling a threat worthy of his goal.

He did in fact almost come to grief as he entered the town, where the arrow pointing to left warned of the imminent curve to the right. From time to time he had taken one hand from the wheel, to draw across his nose, which is just what he was doing at that moment, and for uncountable terrifying instants he wove between the Civil War monument and the Depot Tavern, as though choosing which to demolish, an experience which the most worthy of goals could scarcely redeem, and explains why he had to be helped from his car upon arrival at the church.

Things had been set to rights as far as was possible, the pulpit replaced, the damaged pews straightened out, and the windows unboarded, largely through the efforts of the burly man and his buddies. He stood now to the back of the unsteady gasping congregation, looking quite indignantly about him, and above, from an eye already greatly swollen and discolored. There were others as severely marked, better than a half-dozen of them, and he turned to one now, whose shirt hung in tatters under his torn jacket, to mutter, —We got him there all right, the doc gave him a sedative, put him right out like a light. Then he turned respectfully to the fore, waiting for the conscript in the pulpit to begin.

The young minister started twice, but the sounds he made could barely be heard above, or distinguished from, the gasps and chirps in the congregation. And the reason for this ferment was that they were, one by one, turning their eyes above them. Although little light came in through the lozenge-shaped panes even now, uncovered, because of the sudden change in the weather, and the electric lights were, like the organ, found to have been put out of order, it was still quite easy to see the figures of stars, planets, the moon in various phases, and a resplendent sun, among other lavish celestial bodies, painted broadcast over the inside of the roof.

Gradually the sound from the pulpit disentangled itself from those rising before it, climbing earnestly from one line to the next of what turned out to be part of the second chapter of the Gospel according to Saint Luke. After that reassuring narrative, the place was quiet but for the sounds of his own sincere pleading, as he went on to Saint John, and that vernal episode involving Lazarus, which he seemed to think might not come amiss. Apparently he was right. They seemed more grateful for resurrection than they had needful of the stable birth; and as his own voice broke and mounted between gasps, and his eyes watered in what, from almost anywhere in that light, appeared an overpowering emotion of belief, many lips on the upturned faces joined his importunate plea, —I *am* the Resurrection, and the Life . . .

It was a simple service. He hoped by now to do little more than read a psalm, solicit a hymn, a cappella, and during that exercise recover enough voice himself to get through benediction; but he had hardly launched Psalm Number 89, —Till I thy foes thy footstool make . . . when there was a resounding crash which, though apparently some distance off, in the direction of the railway station, lost none of its impact on this convalescent throng. With great presence of mind, he called for *Rock of Ages*, and with equal fortitude led two stanzas of it himself, so that the benediction, when it came, was accepted as a minute of silent prayer by all but a few who could see his lips, and every bit of his face, straining over it, until, with the lowering of his unsteady hand, it was all over, and no one there ever saw him again.

He left that town the way he had come, though more slowly, and more slowly still as he approached the built-up end of the curve which had almost saved him from the experience he had just been through, in the same manner that someone else, a complete stranger as the barbarian license tag showed, had just been delivered from the cares of this world to the chimera of the next. The Depot Tavern was ablaze; and the car radio, which was well inside with the whole front end of it, was playing the rondo from Mozart's *Eine Kleine Nachtmusik*, to the silent passenger, and the twelve-point buck, knocked slightly askew up there as though he had cocked his head, listening, and in spite of the red Christmas tree light dangling at the end of his nose, watching with a dusty eyeball and an air of imperturbable serenity.

The real storm came, shrouding Mount Lamentation and then obliterating it altogether. The wind blew with a peculiarly terrible quality, broke here and there in the town a few windows, vindictive, viciously fingered where there was anything to destroy. It swept over the empty carriage barn, and cracked a blotched pane of that window tucked high on the house where Janet had been found, blue and rough-faced, weeping, and slavering —never never never never never . . . see him . . . more . . . , which some coarse unimaginative mind later publicly interpreted as a reference to a figure he'd known only as the sexton, found then in answer to the whine of a dog from behind a locked door, in bed, clutching a piece of paper, as the coroner, displacing the top button of the underwear for a token touch of his stethoscope against that empty chest, said he had probably lain for a day or two.

(Downstairs, in the defaced study, the coroner even got to his knees on the floor beside the carcass flung there at full length, to note and comment on the single fatal wound in the bull's neck, inflicted while it lived, as one could see from the round and gaping nature instead of its being drawn in a slit, as such a wound would have been otherwise.)

And the darkness came in like a substance driven on the wind which filled every crevice with it, and still did not relent where it failed in destruction, wailing round corners and shrill in the timbers erected awry but steady there at the foot of the hill. As for that platform, it would take three men as many days to dismantle it; but, although a number of curious things were to turn up around the place within the next few months, no one ever came upon anything that might have been a balloon.

A number of curious things turned up during the first few months of the new minister's tenancy, though that barely lasted the spring. He did "dig right in" (that was one of his expressions) to try to make the place "cheery" (another) and even "cozy" (...), choosing, first off, a bright upstairs room for his study, where it was not until one day when he lay on his back on the floor exercising with dumbbells (that was one of the things he did) that he discovered the wall to be papered with roses, and all of them upside down. Heretofore the pattern had not disturbed him, for he'd never tried to make anything of it; but now!... He was on his feet immediately, and had that taken care of, re-papered, that is, with something (as he said) of a more masculine character, a repetitious series of what for him represented fox hunting, not unlike the paper he had used in a darker downstairs room, after its floor had been sanded to remove the stains, and its walls and ceiling scraped of the brilliant colors with which they had been heavily painted, that and a half-dozen repairs to the walls where they looked to have been kicked in.

From a small room at the end of the upstairs hall, he'd had removed a print-ing press, its jumble of type, and a bundle of printed matter of which he could not make head or tail; not that he needed the room for anything, but he saw no *reason* to have a printing press in it at the foot of the narrow bed. From a chest of drawers in another room, he had a quantity of empty bottles removed. Not that he needed the drawers. He took down some paintings, whose subject matter was neither cheery nor cozy, and stored them along with a damaged statue, whose presence was certainly neither of those things, in a closet where he had come upon a jumble of books and some pieces of dark wood each mounting a small broken mirror in the end, which he took to be the remains of a curious picture frame, though he did not consider trying to have it restored.

At one point he opened a small closet and found in it oatmeal tins, noth-ing but empty square oatmeal tins stacked from floor to ceiling.

Then there were the books. Dumped in another closet he found such titles as *Malay Magic* and *Libellus de Terrificationibus Nocturnisque Tumultibus* in a cascading disarray, and forced the door closed on them again immediately. From a dim room presided over by a needlepoint NO CROSS NO CROWN (which he gave to the Use-Me Ladies) he rescued a few sober titles for his own shelves, where Baxter's *Everlasting Rest* and Fisher's *Catechism* lent an air of permanence, stacked against Dale Carnegie's *How to Win Friends and Influence People*. Andrew Jackson Davis's *Penetralia* was of course relegated as a curio, for "Dick" (as this young man encouraged people to call him, since his Christian name was Richard), had no interest in seeing the interior of objects. That, along with Buffon's *Natural History*, which actually sprang open in his hand when he took it down, and he found himself staring at a hand-tinted picture of an ape.

There were even books in the room where he'd found the drawers full of bottles. He kept two volumes, Tissandier's *Histoire des ballons*, not that he was interested in balloons, or could have read them if he were, but they were bound in green, and matched the motif of the new wallpaper. As for the others, two volumes of Lew Wallace, and Jules Verne's *Tour of the Moon*, *Round the World in Eighty Days*, and *Five Weeks in a Balloon*, those he gave to the American Legion, with whom he was co-operating in the great nation-wide Spiritual Crusade which they were sponsoring.

In the community, "Dick" also sang (he had a very agreeable "white tenor"), and conducted the Boy Scout troop.

There were, among the local mothers of fourteen-year-old boys, a few who felt they understood "Dick" very well, and cherished him accordingly; there were on the other hand a few elders who did not understand him at all, even to one sturdy old man who complained at the new minister's pronunciation. —Don't like the way he says *Gawd*... said that gray eminence, with the petulance of a man defending someone in his immediate family, and he never entered the church on his own feet again.

The ladies of the Use-Me Society found "Dick" a very agreeable listener; and he soon had some idea of how matters had gone before him, how the church (where he took one look and said, —Gee, we'd better dig right in...) came to demand such extensive refurbishing, and so forth. —And don't you know... said one of the ladies (who already referred to him as "Our 'Dick'"), speaking of the late sexton, —I once heard him say, It's only we that have no care for dying who never manage it... And from other things she, and her companions, said from time to time, their relief at having been delivered from the prospect of burial by those hands was evident, as though he might have laid them in askew, to hamper that mighty leap when the Trumpet sounded.

"Dick" heard of the demented girl who had lived up there, since taken to a state institution where she should have gone in the first place (for her own good) but for the Reverend's charity (which often extended too far), that she had rewritten the Bible and was in the act of printing it herself when "everything came to a head." Even the reliable details of her rumored cure of the sexton's paralysis were brought from these rotting-rooms and aired quite solemnly: the old man had got both legs into one leg of his pajamas one night on going to bed, cried out, —A stroke! ... or —Paraplegia! ... or some such, and she had come down the hall to the rescue. Though where they had gained this intelligence, or that she never left the house because she feared falling through the cracks in the sidewalk, they did not disclose.

As for the Reverend himself, it was generally admitted that his efforts and accomplishment, especially in those two final days of his dominion, had been prodigious, and, for one man, incredible; as it was generally agreed that he had, in his lifetime, suffered severe trials, and in sharing the magnanimous aggregate of their own troubled pasts, they were able to concur in granting him the right to a prolonged, confined, rest, in a private institution, where what remained of his own funds after the cost of repairs to certain community property, and his neighbor's bull, had been deducted, would suffice to maintain him until he was delivered (or summoned: there were two distinct opinions on this) by the Lord; and where "Dick," being of an earnest, responsible nature, decided to visit him.

And he did manage to emerge with the consolation that the familiar figure whom their community of kindness had enthralled showed no signs of breaking out to return and violate them with signs of appreciation, and appeared, if not grateful, distantly resigned to what, in the compound agreement of their own, they were pleased to call the Lord's will.

Happymount had been built originally as a natural history museum, by a philanthropist who felt that such things should be located in the country. When, eventually, it became evident that people were unwilling to make this excursion simply to see stuffed animals and stuffed Indians, it was suggested that they might come out to see human specimens, especially if they were relatives. The lighting inside was very bad. Beyond an iron palisade which separated it from the cares of the world, Happymount rose on a sea of green lawns tended by lonely lunatics: what could be more restful and rewarding than following the lawnmower up and down the green swathes day after day, and by the time one reached the laundry it was time to start at the front gate again.

The grassless winter proved a problem.

—Then you are the son? The doctor stared brightly through gold-rimmed glasses. He had proved, when he stood behind his desk a moment before, to be a good head shorter than "Dick," who was himself barely average height.

—The what? I? . . .

—Miss Inch, the doctor called, and a nurse appeared in the door. —The son . . . the son . . .

—It's a beautiful day, doctor.

—Ward G . . .

—Wait a minute . . . wait a minute . . .

It is true, the grassless winter proved a problem for everyone. Once outside in the sunshine, the nurse said, —You must not mind Mister Farisy. We have put him to sharing quarters with Mister Farisy.

Mr. Farisy's dossier at Happymount was a slim one: it detailed little of his successful years as an eminent anatomist, did not, in fact, even mention the process he said he had perfected for curing hams while still on the pig. It commenced in volume only at the point where (according to his own testimony) he had been appointed by the Congregation of the Sacred Rites, at the Vatican, to investigate early methods of crucifixion: were nails driven through the hands? or the wrists? As a scientist, Mr. Farisy had always relied on empirical methods, and found no reason to abandon them now: twenty arms were delivered to his laboratory. He nailed each right hand, and each left wrist, to the wall, and attached mobile weights driven by a system of bellows which he'd removed from a player piano, to simulate the rising and falling motions of the breathing human being. Then he set the thing in motion: weights rose and fell; wood creaked; flesh tore; bones split; and something snapped in Mr. Farisy's head. Next day he called for two dozen arms, then a gross, and silence followed: he said he had been brought to Happymount soon after he'd been discovered swinging hand-over-hand in the trapeze of intricate and grand proportions he'd fashioned in his laboratory. (But then, he also said he was descended from Attila the Hun.)

—Humm . . . ho . . . did Barabbas go free? Listen, I had a dream last night, a most ghastly nightmare. Do you want to hear it?

—No.

—I was on a mountaintop beside a little shed. I don't know how I could tell I was on a mountaintop, because I couldn't see the mountain. I couldn't even see other mountains. It was just because I knew I was on a mountaintop, so there! Ahhp . . . don't interrupt or I won't tell you any more. Maybe it was the light. The quality of light is different on a mountaintop, you'll see, thin, rarefied, the quintessence of purification.

—Be quiet. Go to sleep.

—The shed was an old board building. Weatherbeaten. Well, why shouldn't it be weatherbeaten, on a mountaintop like that, so there. The sun...

—Hmmnph...

—Yes the sun was behind me, covering me with its quintessential light, so there. I had him under the arms, with his back up against the shed but he was much bigger than I was, so much bigger I could hardly lift him. I decided the only way to do it was to nail one hand to one board and the other to a board higher up, then take the first nail out and put it in two boards higher, and then the same with the other hand, left hand, right hand, left hand right hand left hand...

—Stop it. Stop it. Stop it.

—Right up the wall. And why that's exactly what I was doing when I saw the hands were tearing to pieces. He was too big. I couldn't keep it up or the hands would be all torn to pieces by the time I got him up there. Oh, oh, oh, oh, it was terrible, and terrible, and discouraging from a scientific point of view, the way the nail just tore it apart, left hand, right hand... maybe I should have used smaller nails? That's the way I left him, with his trouser-cuffs dragging in the dirt.

—Stop it.

—There we were, in the pure quintessential light of the sun.

—Hmmmnph...

—On the mountaintop.

—...

—Transmogrification.

Then, —Look! came in Mr. Farisy's hoarse whisper of confidence. —See? the hammer? I keep it all under my mattress. See the nails? Nails! one by one. I've taken them from the shop, one by one by one, ten-penty, twenty-penty one by one. We'll do it on the door frame, I measured it. I know how much you weigh. I looked at your chart. We'll do it scientifically. If they burn you afterward, one by one, ashes don't show scars, left hand, right hand, twenty-penty, thirty-penty, clink, clink, ... listen!

—Mabutone, said Miss Inch the nurse, —or Methyltestosterone Mucorettes, between the upper lip and gum above incisors.

—Oops!...

—Take his arm.

—Luminal?

—Sedamyl.

—You have a guest. Your son...

—He's not big enough.

—Not you, not you. Doctor?...

—Try Palagren or Passiphen, or Pento-Del or Phanodorn...

—Reverend, your son?...

—Ooops!...

—The sun?

—Seconal or Sedamyl, Tolyphy or Tolyspaz...

—Wait a minute...wait a minute...

The refurbishing job which "Dick" had brought about in the church had been an extensive one. To begin with, the bell had been replaced with an electrically driven sound system which not only rang out the hour in more dulcet tones, but summoned the congregation on Sunday mornings by playing familiar hymns especially recorded for the purpose, and broadcast from the church spire in lively resonant notes originally drawn from a novochord, or something similarly up-to-date (it is true, there were days when the wind behaved badly that it sounded like a Hawaiian guitar).

The hole in the roof had, of course, been repaired; and the interior done over in taupe and white. The gilded organ pipes had disappeared; and so had all of the harsh angles of woodwork; instead, eyes and voices were lifted to smooth turns and flexures in taupe, and two bullet-shaped chromium lights trained on the pulpit, whence the President of the United States was exhorted with benedictions for the first time since the assassination of James A. Garfield. The oaken boards, where hymn and verse had been posted during services, were no longer necessary, for programs were now printed up every Sunday, detailing not only the service but other church activities. The programs sometimes ran to three or four pages, not counting the front which bore a "nice" (slightly Gothicized) likeness of the church itself.

Sturdy brass basins had taken the place of the wicker baskets for the offertory (not, in this illuminated Protestant world, of course, the tendering of bread and wine for Divine approval before their consecration; but here, according to custom, that equally exquisite and perhaps more realistically inspired moment of communion, when "Dick" received the brimming basins from the ushers, and solemnly held them up somewhere over his head in a gesture of intercourse of the most intimate dimensions imaginable to those who had contributed).

On the whole, the congregation looked rather younger; and it is just possible that "Dick's" "bad habit" might have had something to do with this. It seemed he had, at the outset, perceived that an entirely virtuous man, even one of the cloth, occupies an untenable position in society; and sensed the wisdom in giving one's neighbors some small vice upon which to latch their rancor at the absence of larger ones. Had his wisdom grown of years as well as wit, he might have gone a step further with his logic and had the good sense to conduct this vice in private, thus giving it the aura of secrecy, and so something to be spoken of in whispers among the townsfolk: but no. He did not give them that satisfaction. He let himself be seen in public, smoking his small cigars. Now for one thing, there were certainly members of this community who did believe an entirely virtuous man possible, men who themselves had shrunk to those proportions; and then among the ladies, there were some who had no intention of considering this a minor vice, but felt every bit as strongly about tobacco as did England's first, and Scotland's sixth, King James, whose Bible they retired to read in the clear dry air of their fathers, and the fathers before them, piqued in their solitude, it is true, on occasional Sunday mornings when the wind was wrong, and that air shimmered painfully with crystal tones and clear glissandos from the chaste spire turned campanile, where the new minister, whose forebears, it was generally known, sprang from somewhere in New Jersey, prepared to lead off with Hymn Number 347 in the *Pilgrim Hymnal*, —O God be-neath thy guid-ing hand... Our ex-iled fa-thers crossed the sea...

Still, a number of gray petrous visages continued to appear, drawn on by a habit which they called duty, and perhaps, though none would have admitted it, a sort of perilous curiosity roused by this young man who invoked flesh and deity alike in whistling tones which bounced off their northern souls like shiny stones scaled over still water. As for those whistling punctuations, they were first credited to some electrical distemper in the public address system, for there was now a microphone mounted on the pulpit through which "Dick" managed to convey, if not severe awe, moments of anxiety, and if not wonder, moments of acute embarrassment; if he could not tender mystery, he could arouse curiosity, rewarded with ceremony if not ritual, inspiring, if not hope, then sincere desire, if not faith, allegiance, if not charity, tolerance.

In keeping with the general spirit of refurbishing (for even the arrow at the entrance to town had been changed to point the real direction of the imminent curve, a kindness to strangers though it caused some confusion at first for the natives), the weathercock atop the spire had been exchanged for a cross, and "Dick" ministered wearing a pallium (he called it a "surplice"). All this, what elders were left him bore very well; and he was quite popular among the young people. They asked him weighty questions: one young lady, whether he would approve her reading a current novel, entitled *SENSATION* (it was one of those books called "bitter satire" by those who think life better than they find it, and "inadequate" by those who find it a good deal worse than they had thought); and he did not say no. (He was waiting, and would in vain, for it to appear condensed in the *Reader's Digest*.) It was the same girl who had asked him earlier if a passage she showed him from Katherine Mansfield were sacrilegious: something which mentioned the soul being "set before its Maker, hatless, disheveled and gay, with its spirit unbroken..." And though this was a sensation which had certainly never occurred to him, "Dick" indulged it in what he, with Saint Peter, regarded as the "weaker vessel."

In spite of all "Dick" had done to brighten things up, the parsonage held a sense of bereavement about it. His heels clicking on the floors (for he wore metal taps, to save leather so he said) echoed sharply and came back to him in creaks in the woodwork. And he found himself, when he should have been busy culling a sermon, standing instead at the window of the dark downstairs room which he never used, staring through evergreen branches at a distant shrouded hill; or, as he sat quietly going through letters, or the church's business, bent forth from his chair, listening, staring at nothing, listening to and then for, creaking sounds from other parts of the house. And one afternoon in the bright upstairs room he had chosen for his study, he dozed off, in the midst of considering plans to co-operate in a large (interdenominational) campaign to dispatch airborne Bibles, via hundreds of free-floating balloons, to a part of the world where they were, presumably, desired. He awoke at dusk sitting bolt upright, startled by silence, looked around where nothing moved, unable even hours later to shake from his head (which he literally tried to do) the sound of a child crying, which he thought he had heard.

He had already considered removing, to a neat white house only two doors from the church itself, nearer "the center of things."

That happened before the winter was fairly out, soon after the death of his predecessor, whom "Dick," being of a responsible nature, followed to the crematorium with that somberly vacant mien composed for such occasions with as much care, and similar in result, to the face the lid is closed upon once it has been drained of any suggestion of death, life, or familiarity. For the ashes, however, he had no idea what to do with them but leave them behind, until a fortunate incident occurred when he went to the cascaded books in the closet, seeking material for a memorial sermon. He settled down to what he would refer to as "these quaint and curious volumes of forgotten lore"; and though startled at the outset to discover the cavity cut in *The Dark Night of the Soul*, and about to lay that pleasantly scented curio aside, a paper fell from it which proved to be his predecessor's last will and testament. In that, he found the request that "the remains be laid to rest" (that phrase was "Dick's") with those of "the wife of the deceased" (so was that). It was fortunate in more than one way, for it gave "Dick" occasion to congratulate himself on his procrastination in another matter, which he could now call "foresight." In a kitchen closet he had come upon a large package of food staples, loosely tied in already-addressed wrapping paper, which he'd meant to send off and generously pay the postage himself. The operation which followed was a rather hurried one, for this red-blooded young man had an instinctively healthy distaste for death. Remembering the sturdy oatmeal boxes in the upstairs closet, he got one, transferred the ashes from the delicate urn in which they'd been delivered, and clamped the round top in tight, noting as he did so that it carried the family name stamped in the tin. This he put into the parcel already bound for Spain, sent it off (by ordinary ship post, since he was paying the charges himself), and only when he sat down to write the covering letter did he realize that he'd forgot to take the name of the monastery where it was bound. In an almanac, he found a prominent monastery located at Montserrat, and so he addressed his letter, in cordial English (on a church letterhead) there, considering that if it were not quite the right one, things would be straightened up at that end, where they were, after all, all Spanish, and after all, all Catholic.

Before Sunday came by, he'd spent time thumbing through Tertullian and Origen, Sozomen and Zosimus, and the evidence in the *Avesta*, noting down marked passages, all of which would serve as batteries for exposition, but the text itself of course, must come from the Bible. He sat back in a deep chair and smoked his way through a small cigar.

It was in this inert position, and with no change in his expression at all (as a matter of fact he had finished the cigar and was picking his nose), that "Dick" was inspired to take his text from I Corinthians, "the foolishness of God..." what was it? "Hath not God made foolish the wisdom of this world?" He got up mumbling —"Unto the Jews a stumblingblock, and unto the Greeks foolishness..." looking for the familiar gold-lettered black spine, —"But God hath chosen the foolish things of the world to confound the wise..." His blank look gradually focused as his lips, pursuing "Because the foolishness of God is wiser than men..." slowed and went dead. There, on the maple table, lay one of seventeen and a half million copies of the latest issue of the *Reader's Digest*, in which he became so engrossed, that he took it to bed with him.

—And don't you know, said one of the Ladies, going on from shaking "Dick's" hand out into the sunshine of the newly graveled drive before the church, —I even felt that it was a little impertinent...

For the sermon was not a great success. In spite of "Dick's" earnest and refreshing manner, and the trouble he had gone to, combing through the marked passages in the books jumbled in the closet, to make Mithraism sound unattractive, several people felt as that Lady did.

Nevertheless, on this particularly fine morning it would have been difficult to harbor any sense but one of well-being. "Dick" was, this morning, behaving with even more than his usual bonhomie, even showing some cordiality to the sexton of whom he did not wholly approve, for it was known that the small modest man, formerly the station master, liked his daily glass of beer, could, in fact, sit over it an entire afternoon below-stairs: a comforting figure to many in the community for all his small beer, not likely, on his small stipend, to be found rolling lopsided down Summer Street at odd hours of the night, singing unchristian songs.

If "Dick's" bonhomie was, as it appeared to be, exaggerated after service, it was because with his penetrating insight he had sensed something wrong, about halfway through his sermon, a restlessness which commenced with his passage from I Corinthians, and seemed to rise especially among the older faces, as he went on into the contents of the "quaint and curious volumes of forgotten lore," doing his best to show Mithraism in its "true" light, and its most recent propagator, if not demented, certainly misled. Supported by the battery of purloined mercenaries, Justin Martyr and Tertullian, Origen, Arnobius, Firmicus Maternus, Augustine Bishop of Hippo, Paul of Nola . . . "Dick" could hardly fail in his unnecessary cause. Reading from the ex-Manichee Hippian bishop, he had reached this point when he noticed lips moving here and there, as though minds were already wandering: —"For evil spirits invent for themselves certain counterfeit representations of high degree, that by this means they may deceive the followers of Christ . . ."

—But don't you know . . . as one of the Use-Me Ladies said later, —there was something . . . She sniffed. —Something . . .

For "Dick" had brought to the pulpit all of the notes he had made; and this panegyric upon Julian written by Himerius, was among them. Antagonistic as it might be to the original Corinthian epigraph, he found it in time to change his course and, that abruptly, come in on still water with the wind at his back, for he did read it very well:

"He by his virtue dispelled the darkness which forbade the uplifting of the hands to the Sun, and as though from the cheerless life of an underworld he gained a vision of the heavens, when he raised shrines to the gods and established divine rites that were strange to the city, and consecrated therein the mysteries of the heavenly deities. And far and wide he bestowed no trifling grants of healing, as the sick in body are revived by human skill, but unlimited gifts of health. For with a human nature akin to the Sun he could not fail to shine and illuminate the way to a better life."

Soon after that day, the new minister moved down to the neat white house "nearer the center of things."

From his back yard, partly tilled as a garden, Mount Lamentation still reared in the distance, and more distant when it withdrew, shrouding itself in time of storm. He seldom looked toward the old parsonage, unless at evening watching birds gather and compose their course toward that eminence already dark, where a tree had fallen through into an upstairs window and leaned there so, where so many curious things had turned up, and would turn up, even, in some digging after the carriage barn was leveled when it threatened to collapse, to a small skeleton, and don't you know the story gained ground, that this was the son? though some thought they remembered him grown older, bigger than this evidence, as time passed and no one ever saw him again, the story remained, with the parsonage to witness, a place with a sense of bereavement about it, though no one has come or gone in a long time.

PART III

I

"There are many Manii at Aricia."

IN PATIENTLY prolonged collision with the sea (to such an untropical degree of frankness that a concrete length of seawall is necessary to separate them), and then retreating up the hills, lies the Central American port of Tibieza de Dios. Shiploads of iron beds, houses of broken bannisters whose paint is unable to tell to the querulous eye of the foreigner (for no native would question) what was its original color, indeed has forgotten itself, the streetlights bare electric bulbs strung on wires, it has the transient air of a ragged carnival never dismantled. The population is largely black. It is governed by descendants of Spain who live on the central plateau, given work by an American fruit company whose white employees live between ten strands of barbed wire and the sea, and its modesty and sophistication are at once satisfied in acres of brilliant calico provided by the Tibieza Trading Company, a family of seventeen Chinese, all male, and all different shapes, whose veranda card game never ends.

Traffic often consists only in the gay orange garbage carts, passengered by black vultures who ride rocking in mistrust on top, or follow running, half in flight, behind. In the postprandial heat of midday no human inhabitants may be seen at all (except for the card players) and passers-by in the streets hardly nod acquaintance, for they are dogs, vultures, and occasional horses moving with easy poise, looking neither right nor left, as though on their way to appointments as casually futile as the tides. When the afternoon rain is over, black stirrings begin again, and the natives appear in such states of disintegration that a bit of string knotted round the wrist or neck seems to indicate that even these parts would be lost unless tied on.

Drift in suspension, the only sounds were the dry bird-calls of old men selling peanuts, —*Mani ... mani ...* that and the sea. Now, after three days of rain, it was brown, green further out, and the horizon a hard line of blue against the gray sky. The steel braces of the pier were rusted to ankle thinness at the water line, and the sea crashed in around it against the seawall with merciless finality, piling its fullness into reckless weights of water and hurling that in, tirelessly. At first sight, that seawall looked ridiculous, a pitiful barrier which the sea could easily swarm over to obliterate this frail town. But again the water was abruptly smashed into whiteness and hurled back upon itself.

Otto, though as yet he did not know it, was on his way to Tibieza.

At that moment his airplane sat like a great sow on the field at New Orleans, bulging from end to end and barely containing the weight of its long belly from the ground. Otto was an even color of yellow. This was interrupted in his clean-shaven face by the two ghastly pits of his eyes, staring out in exhausted possession. His hands, both free and one noticeably whiter, both shook. He had imagined, at other times, himself outwitting scores of the finest minds of international detective forces, casually committing deeds of stupefying audacity, of inhuman daring... (just then, as a uniformed porter passed, his hand shook so raising a cigarette to his lips that he rested it on his knee, and turned again to stare at the book he held propped against the chair arm).

He pressed his wrist against the bulge of his wallet, to assure himself that the crammed wallet, and his ticket for Balboa airport, in Panama, were still there. His flight was announced. He went out to the field. Mail was loaded. Luggage was loaded. A white-crated dog, spurting with excitement, was loaded. Startled by the immensity of the airplane as he stood beside it, the air and his whole inner body were suddenly shaken by another airplane taking off before him. Abruptly, then, the fury of the other rising airplane was gone; and a frail bird flew by, in silent dignity, and in the opposite direction.

Otto noticed that one wing of his airplane looked curiously bent. A man in uniform passed. Otto almost spoke to him about it, then caught himself. Or perhaps the man in uniform knew the thing was bent suicidally? did not intend to do anything about it? It would be quite a job, straightening it. Otto looked at his watch. Obviously there wasn't time. It looked tremendous.

The great body throbbed on the ground. He sat in the womb of this furious animal. Then worse, it moved across that ground with desperate purpose, angry to leave it. Something lifted it, and it roared away from the sane hardness of earth into nothing. Smoke swirled past the windows: not smoke, but a cloud. There were the clouds below, moving restlessly over one another while the absurd silver animal hung above them motionless. From it, Otto looked out on the white fields below in a nervous exhaustion at being so enclosed, as though, could he get out there and sit down for awhile, everything would be solved. But it went on, hanging without self-consciousness as though it had forgot this preposterous thing it was doing. Heavier than air, it tore into a cloud, angrily shook itself through, conscious again. Frail, wings quivering with effort as unnatural as the bird's glide is harmony, it shifted, dropped, scaled over shallow green water and came down on Mexico for a rest, recollected its fury, gathered it, and tore away from the ground again with the frantic speed of one possessed, afraid to look back, as though to hesitate, to doubt for an instant, would lose all that illusion was making possible.

Below the sea lay still and hard as a field of lead.

Otto looked behind. Reassuringly, the tail assembly was following, though he could not see its full profile broken by the figure clinging to it, throwing the plane off balance. Beyond lay that giant curve, two colors, nothing more, separated by the surface luster of their meeting: the quiet limit of the world? It went on suspended up there, finally over Guatemala, whose twisting highways looked to him like the course of his own life. Then on the right, alarmingly close, stood a volcano, losing its quiet smoke against the green sky. It stood out of space, in time like a thing seen in memory. Not to be touched or known in any way, it ignored him, beauty which would admit no tampering, to be lost in the horror of intimacy. With every effort of his eyes it grew less real, more distant, as the airplane flew on, like a fragment of time itself scrambling through eternity.

Several thousand sensible feet below, on what had appeared a surface of lead, the *Island Trader* trundled south-by-west on the surface of the Caribbean sea. This vessel was a bare two hundred feet long, and its dirty hull, which kept it to a speed of seven knots, drew thirteen feet of water. Twin screws labored it forward. It had been built in Copenhagen in 1924 as a private yacht. Some time since it had seen the Atlantic, or even the North Sea: sheltered by the chain of the Antilles, it fared nobly upon a sea whose surface was like glass, as the Caribbean was now. The *Island Trader* was returning from Florida, where it had carried seven thousand stems of green bananas. The Honduran mess boy stood on deck watching the sun set. Jutting from the porthole beside his head, long toes of one black foot engaged those of another in contest, tugging at one corned toe whose compatriots were busy protecting it. The boy seemed tempted to leave the sunset and attend this contest for the winner. From inside, a voice sang, —*Littel girl, please leave my bachelor room . . .*

The sun had melted into the shape of a keyhole on the horizon, and the *Island Trader* moved as though enclosed by the sea and the dull beauty of the sky, with only a glimpse, through that open door, of the outside, real world of fire.

A shout of the mate's voice and the contest ended, abruptly the feet were withdrawn, to reappear a moment later in the door frame where Fuller paused to press them into shoes. —He callin me, Fuller said. —Mahn, I hope he not goin to be vexed again. This was because Fuller sat next to the mate, at the end of the table, at meals. Though immense bowls of mashed potatoes, platters of meat and fish, chops, croquettes, and many vegetables were served, the mate's diet never varied from pigs' feet, cooked roots, and banana chips. This choice was all that reached Fuller, unless he interrupted the silent prandial industry beside him to ask for something else. When the mate was vexed, Fuller dared not hazard this interruption. He did his best with what was left in the three serving bowls, when the plate beside him had been loaded with pigs' feet, cooked roots, and banana chips. Such fare was difficult, for Fuller had no teeth. He had sold them in Tampa, Florida, to a rising young buck with social aspirations, left behind, like Crassus below, admonished, —Say, did the taste of gold make thy mouth good?

In response to the darkening sky, the sea changed its surface from glass to marble, the Breche rose marble of Italy reflecting the broken color of the sun, and losing that, to the gray-white Piastraccia, reflecting light from nowhere, veined with shadows.

The sun sank over the sharp edge of the marble sea. The shout sounded again from above. Nevertheless, Fuller paused there at the rail for a moment, that momentary sense of something lost, that sudden moment of emptiness which pervades everywhere the instant the sun has disappeared.

There was trouble in Tibieza. No one there wanted it. It came from the capital, up on the central plateau, where brisk weather encouraged that troubled intelligence necessary for revolution. It was all very well for *them* to run about the hills firing old Springfield '06 rifles, ponderous brass French Hotchkiss machine-guns whose clips jammed after the first few explosions, heavy American water-cooled Brownings and delicate Italian Bredas: that stock of arms which has been floating about Hispanic America for decades, whereabouts totally unknown until necessity produces it with revolutionary magic in any one of the sister republics. All very well for the educated people up on the plateau to blow each other to bits, but for Tibieza . . . except that Tibieza de Dios, in fact its only reason for existence, was a port, and one of few. Therefore it must be taken. First, it was necessary to settle who held it. This was arranged one early morning, when three men suspected of belonging to the revolutionary party, and known to have participated in shady deals (an easily made and always justifiable charge) were shot over their morning coffee, in reprisal for removal of the local priest who had been found garishly made up with lipstick, and castrated, sitting on one of the petrified sponge-like rocks at the end of the seawall in an attitude of repose, with a hole in one side of his head where an ear had been, and out the other.

After that, even the veranda card game moved indoors.

The cathedral, in a state of such genial collapse that it looks never to have been built stone by stone, its arches chipped and smooth so that no one stone stands away from another, its saints armless and headless waiting, smoothed and quietened by the rain, in open niches, its towers hanging heavy with the silent bells, stands to one side of the central plaza, behind a pitted concrete wall. These pits, obviously due to poor contracting years ago, were now circled with chalk, and scribbled beside them, "Calibre .45 para los niños," though actually no children were known to have been blown up in some time. Across that plaza stood the Hotel Bella Vista, girt with a rickety balcony, and leaning, as though rickets were familiar throughout its frame, like a hipshot elder, toward the sea. There were a few large trees in the plaza, which was surfaced with concrete. Just around the corner, toward the beach, was the office of Doctor Espinach, whose sign told that he had been educated in the United States of America.

It was upon this strip of beach that Otto's mighty airplane careered to an ungainly stop. The passenger who had caused this aerodynamic embarrassment, by riding outside instead of in, was so cold that he remained fixed to the tail assembly as the others got out to see why their giant had hesitated, what engine of human frailty had interfered with the miracle so preternatural that they took it for granted. The other passengers were a fairly dismal group, except for a handsome lady with an armload of orchids, and a small man whose clothes bulged suspiciously, both of whom seemed delighted to be put down right where they were. The fresh-air passenger had boarded in New Orleans, so he said, in Spanish, for that was all he spoke, with lips which were the only thing about him that he could move. —We would have seen you when we stopped in Mexico, said the co-pilot, who allowed miracles only a reasonable breadth. —Dios . . . dios . . . said the passenger. The plane might have waited until this problem was disposed of, but its arrival had caused some consternation, and delight, in the town. At that moment seven carloads of men were racing toward it, believing it had brought arms from the capital. Two of the cars were loaded with revolutionaries, four with loyalists, the last undecided, but armed. All stopped behind the dunes. Before he knew what was happening, the co-pilot was knocked awry with a bullet in his calf. He and the pilot consulted in decisive profanity, and a minute later the airplane roared down the beach and veered away into the sky, slightly cockeyed, its topside passenger so occupied holding on that he did not raise even a paralyzed arm in farewell.

The proprietor of the Bella Vista was a man with a heavy bunch of keys which rattled against his thick thigh as he strode up and down the first-floor veranda, avoiding the place over the dining-room door where the boards had gone through one night during a visit from United States Marines. He wondered what the airplane's mission had been, what all the shooting was about, and it was oafishness rather than courage that permitted him to expose himself as he was doing. All he saw, however, was a draggled figure in gray flannel crossing the empty plaza toward his door. Everything was silent but for a distant hum of song, punctuated by thuds, from the direction of the Baptist Church where a prayer meeting was in full sway. They were using their new bass drum to rousing effect, its clamor enhanced by the resonance of the roof, which was pleached of flattened oil tins.

Past the sign of Doctor Espinach, a tempting swinging target with three holes in it already, he came on looking slightly dazed, to be given a room with one window facing toward the sea, hung with forlorn curtains in the middle of a sagging string. Two doors led to nowhere, and the louvers in the outside door were broken. The wire to the electric bulb swung free on the wall. The sink gurgled like the plumbing on a ship. There were large pictures of blond girls on the wall, one holding daffodils for Carr's English Biscuits, the other, suffering a running jaundice brought on by a leak in the ceiling, presented a tray of Canada Dry. With a cigarette, he lay back to consider that modest portion of the ceiling which was painted, just over the bed, and his own, a swelling weight on his chest where the wallet lay empty of anything but uncounted bills. He had escaped twice, this second time from the certain difficulties he would have had upon reaching his destination and being asked to produce identity papers and a visa. He had escaped, where, he did not know, he did not think, he had not thought since Christmas Eve, and when thought or memory intruded he forced it off with calculation drawn to one purpose: to keep moving, with money no object but to spend his way through it, to keep moving and live it through, without looking back. He reached out on the floor and drew the chamber pot nearer, to use as an ashtray.

In the afternoon, it seemed that the loyalists were in full control. Police, at any rate, rode into the plaza, though no one was certain whether they were on the payroll of the loyalists or the revolutionaries. They were armed with pistols and carried sabers. This was because there was to be a demonstration, fomented in the local school and forbidden by the mayor, whose measure for peace and quiet was understood as a challenge to liberty.

The demonstration began on time. Boys marched into the plaza carrying placards which read, "Mothers! Your children have the right to be free!" and "Calibre .45 para los niños." Someone threw a rock at a mounted policeman.

Someone else threw another. The horses were having difficulty keeping their feet on the slippery concrete.

After a ghastly lunch served by a black girl sheathed in one spotted white garment, Otto wanted coffee. He waited. The dining room was festooned with fly-blown streamers of colored crepe paper, each leaf of which had lost most of its own color and borrowed some of its neighbor's. In the middle of the room, a fruit bowl stood on a table, a luxurious economy, for the bananas were so near rotten that no one ever took one, or at best, never took another. —No coffee. She burned the milk, the girl said. Otto lit a cigarette, and went out. He had got as far as a café across the plaza before the demonstration began. From there, he watched it progress. It made no sense. He started back toward the Bella Vista. The demonstration was noisy, but he looked on it with a tired eye, refusing to be taken in by such foolishness. Until a policeman rode toward him, swinging a saber; and the policeman's neck was covered with blood.

That suddenly, it was real. And as suddenly terrified, Otto looked frantically for sanctuary. The cathedral, with its protecting wall, stood waiting. He looked wildly round him but saw nothing as he started to run toward it. From behind the bandstand, a policeman rode, he and his mount looking in every direction, the man's and the horse's eyes matching in bloodshot apprehension, dodging the rocks that found them from above.

Just then a white bird came down in an arc from a branch, down falling like a stone before it ascended, and the policeman, dodging the threat, threw his weight over, his horse scrambled for a moment on the concrete and went down, and the falling flank caught Otto as he ran without seeing toward the church, spun him round and pinned him on the concrete, unconscious.

The vulture on the outside roof fussed for a moment, one wing extended, impatiently like a dignitary fully dressed for an appointment looking at his watch. Then the wing came back somewhat askew, as though he'd buttoned the coat up wrong, and not noticing it in his impatience stood rocking from one foot to the other.

In the street outside a little boy held up a male dog, exposed, for a female to investigate. His mother said to another and larger black woman, —Tomorrow morning, soon soon . . . Other little black boys passed, wearing men's hats. The card game was back out on the veranda.

Near the only occupied cot, in the schoolroom which had been used as a hospital, was posted a stuffed fox whose snarl exposed a pink fly-blown tongue. The doctor stood beside the cot looking down at the face. Nothing moved there but a fly. It rummaged a cheek for a moment, studied the caves of the nostrils, hurried across the bandage to the cleft of the chin, from that eminence sighted the convoluted marvel across the way, and leaped silently to the ear. The eyes flickered, and closed tightly as though to recall the long night and the wonder of nonentity it had permitted: recreation not for the body, nor the soul, but opportunity for circumstances to refurbish themselves, a hope untempered by ages of experience where morning brings no change, but only renewal of conflict on the terms it left off. The lips moved, drawing up twice on, —I know it . . . I know it . . . and then tightening to know sleep only, and there animate circumstance with the good intentions which had already brought it low in present disaster; and then descending, a little lower, only to belabor those good intentions, vicarious opiates laboring in half-consciousness to fall away before the pursuit of dreams, dreams ravin in tooth and claw, while the beard grows against the pillow in darkness.

The fly returned to course the warm terrain of the eyelid, moving with the careless persistence of diabolical things, and both eyes came open.

—What happened?

—I was going to ask you the same thing. They just brought you in here in pieces, and . . .

—I feel sick.

—Well you are sick, so it's a good thing you know it.

—I can hardly hear you.

—You're lucky you can hear me at all. Ever have ear trouble?

—Yes. No.

—Well, you do now. You might even have a deaf ear before you're through. Just like Julius Caesar, that would be nice, wouldn't it. Who are you? You're very young to show up with something like this. I might even say tragic if I knew who you were.

—Wait, I . . . I can't move my arm.

—That's partly because it's broken. Do you remember trying to walk yesterday? Please excuse my shouting at you.

—But what is it? what is it?

—Like a drunkard. Staggering around like a drunkard. Of course I might not say that if I knew who you were. We didn't find any papers on you at all. Just money. Money. Lots of it.

—Where is it?

—Lie back now, it's safe. All that money! But you can't run around spending it now. Don't be impatient. Why, look at me, I have a right to be impatient. I was sent down here to help these nig . . . natives with their drainage problems, and now look at me. They keep promising to transfer me to Barbados, but they never do. A special health project in Barbados... He had walked over near the window, and looked out. —I've sent for some more medicine for you. Of course I know all the time that I'll have to go get it myself eventually, this tattooed idiot who's supposed to work for me... Then he shouted out the window, —Jesse...! Jesse!... There, you see? He's nowhere to be seen. Worthless, useless, tattooed idiot... of course I wouldn't call him that if I thought he could hear me. This is the third time now that I've put in for a transfer to that special health project among underdeveloped... oops! Wait, don't throw up on the floor. Here... here we are. Ummmp! That's better. Feel better?

—But... what... what is this? Who are you?

—What are either of us doing here? Who are you? Tsk tsk, excuse my shouting at you.

—But you... you must tell me...

—I suppose I must. The doctor should not discuss the case with the patient, but who else can I discuss it with? Well, after your little accident, something set in. Something.

—Something what?

—Don't be hasty. Something. Maybe something entirely original. Do you hear noises in your ears?

—I hear you...

—I have to shout, or you couldn't hear me. Dizziness, nausea, vomiting, staggering, and down you go unconscious. It doesn't sound very original, does it. How would you like to have a disease named after you?

—But I...

—Well, I'll tell you a secret. It may be Ménière's disease. It may be. You'd accept that, would you? Because if it is we couldn't name it after you. We'll see. I've given you a little nicotinic acid. Do you work for the fruit company here?

—No... no, I...

—It's all right, don't explain. I'm on the outs with them too. If they knew I had you here they'd try to get you for their patient.

—No, I... now I...

—That's the spirit. Now you just wait here. If anyone comes in, cover up your head and moan. I'm going over to the fruit company dispensary, and try to get some Diasal for you. Diasal or Lesofac, Amchlor or Gustamate. If it is Ménière's syndrome, we'll have you up staggering around in no time. Of course I don't know where you'll stagger to, with no papers. What's your name? We can't name a disease after you if you don't have a name.

—But I... I...

—My name is Doctor Fell. There. What's yours?

—...Gordon. Gordon. My name's Gordon.

—All right Gordon. Don't throw up on the floor while I'm gone, Gordon. Gordonitis? tsk tsk...Get some sleep Gordon.

—But you...

—Roniacol or Dramamine...

The door banged. Outside all was quiet, except for the distant dull crash and recession at the seawall, where the rehearsal continued. The sun shone.

On the ridge of the tin roof across from the window, the vulture strode up and down, wings drawn back in a black mantle and head darting forward, like an old man thoughtful of money, hands restlessly grasping under the wings of his tailcoat. Then from somewhere an old man in a dry bird voice cried out, —Mani...mani...

II

"Miss Potter, where is God?"

"He is everywhere," replied Miss Potter with dignity.

"But, my dear Maiden," exclaimed His Highness, planting himself firmly on one of the chairs, "what good is that to *me*?"

—ACKERLEY, *Hindoo Holiday*

—A PATRON saint?

—It's a natural.

—What does she do?

—She intercedes.

—What do you mean, she intercedes.

—I don't know, but that's not the point. Look, they've dug up this Saint Clare. She's going to be patron saint for the whole industry.

—Where'd you hear all this?

—Story conference. Somebody read about it in the paper. They've already run up a rough script on it. She had a vision once, at a basilica, where she saw the whole Christmas thing appear before her eyes. It was sort of the first TV show, you might say.

—What's a basilica? What was she, Eyetalian? They didn't teach Eyetalian at Yale.

—I guess so. It's where Saint Francis of Assisi lived. The poor one. A place called Portiuncula.

—How come they call him Saint Francis of Assisi if he lived in Port...

—I don't know, but that's not the point. Look, for the program that inaugurates *The Lives of the Saints* on TV, this is a natural. The story line is terrific. This poor girl, she lives near Saint Francis, and finally she went around to ask him how she could be a saint too, like he was, except to start one for women. So he said...

—Start one what?

—Like a nunnery, but that's not the point. So he gave her this hair shirt, and told her to go out and beg for awhile, and then come to his place at Portiuncula dressed like a bride. So she did. It's a natural. This scene where all these monks meet her with lighted candles and walk her up to the altar.

—Then what. They get married?

—I guess so. Why else would she come dressed like a bride?

They walked in thoughtful silence for a moment. The long bare corridor was brightly lighted and empty, until a young man with a thin face, a slightly crooked nose, and a weary expression which embraced his whole appearance, passed them. —There, there's the guy who was working on this, he's one of the writers. Hey, Willie... But the weary figure went on. He was carrying two books, one titled, *The Destruction of the Philosophers*, the other, *The Destruction of the Destruction*. He rounded a corner away from them muttering, —Christ. Christ, Christ, Christ, Christ, Christ.

—It would be nice if we could get some kind of testimonial on this.

—She's dead, this saint.

—I know that, for Christ sake. I mean from somebody like the Pope. It would make a nice tie-in.

They walked on in thoughtful silence for a minute.

—Ever since the Vatican pulled that stunt of telling Catholics that seeing Mass on TV wasn't enough, that they still have to get out and go to church, when right in the comfort of their own living rooms they could...

—Ellery...!

—Morgie!

—You two guys know each other? Ellery, this is Mister Darling, he's the account exec handling Necrostyle...

—Know each other! Morgie's an old Skull and Bones man. The whole industry's being taken over by the Ivy League. How the hell are you, Morgie?

—I was saying the same thing at a party last night, Morgie said. —We all used to end up in the old man's brokerage, and now... you can't tell me advertising isn't the new Wall Street. He and Ellery walked down the bright corridor with their hands on one another's shoulders. The third man said, —The highest paid business in the U.S. today... and fell in behind them. He was an old Alabama Rammer-Jammer man.

—I just came up for a look at our new morning show, said Morgie. —But why you've got a kids' ballet school on for Necrostyle, now what the hell Ellery, with kids' shows like the *Saints*...

—That's how you reach them, Ellery said, —through the kids. There's something about kids. People trust them, you know?

—But a ballet school! We want...

—We know what you want, Morgie. Just be patient, we know what you want.

A girl in a wedding dress stood outside a door in the empty corridor. She was very young, and the heavy make-up on her face almost hid her bad case of acne. She smiled uncertainly as they approached. —Lost, baby? Ellery asked her. She nodded and sniffed, up this close she looked about to cry. —You're on the Let's Get Married program? Ellery winked at her. She nodded and sniffed hopefully. —Look, down there, quick, see that guy in the skirt coming out of the men's room? Quick, follow him. It's studio thirty-seven, he called after her as she ran, hampered by her tight wedding skirt, her sharp heels calibrating the silence of the corridor, away from them.

The third man turned and watched the restricted motion of her thighs. At present he had a single modest ambition: he was trying to get a line he had heard somewhere into the script of a highly paid comedian. The line was, It looked so nice out this morning I left it out all day. The censors would not have it: they said it was immoral. Nevertheless, he thought it was one of the funniest things he had ever heard. He also had a salt-shaker which he carried and used in public places. It was a crude plastic reproduction of the Venus de Milo. The sign in the place where he had bought it said, *Because of the amusing way in which these shakers pour, better hide them when Grandma's around.* He was becoming a "character," which was exactly what he wanted. When he went out he wore a cap. The person who had sold it to him had told him that he looked like the Duke of Northumberland in it. Now he said, —What a nice tight little can.

Morgie looked at the girl too, over his shoulder. —You couldn't get into that with a can-opener. It's a crime the way they tie it in.

—No disparaging remarks.

—What d'you mean?

—We got the Kanthold Korsets account.

—What's the tape over your eye, Morgie? Did she bite you?

—This party I was at last night. A bunch of scared intellectuals, you know? A bunch of goddam unamericans.

—But you told them, didn't you Morgie. Ellery turned to the third man. —Morgie's serious as hell. He was always serious, even in college.

—This is serious, goddam serious. Don't kid yourself, Morgie said. —They corrupt, these goddam intellectuals do. They corrupt.

—I told you Morgie was serious, Ellery said, and grinned. —See what he got defending his country?

—Don't kid yourself. Some bastard started in on how New York would change if prostitution was legalized. Clean honest whorehouses, see?

—In that case, you'll have to consider me unamerican too, in Alabama ...

—No, the point was sublimation, see? This is the whoring of the arts, and we're the pimps, see?

—You should have hit him.

—I did. That's where I got this. Morgie pointed to the tape above his eye. —No matter how much you talk to them, they don't get it. It's too simple. It's too goddam simple for them to understand. They still think their cigarettes would cost them half as much without advertising. The whole goddam high standard of American life depends on the American economy. The whole goddam American economy depends on mass production. To sustain mass production you got to have a mass market. To sustain a goddam mass market you got to have advertising. That's all there is to it. A product would drop out of sight overnight without advertising, I don't care what it is, a book or a brand of soap, it would drop out of sight. We've had the goddam Ages of Faith, we've had the goddam Age of Reason. This is the Age of Publicity.

—O.K. Morgie, you believe in it. Come into the control room and see your dancing girls.

—Goddam right I believe in it. You got to regard advertising as public information, that's what it is.

—O.K. Morgie, relax. Put out your cigarette.

Morgie dropped his cigarette on the floor, and stopped to put it out with his shoe. —I know it, but I get browned off the way some people talk. They talk as if we weren't respectable.

—It's the highest paid business in the U.S., said the old Alabama Rammer-Jammer man.

A man in shirt-sleeves came through the door. —You seen Benny? Ellery asked him.

—Benny who?

A girl going the other way heard this. —I know who you mean, she said to Ellery. —He's in OP, nobody around here knows him. I know who you mean, he was here earlier and he left.

—Thanks, said Ellery; hunching up one shoulder he dropped his cigarette, put it out, and watched the girl go down the hall as he held the door.

—You've only got two cameras up there? Morgie asked. They stood looking at three selective screens. Ellery nodded. —I don't think I'd call this even a B show, even for morning, Morgie said. He was watching the close-up screen where a four-year-old girl, extended at the practice rail, smiled a personality smile into the wrong camera. Ellery looked at his watch.

—And look. What the hell are they doing now, is this part of this show? Ellery was watching that screen, where the façade of an ugly church quivered into focus. The image moved to the squat steeple, and turned up to follow the spire to its top. —There's a guy up there, there's a guy climbing up it ...

Someone handed Ellery a telephone. —That's right, telephoto on number one as soon as you get number two camera set up down in the street, got me? Cut an announcement in right now, got me? First-hand coverage of a stark human drama, take it from there. Get the church in, nice if you can get a shot of the service going on but don't bust *that* up, got me? That's it, that's it ... he went on, watching the screen. —Lift it a little, get the bells in ...

—See if they can get the whole goddam cross in, Morgie whispered.

——Ladies and gentlemen, Necrostyle, the modern scientific aid to civilized living, interrupts its regular program, *Today's Angels*, to bring you on-the-spot coverage of a stark human drama ...

The close-up screen flashed into life again with the figure of a man mounting the shingled spire toward the cross. Ellery stood silent, gripping the telephone. —But wait a minute, he said. —Wait a minute ...

—Let it roll, let it roll, Morgie said beside him. —It's terrific.

—Wait a minute ...

—You can almost see the sweat on his face, Morgie said beside him. —Coming over like a dream.

—It's too bad they didn't get some pancake on him before he went up, said the old Alabama Rammer-Jammer man. —But that light blue necktie ...

—That light blue necktie ...

Morgie took a step closer to the screens. He held his breath. When he realized that the man beside him was holding his breath, he commenced to breathe self-consciously. The man beside him realized this, and he commenced to breathe self-consciously.

Then at the same instant they both stopped breathing again.

——Our camera seems to be having some difficulty ... We're sorry, friends, but because of the crowd which has gathered in the immediate vicinity there on the sidewalk it looks like we are going to be unable to bring our camera in for a close-up ...

—Like a dream, said Morgie, as they breathed again.

When the scene was obliterated in favor of a sleek-haired oily countenance, they turned to one another. —Where's Ellery?

—— ... brought to you through the courtesy of Necrostyle Products. And so friends, don't forget, *Necrostyle*, in the vanguard of modern civilized living. Ask your favorite druggist for the *Necrostyle* product that meets your needs. *Necrostyle*, the water-shaped sleeping pill, no chewing, no aftertaste. *Zap*, the wonder-wakener. *Cuff*, it's on the cuff. And *Pubies*, the newest ...

—Where's Ellery?

In the background, an electric organ played *The End of a Perfect Day*.

——...no harmful after-effects. For men *and* women over forty, start living again, with *Pubies*...

—He must have gone out, do you think it got him down?

——And so remember, friends, when *you* come to the end of a perfect day...

They went out to the bright corridor where, after a moment, Ellery appeared from an office. He was walking very slowly and staring at the floor. —I just had to see B.F. for a minute, he said when they joined him, and he stood there by the door and lit a cigarette.

—Like a dream, Morgie congratulated him. But Ellery did not raise his eyes. From the office they could hear a voice. It was B.F. on the telephone. —Hello, hello Ben? Listen, there was a jump a few minutes ago, it...what? No, this was a man, off a church up in the Bronx, he...Yeah, that's the point, it was one of our own men, a guy named Benny...what? I don't know, something must have went wrong. I know you can't hush it up, but try to keep us out of it...Yeah, they can play up this other one then, the woman...Inside the office B.F. hung up the telephone. He stared vacantly for almost a full minute. Then he clicked his lips and took out a cigar.

Ellery blew a heavy ring of smoke toward the floor. It rolled, getting larger, dropping more slowly, and settled round the toe of his shoe.

All this time Morgie was talking. —You handled it beautifully, it came over like a dream. But look, what's the matter, did it upset you? A thing like that? Look at it this way. Those things happen. This happened. We happened to be there. What the hell, it's all in a goddam day's work. Come on, he said as they started to walk down the corridor. Ellery dropped his cigarette and paused to step on it. —Come on, I'll buy you the best lunch in town. You'll bounce back.

—Twenty-one? said the Alabamarammerjammerman.

—Twenty-one Ellery?

—Twenty-one.

One after another the flashbulbs burst and, in the gray light of that day, seemed each time to arrest an instant of riotous motion as lightning freezes motion and then, in the dark again, the persistence of vision retains that image of abandon which could not have sustained itself, as it did here, on the winter pavement, after the newspaper photographer had bundled up his equipment and hurried into the hotel, hoping to make the sporting final.

The morning mail was late, for the falling body had struck the mailman, setting off a pattern of inconvenience which intruded upon many routines. Outside that hotel of faded Edwardian elegance which, having become a landmark, was about to be torn down, the body lay in a pose of reckless flamboyance, a gratuitous gesture annoying such passers-by as the tall woman who was leading a poodle and saying to a friend, —Her name is Huki-lau, that means fish-picnic in Hawaiian, isn't that cute? She used to bite her nails right down to the quick, analysis is doing her a world of good. Oh God! Look! No, don't look.

Discovered breathing, she was taken away on a stretcher instead of the pinewood crate which was already half unloaded.

The hotel room itself proved so rewarding that the newspaper photographer telephoned for more flashbulbs, and asked the city desk to send over somebody with shorthand. He said the reporter with him had just been taken sick by the fumes. Then he hurried back down the hall, took a deep breath, and entered that mélange of smoke, whisky, and roses, where he paused only to sweep some of the letters into a pile with his foot as graphic witness to the story which would say that they were ankle-deep all over the room. The bottles he did not have to rearrange at all, their hollow necks protruded everywhere. As for the roses, he could not have done a better job if he'd taken a month to it. They were festooned dead, dying, and two or three dozens still in bloom, wherever that desperate ingenuity could contrive, and the hand reach. —Roses ... he would say later (when someone was trying to recall a line of poetry that contained "Roses, roses..." to use in the caption), —Roses till hell wouldn't have them. The bathroom, especially, was entirely transformed. There was no place to sit down at all.

But when he returned to his office, the newspaper photographer found an atmosphere of tense gloom which even his prize plum could not dispel. The managing editor, the feature editor, and the foreign editor were all gazing at a story from their own columns. There were two pictures: in one, a little girl in long white stockings; but they were looking at the other, a man with a round face whose limp flabby quality was belied by an exquisite mustache and penetrating eyes beneath a sharply parted widow's peak. —That bastard, one of them muttered, and which one was not clear, for all of their expressions reflected the same feeling. —That dago bastard.

—All right, how much is four million lires? What are lires, Spanish or Italian?

—Eyetalian.

—What do these spies want with Eyetalian money? for Christ sake.

—That's their business.

—Six thousand six hundred sixty-six dollars and two-thirds of a cent, a junior reporter reported, after careful miscalculation.

—Lemme see that God damn letter again. "A respectable business man and professor," for Christ sake. "A mere child in arms when this unhappy incident occurred," for Christ sake. "Reparations ... my unblemished character ... four million (4,000,000) lire ..." for Christ sweet sake.

—You're a Catholic yourself, aren't you?

—Christ yes, but not one of these ignorant spic Catholics.

—So?

—So we're screwed. We'll settle for three million. How much is that? ... And what the hell is all this?

—These are some of the letters from that hotel room where that dame jumped out the window, the photographer said, and continued pulling them out of a bulging pocket. —You didn't send me a speedwriter down so I just brought some along before the cops moved in.

—Any good reporter would have done that in the first place. Why didn't you bring them all?

—I would have needed a truck ...

—So you just left the rest of them there, for every other paper in town to sift through ...

—I mailed one of them.

—You *what?*

—There was a thick one all sealed, with the name of this Doctor somebody on it, so I just looked his name up in the phone book and wrote an address on it ...

—You stupid bastard. You stupid stupid bastard. What address?

—I don't remember, the first one I saw under his name, I think it was somewhere on Fourteenth Street ...

—Oh you stupid bastard.

—I just thought I'd do her a favor, I ...

—You just thought ... Christ! How did you get onto this paper? How did any of you get onto this newspaper? And how much is three million lire, didn't you figure it out yet?

—All I get is sixes, six six six ...

—All right, shut up. And now what's this?

—A watch. I found it on the pavement beside her.

—Jesus Christ. The battered thing dangled between his fingers. —Even Minnie wouldn't know him.

It was roses, roses, all the way

And like an avenue of flags unfurled, the newspapers quivered in the hands of passengers whose faces reflected costive content and requited destitution,

prodigies of unawareness, done with plotting against life, secure in disenchantment, recovered from the times when Cleopatra's gnathic index, or Nefertiti's
cephalic index, might have made a difference, while the train shook only negligent response from attitudes which flouted the aesthetician who devised the
divine proportion of seven to one from the dimensions of the human being.

All save one: for there was an alertness about Mr. Pivner's attitude, as there
was an eagerness in his face, which distinguished him, hurrying home now
under the ground. Eddie Zefnic was coming over again this evening, and they
were going to listen to something on the radio which Eddie said was very
worth listening to.

Above ground, he hurried, scarcely pausing at curbs, scarcely pausing to
greet Jerry when he got his paper, almost run down at his own corner where
a truck swerved past bearing before his eyes a primitive family pictogram and
the legend, "None of us grew but the business." Even near his own door he
scarcely paused when he dropped a coin into the tin cup of the blind accordion
player who had been stationed there the last few evenings.

Once inside he did not waste a moment, did not even pause to lock the
door behind him, entered in darkness straight across the room to the floorlamp,
which he turned to its highest brilliance. He ate with no sensation but of what
was too hot, what too cold; looked three times to make sure of two quart
bottles of beer in the icebox; took his injection with professional dispatch;
and then, his shoulders drooping in weariness, squaring again with pride, he
drew on his dressing gown, pulling its generous folds tight: for he still had
the sense that it had been a gift from the guest he expected. He turned on the
radio and it responded with *The Bells of Saint Mary's*, played by the Department of Sanitation Band. Uncertain just what it was that Eddie had said
would be very much worth listening to, he left it at that and sat down with
his newspaper.

THE GHOST ARTISTS He read the advertisement automatically.

We Paint It   You Sign It   Why Not Give an Exhibition?

He gazed at it a minute longer without understanding, and then went on to
an article which said that Swedish scientists hoped soon to be able to breed
men ten feet tall.

He could not concentrate. It was not that he was without his glasses, which
he had hardly worn since Christmas: he could read clearly enough. It was not
that the newspaper was less provoking than usual: quite the other way, in fact.
In addition to the front-page story, where he read fragments from the letters
found in "ankle-deep" dispersal in the hotel room (including a proposal of

marriage addressed to a man executed for murder some time since, a discrepancy accounted for with evidence of a crumpled news item torn from an old paper used to wrap the roses), there were other diverting tribulations: the bones of Sitting Bull, buried in North Dakota, had been dug up by unauthorized persons and buried in South Dakota; a man apprehended on a charge of engraving ten-dollar bills said that it had grown out of etching nature studies, he had "just drifted into counterfeiting from a hobby of fooling around with engraving copper plates"; a Reverend Gilbert Sullivan had been arrested for practicing phrenology without a license and, on the side, distributing literature which described his South African kingdom, holy water from the spring of Nebo, Uncle Ned's Black Cat bone dust, Eagle-Eye Joe's controlling powder, Aunt Sally's Black Cat pussy-foot oil, and Mother Duck's holy No. 8 oil... then the doorbell rang.

—It's *The Messiah* by Handel, Eddie said after they had exchanged slightly embarrassed greetings, and he put down his armload of new books. —It's on this real little station, he went on, approaching the radio with a businesslike air, the slight apology in his tone articulating the expression on the face of the owner of this modest plastic affair who stood behind him, one hand clasping the other anxiously.

——What have I *du-un*...and so friends to get your free...managed to hold onto the ball...en este momento...and now in a brand new...

—Is it...time for it yet? Mr. Pivner asked hesitantly, prompting, self-conscious, a shyness reflected in the face of his skinny earnest guest as a hand dug into a pocket and the gold watch snapped open, and Mr. Pivner looked at him, and into his future with the thrill he had once known contemplating his own.

—I don't get much chance to listen to music any more since I'm studying so much, Eddie said, standing over the radio with an uncompromising look on his face, and like Pandora's box, the stream of things shut up in that marvelous creation poured out as he turned the dial. —It ought to be right here, he murmured, as though indeed seeking the one beneficence which remained behind when the lid was lifted and all of the torments and absurdities lying there in wait rushed forth, to inflict themselves with such thoroughness in man's life that he came to take them for granted as a part of it. —There's no...hope, Eddie muttered, as brackish laughter, turned on like a tap, burst in his face.

—Eddie...

——Owners of television sets in the metropolitan area witnessed a stark human tragedy in their own living rooms, when...

—Listen...!

The Messiah was trying to squeeze through an infinitesimal aperture, where it was being jostled, shouldered, pushed aside and out of shape by an acrobatic contest among violins performing Paganini's *Perpetual Motion*, on one side, and a cordially inane voice addressing friends, finally a quiz program where a house was being given away among much disciplined merriment.

Mr. Pivner listened with all his attention, faintly able to follow

——He was despiséd ... rejected ... a man of sorrows ...

But he found himself following the quiz program, where a Mr. Crotcher had just answered a question concerning a fable with an ant for its hero, and won a completely furnished house in a popular suburban community called Arsole Acres.

——A man of sorrows and acquainted with grief ... while the voice described the joys of the suburban community (its singular name derived, it appeared, from the Latin *ars* meaning art), and the doorbell rang.

There was something familiar about the man standing behind the one who flicked open a hip-pocket wallet with one thumb, to flash the star of the Secret Service as they entered.

—And who's this?

Eddie Zefnic was standing, as wide-eyed as his host.

—This? a ... young friend of mine, he ... what is this, officer?

—You better come along too.

—But what's this about?

—You can tell us what it's about, when we get downtown.

—But ... where are we going?

—The corner of West and Eleventh Streets, the Treasury man said patiently. Then, —Wait a minute, let's have a look at this bathrobe.

—But this, I ... Mr. Pivner commenced, getting out of it.

They looked at the label. —This is the one, all right ... and rolled it up. —You're going to tell us you didn't know it was paid for with queer money?

—But ... Mr. Pivner was getting into his jacket, his coat, his green muffler. Eddie Zefnic was picking up his new science textbooks.

—Wait a minute, where you going?

—Just to ... to get my glasses, Mr. Pivner said, and the man who had been silent accompanied him into the bedroom. Only as they were about to leave he spoke,

—You might as well turn off your radio, you won't be back here tonight ... and Mr. Pivner recognized him, as he hurried back across the dark room while they waited in the door. It was the blind accordion player.

—O.K., let's go ... But even now, habit did not desert Mr. Pivner. He waited until the radio announcer had finished his sentence,

——And now friends, stay tuned for drama with the impact of reality.

*

The program was introduced by *Beautiful Dreamer*, played on the studio organ. Somewhere, distant, spectral, came the tender alleluias of a sixteenth-century processional, written by Gabrieli, to be led across the plaza of Saint Mark's, where he was organist.

——I came here from another state thinking I would be more happier with my father and . . . an insistent quailing voice commenced; and the apparitions on the plaza of Saint Mark's retired. ——Now just a minute, dear, how old are you? . . . With preternatural and delicate strength, the specters reappeared, for an instant directly the viscous voice left off, and then, ——Twelve years old and I came here from another state thinking I would be more happier with my father and my father start drinkin again and beatin up on my step-mother . . .

There was a crash. Stanley stood, and withdrew his foot from the front of the plastic radio, which was on the floor. He stood, staring at it, unable to believe that he had done such a thing: but there it lay in a mute tangle at his feet. Then he looked over his shoulder, alarmed as though he might have been seen by someone (the owner of the borrowed radio, for instance). Round him, everything in the room was packed in readiness, everything but the crucifix over his bed. Stanley's eyes reached that, and rested on it. His tooth began to ache again, the same one that had been aching the hour his mother died; and with that dull throbbing pain that memory returned, throbbing as vividly. Then Stanley squared his shoulders. He stood up straight, a movement which drew breath into his chest. He closed his teeth together hard, and then turned off the light without a glance at the bundle which held his almost completed work, palimpsests bound together with clean scores which he hoped to alter and copy on the boat; and he went out the door without stopping at the communal hall bathroom, as he'd meant to, pause there and correct that multiplication problem for the thousandth time, out on the street with no idea where he was going. He soon arrived at that place where everyone else who had started out as aimlessly decided was the place they'd started out for.

The juke-box was playing *Return to Sorrento*, and Ed Feasley, whom he did not think he had ever met, greeted him with, —Hello . . . Chr-ahst, and handed him a glass of beer.

A weary atmosphere hung over the place. People stood about at odd angles, like clocks which must be stood at odd angles to keep running, finally all that is expected of them, for they seldom tell the right time, cracked faces kept around for familiarity as long as they keep some track of day and night.

—And so then she broke right out in Braille . . . someone said.

And Hannah asked Ed Feasley to buy her a glass of beer. While he was getting it she turned to Stanley and said, —I hear you're going to Rome and be a Pilgrim. Where you getting the money?

—My mother . . . left it.

—Insurance? you can't get insurance if you . . .

—No, it was . . . she had it pinned in her clothing, in her underclothing.

—I hear your lady friend with the white fingernails went out a window too.

—What? Stanley looked at her aghast.

—Didn't you hear? Max was in here, he had a newspaper. It's all over the front page. She jumped out a hotel window.

—No but, she wouldn't have jumped, she might have . . . fallen, he faltered. —She wouldn't just . . . to kill herself . . .

—She jumped, don't be . . . that way about it, she jumped. And she didn't kill herself, she just smashed herself up. She's in Bellevue the paper says. Hannah accepted her beer, sipped it without a word, and turned, —Hey where you going?

—Well I thought I might go over there, over to Bellevue . . .

—Come on, for Christ sake, you can't go in there this late. You probably can't visit her anyhow. She's probably all strung up there . . .

—Please . . . Stanley said, looking up with sudden appeal at Ed Feasley who stood staring at the floor, silent.

They were all three silent for a moment, looking down, and Don Bildow's plaintive voice reached them. —She's all swollen up, and just before I sail. I don't know if I should go with her like this.

—Dropsy?

—How could a six-year-old girl have dropsy? Bildow moaned, fingering the yellow and brown necktie which seemed to support him.

—I mean Chrahst, what happens to people? Ed Feasley asked finally. Stanley stood looking numb. —And I mean Chrahst, everybody's leaving, everybody's going abroad. I haven't been in Paris since I was seven years old, Chrahst to go there now! I mean to Saint Germain des Prés where they're imitating Greenwich Village and here we are in Greenwich Village still imitating Montmartre . . . I mean Chrahst. Hannah had been watching him narrowly, noting the strain in his voice, the forced way he spoke and looked away. When he looked up and saw her he started to speak again, sounding more forced and talking about Max in order to avoid talking about something else. —And I mean did you see that fistful of Confederate money Max had? All these old ten and twenty-dollar Confederate bills, he said he picked them up for almost nothing, I mean what does he want with that if he's going to Paris? I mean, you know? Chrahst. And I saw him talking to Bildow, I mean how come he gets along so well with Bildow after that poem thing, that poem Bildow published . . .

—He explained that, Hannah said. —He didn't steal it, he said that skinny girl, you remember the one, she used to write poetry, or she told everybody she did. Max said she gave it to him and asked him to have it published under his name. I guess she pretended she didn't want to use her own name in case people didn't like it. That was a lousy trick, getting Max in trouble like that. She was probably high. They picked up that junkie she had hanging around.

—What happened to her?

—I don't know.

—I mean Chrahst what happens to people. You know? I mean, like Anselm, did you hear about him? He joined a monastery Max told me. I mean Chrahst I'd just as soon be dead. Look out, you're spilling your beer.

—Did he . . . is that true? Stanley asked.

—I mean Chrahst how do I know? Ed Feasley said impatiently. —It's what Max told me. Some silent order out west.

—I always thought he was queer, said Hannah.

—But . . . is that true? Stanley repeated, staring at Ed Feasley.

—How do I know! Ed Feasley burst out at him. —I mean, I told you . . . I'm sorry but, Chrahst, I mean haven't we all had enough of all this? They looked at him with surprise, because his voice was that different, it almost broke; and then he recovered without looking up at them mumbling, —Because Chrahst I mean you can't just you know I mean Chrahst . . .

—I heard you bought an airplane, Stanley said after a moment. Ed Feasley nodded but did not look up. And then Hannah asked him,

—Was that true? what we saw in the paper? Was that your father in the *Times* this morning?

—How do I know, I don't read the *Times*. Chrahst. I suppose it was. Then he looked up. —Have you got a cigarette? They both looked blank. —What do you mean? he broke out again. —About all this . . . these charges of collusion with a foreign government, and the whole works going to hell, and then my old man has a stroke on top of that? Is that what you mean? I mean Christ say what you mean.

—She . . . she didn't mean anything, Stanley said putting a hand out.

—Well Chrahst nobody means anything, Feasley drew away muttering, and stood rubbing the floor with his shoe.

—But you . . . you're all right, about money? you did have plenty of money, if you could buy an airplane . . . ?

—That thing, it crashed in Florida. Were you ever in Tampa? I mean to Chrahst what a lousy town that is, Tampa. They were nasty as hell about it.

—You crashed? in a plane crash?

—I was taking off, I hit this flock of lousy birds.

—But you got out all right? you weren't hurt?

—Chrahst no, I never knew what happened after I saw those white birds right in front of me. I was drunk. I mean Chrahst, what a Chrahst-awful mess everything is, everything at once.

Ed Feasley stood watching his toe rub the floor board, grinding a cigarette stub there into the wood, and would not look up until their continued silence provoked him. He looked up, and they looked down.

—I mean, my old man, Chrahst I never liked the old bastard, but I...I hate like hell to see him like this, just...just sitting there and he can't move a thing, he just sits there.

When Hannah started to speak, Stanley looked at her apprehensively as though he expected some note of acid triumph (and she had, at that, been referred to in a news item on her arrest the night she was doing her laundry in the subway washroom, as a Stalinist, or Trotskyite, or the parent that combined them both, some such); for each of these two seemed to feel that they had suddenly lost a friend, or at the least an affluent acquaintance upon whom they could call in some moment of extremity, as indeed they had: or say that someone of those dimensions had simply gone out of their lives, and someone else, bearing superficial resemblances, come in. So Stanley was surprised to see the same expression on Hannah's face that he felt on his own; and her tone, which could not help but be bitter, perhaps the more so for all this, was a relief for she changed the subject abruptly with, —Do you remember that fucking faggot that knocked me down at Max's party that night? Have you heard about him?

—Herschel...what?

—He's a movie star.

—Him?

—He's a movie star. He's the new most eligible bachelor in Hollywood.

—Good Chrahst.

—He's going to be Saint Sebastian in a movie about the Virgin Mary.

—But he was...Saint Sebastian was third century... Stanley complained feebly.

—Good Chrahst. I mean, this is like a post mortem, like the night that Otto and I...Chrahst. I don't know. Ed Feasley looked round him. —I mean when I come down here all these people remind me of parts of me that never grew up.

—We live in a country that never grew up.

—We live in a whole God damn world that never grew up, said Ed Feasley. —And everybody's leaving. I mean, he looked round again, —everybody's gone. Where are they going? What are they going to do when they get over there?

—Bildow's going over to get laid, said Hannah.

—I mean Chrahst, I almost don't blame him. You know? The only use I ever found for a condom was to fill it up with water and roll it around on the floor. We used to do that in college. I mean you'd be surprised how tremendous they get. It's like a big piece of water with nothing around it rolling around.

—Do you think there would be so many queers around if there were a few good whorehouses in town? Hannah demanded sharply. —No, here they'd rather see their boys go to bed with a picture of some movie star with big boobs, and go on a five-fingered honeymoon like Anselm used to say, with a movie star.

—I know. I mean Chrahst, every time I've gone out to bars looking for a girl I end up drunk talking to some old man.

All three of them stood staring at the floor.

Don Bildow left, looking as vengeful as plastic rims would allow. He had just learned that someone he knew had been arrested trying to charge a three-hundred-dollar suit to the account of someone neither of them knew. Someone else discovered that the old man in black coat, black hat, black rubbers, and black umbrella, was not the art critic for *Old Masses* at all, but had been hired to go round to galleries because he looked the part (and could keep warm this way); the columns were written by someone in Jersey City, who mailed them in because she never came to New York. The old man left, carrying a glass of beer with him. And down the bar, the Big Unshaven Man was offered a job writing the lonely-hearts column for a newspaper in Buffalo.

—What I get a kick out of is these serious writers who write a book where they say money gives a false significance to art, and then they raise hell when their book doesn't make any money.

—Here, put this in the juke-box. Play *Return to Sorrento*.

—That's what's playing.

—Play it again.

—Chrahst I wish they'd stop playing that and play *On the Sunny Side of the Street*.

Stanley had been simply standing there dumbly, staring at the dirty floor, until Hannah asked him what he was going to do next day.

—Well first I, I guess I'll go over to Bellevue, he said. —Why?

—I thought maybe you'd go with me to get a passport.

—But you, you're going too? To Rome?

—Rome, for Christ sake? I'm going to Paris. All he could say was, —But . . . looking at her. Hannah looked straight up into his face; and then as suddenly as he had turned, she stood on her toes and kissed him. —Because I may not see you again, she said, and was gone. He stood there, his mustache trembled, and he pressed a finger against it where she had kissed him.

—You know? said Ed Feasley beside him, —I mean I feel like I've left little parts of me all over the place. Like I could spend the rest of my life trying to collect them and I never could. These pieces of me and pieces of other people all screwed up and spread all over the place. I mean there are people you... do something with and then you never see them again. Like Otto, you know? Where the hell is he?

—I don't know, Stanley said clearly, but he continued to stare at the floor.

—I mean he's probably raising hell and having a good time somewhere, you know? But Chrahst, a good time! I mean like the night we went to that party up in Harlem with all the queers, that seems like ten years ago, that little nigger in the lavender dress standing at the next urinal. And then there was this blonde, a woman, I mean I can still hear her singing, If you can't get Maxwell House coffee by the can get Lipton's tea by the balls, I mean Chrahst I can hear it now. I never got over that night somehow, it got me somehow, I even remember what the soap smelled like, this kind of medical smell, I mean why does the soap always have a medical smell in a place like that? You'd think it would be scented. Where you going, you leaving already?

—It's late, Stanley said. —I'm going home.

—Yes but home, I mean late, and then there was this marathon walker, but I mean Chrahst I mean, how long?

—Half an hour, Ellery said thickly. —I'll meet you there.

—One of us better go with you, Morgie said. —You can hardly walk.

—I told you, like I told you, I told you I'm just going to drop up there alone for a minute, I'll meet you at the whatever the nightclub I'll meet you.

They helped him into a cab, which got him to Esther's address before he went to sleep in the back seat. He had difficulty getting out, but he managed, staggering into the doorway, and pushed the first button his thumb found. Then he climbed, stopping every now and then to try to count the number of flights he'd come up, and finally knocked at the door halfway down the hall. There was no answer. He put his hand on the knob, it turned, and there stood a little girl with a fly swatter.

—Rose? She stared up at him. —What's the matter, is she asleep?

—Yes, the little girl said. —She's still asleep.

He followed her in mumbling, —Rose, Rose, you're like a kid, Rose. There was a strange smell in the place. It became stronger as he approached the bedroom.

—See? She's still asleep. The little girl pointed with the fly swatter at the figure in the bed, and repeated, —She's still asleep.

The smell was overpowering. Ellery almost fell on the bed; but he steadied himself and stared. He got out a cigarette, but dropped it.

—She's still asleep, and I'm keeping the flies off her.

—Rose. Christ. Jesus ... He turned away heaving.

—They say at school there aren't flies in winter, the little girl went on, while he was sick over the back of a chair, —but there are, and I'm keeping them off her.

He hung there for a minute, and then pulled a dresser scarf close enough to wipe his mouth on it.

—Because there are flies in winter, here there are ...

He turned slowly holding his head in his hand, staring at her, and then pulled himself up and started for the door, where he fell against the door frame turning to look at her again. —Rose, listen, Rose ... Breath was pouring into him and out of him. Then in one motion he turned himself out the door and reached the stairs. He stopped three or four times on the way down, to prevent himself from falling headlong, and finally did fall about three steps at the bottom. It was enough noise to bring out the janitor, who helped him up and demanded, —Do you know anything about fifty tons of sugar?

Ellery just stared at him. Then he raised a hand and pointed up the stairs.

—Somebody's been trying to deliver fifty tons of sugar here all day.

Ellery let his weight go back against the wall, still pointing up the stairs. Then his hand dropped as though too heavy a weight to hold suspended so, and he got out the door, found a cab, and finally got to the nightclub, where some of the movie people had also come, for it was still comparatively early.

—My, that really was a verklärte Nacht, said Mr. Schmuck's musical director. —It was bad publicity.

Mr. Schmuck was tapping his fingers impatiently on the table, waiting for his order while beside him Mr. Sonnenschein engaged a Baked Alaska. Mr. Schmuck had simply ordered filet de mignon.

—I told you we'd ought to have just bought our pictures and gotten out of there, said Mr. Sonnenschein, blowing a delicate meringue filigrane across the table through the word pictures.

—A real Walpurgis ... Mr. Schmuck's assistant commenced.

—Shut up, said Mr. Schmuck, —so I could see the lady singing.

—Si-hilnt nite. Holy-y nite. Alll is calm ... she sang, in a blue gown with sequin-studded bolero jacket to match, filling a selective circle of blue spotlights with a song which had proved such a favorite Christmas Eve that she was singing it again.

In the reverent shadows, the Alabama Rammer-Jammer man salted a steak with Venus de Milo. Morgie pushed a glass over to Ellery. —Drink that and you'll bounce back.

Ellery mumbled, staring blearily into nothing. From a mouthful of steak across the table came, —Come on, if you can't eat you got to . . .

From a nearby table came, —We were here Christmas Eve too. We tried to get into Saint Pat's for the High Mass but you should have seen the mob.

And from the floor,

hea

—Slee pin   vun   peece . . .

lee

—What happened this morning? It's like it was a thousand years ago, Morgie said, and added to Ellery, —It's the first time I ever knew you were so goddam sensitive.

—And that, Ellery mumbled, going on despite the floodlit applause. —His face, I just keep seeing those beads of sweat on his face, understand? like a God-damned wreath of . . . beads of sweat around his forehead, do you get me?

—Tonight we have with us that famous star of stage and screen . . . Spotlights fought each other over the surface of blank faces. —It's a little late, but I know everybody still has some of the Xmas spirit . . . how about a word of Xmas cheer for everybody . . . ?

Hanging onto the microphone, the star entertained: —Merry Xmas everybody. Glad to see everybody making merry. Just watch out Mary don't go home with somebody else. He paused for laughter, and breath, swaying. —It was the most beautiful Xmas I ever saw . . . when I got up Xmas morning . . . it looked so nice out I left it out all day . . .

—That bastard!

—I've got a broad waiting for me down at the Fritz-Carlton . . . the star babbled on.

—That bastard! He killed it! said the Alabama Rammer-Jammer man, but neither of his companions appeared to notice. Ellery was trying to sit up straight and drink. Morgie stared dully into his glass.

—Look, what did Schmuck's number-one boy want over there, when you stopped and talked to them.

—They made me an offer. Ellery's shoulders sagged again. —The life of the Virgin Mary. They're shooting it in Italy. They want me on publicity.

—Look Ellery, for Christ sake, you're a swell guy. I'd hate like hell to see you get mixed up with the movies.

—What the hell, Ellery said. —You have to make a change once in a while.

—A change? You think it's going to be any different out there? It's the same goddam thing only it's worse. Here at least you know the people you work with, they know who you are, you got friends. Out there nobody knows you. Morgie was staring at the same blank place on the tablecloth where Ellery was staring. —You got to stop trading in some time. You trade in your goddam car, you trade in your goddam wife, and the minute you get used to the goddam thing some bastard puts out a new model. Just go to the goddam bank. Eye-bank. Blood-bank. Bone-bank.

—That's a nice idea for a show, the old Alabama Rammer-Jammer man interrupted. —Banks as a symbol of progress. Money-banks. Bone-banks. Eye-banks. Blood-banks.

—We just bought a canned show on the march of science, Morgie said, speaking slowly. Neither of them had raised his eyes. The plaintive quality in Morgie's voice was that defiant disappointment in the radio voice which has predicted *clear* only hours before, and returns to admit the possibility of scattered showers unhumbled by the fact that his listeners are staring through closed windows at driving rain. —Did you know that a handkerchief and a cannonball fall at the same goddam speed in a vacuum? Well that's where we are, in this great big goddam vacuum where a handkerchief and a cannonball fall at the same goddam speed, you know what I mean?

Their companion was watching the floor, the hollow plastic figurine clutched in his hand. His thumb moved from one salt vent to the other and the lights dimmed again and went out. A ghostly emanation took their place, withholding reality, as an undelineated naked woman came forth, a pair of pink hands described in phosphorescence cupping her buttocks, which she ground at her audience as though the heavy hands of love (fleeting, groping, failing under other tables in the darkness) were kneading them in orgiastic violence.

—He's on, said Mr. Schmuck's assistant to Mr. Schmuck. Then he turned to Mr. Schmuck's musical director. —You're right. Verklärte . . .

—*You're* right. Walpurgis . . . Mr. Schmuck's musical director commenced.

—Shut up, said Mr. Schmuck, —so I could see the lady dancing.

Out there, she turned and bobbed an undulant front, blossoming at its tips in phosphorescent roses.

—What do you want to get mixed up in that for? It's the same goddam handkerchief and the same goddam cannonball in the same goddam vacuum.

—Travel, Ellery muttered. —See why the other half lives.

Six months: *Elmira* was one postmark, and her lips formed the words silently. The marking on the other letter was indecipherable, though the stamps were Spanish, and she held it up to the light, lips tightening as nothing interrupted the translucency but the jumble of a florid hand. There was no return on it.

She put it aside, and took the first letter with her on her trip across the room, there to press it up under her armpit as she adjusted the radio with one hand, and tuned in her new hearing aid with the other. Then she sat down, resting her head back, lips twitching again on "six months," the letter gripped still unopened in her hand as the radio warmed up to *Sweet Betsy from Pike* sung in Yiddish, and she stared at a crack in the ceiling.

By daylight, the crack appeared to have just lengthened another whole inch or even more, and Stanley almost bounded out of bed for his string measure. Then he sank back under the blanket (his sheet was packed), closed his jaws tight on the throbbing tooth to hold off the image it conjured as well as the pain, and then lay waiting, as though for instructions from above on something near at hand which he could not quite grasp, and with little time remaining him to do so. His forehead creased with the effort of trying to think clearly what it might be, and as the effort rose to that part of his face his jaws relaxed and immediately the pain in the tooth penetrated him sharply, and the image, close upon it, intruded.

Within the half hour, he was wandering among hospital corridors.

—But baby, taking *that* one to *Is*chia would be like taking an ow-wel to A-thens, he heard, approaching her door, and he stopped. —And don't permit me to leave without the key to my *box*, all those brrrr-beautiful things, I just couldn't show up over there na-ked.

He heard someone say, —Agnes, I'm glad you're all right . . . and then,

—Baby do you call that all rwight? all strung up like an exhibition in a shop window! Cru-wel boy!

Stanley stood there, after a glimpse at the group round her bed, pressing the deep pain in his jaw, listening.

—Arny baby you must try to stand up, or they'll put you in a little box here and you'll never never never see the normal outside world again. Arny-marney-tiddley-parney, what *have* you got in your pocket?

Then he heard her voice, giving someone an address, her mother's address, on the Via Flaminia in Rome.

—Rubbing alcohol! You should be spanked!

Stanley turned away with sudden resolution: he had heard of there being a chapel in Bellevue, and set off to look for it, rescued from the prospect of actually seeing her, by the more abiding, and surely more prudent reflection, that he might burn a candle for her recovery. And he was well on the way to doing so, moving through the corridors with apprehension, as though afraid of being hustled into a ward, or a straitjacket, himself. But as he came down that hall, where the three western faiths have their depots, he was stopped dead by an apparition in a red and white candy-stripe bathrobe emerging from the synagogue, her face so abruptly familiar, delicately intimate in the sharp-boned hollow-eyed virginity of unnatural shadows, like those priestesses of Delphos in subterranean silence transfixing what might have been fear on a face in the light but there paralyzed in prophecy (until one of them was raped: then they were replaced by women over fifty). —Hello, Stan-ley, she greeted him as she had always, as a stranger whom she knew.

—But... I didn't know you were... Jewish? he said, and looked even more surprised, having meant to say, —I didn't know you were here...

—It is so beautiful in there, she said, and smiled, as one foretelling death by falling pillars, death at sea.

Zealous, importunate, he pressed her. —But here? he recovered.

—She has always been just here, but just here, Stan-ley, she said to him; and then lowered her eyes and turned her face away. —But now they are going to send her away.

—When? he asked quickly.

—Yesterday, or today, so soon. She looked at him, in an instant looked about to cry.

—Where? Stanley asked her; but she looked at him. —Wait, he said, and started to speak rapidly. —You, you see you can come with me, yes, can't you, you can come with me. He took her wrist, and she looked at him. —You see because... yes and then everything, then you'll be save... safe I mean, you'll be safe... Now... wait, first... He pressed the pain in his jaw, as though to communicate its urgency. —This, I have to take care of this first, I have to go to a dentist but then I'll come back and we, and you'll be... all right. You see I... we're going away... The question lay only in his eyes, searching the large still pupils of hers.

After that he moved with compulsive certainty. And only on going through the pales outside, pressing his jaw but carrying his head up, and passing the delegation which had forestalled his intended visit, he remembered that he had not asked for his glasses and then, that he had not lit a candle.

—Arny-parney-tiddly-marney, he passed quickly, —stand up! What ever made you try and telephone your *wife*, even if the line *was* busy?

The telephone was still ringing when Maude got in. She'd heard it from the hall, and almost broke her key trying to fit it in upside-down.

—Yes, what? she said breathlessly into it, —I? Me?... As she spoke her eyes rose slowly to meet those of the figure gently swinging in the bedroom door.

—But you . . . why did you choose me? she brought out finally. —But no, no . . . no, she cried, and even with the last word the telephone was back silent where she'd got it, and she stood with her weight on it staring and still, as though supported by those eyes which held her across the room. It was only in wilting, as the energy which the telephone, so long silent, had flooded her with, ebbed away, and she came to rest in her spinal support with a twinge, that the bond of their eyes broke, and she ducked round the suspended figure, into the bedroom to take off her coat. And the baby hung there, sitting silent in a sort of breeches buoy which she had made from a pair of Arny's shorts and some cord, a breeches buoy pulling neither to ship nor shore, moving gently, never more than enough to intensify the repose of its occupant whose only activity was to fix Maude and hold her with clear blue eyes.

In the bedroom she stood looking vacantly at the thing curled on the dresser top: only that morning, trying to find her bank in the telephone directory, she had come helplessly upon the *Guarantee Truss Company*, thrown the book down, and never called to find what remained of her tiny bank balance. And here the thing lay, a circle of swathed steel tapered, to broaden an end in a cushion which rose just enough from the top of the chest to liken it to an open hood, and the whole tensely coiled length a cobra in devious wait: and she hurried past it jabbing a hand to the light switch.

The kitchen sink was stacked with dishes. On her way in there with the baby, she tripped over a pair of Arny's shoes which she kept out, empty, in the middle of the floor.

—The most popular hostess of the week . . . ! she said in a faint tone as she washed, first a dish, then a tiny foot, then a cup. —They telephoned me to ask me if I would like to g-give a luncheon for my . . . and they would bring everything and do all the work and afterward s-serve . . . s-sell their lunchware to my . . . my . . . And I asked them how they picked me and she said we blindfolded a girl, and found your name in a telephone book, it's a great . . . a great honor to be . . . to be chosen the most . . .

The eyes did not move from her. The baby's head was not conical nor, looking at it, did one have that impression; but immediately upon looking away such an image formed in the mind, and no amount of looking back, of studying it from strategic angles, served to temper the placid image which remained. When most of the dishes were done she had reached the neck, and suddenly she applied both thumbs at the base of the baby's head. —It should go in more *here*, she whispered, then applied the heel of a hand there, and finally stepped back and turned away from the fixed gaze as though breaking fetters. She left the baby there in the sink with what dishes remained and went into the living room, where she turned the radio on, tripped again over the empty shoes, and stood thoughtfully for a moment before she picked up the telephone and dialed, reading the number of the druggist written on a bottle in her hand.

——Friends, the time to sell your diamonds is now...

—Hello? Could I buy some morphine from you? What? No, I mean just some plain morphine...?

It was a long struggle, as though the image itself were holding him back in the chair while the dentist worked. And there was time for the agony of remorse, since Stanley had simply got off the crosstown bus and gone to the first dentist whose sign he saw, up a flight, someone he had never heard of and who had, surely, never heard of him. They strained and tugged at one another, Stanley at the chair, Doctor Weisgall at Stanley, and the longer it went on the more alarmed Stanley became, for the dentist seemed in an unsettled state himself. He had heavy arms, was in need of a shave, and perspired freely in his white coat. And then, while Stanley still lay back, gripping the arms of the chair in a rigidity of concentrated terror, he heard a voice and opened his eyes to see the thing held before him in a pair of heavy pincers. —Is it out? he tried to say, —Is that it? But he could not control that side of his mouth. Nonetheless he asked for it when he left, to take with him wrapped in gauze and a piece of newspaper. Out on the street, the dead side of his tongue nudged the numb hollow on his jaw, and he stopped to spit blood in the gutter. Passers-by glanced at him with distaste, the contempt bred of Fourteenth Street's familiarity with such exhibitions, for he made a bad job of it, a stream blown against his chin, hung dripping from the uncontrollable side of his mouth, for he had no handkerchief.

In the window above, Doctor Weisgall watched him stagger, collide with a trashbin, a child, another staggering figure who tried to embrace him as a companion in arms, and finally disappear from sight. Then he took off his white coat and stood there rubbing his chin for a minute. Then as though he had put off for long enough some alien, fortuitous, but no less constraining duty, he picked up the letter he had received that morning, opened it, and stared at its pages as he called the police to report this anonymous persecution:

Dear Doctor Weisgall.
The I, what does it stand for? your first name, what is it? The book I am going to write will be called Flowers of Friendship, because do you remember Before the flowers of friendship faded friendship faded, well that is what my book will be about.
We are the great refusal, doctor.
Why do they love us and trust us for all the wrong reasons, reasons often we know

nothing about and then they are disappointed. They are always disappointed. Sometimes I want to just stop, just stop everything and thank everyone. What they do, they free us when they betray us. Is that too easy, doctor? Is it because we can share a part of Ourself with each one we know, the part he demands for the rest we do not offer because he would not recognize the rest and more important even would not believe it is us, so we think better perhaps to simply put it away and do not bother him with it. Then see him, with all his might and main and all of his necessity he builds a whole Us out of his fragment, an Us we may have trouble to recognize too but respond kindly to it but better fearsomely, better beware and afraid for one day he will face us with it and then who can say, This is not us at all, why he has depended upon that Us he made with such loving care did he not? Oh surprised he is and disappointed! How we failed how we failed! He is angry and deeply hurt, betrayed! Betrayed! Do not trust Us, flowers of friendship. All the while we search beyond him for what he thinks he has offered so honest, so honest is he, so honest. Finding in him and everywhere some where where we may share a part but no more, is there anyone you can share nothing with? Is there then who you can share everything with? No no no no— but they do not understand. There were too many of them, doctor. There, there, you see? Your kindness is hypocrisy. They gave you everything, he shared everything he had with you. Did you ask him? No, he gave it so honest is he and so sincere. And some day he finds, you never did accept from inside do you understand? Only outside like a handshake you accepted. He is angry and reduced, not for you now but of you then who pretended to share, and did not share but gave, and gave in the giving only a fragment in exchange you see. How little of us ever meets how little of another. As one day he recalls his confidence to you as weakness, and to cast it out he will cast you away because you did accept it from him, so you served him well, and he is older now, and better unfriendship and weakness so cauterized than friendship which remembers.

Why after this long time have you not answered me? What do you demand?

Why do you treat me as they do, as though I were exactly what I want to be. Why do we treat people that way? But we do, everyone treats anyone that way, saying I have had these defeats and disappointments, but you whom I encounter you know what you will say, moving, in accord with your nature which is here in bloom, but I do not yet understand, I, for myself, do not yet understand. Since my problems are not yours therefore you must have none, but live alone inside yourself, therefore here are my problems and we shall share them. So honest are they, picking the flowers with such ease and such concern.

If you have walked out in a summer night, you will understand this, walked out with your face bared to the darkness and then, a spider's web hung heavy with moisture between magnolia and the yew claps its sodden delicacy over your face, then you will know what I mean. Here, he makes friendship in spite of things, worming confidences as they say, he does lose no opportunity to find your frailties, where you fail and how weak, nor lose opportunity to make you know he knows these, at last to lose no opportunity to assure you of his friendship in spite of them, and always in spite of them and so how fortunate you are to have him a friend! feebly saying nice things about you behind your back.

Or elsewhere, never live at the end of a straight road lest you be always looking down it. There in the distance two meet and do battle, where are you? They do battle about you, faded, faded, One says, That is my friend, but you and I are so different, that That cannot be your friend too, then each says secretly, if That is his friend That cannot be my friend too, then they look at one another saying this, We are so different (they say because they do not know each other) that That can be friend to neither of us, but shall be our common hypocrite, and nevertheless and recognized now must be thanked nevertheless for bringing us together and we, being different we shall be friends but honest friends, for you see there are things we do not share.

O doctor, how the meek presume.

Then why after so long have you not answered me?

It is forbidden to enter the garden with flowers in the hand. That was a sign in french at the gate of a french garden, you see, and read it well and you will understand. As though to understand were to forgive! We find the ones with whom we can share nothing. Oh, hold them up and cherish them for they will never come saying, I have found you out! Oh. Oh. They will, doctor. Even they, they will come saying, I have found you out! for from the first you knew we had nothing to share, and that is what we shared, not the nothing but the knowing we had nothing, that I shared with you, but you, what did you give me in exchange but the nothing: I have found you out! They will murder you for that they will. So good doctor do a favor to your friends and go away and die and so unite them.

It is all going to get much worse before it begins to get better, doctor. Glowing they gave you things you did not want, their scarcest treasure. We will not tell, we will not tell, until one day they take it all and nail it frabjously upon another, and your betrayal will be another nail in the coffin of love.

The satisfaction of being found out. It is a very relaxing satisfaction. Oh I have read so much, doctor. So many sensitive things, how sensitive they are, the ones who do not suffer. They wish themselves very well, sincere people. Not with trumpets, doctor, but I see the Lord of Hosts putting his enormous head round a promontory on the northeast end of the Island where a point rises from the water, and here all of us are on the beach, somewhat sheltered. They will all know what to do, the others on the beach, for they will recognize Him and follow some satisfactory prescription but doctor you and I, what will we do but look surprised, look up from a paper-backed edition of something that sold well twenty years ago, or the serial story with no beginning and no end in a magazine found on the veranda, the sole of a beach shoe needing mending, that or the cigarette lighter which won't work for the sand in it or the face of the dollar watch we always take there which tells the time with sand in it, look up and look surprised and mildly so at that. You and I doctor, on the beach.

He speaks of you and wonders where you are. Calls you Indy, in his selfish voice which is mild with disappointment. Why are the meek so selfish?

You would be surprised how important bars are to people who don't read books, doctor. Sometimes I could weep, and other times I do. I remember The Deserter, a drama acted by dogs and a monkey at Sadlers Wells in 1785, and I could weep. I remember Freddies Football Dogs, and I could weep. I remember the round of names, names taken from popular books for naming of children, and taken back from them grown-up for books which no one reads, and I could weep. Somewhere in Africa I believe they made a mermaid from a monkey and a codfish, I have seen its photograph.

I remember the dampness there. I remember cherries in a blue ceramic dish, specked with water and mold, the cigarettes were delicate to smoke, specks of brown appeared on the white paper as it burned, and left a wet line on the stone tray and all the while the green working outside like a blanket, the grass, honeysuckle, clematis, ferns, tall weeds including Queen Anne's laces, the rosebush and the blackberry out of control without flowers or fruit so busy growing, and tomatoes fallen into the high grass, cobwebs formed and hanging heavy with dampness, the clothes clinging with dampness and without stockings the shoes hollow and damp. Every surface needed paint, and the damp wires sent electricity free through the lampstands. Dust worked into pages of the books left open for them. We invited them, they did not come but they remembered the gesture.

Doctor, eventually the importance of breeding.

Do you remember Rue Gît le Coeur?

What did he say? What did she say? Three of them are there, which is intolerable. Witness three must leave the room so that ambiguity may enter, and in such company one talks assuredly to two since they are now safely alone with mistrust.

Names are very important.

How can you deal seriously with a person named ——? they ask me.

If I owed you money, then you would be interested in me, then you would follow my career with interest. I have thought of that, doctor. For upon contraction of debts, you must expect to pay. You will have to, and probably in a way worse in proportion to the ease and faith with which they were contracted. Do you understand her, doctor? Raped across three state lines, in a back seat in her uncle's car for her uncle with whom she lived was dead on the kitchen floor, raped in an empty movie house and in a cornfield where the police finally cornered him and killed him with a hail of bullets and rescued her, she protested, I only wanted Romance, doctor. And even then no matter how you love, you cannot repay the debts contracted in the loved one's past, nor interfere with how the loved one tries to repay them. But you must pay, you do though you cannot.

Doctor, your honesty's showing.

Well then, do you know the worst thing? When he confirms your accusations. You accused him, then how violently he sets upon you to prove otherwise, then you can do no more than stand and watch, in spite of himself watch him work out all of the things of which you accused him and did you, all the while, hope he would prove you wrong? Watch him unable to leave the scene without making it worse, and the more he insists upon his right the more he disintegrates it until it ends in all he feared most, he recreates and proves you right.

How helpless you are when you are right.

For hard times and difficulty do not make a stronger person as they told us children, good fortune makes him stronger but the others make him weaker and more crafty you see, and they make his circumstances which when good fortune comes he will resist by making circumstances which will make him what he is neither good nor strong. That is what happens from hard times and disaster. Those bad circumstances are the only ones where we can recognize ourselves, and when good fortune comes away, away, we cannot face it, to see ourselves abroad in good fortune and there is no alternative, there is none but in the face of good fortune to flee, and in the terrifying comfort of solitude find the devices to construct the familiar landscape of bad fortune where we step forth in certainty, so it mounts, gets worse and in spite of ourselves we see ourselves more fully and there we are precious again.

What would I have done in his place? People say that, and they mean it because they do not understand it. Sometimes I clean my pocketbook, and that is a wonderful feeling though a task. That is why I do not telephone you, telephones are dangerous things, they separate us from one another and is that simply because we put them to the wrong use? Human, we treat them as we treat others, take for granted services to which they did not pretend. But we force telephones to corrupt intimacy while they pretend to preserve it by keeping alive only its dangerous immediate symptoms. Say a word, say a thousand to me on the telephone and I shall choose the wrong one to cling to as though you had said it after long deliberation when only I provoked it from you, I will cling to it from among a thousand, to be provoked and hurl it back with something I mean no more than you meant that, something for you to cling to and retreat clinging to. There, now we are apart! Doctor? That is why I did not telephone you, send only a symptomatic fragment of me to you in my voice where you cannot see my face but instead sit and stare upon matters of your own intimate self arranged like furniture but not my face which I have been so long in forming for just this moment, writing you a letter where you will see my face doctor and all of me laid out, what can I give you more for forgiveness? That's all right, we serve them better than they know, if only we exist for them to reject, for they do not understand as you and I do, doctor, and to be certain of accepting one thing they must reject another. I remember, we serve them well. Many of them must make you unhappy before you will take them seriously, so honest are they. Do you remember envy when it called itself admiration?

We serve them well, icons of their desperate and idle manufacture, and Oh! when we betray them by being other selves, and the icon is broken, doctor, do they grow? Or fashion it again and elsewhere, so detailedly the same, different only enough to prevent their recognizing it for what betrayed them once. We serve them well, doctor. That is what I did, extended my vanity where I thought it would be held in trust, and found it taken with desperate seriousness in all the confidence that envy engenders. Then you have accepted a confidence, and laid ground for mistrust. Do you read, doctor? Do you read so far? Are you, too, always certain that you have found the answer at hand, demanding it so, articulate and incarnate? and then you are betrayed? and who betrayed you? How many have you around you, who have never feared you? nor mistrusted you for fear of your being more than one? How many who will share what can be shared but do not fear to expose, simply expose without confidence, nor the secret sharer, those other things which must be worked out alone in privacy, knowing they exist but respecting you for respecting that privacy as the matter of fact indeed it is, doctor have I trapped you?

Are you there, an island in their past, afloat, or a rock shoal, and sailing back do they sight you with cries of happiness and recognition? Indeed, do they cruise back just to reach you, to land and enter the same pleasance with recognition even delight, share it with others who have languored there, or meet those others upon the beach and do battle? Or cruising somewhere else beyond do they sight you casually, remark your presence with a smile, or do they mark you severely upon the chart and sail by far to leeward and out of sight, to meet further on others bound forward and warn them of your dangers where you lie in the past there though it is for these bound forward the future and they will set their course accordingly. Or sailing back do they sail past however near or far offshore with a shrug and a glance of dismissal recalling nothing but an arid coast. Or do you float, as they told us the Sargasso Sea floats partly under the surface and none is certain exactly where, necessitating vigilance and uncertain anxious care.

Have you ever thought about this, that right now this instant every one of them is somewhere being real? The Pope and the President and also certain surviving kings, the people whose secrets we know and the ones of whom we know no more than the newspaper confides, all the people you have met and all the people you will meet, and all you have never met and will never meet, all of them they are somewhere now right this instant being real. Even when you are not talking about them, not thinking about them perhaps not even remembering them in spite of these insults they are somewhere being real. As though they did not care! At the very same instant they are being real right now. It is too much to comprehend that, still they dare it, but it is too much.

From the train window I see places I have never been, a street corner with the streetlamp on one evening in New Britain Connecticut, and I wept. For it is worse being alone without someone than just being alone. Why I remember green, that color, when color was more than itself, green at sundown after a rain when it was blinding with life, doctor should I have been a drunkard or a nun, for they will not love us as we want to be loved, and a nun or a singer, a singer or a child, doctor or only unborn? For when she lay alone making love, do you think as that ring slipped round her finger, and breathing in the feverish dark do you think she fancied his breath upon her? visioned his beauty? or her own, and only the beautiful woman she will be— Now you have tricked me! coming into the garden so, carrying cut flowers in your hand. In spite of the prohibition which even you could not help but see, so you were deliberate? Yes, I understand, why you cannot forgive, love and forgive, if forgiving restores our innocence and being loved confirms the beautiful things we want to be, and loving is always forgiving that we are not. Why love is divine, because only divinity can restore innocence. You knew the secret I had, didn't you, coming in with a nosegay, love-in-a-mist, love-in-idleness, love-lies-bleeding, you knew the worst thing didn't you. But there wasn't time. The honeysuckle grew and covered everything like a blanket and smothered it. The grape arbor collapsed, not with the weight of the fruit for the birds had taken the grapes away, but under the weight of the vines. I remember the holly trees, where the female stood alone out on the front lawn, and the male cringed away upwind, did you know that doctor? Everything grew too fast then, it was no use trying to keep it down. Everything grew too fast.

But in reading it, the hand had defeated its own purpose: for those lines written in frantic haste took time to interpret; while it was quick work to go through those written with careful painful pauses, written slowly, to compel the reader to read slowly and attentively, a habit she might have made in conversation.

—Plain morphine, doctor?

—Better give her a half-grain.

—I don't think there's any on this floor. We've been using Pantopon.

—All right. A forty-milligram dose.

—Surgery recommended Trilene, with an inhaler?...

—To hell with Surgery.

—Yes doctor. And now... the nurse went on, turning, —Miss Deigh, or Mrs. Deigh, Mrs. or Miss?... which is it? I'll just bet it's Mrs. she said coyly, seeing a letter there on the night table addressed *Mrs.* The letter was from an insurance company, to inform her that upon receipt of her signature on the enclosed waiver, they would make payable to her the sum of twenty-five thousand dollars ($25,000.00) in life insurance on her husband, who had fallen off a bar stool in Hollywood.

—And wasn't that an interesting young man that came to visit you tonight! Why, I think I could turn into a Buddhist myself with him to talk to me. The Four Noble Truths! and the Eightfold Noble Path! Why, life *is* suffering, isn't it... you just try to lie still now. The nurse finished tidying up the bed and went out of this private room, where the patient had just been moved, mumbling, as she passed a ward, —But to say suffering is caused by *desire?*... and that story he told about Bishop...Whutley?... which she repeated to the nurse in the drug room, —And so this Bishop says to the man praying there in front of this little wheel, who are you praying to and what are you praying for my good man? and the man says, I'm not praying to anybody and I'm not praying for nothing...

But that nurse shrugged her shoulders too, handed over the prescribed Pantopon, and went back to straightening the gay handkerchief pinned to her blouse, and untangling the plain gold cross whose chain had got caught on a button.

The night nurse paused on her return to reprimand a shapeless figure huddled half out of bed in the dark to receive this confidence from a low-tuned radio, ——Another case of homicide. And so for really top-notch entertainment, listen in...

—All right now Mister Jenner, tomorrow's another day. And she carried her cheer, and the drug and a clean glass back to the private room. She turned on a bright light and started to speak, but the whistle of a boat, very near on the river, startled her, and she waited, pouring water into the clean glass on the night table, beside the flowers.

—Isn't this the nicest plant! she said, and her patient turned: until that moment the anthurium had really looked rather obscene.

About the only person whom the blasts of the whistle did not intimidate into silence was Arny: it brought him round just enough to raise his head, and speak for the first time in two hours. He said it was getting late, and he thought he should call his wife. But he did not speak distinctly, and the blasts of departure drowned out every other sound.

He was part of a gay throng on a promenade deck, where someone fluttered up to ask, —Where's Rwu-dy?

—Baby you'll find *that* one in the bridal suite. *Alone.*

The whistle blasted them into silence again. Arny alerted, and spoke.

Up above, the tall woman said, —My God, what do you suppose we've got next door *this* trip...will you listen to that?...pouring-on party?

Her husband put down his glass and stared at the passenger list for First Class. —Two United States Senators, he said finally, and got his glass back.

Aft, as near as he, could get to his wife and the two with her who had come down to see him off, Don Bildow waved again and straightened up. His wife cried something out to him. He waved. It was past midnight.

—If you can't be good, be careful, she repeated. He waved. Then, —Oh! Oh! Oh! Look!...he forgot and left his Methyltestosterone tablets, he won't be able to do *any*thing without them. Look, he left his Methyltestosterone tablets...

He waved. With the other hand he held on his plastic glasses. The wind stirred his brown and yellow necktie. From down below, he looked like he was being abducted.

The whistle blasted again.

—Baby you were sweet to come see us off but you'd better get back on sho-wer...we're going to *sail.*

—But I'm coming *twoo.*

Lines were cast off, and the ship, as large as a country town, commenced a grotesque rearward motion, now as though embarrassed at its size, like a football player backing out of a doll house. Finally, faced in the right direction by six tugboats, it recovered its dignity in imperious puffs of smoke and a shrill blast of steam that lowered enough to sound, to penetrate chasms ashore and be rendered back in particles, each one more faint, as though the island were loath to let it go.

Well below the water line, Stanley opened his door and looked into the passage. —It's all right, he said, —come on out.

Other Pilgrims were already apparent, and Stanley had, a few minutes before, met a priest whom he liked immediately, a man with a plump face which carried joviality easily, but could instantly recover a medieval sternness which, one realized, was there all the time. His name was Father Martin, and he accounted for the large number of Pilgrims, some of whom he was shepherding toward the impending Canonization ceremonies in Rome, which

Stanley forthwith hoped, somehow, to attend. They had quite a chat in that minute or two.

—Come...he said again, and took her arm. —Don't you have any coat? You didn't bring any coat at all?

She looked at him and shook her head, her eyes impossibly large it seemed to him as his own widened. Then as though aware of the warmth of her elbow in his hand, he took her hand which was cold and led her up to an open deck.

She'd brought no luggage, only a sort of bundle, and what was tied up in it he had no idea, except for a paper book tied on the outside. It was labeled *The Story of Barbara Ubryk*. There was a picture on the cover captioned, *Smothering a baby*. And below, *Why nunneries are within high walls, barred windows and bolted doors.*

—But...where did you get this?

She had looked at him with these wide eyes, instantly frightened at his wrath but with no challenge, no question but that it must be justified. —An-selm, she answered him; at that he'd looked away quickly, put the thing back, its cover turned down, and stood looking away unable to confront the sad hope that had suffused her empty face for that one moment, and the bright pleasure her eyes had almost dared over this thing they were to share, that he had brought her to.

She hardly spoke, except when he spoke to her and even then, only if he addressed a question, which she would answer very slowly, deliberate and brief. Though once she had burst out with, —Then do Pilgrims need a passport too? Or I shall wear a cockleshell, and he will know me and he will know me well...Which disarmed Stanley: what could she know of Santiago de Compostela? or when with the same light about to break in her eyes, waiting only his confirmation, she had asked whether it were true, Did the mice eat Saint Gertrude's heart? —For she is patron saint of them...

As now, he took his hand from her and stood, staring at the lights of the Jersey shore, unable to believe that this was New York, and he was leaving it; and as dreadfully convinced that it was.

Even now the name Anselm threw him into a whirl, the more so now if what they had said a few evenings before, what Hannah had said and they had accepted, if it were true: and if it were true then everything else was true.

With one hand in his pocket he clutched the gauze-and-newspaper-wrapped tooth, as Anselm's dream, —I dreamt about you last night...I'm sure it was you...and the tooth almost came through to bite into his palm. At that the other hand came up in reflex to take her arm, and missed, though her arm did not move at all there on the rail: missed only so that his knuckles rubbed her bare arm and she turned that anticipating vacant beauty upon him, her eyes unblinking though the wind was rising and came round the upper decks full upon them now, as she waited, awaited his temper: and Anselm persisted, the more strongly, on the floor, ritu quadrupedis, —Succubus...

The daring instant of a smile on her face provoked him, —Aren't you cold? Until he asked her she might have been anywhere; now with his prompting question the smile and, if it had been warmth, left her. She shook, three times or four, sharply as though to atone for a multitude of slight shivers.

He looked away, not toward the shore, or where the shore might be, but up forward; and saw only a man on the deck above leaning at the rail, a man in a Chesterfield with the collar up, a black Homburg hat and a long face which seemed to empty through the triangular chin, that, and a glint of gold, at the cuff was it? a finger?

—Don't you want to come in?

After a moment he left her there, and with a shudder of cold went below himself. Roll and go, the motion of the ship was becoming familiar and inevitable to hundreds of people, the sole reciprocation that bound them together.

Already through the Narrows and into the Lower Bay, past Sandy Hook, and into ten fathoms of water when Stanley realized that it was some time since he'd left her out on deck, and hurried up stairs and passages again with an anxious look on his face.

She was not where he'd left her. But he was confused enough with the unfamiliarity of it all to be uncertain that this was where he'd left her, where he stood at the rail and started to call out, at the moment a wave hit the side and threw up spray, and knocked his voice right back into him. He swung round and looked at the water, terrified.

He heard her call him; and he looked still more alarmed.

She was up on the deck above, and waved to him. He saw her there with great relief, finally, and saw a shadow that had been standing near her turn and disappear in the dark. When she came down, he could not scold her for the fright she'd given him, and so he reprimanded her, —You shouldn't go up there, that's First Class... and he pulled the door open with more effort than he would have thought necessary.

—Was there somebody up there with you?... were you talking to somebody?

—Only to the cold man.

—Well you... you ought to be more careful, you can't just go talking to people.

—That is what he said, when he heard her singing.

—Who?

—The Cold Man.

At the foot of a staircase leading to First Class, Stanley saw Father Martin descending, and let go her arm. Then as abruptly he took it again, up high where there was some sleeve, and came on resolute, slowing his step and so hers, for the greeting, the introduction, the explanations: but Father Martin passed, looking him straight in the face, without a word, without a shade of recognition, the medieval lines of his face standing out livid as though he had seen a ghost.

Off Ambrose Light, there was some commotion. The ship almost ran down a rowboat in which a Chinaman, equipped with three New Jersey road maps, was setting out confidently for home, and had already got this far from the land into which he had been smuggled so many years before.

But Stanley didn't hear of the incident until a day or so later. Down a passage before him, she commenced singing, her voice very low,

—Blessed Mary went a-walking... Over Jordan river...

—Where did you learn that? he demanded.

—The song you taught her?

—But I... I never taught you that.

—Stephen met her, fell a-talking...

—Who is this... cold man? he interrupted her again.

—The Cold Man, and he carries his arm like the boy did.

—Like... what do you mean, in a sling?

—In a black one.

Inside, Stanley stood looking vacantly at *The Story of Barbara Ubryk*. Then he took her bundle from the chair where he intended to sleep.

—Blessed Mary went a-walking...

—Come... he said, knelt now beside the bed where the yellowed crucifix was already hung, already muttering the *Pater noster qui es in coelis* he intended to teach her, the metal deck cutting his knees. The engines sounded in a constantly renewed heave forth, as her knee where she stood beside him, brought her weight against his arm, and away, and against him the more heavily as the prow far ahead shuddered into a trough, into twenty fathoms of water, and without a word he drew her down.

III

THE LAST TURN OF THE SCREW

¡Así por la calle pasa quien debe amor!
—LOPE DE VEGA, *Amar sin saber a quién*

SPAIN is a land to flee across. Every town, and every capital, is a destination; and the names which ring with refuge to the fugitive mount with finality to him traveling relentlessly unpursued, setting destinations one after another whose reasons for being so cease upon arrival, and he must move on, to provide that interim of purpose with which each new destination endows the journey however short, and search each pause with reasons anxiously mistaken drawing nearer, with each destination, to the last.

Trains do not depart: they set out, and move at a pace to enhance the landscape, and aggrandize the land they traverse, laboring their courses with the effort of journeys never before made, straining the attention on sufferance of minutes passed separately until concentration is exhausted, and no other pace conceivable. The very distances become greater, through landscape irreplaceable by the exhausted fancy, unaltered by the most resourceful imagination, impossible at last any other land, oppressed by any other sky.

Five miles behind lay Gibraltar, crouching across the bay from Algeciras heavy-buttocked and dumb, the hulk of an animal in immense malformity with lights stacked glittering at its base like suppliant candles round a monstrous idol.

This time of the year, the levanter blew in its chill from the east, shrouding the rock and bringing dampness and an overcast to the sky. Algeciras showed no light but what was left over from day, and when even that was gone dull glows appeared at last in the narrow cobbled streets leading up to the plaza where trees bore oranges among benches tiled orange and white and blue round a dry fountain. There, when the one-arm church sounded the flat plannng of its bell, and the dim lights of the plaza, burning an hour or two now in lusterless illumination of the quiet, failed and went out, that quiet proved not what it had seemed, not an immanent thing at all, but imposition: back down those narrow streets the town seethed behind shuttered casements with music and the violence of voices in strained extremes, driven on frenzied patterns of clapped hands, broken by the disciplined clatter of castanets. Café Pinero was betrayed almost two blocks off by the strident crash of the girl's heels on the frail wooden stage. A mute idiot winced in the single door where an unshaven man in a lambskin jacket and dirty white turban pushed him aside to enter, and leave him standing spent in masturbatory gestures for the dancer beyond the round tabletops and coffee cups, turning when she was done, twisted, with a whine, away from the glasses and smoke, frantically hopeless back to the narrow street, drawn by the heels of a passer-by loud on the stones going down the hill unsteadily, with a pause of distress to brush a spot of moonlight off the sleeve, pursued once more by the wail, —sangre negra en mi corazón ... down, toward the bay again and a hotel whose high-ceilinged rooms drown the transient overnight among sunken ribs of ponderous furniture, to surface him rapidly with dawn among tiles of differing intent, exaggerated on rising, distorted in mismatching deep and then not as reflections underwater, bold below as a public lavatory, consumed on shallowing in Moorish intricacy as light separates the louvers and the train sets out before sunrise for Madrid.

It enters upon the surface of an inland sea, so that land is, as empty and apparently trackless and vast, harboring briefly in indistinguishable ports along a course charted over barren swells, past trees as alien here as things afloat, and the apparitions of isolated ruins condemned like the specter-ships of the sea to sail forever unable to make port.

It was cold, and one of the soldiers sitting by the broken window in the old second-class coach bundled up a coat and stuffed it into the opening. The seat they had taken was broken too, and every time one of them fixed it, it collapsed again, until they stacked two wooden suitcases under it. Then one of them passed round a leather wine skin, and another brought out a trumpet. He played *Dinah* twice, and each time left out the line, —change her mind about me ... as the train paused at a village, and went on among stripped cork trees. A vendor came down the aisle with a tray of peanuts and inedible-looking confections. He was stopped by a handsome boy about twelve years old, who paid for three peanuts with a ten-centimo piece delivered with some difficulty from a deep pocket. The boy had a black corner stitched on his lapel. He gave a peanut to each of the younger children, both girls, and offered the third to his mother, who watched him all this time, her own grave eyes excited and shining with a strained surprise which the children reflected, when they looked at her, and all four were caught in the silence of being left alone which none of them tried to dispel with feigned pleasantry or false cheer. But they asked him the time often enough, to provoke the solemn exercise of taking out the watch whose face he studied with such sober attention that years mounted upon his own; and the woman, turning her eyes with something fierce and proud in them from the boy, stared for a rude moment at the man sitting alone across the aisle who was looking at them all with an expression which was not a frown but had happened as an abrupt breaking of his features, until that instant apparently cast for good as they were but even now, in this new constriction, renewing an impression of permanence, as molten metals suddenly spilled harden instantly in unpredictable patterns of breakage. She did stare, with the face of someone looking at a wound, until discountenanced, and when she turned away held a hand to her temples. She was not more than thirty, and in black. Now the train was moving so slowly that every stripped cork tree drawn past stood out in nakedness, writhing the red agony of its flayed trunk toward the waste of heaven.

Between the land and the still brilliant blue and white of the sky moved gray clouds with torn edges.

An old man with a battered guitar entered at the upper end of the coach. He had two tunes, one a vaguely recognizable paso doble, the other a hapless *La Tani*, which could only be heard in his immediate vicinity, with such meticulous care did he work what strings remained. The soldier played *Dinah* in another key, on the trumpet, and the old man tried to accompany with his paso doble. —Aïe... they passed him the bota, and he did not spill a drop.

Past noon, the woman asked the time, and they waited with proud patience through the grave ceremony of finding it. Then she stood to their baggage in the rack, all cloth bags and paper packages, baskets and bottles, and a silent bird in a cage. She had already sat down and opened some cheese, while the boy broke open a loaf of bread, when she glanced up to see the man across the aisle staring at all of them feverishly. She was quick to get some bread under the cheese, and with no hesitation offer, —Quiere comer?

He grimaced, and mumbled, appeared to try to smile, shaking his head. He looked eager, but nonetheless surprised, even shocked at her invitation, even her recognition, which she withdrew from him, and returned to the children, the bread, cheese, and fish.

He sat turned away staring for some time through the glass, or possibly no further than the image the dirt on the outside of the glass made fleetingly discernible, and unchanged; until eventually his own meal appeared, part by part, oranges, a banana, bread, a bottle of wine, a cucumber, an onion. Then he smoked, until the cigarette came apart between his fingers.

Toward evening, mountains far ahead posed impassability.

—Una y una dos . . . dos y una tres . . . the soldiers sang up ahead, *La Tani*, though the old man with the battered guitar was gone. —No sale la cuenta . . .

The mountains turned dark, their features flattening and their shapes ahead black and two-dimensional against a sky suffused with faint green: and suddenly the train burst out upon the open blue plateau, into a haze which still held the spent lust of the sun clinging over the barren plain of New Castile, where the train rushed forward into the approaching darkness, toward its destination, Madrid.

The haze settled on the city in the early morning conveyed that remarkable cold which they say will kill a man and not blow out a candle, motionless cold which seems to come from inside, and be diffused through the body from the very marrow of the bones. That early, the streets were desolate. Here and there old women fanned kindling fires in brazier pans, standing one foot in gutters then being swept clean. Men hosed down the streets, as they did whatever the weather; and those who passed hurried, only the glint of eyes between the drawn beret and muffling throw of a cape. Over all this the Spanish sun hesitated, would not rise until forced by expectant activity, then with a great red flush it appeared from the haze beyond the Atocha station.

And soon enough, the streets were filled with cries, men selling brooms, or buying bottles, women selling *España*, *Arriba*, *ABC*, tobacco, lottery tickets, —Dos iguales para hoy! . . . Their cries rose like the sounds of people in agony. And soon enough, the blind boy was posted at the corner near the Plaza Santa Ana, with lottery tickets pinned to his coat, to pass the day there, and be taken away at night.

In a nearby alley, identified on a tiled wall as Alphonso del Gato, a spotty unshaven man with cigarette burns in the robe he had wrapped round him, stood on a narrow window balcony looking down at the figures hurrying below in carpet slippers on the cold pavement. Two members of the Guardia Civil appeared, and he retired quickly, closed his windows, and went on with his work at the mirror. On the dresser top before him, a passport was propped open with a bottle of oxalic acid, which he had used to make a few alterations in the lavender stamp-ink, and now he was trimming his tinted mustache in accord with the passport photograph. There were in fact two passports, one Swiss, and this one opened, Rumanian. He had studied the Swiss face and particulars often and regretfully, and finally given it up in favor of the other, though there were, as he knew, certain inconveniences attached to being a Rumanian. One was that he did not understand a word of the language (though somewhere, among the litter of newspapers and bottled chemicals, there was a copy of I. Al. Bratescu-Voinesti's short stories, *In Tuneric si Lumină*, which he carried occasionally and appeared to read in such places as customs sheds and police stations). By adding ten years to the life of Mr. Yák (whose passport, along with the Swiss one, he had been working on in New York before his sudden departure) and, with the tinted mustache and a shock of black hair, subtracting ten years from his own, he quite fit the unknown Rumanian whom he had recently become. He did, in the habit which years of application had instilled, think of himself as Mr. Yák; and any other name, or life he had borne, was almost forgotten: almost, that is, but for the one thing which had driven him to this unobtrusive retirement from his former profession, into the historical asylum of Iberia. Among the scattered periodicals, there was one particularly thumbed, creased, and soiled, a recent copy of *The National Counterfeit Detector Monthly*. Page one, headed *The new counterfeits*, was the most soiled, creased, and thumbed: "Check letter A, face plate No. 95, back plate No. 475, series 1942B...The Jackson portrait is exceptionally good..." —How? he would murmur whenever he read it over, —How did they catch it? He would go on to read the other current reviews, "The Hamilton portrait is smutty...Nose lines broken, right eye too narrow... Crude reproduction on poor paper...This is a counterfeit of average quality... Dark expressionless eyes..." but he always came back to the top one, and muttered —*How?*

All this made him quite restless, as the chaos of newspapers showed, *ABC*, *Oggi*, the *Continental Daily Mail*, through whose pages he sought some new challenge to erase the indignity of this recent defeat. This was the first vacation he had ever had in his life, aside from enforced recreation periods prolonged at Attica, Atlanta, and other resorts where he was familiar. He had plenty of money, the local currency that is, having sold the remaining packets of his last work to a Levantine who did business in Tangier. Still he could not relax. He was beginning to look like a remittance man, though, with some success, he tried to melt into the people around him, and look like the other men staying in this pensión, dressed with spruce seediness, as they were, nervously alert, as they were, and even a plexiglas collar, as they wore. Everything was in order. Even his stomach had settled down, after its first horrendous adventures with the fare in the Pensión Las Cenizas.

Still he could not relax. Small things upset him. The mustache, for instance: he was unused to wearing one permanently, and when he came into the room alone and locked the door behind him, reached up to pull it off and toss it into a drawer. And the room was cold. When he complained about it, to the dueño, or the girls in the kitchen where he went to warm his hands, they behaved as though winter had come for the first time to Madrid, and spoke

of the cold in terms of a vague wonder which they managed to sustain annually until spring. There was a radiator, a cold, absurd, mocking piece of furniture in one corner, for there was very little coal anywhere in the country;
and so he was at last given a brazier whose surface of gray ash remained warm
to the touch for some hours. He spent a good deal of time sitting a knee on
either side of it, cleaning his nails with the end tooth of a comb. He had tried
to read, something more sustained than the papers, but that got nowhere.
There was nothing there for him. The same for the paintings of Velasquez and
Goya, Dürer, Bosch, Breughel, for he'd even been to the Prado seeking challenge, but there was nothing there for him.

He picked up the *Daily Mail*, and under "Teddington's Good Win," read
again of a distant hockey game. He read again of the visit of four rare (Bewick's)
swans at Penns Pond, Richmond Park. He read again of betting law reforms;
and a seven-year-old girl killed by a shotgun blast. Under "Today's Arrangements" of an organ recital by Mr. W. J. Tubbs at Holy Trinity, Marylebone;
a meeting of the Victoria Young Conservatives, the Johnson Society of London, the Friends of Uruguay Society. There was nothing there for him, and
he threw the paper down, but with no alternative, than to pick up another.

A minute later, his brows knitted over an open page. He sat forward, and
Digame quivered in his hands. He looked up from it, and stared abstracted
for a full minute at an Andalusian love scene on the wall, then back at the
page, his sharp darting eyes glittering with excitement. Pictured in the paper
was a face beaming malevolence over a black beard, identified as Señor Kuvetli,
a prominent Egyptologist stopping in the capital in the course of his work,
which now centered about a search for the lost mummy of a young princess,
possibly to be found somewhere in Spain, brought here as a talisman by a
retreating band of Gypsies centuries before.

He laid the paper aside and commenced to pace the floor. Then he sat down
over the brazier and commenced to clean his nails. The residue from this task
dropped on the surface of gray ash, where it sank and burned with a slight
puff and a noxious odor which rose to him until suddenly, as though inspired
by some divine flatus, he leaped to his feet, and in a matter of minutes was
shaved, dressed, and generally caparisoned for the streets.

Before he left his room, however, he took time for a quick look in Baedeker's
Spain and Portugal, which he had in two volumes, the original having split
into two, and then went to seek the dueño in the dim halls of the pensión,
after giving the shock of black hair a toss with his broken comb. As he stooped
to lock the door, Marga came hurrying down the dark passage, bumped him,
and with a flash of her eyes, blond hair, and a blue angora sweater, begged his
pardon and was gone inside her own door.

Now there are some women, of retiring nature and modest comportment, who if seen, say, wearing a fur-trimmed cloth coat, are remembered after as having been dressed in the simple cloth coat of whatever color it may have been; and there are others, seen in that same coat, who are recalled sheathed luxuriously and entirely in the fur, and Marga was one of these latter. She was a guest here, and though she had never importuned this exotic neighbor of hers, now adjusting his hair in the dark passage, the mere fact of his avowed origin made him interesting, and she was always exceedingly bright with him, as she was with others there who knew more of her private habits than Mr. Yák might be expected to, keeping to himself as he did quite strictly, but for the dining room, and speaking only when spoken to, in a flow of Spanish which was difficult to follow, was in fact a stiffened Italian from which he pruned the luxurious curls and Neapolitan tendrils as he went along, though as far as that goes neither Marga nor the dueño had ever been to Italy, and neither had ever seen a living Rumanian in their lives.

As for this one she'd just left behind in the chill corridor, he was quite spry this morning, now following a girl laden with two chamber pots toward the kitchen, where two other girls sat picking over a pile of lentils on the metal table top, and the one he had followed went on next door to empty her charges, and rinse them in the bathtub.

He found the dueño there too, in checked carpet slippers, soon had the information he wanted, and left down the linoleum, banging the heavy door so that its bell jangled, moving with a sprightly vigor which might have been surprising even in one of the age he appeared now, the shock of black hair dancing over his forehead as he hastened toward the Estación del Norte, where he was in time to catch the morning express to Segovia, along whose route his destination lay not far distant.

San Zwingli appeared suddenly, at a curve in the railway, a town built of rocks against rock, streets pouring down between houses like the beds of unused rivers, and the houses littered one against another like boulders along mountain streams. Swallows dove and swept with appalling certainty at the tower of the church, as the morning visitor climbed the hill toward the town, touching now and then at his mustache, as though to make certain it was on straight. He walked with a briskness, and a light in his eye seldom seen today but in asylums and occasional pulpits, the look of a man with a purpose.

With this spring in his step he was soon up behind the town, where the sound of running water nearby, the braying of burros and the desultory tinkling of bells, and the distant voices of people below reached him where he paused to sniff, and then stood still inhaling the pines above him and the delicious freshness of cow manure, like a man rediscovering senses long forgotten under the abuses of cities. Then he was off again, and when he reached the road bounded by cypress trees, he hardly paused to cross himself at the first station he encountered as he hurried up the hill toward the white walls of the cemetery.

The forecourt, as he entered, was flooded with a riot of flamenco music from the radio in the house of the resident watchman, to one side there and almost hidden behind the unfurled hilarity of the week's wash. Nonetheless he could hear voices beyond the next gate, where a small stone crucifixion drew his eye as he approached and went through, with a quick glance up at it and a stab, more a parabola than a cross over his chest, for the figure carved in what appeared at that moment full abandon to a dance which the music accompanied. Within, the bóvedas mounted on both sides, three, four, five vaults high, decorated with bead flowers and metal wreaths, icons and wilted nosegays, broken glass protecting photographs, and all of them numbered, with names, and ages caught up in infancy and childhood, many between fourteen and twenty, and few to sixty. Straight ahead stood a separate mausoleum, a cross atop it, surrounded by a chain and four corner columns mounting stone faces, the girl, the woman, the hag, and the skull.

—Ausculta...

—Mira señor... aïee...

The argument going on in two languages would hardly have made sense in one, and the newcomer arrived to enter with what sounded like a third, for one of the men was the watchman whom he'd come to see. The other was a feverish-eyed man whom he studied sharply for fear, as he confessed later, that he might be a Rumanian, since the language he spoke sounded as if it might have been anything. (It proved to be Late Latin, being garlanded with whatever tendrils and sprays came to hand.) Both were waving their arms at the bóveda beside them, where an unmarked vault and one containing nothing but the wet end of a broom stood side by side.

—My father doesn't make mistakes! the feverish-eyed man suddenly burst out.

—Ah... speaks English?

—Yes, I... you, who are you? Listen, do you speak... can you talk to him? My mother's in there, and I... he tells me... Here, you talk to him. Here she is, I've written her name down, here, he went on rapidly, and handed a rumpled card to the shock-haired man, who stared at it. —Yes, yes, there that's her name, she... What's the matter, can't you read it?

—This... this is your mother's name?

—Yes, can't you see? And she...

—But...what's she doing here? How'd she get in here? The card quivered, and became damp in his hand. He reached up as though he were going to smooth back the shock of black hair, but his raised hand dropped and he crossed himself as he handed the card back, and crossed himself again.

—Well that's what I want to know. I mean, there's no name on this vault, there's no mark, there's no way to tell...

Then the sacristán started, and spoke as though he could not stop: *la guerra* was the word to occur most often; next to that, *los rojos*. All this time Mr. Yák studied the figure beside him closely, as though it might be a ghost, or the leavings of one, the thin lips and nervous blinking eyes, hands at his sides opening and closing on nothing. Mr. Yák was agitated enough himself, tugging at his mustache as he listened to the sacristán, and then pressing it anxiously back in place, searching the face beside him for some resemblance he hoped not to find, while the other simply stood, blinking at the unidentified vault and then up at the brilliant sky where low-flying gray clouds exaggerated the vastness of the sheer blue and white beyond.

—España...no hay más que una! burst the music in the court, as the sacristán gasped for breath, and Mr. Yák turned to interpret, —In this war they had, these reds came in and turned everything upside-down, some places they even opened up some coffins and stood the bodies up all over the place... even down in the church he says they turned everything upside-down, even the párroco, the town priest here, they turned him upside-down too...

—Coño, mira...The sacristán recovered his breath, and with it his stream of Andalusian enthusiasm; but he was interrupted by a proposition which left him wide-eyed and open-mouthed: Mr. Yák had, after all, come here on business himself, and now, to show his calm as he spoke of it, he reached to a niche nearby to pluck a boutonnière. He had some difficulty in breaking the wire stem, but by the time he'd done speaking he had the spotted paper rose in his buttonhole, and the sacristán, though he was staring transfixed at this gay embellishment, seemed not to see it for the horror of what he heard. Even the wad of five-peseta notes which reached his hand did not break the sacristán's cataleptic stance, though it loosed his tongue enough for, —Ya no! Ya no!... and he commenced to chatter on about the párroco, and a funeral cortège which was imminent, to listen, while he caught his breath, and then bound round the corner of the bóveda, pointing, —Ya viene! Ya viene!

Sure enough, below, and as yet beyond the first station of the cross, the coronation approached. Still Mr. Yák seemed in no hurry. He said a few more words to the sacristán, and then sauntered off among the bóvedas, reading ages and dates on the tiers of vaults like a man on a shopping tour. The paper rose, slightly disintegrated and faded in spots by drops of rain, added a jaunty note to the general trimness of his person, which the plexiglas collar so nicely defined. He might have worn a hat, but for fear his hair come off with it when it was removed, and now, as the sacristán watched them out the first gate, the wind stood his black hair up on end, and he grabbed for it. As for the figure beside him, the sacristán had earlier noted how the man's coat stood out on both sides like a pack-saddle, but said nothing, only stared, as he did now after them: seen from behind, as they passed through the second gate, they looked like two old men.

The funeral pomp was black, led slowly up the rock-studded road by the párroco, an old man with a boy on either side carrying their standards. The horses wore black plumes on their harness and black net halfway to the ground, and the open carriage they drew mounted to a black cross pinnacle over the exposed casket. The man seated before, driving the horses, and him up behind between the wide rear wheels, both wore black hats square over old unshaven faces, derelict decorations like those awaiting them above. The men who followed carrying their hats, and their heads bowed, stepped round the horses' droppings which were left behind steaming in the sun. Mr. Yák crossed himself, three times, as the procession passed.

Part way up the rough road a little girl in a green dress followed on a cycle, which she turned in uncertain circles before the two figures descending, and looked them over curiously before she went back down slowly before them. —How old do you think she is? Mr. Yák demanded suddenly, studying her with a strange appraising look.

—Ten, maybe.

—Yes. Just about. Just about. His companion shuddered beside him. —What's the matter?... it's not your funeral. They passed the sixth station silently. —What's that you've got in your pockets, they stick out like that.

—Oranges.

Mr. Yák nodded, as the oranges bumped against him. At the second station he brought out, —So that's your mother up there, you came all the way to visit her grave?

—There's no mark on the vault. It ought to be but there's no name on the vault.

—It's probably her in there, you wouldn't have any way to know if it wasn't anyway.

—Well I...I might...I could...

—You wouldn't want to go prying around in there.

—What?

—I mean you wouldn't want to go looking inside. She's been in there thirty years, you wouldn't want to...

—How do you know she's been in there thirty years? The man stopped beside him, bumping him round with the oranges. —You...what do you...

—I just said that, Mr. Yák answered with quick constraint, putting a hand on the arm beside him to draw the man on. —You know...here, what's the matter?

—I just don't like people's hands on me, that's all.

Mr. Yák drew his hand back quickly, and pressed his mustache with a finger. —That's a nice ring you got there. Diamonds? He had no answer. Then his companion stopped as abruptly as before, but he was looking far beyond, to the east where the snow-capped peaks of the Sierra de Guadarrama emboldened the sky.

—What's the matter?

—Matter? I...nothing the matter. Those mountains, I just noticed them.

—Oh them. Mr. Yák sounded relieved. —They been there a long time.

A barrel organ sounded defiant gaiety in a side street as they entered the town and approached the church.

—It's nice you came to see your mother's grave like this. Mr. Yák paused outside the heavy door, its opening covered inside with a hanging which a girl pushed aside, coming out, and took the handkerchief from her head. —You're not coming in?

—In there? The man looked up for the first time since he'd stopped to gaze at the distant mountains, but the same look in his eyes, as though he were looking at something far away.

—To burn a candle. You know. You can have a Mass said for her. If you come all the way here...

—But I...look, what is all this? Who are you, anyhow? You...what does it matter to you if I...if I burn a candle or burn the whole church down for her?

—All right! Mr. Yák took a step forward. —Then as far as that goes, how do I know that's your mother?...that name on that card you showed me.

—Damn it, now, what...

—Look, can't you read that sign? The shock-haired man pointed to a sign beside the door. Further down the wall, near the street corner, was pasted a once-colorful poster for a seven-year-old American movie. —Hace años que los Prelados de la Iglesia vienen repreniendo la bochornosa...see? You shouldn't swear...

—Damn it...

—Que ya no se respetan ni la santidad del templo, ni los misterios más augustos y sagrados en cuya presencia...

—Goodbye.

—While you're here you could at least have a Mass...

—Good God, I...what makes you think she's still in Purgatory? You... look this...this is idiotic, she wasn't even...Wait, I thought you were going in there, in the church.

—I just remembered, the priest, he's up at the cemetery now.

—Yes, I...he'll be back. Goodbye.

—Are you going for some coffee? We can have some coffee.

—I'm going for a drink.

—You don't want to drink so early.

—Good...God! If I want a drink, damn it...

—Look out!...

The empty funeral carriage came careening around a corner. Both men aboard it had their hats pushed back, and were smoking.

—That was almost your funeral.

—Yes, well...listen, every time a funeral passes, it's your own passing. Now let me go. Thank you. Now let me go, will you?

Mr. Yák took his hand from the man's arm, but hurried along beside him. They followed the barrel organ to a bar called La Ilicitana.

Inside, Mr. Yák ordered two coffees. The man beside him clutched one hand in the other on the bar silently, as the bartender escaped with the order. Then looking straight ahead at the bottles behind the bar, he took out a torn green and black paper packet, and from it a yellow-paper cigarette.

—You don't want to smoke that. The tobacco here's one-third potato peelings. Here...

The man's hand trembled slightly as he lit the yellow-paper cigarette, raising his elbow to ward off the cellophane-covered packet being thrust at him.

—You can get real cigarettes here. Rubio, you call them. Tobacco rubio... here.

The man exhaled a cloud of acrid smoke, and as the bartender appeared with two cups of coffee he began to gesticulate and mutter, —Vino...albus. Bianco...

—Here, I already ordered coffee...

—Damn it, I don't want coffee, I...

—I can't drink two cups of this stuff. One of them will get cold...

—Now listen...

—All right, what do you want. Wine? White wine? Un blanco, he said to the bartender, watched until a glass was half filled and then interrupted, waving a hand. —Manzanilla. The bartender stopped, and poured back what he'd poured out. —See? Manzanilla, Mr. Yák said to the man beside him. —I'm ordering you the best.

—Yes, I . . . how did I forget that name? he whispered to himself.

The excellent stuff appeared in a stemmed narrow glass, which was quickly emptied and pushed forth again.

—You shouldn't drink it down so fast like that, wine like that you want to sip . . .

The man looked up, as though about to speak, or shout; but his host was sipping his coffee, careful not to dip his mustache. A small dish of fried blood and potatoes appeared, and neither of them touched it. Outside at the door, the barrel organ was straining its way through *La Sebastiana*. The bartender obliged the silent grimace of the man to his left with another glass of Manzanilla; and collected a blue note from the man to his right.

—Now here, don't you pay for this, I . . .

—I invited you for some coffee.

—Well there, I'm not having coffee. You don't owe me anything, you . . .

—How do you know, maybe I do.

—What do you mean?

—Sometimes you just like owe somebody something. Mr. Yák dusted at his boutonnière. One of the spotted petals came off. The bartender returned his change, in coins scarcely more than the weight of paper and bits of paper that looked like a handful of dead leaves. —That's what depresses me about a poor country, he said, trying to fold the brown one-peseta notes together. —All the small denominations, it gets so dirty you can't hardly recognize it. Then he spread one of the notes out on the bar with his thumb, and shook his head with professional disapproval. —Just look at that. Startling him, the hand mounting the diamonds snatched the note from under his fingers. —What's the matter?

—Nothing. This. I just noticed it. He bent close over the note. —This beautiful thing, he whispered.

—What? . . . this thing? Mr. Yák demanded. —Why, I . . . a child could do better than that.

—No, just this. The picture on it, the Dama de Elche. It's a . . . a beautiful thing, that . . . that head, the Dama de Elche. Then the note was pushed back as abruptly as it had been taken, and the man put an elbow on the bar and gripped his face across the eyes, his thumb and a fingernail going white where they pressed his temples.

Mr. Yák picked the note up again and studied it with distasteful curiosity; then he shrugged and folded it, face forward and right side up, with the others. —A cheap engraving job, he muttered, putting the wad into his pocket. Then he craned his head round and said, —That's a nice ring you got there.

They're real diamonds. No answer, and the hand did not move away from the eyes. —Why do you wear it on your middle finger for?

The hand came down and almost caught him across the face. —Because it's too damned small to get around my neck. Now will you...will you...The hand with the ring hung taut and half closed in the air between them, then came back slowly and the man drew it across his feverish eyes, and turned away again, to stare down at a plate of sardines.

Mr. Yák picked up the small fork from the cold fried blood and potatoes, and commenced to clean his nails with a sharp tine. —You don't look very good, he said.

—I...I don't dress to please you.

—I don't mean your clothes, you don't look well in your face. You haven't even told me your name, your first name.

—My Christian name.

—Yeah, you haven't even told me that. My name is Yák. My first name... He paused to press at his mustache, thoughtfully. —Never mind that, it's not a real Christian name, you might say. Just call me Mr. Yák.

—All right, you...Mister Yák, you...The face suddenly turned up with a look of terror in the eyes, which spread quickly from the lines around the eyes over the whole drawn face. —What do you...what are you so damned interested in me for?

—That's all right now, that's all right, said Mr. Yák, putting a hand out to the arm which was instantly withdrawn. —I can tell you're not a bum.

—What if I am? What does that...to you?

—Never mind, you're not a bum. I can tell that. See? Mr. Yák's voice was almost gentle, and this time, when he put his hand on the wrist before him it was not withdrawn, but stayed quivering there. —Maybe there's something I can do for you.

—You...you, what do you think you are, my guardian angel? Listen... The voice shook, sounded exhausted, though he continued to stare at the plate of sardines. —Listen...he repeated hoarsely.

—Are you wanted? Mr. Yák asked him in a low tone.

—Wanted?...he repeated dully. —Wanted? Wanted?

—What do they want you for?

—What do they...what does who want me for? What do you want me for?

—The police. You got the police after you, haven't you? I know how it is, see? Have you? What do they want you for?

The man stared at the sardines a moment longer, then threw his head up and started to laugh. He jerked his arm away, looking Mr. Yák straight in the eyes for the first time. —Murder. Eh? Damn it. I stabbed a man and left him there for dead. Now, is that what you wanted? The laughter broke off, and he hung there staring at the man before him who said quickly,

—Yeah but don't tell everybody, be quiet. That's not the kind of a thing you broadcast. You can't tell who's watching you, even in a dump like this.

—Yes…well they're watching us. They're watching us, the voice took up its dull tone again.

—Who? Where? Who? Mr. Yák grabbed the man's arm again, and it lay there still on the bar.

—Don't you see them? he whispered. —See their eyes, watching us?

—You mean these…these fish here? Mr. Yák's grip relaxed, as he looked where the other eyes were fixed.

—Yes, see them watching us?

—Look, Jesus…don't give me a scare like that again, will you?

—See them watching us?

—All right now, forget it. Pressing at his mustache, Mr. Yák stepped back and spat on the floor. Then he looked up, studying the profile before him narrowly, as though he were looking over glasses. —You didn't tell me your whole name yet, he said finally.

—Sam Hall. Now…leave me. Leave me. He signed for another glass. There was a tapping at his elbow.

—Get out! Vaya! Fuera! Mr. Yák broke out. The man beside him spun around, to see the ragged staring wretch who accompanied the barrel organ, holding out a hat which was the only whole piece of clothing he had.

—Wait…wait a minute. Here.

—Wait! Mr. Yák tried to stay his hand. —Five pesetas, you can't give him that much, five pesetas?

The cringing figure took the bill and scuttled away.

—You don't want to give them that much every time they…

—I like the music, that's all. Now leave me alone.

—Listen, get hold of yourself now, relax, said Mr. Yák up close to his elbow again. —Maybe I'm your gardeen angel like you say. Maybe I can help you out.

—Out of what.

—You need papers. You need a passport, don't you? Mr. Yák went on in a low tone.

—No.

—Yes you do. You can't move here without them. How would you like to be a Swiss?

—Less than anything I can think of.

—You'd make a good Swiss, I just thought about it.

—A good Swiss? The man snorted behind his hand. He took the Manzanilla as soon as it was put before him, and drank half the glass. —Women cross themselves when they meet me in the street. Dogs in the street bark at me. A good Swiss!

—You wash up and shave and you'll be fine. I just thought about it. I have this passport, see? This Swiss passport, I didn't have time to alter anything on it before I left, I didn't even change the picture on it yet, see? And I just thought about it, that's why I say this, see? This picture looks like you, this Swiss, it's got short hair and a square face like you, all knotted up like around the eyes. See? I'm not kidding you, it's a natural, this Swiss. And you can be him, see? Mr. Yák was talking more rapidly, but in the same low tone of confidence. He had a hand on the man's arm, and followed the half-step the man drew away from him, staring straight ahead. —What do you say? Listen, I know how it is, see? And this way you'll be safe as a nut. Still he had no answer, pressing close so that the man slipped another half-step's space between them, which Mr. Yák filled, speaking in a slightly different tone now, —Maybe I'm like in the same spot you are, see? he said. —Only I'm being a Rumanian. You can make as good a Swiss as I am a Rumanian.

The man took another half-step away to turn and look at him, speaking with something near interest in his voice for the first time. —You've killed someone?

—No, nothing like that. You wouldn't find me doing something that crazy. Mr. Yák filled the space between them, and pulled his throat up from the plexiglas collar. —Anybody can stab somebody. I'm not a bum to do something like that, that crazy. I'm a craftsman, an artist like, see? That's what happened to me, see? he finished, his eyes glittering.

—No.

—No what?

—What happened to you?

—I just told you. There, see? I knew you'd get interested. I'm not a bum either.

—I didn't say you were. What happened?

—I told you. I'm an artist like, a craftsman, see? . . . and they got jealous of my work.

—Who did?

—Well never mind, never mind that right now. And Mr. Yák snorted, and began drumming his fingers on the bar, looking down himself. After a few moments' silence, during which his companion finished his wine, Mr. Yák took a deep breath and spoke again, briskly as though opening a new subject. —Just never mind who right now, he said.

Another half-step, and they'd passed the staring sardines.

—What do you say? Mr. Yák demanded of this companion in whom he'd at last roused interest; but it was gone again, he'd pushed his glass forth and stared vacantly resting an elbow on the bar, and his rough chin in his hand. Mr. Yák looked about to climb up his shoulder. —What do you say, now? This is no joke, I can fix you up with this passport. This is what you want to do, see? Like putting off the old man, you know what I mean, see?...like it says in the Bible, that's it, see?...that's what you want to do, put on the new man, like it says in the Bible. What do you say?...All right, listen. Shall I just leave you here then?...

—Yes.

—Listen, I can tell when a man's not a bum, see? Like you, see? Listen, you can have this Swiss passport. You can have it. I'll give it to you, see? Then you're as safe as a nut. This guy's name, this Swiss, I forgot his name. That's all right. It's something Stephan. Stephan something. See? All right, I'll call you Stephan, all right? That will help you get use to it, see? See, Stephan? See?...you're getting used to it already, see? See Stephan? Then after a while you think of yourself as Stephan like I think of myself as Yák, as Mr. Yák, see? In case they pull any fast ones on you, see? See Stephan?

They had gone about three full steps, and almost reached the wall by this time.

—See, Stephan?

And Stephan finally turned to him. —Haven't you got anything else to do?

—I'm here on business, Mr. Yák answered immediately, and took quick advantage of what he interpreted as a renewal of his companion's interest. —Listen, do you...listen Stephan, I'll call you that so you'll get used to it, just out of curiosity have you ever heard of mummies?

—I feel like one, said Stephan with his back against the wall.

—Good! Listen...you know what they are then? You know about them? Listen, how much do you know about them. I knew you weren't a bum. Stephan.

—What do you want to know about them?

—Good! Listen, have another glass of wine. Stephan. Listen, do you... Listen...Mr. Yák brought his voice down with difficulty. —Suppose, now listen, just suppose somebody wanted to make one, see? A real craftsmanshiplike job, to make one up. Now I know something about it, see, you wouldn't want to use a new...you wouldn't use somebody who just died a little while ago... Mr. Yák thrust his face into the one before him to confide, —A doctor pulled that one in Vienna and it began to smell, see?

—How old do you want it to be?

—Real old, so it looks real old.

—What Dynasty? Stephan asked grudgingly.

—What what? Oh...now wait. Wait a minute, it was, wait...Mr. Yák pressed at his mustache with the length of a forefinger, looking down. When he saw his foot on the floor, he started to tap it. —Wait. The Fourth. The Fourth? he repeated, looking up.

—That's quite early.

—Yes, it's real old.

Stephan had lit another harsh yellow cigarette, and the smoke he exhaled separated them a little. He let the smoke settle, and then said, —If I tell you, will you go away?

—Yes, I have to...I have some business here I want to take care of pretty soon, Mr. Yák said impatiently. —Go on.

—Well, I should think...

—Stephan.

—What?

—No, no. go on. I just called you that so you'll get used to it. Go on, Mr. Yák said bridling both hands before his companion. —Stephan.

—If it's that early...you'll go away if I tell you?

—Yes, yes, go on. Go on, Stephan. Mr. Yák stepped back and spat on the floor, then brought his glittering eyes up in enthusiasm, though the voice he heard was level, even forced, the words spoken rapidly, as vacantly strung together as a recitation.

—The body is extended, make an incision in the left flank and take the internal organs out, except the heart. Fill the vacant cavity with linen and resin, saturate the outer wrappings with resin and mold them to the shape of the body, then emphasize the details with paint on the outside.

—That's all?

—That's all.

—But what about wrapping it up, all those linen bandages around it?

—That's quite complicated, the series of bandages. And leave the brain in, they didn't take the brain out until very late. And the heart, don't forget the heart, leave the heart in.

—What about the bandages, do you know them?

Stephan said nothing, but nodded vaguely.

—And the paint, what kind of paint do you paint it up with.

—I don't know. Red ochre I suppose, he answered wearily, as though the recitation had exhausted him. He turned to his empty glass.

—All right, all right for now, Mr. Yák said in a sudden hurry. —But later you and me, we can work it out. You and me... He stopped speaking. The burning green eyes were fixed on him.

—You and me... what?

—Never mind, never mind now, Stephan. We'll work it out, you and...

—Good God... will you... aren't you going?

—Yes, but later...

—Wait.

—What's the matter?

—Here, do me a favor will you? Get one of those... get me a fresh clean one-peseta note if he has one, will you?

—You haven't got any money? You want some money?

—Yes, damn it, I have some money. I just want a look at a fresh one-peseta note, I want to look at the picture on it.

—Listen, I'll lend you...

—Damn it, never mind. Never mind. Go away.

Mr. Yák examined the dirty wad from his own pocket, then called the bartender and explained what his friend wanted, —por el dibujo sabe?... quiere ver el dibujo.

The bartender's expression did not change. He found the freshest one-peseta note he had, and put it before the man at the bar, watched the one with the blown rose pat his arm, heard him say, —Goodbye Stephan, I'll be back, I won't be long, be careful... and when that one had clattered out the door, pressing his mustache with one finger, smoothing the shock of black hair with the other hand, the bartender managed to look a little relieved, not having understood the parting threat. He crossed his arms and sighed, as though a party of twenty had just gone out the door, leaving one numb member behind, standing now, gazing, not at the bad engraving of the Dama de Elche, but returning the vacant stare of the sardines.

In that quiet village, stacked three thousand feet above the sea against the southwestern slopes of the Sierra de Guadarrama, the province of Madrid, and the kingdom of New Castile laid out barren at its feet, there are thirty-seven bars, where, as in most of that country, the visitor is free to enjoy that privilege which distinguishes him from the natives to such advantage, and get morbidly, or helplessly, riotously, or roaring, drunk. No one minds. He is looked upon as a curiosity, one who has, perhaps, worked out an ingeniously obvious solution to unnecessary problems, and is mortgaging a present which is untenable to secure a future which does not exist. All but three (and they are known but to the learned hand), before that sunny day was out, became familiar with the draggled man whose greeting, and entire store of conversation, lay in the word *Manzanilla;* with the tune *La Tani* on the local barrel organ, which at first he trailed from one to another, and then, finding a tattered duro waiting at each stop, it trailed him; and finally, with the vociferous shock-haired figure whose boutonnière, by the time he found his comrade in Mis Niños, was no more than a twist of wire flying a shred of spotted pink paper, and his mustache awry as though stuck on in a hurry, for he adjusted it before each threshold he crossed. He also sported, by now, a cord of yellow and purple intertwined, knotted under the plexiglas collar where his tie had been, a manifest, as he hastened to explain to his glazed friend after his first recriminatory greetings, of a pledge made to Saint Anthony in return for the Saint's assistance in this impending project.

—No. No. Good God.

—Where have you been? I've looked all over the town for you, all afternoon. You said you were going to wait for me back...

—I thought you'd wrapped yourself up...in a mummy.

—What?

—No.

—Listen...what's the matter, you hiding from somebody?

—Yes.

—Who? Where? Where are they? Mr. Yák looked wildly round. —Hmmn? Come on. Stephan? Stephan, come on. Hmmn? At the door, *La Tani* played in thunderous broken chords. Mr. Yák finally brought his eyes round to find the two faintly green ones fixed on him. —All right. You all right? There was a withering crash as *La Tani* finished, something dodged between them, plucked a green duro from the hand hanging off the bar, got out, —Dios se lo pague señor...in one word, and was gone.

—Listen now, it's almost dark, and we...

There was a shimmering crash at the door: it was the opening chord of *La Tani.*

—Listen...Jesus! Mr. Yák brought his fist down, got to the door in two steps, and started to shout above the music, which continued, skipping notes it had lost during the day, but parading what remained with frenzied exultation. Mr. Yák finally managed to halt the spinning handle, and returned a minute later looking even more done in, after an argument which had become as deranged as the music it had sent packing.

—Una y una...tres. What do you want now?

—Listen, it's almost dark by now, did you know that? What are you doing here, anyway?

—I tried to leave. No trains.

—No, I mean in this dump. Mr. Yák looked around. It was a modest place, to be sure. There were barrels, bottles, and dirty glasses recklessly arranged behind the bartender, who put a dish of olives before them, and awaited Mr. Yák's order. When he realized that someone was eavesdropping, Mr. Yák spun round with, —Nothing! Nothing!... niente! Nada!... He was quite agitated, and returned to his comrade, propped before him. —I ought to just leave you here like you are.

—That's the spirit.

—Now listen, said Mr. Yák, taking a step closer, and he put a hand on the reposing arm on the bar. A crafty look came to his face as the sharp eyes narrowed over the expression which was almost a smile before him. —How would you like to make sure? he asked in his low confidential tone.

—Sure?...

—Sure listen... how would you like to go up with me, up the hill, see?... And look in and make sure that... that that's your mother's... resting place.

Some recrudescence mounted to the face before him: the smile fell away, at any rate, leaving evidence of sharp consciousness scattered in fragments of complete confusion, which the muscles of the face seemed to try to draw together into some single question.

—Listen, see?... I have to go up there anyway, on business. You can come up with me. Then you and me can...

—Damn it just... stop saying that. That you and me. Will you? Damn it. What do they want me for? What do you want me for? Damn it, what do they all want me for?! he burst out.

—Listen...

—Damn it. Damn them. And you... you...

—Come on out, we'll get some fresh air outside.

—They all... they all... want me, they want... damn it! What do they want? he cried.

—Come on. Come on. Mr. Yák put an arm round his shoulders, and led him toward the door. The bartender called, but not loudly, —Señor... se olvida... He held up a fresh one-peseta note, and Mr. Yák waved it back in a munificent gesture with his free hand.

Clusters of lights stood out on the mountain slopes like the lights of ports driven uphill by the sea, for it was yet light enough that the barren plateau stretched away levelly blue under the haze. They made their way up behind the town, and as they climbed the stone streets shocks of consciousness, and consequent revulsion, ran through the figure Mr. Yák supported, and pulled away from him, to come back the more heavily. Meanwhile, Mr. Yák talked. He explained the purple and yellow cord hanging from his shiny collar, and the debt incumbent upon Saint Anthony. He said he had made full confession, but in Rumanian, so the old párroco, who had not understood a word of it, had given him a light penance, —not like Rome, at Saint Peter's they can confess you in half a dozen languages, they got you going and coming. He said he had turned in three per cent of his money to the church, —to be devoted to pious uses, like it says, see? And he said the párroco was real old, —it won't take much to bring him around where we want him, I've got some ideas right now, see? . . . because I already gave him an idea I've got an in on the sacred mysteries, see? But there's this one guy I got to watch, we got to watch, I met him the last minute there . . . and as they trudged toward the rock-studded road up behind the town, Mr. Yák went on to describe Señor Hermoso Hermoso, who —had this real holy attitude about everything, see? Because they're getting this patron saint and he acts like he arranged everything, and he's not even a priest or anything, he runs a drugstore sort of, and that's one reason we got to watch out for him, see? And he speaks English, so he told me all about this patron saint they're getting. When they took her out of the graveyard here to put her somewhere else when she was beatified they thought she looks kind of big for an eleven-year-old girl, but the way the body was preserved after forty years almost, so that made them sure it's a saint. But that long, even no matter how well it's preserved they probably make a new head out of wax. Anyway that's not so long, you don't eat anything but beans all your life like these people around here they haven't got enough money to eat anything but beans all their life, then you don't decay so fast. Mr. Yák paused, but took up again almost immediately as though harried by the silence of his companion.

—Anyway so he told me all about the cures she effected, by her intervention, you know, like there was this one old guy who's deaf for six years, and so he prays to her for intervention and he gets over it just like that, what it was, it was an earwig that was in his ear all that time, you know? . . . and when it comes out all of a sudden then he could hear again. And then about this old guy who raped this girl, or he tried to rape her, see? . . . when he was young, he's real old now, he gets out of prison and he goes to this monastery where he's some kind of a penitent, you know? He's sort of like a janitor there . . .

Mr. Yák finally silenced, mainly for the exertion this walk was costing him. It was dark now, as they reached the hill and started up it. Then Mr. Yák heard something behind them, and stopped. He looked back. —What the . . . well I'll . . . that barrel organ, they been following us. A square shape, with two shapeless conductors, had stopped at the last corner behind them, and reluctantly turned back into the streets of the town. —See? See? Mr. Yák shook his companion as they climbed. —I told you not to go giving them money like that, they'll follow you around the world now.

About halfway up, as he stepped out of a soft mound in the middle of the rough road, Mr. Yák stopped. —Listen, why don't you just wait for me here? You don't have to come up, you just sit down here a minute and wait, I'll be back in a minute, see?

At that, the man he was supporting suddenly came to life, and stepped back, almost falling over. —No, no, no, he said clearly. —I'm coming. I'm coming now.

—Listen there's no reason you should bother to come, see? And what I said before, I was just kidding, you don't want to go prying around up here, you just sit and wait here for me a minute, you . . . wait . . .

But the figure was already steps ahead up the hill in the dark, and Mr. Yák hurried to overtake him.

A light shone at the gate, piloting an unseen figure. It was the sacristán, and he groaned. —Quién es? he asked the specters, though he knew well enough, and turning without an answer, led them in. They passed through the inside gate, and the light from his lantern glanced away from the white bóvedas and here and there caught a beaded wreath, the Virgin stark in an icon looking like a playing-card queen, the Infant with a hand out as though hailing a passing cab.

The sacristán was pausing, helplessly, waiting for word from Mr. Yák, who was bending down along the way to look at ages and dates on the vaults, when they both realized that the man with them had gone on ahead. They found him, there where they had all met in the sunlight.

—Look, you don't want to go prying in there . . . Mr. Yák commenced, but too late, he'd already started to pull the unmarked vault down himself, when the light showed him where it was. Mr. Yák was trembling too, turning his face as though he did not want to look when they lifted it down; and they were all surprised at the lightness of it as they lowered it to the ground. Of the three, the sacristán appeared most distracted now, trying to loose the top with one hand, holding the light up with the other, and he kept looking up as though in fear someone, or something, might appear. When it came open, not with a wrench, but breakage of the wooden top, it was he who was first to shatter the pattern of shock which gripped them together, staring in at the dark, withered, and childish-figured contents.

—Coño! . . . Dios! válgame Dios! He banged the broken cover down and stayed, quaking on his knees beside the little girl who had been left behind. He raised his eyes slowly, beyond them to where their shadows were sundered over the sills of the empty compartments next to one another high in the bóveda. And Mr. Yák, still motionless, felt a shudder beside him, one which persisted in the shadow thrown flickering past the broken broom, back into the hollow depth bereft of the alien presence who had waited so long unchallenged by earth, through war, and profane seizure, and the destruction of names more ornate than her own, among decayed floral tributes and wreaths made of beads, to be removed at last from this domain of broken glass façades and rickety icons, and enshrined, to work miracles.

The sacristán crossed himself: and the leaping shadow was caught and reflected, twice, in the arms of the men standing above him. Mr. Yák turned, startled at that motion beside him. The hand he put on his companion's shoulder was not rejected, and he whispered —There Stephan. I told you, you weren't a bum.

The sacristán was struggling to his feet. Suddenly Mr. Yák's eyes were glittering again. —Now, see? back to the work. She ... this, he motioned at the box without noticing the paper torn in trembling hands seeking a cigarette beside him. —This is just what we want. See? Stephan? You all right? Mr. Yák looked at him.

There in the broken moving light from the match and the lantern, his face appeared darker, and everything seemed to move in it though nothing moved there at all, lines drawn down from the nose holding the jaw up rigid, lines which broke the flat cheeks sinking away from the high-boned lines of the face. Then the sacristán was assailing them for help, to get the thing back up where it belonged before they were discovered, and Mr. Yák got hold of one side, but the third of them simply stood staring into the empty space where there was nothing but the wet end of a broken broom. When they got it back in place, he was gone. They found him a few minutes later, sitting outside the front gate on a stone, eating an orange in the dark, and looking at the moon which had just come into view beyond the mountains.

—Come on, Stephan. It's cold, Mr. Yák said taking his arm down the hill. —We want to make that train. His voice sounded loud on the night air, and he lowered it as though talking to himself to add, —We'll see about this thing tomorrow, when we get the old párroco in line, eh? He felt the figure beside him shrug, and said no more, busily planning in his head the immediate future. Neither of them spoke all the way through the town, where single lights cast clear separate shadows, stood doorways up vertically, none of the lights close enough to one another to confuse the night with multiple and exaggerated shades, or the shadows of these two moving figures behind with those before them.

They reached the railway station without speaking. On the empty platform, Mr. Yák shivered looking at the sky. —Look at that, that moon, he said, hunched up with his hands thrust deep in his pockets.

—Yes ...

—What? After a pause, Mr. Yák muttered, —It looks so close there, don't it...Then he shivered again, and looked back over his shoulder to where a dull glow hung over the sign *Urinarios*. —Hey, Stephan? I got to go over here a minute, he said. —Stephan?

—Oh yes, do you know?...charms can even bring it down...

—What?

—Down from heaven?

Mr. Yák waited, half turned, and then his shoulders relaxed a little and he said, —I forgot to tell you, hey?...I had a Mass said for your mother, up there at the church today. He waited another moment, swaying with his knees together. —See? he added. But from where he stood, it looked to him like the lonely figure there, drawn back from the empty platform, was trying to brush a streak of moonlight from his sleeve, and Mr. Yák turned and went on in the direction he'd started. When he arrived and stood, occupied, staring above him at the sky, the silence of the country, that silence which keeps city ears awake, alert, provoked him to speak aloud, as though to hear what he said confirmed. —This poor guy, he's as crazy as an eagle...Then he sniffed, cocked his head, and seemed to hear the rush of the barrel organ pounding inside it. But everywhere was silence, and as a matter of fact, *La Tani* has not been heard through those streets since that sunny day.

The Andalusian maiden looked down from her balcony, next morning, past her wooer, upon a scene of considerable activity. The air was enhanced with smells, mutterings, and occasional puffs of smoke, as Mr. Yák bustled among the confusion of newspapers so engrossed in his work that he almost dropped the glass test tubes he held in either hand when the dueño knocked at his door.

—Su amigo, señor...The dueño stepped back to introduce the bedraggled figure in the hall beside him, and Mr. Yák, who had put down the test tubes and pulled on the shock of black hair slightly askew, stepped back and said, —Come in, Stephan. Come in. Sit down...here, let me move this...there. Sit down. Now watch. Watch this. And he grabbed up the test tubes again. He began to pour the clear liquid from one into the other which was apparently empty, but the hair had slid over one glittering eye. He reached up impatiently, caught the black shock, tore it off and flung it across the room to the bureau top. Then his hand returned to his face in a reflex and gave the mustache a sharp tug. He yelped and almost dropped the test tubes, but recovered his purpose quickly. —Watch...The colorless liquid poured into the empty test tube, where it became bright red. —Now, what do you think of that?

—It's very nice, but tell me...

—Wait. Watch . . . He poured the red liquid into another test tube, and it became colorless again.

—Just tell me . . .

—Water into wine, wine into water. I can change it into milk too. Add a little sodium bisulphate . . .

—Will you please tell me . . .

—Here's another one. This one's even better. Water into blood, blood into a solid. Remember the miracle at Bolsena? Watch. A little aluminum sulphate dissolved, a few drops of phenolphthalein, and now . . . watch. Sodium silicate. Watch. See? Look at that, blood. Watch. See it? See it congeal?

—Yes, yes, but . . .

—What do you think of that?

—All I want to know is . . .

—I can eat fire too, if I have to. Mr. Yák hopped off among the flurry of newspapers, to see where some wads of blotting paper were drying on the sink. —See? he said, holding one up. —You just light it and wrap it up in cotton. And then, whoof!

—If you'll just . . .

—Whoooft! Sparks all over the place. Hey? Mr. Yák's eyes shone eagerly across the room, as he awaited some confirmation of his enthusiasm. But his guest simply stared at him. —Hey Stephan? What's the matter?

—Will you just tell me where I am? and how I got here?

—Where are we? We're in Madrid, where else would we be. This is the pensión I'm living at, I got a room for you here last night. You were drunk last night, you don't want to drink so much. I gave your passport to the dueño, he has to show it up at the police station, see? I told him you're a friend of mine from Switzerland worn out by the journey here, that's why you couldn't walk I told him, see? Now everything's O.K., you're safe as a nut. Stephan.

There was a tap at the door. Mr. Yák snatched up his hair and put it on. His excitement had brought color to his face, and while it might not be the blush of youth, he did look younger this morning, and capable of almost anything.

—It's backwards.

—What?

—Your hair. You've got your hair on backwards, said his guest, folded up there in the corner among the newspapers, speaking in a tone which reflected the look in his eyes, one of patient, but wary, curiosity. He pulled a yellow cigarette from the green and black paper of Ideales.

—Oh! Oh! Oh! Mr. Yák spun the shock of hair round on his head, and opened the door the margin of an eye.

—Señor Asche? said the dueño from the dark passage. Mr. Yák started to make wild gestures of beckoning behind the door. His guest stared at him. —Su pasaporte . . . Finally Mr. Yák reached through the opening to snatch the Swiss passport, with a muttered —Gracias to the dueño, and he closed the door and bolted it. —Señor Asche, that's you, he said crossing the room. —I wanted you to come get it from him, your passport. Stephan Asche. See? He handed the Swiss passport over the newspaper barricade. —There, Stephan. Like I said, see? Safe as a nut. Look at the picture in it, go ahead. It's just like you, just like I said, that square face all screwed up around the eyes, see? Now you just want to wash up a little and get a shave. And he bounded off again, across the room toward the mirror over the washbowl, where the drying wads of blotting paper caught his eye. —Do you want to see me eat fire? he brought out, leering into the glass at the image of the man behind him. The image of Stephan Asche did not move. Nothing moved there, but the smoke rising gently behind the disorder of newspapers, the untended trail of a fire smoldering in a pile of debris where nothing retains its original shape, or purpose, among broken parts and rusted remains of useful objects, unidentifiable now, indistinguishable from other fragments of the past, shapes and sharp angles of curious design and unique intention, wasting without flame under the litter of news no longer news, pages of words torn by the wind, sodden with rain, words retaining separation, strung to the tear, without purpose, but words, and nothing moves but the smoke, rising from two bright embers.

—Stephan! Mr. Yák bursts out, turning from the washbowl. —Wake up! . . . you . . . you went to sleep with your eyes open it looked like, you . . . listen . . .

—Look . . .

—Listen, you don't want to smoke that stuff, see? It smells lousy, it makes the whole room here smell like the town dump. It's a third potato peel, the tobacco here . . . See? Listen, you want to wash up and shave.

—But I don't.

—Yes you do. Come on . . . what do you want to do?

—Nothing.

—You can't do nothing. See? There's work to do. See? All this . . . All this . . . The spotted cigarette-burned robe comes off in a swirl: Mr. Yák's neck is quite a long one, springing out of the neck-band shirt, caught, constricted with a preposter's dignity, in plexiglas, roped and drawn with Saint Anthony's earnest, Saint Anthony's hostage draws it tight to the throat. —The water into wine, and the wine into water, the blood that congeals and turns into stone, that's all for the old párroco, see? To bring him around to where he'll agree to sell us that . . . sell us the thing for the mummy. Nothing? You don't want to do nothing? That's the way you get into mischief. You get into mischief, doing nothing.

—Dies irae, dies illa, solvet saeclum in favilla...Tell me, did they sing that out here?

—Where?

—The Mass, you said you had a Mass sung for the dead. They sing that sometimes, in Masses for the dead, swinging the censer to kill the smell of the living. Look, what was that blonde I met in the hall?

Silence submits to the thud of an Ideal ash hitting the floor. From the wall, the Andalusian maiden stares down over her sturdy balcony, over the shoulder of him in the guitar's embrace, to coquette with her host, who disdains her directly their eyes meet, turning as though yanked to by the lead at his neck. —Just what you say, a blonde. Forget her.

—But I don't even know her yet.

—So that saves you the trouble. You don't want to get mixed up with that flashy piece of goods. See?

Somewhere, a clock struck. —See? Mr. Yák repeated, taking a step toward the darker corner, his head lowered, chin jutting forth, he looked searchingly where the smoke rose like a man looking on a refuse heap, finding a nondescript necktie worn and discarded among the cinders, some rags, two shoes which will never fit anyone else, still he looked searchingly, and his eyes caught a glitter. —You're here to get mixed up with some blonde that'll take them diamonds right off your finger? Then why are you here then?

—Why am I here? I'm here because I'm not any place else. Now look...

—Now listen, you and me...Wait! What are you doing? You don't want to open the windows...

Nevertheless, the floor-length windows were swung open, and the sounds of Alphonso del Gato rose to them, mounting on a chorus of *Francisco alegre*...ole!

—You don't want to get mixed up with that flashy piece of goods down the hall, Mr. Yák repeated, addressing Stephan's back, at the windows. —See?

Nevertheless, awhile after everyone else had lunched on garlic soup, a simple cocido, dead fish, and an orange, and the blue angora sweater nowhere in sight in the small dining room, Mr. Yák, slipping down the passage between doors closed upon afternoon slumber, glanced in the dining room, and there saw his friend at a table, the blue fluff catercorner. She was biting his thumb.

Reproach filled Mr. Yák before he knew it, and he almost mistook his step;

but there would be time enough for all his words of rebuke, warning, and censure: now there was work ahead, and he hurried toward it, feeling chilly and grown old.

As for Marga, she was a discreet person: there was a building in the Calle Ventura de la Vega where, up a flight, a dim shuttered room afforded but one furnishing above necessity, a mirror, mounted along the length of the bed, which that afternoon reflected with a fertile vigor undiminished by repetition liberties taken upon every natural part of her but her coiffure, though that, to be sure, was a crown of artifice whose consequent fragility she had good reason to protect: only in descent from the exposed and cultivated brow did the remontant powers of nature prove how, as the poet wrote, the natural in woman closely is allied to art.

—I saw you ... Mr. Yák said that evening, standing in the spotted robe, holding his hair in his hand before him, and he looked weary. His day had been a busy one, inveigling the old párroco on the one hand, fending off the importunate Señor Hermoso Hermoso on the other. But more than the day's fatigue showed on him. The instant he pulled off that shock of black hair, a heavy decade of years weighed his shoulders down, and now his eyes, as though another day's application had exhausted their glitter, showed with a dullness which, but for the impatient promptings of his voice, might have been construed as disappointment. —Listen, we ... we have work to do, and you, behaving like this, it's like cutting your nose off in spite of your face, he said. —You're not a bum.

— ...

—Stephan.

—What?

—No, I ... I just said that, I just called you that, so you'll get used to it. Mr. Yák lowered his eyes wearily, to the floorboards whose different lengths effected an unsteady parquet.

If the orange-colored cloth of that coat could be so quickly supplanted in memory by its leopard collar at full length, both disappeared from attention and memory alike when the coat was drawn open and nothing but Marga beneath it, for she wore it as a robe de chambre, or rather de couloir, on that last-minute trip between her room and the toilet, managed, like all of her public appearances, with a decorum which greatly enhanced her license in private. There, except for the armoire across the room mounting something the proportions of a pier glass which would have demanded taxing, if not unnatural, exertions, for its full employment, there was no mirror in her room to confirm one sense in what four others were making possible, no confirmation for that most immediate sense, that most used, most depended upon, most easily deceived, none but her lips too close, separated, teeth biting silence, and eyes demanding correspondence in closing.

—I heard you . . . Mr. Yák said next day. —I heard you in there last night. And now look at you, look at your eyes, you're getting this French influenza like everybody's getting, that ought to put you in bed a while and take care of yourself, see? Because in a day or two we're going to bring it in, for the mummy, see?

If she heard the heart pounding in the dark, or felt it shaking the whole frame she embraced, every beat splitting the head she held between her hands, the jaw rigid then shivering on gasps for breath, while every beat of the heart surged the flow more weakly and ebbed to withhold the life she drew forth, she gave no sign of knowing in the dark, the first time, the second, the third and her knee raised to manage gently insistent manipulation with her toes, to continue the rehearsal and then in a rush repeat the performance, no more sign than the animal trainer putting the sick dog through its paces.

Two days later, when Marga had left for the country (a family wedding), Mr. Yák had his arrangements almost made. The párroco in San Zwingli was properly awed, the sacristán thoroughly intimidated, and Señor Hermoso Hermoso, convinced with such happy importance that he knew what was going on, had given up trying to find out. He had even at one point, and quite unwittingly, put Mr. Yák onto something most pertinent to the project, in a casual café conversation which turned to a local method for aging fine lace, a process Mr. Yák now considered employing to add some dozens of centuries to the linen bandaging, before it was finally baked on.

   —So what we want to do, we want to bury it somewhere, in the ground, see? Listen . . . are you listening, Stephan? How do you feel, you feel better? Listen, then what you want to do, you go there where it's buried, and wet it down, see? You know what I mean, wet it down? I mean, like . . . like you stand over it and wet it down, see? You do that a lot of times, then you dig it up and hang it in the sun, and it's got that nice yellow aged color that makes it look real old, see? You listening? Come on, get your head out of under the covers. You got to come out with me and buy this linen bandaging so we get the right kind. See? Come on. You feel better. You're all well now. Come on, get your head out of under the cover.

The mound on the bed shifted, but remained silent, and Mr. Yák leaned forward to put a kindly hand on what he believed to be a shoulder. There was a growl from inside.

—Come on, you want to come out in the fresh air will do you more good than this here ... Mr. Yák shook the mound, and the growl grew louder. Finally a cautious aperture appeared, with an eye behind it, and a clear voice said, —Go away.

—Good. You're not in a delirium any more anyway, Mr. Yák said, letting go the shoulder, and he sat down beside the bed, relieved. For these past two evenings, Mr. Yák had returned wearied enough with the work of the day, to the even more taxing demands of this friendship he had formed from the depths of what he could by now believe to have been the kindness of his heart. And just as there could be no doubt, after touching his forehead, but that Stephan had been ill, there was even less doubt of his delirium after listening to his conversation: Salamanders and Sylphs, and Mermaids, a regular Carnival, but wait, not carne vale ... Ave carne! ... Salve! ... macte virtute esto! —Did you want me to end like Descartes, then? Larvatus prodeo, retiring to prove his own existence, and he kept a Salamander. She came to visit him like mine did then. But now ... Copulo, ergo sum. Eh? Carne, O te felicem!

And Mr. Yák had shaken his head, and muttered something about "that flashy piece of goods down the hall," at which he was instantly threatened with blindness as happened to Stesichorus, —for slandering Helen.

—What an affliction, Mr. Yák muttered, but to himself, and thinking of himself, not Stesichorus.

—Why, proving one's own existence, you'd be surprised what a man will do to prove his own existence? ... pursued Mr. Yák out the night before, crossing himself. —Why, there's no ruse at all that people will disdain, to prove their own existences ...

—Get some sleep, Stephan.

—No ruse at all ...

Now, Mr. Yák gave up once more, with a glance up at the Andalusian love scene on Stephan's wall, and returned to his own room where now hung the picture he had traded for it, Jesús del Gran Poder, which he had found leaning face-to against Stephan's wall. He stood looking absently at the dark bowed head of Christ under the weight of the Cross, and, after a full minute, cocked his head at a sound in the hall. A moment later he found Stephan trying to slip out of the pensión. He let him escape, followed, and then caught him up in the street below as though by accident. There they exchanged their usual contentious greetings, and Mr. Yák took him off to buy forty meters of linen bandage, on the promise that they go to a bar immediately after.

The comradeship between these two men by now had something inevitable about it. They were in ways mutually dependent, and at constant cross purposes. The older man seemed interested in what the younger did only in order to disapprove of it; and the younger man's total lack of interest in the elder's activity only spurred that one on to redouble it. They seldom entered a bar together, but that Mr. Yák ordered two coffees, and his companion stood, restraining one hand with the other, until he could get one of them on a glass of wine, or, more frequently now, coñac. What is more, there were moments when they strongly resembled one another, though that, perhaps, was only in an expression round the eyes, a tense look, glittering with impatience, a sort of alert vacancy, ready for flight.

Their pursuits were by now so mysterious to one another that neither showed surprise at anything the other did or said, each, in fact, depending more and more heavily on the other for encouragement, an arrangement somewhat similar to that magic formula of modern marriage, whose parties are encouraged by disapprobation and disinterest respectively.

Their present careers were reaching the first peaks at about the same time: just as Mr. Yák was ready to bring his purchase from the rural cemetery into town and commence actual work on it, his partner had passed the last lap on a Marathon of drink, and appeared to be scaling the heights beyond.

—What's that spilled on the lapels of your coat like that? Mr. Yák demanded, catching up with him at one point.

—I'm learning to drink from a bottle with a spout, you don't touch it to your lips. Getting it up there's easy enough, it's when you try to stop that it gets on you like this.

—What's that, those marks on your shoulders?

—That's from sliding down between the casks.

—You don't want to spend money like this.

—You told me it's so dirty it's unhealthy to carry around.

—Why weren't you in at supper tonight?

—Not after that gray artichoke. And that woman at our table, I can't tell whether she's crossing herself or fixing her napkin, it goes on all the way through the meal. And that woman at the next table, suckling the baby.

—What's the matter with that?

—Nothing the matter with it, it just takes my mind off the bread soup.

—You're not mixed up with some woman now, are you?

—What's the matter with women?

—I got nothing against them, it's just that no one of them can last a man his whole life.

—Good God! What, do you think I suggested that?

—No, but they will. I never knew a woman yet that the minute she came into the room I wasn't waiting for her to leave it. Try getting married some time. I even had a wife once myself.

—What did you do with her?

—I tied the can to her. What do you think I did. Listen, tell me something...

—The joke about the five Jones brothers? Have you heard that? Los cinco-jones?...

—We got work to do, why do you get drunk like this?

—Well I'll tell you, I have five monkeys in my stomach and four chairs in my head, do you know that one? The first coñac and one monkey goes up and sits down. Second glass, another one goes up and sits down, the third...

—Listen...

—The fourth...

—Listen...

—And when the fifth monkey gets up there, there's no place for him to sit down, so...

—You're picking up the language? Where.

—Marga taught me all I know. That's love. Or say, I'm encoñado.

—What's that encoñado?

—That's a local invocation to call men into bed.

—Where do you think you're going now?

—I'll go to sleep if I can. If I can't I'll go down and dance with the gypsies.

—You keep away from them down there. Tomorrow...

—Good night.

—Tomorrow...

But Mr. Yák was restless. It was barely eleven at night, and a good deal of noise came to him from Alphonso del Gato below. He went out alone for coffee.

The streets were thronged with people very different from those of early morning, the girls and old women in black, the line before the charcoal seller's. But the cries were the same, —Cien iguales me quedan!... Cien iguales para hoy!... The sound of English in the street was startling, a blond boy on the arm of a man, —But I'm not even sure where Spain is... A tall woman passed, speaking to her husband, —I've gotten used to poverty by now. —You mean other people's? —Yes, it doesn't bother me at all like it did, remember when we got here yesterday and I was giving money out everywhere?...

Mr. Yák found he had walked in a large circle, and returned to the Villa Rosa. He entered its Moorish interior, ordered coffee, looked sharply away from two girls, and was raising his cup when he heard something familiar from a room down the back hall. It was *La Tani*.

He found Stephan presiding at a juerga. There were bottles of wine on the table, three people were eating, a man was tuning a guitar, and the girl on Stephan's knee smiled uncertainly at Mr. Yák. Now, if Marga had put him off, Pastora stopped him dead. Her coarse black hair stood out round her dark face. And her large and dark eyes were gravely excited. They shone with a strained surprise, reflected in the face so close there, and she turned them up with something fierce and proud in them. Her teeth were large, her nose slightly flattened, and her shaded upper lip was curled in what, on another face, might have been a pout, but here lay tinged with ferocity, suggesting the savage gifts her voice assured, and her quick simple movements confirmed. Her faded cerise blouse had pulled out of the skirt whose zipper was apparently broken, as was one of the straps on her high-heeled sandal, and she could not have been more than nineteen. From the hostility of the smile with which she greeted Mr. Yák's intrusion, her acquaintance with the man whose neck she got an arm round now was apparently not too recent.

—How long have you had this one? Mr. Yák demanded, sitting down. She watched him mistrustfully, understanding nothing but the tone in his voice, and sulked miserably when she was put down. —I see you still got your diamond ring, anyway, Mr. Yák said.

—Es un amigo tuyo? Pastora brought out, her voice harsh, uncertain.

—Tell her, she wants to know if I'm a friend of yours, Mr. Yák challenged. —Come on, what are you grinning about, you that drunk already?

—Krishna seduced sixteen thousand maidens.

—Listen, tomorrow...

—You'll believe me if I tell you... Krishna was the sun, and they... they were dewdrops.

—Tomorrow we've got work, do you hear me? You don't want to do this, you don't want to let yourself go to hell like this, do you hear me?

—No, he whispered, leaning abruptly over before Mr. Yák's face, —It's just the other way, he whispered, looking up craftily at Mr. Yák's eyes. —Have you ever heard of the... I am... encoñado, and she... she's acara... acarajotada, un... understand? Known in vulgar English as... as being in love, understand?

—I'm not going to stand by and see a tramp like this...

—They let the path stay dirty, you ... you see? To fool people, to fool reasonable people, like you. But I ... I ... His head swayed, and he blinked his eyes in Mr. Yák's face. —See? he managed to add. Pastora got up suddenly, and stood beside him. The guitar broke a chord at the other end of the table. Someone there commenced to clap. Pastora put a hand on his opposite shoulder, nearest Mr. Yák, all the time watching Mr. Yák with animal alertness, even as he stood and reached to dislodge her hand and help his friend away.

—Déjame! she snarled across the sunken shoulders, and then in her hoarse whisper, —Déjale! ... sounding that j with the guttural intensity of the Arabs' ج.

—Hoy los novios se van a casar ... someone at the end of the table began singing. Mr. Yák withdrew his hand slowly, and lowered his eyes to the figure slumped at the head of the table, where he stared for a moment while Pastora watched him and did not move. Then he looked sharply up at her. —Ten cuidado, he said, warning her, and before she could answer he turned away and was gone, past the diners, the guitar, the bottles, the heels, the singer's —No sale la cuenta porque falta un churumbel.

Pastora, at every instant with him as near to joy as to woe, waiting to be told, for joy to burst over her at the slightest assurance, despair at the first slight, tears of helpless anger at indifference, recovering in surly contempt, but still waiting to be told, —Me quieres? She with nothing of her own, not even her words but in question, until forced to cry out at last, —Yo te quiero y tu no me quieres.

They kept on there until the wine was gone. Then she lit one of the harsh yellow cigarettes and put it to his lips. —Vámonos ... Esteban! Vámo*nos?* ...

At night, —Vida! ... Cielo! ... no termina ... mi vida! And still in the dark, and in fun so she means it to sound, —Vamos hacer un niño! ... gone unanswered, Pastora listening in the dark, no answer but the sound of the bed and she goes limp through her thin body under the steady silent weight, or a hand at the brown nipple of her small breast, and flings up her arms to pull the weight closer, her head back, sobbing, sobs shaking her occupied body and that part so full, still unfulfilled, forgotten for this anguish, her face wet, turned away from the silent lips she has drawn down to her, waiting, to cry out at last, —Me quieres? ... Díme lo, aunque no es verdad! ...

Pastora woke alone in the damp bed, the sheets twisted, to call, —Esteban? ... and hear nothing but her own breath in the dark. She got up naked and opened the inside shutters, and daylight separated the louvers of the outside. A blanket and her skirt lay on the dirty worn tiles of the ground floor.

She put on her slip, her skirt, her shoes, shook the pitcher, found it empty, called loudly for water, and when it was brought she poured some in the basin, rinsed her face, wet her hair, and combed its coarse strands down with a comb from her purse. On the table by the bed, as she put on her blouse, she found an empty Ideal packet, and another one-hundred peseta note.

Mr. Yák was out of bed and dressed before his morning coffee was brought. He did not wait for it in fact, but locked his room, tapped at the door down the hall, opened it and found the room empty, and interrupted a girl on a trip with two chamber pots down the chill front passage. She opened the front door for him, smiling, —Vaya Usted con Diós . . . and he went out, down the stairs and into the street, his hair square on his head and his mustache set stiff with purpose.

He passed the blind boy with the lottery tickets pinned to his coat, the line of women in black, before the charcoal-seller's, children carried by bundled like Eskimos, men in bedroom slippers, cloth hemp-soled shoes, berets, mufflers drawn over the chin, capes out of Goya across half the face. The sound of English in the streets was startling: the same tall woman passed, pointing to a tattered old man before her, —Now there, I want some sandals like those, see them? —Those aren't sandals, mumbled her husband beside her, —those are his feet.

Mr. Yák made a circle, looking in at every bar and café, from the Puerta del Sol back down the Calle de Atocha. It grew later, and his expression of impatience became more stern, entering the Plaza Tirso de Molina, watching, listening for *La Tani*, he stopped in at Chispero's for coffee, still searching every face for the one he sought, searching faces as though the great city were a perpetual masquerade, where every face, like his own, hid another, so that at last it was not that specific square face knotted about the eyes in mild surprise that he sought, but familiarity to emerge from this world of shapes and smells, the amber color of Genesis coñac, the green of the bottles, the fixed stare of the silver fish on the bar, the smell of oil, dark squares of fried blood on a plate, shreds of liver, the seat of the emotions roasted, cut up, served beside the tall stemmed glass, waiting, watching for familiarity to emerge from this world of shapes and smells, clad against the cold reality of the outside in the yielding armor of drunkenness. An elderly man stood against the wall opposite, drinking coffee beneath a picture of Adelita Beltrán who would appear later on the stage inside, to dance, pounding her heels, brandishing her skirt to *La Sebastiana*, to sing *La Zarzamora*, and Mr. Yák looked away from the old man quickly, aware that the resemblance he had sought and found in that face was his own. The coffee in his glass floated yellow globes of oil at the rim, and he drank it down and went out, pressing at his mustache with two fingertips.

It was not in a bar that he finally did find Stephan, but standing unsteadily outside one, a place called La Flor de mi Viña, where a car had just run over his foot, slowly, nudging him insistently from behind like a clumsy animal sidling up, leaving him with that expression of mild surprise confirmed in his face. And the only reason a policeman appeared was that one happened to be passing, and a handful of unoccupied people had set up a clamor. It happened so slowly. That gentle nudging might have been one of the burros that stand harnessed to trash carts in the streets of the city. The policeman was very polite, as Mr. Yák appeared, rescued his friend and set off with him in the direction of the Estación del Norte, walking briskly not speaking after his first reproof, —What did you want to tell the cop you're a...what did you tell him? A Pelagian?...he just wanted to know what kind of a nationality you are, can't you just say swisso? What if he asks for your Pelagian passport? Have you got your passport on you? What if I didn't come along just then? The day was heavily overcast, and they walked on without looking up at the even unchanging gray of the sky. —How long you expect to keep this up, anyway? Mr. Yák muttered, expecting no answer, and he got none. They'd walked some distance before he commented, —This place is getting on both of our nerves.

They reached San Zwingli without incident, and very little conversation after Mr. Yák had outlined their plan. —We can't take it away in the box, that's too bulky...but if we leave about at dark...Then he looked closely at his companion, as though to see if he would be capable of carrying out his end of it when the time came. —How many monkeys you got sitting down up in your head now? he brought out finally, as they climbed the hill from the railway station.

—I? I haven't had a drink all day.

—Where you been all day then? Mr. Yák's tone was truculent, possibly to hide the surprise he felt at this answer. —I looked all over the place for you, he added, muttering, returning his eyes to the stones of the road. Up in the town, the bell of the church sounded, and both of them raised their eyes for a moment, then lowered them immediately as though in embarrassment, as it went on striking, and they continued side by side up the uneven grade, out of step, and so close they bumped each other. —Where were you all day? Mr. Yák asked again, when they bumped the second time.

—The Prado.

—The art museum? Mr. Yák shrugged. —What did you do there? He glanced up at the face beside him, and said, —You don't look like you liked it much. The art there.

—Well they... the El Greco, his companion began, as though called upon to comment, and he drew his hand across his eyes. —They have so many in one room, they're almost hung on top of each other and it's too much, it's too much plasticity, there's too much movement there in that one room... He suddenly looked up at Mr. Yák, holding a hand out before them which appeared to try to shape something there. —Do you... do you see what I mean? With a painter like El Greco, somebody called him a visceral painter, do you see what I mean? And when you get so much of his work hung together, it... the forms stifle each other, it's too much. Down where they have the Flemish painters hung together it's different, because they're all separate... the compositions are separate, and the... the Bosch and Breughel and Patinir and even Dürer, they don't disturb each other because the... because every composition is made up of separations, or rather... I mean... do you see what I mean? But the harmony in one canvas of El Greco is all one... one... He had both hands out before him now, the fingers turned in and the thumbs up as though holding something he was studying with a life which Mr. Yák had not seen in his face before. But he broke off abruptly, and his hands came down to his sides.

After a pause, Mr. Yák said more quietly, —I didn't know you ever went there.

—I... I go there every day.

—You spend the whole day there? Mr. Yák turned on him in amazement.

—Well, I... not today, I... I had the strangest dream today, I... when I came back. And I woke up and I thought... it was almost dark, but I thought it was dawn and I thought I'd slept there all night, and all I heard was... I heard a child crying somewhere, that was all I heard. But I thought I'd slept all night and it was dawn. Then I tried to use my right arm, I reached out for a cigarette and it wouldn't work, my arm wouldn't work, it just hung there and fell over, and I... and all I could hear was a child crying somewhere.

They had reached the town. Mr. Yák glanced at him again, shrugged when he did not go on, and as they approached the doors of La Ilicitana muttered, —I just hope that barrel organ don't catch us out, as they entered, and his order for two coffees was not countermanded, or even qualified, by his companion, which, after the revelation concerning the Prado, brought Mr. Yák to observe soberly, —I even said you weren't a bum. Eh Stephan?

That brought a smile to Stephan's face for a moment, though it was one of detachment and when it faded away, left a vague abstracted expression.

—That girl you were with last night, Mr. Yák commenced, pressing his mustache and speaking with the ease of someone mentioning an event long forgotten, —I was glad to see you got away from her with your diamond ring.

—But you ... wait, you don't understand, you see she ... I don't know, never mind.

—You paid her, didn't you? Forget her. Mr. Yák shrugged, sipped his coffee, and asked, —That blonde, did you pay her anything?

—Well, I ... that's just it, you see I ...

—Forget it. That's nothing, forget it.

—No, because the blonde didn't ask for anything, at first she didn't ask for any money, I thought, she just came with me as though she wanted ... to. But then after a few times, then she borrowed some money from me just before she went away and I thought, I lent it to her. I would have given it to her except I still thought she'd come with me because she'd wanted to, and I lent it to her.

—Never mind, forget it. The kind of tramps you're picking up now you're lucky you still got your diamonds.

—No no but that's the point! when the blonde pretended she didn't come with me for money but all the time she ... don't you see? And this one, this ... Pastora, she ... with her it was money right from the start, and now, she couldn't afford to pretend because she needed the money, she really needs it but now, now with me what she wants ...

—I know what she wants ... Mr. Yák drew back as the diamonds came up in his face. —You gave her those rhinestone earrings?

—Those cheap things! Twenty pesetas. When I gave them to her I told her that, how cheap they were and she nearly cried just because ...

—Just because you didn't go get your diamonds made into earrings.

—No, listen, look, those cheap clothes she wears coming apart at the seams, she doesn't mind, if they're clean, if I ... if I tell her she looks good, but if I say anything like ...

—You make quite a couple in the street, said Mr. Yák.

—Yes, he laughed himself quietly, looking down. —I was walking with my hands in my pockets, and all of a sudden she stops right there on the sidewalk, she was furious, Si tu no me coges ... she wouldn't walk a step further with me if I didn't take her arm. He stood there looking at the floor and almost smiling, until Mr. Yák said,

—You could do better, if you're going to get mixed up with ...

—Better? He brought his eyes up again, their vacant quality restored.

—If you're going to pay good money ...

—But it isn't ... paying!

—I get it. You just give her some money afterwards.

—Yes but, listen...

—You're going to catch something, you probably caught something from her already. Those kind of tough girls you meet like that...

—Tough, yes, the scars on her belly and down one leg, listen...

—You probably caught something from her already.

—Caught something...? His hand was up between them again, squared fingers closing upon nothing; and he was staring there. —I was, I had her breast and I was...she, all of a sudden she said, No, son para la niña, she didn't want me to...to take what was...wasn't mine.

Mr. Yák shrugged. —If you were getting what you paid for...

—But that's what I'm trying to tell you! right in the middle of it, when I was still...His closed hand quivered between them. —All of a sudden crying out, she burst out crying, Me quieres? me quieres? Díme lo...que sí! aunque no es verdad...

Mr. Yák finished his coffee and studied the face before him with the composure of a man examining something unobserved. Then he shrugged again and said, —You get one every once in a while like that, they have to cry right in the middle of it. So you told her yes, you loved her? even if it wasn't true? He got no answer, put down the cup he'd been holding, and shrugged again. —You ought to have told her yes. A time like that, it's the only thing you can do, if you want to get your money's worth.

The town was quiet in the late afternoon. Mr. Yák tucked the purple and gold cord into his front as they came out on the street, and reopened the conversation on a more promising note. —Wait till you see this mummy thing when we get through with it, it will be so terrific it'll make your nose bleed.

The sky was unchanged, except for seeming closer to the earth, more oppressive upon the mountains, as the light of day drained from it. The two men approaching the rock-studded road up behind the town did so in silence, the one swinging his arms as he walked, allowing sounds of anticipation to escape him, the other hands clasped behind, watching every detail of the pavement they followed. It is true, Mr. Yák's gait was somewhat irregular, his head bobbing up to the challenge ahead, then down, and aside, as the past threatened in the dull intent profile beside him. He wondered, if this climb would recall its earlier end, when they'd met over a past beyond them both, if this prolonged gesture of atonement of his should suddenly shatter between them while the future yet promised, if he should mention any of that simply to hold it at bay, before it attacked of itself.

—Good God!...

—What's the matter with you? Mr. Yák asked before he looked for reason, finding, for the first time, this hand on his arm.

A white carriage, all white, drawn by horses strung with broken white netting, mounting a small white casket beneath the white coronating cross, climbed before them, —Christ! are they always held at the fall of the day? Another one, up that broken road to the cypress trees, and the men follow, carrying their hats, and that girl on her bicycle, in her green dress, making the stupid windings of life in the road behind it, and she'll be back down the hill before they unload the box ... As though that child had ... chosen this time to die.

His hand had fallen away, and Mr. Yák caught his arm. —Listen, Mr. Yák said quickly, —you go back there and wait for me, go back to that bar and wait for me, see?

—Well I ... then you'll have to lend me some money.

—You're broke ... you've spent ... you don't have any money?

—Point d'argent, point de Suisse ...

—Listen, I don't want to let you ... have you got your passport? Mr. Yák had pulled out a wad of paper money. —If they ...

—It says I'm from Zurich. Quick! I'll speak to them in German ... aber die jüngste war so schön, dass die Sonne selber ... Quick! ...

The procession gone up the hill had been drawn by two horses, and now, down through the town, came a cart drawn by one, loaded with refuse from the factory nearby. Watching it with the same apparent interest as she had watched the other, an old woman withdrew from her railed balcony, leaving her husband in his chair, put out there in the afternoon for the sun, to look and cough, with his piece of bread, waiting. And the sun, which had kept so close all the day, sought before leaving it to fill the sky with color, a soft luster of pink, and then purple, against the pure blue, color which refined the clouds to their own shapes and then failed, discovering in them for minutes the whole material of beauty, then leaving them without light to mock the sky, losing form, losing edges and shape and definition, until soon enough with darkness, they disappear entirely.

—Allí se mueren, said the man behind the bar of La Ilicitana. He placed a glass there, and brought down the bottle of Genesis, answering a question with his voice, and an order with the bottle of coñac. —En invierno no, pero quando vienen las hojas por los árboles, allí se mueren.

It was dark out of doors when the bartender at La Ilicitana leaned forth to direct his only client's attention to the couple waiting outside. Mr. Yák stood just within the dim shaft of light, beckoning. Beside him, in the shadows, a small figure draped in a shawl waited patiently; and a moment later, the man behind the bar there watched the three of them leave with no misgiving curiosity in his face at all.

—Take her arm, said Mr. Yák in the street. —But be careful. You're not drunk, are you? Are you? You got enough chairs for the monkeys? Come on. Be careful. We pretend it's an old woman, see? Only when we get on the train she's real stiff in the joints, see? But these Spaniards here are very reverent for an old woman, like it's somebody's mother, see? So be careful . . .

He was right.

The conductor even threatened to help the stiff figure aboard the First Class coach, but Mr. Yák was impressively filial, and they were soon seated abreast in a compartment. Mr. Yák pulled the shades down upon the aisle passing outside, for the figure between them sat stretched out at an uncomfortable length for her size, and there was no relaxing her into the cushions, —because we don't want to break nothing.

The moon, in its last quarter, had not yet entered the sky, waiting to come in late, each night waiting nearer the last possible minute before day, to appear over the distant gate more battered, lopsided, and seem to mount unsteadily as though restrained by embarrassment at being seen in such condition. And so the train rattled out into the rock-strewn plain in darkness. Mr. Yák stood up, slipped the door open enough to peep into the corridor, and then displaced the glass and removed the light from above the seat across from them.

—You're afraid the light will hurt her eyes?

—No. In case somebody should come in here with us so it don't shine in her face, Mr. Yák answered earnestly. —See? he added as he resumed his seat and leaned forward, solicitously arranging the black shawl, tucking its long ends round the extended feet. Then he straightened up and said, —There! . . . patted down the shock of black hair, pressed the mustache, and cleared his throat with satisfaction. The acrid smoke of an Ideal commenced to rise from the window side of the compartment, and they rode on, seated backwards, facing the place they'd come from, and looking in what light there was through the smoke like a weary and not quite respectable family.

The conductor, at any rate, showed no rude curiosity when he tapped at the glass panel, slid the door open, and took three tickets from Mr. Yák, who had bounded to his feet to meet him, with such zeal, in fact, that part of the shawl came along with him, exposing hands clasped one over the other on the sunken basin of the pelvis, above the wide separation of the lower limbs, and the head, tilted forward slightly, the surface of the face unbroken by a nose, the eyes sunken, the jaw dropped. But the conductor was gone.

—Come on!... cover it up! Mr. Yák burst out, getting the door closed, but the face he saw was a reflection in the glass. He pulled the shawl up quickly round the stiff figure, and drew it in a deep hood over the nodding head. —You got to keep alert, doing something like this, he went on when he got his breath, —you can't just sit looking out the window, you... Are you drunk? Hey? Stephan? How many monkeys got upstairs while I left you there? Did you? Are you?

With no answer, and nothing of his companion but the back of his head and the steady image of his face in the glass, Mr. Yák recovered from his impatience, sat down again, and turned to the figure between them. —You wouldn't think she's only a little girl, would you have. He stared abstractedly at the flat lap for a minute, blinked, rubbed his hands, said, —Now we can really get to work, and sat back.

But he could not sit still. His foot commenced tapping on the vibrating floor. —What we want to do first, we want to find a place to bury that linen stuff awhile, so you can go there and sort of wet it down, see? Then I got to get into touch with this guy, this Egyptianologist, so he don't give up hope and leave town. Then all I got to do is keep out of his way till it's all set. See? Then we... Are you listening to me? Mr. Yák leaned over and tapped a far knee.

—What's the matter?

—Are you listening to me? What's the matter?

—Nothing, I... Nothing.

—Nothing? You...

—Nothing. I was just thinking about something.

—What?

—Nothing.

Mr. Yák snorted, and tapped his fingers on his knee. Then he turned abruptly and his neck shot out of the plexiglas collar. —Listen, he said, —I feel like I'm alone in here with this... with this. He nudged the figure beside him. The face beyond did not turn from the window. —See? So...

—What do you want me to do? Get up and dance?

—No. The vagueness of the tone irritated Mr. Yák. —But we...

—Shall I sing something? Una y una dos, dos y dos son tres...

—Listen, we...

—No sale la cuenta... Porque falta un churumbel. What's churumbel?

—That's a gypsy word here, Mr. Yák answered, the irritation still in his voice, speaking to the back of his friend's head. —The bill doesn't come out right because there's a kid missing. It means a kid. His tone was belligerent, but he answered rather than have no conversation at all. —See? he added, paused, and prompted, —See?

—They don't die in winter, the voice murmured from the reflection in the glass, which held the blackness of the night right up against it.

—What?

—But when the leaves come to the trees, the bartender told me, then they die, quando vienen las hojas . . .

—That's t.b., they got a lot of t.b. here. The kids especially. Now listen, when we get into the station . . . Look out! Look what you're doing! . . . Mr. Yák bent down so fast he almost fell. —You throw your cigarette on her feet like that, she's liable to go up in a cloud of smoke. See? When he straightened up from blowing the ashes away, he went on, —Now from now on, we've got a lot of work to do, see? And you got to settle down now and be more . . . more serious, see? All this drinking, and these girls, you want to forget all that, you're not a bum. All that kind of thing, he continued, with no response, —it's a waste, it's sinful, living like that.

—Yes, I know. I know . . .

—What? See what I mean? It's sinful.

—I know.

—See? And if you go on like that . . .

—But . . .

—What? . . . See? What fun is it.

—But . . . it's not the sin itself that's what is . . . Good God . . . the voice went on dully, and distant, —staggering into one after another . . . and then . . . and lying in the dark knotted up in wet sheets, and . . .

—See? What good is it? Mr. Yák demanded, leaning across and resting an elbow on the brittle lap between them for the moment before he realized it, then he drew up, —it's always the same, isn't it, so why do you want to do it again.

—Yes, but . . . it's not the thing itself, it's not sin itself. It's never the thing itself, it's always the possibility that . . . It's always the prospect of sin that draws . . . draws us on.

Mr. Yák straightened up from his strained position, peering round the back of the head as he'd been doing, trying to reach the face if only in its reflection against the black surface of the night. —See? he confirmed. —After awhile you get tired of it, after awhile you get to the place where it doesn't satisfy anything inside you like. You get to the place, he went on, staring at the shivering floor, —where no matter how much you've got mixed up with all kinds of the wrong things, that they don't gratify you any more to do them, see? So then you have to kind of look up, and look for something bigger. See? See what I mean? He looked anxiously up at the window.

—Yes but... if you've done things... if you've done things to people, and they... and you can't atone to them for... for what you've done...

—No, you can't! You can't!... not to them, but you... if you've like sinned against one person then you make it up to another, that's all you can do, you never know when you... until the time comes when you can make it up to another. Like I once... this woman, I...

They paused, rocking together all staring in different vacant directions of the past.

—What?

—Nothing.

—What woman?

—You... Mr. Yák jerked his head up, to see only Mr. Yák's face on the glass. —I'm going out to the gents' a minute... He faltered a pause in the door to the corridor. —If anybody comes in to sit down, you want to kind of talk to her, see?... Then the door slid closed, and he left them together, steadying himself down the corridor like an old man.

Almost immediately, lights appeared in the darkness outside, moving past the windows slowly, lights so dim that they seemed to do no more than illuminate themselves. The train stopped.

—Well *I* would have thought the name of the town was Urinarios, a tall woman said getting on, —it's the only word you can see on the station out there. She stopped while her husband opened the door of a compartment, and they went in. They sat down side by side, and she stared at the couple sitting side by side across from them. —So much *smoke*, she whispered to her husband. He offered her a cigarette. The train started. —And if we ever go all the way to a town like *that* again, if you could call it a town, just to see a church or whatever it was... I don't see how you ate a bite of that lunch. You'll regret it too, she added, trying to arrange her feet round the wrapped legs stretched before her. The spike of her heel caught the edge of the shawl, and she gasped. At that, the man across from her appeared to recover some long-lost consciousness, and he did so with a wild light in his eyes, darting down as though he were going to grab the tall woman's feet and pull her off her cushion. But he very busily brought the ends of the shawl back where they'd been wrapped, and then, lighting a ferocious-looking yellow cigarette, started chattering to the hooded figure beside him. —Díme lo, he said, —aunque no es... díme que tu me quieres, aunque no es... The tall woman cleared her throat, drew her feet together carefully, managed a prim smile across the way, and gripped her husband's arm. —Let's get out of here, she whispered, —this...

She stood, straining her smile, sustaining it until her husband was up, fomenting it with embarrassment of being polite, whispering, as the door slid open, —And my God!...did you see her face? —Syphilis, her husband said, —they've got a lot of syphilis here, even in the children, it's inherited...as he closed the door, and Mr. Yák, coming down the corridor behind him, opened it and entered.

—Who was that? he asked, seating himself, squaring his hair as he did so.

—I told you, people...people will disdain no ruses, no ruse at all to prove their own existence.

—Listen, you...But Mr. Yák found that he was again speaking to the back of a pair of shoulders, and he wilted back.

—Good God, the desolation of that place, that station we just stopped at. The window again held off the black surface of the night.

—I feel like we been riding on this thing all my life.

—Yes, yes that's it, that's it, you know? It's like...like being at sea. Somebody's said that going to sea is the best substitute for suicide. Why, in this country...in this country...

—Suicide?...

—Look, what if we're caught?

—With this? Mr. Yák shrugged. He had recovered his composure.

—No, I mean...whatever you...whatever we're...wanted for.

Mr. Yak looked up quickly, to see him turning back to the window. —What's the matter, you scared now? he said, and then repeated, —Wanted for?

—Yes, I...I am. I am scared.

—Sometimes I think I ought to have gone to Brazil. But that's the thing, a place like that, Brazil, everything's too new, what you want to do, you always want to go to the mother country of the place you maybe should have gone to...His voice tailed off. He had recovered his composure, but he looked weary, and older, jouncing back against the seat cushion, his hair slightly crooked on his brow, staring vaguely straight ahead, and the shaking of the train kept him nodding thoughtfully. —But now you go one place, and then you go somewheres else...His own tone was vague now, as he turned his attention to the reflection in the glass.

—Sail on, sail on, like the Flying Dutchman. Why good God, in this country...

—Who?

—It was Herr von Falkenberg, sailing without a steersman around the North Sea condemned to never make port, while he and the Devil played dice for his soul.

Suddenly they were face to face, and Mr. Yák found the hand mounting the two diamonds clutching his wrist. The eyes he stared into were burning green, the face even more knotted than that first day he had seen its confusion in the cemetery, and the voice more strained with desperation. —Why, in this country you could . . . just sail on like that, without ever leaving its boundaries, it's not a land you travel in, it's a land you flee across, from one place to another, from one port to another, like a sailor's life where one destination becomes the same as another, and every voyage the same as the one before it, because every destination is only another place to start from. In this country, without ever leaving Spain, a whole Odyssey within its boundaries, a whole Odyssey without Ulysses. Listen . . .

—You . . . anyways, Mr. Yák interrupted, trying to break away from the eyes fixed on him and even to withdraw from the hold of the hand he had sought so many times, —anyways you couldn't drownd on the land.

—You couldn't! Well it's . . . it's like that. It's like drowning, this despair, this . . . being engulfed in emptiness.

The grip on Mr. Yák's wrist quivered with intensity, as did the eyes and the whole face as though waiting for some answer from him. Mr. Yák broke the hold of the eyes, lowering his own to the hand there, and the diamonds glittering over the flat lap which separated them. —What you'd want to do maybe, he commenced, —you might like go to a monastery awhile, you don't have to turn into a monk, you're like a guest there, you . . . he faltered, staring at the hand, and the two diamonds, —you . . .

—Do you want it?

—What?

—This ring, this diamond ring? It's yours. It's yours now, if you want it.

Mr. Yák snatched his arm away and almost lost his balance. He looked helpless for a moment, and then managed to say, —No, no I . . . I didn't ever want it off you . . . He looked away from the hand there, to several places before his eye stopped at the extended feet between them, where the shawl had come off again, and there he bent down to pull it together. —We can get down to work now, he said from the shaking floor, —and then, when you have your work everything is . . . He was trying to knot the ends of the shawl, but it kept coming undone. He heard his own voice speaking with the tone of another, —And then all the love you've hoarded all your life, for your work . . . listen . . . His hands were shaking, and he could not make the ends meet to knot. —Have you got a knife, so I could cut this thing and tie it? Still he did not look up, aware that the figure was standing over him steadily on the shifting floor, and the square hand held a penknife before him. He reached up for it, raising his eyes at the same time. —Listen, he said, —listen, did you . . . really kill? . . . did you really kill somebody?

The train jolted, and he lost his balance on the floor. —Look out! Look out for her!

They were in Madrid.

In the railway station, what they wanted to do, according to Mr. Yák, who was moving and muttering like an old man talking to himself, they didn't want to be in any big hurry, and they didn't need to act suspicious pretending they were having an easy time with their charge, —because if people think you're having any trouble then they don't bother you, they try to look the other way. Except here, he added, annoyed, looking round the station. —They're better in New York that way, here somebody's just liable to try to help you out, that's because they're used to old people here, in New York they pretend they don't know there's such a thing... and he went on muttering, in time with his shuffling steps, when his words were no longer distinguishable.

Near the luggage check-room, they paused and Mr. Yák said, —Wait here, I'll get a cab. We can't carry this all over town like this. His eyes darted about as he spoke, and then he muttered, —All these cops, these Guardia Civil... and he hurried away.

He was in more of a hurry, his eyes still jumping from one black patent-leather tricorn to another as he avoided the Guardia Civil, when he returned. He was in such a hurry, in fact, that he went right past the woebegone couple standing against the wall near the luggage room. A moment later he returned, looking more harassed, glanced up, away, and stopped dead. He turned his head slowly, to see the patient shawl-wrapped figure standing right where he had left her, but now she was waited upon, at a respectful distance, by a creature not much taller, apparently not much younger, and despite his activity, in an inferior state of repair. The numbered metal tag on his dirty cap shone like a diadem in the battered crown of this martyr to unkemptness, and identified him as one of that villainous horde who, for a nominal fee, will spare no effort in making the first moments of the traveler's arrival in these capitals a faithful foretaste of the worst possibilities for helplessness, confusion, misery, anger, blasphemy, and acute hatred, that may lie ahead. A single tooth appeared and fled from sight in the midst of the dirty field of stubble on his chin, pursuing words which leaped out the more exhilarated by Mr. Yák's incredulous approach. He had a strap for binding the handles of bags together, and this he waved in the air, spurred on, and still held to his proper distance, by the stiff reserve of the figure he was regaling.

Braving the threat of the flail, Mr. Yák stepped between them, put a dutifully protecting, and steadying, arm round the shawled shoulders, and with something near his last bit of energy turned to face his opponent who, far from being daunted, was carried to new heights of clamor by this doubling of his audience, and did not stop until he gasped for breath. It turned out that the Señorito who had stationed him here had, upon leaving, instructed him to talk to her, —la vieja ... and he indicated the silent shawled figure with his strap, should anyone approach. And the Señorito had gone? —Sí Señor. Where had he gone? —Yo no se, Señor, yo, mira Usted ... That riot of gestures proclaiming a triumphantly total lack of responsibility for the vagaries of others commenced again; and it was some time, and with some effort, that Mr. Yák learned the police were on the lookout for someone, —Un extranjero, entiende, un norteamericano, sabe Usted ... —Per ché? —Claro, mira Usted, un norteamericano ... —Por qué? Mr. Yák demanded, gripping the shoulder he supported, mumbling, —Why? ... what ... ? ... for murder? —Claro que sí, Señor, un falsificador, m'entiende? Un norteamericano, sabe Usted, un falsificador...

—Falsi-ficador ... Mr. Yák mumbled, repeating it, —but ...

—Sí Señor, mira Usted ...

It turned out that the Señorito had asked the same question, and fled directly he got this same answer, leaving this mozo behind, to chat with her, —con la vieja ... all of which the mozo had accepted, apparently, without it ever occurring to him to wonder about the Señorito, and his sudden flight, any more than it might occur to him to question the Señor whom he was serving at this moment, so used was he to the transient rewards of blind loyalty, and a life sustained by a blind faith in the innate depravity of human nature. And now he stood, wadding the first five-peseta note he had seen for some time into the depths of the only whole part of his pants, while he held out his other hand for another, leering at Mr. Yák from a face which only the heritage of centuries of ignorance could redeem, for there was enough guile in it to rule an empire.

It was like a night at the fall of the year, a chill borne on the air in light rain, out where the mozo installed the elderly couple in a taxicab, which looked, and set off, like something the age of all three of them and the driver together, a Renault fitted with a charcoal burner, whose few undefiled surfaces might still maintain, in strong daylight, that they had once been painted red. Heaving and shuddering, this intrepid equipage passed the wet palace gardens and the palace itself, picked up speed and careened past the Opera, toward the center of the capital, that storied arena the Puerta del Sol, once a gate of the city opened on the rising sun.

In spite of his weariness, Mr. Yák managed to introduce his guest into the Pensión Las Cenizas unnoticed, down the dim passages and to his own room, which he locked and hurried to tap on the door down the hall, though he could see from the frosted glass panel it was dark. Past ten o'clock, he went to the dining room, dipped two spoonfuls of the garlic soup taking his usual care to avoid the sodden chunks of old bread afloat there, though he needn't have bothered for he didn't eat the soup, but just looked at it until it was taken away and four dead fish, gripping their tails in their burnt jaws, appeared, and he got no further than breaking one of the warped spines with his fork. The woman beside him was busy with her napkin, or crossing herself, it was difficult to tell which, and he looked away, crossing himself surreptitiously a moment later, for he'd forgot when he sat down, the first time since he could remember. And then a new guest entered, looked uncertainly about, and was seated at the empty place across the table. He was a stout man, and he filled his bowl with the garlic soup, whose thin surface reflected in orange-colored globules, and set immediately to eat. Mr. Yák looked up, to his left where a mirror on the sideboard had so often reflected the vivacious decorum of blond hair and the blue angora sweater that it was empty now as though it could contain no other. Then his eyes came down to the nursing mother, half his age, and he stared at her full breast. The man across the table finished his soup, sat back, and the sounds from inside him, like huffy pigeons in the open, brought Mr. Yák round, and to his feet. Without repeating his usual courtesy to the diners left behind, he hurried out, down the chill corridors, past his own door, to the dark panels beyond, and he opened that door without knocking, and reached above him until he caught the string on the light.

It was not the bright bare bulb he was accustomed to in his own room, but dimmed with the translucent paper wrapper from a coñac bottle. Atop the armoire there was a small forest of bottles, transparently green with emptiness. Its long mirror endlessly reflected one smaller, across the room over a single-spigot washstand, where a glass stood corroded with unfinished coñac whose smell hung in the room, rose to the molding of plaster garlands round the high white ceiling. Above the silvered bed (—a regular whorehouse bed, he'd called it himself once), the Andalusian maiden coquetted over her balcony and the shoulder of him in the guitar's embrace, hung at length across a faded vertical space where Jesús del Gran Poder had made way for her. Then noticing the cold radiator he remembered he'd meant to ask the dueño to put a brazier in here. He stepped from the carpet, a piece gray-blue and orange cut by the yard laid here on the uneven lengths of flooring, to a wicker table where a wicker chair with a red and black Indian-style cushion was drawn up, an empty coffee bowl and a stump of bread before it, and stepping, his foot rolled on something, and he stooped to pick up a .32 cartridge. It lay in the palm of his hand, the rim of the case cut in for use in an automatic pistol, and he weighed it there with a confused expression on his face, an expression which he snorted away as he pocketed the cartridge and returned to the table. A half page from a book lay beside the stump of bread, torn from Calderón's *La Vida es Sueño*, and it was torn evenly along the line, "El delito mayor del hombre es haber nacido..." and this too he seemed to weigh in his hand, before he put it back by the stump of bread, and a crumpled one-peseta note on the wicker table, pausing, as though he heard something, that voice, and —Oh yes, was it? the greatest sin of man, being born? hehehehe... and then that broken laughter. —No, because there's more to do, more work, more work if it's true that even the gods themselves, can't recall their gifts. Because there's a moment, traveling. Quiere comer? they offered, shelter. Coming up to Madrid, it's a destination, Madrid. You can tell by the name. Quiere comer? Everyone used to offer shelter to travelers, who knows it might be a god in disguise. The whole family there, eating, the whole... all the family... Quiere comer...? No, no I'm smoking, there's still so much work that's necessary, I'm smoking, I'm alone because, not hungry, because if it's true, then the love had to be hoarded for the work, locked up, there, there! is there a moment? traveling when, love and necessity become the same thing?

Then his eye caught the Swiss passport, thrown open on the floor.

—Aïe no, que no lo come, there, no don't eat that... son para la niña... tell me, for the love of Christ now will you leave me alone?

The outside shutters were almost closed on the narrow balcony, but sounds came up from Alphonso del Gato, the sound of voices and a barrel organ somewhere in the lame joy of some indistinguishable tune, through the shutters and the imposition of joy in the red-figured drapes that hung there motionless. Before him the mirrors, from the one tall and narrow mounted in the armoire to the small square one over the one-spigot washstand, and back, embraced one another's images, as the rain took up against the shutters, and reached the glass, and he stood there, chilled, his memory frantic for something precious left out in the rain, or a window left open, the rain pounding in, in the dark, engulfing a consciousness alert now in all the sudden perspicacity of terror, deepening round it so that it seems to have been falling all the time: sounds came from a great distance, a strange city, in a foreign land, and the sense he'd just been put down here this instant, alone, and for the first time, engulfed in the sense of something lost. He spun around on his feet, to confront who had come in the door behind him, but he saw no one there. He stood, off balance but still for a moment, and then he moved sidling toward the door, as though she were waiting for him to get out before she could enter, and once at the door he left like a crowd leaving, and the door open behind him.

—Vaya Usted con Dios... y que no haya novedad, Jacinta said opening the front door and wishing him off, and Mr. Yák repeated that phrase as he came out to the wet street, to crowd out other things from his mind. Novedad?... novelty, newness, change...That you go with God, and have no...novedad. He hurried down back streets, and then out past the Cortes, to the Palace Hotel, to leave a reassuring note for Mr. Kuvetli, saying that he had located what Mr. Kuvetli sought, and for a reasonable sum could see to its turning up within a few days; but he had forgotten his passport and was unable to remember his full name, though he did know the initial to his Christian name was J, and so he signed it J. Yák, and returned quickly to the streets.

The streets were thronged with people wherever he turned, crowds parading with such animation that one might at first think some major holiday, or grand catastrophe, had brought them out. He found himself approaching the Plaza Tirso de Molina, saw a blond boy pass on the arm of a man and someone said, —Los turistas, sí... pero los maricones... He bought some raisins from a cart, an unidentified flower for his buttonhole, and stopped in at Chispero's for coffee, glancing round him all this time but without much hope in his eyes of seeing anyone he knew. From the stage in the hall beyond the bar he could hear heels pounding, where Adelita Beltrán sang *La Sebastiana*, and he found himself mumbling along with the words, —Aunque tiene siete colchones... as he returned to the street, more nervous each minute at putting off his return to the pensión, and his work. —Un falsificador? he muttered, bumping people in the Calle de Atocha, —even though he has seven mattresses, la Sebastiana can't sleep...? How...?

—Adiós...

—Dios...

People passed in the wet recommending each other to God, instead of God to each other.

—Y que no haya novedad... he repeated to himself, approaching the Plaza Santa Ana, and glanced down in the shaft of light from the Villa Rosa. It was the remnant of a rose in his buttonhole. He brought his hands up before him to clap for the sereno, and they hung there, as he did, standing unsteadily, overwhelmed in the chill rain at being engulfed in Spain's time, and that like his guest awaiting him upstairs he would never leave it.

—Adiós...

—...?

Pastora stood in the doorway of the Villa Rosa, the strap on her high-heeled sandal still broken, the cerise blouse pulled and protruding from her skirt where the zipper was broken. —Buenas noche, Señor, she repeated timidly, her coarse black hair standing out round her face, and her lip drawn back from her large teeth no longer in the snarl he remembered, though it was the same expression but now pathetically defiant, waiting, alone, staring at him and waiting. He moved his arms with a quick shrug of his shoulders, and clapped for the sereno who came stumbling up with the keys and the usual observation on his job, —The worse I do my work the more people clap for me . . . and the street door came open.

—Adiós . . . Pastora repeated, desolately, without a look from him as he entered and climbed the stairs, muttering against the hollow sound of his feet on them. Jacinta let him in, and he hurried down the dark passages to his own room, still muttering something about the *work, the work.*

He pulled on the light and stared at the figure laid out on the uneven parquet of the floor. —Why would I have said . . . a thing like that? he mumbled, motionless, —The love hoarded all your life . . . for the work, and his lips still moved silently over that last word as he locked the door behind him, and continued to move, repeating it, until he saw them moving in the mirror where he went to pull off his hair, tug at the mustache, and startle when it failed to come off. He turned away from the glass to remove the plexiglas collar, though the gold and purple cord remained strung at his throat, and he crossed himself when his eyes fell on Jesús del Gran Poder hung upright over a faded length on the wall, forming a cross so. —All this, he muttered, and drew his hand across his chin. —Y que no haya novedad . . .

Then he snorted with impatience. A light came in his eyes, as he picked up the penknife and knelt at the left flank of the figure laid on the floor. As he commenced to work the light became brighter, until his eyes shone as though alive with sparks. Sounds still rose from below, the measured clatter of heels and palms, a voice in a constricted wail, from the Villa Rosa, and still he worked.

Then the blade stopped: the heart, was it? or the brain?

Until at last the only sounds were from the ends of the empty alley below, where the tapping sticks of two blind people approached each other in the darkness, that, and the scraping edge of the penknife, as the hag of the moon, the dark winnower, rose in its last quarter.

IV

If the sun and moon should doubt,
They'd immediately go out.
—BLAKE

—BLESSED Mary went a-walking...

The prow of the ship lifted from a swell, remained suspended and then dropped into the trough that followed. Everything shook.

—Over Jordan river...

—Please, don't sing that, Stanley interrupted. —Not here, not right now anyhow. Clinging to the rail, he looked uncomfortably over his shoulder, where Father Martin paced the deck reciting the appointed section of his breviary. She stopped, and gazed silently out to sea. Stanley looked at her face, the only one which (next to Father Martin when he was engaged in such supramundane pastimes as the one occupying him now) had preserved its equanimity throughout the voyage thus far.

It was not proving an easy crossing: several times Stanley himself had felt the saliva mounting in the back of his mouth, and tried to put his mind on something sublime and far away, or at least extracorporeal; but sounds and signs of adjacent suffering usually recalled him to the immanent prospect of his own, and he swallowed with great effort. He did so now. Behind him, beyond Father Martin's path, a mound of human misery heaved in a deck chair, clutching a small machine which clicked at regular intervals. It was a woman who had several times made the flat reasonable demand that the captain halt the ship. She was one of the Pilgrims; and as such, firmly convinced that the sea was aroused specifically for her and her fellows, whom she was ready to inform, at one moment, that infernal hands were responsible, working from anfractuous residencies far below to hinder them on their pious mission, and at other moments quite prepared to accuse the very Deity this voyage was designed to placate. In that case, He was certainly intent upon making it as memorably uncomfortable an excursion as any those medieval pilgrims enjoyed, setting off from Venice in the most deplorable conditions that could be arranged, which, for their times, is saying a good deal. Right now, the sky was blue and brilliantly clear, permitting a moment of hope, until the ship rolled and the boiling sea was raised before her eyes, which she closed forthwith and tried to dwell on the felicitous snarl of misconceptions which she had, over many devout years, managed to accumulate about her destination. They were not, after all, going to Jerusalem, and once landed did not run the risk of being stoned by Saracens, or offered for sale such articles of commerce as the bodies of the Holy Innocents. Neither the prospect of getting hold of a shred of the True Cross, nor a casket containing the tears of the Virgin, nor even the toenail parings of some venerable ecclesiastic, all opportunities of which their earliest forebears had taken full advantage, drew them forth: but rather the reward of indulgences. That, and the spectacle of the canonization of the little Spanish martyr, whose reputation a number of these Pilgrims, and this woman foremost among them, were importunately trying to enhance by seeking her intervention in this present misfortune.

It is true, there were others on board prey to less disciplined superstitions who agreed that this plight might well be a visitation on the Pilgrims, and were inclined to be quite rude about being so freely included. The Swede was one of these. Dressed in a becoming wrapper, he lay indoors sucking a lemon, and brushing aside objections. —But Anna, baby... —No, don't argue with me now, it's those hideous vulgar Pilgrims. —But baby the reason *you're* coming is to join the Church yourself... —You know very well why I'm coming, because the only way I can possibly get *hold* of little Giono is to *adopt* him, and I have to be a Catholic parent or they won't *give* him to me. —Don't you want to come out in the fresh air for a little?...you'll feel just *tons* better. —I can't go out in *this*. The Swede held up a pink satin hem. —Baby why did you give *all* your clothes to those stowaways?...

And among the lower echelons of the crew, those encountered mopping passages and lavatory decks, there appeared paper hats of crackled gilt and blemished colors, remnants of an exhausted carnival at some lost latitude whose banter still rode on smells and stains below the surface.

—Isn't there any more Dramamine? The tall woman raised her head from the pillow, seeing her husband enter. Then she lay back. —Poor Huki-lau, she's biting her nails again... breaking off her analysis...

And on deck, from the mound stacked heaving in a deck chair against the bulkhead, the clicks continued at somewhat irregular intervals. Almost gone inside her hand was the Machine, a "Recording Rosary," with the button under her thumb to be pressed each time she reached the Gloria, and an arrow

("Keep tabs on Mystery!" the ad had said) which pointed to the next bead to be prayed.

—Why do you keep singing that? Stanley broke out, seizing her wrist at the rail. Then he loosed his hold and apologized for startling her so; and a moment later a cry escaped him, and he lunged. Beneath him a book washed up on a crest, was gone, and reappeared in the white foam. He stared at that invitation to mortal sin being borne away by the sea, and then raised his face to the sea itself, as though to try to bring it all into his vision, and he said something like that to her, something about its immensity. He looked at her. She was looking at the sea. And then she said, but not to him,

—For some fishes the sea is a great big sky.

Stanley clung beside her. Then he turned, —Where are you going?

—For a walk.

—Yes, but... all right, but you're not going up to see... up to First Class?

—And see the Cold Man? She smiled to him; and Stanley lowered his eyes from hers. Who the "Cold Man" was he did not know, had no idea but of a tall figure he had seen, and then only at night, standing at the rail above, the left sleeve of a Chesterfield coat tucked empty in the pocket, the face motionless, obscured under the rim of a black hat. For Stanley was still pursuing the course he had set himself, asking no intrusive questions, making no demands upon her willingness which was, every moment she was near him, so candid in its expectation, so attentive to his wishes, as in the only renders he exacted of her, the devotions she secured with such care, and practiced with such grace.

Everything was going exceedingly well.

And her eagerness to learn the preparations he had set himself to teach her was sometimes pathetically touching, and sometimes it frightened him: touching, delicately absurd for there was no mockery in her when, for instance, she affirmed the dogma of the Assumption of the Virgin with that of Little Eva in *Uncle Tom's Cabin*, as the only historical parallel she knew; frightening, when she brought from nowhere the image of Saint Simeon Stylites standing a year on one foot and addressing the worms which an assistant replaced in his putrefying flesh, —Eat what God has given you... Or her frank familiarity with the career of Saint Mary of Egypt: seventeen years of prostitution in Alexandria, talents put to good use when she was converted and paid her boat passage to Jerusalem so, all expiated by wandering unwashed in the woods for the next half-century. Or how she might ever have known of the seventeenth-century Sicilian girl Ana Raguza, who called herself the Bride of Christ and could, so she said, actually smell out sinners. Or that the right foot of Santa Teresa de Jesús is venerated at Santa Maria della Scala in Rome. Or that the pus of Saint John of the Cross smelled strongly of Madonna lilies.

Things seemed to be going exceedingly well, better than Stanley would have imagined had he paused at the beginning of this undertaking to consider the practical difficulties it would so surely involve. Her passage, for instance: he was prepared to pay it, but no one had asked him to. And though he was relieved at the apparent lack of curiosity on the part of the other passengers, it had commenced to trouble him. No one, not even Father Martin, had asked her name; and though the fat woman had, at one point, risen in a gesture of myopic kindliness to include him in her own generation, asking if the "charming young creature" were his daughter, she had as quickly relapsed, clutching a shiny-surfaced paper book stamped with the *Nihil obstat* and *Imprimatur*, and entitled *A Day with the Pope*, and entirely forgotten that such a question, or any provocation for it, had ever entered her busy head. Licking her finger to turn each page of pictures, she visioned herself trundling in Vatican corridors, in the Court of San Damaso, and who can say where else? when she looked up to the boiling surface of the sea rising before her, and reached for a paper bag beside her deck chair.

Nevertheless, it was working out. Though Stanley, left alone below with his stack of palimpsests, and the clean scores onto which he was copying, made more mistakes than he had ever before, some of them maddening, copying the same bar twice; some strange, for here and there he found himself inserting grace notes which broke the admirably stern transitions, slipping in cadenzas which had nothing to do with anything, and, just this morning, writing in a throbbing bass which, as he realized when he stopped, was the steady vibration of the engines.

He could not get her out of his mind. When they were together, her smile, or often when she did not know he was looking the empty sadness of her face, forced him to lower his eyes, and fumble for something to handle, or something to say; and he usually found that tooth in his pocket, as he did now, and said nothing.

At all events, nothing had gone wrong yet. Even below, where they were at close quarters when they were together, being with her in illuminated silence or in prayer proved, in fact, less difficult than he had pictured, never having known temptation as it is usually succumbed to. And even at rising, or her going to bed, he found no temptation to touch her, or to tell her she was beautiful, though the warm brush of an elbow shocked him sometimes. But directly he was alone, it was all entirely different.

Directly he was alone, he was assailed by her simulacra, in all states of acute sorrow, or smiling, of complete abstraction or painful animation, of dress and undress, as he had seen her these last few days: directly he was alone, the images came to mock everything he had seen. Her sadness became shrieking grief, and her animation riotous, immodest in dress and licentious in nakedness, many-limbed as some wild avatar of the Hindu cosmology assaulting the days he spent copying his work on clean scores, and the nights he passed alone in his chair where, instantly the lights went out, everything was transformed, and the body he had seen a moment before with no more surprise than its simple lines and modest unself-conscious movement permitted, rose up on him full-breasted and vaunting the belly, limbs undistinguishable until he was brought down between them and stifled in moist collapse.

He woke in the morning exhausted; straightening his damp disarranged clothes, and there she lay, cool and unconsciously breathing and often uncovered; and when that was the case he covered her when he stood, no more allured to try her with his hand than he might have been a flesh-tone on canvas, and went out without washing, and up without even a pause on deck for the air of day, straight to breakfast. For there was that: he found himself with a great appetite, and sometimes he went to two sittings.

As yet, things were still under control, though he found himself avoiding Father Martin as carefully as he did the fat woman who sat drawing an enamel-nailed finger down her tongue each time she turned a page of a shiny-surfaced paper book stamped with the *Nihil obstat* and *Imprimatur*, and the title in yellow, *The Vatican and Holy Year*. (She had caught him at breakfast, starting off the day with a covetous reference to "the lily-white flower of her virginity" which the little Spanish saint-to-be had died protecting.) Now Father Martin passed behind, engrossed in what sounded in his murmurs to be a Psalm of David. With him, Stanley had formerly led off a number of interesting conversations: the etymology of "atonement" (at-one-ment); the Augustinian doctrine (this did not get too far) of the Crucifixion as a ransom paid Satan to release man from his power; of the decline of Satan (this got nowhere at all) from God's official tempter to His arch-enemy. But now Stanley avoided him, as though afraid he would blurt out some betrayal of his state of mind, some image of its nature.

As for the *Story of Barbara Ubryk*, he had slipped that away and dropped it overboard, only to find her with Margaret Shepherd's *My Life in a Convent*. "Wronged by a priest through the confessional" (he read), "when but a young girl, married to a priest, thrust into a convent with her baby and abandoned by the priestly brute who had promised to stand by her. It will hold you in its grip until through tears and heart-throbs..." That went overboard too, and was followed by the tale of Rosamond Culbertson (an American girl at the hands of Popish priests in Cuba), and Rebecca Reed's *Six Months in a Convent*.

And each time this happened, she looked up at Stanley with the same dismay anew, which sounded in her voice when she asked, —But isn't that how it's going to be?...

He swallowed with an effort at constriction which ran right down through the hand clutching the wrapped tooth in his pocket, gazing below at the shifting surfaces of white foam, and startled to see that he was not watching *Paradise Lost*, but a man's hat afloat down there.

The touch of her hand on his clutching the rail startled him to withdraw it, and he watched her go down the deck, swaying with motions scarcely incurred by the roll of the ship, or even compatible with it, nothing at all to do with the sea, this brilliant unbroken expanse of sky and the sea bound only by one another, by now reality's only terms: she walked off with the gait of the desert, the movements of a gypsy, or the ease of those women (though he had never seen such a company) who follow camels, and acquit the camels' grace from behind, as they share the features before, with their own.

Stanley followed her. It was an abrupt decision, and he kept well behind and out of sight, hesitating round corners, behind ventilators, too heated to know if he feared being seen, or feared what he would finally see himself. At one turn he paused too long, and he lost her. He took a moment to congratulate himself on giving up such a reproachful pursuit, and then set off again frantically. He ran aft until he reached the set of outside steps leading up to First Class, and had already started up them when he saw her. She was standing alone at the rail below and she did not see him approach, nor see his humiliated retreat, for she was weeping.

Stanley went inside, and wandered vaguely through the Tourist Class smoking room. He stopped to read the weather report again, and he reread the same news bulletins that had been posted there in the morning. He had read the third item, a cargo ship which had broken in half and gone down off the Azores, twice, before he realized that he had read it earlier, and was only standing here, instead of working, waiting for first call to luncheon.

For the first time on the voyage, he drank down a glass of wine before a bit of food appeared; and during the meal he filled his glass four times from the carafe on the table. When he went below, he found her lying down. She appeared to him to be asleep, her face turned to the wall. Her figure lay entirely still on the bed, with no evidence of her breathing nor even any apparent response to the motion of the ship, which kept Stanley replacing his feet while he stood over her.

On the floor was a small folded card, lavishly decorated. It was something which had belonged to his mother, used here to the best purpose, making up to her those damned and absurd books he had thrown overboard, and now he leaned over to pick it up: *A remembrance of the venerable shrine of Saint Mary of the Angels*, with a picture on the outside of Saint Francis receiving the Indulgence of the Portiuncula. Inside, on the one hand were glued three infinitesimal particles, labeled as a piece of the door of the cell where Saint Francis died in 1226, a piece of the Portiuncula, the church itself, and a piece of the pulpit where the Indulgence was proclaimed by Saint Francis and seven bishops; on the left hand were four leaves from the miraculous rosebushes of Saint Francis of Assisi, and beneath the marvelous history of how "One bitter winter's night, Saint Francis being sorely tempted by the Devil to lessen his austerities overcame the evil one by throwing himself into a thicket of briars... rolling himself in it till his body was all torn and bleeding..." at which juncture the briars became full-blooming rose-trees, and in a heavenly brightness angels appeared to lead Saint Francis to the Portiuncula, where Our Lord with His Mother and a Heavenly Host granted the Indulgence, a "Plenary Indulgence which, after the devout reception of the Sacrament of Penance, can still be gained daily as often as one enters the Portiuncula... This indulgence can be applied to the souls in Purgatory."

The card now was curled and still damp, as though she had been clutching it in the hand open palm up beside his face as he started to stand, and the roll of the ship moved him toward her, off balance and his cheek touching her hair. For a moment he hung there, as motionless as she; and then he moved his cheek very slowly, and back, against her hair. In her hair he felt his own hot breath. Her hair held it and burned his cheek, and he came down on one knee, turning his face into her fine hair and breathing more heavily, his eyes wide open. His whole face was burning, but he became aware of something else; and then of nothing else but the beat of his heart, pounding unevenly in a gigantic shape which grew from the depth of his chest to his neck, and with each beat, going more slowly.

She moaned, and came over on her back; but he could not move. She moaned something almost articulate, and then her lips stayed open, and loosened, and the lower one was drawn in. Her tongue showed at a corner of her mouth, and her lips closed, still showing the tip of the tongue as her jaw became rigid and her chin rose, and her whole body heaved up from the bed and came back delicately taut, and distended rose again, and returned with gentle force as she breathed so heavily, her face thrown back, that it seemed to empty the whole upper part of her body. Her breath felt as hot as his own, pouring over her ear which touched his lips now: still he could not move, still on one knee, gripping the side of the bed with both hands and his eyes still wide open, all his senses confused into the one he projected, listening. Because he was listening for the beat of his heart, which had not seemed to him to fill that whole room until he became aware that it no longer did, and waited, each throb heavier, and separated from the last by a dreadful distance.

Nothing moved, and he heard nothing. The metal plate under his knee was still, and he heard nothing at all, not even the engines; not even the engines which had paced his heart day after day and sustained it at night while he slept, so that its beats had vibrated through the whole ship, driving them on when it went faster and paced the engines with anticipation. Then the ship lurched, and a great surging sounded from behind. The engines started; and Stanley's heart doubled their measure as he stood, lost his balance and fell back against the door.

She came up on one elbow, eyes open with alarm as though they had never been closed. —What is it? she cried out.

—I don't know... he gasped, and pulled himself up against the door.

The engines had been reversed, and slowed now to a dull and far-off sound, as the ship rocked slightly and appeared to be still.

—Are we there? she burst out.

—There?... there? Where? he answered helplessly. Then he got hold of the door handle, and pulled it open.

In the passage, the fat woman had just reached that point. Her Machine came one way, a small three-penny paper book titled *A Modern Virgin Martyr* another, and she fell in at his feet. —I just know... she cried, —I just know... I just know...

Stanley stood there, staring dumbly at the wool-knit knee warmers drawn askew over knees the size of his own waist. —Cut armholes and I'd have two nice sweaters... He almost said that out loud, staring now with the glazed look of plain lunacy. Then her hand caught his knee, which almost broke, or gave way, and instead of reaching down to help her he grabbed with both hands for the door frame.

—I just know... She started to sink, and mumbling something he reached for her hand before she could seize his knee again. Everything seemed to be happening very slowly. He studied the inadequate ring on the hand he held, doubly miserable for having two mean pearls mounted at an angle to the thin line of gold which had almost been absorbed in the flesh: had she been given it when the ring and her hand still complemented one another? or bought it...

—*Water!*...

Sure enough, there was about a saucepanful of water in a quiet pool, with neither source nor destination apparent, there in the passage.

—*My rosary!*...The Thing glittered near his feet.

Stanley retrieved it, finally closed the door upon his guest, and came back and sat down. His shoulders were just beginning to sink when he leaped to his feet again. —What *has* happened? he cried out, losing balance again and coming down beside her on the bed. He took her hand, and together they hurried out.

The surface of the sea was blinding on the port side where they came on deck, and where other passengers already lined the rails. The days lost count of by now, people stared stupidly at the sea. Conversations inclined to tail off and disappear, as eyes were raised to that expanse of heaving indifference, as inevitable as it had been novel the first day out, and the face of one who talked, and one who listened at the rail turned from one another and lay as open and destitute of past, or future, or anything to give, as the vacant face of actuality they looked upon.

Stanley lifted a hand from the rail to hold the white hand which had been holding his. He looked at his wrist watch, then at her face, and then looking below again he simulated her expression, subdued but troubled, curious but not to know too much.

Lines were flung out, men's voices rose to them, and directly beneath a loading port was opened in the side of the ship. There were six figures in the lifeboat that was finally pulled up to the side, men in torn shirts with blackened faces looking up without the particle of interest exciting the faces that looked down on them. Their boat rocked as they drew on the lines, caught the end of a rope ladder, moving with agile assurance, all but one. He was laid out across a thwart, and when a canvas sling was lowered two men got him in it, and held the sling back from bumping the side as it was raised. It came up slowly, toward Stanley who was directly above, and then, almost to the port, there was a hitch in the line which caught, jerked, and one end of the sling came open. Passengers participating breathlessly shared a sound of shock, a sharp intaking of breath as the head fell back and hung from one end of the sling. The face was dark, and covered with oil-slick which shone in the sun bringing out, even at this distance, the square high-boned lines of the face, the jaw set rigid as though held by the lines drawn down from the nose, breaking the flat cheeks, and the eyes, even closed in unconsciousness, held tight as though with effort.

—You wouldn't think... Stanley commenced, turning to her. She raised her face from the one below slowly to his, paling, all the color gone from her lips which quivered round a word, and she fainted.

Stanley caught her against the rail and looked up for help. He met square with a face a deck above, looking down beyond him with eyes which had their color and their substance from the sea beneath but too light, and even as Stanley looked, too watery, for the glare of the sea in the declining sun had turned to a vast surface of molten metal. The face up there was as pale as the one Stanley supported against his chest, and the figure, in a dark blue striped suit, one arm in a black sling rested on the rail, withdrew and disappeared.

—Now *he's* cute . . . came from further along on the promenade deck above, and Stanley, still craning, could see through the grating a tall blond creature in an overcoat, a bright pink hem hanging out beneath it, toes of a bare foot peeping through the scuppers. —If I'd only brought just *one* of those Boy Scouts . . .

—My dear boy, isn't this a divine miracle? The fat woman's voice brought Stanley back to himself, and the weight he was supporting. He held her still against the rail, and raised her face. Her eyes were still closed but a smile moved her lips.

—Now there's something, the fat woman said, —something I wanted to ask you. An American candy bar was flourished in Stanley's face for a tempting moment by the pearl-laden hand. —Would you like some? he was asked as though he were standing there empty-handed himself.

—No, I . . . please, please excuse me . . .

—Now what could it have been? . . .

Stanley turned to the face close to him. —Are you . . . can you walk now? he asked, and got no answer but the unsteady lifting of her weight from against him. He supported her with an arm round her waist. She walked with her head down, did not raise her face until they had reached the foot of the first flight of steps.

—We are going to him? she asked. Stanley mumbled something, —Mmhmm, pretending to be engrossed in the effort of helping her. They finally reached the passage where the pool of water moved from one side to the other with the roll of the deck, and not until he opened the door and closed it behind them did she utter a little cry, and then, looking round, —Where is he?

She asked with a smile, as though Stanley were playing a game with her, but he said,

—Now, lie down. Lie down. You lie down for a minute . . .

—But where is he? the smile left her face as she looked at him.

—Now you lie down for a minute . . .

—Where is he? she cried out.

—Who? Stanley brought out finally, standing as though afraid to approach her for she had come more alive than he had ever seen her, ever, he realized, except at night when the lights had gone out.

—The man . . . they took out of the sea? She became unsteady for a moment, appealing to him.

—Why they . . . he . . . the one they brought up in that thing, he's probably in the ship hospital, he . . . but you . . .

—Oh yes . . . she whispered hoarsely, —take me. She came toward Stanley, toward the door behind him. —Take me there, take me to him.

—No you . . . now you lie down. He seized her arm and they struggled. Her strength was remarkable, more than his, but desperate and unable to sustain itself, while Stanley fought to hold her away from the door, to hold her back and away from himself, as though he knew from experience what he was doing, though even this did not mitigate the terror in his eyes, struggling with certainty, and the certainty that he would finally lose: for he was shocked at her strength, but not with surprise, shocked with familiarity. It was the same strength he fought at night: the same dreadfully familiar twisting body, the same hard fingers twisted in his, nails cutting the backs of his hands bending them back, drawing them down, the same leg wound around his, the shoulder wrenching away and then dug sharply into his chest, the same arm suddenly flung round his neck, the same hot face, and hot breath, and the hair blinding him, suffocating him, wet with his own sweat and burning with his own breath, until now he got two arms under hers, and with his hands up on her shoulders from behind held her away, her head flung back, fingertips digging into his arms, he stood unsteadily with a leg through between hers and her body still twisting against his where they met.

He was weak, and he clung to her. All this time the motion of the ship had kept them up, where one who might have lost balance on a level floor and gone down was buoyed up from behind as the deck rose, but now, as the port side came up again, and no struggle to sustain them, they went down. His balance gone, Stanley managed to push one more step toward the bed, and there came down on top of her.

—Let me . . . take me . . . she whispered, almost piercing his shoulders with her nails, as he still held her, and could not let go. He could not move, though she writhed under him; he could not breathe, though her breath poured up at his face and was withdrawn sharply, raising his chest on hers; and though her eyes were closed he could not close his own but stared at all this, familiar and dreadfully light. Then Stanley's shoulders shook, and he twisted hers back in his hands. His elbows dug into the bed and his chin came up, his legs hardened and his feet lapped one over the other came rigid and straight to the toes, the rigor of death setting into every extremity as life went out of him, dissolving his senses, melting everything in him until it was drained away, and his head dropped, eyes closed on the pillow.

He recovered suddenly, pulling himself up on his elbows, the same shock of consciousness that woke him every morning. It seemed a full minute before his heart took up beating, and then pounded relentlessly. He threw his face down into the pillow, and pulled the pillow up on either side of his head, his whole frame shaking. Then he raised his head and looked round the empty room. He threw his feet over the side of the bed and stood up, caught his balance on the back of a chair, started a step and then, his eyes fallen on his unfinished work, palimpsests on one side of the table and clean scores on the other, but vacant, staring eyes, he hung there, suspended, —Anathema . . .

Then he moved slowly. Stepping with feet wide apart he gained the chair, where he sat down and drew off his trousers and then, without looking down, his drawers. Then he got up and wet a towel and, looking away from what he was doing, saw first his face in a cabinet mirror, turned quickly to escape it from that to the wall and saw there the yellowed crucifix, moving gently on its nail. He closed his eyes and stopped, a hand to his forehead, and there was a knock at the door. He waited, his shoulders drawn tight, paralyzed. The knock sounded again. He stepped to the door, not knowing whether he was going to open it or hold it closed.

—My dear boy! . . . he heard from the passage, and waited, holding the door, until there was a snort, and heavy footsteps, receding. Then he opened the mirrored cabinet door, got out a pair of clean drawers, gazed at the blue suit unworn since his mother's funeral, hanging there, swinging gently as though to recall him to it, and turned his back quickly. He got on the clean drawers, hopping about on one foot and then the other, informally, as though pursued by puffs of wind from different and unexpected directions. He hesitated over the trousers he'd been wearing, fell back on the bed pulling them on, and was out and up the passage a moment later, the drawers and the wet towel wadded into a bundle which he threw over the side when he reached the deck.

It was dark, night swelling and falling around him, and there was a moon. He clung there staring at it. And in its light the ship seemed to fleet over the surface scarcely touching the water but to break its crests, a spectacular un- reality which sent a shudder of excitement through his emptied frame, fleeing with no more weight than the weak ship's lights above him. He clung as though to save himself from going over, not falling, but simply going over the side and out onto that swarming brilliance where everything would be all right at last.

When he would look back over it all, what had happened, and what was yet to happen, this was the last moment of the voyage that he honestly, clearly remembered.

Father Martin's face was illuminated full from an uncurtained porthole, standing with his back to the rail on the First Class deck. Up the steps, Stan- ley started to rush toward him when a light sprang up in the face of the man talking to the priest, a light cupped in one hand against the wind, to show the face strong in profile, the eye shining from its surface. The light went down, drawn by a cigarette, flared up as the man shrugged, and went over the side a red speck. —Of course I still am, my dear fellow. We're both probably working on the same thing now.

—You haven't changed, the priest said after a pause.

—Semper aliquid haeret . . . you remember?

The priest turned his back and went up the deck. Had he followed him, Stanley might sooner have found what he was after, for a few yards on Father Martin was stopped by a hospital attendant to whom he listened for a moment and then followed quickly. But the shadow remained at the rail and Stanley turned away from it, and soon got lost.

In a bar, Don Bildow caught his coattail. —I didn't know you were on board! . . . I want you to meet Miss Hall. Mrs. Hall? Mrs. Hall.

—How do you do, excuse me I . . .

Don Bildow, in a threadbare light brown suit, yellow and brown necktie, and plastic-rimmed glasses, stood up looking translucent. —Wait . . . he said, turning his back on Mrs. Hall.

—But I can't, I . . .

Don Bildow was clutching a recent copy of the small stiff-covered magazine which he edited, and, from the stains on the cover, it looked as if he had been carrying it for some time. From his eyes, it looked as if he had had a good deal to drink. "Mrs. Hall" was watching him critically from behind. —Listen Stanley, I've always thought of you as a . . . somebody I can . . . somebody I share a lot with . . . said Don Bildow with a hand on Stanley's shoulder, appraising him for some mutual infirmity, —and I . . . listen Stanley, have you got any Methyltestosterone? I'm with this girl, see? This Mrs. . . . . this girl, and she . . . you know she wants me to go up to her cabin with her now but I haven't got . . . I didn't bring any Methyltestosterone, I mean I had some but my wife . . . I left it . . . Have you got any?

—I . . . excuse me, I don't even know what it is, I have to go. Stanley broke away from the limp grasp, and turned a few feet away recalling, thinking he might have asked Don Bildow if he had seen her; but Don Bildow was back deep in conversation, telling "Mrs. Hall" about —My little daughter, she's only six and she was all swollen up when I left, I shouldn't have left I know it, I have terrible guilt feelings about it, all swollen up in the middle . . .

—And you're the young man who wanted to trade some Dramamine for some Phenobarbital?

Stanley turned to the tall woman, automatically held out his hand as he was accustomed to do when something was offered.

—But what do you need them for, you're all right, the tall woman's husband demanded. —You can walk, I can't even walk.

—They're not for me, she said to him, —they're for Huki-lau... now where did that boy go?

At the door, Stanley had to wait a moment.

—After you, Senator.

—After you, Mister Senator.

—Senator, you'll be doing me a great service if you'll go first and help me out, I can't even see the door, sir.

Stanley saw her pass, outside on the deck, running. —Excuse me, I...

—What?... Senator?

—Excuse me, sir, I...

—Oops!...

—I'm sorry, I...

She was not in sight, but Stanley hurried in the direction she'd gone. He dropped the sticky pills into his pocket, found the tooth, and ran clutching it. Rounding another corner, he saw her feet through a flight of steps; but when he reached them, and got up them, she was gone again. He stopped to get breath. A man in a dinner jacket approached, and Stanley, thinking, stopped him to ask for the ship's hospital.

—You don't look ill, my boy. Stay out and get a little air, thet'll straighten you up quicker than all the ductors...

Stanley ran on over the metal plates, and finally he did reach the ship's hospital, but she was not there. At any rate he did not see her when he came in. Few of the beds were occupied, and round one stood a screen against which shadows moved, and he went there.

From within came the steady murmur of Spanish, interrupted but unbroken by subdued words in Father Martin's voice. Stanley stood listening to the confession, bound, not understanding its features but only what it was. Then the murmur subsided, broke in a cough, took up again more rapidly and abruptly ceased. There was silence. The shadows on the screen moved, and then Father Martin's voice took up, a monody hardly breaking the reciprocal sounds which bound the ship in motion, no more pressing or importunate, and no more faltering than the movement of the ship itself into the darkness. Bells sounded somewhere, clear tones which penetrated the misereatur, hard separate sounds which signaled the Latin syllables with consequence: Stanley was counting them. For no reason, he had never learned the simple system of ship's bells and seven might be any hour; but now each one pinioned his tension, waiting for the next, listening, as he waited watching the shadows, for one of them to take form and move of itself. Then the bells stopped and left him swaying on the firm undulations,

—Per istam unctionem, et suam piissimam misericordiam... He smelled oil, or it seemed, burning oil, —indulgeat tibi Dominus . . . the shadow of an erect thumb drew out elongated on the screen. —Quidquid deliquisti per oculos . . . Then he saw her, moving slowly and more clear as she approached the light, her dress wrinkled and torn at the bosom, hair in disarray, and catching light her eyes were wild. —Deliquisti per aurem . . . the voice came on with intolerable slowness, and that because its progress seemed to draw her on and restrain her at once. —Deliquisti per manus . . .

When she broke and ran toward the screen Stanley stayed her no more than a shadow thrown across her. Nor did her body when she flung it forth heaving with sobs, seem to disturb more than a shadow so suddenly fallen upon him the figure laid out there, exposed for the last touch of forgiveness upon the flesh where all of its impulses reared in one. And like a ragged shadow her hair almost covered his lined face, and her left arm round his head and his shoulder in her other hand so forcefully that it appeared to rise slightly from the bed, nothing moving but her lips on his ear, —Oh yes . . . her voice broke but she would not leave it, —Oh yes, oh yes . . . Oh yes . . .

The left hand of the man on the bed came up slowly. It moved as though with life of its own into the shadow of her thigh, and there under a final hieroglyph of veins it came to rest.

Then there was no sound, of voices nor of any voice: and without, her shape flung down there appeared no longer dirigible. The only thing to bind time together was the reciprocal motion of the ship: yet in the moments of the prow dropping forth into a trough far ahead and shaking the fragments of its advance down in shudders all about them, Stanley had long since begun, repeated every motion of battle, every twist of the past convulsed nights, every skirt and dash in this sciamachy brought up firm now with Father Martin's hand on his shoulder until he straightened himself back to its force, straining away at last, rending away his spoil and leaving a dead man laid out in the light.

Together they staggered down decks, down steps, companionways, passages, nearly fell in the pool shifting just before their own door, and once inside it was as though they'd never left: buff-painted metal walls studded with double rows of rivets, metal above transected by a steel I-beam, steel under foot in plates lapped with rivets, the closed door flush and no way out but the ventilator, and this whole severe enclosure of angles driven by vibrations, in motion with no direction, it was more than as though they had never left it, as though they could never leave it, and had never been anywhere else. Stanley looked at his wrist watch, as though knowing what time it was might confirm something.

—Why did you take me away from him? she asked quietly.

Stanley looked up from the watch face to hers, and gaped at her. —But he wasn't...he isn't...you...That's all he could say; but she was still waiting, standing still against the roll of the ship and staring at him, her plain dress wrinkled and torn at the breast where he'd torn it, and on her face a look like she'd had that day he found her in the hospital, a day in his childhood it struck him now. He took one step toward her and raised his hand. —Now...and he stopped as though something had caught in his throat: he had started to tell her to lie down, as though that could ever be an innocent proposal again, and a pain of a novel and intimate sort shot through him from behind to confirm the cleaned empty feeling his weak legs supported in witness.

—Why?

Stanley recovered the step he had taken forward, back. He saw streaks glistening on her face, but not tears. They were streaks from the anointed face she had thrown herself upon. And throwing both hands before him Stanley burst out, —But why did you...who was he?...how did you know who he was?

—He was?...she repeated, and —Oh, he was. She put fingers to her forehead and lowered her eyes, and then let her hand go down to an ear and stop at the empty lobe. —For he knows who I am, though he had so little to share... so precious little. And did you never know him? she asked, raising her face to Stanley, —his eyes, not the eyes of a lover, no, never but once. He brought lilies when selling them was against the law. Against the law?...to sell lilies? Still touching the lobe of her ear, she was looking away from him now, and went on, her voice low, —Not a lover, not looking to find what was there but for what he could put there, and so selfishly take it away. But he didn't! He didn't! He didn't! she cried, and she threw herself on Stanley.

He fell back against the door, and his arms raised, prepared of their own accord to fight, for he was not, found themselves supporting her, sobbing in weak broken cries which were caught up in desperate gasps for breath. But even these sounds so close that his own chest shook with them seemed far away as he dragged her across the steel plates, staggering, catching his foot on a riveted seam, and ready to smash his head on the floor before her weight could pull him down on the bed with her distant sobs, for the sound of his own heart engulfed them both, the steel room shuddered with its pounding, a half-measure and then a full one, and both of them shut inside it, locked in the riveted steel enclosure, a heart in motion with no direction.

—Let me out! she screamed, and he pushed her, catching himself on the sharp corner of a metal bureau as she fell back on the bed, the port side rising behind him, and she hit her head against the rivet row, and the crucifix fell and stabbed her shoulder.

It was the crucifix Stanley recovered first, and he stood there with it in his trembling hand staring at the drawn yellowed legs, rigid, hard-muscled straight to the toes, and then, the chest raised stiffly motionless, the chin thrust up and the unseeing eyes wide open. He had stopped breathing. The trembling crucifix lowered from his fixed gaze and he was staring at her, only a blur before him.

Her head lay over on one shoulder, lolling gently against the steel behind her, eyes closed, and she whimpered. Faint streaks and blotches had begun to show on her pale face, and Stanley bent over her. He started to talk loudly as his heart took up again with the engines and the whole thing of metal angles straining against each other enclosed overtook him, —Listen, listen . . . listen to me . . . He dropped the crucifix beside her and took her shoulders. Her head fell forward. —Listen to me . . . He laid her back on the bed, got her legs up, and then pulled the crucifix out from under her and put it over beside her head. He stared at her still face for a moment, then got up and got a glass of water. He looked for a towel, found none, and so he dipped his fingers in and drew them over her forehead, saying now, —Listen, you can't have . . . I didn't mean . . . you can't have hurt yourself, you . . . listen . . .

She opened her eyes staring straight at him, and said finally, —Will you always keep me here?

—No, no, I . . . because even I, I can't stand . . .

—Will we go to him now?

—Yes, I . . . no, you . . . now, now you have to rest for a minute for a little while. Now we, listen, both of us have to . . . where did I . . . Where did you put that . . . that rosary I gave you, that . . . those silvery beads I gave you, where are they? . . . because we . . .

She just stared at him. Stanley got up and started looking frantically round. In a pocket, a hand as frantic as his eyes found the tooth, and two sticky pills clinging to its wrapping.

The rosary was Italian, of silver filigree beads, with a filigree cross at the end of it. He saw it in a heap on the bureau where he'd just come from, and brought it back to her, going down on one knee beside her. —Listen, now we both . . . after what we've both . . . listen, the Angelic Salutation. The An-gel-ic, Salu-tation, do you remember it? Ave . . . listen, repeat it with me. Take this . . . He thrust the rosary beads into her hands, still on her belly. —Ave Maria . . .

Her torn dress was pulled to the tip of her breast, which lay still as though she were not breathing. The beads lay over her motionless fingers with their colorless nails. She stared at him.

She stared at him through four repetitions, her breast just as still, the beads unmoved by her fingers and their colorless nails, the streaks on her face reddening. Then she burst into laughter.

The port side came down with a shudder; and Stanley went back on his heels: he'd never heard such a sound, thrown down on him from every side from the metal walls. All he could say was, —No!... No!... until he did manage to get hold of the crucifix. —No, now... now listen, you... Him who... He who... whose love was so great... whose love for us was so great that He gave up His life... He... He...

—He!... she cried out, —then take me to him!

—No, I mean, not him, I mean... here. Stanley thrust the crucifix into her hands raised before her, the beads in a heap in her lap. For the moment his hand held it, his fingers trembled on the rigid yellow figure. The new significance his own body had given it made him dizzy, and he swallowed with the effort sea-sickness cost him.

She was staring at it too. Her eyes shone brilliantly, and she gripped it with great excitement. Stanley stood up before her. He watched her, waiting for her to confirm him in some transfiguration of faith, what, he did not know. She raised her eyes. They were glittering from her hollow face.

—This h-horrid thing, she said, and threw it at him.

Stanley reached automatically to catch it, but the instant his fingers touched it, they stiffened and it fell.

—Your terrible little man with nails in him, she cried, —your muttering and your muttering, and that... terrible thing. She stood up. —For love? For love? Oh never, never, never. I know whose love must save me as I must be for love. And you cannot keep me from him. You cannot keep me from him. You cannot, nor Him dead with nails in, not for love.

There was a knock on the door, and before Stanley could open it or hold it closed, there was the fat woman filling the doorway. —My dear boy, my book, I lost it and I must have lost it here. My book about our little Spanish saint?

She stared at Stanley and beyond him. Stanley found the yellow three-penny pamphlet on the floor, and got it.

—But I won't take it if you're reading it, the fat woman said, standing curiously still in the rocking doorway. —The lovely child!... preferring death to sin. I liked the part...

—Here, take it! Stanley said.

—I liked the part like where she's getting ready, for First Communion? "Take care of your tongue," the priest told her, "for it's the first part of you to touch the body of Our Lord..."

The fat woman stood there, filling the doorway. She had a small mouth, lips lined with a coral shade, which she pursed impatiently. She stood there, curiously still.

The rosary flew through the air.

—Go fuck yourself!

Stanley turned his head slowly. He saw no features, only livid red streaks. The silver filigree beads rolled all over the floor. He leaned over to pick up the crucifix.

—You are possessed, said the fat woman. Stanley brought his head up slowly before her, as he recovered the crucifix, afraid of the expression on the coral lips, afraid the fat woman would knock him down in an attack on the figure behind him, whom she'd just judged: but the fat woman was looking straight at him. She watched what he was doing, and as he stood, fixed her small eyes on his. The coral lips continued to twist silently. Then she turned from the doorway and went up the passage, the yellow three-penny pamphlet in the hand with the two mean pearls.

Stanley bolted the door, and turned his back against it. The cross he held was whole, but the figure mounted there was broken across the knees, and the chin was gone. He laid it face down on the bureau and turned with a hand in his pocket, where he felt the tooth and the two pills stuck to its wrapping.

Then he was grappling with her again. At one point they were thrown a hand or two apart, and Stanley looked up to the mirror in the cabinet door for reassurance, but he saw only himself. The ship heeled over, the door swung gently to, and the mirror embraced them both again but he did not see, for at the moment he was forced to renew the struggle, with the single mirror image before his eyes.

Her strength gave out suddenly; and he finally managed to get her to take the two sleeping pills, thinking, as the second one disappeared, that he might have kept it for himself. Then he started to pick up the filigree silver beads. He found the Portiuncula card torn in half, and paused, piecing it together, but his shaking hands could not make the edges meet. He gave that up and laid it with the crucifix, stared for a full minute at the bed, and the silent figure he saw there, then looked wildly about as though indeed himself seeking a briar patch. He shuddered as though with cold, and went back to hunting the beads.

Each time he reached for one it rolled away from his hand, as he concluded a Gloria Patri on the last. Mumbling Aves in between, each time he caught one he renewed the devotion with a Paternoster, recovering, after sixteen centuries, the pebbles which the hermit Paul threw away to keep count of his daily three hundred prayers.

The stem broke a path in the water as the ship ground its way into the night, and the sea washed well below the nineteenth-century monogram on the side, a more intricate device than the cross painted at the load line on those Pilgrim Galleys carrying devotees on their quest for relics, to Jerusalem for stones from Saint Anne's church, for pregnant women, reeds for women in labor from Saint Catherine's fountain at Sinai, and for barren women, roses from Jericho.

Asleep in the chair, Stanley had a bad dream, the worse for its dreadful familiarity, though, waking in the dark, he could not remember what it was. But at hand he heard twisting, turning, moaning —Yes, if there is time yes, oh yes...Oh yes...

Stanley found himself perspiring freely. His clothes were damp and his drawers almost wet, still he did not dare turn on the light, fearing its confirmation of everything he imagined the darkness to hold in abeyance as he pulled a coat round him and shivered, listening, to her sounds, and the pounding of his own heart driving them forward toward Gibraltar and the inland sea, as hearts have driven them down through centuries, from the ones peering into the cave at Bethlehem where the bodies of the Holy Innocents were hurled (and more than willing, upon turning round, to pay a hundred ducats for the knife-slashed body of a still-born Saracen child), to their descendants gathered at the burning of a celebrated poisoner of Paris, the Marchioness of Brinvilliers, her gifts thus solemnized at the stake, and her ashes sought as preservative against witchcraft.

Dawn broke, in the full glory of the dawn at sea. Some white birds had appeared. They hung behind the aftermast, breaking now and then to come down to the water for a look at anything thrown over the side. The rising sun found Stanley running damp and disheveled down a starboard deck. He paused at a ladder, hung on its wet railing to get breath, and then buttoned himself up in a number of places. He looked slightly surprised at the sun, as though it were an intruder, and might be a helpful one; but soon gave that up and carried on. His mustache looked like something he had fallen into, and his hair stood out in a heavy tangle behind. A waiter from the Tourist Class dining room stood to the rail out of his way, apparently taking for granted that Stanley was being pursued. But Stanley slid straight up to him, making a grab for him with one hand, waving the other,

—Have you seen her? Have you seen her?

—Ma signorino, che...

But Stanley was off again; and the waiter stood there at the rail for a good half-minute looking in the direction Stanley had come from, with the unhealthy expectancy of someone who has seen a number of American moving pictures.

Stanley covered a good part of the ship. At one point he almost made the chart room. At another he skidded into a tall white-haired man in a blanket robe and straw slippers, with the same question.

—Heving a bit of a run, eh? Good thing, better for you then all the ductors … good heavens. Ghood heavens! …

Stanley caromed off the rail, made another ladder, and was up it. In the ship's hospital he found the bed which had been a center of activity the night before, empty. Though Stanley could hardly know it, waking as he had, alone and moist, to jump up and spill those silver filigree beads all over the floor again, she hadn't got much head start on him, and perhaps as little idea, he did realize when he found her still running, of where she was going as he had.

And —Dead! she said when he did find her, and caught her wrist to hold her back.

Up the deck, now a covered one and near the water line, a group of silent men surrounded a long canvas sack, where Father Martin presided, a book in one hand, raising the other at the regular somnambulistic intervals of ritual.

—Dead! … and that damned black andro-gyne. He did it.

—But now you … now you … now …

—You know, you saw him, too, apply the poison, and the envenomed words …

—Now now now …

—No! … don't hold me here …

—Some Spaniard's all it is, I heard him talk. I heard the Viaticum last night and heard him talking Spanish.

—Let me go!

Upwind on the deck, none of them heard her cry out, none of them turned at any rate; and holding her, Stanley finally realized that she was making no effort to escape him.

With a sign, Father Martin was still, and the other figures took up his motion, as slow and as careful, they slid the weighted canvas bundle over the side.

With the splash, the birds came down immediately. The men and the priest had left the rail and gone forward, for the dawn was very bright on the water, and dazzled the eyes. Then she broke away from him and ran toward the rail. Stanley hesitated in surprise, and then started after her to hold her before she could jump.

But she stopped, and stared down at the dazzling sea.

Stanley stopped, and recollected enough to cross himself. Then he looked out, at the glare of the sea stretching everywhere the sky was not, and the notion of land as impossible to him as daylight on wakening from a nightmare, the sea the man had come out of, and gone back to. Then he recalled his dream: he had been crossing the street, carrying a tiny shawl-wrapped figure, and he met Anselm.

—No! . . . she cried out at the rail; and Stanley shut his eyes on the dream, opened them again on the sea, which had lost the glare of sunrise. The sea, romantic in books, or dreams or conversation, symbol in poetry, the mother, last lover, and here it was, none of those things before him. Romantic? this heaving, senseless actuality? alive? evil? symbolical? shifting its surfaces in imitation of life over depths the whole fabric of darkness, of blind life and death. Boundlessly neither yes or no, good nor evil, hope nor fear, pretending to all these things in the eyes that first beheld it, but unchanged since then, still its own color, heaving with the indifferent hunger of all actuality.

Stanley looked down, to steady himself as he took a step toward her, and the lines in the grain of the wooden rail swam over against themselves in imitation of the surface of the water, stretching like this beyond the morning mists which belied the horizon to where Africa lay, unknown to the senses, but borne in insinuations on the wind from the south. The ship heaved, shuddered, dropped its bows on the water. Down below, the white birds, finding nothing, startled by the clap of the hull, fled coming up all together, and away, like the fragments of a letter torn up and released into the wind.

—O Christ, the plough . . .
    —O Christ the what?
    —the laughter, of holy white birds . . .
    —What you reading? a poem? You know, you don't look so good. The man at the rail held out his glass. —Take a swat at this? He shrugged at the look of horror with which his offer was received, but continued to stare at the figure in the deck chair, a man who, in any other circumstances, might have been described as of comfortable middle age. Engulfed in the flow of a tartan lap robe and folds of Irish thorn-proof, he stared fixedly at an open book and moved his lips with precise effort.

The man at the rail took a bottle from his pocket to replenish his glass, and stared out over the water, through the morning mists toward the indistinct mound on the horizon. —That broken-down bump doesn't look like a life-insurance ad from here, he muttered, spat over the side, and wiped his chin. He had appeared on all fours, though somewhat taliped because of the glass he maintained upright in one hand, growling at a dog leashed to a tall woman who passed in the opposite direction, —a Hawaiian poodle dog, he explained. —Did you see what it's wearing? I asked her what the hell it was. A chastity belt, it's made out of plastic. Made in England. Huki-lau will need it among those naughty Spanish doggies, she says to me. Jesus. Grrrr-rouf! he lunged after the dog. —You getting off at Gib too? The figure in the deck chair responded with a feeble sound, amended with a nod. —Me too. Some spic sued my newspaper, they pay the bastard off and then send me all the way the hell over here to see what the hell is going on. They think he's blowing the money on a patron saint. You know, you don't look so good. He had straightened up and leaned back against the rail, sipping. —What you got in the paper bag? To be sick in?

—Bread.

—Bread?

The figure in the deck chair made an infirm gesture overhead.

—Oh, for the birds? The newsman steadied his glass at the rail and got a handful of bread out of the bag. —You look fermiliar somehow, you know? It's the first time I've seen you on deck the whole trip. The man in the deck chair made a vague gesture, down. —Oh, you been sick in your cabin? You missed all the fun then, you hear about it? the shipwreck? The man in the deck chair startled visibly. —We picked up these poor bastards in a lifeboat, one of them died yesterday and they dumped him back where they got him. An old tub called the *Purdue Victory*, it busted right in half. He paused to dip a bit of bread into his glass, and throw it at a seagull. —A foot of barnacles on the hull, salt water leaking in the fresh water tanks, rust flakes like your fist painted right over, they get in this storm and the rudder chain snaps, the sea swings it right around like a fighter turns a guy around in the ring when he's groggy to finish him off. Pow! The damn thing broke in half and went down in two minutes, both ends of it. They were going to scrap it anyway after this trip, you know? But that company's got a good lobby in Congress or it would have been scrapped ten years ago. So now with deep remorse for the guys who were drownded they collect a quarter of a million bucks insurance. Breaks your heart. He flung another whisky-soaked wad of bread heavenward, and watched his new deck companion labor a deep swallow and return to the printed page. —Whose poems? He squatted to look at the cover. —John Mansfield? You get them out of the First Class saloon? The man in the deck chair nodded. He tried a smile but it was obliterated by a grimace of swallowing.

—Sail on! sail on and on, you remember that one? Columbus? Behind him lay the blue Azores, behind him lay the Gates of Hercules, you remember that poem? Speak, brave Admiral, what shall I say? Why say, sail on, sail on, sail on, sail on... The newsman struggled to an almost vertical position against the rail and drank off half his glass. —He knew where he was going all the time, Columbus did. Did you know that? he confided. —Sail on, sail on, he knew he wasn't going to India. You know how he knew? Because the Portuguese already discovered America. The King of Portugal took one look at it and said to hell with it. You know who his mapmaker was? It was Columbus's brother. All the King of Portugal wants to do is get the spics the hell out of competition in the spice trade, so his mapmaker slips Columbus these maps so he can go discover America for Ferdinando and Isabella, give them something to keep them busy and get the hell out of the spice trade. The stout mate said, lo! the very stars are gone. My men grow mutinous wan and weak... And all the time Columbus is keeping two sets of logs on the ship, he fakes a set to pretend they're only half as far out as they think, while he knows they're going to America all the time. You know what Columbus discovered in America? Syphilis. They all crossed the ocean to get laid. Now speak brave Admiral, what shall I say?... With a full slice of whisky-soaked bread, he lunged into —Sail on!... tripped over the foot rest of the deck chair, and caught a foot under the rail. The bottle flew from his pocket, slid down the scuppers and smashed. He lay for a moment staring at the glass still gripped upright in his hand. Then without changing his position he raised his chin from the deck and drank it down, struggled to his feet, and calling out, —Here, chum, to a seagull flying as though hung suspended beside the ship, threw his empty glass at it.

The man in the deck chair opened his eyes. The hulk of Gibraltar was closer. Direct above, a white gull fixed him with a cold eye. He looked back at his book, and a few minutes passed while he looked up nervously and back at the page, until finally he got the paper bag and with an indecisive gesture attempted to toss a bit of bread up. The bird swooped.

—What's the matter, scared you?

—Up there flying, they're beautiful, but so close...

—Scared you, huh? The newsman recovered the rail limping, and pulled up his trouser cuff. —It's going up like a balloon, he said looking at his ankle. —Look at that broken-down rock, they ought to sink it. But oh no! Not the limeys. That would make too much sense. Instead they have this crazy superstition about these baboons that run all over the place there, that they'll lose Gibraltar when there aren't any more. So what do they do, they fly these sunset-assed baboons in from Africa when the stock gets low. They run all over the place there. How would you like to look up and see some sunset-assed baboon looking in your bedroom window? he challenged. —They don't hurt anybody, you know. Except the Y.M.C.A. It's yellow, the building. It makes them mad as hell. They come down and throw rocks at it. How'd you like to be a member of the Gibraltar Young Men Christians Association with a bunch of sunset-assed baboons throwing rocks at you? Favoring his swelling ankle he leaned on the rail and gazed back at the wake of the ship. —Behind him lay the Gates of Hercules. The blanched mate showed his teeth and said, brave Admiral, speak!

The man in the deck chair mastered a liquid swallow, and heaved slightly fixing his eyes on *The Everlasting Mercy*, reading under his breath in precise gasps, —Chra-hist, the laughter of hu-ho-white birds flying...

—A light! A light! Sail on, sail on. The son of a bitch knew where he was going all the time.

Stanley woke to cold hands opening his pants from behind, and lay there with his eyes wide open for a moment as the fingers became more intimate.

From somewhere, there came music. It was the tango, *Jealousy*.

Then he almost leaped out of the bed. —What are you...who *are* you? he cried, turning on the woman in white. She had a generous Scandinavian face. —Now wait, now wait, now wait...

—Now you lie down, she said. —You just lie down. I want to give you this suppository, sonny.

—This what? He stared at the cone between her fingers. It was Nembutal sodium in a cocoa-butter base. Then he stared at her. She smiled, and got his shoulder in a bone-breaking grip. Then he looked round him. The place was rocking gently. —I'm in the ship hospital? he asked. Then he looked at his wrist and said, —Who stole my watch?

—You'll be all right, now you just roll over and let me give you this suppository...

—Get me out of this bed, he burst out.

—You have to stay in bed for a little while longer...

—No but not this bed, not this bed...look all the other beds are empty, put me in another one, put me in that bed but not this bed...

With a pleasant smile and a turn of her wrist, she spun him round and his face went into the pillow. —But you...can't you...wait...

—Just relax the buttocks now...tha-at's it...

—But can't you...ummp!

—That will help you rest, sonny.

—But I don't want to rest. You can't just keep me here. Where's my watch? What day is it? And where...where is she?

The woman looked concerned for the first time, and she said, —Now we mustn't start that again, must we.

—Start...what again?

A waiter entered and started to approach with some food on a tray. Then he saw Stanley was sitting up, with eyes wide open. He put the tray down a safe distance away, and said, —Coraggio...

—Now what was that? Stanley demanded as the waiter got out the door.

—He's the one who saved you from jumping over the side.

Stanley lay back slowly. —The side of what? he murmured, but she did not hear him. She was busy unmaking a bed.

Spots of sun danced brokenly off the ceiling and down one wall. Stanley's head came back to rest against a metal bar of the bed. —But no... why would I... he commenced, raising a hand to his face. He touched his cheek, then his chin, pulled his hand away and stared at it, then began to rub his chin again. It was rough with stubble. —But how long have I... how long have I been here?

—Lie back and don't try to remember everything now, sonny boy, said the woman in white. —Lie back and get some sleep. She emptied a pillowcase briskly.

—But I do, I remember everything. I remember everything perfectly. Everything except... except that, if I did that, but I... I wouldn't do that. No!... He came up on his elbows again, —No it wasn't me that tried it, it was her, don't you remember? But wait, listen, first put me into another bed, I can't stay in this bed. Any of the other beds, they're all empty and it doesn't matter but... Then he stopped. There was someone two beds away from him. A face, clean-shaven but weary looking, rested on a doubled-up hand, the elbow dug into the pillow, watching him with patient curiosity. The covers were pulled up over the head, so that only the face showed. —What do you think I am, a seagull?

—Oh no, I'm... I'm sorry, I didn't see you, I hope I didn't disturb you but I... I didn't see you.

—That's all right, chum. I been listening to you for a long time now, I'm used to it. Have a swat at this? A bottle appeared, from under the pillow.

—Oh no, no thank you, no but listen...

—Play cards?

—No but listen, what do you mean you've been listening to me for a long time?

—Right up until you were excommunicated, since then you been real quiet, you know?

—Since I was what?

—You got excommunicated, right up at the high altar with a bishop and twelve priests, don't you remember? It sounded pretty swell, all of them carrying lighted candles and talking Latin, you know? And then they all shouted Fiat! Fiat! Fiat! and threw their candles down. And then she gave you a shot.

—Who? Stanley asked helplessly.

—That squarehead. She's got a nice ass, hasn't she.

The woman in white was approaching again from the far end, carrying some linen. She stopped to put the tray in front of the man two beds away, and smiled threateningly at Stanley, who sank back.

—It sounds like you were in trouble with some dame, said his neighbor, trying the mashed potatoes with his finger. —Just tell me one thing, will you? Who the hell is Saint Mary of Egypt?

—Why she . . . that's when I came down and found her in front of the mirror making up her face with make-up and lipstick and everything, and black around her eyes, and she had those streaks on her face, from the poison, I mean that's what she said, from the poison the black androgyne, I mean that's what she called Father Martin, the poison Father Martin put on him and it came off on her but only on her face. Because she said, See? and pulled up her dress to show me her . . . to show there weren't any marks on her . . . anywhere else on her body.

—You mean on her snatch?

—I mean then she said, This was covered when she lay with him, for he was poisoned here and so he died, but she shall not. That's what she said and then she said we're going to the Holy Land and she's going to be Saint Mary of Egypt going to the Holy Land on the boat.

His neighbor looked at him a moment longer, and then started to eat, saying —Thanks, through the first mouthful. —That clears up everything.

—And talking . . . Stanley mumbled, looking down with a fixed stare, —about the beast with two backs, he mumbled to himself, —about . . . making the beast with two backs.

It was quiet for a minute, except for the sounds of his neighbor's eating, and the distant radio playing something Italian. Then the blond woman loomed over him, and Stanley jumped as though she were going to strike him.

—Now you just lie back and try to get some rest, sonny boy. Don't try and remember everything.

—But I do, Stanley whispered desperately, —I remember, I . . . because all that time I repeated the Angelic Salutation and then I repeated the Apostles' Creed, and those beads were rolling all over the floor and the . . . the crucifix was . . . I couldn't hold it because . . . and then Father Martin came, you can ask him, he came in, that fat woman must have sent him because he came in and he put a hand on me and said something, and she was laughing. And I said thank God you've come Father she needs you and he just looked at me and she kept laughing. She called him a funny old hermaphro-ditic and asked him if he could relieve a possessed camel like Saint Hilarion did once. And then he held up his crucifix and she changed all of a sudden and said, Take him away he's hurting her, and she spat at him. But he kept looking at me, and he had his hand on me and I said, Do something for her, Father, I kept saying that, but he didn't pay any attention to her. He sprinkled some plain water around and nothing happened and then he sprinkled some holy water around and she started to cry then and she said her shoulder hurt her.

Stanley shivered, and stopped speaking. The woman in white had turned away, and was walking with a firm silent tread toward the other end of the place, down the aisle of beds. The man two beds away spilled the last forkful of his lunch in his lap, and swore.

—And then when I confessed, all the time I was kneeling, she kept...

—You better have a swat at this, said the other man, getting the bottle out again. He took a long swat himself, and offered it.

—No, because listen... Stanley commenced again.

—How about a hand of casino?

Stanley sat in the bed with his knees drawn up, and he let his head fall forward on them. He swallowed, and started to talk again, more rapidly, less loud and, with his head like that, less coherent, —Because when he said, "I exorcise thee, Stanley, being weak but reborn in Holy Baptism, by the living God, by the true God, by God Who redeemed thee with His Precious Blood, that thou mayest be exorcised, that all the illusions and wickedness of the devil's deceits may depart and flee from thee together with every unclean spirit, adjured by Him Who will come to judge both the quick and the dead, and who will purge the earth with fire. Amen. Let us pray..." when he said that she just looked at him and I could see her there, and she looked... she looked...

The blond woman had returned with a small tray full of bottles and syringes. She stopped at the other bed to clean the mashed potatoes off the counterpane, and the man slid a hand round her waist and ran it up and down her starched thigh. As she bent over him he blew into her ear.

—"to bestow Thy grace upon Thy servant who suffereth from a weakness in the limbs of his body," Stanley mumbled on, —"that whatever is corrupt by earthly frailty, whatever is made violate by the deceit of the devil, may find redemption in the unity of the body of the Church. Have mercy, O Lord, on his groaning, have mercy upon his tears..."

—In a minute, said the woman at the next bed, pulling away with a giggle and a snap of elastic.

—You see? I remember all of it, even all the words, Stanley burst out, as the woman in white put the small tray down on his night table and pulled one of his arms out straight. —And then...because then the streaks, those red streaks she had on her, it seemed like they were leaving her face, like they just sort of disappeared and she was as white as...as this, and then he said, "Therefore, accursed devil, hear thy doom, and give honor to the true and living God, give honor to the Lord Jesus Christ, that thou depart with thy works from this servant whom our Lord Jesus Christ hath redeemed with His Precious Blood. Let us pray..." and she...she'd started to talk too, and she was crying too, and she said, She will be a nun and sweat blood too, and sweat blood like Blessed Catherine Racconigi, and like Saint Veronica Giuliani and like Saint Lutgarde of Tongres, yes and like Blessed Stefana Quinzani on every Friday the sweat of blood, and conceal the Four Wounds, and hide the Crown of Thorns under her veil like that Poor Clare of Rovereto...*Owwwoww!*...Stanley screamed.

—Jesus Christ, chum...

—Now hold still, sonny boy, this doesn't hurt, just a little needle.

—But you...but you...no, listen! No! No, because I'm...don't! He cowered back at the head of the bed, away from her. The sun no longer danced off the ceiling and down the wall, but it shone in a steady weakening light of its own, no longer reflected off the water, but shining in through a porthole upon a heavy glass ashtray on another table, where he stared. The corner of the ashtray caught the sunlight and broke it into colors which changed slowly before his eyes, red, to green, to violet, to green, as the ship rocked gently. —Listen!...Stanley whispered hoarsely, drawn up rigid against the bars of the bed, the tendons in his neck standing out, —*Listen...*

There were distant voices, indistinct, broken by shouts from closer by, and sounds totally unfamiliar by this time, all sustained on the throbs of a dull pulsation, which went on, and had been going on all this time like the beat of another heart, but not his own.

—Listen...he repeated weakly. Then he appeared to fall off the end of the bed; but he was up, and with energy not his own, so far as he knew, for he knew his heart had stopped, he got to the door and pulled it open. What he saw stopped him. He staggered, and fell in two or three steps toward the rail where he caught himself.

He stared at the static landscape. It would not move, and he could not accept it that way, not moving, and so crowded. Here and there fragments moved sharply and separate, small boats offside, and people on the dock, cars moving slowly but steady against the hard land, and everything separate; even the noises rose with the discordance of differences, whistles and sharp cries, bells and motorcars breaking their edges against one another.

—Where are we? he said, as the woman in white caught him there at the rail.

—Naples, but you...

—But Naples, I have to get off, I have to get off here, I have to get off at Naples, tell them...wait...

—All right, sonny boy, you come back in to bed, we'll stop at Livorno and Genoa, and you can...

—Wait wait wait look look there she is, there she is, don't you see her? Look don't you see her?

He twisted out of the grip on his shoulder and almost went over the rail, pointing to the figures on the dock below. —Look don't you see her?...there she is, don't you see her?...with that man, don't you see her with that man, with that man in the black hat and the black coat and the...with the sling, don't you see them? Don't you see her? Wait! Wait! Wait! he cried, over the rail. —Wait...wait for me!...

The woman caught him by both shoulders, and dragged him back on his heels, back from that sudden landscape so crowded with detail. The ship's whistle shivered every fixture aboard. Stanley was heaving helplessly when she got him back inside. His eyes were closed, but he kept mumbling, —Now wait...now wait...now wait...as she filled the syringe again and thrust the point of the needle into his arm.

He lay shivering in the dim light, the sheet drawn perfectly straight across his shoulder, trying to speak but even as his lips moved, he could not make a sound. In his staring eyes, the image of the woman in white came up the aisle between the beds, carrying a screen, up the aisle. His lips formed, Now wait, not this bed, any other bed but not this bed, now wait...But he could not make a sound. He choked on a scream, Not this bed...but he could not make a sound. He felt for his pocket, but he had no pocket. He found his left wrist with his right hand, and all he felt was the naked wrist.

—Not here...not this bed...not yet...he whispered; and the screen stopped there two beds away, and came open.

Stanley listened: he thought he could hear the beads rolling on the floor; mounting, pausing, rolling back. —Pater noster, he whispered as they rolled, —qui es in coelis...His tongue found the hollow on his gum. —Qui tollis peccata mundi...no I mean qui...qui...who...

He coughed, and tried to say, Wait!...but found he was throwing up, and put his head over the side of the bed. Then he put a foot out, and it touched the cold floor. The sound of the engines rose, and with that his heart took up beating heavily, and he caught his breath and was able to breathe. Both feet on the cold steel floor, he steadied himself with a hand on his night table and tried to whisper Wait … but he heard, —What? … what am I … doing here? all I have … all I have lost … He was dizzy, standing.

The ship bumped, and shook. He held to the foot of the bed, and held the more tightly when the whistle sundered the only sounds he had, and failed, coming back from the harbor in fragments to augment them: the steady energumenical force of the engines, filling his heart to a shape rising from his chest to burst the bounds of his throat, and the squeaking, squeaking, squeaking behind the screen. That sound had begun unevenly, and then stopped, and commenced again with the regular mounting thrust and withdrawal of the engines and of his heart, faster, all of them as he came closer to the shadowless screen and behind it a moan, and gasps, the wary and then attacking steps and panting of the beast he approached silently, whispering unheard, —Wait … don't … don't … leave me alone.

It was nearly dark. The whistle sounded again, halting everything. Even the reversed engines stopped; then there was a consummate pause, and the engines, and his heart, took up slowly, as the starboard side rose, and he took another step forward. He had seen Naples.

V

Run now, I pray thee, to meet her, and say unto her, Is it well with thee? is it well with thy husband? is it well with the child? And she answered, It is well.

—II Kings 4:26

DAY DID not dawn. The night withdrew to expose it evenly pallid from one end to the other as a treated corpse, where the hair, grown on unaware of the futility of its adornment, the moment of the brown spot past, is shaved away like those early hours stubbled into being and were gone, and the day laid out, shreds of its first reluctance to appear still blown across its face where dark was no longer privation of light but the other way round as good, exposed passive and foolish at the lifting of chaos, is the absence of evil. The day existed sunless, its light without apparent source, its passage without continuity, not following as life does but co-existent with itself, and getting through it was to blunder upon its familiar features, its ribs and hollows, impotent parts and still extensions, with neither surprise, nor hope, like the blind man identifying with a memory-sensitized hand the body of a familiar in what they had both called life.

The sound of the bells sank on the air and was gone, while the clouds in shreds of dirty gray, threatening like evil recalled and assembled hurriedly, blew low over the town clinging for refuge to the embattled walls of the Real Monasterio de Nuestra Señora de la Otra Vez.

In the muddy plaza open beneath the wide porch of the monastery church, whose gothic façade and unfurnished rose window overlooked it, the village fountain spouted, and women with stone and copper jugs came to fill them. Their voices rose on hard sounds whose delicate edges went quickly to pieces and the words were lost, recovered and composed in that gentle mitigation, —Adiós . . . and gone on the soft monotonous confirmation until it was repeated, and every minute repeated, —dios . . . an expression of sound so much a part of that harsh chill and gray tranquillity that only lacking would it have been remarkable.

With the church doors unlocked, the porter stood a full minute on the wide stone porch, tapping the keys which he'd got strung to one end of a stick, most of them the length of his hand, and he was a big man, with long hands. He was old, and his face was scarred with memories of a disease half a century gone, a heavy face broken by ridges like the land before him where walls were built everywhere to clear small spaces of the stones. He wore a black cloth jacket closed with a single button at his throat, and after standing a full minute looking on the muddy plaza, he turned his bare head back to the walls of the monastery, and disappeared from view.

At that, the figure watching from above turned from the window, was gone the time it took to pace the length of the room and back, and then stood there again, staring down at the muddy plaza. There was a narrow balcony before him, and the window itself was set in the façade of the church, though it was a guest room. He raised his eyes, over the roofs of the town, and fixed his vacant stare on the cloud-steeped mountains. He was a comfortable man of middle age, dressed in an expensive suit of Irish thorn-proof, the last two buttons of the vest undone, or rather, never done up at all, in token of the casual assurance he afforded himself as a novelist successful enough to be referred to by his publishers as distinguished. At this moment he wore an expression of intent vacancy, his face that of a man having, or about to have, or at the very least sincerely trying to provoke, a religious experience: so it appeared to him, at any rate, when he passed the mirror and confirmed it.

He stood now, staring down at a boy poised on the balustrade of the church porch below, a boy big enough for the Boy Scouts, constricting his person to see how long a stream he could send out into the muddy plaza, where a sow and three pigs were passing in a dignified procession of domesticity. The distinguished novelist stared, to see, he was bound to admit to himself afterward, if the stream would reach, when a bird flew up against the glass square before his face, and continued to flutter there as he staggered back and almost lost his balance on the bricks of the floor. He recovered, returned the length of his room, and sat down on the bed. Notes for the magazine piece he'd begun lay on the table beside him. He saw them there and looked away. The moment of religious experience was gone again. The boy directing his stream from the very porch of the church had upset it; the bird had dispatched it. The distinguished novelist clasped his hands between his knees, and wondered if it were a mealtime.

The room was large and, in spite of not being especially warm, a comfortable one. On a white wall to his left hung a color print of a Raphaelite Madonna;

on the wall to his right, a picture of his hostess in stiff dark effigy, Nuestra Señora de la Otra Vez, the features of her deeply browned face marred and irregular from years spent underground during the Moorish ascendancy. In this picture, he could barely make out if she had a nose; he certainly could not tell if she were returning his stare, so he withdrew it and sent it elsewhere, wrinkling his nose with the sniff of impatience which had become more and more frequent the last day or so. He began to look uncomfortable.

The bed was set in an alcove. It was one of the softest he would find in the country, made up with a blanket of rich wool, and in this clandestine arrangement highly suggestive of pleasures beyond the walls, reminiscent of illustrations in Boccaccio, stimulating to every sense but the ascetic. He stood up abruptly, looking severely uncomfortable. And he was. He had come all the way from Madrid, along roads which got worse at every turn, changing his bus at almost every town for another more battered until the one he arrived in appeared to have been rolled to its destination over the mountain rocks like a barrel. That was a promising start, and it might have been difficult to know what his thoughts were as he approached the gray walls whose greatness gave way to delicacy in the gothic tracery of the spandrels over the arched doorway where he knocked. It might have been difficult, that is, had he not written some of them down before the spell was broken by the old woman who showed him to this guest room. ("Since it was well known that people from the world without seldom if ever win admittance to this almost inaccessible retreat, I felt throbbing within my breast the thrill of a deep emotion which I was powerless to describe, as I approached the soaring walls after an exhausting climb, and reached up to pull the cord of the centuries-old bell. Its gentle voice, sounding distantly just as it must have on that sunny day (snowy night &c) when Saint X (fill in) appeared at this same door, quickly summoned a lay brother of the Franciscan Order, who opened to me. He was still young, a slim yet virile figure, in the depths of whose piercing gray eyes I could read a message of patience and kindness seldom seen out in the bustling world of affairs...") The old woman, who had delayed opening to him, explained it by saying that they had to be careful of beggars. Since she spoke in Spanish, which he could not understand, he acknowledged her greeting with a few words in English, mustering an expression somewhere, he believed, between humility and beatitude. Seeing what appeared to be signs of illness rise to his face, she hurried away, and returned with a young monk who had been plaguing him ever since.

Fr. Eulalio was in his twenties, a fact which he never allowed to interfere with those exercises of gravity so necessary to his profession, which was not so much being a monk, as being a Spaniard. —Somos españoles, he would repeat with stern grandeur, —que es una de las pocas cosas serias que se puede ser en el mundo. And with these words of his, and indeed everyone's hero, José Antonio, on his lips, he had made that historic choice between church and state because, under present conditions, there were few other choices to be made. There was not much more to it than that, each occupation alleviated somewhat the miseries which the other magnified, and, in the absence of either, took possession. It was certainly no question of fear, or bravery: a recent civil war had shown the cowl as dangerous costumery as the uniform. And, in the case of Fr. Eulalio, neither would have smothered his busy curiosity with whatever came near him, his simple ambitions, and the naive audacity which led him to consider people from the outside world, outside Spain that is, as objects of rare interest, and present himself to them as the living breathing spirit of this land they were visiting. He came from somewhere in Andalusia. He had that primeval way of becoming friends, which was to go through the possessions of any new acquaintance, busy with comment on anything he recognized, questions for what he did not. The first thing he noted among the equipment of the distinguished novelist was a handful of books, and his first question, upon attacking them, was if there was among them a copy of *Como Ganar Amigos y Vencer Todos los Otros.* He spoke broken English with enthusiastic effort. Then he saw the typewriter, and he gazed at it with an expression much like its distinguished owner tried to muster when he saw the original figure of Nuestra Señora de la Otra Vez, in the chapel. He had already rolled a cigarette and offered it to the guest, who did not smoke, so he lit it himself, spat on the bricks of the floor once or twice to indicate that they both might consider themselves at home, asked how high the buildings were in New York, how many Catholics there were in America, and the amount of an ordinary laborer's weekly wage, when he put the cigarette out with a sandaled foot and hurried away. The distinguished novelist was just about to settle down and seek a blank spot on the wall to stare at, in an act of contemplating what he would describe as being "overcome by this overwhelming solitude" when, with a precipitant tap and a whispered, —Se puede?... Fr. Eulalio burst in carrying a large volume under one of the brown arms of his robe. The older man folded one hand over the other, assumed a somber air before what he gathered would be an exposition of the history of the monastery, or the Order, or some such, so carefully did the young monk handle it, and found himself gazing at the large pages of a private scrapbook. One after another, the breathless owner turned the pages, slowly enough that each might be thoroughly perused. They were all pictures of typewriters.

Neither the gray sky, nor the darker shapes of the landscape which lay beneath and seemed to have sunk there out of mere heaviness, had changed since the distinguished novelist had looked out at them a few minutes before. He had no idea of the time, for he had let his watch stop in a gesture of submission to the "lonely abyss of eternity" on whose edge he had expected to perch here. He turned his back on the window, and pounded a heel on the floor as though testing it for hardness. After a vexatious look at the bed, that is, as a matter of fact, exactly what he was doing, and he did it again, though the second time he used less force, and brought forth a less alarming ring. For somewhere, in this vast pile, were the plank beds, or straw pallets at the very least, which he'd expected to have been led to, and laid out on, there to glimpse the world these "good monks" lived in for long enough, at any rate, to pass it on to his fellow man. He struck a brick in the floor with his heel: obviously, he owed them something.

The sound of the church's bells reached him from outside, and he turned and struggled with the catch on the window, the gates of his heart already flung open, and its humble furnishings waiting to be flooded and swept away on the sonorous waves of those sentinels' voices ringing out their message of faith, to... He pinched his finger in the catch, and muttered something.

For he was not here to be converted. Neither did he have any intention of trying to convert his fellow man, or those earnest women, at home. He was not a Roman Catholic, or any other kind, and had no idea of becoming one. He considered himself, quite free and simply, Christian. If pressed, he might have been called Protestant, simply because he was not a Catholic. He limited himself to no special denomination, subscribed to no segregated cult, but held them all in equal esteem. As his writings showed, he found his duty to his fellow man in proselytizing for those virtues which bound his fellow man's better selves together, favoring none over another among the systems of worship he saw round him, honoring all, advancing in the name of some amorphous, and highly reasonable, Good, in the true eclectic tradition of his country, a confederate of virtue wherever he found it, and a go-between for the postures it assumed, explaining, not man to himself, but men to each other.

All of which meant that he reached his fellow man in large numbers, as his serene face (on the dust jacket), and his royalties, showed.

The windows burst open as the last bell faded from the air, and he found himself listening to the strident raucous tones of a barrel organ, pursuing some vulgar tune through the wet village streets below. The distinguished novelist banged the windows to, could not close them tight, and retreated toward the other end of the room clearing his throat. The bed reared before him, and he spun on his heel and sat down at his writing table, to stare at the papers, the few books, and the sign hanging before his eyes. The books included, instead of a dictionary, a Thesaurus of the English language, well thumbed;

a book of quotations, which stood him in the stead of a classical education; Baedeker's *Spain and Portugal*, the most recent edition (1913); and the Holy Bible, which he inclined to leave out, and opened, in token of the sanctity of his purpose here. One of the books had some pages missing, after a sudden attack of dysentery brought on by the oil used in the cooking; and as his eye fell on it and he realized again which of the books it was, he looked up quickly, and stared at the sign on the wall, composing his embarrassment by rereading these words he could not understand: *Se ruega, por lo tanto, a nuestros visitantes la más estricta moralidad y compostura en todos sus actos y conversaciones, y se recomienda a las Sras. que en el vestido se atengan a las prescripciones de la modestia cristiana.*

He made out the last word there, and the small initial troubled him. Then that look of intent vacancy spread over his face once more. True, he would have been more startled than anything else, if the Raphaelite Virgin on the wall above had rolled her eyes (like that Virgin of Rimini, first up and down, then laterally, then in opposite directions); or if the dark featureless figure on the wall behind him had spoken, or beckoned, or reached out and knocked him to his knees. Yet in a way it was something of this order that he awaited, something less threatening, less sectarian that is, for he could hardly admit to having come, like a vulgar Greek, seeking a sign: no, it was rather some vague, exotic manifestation of some equally vague and exotic Presence, a mystery of euhemeristic proportions and, brought forth in his own prose, amenable to reason.

The bird hit the glass. He jumped, and the vacancy left his face as details of irritation crowded to fill it. The bird was fluttering at the partly opened windows, and he hurried over to try to shut them again. This time he managed it, and stood there once more looking down. A young monk in the brown Franciscan robes was leading the bent figure of the prior of the monastery, Fr. Manomuerta, who was almost blind, across the porch toward the doors of the church. The old porter appeared briefly, dropped his shoulders and made a sign between his chin and his chest, and waited for them to pass. The prior was dressed in flowing white vestments which barely cleared the wet stones. All of which made the middle-aged man in the window above clear his throat behind the glass, and shift his weight from one well-shod foot to the other, as though caught intruding. He watched the doors close upon them with that self-conscious look which he meant to be read as respect, the look he wore when they opened drawers and showed him chasubles worked with thread of gold and studded with seed pearls, the wall where the chains of freed Christian slaves were hung, the exquisitely carved rail of the choir in the church, the superb retablo behind the main altar (which did impress him, for it was sixty feet high), the paintings of Zurbarán, an El Greco, and two or three sixteenth-century Italians in bad states of repair, in the sacristía, the marble penitent Saint Jerome by a Milanese, the tomb of a king of Navarra, the Moorish cloister, with orange trees, the gothic cloister, with boxwood. They had showed him all these things quite freely, and answered his intelligent questions readily (they, that is, through the person of a reserved man about his own age, and similarly built though the brown robe showed his prosperity to better advantage than Irish thorn-proof, and he spoke a few peremptory words of English). Even the prior, Manomuerta, who appeared and then disappeared with the silent ease of a ghost, smiled and bowed the head to him with a brief greeting. In short, he was treated on all sides (but for the forays of Fr. Eulalio) with a kindness and consideration which kept him a good arm's length from any of the revelations he had come all this distance to explore. There was, to be sure, the language barrier, which persisted almost everywhere but for that breach made under Fr. Eulalio's assaults, crashing through to ask the price of a suit in the United States, or after that book he so wanted, *How to Procure for Friends and Vanquishing of Everybody*.

So it went on, day after day. And now, if truth were known, he had prepared himself in advance to guard against any wiles which might be designed toward his conversion: but no one was trying to convert him at all. The meals were excellent, and this room, this bed . . . but no one seemed faintly concerned with his "spiritual side" as he called it in his fellow man: no one, in fact, even seemed to notice that he had one, however diffidently he approached. They treated him with the same gentle formality, from the same courteous distance of gracious condescension, that he had come prepared to treat them with.

He stood still at the window, staring through his own faint image in the glass. It is true, he did enjoy novel burning twinges on odd parts of his body at night in that bed, which might be a manifestation of some sort, though he suspected the coffee (for he did of course abstain from wine at table). In the same bed, he had developed a sort of dream, though it seemed he was but half asleep when it occurred to him: he was walking somewhere unremarkable when suddenly he tripped, or almost put a foot off something, or into something, and drew his foot back with a violent start, which woke him. That was all. And that too might be the coffee, for he did not smoke.

If he had, he would certainly have lit a cigarette now, as the sight of a soiled limousine parked up the street and almost filling it, clouded his face with the memory of the girls from the American Embassy in Madrid who had rolled up the day before. They got quite a kick out of the place, they said, and offered him American cigarettes which they were going to give to the Embassy chauffeur anyhow, if no one else wanted them. They left right after lunch, but their chatter and blank interchangeable images stayed behind well after dinner. —Well why are you in Spain?...if you don't especially like it? the distinguished novelist asked, once recognized and trapped. —A job's a job. —And you wish you were back in the States? —That's all we ever talk about, going home, but a job's a job.

His eyes followed the only moving thing in sight now, the slight unsteady figure of a man who had come out of the bar across the plaza, and was approaching the walls. He moved with uncertainties in his gait, hesitations before mud puddles as though unsure which way to take round them, though at that he often did not stop until he'd already got a foot into the water. There was none of the swaying vacillation of drunkenness, but a nervous combination of insistence and uncertainty.

Then the plaza was still, and he raised his eyes to the profiles of the mountains where the clouds had lifted, exposing the same gray sky at the horizon as the one stretched above. The distinguished novelist turned resolutely back to his writing table, sat down, sniffed, and wrote, "High in the brilliant sunshine of the Sierra de G——, weary and footsore after climbing the bridle path ~~from the peaceful which wends~~ wending its way ever upward from the peaceful valley town of Logrosán (?) into the forbidding landscape of Estremadura..."

A knock sounded at the door, and —Se puede? in a hoarse whisper.

—Fra Eulālio?...he gasped.

The door came open enough to permit the old woman to show herself pointing down her throat with her thumb, as though there were something lodged there. —Café, she whispered, sounding as though there were, and disappeared back into the dim tortuous passage leading to his apartment. He got up, put on a black necktie, let the ends of his mouth, and his eyes, sink, and set out. But in the door he stopped to look back, as though afraid of missing something. He had, after all, been here, waiting, for three days.

—Oh my God!...

—Whmmp?

—She wet on that...whatever you call it. Bad doggie! Bad sacrilegious doggie!...

—This would make a nice place to throw a party, said the tall woman's husband, pausing to look round him, as the poodle strained in the harnesses encumbering it at both ends, and pulled her toward the boxwood hedge.

—Parties, my God!...don't start that. What did we come all the way over here for? I hope I never see another party. She jerked the dog away from a gothic column, and added, —All you've been talking about is drinking ever since we landed.

—Well all you've talked about is eating.

—I have not, I'm dieting and you know it. What else can you do in this country but diet?

—Well, when you don't talk about eating, you talk about not eating. It's just as bad. He stood gazing round the gothic arches of the cloister. —Anyway, he murmured, —the food's usually better in these places than in a lot of the hotels.

—I still don't see why you wanted to get here at the crack of dawn.

—You would if you were paying for the car. And there wasn't any dawn, as far as that goes. Look at it. It might as well be . . . cocktail time.

—See? . . . there you go. They ambled on in silence, until she pointed with a scarlet-tipped finger, —Look at those old chains hanging up there, they save anything they can get their hands on. And look! . . .

—What?

—That man, isn't it . . . in the tweed suit, did you see him? I know I've seen his picture on book jackets.

—Yes, him. I saw him. Might have known you'd find him hanging around a place like this.

—I've heard things about him, that he was . . . Is he?

—What.

—That way?

—I don't know. He hasn't touched a woman since his third wife left him.

—He's gone, I guess he didn't see us. What do you think he's doing here? I've heard things about life in monasteries.

—He hasn't got that much imagination. He's probably writing another book.

—He's written fifty of them. If he had anything to say you'd think he would have said it by now. Why do they keep publishing them?

—Because he keeps writing them. And it costs a publisher more to lay off than it does to keep his presses running, so they feed anything in. A morose note of reminiscence had crept into his voice.

—Now come on, the tall woman said, taking his arm in five scarlet nails, —we're going to forget all about all that. She looked round for something to comment on, and her eyes fell on the dog. —Don't you think she *should* wear her belt when she comes into a monastery?

He laughed, or moaned, it was difficult to tell.

—Just the same, I saw a bad goat out in the street give Huki-lau a very suggestive look.

But her husband was not beside her. He had stopped to gaze back on the cloister.

—What are you thinking about now, turning into a monk, for God's sake?

He turned to follow her obediently, and mumbled when he reached her side, —Oh sure. A monk. I'd just as soon be dead.

But the man in Irish thorn-proof certainly had seen them and, for perhaps the first time in his adult life, he did not want to be recognized. He backed away from the colonnade, along the wall until he reached a door, and he backed through that. He went through a gallery, out into another court, was almost run down by a perambulating figure in the ubiquitous brown robe busy with the breviary, caught a hand in the swinging tassel and almost went over in a reeling attempt to avoid mashing the bare toes protruding from the sandal, grated out the first words of an apology and was silenced by a sweet and gelid smile, narrowly escaped falling backwards into the Moorish fountain, tucked in his black necktie and at last, coming sideways through the door, found himself entering the sacristía at one end as a man, the same he had seen making his unsteady way across the plaza earlier, disappeared from the other carrying something large and unwieldy under one arm. The distinguished novelist was, by now, not only breathless but excited to a considerably alert degree, and it took no more than a glance at the wall for a square unfaded expanse to assure him that a painting was missing. Whether it was the desperate hope of managing some measure of atonement for the collision of a moment before, or the sudden opportunity to repay the complacent hospitality shown him here, or just the chance to get into things, he did not stop to consider, but rushed the length of the room trying to get enough breath to cry out. Now although he had seen the man clearly, even clearly enough to be able to swear that he had screwed his already knotted-up face into a leer as he escaped, upon arrival at the far end of the sacristía the pursuer did not know which of the two doors he'd gone out. He did not stop to consider that either, but pulled open the first door to hand, summoning enough breath to call, —What are you doing there! . . . into the depths of the church. Whether his cry was heard over the *Te Deum*, he did not stop to consider, but got that door closed as fast as he could, and the other open. The stone passage was almost dark, but a bulb glowed at the far end, and he hurried toward that, bringing forth, with what breath he could spare, —Where are you going with that! Who are you?!

—Yes, what are you doing with that? . . . Where are you? he repeated, when he reached the hanging bulb, whose glow barely cast his shadow on the stone floor. He paused, and thought he heard nothing. —Where did you go? Where are you? he demanded of the walls. —Here now! He looked down at the hand he held before him. It was quivering. Then he thought he heard a faint scraping sound, and he followed it on tiptoe until he reached a small room whose sole illumination came from the space of gray sky in the window well out of reach up the wall. And there, sitting on the floor with the painting propped up before him, was the man.

—Here now, you... what do you...

The man looked at this intruder hanging in the doorway with a hand on either side of the door frame, steadying. He stared attentively, but from a face with no expression at all, neither surprise, nor curiosity, nor interest, nor any betrayal of intelligence at all. Then he returned to the painting, and the blade in his hand made scraping sounds on the canvas, barely more distinct than they had been from farther away.

—What are you doing to that picture? You there!... But the Irish thorn-proof was already beginning to sag precariously, with doubt, or possibly plain weariness. The delicate scraping continued. The painting showed a man in religious habit kneeling before a crucifix suspended in midair. —Do they know you took that picture? Do they know what you're doing?

—They? the man on the floor repeated dully, without looking up.

—They, the... the monks, the brothers up here, up there, they... I thought... The protest began to fail, as the intruder got in against the wall and quieted his breathing. Finally he brought out, —You don't have very good light. He stared at the moving blade. —Do you.

—That's all right. The blade went on, removing the corner of a windowsill, a high small window much like the one in this room. There were no chairs, but a table against one wall was laden with pots and bottles, sticky pools and spots and some bread. —I can't see very well anyhow.

—But... but you... isn't it cold?... to be sitting on the floor? The scraping continued. —And you... who are you? The scraping continued. —I... my name... my friends call me Ludy. People who know me call me Ludy.

—That's all right, said the man on the floor, still not looking up, his voice dull and even. —People I've never seen before in my life call me Stephen.

The Irish thorn-proof hitched slowly down the wall, and Ludy came to rest on his heels, squatted inside the small room.

When the damaged portion of the windowsill had been scraped away, Stephen turned and stared at him again, but with no more interest than before. Once turned so, his eyes did not move after details, but stared lifelessly for a good half-minute before he turned back to his work. After studying the painting with this same look, he commenced a meticulous attack on a table leg there. —Are they after you?

—Are who?... after me. Who?

The man shrugged over the picture. His lips were drawn tight, as though in concentration on his work; nonetheless there was something regular and mechanical about his movement, as the blade moved and its sound was the only one in the room.

—Who?... after me.

He stopped and put the blade down on the floor, rummaging in pockets until he found a bent cigarette wrapped in yellow paper. He lit it, and asked, —You're not wanted? The thick smoke rose over his face. It clung to the squared hollows of his cheekbones and curled slowly in the hollows of his eyes. He shrugged again, and returned to the painting. Blue smoke from the coal of the cigarette ran up its yellow length, broke round his nostrils and rose over his eyes, still he made no move to take it from his lips as he worked.

Ludy came forward, elbows on the thorn-proof knees. —Wanted? he repeated. —I?... I don't understand. I... I'm afraid you don't understand. When I followed you I... I took you for a thief.

—That's all right, Stephen said quietly, and no expression appeared on his face through the smoke. He went on working at the table leg in the painting, but he muttered —A thief... under his breath.

—But of course, now I see... you're an American too, aren't you. I started right out, calling to you in English, it's funny, I never thought...

—It's all right, Stephen brought his voice up enough to say. —I'm lived as a thief. Don't you know? All my life is lived as a thief.

—But you're... you're working. You're an artist?

—Yes, and lived like a thief. Then he turned his face up again, abruptly, though the cigarette retained its ash. —You're looking at my diamonds, aren't you.

—Well, I had noticed them. Ludy cleared his throat. —They're very nice, aren't they, he managed to say.

—They were a present, this ring. A present from the Boyg, was it? Yes. There. Why did you come here? What do you want of me?

—Well, you know, a little conversation in English for a change. And the tourists here. I didn't expect tourists. Women.

—Girls...

—And those awful girls from the Embassy. Coming right in. Right into the monastery. Eating here. They ate here. Did you see them?

—One of them gave me some cheap cigarettes.

—But you, being here this way...

—What way?

—Just...just working here, I mean. Living here, Ludy said looking round the stone walls again. —Do you live down here?

—No.

—Am I disturbing you? Your work?

—No.

—And...how long have you been here? Finally Ludy got no answer but the scraping. The leg of the table was almost gone. —You see, since you... since you're familiar here, I thought you might tell me some things about the place, since you speak English. It's a very wealthy monastery, isn't it. Why, I've seen cloth of gold, and seed pearls...

—The lay brother Eulalio speaks English.

—Him! I know it, but he...I didn't come here to talk about typewriters.

—Why did you come here?

—Well of course, something...an experience of a spiritual nature...possibly. Stephen looked up at him blankly. —A need for spiritual...something more spiritual than typewriters, Ludy finished, and shifted his hams on his heels. He cleared his throat and lowered his eyes from the blank gaze. —And when he does get enthusiastic about something spiri...something about the place here, this Brother Eulálio, it's even worse, he went on petulantly. —You can't explain to him that you don't shout about beautiful things, you don't try to...you know what I mean.

—You suffer them, Stephen said evenly, and the blade went right on, and the smoke rose against his face filling its hollows.

—Yes, why I was listening to the bells out there one morning, the campanilla, and he showed up and tried to raise his voice above them to tell me how beautiful they were. He's up and about early, isn't he. Why, he was showing me a chalice of some sort and he got so excited about it I thought he was going to jump on my shoulders. I couldn't appreciate it properly after that, of course. I wonder if they know what a nuisance he makes of himself, just because he speaks English, if you can call it that, prying around everywhere. Smoking. I didn't think that was right at all, a monk smoking cigarettes in my room. I almost reported him. Prying around...I suppose he's been through all your belongings too? Waving them in the air and spitting on the floor...

—That's how he found the pistol.

—The what? Found what, did you say?

—In the drawer. I had a pistol in the drawer, and he found it that way.

—A pistol?...Well, that...that must have put him off, a...a gun?

—He looked quite disappointed.

—Scared him, yes a...a gun like that...in a monastery.

—Oh no, no. He just looked shy, and then he looked at me and closed the drawer. He didn't say anything. He just looked disappointed.

—Yes...yes, I...I see. Ludy cleared his throat, and looked up so sharply at the profile before him that the impact of his glance seemed to knock the long curve of ash from the cigarette, for nothing else moved there. Then he looked down at the painting, and asked who it was.

—Navarrete...Juan Fernández.

—Oh...yes.

Stephen had leaned back from it, to spit the cigarette on the floor and reach for the bread on the table. He sat there chewing the bread with no more apparent sense of what he was eating than showed in his eyes for what he was looking at, though the half-loaf was gone quickly, and he was back at the picture with the blade.

—Navaretty, he was a monk too, was he? Ludy showed his interest in this religious by bringing his weight from his hams forward on his toes.

—He studied with Titian, the man bent over the painting muttered, working the blade more busily now. —Titian's paintings in the Escorial, he saw them when he went there to paint for the king, and his whole style changed. He learned from Titian. That's the way we learn, you understand.

—And you, you're...restoring this work? Ludy bent closer, got no answer, and went back on his heels against the stone wall. —You ought to have better light for such delicate artistic work, he said. —Especially if you can't see very well.

—Yes, ver-ry careful, it's very delicate... Stephen hunched more closely over the picture with his blade. —But that's all right. That's what they say about Leonardo now. Doctors say it, eye doctors. You'd be surprised. That's the secret of her enigmatic smile.

—What? Whose?

—The *Mona Lisa*, the *Mona Lisa*...whose! he muttered impatiently, without looking up. —Science explains it to us now. The man who painted her picture couldn't see what he was doing. She didn't really have an enigmatic smile, that woman. But he couldn't see what he was doing. Leonardo had eye trouble.

Ludy watched the blade approach a bare sandaled foot.

—Art couldn't explain it, the voice went on clearly, but low as though he were talking to himself, as he worked the blade. —But now we're safe, since science can explain it. Maybe Milton wrote *Paradise Lost* because he was blind? And Beethoven wrote the Ninth Symphony because he was deaf. He didn't even know they were clapping for him at the first performance. They didn't have an applause-meter, you understand. Somebody had to turn him around to the audience so he could see them clapping for him. Then Stephen turned his face up abruptly. —I have passed all the scientific tests, you understand, he said earnestly, his voice taking tone for the first time. But when he repeated, —You understand ... stopping his work to reach down another of the small loaves of bread, he spoke with the same dull voice. Though the loaf was hard-crusted, it broke easily between his fingers. The bread crumbled because of its fine gray texture. He crammed half of it into his mouth, offered the other half to Ludy, who shook his head quickly, and then threw it back up on the table. As he chewed, a thoughtful expression came to his face for the first time. Though he may only have appeared thoughtful because his eyes, directed at the painting, were focused far beyond it. He chewed on.

—There was a Beethoven Street in my home town, said Ludy. —We pronounce it just like it's spelled. Beeth-oven.

—If you're going to make loaded dice, you have to make them perfect first. You can't just load ordinary dice, they have to be perfectly true, to start with.

—Ahm ... yes, what I meant to ask you ...

—I've passed all the scientific tests, Stephen murmured, picking up the blade again and bending over the picture. —With science you take things apart and then we all understand them, then we can all do them. Get things nice and separated. Then you can be reasonable. Leonardo just needed glasses. That's the enigma. He got busy with the scraping again.

—I meant to ask, who's this a picture of?

—This is Saint Dominic. He thrashed himself three times a day.

—What?

—He invented Rosaries. Our Lady revealed the Rosary to him.

—You're Catholic, then?

—Once a possessed person confessed that anyone who's constant to the Devotion of the Rosary will surely be rewarded with life eternal. But you've probably read Ganssenio's *Vita Dominici Ordinis Praedicatorum Fundatoris*.

—Why no, I ... I'm afraid I haven't ... run across it.

—You may have forgotten it, Stephen reassured him, going on busily. —It's all in chapter five, De auctore Sanctissimi Rosarii, ejusque efficacia. Now do you remember?

—Ahm ... vaguely, but ...

—He enclosed nuns too, he went on without looking up. —Strictly cloistered. Most of the Inquisitors were Dominicans.

—Ahm ... this, Ludy commenced, bringing his weight forward again to inspect the picture, —this little figure of ... the figure on the cross here is interesting, isn't it.

—That's Jesus Christ.

—Why...yes, yes of course. What I meant was...Ludy cleared his throat. Stephen straightened up, and held the blade before him as though it were a brush, and he was sighting some line along its tip before adding another touch to the canvas. Ludy sniffed helpfully. —This crucifix, what I meant was, the figure isn't...it looks alive...He sounded embarrassed, at having got into this, but he went on, —A little...almost a live little mannequin...ahm, responding to...ahm...you see a great variety of ahm in paintings of the Crucifixion, the expressions on the face, don't you, some of them show an agony that is downright ahm...you can hardly say human, but...and then some of them...I mean to say, others...

The man sitting on the floor brought out another yellow paper cigarette and lit it. —In some of the cheap prints He just looks bored, Stephen said, and got back to work with the blade. —Have you seen El Greco's?

—I...I don't think I've come across it. Ahm. There's an El Greco painting here, isn't there. Here in the monastery, up in the...one of those rooms, a picture of ahm...there's a white bird coming down...

The blade stopped. Stephen darted a look at him, an instant in which the same leer Ludy thought he had seen on his face reappeared, but he got immediately back to work, even more busily, the cigarette smoke clinging to his face. —The *Descent of the Holy Spirit*, he said, a suddenly hungry tone in his voice. —He studied with Titian too. We all study with Titian.

For almost a minute, there was nothing but the rapid scraping of the blade, and Ludy came forward further and further until he almost went off balance. —But...he finally brought out, —the foot here, it's almost gone. You...why are you taking it away, it...this whole part of the picture here, it's not damaged.

—Yes...Stephen whispered, —it's very delicate work. Why you can change a line without touching it. Yes..."all art requires a closed space," ha! remember Homunculus?

—But wait, stop! What are you doing? Ludy brought a hand up as though he were going to interpose. —You can't...

Stephen turned to him sharply. —Be careful now, he said, as Ludy dropped his hand and sank back against the stone wall. —I've passed all the scientific tests, you understand. And I have a lot of work here, very delicate, strength and delicacy...

—But you can't...Ludy protested weakly.

—That El Greco up in the Capilla de los Tres...

—Yes...?

—I'm going to restore it next.

—But you ... there's nothing wrong with it at all, it's ... it's in fine condition, that painting.

—Yes, he studied with Titian. That's where El Greco learned, that's where he learned to simplify, Stephen went on, speaking more rapidly, —that's where he learned not to be afraid of spaces, not to get lost in details and clutter, and separate everything ...

—But you can't, they won't let you just ... take that painting and ... and do what you're doing ... Ludy was rising slowly, the Irish thorn-proof back against the stones, sliding upward with his weight as he drew away from the figure on the floor, still busily working the blade. But his stare was transfixed by the squared hands, one of them gripping the picture with the long thumb along the top, the other blinking the two diamonds from the middle finger as the sound of the blade went on. Ludy closed his eyes, and opened them again, as he neared his height, and sniffed. —You ... He was looking at the face, where nothing moved but the curls of thick smoke against its hollow surfaces. And then he cracked his head against the stone wall behind, so startled that he threw both hands up before him.

Stephen had jumped to his feet. —Do you want to see ... see one I've already restored?

—But you ... you ... The Irish thorn-proof, the back of his head and his hands drawn back,. Ludy stood flattened against the stone wall. He stayed so as though pinioned there, staring at the moving figure before him in the dim light, as the table was dragged away from the opposite wall, all the while Stephen was talking in a voice which was strangely breathless and at the same time unexcited,

—A painting ... a ... a Valdés Leal, I worked a long time on it, it ... yes there's warmth in it, I worked a long time on it, you'll see that. Venice, Venice ... we all studied ... yes Titian, you'll understand, we all studied ... with Titian, working out this ... harmony, yes, it ... you'll understand when you see it, this ... this picture.

Holding to the end of the table with both hands, he stopped and stared at Ludy, who had begun to wilt against the gray wall. And when he repeated, —Yes, in a hoarse whisper, the same shock of a burning showed in his eyes, but he turned back to the table quickly, looked there uncertainly and mumbled something, grabbed up the half-loaf of bread he'd tossed there a few minutes before, and went on, looking behind the table and talking and chewing at the same time, so that his words were at once muffled and disconnected.

Possibly if he'd been still and talked evenly, Ludy would have turned and got out the door; but now he stood against the wall, moving his lips slightly as though trying to finish the sentence which would dismiss him, bringing his hands out loose and empty to press them back against the stones immediately, then bringing them out again if only the distance of their own warmth from the wall, to complete the gesture which would allow him to escape.

Meanwhile Stephen was muttering and he kept looking up as though he were talking to people in all parts of the small room, at one moment looking over Ludy's shoulder and hemming him in that way, then addressing an empty corner, or the table itself, with things like, —Separateness, that's what went wrong, you'll understand . . . or, —Everything withholding itself from everything else . . . and the moment Ludy started to turn away the eyes caught him again and he sank his weight in Irish thorn-proof back against the gray stone wall, as the voice broke out,

—You'll say I should have microscopes for this . . . delicate work. Yes, egg white, egg yolk, gums, resins, oils, glue, mordants, varnish, you'll be surprised how they're put together just to bind the pigments. We could take X-ray pictures, infra-red, ultra-violet . . . Layers and layers of colors and oils and varnish, and the dirt! The dirt! Look at that, that picture there, look at the crackle on the surface, that's from the wood panel expanding and contracting and the paint crackles when it gets dry. If we had a microscope with a Leitz mirror-condenser, we could turn it up to five hundred diameters, put on a counting disc and make a particle count of the pigment. Then we measure its thickness with a micrometer, put the Micro-Ibso attachment on the camera and you . . . If we had a micro-extraction apparatus we could bore holes in it too and get some nice cross sections out, put them in wax and then you slice them in half just like that with a microtome knife. And when you get that under a microscope with polarized incident light then you can really see what's going on with a carbon arc lamp, you'll see when we get into the high oil immersion series of lenses. You'll see, if we can fix a microscope up with polarized light and put a particle of the pigment under it, we can see whether it's isotropic or anisotropic, for that we use nicol prisms. Then we determine the refraction index of the particles of pigment and then, well then of course, then we know exactly . . . the dirt that collects, and one layer of varnish after another, and the dirt that collects in every little ridge and crack century after century, then we'll know. Here's the secret, laying transparent oils on heavy thick ones. Bosch . . . not Bosch. The transitions . . . Leonardo put on wet paint with the palm of his hand . . . dark brown underpainting all the way, and . . . that plasticity, that plasticity. And . . . and . . . if we can get a good reliable particle count, the refraction index on each particle and whether it's isotropic or . . . when you get down to the gesso, you . . . what was it? What was it? . . . You . . . yes, the El Greco, I . . .

—No, you . . .

—Next.

Ludy still stood with his back flat against the stone wall, and it was not only the eyes, each time they darted at him, which held him there, but the stifling sense, which increased every instant, that the doorway was not open, that there might be no doorway at all; and inching in fear of confirming such a possibility, his hand moved as slowly as he could let it, toward the door frame.

—Yes, the El Greco . . . that . . . using carmine for shadows, and . . . the red and yellow ochre for the flesh . . . the flesh, the . . . hematitic . . . painters who weren't afraid of spaces, of . . . cluttering up every space with detail everything vain and separate affirming itself for fear that . . . fear of leaving any space for transition, for forms to . . . to share each other and . . . in the Middle Ages when everything was in pieces and gilding the pieces, yes, to insure their separation for fear there was no God . . . before the Renaissance. He stopped speaking with the effort of lifting a panel from behind the table, and he rested it there, its face turned to the wall. But once he got it there he commenced to mutter again, —Everything vain, asserting itself . . . every vain detail, for fear . . . for fear . . . Then he snatched up another of the small loaves of bread in the hand that bore the ring with two diamonds, steadied the panel with his elbow and tore the loaf in half.

Ludy's hand had reached the door frame, and his fingers began to curl against it, pulling his whole weight in that direction of escape, when they touched cloth, and stopped.

—Yes, do you remember, Cicero, in the *Paradoxa?* . . . and he gives Praxiteles no credit for doing anything more than removing the excess marble, until he reaches the real form which was there all the time. It was there all the time, and all Praxiteles did was to remove the excess marble, and here . . . here this is the . . . the one I just restored, the Valdés Leal . . .

—Hahauuuu! . . .

—You . . .

—Who? . . .

—He? He's been standing there, Stephen said calmly, as calm as he had sounded when first intruded upon. —Didn't you know he was standing there? Stephen asked, with the same simplicity he had shown when he was discovered at work. —You know him, don't you?

—Yes, he . . . he's the janitor here, Ludy got out, staring up at the porter who filled the doorway, and with apparently no idea that his presence had provoked any more than mere notice, showed no sign of moving. He stood there a good head taller than the figure in Irish thorn-proof, and seemed to stand as massive and motionless as the walls, out of respect for the engagement he had interrupted.

—Casa con dos puertas, mala es guardar, eh? Stephen addressed the old man easily, and pleasantly. The porter answered him in the same familiar manner, and shrugged his heavy shoulders. He lowered his head, and a smile commenced to break the lines on his face, pressing the disease scars away until they were almost out of sight in the flesh. But the smile stopped there: the lines restrained it, and the scars showed out.

—He's like all the old men I've ever known, Stephen said quietly, as the panel under his elbow came slowly face down on the table.

Ludy stared at the square of gray sky in the wall above while they talked in Spanish, pressing his heels against the wall as though he were going to leap for it, though their voices were low and casual, and Stephen shrugged and almost smiled as he spoke, a shock which brought Ludy down full-footed on the floor, slowly, but looking at the figure standing by the table with incredulity as though he had emerged from the stone. Nonetheless Stephen's smile stopped where the other did, unrestrained by deep lines and scars, but it stopped.

The old man was talking, and Stephen, looking at him as though listening, said in a low tone, —He comes to watch me work sometimes . . . and got out a sharp constricted sound near a laugh as he picked up the remaining loaf from the littered table. —He says it's like Sigismundo in the cell. You've read that haven't you?

—No, Ludy answered helplessly, looking down at the space between the leg and the door frame as though he might try to slip through it.

—You haven't read about Sigismundo in the cell? "Vive Dios, que pudo ser!" . . . falling off a balcony into the sea, though there's trouble there because Poland has no seaports. Vive Dios, que pudo ser! You haven't read *La Vida es Sueño*? Here . . .

Ludy saw a piece of bread held thrust before him. He took it and stood holding it. He could hear the old man chewing beside him. The two figures seemed to be crowding him to the wall.

—He is a penitente, Stephen said, close upon him, —when he came out of prison. Though think! . . . for him she's still a child, and beautiful in wax, while his face is old and broken like the ruins everywhere here, the past left where it happened. There's a permanence of disaster here, left where we can refer to it, the towers of the Moors lie where they fell, and you'll find people living in them, whole cities jealous of the past, enamored parodies weighed down with testimonial ruins, and they don't come running to bury the old man, but give him the keys to the church, and he rings the bells. He says she comes to him carrying lilies that turn to flames when he takes them. You see how I trust him.

Ludy looked down at the bread, which was crumbling in his hand. —I ... I have to ... go ...

—I have to trust him. That it comes to this, envying an old man. Why, two thousand years ago, thirty-three was old, and time to die. "A curse on youth, that age must overcome; a curse on health, that illness destroys; a curse on life, which death interrupts!" You know Buddha's immaculate conception, and dead of an indigestion of pork? "Age, illness, death, could they be forever enchained!" I have to trust him, for we're here together now, and penitent for rape and murder.

—You've ... killed someone? Ludy said looking up at last from the bread crumbling in his hand, to see the lines round the same dull eyes draw into the beginnings of a wince, so close he could see the clotted buds of veins broken beneath the skin of the eyelids, as the lips tried to force the wince into a smile but only become tighter and tighter as Stephen spoke, breathless but not excited, a purely physical halting of his voice, as though there were not enough breath at once to finish all that he had to tell.

—In Africa, Algeria, the bullet went right through and broke his neck, in Sidi-bel-Abbès, I'll tell you. *J'ai le Cafard* he'd got tattooed across his forehead, in the broken letters of a child's hand ... He paused, looking into Ludy's face anxiously, an appealing moment, until he brought up the last of the bread and bit into it fiercely, hunched to catch the crumbs in his empty palm.

—"Mon Légionnaire!" A ghoum, simpering up to the table where we sat, I and the poor policeman arguing if daylight time was black upon the moon. "Et toi, divine Mort, où tout rentre et s'efface, accueille tes enfants dans ton sein étoilé ..." The poor policeman read Leconte de Lisle. And he called me romantic! for planning escape to the desert. "Shave and clean up a bit," he says, "or I must arrest you." No money, no papers, it's more shameful than being naked out in the streets in daylight. But at night we talked, the girl gashed with tattoos in Djelfa, or her in Biskra wearing louis d'or at her throat and a safety pin in her ear. "The desert is well patroled, and you're dead in four hours without water. It's romantic! I won't permit it. I have my duty to do. You speak of reality. No, I know these stunts," he goes on, we were friends, understand, "hiring a camel and setting off in secret, to journey a night and a day and turn your mount loose in the desert, and lie down and wait for the dawn. 'Affranchis-nous du temps, du nombre et de l'espace, et rends-nous le repos que la vie a troublé.'" Then he looks at his watch. We were friends for some time there. The blue gash down her forehead, and up the chin and the heels, three hundred francs in Sfax on a Saturday night, the gold louis d'or and the feathers and bars in the door. Or tea in Bou-Saâda, she offers it bristling there on the rug on the floor, the porches ready to fall from the fronts of the houses, and her mother stays in the room, guarantee that she's Ouled-Naïl for the dance that shocks the French tourists, the musicians play to the wall and it jumps like something was living and jumping inside, in town, while their stripes stretch over the edge of the desert near the shells of colonists' houses. But here where the Legion's quartered, the black beard grows, "Défense de raser," she tells me, "les médicastres français s'entendent," encouraging crabs. And the guards wilt with bayonets fixed in the street. So here's Han, in the Legion, a ghoum, coming up to our table on the walk outside the café. Le Cafard tattooed on his forehead, but wait. That's nothing, you'll see, when they took down his pants. He stops to spit on the road, and looks up like an animal, "You! You have come here to join us! What pleasure this is, to see you, at last, here, to join me again. Hey? . . . how fine it will be now, together. Where have you been all this time, since Koppel, remember? Do you remember? The old fool he was. And Frau Fahrtmesser, and Minchen, the pig and her daughter, remember? How happy we were! Die Jungfrau? And how young! Do you remember all that? And now! my dear friend, how fine it will be, together. At first it is hard, but I can watch out for you, hey? At first the Legion is hard, but with me, you and me, you . . . but you . . . but that's why you're here? to join us? to join me in . . . this? . . ." And he holds up his khaki shirt bunched in a fist, standing over me. "Yes, no other reason for coming to bel-Abbès, but to . . . come in . . . with me?" So the sun had gone down, and when I drew back and said "No," he stared for a minute. He stared, and he hissed, "And now you! We were cheated, now you . . . I will tell you both how we were cheated. They betrayed us, and now . . . I will tell you." He spoke low, he was gathering force that might have escaped in his voice, and his shoulders climbed higher restraining, until he could say, "I hate you. I hate you very much. Do you understand how I hate you? Even then, I hated you . . . there was something missing, and I always hated you, even then, or . . . it wouldn't be so missing." Then he rushed at me. The bullet caught him right through, and broke his neck. Sir-reverence, the bastard was dead. And since then, I've been wandering. The policeman turned up his face with the toe of a boot, and then let the blue letters roll back in the dirt, and the wind blew the blond head full of dirt from the street, and since then I've been traveling. "Get away! You were not even here! Do you understand? Get away!" And what could I do? The policeman . . . we were friends for some time there. He stood over that thing in the dirt with his gun in his hand, and when two or three people had seen it he put it away unfired, and looked at his watch, and since then I've been moving. He knew. We'd talked so much together, he knew he was sending me on, and since then I've been voyaging, until I came here. It's a place here to rest, to rest here, finally, a place here to rest, and the work, to start it all over again, alone . . .

—But these things…don't happen…I have to go.

—But wait! Wait! I haven't told you, when they took down his pants he's a face tattooed on his fundament! There's homage for a whole coven, wide eyes on the cheeks. Wait!…there's a kiss he'll remember. Ehh? And I knew it, going around with a bum like that, blue eyes…Wait!

Fr. Eulalio, his eyes fixed reverently on his toes flattening in the sandals at each step, emerged first from the Capilla de los Tres with a measured tread, one which he was, however, seldom able to measure for more than ten paces. At that point, some enthusiasm usually took hold, and he inclined to break into a disciplined but irregular dance, no matter how retiring his partners proved, so they were from Outside. At this moment he even had his hands clasped, and for a parlous moment, stood stock still at the door.

—I don't know whose tomb it is, but we might as well go the whole hog while we're here and take it in, said a woman, emerging.

—Boy, that big picture was some mess wasn't it, the Rubins, said a fat man in a brown suit and yellow necktie, who had apparently joined them. Two cameras swung from his neck, and a light meter, all in new leather cases. —Rubins, was he a Spaniard?

—Look at his name, Peedro Pablo, where else do you get a name like that? the woman with him answered. She was totally undistinguished, but for the ring she wore. It was gold, and large, and very modern, and suggested those articles which are advertised as "silent defenders."

The tall woman waited for her husband. Fr. Eulalio stood entranced with the morning's haul. But looking up, he commenced to vibrate, as though a marvelous set of springs were concealed under his robe; and if anything was required to set them in motion, it was the sight of the figure he saw now in fleeting glimpses of Irish thorn-proof, dodging behind the Moorish columns which surrounded them. For next to introducing himself to Americans, nothing gave him greater pleasure than introducing Americans to each other, and the opportunity of introducing four to one, and that one a noted writer, —un escritor muy distinguido, muy culto…He almost sprang across the Moorish fountain.

The distinguished novelist saw there was nothing for it but surrender, and tried to compose himself as he was led forth, if only for that minute of courtesy which his position demanded. He came out wiping his hands on the seat of his trousers.

—We didn't know you were Catholic! said the woman with the ring, delighted, extending that hand, and withdrawing it more slowly, separating her fingers and glancing down surreptitiously to see what the sticky gray matter lodged between them might be, while her husband, bobbing amid the leather cases, lost his good-natured grin as he shook hands, and retired to wipe his on the seat of his pants.

—Well, you see . . . the distinguished novelist commenced; but he was unequal to it. He tried to arrange his debilitated features into a smile, and turned to the tall woman with a weak inclination which he meant as a bow.

—We're going to see a tomb, she said, —the tomb of . . . somebody or other, have you seen it?

—Yes, he answered instantly, and stared at her so oddly that she turned to her husband and said,

—We can't just leave poor Huki-lau out there all alone, even if she is wearing that . . . protection, you never know.

Fr. Eulalio, meanwhile, moved busily enough among them to give everyone the feeling that they were in a crowded room, and as though for reassurance that this was not the case, the tall woman's husband turned his blank gaze up to the shreds of gray cloud which fled over the Moorish cloister. The distinguished novelist excused himself: he had a little work to do before lunch, and he got away.

—It was him, that stuck his head in the church and asked me what I was doing there, the woman with the ring announced. —You wouldn't think he'd act that way here in a place like this.

—Maybe he's just playing a game, the tall woman said vaguely, preoccupied with a high heel caught between the teeth of a broken mosaic. —My God . . .

—It's hardly worth all this walking around everywheres, the woman with the ring said, —We haven't got any color fillum in the camera at all, they don't have it here.

Fr. Eulalio, meanwhile, explained that the distinguished novelist had recently suffered the death of someone very close to him, a sobering conclusion which he had drawn from the customary manifest of the black necktie.

Thus they were all slightly put off when the distinguished guest appeared in a calming Glen Urquhart plaid suit, and the necktie of the Honourable Artillery Company, though none of them knew its signification any better than he (for he'd just picked it out one day, passing Gieves's window in Old Bond Street, in London where he'd gone for first-hand experience of quite a different nature). It was a bracing pattern of jagged dark red strokes on a blue ground, and he looked quite restored.

It is true, he was happier taking lunch in the chill room at that small table near the windows, knee to knee with a calm lay brother appointed to the task, the heavy red cloth drawn over their laps and warm to the waist from the brazier underneath, with a cage over its coals to protect toes protruding from sandals, an arrangement rather like a communal Persian bed he had seen somewhere (not Persia).

—We've had plenty of experiences to write home about already, said the woman with the ring at the long table where lunch had just commenced, presided over by a placid Franciscan who spoke no English. The tall woman closed her pill box with a snap, as her husband poured his second glass of wine, and the woman with the ring crossed herself and got her napkin in place in one utilitarian gesture.

—We even got held up by a highwayman, her husband confirmed.

—It was on a train.

—You still call it a highwayman anyway, her husband said patiently, smiling his cheery smile. —And he even talked English.

—It was broken English. And what do you think he told us? That we're just as much to blame, because we're there, that the victim abets the violence just by being there, he said, and he even made a quotation to prove it.

—From Dante he told us. He took all our money, at gun-point.

—Every peseeta we had on us.

—But he didn't take the cameras, the fat man said, —I guess he didn't know how much they were worth.

—He said he ought to do us a favor and throw them out the window, can you imagine? My... don't they keep it cold here, she shivered.

Her husband got out his billfold and found a scrap of paper. —Here's a souvenir of it. He made me write this down so I'd remember to get this book and read it. *Transcendent Speculations on Apparent Design in the Fate of the Individual*, that's a mouthful isn't it. I wrote this down at gun-point.

—Can you imagine? she demanded of the distinguished novelist, and he shook his head as though indeed he could not. Then he turned to the soup which the old woman put before him, and commenced to eat with a look on his face as though, perhaps, he could.

—Well you can't complain, said the fat man good-naturedly, —when you set out on an adventure trip in a country like this, like Mamie and me here with nothing but the clothes on our back. Right, Mamie? Then he lowered his attention, to wipe a spot from his yellow tie on the edge of the tablecloth.

—We didn't even bring a car over this time, said the woman with the ring. —We're going right down to the Holy Week in Seville as soon as we leave here. I wanted to see the big fair they have in Valencia too but I don't know how long we're over here for, it's not till later. They call it the Fallas, it's all fireworks. Then she turned to the tranquil figure at the table head, and addressed him in what she believed was his language, for she, with some of the girls back home, had taken a course, preparing for exactly such opportune exigencies as this. —Cuando tiene las Fallas en Valencia? she asked, and repeated, —las Fallas?...but since she pronounced it phallus, the good Franciscan answered with a gelid smile and offered her the bread.

The tall woman cleared her throat, passed the wine decanter in answer to no one's request as far up the table as she could reach, and said that somewhere she had read that in this very monastery a monk had been put under a pot for refusing to go out and beg, and that he was still there. Had anyone seen it? —The pot, I mean.

No, but when the woman with the ring and her husband were in Granada, a guide took them on a tour through the Hospital de San Juan de Dios, and they had had to look at the crippled and deformed orphans, —which wasn't really the kind of thing we came all the way over here to see, we didn't know where he was taking us.

—That cathedral they have there, it's the biggest one I ever saw.

—And the sound when that gypsy boy's head hit the pavement...

The distinguished novelist remained bent over his plate; and whether or not he appeared as contemplative as he believed, he did at least thus thwart any attempts to draw him into conversation, until, that is, someone asked him directly if he liked the art here...

—Ahm...

—Like that big El Greco, the picture of the...

—What? Is it safe? Is it still... he broke out, looking up abruptly.

—What?

—No...nothing, I...I was thinking of something else. The...ahm, yes it's a...an excellent picture, the ahm plasticity of the modeling, the transition of ahm the heavy oils laid on transparent ones, a great clarity of ahm religious purpose without getting lost in a maze of details, of ahm...for fear that there may be no...Ahm...

—I've seen another picture of his, they make me nervous, everybody seems to wiggle too much in them.

—We saw a big Pietà in Granada, I like him better. Aren't you chilly?

The distinguished novelist attacked the fish on the plate before him. It stared up with one round insolent eye, and he severed the head at one blow. The world of art settled, that of religion reared intrepidly.

—That was probably the village idiot.

—But won't they let him in church? the tall woman demanded. —In our church at home, of course I haven't been in it recently but we used to have one, an idiot I mean. Every small town had one, just like they had a town drunk and a Jew, but of course we didn't have any of these little boys in red sleeves to get him out the door. And that boy swinging that brass thing on the end of the chain made me frightfully nervous. It looked like it was going to blow up any minute.

The fat man looked self-conscious, and stopped to rub another spot from his necktie.

—And were you in the sacristy when they were getting that old priest ready to send on? I don't know, all that lace, and the way those little boys flit about . . . She saw the distinguished novelist looking at her uneasily, and went on hurriedly, —I don't mean to say they're that *way* or anything but . . . one hears things, she murmured, looking down at her plate. —Tell me, she whispered to the woman next to her, —what are these perfectly weird little things we're supposed to be eating.

—Lentils. Haven't you ever eaten them?

—I've read about them, the tall woman said and put down her fork.

—To tell the honest truth I don't really see how they eat like this all the time. I've had the johnny-trots ever since we got here. From all the oil. Do you have . . .

—I take reducing pills. You swallow one before a meal and it blows up like a balloon in your stomach. You lose your appetite. Not that one wouldn't here anyhow. Have you looked at the bread? I don't mean tasted it, but just look at it. It's practically turning red.

—My husband would know what it is, said the woman with the ring, examining a piece of the bread. She broke it, and the fine gray texture crumbled. —My husband's in food chemistry. He studied toxicology at Yale. Her husband took the bread from her and examined it with a pocket magnifying glass. —He's with the Necrostyle people, she said, —you must know their products? Then she nudged her husband, and whispered that maybe he was being impolite, —because they're very sensitive, these people. Even if they're monks.

—Micrococcus prodigiosus, he pronounced, snapping the glass closed and looking up with his cheery smile. —It forms sometimes on stale food kept in a dry place. Looks like blood, doesn't it.

—He's giving you a funny look, the woman with the ring said to her husband. And when at a sign from the figure at the head of the table, the bread was taken unobtrusively away, she whispered, —Oh dear, I wonder if we hurt his feelings . . . And she'd just started to speak to the tall woman, in a very low tone of frank confidence, —They're pretty behind the times over here, when we landed the customs almost arrested me, they thought my Tampax was incendiary bombs...Then she realized that the figure at the head of the table was addressing her, in slow careful syllables.

—He's explaining about the bread, she whispered aside, listening, —why it's funny. Concentrating, her lips moved as though to wrest the words from his, syllable by syllable while he spoke, and turning to explain when he paused, —because it's real hard to get flour over here, especially if you're poor like monks, they have to get it off the black market. That isn't exactly the way he put it, she amended when his silence unleashed her full confusion. —He says they even get food packages from America, like there was this Protestant minister who came here on a visit about thirty years ago and he always sends them these packages of food, they just got one lately. Then this is where I got sort of mixed up, she confessed, while the figure at the head of the table watched her querulously. —I think it's something he wants me to explain to him, because in this last food package they just got there was some kind of powdery stuff in a tin box they mixed with the flour when they made this bread, and it came out funny. Maybe it was cereal, except I'm not sure what's the Spanish word for cereal. Maybe it was wheat germ, my husband could probably explain it to him, like enriched bread like we have home, except I don't know what's the Spanish for wheat germ. She sighed, looking almost wistfully at the scrap of bread by her husband's hand on the table, a hard crust, the crumbled fine gray texture flecked with spots "like blood." —Home, she repeated —Now, with it's almost Easter...She sighed again, and smiled pensively, looking far away and rubbing the slight hair shade on her upper lip. —Isn't it nice we're all merkins.

At the head of the table, the figure nodded to her his thanks for her explanation to the other exotic guests and she, seeking to please him still further, was fishing for something in her bosom. The ring got caught, and finally she extracted it along with a string of beads which proved to be a rosary. —And see this here? she said to the others. —This little heart-shaped thing in the middle is full of Lourdes holy water, see it's stamped right on there, certified. She passed it up the table. The Franciscan looked at it with the polite interest he might have shown for a Zuñi prayer stick, and returned it as she went on, —My family's in religious novelties. Mostly plastic ones. Last year we got out a plastic shofar, for Yom Kippur. It was filled with candy. It went real well. Show them your key chain, she said to her husband, digging him with an elbow. —See? she said, showing it. There were a good many keys, but she got the plastic-enclosed picture free. —See? you just move it a little and his eyes open and close, see his lips move just like in prayer? And the hand he's got up in a benediction even wiggles a little, see? See the halo move when you tip it?...These go real well. It's a whole series of art-foto key chains. She started to pass this devotional object up the table, but the good Franciscan appeared to be absorbed studying his thumbnails.

—Of course, not being Catholic ourselves, the tall woman said to her, —my husband and I don't always appreciate these things, you know. I'm sure he thought he was going to get a free drink in church.

—Well we're converts ourselves. You catch onto things after awhile. She lowered her voice and looked vacantly past the ceramics on the wall. —The spiritual meaning of the Mass, the elevation of the Host, and the when they break the bread...

—Well of course in our church we had the Lord's Supper...

—And everybody got a drink, the tall woman's husband came in. He'd recovered the decanter. —This morning the old man in the middle up there got three drinks, he mumbled, —and nobody else... could you understand him?

—Well, they do it in Latin, the woman with the ring said soberly.

—It sounded to me like he was singing, I can play dominos better than you can...

The tall woman rescued the decanter and started to pass it back up the table, but put it down because it was empty. —To tell the truth, she said to the woman with the ring, —my father was born one, but of course he never told anybody at home that, you have to be so careful in a small town. He had an awful time, he even had extreme unction.

—When he died?

—Oh God no, he's still alive. That was before my brother was born.

—But once you have extreme unction administered to you, then if you recover you have to eat fish and... renounce matrimonial relations.

—Then it must have been something else he had.

—I can play dominos better than $_{you}$^{oo} cannn... came in a cooing chant beside her.

—Frankly, she said in a low tone to the woman with the ring, —I don't want to see *him* getting mixed up with any of this. He's already got two analysts waiting for him when he gets home.

—better than $_{you}$^{oo} cann...

—You can see what I mean.

The figure at the head of the table rose, and the woman with the ring, brandishing it like a weapon as she undid her napkin and crossed herself, turned to him and said with oppressive clarity, —La comedia está muy bien. And the Franciscan, who had not been to the theater since he took orders, inclined his head to acknowledge her kind manner, though she could not see if he wore his kind smile because he held a napkin over his mouth with one hand, picking his teeth behind it with the other.

When they got outside, Fr. Eulalio, who had been confined somewhere in the depths of the great fortress this past hour or two for reasons best known to his superior, joined them again, and hoped they could find room to take him to Madrid. It was something urgent. If he went now, he believed he could get a ride back somehow that night, or early next morning (he was going to see about flour on the black market). The distinguished novelist excused himself, looking haggard and unsteady despite the bracing stripes of the H.A.C. He tripped on the stairs.

—My, he is odd, isn't he. One almost wonders . . . The tall woman's voice tailed off, as she looked abstractedly up at the walls, and murmured, —My God, you'd think they were expecting the Russians. Then she recovered, adjusting her hair with her scarlet nails. —You know frankly, I haven't seen a soul around here who looked frightfully holy. They all look quite easy-going.

—They've got the life of Reilly, her husband said, licking his lips.

—Here, we ought to leave them something, an alms or whatever you call it, to pay for the lunch. Have you got some of those big brown bills? And there's the old porter out on the front porch, should we give him something? They always show up like this at the last minute . . .

She came back looking quite confused. —He wouldn't take a penny!

—They're very proud, said the woman with the ring, —even the poor ones.

—Well he has so few teeth he certainly can't eat much, but I thought he might buy himself a drink, he probably drinks, and from those marks on his face you can see he probably *has* something . . . she went on, closing her pocketbook, turning toward the soiled limousine where Fr. Eulalio was already climbing in. —And that one asked me what Huki-lau's belt was, my God! What *could* I tell him? Nevertheless, she added as she watched the brown robe disappear inside the car, —I *am* glad she's wearing it.

—Goodbye . . .

—We may get down to Holy Week in Seville ourselves, it sounds a riot.

—Or if you're still here, or maybe next year, Valencia . . .

—Next year we *are* going to Hawaii for the Narcissus Festival.

—For the Fallas.

—Goodbye . . . Isn't it a God-awful day . . . The soiled limousine rolled, choked on the hill, barely missed a mule approaching the fountain with solitary dignity, and a child squatted in the gutter, and turned from sight.

—Look! Bernie, look! said the woman with the ring, waving it toward the porch on the gothic façade, —that man, that funny man talking to the janitor, don't you see him? Haven't we seen him before? on the train? at gun-point on the train! Wasn't it? Look, or . . . wasn't it?

Her husband was turned in that direction, but he was busy. The yellow necktie, which appeared to have pictures of brown sailboats on it, kept blowing in his face, and he was trying to adjust a light meter to the bleak even color of the day.

"The world is too muhvh with us, late ans soon, gettijg and spendinf we lay wasre . . ." The distinguished novelist glanced up to read what he had written. The ribbon was sticking. He pulled it. Something snapped. He sniffed. A soft scent of perfume reached him. He raised his hand, and sniffed. It was the tall woman's perfume.

He did not leap to his feet, but sat there at the writing table a minute longer, gazing at the machine, the papers, the spines of the books, and the sign. He sagged, and the bold strokes of the Honourable Artillery Company appeared to support him. There, at his elbow, were the notes he had made toward a touching and inspiring novel about the Children's Crusade, that deeply moving episode out of religious history which served incidentally to disembarrass the South of France of the remnants of the Albigensian purges. There was also the list of those concepts he tried to keep before him while he worked, and pass on to his fellow man. The separate words were in capital letters, and included: FAITH HOPE CHARITY CONSCIENCE FAIR PLAY COURAGE and HUMBLE.

Both hands braced on the table, he rose, poured cold water into the basin, washed his hands, and pulled out the stopper. The water fell loudly into the pail below. Then he lay down on the bed and pulled the soft cover over him, noting it had begun to rain lightly outside. His foot twitched once or twice, and then nothing moved in the room for some time.

Dull patches of the olive trees tempered the deep green mountainsides. Columns of smoke rose straight up. And everywhere were those blue tones which Leonardo observed in nature, and warned the painter against as an optical illusion.

The muddy plaza was as busy as any local at the end of a work day. Mules and burros arrived, singly and in pairs, horses appeared at a trot, shied, threw up their heads, illustriously horned cattle sauntered up, some for a quick drink at the fountain and they were off home, some hung around for another. A sow and three pigs went up the street and in at a doorway. Goats climbed to the porch of the church, butted each other through the, balustrade, and left pebble-droppings on the steps. Smoke from the pitch-top chimneys of the village carried the kindred discord of their bells over the tiled roofs. For a minute or so, there was not a human being in sight.

The distinguished novelist waked with a start, as though someone had yanked his foot. The room was dark. He huddled there for a minute with his eyes wide open, and pulled the soft wool blanket over his shoulder protectively. Then he turned his head slowly, to see who had roused him. There was no one there. He sat up, sniffed, licked his lips, and then threw off the blanket and hurried across the uneven floor to the windows, which he pulled open. At first all he saw was the moon, a sharp shape in the clear sky waiting in continent ambush. Then he made out the jagged black rim of the mountains, and he smelled the smoke loitering in the valley. From somewhere, he thought he heard music. And then, from the very doors beneath him, figures appeared, to form a procession. Led off by a boy in white, two lines of women in black came adjusting their veils. Between them, two boys with candles enclosed the tall white-figured priest. He watched them down the steps, past the dark fountain, singing softly into a narrow street where lights appeared at windows on their way. He watched them out of sight, and then hurriedly closed the windows, pulled on the light, sat down at the writing table and cleared his throat, trying to clear his head of all he had seen and heard during the day, from the worldly pastimes to those which he could, at this distance, be assured had never happened.

"As the brilliant spring day drew to its peaceful close, I stepped forth from the cell to which I had been assigned by the spare yet virile old prior, and where I had come to know unwonted pangs of loneliness, sleepless nights and Spartan fare..." He had to type with one hand, for he was pulling the ribbon along with the other, so he worked with reverent slowness. Through some vent in that vast stone pile, exhalations of the organ reached him, and the overhanging light, dim at its best, went dimmer each time the organ rose. Beside him on the floor where he'd thrown it, lay the crumpled writing of a day before, the delicately telling description of the preparations in the sacristy before a high Mass, which, upon rereading it after overhearing the tall woman's remark, appeared too delicate and too telling, and he realized it might be misunderstood. (It was that sniff of her perfume that did it.)

"Beneath the clear star-studded canopy of the spring night, the darkness was transfigured by the voices of these men raised on high in a shining message of faith to all men mankind. At this moment I recalled the simple candor in the face of Saint ~~Dominic Francis Dom~~ a saint painted by ~~the great Span-ish artist El~~ an unknown Spanish artist of long ago, and it was this same glowing faith that showed in the ~~figures~~ cowled figures before me, moving into the shadows without a faltering step. One felt, at that glorious moment, that their faith lit the way before them, escorting the Eucherist to their beloved Superior, who lay now hovering between life and death. The same Gregorian chant, perhaps, that rose to these very walls some ~~thousand~~ centuries agone, ~~rose~~ came gently forth ~~once more~~ yet once more, too soft to echo from the stones. Rather, there was the inspiring suggestion that the simple and beautiful melody lived on in the stones which had witnessed and overheard devotions from time immemorial, and the ~~diving~~ divine errand passing before them now drew it forth. Their pace did not hasten, despite the crucial nature of their ~~divine er~~ purpose, but moved at once inexorable and resigned to the will of Him who drew them forth ~~on this divine~~, carrying the Eucharest to that ~~beloved~~ humble ~~man~~ figure even now being delivered from the life that bound them together, even as did their singing in this darkness on the earth they trod. So it was that late that night, when the ~~beloved old~~ venerable man had passed across the veil to his Heavenly Reward, I lay back upon my hard pallet and considered the world whose sounds still rang in my ears, and where I must, perforce, so soon return, the world he had voluntarily shut out so long before, the world of vanity and selfishness, of lies and deceit, of wars and rumors of wars, of men devoting themselves to the service of both God and Mammon ...”

He stopped, to gaze at the wall showing blank between the machine and the reproving sign hung above the table. The light dimmed almost to a mere color, and rose again, at which the bird outside struck the glass, and fluttered against the pane; but he saw nothing and heard nothing, preparing himself for the leap:

“And then of a sudden, my heart ~~started~~ sprang up in my breast, as I ~~un-derstood~~ found the true meaning ~~in of~~ in the message ~~brought~~ held forth ~~for~~ to all mankind, of all faiths, and creeds, and color, in this symbol of life eternal. My bones no longer seemed to cut through the flesh into the hard pallet where I lay, the night air engulfed me but it was a night in spring, and it raised me up. For as the lights of their tapers shown so small against the gigantic darkness of the night, still they shown from afar off, as they lives they ~~led~~ lead shine ~~in atonement~~ before Him ~~wh~~ Who created all, in atone,ent for the dark deeds of the world ~~they~~ today. No, I thought, such lives as these cannot be in vain. And as the fresh life ~~of~~ in the air rose everywhere about me, the symbol which these good men bore to one of their number soon to be taken from them ~~among them~~ amongst them became a part of ~~it the~~ it.

The deep thrill of the Spring, and of all life reviving, paralyzed me for that instant as, ~~w~~ even now, Easter week approached, and with it, the message of life beyond the grave, and to all ~~mankind~~ humanity, that hope which springs eternal in ~~the human breast~~ every human breast that opens its portals to its fellow the service of ~~its fellow~~ man., and in this expression of ~~His~~ the divine will, ~~no longer~~ fears death no longer, but ~~procures acquires secures insures obtains nears~~ draws nearer to Resurrection."

He sat back, and drew his fingertips across his forehead. Then he stood abruptly, and turned away from his achievement. His chest, which had caved during this exercise, filled with a deep breath, and the bold strokes of the Honourable Artillery Company stood forth, as he strode across the room to the windows. He had had faith, but he realized, looking down now on the drift of roofs below, broken in genuflection, from the facade pitted by five centuries, it had simply been a question of time. At that moment the bird fluttered against the glass. Its wings beat the panes, and it clung with its delicate talons to the leading which separated them. It struck at the glass, at the same time turned its head from one side to the other so that its beak did not strike, its tail spread in balance. If it was the light that attracted it, that was soon turned off; for the bird was gone when he took the blanket over near the windows, and lay down to sleep on the floor. He felt he owed it to them.

Nor was it difficult, waking next morning in the sensual shelter of the bed, to believe he'd slept on the hard bricks. He had spent a numb quarter-hour there and now, hurrying over to stand before the windows, the inspiring hardness of the uneven floor beneath his feet erased the night in bed (for if he'd dreamt there, he could not remember), and he looked out at the dawn with eyes as clear as the early sky itself, and features as reasonably detailed and separate as the illuminated composure of the landscape before him, where the world had emerged from that dangerously throbbing undelineated mass of the unconscious, to where everything was satisfactorily separated, out where it could all be treated reasonably.

He looked relieved, and got the windows open. The voices he heard came from directly below, where he saw Stephen and the old man arguing on the porch of the church. What it was he could not make out, since it was all going on in Spanish. They would come nearer the doors of the church and then the old man would back him away, waving the keys he had there on the end of the stick. Once or twice it looked as though Stephen were going to seize them, but the old man got them up out of his reach, and then, the third or fourth time that happened, the old man closed with him. From above, they looked about to grapple, but the porter had an arm round the younger man's shoulders, and as he talked led him over to the steps, where he went on talking to Stephen in lower tones, gesturing now and then with the rod away toward the mountains.

In the window, the distinguished novelist turned away once or twice himself, as though caught, or fearful of being caught, eavesdropping, but he kept looking back down at them. Finally he did go over to the writing table, and turned papers up there for a minute distractedly. And when he got back to the open windows, he saw the old man standing down there alone. He looked where that one appeared to be staring, saw nothing but an empty street ascending out of sight behind the walls of houses, where, a few minutes later, he was climbing himself.

He'd looked over the seat of the Irish thorn-proof trousers, found it in need of no more than a brushing for the gray matter dried there, put on the suit and come out for what he'd have called a meditative walk, by which he seemed to mean aimless wandering amid unfamiliar scenery, qualified now by the consciously exerted realization that he was now, after his period of enclosure, outside the walls.

Like everything else, the road was flat stones turned up on edge for footing, and he was soon up behind the town. The only sound to reach him where he'd stopped was the regular tinkle of a bell, resting up against the jaw of a burro chewing somewhere near. He stood there as though this betrayal of rural tranquillity had engaged his whole attention, as though some innocent line from the *Eclogues* had turned up for the first time since he'd left Vergil behind in a dusty schoolroom and never read Latin again anywhere but on public buildings. It was an expression of rapt, almost beatified innocence, one seldom seen but on the faces of men carrying on some vile commission underhand, or something which they, for childhood's shame, consider vile. Then he realized that he was being watched.

An encounter with a lunatic in the wilds of Portugal is described somewhere by George Borrow, the figure discovered sitting alone, on a stone, and staring, as the most vivid interview with desolation that that intrepid spreader of the Gospel ever suffered: something like this froze the distinguished novelist now, looking up from the small cloud of steam he'd raised before him, to the figure seated motionless up the hill, outside the arch of a four-door square gothic ruin. It might once have been a tower, or a chapel, at this remove from the monastery below, or nothing at all to do with it. And sitting there staring down was Stephen. He hastened to button up the Irish thorn-proof trousers and approach with a greeting to belie his embarrassment.

—Look!

Startled, Ludy turned to look. Seeing nothing, he asked, —What?

—The sky. If no one ever painted it until El Greco did? Look at it, the Spanish sky.

And glad of an opportunity to escape the strained face and the eyes, Ludy stared out at the sky. He stared; and found himself trying to find something to fix his eyes upon, but every line led him to another, every shape gave way to some even more transient possibility. And he stood there trapped, between the vast spaces before him and the intricate response behind to which he almost turned, seeking some detail for refuge, when the voice in strained calm over his shoulder stopped him, gave him, at any rate, separate fragments to hang one sense upon while he suspended the torment of loss through the other.

—The Pleiades are rising, now, now is the time. The Greeks put to sea now, in their system of navigation this was the time they put to sea, with the Pleiades rising, and I have to go on. It wasn't so simple,

—I see, you're ... going away somewhere?

—My father was a king. Did you know?

—Oh? ahm, yes and ... Ludy fumbled. —Ahm, and where is he?

—Yes, where is he? "Kings should disdain to die, but only disappear" somebody said. He took me up like this once, and he showed me the world like this. Yes once, remember "I was that king, and all these things were mine! See, Ananda, how all these things are past, are ended, have vanished away..."

And with this, Ludy was suspended, doubly bereft: the silence, untroubling a minute before, became as empty as the sky; and as he'd sought the sky with his eyes for something to fix them on, now he did that and listened too, for something to break through the fearful vacancy which was tolling his senses one by one until, in this absurd anxiety mounted in him from the consciousness at his back, he abruptly saw himself darting his eyes' attention everywhere, sniffing, clutching at anything, even grass, to taste, speaking to hear. —And where was that? he brought out listening. —Yes, where did you live? he waited, for any answer and getting none twisted about, ready to repeat the question with no reason but to rescue them both from silence, as a sound broke in his throat, to be swallowed, and he listened.

—I? in a world of shapes and smells. The things that were real to other people weren't real to me, but the things that were real to me, they...yes they still are.

And listening, the strain in the voice was there but it was different, an extreme concern but without anxiety, intent, but without those shocks of frenzy which had backed him against the stones yesterday, in that cold cell where the eyes turned up from the canvas struck him back into the arms of the old man in the door. —I saw you this morning, looking out my window, what happened down there?

—I woke up and I thought it was evening, Stephen answered immediately, but then he paused, as though still uncertain and trying to remember. —And there was a sound of clanking and scraping, it sounded like the port of a ship swinging open and closed. It was strange, a strange feeling, I could almost feel the room roll and go. Then I reached out my right arm to straighten the shade on the floorlamp, it was crooked, but half the arm was asleep. Right along its length, and the tingling made me drop it, but I got it up again and I straightened the shade. But the shade kept quivering. When I let it go it kept quivering and that made me nervous, so I reached out to stop it again. But it kept quivering. I watched it, and I began to realize that it was quivering with a regular rhythm, a regular beat, and beat, and beat running through it, and I felt my heart pounding in the back of my head with that same beat. And then the whole table began to throb. When I looked at it it stopped, and when I looked away it began again. I closed my eyes. The only thing I knew was my heart beating as though it would break through my collarbones. And then I came out. I came out and the sky wasn't getting darker, it was getting light. I'd slept the night through there.

—Yes, you ... look rested. Ludy said that looking up at him intending, with the look confirming the word, to escape both; but the word —Rested! repeated, closed on him and he stared lost darting among the contrivances of the face before him, until it turned away, and released him on a hoarse whispered, —Rested?

—Yes, you were going into the church this morning? and then, the old man...

—He wouldn't let me in.

—Yes but. I shouldn't think he could tell you...

—Standing out there on the porch with his keys, he was looking at the dawn himself, and he wouldn't let me in. Rested? when I thought I'd found a place to stop. But he wouldn't let me in. What did you think we were doing, arguing, if he wouldn't let me in.

—Well to tell the truth...

—All right, that's a way of putting it. "To tell the truth." All right but, finally if the things that were real to other people, weren't real to me? and if... never mind. But it almost ended that way. If he'd let me in it might have, ended that way.

—Why wouldn't he let you in?

—No, you don't understand? being real just like that? It wasn't so simple.

"To tell the truth," I like that though. "To tell the truth…" Listen, here's part of it: He sent me on. Go where you're wanted, he said.

—Yes, if you've … killed a man … Ludy withdrew slightly, —to give yourself up…

—Killed a man! that? That, that, there's no fruit of that. Killing a man, no that's got nothing to do, it ends right there. Stephen was looking down into the palms of his hands, trembling opened before him, the thumbs crooked in and the skin drawn tight bringing color to the lines: he looked, as though searching evidence for acquittal in hands which like the heart, knew their own reasons.

—I didn't mean…

—What?

—But there was something else I meant to ask you, I…

—In a killing like that, you don't get permission, you don't seduce, you don't agree. You don't even touch. So there's no breaking faith there. In a killing like that, they don't consent, he finished in a harsh decisive whisper, dropping his hands slowly, and then taking up again, his voice became clearer, the words more rapid working out their own logic. —Go where you've sinned, and give yourself up, do you think I mean the police? Why do you think he sent me away then, just like the old man sent me on. Do you think it's that simple? I did. And it wasn't. They wouldn't let it be, they weren't … children. And now, to start it again. I've been a voyage, I'll tell you … "To tell the truth … ?" yes, but not yet. I've been a voyage starting at the bottom of the sea. I willingly fastened the tail to my back, "I'll scratch your eyes till you see awry, and all you see will seem fine and brave…" Good God, what a luxury he was! A journey like him sailing off the Cape forever, the Germans dressed that up, though, with a woman, but it's not that simple. Come into Toledo at night, it's monstrous, with only the stars, the heaps of broken buildings, all weight and shadow, and you'll never see it that way again, after you've waked the next morning and walked through the town all laid out under foot in the daylight, and where were you wandering the night before? It's all different by daylight. Find Valencia, with the sky brocaded with fire, in the heat of the summer, there's a telephone exchange there *Sangre*, I liked that. The women fanning themselves in the trains, fanning down into their crowded bosoms, that old woman's face like La Mancha after the July harvest. There are pieces spread everywhere. "A souvenir of New York," he'd ask me for, or "Give me some money for medicine," always medicine, and he'd show me a swollen leg before he'd play the guitar, and say it was his heart gone bad, that old gypsy looking at my frayed cuff, and he said he could have it fixed nicely, he'd a

friend a tailor. It fit him, too. Hiding money in another pocket at the last
conscious minute, and then the next morning searching everywhere for it, the
shame of it! . . . and then finding it, so carefully put away, and out to celebrate
the husbandry of the night before. Commuting between disasters, and always
the land and the sky, and now, starting it again? I'll tell you how cold it is
in the desert at night, and they think Africa's only the heat of the sun! I was
only there because I wasn't anywhere else. You'd see a town with two walls
overlapping, and a man disappear into the wall, everything regulated to the
gait of a camel, an ass hobbled on a brown rock hillside and palms at the bottom. Do you wonder why I'm telling you all this? Do you believe me? Here . . .

He got up and rummaged in his clothes, and came out with a fragment of
clay pottery; some other things dropped but he didn't look down after them.
—That's from Leptis Magna, it's not pretty is it, you can still see the thumb-
prints on it, from molding the edge here. What do you keep a thing like that
for, from Leptis, and Arabs crouching making tea over sheep-dung fires on
the marble floor, the temple of Hera, and the lilies sprung from her milk, and
the Roman's ruins run right down into the sea.

Ludy stooped to pick up what had dropped, some crumpled one-peseta
notes, and a raggedly cut out picture on canvas stiff with the cracked paint,
a sharply detailed figure of an old man drawn out, being flayed by detached
hands. —This, he said, holding up the likeness, —it's the old man, the porter
here, is it? The face . . .

—Old men, he's like all the . . . old men, Stephen said, starting to reach for
it, then he waved it away. —He told me . . . look at their difference in ages, he's
sixty and more, and she's still a child, and they're still in love. It's . . . that, now
do you understand? It's here he can be closest to her now, while he's waiting.
But for me? That's when he said no, and sent me on again. He's here, a penitent? . . . but it's different, for she comes to him here, and . . . all this time he's
carrying on this love affair, being loved. But for me, that's why he sent me on,
to find what . . . what he has here.

—But . . . after what he did . . .

—After what he did, and he learned only through her suffering, Stephen
brought out more loudly, —Now . . . If she comes to him carrying lilies that
turn to fire? And the fire, what do you think it is? If that was the only way he
could learn? So now do you see why he sends me on? If somewhere I've . . .
done the same thing? And something's come out of it, something . . . like . . .
he has. While I've been crowding the work alone. To end there, or almost end
running up to the doors there, to pound on the doors of the church, do you
see why he sent me on? Look back, if once you're started in living, you're born
into sin, then? And how do you atone? By locking yourself up in remorse for

what you might have done? Or by living it through. By locking yourself up
in remorse with what you know you have done? Or by going back and living
it through. By locking yourself up with your work, until it becomes a gessoed
surface, all prepared, clean and smooth as ivory? Or by living it through. By
drawing lines in your mind? Or by living it through. If it was sin from the
start, and possible all the time, to know it's possible and avoid it? Or by living
it through. I used to wonder, how Christ could really have been tempted, if
He was sinless, and rejected the first, and the second, and the third temptation, how was He tempted?...how did He know what it was, the way we do,
to be tempted? No, He was Christ. But for us, with it there from the start,
and possible all the time, to go on knowing it's possible and pretend to avoid
it? Or...or to have lived it through, and live it through, and deliberately go
on living it through.

He took a few steps down the hill, and stood looking over the valley, where
smoke was rising from the drift of roofs of the town, and further on the
mountainsides.

He looked fragile enough there, blocking the path before the figure in Irish
thorn-proof, which loomed larger for being slightly uphill. Still Ludy saw no
way to get round him, but stood unsteadily awkward waiting, trapped once
more, seeking some detail of sight or sound, threatened again with the torment of loss tolling his senses one by one, while somewhere unseen the bell
against the ruminating jaw jogged the silence. —You can't go on this way, he
broke out at the back turned to him, —this wandering...and he amended,
—I mean, I travel a good deal myself, but...

—Listen! there's a moment, traveling...

—But I...

—Offered shelter, there they were, all the family at dinner...

—Usually working on something...

—But she didn't wear her breasts around to be chewed by strangers, when
she said...

—Without...reproach...

—her daughter...

—What? Ludy came down upon him, —You said, you have a daughter
somewhere?...

At that he came round so quickly in the path that Ludy startled off it and
the instant his foot went into the deep grass a commotion burst there. Another
step back, Ludy stumbled and fell, and the bird which had fluttered up was
caught in Stephen's hand above him, where it beat its wings frantically.

—A daughter, yes.

—I've cut myself, Ludy said from the ground.

—Yes, Stephen laughed suddenly over him, holding the bird, looking down, where a streak formed on Ludy's hand.

—But I'm bleeding... don't, why are you laughing?

—Yes, who would have thought the old man to have had so much blood in him...? Stephen stood there looking down, and he covered the bird in his hand with the hand mounting the diamonds. —But you can't quiet it, you can't comfort it, it would die of fright.

—It frightened me, so close...

—See, how it's made...

—No, no... from far off, flying, yes, they're beautiful... Ludy struggled up on his elbows. —But no, not this close, like that, they make my blood run cold... He looked at the faint streak on his hand and repeated, —I'm bleeding...

Stephen burst into laughter again, more loudly, standing there with the bird. —Yes, yes, who would have thought, the old man... he laughed more loudly, at the slight and so faintly colored streak, —to have had so much blood in him!...

—But what is it... no, Ludy shuddered on the ground and unable to rise while the bird was held over him there.

—A daughter, yes! and born out of, not love but borne out of love, when it happened, the bearing, the present reshaped the past. And the suitor? Oh Christ! not slaying the suitors, no never, but to supersede where they failed, lie down where they left. Where they lost their best moments, and went on, to confess them in repetition somewhere else without living them through where they happened, trying to reshape the future without daring to reshape the past. Oh the lives! that are lost in confession...

—I'm bleeding...

—To run back looking for every one of them? every one of them, no, it's too easy, Penelope spinning a web somewhere, and tearing it out at night, and waiting? or to marry someone else's mistake, to atone for one of your own somewhere else, dull and dead the day it begins. You'd see, listen, listen, listen here if the prospect of sin, draws us on but the sin is only boring and dead the moment it happens, it's only the living it through that redeems it.

—Where are you going?

—I've an early start, I've come this far. Hear the bells! the old man, ringing me on.

—But the bird...?

—There are stories, I could tell you about Saint Dominic plucking alive the sparrow that interrupted his preaching...

—Just take it away, just, and let me get up, I'm bleeding.

—I told you, there was, a moment in travel when love and necessity become the same thing. And now, if the gods themselves cannot recall their gifts, we must live them through, and redeem them.

Stephen had knelt slowly beside the older man down on his back in the path who had retreated as best he could, shifting his weight away elbow to elbow, still prone with the bird's brittle torment so close, bursting out, —But why are you doing this to me?

—Doing? what. You asked me, where am I going?

—But I'm bleeding.

—Listen, whoever started a journey, without the return in the front of his mind? The bird fluttered there in the austere hand almost closed on it. Stephen watched it with calm, as he spoke only instants of intensity in his voice showed hardening lines stand out on the hand, which the man on the ground watched, the hand's shape broken only by the darting beaked head of the bird while from above Stephen watched its soft fluttering mantle, and his hand only a shape to contain it. —If it leads back into the wind blowing in off the desert, there's Biskra. Or Nalut, and the crescent moon hung in the sky there, it's all mine, I remember. When something you hadn't planned happens, where you hadn't planned it to happen... from north the Atlas stands up out of the earth, at sundown all of it looks like the world after the Deluge, then the darkness comes in. There's no horizon to separate fires on the mountainside from the low stars in the sky. The only way you know, a man passes between you if it's fires there, you've that moment's witness of goat hair passing between you it wasn't a star.

—Please... said the man on the ground, making movement to rise, but his own eyes pinioned him on that bird, —don't...you'll kill it holding it, that tight? And as he watched, Stephen's hand closed, only enough to stand out its tendons, and a whisper as tense,

—Yes yes yet should I kill thee? with, much cherishing?

And as the bird stilled in his hand, Stephen looked down, before him, at the old man on the ground. —What was it? he asked.

—But what, was what...

—Yes, something you wanted to ask me? Oh, remember? varé tava soskei me puchelas... much I wondered... but no. Stephen smiled down at him.

—Nothing, but... nothing, you see I I've been writing something here but I it's it concerns an experience of a an a religious nature and the prayers, I wanted something from the service but the Latin... of course I studied Latin, I went through Vergil but hearing it, since I'm not Catholic, the Latin, I wanted something to, sort of round things off? And that old man, the prior? at the end of the service? whatever...

—From the service?

—But Latin...

—That ex-Manichee bishop of Hippo...

—Oh? is that the old man? the prior?

—Do you have a pencil? Then write this. Dilige et quod vis fac.

Stephen rose slowly above him, standing, watching the pencil move.

—e . t . . qu . o . d . . v . i . s . . fac, and what does it mean? I studied Vergil but I've forgotten...

—Love, and do what you want to.

—What...?

Stephen stood, looking down at him.

—What? is that part of the service?

The bird was still warm in his hand. He opened it, and the bird moved against his fingers, as he stood looking down.

—I can look it up later. Dilige...The man on the ground moved up on his elbows.

—Yes, much I pondered, why you came here to ask me those questions, Stephen laughed above him, stepping away. He opened his hand. The bird struck it and went free. —Hear...? Bells sounded, far down the hill there. —Goodbye.

—You're going? The man on the ground raised himself from his elbows, staring at the slight streak of his blood.

—Yes, they're waiting, Stephen said to him. —They're waiting for me now, they...With his own eye, in the dawn, he caught the sparkle of the diamonds. —Her earrings, he said, —that's where these are for. Did I tell you?

Stephen's throat caught, looking down at the figure on the ground struggling to get up. —Yes... His eyes blurred on the figure older each instant of looking down at that struggle, and the hand where the blood lost all saturation. —Goodbye, hear? the bells, the old man ringing me on. Now at last, to live deliberately.

—But...

—What!

—You and I...

—No, there's no more you and I, Stephen said withdrawing uphill slowly, empty-handed.

—But we...all the things you've said, we...the work, the work you were, working on...?

—The work will know its own reason, Stephen said farther away, and farther, —Hear...? Yes, we'll simplify. Hear?...

—But...
—The old man, ringing me on.

The man in Irish thorn-proof did look a good deal older, by the time he'd picked himself up and got back to his room behind the walls. He meant to wash immediately he returned, but came in fumbling in a pocket with a wad of paper, which he brought out, saw there in his own hand, *Dilige et quod vis fac*, which he took out only long enough to annotate, "What mean?" and would, before his stay was out, find, as an unheartening curiosity, and drop on the floor (since there was no wastebasket).

He had left his windows opened, and the bird was sitting on one of the framed pictures when he came in, and closed the door behind him.

But he had already paused to make his notation, "What mean?" before he saw it, when it fluttered across the room to the other picture, and though he tried frantically to chase it toward the front, toward the windows and out, it fluttered the more frantically from one picture to the other, and back across the room and back, as he passed the mirror himself in both directions, where he might have glimpsed the face of a man having, or about to have, or at the very least valiantly fighting off, a religious experience.

Aux Clients
Reconnus Malades
l'ARGENT
ne sera pas
Remboursé

—Notices posted in brothels, Rue de l'Aqueduct, Oran

STANLEY was sprayed with green paint and had a finger broken on his first day in Rome. It happened when the band of Pilgrims he accompanied visiting the Basilica of Saint John Lateran was mistaken by alert police for a demonstration by a notorious political group, and set upon with as much ardor as the Saracens showed mauling those early Pilgrims to the Holy Land. Lonely, already tired before he started, unnerved by that violence, nettled to the extreme even by such small things as his constant re-encounters with the trundling, enamel-nailed, clicking (keeping tabs on Mystery!) fat woman, when he overheard mention of the Via Flaminia he remembered overhearing it named once before, lurking lonely in hospital corridors as he lurked now in Rome. He sought Mrs. Deigh, and reached her with less trouble than he might have expected. She sent the Automobile for him immediately.

Like other monuments of antiquity in the Eternal City, the Daimler stood at an impressive height, and moved, when it did so, with all of the dignity possible under such vulgar circumstances as locomotion. Stanley sat up front with the chauffeur; and though they rolled imperiously past streets and buildings which he'd crossed the ocean to see, he spent most of the ride gazing over his shoulder into the empty interior behind him, and the single seat there. Eventually, Mrs. Deigh might well insist that she'd got the car straight from the Vatican garage after the ascent of Benedict XV to a landscape where he would have no use for it (for, as an eminent Spaniard supplies, mortal man must triumph over distance and delay because his vital time is limited: among the immortals, motorcars are meaningless). But she was generally the first to admit responsibility for installing the stained glass windows herself.

Once arrived, the silent chauffeur let Stanley in, rang a bell, and left him standing quite forlorn beside a piece of bronze statuary. But only for a moment. A blond figure in organdy and white fox swept up, extended a muscular arm which, on a man, might have been called brawny, froze Stanley with what, man or woman, was most certainly a wink, and was gone. Stanley wilted against the bronze, and dropped the hand he had held out in greeting. Then he straightened up and pretended to be inspecting the voluptuous nineteenth-century triumph of Judith over Holofernes, as he heard footsteps in the hall behind him.

—So this is Stanley!... and he's already admiring our Donatello... he heard, and turned. —It's his Salome... but then you knew that, of course. Are you all right, dear boy?

Mrs. Deigh was a stout woman. She wore a knee-length fur cape, a green summer cocktail dress with a scalloped hem, what appeared to be gold paper stars pasted on it, and décolletage which exposed a neckline of woolen underwear. She advanced with a distinct rattling sound, held Stanley's hand in hers, and led him inside where, amidst deep red hangings, marble surfaces, heavily ornate gold frames enclosing obscure squares and rectangles, and more Victorian bronze, she sat him down to tell his story.

Encouraged by such exclamations as, —We are so grateful that He sent you straight to Us!... Stanley told haltingly of the circumstances of his voyage, though he did not get round to mentioning that he had accomplished it any other wise than alone.

—But you did land all right. At Genoa?

—Well yes except...

—What, dear boy?

—Nothing. A man got off at Genoa, and they found a... in one of his suitcases they found a body all chopped up.

Mrs. Deigh gasped, and drew back with more rattling and a distinct clank.

—He said it was only... only some Holy Innocents.

—And was it? she demanded, sitting forward noisily, with interest.

—No, it was... he confessed it was only his best friend.

—Oh! said Mrs. Deigh, with relief and a slight sigh of disappointment. Then there was a distant sound of breakage. Mrs. Deigh looked pained.

—Oh, dear Dom Sucio!...she murmured, as Stanley went on, in answer to her questions about his work, to tell of his interest in music, and mention his ambitions for Fenestrula.

—But did...then has your daughter written to you?...about me?

—Oh no, dear boy! No! She never writes to me, we don't correspond.

—But she...you know she...

—She's all right, we know the Lord is watching over her in His own way. Mrs. Deigh smiled a smile which seemed to settle her into the chair, and the brow of a lavish mother-of-pearl crucifix climbed from her bosom. It was finally evident that most of the rattling about her came from the long chain, supporting something like a large egg pendulant when she walked, and nestling somewhere in her lap, as it did now, when she sat. Like a Russian Easter Egg, this Thing had a tiny window in one end fitted with a magnifying pane but, viewing, instead of a crèche or a landscape, one saw only a highly enlarged shred of Something: last year, it had been a splinter of the True Cross (which, as Paulinus attested, gave off fragments without itself ever diminishing); more recently, a splinter of Saint Anthony's femur. There was a faint oriental look about her eyes, as though the skin might have been drawn back and tightened, which heightened her quelled expression with its sense that some enthusiasm might burst forth there, but for fear of cracking the extraordinary likeness to the face beneath, which she had managed to create with make-up. She always appeared cheerful, excepting devout moments when a soulful vacancy spread over her face, or moments of concern, when other features mounted anxiously toward the prominent nose, as they did now at a sound of moaning from somewhere. She excused herself saying, —Poor Hadrian, he needs Us...and got off in a clatter, leaving Stanley to clutch the tooth he'd found in his pocket and look about the room.

The paintings in the gilded frames were hallowed by numbers of coats of varnish, each darker than the last for the dirt collected on the one before. Thus it was difficult to tell what they depicted, but obligingly so since, for Mrs. Deigh, each one was a religious episode to which she assigned both the subject and the master's hand it had come from. Even now, Stanley stood impertinently close to inspect a small *Annunciation* by Tintoretto, with the notion that he saw a dog carrying a game bird in one corner. Then the sound of busy footsteps turned him round. —That is...he commenced, looking up at eye-level, and it seemed a full minute before he could bring his eyes down to meet the sharp glance of the figure scuttling through the room behind him. At that instant an arm shot out and Stanley recoiled from what, he realized afterward, must have been a sign of benediction, as the cassock came up and the little figure disappeared in the swirl of a black mantle.

—Dom Sucio!... Mrs. Deigh called, hard on his heels. —Did Dom Sucio pass this way? she asked when she appeared.

—Something did, Stanley brought out.

—Oh dear, he's gone again. He is so busy, she said, sagging slightly until she sat down. —He is such a dear.

—Is he a...a...

—A Dominican, and he is so kind to Us. So protective...and she subsided into the chair with, —Now you must tell Us more about you.

And so Stanley told her once more of his interest in music, dwelling modestly on the organ work he had composed (which, as he said, might have been a Requiem Mass had he done it three centuries ago), and reiterating his wish to visit the church at Fenestrula, and possibly...

—Play the organ there? But dear boy, nothing could be more simple. It was the gift of an American, and so of course they will let you play on it, an American whom We knew quite well, quite well indeed...

After that, Stanley could hardly keep his mind on their conversation. Everything else seemed unreal, as this one vision soared before him. His eye fixed on a gold telephone across the room, and the tooth clutched in his pocket so that it almost bit his palm, the pain disappeared from his bandaged hand, and he scarcely heard Mrs. Deigh describe how, as a girl in school studying French conversation, lunching, and the mandolin, she had known all that while that greater things lay ahead, though what they might be she'd no idea until one day, floating naked on her back in the blue waters off Portugal, she was discovered by some peasant children who took her for an apparition of the Virgin, and since then, of course, her path had been clear. In fact, it was not until he was about to leave that he even noticed her wrist watch: its four gold hands mounted a delicately contrived figure, and those pointing to III and IX were apparently stationary. The other two told the minute and the hour, and since it was just ten minutes after four when he left, he had no thought for what it might be until he came for lunch next day, and was greeted by his hostess promptly at twelve-thirty.

Stanley had hung his own crucifix, broken though it remained, on the wall over his bed in the room he had found in the Via del Babuino. It is true, every time he looked at it his own knees went weak, and when he addressed it, a sense of emptiness quivered and then surged through him, until he dropped his face on his clasped hands and with all the concentration that makes images from the past the more vivid, tried not to remember. But if he stayed so for long, on his knees beside his bed, the floor itself seemed to rise, and fall away driven on by his pounding heart where the ship's engines echoed, his own gasps of nausea as he staggered up echoing the gasping moans of the beast he had fought all his life. He closed his eyes against the Christmas card he had seen in that uptown bedroom, and the image stood out the more vivid on this dark tapestry of memory; he opened them on the yellowed rigid thing itself, its drawn legs hard-muscled straight through the broken knees, and turning away unsteadily he resolved to get it repaired next day.

But there was always something else. First, of course, he must procure his identification booklet, guide to Rome, prayer book, and the pin to wear and identify him as a Pilgrim. He wore it on the lapel of his second-best suit (it had been his third and last, fortunately, that suffered the green-paint episode, and his best blue suit hung unfolded, unworn since his mother's funeral). It was in this same second-best suit, pressed between mattresses during the voyage, and donned with self-conscious anticipation under a porthole suddenly filled with a static landscape instead of the sea and the sky, that he had emerged from the boat, with that shiny flattened look of sailors ashore.

Still, making the round from Saint John Lateran to the tomb of Saint Peter, the Basilica of Saint Paul, and Santa Maria Maggiore, required for indulgences, he looked lonely. Crossing the Ponte San Angelo, where Pilgrims had already been suffocated and died in the crush, he looked lonely. Passing through the Gate of the Bells, entering the piazza before Saint Peter's and gazing up at the Egyptian obelisk and beyond it to the Apostles on the roof, and Michelangelo's dome, he looked lonely. His hair still stood out thickly on the back of his head, and had begun to curl near the neck. He had trimmed his mustache, but it was uneven, and he kept catching ends of it with his teeth anxiously. If anyone had stopped him and asked him what he thought of it all, he would have answered with his surprise at finding Rome so yellow… but no one did. One after another he visited the places he felt bound to visit, and, it is true, he often found upon returning to the Via del Babuino that he could not remember which was which, that he was not sure whether he had seen the *Laocoön*, though here was a familiar picture of it before him, that he even, at one point, confused the Sistine and Pauline chapels, and finally both of them with the Vatican library, where he was quite sure he had not been at all. As for the statue of Saint Peter, with its foot worn smooth by kisses, he did not mention to Mrs. Deigh that he had wiped his lips after kissing it himself. He usually reported his excursions to her, as he did one day entering to interrupt her petulant murmurs over the newspaper, —He is wearing that heavy fisherman's ring back on his right hand again, which must mean his arthritis is better. Of course We have requested the Blessed Virgin Mary…

She thrust the paper away, showing a new book titled *Le cinque fonti sanguinose* nesting in her ample lap.

—San Clemente! she repeated fervently. —But it was the *upper* church you visited? Yes, with its lovely ceiling. We knew Prior Mullooly so well, you know. It's comforting to know it's all owned by Dominicans. Poor man, martyred by being thrown into the sea with an anchor tied around his neck. But we hope you did not descend *all* the way? because someone (and she often spelled out words which she considered unsuitable when Hadrian was anywhere near), —someone has built a p-a-g-a-n temple right square underneath it. A smelly damp dark little stone room where they went to worship the sun. Wasn't that stupid of them? But of course, they were all repressed, weren't they...

Here and there he saw the fat woman from the boat, clutching her threepenny pamphlet on the Modern Virgin Martyr, that or some other, clicking her Machine, and though he was relieved enough when she fled at the sight of him, he wished it might be with something less than the look of terror she wore when she did so. Once he saw Father Martin, coming out through the Bronze Door, and almost hailed him. But Father Martin was at that moment joined by another priest and the two went off with their heads nodding and bowed in convocation, leaving Stanley to stare at a pale girl carrying a copy of Forster's *Where Angels Fear to Tread*.

He might have got down to work. He should have, since the day he hoped and now could plan on for playing his composition for the first time, in the church he had dreamt of unnumbered times, lay not far off. He even tried, once or twice, to sit down at the practice keyboard and go through the copying he had done on the trip over: but a minute after Stanley had sat down to the printed keys, staring at an empty wall in the room in Via del Babuino, the whole place seemed to sway, the flat keyboard to rise under his fingers, the wall itself to be studded with rows of rivets binding its overlapping plates. The fingers of both hands drew up in frail fists, and a rash of irrelevancies crowded his mind to obscure the idea that possessed it. Sensing mistakes in the work before him, he did not find them. He did not really seek them out in fact, but might suddenly look up with some memory in his mind like that of oriental carpets made with a conscious flaw, in order not to offend the creator of Perfection by emulating his grand design.

Thus the one hollow face his memory tried to force upon him was always promptly transfigured, quickly weighed with flesh to come up the fat woman, or something enough like her, refusing him, and leaving him with his anathema on his own lips, —et eum a societate omnium Christianorum separamus...

Or Father Martin, turning away, —et a liminibus sanctae Matris Ecclesiae in coelo, et in terra excludimus, et excommunicatum...

—But dear boy, you can't want to go *that* Sunday, why that is the day of the canonization, this little Spanish martyr, and We have tickets...you can't want to go to Fenestrula *that* Sunday.

—But I do, I...that...that's the day I want to...to celebrate my...the canonization in my...in this way with my work, I...you understand, he finished abruptly with the appeal which never failed to her, for in a last resort of charity, Mrs. Deigh always "understood." He found himself spending more time at her place in the Via Flaminia; for though with her prominent nose she did not really resemble the fat woman from the boat, whose mean features clung desperately together as though in fear of being lost in the expanse of that face, there was a fullness in Mrs. Deigh's acceptance which counterbalanced and finally outweighed altogether the distant rejection of the fat woman.

Stanley shifted on the edge of a Queen Anne chair, and hitched his shoulders up. The scapular which Mrs. Deigh had made herself, and given him, itched under his shirt. He caught the glare of Mrs. Deigh's wrist watch, and looked down at his own.

—Of course, dear boy, if it's what you want, she said, and sighed. —We know how important your work is, and that is as it should be, but We had hoped...The chain rattled.

—Yes, I...

—Well then, perhaps this afternoon We shall drive together to see Cardinal Spermelli, he was acquainted at Fenestrula. If We dare leave Our Hadrian for that long a time...she added, and shook her head.

Hadrian was not, as Stanley vaguely suggested one day (thinking about something else) her son, but an aging bull terrier, once white, and now suffering a severe skin infection he'd got from a dye she used when she tried to make him match a yellow velours gown she often wore in public. Stanley had learned to watch his step around the place, after almost trampling the poor old fellow one day he was up and around, for though Hadrian wore a hearing aid and so certainly heard Stanley coming, he moved with that perilous assurance of old age everywhere, taking for granted that way would be made for him. Not that Stanley did not watch his step anyhow: he'd also come near enough to trampling Dom Sucio, and the look he got for that was tempered by anything but senile infirmity. It was in fact quite venomous. Now whether Dom Sucio had seen him, when he saw the little figure cavorting in a window display in the Corso Umberto costumed as one of the Nibelungs, in some sort of Wagnerian panorama got up for German and Scandinavian tourists, Stanley did not know, any better than he knew if he dared report it to Mrs.

Deigh; for the little man certainly guarded his interest in her with as much jealousy as the Nibelungs showed for their treasure hoard, and he never failed to fix Stanley with a look which sent shivers down that un-Siegfriedian spine, as he did now, entering.

—Dear Dom! she cried, —We are off to see Cardinal Spermelli, We think Stanley will like him and We know he will like Stanley, he always likes young boys, especially musical young boys. Stanley simply cannot wait to see his arca musarithmica. Is he well?

—His what? Stanley got in.

Dom Sucio sat down on a needlepoint footstool and shook his head gravely. —White ants, he said.

—What?

—White ants, dear lady.

—But Dom Sucio...you told me that white ants had invaded the Vatican, the very Papal archives, but...

—They have eaten through the six-foot thick wall of the Cortile del Pappagallo, they have eaten a number of books and a cardinal's ceremonial cape, and the Swiss guards have reported the spearhead of a new attack swarming across the very piazza of Saint Peter's.

—But Cardinal Spermelli?

—He complains of a feeling of burrowing in his right leg. He has worked for so long you know, dear lady, always seated in the same chair. The chair collapsed yesterday.

—Oh! Mrs. Deigh moaned, rising, —We hope it will not be as bad as the time he had the bee in his stomach. Come, come dear boy, she said to Stanley, and he followed her out.

—We do wish that you would get your hair cut, dear boy, said Mrs. Deigh as they set off.

It seemed advisable, under the circumstances, that Stanley wait for her in the Automobile. She was gone for a good half-hour inside the yellow portico where they stopped, and he sat patiently licking the ragged edge of his mustache in the Automobile's kaleidoscopic interior. At the foot of the large single seat, facing the peep-hole and oncoming traffic over the chauffeur's shoulder, was placed what appeared to be a prie-dieu. Its petit-point seat was even worked with the initials I H S, but this, Mrs. Deigh told him, was Hadrian's "little chair," and it was here that Stanley sat now, as the chauffeur helped her back into the car, and they set off again for the Via Flaminia.

After she had got settled, Mrs. Deigh handed him a letter, —for Fenestrula, dear boy...And he could hardly thank her. But she sat staring up at the damask ceiling, clicking her teeth, so he tried to look out through one of the lighter portions of stained glass. Finally settled, with his knees drawn up under his chin, and staring as best he could through the Saint's breechclout in the martyrdom of Saint Stephen depicted on his right, as the car slowed, and halted in traffic, he suddenly cried out and almost went through the damask roof.

—There she is! There she is!...

—There who is?...dear boy...

—There she is!...sitting at that...at that table at that café...

—Dear boy...

The Automobile swept on, and Stanley recovered himself somewhat.

—Nothing, I...someone I...someone I knew...once.

—But dear boy, you're so pale...She reached forth for his hand, quivering with the letter to Fenestrula, and brought her wrist watch directly under his gaze. Vividly recalling the topsy-turvy contortion there afterward, he would also remember the time: it was just six.

—Well we got used to poverty in Spain, so we don't really mind it here, said the tall woman sitting on the café terrace next evening. She drew away from the figure standing over her and gazing at the tables beyond. It was Stanley, and he was scratching himself up under his coat. When he moved on, she leaned across and whispered to her husband, —Do you itch? Maybe it's just my imagination but ever since we left...none of those monks looked like they'd really bathed in literally years.

—So if you didn't want to go to bed with me I just naturally took it for granted you didn't go to bed with girls, so I just naturally took it for granted you were queer. What are you doing here, are you Catholic? The girl at the next table looked up at Stanley as though he were intruding, but he stood gazing searchingly beyond them.

At the table to his left, an American Protestant minister in rimless glasses tasted Cinzano for the first time, made a wry face, and said, —It's just part of this big job we're all pulling together in. Do you know this new word, *Caprew*...? It's made up of the first two letters of Catholic, Protestant, and...

—Me Catholic? Christ no, I just came over to see the art here.

—Well you sure picked a lousy time, the girl said, watching Stanley recede among the tables. It was just six.

—Why do they get excited about the ruins in Rome here, Berlin is just as good now.

—You can always see an ancient city better when it's been bombed.

Stanley looked on. He saw the pale girl he had seen before, outside the

Bronze Door when he sought Father Martin; and as her face had taken the place of his then, Father Martin's face rose before Stanley now, and turned away, as Stanley turned away from her. She was sitting alone, and reading *A Room with a View.*

—I've really practically finished this novel, all I have to do now is put in the motivation, said a young man at the next table he stopped near. —I've been reading Dante trying to get some ideas.

Then Stanley thought he saw her, at a table with a number of faintly familiar figures, halfway across the crowded terrace. He tried to hurry in that direction, his mind again filled with the rash of irrelevancies flooding in as Father Martin's face bowed and was banished by that of the fat woman, pursing the small lips silently, losing flesh, the eyes widening, hollows deepening, to become the face he sought now and believed he had just seen, except, he considered, bumping tables and chair backs in his haste, weak-kneed, except for what she appeared to be wearing: a white turban knotted with a flair over the forehead, white cuffs and a broad white collar over her shoulders, her lips brightly colored and the glimpse of a narrow long black skirt.

—Stanley!

—Wha...haa?...

Don Bildow had his wrist in greeting. —I wondered what happened to you when you didn't get off at Naples...

—Yes, I...I'm in a hurry, I...

—So am I, wait, listen...Don Bildow looked appealingly through his plastic rims. His hair looked thinner, and his brown suit more threadbare. The brown and yellow tie was getting soiled about the knot. —Just one thing, if you've got any...

—I...I have to go! Stanley broke from his grasp saying, —And I don't even know what that stuff was that you asked...

—No, that's all right, said Bildow catching his arm again, —the Methyltestosterone, I got that, the nurse on the boat was fine about it when I...but listen, now I need...Do you know the Italian word for contraceptive? There's a girl waiting for me and I...Wait!...

When Stanley reached the table across the terrace, there was no one there he knew. A blond boy had just finished saying, —I don't care if Saint Joseph of Copertino *did* fly around and perch in trees, that hasn't a thing to do with it!

—I saw you! said a voice from a vaguely familiar face, and a large red forefinger was rested on Stanley's hand.

—But...where? he asked, taken aback, for in spite of the dark blue suit and short blond hair, the heavy face was familiar.

—Chez that perfectly obvious woman, you came in as I went out.

—But it was...

—Me. I called to ask about a shop where I could buy undies. But what was a boy like you doing there? I won't think. Then the finger slid away as he turned and introduced Stanley to the rest of the table with, —I'm afraid, my dears, it's one of those odious Pilgrims, and he's already been stoned in the streets, see his hand. But it's only a finger? What naughty game were you playing?...

—But I...

—And as I was telling you, this morning I'd gone to this brazenly recherché little church, since they're supposed to have an honest-to-God Titian hidden there somewhere. Of course there was a line, so I waited my turn, and do you know, I found myself on line for benediction as a pregnant mother?

—Was there a girl here? Stanley broke in.

—My dear boy stop being indecent or you'll have to go away. What *is* the matter, do you have lice? You're scratching like Thomas à Becket.

—Look!

—Why it *is*, it's Herschel. Now do you see what he's married to? His studio paid her ten thousand dollars. Something named Adeline.

—But does he have to take her everywhere?

—That's why they paid her ten thousand dollars. Of course he doesn't have to take her to *bed*. Have you heard he's not to play Saint Sebastian in this film after all? In the martyrdom scene you know, he has to be practically naked when they shoot all those horrid arrows at him, but one look at the divine tattoo on his...

—Please, Stanley interrupted again, —don't any of you...

—And think, they won't let me have little Giono until Wednesday, when I'm *received*. Why I'm in a state of Grace this very moment.

In a moment of silence, as Stanley got his breath, a feeble falsetto across the table rose with, —Blessed Mary went a-walking...

—That's her! you... that's a song she sings, she...

—Baby, do you know her?

—Yes, you... where is she? She was here, she... wasn't she? Wasn't that her wearing that funny...

—Careful, baby. Rudy designed that specially for her. It's her brwidal gown.

—Her... what?

—I should say, her trwousseau.

—But you... she... she's... getting married?

—Baby, didn't you know?

—But to... who? Who's she going to marry?

—Maybe it wouldn't be descrweet to tell.

—But you must, she ... I ...

—All rwight, we won't *name* the grwoom. You can guess. We'll just tell you she's going to become a nun. Now, can you guess, Who?

—But you ... huuu ... Stanley could only breathe in gasps.

—Baby, don't take on so, we don't want any jealous suitors.

—Huuuu ...

—Isn't Rudy's habit sweet on her? I mean the habit he designed. She has a very trim body anyway, you know. Not all round and plumpy like women.

—An ... nnn ... nun?

—Rwudy said he trwied to make it look as Do-*min*ican as possible. And imagine Rwudy marrwied!

—She's ... marrying ... Rudy? Stanley brought out.

—It's no one you know, silly. It's no one anyone knows, no one can see what he sees in *that* one, who shall be nameless. A piece of trade. Ordinary, common, vulgar ...

—But wait, I ... she ... where did she go? Stanley demanded looking round helplessly.

—Rudy designed another with the most divinely inspired halo hat, and the longest swishiest magenta sash with oodles of gold, why I could have taken vows myself when I saw *her* in it. But did you hear her talk? about stigmata, and a lance tipped with golden fire piercing her heart, and pus-filled holes in her forehead smelling like lilies and all sorts of the *most* gory details. Oh no! "Lilies without, roses within." But not that. Oh no! On her face ...

—Pure Caravaggio. I told her I knew I'd seen her before, but I refused to ask her who she knew in New York, I never want to think of that rude vulgar nightmare again, ever. I said, I'll just pretend I've met you in a painting. Pure Caravaggio. But did you see *my* Raphaels this afternoon? Benito is only seven! and you should hear him chatter with that exquisite little pink tongue ...

—Please, tell me ... Stanley said now, getting his voice down where he could almost control it, —where did she go?

—*Do* stop scratching! Simply all she talked about was going to Assisi, to run in and out the door of the Portiuncula church there and get just oodles of indulgences for someone she knows in Purgatory, someone who came down into the celestial sea on a rope, I don't know, she made it all sound just too camp.

—But she's ... gone there now?

—She wants to go just more than anything, but she has no way to get there. I told her to simply go barefoot. Put your faith in God, baby, I told her. She'll protect you.

—But she . . . then where did she go?

—She went off with a vulgar person in a green silk necktie, who said he was going to enter her in a movie contest. That's simply all I know. There. There, do you see that rather clumsily collegiate person over there? with a green silk necktie? sitting with that odd little . . .

—Thank you, Stanley said, turning away, and he hurried off.

—Is it trwue that the Cardinals can roller skate between the sala ducale and the cappella Sistina?

—I don't care if Moses is accused of witchcraft in the Koran, who reads the Koran?

Stanley caught up with the man in the green silk necktie at the terrace edge, as he was leaving, and immediately got across a pertinent description.

—Do you know her too? She's terrific, isn't she. I didn't even know she was a-merican, except for whatever the hell she was wearing, she looked like a regular eye-tye madonna, do you know what I mean?

—Yes but I . . . where is she?

—Well I'm here doing publicity for this movie on the life of the B.V.M., and we're running a competition for the lead. She's a natural for it. You know, I came up to her and I said, Spikka ing-glish? like that. I never learned Eye-talian, they didn't teach it at Yale.

—But she . . .

—Not that I ever knew anyway. So I ask her if she was ever in the movies, and you know what she said? She said once she went and saw a picture about a funny man in a round black hat and a little mustache . . .

—But . . .

—Another time she saw *Uncle Tom's Cabin* where Little Eva gets pulled up on ropes to heaven, so I said, Not going to the movies, I mean ever acted in one. We've got a six-language sound track on this life of the B.V.M., we've rented a whole town for it.

—But . . .

—We rented all the people in the town too. It's color. She's a natural for the B.V.M. What'd you do to your hand?

—Well that, I . . . there was a sort of a riot . . . Stanley faltered.

—You in that too? Look. My checkbook, see? See that? A bullet. It stopped a bullet for me. I have to go. It's nice meeting you. See that little jerk who's with me? I have to have dinner with him, he's an ex-king. He wants a good publicity man to help him get his throne back. So long. It's nice meeting you, if you know her too. She's terrific. A natural . . . the B.V.M. incarnate . . .

—But where *is* she? Stanley asked desperately, clinging to the hand which had seized his in an automatic gesture.

—Now? You got me. I tell you, all she talked about was she wanted to go up to some town into some rose garden, and see some guy up there who came down to the bottom of the ocean on a rope. I didn't get it, to tell you the truth. We barely had time to get a few stills of her. She's terrific, even in 3-D she'd be terrific, so I told her I'd send a studio car around to take her wherever the hell it is, this rose garden. She's going to call me. So long.

—Yes, I . . . so . . . so long.

Stanley stood scratching under one arm, and watched the lime-green convertible car roar away. Behind him, someone said,

—Of course the Vatican is abject poverty, after Delphi.

—Dear boy, thank Heaven you are all right. I've been praying.

—But . . . what?

—A young man jumped from the inner dome of Saint Peter's, and I thought it might . . . Oh! His body landed right in front of the high altar, right in front of all those tourists, and I felt . . . though the paper does say he was a well-dressed young man.

Stanley followed her into the crowded room, where she sat down looking distracted. The chain rattled as she cocked her head to a distant sound of breakage, which reached them somewhat muffled by the red hangings. —It's been such a day, and poor Dom Sucio, he's being plagued by a gross German woman who wants her daughter canonized. She actually came *here* today looking for him, and We had to hide him in the harmonium. A Frau Fahrt-messer, Mrs. Deigh pronounced forcefully, —and she says she has her daughter with her, in the baggage room at the Stazione Termini. Then Mrs. Deigh gazed for a minute at Stanley, who shifted apologetically in his jacket. She shook her head, made the familiar chucking sound with her lips, and repeated, —Thank Heaven you are all right, as she picked up the newspaper. —Our scapular protected you, thank Heaven. She lowered her eyes to the paper, and shook her head over that. —We do hope they find them, she murmured.

—What?

—Saint Peter's bones. They've been after them for so long, she murmured, and continued to shake her head. The room was very warm, and Stanley sat forward on the edge of the Queen Anne chair with his hands clasped between his knees, staring at the floor. Once or twice he looked up about to speak, and finally he leaned back and rubbed his shoulders against the chair.

—I wanted to . . .

—The newspaper never tells Us nice things. Sometimes it just pipes in more blood than We think We can endure. And when you mentioned Our daughter, didn't you. We knew there was something, and now We remember. I was sure I'd read in the newspaper that she'd been hung for murder. Murdering her husband! And that is a little too much to endure, even for one's own flesh and blood. And in Mississippi.

—Yes, she... but you should know, she...

—She was always a willful girl. We did all We could, but We saw signs of her drifting away quite early. And when she confessed to Us that she chewed the wafer... Mrs. Deigh looked up sharply, down again, and shook her head. —How sad We are that you will not be here for the canonization ceremonies of the little Spanish martyr. There will probably be fifty thousand people, and it will be the very first one to be held out of doors. We have tickets in the colonnade, you know. Why, there will probably be at least a hundred bishops, and His Holiness will wear the red mantle of martyrdom.

Stanley sat scraping the rug with the edge of his shoe, looking more apologetic, until the next thing she said, when he straightened up and almost brightened.

—And We have taken a vow to remain indoors until that glorious day.

—Oh, I... I wanted to ask you if I could... if I wanted to go somewhere if the Automobile could take me?

—You would have to tell Us where, she answered, and the chain rattled a slight reproach. —If only so We could give instructions to Orlando, since he cannot understand you.

—Well, to... to Assisi, I thought I... want to go to Assisi.

—The birthplace of Saint Francis! Of course, dear boy. That gentle, heavenly figure, so many stories have come down to us. To visit the Portiuncula, where he threw himself into the thorny rosebush in dead of winter, to overcome his passion... or We should say, the temptation to lessen his austerities, for it is his passion that we worship, is it not. It is almost time for the roses to come into bloom now, and you will see their little leaves spotted with his blood. Tell Us, dear Stanley... She inclined toward him. The egglike object slipped from her lap, and swung on the chain to the floor between them. Stanley got it and handed it to her. She accepted it without a glance, looking into his face. —Do you consider taking Orders? For We have read in your sweet unselfish nature...

—Well I... I... he commenced, when she left her words unfinished.

—And that is why you want to visit the shrine of the most selfless of the saints, the most humble? And see the very spot where he fought off the temptations of the Evil One?...

—Well I... it isn't exactly for myself, I... Is Orlando really mute?

—Why yes, dear boy, but why do you ask that? And what do you mean...

—Well I mean, I mean not for myself, I mean, what I mean is not just for myself, I mean . . .

—You mean not just for your physical self, your senses, she said helping him forth from his confusion. —You mean for your spiritual self too, of course We understand, dear boy. Of course.

—Yes, I . . . yes, Stanley said feebly, and sat back. Mrs. Deigh was silent. He looked up guardedly, ready for her eye on him, but she was gazing at the newspaper and shaking her head.

—And here is a poor unfrocked Jesuit priest, she commented regretfully, as though continuing the conversation, —who is trying to start a world crusade against the Pope. She made the chucking sound once more. —And he is already excommunicated, not just toleratus, but vitandus. If he enters a church, service must stop instantly. But what is toleratus? she asked Stanley, looking up abruptly.

—Well that . . . that . . . he faltered, —toleratus is when someone has not yet been . . . been publicly denounced, when . . . and they can't . . . put him out unless he tries to . . . to take part in the Mass.

—And where did you go to morning Mass today? she asked, as though now changing the subject.

—I . . . I didn't go.

—You . . . but my dear boy! You mean you didn't go to *early* Mass. We understand, she said, settling in the chair so that the mother-of-pearl crucifix rose above the wool border of her bosom. Stanley stared at it. He stood up, and his knees were weak.

—I should . . . go home, he said. His hand caught the tooth in his pocket. —Tomorrow . . .

—Yes, dear boy, until tomorrow. She smiled up at him, and then pursed her lips silently, almost like the fat woman. Stanley tried to smile but turned away, rubbing his eye with one hand, and murmured a good night. Then he heard her voice, and turned to look back. She was gazing at the paper once more.

—Find what? he asked, as the glitter of her wrist watch, and the soft gleam of the pearl-white crucifix caught him again, weak-kneed with the words running through him, —et anathematizatum esse decernimus, et damnatum cum diabolo, et angelis eius, et omnibus reprobis in ignem aeternum indicamus . . .

—Some Americans on Mount Ararat. They're looking for Noah's Ark.

Next day an American picture magazine, whose insidious pretense to simplicity earned it a large circulation, gave a full page to a picture published earlier in *Osservatore Romano* in substantiation of the sun's antics over Portugal at the time of the Virgin's apparition there. The Pope himself (who had spent part of today blessing drivers at a motor-scooter festival, whom he praised for their "courage and agility") had, on another inspired occasion, received "silent and eloquent" messages from the "agitated sun," and witnessed "the life of the sun under the hand of Mary." And here, as proof, was the picture (of "rigorously authentic origin") of the sun near the horizon at 12:30 P.M., where it might well have been photographed if the horizon were Portugal, and the hour, Barbados, for even now it was near noon in the Caribbean as an evening Angelus bell sounded somewhere over Stanley's head and he entered the Piazza di Spagna looking weary and disquieted.

—Oh no! he found energy to say, as Don Bildow caught his arm and, at the same moment, he saw the tall figure he had not seen since the dock at Naples, the black homburg hat drawn over the forehead, the arm no longer in a sling but resting in a pocket of the Chesterfield coat.

—I just came for my mail at American Express, Bildow said, not letting him go. —What's the matter? Aren't you all right?

—I... I have to...

—I guess I look pretty seedy myself, Bildow said looking him over, —but I've just been to this tailor, he's making me a beautiful suit, forty thousand lire, I'm going to throw this one away when I get it. Everything else I have got shipped right to Paris, I'm going on up there in a few days. I'm going to throw this suit away and wear the new one so I don't have to pay duty on it. Have you seen this? He held out the book he was carrying. —I just saw it at Piale's. It's Anselm.

Stanley, who had been looking anxiously after the figure he knew only as the Cold Man, startled and looked down at the book. —Anselm?

—His confession. I'm in here. You're in here too. We're all in here.

—I... really? Stanley said, staring at it. —But I thought he was in a monastery?

—He is. This is his confession of what drove him there. I'd like to... get my hands on him, Bildow added, clutching the book in a soft fist.

—Could I borrow it? Stanley asked suddenly.

—Why... why sure, if you want to. I haven't read it yet, I just looked in it. We're all in it. I don't want to read it yet, he added, handing the book over, and Stanley took it in both hands, his broken bandaged finger across the title.

—And do you know what happened to me last night? Bildow went on, sounding slightly incensed. —I can't wait till I get to France. That girl I had, waiting for me, you remember?

—I have to go, Stanley said quickly, holding the book up against his chest as though to shield himself.

—I took her up to the room, and at first she wouldn't take off her brassière. She had everything else off but...

—I have to go, goodbye, thank you for the book... Stanley had caught another glimpse of the Cold Man.

—And you know? You know the kind of a trick she was pulling on me? One of her breasts was wooden.

—I...I don't want to hear, let me go, goodbye...

—Are you still in a hurry? What do you think of that, though, one of them was wooden, it was made of wood, just like...hey, when will I see you again?...

But Stanley was out of earshot. He hurried along the pavement with the book under both forearms against his chest, darting looks ahead, unsure where he had seen that same strong profile and narrow chin, and the watery blue eyes, but certain now he had seen it long before the *Conte di Brescia*. But with some question far more important, more immediate, burning in his face, Stanley followed him to a café where he entered, looked round quickly, and sat down alone, putting his hat beside him, smoothing the ends of his hair with his fingertips, then resting his chin on his hand, turned in so that he appeared to be biting the gold seal ring there. Stanley stood uncertainly near a pillar behind him, catching the ragged ends of his mustache as though to find the words of address he sought in that way.

—The whole cabin was filled with the most God-awful stench, said the tall woman sitting over an apéritif nearby, —simply all his vitamin B pills had melted. He takes them for hangovers.

A girl to his right said, —All the drawers were full of empty Bromo bottles when she left. Have you read this? It's Firbank.

Then just as Stanley was about to step forward, a man with a smooth unpliant oriental face, tight but not tense, and moving only faintly at the corners of the mouth as he approached, came forward from another table. He was quite short, and wore a trenchcoat. They greeted one another with apparent surprise, and the man in the trenchcoat started to speak as he sat down.

—Fenn és...

—Speak English, you idiot...

At the sound of that voice, even muffled as it was behind the clasped hands, Stanley remembered, and his lip trembled. The whole night came back to him, and he lowered his face and sat down half behind the column, opened Anselm's book and stared at a page: "If we had stopped for even a minute then, a minute of silence..." He closed his eyes tightly, and his head was filled with the roar of the subway train. Now he almost drew his hands up to find if his shirt was unbuttoned, to button it as he had been doing then; instead he only shivered, as he had been shivering then, and as a woman's voice near him came out with, —There are little electric lights on the graves, and you pay by the hour, just like they were candles burning down... Stanley heard echo the voice of the woman on the subway embracing him and the man who stood with the handkerchief before his mouth, as he sat with hands clasped there now. —Up where Keats is buried, or is it Shelley?... Her voice, and the tangled mass from under her skirt embracing them both in the intimacy of horror, out onto the platform where the liquid blue eyes froze above the white hand-kerchief: —Those, my dear young man, are the creatures that were once burned in witch hunts...

—The stench, everywhere...

Stanley wiped his face with his hand, as he had done that morning, waking suddenly, looking at the palm, dropped it, and listened.

—It could not have been more simple, more inviting, the man in the trenchcoat was saying in a low tone. —He invited me there, in fact, to see the mummy. He had made one himself for me! Oh, but with such ingenuity, it was really a masterpiece...

—Really, my dear fellow...

—I confess I did not have heart to finish our business so immediately, I spent a few minutes congratulating him. He became very angry when I appeared to question the... authenticity? of this thing, but he was very proud. I saw in his eyes, he was very proud, when we finished our business together.

They sat silent for a moment, and the man in the trenchcoat twitched a little at the corners of his lips, gazing at the ceiling, as though he were fondly recalling some pleasant encounter with the past. Then he shrugged, and added, —The Spaniards, however, they are not... sane, of course.

The man with him had hardly moved, except to shift an elbow to make way for a glass on the table before him. He sat staring past the door of the café from vacant light blue eyes.

—You don't look well, said the other. —You are more haggard than when I saw you, over there.

—I don't sleep well.

—You did not sleep well then.

—Even as well as... then.

—Cigarette?

—No.

—You no longer smoke.

—No.

After a minute of solicitous silence the man in the trenchcoat said, —And you do plan to go back? He got no answer but a faint nod. A waiter appeared with more wine, and some Gorgonzola cheese. —Yes, you are then? certain you want to go back? For there is still time...

—What...business is it of yours! Certainly I'm going back. Still he barely turned his face from the hands clasped before it, for this outburst of impatience, and quickly muffled them there again.

—Your lip is badly scarred? The man in the trenchcoat twisted again round the ends of his mouth. —You know it can be fixed, of course, he murmured, listening, watching with glittering eyes.

—What did you mean by that? Going back, why not. What did you mean? The shoulderstraps on the trenchcoat shrugged slightly. —Nothing. Of course, rumors?

—Yes, yes, yes, the other whispered with sharp impatience behind his hands. —And after your reports, eh? Watching over me...yes, little things like, the moment I show some dismay over our paintings being dumped for dollars, did you tell them that too?

—Please, of course...

—Yes, which proved conclusively that I must be working for the restoration of the crown...aphhh...this kind of logic...Certainly I'm going back, why not? where...what else? he whispered staring straight ahead. Then he lowered his eyes slowly, and sat studying the cheese on the plate at his elbow.

—Of course, I meant to say, I understand you...

—Of course, you explained that once. No...

—I meant only to say, things there are not going well, nothing is going well there. Everything there, the corruption has spread...His voice tailed off, he sat silent with his small glittering eyes, startled when the cheese was suddenly pushed toward him with an elbow.

—There, try some of that, taste it, corruption put to good use...

And they were silent again, the man in the trenchcoat did not touch the Gorgonzola, finally he said, —Tomorrow? There is one more? they told me, a priest?

—Dressed like one.

—And you, you will indicate him to me, you will not mistake him?

—Yes I, I'll point him out to you. I won't mistake him, his companion muttered behind his hands, drew them aside and appeared to spit something from the end of his tongue. —If you think you can take care of it then, on the street, in daylight?

—Of course...the man in the trenchcoat murmured, then, —*A Véres költö*...you remember that...?

—You? The clasped hands fell away for a moment, with a sparkle of gold, and the scar on the lip drew it into what appeared to be a sneer. —The poet stained with blood!... He drew his hands up again.

—Or...you?

—Enough...

—You will be on the train tomorrow night?

—Yes.

—I should like a last good dinner, before we go back. Eh? The Piccolo Budapest? Eh?

—Yes. Early. About seven.

—You are ... going back, then? the man in the trenchcoat said, and studied the profile beside him.

—Yes, yes, and now good night. Good night.

—The personal affairs no longer take precedence, eh? Good night. Until tomorrow? Under Saint Peter's Umbrella ... eh?

Stanley looked down at his book quickly.

—And have you ever seen anything so frankly hideous as this, the tall woman's voice took up. —A piece of dirt enshrined forever in clear lifetime plastic. My God!...with a certificate of Miraculous Origin and the Seal of the Church. A piece of dirt from the church of Cana in Galilee, where they turned wine into water, my God. My husband's picking up all sorts of things, you can see the state he must be in after what happened to Huki-lau...

A distant voice said, —I don't care if Joan of Arc was a witch, that hasn't a thing to do with it...

And another, —Of course everyone knows that the Franciscans were canonized for the very things the Waldensians were burned alive for...

And then Stanley looked up as though he had been struck. A waiter stood before him, and he whispered, —Café, hoarsely, trying to look round the dirty apron to where the voice had come from he had so certainly heard. When he saw her, she was already seated, and although so close, in the chair which the man in the trenchcoat had left, she had not seen him, and she did not look round, but down at her hands on the table. At that instant Stanley might have leaped up, or cried out, or simply spoken beginning with some overladen conjunction, as though to continue a conversation of minutes or hours before: and it was not her company that stopped him but the absolute, absolved quiet on her face, in spite of the small sore which disparaged the delicate line of her lip.

—Something bit her, perhaps, she said at that moment, answering a question from the man half turned from Stanley, and a reproachful smile touched her face, still looking down. Then they were both silent. He only appeared to have glanced at her, and he went on, staring straight ahead.

—Of course Huki-lau isn't dead, she's ... The tall woman whispered something. —Which is just as bad. *I* don't see how it happened, she's had her belt on every minute she's been over here. There was a goat, in Spain, though, with designs on her. You could see in his eyes.

—How tired you look, like he looked sometimes, like an old man, with nothing left before you to regret. And are you old? or are the scars still unhealed down your front. Raise your left hand ... you can't, it sits there relishing another scar. She laughed, a sharp sound, and left it between them, looking at her own hands on the table. She was wearing a simple dark gray suit, with a long unbroken skirt and a short cape. She had nothing on her hair.

He muttered something.

—What? You're joking. And she laughed again. His right hand had come down on the table, and she took it in hers, and laid her left hand over both. Still, he appeared to bite the gold seal ring on the other, staring ahead.

—Still ...

—Today? In Assisi, she went through and through and through the gate. No one appeared in person, granting indulgences. No one, in a "heavenly brightness shining," no one, do you remember? When no one was at the door? Now granting indulgences, O friars minors, is he in Purgatory if he drowned? Down, on a rope, did he tell you that story? Drowned, in the celestial sea come down the rope to undo the anchor caught there on a stone with no one's name on, and a date, inclined against the bottom by the darkness, and so no wonder that the anchor caught, and he came down the rope. If there were time ...

—Listen. Just tell me ...

—More you know? His blood on the leaves, I saw it. But no thorns? that's someone else then, for I saw him delivered, down. Yes, streaked with no one's oil and delivered, down, that damned black androgyne who held him back and lost him, down ...

—I may not see you again.

She did not raise her eyes.

Stanley swallowed with self-conscious effort and pretended, to himself, to find his place in the book before him. At another table, a group had settled to worry the most recent dogma, that of the Assumption. One of them said, —There's a perfectly good scientific explanation ...

—And then when we drove back, a monk drove with us. She had her belt on then, but I didn't *watch*...

—She would have died of asphyxia at fifty thousand feet.

—You hear things, about life in monasteries.

—Or if she'd gone fast, burned up like a meteor.

—Will you marry her?

Stanley looked up at that, eyes wide but the lids drawn upon them in disbelief, as though trying to hide what he heard from himself; and hide what he saw, for her eyes were wide, and no lids discernible.

—Marry you! the man said, and he withdrew his right hand from under hers.

—All right, Mary was a Jew, wasn't she? A Jewish woman, if she went bodily to heaven, how does she eat?

—This little piece of dirt, enclosed in lifetime plastic forever. Does a plastic lifetime last forever?

—Is there a kosher kitchen in heaven?

—You see, he put it there, and he did not take it away. Stanley stared at her. His own expression, and even the movement of his hands, commenced to follow hers, then those of the man when he answered, then his face hers and his hands those of the man, except intricate muscles tried round the edges and round the eyes, and the corners of his mouth, to rescue his own face from that unguarded openness, and his hands quivered.

—Marry you! Me!

—For he put it there, and did not take it away as he promised, as he always had done before, as he promised.

—Me!

—Take the dogma of the Immaculate Conception. You try to preserve Mary from the taint of Original Sin, then what about Elizabeth? You can go all the way back.

—Of course we met the people who make these things. Religious novelties, and mostly plastic. And she even admitted openly she was a convert. But my husband can tell a Jew a mile away.

—So Mary Herself told Saint Anthony of Padua her body remains incorruptible in Heaven.

—Saint John of the Cross said . . .

—Listen! Listen . . .

—Where there is no love . . .

—This is the last time I will see you.

—But why do you do the things you do? Why do you live the life you live?

Stanley watched his shoulders hunch forward, watched one hand grip the other, and though he could not see the watery blue eyes, his own by now lay open with the same implications of desire as those wide dark eyes he sought.

—Because . . . do you understand? the Cold Man said, speaking with quiet clarity for the first time, —because any sanctuary of power…protects beautiful things. To keep people…to control people, to give them something… anything cheap that will satisfy them at the moment, to keep them away from beautiful things, to keep them where their hands can't touch beautiful things, their hands that…touch and defile and…and break beautiful things, hands that hate beautiful things, and fear beautiful things, and touch and defile and fear and break beautiful things…

—Oh no, she said to him.

—Because there are so few…there is so little beauty, there are so few beautiful things, that to preserve them, to keep them…

—But to make more…beautiful things?

As they looked at each other, Stanley looked at them both, helplessly suspended between their eyes, waiting for what each sought in the other.

—Now…if there were time…she said softly.

—And you are going into a convent, you are going into that…that life, he insisted suddenly, and she shrugged her shoulders, looking down once more.

—Or what other? For there she will become a bride.

—Tomorrow, yes it's arranged, an audience, it's the best thing, tomorrow.

—So soon!

—Tomorrow, yes. It's all arranged.

—Tomorrow she will…kiss the Fisherman Ring? If there were time, to ask him questions about Purgatory.

—I had a book of his once, by mistake…

—To kiss Saint Peter in the Boat, tomorrow?

—Here you are! Listen, listen to this, this letter from my wife, Don Bildow burst out, dropping square in front of Stanley at the table.

—No, no, no…

—Listen. My daughter was all swollen up when I left, remember? And we thought it was…we didn't know what it was, remember? Well do you know what it was?…what it is? She's pregnant! That's what this letter from my wife says, and she's only six. Do you hear me? What am I going to do? What are you looking at me like that for?

Stanley was silent, he was staring at Bildow's face, but vacantly, as though far beyond it.

—It's the *Eccentricities of Cardinal Pirelli*.

—But have you read *Justine?* In that he desecrates the wafer right inside her.

—Give me that! Give me that thing! Don Bildow snatched the book from Stanley's lap.

—My husband's sitting up in the hotel room now, with a book by some laousy Chinaman, and a bottle of Scotch.

An Italian boy entered and joined the next table, where he offered a group of American tourists for sale.

Further on, two American senators were drinking whisky and arguing whether or not Sweden had a king.

—He says he's practicing the gentle art of sitting and forgetting. My God, I'm tired.

Don Bildow was trying to tear the book up. First he tried to break the spine, but he could not. Then he got half the pages in one hand, but he could not tear them. Finally he held the book against him, and started to rip out about ten pages at a time. The table behind his narrow back was empty, and then Victoria and Albert Hall, and Rudy, and Sonny, and Buster, and Big Anna, the Swede, and two others descended on it, and set to discussing the problems of the train trip to Paris, if Rudy and Frank were both in states of Grace they could not share the same compartment. The pages continued to rip. A faint male voice protested, —Caprew... A woman's voice said, —Kike. Don Bildow sat at the table ripping the pages out of the book, about five at a time.

From behind, when she stood still in that yellow velours gown, Mrs. Deigh rather resembled an uneven stack of sofa cushions. At the moment only Dom Sucio had this coign of vantage, and he did not stop to enjoy it, but turned and hurried down a dark hallway hastily adjusting his mantle, as she opened the door to Stanley. He paused, upon entering, to support himself on Judith's sword-arm: Holofernes' head swung toward him, and the whole thing almost came over.

—My dear boy be ... be careful of our ... Donatello, Mrs. Deigh gasped as the bronze righted itself. —It's his ... David, his famous David, she murmured nervously, addressing the still gently swaying head, as though apologizing to it. She continued to murmur nervously, wringing one hand in the other, as she led him into the crowded room. —We do wish you would have your hair cut. Stanley sat down on the edge of the Queen Anne chair, and she stood over him for a minute. —What is it? What is troubling you, dear boy?

—Nothing, nothing, nothing, he said quickly, and pulled his shoulder from under her hand, and the glitter of the wrist watch at his cheek. She withdrew looking injured, and sat down almost silently in the big chair. There she commenced the familiar chucking noise.

—I ... I'm sorry, I ... I'm tired.

—It has been a trying day for everyone, she said, somewhat distantly, and went on looking at the ceiling. When he continued silent, hands gripped between his knees, she said in the same tone, —We had a very trying visit from some British Israelites. And poor Cardinal Spermelli, the white ants have completely destroyed his chess-playing machine. All he talks of now is going to Venice, where he can be conducted to his last resting place in the dignity of a pompa funebre, though those little Coca-Cola motorboats ...

—Is he real? Stanley brought out suddenly.

—Is he what? my dear boy?

—No, no, but if he's a Cardinal he should be ... nothing. Nothing.

—You are upset, are you not, she said looking sharply at him as he lowered his eyes once more, and she looked back to the ceiling. —We knew you would like him, he likes young boys so much, especially musical young boys. But his arca musarithmica, alas ...

—What is that?

—Don't you remember it, dear boy? The seventeenth-century machine he showed you, that composes music automatically. Alas, you will never see it again. The white ants ... what is it? What's the matter? Are you having a chill? ... She stared where he was staring. —Ahhhh ... she sighed with sad affection, but she did not get up. —It's one of his days up and around, she murmured.

The lean figure had emerged unsteadily from one of the dark doorways, and stood resting at a precarious angle against the leg of a figure in a bathing suit, a bronze (labeled *Hercules*, by della Robbia). The dim light cast a faintly yellow sheen over the velutinous patches left on his back. A twist of insulated wire led from one ear to the object hung at his collar. Mrs. Deigh made the chucking noise again, but nothing moved. —He has not looked so discouraged since he fell into the baths of the Emperor Tiberius at Capri, and we had to hire an Alpinist to rescue him. She looked slowly round at Stanley. —Do you recall asking me about the initials on his little chair in the Automobile? the little chair where you sit? I asked Dom Sucio, and he told me, of course. Impubis Hadrianus Semper. Then she cleared her throat. The chain rattled as she leaned forward and spoke more gently. —Dear boy, your teeth are chattering. Perhaps ...

—No, no, I ... I'm all right, I don't ...

—We understand. Perhaps you caught a chill at Assisi? ... We won't ask what is burdening your soul. We understand. Perhaps it will take your mind off it to tell us about Assisi? It is so long since we have walked among those roses, and touched the very spot where ...

—She asked me to marry her, Stanley blurted out.

—What? to what? Who?

—She asked me to marry her, yes, and ...

—But ... my dear boy, you ... you never told me there was a ... a girl?

—Yes...

—And you...you didn't take her up there with you? To that...that holy spot...? The chain rattled, the objects strung to it went to the floor. Neither of them retrieved it.

—She...she kept going through the gate of the Portiuncula, she...to gain indulgences for...she...

—Dear boy! dear boy! Mrs. Deigh had come forward, half unseated, half to her feet.

—No, she...If only there were time, she said, over and over. She's pregnant.

Mrs. Deigh went back in the chair, got firm hold on the arms as the mother-of-pearl crucifix climbed out of her bosom, and it dropped back in as she stood. The chain came up with her.

—You...you don't understand, she isn't just a...a who...a wh...

—Dear boy, don't weep, We...

—If she...she wanted to share her beauty with anyone...with everyone, she...if she...

—We understand, dear boy, We understand, Mrs. Deigh said with a warm hand on his neck, patting him there gently, as she did for a minute broken only by his sobs, until finally she said to him, —And of course you said, No. No? We hope you said No, when she asked you...that. We hope you said No, and told her that you are going to Fenestrula, for your work, your work is what matters, your work is all that matters isn't it, isn't it dear boy. And you did say No, did you not.

—Ye...hes. No.

—There. Of course you said No.

—Yes, it...everything is in pieces. I...Stanley got to his feet, and drew both hands down over his face. Then he turned to her and burst out, —And your...Dom Sucio, he...did you know he...he isn't real?

—But dear boy, Mrs. Deigh said gently, —he is as real as we are.

—No, what I mean is, I mean a monk, a real monk, I saw him...I...did you know that?

—Of course, dear boy.

—But you...you knew all along, there's no...no special Order for...for little people? And he...the contributions you give him, he...yes, you told me, people turned to look at him in the street and he...he was sensitive, but I...that they mistook him for a wandering child, but I...I...

—Dear Stanley, Mrs. Deigh said, and came close to put an arm round his trembling shoulders. —You are such a...dear boy.

For a moment, it looked as though Hadrian were going to improve his position against the bronze leg. With great caution he commenced to raise one foot from the floor. The instant he started to sag in that direction he planted the foot where he'd got it, but too late to do more than save himself from going down altogether, and so he stayed that way, the moment of daring, and all memory of it, gone.

—Will you join Us in prayers, in our little private chapel, Stanley? she asked as they separated, slowly, each with a look of wary interest, close enough to smell one another for the first time.

—Ye...yes...

Then she moved quite briskly, first to Hadrian, making the chucking sound. Hadrian did not raise his head. —We must confess, Hadrian and Dom Sucio are not the best of friends, she said with some asperity, setting Hadrian square and working at the box on his collar. —Dom Sucio turns his hearing aid off, and sometimes he doesn't hear a thing for days. As she straightened up murmuring, —Now there was something else...Hadrian sagged back against the bronze calf. —Oh, from Our daughter, something she sent, I meant to show you.

—A letter?...

—Not precisely a letter. Here. Here it is. She took a folded paper from behind a picture frame and handed it to him. —We shall return in a moment, dear boy. For prayers. And she left him with this:

PLEASE HELP IMMEDIATELY
This lady knows that you need this Ritual
The Ritual

Jehovah God
Before me Saint Raphael
Behind me Saint Gabriel
To my right Saint Michael
To my left Saint Auriel
Behind me shines the gold star
And above me shines the Glory of God.

Pray for this sick lady, for her hair to be thick and black, for her eyes strong, and clear eyesight, for her nose to grow one inch longer, big, thick and healthy, her teeth and gums to be strong and healthy, also pray for her eyelashes and eyebrows to be thick and black, and skin healthy and white, and for all her Health, all her Reconstruction, and her husband.

Please help this lady; pray hard and strong for her. This Ritual comes from India to help this lady and to save and uplift humanity.

Please pray hard for her to get to India to help humanity. Please spread this Ritual for her and her husband. Please use this Ritual or you will be sick and poor. Please get this lady a lot of helpers and help her to live in India.

After you say this Ritual, pray in your own way all you can. Help this lady or you will be sorry. If you do this Ritual you shall have everything you need in this world. Send this Ritual to all your friends and to the children and to the relatives. You must do this work or everyone will get sick and poor and the world will shake to pieces.

TRANSMUTING

You need to know this added higher law of the transmuting of power within mankind, within your own system.

You already know that all of our mental power must be used to help. Also all of your creative power must be used to help.

Instead of wasting this creative power of the genetalia, it must be used with the Ritual, praying out the power to help this sick lady for her health and her reconstruction, out of suffering.

Also you should get the men to transmute power to their sick wives so that their wives can be strong and healthy and so that their wives can pray for this sick lady.

Also you should get all the men and all the women and the older adolescent children to send out their power both ways to help this sick lady. This has to be done quickly to save this lady and her husband and to save and uplift humanity, to the next teachings, which you all will receive thru some sort of world publicity.

Please send copies of this Ritual and letter to all Doctors and Dentists and Lawyers and everybody that you can all over the world.

Stanley twisted his shoulders against the hot nettling sensation under his shirt. The rattling chain sounded distantly, muffled by the red hangings, and his bandaged hand sought the tooth in his pocket. Then the heat became more sensible. It was drenched with the scent of roses, and a soft glow illuminated the paper he held before him. —We always say our prayers this way... since Portugal... He looked up slowly, past the figure of Hadrian, sagged forward again silently, petrified there about to spring upon something long since gone to earth, the light from behind bringing a soft sheen to the yellow patches of pubescence. —It makes Us feel, somehow, closer to Him. She had two lighted tapers and held one of them forth, in the hand springing from the gold circlet of the wrist watch, and that, with the ellipsoid still swinging gently on the end of the chain, was all she was wearing, though the attar of roses clung to him as he passed the tendered head of Nebuchadnezzar's general, slipping, near being pinioned on Judith's sword, and made the street where a car swerved to a stop, so near running him down that he found himself standing stricken in the dark gap between its headlamps, his empty hand against its grill, where he read the word FIAT.

—Of course I said . . . No, he whispered. Bells sounded somewhere.

It was sundown in Barbados.

Doctor Fell stood on his veranda with one hand down the front of his pants, scratching. In the other he held a letter which commenced, —Dear Doctor, In cases of gastric hyperacidity, the commonest symptom is the sensation of a bonfire in the stomach . . . He was not reading the letter, however, but looking down the path which led to the rest of the Pilot Project and the native bungalows. Shadows were already gathering, and Doctor Fell appeared concerned, for he knew what difficulty his assistant had keeping his balance in the dark.

—Gordon! . . . he called after a moment. He saw nothing but the palm trees one way and the rim of the sea the other way. He heard the sound of the surf. —Gordon! he called again, and then sheltering his eyes from the lack of brilliance above with the letter, he peered down the path. Scarcely more steady than the shadows themselves, a figure took form, and emerged. Doctor Fell stepped down and came to help him with his load of little white boxes. Gordon could only carry one armload, stacked up to his chin, since the other arm was in a sling.

—Tsk tsk, said Doctor Fell, —how heavy they are getting . . . Gordon followed him in. When the little white boxes were all locked in the freezing unit, Doctor Fell turned and said, —How do you like the work by now, Gordon? You don't mind it so much, do you Gordon?

—No. But they . . .

—Who?

—The men down in the field, Ed and Max, and Anselm and Chaby . . .

—You mean the natives?

—Yes, they . . .

—What do you call them Ed and Max and . . . what do you call them names like that for, Gordon?

—They . . . they just . . . look like them, by now.

—You'd better have some Dramamine, right now, Gordon. Doctor Fell opened a tremendous cabinet. All the shelves were filled with bottles. —It's also good for fenestration procedures, labyrinthitis, and vestibular dysfunction associated with antibiotic therapy. I read up on it today. It's even good for pregnancy. Do you ever feel like jumping out of windows, Gordon? Tsk tsk ... you can here, of course, but it wouldn't be any fun. It wouldn't be any more fun than falling out of bed. Do you still fall out of bed?

—I ...

—Here we are, Gordon. Ahmm, tsk tsk, this is the last of the Dramamine. How do you want it administered, orally or rectally?

—I ...

—But don't worry, Gordon, we have lots of things here, said Doctor Fell, rummaging among the bottles for the jug of saline solution. —Tomorrow we'll start on Roniacol, and when we run out of that there's Lesofac, Gustamate, Diasal, Amchlor ... Oh they've sent us everything. The Nicotinic acid was the best, wasn't it, in spite of its evanescent reactions, the tingling, itching, burning of the skin, dizziness, faintness, sensations of warmth ... bend over now, Gordon ... gastric distress, cutaneous flushing, the increased gastrointestinal motility ... ah ... mmmp, there we are, Gordon. You'll feel better in no time. It's due to a vasodilating action.

—Do you think there will be a scar ... ?

—What do you suppose vasodilating means? ... a what? a scar? where?

—When you take these bandages off my arm?

—Oh certainly, certainly Gordon.

—But ... like this one on my face?

—Oh, bigger. That one you could cover with a mustache. You'd be cute in a mustache, Gordon. Wait, don't go yet. Doctor Fell had fitted an ophthalmoscope to his head, and swung the mirror down over his eye. —Have a look at the bloody labyrinth, he went on talking as he worked. —Oh, I'm not being profane now you understand, tsk tsk, I'm referring to the hemorrhaging in the labyrinth of the ear, your ear of course ... Can you hear me? can you hear me in this ear? Yes, you're getting better, I think it's all over now. Why, I'll lose you before too long, won't I ... with all that money you can be off, you can fly to the moon if you want to, can't you. I've worried about you, you know, you seemed like a very sensitive young man, and I've wondered how this sickness had done this to you, just left you with your eyes glazed and no interest in anything but your work. Tsk tsk, maybe something better will come along? You can't really enjoy going out with the vitamin samples in the morning and bringing in the ... the specimens in the evening. But that's what life is, isn't it, yes, tsk tsk ... Ooop ... be careful, Gordon, watch where you're going. Keep your eyes open. Do you want me to walk back with you? No? All right, just be careful, keep your eyes open. Yes ... and now where do you suppose that tattooed idiot is? He's useless, worthless, all he does is drink and talk about shark fishing and trim his little mustache, I don't trust him at all. I'd think he'd followed us here, but I can't imagine why anyone would follow anyone here.

—No... N O. Tresp... Oh Chrahst give it to me, I'll do it, I mean Chrahst I'll do it, I have to do everything here myself anyway sooner or later, and it's too late to put it up anyway. But I mean Chrahst give me the paint, will you just let go of it, Otto? I mean just let go of the handle. Now give me the brush, I mean Chrahst just hand it to me, don't throw it on the floor. I mean look at Hannah over there, the way she's working waxing it, you know? I mean Chrahst, she's going to go through to the cellar in a minute. Now go away, will you? I mean after a day like this I want to relax a minute, you know? I mean Chrahst, before I fix supper for all of you. Up in the ballroom, you know? The green room with the three chandeliers, go up there and wait for your supper while I bring the rest of them in. And look, I mean when you pass give Hannah a shove with your foot, will you? She's going to wax my old man right into the floor, and... Oh Chrahst, I have to do everything myself. I mean look at him sitting there staring at the clock with the sun on his face, like he was going somewhere, and Chrahst I mean the best he can do is pick up the telephone and dial and by the time I get there he's just sitting holding the telephone and he wonders who's calling him. Chrahst. I mean he'll never hang his hat on that buffalo horn in the Harvard Club again, and sit down and eat an omelette with a spoon. Now Chrahst, where are they all. Max is still mowing the lawn, even if there isn't any grass there yet, when the grass comes up I'll have to keep moving him along or he'll mow the same strip until he gets right down to rock. And Chrahst look at Stanley painting that pillar on the porte-cochère, I mean he must have about fifty coats on one side of it by now. And where the hell is Anselm, or did I leave him washing the clothes. He's scrubbed holes in everything we've got by now, he can go through a shirt in half an hour if you don't take it away from him and put something else in his hands. But Chrahst I mean how many clothes can you wash at once in a couple of lousy cut-glass punch bowls. And Chrahst I might as well have another drink and another cigar, because that's all there is in the house, and they can't expect me to eat the kibbled dog food I feed them when I know the state inspector isn't coming around, I mean Chrahst he can't expect me to feed them anything else and pay the taxes too, at forty dollars a month a feeb. And I have to tie up another package for my mother to open before dinner, she's been waiting for it all day again. And what a letter to get, Dear Classmate,

We realize this letter, our second appeal to you this year, comes at a time when you have recently been solicited for reunion funds, I mean Chrahst. Many classmates have wondered how much money has been raised toward the 1975 goal of $100,000. Chrahst, listen to that record, you can hardly hear the tune any more it's so scratched, I mean it's just as good as having an automatic record-player to have a feeb sitting there starting it over again every time it ends. *The Sunny Side of the Street*. But Chrahst. I mean, 1975. I mean, Chrahst.

Dear Mr. Pivner... Eddie Zefnic wrote.

Gee you would really be interested in the work we are doing here now, and I guess I
   won't ever really be able to thank you for all you have done giving me a start, and
   treating me practically like a son and all, I mean by helping me go on with my
   education to where it really comes to grips with humanity and learning all about
   things in science like in the work we are doing here. I'm sure glad you had your
   operation, and believe me I sure did everything I could so you would even after I
   talked to you and I guess finally convinced you that it was a good idea, because
   now modern science knows what these things are and how to fix them, not like
   the Dark Ages. So maybe by convincing you to go ahead with it and have the
   operation, and while all along I'm working here right in the forefront of all that
   kind of things, maybe in that way I'm repaying you.
Let me tell you about the work we are doing here now, first we are studying anxiety
   neurosises by giving some animals a nervous breakdown. Like we have a whole
   bunch of kids (ha ha I mean little goats) which are hooked up so that when the
   light dims it gets a shock, so after a while then the minute the light dims the kid
   backs into the corner and gets tense so after a while of that he gets anxiety neurosis, because at first he's only tense but then when we change the signals around
   on him then he gets the real anxiety neurosis. Then you do that about a thousand
   times on him, you should see them kicking out their both hind legs so they won't
   get the shock except waiting for it when they don't know it's going to happen at
   what moment then they get the anxiety neurosis which is a breakdown, while all
   the while we measure everything so that we know. So after about a thousand times
   then we try to get them out of it, and everything is recorded real close by the lab
   and then we go over all that and try to get them out of it, you can see it's real interesting and how much good it will do.
You must have a real nice nurse up there, to write me your letter like she did and all.
   I have been in the laboratory here where they took a sheep's brain apart so I could
   see what it must be like having those nerve tissues between the frontal lobes of

the brain severed off of the mid-brain which is where you have the emotions, so I can see where the prison psychiatric doctor said how it might be a good thing because things like counterfeiting and forging arent crimes of violence but more something emotional maybe that gets mixed up so if you sever it off then it can't get mixed up any more and you don't want to do things like forging and counterfeiting any more. Which even though they aren't crimes of violence they sort of mean something's wrong somewhere.

Like I already wrote to you the last time mostly what I do here still is things like cleaning the pens of these kids and feed them if their being fed if we're not testing something on them or something, and all things like that, which keeps me pretty busy because the rest of the time mostly I spend reading these books so I even haven't been to church for a while now, and even the radio I don't turn on listening just to music but only the news broadcasts, because there is all this I want to learn and the scientists here are real nice about if you want to ask them questions how they'll explain everything to you, so I keep studying so I can too some day, I mean explain everything.

That's too bad about like you're having this child to play with and like being trained all over again about things like going to the bathroom but gee we took care of the main thing didn't we, and gee if I have repaid you by convincing you to have that operation when we talked in the prison, gee you know how much I appreciate how much I owe you and all, and I guess you sure must know I didn't ever think anything bad about you when that happened, I mean that you were a criminal or like that, but just something was wrong somewhere which wasn't your fault but a good scientific explanation for it, so If I have repaid you that way and by studying hard like I am and all, then I guess that's the best I can do to show you how much I appreciate all you've done for me and all, and I sure study every minute, like last night this friend came by he had tickets for some concert when I was studying and he tried to keep asking me to go and I said no.

Yours very truly,
EDDIE

P S I'm enclosing something I saw in the newspaper about this man who was a counterfeiter which they were trying to catch for a long time, I guess he was pretty good at it too which just goes to show you there was something wrong somewhere, like they found him in this hotel sort of in Spain it looked like he took his own life there, so I guess we took care of the main thing didn't we, I mean if a counterfeiter has to take his own life like that, and thats one thing, I mean restoring life after death that science hasn't figured out yet, but we're working on it.

Dear Friend ... Mrs. Sinisterra read on a postcard,

We have not yet heard from you regarding the plastic newspaper clipping which we sent you recently. If you would like to keep this "permanized" clipping just send one dollar in the self-addressed stamped envelope which was enclosed for your convenience, or mail your payment with this card enclosed for proper identification and credit.

We can obtain additional copies of this item or items from other newspapers and permanize them in plastic at $1.00 each. If you can furnish the clippings, the charge is only 75¢ each. Thank you for your courtesy and patronage.

MEMENTO ASSOCIATES

She tore the card in half and went up the stairs alone. When she got inside, she clung to the edge of the sloped sink for a minute, her body hunched as though in pain and her head up, listening; she turned the plastic knob on the box pinned to the collapsed folds of her bosom, her head still up, as though listening. Then she went to a medicine cabinet at the end of the sink, opened it, and took the same attitude. —You! . . . she called out. There was a disagreeable sound of response from somewhere. —You took my . . . Then she stopped, and held her forehead in a hand.

"Deft, moving, genuine, at once tough and compassionate . . . one does not often get from autobiography so satisfying an experience." "Told with sensitivity which is fresh, combined with masterful insights, moving at a swift yet leisurely pace . . ." "A tingling narrative style, which touches deeply in its moments of swiftly known pathos, and breathes into memories of worldly experience insights into great truths almost worthy of the author of the *Confessions* . . ." —You're trying to tell me these are reviews of your book?

—Yes, yes, said Mr. Feddle eagerly, snatching the ribbons of paper back, and returning them to the book under his arm. He'd met the hunched critic in the green wool shirt plodding up Sixth Avenue as though in deep snow, a heavy book under his own arm, about to enter a tailor shop to have two buttons sewn on the front of his pants. —How come I haven't seen it then?

—It's out. It's out, it just came out, said Mr. Feddle retreating.

—I thought it was poetry, how come these say . . .

—Poetical autobiography, Mr. Feddle said quickly.

—How come all these reviews have the name of it torn off the top?

—Oh, oh that's my . . . being modest . . .

—You being modest? Don't try to give me . . . is that it? Under your arm there, is that it? Lemme see it.

—Yes, but ... an advance copy, Mr. Feddle said retiring further out of reach, moving the book under his arm only enough to show his name on the jacket.

—Here, lemme see it, you ... all right, you stupid old bastard, don't, I don't want to see it.

—But you ... aren't you even going to buy me a glass of beer?

—Go on, you crazy old bastard. Do you think I don't know what those reviews are? You think I don't know the book those reviews are written about?

—Oh did you ... read it? Mr. Feddle asked helplessly.

—No, but I knew the son of a bitch who wrote it, said the critic, turning away, into the tailor shop where he found his friend the stubby poet sitting debagged in a waist-high booth.

—What are you doing here?

—Having the zipper on my fly fixed.

The critic undid his waist and sat down in the next booth. —That crazy old bastard out there, showing me reviews of Anselm's book he's trying to say are his. Anselm ...

—Anselm, the Church really had him. I laugh every time I think of him, retiring from the world and they make him publicity agent for a monastery. And the importance he tries to give himself by talking about what a sinner he was, he has to bring in every saint from Saint Augustine to Saint ... some other saint to back him up, for Christ sake, publicity agent for a spiritual powerhouse. How'd you come out in court today?

—That snotty kid swore he'd never met me, so how could he have used me in his novel. But we're proving he took incidents right out of my own life ...

—So what good are they to you ... ? The tailor came out with a pair of pants over his arm. The poet put on his pants and the critic took off his pants. —Tell him to hurry up, we have to get uptown to meet this guy who's going to put up money for a new magazine.

—I can't go without my pants, for Christ sake. Give him a couple of minutes to sew the buttons on.

And then they silenced, each bending forth, closer and closer, to fix the book the other was carrying with a look of myopic recognition.

—You reading that? both asked at once, withdrawing in surprise.

—No. I'm just reviewing it, said the taller one, hunching back in his green wool shirt. —A lousy twenty-five bucks. It'll take me the whole evening tonight. You didn't buy it, did you? Christ, at that price? Who the hell do they think's going to pay that much just for a novel. Christ, I could have given it to you, all I need is the jacket blurb to write the review.

It was in fact quite a thick book. A pattern of bold elegance, the lettering on the dust wrapper stood forth in stark configurations of red and black to intimate the origin of design. (For some crotchety reason there was no picture of the author looking pensive sucking a pipe, sans gêne with a cigarette, sangfroid with no necktie, plastered across the back.)

—Reading it? Christ no, what do you think I am? I just been having trouble sleeping, so my analyst told me to get a book and count the letters, so I just went in and asked them for the thickest book in the place and they sold me this damned thing, he muttered looking at the book with intimate dislike. —I'm up to a hundred and thirty-six thousand three hundred and something and I haven't even made fifty pages yet. Where's your pants?

—Wait a second, he'll be right out with them. I got a card from Max.

—Did he hear about Charles Dickens yet?

—I wrote a note to him about it on a review of his book I sent him.

—Your review? He'll thank you for that.

—They cut it on me, for Christ sake, you know that. The hell with them, anyway, they're all of them fucked and far from home, sitting over there right now pretending they're in New York pretending they're in Paris ... hey wait, wait ...

—I can't, I can't miss this guy, I'll see you later, the Viareggio.

—That place, for Christ sake, it's taken over by fairies. Wait ...

Out on the sidewalk, Mr. Feddle hurried up fluttering the ribbons of newspaper. —Beat it, screw, go on you crazy old bastard, I heard all about your book ...

—You did? you did? You've heard about it already? Yes, a beer? a beer to celebrate ... ? And in his enthusiasm Mr. Feddle came too close. The book was snatched from under his arm and he fluttered here helplessly, listening to the laughter, and an instant's more hope that it might not be opened, that the dust wrapper he had made so carefully, lettering his name with such meticulous clarity on the front, pasting a picture of himself taken forty years before on the back, might yet sustain it. Then pages flashed, the laughter broke. —*The Idiot*? That's the title of your book? *The Idiot* ... the laughter came on, —by Feodor Feddle ... ?

"'Did you imagine that I did not foresee all this hatred!' Ippolit whispered again ..." Mr. Feddle wiped his eye, sitting at an empty cafeteria table a few minutes later, over a tomato cocktail he had made with catsup and water, trying to hold together the torn dust wrapper so that his picture and his name might be seen whole by anyone coming near, the book balanced upright as pages slipped under his thumb, and a smile as of satisfaction fixed to his lips, weary satisfaction for a work completed, as the last page turned and the last paragraph swam before his eyes. "They can't make decent bread anywhere; in winter they are frozen like mice in a cellar ..." He touched at his watering eye with the crook of a finger. "'We've had enough of following our whims; it's time to be reasonable. And all this, all this life abroad, and this Europe of yours is all a fantasy, and all of us abroad are only a fantasy... remember my words, you'll see it for yourself!' she concluded almost wrathfully..." Someone approached his table. He swallowed hard, preparing to speak. It was a Puerto Rican busboy, with a hair-line mustache. Pages retreated under his thumb.

"'Pass by us, and forgive us our happiness,' said Myshkin in a low voice.

"'Ha, ha, ha! Just as I thought! I knew it was sure to be something like that! Though you are...you are...Well, well! You are eloquent people! Good-bye! Goodbye!'"

On the terrace of the Flore sat a person who resembled the aging George Washington without his wig (at about the time he said farewell to his troops). She was drinking a bilious cloudy liquid and read, with silent moving lips, from a small stiff-covered magazine. Anyone could have seen it was *Partisan Review* she was reading, if anyone had looked.

Paris lay by, accomplished. Other cities might cloy the appetites they fed, but this serpent of old Seine, pinched gray and wrinkled deep in time, continued to make hungry where she most satisfied, even to that hill where by night, round corners, she fed on most delicious poison, where, with, —Hey Joe, you see ciné cochon? deux femmes fooky-fooky? the vilest things became her still; where by day picturesque painters infested picturesque alleys painting the same picturesque painting painted so many times before: the spectral bulbiferous pyramids crowning the ascent where the first bishop of the city had approached carrying his head under his arm in a two-league march which centuries later would provoke a comment worthy any thinker before him, in a woman's pen whose shrewd instant would, ever after him, define and redeem the people whose patron saint he became.

Now, her whole mien no more changed after another great war than those of her daughters parading the Grands Boulevards, quickly restored with cosmetics after their own brief battles, murmuring, like them, —Vous m'emmenez?... Paris prepared to celebrate an anniversary. It was her two thousandth anniversary, and that not one of birth, but of the first time, under another name, when she was raped: a morsel for a monarch, Lutetia succumbed after a struggle, and later on, like her daughters parading now between the Madeleine and the Café de la Paix, took a more gaudy name for her professional purposes, shrining the innocence of the maiden name in history.

Thus brilliant in flowered robes, like those Greek law decreed for courtesans, Paris soon gained the ascendancy, soon stood out like those prostitutes of

Rome who, it was said, "could be distinguished from virtuous matrons only by the superior elegance of their dress and the swarm of admirers who surrounded them." As fashions have originated with courtesans throughout the ages, she soon became their arbiter. And since she was, like the better class of whores in ancient Greece, a trained entertainer, no more opprobrium attached to distinguished men visiting her than fell to Socrates visiting Aspasia: statesmen and generals came too, as Pericles came to Aspasia, and even after she had ruined him, and found herself accused of impiety, the great man appeared at her trial as her advocate, only to find his eloquence to fail him in court: "he could only clasp Aspasia to his breast and weep."

Other lands were not slow to credit her reputation as the author of all civilized innovations in the western world, and as much as five centuries ago the English, Italians, and even Turks, readily acknowledged that civilization had been enhanced with syphilis by the French. Paris exiled her overcivilized members across the river to Saint Germain des Prés, which had now once more become a haven for those crippled by novel and contagious disease. They behaved in this sanctuary very much as they had then, prohibited, as they were in the fifteenth century, "under pain of death, from conversing with the rest of the world."

On the terrace of the Flore, a passably dressed man who had compounded a new philosophy sat surrounded by some of the unshaven, unshorn, unwashed youth who espoused it. Four ruthlessly well-organized Hollanders, in the picturesque dress of their native land, sang *Red River Valley* from the sidewalk, and passed a cute wooden shoe among the captive audience. Someone whispered, —I'm actually going to join the church, the Roman Catholic. Someone else warned that the Pope and the whole works was going to Brazil. Someone else said that the Polar Icecap was growing, and would soon tip the earth over. Across the street on the terrace of the Brasserie Lipp, two pin-headed young men in gray flannel compared shiny green passports, thumbing forty-one blank pages. They were with two square-shouldered girls, whose small breasts were attached quite low to accommodate the fashion which the dresses imposed. One of the girls said, —I think my conçerage is returning all my mail marked ankonoo because I only gave her a thousand francs poorbwar. Behind them, another young man in gray flannels said he had known one of the girls, she was on the Daisy Chain at Vassar. On the terrace of the Reine Blanche next door, a golden-haired boy said, —I just want to say that being in Paris is a big fat wonderful thing... and beside him a youth whose plume of hair stood uncombed with painstaking care laid a hand on his and said, —Be-t tout nô ônelé etheur boïze frem dthe younaïtedd stétce in Paris is laïke kemming tout a bagnkouètt and bring yoûrze ône lennch.

On the terrace of the Royale Saint Germain, Hannah was told that a friend of hers was coming up from Italy, Don...what-was-it? And she responded, —Hey diddle diddle It bends in the middle, can you buy me a beer?

—I heard they hung one of Max's pictures upside down at his show.

—So what, Hannah said and she sounded morose. —Nobody noticed it until today, it's a real compliment to the coherence of the design. She was sitting at a table with an Australian sculptor who made leather sandals, a colored girl in the Stuart tartan, and a professional Mexican, who looked blank. Hannah was staring at a ribbon of newspaper, with a note scribbled in the margin.

—Who was that guy Charles that Max was talking about? He said he finally made it? under a subway? that he held up the IRT for twenty-five minutes...

—Will you shut up about it? Hannah responded, to amend her tone with, —and buy me a beer?

The Australian sculptor who made leather sandals said that Beethoven's duet for viola and cello sounded to him like two bulky women rummaging under a bed. Behind him a girl said, —Of course I like music, but not just to listen to.

—And you know how he paints them? He climbs up a ladder with a piece of string soaked in ink, and he drops it from the ceiling onto a canvas on the floor.

—We've just bought a lovely big Pissarro...

—My uncle had one, it was so big he couldn't park it anywhere.

—Max got good write-ups on his show. The critic in *La Macule* said...

—Why shouldn't he? Hannah interrupted. —They came around asking for a ten per cent cut on anything he sold if they gave him good reviews, sure he said yes, any good publicity agent charges ten per cent.

—Look, is it true what I heard about Max? that his mistress is the wife of... (and here the name of a well-known painter was whispered in Hannah's ear) —...who slips him her husband's unfinished canvases that he's discarded and forgotten about, and Max touches them up and sells them as originals?

—My uncle finally smashed it up one night, somebody on a motorcycle thought he was two motorcycles and tried to go between them.

—And then he told me he spent two days in bed with this real high-class whore he picked up in the Café de la Paix, after he told her he couldn't pay in francs, all he had was dollars, and he flashes this roll of tens and twenties and fifties, so she paid all the bills at the George Sank and gave him a terrific time for a couple of days and then rolled him, he said he'd like to see her trying to change Confederate States money in the Banque de France. What's this, a review of his book?

Hannah pushed the ribbon of paper forth saying, —The poor bastard who wrote it sends it over to him. Read it, you can see he misses the whole idea. Somebody in the *Trib* compared it to *Nightwood*.

—Here he comes now, isn't it?

Hannah looked up, to see Max approach, smiling; to ask, —Hey, can you buy me a beer?

At the next table a girl said, —Plagiary? What's that. Handel did it. They all did it. Even Mozart did it, he even plagiarized from himself, just look at the wind instruments in the dinner scene with Leporello. Someone said he'd been knocked down by a priest riding a bicycle with a red plush seat in the Rue Zheetliquer; someone said she had been knocked down by a nun on a bicycle in Rue Dauphine street: someone with a beard said he had never seen either a nun or a priest on the left bank, and added, —I just got a new holy man myself. —A what? —You know, an analyst. Have you been up to the exhibition of paintings by nuts up in the Saint Anne hospital? We got a nice section, the ones by American nuts. Some of them are dirty as hell.

And someone said, —Nothing queer about Carruthers...to conclude, once for all, the story of that subaltern and his mare.

—Maricones, muttered the man in the sharkskin suit.

—Wie Eulen nach Athen bringen...

—Maricones y nada mas.

There, on the terrace of the Reine Blanche Rudy and Frank held hands under the table, and talked about the wedding banquet: Caviar Volga, consommé Grands Viveurs, paillettes, homard au whisky, cœur de Charollais Edouard VII, perdreau rôti sur canapé...champagnes, Mumm 1928, Château Issan 1925... —And in the ceremony we just told him to leave out that vulgar part about the bodies of man and woman clinging to each other. They said afterwards that I was quite dewy-eyed.

—Sonny's terribwy upset, so *jealous*! He trwied to do *away* with himself, did he tell you?

—How?

—By hitting himself *savagewy* in the temple with a fountain pen. But where was Big Anna? Is that one jealous too?

—No baby, Big Anna telephoned from some absurd place in Italy. They were going to drive up in some nameless person's new Renault, and they were somewhere in the Fremola valley when it didn't go right, so they opened the hood to look at the engine, and there was nothing in there but an old tire, they must just have dropped the engine right out. So they just left it there, it was the only thing they could do. In the Saint Gotthard Pass, it was the only thing they could do.

—Rudy has the sweetest flowered toilet bowl, but he lent it to someone before we found this place on the Quai d'Orsay, and they just won't give it back. They're growing something in it, and we want to *use* it.

Across the river, up Montmartre, that hill whose name had been so many times ransomed since Saint Denis showed up carrying his head, an immense lopsided Negro in epaulettes guarded a bar where a heaving hunchback played an accordion like a beast lovemaking, a girl heaved as though about to be sick, and her girl friend said enticingly to a lone stranger, —She dancing, wonderful dancer. You dance? —No. —You pay me drink? —No. —You ingliss? —No. —You swiss? —No. —You jermn? —No. —You hollandais? —No. —You dance? —No. —You pay me drink? The hunchback would go on heaving over his accordion, the girl over the bar, the huge doorman at the door, but they would not see Arny again, stumbling in from his hotel in Rochechouart with his shirt on inside out and the hem of his coat pinned up, for even Henry's Hotel was no longer standing: the day had been a sunny one, and Arny, finishing a bottle about breakfast time, put it empty in the window-sill and sat down to try to write a letter. —Dear Maude, I am just trying to figure things out . . . it commenced, and got no further, for he was soon asleep over it, his head down on his folded arms. The sunlight filled the room, and the wallpaper looked like it was going to descend and devour him. Still he slept. The sun caught the bottle, which drew its light and heat to a sharp point on the bedclothes. Arny woke to find himself engulfed in smoke. Before he could stand, it was flames. He got to the window, where there was a sign pasted, possibly by some jester: *On est prié de n'ouvrir pas ce fenêtre parce que le façade de l'hôtel lui compter pour se supporter* . . . Arny did not read French, even when it was written by an American. With some effort he opened the window, smoke billowed out, and the façade of Henry's Hotel collapsed.

In the more fashionable part of town below, tourists continued to stroll the Grands Boulevards, marveling at French cooking, côte de veau, côte de porc, entrecôte, biftec, bistek, pommes frites, pommes frites. The two small-headed youths had brought their young ladies back to the right bank for supper, and they advanced up the Boulevard des Capucines like the horses in a chariot quadriga, stallions on the outside. —Why don't you go up ahead, Charley, see if one of *them* will approach you, pretend you're not with us, go ahead, I want to see how she does it . . . None did. They came on, spavined stiff with formality, spaved and gelded, to a small restaurant whose small sign said, *Son menu Touristique 400 francs, You Speack English.* —Hors d'oeuvres veryay pertoo, puis boeuf à la sale anglaise. —Comment, m'sr? —Boeuf à la sale anglaise. —Com*ment*? —Ici, damn it . . . He pointed to the menu and repeated. —Ahh oui, boeuf salé à l'anglaise, oui m'sr . . . —That's what I said, damn it,

I mean Christ, he added when the waitress was gone, —they can't even understand their own language.

But on most hands the French were still being taken at their own evaluation. They were still regarded as the most sensitive connoisseurs of alcohol. Barbaric Americans, the barbaric English, drank to get drunk; but the French, with cultivated tastes and civilized sensibilities, drank down six billion bottles of wine that year merely to reward their refined palates: so refined, that a vast government subsidy, and a lobby capable of overthrowing cabinets, guaranteed one drink-shop for every ninety inhabitants; so cultivated, that ten per cent of the family budget went on it, the taste initiated before a child could walk, and death at nineteen months of D.T.s (cockeyed on pernod) incidental; so civilized, that one of every twenty-five dead Frenchmen had made the last leap through alcoholism.

They were still regarded as the arbiters of fine art, and Commissioner Clot of the Sureté Nationale could prove it by pointing to the walls of his office which were festooned with evidence: the best modern French painters brought such high prices, changed hands so freely, were so much easier to copy and, most ingratiatingly, had no histories, that no one need bother producing "old masters." Deluged as he was even now with the work of someone who was buying originals, making and selling (perfect) copies, and selling the originals later elsewhere, Commissioner Clot remained confident of his prey: "If forgers would content themselves with one single forgery, they would get away with it nearly every time ..."

To the end, the world's most exemplary models of free men (as their vigorous succession of governments, and singular adroitness of tax evasion, witnessed); of thrift and provident husbandry (with three or four billion dollars' worth of the world's gold dead and interred in back yards); of sophisticated modernity (one had only to dial Odéon 8400 to get the time, the dissection of the latest minute scarcely understandable but, badly worn as it was, recorded by a famous French comedian); and still the favored child of the Church ...

—Well *she* says she got athlete's foot in one of the baths at Lourdes, said someone entering the Louvre; as an Italian coming out observed, to no one, that the sculptures of Michelangelo he had just seen inside were placed —coll' arte ben conosciuta di tradimento francese.

Back on the left bank, the philosopher on the terrace of the Flore had been superseded by a blond woman with a fake concentration camp number tattooed on her left arm, who was supervising a discussion on Suffering. To one side, a chess game progressed with difficulty, for there was argument as to which tall piece was the king, which queen. An American who had been motoring in North Africa said, —Don't laugh, it isn't funny. We hit one.

There are about thirty-five a day in Casablanca, they just don't understand machines. It cost me thirty-two thousand francs to get my car fixed, I should have hit him square. They even found his teeth in the muffler.

One end of the Deux Magots was honoring a painter who had been discovered by an American fashion magazine: until 1916, he had painted nothing but bottles. His artistic revolution came in 1930. He discovered white.

Max had left the Royale. —How does he make it, does he work somewhere? —He lives out in a suburb called Banlieu, Hannah said, —he paints pictures for a well-known painter who signs them and sells them as originals. —But they are originals... Twelve Arab children sold peanuts from the tops of baskets and hashish from the bottom. Someone said there was a town in France called Condom. Many of the young men wore beards. —I never did understand Italian money while I was there, it was like confetti, rarther expensive confetti... Hannah said she had to go to work. She read her poems aloud in a local cave, naked. —I'm studying art here on the GI bill, one of the beards said, —I've found a school where all you have to do is register. Someone recited the Malachi prophecy concerning the Papacy. —There are only seven more to go, counting this one. —Do you think Paris is worth a Mass? someone asked, clutching a book titled *Les cinq fontaines ensanglantées*. —Nostradamus predicts it will last until 3420. AD that is.

On the terrace of the Reine Blanche, the blond boy said, —Next week he's promised to take me to Paris... —But baby, this *is* Paris. Rudy and Frank had left, to return to their new flat overlooking the Pont d'Iéna with some of their gay party, all of whom stopped in the foyer to admire the large painting which had been a wedding present from a well-known artist. It portrayed a tall man standing, and a youth reclining at his feet, gazing up at what, upon close inspection, proved to be no more than a tear in the tall man's trousers. Then one of the guests started to open the drapes at the long windows, and was stayed immediately from it. —Because Rudy just looked and looked for months for a place just like this, overlooking the water, and the very first night we were here, standing right here in this very spot looking out at the lights and the Seine, a girl went out on the bridge and took her shoes off and jumped, right before our eyes, and that's just ruined the view ever since for both of us... Then Frank was excused to write a letter home to Ohio, while the rest sat down to friandises served on modern Finnish glassware, to light cigarettes from match books stamped *Rudy and Frank*, and talk of Copenhagen. —Dear Mummy, Frank wrote, in the bedroom, —I know you will understand why I want to be with him always, Mummy. I know you will understand when I tell you that I love him the way you loved Daddy...

—"Time is a limp..." Hannah read under the pavement, her words rising despumated on the smoke and desultory commingling of languages, —emmerdant... —les americains, alors... while the city might seem to try to sleep out this great gap of time, asking, —Hast thou affections? —Yes, gracious madam. —Indeed! —Not in deed, madam... yet have I fierce affections, and think what Venus did with Mars... The thirty-third person leaped from the Eiffel Tower (though unofficial figures had it nearer a hundred), this time from the 348-foot second platform, and after a twenty-year investigation the Friends of Cleopatra found that the remains in her grave, in the library garden of the Louvre, were not that queen at all, but the body of an Arab soldier killed in a Paris café brawl, and the mummy, looking like a tight bundle of rags, gone to a mass grave eighty years before, and all joy of the worm. —Et toute nue... quelle envahisseuse! —"Time is a limp..." she commenced again.

Behind the clattering bastion of saucers, the aging image of the wigless father of her country read on, and someone said she could sit like that all night, because she wore a Policeman's Friend. Someone on the terrace of the Deux Magots said a balloon race had begun that afternoon in the Bois. Someone read the message on a card from a friend touring the Holy Land, —I've just visited the Wailing Wall, and had a good cry. In the men's toilet downstairs, someone scrawled *Vive le Pape* over the urinal.

> America
> My contrey tears a dee
> Sweat land a liberty
> of D.I.C.
> Landwert ar fater dye
> Land of thy pildrem bride
> From every mountain sides
> Every dumb breed

wrote a student at the Essex County Boys Vocational and Technical High School in Newark, New Jersey.

The ooth person leaped from the Empire State Building in New York.

In San Francisco, seven strands of barbed wire were strung at the jumping-off place on the Golden Gate Bridge, which one hundred and fifty people had chosen as a point of departure from this world since the bridge was opened in 1937.

In Moscow, *Pravda* announced that Hawaiian guitar music had been banned in Russia.

Was the long winter really done? and "the fireside, the slippers and the waiting bed" no longer there to "protect the depressed person from himself... This line of retreat recedes as the day grows longer," the World Health Organization reported, finding, in these verdant expressions of springtime's acceleration, "the never-ending daylight difficult to bear, ... and the glorious sun becomes a curse."

Any city that calls herself modern anticipates all her children's needs, even to erecting something high for them to jump from: the Eiffel Tower went up more than half a century ago; but everywhere the rural population must make shift to civilize itself with what it has. In southwestern France, within the neighborhood of Landes, forty-eight hours in the Easter holidays saw a woman hung in a farm barn, two men in a forest, one into a river, and another into the sea, while Deauville was already preparing to celebrate Pentecost, some seven weeks hence, by issuing five-hundred-thousand-franc chips in the casino, for the first time.

"Plage a allengas to are flag," wrote the New Jersey high-school student, hardpressed by his progressive education: "i plegance to are flag of the united states of American / An to the republican for region stands / One machone in the viguable / witch libryt an justest for all"...

Libryt and justest, Los Angeles police confiscated a hydraulic press, dies, and the plastic rubber compound with which the three arrested men were counterfeiting poker chips, to be cashed in the gambling palaces across the line in Las Vegas.

In the viguable, the machone's customs agents were importuning a Hollywood movie producer for duties on a "Study by Candlelight" by Vincent van Gogh. The purchaser said it was an "original" and therefore should enter the machone duty-free, witch libryt an justest guaranteed to any genuine work of art no matter how valuable; but the guardians of the viguable demanded a healthy cut (10 per cent) of the purchase price ($50,000.00), enforcing the tariff this sweat land levels on an "imitation or copy" whose entrance threatens the livelihood of the inspiration even now ringing from every mountain sides.

Lovers of beautiful things were thick as thieves. Some of the six hundred seventy-five thousand dollars' worth of paintings stolen from a cathedral in Bardstown, Kentucky (including a *Descent of the Holy Ghost* by Jan van Eyck), were found in the trunk of a car in Chicago. Far across the sea, the axiom that aesthetic value is not enhanced by ownership was once more disproven: a caretaker of the Victoria and Albert Museum had in twenty-three years taken home nineteen hundred and sixty objets d'art hidden in his trouser-leg.

Spring came everywhere, as though for the first time.

And for the first time, civilized use was found for the Great Pyramid of Cheops in Egypt, where a native son hurled himself effectively down the slope of two-ton blocks. In South America, with seventeen dead and 4,990 in need of medical attention after Rio de Janeiro's pre-Lenten festivities, Holy Week itself moved toward a comparatively peaceful close. Three hundred lepers were reported marching on the capital city of Colombia from their colony at Rio Agua de Dios. Nine Pilgrims were trampled to death, and twenty-five injured, jamming the gates of the Shrine of Chalma in Mexico. A Baptist minister in Rocky Mount, North Carolina, burned two copies of a new revised version of the Bible because it substituted the words *young woman* for *virgin*, and a Lutheran minister said they were both wrong: the word should be *maiden*. In Chicago there was a crime every 12.5 minutes. Some chickens exploded in a town near Hanover, Germany (they had eaten carbide dropped by British troops on maneuver and drunk water). The Sheik of Kuwait asked that posters portraying the Venus de Milo not be shown in his domain, not prudish about her undraped bosom, but because Islamic law punishes the thief by chopping a hand off. The right arm of Saint Francis Xavier arrived in Japan by air. In Moscow, *Pravda* asked, Where has Noah's Ark disappeared?

In Hungary's capital, the newspaper *Esti Budapest* complained that children were not being taught to read and write in the state welfare schools: a painful confession, in the face of the strides being made in progressive education by her most redoubtable political antagonist, so far off, in the New World, where that intrepid young patriot at the Essex County Boys Vocational and Technical High School in Newark, New Jersey, soared to new heights of enthusiasm when asked to write his country's national anthem, ... the Stears Sbangle baner.

Oho see can you sing by the doon ter lee rise
Who's so brightly prepaid as the twiylight least evening.
Who saw stars and bright strip threw the merilla fite
Where the ram what we watch where so ganley strening
And the rock that red clar bom boosting in air
Gave thru thur the nite that are flage was stild their
Oo sake of that stear sparkle baner yet quake
Over the home of the free and the land of the grave.

In a corridor outside a private room in the Z—— hospital in Budapest, two doctors talked.

—Napok óta nem aludt.

—Hetek óta.

—Seconal, Luminal, Somnadex, mindent megpróbáltunk. Még amerikai szereket kényszerüségükben.

—And you still do not sleep? said the man in the trenchcoat, inside.

—No.

—Your voice is clear, not strong perhaps but clear. He stood with his plump hands clasped behind him, looking out the window, his back to the figure on the bed. When he turned, the round flare of the trenchcoat's skirt broke unevenly in front with the weight of the pistol in the pocket. —And the eyes are clear, he went on, —not strong perhaps, but clear.

—Yes, the eyes, the voice... my mind is clear, everything is clear but if I, cannot sleep? Everything is clear, my mind has never been more clear, do you hear me? My mind has never worked faster or... or more clearly, but this... this... without sleep, thinking, thinking, but none of it... without sleep?

—They say it cannot last very much longer, the man in the trenchcoat said, and shrugged his shoulders slightly. The corners of his lips twitched, but otherwise his expression did not change at all.

There was no pillow on the bed, and the head lay back, the chin thrust upward and the whole profile sharp and hard in its features. The hands lay separate on the counterpane.

—Nincsen oka... the words of one of the doctors drifted in.

—Yes, there's no reason, it isn't reasonable that... there's no reason, no reason! he brought out gasping, the watery blue eyes still on the white ceiling, a vein at the temple showing itself in throbbing. —Someone laughed, he gasped after another moment, —the Hapsburg lip, yes! We did our work there, you did didn't you? You did meet Martin, in Rome?

—On the street "in broad daylight." It was the work of a moment, the man in the trenchcoat shrugged again, rounding out the circle of his skirt as he lifted the weight in the pocket, coming closer to the bed. —How loose the ring is on your finger, he said. —You will lose it.

—Don't... touch me, don't... don't be so close!

He looked down for a moment longer at the face almost full before him, the strength in the profile gone, drained out through the narrow chin. Then he returned to the window murmuring, —A pretty thing, the ring, the gold. And your family crest, in America?

—My family crest in America is... hahhgh, my family crest, eh? Eh, my dear fellow? Remember? remember saying "Thank God there was the gold to forge"?

—You should not try to laugh so, said the man at the window.

—Eh? eh? my family crest in America, eh? Aetas parentum pejor avis tulit nos nequiores... eh? We cannot insure against inherent vice. No, damn it, I'll have it through, this time. You see? You see how clear... how clear my mind is? But still with no reason... no reason, it can't... t... He had struggled to raise his head; and then he cried out rigid with terror, gripping the neatly folded counterpane at his chin. —There! there! take it... His voice abruptly regained peremptory control, but he spoke the three words as one, —Take-it-away... take-it-away...

The man in the trenchcoat stood over him. —But...what? All he saw was a delicate coil of hair on the white sheet drawn quivering up to the chin, and idly he reached to remove it.

—Yes yes that, take it away take it away...

With his other hand the man in the trenchcoat signaled the figures in the door, where a doctor spoke to the priest who had just entered, —Nincsen oka nem aludni...

—What is it, what is that smell, oil? oil? what is it, where is it?

—Of course it has not been easy, but we have arranged that a priest comes to see you.

—Yes, yes here, here he is, yes but no reason, it can't...no! no!

—Nézzen rá, nézzen a szemére...

—...indulgeat tibi Dominus...

—Do you remember? Aut castus...Martin? Martin? damn it, damn you, do you remember! Aut castus sit aut...aut...yes, sit aut pereat, you see? how clear my mind is? Aut castus...you see?

—Nincsen oka, nincsen oka, nincsen oka...

—...deliquisti per oculos...

—Martin! Martin! Damn it! Damn you! You see, how clear...do you remember? Be pure or perish, aut...aut pereat, do you see?

—Quidquid deliquisti per manus...

—...et pereat! do you see?

On a caned veranda, Fuller blew a slow cloud of cigar smoke at the rising sun. From this bungalow, situated at an extreme end of what had recently become the Pilot Project, he could see the sun both rise and set, and greeted both occasions in this same manner.

But finally the sun was full in the sky, and still the usual figures did not appear, the pale young man with an arm in a sling who set his helpers a slow pace, approaching —with the vitameen pills and the littel wite boxes...in the morning; and at evening appearing once more, to accumulate from one after another of the bungalows, the specimens, —a peculiar thing to go about collectin, still he conduct it all very proper and decorous. Seem I recall the face of this young mahn so put upon with the littel wite boxes. Once I have a mahn in my eye, I do not forget him.

For a commotion had arisen, at daybreak, in the heart of the Pilot Project, where Doctor Fell rushed to the bungalow of his assistant.

—I knew it! I knew it! And I warned you, didn't I? Warn you not to trust that...that tattooed...I won't say it, but didn't I? Warn you? And now he's gone, he's stolen all your money and gone. He did follow us here, he followed you here, just to steal your money. Yes, didn't I warn you? Thousands of dollars, wasn't it, didn't I warn you? What are you smiling about? Are you all right? Gordon? Gordon! Are you all right? Now you'll have to start all over again. I knew it. He knew you had trouble in the dark, didn't he, that tattooed...idiot, he knew it didn't he, that's how he took advantage of you, and now he's gone and stolen all your money. What are you going to do? There's nothing you can do. What are you going to do now? You'll have to start all over again. Gordon!...what is it? what are you smiling...Gordon! stop it, you can't tear off your bandages like that, you can't...you poor...Sit down! stop laughing! stop...tearing off your bandages, stop...think! You can... you must...start all over again.

There was a soft wind from the south, and the bells ringing a morning Angelus sounded all the way up the coast from Bridgetown.

It was near noon in Rome, where peace had come, if nowhere else the night before, to the rooftops of the Vatican, with the death of the black tomcat belonging to the Cardinal librarian and archivist, and the gray mouser owned by a Monsignor Gentleman-in-waiting to the Pope. Newspapers reported that they had struggled for preeminence for some time, and their bodies were found "still locked in mortal combat" in the Belvedere Courtyard seventy feet below.

Rounding a corner into the Via Umiltà, Stanley looked a good deal more frail than he had in some years. He even glanced up nervously himself whenever he saw a reflection, for the haircut, his last concession to Mrs. Deigh, seemed to take pounds, and a year or two, from his appearance. Nonetheless, a new quality of intensity showed in his face; and if it was the despair and conquest which had raged through him in the events of the past few days, or simply the haircut, he himself might not have said immediately. But possibly the very possessed way in which he now spoke of his work, especially that part to be played so soon at Fenestrula, betrayed the depths made real to him for the first time by the experiences which had suddenly brought him into his new estate, experiences which had raised the childish masks of anxiety from the face of the resident dread, exposing conflicts he did not yet understand, posing questions he could not answer now, and he sensed, might never. The two tragedies had occurred so close that they might have been coupled; so they were, in him, and here was the unforeseen conflict in the demands of his new manhood, in that he had suffered directly from neither.

Ashamed at having run out of the place in the Via Flaminia that night, after all she had done for him, the weight of the letter to Fenestrula she'd procured for him heavy in his pocket with his show of ingratitude, he'd pulled himself together and gone back, though this time it was the woman who wept through his broken apologies. First thing, he'd got his hair cut, to please her.

It was that same day he learned of the first tragedy. With it, all of his anxieties returned redoubled, his uncertainties flared in every direction, his fears for every moment of the past and future worked upon each other, and his guilt reared through him more oppressively than it had ever. In one of the first moments of distraction, whether to confirm the one certain prospect he had left, or to confirm the apprehension he suddenly felt for even that, he opened the letter to Fenestrula himself, and found there nothing but a grocery list. At that point he tried to force himself to think of nothing, to try to understand and solve nothing, until he could find Father Martin, as he was fortunate enough to do, and he confessed everything which his evasion of just such an encounter had intensified in every detail of the past few weeks. The priest was obviously busy, and it was quickly apparent that his work concerned more than mere shepherding of Pilgrims from one shrine to another, that the questions which concerned him embraced broader problems than the confessional. Still an hour passed, possibly two, as Father Martin listened, his face losing its joviality, recovering it for a moment, returning to its lines of medieval sternness, while Stanley told him of every detail he knew since he had boarded the *Conte di Brescia*. Every detail, even to the broken crucifix, the beads rolling on the floor, the fat woman, Stanley's teeth chattered sometimes while he talked, and in the midst of narrative he might break off for some urgent incoherence like, —Sorcery, maléfice, is it from maleficiendo, is that from male de fide sentiendo, I mean does that mean is ill doing from ill thinking on matters of faith? . . . And now this last tragedy; and his work, and Fenestrula.

Father Martin listened to him, and talked to him, with an extraordinary gentleness and sternness at once, with a calmness which was never complacent, a strength of understanding (though he never said he understood), an interest which was not patent curiosity to excuse pat answers (for he gave none), and a patient sympathy with the figures Stanley spoke of, a quality which showed itself the deepest aspect of his nature, the most hard earned and rarely realized reality of maturity, which was compassion. He was an extraordinary man, as the later event might attest. The longer Stanley went on, the more frequently he returned to his work, and its importance to him. Father Martin did not come all out in encouragement, though finally he said, —We live in a world where first-hand experience is daily more difficult to reach, and if you reach it through your work, perhaps you are not fortunate the way most people would be fortunate. But there are things I shall not try to tell you. You will learn them for yourself if you go on, and I may help you there. He arranged things for Fenestrula immediately, and Stanley left with that assurance to steady the bewilderment of his heart at everything else, a bewilderment exactly doubled, as Fenestrula became the only possible position left, when Father Martin was shot and killed in broad daylight, later in the day.

Even now, as he entered the Via Umiltà, a song danced through his bowed head and he could not shake it out. Every word brought with it the shades of anxiety in the sea washing up to him again, the shuddering decks, and even now, walking, he sought the tooth in his pocket and remembered it was gone: in an instant, the end of his tongue found the healing hole on his jaw, and someone leaped from a lime-green convertible at the curb and caught his arm.

—God damn it, I'm glad I found you. It was the man in the green silk necktie, though today, the silk was yellow. There were pictures of nuts and bolts on it. —I've got to find that girl, that kind of skinny girl you were looking for that night, I've got to find her. Where is she?

—She's dead, Stanley said clearly, and the two of them stood there for a moment looking at each other as though someone else had said it.

—Wait, she can't... What did you say?

—She died. Stanley spoke more faintly, and he looked down from the man's face to the nuts and bolts.

—She... she can't do that. I've got to find her, she won this contest for the B.V.M., just like I told her she would, she can't... just... skip out, she... she have an accident?

—An accident? Stanley repeated. The strain of calm in his voice, instead of breaking, had driven it down to a dumbness. He stared.

—This is serious, now listen, she...

—She was going to marry me.

—O.K., but a chance like this, she couldn't just... she would have been made.

—Made?

—I told you, I told her, she... we've rented a whole town for this thing. Even if they changed the story line around on us a little, they're going to make it the *Divine Comedy* by Dante now, instead of a straight life of the B.V.M., see? So maybe she'll only have a bit-part at the end, but that's all right. The whole thing builds up to that anyway, see? Where he meets her at the end. I haven't read the script yet, but they got a shooting script all ready for this thing, see? This *Divine Comedy* by Dante...

—She's dead, Stanley insisted suddenly, then was silent again.

—But...what happened? What happened?

—She died, she...she had a place on her lip, a sore, a...and it got infected, it was something like...staphylococcic infection, and it happened just like that almost, in a couple of days, she...

—How'd she pick up something like that just like that, she...

—She wasted away, so quickly as though she...she had no will to live, and she...she said, Stanley shuddered, —from kissing Saint-Peter-in-the-Boat, she said, For some fishes, the sea, the sea...

—Come on, get hold of yourself, you can't...The man took his shoulder, nodded and muttered, —Yeah, she...God damn it. He looked at Stanley, who stood staring dumbly at the pictures on the silk necktie. —And...God damn it, we've got it all tied in, this contest, we've got it all tied in with this canonization that's coming up, and this Assumption thing, all this God-damned publicity for this contest, God damn it, she was the B.V.M. incarnate, she had it in the bag. Now it's too late to do a God-damned thing. Then as Stanley's eyes remained fixed on a brown silk nut, he took Stanley's shoulder and said, —Christ. Come on. Come in and have a drink. We'll bounce back.

—No, I have to leave. I have to get a train.

—Come on in for one drink. Christ. Look, this little jerk in the car with me, he's this ex-king who wants his God-damned throne back, I've got to have lunch with him. But come on in for a drink with us. You can meet the little jerk. It's lousy luck. You'll bounce back...Then he looked down at the pavement between himself and Stanley. —God damn it, he said, —I had a friend, a guy who was in college with me, he just got killed in a plane accident, he used to say the whole thing is like this handkerchief and this cannon ball falling in this vacuum, they fall the same speed, you know? And every God damn place you go, and every God damn thing you do, it's still this same God damn handkerchief and this same God damn cannon ball falling in this same God damn vacuum.

On the afternoon train, Stanley saw Don Bildow too late to avoid him. Don Bildow had a big box under his arm. He stayed Stanley for long enough to tell him he was on his way to Paris, and ask Stanley where he was going, but gave him no chance to answer. —That was lucky, he went on, —the boy from the tailor just got to the train with this in time, this is my new suit and I almost missed the train. I'm going to put it on before we get to the Swiss border so I won't have to pay duty.

—Yes but, excuse me, Stanley said, possibly the first time he had ever spoken to Bildow with such sharp dismissal, —I'm tired. Excuse me.

—What's the matter? You, I'm surprised you're not staying in Rome, for that thing tomorrow? The canonization of that saint?

The train roared northward. Second Class was no dirtier than most trains, but Don Bildow kept on his spotted threadbare old suit, dirty shirt and tie, until the last bit of Lago Maggiore disappeared from the passing landscape. Then he went into the men's room, and got out of his clothes. He washed as best he could, though his plastic-rimmed glasses kept falling down into the basin. Then he put on a new Italian part-silk shirt from a small rolled package in his pocket. All his property: his money, passport, testosterone tablets and contraceptives, and a few letters, was folded into a copy of a stiff-covered magazine on the floor. He had got a new yellow and brown tie looped round his collar, when he realized he must dispose of the evidence of the old clothes somehow. The window would not open, so one by one with his new sleeve rolled up, he pushed them down through the hopper. By the time he reached his jacket, it went through quite easily, for by then the hopper was fairly clean. Then he opened the box from the tailor in Rome. All it contained was a sailor suit made for a boy of seven, with short pants. Nonetheless the hand stitching was fine, the double seams drawn with exquisite care. There was even a little round hat with ribbons, and the name of the first Italian dreadnought, *Dante Alighieri*, embroidered in gold round the band.

—Maybe . . . he gasped, looking at it. Then he put on his glasses and looked at it. —Stanley, maybe Stanley would . . . have something . . . But his friend had got off some time before, at Milan, to change for Fenestrula and he stood unsteadily on the shifting floor, holding the blouse at a rolled-sleeved arm's length, and staring at it through the plastic rimmed lenses. The whole outfit was made as carefully as any tailoring for a real grownup, he could see, even in that light, as his train roared toward the Simplon.

In the next morning's light, the church looked much smaller than he had imagined it would be, and different than Stanley had pictured it the night before, when he arrived in the dark and walked up to look at it immediately after he'd got his few possessions settled in a pension room in the town. The whole town was different than he'd imagined in the darkness. The masses and shadows were gone, and he found nothing to suggest what they might have been. In one entirely different direction from where he thought he had walked, he came upon what he had taken for an enclosed, dimly lighted and possibly private chapel of some sort: it turned out to be a public convenience. And the church itself was a good deal smaller, its single spire a good deal more modest against the vast consciousness of the lighted sky, than undefined shadows had raised it at night, and as, once he'd seen it in daylight, he realized he would never see it again.

The walls of the church were heavy, and furrowed apart in places. At one end near the ground, he could see the rubble core.

Stanley was dressed, that morning, in his best suit, the blue one, and the second time worn. He walked with hands clasped low in front of him; for, putting on the trousers, he'd been dismayed to find moth holes round about the crotch. He wore a white shirt, and a red necktie, and there was nothing, absolutely nothing, the way he had thought it would be.

He came back to his room from early Mass, where he had also got a look at the gigantic organ (for it was the gift of an American), and confirmed his arrangement to play it later in the morning, and also, or rather first off, sought the intervention of that saint still to be rung in that morning on behalf of three souls equally dear, and equally beautiful.

And it was those he thought of, and not the work he thought of, as he stood alone in his room and looked at the work, which was all that was left. He looked at it with sudden malignity, as though in that moment it had come through at the expense of everything, and everyone else, and most terribly, of each of those three souls: but there was this about him, standing, running a hand through his short hair, pulling up his belt, and staring at that work, which since it was done, he could no longer call his own: even now, it was the expense of those three he thought of, and not of his own.

He was standing as though he expected something to move; and nothing did. Nothing moved in the room, until a chill shook his shoulders, and he turned to look behind him, his lips ready to speak, but no one was there. Nonetheless, he was still standing, poised, half turned, waiting, when the bells released him, and he quickly gathered up the pages he needed, and hurried down to the street.

He carried them clasped before him, and did not look up until he had reached the church itself. There he explained he had come early, to play through this one part he would play later, explained as best he could, that is, with his hands, the pages, pointing to the organ, to himself (the red necktie), for this priest understood no English, and spoke to him in Italian, a continuous stream of it as he conducted Stanley to the keyboard, leading him with a hand on his arm, then on his shoulder, and Stanley came on head bowed, closely attending the words he did not understand, as he seated himself and touched the keys, pulling out one stop and another as he listened, and why the priest shook his head and pushed two of them back as he spoke, Stanley did not understand (and he pulled them back out when the priest was gone, apparently in a hurry to be off somewhere before the next service called him back). —Prego, faccia attenzione, non usi troppo i bassi, le note basse. La chiesa è così vecchia che le vibrazioni, capisce, potrebbero essere pericolose. Per favore non bassi… e non strane combinazioni di note, capisce…

When he was left alone, when he had pulled out one stop after another (for the work required it), Stanley straightened himself on the seat, tightened the knot of the red necktie, and struck. The music soared around him, from the corner of his eye he caught the glitter of his wrist watch, and even as he read the music before him, and saw his thumb and last finger come down time after time with three black keys between them, wringing out fourths, the work he had copied coming over on the *Conte di Brescia*, wringing that chord of the devil's interval from the full length of the thirty-foot bass pipes, he did not stop. The walls quivered, still he did not hesitate. Everything moved, and even falling, soared in atonement.

He was the only person caught in the collapse, and afterward, most of his work was recovered too, and it is still spoken of, when it is noted, with high regard, though seldom played.

AFTERWORD

HE HAD been a floorwalker at Bloomingdale's. That was one rumor. He was presently writing under the *nom de plume* of Thomas Pynchon. That was another. He had had to pay Harcourt, Brace to publish *The Recognitions*, and then, disappointed and peeved by its reception, he had the unsold stock destroyed. He died of dysentery or some similarly humiliating and touristy disease at forty-three and had been buried stoneless-in-Spain under a gnarled tree. Among the more absurd was the allegation that he had worked as a machinist's assistant on the Panama Canal and served as a soldier of fortune for a small war in Costa Rica. He had no visible means. What he did do was traipse. He became a character in books which bore a vagrant's name. No. He worked for the army and wrote the texts of field manuals. No. He scripted films. They told you/showed you how to take apart and clean your rifle. A rather unkind few suggested he had been a fact-checker at *The New Yorker*. Not at all, argued others, he was born a freelancer. And became a ghost who moved corporate mouths while gathering material for a novel he would write one day about America and money. When John Kuehl and Steven Moore edited a collection of essays about him, the honored author turned artist and, for the title page, self-drew himself suitably suited and bearing a highball glass. The figure has no head.

In 1976, when his second novel, *J R*, won the National Book Award, his admirers, confused by William Gaddis's previous anonymity (very like the chary pronouns above), by the too sensibly priced fumé blanc, and by the customary babble at celebrational parties, frequently miscaught his name, often congratulating a fatter man. Even *The New York Times*, at one low point, attributed his third novel, *Carpenter's Gothic*, to that self-same and similarly sounding person. Yes. Perhaps William Gaddis is not B. Traven after all, or J. D. Salinger, Ambrose Bierce, or Thomas Pynchon. Perhaps he is me.

When I was congratulated, I was always gracious. When I was falsely credited, I was honored by the error.

These mistaken identifications turned out to belong to William Gaddis's book where reality already had been arrested; for what can be true in a world made of fakes, misappropriations, fraud, and flummery? Only this: that, if we had two doorsteps, on one would stand a hypocritical holy man, on another a charlatan dressed as a statesman; that among our most revered relics, if we had some, we'd find out our local saint's pickled thumb belonged originally to a penniless neighborhood drunk, that our museum's most esteemed painting was a forgery, that the old coins we'd collected were inept counterfeits, and the fine car we'd just bought a real steal. What Rainer Maria Rilke wrote of Auguste Rodin is certainly true of the man in that headless sketch: "Rodin was a solitary before fame found him, and afterward perhaps he became still more solitary. For fame is finally only the sum of all those misunderstandings which gather round a new name." In our oddly clamorous yet silent times, to be a famous author is to be unknown all over the world. Similarly, *The Recognitions*, the work which wrapped William Gaddis in the cloud of its carefully adumbrated confusions, remains widely heard about, reverently spoken of, yet narrowly read. It seems to lead, like an entombed pharaoh, an underground life, presumably surrounded by other precious things and protected by a curse.

Like Malcolm Lowry's great dark work, *Under the Volcano*, *The Recognitions* needed devotees who would keep its existence known until such time as it could be accepted as a classic; but a cult following is not the finest one to have, suggesting something, at best, beloved only by special tastes—in this case, the worry was, a wacko book with wacko fans. In fact, a cult did form, a cult in the best old sense, for it was made of readers whose consciousness had been altered by their encounter with this book; who had experienced more than its obvious artistic excellence, and responded to its neglect not merely with the resigned outrage customarily felt by those who read well and widely and wish that justice be accorded good books; it was composed of those who had felt to the centers of themselves how much this novel was indeed a recognition and could produce that famous shock: how it revealed the inner workings of the social world as though that world were a nickel watch; how it combined the pessimisms of its perceptions with the affirmations of the art it, at the same time, altered and advanced; more, how its author, though new to the game, had cared enough about himself, his aims, his skill, to create greatness against the grain, and, of course, against the odds.

Begun in 1945 without really knowing what or why, and continued in bursts from 1947, *The Recognitions* was published in the middle of the fifties, a decade so flushed with success it could not feel the lines of morbidity which were its bones. A typesetter, it's said, refused to continue work on the text and sought advice from his priest, who told him he was right to desist. Naturally the novel, when it appeared, won an award for its design.

Its arrival was duly newsed in fifty-five papers and periodicals. Only fifty-three of these notices were stupid. But the reviewers' responses to the book confirmed its character and quality, for they not only declared it unreadable and wandering and tiresome and confused, they participated in the very chicaneries the text documented and dramatized. It was too much to expect: that they should read and understand and praise a fiction they were fictions in. You, too, can let your present copy rest unread on some prominent table. A few critics confessed they could not reach the novel's conclusion except by skipping. Well, how many have actually arrived at the last page of Proust or completed *Finnegans Wake*? What does it mean to finish *Moby-Dick*, anyway? Do not begin this book with any hope of that. This is a book you are meant to befriend. It will be your lifelong companion. You will end only to begin again.

It was wrong in someone young to be so ambitious, the reviewers thought; the result was certain to be pretentious, full of the strain of standing on tiptoe. If the author works at his work, the reader may also have to, whereas when a writer whiles away both time and words, the reader may relax and gently peruse. Well, *The Recognitions* will lie heavily in any snoozer's lap. (What is the weight of the one you are holding? You can compare it to the 956 pages of the first edition, which comes into the ring at 2 lbs. 7 ozs., in order to discover how much of its substance has been leached out. Add an oz. for this intro.)

Well, it was ambitious certainly, dense, lengthy, complex. Its author is a romantic in that regard, clearly concerned to create a masterpiece; for how else, but by aiming, is excellence to be attained? It's not often one begins a sandcastle on a lazy summer morning—pattybaking by the blue lagoon—only to—by gosh!—achieve—thanks to a series of sandy serendipities—an Alhambra with all its pools by afternoon. The book was about bamboozlers, the slowest wits could see that, and therein saw themselves, and therewith withdrew. This was not to be a slow evening's soporific entertainment, it was to be their indecent exposure.

They cribbed from the dust jacket. They stole from any review appearing earlier. They got things (by the thousands!) wrong. They condemned the subject, although they didn't know what it was; they loathed its learning, which they said was show-off; they objected to its tone, though they failed to catch it; they rejected with fury its point of view, whose criminal intent they somehow suspected. They fell all over one another praising Joyce, a writer who, they said, was the real McCoy, whereas . . . yet had they been transported to that earlier time, they would have been first in line to shower Ireland's author with deaf Dublin's stones.

Many think that it is reviewing which needs to be reformed, but I believe the culprit is the species, which surrounds itself with lies, and calls the lies culture, the way squirrels build their nests of dead twigs and fallen leaves, then hide inside. In any case, as the German philosopher Lichtenberg observed, when reader's brow and book collide, it isn't always the book that is lacking brains.

Following the hubble-bubble of its initial reception, *The Recognitions* was left in a lurch of silence, except for those happy yet furious few who had found this fiction... about the nature, meaning, and value of "the real thing"... found *it* to be the real thing. The rumor was that William Gaddis himself had published a pamphlet excoriating the reviewers of his book and citing their malfeasances one by one. The truth, when it lies down among lies, such as those falsehoods, slanders, and distortions with which I salted the opening of this intro (for "yes" becomes "no" in oleo), takes on their odor, and is soon not distinguishable from them. Gaddis did check facts for a living once. He did banana-boat out of Central America. It would scarcely matter except that contexts corrupt. Bedfellows bite. Turncoats will steal from their own pockets and betray even linings. *Cozenage est une dangereux voisinage.* Actually a pseudonymous New Yorker named Jack Green published three articles on the qualities of the book hacks who had inflicted their skills upon *The Recognitions*. He called it, rather directly, "Fire the Bastards!" and the Dalkey Archive Press has recently reissued it in fine form. There, in addition to much of the data I have already used, I learned that one of these gentlemen attributed the book to William Gibson.

So a slender ring of fans kept the work afloat for the next twenty years, but its neglect, I think, was due to factors having little to do with its alleged difficulty or the dubious distinction of having a cult following. If you are to remain known while writing books (for the books themselves are likely to have a mayfly's life), you must either court the media and let publicity be your pimp, like Truman Capote, or cling like old ivy to the walls of the Academy, passing your person around from campus to campus like a canapé on a party tray. One way or another, you are thus able to appear in public often and collect the plaudits of hands which might as well clap since they are otherwise empty. You read your book with histrionic polish, or display a practiced wit, and your increasing ease, on talk shows. You review. Yes, you do, you descend to your opponents' depths, where you'll be seen as just another shark. You sympose. You give interviews. All of it adding to the stuff about and by you which a student, a critic, a scholar must consult. For you are as large as your library's catalog entries. Meanwhile you instruct beginners on how to be a genius, giving selected students a professional boost, and forming around your tutorial self, over the years, growing rings of gratitude: your career likewise enlarging as steadily as the trunk of a weedy tree.

William Gaddis, a.k.a. Gibson, a.k.a Green, a.k.a. Gass, did none of these customary career-enhancing things, remaining, as the politicians' escape-phrase always conveniently claims, "out of the loop." Out of the network. Not in the swim. Nor did he write a new book every fortnight just to prove how easy it is, for we all know how easy it is, and how desirable, for that way you can continue to feed your new friends what they are used to, and there are publisher's parties to go to, and more and more nice notices, even raves, since now aren't we all old friends? We must remember that the same hacks who condemn, for a price also praise.

Silence became his mode, exile (in effect) his status, cunning in scraping by his strategy, while compiling data and constructing other people's niggling or nefarious plots, building another long book out of our business world's obsession with money, manipulation, and deception, composing a hymn to Horatio Alger, music made of inane, conniving, sly, deceitful speech. *J R* did OK at the store for a time, and gathered in the National Book Award, but I think it was less read than *The Recognitions*, less enjoyed, and could not produce, of course, the same surprise. Furthermore, although clearly created by a similar sensibility, and expressing a common point of view, *J R* was as different from the earlier novel as Joyce from James. But do not put down what you have to go to *J R* yet, even if it is almost as musical as *Finnegans Wake*, a torrent of talk and Tower of Babble, a slumgullion of broken phrases and incomplete—let's call them—thoughts; because there is plenty to listen to here; because we must always listen to the language; it is our first sign of the presence of a master's hand; and when we do that, when we listen, it is because we have first pronounced the words and performed the text, so when we listen we hear, hear ourselves singing the saying, and now we are real readers, we are participating in the making, we are moving the tune along the line, because no one who loves literature can follow these motions, these sentences, half sentences, of William Gaddis, very far without halting and holding up their arms and outcrying hallelujah there is something good in this gosh awful god empty world.

Which is almost the whole point of what we do.

And accounts for the purity of Gaddis's artistic intentions, and the reality of the work, for he actually makes grace abounding out of fakes astounding. Furthermore, the progression from the concerns of *The Recognitions* to those of *J R* is completely reasonable. *The Recognitions*, indeed, tackles the fundamental questions: What is real, and where can we find it in ourselves and the things we do? But a generation later there are no fundamental questions to be posed. *J R* creates a thoroughly descendental world. It is a world of mouth, machination, and money. A few reviewers of *J R*, more perceptive than most, longed for the spiritual struggle of the earlier book, but—reader—just look around: that struggle has been lost. The large has been smothered by the small. Be petty enough and the world may make you a Prince. The cheat, not the meek, has inherited the earth.

Yes, we must follow the instructions we are given at the conclusion of *J R*:

> ...remember this here book that time where they wanted me to write about success and like free enterprise and all hey? And like remember where I read you on the train that time where there was this big ground-swill about leading this here parade and entering public life and all? So I mean listen I got this neat idea hey, you listening? Hey? You listen-ing...?

Then, if we are properly obedient, we shall have scarcely reached the second page of *The Recognitions* before we have the hearing of a paragraph like this, which introduces us to Frank Sinisterra, at the moment masquerading as a ship's doctor, but a counterfeiter by trade:

> The ship's surgeon was a spotty unshaven little man whose clothes, ar-rayed with smudges, drippings, and cigarette burns, were held about him by an extensive network of knotted string. The buttons down the front of those duck trousers had originally been made, with all of false economy's ingenious drear deception, of coated cardboard. After many launderings they persisted as a row of gray stumps posted along the gaping portals of his fly. Though a boutonière sometimes appeared through some vacancy in his shirt-front, its petals, too, proved to be of paper, and he looked like the kind of man who scrapes foam from the top of a glass of beer with the spine of a dirty pocket comb, and cleans his nails at table with the tines of his salad fork, which things, indeed, he did. He diagnosed Camilla's difficulty as indigestion, and locked himself in his cabin.

I particularly like the double *t*s with which our pleasure begins, but perhaps you will prefer the ingenious use of the vowel *i* in the sentence with which it ends ("which things, indeed, he did. He diagnosed Camilla's difficulty as indigestion, and locked himself in his cabin"), or the play with *d* and *c* in the same section. But these are rich streets and should be dawdled down, not simply to admire the opening alliteration, but to enjoy the fact that this paper money man is made of paper, or to visualize the gesture, as suitable as a finger's, and certainly as unclean, which sweeps his pint's excessive foam away, or above all to appreciate the hidden pun that runs from "foam" to "comb," contriving the de-combing of Frank's beer's head.

No great book is explicable, and I shall not attempt to explain this one. An explanation—indeed, any explanation—would defile it, for reduction is precisely what a work of art opposes. Easy answers, convenient summaries, quiz questions, annotations, arrows, highlight lines, lists of its references, the numbers of its sources, echoes, and influences, an outline of its design—useful as sometimes such helps are—nevertheless very seriously mislead. Guidebooks are useful, but only to what is past. Interpretation replaces the original with the lamest sort of substitute. It tames, disarms. "Okay, I get it," we say, dusting our hands, "and that takes care of that." "At last I understand Kafka" is a foolish and conceited remark.

Too often we bring to literature the bias for "realism" we were normally brought up with, and consequently we find a work like *The Recognitions* too fanciful, obscure, and riddling; but is reality always clear and unambiguous? is reality simple and not complex? does it unfold like the pages of a newspaper, or is the unfolding more like that of a road map—difficult to get spread out, difficult to read, difficult to redo? and is everything remembered precisely, and nothing repeated, and are people we know inexplicably lost from sight for long periods, only to pop up when we least expect them? Of course; the traditional realist's well-scrubbed world where motives are known and actions are unambiguous, where you can believe what you are told and where the paths of good and evil are as clearly marked as highways, that world is as contrived as a can opener; for all their frequent brilliance, and all the fondness we have for these artificial figures, their clever conversations and fancy parties, the plots they circle in like carousel'd horses, to call them and the world they decorate "real" is to embrace a beloved illusion. The pages of *The Recognitions* are more nearly the real right thing than any of Zola's or Balzac's.

There's no need for haste, the pages which lie ahead of you will lie ahead of you for as long as you like them to; it is perfectly all right if some things are at first unclear, and if there are references you don't recognize; just go happily on; we don't stay in bed all day, do we? just because we've mislaid our appointment calendar. No, we need to understand this book—enjoy its charm, its wit, its irony, its erudition, its sensuous embodiment—the way we understand a spouse we have lived with and listened to and loved for many years through all their nights. Persons deserving such devotion and instinctual appreciation are rare; rarer still are the works which are worth it.

It may be helpful, however, to place *The Recognitions* in the center of all stories where it belongs, in order to get a grip on the novel's basic strategy. First, a model archetypal plot:

A baby boy is born. In former times, before equalization was achieved, the parents in our history would have been important—they were gods and goddesses, heroes and their consorts, kings and queens—because what happened to them had to be significant not just for themselves but for the whole of their society. So this child will be an heir, and, as Joseph Campbell has pointed out, he will have a thousand faces. Signs of several sorts—omens, portents, the prognostications of soothsayers—warn the father (the King) that the birth of this son endangers him, so the King has his child taken away and exposed to the harshness of the wilderness where he will surely perish, but perish at Nature's hand and not at the hand of his father (a sophistry our signers of death warrants still practice). However, if the father in question is as forthright as Chronos (or Saturn, if you like), he simply swallows his rival. The first recognition belongs to the parents, and it is that the new generation will one day assume the position and powers now possessed by their elders. Although passing away is as important as coming to be for the health of the species, it is rarely welcomed, and is usually postponed as long as possible.

At the time the infant is borne off, if it does not already possess a mark of identity it is inadvertently given one. Oedipus, you recall, had his feet pinned as though he were being trussed like a bird for the spit. Whether left on a doorstep, set adrift in a basket, or abandoned on a hillside, the child is found by a totem animal and raised as one (Romulus and Remus are brought up by wolves), or he is rescued by a shepherd or a fisherman who becomes his foster parent. It is in this period of exile, during which the boy grows up in a foreign land, that the second recognition occurs, either through a slowly increasing inner conviction that he is "other" and important and has a destiny, or because, at some point, his foster parents tell him something of his history. This is our "hero's" first recognition, and it is primarily negative; put crudely, he says: I am not a wolf; I am not a bear; I am not of peasant stock. "What am I doing in Akron, Ohio," Hart Crane wonders; "Utah," Ezra Pound insists, "is not my middle-name."

Soon he sets out in search of his true homeland and his real identity. This part of the tale is in the form of an odyssey: a lengthy journey during which the young man overcomes a series of obstacles which test his character, certify his skills, and establish his stardom, as do the labors of Hercules, or any *Wanderjahr*. His final trial, it turns out, is usually the solution to some sort of conundrum, and is a spiritual or intellectual trial rather than a physical one (Oedipus solves the riddle of the Sphinx).

Much later, after Oedipus has been rescued from his fate by his foster parents, and has wandered through the world in search of his true home (his Odyssey), he arrives in a place he has no memory of, and by chance (that is, by Fate) encounters the King, his father. His maimed feet determine his identity, the King is appropriately alarmed, and in a kind of contest (the agon) the son defeats him, and receives his reward, the hand of the Queen. This recognition could be mutual, and the contest, consequently, clear-eyed, but the recognition is often put off, as in Sophocles's version of the Oedipus story, until many years have passed. The first arc of our narrative is now complete. It begins with a boy's birth and ends with his marriage, or comus; hence it is called a comedy.

The second part of the story repeats the first but from the father's point of view, for marriage means a new rival will soon appear upon the scene. If we stay with our original protagonist, there follows for him a period of peace during which time he establishes his rule and prospers along with his people. Meanwhile, in another country, his banished child grows restless and continues his searches. It is important to realize that from one point of view our "hero" is precisely that, from another point of view he is an unredeemable villain, and that the crimes of banishment and usurpation are repeated one generation after another without remission. The story's second arc ends, then, with the death of the hero at the hands of the son he has wronged, and it is called, of course, a tragedy.

However, a hero who is overthrown and dies is hardly a hero, especially when, as so often happens, he is torn to pieces or sacrificed or eaten. Clearly, he would not have lost the contest, the battle, the election, the war, the woman, unless he was betrayed, as Germany was by the Treaty of Versailles, as the South was in the Civil War, as every loser always is: by bad officiating, rotten luck, corporate scheming, political cabals, racial plots. We may have dropped the ball, but we did so because we were stabbed in the back. So there is usually a Judas or two hanging around, waiting to do some dirty deed, an Iago with a hankie up his sleeve. We can disloyally switch our allegiance to the new ruler: the king is dead, after all, so long live the king; but if we remain with our original character, what have we left but scattered bits of a disgraced corpse or a sealed tomb to pass a lifetime's vigil by? Well, the bits get put back together one way or another; the hero rolls away the stone which stoppers his grave; the followers of the betrayed and crucified king recognize him as restored and alive; whereupon, like Dionysius (his history now complete), he is pulled from the plot like the first gray hair, his name is given to a constellation, and he goes to dwell in the company of the gods.

And we—you and I—insofar as we are able to identify with the nature and life of this heroic figure, will overcome death and be redeemed as he was;

for he, and the ups and downs of his career, merely embody the uncertain cycle of the seasons. "In the juvescence of the year came Christ the tiger."

There is another section of this tale which might be mentioned, although it tends to be heretical in its content, popular rather than ensconced in any canon. While the hero of one cycle is enjoying his Queen and ruling his kingdom, you remember, the son (the hero in another version) was in exile and on his odyssey. Similarly, when the King is slain, and a new King assumes command, the dead lord can be imagined as living in exile in the country of death—in the underworld—and there he will undertake another trip, and face other trials, while awaiting his resurrection. The Christian tradition describes a "harrowing of Hell": a struggle between the crucified Christ and the Lord of Hell—there, like two cocks, in the pit itself. And this phase will possess its own set of recognitions.

Poets, novelists, mythmakers, rarely try to narrate the entire tale but usually will decide to focus on one element of the story, and elaborate it (odysseys provide many such opportunities), or they will alter the ontology of the enterprise, as Sophocles does, making not action but understanding the central theme of the cycle. Because Oedipus's deeds have been so heedlessly performed, he blinds himself, once his eyes have been opened to what he's done, with a brooch taken from his lover-mother's garments. This physical blindness is, of course, a prerequisite to his now powerful inner sight.

Suppose, now, I reenact this tale, furnishing it with details which will suit my place and time and special interests, as if none of its features had ever been seen before, as if none of its acts had ever been performed, as if none of its aims had, in any previous place or period, been realized. My rituals would be make-believe; they would be counterfeits; and their effects would depend upon the suppression of the original "once upon a time," and its replacement by my later sly reenactment. My story would be a usurper unless it recognized its kinship with all earlier versions, and it would risk overthrow the moment acknowledgment of that kinship were forced upon it. The long and unique quotation from Sir James Frazer's seminal book *The Golden Bough*, which Gaddis inserts in *The Recognitions*, permits us to recognize (although we have now known it for some time) that the practice of scapegoating is ancient and happens often and has seasonal motives. If crucifying a monkey or a rat has an air of superstitious desperation, what quality are we to assign its Christian counterpart?

There are suppressions and recognitions, then, which are inherent in the traditional myths and tales which anthropologists turn up, and which constantly occur as a part of the mechanism of their unfolding (among the suitors surrounding Penelope, it is only Ulysses's dog who recognizes him in his beggar's rags); and there are recognitions which the characters in this novel experience, too; as well as those which we readers will have, as we pursue its complicated course, a course whose origins it constantly alludes to in the manner of "The Waste Land"—references which make for much of its richness. Among these "epiphanies" is that special one of which I have already spoken, namely of what it is to be a genuine work of art, and what, being genuine, "touches the origins of design with recognition."

We shall live for no reason. Then die and be done with it. What a recognition! What shall save us? Only the knowledge that we have lived without illusion, not excluding the illusion that something will save us. For the temple of our pretenses shall come down at the end in a murderous fall of its stones (just as it does at the conclusion of this novel), not from the brute blind strength of a Samson shoving great pillars out of plumb, but from an art, a music, realized in the determined performance of an organ whose stops have been pulled out to play, at last, with a reckless disregard for the risks its reverberations run it, till every stone in the vicinity trembles.

The reviews which struck William Gaddis and his book were indeed stones from an old order, but, as *The Recognitions* concludes, such genuine work "is still spoken of, when it is noted, with high regard, though seldom played."

So turn the page . . . and change that unfortunate frequency.

—WILLIAM H. GASS
1993
Washington University, St. Louis

OTHER NEW YORK REVIEW CLASSICS

For a complete list of titles, visit www.nyrb.com or write to:
Catalog Requests, NYRB, 435 Hudson Street, New York, NY 10014

RENATA ADLER Speedboat

KINGSLEY AMIS Lucky Jim

IVO ANDRIĆ Omer Pasha Latas

WILLIAM ATTAWAY Blood on the Forge

EVE BABITZ Slow Days, Fast Company: The World, the Flesh, and L.A.

J.A. BAKER The Peregrine

VICKI BAUM Grand Hotel

WALTER BENJAMIN The Storyteller Essays

HENRI BOSCO Malicroix

SIR THOMAS BROWNE Religio Medici and Urne-Buriall

INÈS CAGNATI Free Day

EILEEN CHANG Love in a Fallen City

JÓZEF CZAPSKI Inhuman Land: Searching for the Truth in Soviet Russia, 1941-1942

ALFRED DÖBLIN Berlin Alexanderplatz

CHARLES DUFF A Handbook on Hanging

CYPRIAN EKWENSI People of the City

J.G. FARRELL The Singapore Grip

FÉLIX FÉNÉON Novels in Three Lines

WILLIAM GADDIS The Recognitions

MAVIS GALLANT Paris Stories

LEONARD GARDNER Fat City

WILLIAM H. GASS In the Heart of the Heart of the Country and Other Stories

JEAN GENET The Criminal Child: Selected Essays

JEAN GIONO A King Alone

ROBERT GLÜCK Margery Kempe

ALICE GOODMAN History Is Our Mother: Three Libretti

HENRY GREEN Party Going

WILLIAM LINDSAY GRESHAM Nightmare Alley

VASILY GROSSMAN Life and Fate

OAKLEY HALL Warlock

ELIZABETH HARDWICK The Collected Essays of Elizabeth Hardwick

ALFRED HAYES The End of Me

MAUDE HUTCHINS Victorine

TOVE JANSSON The Summer Book

ANNA KAVAN Machines in the Head: Selected Stories

RAYMOND KENNEDY Ride a Cockhorse

DWIGHT MACDONALD Masscult and Midcult: Essays Against the American Grain

CURZIO MALAPARTE Diary of a Foreigner in Paris

JANET MALCOLM In the Freud Archives

JEAN-PATRICK MANCHETTE No Room at the Morgue

ROBERT MUSIL Agathe; or, The Forgotten Sister

IRIS ORIGO The Merchant of Prato: Francesco di Marco Datini, 1335–1410

J.F. POWERS The Stories of J.F. Powers

GRACILIANO RAMOS São Bernardo

ANNA SEGHERS Transit

GILBERT SELDES The Stammering Century

VARLAM SHALAMOV Sketches of the Criminal World: Further Kolyma Stories

SASHA SOKOLOV A School for Fools

BEN SONNENBERG Lost Property: Memoirs and Confessions of a Bad Boy

MAGDA SZABÓ The Door

SYLVIA TOWNSEND WARNER The Corner That Held Them

MAX WEBER Charisma and Disenchantment: The Vocation Lectures

JOHN WILLIAMS Stoner

HENRY WILLIAMSON Tarka the Otter

STEFAN ZWEIG Journey Into the Past